10/2018

Madeleine L'Engle

The
KAIROS NOVELS
Madeleine L'Engle

The
POLLY O'KEEFE
QUARTET

**THE ARM OF THE STARFISH
DRAGONS IN THE WATERS
A HOUSE LIKE A LOTUS
AN ACCEPTABLE TIME**

LEONARD S. MARCUS, EDITOR

THE LIBRARY OF AMERICA

Published in the United States by Library of America.
Visit our website at www.loa.org.

The Arm of the Starfish copyright © 1965 by Madeleine L'Engle Franklin.
Dragons in the Waters copyright © 1976 by Crosswicks, Ltd. *A House Like
a Lotus* copyright © 1984 by Crosswicks, Ltd. *An Acceptable Time*
copyright © 1989 by Crosswicks, Ltd. Published by arrangement
with Farrar, Straus and Giroux Books for Younger Readers, an imprint
of Macmillan Publishing Group, LLC. All rights reserved.
All other texts published by arrangement with Crosswicks, Ltd.

Interior design & composition by Gopa & Ted2, Inc.
Interior & endpaper illustrations by Kimberly Glyder.

This paper meets the requirements of
ANSI/NISO Z39.48–1992 (Permanence of Paper).

Distributed to the trade in the United States
by Penguin Random House Inc.
and in Canada by Penguin Random House Canada Ltd.

Library of Congress Control Number: 2017962765
ISBN 978–1–59853–579–2

First Printing
The Library of America—310

Manufactured in the United States of America

Contents

THE ARM OF THE STARFISH

For
Edward Nason West

ΚΑΙ ΟΣΟΙ ΤΩ ΚΑΝΟΝΙ
ΤΟΥΤΩ ΣΤΟΙΧΗΣΟΥΣΙΝ,
ΕΙΡΗΝΗ ΕΠ' ΑΥΤΟΥΣ

1

A HEAVY summer fog enveloped Kennedy International. The roar of the great planes was silenced but in the airport there was noise and confusion. Adam wandered about, trying not to look lost, keeping one ear open to the blaring of the loudspeaker in case his flight to Lisbon should be called or canceled. His bags had long since disappeared on the perpetually moving conveyor belt, and he was too excited to sit anywhere with a book. All he could do was walk about, looking and listening, caught up in the general feeling of tension.

An extra load of business was being conducted over the insurance counters and at the insurance machines. Adam debated between a machine which would give him insurance and one which would give him coffee, and chose the coffee. Holding the paper cup in one hand, and his battered school briefcase in the other, he walked through a crowd of agitated people who had come to meet planes which were now being deflected to Boston and Philadelphia.

The hot, sweet coffee finished and the carton disposed of in a trash can, Adam headed for a row of phone booths, but they were all occupied by frustrated people whose plans had been changed by the July fog, so he decided against trying to call any of his friends. Probably no one would be home, anyhow; they were either away for the summer or busy with summer jobs.

So there was no point in trying to impress anyone with *his* job which had come up suddenly and gloriously after he and his parents had moved to Woods Hole for the summer and he was already set in the familiar routine of sorting and filing for Old Doc Didymus.

Doc might be ninety and doddering, but it was he who had said, the second day Adam reported for work, "Adam, I'm letting myself get dependent on you in the summer and this isn't good for either of us. My young friend, O'Keefe, is doing some rather extraordinary experiments with starfish on

3

an island off the south coast of Portugal, and I'm sending you over to work for him this summer."

Strangely enough it was almost as easy as it sounded, parental permission, passport, inoculations, and a ticket to Lisbon.

Adam, like every biology major, had heard of Dr. O'Keefe, but the scientist was only a name in the boy's mind. To work for him, to see him as a person, was something else again. He was full of questions. 'Young' to Old Doc meant anywhere between eight and eighty, but Adam had early learned that one did not ask Old Doc anything that did not pertain directly to marine biology. Adam's father, who had also worked for Old Doc in his day, knew this, too. He said only, "If Doc thinks you're ready to work for Dr. O'Keefe then it's the thing for you to do, and I'd be the last person to hold you back. O'Keefe has one of the extraordinary minds of our day. Your mother and I will miss you, but it's time you got off and away."

Over the loudspeaker Adam's flight was postponed for the third time. He started for an emptying phone booth, but a woman with three small children beat him to it. The children huddled together outside the booth; the eldest, bravely holding on to the hands of the two littler ones, began to cry, and Adam, to his own indignation and shame, felt a strong surge of fellow-feeling with the child.

He turned quickly away and walked up and down the large, noisy main hall of the air terminal, trying not to be disturbed by the loudspeaker calling, people rising from couches and trying to listen, annoyed men heading for the bar, mothers trying to coax babies into sleep with bottles of milk or juice. The main thing, he finally acknowledged to himself with a feeling of deep shame, was that he'd always had someone's hand (figuratively, of course) to hold, his family's, or Old Doc's, or the teachers', or the kids' at school, and now for the first time (for shame, Adam, at such an age), he was on his own, and just because his flight kept being postponed was no reason for him to start feeling homesick and to look around for another hand to hold.

Adam Eddington, sixteen, going on seventeen, out of high school and set for Berkeley in the winter, had better be ashamed of himself if a crowded airport, heavy with fog and tension, could put him on edge now.

It was after his flight had been delayed again (but not yet canceled) that he became aware of one person in the enormous, milling crowd, a girl about his own age. He was aware of her not only because she was spectacularly beautiful in a sophisticated way that made him nervous, but because she was aware of him. She looked at him, not coyly, not in any way inviting him to come speak to her, but coolly, deliberately, as though looking for something. Twice Adam thought she was going to come over to him; it was almost as though she had some kind of message for him. But each time she turned in another direction and Adam decided that he was being imaginative again.

He started to go for another cup of coffee, then looked back across the echoing hall, and now not only was the spectacular and enticing girl looking at him, she was walking toward him, and as she came closer she smiled directly at him, and held up one hand in greeting. His palm was slightly moist against the handle of his briefcase.

"Hi," she said. "I know you."

Adam gave what he felt must be a rather silly grin and shook his head. "No. But I wish you did."

She frowned. "I *know* I know you. Where?"

Adam was aware that this was a rather outworn opening gambit. However, he felt that this girl really meant it; she wasn't just casting around for someone to amuse her until her plane should be called or canceled. With her looks in any case she could have had any man in the airport with the lift of an eyebrow; Adam saw several men looking admiringly at the naturally fair hair, that particular shining gold that can never be acquired in a beauty parlor, and which shimmered softly down to slender shoulders. She wore a flame-colored linen dress and spike-heeled pumps. A leather bag was slung casually over one shoulder, and Adam no longer felt even the smallest need to hold anyone's hand, except perhaps the girl's, and that would be a different matter entirely. He was overwhelmingly proud that out of this vast conglomeration of people she had singled him out for her attentions.

"I'm Adam Eddington," he said, "and having met you now I'm not likely to forget it."

The girl laughed, with no coyness. "I admit I'm not used

to being forgotten. I'm Carolyn Cutter, called Kali. Where are you off to? That is, of course, if we ever *get* off."

"Lisbon first."

"Oh, sharp! Me too. Where next?"

"Well, I'm going to be working on an island called Gaea. It's somewhere off the south coast of Portugal."

As he said 'Gaea' she frowned slightly—perhaps she was thinking of Gôa—but she said, "What on earth kind of work could you possibly find to do in Gaea?"

"There's a marine biologist working there, Dr. O'Keefe. I'm going to be assisting him."

Now the girl definitely frowned. "Oh, so you know O'Keefe."

"No, I don't know him. I've never met him."

Kali seemed to relax. "Well, *I* know him, and if you'd like the lowdown I'll give it to you. How about going into the coffee shop and having a sandwich and a Coke or something? I was counting on eating on the plane and heaven knows when we'll get on *that*. I'm starved."

"Me, too. Great idea," Adam said. He put his hand against the firm tan skin of her bare arm and they started across the hall to the coffee shop. Suddenly Kali stiffened and veered away.

"What's the matter?" Adam asked.

"I don't want him to see me."

"Who?" Adam looked around stupidly and saw a middle-aged clergyman holding on to the hand of a gangly, redheaded girl about twelve years old.

"Him. Canon Tallis. Don't look. Hurry."

As Adam ran to catch up with her, she said, under her breath, but with great intensity, "Listen, Adam, please take this seriously. I'm warning you about him. Watch out for him. I mean it. Truly."

Adam, startled, looked at her. Her lovely face was pale with emotion, her pansy eyes clouded. "What—what do you mean? Warning me? For Pete's sake why?"

She tucked her arm through his and started again toward the coffee shop. "Maybe the simplest thing to tell you is that he's a phony."

"You mean he isn't a—a—"

"Oh, he's a canon all right, you know, a kind of priest who floats around a cathedral. He's from the diocese of Gibraltar. But I didn't really mean that." She turned her limpid eyes toward him, and her hand pressed against his arm. "Adam, please don't think I'm mad."

"Of course I don't think you're mad," Adam said. "I'm just—well, for crying out loud what *is* all this? I don't know you, I don't know your canon or whatever he is, I think you've got me mixed up with someone else."

"No," Kali said, leaning rather wearily against the wall. "Let me tell you about myself, and then maybe you'll understand. But first I want to know something: how do you happen to be working for O'Keefe?"

"I'm majoring in marine biology," Adam said. "My father's a physicist, teaches at Columbia, but we've always gone to Woods Hole for the summer and I've worked for Old Doc Didymus there ever since I was a kid."

"Didymus?"

"You've probably read about him in the papers and stuff," Adam said with some pride. "He's one of the most famous marine biologists in the country, and he's still going strong, even if he is ninety. Anyhow, he got me this job. It's a marvelous opportunity for me."

Four people at the head of the line were beckoned to a table and Adam and Kali moved up. Kali looked around at the people ahead of them and behind them, then said in almost a whisper, "Oh, Adam, it's terribly lucky I met you! I've absolutely *got* to talk to you. But there's no point here—you never know who might be listening. Maybe on the plane—. Anyhow, I'll tell you something about myself now, because at this point if you thought I was a kook I certainly wouldn't blame you."

Looking at Kali standing beside him, at the pale radiance of her hair, at her hand resting lightly on his arm, Adam did not think her a kook. As a matter of fact, it didn't make the slightest difference whether she was a kook or not. She was a gorgeous girl who for some unknown and delightful reason had chosen him out of all this crowd, and what she was saying was only a soprano twittering in his ears. Most girls' conversation was, in his opinion. She chattered away, looking up at him confidently, and he sighed and tried to give a small, courteous amount of attention to her words.

He had always, with a degree of arrogance, considered himself sophisticated because he had grown up in New York, because his friendships cut across racial and economic barriers, because he could cope with subway and shuttle at rush hours, because the island of Manhattan (he thought) held no surprises for him. But, trying to listen to Kali, he saw that his life, in its own way, had been as protected and innocent as that of his summer friends who lived year round at Woods Hole, and with whom he had always felt faintly worldly. Kali, it seemed, crossed the ocean as casually as Adam took a crosstown bus. She knew important people in all the capitals of Europe, and yet she talked about them with an open candor that kept it from being name-dropping. Her father had extensive business interests in Lisbon and on the west coast of Portugal; they had an apartment in Lisbon and were intimate with everybody in the American and British embassies. Because Kali had no mother she acted as her father's hostess for all his entertaining. "And we do lots and lots of it," she said. "Daddy's a sort of unofficial cultural attaché, only lots more so. I mean he's ever so much more important. Good public relations and stuff. Fine for business, and fun, too."

As Adam listened, his mouth opened a little in admiration and awe. Her light, rather high voice, fine as a silver thread, spun a fine web about him. He felt that at last, here in the international atmosphere of the great airport, he was truly entering the adult world in which Kali already trod with beauty and assurance. She gave him a sideways glance, and her fingers pressed lightly against his arm. "I do love being daddy's hostess," she said, "and I really do very well by him. I mean I have a flair for it. I'm not bragging or anything; it's just what I'm good at."

Adam could easily picture her being gracious and charming and radiant and having every man in the room at her feet.

There was a group of six young people ahead of them, three boys and three girls. Adam felt that the boys were conscious of Kali's exotic beauty and envious because it was his arm she held, and that the girls were conscious of the boys' consciousness, and annoyed by it— Those jerks, he thought. —I wonder what they're doing here anyhow?

The harassed coffee shop hostess moved through the crowded room toward the line and held up her fingers. "Two?"

"Oh, good, that's us," Kali said. "Come on, Adam."

They were taken to a dark table in the corner. A waitress wiped off the wet rings and crumbs and stuck menus at them. Kali ignored the menus. "I just want a cheeseburger and a Coke. That okay by you, Adam?"

"Sure. Fine."

Kali waved the menus and the waitress away with an airy command that just barely missed rudeness. She leaned over the table toward Adam. "This was luck, getting a corner table like this. I guess we can talk a little if we keep our voices low. This—what's his name?—Diddy—"

"Didymus."

"You're sure he's all right? You can trust him?"

"Of course! We've always known Old Doc. He's—he's like my grandfather."

She pressed the tips of her long, lovely fingers together thoughtfully. "I wonder."

"What?"

"I wonder how well *he* knows O'Keefe. If he's ninety—"

"There are no fleas on Old Doc. You'd never take him for over sixty."

"O'Keefe has a reputation all right," Kali said. "I mean, he's a scientist. That's no front."

"Why should there be a front?"

"Oh, Adam, it's so complicated! We *are* on the same flight, aren't we?"

They were not.

Adam was going Swissair and Kali, Alitalia. She looked at him blankly. "How long are you going to be in Lisbon?"

"I don't think at all. I'm being met there and flown right on to Gaea."

The waitress plunked their orders in front of them, slopping their Cokes. Kali looked at her sweetly. "I'm so sorry to trouble you, but would you mind wiping the table, please? Thank you *so* much." Then she looked somberly at Adam. "This is bad. I've got to see you somehow. Do you think you'll be coming to Lisbon at all?"

"I don't know. I rather doubt it."

"Then I'll get to Gaea. I'll manage. Because I can't—" She held up her hand for silence as the loudspeaker blared. "That's my flight, Adam! The fog must be lifting. Come with me quickly, and I'll tell you what I can."

They left their untouched food and Adam picked up the check. Kali waited impatiently while he paid and got change.

They hurried along the echoing corridor. "Listen quickly," she said. "I can't really tell you anything now, but just watch out for O'Keefe, Adam. He's in thick with Canon Tallis. That's O'Keefe's kid with Tallis now."

"Dr. O'Keefe's!"

"Yes. I *told* you they were in cahoots. He has dozens of kids. O'Keefe, I mean. O'Keefe and Tallis are against us, Adam. Don't let them rope you in. I'll try to get you to meet daddy somehow or other as soon as I can. I'm not being an alarmist, Adam. I know what I'm talking about. Believe me."

Adam almost believed. In spite of the wildness of Kali's words there was something about her that carried conviction. And Kali, with her sophistication and beauty, did not need to invent stories to get attention.

They reached the Alitalia gate and through the window Adam could see the big jet waiting in the rain that had driven away the fog. Kali took her ticket out of her bag, turned anxiously, and, to Adam's surprise, kissed him quickly on the cheek, saying again, "Believe me."

Adam stood watching as she hurried through the door. People brushed rapidly past him. He looked vaguely for the canon and the redheaded child, but did not see them. Oddly enough he felt excited and elated as well as bewildered. He did not have the faintest idea what Kali had been talking about, or what she was warning him about, but this was adventure, adventure in the adult world. He had graduated, all right!

He stood watching, bemused, as Kali's plane wheeled around and moved like a cumbersome bird down the runway. He could hear the blast of the jet as it slid out of sight into the rain. Slowly he walked from the Alitalia gates to the Swissair waiting room. There he saw Canon Tallis and the tall, gangly child, Dr. O'Keefe's child, standing with silent concentration licking ice cream cones, side by side, each bowed seriously over the ice cream.

 **2**

ADAM studied the clergyman and the child surreptitiously. The only extraordinary thing about Canon Tallis was the fact that he was completely bald, even to having no eyebrows, and had the look, somehow, of an extremely intelligent teddy bear. The girl seemed to Adam no different from most children who have suddenly shot up in height and not caught up with themselves in any other way. Only the flame of her hair and the open clarity of her blue eyes hinted that there was something for her to grow up to.

She looked at him over her ice cream cone and Adam shifted his gaze, for he wanted neither the canon nor the child to know that he was observing them. He took a book out of his briefcase and pretended to read it until his flight was called.

He started to the gate, and saw out of the corner of his eye that they were following him.

Because it was the height of the tourist season the plane was crowded. Adam had been assigned a seat by the window in the tourist section, and though the wing partly obscured his view he would still be able to see a good deal. Across the aisle, next to the window, sat the child, the canon beside her, and a lady with lavender hair in the third seat. The places next to Adam were occupied by two businessmen with attaché cases.

It was ten o'clock at night by Adam's watch when they took off. He had flown in from the Cape in the morning, but this was his first trip in a jet, and the pull of the gravities took him by surprise as momentarily he seemed to be pinned back in his seat. Then, with a smoothness he had never felt on a prop plane, they were airborne, rain drenching against the windows. And suddenly there was a star, and then another and another. Adam tried to watch as the plane flew high and clear of the clouds, but the lights in the cabin turned the windows into mirrors so that he saw his own reflection thrown back at him.

He looked warily about the plane, trying not to let his gaze linger on the dark figure of the canon, who was talking to the child, his face quick with interest and intelligence. But was it a malevolent or a benevolent face? Adam could not tell. The child laughed, openly, spontaneously: Dr. O'Keefe's child. Adam gave a shiver of excitement. Already, and before he had even met Dr. O'Keefe, the job promised to be far more than a summer job with a well-known scientist. Adam, crossing the Atlantic for the first time, dazzled by the international atmosphere of the great jet, felt ready for anything.

There was the click and buzz of the loudspeaker, and, while an attractive stewardess demonstrated, a voice explained, in English, French, and German, the emergency use of oxygen and how to put on the life belts just in case the plane should have to be ditched in the middle of the Atlantic. The captain, also using the three languages, introduced himself, and described the flight route and the altitude at which they would be flying. All of this and Adam hadn't even noticed that the NO SMOKING and FASTEN SEAT BELTS signs had blinked off. Feeling a little foolish, he undid his belt, noting that his companions had already unfastened theirs, and tried to relax and look world-traveled. But he was too keyed up for the tautness to leave his body.

Dinner was served, a full and delicious meal in spite of the hour, and Adam, having had none of his cheeseburger in the coffee shop with Kali, ate ravenously. After the trays were cleared the stewardess came around with pillows and blankets, and Adam, like the older men beside him, leaned back in his seat, loosening his tie and belt. He knew it was important to try to sleep as soon as he could because the difference in time would make it a short night. When they landed in Lisbon at eight-thirty in the morning it would still be only three-thirty in New York.

But his mind would not shut off. He found himself remembering a trip to the Hayden Planetarium. He loved the Planetarium and went there often to see the dome come alive with stars. He thought now of a lecturer who had said, "Of course you never see stars like this in New York. If you want to see stars you must go out into the country where there are no lights to dim them. But if you *really* want to see stars then you must be out in the middle of the ocean. Then you can see them as the sailors and navigators saw them in the days when stars were known as very few people know them now."

Adam, wakeful, remembering these words, glanced at his seat companions. Both had their eyes closed, so very gently he drew back the curtains at the window. The lights in the cabin had been dimmed; the window was no longer a mirror, and he saw that the Planetarium lecturer had spoken the truth. Never had there been stars as he saw them now, not at Woods Hole on the beach, nor even out in a sailboat at night. The stars—how many miles out over the Atlantic?—were clearer and more brilliant than anything he could have imagined, glorious myriads pulsing and throbbing about the plane. With his face turned toward the window he dozed, never sleeping soundly, but over and over again opening his eyes to the stars.

Then, very slowly, in the east, straight ahead of him, the sky began to lighten faintly, the stars to seem just a little less clear. A pale red warmed the horizon, but what made it different from sunrise seen from the land, or even from a ship, was the plane's great altitude, and the most extraordinary sight came surprisingly from behind the plane, in the west. They were flying east into sunlight, but the western sky was a strange, deep blue, with a haze of rose spreading out below and pulsing slowly upward.

By now he was completely awake, looking out the window before him, behind him, below him. The plane was so high that he did not see the ocean as ocean, but as great patches of purply-grey darkness among the scattered whiteness of clouds. As the light brightened, so that he was afraid his seat companions would ask him to draw the curtains, the clouds thickened beneath the plane, though it was flying in dazzling sunshine.

He leaned back in his seat, saturated for the moment with beauty, and looked around the cabin. Most of the passengers were still asleep. A portly gentleman moved stiffly up the aisle past Adam to the washroom. Across the aisle the canon and the O'Keefe child were eagerly peering out the window, the priest leaning over the child, his arm around her. He seemed very avuncular and not in the least sinister, and for a moment Adam wondered if he could have dreamed Kali and her warnings. In the aisle seat next to the canon the lavender-haired lady snored delicately.

Then, at three o'clock in the morning New York time, all the lights were turned on in the plane cabin, and breakfast was served, which, Adam felt, must have been a little hard on those passengers going on to Geneva and Zurich, though he himself was more than ready for food, and the hot, fragrant coffee made him forget his lack of sleep.

He was starting to wonder why they were not beginning the descent for Lisbon when he heard the buzz of the loud-speaker: "Ladies and gentlemen, this is your captain. We have just passed over Lisbon. Because of weather conditions we are unable to land and will proceed to Madrid." The same message was repeated in French and German.

The man next to Adam rang for the stewardess and asked about visas in Madrid; if they were being forced into Madrid he wanted to do some sightseeing; he wanted to go to the Prado.

It would be perfectly all right, the stewardess assured him; if the plane was held in Madrid for any length of time those passengers wanting visas would be issued them.

This struck Adam as an unlooked-for piece of luck; a glimpse of Lisbon and then the island of Gaea were all he had expected to see. A day in Madrid was a wonderful and added adventure. The Prado, he knew, was a museum; if that was the place to go, go to it he would.

Within a few minutes the clouds dispersed as they started their slow descent, and he could see the countryside of Spain beneath them. It was all he could have hoped for in his most romantic dreams: it was as though the plane had taken them centuries instead of miles out of their way. In the distance were snow-capped mountains. Below him were fields of all shapes and patterns and in all shades of green and brown. He thought he recognized olive trees, but the plane was still too high up for him to be sure. There were hills with ancient forts built around a square; there were hills with turreted castles. He had heard of castles in Spain; now he was seeing them. Suddenly he saw great bare circles of some kind of modern military emplacements; he was not sure what they were; perhaps Nike sites. Strange, bleak pockmarks on an ancient rural landscape, they jerked him out of the middle ages and into the present.

FASTEN SEAT BELTS flicked on. Across from Adam the canon and the child slowly sat back in their seats.

The landing was effortless and the great plane taxied down and around long runways until in the distance Adam could see a large, cold-looking modern airport; there were many men in military uniforms moving about. As soon as the plane had stopped, the rolling steps were pushed up and the passengers herded out and into a waiting bus, although the jet was only a few yards from the terminal. Probably, Adam thought, they're taking us to some other entrance where they can fix up our visas and tell us when we can get to Lisbon.

The bus was all part of the adventure, it was so definitely not an American bus. There was something almost institutional about it, as though it were not a bus for which one ever voluntarily paid a fare to take a ride; it was like a bus in a dream into which people were thrust, as the jet passengers were now, like it or not, and taken to some impersonal destination, probably unknown.

About half the passengers were able to sit on the seats which ran the length of the bus; the rest of them, including Canon Tallis and the O'Keefe child, and, of course, Adam, stood as the bus jounced the few yards to the air terminal: no more. They were as drenched by the rain that had suddenly started as they would have been if they had been allowed to run the short distance between plane and port, and why they hadn't been Adam could not fathom; but since nobody else was remarking on this he kept his mouth shut.

From the bus they were urged into the terminal where one of the stewardesses smiled with professional cheer and confidence and said, "Wait."

This must be tough, he realized, throwing the whole flight out of schedule; for the plane personnel it was not the adventure it was to Adam and to some of the passengers who were already making sightseeing plans; others were yawning openly and talking about getting to a hotel and catching some sleep.

There was also some speculation as to what kind of hotel they were being taken to, and one of the more traveled passengers said that probably it would be the Plaza, since the Swissair offices were in the same building, and that, though there was nothing wrong with the Plaza, it bore no resemblance whatsoever to the Plaza in New York and no one had better expect any such luxury.

The interior of the terminal was as modern and cold and bleak as the exterior, and as filled with men in uniform, though these at least were keeping dry. As Adam looked at their dark, stern faces he felt some of his optimistic sense of well-being and grownupness beginning to fade, but shook himself, remembering that he had not had much sleep for two nights now, and lack of sleep always tended to make him edgy and apprehensive—one reason he never sat up late studying for exams. If he didn't know it he didn't know it.

In the big, chill room some of the passengers sat wearily on wooden benches, others chatted desultorily, making tentative plans. Canon Tallis stood holding the hand of the child, who was beginning to look white with fatigue, but neither of them spoke. It seemed a long time before one of the stewardesses reappeared and said that they would now be given visas and would then be driven to a hotel in Madrid. She herded them into two lines, telling them to have their passports ready for inspection and stamping.

Adam asked her anxiously, "I'm being met in Lisbon. Will they be notified there?"

"Certainly, sir, but we'll be glad to send a telegram for you. To whom?"

"I'm not sure who's meeting me. Could you just notify Dr. O'Keefe on Gaea? My name's Adam Eddington."

"Of course." She made a note, smiled again, and excused herself charmingly.

In the other line, with his passport already being inspected, stood the canon, and Adam realized that the older man had overheard him and was now looking at him in an intent and curious way. As the priest took his passport and the child's and walked off toward the exit he turned and looked back at Adam.

The lines moved quickly. The passport was given to one man, who checked it. Then the passenger was moved along to another man who stamped the passport with the required visa and returned it. It was all brisk and uncomplicated.

Until it was Adam's turn.

The officer at the window took Adam's passport and flipped casually through it, then turned back to the beginning and began to go slowly over each page. Finally, in heavily accented English, he said, "Your name, please."

"Adam Eddington." Then the boy spoke in Spanish, since he had had four years of it in school, and Juan, one of his closest friends, was a Puerto Rican, school track star and prize chemistry student, whose family spoke no English. "Aquí tiene usted todo escrito en el pasaporte." —It's all there, right in the passport.

The officer looked at him sharply. "You have been in Spain before?"

"No, sir," Adam said.

"Then why do you speak Spanish?"

"I learned it in school."

The officer looked at him unbelievingly. "Americans do not make a study of languages."

"Oh, yes, sir. Some of us do." Adam made the mistake of smiling as he remembered Juan's initial struggles with English.

The officer stared darkly at Adam with hard black eyes; his hair, too, was black, wavy, and highly polished. His chin had a dark shadow on it that would never disappear no matter how recently he had shaved. Looking at him Adam began to feel distinctly uncomfortable. Maybe speaking Spanish had been the wrong thing to do, but he had only intended to be polite.

After giving Adam the silent treatment for almost a full minute the inspector returned to the passport, his eyes flicking from Adam's photo to his face to the photo again. Finally he said, in deliberate English, "Your destination?"

Adam did not try Spanish again. "Well, Lisbon."

"And from there?"

"Gaea."

A cold flicker seemed to come into the man's eye. "Why Gaea?"

"I have a job there for the summer with a Dr. O'Keefe."

"O'Keefe," the inspector said thoughtfully, tapping Adam's passport against his teeth. Then he slapped the passport sharply on the palm of his hand and stood up. He spoke to two other officials who were behind him, but in Spanish so swift and low that Adam could not catch it. He turned to the boy: "Be so kind as to come with me."

"Now, look here," Adam said indignantly, "what business is all this of yours? I was supposed to land in Lisbon, not Madrid. The only reason I'm here is the fog, and I didn't have anything to do with that. If you don't want to give me a visa to go into Madrid, that's your business. But I'm not trying to get a job or anything in Spain and I don't see why any of this has anything to do with you."

The inspector listened impassively. Then he jerked his head. "Come," he repeated.

Adam opened his mouth to protest again, but something in the inspector's visage made him keep quiet. Stomach churning, he followed the inspector past the line of passengers, through the airport hall, down a corridor. Until the corridor turned he could feel the eyes of the other passengers on him. He had a moment's impulse to shout at them not to let him be taken away like this, but he controlled himself. It was probably something not quite right about his vaccination certificate, at which the inspector had glared for several seconds, or something silly and simple like that.

The inspector led him into a bare room painted a dark, oppressive grey. There was an unshaded light glaring from the ceiling, a desk with a chair before and behind. The one small, high window was barred. Adam, his knees suddenly feeling weak, went to one of the chairs and sat down.

"Stand," the inspector snapped.

Adam stood. "What is this—" he started to protest again, but the inspector cut him off.

"Silence."

Adam shut his mouth.

The inspector went with deliberate pace across the room, behind the desk, sat down. He looked at Adam again from head to foot, as though he did not like at all what he saw. With a gesture of his dark chin he indicated that Adam might sit.

This time Adam decided that he was happier standing on his own two feet.

"SIT," the inspector barked.

Adam sat.

For a full minute the inspector looked at him in silence. Then he said, "Why are you working for Dr. O'Keefe?"

"Well—it's—it's just a summer job," Adam said. "I've just graduated from school and I'm going to Berkeley—that's in California—in the winter."

"So why a summer job? Why is this necessary?"

"Most of us kids have to work in the summer to help out some with our education. Besides this was a big opportunity for me."

"Opportunity? How?"

Adam tried not to let his eyes falter as the inspector pinned him with his stare. He thought of saying that one does not treat law-abiding American citizens in this way, but decided that it might just get him into more difficulty, so he said nothing.

Because of the placement of the chairs the sharp light fell directly on Adam, but the inspector did not entirely escape the glare which glinted against a gold tooth in his stern mouth and threw back a tiny gleam of light. "Opportunity, *how*?" he asked again.

"Well—to work with Dr. O'Keefe—and I've never been in Europe before—"

"And now that you are here you intend to do what?"

"Well—just work for Dr. O'Keefe."

"What kind of work?"

"I don't know exactly. Just whatever I can to help out, I suppose."

"Such as?"

"Well—there may be experiments with starfish or something I could check on."

The inspector looked at him sharply, as though the boy had said something unexpected. He opened his mouth to speak but was stopped by a knock on the door. He snapped, "Come in."

The door opened and in came one of the uniformed men, followed by Canon Tallis, looking grim.

Adam suddenly remembered with horror all of Kali's warnings. He realized that they had seemed part of an adventure that was somehow make-believe; he had not taken them very seriously.

He took them seriously now.

THE canon did not look at Adam, but went straight to the inspector, bowing and saying, "Good morning." Then, in precise British accent, he said, *"But yield who will to their separation . . ."*

There was a pause as the inspector looked at the canon. His visage, too, was grim. Finally he replied, *"My object in living is to unite . . ."*

The two men remained looking at each other, not speaking, until the inspector got up from the desk, nodded at the canon, came around to Adam, and handed him his passport. "I find your papers are quite in order after all," he said. "You may go. I believe the bus is still waiting."

The official who had escorted the canon opened the door, making a respectful obeisance. The canon looked at the inspector, bowed slightly, turned to Adam, saying, "Come."

Adam followed him. The priest moved with the ease of familiarity through the maze of passages until they were at the glass doors. Outside the bus was sitting greyly at the curb. The driver opened the doors. The canon got in. Adam climbed in after him. Someone had given the redheaded child a seat and she was asleep, her head down on the shoulder of a middle-aged, motherly-looking woman, who looked at the canon, saying, "She's all tuckered out. Let her sleep."

The priest smiled at her. "Thank you, Martha."

Adam knew that he, too, ought to say 'thank you,' since in some way the canon had been responsible for the escape from the inspector's inquisition, but the boy's mind was in such a turmoil that he could not speak.

It was obvious that the passengers, who had been kept waiting in the dark bus all this time, were intensely curious. A young man turned to Adam. "What on earth happened? Why did they drag you away like that?"

The canon answered quickly for him. "Just the usual passport confusion. There's one in every busload. You'll get used to it."

Now at last Adam said, "Thank you very much, sir." But he was not sure just how grateful he was. Although the canon had an easy and relaxed expression, reminding Adam once again of the intelligent teddy bear, there was still the memory of the grim look with which Tallis had greeted him in the inspector's office.

The bus started with a grinding of gears and a series of jolts. Adam felt surprisingly weak in the knees and would have liked to be able to sit down, but he clutched the aluminum pole firmly and braced himself so that without bending down too far he could look out the window. The trip into Madrid somehow surprised him. Spain seen from the air had been, except for the emplacements, everything that he had pictured it in his imagination; the outskirts of Madrid were a strange and unexpected conglomeration of old and new. There were many bleak housing developments like the projects in New York or those pictured in articles about Russia. Ugly apartments crowded upon beautiful old houses with walled gardens. Some new buildings were finished as far as the scaffolding, but seemed abandoned. Outside both the old buildings and the new laundry was flapping in the breeze. There were many billboards, well over half of them advertising American products, Pepsi-Cola, Coca-Cola, toothpaste, Singer sewing machines. The city itself was modern, commercial—buses, trolley cars, taxis, booths advertising the National Lottery, priests, nuns, young people on bicycles, old women with long black skirts and black shawls over their heads, girls with bright skirts high above their knees, newsboys calling, lottery boys calling— Adam's mind whirled. The impressions were coming too thick, too fast, events had been too confusing from the moment he had reached the fog-bound airport in New York for him to assimilate and sort out any of it.

Canon Tallis reached down and wakened the child. "Poly. We're here."

She opened her eyes and yawned as the bus drew up in front of the Hotel Plaza with another sickening jerk that almost threw Adam and all the standing passengers off their feet. As they surged toward the exit Canon Tallis said to the boy, "I'll see you."

A pleasant Swissair representative was waiting for them and herded them quickly out of the bus and through the revolving doors into the hotel. The Hotel Plaza, at least, seemed to hold no startling surprises for Adam; it was very much what he had imagined a middle-class European hotel would be like.

The passengers were lined up at the desk, where their passports were collected. Adam's was given no more, no less attention than anybody else's. They were assigned rooms. The man from Swissair explained that, because of the fog that gripped Lisbon now as it had New York the day before, they would not be able to leave Madrid until five in the afternoon, when weather conditions were supposed to improve. Precisely at five they were all to be in the lobby of the hotel and would be driven back to the airport where a plane would be waiting for them. Meanwhile they were free to sleep or to do some sightseeing around Madrid.

Adam went up in the elevator to his room not knowing exactly what he was going to do. He was wavery with the desire to sleep, but he was determined not to waste the day. He decided that a shower and some food would refresh him, and then he would find a bus or trolley to take him to the Prado and maybe some other places of interest.

His room, a small one with an enormous bathroom, faced the back. If the view from the front of the hotel was definitely twentieth century, the view from the rear flung him into the Middle Ages. He looked down into a courtyard filled with strutting black geese. In the center was a stone fountain. The rooftops, in a confused jumble of levels, were warm red tile. The houses were oyster white, with crooked, unmatched windows. The geese strutted about, their heads jerking awkwardly in and out of the downpour. An old woman, almost completely covered by an enormous black shawl, came out of a door and threw the geese some grain, toward which they scurried, gabbling. The woman stood, one hand holding the shawl about her face, watching them; then she disappeared into the house.

Adam felt his eyes gritty with sleep. If he didn't take that shower and get some more coffee and some food he would succumb to the temptation to lie down on the brass bed, and that he was determined not to do. Who knew when he would ever have another day in Madrid?

The water was hot and he steamed happily, then turned on the cold; he was shivering under its stinging needles when he became aware of a tapping on his door. He turned off the shower and called out, "Just a moment, please."

The hotel towels were fluffy and white and voluminous enough to wrap around him as a kind of bathrobe. Some instinct—or was it Kali's warnings?—made him call, before he opened the door, "Who is it?"

A pleasant British voice replied, "Canon Tallis."

Adam fought down a desire to say, 'Go away. You're dangerous. Kali warned me.' But after all the canon *had*, by no matter what devious means, rescued him. So he said, "If you'd wait a minute, please, sir, I'm just out of the shower. I'll throw on some clothes."

He dried and dressed as quickly as he could, then cautiously opened the door. Canon Tallis was standing, hands behind his back, staring upward through the ceiling at some inner vision. He smiled, the faint ridges where he should have had eyebrows rising slightly, followed Adam into the small room and sat on the one chair. Adam sat on the bed. The canon looked at him for a moment; Adam was getting distinctly tired of being looked at.

"So you're the young man who's going to be working for Dr. O'Keefe this summer." It was a statement, not a question.

Adam responded with a terse "yes." He was giving out no information. He began to wonder if Old Doc might not be getting senile after all, letting him in for this kind of thing. And as for his parents, they had no right to allow him to go off into the unknown like this. Of course there had been correspondence between his father and Dr. O'Keefe, and a couple of transatlantic phone calls, but Adam felt that none of the disagreeable things that had happened should have been allowed by parents who took a proper concern for their offspring. He forgot that he had been elated at first by Kali and her warnings.

"Tired?" Canon Tallis asked.

"No." He bit the word off and did not add *sir* or *father* or whatever it was one was supposed to call an English canon.

"Not much sleep last night."

Adam could not help adding, "Nor the night before."

"Planning to catch up on it today?"

"No," Adam said briefly. "I'm going to the Prado." Then, because his training in courtesy had been thorough, he added in a more reasonable voice, "I've never been in Spain before and I don't know when I'll get another chance. I didn't think I ought to waste it."

Canon Tallis nodded. "Poly's taking a bit of a nap, but then we're going to the Prado ourselves. Meanwhile I need a cup of coffee and a bite to eat. How about you? Dr. O'Keefe's a friend of mine, and maybe I can brief you a bit. Also I want to ask you a favor. I find I am going to have to stay in Madrid for a few days on business that would be very dull for Poly. She's the O'Keefes' daughter and a bright child, and perfectly capable at this point of traveling alone, but I'm responsible for her, and I feel rather badly about cutting her little vacation short, so I thought, since we've happened to run into each other, that I'd ask you to be kind enough to let her travel back to Lisbon with you."

What was there to say? There was no possible grounds for refusal of this perfectly reasonable request, so Adam nodded with a mumbled, "Yes, sir."

The canon stood up and yawned amply. "Two sleepless nights haven't given you the best preparation in the world for seeing the Prado. Nevertheless you may find it rather impressive in its own modest way."

When they reached the lobby the priest, instead of heading for the revolving doors, went to the desk. "Passports for Canon Tallis and Adam Eddington, please," he said in fluent Spanish. There was a brief wait, during which Adam felt himself getting nervous again. But the passports were handed to them without question.

"Be careful of it," the canon said. Adam did not mention that the advice was unnecessary. "Let's just go into the dining room here, shall we? No point in getting soaked again before we have to."

They went into an almost empty dining room with white-naped tables, and the canon ordered café au lait and an omelette.

Adam told the waitress, "Está bien para mi, también."

As she left the canon said, "You speak excellent Spanish."

"I had it in school," Adam found himself explaining again.

"Any other languages?"

"A bit of French and German."

"Portuguese?"

"No."

"Too bad. Russian?"

"No. I'd have liked to, but they stretched a few points for me with the ones I took."

"Poly's our linguist," the canon said. "She speaks all of those, plus Gaean. Now she wants to tackle Chinese. Sometimes it's a bit hard to hold Poly down." He seemed to be looking at Adam as though searching for something. "Poly's the oldest of the O'Keefe children, and she helps her mother a great deal. This is the first real vacation she's had. I had to give a couple of lectures in Boston and it seemed a good chance for her to get away. Then I was to have gone to Geneva for a few days and I'd planned to take her with me there, too. Too bad this fog had to come up and spoil her little treat for her. I must ask you, Adam, please to stay close to her. It is not that Poly isn't capable of taking care of herself. But there are some—shall we call them undesirable characters?—who are far too interested in Dr. O'Keefe's experiments. I will see to it that you both get on the plane, and Dr. O'Keefe will be at the airport to meet you. But please do not let Poly out of your sight. Will you promise me that?"

"Well—yes, of course," Adam said. "But I don't understand."

The priest looked at him thoughtfully. Adam looked back. —I'm going to do some of the staring, too, he decided. Grey eyes looked steadily into grey. Finally the canon said, "Adam, I wish I could tell you the things that would make you understand. When you start working for Dr. O'Keefe you'll realize for yourself the importance of his work, and its implications.

But for now I must simply ask you to trust me, as I must, in my turn, trust you." His face again looked grim, though it was a different kind of grimness from that in the stark and frightening room in the airport.

—But I don't trust you, Adam thought. Not after Kali. Not after you seemed to be so in cahoots with a fink like the inspector. People you can trust simply aren't *in* with secret police kind of people.

The waitress brought their coffee and omelette, and crisp, crunchy rolls each wrapped separately in tissue-like paper. The omelette was delicious, though the coffee was bitter, and stronger than any Adam had tasted before. He watched the canon take the hot milk pitcher in one hand, coffee pot in the other, and pour simultaneously, and so he did the same for his second cup and found it considerably improved.

Finally, leaning back and lighting a cigarette, the canon said, "There. That's better. I hear that you have the makings of a fine scientist."

"Well—it's what I'm interested in," Adam said. "Marine biology."

"Yes. I saw the letter Dr. Didymus wrote Dr. O'Keefe. You will, I trust, like working with Dr. O'Keefe, Adam. He's a very great man, far greater than Dr. Didymus, fine though he is—"

"Old Doc—" Adam started indignantly.

"Old Doc would be the first to acknowledge it," the canon said sternly. "If he didn't think you had the makings of—somebody worthwhile, he would never have sent you over here."

Adam flushed with pleasure, then remembered Kali's warnings, superimposed on a few Grade B movies. —Flattery, he thought. —He's trying to get around me with flattery. And just because he looks like Winnie the Pooh. . . . Yukh: I've got to watch it.

Canon Tallis pushed back his chair. "Let's go wake poor Poly up, and then we'll be off to the Prado. You'll come with us, of course." This, again, was a statement, not a question.

Adam's first instinct was to say, "Of course I won't." But then he thought, —If I go with him I can keep an eye on him.

And if I have to drag this kid to Lisbon with me I might as well see what she's like, too.

So all he said was, "That will be fine, sir."

They went up in the elevator together to the top floor. As he reached for his keys the canon whistled the first few measures of a melody. Behind the closed door the melody was returned. Adam recognized the tune, but in the fatigue and confusion of the moment he could not place it. Canon Tallis unlocked the door.

Poly was sitting on the edge of the bed, reading. She looked up, indignantly. "You locked me in."

4

"No, Poly darling," the canon said. "Just others out."

"Oh. Oh, okay, then."

"Adam, this is Poly O'Keefe. Poly, this is Adam Eddington, your father's new laboratory assistant."

Poly stuck out a lean brown hand and shook Adam's. Her grip was firm and confident. "Hello, Adam. Actually my name's Polyhymnia. Isn't that an awful name to give anybody? And it's all Father Tallis' fault. He's my godfather and he christened me. It's surprising that I still love him, isn't it? I tell you all this so that you'll know that if you ever call me anything but Poly I'll jump at you and kick and scratch like a wildcat."

"All right: Poly it will be," Adam said.

Canon Tallis said, "Get your coat and hat, Pol."

Poly looked out her window, which faced front on the modern street. "Nasty, stinking, foul old rain," she said, crossly, wheeled and took a navy blue burberry and a beret out of the closet.

They stopped off on Adam's floor while he picked up his trenchcoat, then went out into the street where the canon hailed a taxi with his furled umbrella.

"A lot of good it does us *that* way," Poly remarked.

They got in the taxi and the canon began pointing out places of interest. "If we have time this afternoon we'll go to the Plaza Mayor and you can walk around a bit."

"That's where the Spanish Inquisition started," Poly said, "and bullfights, and all kinds of icky stuff. It always gives me the shivers. Do we have to go there, Father?"

"Don't you think Adam ought to see it?"

"Oh, I suppose so. But I always seem to hear screams still quivering in the air. And smell blood." She looked defiantly at Adam. "I am *not* morbid."

"It's all right," Adam assured her. "I think that places hold atmospheres, too."

"You're nice," Poly said. "I shan't mind flying to Lisbon with you after all. At least Father said that that's what I'd be doing if it's all right with you."

"It's fine with me," Adam said. She was a queer kid and he couldn't very well hurt her feelings. Something in the tone of his voice, though, seemed to make her dubious, so he added, "Now I won't have to worry about recognizing your father."

Poly laughed, a warm, deep chuckle. "I look *exactly* like daddy. Stringbean aspect and all. Some of daddy's assistants have called him a long drink of water. That's me."

"The red hair and blue eyes, too," Canon Tallis said, "and with a little bit of luck the looks of your mother and maternal grandmother."

"Oh, I don't really care about being beautiful," Poly stated. "At least not yet."

As they neared the Prado, which was a longer drive than Adam had anticipated, Canon Tallis explained that although the museum was now in the city of Madrid, it was not too very long ago that it had been out in the country in the middle of fields.

It was not at all what Adam had expected of one of the most famous museums in Europe. Not only was it utterly unlike the Guggenheim or even the Frick, which was only natural, it also bore no resemblance whatsoever to the Metropolitan, either in the building itself, or in the display of pictures. He was amazed to find it an enormous, dirty, badly lighted place, the light even worse than usual now because of skies dark with rain. In room after room there was a great jumble of masterpieces, El Grecos, Murillos (many of these looking like cheap religious Christmas cards), Velásquezes, Goyas, Raphaels, lesser known painters, unknown painters, early work, middle work, later work, good painting, middling painting, bad painting, finished and unfinished painting, all thrown at the wanderer in one great saturating splash. Canon Tallis was obviously familiar with every inch of the place, separating, sorting, explaining, ostensibly to Poly, but also for Adam.

Poly stood in a roomful of El Grecos and turned round and round, slowly. Then she stopped in front of a large painting of St. Andrew and St. Francis, the two of them standing together in obvious and direct communion. "I'm staggered," she said, "absolutely staggered, Father. Why haven't I seen it before?" She contemplated the picture again for a time in silence, assuming a junior version of Canon Tallis' stance, her legs braced slightly apart, her hands behind her back. "Of course it's impossible," she said.

"What?" Adam asked.

"That they should be there, like that, standing, talking together when they lived eleven hundred years apart. But I'm so glad they are. It does make time seem unimportant, doesn't it?" She turned to Canon Tallis and smiled. "I'm sorry I was horrid about not going to Geneva with you. But we'll do it another time, won't we?"

"Yes," he said gently. "Yes, we'll do that, Poly."

Just as Adam felt super-saturated, they paused for lunch in the museum cafeteria. This, at least, Adam found not unlike the cafeterias in the Met or the Museum of Natural History, except that it was much smaller, and most people automatically ordered a bottle of wine with lunch.

Here, for some reason, the canon and Poly switched into Spanish, so Adam joined them. Poly smiled at him warmly, "Oh, good, I'm so glad you aren't one of these Americans who refuses to speak anybody else's language. You speak awfully well."

"Thank you."

"Adam, do have a hamburger. Spanish hamburgers are the funniest things. The meat even is different. People who want some good Amurrican food order them and then go into a state of shock. Then they say it's bad meat cooked in rancid oil." She grinned at the canon and slapped her own hand lightly. "I'm being judgmental again, aren't I? I'm sorry. But do try one, Adam. I find them absolutely *cordon bleu*."

The hamburger was indeed unlike an American hamburger; Poly's milkshake, too, bore little resemblance to anything Adam had had at home. He and the canon had coffee; without it Adam by now could not have stayed awake, and fatigue multiplied the already existing confusion in his mind. Poly, like the hamburger and the milkshake, was unlike any American child Adam had ever met, but she had evidently spent most of her life abroad. It was obvious that she adored Canon Tallis, and he, in his turn, seemed to love her deeply, but Adam was still very unsure of the canon. After all, a man in ecclesiastical garb could get away with murder—well, perhaps not murder, exactly—a lot more easily than anybody else.

After lunch they wandered around the museum for a while longer. Adam's legs were beginning to ache with fatigue. He now felt only irritation at some of the pictures which were so badly hung that they could hardly be seen for the glare; at others Adam found he was squinting, one eye closed, his nose almost touching the canvas. In many of the rooms were smocked art students copying paintings. The canon stopped by a young girl who was copying a baroque Annunciation. She turned around and smiled at him, brilliantly and warmly, in recognition. He pressed one hand briefly against her shoulder, but neither of them spoke, nor did he seem to consider introducing her to Adam or Poly. They moved on into a large rotunda full of statues watched over by a uniformed guard. As Adam and Poly followed the canon in, the guard moved over to them quietly, saying in English,

"*My avocation and my vocation—*"

"*—As my two eyes make one in sight,*" the canon replied. The exchange was so swift, the voices were so low, that no one but Adam, and perhaps Poly, was aware that anything had been said.

Adam's retentive memory, the envy of his friends at school, came to his rescue now. For a moment he seemed to be back in the secret police room in the airport with the grim-faced canon speaking to the inspector.

—They rhyme! Adam thought suddenly. —What he said with the inspector then, and with the guard now. I don't remember the words, but I'm sure if I could get them and put them together and make four lines of them, they'd rhyme. An ABAB rhyme scheme.

He looked at the canon. The canon looked at him. Neither of them spoke.

—It's familiar, Adam thought. —It's vaguely familiar. Maybe

something I had at school. If I could only figure out what it was I'd know more what I think about him.

The canon pulled out a very plain gold watch with a Phi Beta Kappa key on the chain. Something clicked in Adam's mind. —But he's English. He shouldn't have a Phi Beta Kappa key. Not unless he went to an American university as an undergraduate. Not likely. So then he *must* be a phony, the way Kali said. Unless—well, it *could* be honorary, like Churchill's. I don't know.

His eyes flickered back over the canon. For the first time Adam noticed that the plain black of the priest's clothing was broken by the tiny red sliver of the French Légion d'Honneur ribbon in his lapel. This was possible. Old Doc had one, too.

"Time to go," Canon Tallis said briskly.

Perhaps because of Poly's words Adam was not too happy with the Plaza Mayor. Then again it may have been simply the rain which dripped down the collar of his trenchcoat, though Canon Tallis tried to shield the three of them with his big black umbrella as they walked slowly about. The Plaza Mayor was a great, beautiful square, cobblestoned, with magnificent buildings, horses sadly pulling wagons, arches leading to narrow, winding streets with shops and restaurants and laundry hanging out even in the downpour: perhaps it was the sullen stream of rain which was responsible for the dark aura that Adam felt as he looked across the vast, echoing space of the square.

It was almost five when they got back to the hotel, and Adam went up to his room to collect his things. When he opened his briefcase, which he had not taken to the Prado, he was quite sure that someone had gone through it while he was out, that his books were not as he had left them. His first thought was to rush to Canon Tallis with this disturbing news. Then he realized, with a sudden jerk of the stomach, that the trip to the Prado might have been engineered by the canon simply to get him out of the room.

Adam went through the briefcase again, carefully. Nothing had been taken, but he was quite certain that its contents had been examined and then replaced as accurately as possible.

—When I get to Lisbon, he thought, —I'll make some excuse at least to telephone Kali. If I see her again now maybe I'll be able to sort things out.

Downstairs the Swissair man and almost all the other passengers were already assembled. Those who had been going on to Geneva and Zurich, with the exception of Canon Tallis and Poly, had left, so it was a smaller group gathered together in the lobby. The perpetually pleasant Swissair man told them that the bus was waiting, that they would be taken to the airport and flown to Lisbon, and would be there in time for dinner.

Since the canon was staying in Madrid instead of going on to Geneva, as originally planned, or even to Lisbon, there seemed to be some question about his being allowed to go in the bus with them to the airport. Adam felt like saying that he could take care of Poly perfectly well by himself, but at this point he thought it wiser not to cross the older man who was talking in a quiet but most determined way to the Swissair man, who finally smiled and nodded, shook hands with the canon, and then ushered the passengers out into the rain and onto the bus.

At the airport the Swissair man, still smiling, but beginning to look tired and harassed from all the questions being thrust at him, took them into the dining room where he told them to order refreshments, compliments of Swissair. Adam sat at a large, round table with Poly and Canon Tallis and five other passengers, so that conversation was perforce general, and mostly about the weather. Bits of gossip flitted from table to table as the Swissair man would appear, speak to one group, then hurry off: the airport in Lisbon was still closed; the airport in Lisbon was open; the airport in Lisbon was open but might close at any moment; the airport in Lisbon was closed but might open at any moment. Strangely enough the downpour in Madrid never seemed to be any concern.

After a little over an hour had gone by the Swissair man came hurrying in and told the entire group, in a voice now slightly hoarse, that they would be served dinner since the airport in Lisbon was definitely still closed down.

There was a small, smug, middle-aged couple at Adam's table who decided that they would like to stay on in Madrid and were furious when the Swissair man wouldn't pay for their hotel or passage to Lisbon unless they traveled with the rest of the group. Adam was embarrassed by their rudeness, and ashamed that they were American. Poly leaned sleepily against Canon Tallis who sipped at a small glass of Tio Pépé.

The Swissair man disappeared again and the table was quickly set and a full dinner served, soup, omelette, chicken, fruit, cheese. Adam discovered that he was starved. They were finishing their coffee when the Swissair man appeared again, beaming like the Cheshire cat. A Spanish plane would take them to Lisbon where the airport was at last open. He hurried off; in a few minutes the plane was called and everyone trooped to the gate where they were completely unexpected. Canon Tallis was trying to sort out the situation with the Iberian Airlines official when the Swissair man came panting up. Wait! A plane was being flown in from Geneva for them.

It was well after ten when they were finally herded through the gate. Canon Tallis stood watching after Poly and Adam as they paddled out into the rain and onto the bus, stood watching until the bus was driven off. This time it was more than a few yards to the plane. The bus began to gather speed and although the rain was letting up and the atmosphere was lighter it was not long before the dark figure of the canon had disappeared.

Poly turned anxiously to Adam. "You *will* stay right with me, won't you?"

"Yes, if you want me to. Why? Are you nervous?" Adam asked, hoping to get some information out of her.

Poly contemplated him as the bus jolted along over the wet ground. Finally she said calmly, "I have never traveled alone before, and, after all, I am still a child."

Adam felt like crying, —Okay, child, why are *you* holding out on me, too?

But if he ever wanted to get anything out of Poly it would not do to antagonize her now. Granted she was an odd kid, but she was obviously a bright one, and he liked her, and he knew that she liked him, despite the deliberate evasiveness of her last answer. Sooner or later she would talk to him, as long as he didn't push her. Most people did seem to talk to Adam, which may have been one reason he wasn't more surprised at Kali's confidences or at anything else that had happened.

Giving him a wary look Poly put her hand in his as they left the bus, and held it firmly until they were safely in the plane. "A caravelle," Poly said. "You don't mind if I sit next to the window, with you on the aisle, do you, Adam? It's just because I like to look out."

"Is that the only reason?" he asked her, stowing her small blue case and his briefcase under their seats.

"Isn't it reason enough?" she asked as he sat down beside her.

It was to be a short flight, they were told, about forty-five minutes. After they had been in the air less than half an hour Poly said, "I have to go to the washroom, Adam."

He moved his knees to let her go by. At the aisle she stopped, started to say something, walked on for a couple of rows, then came back. "Watch after me, Adam, please," she said tensely, then hurried up the aisle and disappeared into the washroom.

Adam had looked over the passengers and a more normal lot, he felt, could not have been found. The original group was all American, vocal, and eager to be on the way. Only a handful of new passengers had been added, and none of these looked in the least sinister or even curious. The only figure who was even faintly colorful was a rabbi with a long, luxuriant growth of brown beard. He had a look of quiet dignity, and sat, isolated in contemplation, until he turned to a book which Adam could see, by straining, was something by Martin Buber.

Poly's small voice as she had turned back toward him made him a little tense, but after all she was only a kid, and a girl, and girls are apt to be hysterical, and that doggoned canon had evidently frightened her about something. He shook himself and settled back to read an article on starfish which Old Doc had stuck into his hand that last day in Woods Hole. Adam could usually concentrate but his eyes now kept flicking to the face of his wristwatch. After Poly had been gone a couple of minutes he began to look back toward the washroom door every few seconds. After the hands showed that five minutes had passed he put the starfish article aside and did nothing but look at the washroom. After another minute he felt a distinct queasiness in the pit of his stomach, and went to the back of the plane.

The steward looked at him, saying courteously, "The other washroom is empty, sir."

"Yes," Adam said. "I'm traveling with a little girl and she's been in there several minutes and I'm afraid she may not be well."

The steward tapped lightly on the door. Nothing happened. Adam knocked, rather more loudly. "Poly!" he called.

Nothing.

"Not so loud, please, sir," the steward said. "We don't want to disturb the other passengers. Just a minute and I will unlock the door from this side."

He took out a key and after a certain amount of manipulation the door swung open.

The washroom was empty.

5

"YOU must have been mistaken, sir," the steward said.
"I saw her go in."

"Then she must have left without your noticing it."

Wildly Adam looked round the plane, but his hope of seeing Poly safely in her seat vanished. "Find her for me, then," he said, angrily.

"What does she look like?"

"A tall, thin child, about twelve. Red hair and blue eyes."

The steward went methodically up and down the aisles, even looking into the pilot's cabin. When he came back to Adam he spoke soothingly. "Are you absolutely certain, sir, that any such child came onto the plane?"

"Get the stewardess to check the records," Adam suggested.

The steward summoned the stewardess, speaking in Spanish. "This young idiot," he said, "seems to think he brought some kid on the plane with him, and now he's lost her. He has a wild idea she's been flushed down the toilet or something. Just another American crackpot. But check your records." Turning to Adam he said, in English, "Her name, please."

"Polyhymnia O'Keefe."

Adam stood, seething, until the stewardess looked up from her papers. "No O'Keefe got on the plane."

Adam burst into Spanish. He had learned a good deal of picturesque language from Juan and his family and he let it all out now. Up and down the cabin passengers roused from snoozing and turned their heads in curiosity.

Adam thought he saw the steward press some kind of signal. In any case the FASTEN SEAT BELTS light flashed on and the stewardess moved briskly through the cabin, seeing that the passengers, many of whom had risen at Adam's flow of invective, were seated and their seat belts snapped on.

The steward turned to Adam. "We are going through some turbulence, sir," he said, though this time in Spanish, seeming not at all abashed that Adam must have understood his words to the stewardess. "You will have to go to your seat."

Adam did not move. "*I'm* going through turbulence all right. I was put in charge of the child and I am responsible for her. I saw her go into the washroom."

"Sir." The steward sighed in resignation at Adam's idiocy. "No child came onto the plane with you. You saw us check the passenger list. I must insist that you sit down, and in Lisbon— are you being met, sir?"

"Yes," Adam snapped.

"Then perhaps you should see a doctor." The steward's hands shot out with unexpected suddenness and strength, grasped Adam's arms, and forcibly propelled him down the aisle. He was put into his seat with a quick shove, and the belt tightened around him.

The loudspeaker coughed. "This is your captain. We are now beginning the descent to Lisbon."

The stewardess walked up and down the aisle, adjusting a pillow here, asking a passenger to put out a cigarette there. The steward stood lounging by Adam's seat.

"Listen," Adam said, "if you don't believe me, the blue case under the seat belongs to Poly. How did it get there if she didn't come onto the plane?"

The steward spoke gently. "There is no blue case under the seat."

Adam looked down. His briefcase was there, but not Poly's little blue bag. "Hey!" he called wildly, looking up and down the plane. "I *did* get on with a redheaded kid, didn't I?"

The steward's hand pressed against the boy's mouth as he explained apologetically to the passengers that Adam wasn't well, that a doctor would be found as soon as they had landed in Lisbon, that there was no cause for alarm. No one need worry. Over the steward's hand Adam looked frantically at the passengers, but nobody said anything or moved to rescue him. He heard one woman say, "I thought I saw a child, but maybe it was at the hotel with that priest. I'm so tired I just don't remember which way is up."

The steward removed his hand. If Adam had thought it

would do any good he would have started a physical battle with the man. But that course would, at this point, seem to lead into worse trouble than already surrounded him.

"If you will stay quietly where you are until we land," the steward said, "everything will be all right." He walked back the length of the plane to his post.

Again Adam looked up and down the cabin, though he did not move in his seat or turn his head more than necessary. Surely they must have heard him; surely someone must have noticed Poly and would come to tell him so.

The rabbi was sitting with his hands in his lap, his book evidently put away in his briefcase. His head was back against the seat rest and he appeared to be contemplating the ceiling. To Adam's surprise he began to whistle thoughtfully.

Adam almost jumped out of his seat.

It was the melody Canon Tallis had whistled for Poly at the Hotel Plaza.

He kept his eyes fixed on the rabbi, but the rabbi continued to look upward. Although Adam still could not place the melody it was familiar enough to him (had he sung it in school? in choir? was it something his parents knew?) so that he in his turn could whistle a measure. The rabbi stopped. His eyes moved slowly from the ceiling. He turned, looked at Adam, nodded almost imperceptibly, then turned away and studied the ceiling again.

Adam was too upset and confused to look out the window as the plane descended toward Lisbon. He kept looking up and down the cabin, with his gaze coming to pause again and again on the rabbi. But the rabbi did not move. Adam felt, after a while, that he should not stare, that he should not let the other passengers, and certainly not the steward, know that he had had any kind of communication with anybody in the plane since Poly's disappearance.

He was startled to feel the touch of wheels upon runway, to know that they were earthbound again. The loudspeaker buzzed and the passengers were told the disembarking procedure. It would all be very simple. Except, of course, for Adam.

The FASTEN SEAT BELTS sign blinked out, though the NO

SMOKING sign remained lit. The passengers rose and took coats and bags and began moving to the door. Adam pushed forward as quickly as he could, almost knocking into the rabbi who was just ahead of him. As they waited to get out Adam touched the dark sleeve gently and the rabbi moved his head just enough to let Adam know that he was listening.

"I *did* have the child with me, didn't I?"

The rabbi gave an almost imperceptible nod.

At this quiet confirmation Adam was again able to think coherently. By the time he reached the exit he knew what he was going to say and do. He spoke to the steward with cold control. "I will have to report this to the authorities. I have taken your name and that of the stewardess."

The steward shrugged indifferently. "As you like, sir. You will be yourself again soon, I am sure."

The stewardess simply smiled blandly at him as she had at the other passengers, saying, as though there had been no trouble, "I hope you enjoyed your trip."

Adam brushed by her and down the steps after the rabbi.

At the passport counter, despite, or perhaps because of his hurry, Adam found a number of passengers ahead of him; he was in the middle of the line. He looked ahead and saw the rabbi collecting his passport and disappearing. Adam was shocked and disappointed at this complete abandonment. For a moment he had felt that the situation was under control, that everything would be all right as soon as the proper authorities were spoken to. Now he felt blind panic.

The line here in Lisbon moved more slowly than it had in Madrid. When Adam's turn came he handed his passport across the counter saying, "I want to report a missing child. I got onto the plane with a twelve-year-old girl and she went to the washroom and never came out."

The official looked at him incredulously. "But sir, that is impossible."

"Yes," Adam said. "Nevertheless it happened."

"Why didn't you speak immediately to the steward or the stewardess?"

"I did. They were not very helpful."

"Oh, but sir, the personnel is always—"

Adam interrupted. "They said the child had not come on to the plane with me."

The official relaxed. "Well, then, sir—"

"But she *did* get on the plane with me. If you will get in touch with Canon Tallis in Madrid—"

"Yes?" the official asked helpfully. "His address, please? Or perhaps you know his phone number?"

Adam realized that he had no way of knowing where in that enormous city the canon might be. He thought quickly, then said, "I don't know where he is staying, but if you call the English church they would be able to tell you there."

"Sir," the official said, shaking his head sadly, "I'm afraid I cannot possibly help you. I will see that you are conducted to my superior, and you can tell your story to him." He summoned a young boy in a page's uniform, and spoke to him in rapid Portuguese. Adam had hoped that Spanish and Portuguese would be close enough so that he would be able to understand, but they were not.

The page said, "Kindly follow me, sir." Adam started to move away from the window when a voice said, "Don't forget your passport."

Startled, and furious with himself for having almost done exactly that, Adam wheeled around and there was the rabbi, together with a tall, blue-eyed, redheaded man. The resemblance to Poly was plain; it could be none other than Dr. O'Keefe who came up to the window and spoke in slow, clear English. "Mr. Eddington's passport, please. He has had an unfortunate experience and is a little—upset. I will take care of everything."

Adam started to turn on Dr. O'Keefe in indignation, but something in the older man's expression stopped him. The official at the window handed Adam the passport, saying, "Certainly, and my sincere thanks, Dr. O'Keefe."

Adam found himself hustled out of the airport and into a waiting taxi. As the door was slammed and the taxi pulled off he realized that he was alone with Dr. O'Keefe; the rabbi had again disappeared. "But Poly—" he started.

"Not now," Dr. O'Keefe said. Adam looked at him and

could see that the older man's face was white with strain. His complete quiet and control was costing him an enormous effort. After a moment, as though to break the silence, he said, "We managed to get your bags. Fortunately you had them well labeled. They're in the trunk of the taxi."

"Where are we going?" Adam asked.

"The Hotel Avenida Palace. We will have to stay there until—"

"Sir," Adam started, "sir . . ." and then stopped because he found that he could not go on.

Dr. O'Keefe said quietly, "You are not to blame yourself for this in any way. It was nothing you could have prevented. We thought getting Poly away would be the best thing. But—" again he broke off.

Adam saw little of Lisbon as they drove in, though, in order to gather himself together, he turned his face toward the window as though he were looking out. Lisbon was, even to his confused eyes, completely different from Madrid. Madrid was a cold city, Lisbon a warm one, full of buildings painted sun yellow, deep blue. There were squares with fountains, statues, gardens, a sense of space and color everywhere.

The Avenida Palace was an old hotel, a beautiful building which at any other time would have delighted Adam; but he was now so tired with the events of the past hours as well as with lack of sleep that he followed Dr. O'Keefe like a small child. A porter took his bags out of the taxi's trunk, and Adam went with Dr. O'Keefe into the hotel.

"Your passport, please, Adam," Dr. O'Keefe said, and registered for him. The passport, as in Madrid, was retained, but Dr. O'Keefe explained that this was routine procedure, and, unless there were trouble with the police they would get it back shortly.

They were taken to a great square corner room with four shuttered and curtained windows. There were twin beds, an octagonal table with easy chairs, a desk, a crystal chandelier. The bathroom was large and all of marble.

"We look out on the Place dos Restauradores and the Rue Jardim do Regedor," Dr. O'Keefe told Adam as the page put down the suitcases. "There's a rather interesting view of the Fort up on the crest of the hill." He gestured to one of the curtained windows, but made no move to pull back the draperies. He locked the door carefully, checked the cupboards.

"Poly—" Adam started desperately.

Although Dr. O'Keefe's rigid control had not lessened, he dropped, now that he and Adam were alone, the public manner, answering with the one word, "Kidnapped."

"But—"

"But why? Old Doc may have told you something of my research."

"Just that it was interesting, and—unusual."

"I've stumbled onto something. Something that *is* unusual, desirable to many people, and important. It was wise of Old Doc not to tell you anything about it. What you don't know, you can tell no one. Therefore, if you will forgive me, I will not tell you yet. But Poly knows too much for her own good. Therefore, Adam, I will have to ask you to stay here in this room until I return. Are you hungry?"

"No, sir."

"But tired, I imagine."

"Yes."

"Then this will be a good opportunity for you to sleep. You should answer the telephone if it rings. But under no circumstances open the door, and when I go please double-lock it from the inside. The best thing you can possibly do now is to catch up on your sleep. When I find Poly and we get to Gaea I will be able to explain things more fully to you."

Adam said, "But, sir, what are you going to do?"

"There are only certain things I *can* do. First I'll go to Interpol—the International Police. But there is only so much, at this point, that *they* can do. Then the Embassy. Then to a man I know and trust in the police here. But for Poly's sake nothing must be done wildly or without thought. Don't be worried if I'm not back immediately."

Adam nodded numbly, taking courage from the fact that there was not a hint of a suggestion that Poly might *not* be found.

When the older man had left he undressed and took a long, hot bath, followed by a shower, as though to wash off the evil aura of the steward and stewardess who had tried to make him believe that Poly didn't exist. He put on his pajamas, turned down one of the twin beds, and got in. The telephone, a rather old-fashioned instrument, stood, silent, on the table between the beds. Adam looked at it, felt his eyelids sag. He had thought, while bathing, that he was much too upset to be able to sleep, but the moment his head touched the pillow his exhausted body took over and he blanked out.

He did not know how long he had been lost in sleep, sleep so deep that it was dreamless, when he became aware at the edges of his consciousness of a soft but persistent tapping on the door. He had no idea where he was, his sleep-drugged body feeling that he was back in Woods Hole and that his mother was trying to rouse him to get him to Old Doc's on time. "All right, Mother, all *right*, I'm *up*," he mumbled irritably.

The tapping continued.

Finally it penetrated into Adam's mind enough so that he knew that he must drag himself out of his stupor and do something about it. He pulled open his eyes to absolute darkness. His room at Woods Hole, many-windowed and curtainless, had always been full of light. He could not be there. Where was he? Slowly his tired mind began dredging up the events of the hours since he had first gone into the airport in New York, though it was several moments before he was able to waken sufficiently to remember that he was in Lisbon, in a hotel called the Avenida Palace, that the windows were heavily shuttered and curtained, and that this accounted for the sultry darkness. He fumbled around until he found the bedlamp and turned it on, a bulb of wattage that would be thoroughly inadequate for reading but did suffice to show him the face of his watch. It was almost four o'clock. In the morning or in the afternoon? He looked across to the other twin bed and it was empty. In this closed-in room there was no telling the hour of day or night.

The tapping on the door persisted, never getting louder, just going on and on, like a branch in a light breeze knocking constantly against a window.

It should have made him afraid. Alone in this dark, timeless place with someone—who?—softly trying to penetrate his consciousness and then his room, he should have been weak with terror. But he was too tired to feel anything but regret for his lost sleep.

"Wait!" he called, shoving back the sheet, getting out of bed, crossing to the nearest window, dragging back heavy folds of curtain, opening creaking white shutters. A welcome breath of cool, damp air came in. Street lamps shone waveringly onto dark, rain-wet pavement.

Four in the morning, then.

He went warily to the door, put his hand on the knob, then drew back as if the door were hot, and called softly, "Who is it?"

He half expected to hear the voice of the steward from the plane, or even Canon Tallis; but it was a girl's light voice. "Adam, it's Kali. Let me in."

Adam felt weak with relief, but just as he started to unlock the door his hand drew back again. "Just a minute." He stood there in the dimly lit room, trying to marshal his thoughts. He was still not all the way out of sleep; his mind circled and would not focus.

"Adam, what's the matter?" Kali's voice came softly, urgently.

"Just a minute," Adam said again. If he could have slept a little longer he would know better what to do. In spite of the urgency of the moment he could not control an enormous yawn. Finally a question that seemed reasonable came to him. "How did you know I was here?"

"O'Keefe always stays at the Avenida Palace. Adam, let me in. I have to talk to you. We have work to do."

"Just a minute," Adam said for the third time. He went into the bathroom and splashed cold water on his face, over and over again, until his thoughts began to clear.

If Kali was right, then Canon Tallis was wrong.

This was the primary fact he had to work with.

It was not difficult for him to believe that Canon Tallis was wrong. But if Canon Tallis was wrong, then so was Dr. O'Keefe. This, too, was perfectly possible to believe. Hadn't

Dr. O'Keefe acted in a rather strange way at the Lisbon airport? Wasn't this whole setup at the Avenida Palace peculiar? But then: if Canon Tallis and Dr. O'Keefe were wrong, then so was Polyhymnia, and right or wrong, Adam was responsible for Polyhymnia.

He went back to the door. "Kali."

"I'm *waiting*, Adam."

"Why are you here, and at such an hour? It's the middle of the night."

"I'm here because of *you*, of course. And I had to come while O'Keefe was out."

"How did you know he was out?"

"I was at a party at the Embassy with daddy, and he came in."

"To the *party*?" Adam's voice soared and cracked as though he were an eighth grader again. If Dr. O'Keefe, with Poly vanished, could go to parties, then there was no doubt on whose side Adam had to align himself.

But Kali said, "To *see* someone, silly. I don't suppose he'd even been invited to the party. Adam, I can't help you if you keep me out here in the hall. Someone's bound to come along."

"How are you planning to help me?" Adam asked.

"Don't you want to find the redheaded kid?"

"Why should I need to find her?"

"Because you know as well as I do that she's been kidnapped. Adam, I'm not going to stand out here any longer. Either you open the door and let me in, or I go and you can just get out of this mess on your own."

You should answer the telephone if it rings, Dr. O'Keefe had said. *But under no circumstances open the door.*

"Wait," Adam said sharply to Kali. Never had his mind functioned at such a snail's pace. He usually made decisions quickly; sometimes too quickly. At school he had been president of Student Council and often decisions had been forced on him, and occasionally decisions that seemed on first sight to go counter to the rules.

'Rules are made for people, not people for rules,' he had once said in defending one of his actions. 'If you accept any position of authority you have to know when to break or circumvent a rule. It's the knowing *when* that's important.'

But now he was in no position of authority.

No. But one of responsibility. He was still responsible for Poly. She had been in his care when she disappeared.

He pounded one fist into the palm of his other hand. Then he unlocked the door.

6

KALI came in. She was dressed for evening, and Adam drew in his breath sharply because he had forgotten how beautiful she was. Her shimmering hair was drawn softly back with a filigreed gold tiara. Her dress, of a material that Adam, being a boy, could not place, was the color of champagne. Her feet were in gold sandals. She gave him a scowl which managed not to wrinkle her brow. "And about time, too," she said, going over to the octagonal table and sitting in one of the easy chairs. "Now tell me everything."

Adam sat on the side of his rumpled bed. "You seem to know everything already."

Kali sighed with resignation. "I know your plane was rerouted to Madrid. I know you didn't get to Lisbon till tonight. I saw O'Keefe come in to the Embassy and go off with the Ambassador. I happened to walk by the door of the library, looking for the ladies' room, when O'Keefe mentioned his child. That was a lucky break, hearing that; it gave me some idea of what we're up against and how I can help you. Get dressed and I'll take you to daddy."

"To help me find Polyhymnia?"

"Of course."

"But why me? Why didn't you go right to Dr. O'Keefe?"

Kali sighed again. "Adam, you are really very slow. It's in O'Keefe's own interest that the child be gone. Don't you see he's in on the whole thing? What we have to do is get her to daddy. Then he'll take care of everything."

"Okay, I'm slow," Adam said, "but even on not enough sleep that's logic nohow contrariwise. Why under the sun would Dr. O'Keefe be in on the kidnapping of his own daughter?"

Kali got up and went to the one uncurtained, unshuttered window, and stood looking out. "Adam, my sweet, you aren't in your little backwash of a Woods Hole now, or your ivory tower of school. This is Lisbon. Lisbon."

"Yes," Adam said. "I'd figured it might be."

"Has it never occurred to you that we do *not* live in one world? That there are certain nations interested in the private businesses of certain other nations? If this primary fact has never occurred to you, living in New York—and for heaven's sake, kid, haven't you ever even taken a tour through the UN?—it can hardly escape you in any of the capitals of Europe. Don't you know we're in a war, Adam? Aren't you aware of it?"

Adam had taken College Boards in Modern European History. But that was history.

Kali continued: "Of course his going to the Embassy was a front, and a rather clever one, I must admit that. But never make the mistake of thinking O'Keefe's a fool. He isn't. What he wants to do is keep the child out of the way until. . . . And he's ruthless, Adam. If something happens to her then something happens to her. When I think of daddy and me— Well, O'Keefe gives me the shudders. Now come on, Adam. Get dressed and let's go. I hope I have made myself clear."

"As mud," Adam said. "But I'll get dressed. Let me take a quick shower. It'll help me wake up a bit." It seemed he had been doing nothing but take showers to wake up since the bus had taken him to the Plaza Hotel in Madrid.

When Adam and Kali emerged onto the sidewalk dawn was beginning to lighten the sky; the dim street lamps became even dimmer. The rain had stopped but the air was wet and heavy. A dark limousine was waiting in the courtyard of the hotel and Kali walked quickly toward it. A uniformed chauffeur climbed out and opened the door for them.

"Take us home, Molèc, please," Kali said. She sat back in the upholstered seat as though she were very tired. "I don't know why I'm taking so much trouble about you, Adam, I really don't."

"Well, why are you, then?" Adam demanded.

"Not for your own sake, I assure you. At least not to start out with, I wasn't. But you're like a half-grown puppy. There's something endearing about your clumsiness. I have to admit that I *am* doing it for you, too. But that's wrong, of course."

"Wrong?"

"Adam, we simply *cannot* let people matter to us or we won't get anywhere. Letting people matter is nothing but sentimentality."

—Then I have become rather quickly sentimental about Polyhymnia, Adam thought. —Only there's something wrong here. 'Sentimental' is not the right word. If only I could have slept a few hours longer.

He tried unsuccessfully to stifle a yawn.

Kali put a hand on his arm. "I'm sorry I had to wake you up. But you do see, don't you, how desperately urgent it is?"

Yes, he saw, though there was something wrong with this, too.

The limousine drove a narrow and winding way. Some streets were barely wide enough for the car. Others were as steep as San Francisco. They went under arches, into streets wide enough for buses, under more arches into alleys, finally drawing up before a whitewashed wall. The chauffeur, Molèc, got out and opened the door, and Adam climbed out after Kali. She opened a gate in the wall and went down a steep flight of steps to a pale pink house with a deeper pink door which she unlocked. As she shut the door behind them she held her finger to her lips and took Adam down a softly carpeted hall.

The room into which she led him was already beginning to fill with light which flooded in from a great sweep of windows overlooking the harbor and the dawn. The view was so enormous that at first Adam did not notice the room itself, a room striking in stark blacks and whites. The long wall of windows was curtainless, but the opposite wall was hung with black velvet. Against the background of velvet was only one thing, a picture, an unframed portrait (for the great sweep of velvet was the frame) of the most handsome young man Adam had ever seen. It was a young man with the bearing of an angel, hair the same pale gold as Kali's, heavily fringed eyes, the mouth slightly opened as though in eagerness to meet life.

"Adam," Kali said, and he turned from the portrait to follow her across the black marble floor.

Silhouetted against the dawn was the dark figure of a man

who stood, motionless, staring out across the bay, a man big in both height and bulk.

"Daddy," Kali said, and the man turned around.

Because he stood between Adam and the light he was still only a silhouette as he stretched out his hand in greeting. "Adam, you're safely here." He took the boy's hand in a grip of steel. His voice was high, and light for the bulk of his body, but it, too, had the quality of steel, the steel of a spool of fine wire. He dropped Adam's hand and crossed to a desk made of a great slab of black-and-white marble, and sat in a black leather chair, leaning back so that at last the light struck his face. It was a powerful face: there were pouches of fatigue under the dark eyes, and the thin lips were closed in tight control. He impatiently pushed back a strand of thinning, pale gold hair. Involuntarily Adam glanced at the portrait.

"That's daddy," Kali said, with pride. "Wasn't he beautiful?"

The man laughed. "Yes. Nothing of Dorian Gray about Typhon Cutter, is there, Adam? I am marked by the inroads of time. Time and experience. And this is something you lack, is it not?"

"I'm getting it," Adam said, warily.

"And learning from it?"

"I hope so."

Typhon Cutter looked thoughtfully at the portrait. "The years make their marks on ordinary, hardworking mortals, and I can assure you that my work is hard. And now you have become part of it." He looked from the portrait to Adam, and Adam looked back, saying nothing, swaying slightly with fatigue.

Typhon Cutter picked up a black marble paperweight and appeared to study it. He crossed his legs, and as he did this Adam realized that although the great body was ponderous with weight, the arms and legs were thin and bony, but again giving the effect of steel. Typhon Cutter, sitting at his desk in a black satin dressing gown, was one of the most extraordinary men Adam had ever seen.

"Tired?" Cutter asked in his surprising tenor voice.

"Yes, sir. I haven't had much sleep."

Typhon Cutter motioned to a stiff ebony chair on the opposite side of the desk. "You may sit there as long as you stay awake. I'm sorry not to be able to let you sleep, but there's no time now for anything but business. And we *do* have business, you and I."

In a daze of fatigue Adam staggered to the chair. Typhon Cutter leaned across the desk and snapped his fingers in the boy's face. "Wake up."

"I'm sorry," Adam mumbled.

"Kali, see about coffee."

"Yes, daddy." In quick and loving obedience Kali slipped from the room.

"Now, Adam."

"Sir?"

"How much has Kali told you?"

"That you'll help me to find Poly—Dr. O'Keefe's daughter."

Typhon Cutter nodded, for a moment speaking almost absently. "Yes. We'll cope with that." Then, sharply, "Wake up. What else?"

"About what, sir?"

"How much has Kali told you? Perhaps you may have thought that she seemed a little wild, or even a little hysterical, but she never does so without cause."

"I didn't think she seemed hysterical, sir."

"Good boy. I assume she warned you about Tallis and O'Keefe?"

"Yes, sir."

"Did you take her warning seriously?"

"Mr. Cutter, I'm too confused to know what to think. I'm too tired."

Again the fingers were snapped in Adam's face. "Wake up. Why did you come with Kali now, then?"

"Because I have to find Polyhymn——"

"Yes. All right, Adam, try to stay awake while we get down to business. You are to be working as laboratory assistant to O'Keefe this summer."

"Yes, sir."

"O'Keefe is a great scientist. In that respect you are very privileged."

"Yes, sir," Adam responded automatically, knowing that each time Typhon Cutter paused he was expected to make a response to prove that he was awake, that he was listening.

"Do you know what your work will be? I mean by that, do you know the experiment O'Keefe is involved in?"

"I believe it's the regenerative process of the arm of the starfish, sir."

"Explain yourself."

"Well, if a starfish loses an arm it can simply grow one back."

"How?"

"That's the point. No one knows. I mean, the starfish is still pretty much a mystery even to the people who know most about it."

"That is true. I, for instance, know as much about the starfish as any layman, and I am the first to admit that this is not much. But I fancy you'll find that the starfish is less of an enigma to O'Keefe than to anybody else in the world."

The door opened and Kali came in followed by a white-jacketed servant bearing a silver tray which he set down on the desk. Typhon Cutter waited until the door was closed again, then picked up a silver coffeepot and poured. He handed a cup across the desk to Adam. "I don't know how you usually drink it, but this time it will have to be black. You *must* wake up."

"Sorry, sir."

"All right, Adam. Now tell me something. If O'Keefe is learning new things about the regenerative process of the arm of the starfish, why is this of such importance?"

"Well, sir, in the evolutionary scale man comes pretty directly from the starfish."

"Go on."

"Well, man is a member of phylum Chordata, and we developed directly from the phylum Echinodermata, or the starfish. We both had an interior spinal column and the same kind of body cavities."

Typhon Cutter pressed his thin, strong fingertips together,

nodding in satisfaction. "Good. Good. Of course one goes on the assumption that if O'Keefe is willing to employ you, you must have a certain amount of intelligence. Let us proceed to the next step. What is the implication of O'Keefe's experiments?"

"Well, sir, that anything he finds out about starfish might also apply to people."

Kali perched on the arm of her father's chair. "Why? Just because we have the same great great great grandpappy? I should think you'd need more than that."

"You do," Adam told her. "We have the same kind of complex nervous system, and we're the only ones who do—echinoderms and chordates—people and starfish."

"So?" Typhon Cutter asked.

"So if someone could find out how the starfish regenerates then maybe this knowledge could be used for man. But—"

"No buts," Typhon Cutter said. "Don't try to evade what you've said. The implications are so staggering that most people will tend to turn away from them or refuse to face them. You're a bright boy, Adam, and a brave one, or you wouldn't be here in this room, now. You can be of great help to mankind if you will."

Adam's mind was gritty with fatigue, but he said, "I think I have to know how I am to help."

"A perfectly reasonable attitude. Kali has perhaps told you something about me?"

"That you have business concerns in Portugal—"

"And—" Typhon Cutter reached across the desk and poured more coffee into Adam's cup.

"That you know a great many people at the Embassy."

"There's the key, boy. My business is—business. And a very lucrative one, I might add. But it is also more than business. Just as you are in a position to be useful to me, I am in a position to be useful to the Embassy. More than that, I have been asked by Washington to assist the Embassy and to keep my eye on a group there whose loyalty is not entirely unquestioned. There is nothing I care about more than my country and I hope I am not wrong in assuming that you feel the same way."

"Well, of course, sir—" Adam started, and stopped. Abruptly. Listening.

From somewhere deep in the house he thought he heard a faint, thin wail. A child's wail.

7

Typhon Cutter held up his hand. "It's all right, Adam. She's here. We have her, safe and sound."

"But—"

"Wait." The word lashed at Adam like the flick of a whip. "You will see her in a few minutes. But there are certain things you must know first. Drink your coffee. Wake up."

The wailing continued.

"She is all right," Typhon Cutter said. "She has only had a frightening experience. She is caught in a web of events that she is too young to understand, and she is being used as a pawn. You will take her back to her father, but you will not say from where."

"But—"

"Be quiet. Listen. I have told you that O'Keefe is a great scientist."

"Yes."

"But, like many other great scientists his wisdom does not extend beyond his work. You yourself know of scientists who have been spies, who have sold their country down the river."

"Well, yes, but—" Abruptly the crying stopped. "*Please*," Adam was determined this time not to be cut off. "Why is Poly here? How did you get her?"

Typhon Cutter held up his hand, speaking tolerantly. "Hold it, boy. One thing at a time."

"But how did you get her? Did you get her from the plane?"

"Not very likely, is it? Has it occurred to you that you may not be the only one interested in her safety?"

"Her father is! He must be out of his mind with worry."

"Oh?" Typhon Cutter gave a thin laugh. "I hardly think so. It was her father and his inconsistencies we were talking about when you interrupted me." He paused, as though to give the boy a chance to say, 'Sorry,' but, as Adam was silent, he continued, "Let us simply say that we managed—and with no little difficulty, I might add—to rescue her."

"From whom?"

"Don't you know?"

"No, sir. I don't."

"Then you'll have to find out, won't you? I can hardly spell it out for you more clearly."

"But—"

"This is not, at the moment, the point. The point is what it means—what *all* of it means—to the United States. To do O'Keefe justice, I do not think that he would betray his country deliberately. But I have been instructed to see that he does not do it even inadvertently. I am asking you to help me."

Adam nodded, and took another swallow of coffee.

Typhon Cutter looked at him and smiled tightly. "It has come to my attention that I am sometimes compared to a spider. I do not find the comparison entirely invidious. It is my intention to spin a net and to pull it tight around anyone who does not put the interests of our country first. As for you, my boy, the moment you were chosen to work for O'Keefe you became important. You were important enough to be watched by both sides—our own, and the enemy's—from the moment you entered the airport in New York. I sent Kali as my personal emissary. I have every faith in my daughter; she has never let me down. I hope that I will be able to say the same thing about you. You *do* care for your country, don't you, Adam?"

"Of course, sir."

"Then you must do as I say." The thin cry came again, and ceased. "I have told you that O'Keefe's child is being used as a pawn. For the moment she is safe. She does not know where she is, and she is being blindfolded. This is for her own protection as well as ours. And yours. You are far more useful to us alive than dead, my boy, and I think perhaps you are not quite aware of how many people are aware of *you*, and the fact that you are going to Gaea. If you will do as I say I think that I can protect you. If not—" Typhon Cutter shrugged.

—I am half dead with sleep, Adam thought. —I don't understand anything. I don't want to understand. I want to sleep.

Typhon Cutter's high voice probed like a needle into his fatigue. "Are you going to help us, Adam?"

"I—"

"Think. Think about the child."

"I am."

"If you could not trust me, do you think I could trust you with the child?"

"But she's not your child."

"No, she's a pawn of dangerous, ruthless men. As I have said, I do not think that O'Keefe is fully cognizant of what he is doing. But there are others. Men like the egregious canon."

"Well, what about him, sir?"

"Do you think highly of someone who would deliberately send a child onto that plane?"

"But if she hadn't gone into the washroom—"

"Don't be naïve, boy. That simply made it a little easier."

Adam looked at Typhon Cutter. Yes, there was indeed the resemblance to a spider. Then he thought of Canon Tallis, the body portly but firm, the piercing grey eyes, the bald head. . . .

—But you can't go by people's looks, he thought groggily. —Just because I prefer teddy bears to spiders. . . .

"Why does Canon Tallis have no eyebrows?" he asked without thinking.

"I believe he does what he can to broadcast some story of losing all his hair after some extraordinary physical bravery in Korea; this kind of thing does happen occasionally, I believe. However, I am inclined to doubt it. Tallis, you will find, likes to take the easy way and to receive credit for daydreams. If he has done anything braver than kowtow to the bishop of Gibraltar I have yet to hear of it. Now Adam: I know that you are tired and so for the moment my instructions will be simple. You are to take Poly back to her father at the Avenida Palace. You will be driven to a central point from which you will be able to find your way to the hotel without trouble. I cannot risk taking you directly there, since my chauffeur, Molèc, who is one of my key men, would be recognized. You will tell O'Keefe that you were half asleep when you opened the door to loud knocking, that you were grabbed and blindfolded, that you were taken you know not where, and interrogated. Since you knew nothing—and what you know *is* nothing, I assure you—

there was very little you could tell. You were not in any way abused. You were put into a car, and when you were ungagged and unblindfolded you stood on the street with Polyhymnia O'Keefe. Understand?"

"Yes, sir."

"Take her immediately to the Avenida Palace. From there I presume you will proceed to Gaea. Kali or I—probably Kali—will get in touch with you there and give you further instructions. In the meantime you are to learn as much about O'Keefe and what he is doing as possible. Since you will be working with him directly on the starfish experiments this ought to be a good deal. Don't be afraid. The Embassy knows where you are. If you do as you are told you will be perfectly safe. If you do *not* do as you are told I cannot answer for the consequences."

Swaying, Adam finished the bitter dregs of his coffee. —But I have *not* done as I was told, he thought. —I opened the door. I let Kali in. And whether I did right or wrong I don't know. Whether this man is right or wrong I don't know.

His eyelids started to droop.

Typhon Cutter rose. "Take him to the car, Kali. The child is already there."

"Am I to go with them, daddy?"

"No. Molèc will take care of it. Goodbye, Adam. Remember what I have told you. We will be in touch with you soon."

"Yes, sir," Adam said. "Goodbye."

As he and Kali reached the front door she stopped and turned to him, putting one hand lightly on his arm. "Adam—" Then her arms were around him, her face tilted upward, her lips against his.

Kali was not the first girl he had kissed, but now he was no longer a schoolboy; he was a man. His arms tightened around Kali's slender body.

She turned her face away. "We have to go now, Adam." Holding his hand, she took him out of the house, and up the steps to where the limousine was waiting for them. The chauffeur murmured something to Kali, who turned to Adam, saying, "You are to sit in front with Molèc. The O'Keefe child mustn't know you're in the car until you're let out." She paused, and then whispered, "Adam, oh, Adam darling, you must *not* move or speak or in any way let her know you're in the car. Molèc will silence you if you do, and Adam, you wouldn't like it."

The chauffeur opened the front door of the car and shut it on Adam with efficient quietness, climbed in behind the wheel, looked darkly at the boy, and put his finger in warning against his lips.

Kali echoed the gesture, then turned her hand and put the tips of her fingers against her lips.

There was a grinding of gears and the car moved off.

Molèc drove swiftly, skillfully, turning, winding, so that Adam was convinced that no matter how complex the pattern of Lisbon's streets might be Molèc was deliberately making them more confusing, so that the boy would never be able to retrace his steps.

As they moved deeper into the awakening city there were more people abroad and Adam heard the hawking of lottery tickets. Molèc swerved around a cumbersome, double-decker bus, down a dark alley lightened only by high-flapping laundry. As Adam turned to make sure that Poly was truly in the back seat the side of Molèc's hand came down with a sharp thwack on his knee. The pain took him by surprise but he managed not to cry out, though tears rushed uncontrollably to his eyes and he blinked in fury, gritting his teeth. He tried to listen for any sound from behind him, but could hear nothing. He became certain that Poly was not in the car. Out of the corner of his eye he glanced at Molèc. The face under the visored chauffeur's cap was set and sullen; the hands on the steering wheel were enormous and covered with curling black hair. Perhaps Molèc was a useful person to have working for one, but he gave Adam no sense of confidence in the present situation. He had a feeling that it would not displease Molèc to bring that massive hand down in a clip on the back of his neck, that causing pain would incite rather than deter the chauffeur. Adam determined not to move or make a sound no matter what happened.

"Ritz," Molèc grunted suddenly, and pulled the car over to the curb in a quick stop. As Adam saw the great modern bulk of a luxury hotel ahead of him the chauffeur leaped from the front seat with the powerful swiftness of a Doberman Pinscher and opened the door to the back. Adam turned to see him snatching a blindfold and gag from Poly and thrusting her out of the car and onto the street, where she gave a strange, strangled moan.

"Go," Molèc said between his teeth.

Adam did not need urging. He pushed the handle of the door down and out, and, as he slammed it, Molèc shot off down the street. Adam caught Poly as she started to fall.

"Adam," she cried in a choked gasp. "Adam."

He held her firmly, disregarding the stares of people walking down the narrow mosaic sidewalk and having to step around them into the street in order to pass. "Are you all right? Poly, are you all right?"

The child gave a great, shuddering sob and managed to stand on her own feet, though Adam continued to support her with his arm. "It's all right, Poly, you're all right now," he kept saying.

Poly continued the great, choking sobbing breaths, and her hand clutched Adam's frantically, although he could see that she was making a great effort at self-control. Her set, white face was disturbingly reminiscent of her father's.

"Poly," he said, "I'll get a taxi and we'll go to the Avenida Palace."

Poly shook her head, and managed to say through shudders, "Not a taxi, it isn't safe. We're right at the Ritz. Take me in. I know the concierge."

"But your father's at the Avenida Palace."

"We can't go there alone. They might . . . Please, Adam, take me into the Ritz."

In order to calm her Adam nodded in assent and, with his arm still holding her, for he was not at all certain that she was able to walk alone, led her down the hill the short distance to the hotel.

"Good, it's Joaquim," Poly said, as they came up to the doorman. Her voice came stronger, and she said, sounding almost cheerful, what Adam recognized as "Good morning" in Portuguese. In the great lobby she turned left to the concierge's desk. Behind it sat a man reading a newspaper.

"Arcangelo!" Poly cried, her voice rising in a note of hysteria.

The man looked at her, said something in Portuguese, said "Wait," in English, and picked up his phone, breaking into Portuguese again. In a moment another uniformed man came into the concierge's booth, and Arcangelo left, without a word, to join Adam and Poly. "Upstairs," he said, and walked ahead of them to one of the elevators.

"But we shouldn't—" Adam started, as the elevator doors shut on them.

"Wait," the concierge said again.

There was no point now in telling Poly that they should be going, whether by taxi or on foot, to the Avenida Palace. There was no point in telling Poly that they might be walking into some kind of trap. There was no point in doing anything but keeping his mouth closed and seeing what happened next. Never before in Adam's life had situations constantly been taken out of his hands as they had ever since he had left the known safety of Woods Hole. Never had his personal decision seemed to mean less, his intelligence and his will shoved so to one side. Indeed the only decision he seemed to have made in this entire adventure was to open the door of the hotel room at the Avenida Palace to Kali, and whether this was the best or the worst thing he had done he still had no way of knowing.

The concierge led them down a wide hall and unlocked the door to one of the rooms, holding it open for them. Poly entered, taking Adam perforce along with her. They were in one of the most luxurious and beautiful rooms he had ever seen, but very different from the ancient grandeur of the Avenida Palace. Here everything was modern and costly; a great window wall of glass looked over the park, but the concierge quickly swept the gold brocade curtains across, then turned on the lights, which, again in contrast to the Avenida Palace, were soft but powerful.

Arcangelo shut out the light of day at the Ritz with gold brocade. In the Avenida Palace Dr. O'Keefe was barricaded with white shutters and dark green damask. Only Typhon Cutter, standing at the window that overlooked the harbor, seemed to have no fear of being seen. Or was that the entire explanation?

The beds were covered with the same rich material as the curtains; there was a chaise longue padded with pale green velvet, and pale green velvet easy chairs at the round table in a small alcove. The floor was carpeted in what seemed to Adam to be gold velvet; modern paintings hung on the walls; the telephones, one for each bed, were lemon yellow.

Poly let go his hand, flung herself at the concierge, shouting, "Arcangelo!" and burst into loud sobbing. He held her closely, not speaking, rubbing gently between her shoulder blades, kissing the top of her head, waiting until the sobs had spent themselves. At last she looked up at him, saying, "We must speak English because of Adam. Or Spanish, if you like. He's fine with Spanish."

"Not Spanish," Arcangelo said absently, still soothing her.

"French might do," Poly babbled. "I think Adam's all right with French."

"English will do, *meu bem*," Arcangelo said gently. "Hush, now, Polyzinha, hush." He cupped her chin in his hand and looked at her, at the red marks showing where the blindfold and the gag had been. "What have they done to you? What has happened?"

"Hold me, Arcangelo," Poly said. "Tell him, Adam."

Arcangelo sat down on one of the pale green velvet chairs and pulled Poly up onto his lap; her long legs dangled to the floor but she leaned against him as though she were a very small child. He looked inquiringly at Adam, and now Adam was able to look back at the concierge, at a dark, powerful man, perhaps in his fifties, though it was difficult to tell, with a nose that looked as though it had been broken.

The story Typhon Cutter had prepared was for Dr. O'Keefe; it did not work here in this luxurious room at the Ritz for a Portuguese concierge whom Poly treated as though he were a beloved uncle.

"Tell him, Adam," she said again.

"It was on the plane from Madrid to Lisbon. Poly went into the washroom and didn't come out, and when the steward opened the door she wasn't there." He looked at Poly. "What happened?"

She shuddered again, and reached frantically for Arcangelo's hand.

"Not if you don't want to," he said gently.

She shook her head against the blue of his uniform. "No. It's all right. He came in and grabbed me. The steward. He put his hand over my mouth before I could yell. He had some kind of canvas sack with air holes in it, and he put me into it. The washroom was so small that I couldn't fight or kick and he was strong, and he stuck something sweet and sicky-smelling on my nose and it made me all sleepy. He gagged me, too, did I tell you? And it was all dark and horrible and I was too much asleep to try to wriggle or anything and I think I was just dumped on top of the luggage. And then I was in a car and then in somebody's house, I don't know where, because the curtains were drawn. They took off the gag and gave me something to drink and it put me all the way to sleep and then I woke up and I tried to get out but the door was locked and I started to cry. And then that man, the one who drove us, Adam, came in and told me to be quiet and I wouldn't get hurt and I knew he meant business so I was quiet, and he just sat there and watched me, and I sat there and watched him, and I had a headache, and he wouldn't talk or tell me where I was or anything, and then he put the gag back on, and blindfolded me, and told me not to move or I'd get hurt, so I didn't move even when I felt the car start. Arcangelo, please call the Embassy for me." She climbed down off the concierge's lap and went and sat on one of the beds near the phone. "Get them, 'Gelo, and ask for Joshua Archer. I don't want the switchboard people here to hear my voice."

Adam felt that he ought to assert himself, now that Poly's tears were spent and her hysteria gone. "Polyhymnia," he started firmly, but she interrupted him.

"You promised *never* to call me that."

Adam sighed. "Poly. I don't know why you want to call the Embassy, but I think the thing for us to do is to get back to the Avenida Palace to your father. Or, if you want to use the telephone, call the hotel and ask to speak to him."

Poly looked at him as though she were a teacher trying to explain something to an unexpectedly stupid student who fails to understand a very simple problem. "Adam, daddy won't go back to the Avenida Palace without me. He might be at the Embassy. If he isn't, Josh will know how to get hold of him and what to do. We can't go back to the Avenida Palace alone anyhow, and Arcangelo can't get away to take us. Please call, 'Gelo."

Sighing again, Adam waited while the concierge asked for the American Embassy, then for Mr. Archer, then, several times over, evidently to different people, for Mr. Joshua Archer. Finally he held the phone out to Poly.

"Josh," she said. "Yes, it's me. I'm at the Ritz. . . . Yes, he's here . . . well, he was in the car with me when we were dumped here. . . . I was blindfolded, I don't know. . . ." She looked accusingly at Adam. "Were you at the Avenida Palace with daddy?"

"Yes," Adam said.

"Why didn't you tell me?"

"You've hardly let me finish a sentence, you know," Adam reproved her.

Poly scowled at him. "If you were at the Avenida Palace with daddy why did you leave?"

"I can't tell you now," Adam said. "Poly, I'm half dead with sleep." This was not only clever evasion. It was hot now that the sun was higher in the sky, and the air-conditioning unit in the room was not turned on; the heat pressing down on Adam seemed to be pulling on his eyelids. "I haven't had any sleep for three nights," he said.

Poly turned back to the phone. "Where's daddy? . . . Can you get to him to tell him I'm all right? . . . Okay. . . . Okay, Josh. . . . Yes, Arcangelo'll answer. . . . Okay, Josh, 'bye." She hung up, turned back to Adam, demanding, "*Why* haven't you had any sleep?"

Adam spoke with heavy patience. "The last night I was in

Woods Hole there was a party that lasted until the kids put me
on the plane for New York. Then we didn't sleep much on the
plane to Madrid. That's two nights. Then last night I'd just
gone to sleep when I was waked up."

"How were you waked up? How did you get in that car with
me?"

Adam looked around the luxurious room. "I can't talk to
you now. I have to sleep. I have to think."

"Do you want some coffee?"

"I've had coffee. Coffee can't keep me awake any longer."

"Do you want a shower or something?"

"I've had a shower. All I want to do is go to sleep."

"Are you hungry?"

"Polyhymn——Poly—all I want to do is *sleep*."

Poly looked at Arcangelo. "Can he sleep here?"

Arcangelo nodded.

"We have to wait until Josh calls back. He could sleep for a
while, anyhow."

Arcangelo rose and pulled the golden coverlet down off
one of the beds. In a fog of sleep Adam flopped down, not
feeling the softness of the mattress, not even aware of his cheek
touching the fine linen of the pillow. Through a haze of sleep
he seemed to hear the phone ringing, to hear voices, but he
could not rouse enough to listen. He was engulfed in a black
sea of slumber.

8

HE woke up slowly, not because anybody was knocking at the door or in any way trying to disturb his rest but because he had at last, finally, had enough sleep. For a moment, remembering nothing, he stretched, his eyes closed, his body languid, his mind soothed by his body's comfort. Then the events of the past three days came sliding back into his relaxed and unsuspecting brain, so that his body stiffened with the shock of recollection, and his eyes flew open.

He was still in the golden room at the Ritz. Poly and Arcangelo were nowhere to be seen, but a fair young man was sitting on a green velvet chair, reading. As Adam moved, the young man's gaze flicked alertly toward the bed.

"So you're awake," he said.

Adam sat up, every muscle tense and wary. "Who are you?"

"Joshua Archer, of the American Embassy, at your service."

"Are you the Ambassador?"

The young man laughed, easy, spontaneous laughter. "I'm not sure the Ambassador would appreciate that. Hardly. I'm the lowest of the low."

Still lulled with sleep Adam thought that Joshua Archer must be a friend of Kali's and Mr. Cutter's, one of their Embassy crowd. Then he remembered the call Poly had made Arcangelo put through to the Embassy. How was it possible that both Kali and Poly should assume the protection of the Embassy? He looked warily at the young man. "You're the one Poly called?"

"Yes."

"Where is she?"

"On Gaea with her parents. They phoned the Embassy when they reached the island, and the Embassy in turn was kind enough to call me here."

"It seems to me," Adam said slowly, "that I heard the phone ring several times."

"You might have." The young man leaned back in his chair

and smiled pleasantly at Adam. Adam stared back and waited. Joshua Archer was a nicely made young man with a lean face, but nothing in any way conspicuous about him. All Adam saw was light brown hair, greyish eyes, a Brooks Brothers–style suit, a young man who looked like any nice, normal American. Adam's scowl and stare deepened; the only thing he felt might single Joshua out from anyone just through college and starting to make his own way in the world was a look of sadness lurking in the eyes, and this Adam did not consciously identify; all he knew was that there was something about the young man's steady gaze that invited confidence, and this very fact put him on his guard.

"Well?" the young man said, still smiling.

"Well?" Adam asked back.

"Would you like something to eat?"

"Yes. I suppose so. Thank you."

The young man came over to the lemon-yellow phone by the second bed, and called, speaking in Portuguese, so that Adam did not have any idea what was being ordered, or even, indeed, if the young man were really calling room service. Perhaps he was reporting that the dumb kid, Adam Eddington, was finally awake; perhaps he was getting something else awful lined up for Adam's further confusion. If the boy had not had such a full and uninterrupted sleep he would probably have felt very sorry for himself. As it was, he simply tensed up so that he would be ready for whatever happened next.

Joshua Archer went back to his chair and continued to smile questioningly at Adam. Adam became more and more uncomfortable. Finally he said, "What time is it?"

Joshua Archer looked around the room. The golden draperies were still pulled across the windows and no light filtered through. "Around nine in the evening. You went to sleep yesterday morning, so you've had about thirty-six hours. Feeling better?"

"Yes, thanks."

"The bathroom is there," Joshua said. When Adam returned he continued, "Now the problem is what to do with you. You *are* rather a problem, Adam."

"Sorry."

"The Ambassador was all for sending you back to Woods Hole immediately."

Without stopping to think Adam responded bitterly, "You mean I should crawl right back into the Hole I crawled out of?"

Joshua laughed again. "Is it as bad as all that?"

"It might help if someone would tell me just what is going on."

Joshua's voice was smooth as silk, his face as expressionless. "Didn't Typhon Cutter?"

"What about him?"

Joshua shrugged. "Oh, nothing much. Or is there?" Adam was silent. "The last time I saw him was at a party at the Embassy the evening Poly was kidnapped."

"Oh?" Adam asked politely.

There was a knock. Joshua shot a sharp glance at Adam, then unlocked the door. Arcangelo came in rolling a dinner cart. He looked at Adam but he did not smile and he did not speak. He wheeled the cart over to the table and spread a tablecloth, put out silver and plates. From covered dishes a delicious smell rose. When the dinner was set out he looked over at Joshua, who simply nodded. Arcangelo glanced again at Adam, then left, closing the door quietly behind him. Joshua locked the door from the inside, came back to the table and sat down, beckoning to Adam. "Come on. You'll feel better after you've had some food."

"I'd feel lots better if I knew more about what was going on."

Joshua looked at him thoughtfully. "Yes, we all would. But I can't be open with you unless you'll be open with me."

Adam was sitting on the side of the bed still in his travelling suit, which was by now thoroughly wrinkled. He leaned down and reached for his shoes, put them on. As he walked, rather stiffly, to the table, he said, "I'm sorry, but I'm so confused that I don't think I can be very open with anybody." He pulled out his chair, deliberately trying to curb his instinctive liking for Joshua. "I'm just a dumb American kid and the things that have been happening are beyond me."

Joshua ladled some interesting-smelling soup into Adam's dish. "Fair enough. We'll try to clear up what we can. Mind if I ask you a few questions? You don't have to answer if you don't want to, but I'd appreciate it if you'd try. Then I'll know better what to do next. Do you want to go back to America?"

Oddly enough Adam wasn't even tempted. He was in the middle of this thing, and it was a mess, and he hated it, but he knew that he could not deliberately walk out on it until he knew what it was all about. "No."

"Then what do you think you should do?"

Adam swallowed some of the soup; it was delicious and delicate, with a faintly sour, sorrel taste. "I think I should go to Gaea to work for Dr. O'Keefe the way Dr. Didymus wanted me to do."

"And Dr. O'Keefe?"

"What about him?"

"Do you think he wants you?"

"That was the understanding when I left Woods Hole."

"But things have happened since then. Do you think he can trust you?"

"Why not?" Adam asked warily.

"He told you not to open the door of your room at the Avenida Palace, didn't he?"

"Yes."

"Yet you opened it."

"Yes."

"Why?"

"It seemed to me that it was the right thing to do."

"Why?"

"I was alone, and Poly was kidnapped, and I was responsible for her."

"Did you think opening the door would help you find her?"

"Yes."

"Why?"

"I just did."

Sighing rather absently Joshua removed the soup plates—Adam had not quite finished his soup—and put them on the serving cart. Raising the metal dome from a platter of fish

Joshua asked, "Did you just open the door of your own accord and go blundering off in the dark in the middle of the night to look for Poly? Or was someone on the other side of the door? Did you let someone into the room?"

Adam did not answer and Joshua deftly placed a sauce-covered fish on his plate, then handed him a bowl of little, wrinkled olives. Adam took an olive and it was tender and delicious. With the pit still in his mouth he said, "I don't think I can tell you." He looked at Joshua and fought down the temptation to spill everything out to him. Putting the olive pit on his plate he said, "I'd like to tell you. It's just that I have to know more about what's what."

Joshua nodded. "Yes. I see that. From your point of view this is perfectly reasonable. But under the circumstances this entire situation is too potentially explosive for me to be able to do anything until I know more about what happened from the moment you opened that door. I am going on the assumption that you opened it to someone. Unless I can find out where you went and who you were with I shall have no alternative to sending you back to the States." With an expert stroke of his knife he removed the backbone of his fish.

Adam asked, "Do you know what happened up to the time I opened the door?"

"Yes. I have talked at length with Poly, with her father, and, on a closed Embassy line, with Canon Tallis in Madrid. I completely understand how confusing all of this must be for you. And Father Tallis is inclined to trust you, and he's a perceptive old boy. I have a lot of faith in his judgment. He's never blinded by sentimentality. If I'd put Poly in your charge and you'd let her disappear I'd have you on the next jet to New York. Sorry, Adam. I know it wasn't your fault. All I mean is that I'd have blamed you, fault or no, out of my own guilt, and Canon Tallis didn't."

Adam said excitedly, "But then you see why I *had* to open the door, why I *had* to try to find Poly. It was the only way I knew."

"Yes," Joshua said thoughtfully. "I see that. Okay. After we've finished dinner we'll go to my flat; your luggage has been taken there. You can change into fresh clothes, and then maybe it might be a good idea if we go to the Embassy. If there's anyone you'd like to talk to it can be arranged from there."

"Who would I want to talk to?"

"Canon Tallis?"

Adam shook his head.

"Your parents?"

"I don't want them upset."

"Dr. Didymus? I think it might help if you talked to him."

"I don't know," Adam said. "I just don't know."

"Eat your fish," Joshua told him. "Brain food, my grand-mother always used to say."

"You mean you think I need it?"

Joshua laughed. "Don't we all." He removed the fish plates to the serving tray, and helped Adam to meat, rice, carrots. "Still hungry? I've never managed to get used to two seven-course meals a day, so I get around it by not eating any lunch. It's been a couple of days since you've eaten, hasn't it?"

"It probably has," Adam said. "I don't remember. But I *am* still hungry, and this is very good." Then, feeling that perhaps he had been too friendly he picked up his knife and fork. If only he did not have this instinctive feeling that Joshua Archer was someone to be trusted he could be more objective. But if Typhon Cutter and Kali were right then Joshua was the last person in the world to trust.

"Adam," Joshua said, "have you seen Carolyn Cutter since you went into the coffee shop with her at the airport in New York?"

"How do you know I saw her then?"

"I happen to know it from several sources," Joshua said. "The one that might interest you most is Typhon Cutter. He mentioned it at the dinner table at the Embassy."

"You mean the night Poly was kidnapped?"

"Yes."

"You're *sure* Poly is all right?"

"I told you she's on Gaea with her parents."

"How do I know that you're telling me the truth?"

"You don't. You're just going to have to follow your instincts about me one way or the other."

Adam glowered across the table. "But I don't trust my instincts any more, Mr. Archer."

"Call me Josh."

"Okay."

"What's wrong with your instincts?"

"They're just not working," Adam said. "I *do* have a feeling that somebody has to be right and somebody has to be wrong, but I haven't a dream who is which."

"Would it help any if I tell you that I trust you?"

"I don't know. All I can tell you is that if I needed to be taken down a peg I've been taken."

"Because Poly was kidnapped while you were in charge of her?"

"That," Adam said, "but mostly because I can't trust my own decisions or my own thoughts. I used to be pretty sure of myself. I thought I could handle just about any situation."

"You handled some pretty rough ones in New York, didn't you?"

"Well," Adam said, "yes. How did you know?"

"Dr. O'Keefe was kind enough to let me see his dossier on you."

"How did *he* know?"

"His work is too important for him to take any chances. You weren't aware that you were being investigated?"

"No. I guess I wasn't. I thought Dr. Didymus' recommendation was all that was needed."

"Not even Old Doc's word is enough for something as vital as this. What I liked best of what I read about you was the time you and your Puerto Rican friend—Juan, wasn't it—"

"Yes."

"—the time the two of you managed to stop a rumble from starting. Maybe that's what makes me trust you, makes me know that you're fighting on the same side I am. But I think I'd trust you even if I didn't know anything about you. Have some salad?"

"Yes, please." Adam watched while Joshua served. "Could I ask you a question?"

"Fire ahead."

"You say you know I went into that coffee shop with Kali—"

"Yes."

"She told me her father has businesses here."

"That's right. He does."

"And that he knows lots of people at the Embassy."

"Correct."

"Do you know him?"

"Slightly. I'm not important enough for him to bother with."

"What do you think of him?"

"That he's a very clever man."

"Do you trust him?"

"As far as I could throw the bathtub."

"Is this instinct, or do you have reasons?"

"Both."

"Could I know the reasons?"

Joshua seemed to ponder. Finally he said, "He cares more about money than he does about anything else. Money and power. And he doesn't care who's sacrificed as long as he gets them."

"Is Dr. O'Keefe powerful?"

"Not in his own mind, certainly, and only because his mind can run circles around any other mind I've ever met. But power is always subordinate with him. Manipulating people is the last thing in the world he'd want."

"So what do you think about power?" Adam demanded.

"Power corrupts," Joshua quoted. "Absolute power corrupts absolutely."

Adam sighed.

Joshua stood up. "You don't want any dessert, do you? We'll have coffee at my place. I've made my decision about you, Adam, whether you trust me or not."

For a moment Adam felt only relieved that the decision had been made, that it had been taken out of his hands. Then he knew that if Joshua Archer were to try to send him back to America he would have to escape him somehow and go back to Kali and her father.

But Joshua said, "I'm going to take you to Gaea."

9

THEY left the hotel without speaking to anybody, without giving in keys at the desk, without further communication with Arcangelo. Joshua turned to the right and they walked briskly for about ten minutes through the sweet summer darkness. They stopped before a narrow house faced in gleaming blue-and-white patterned tile. "Ever seen the Portuguese tile before?" Joshua asked absently, not waiting for Adam to respond. "It's quite famous." He put his key in the door. "I have the top floor. Modest, but mine. I love this stairway. Pink marble. Beautiful, isn't it?"

"Yes." Adam followed him up three flights.

At the top was a blue painted door, which Joshua also unlocked, saying, "Gone are those innocent days when I didn't worry about keys. I got awfully tired of having my things gone through. So 'Gelo very kindly helped me fashion a lock that is impossible to pick or duplicate."

"Who is Arcangelo?" Adam demanded.

"My very good friend." Joshua flicked a switch and in the ceiling a crystal chandelier sparkled into life.

Adam looked around. They were in a fair-sized room, a room that smelled of tobacco and books. It was, indeed, more of a library than a living room, as there were books not only on all four walls but piled on tables and windowsills. Adam saw in a quick glance a record player and shelves of records, a sagging couch covered with an India print, an old red rep easy chair, a large desk that looked as though it had been discarded from an office. It was a good room, the kind of room Adam had dreamed of having some day. He looked at a Picasso print over one of the bookshelves, a sad-eyed harlequin on a white horse. The harlequin reminded him of someone, and suddenly he realized that it was Joshua himself.

Joshua pointed to an open door. "Bedroom and bath. Go in and make yourself at home. Your stuff's all in there. I'll make us some coffee. I don't have a proper kitchen, just a hot plate, but it does."

Adam nodded and went to the bedroom. It was a small, bare room, furnished only with a narrow brass bed, a chest of drawers, a straight chair. The walls were white and absolutely bare. The room was cold and austere in comparison to the cluttered warmth of the living room.

Adam washed his hands and face. He was not being sent back to America. He was going to Gaea. He could not help liking Joshua. But if he should see Kali again how would he feel? So far he had managed to tell Joshua nothing of any importance, and Joshua did not seem to be going to pursue his questioning.

—Play it cool, Adam, he seemed to hear a voice in his ear. Kali's voice.

As long as nobody knew that it was Kali who had come to him at the Avenida Palace, that it was to Kali's apartment he had gone, that he was expected to work for Typhon Cutter as a—what had Mr. Cutter said? Patriotic duty, wasn't it?—then he had not yet committed himself to either side. And as long as he didn't commit himself he couldn't do anything too terribly wrong. Could he?

—I wish things were black and white, he thought savagely. —I wish things were *clear*.

He remembered his math teacher back at school, a brilliant young Irishman, telling of his personal confusion when he first began to study higher mathematics and discovered that not all mathematical problems have one single and simple answer, that there is a choice of answers and a decision to be made by the mathematician even when dealing with something like an equation that ought to be definite and straightforward and to allow of no more than one interpretation. "And that's the way life is," the teacher had said. "Right and wrong, good and evil, aren't always clear and simple for us; we have to interpret and decide; we have to commit ourselves, just as we do with this equation."

As though reading his thoughts Joshua came and lounged in the doorway. "Don't hold off too long, Adam. The time comes when you have to make a choice and you're not going to be able to put it off much longer. Unless you've already made it?"

"I don't know." Adam rubbed his face with a clean, rough towel.

"The trouble is," Joshua said, "that I can't guarantee you anything. If you decide to work with Dr. O'Keefe I can't in any honesty tell you that anything is going to be easier for you than it has been for the past few days. I *can* tell you that nobody expected things to start breaking quite so soon, or we wouldn't have let you come. You were never supposed to be in any kind of danger. It was pure coincidence that it was this summer that Old Doc decided you were worth sending to Dr. O'Keefe to be educated. Of course neither Canon Tallis nor Dr. O'Keefe believe in coincidence. I'm afraid that I do, and that we're often impaled upon it. Then, on the other hand, I can't help wondering if it *was* pure coincidence that made Canon Tallis finish his work in Boston at just the moment he did so that he and Poly were on the plane with you."

"But if he was lecturing there," Adam protested, "he'd know when he was going to be through."

"Oh, did he tell you he was lecturing? Well, probably he was," Joshua said somewhat vaguely. "The main thing is that if you're worth educating then I suppose you ought to be up to facing whatever there is to face, oughtn't you?"

"What is there to face?" Adam sat at the foot of Joshua's bed.

Joshua did not answer his question. Instead: "Maybe it'll help you if I tell you that it wasn't easy for me, either. I don't know about you, Adam, but I can't look forward to pie in the sky. I'm a heretic and a heathen, and I let myself depend far too much on the human beings I love, because—well, just because. I guess the real point is that I care about having a decent world, and if you care about having a decent world you have to take sides. You have to decide who, for you, are the good guys, and who are the bad guys. So, like the fool that I am, I chose the difficult side, the unsafe side, the side that guarantees me not one thing besides danger and hard work."

"Then why did you choose it?" Adam demanded.

Joshua continued to lean against the door. "Why? I'm not sure I did. It seemed to choose me, unlikely material though I be. And it's the side that—that cares about people like Poly-hymnia O'Keefe." He wheeled and went back into the living room. In a moment the sound of music came clear and gay, Respighi's *The Birds*, Adam thought, following him into the living room. Joshua grinned. "It's the fall of the sparrow I care about, Adam. But who is the sparrow? We run into problems there, too. Now let's have our coffee."

He picked up a battered white enamel percolator from the hot plate on one of the bookcases. "Want to go to the Embassy when we're through?"

Adam watched Joshua pour the dark and fragrant brew. "Why? Do we have to?"

Joshua handed him a cup, indicated sugar and milk. "No. Not if you don't want to."

"I'm not sure it would make things any clearer." Adam put three heaping spoons of sugar in his coffee. "I don't want to telephone anybody. I mean, why bother Old Doc? I think he feels about me kind of the way you feel about Poly, if you know what I mean, so it would just be upsetting to him to have me ask him to help make up my own mind. I mean, I have to do it myself, don't I?"

"When you get right down to it, yes," Joshua said.

"And the whole idea of the Embassy business is very confusing to me. I mean, you working there, and then both the O'Keefes and the Cutters seeming to know everybody, and everybody thinking the Embassy's on their side and it *can't* be on everybody's side. I think I'd rather stay clear of any more confusion for a while."

"Okay," Joshua said. "I follow you. I thought it might help, but I see your point. What about your passport, by the way?"

Adam felt the by-now-familiar jolt in the pit of his stomach. "I suppose it's still at the Avenida Palace. I'd forgotten all about it."

Joshua reached in his breast pocket and handed the thin green book to Adam. "Here. But it's something you'd better remember from now on. Think you could do any more sleeping?"

"You wouldn't think I could, would you?" Adam asked, yawned, and laughed.

"Good. Let's just have our coffee and maybe listen to a little music and go to bed. I'll take the sofa in here; I'm used to it. In the morning we'll go to Gaea. I hope you won't mind flying with me. Actually I'm a pretty fair pilot."

Without knowing why Adam realized that he would feel perfectly safe with Joshua at the controls of plane, boat, or car. It was an instinct that the wariness acquired in the past three days could not shake, no matter how little at the moment he trusted his instincts.

Although Adam protested briefly at the idea of taking Joshua's bed he found to his surprise that he was very happy to get undressed and stretch out. In the living room he could hear Joshua puttering around, changing records, cleaning up the coffee things. The last thing he was conscious of was the strains of a Mozart Horn Concerto. Then Joshua was shaking him; sunlight streamed in through the open, uncurtained bedroom window; and the smell of coffee came from the living room. Joshua, unlike Dr. O'Keefe or Arcangelo, seemed to feel no need to close himself in behind shutters or draperies; or was it just in knowing when and where?

They had coffee, bacon and eggs, all of which Joshua somehow managed with ease on his single hot plate; then they took a taxi out to the airport. This was not the huge state-owned field at which Adam had arrived, but a small, private field with a couple of rickety-looking hangars. The waiting room was a Quonset hut, with a few desks behind which sat the inevitable uniformed men, a row of phone booths, and a speaker system loud enough for Grand Central Station, so that each time a voice came through it the few passengers waiting in the hut were almost blasted out of their seats.

Joshua walked in his usual casual, almost lounging way over to one of the desks, where he stood smiling and speaking fluent Portuguese to the uniformed man behind it; they seemed to be old friends and after a few minutes Joshua turned, smiling, to Adam. "Everything's just about ready for us. Five minutes to wait, that's all. Okay?"

"Sure." What would Joshua have done if he'd said, 'Nope'?

Joshua led him over to an uncomfortable but empty wooden bench and began to talk lightly about Embassy life, of his own job of filing and checking and being general errand boy, all of which, he said, could perfectly well be done by a ten-year-old. Every once in a while he would have to stop as his narrative was punctured by the braying of the loudspeaker. Adam almost laughed as Joshua would shut his eyes against the blast, his sensitive ears seeming to quiver in pain. Adam's own ears pricked up as he heard, "Jhoshuajh Archair. . . . Jhoshuajh Archair. . . ." followed by a message in Portuguese.

"I seem to have a call from the Embassy," Joshua said, sighing. "Please wait right here for me, Adam. Please do not move, I beg of you."

Adam gave a rather lopsided grin. "I won't open any more locked doors."

"Good boy." Joshua ambled off, never seeming to hurry, but covering the distance to the telephones in an amazingly short time.

Adam leaned back on the bench, stretching his legs. Perhaps it was catching up on his sleep that was responsible for his feeling of calm and certainty. —I can't help it, he thought. —I couldn't feel this way about Joshua if he weren't all right. And Poly. They've got to be the way I want them to be. And Dr. O'Keefe and Canon Tallis. I'm making up my mind to be on their side whether I want to or not. It's making itself up for me. Just the way Joshua said it did for him.

"Adam."

He jerked upright, his thoughts knocked out from under him.

Standing before him was a man in ecclesiastical garb.

But it was not Canon Tallis. It was a younger man, taller, extremely handsome, with a head of luxuriant black hair.

"Adam?"

Adam looked but he did not speak. It probably was, it *must* be a friend of Canon Tallis'. But even if his mind was being made up for him there was no being certain of anything any more. Even if it was somebody who knew his name.

"It *is* Adam Eddington, isn't it?" the man asked, in one of the most mellifluous voices Adam had ever heard.

He could hardly pretend to be a deaf mute. "Yes."

"I'm Dr. Baal." Adam looked somewhat startled, and the

man repeated, "Dr. Eliphaz Ball, rector of St. Zophar's, the American church here in Lisbon." A hand was held out toward Adam, a white, clean, well-manicured hand. The grip was strong, man-to-man.

"How do you do, sir?" Adam murmured.

Dr. Eliphaz Ball, smiling pleasantly, sat down beside him. "Your young friend, Joshua Archer, and my friend, too, I am happy to say, has had to go back to the Embassy. Poor lad, when his superiors call he must jump, no matter what previous engagements he may have hoped to fulfill. So he's asked me to see to it that you get to Gaea. I'm afraid I'm no pilot myself, but I've made arrangements for one of the local men to hop us over." Dr. Ball's beautiful voice was smooth and pleasant, his manner easy, as he smiled at Adam. "Poor laddie, we're all more sorry than we can say for everything that has happened to you. It must all have been more than confusing. But once you get to Gaea and settle down to work with the good doctor you'll be able to relax and forget all the unpleasantness. Thank God our darling Poly was returned unharmed, the precious child."

Adam looked at the handsome, friendly face of Dr. Ball and was not happy. For some reason his instinct was telling him not to trust Dr. Ball, but he no longer trusted his instinct. For a brief moment he contrasted the doctor with Canon Tallis. Canon Tallis was brusque, stern, businesslike, formidable. He would never have called Poly a precious child, but Adam knew that it was to the canon that Poly was precious. He knew it. At least he went along with his instinct that far.

"I'm afraid we'll have to hurry," Dr. Ball said. "I think we can manage your bags between us, don't you?"

Joshua had told Adam not to move. Adam had promised to open no more locked doors. "I'm sorry," he said, courteously, "but I'm afraid I'll have to wait here for Mr. Archer."

"But my poor dear boy, I've just explained to you that poor Josh has been called back to the Embassy, and has put you in my charge."

Adam shook his head stubbornly. "I'm sorry. I have to wait here."

The velvet smoothness of Dr. Ball's voice did not alter, nor the friendly look fade from his features, as he said, "Adam, don't you think you've caused the O'Keefes enough trouble already?"

"I'm sorry," Adam said for the third time. "I don't mean to be difficult, but I have to wait."

"Poor lad, I hadn't realized just quite how confused you are, in spite of what Joshua told me. Joshua is not coming back. Please try to understand this. He has been called to the Embassy. Do try to realize that it is absolutely essential for me to get you to Gaea at once. Won't you be a good boy and come with me?" Adam shook his head. "It will be so much easier for both of us if you'll come of your own free will." Adam shook his head again. Dr. Ball sighed and cast his eyes up to heaven. "Dear Lord, be patient with the boy." He looked down at Adam. "I'm sorry, truly sorry, laddie, but I'll have to take you with me. Please do understand that it's for your own protection." He glanced behind him, snapped his fingers lightly, and a burly porter moved up to stand beside him.

Adam braced himself. With a wild and irrational stubbornness he was determined not to move from the bench where he had promised to wait for Joshua.

A second figure appeared beside the porter.

It was Arcangelo.

Adam did not move. Arcangelo spoke in a low voice to the porter, who looked at Adam, at Dr. Ball, shrugged in a vague kind of apology, though Adam could not tell to whom, and trotted off to a baggage cart. A shadow seemed to cross Dr. Ball's brow, but his pleasant expression did not change. He smiled again at Adam, showing his even, white teeth. "We do seem to be running into problems, don't we?" He turned to Arcangelo. "And who are you, my good man?"

"A friend," Arcangelo said.

"Of whom?"

Arcangelo jerked his head in Adam's direction. Then he pointed across the room. Adam looked and saw Joshua coming toward them. As swiftly as he had appeared, Arcangelo left.

Dr. Ball put his hand on Adam's knee. "What an unfortunate incident. I will speak quickly, Adam. I am a friend of Typhon Cutter's."

"He wanted me to go to Gaea," Adam said.

"I am aware of that. Why do you think I am here? I was sent to help you. And to help you to help your country."

"Thank you." Adam turned his eyes to see Joshua's progress across a floor that now seemed endless.

"Not a word to Archer. We'll get a message to you as soon as possible." Dr. Ball's hand pressed harder against Adam's knee. Joshua reached them. Dr. Ball removed his hand, rose, and greeted Joshua. "My young friend, the charming Mr. Archer! How fortunate to meet you here this morning! And how is life at the Embassy?"

"Splendid, thank you, Dr. Ball," Joshua said coolly.

"Keeping you busy?"

"Enough."

"I've had a delightful time talking to your young protégé here. Do take care of him for us."

"I'll do that," Joshua said.

"And give my warmest regards to the O'Keefes."

"Certainly."

"A brilliant mind, O'Keefe's. Brilliant. Our country needs more men like that."

"Right," Joshua said.

"I trust I'll see you around the Embassy, my boy."

"Very likely."

"Do have a safe and pleasant trip. Small craft warnings are out, I believe." Still smiling, Dr. Ball moved off.

Without a word Joshua picked up one of Adam's bags. Adam picked up the other and his briefcase and followed him out of the Quonset hut and onto a runway. A small plane was waiting several hundred yards away. Trotting behind Joshua, Adam could see only a tense, angry line of jaw.

—He said he trusted me, Adam thought resentfully, —so what right does he have to go jumping to conclusions now?

As they came up to the plane Adam saw that it was an old, single-engine, British Hawker Hurricane converted to a two-seater. Arcangelo was standing beside it. Silently he handed Adam, then Joshua, leather jackets, goggles, helmets, and helped them up and into the seats. Joshua, still without speaking (and silence from Joshua, unlike silence from Arcangelo, seemed completely out of character), turned around and showed Adam how to strap himself in, then clipped on his own webbing. Suddenly his face relaxed and he looked at Adam and grinned. "Feel like something out of a World War II movie?"

"Kind of," Adam said. And then, "This guy Ball—"

"Wait till we get going. Silence is golden and all that stuff." Joshua's experienced hands moved over the controls; the engine coughed, choked, finally caught. The blades of the slowly circling propeller merged into a swift blur. Joshua leaned out and waved down at Arcangelo who waved back, then turned and walked toward the Quonset hut. The plane slowly taxied along the runway. "She's a bit bumpy," Joshua shouted above the noise of the engines. "Hold on tight."

Adam held on. After a moment he closed his eyes and gritted his teeth. The plane seemed to buck and strain, to refuse to leave the ground: how could it possibly expect to fly at such an advanced age? The only fit place for it was a museum.

Bounce. Bounce. Jerk. Bounce. A jerk that threw Adam back against the seat. Then a straining upward and a pleased laugh from Joshua. Adam opened his eyes.

They were nosing up, up, higher, higher. They circled the small airport. As Adam looked down he could see Arcangelo leaving the Quonset hut, getting into a car, and driving off.

This seemed to be what Joshua was waiting for. He turned the plane away from the port, away from the land, nosed further and further up. Ahead of them over the rooftops Adam could see water.

"Okay, kid," Joshua shouted back to him. "Everything under control."

Adam shouted in return, "I hope that's not the overstatement of the year."

"I never go in for famous last words," Joshua called. "Don't mind talking in bellows, do you?"

"I'm a good bellower," Adam bellowed.

"Good. Me, too. Nobody listening in but sea gulls. We're over the Tagus now." Adam leaned over and looked down at the rim of Lisbon sprawled along the river. "That's the Jeronymos Monastery," Joshua called back. "It's just about my favorite piece of architecture in Lisbon, except for the São Juan Chrysostom Monastery which is even better. I'll take you there someday." He flew along the coast, pointing and calling. "There's the Belém Tower. Famous Portuguese Manueline architecture. Moorish influence heavy. Makes you think you're in Africa, doesn't it? Lots of Portugal will." And, a moment later, "That monstrosity is the monument to Henry the Navigator, but I've become very fond of it. Now what about Ball?" he asked without transition.

"Who *is* he?"

"Rector of St. Zophar's."

"Friend of yours?"

"I never make friends with the pious."

"What about Canon Tallis?"

Joshua snorted. "He's not pious."

"Did you send him to me?"

"Who? Canon Tallis?"

"No. Dr. Ball."

"Did he tell you I had?"

"Yes," Adam shouted, glad at last to be able to be open about something. He looked down and they were flying over the harbor which was speckled with ferries, small fishing vessels, pleasure craft. "Does he really have a church and stuff?"

"That's right. Very popular gentleman of the cloth. Ladies swoon."

"You don't?"

"I'm no lady."

"Is he a friend of Canon Tallis'?"

Joshua roared. "Hardly."

"But I thought—"

"Adam, my son," Joshua howled over the sound of the engines, over the blasting of the wind, "don't expect any group of people to be all of a kind. The church is no exception. And it is not only because I am a heathen that I say this. So what did the old black crow say to you?"

"That you'd been called back to the Embassy and had sent him to take me to Gaea."

"And you didn't bite," Joshua said. "Good boy."

"I thought you thought I had." Adam looked away from Joshua, over the side of the plane, down at the open water of the Atlantic. Land was only a dark shadow behind them, almost lost in haze. The water was unusually dark, with occasional brilliant flashes as it was caught by sunlight.

"Because I got all furious?" Joshua asked. "Not at you. I thought you'd had about all you could take and I could have strangled him with my bare hands. There wasn't any phone call for me from the Embassy or anyplace else, by the way. He'd bribed somebody to page me to get me out of the way."

After a pause Adam said, "I think I'm shocked."

"Because he's a churchman and stuff?"

"I guess so."

"I had that kind of being shocked knocked out of me when I was in knee pants. Also thinking that anyone in my government's employ necessarily has the interest of my country at heart. This is one of the few reasons I'm of any use in the Embassy. Don't let it get you, Adam. People don't compartmentalize. One bad guy in a group doesn't make everybody else bad, and one good one doesn't make everybody else good."

At that moment the plane dropped. Adam flew up from his seat and was kept in the plane only by the webbing of his harness.

"Whoops," Joshua called, pulling at the stick and nosing the plane up again. "We're going into a spot of turbulence. I can't get above these clouds; we'll have to go through them."

He opened the throttle and the little plane shot into a great, churning white mass. Adam remembered Dr. Ball's smug comment about small-craft warnings. The plane jolted and jerked, dropped and steadied, so that Adam's stomach leapt from his toes to his mouth and back. The noise of the engine seemed accentuated by the swirling cloud, by the unexpected pockets of air into which they fell like a stone.

Adam felt absolutely calm at the same time that he knew that he was as frightened as he had ever been in his life. With each jerk and leap he expected the plane to plummet into the ocean, but Joshua always managed to steady it.

In front of him Adam heard an unexpected sound. It was

Joshua. Joshua was singing, his head flung back, his mouth open, bellowing the joyful last chorus from Beethoven's *Ninth Symphony*. Joshua, Adam realized, was enjoying the battle with the cloud. Beside this supreme happiness Adam's own fears fled. Holding on tightly to his seat, trying not to be thrown about any more than necessary, he watched the young man rather than the blind fury of the cloud.

And then suddenly they were through it and into the blue and gold of the day again. The plane choked and steadied. Joshua turned back to Adam and grinned. "Scare you?"

"At first."

Joshua patted the controls fondly. "She's a good old crate. I'll get you there in one piece. I hope."

They plunged into another cloud and dropped headlong toward the ocean.

10

IT was not precisely a relaxing trip, but Adam caught Joshua's exhilaration; he held on tight and the thought that they might not reach Gaea left him.

"This is better than the roller coaster at Palisades Park," he shouted.

"Rather!" Joshua called back, then burst into song again.

Adam did not know how long a routine flight to Gaea ought to last; it took Joshua, battling through the clouds in the little plane, the better part of two hours before the sky cleared again and there below them was the green of land with a great, curving, golden beach. "Gaea," Joshua called. "Hold on tight, Adam. Tide's out, all's clear, and I'm coming down on the beach."

Joshua accomplished the landing with skill and grace. The wheels touched the hard-packed sand gently and rolled along the water's edge to a smooth stop. He sat for a moment over the controls, breathing deeply, flexing his hands, deliberately relaxing. Then they unstrapped themselves, took off helmets, goggles, leather jackets. As Adam climbed out he realized that his legs were stiff and that, unconsciously, he must have been bracing them against the footboards during most of the trip.

"That was a great ride," he shouted, though the noise of the engine had stopped. "I loved every minute of it."

Joshua stretched, a great wide gesture of well-being. "I love to fly. Heaven, as far as I'm concerned. Adam—"

Adam was looking about, at the ocean, the sand, the dunes, and beyond the dunes to scrub and pine. "Hm?"

Joshua was looking at him directly, questioningly, bringing him back from the excitement of the flight to this moment of the arrival on Gaea, so different from the arrival he had anticipated when he left Woods Hole.

"Josh," he asked, "this Eliphaz Ball creep: what was he up to?"

Joshua stared out to sea, his eyes squinting a little against the brilliance. "I'm not sure. My guess is that he wanted to—well, you might call it indoctrinate you—before you had a chance to talk to Dr. O'Keefe. To get you firmly sewed up in the Cutter camp." He paused, again looking at Adam questioningly, then said, "Before I take you to the O'Keefes do you want to tell me who you opened the door to at the Avenida Palace?"

Adam, too, stared out to sea, his eyes almost closing against the radiance of sun and water. "I haven't told you, have I?"

"No."

"Oh, Joshua—" Adam started, then trailed off.

"You can't make only part of a decision," Joshua said gently. "You have to go all the way."

"I *have* decided," Adam said.

"I know you have."

"Do you know *what* I've decided?"

"To work for Dr. O'Keefe."

"How do you know that?"

"Because you wouldn't come here to work as his assistant and work against him in any other way."

A cloud moved across the sun; its shadow slid murkily over the beach, draining the gold from the sand; the blackness was reflected in Adam's mind. He looked down at his feet, the city shoes darkly incongruous against the damp sand. "Do I have to work *for* him in order not to work *against* him? You don't understand, Joshua. Or *I* don't understand. I don't see why I have to take sides at all. I know I couldn't work against you, and if that means not working against Dr. O'Keefe, then I won't work against him. But I didn't come over here to take sides about anything. I came to assist a scientist in some experiments in marine biology because that's what Dr. Didymus wanted me to do. You said yourself he didn't know about anything else."

Joshua shoved his hands into his pockets. The cloud moved past the sun and the sea was again dazzled with brilliance. "That's quite true, Adam. But you *are* involved, whether you want to be or not. In the end you'll have to take sides, and it'll be easier for you if you don't keep putting it off."

Adam scowled. "It would help if somebody would tell me what I'm supposed to be taking sides about."

"Adam," Joshua said with heavy patience, "if you're as bright as you're supposed to be you ought to know without my telling you that it's because Dr. O'Keefe has, in his work, come across certain far-reaching discoveries that certain irresponsible people are trying to steal."

"But you can't keep scientific discoveries secret," Adam protested.

"You have to try to keep them from being misused."

"You can't do that, either."

Joshua gave a rather wry smile. "That sounds more like jaded old Josh than a kid fresh out of school who ought to have all his illusions intact. If you'd been working for a scientist who was in charge, say, of antibiotics for a hospital, would you have sat back while self-interested men stole them, diluted them, and sold them for high black-market prices to doctors who gave them to children who died in agony as a result?"

"I've read *The Third Man*," Adam said, "and I've seen it on the Late Late Show."

"So don't you see that it's not a joking or a casual matter? You *cannot* be uncommitted, Adam, believe me, you cannot."

Adam's jaw set stubbornly. "I have to be clear about things."

Suddenly Joshua shrugged, and wheeled around from the ocean, kicking at the thin remains of a broken golden conch shell. "Okay. Forget it. Come on. We have a three-mile hike to get to the O'Keefes'."

Adam's scowl settled into stubborn sullenness. He did not understand his own blind lack of decision, but he knew that he hated having Joshua disappointed in him, and he knew that Joshua was disappointed. He was striding across the sand to the dunes; on the crest was a dead and rusty palm toward which he headed. One branch of palm, brown fronds drooping like feathers, seemed to point inland. There was nothing for Adam to do but follow, feet slipping as they reached the deep, soft sand at the foot of the dunes.

Supporting himself on coarse tufts of beach grass Joshua climbed the dune, standing, waiting until Adam caught up. Then he started ahead, moving slowly through what seemed to be no more than an animal track in the undergrowth. Thorny branches stretched across their way, and these Joshua held aside for Adam. Forest creepers looped from tree to tree, and although machete scars showed that the path had recently been cleared, the creepers were tenaciously starting to block the way again. Joshua untangled them, pausing occasionally to see that Adam was behind him. Above them were intermittent flashes of brilliant color, scarlet, orange, gold, and the alarmed shrieks of birds. Shadows moved constantly as the leaves stirred in the slightest breath of air. Joshua was caught in a shifting pattern of shadows, so that his sandy hair, his white shirt, his tanned skin flickered with green, purple, gold.

After a half mile or so of jungle they reached a clearing, a wide savannah of golden grasses. At the edge of the clearing a cloud of multi-colored butterflies hovered. One brushed against Adam's face, startling him so that he jumped. A herd of small animals was grazing placidly in the distance, but ran pelting through the grasses and into the underbrush at the scent of human beings. At the far side of the savannah was a grove of palms, and beyond this a hill, which Joshua climbed without slackening his pace. At the top of the hill there was a plateau where monolithic slabs of stone caught the full blast of the sun, glinting with gold. A large flat slab like a table or altar stood in the center, with smaller stones circling it. Joshua went up to the table stone and put his palm on its sun-baked surface, asking in a low voice, "Not going to be a Mordred, are you, Adam?"

"I've read King Arthur, too," Adam said. The sun beat down on his bare head; his upper lip was beaded with sweat.

Joshua looked at him, seemed about to say something in reply, instead straightened up and spoke in his conversational, social-young-man-of-the-Embassy voice. "This is the highest point on the island. Over there, to your left, you can get a glimpse of the Hotel Praia da Gaea. It's getting a bit of a reputation as a resort in spite of the heat. Sunbathing and tennis, and dancing at night if there's enough breeze. Straight ahead, where you can see a kind of promontory, is the native village. They're a gentle people, a mixture of original islander and Portuguese, with a touch of African thrown in. Some people think these stones were brought here by their remote ancestors and represent a kind of primitive religion. On your right, through the trees, that flash of white is the O'Keefes' house and laboratories. By the way, Dr. O'Keefe happens to be doing his work here with the blessing of the President of the United States, though not many people know this, or are supposed to know."

"Why are you telling me?" Adam asked.

Joshua answered quietly, "To try to counteract some of the things I am going on the assumption you have been told."

"By whom?"

"The people you were with from the time you opened the door at the Avenida Palace to the time Poly fell into your arms on the sidewalk in front of the Ritz." There was no longer any censure in his voice. "Until the hotel was built a year ago there was complete privacy here and ideal conditions for Dr. O'Keefe's experiments. After this summer it will probably be necessary for him to move again. Pity."

"Joshua, don't hate me," Adam said.

"I don't."

"I promise you I—are you going to be staying here in Gaea at all?"

"No. I have to fly back to Lisbon tonight."

"In—in *that*?"

"Wind's quieting down. It won't be a bad flight."

"Is there any way I—I could get in touch with you if I needed you?"

"Yes. I'll give you my phone number at home and my special extension at the Embassy. They're both pretty classified, so keep them to yourself. I don't think you're apt to need me. A few days with the O'Keefes will clear things up for you. I was wrong to try to push you. This is all very new for you. I had no right to expect you to leap into understanding."

"I'd still like to have those numbers," Adam said.

Joshua pulled a small pad out of his shirt pocket, a stub of pencil, and wrote. "Here. But please don't lose them. Keep them with your passport."

"Okay."

Joshua took another sweeping glance around. "All right. Let's go."

A footpath, only slightly wider than that leading through the scrub, took them down from the hill. The sun was heavy and hot and pressed on Adam with tangible weight. It seemed that they were walking far more than three miles. Then, suddenly, they were at a series of low, rambling, dazzling white bungalows, joined together by breezeways.

Joshua whistled, the melody Canon Tallis had whistled in Madrid, the melody the rabbi had whistled on the plane.

"What *is* that?" Adam asked.

Joshua grinned. "The Tallis Canon, of course."

Without being able to control himself Adam burst into laughter. "Of course! What an idiot I am! I *knew* I knew it. We used to sing it in choir when I was a kid." Now that memory had returned he did not see how he could have forgotten. The simple melody Thomas Tallis had written in the sixteenth century had been one of the choirmaster's favorites, and singing it in canon had been like singing a round, so the boys had enjoyed it, too. But Adam's choirboy days had ended in the seventh grade, so perhaps it wasn't too strange that Thomas Tallis' canon had not been remembered.

Joshua joined him in laughter. "Polyhymnia's idea. Naturally." He sobered. "That's the way things come clear. All of a sudden. And then you realize how obvious they've been all along."

Before Adam needed to reply a bevy of scantily dressed children came bursting around the corner of the bungalow and Joshua, calling, hurried to meet them. Behind the children, carrying a baby, came a tall, strikingly beautiful woman, smiling in greeting. Children were climbing all over Joshua, inspecting Adam, and then Poly came running out of the bungalow, holding the hand of a very small child she had evidently been tending, since he was dressed only in a torn white undershirt, and she carried a diaper in her hand.

"Josh! Adam!" she cried joyfully. Joshua was kissed with exuberance, then Adam. "You're late! We've been waiting for ages and ages!"

"We ran into a bit of weather," Joshua explained. "Mrs. O'Keefe, this is Adam Eddington."

Mrs. O'Keefe shook hands warmly, laughing. "Poor Adam, this must seem a formidable welcome. But it *is* a welcome. We're all happy to see you, and that you'll be with us this summer. Poly's told us so much about you. Come on in and I'll show you your room. Are his things still in the plane, Josh? Good. I'll ask one of the boys to ride over and get them." She explained to Adam, "It's twice as long by the beach, but you can't ride a horse through the brush. I expect you found it rather scratchy walking. We're much more primitive on our part of the island than they are at the hotel, but we like it." She led Adam along a breezeway and into the largest of the bungalows. They went into an enormous white room with comfortable and shabby-looking chairs and sofas. One wall was filled with books, another was all windows looking out to sea. At one end was a huge fireplace faced with the same lovely blue-and-white tile Adam had seen in Lisbon. The floor was rose-beige marble. Everything was light and open and clean, and a soft ocean breeze blew through.

"The living room," Mrs. O'Keefe said, "obviously lived in." She went through an arched doorway into a hall off which Adam could see a series of cubicles. "We don't go in for large bedrooms, but everybody has his own. This is the boys' section. Then the doctor and I have our room, and then there's the girls' wing. Your room is nearest the living room. It's a tradition in our family that the rooms go up in age, the youngest being nearest our room. Of course each time we have a new baby the rooms have to be shifted, but that's part of the fun for the children."

She preceded Adam into the first of the cubicles. There was a gayly embroidered spread on the bed, a chest of drawers, a chintz-covered armchair with sagging springs. A small, empty bookcase waited by the bed with a lamp on it, and a bouquet of beach grasses in a glass jar. "Poly's offering," Mrs. O'Keefe said.

Adam looked at Mrs. O'Keefe's tranquil, lovely face. "Is Poly really all right?"

"Yes, Adam. She's fine. And she's very fond of you." Was there a question in the way this was said?

"She wasn't hurt at all?" Adam asked. "You're sure?"

"Quite sure. Only frightened. And you mustn't blame yourself. You had no way of knowing that there was any danger when Tom—Canon Tallis—put you on the plane."

"Is his name really Thomas Tallis, like the composer's?"

"No. It's John. But his last name really *is* Tallis, so of course he gets called Tom. Do you know the Tallis canon?" Again: was there more to her question than the words?

"Yes, but I'd forgotten what it was until just now. Joshua was whistling it and I asked him. It was very stupid of me; we used to sing it in choir."

"Like to sing?"

"Sure, but I've been a bass now for quite a while, and a sort of rumbly one."

"Oh, splendid, we need a bass."

Out of doors Adam could hear the children calling and laughing and then they trooped into the house and in and through the living room. "May we come in?" Poly called. "Adam hasn't been properly introduced."

"Maybe he'd rather wait and get his breath for a few minutes first."

"No." Adam smiled at the crowd of children clustered in the doorway. "I'd like to be introduced."

"May I do it?" Poly asked her mother.

"Go ahead."

"We'll go down in age this time," Poly stated categorically. "After Father Tom gave me my horrendous name mother and daddy wouldn't let him name any of the rest of us, so don't worry. Charles comes next; he's ten, and we're the redheads; we'd given up on having any more carrot tops till we came to the baby, but we haven't come to her yet as far as introductions are concerned."

A stocky, freckle-faced boy in tan shorts and a white shirt shook hands with Adam.

"Hello, Charles," Adam said.

"Sandy comes next." Poly paused for handshaking, "and

then Dennys. This is Peggy. She's four; and Johnny; he's two.
And there's the baby on mother's shoulder. Father Tom was
determined he was going to name her, and if he had it would
have been something awful; he has a weird sense of humor.
We all call her Rosebud, because that's what she is, aren't you,
Rosy? But she was baptized Mary. Lots better than Polyhymnia,
don't you think? Isn't it, Rosy?"

The baby opened her toothless mouth in an ecstatic smile
and held out her dimpled arms to Poly. The soft fluff on her
head was rosy gold and she did indeed have the look of a tiny,
perfect bud. Looking at the baby and the other children Adam
felt a pang of envy: it would have been nice to have brothers
and sisters.

"Not now, Rosy," Poly said. "Mother, may I take Adam out
to the lab to daddy?"

"No, Poly, let Josh do it. Come help María get some lunch
ready."

"But Josh already is *in* the lab."

"We'll just point it out to Adam, then. It's not very difficult,
Pol."

For a moment Poly scowled; then she took the baby from
her mother, holding it up and gently rubbing noses, which
apparently delighted Rosy, who crowed with soft laughter.

"Come, Adam," Mrs. O'Keefe said. "I'll show you the way."

The bungalows, the boy realized, formed three sides of a
square, with the fourth side a cement sea wall. The center
bungalow contained living room, dining room, and kitchen.
The right arm was bedrooms, the left the lab. Through all
of the rooms the salt sea wind blew, and the sound of the
slow breakers was a constant background. Adam left the living
quarters and walked through the breezeway into an enormous
cluttered room; it had the messy maze of tubes, retorts, pipes,
files, bottles, acid-scarred counters with which he was familiar
in Old Doc's lab, and the same smell of the sea beneath and
around the acrid odors of chemicals and Bunsen burners. One
wall was lined with tanks, and Dr. O'Keefe and Joshua were
looking soberly into one of these.

Adam cleared his throat. "Dr. O'Keefe—Josh—"

The men turned from the tank, which Adam could now see contained two lizards. The sunlight was caught and reflected in Dr. O'Keefe's hair, in the brilliant blue of his eyes. Joshua might be able to slip, unnoticed, in and out of a crowd. Dr. O'Keefe would always stand out. Now he smiled at Adam, and his smile had much of the open warmth of Poly's. Adam realized that up to this moment he had seen the older man only at night, only when his face had been pulled tight with anxiety.

"Adam. Good to have you back with us." He made no reference to the Avenida Palace, to Adam's disobedience. "This afternoon I'll show you the setup of some of our experiments, and how you can help me with correlating. Too near lunchtime now, and I'm hungry. Take him for a quick swim, Josh, while I clean up, and after we've eaten we'll set to work." It was a suggestion, but it was also an order.

Joshua looked at him sharply. "Macrina?" he asked.

Dr. O'Keefe gave a barely perceptible nod of assent.

11

"My bathing trunks are in my suitcase," Adam said.

"That's all right," Joshua told him. "There are plenty in the bathhouse. Come on." He led the boy through the big room, into a smaller room, also lined with tanks, and then into a cement-floored room with several showers in stalls. A pile of bathing trunks lay on a wooden bench. Bottles of solution and extra lab equipment were stored in corners.

"Help yourself," Joshua told Adam, sorting through the bathing suits and coming up with zebra-striped trunks. "My favorites. Aren't they repulsive?"

Adam took a pair of plain navy trunks, disregarding several violent-looking outfits.

Joshua laughed. "One of the native bath attendants at the hotel is a friend of the cook's. Whenever someone leaves the island, forgetting his trunks—bathing suits, too, for that matter—he brings them over to us. It's very handy."

They emerged from the dim coolness of the bathhouse onto a cement ramp leading to the sea wall, into a blast of sunlight. At the wall stood Poly, in a faded red woolen bathing suit which clashed with her hair.

"Hi!" she called. "I thought maybe you'd take Adam for a swim before lunch and I didn't want to miss out. What about . . ." she paused and looked questioningly at Joshua.

Joshua nodded. "Your father said yes."

"Oh, good! May I call her?"

Joshua sighed, looking troubled. "Of course. She comes better for you than for the rest of us."

—I have no right to ask questions, Adam thought. He jumped off the sea wall into the deep sand which burned against the soles of his feet so that he hurried, stumbling, across the beach to the damp, hard-packed sand cooled by the waves. Poly was already splashing through the shallow breakers; she threw herself down and started to swim, diving under the waves until she was beyond the pounding of the surf. Adam and Joshua followed. Adam had spent much of each summer in the water, but he had to swim almost to the extent of his energy to keep up.

"Is this okay?" he called to Joshua as Poly continued to cleave her way swiftly and cleanly through the water, out toward the open sea.

"Yes," Joshua called back. "Poly's not allowed to go out this far alone, but she's a natural swimmer and this is as safe a section of beach as you'll find anywhere. They've had trouble with sharks at the hotel, and with undertow, too." He dove under the water, sending up a stream of bubbles.

After a few more yards, Poly stopped, rolled over onto her back and floated for a moment, catching her breath, then started to tread water. She glanced back at Adam, as though about to say something, then seemed to change her mind. Looking out to sea she began to make a series of strange, breathy noises, which she repeated over and over again.

"Look." Joshua pointed out toward the horizon.

Adam thought he saw a flash of silver, then another flash. Then there was the unmistakable joyous leap of a dolphin, coming in toward them.

"Watch," Joshua said.

The dolphin came, leaping through the air, plunging into the water, leaping again, until it had almost reached them. Then it swam directly toward Poly, who swam to meet it with a glad cry. "Macrina!" She, too, seemed to leap out of the water, and then she was flinging her arms about the dolphin in the same way she had greeted Joshua and Adam, and the two of them were rolling over and over together, splashing, Poly shouting, the dolphin making a high-pitched whistle that was a greeting as radiant as Poly's own.

The dolphin started swimming in a slow, graceful circle, with Poly swimming beside her. "Show me your flipper," she commanded.

Obediently the dolphin rolled on its side, waving a sleek, wet flipper. It was a perfectly ordinary dolphin flipper, but Poly kissed it with exuberance, crying, "Oh, Macrina, darling, you're wonderful!"

For a moment Macrina seemed to nuzzle up to her. Then she leaped in a great shining arc and plunged under the water out of sight. It was evidently her goodbye because Poly turned away, back toward Adam and Joshua.

"Does he know about Macrina?"

"Not yet," Joshua said.

"I don't know a *thing* that's happened since Adam went to sleep in the Ritz," Poly complained. "Every time daddy talked to you on the phone he went out to the lab and wouldn't let me come in. He wouldn't even let me talk to Father Tom."

"You're a very inquisitive child," Joshua said. "We'd better swim in now, Poly. You know your father doesn't like to be kept waiting for lunch."

"But isn't anybody going to tell me anything?" Poly wailed.

"Adam's done practically nothing but sleep," Joshua said. "Come on, race you."

It was a close race, Joshua first, then Poly, last Adam. Poly grinned in satisfaction at beating him. "You swim very well, Adam," she said condescendingly, standing on one leg in the shallow water, shaking her wet hair out of her eyes, then jumping up and down to get the water out of one ear.

"That, my dear Miss Polyhymnia O'Keefe," Joshua said, "is how to lose friends in one easy lesson. When you're a few years older you'll know better than to beat a young man in a race."

"Like Diana with the golden apples," Poly said. "Come on, kids, I'm starved."

In the bathhouse they showered, sluicing off the salt, then dressed, still half-wet. Poly and Joshua were filled with such gaiety that Adam found himself relaxing, thinking, —If Dr. O'Keefe asks me about opening the door I'll tell him.

He could not feel, bathed in Poly's and Joshua's high spirits, that there could be any danger here.

As they went in to the central section of the house Charles was standing in wait, calling, "*Hurry,*" and they went directly to the dining room. The dining table was round and the rest of the family was already seated, Johnny in a high chair, and Rosy nearby in a playpen. Mrs. O'Keefe called Joshua to sit at her right, and Adam was taken in hand by Poly who pulled him into the chair by her. Dr. O'Keefe said grace, and then Mrs. O'Keefe and Poly got up and served lunch, helped by a tall, lithe woman with straight black hair and dark skin. The meal consisted of an enormous tureen filled with tiny shellfish, still in their shells, bits of meat and sausage, and the broth in which it had all been cooked.

"One of María's specialties," Mrs. O'Keefe said. "Peggy, how about getting us a couple more bowls to put our empty shells in?" She watched after the little girl, who went to the sideboard and brought two blue bowls to the table. "Joshua, when are you leaving?"

"Low tide."

"About eleven tonight, then. So we can get in some singing before you go."

Joshua laughed. "If Adam can stay awake. I've never seen such a man for sleeping."

Poly defended Adam quickly. "But he was *tired*, Josh, he hadn't had any sleep for three nights."

For a moment there was an uncomfortable silence. Then the phone rang. María looked inquiringly at Mrs. O'Keefe, who said, "It's all right, María, I'll get it," excused herself, and went into the living room, returning to say, "It's for you, Adam."

"But—" Adam started in surprise, pushing back his chair.

"It's Carolyn Cutter," Mrs. O'Keefe said.

"Oh." Adam stood up. "Excuse me." He went into the living room and picked up the phone.

"Adam," came Kali's light, high voice. "I've come to Gaea for a few days, and I'm at the hotel. Isn't that splendid?"

"Yes," Adam said, politely.

"Adam, you don't sound glad to hear from me."

"Well, I am." But he was not.

"Are you where we can talk? I mean are you private or are you surrounded? If you're surrounded just say yes."

"Yes."

"I thought so. Your voice sounds all funny and closed in. Do you think you could escape and come over to the hotel for dinner tonight?"

"I just got here," Adam said, "so I wouldn't think so."

"I was afraid of that. Don't worry, Adam, it'll be all right."

"What will?"

"Everything. I do know it must be awful for you. Come tomorrow night, then. I'll have daddy call and make it all proper and everything. We can't talk now, so I'll say goodbye." Without waiting for him to reply she clicked off.

Adam walked back to the dining room and sat down again, murmuring, "Excuse me."

"I don't like that girl." Poly offered him an orange from a bowl in the center of the table.

Mrs. O'Keefe shook her head, warningly. "You don't know her, Poly."

"I've met her at the Embassy when I've been there with Joshua. I don't like her."

"Poly." Her father looked at her sternly.

"Oh, okay, I'm sorry, but I don't. What did she want, Adam?"

Mrs. O'Keefe said, "If she'd wanted to tell you, no doubt she'd have called you to the phone instead of Adam."

"She wanted me to come to the hotel for dinner tonight."

Poly wailed, "But you're not going!"

"Poly!" Dr. O'Keefe said.

"No, of course I'm not, Poly. Not my first night here."

"Well, thank goodness. I'd have gone green with jealousy."

Dr. O'Keefe rose. "Ready to come to the lab, Adam?"

"Yes, sir." The boy excused himself to Mrs. O'Keefe and followed the doctor out.

In the big lab Adam sniffed hungrily at the odor of fish and chemicals and burning gas in the Bunsens, for there was safety for him in this smell. It was home, it was comfort, and it was, for the moment, escape from confusion. In this familiar room the decisions he had to make would be about what went on in the tanks of starfish, and not choosing between spiders and teddy bears, or between two groups of people, both of whom seemed convinced that they spoke for the American Embassy and therefore for America.

Dr. O'Keefe sat down at a large and ancient rolltop desk. The sunlight struck his hair, firing it. The eyes that looked at Adam were the clear and open blue of the sky. There was, in the smile, the warmth and welcome Adam had come to respond to and to love so quickly in Poly.

Dr. O'Keefe looked around the lab, at the tanks of starfish, at the scarred working counter. "It's a good lab," he said. "I've learned a lot here. I'm sorry to be leaving."

"Because of the hotel?"

Dr. O'Keefe leaned back in his creaking chair. "Yes. This will be our last summer here. It's time to move on." He took up a pipe and filled it slowly. "Sit down."

Adam perched on a rather wobbly stool and waited while Dr. O'Keefe lit his pipe, drawing on it thoughtfully, as though thinking what to say. In the tanks the water murmured and there was the occasional scrabbling sound of an animal moving around.

"We came to the island," Dr. O'Keefe said at last, "because it was, at the time, one of the few places left in the world where I could bring up my family and work undisturbed. We've almost finished what we came for. What we have to do now is to finish it quickly and get out in time."

"In time?"

"When the resort hotel was built here about a year ago it wasn't just because the world is running out of new playgrounds, and it wasn't just one of Typhon Cutter's business ventures—though, as usual, it's been a successful one. It was largely—no false humility here—because of me. Everything I've done in this lab for the past months is now open knowledge." Adam looked at him in a startled way, and Dr. O'Keefe explained. "Therefore everything that's done in this lab is nothing that couldn't have been done by any scientist anywhere in the world: China or Russia, for instance. The important part of my work is neither kept nor recorded here. All right, Adam, enough for now. Let's start you on the tanks and what's going on in them. Your job is to take care of the tanks and keep the daily reports."

Dr. O'Keefe pushed back his chair which gave a loud and protesting squeak. Adam followed him to the first tank in which were several perfectly normal-looking starfish. "Funny," Dr. O'Keefe said. "Here we come from the same family tree and we know so little about these creatures. Presumably," he gave a wry smile, "they know as little about us. Somewhere, a few billion years ago on the evolutionary scale, we chose to develop in different directions. I wonder why?"

"Well," Adam remembered unwillingly his interview with Typhon Cutter, "I suppose Darwin would say it was survival of the fittest and stuff. And mutations."

"Just happenstance?"

"Well, in a way, sir. We developed the way we did because we began to use our forepaws as hands, and stood up on our hind legs."

"Just by accident?"

"Well, I don't know, sir. Dr. Didymus used to talk a lot about free will and making choices and stuff."

The doctor nodded, then pointed to the starfish in the tank. "Do you know how one goes about working with them?"

"Well, it's not easy, sir, because if a starfish feels that an arm is being hurt or threatened in any way he drops it and grows another. So if you want to work with starfish you have to put an anaesthetic solution in the water."

"Standard procedure, yes, and where we've made our first changes. Now, what happens to an isolated arm that drops off?"

"It can't regenerate. There always has to be a piece of central disc, or the starfish can't regrow."

"So one wonders, doesn't one, what is in the central disc that isn't anyplace else? What would your idea be?"

"Well, sir, Dr. Didymus says it's been shown that nerve is very important in regeneration."

"Right. So what we have been doing is taking nerve rings from around the mouth of the animal and transplanting them to isolated arms."

"Wow!"

"Not so spectacular. Not even a very new idea. But it works."

Adam looked not at the starfish in the tank but at Dr. O'Keefe's face, his own face reflecting the doctor's interest and excitement. "What happens?"

"The arm produces its own central disc, and after about four months the familiar five-rayed form is back again. Look. The starfish here have all developed from arm fragments. Perfectly normal, ordinary starfish."

"Wow," Adam said again.

"They've been here a year and we'll continue to observe them until we have to leave the island. You *do* see the implications of all this?"

"Well, yes, sir. If it could be applied to people—"

"Yes. But not too soon. The dangers are so horrifying they hardly bear thinking about. If unscrupulous men got hold of this it would be like letting loose the power of the atom for devastation, for death instead of life. The tiniest thing in the world is the heart of the atom, and yet it's the most powerful. What we are learning from the starfish is just as powerful, and, like the core of the atom, can be either destructive or creative. Misused—it could be like dropping the bomb on Hiroshima." He moved on to the next tank. "Here we transplanted nerve rings about three months ago and you can see that regeneration is well on the way. In this tank we started two months ago but you can see that the starfish is going to grow, that life is going to win. Now here in the first tank you might think nothing is going to happen, but if you'll look carefully you'll see that regeneration has begun."

Adam stared eagerly into the tanks, his excitement at what Dr. O'Keefe was saying pushing the thought of Kali's unwelcome phone call out of his mind. "Why hasn't anybody done this before?" he asked.

"I'm sure other scientists have. Now here in these tanks are frogs and lizards. It's quite openly known that augmented nerve supply stimulates arms to grow on frogs and legs on lizards. The files are here, and I'll show you the file not only for each tank, but for each animal, and it will be your job to keep these up to date daily."

"Yes, Dr. O'Keefe."

"This kind of work interests you, doesn't it?"

"Yes, sir. It excites me more than anything in the world."

"But the exciting things always have implications that we don't foresee. Always, Adam."

"I wish they didn't," Adam said.

"As Poly would remark, if wishes were horses, beggars would ride. Poly has the makings of a scientist, and she's been working with me on this all along. As a matter of fact, I have to keep her out of the laboratory. It's better right now for Poly to help my wife than to work with me here, so I seldom allow her out here until after the younger ones are in bed."

"Is that why she was kidnapped?" Adam asked.

"Because she knows what I'm doing? Yes. But also I think the idea was to use her as a hostage. Then, when you opened that door at the Avenida Palace something new came into the picture. You became more important than Poly. At least this is my guess." He looked at Adam, but Adam looked down at his feet. Dr. O'Keefe sighed.

Adam, still looking down, mumbled, "But you said that none of this was really secret."

"It's not. Most of my lab isn't in a building at all. What's done in here is only the beginning, the going back and working out reasons and proofs. It's the other things, the things that are not here, that are really important. Did you see Macrina when you went swimming?"

"The dolphin? Yes, sir."

"She'll almost always come for Poly. Poly's greatest talent is for loving. She loves in an extraordinary way for a twelve-year-old, a simple, pure outpouring, with no looking for anything in return. What she is too young to have learned yet is that love is too mighty a gift for some people to accept."

"Does she—does she love *every*body?" Adam asked, rather desperately.

The doctor laughed. "As you may have noticed at the table Poly is quite capable of dislike, reasonable or no. Being judgmental is something she knows she has to fight against. But when Poly loves, it simply happens. She loves her family, all of us. She loves Tom Tallis. She loves Joshua. And she loves you, Adam."

At last the boy looked directly at the older man. "Sir. I love Poly, too."

Dr. O'Keefe returned the gaze. "Do you, Adam?"

"Yes, sir. I don't quite know why. And I don't—I don't have

any idea why she would love me. She was—she was in my care when she was kidnapped. I was responsible for her."

"We don't blame you for what happened. Tom says he didn't warn you properly."

"But I was responsible," Adam said. "And I failed. This is why—"

"Why what, Adam?"

Adam looked down and spoke in a low voice. "Why I didn't obey you when you told me not to open the door. Sir. I am very confused."

Dr. O'Keefe put his hand on the boy's shoulder. "All right, Adam. I think you'll do."

"Do for what, sir?"

"Let's just say that I don't think you'll ever betray Poly."

"Dr. O'Keefe, if you ever needed to trust me with her again—if you ever would—I wouldn't fail again."

Dr. O'Keefe nodded. "Yes. I believe you. But you know that I can't trust you with her now, don't you?"

"Why, sir?"

"You must know why, Adam."

"Sir," Adam said, "just let me have a few days to sort things out. If I can just work here quietly in the lab for a while—if nothing here is really secret then I can't hurt Poly or you or anybody else, can I? If I can just get a few things straightened out in my own mind . . ."

"All right. We'll have to let it go at that."

Again the boy looked directly at the older man. "This Carolyn Cutter—"

"What about her?"

"She wants me to have dinner with her at the hotel tomorrow, since I said I couldn't tonight. She's going to have her father call you or Mrs. O'Keefe about it. But if you'd rather I didn't I'd be glad not to."

Dr. O'Keefe shook his head. "No, Adam. If you want to make up your own mind, you'll have to make it up, won't you?"

12

ADAM stayed in the laboratory the rest of the afternoon. He worked with happy concentration on tank and file: here was work he knew; here was safety. He was loath to leave when Dennys, changed to clean shorts and shirt, came to call him.

After dinner the two babies were put to bed. The rest gathered in the living room, Sandy, Dennys, and Peggy in their night things. Poly and Charles were staying up to see Joshua off.

"May we sing until time for Josh to go?" Poly asked.

"It's a must," Joshua said, his arm lightly about Poly's waist. "What first?"

"The Tallis Canon, of course, so Father'll know we're thinking of him. You start, Mother."

Mrs. O'Keefe leading, they sang it in canon, one voice coming in after another.

> *All praise to thee, my God, this night*
> *For all the blessings of the light.*
> *Keep me, O keep me, king of kings*
> *Beneath thine own almighty wings.*

Poly's voice finished alone, light and clear, and full of trust. Adam remembered, unwillingly, the empty washroom on the plane, and thought of Poly drugged, gagged, dumped roughly onto a pile of luggage. He was grateful when Mrs. O'Keefe started the gay "Arkansas Traveller." From this they went into a conglomeration of familiar hymns, madrigals, folk songs, even Bach chorales. Adam had played the guitar at school parties and he knew the bass to much of the music. Joshua and Dr. O'Keefe were both tenors, so he was a welcome addition.

"You're absolutely wonderful, Adam," Mrs. O'Keefe said. "I'm sick and tired of singing bass an octave high. If Old Doc had only told us you could sing it wouldn't have mattered whether you could work in the lab or not. How about 'Come Unto These Yellow Sands'?"

During the singing Peggy, nightgown trailing, came and sat in Adam's lap, at first a little rigid, as though not quite certain of her welcome, then relaxing softly against him, her head on his chest, her breath coming more and more slowly until Adam realized she was sound asleep. He put his arm around the small, warm body, almost afraid to sing lest he disturb her, then relaxing and singing fully. Across the room Joshua, sitting with Poly, smiled at him.

Just as Adam began to feel that he must shift his position, and knew that he didn't want to move, despite his discomfort, for fear of waking Peggy, Mrs. O'Keefe rose and came over to him, saying, "Will you carry her to bed for me, please, Adam? Come on, boys, time for bed."

Adam stood up with the sleeping child. He realized that all evening he had been happy, he had forgotten about Kali, he had felt only pleasure in the children and in the music. He did not want the peace of the evening to end. He did not want Joshua to fly back to Lisbon.

But when the boy returned to the living room Joshua said, "You're coming to see me off, aren't you, Adam?"

"Well, sure."

"I put some riding clothes in your room. Same source as the bathing suits."

Dr. O'Keefe laughed. "It's really not as bad as it sounds. We do make every effort to get the things back to their rightful owners. We'll be waiting for you outside."

Mrs. O'Keefe stayed home with the younger children. Adam set off with the doctor and Joshua, who were both riding stocky, golden-brown horses which Joshua told Adam were an island breed. Poly was on an elderly bay who seemed enormous for her, but was obviously gentle and reliable; Charles rode a shaggy pony, and Adam himself was given a large, white, matronly looking beast, apparently first cousin in disposition to Poly's bay.

The night was bright with a three-quarter moon, and the

horses moved softly along the damp sand at the edge of the water, their hoofbeats almost silenced by the slow, steady sound of the sea. Against the dunes fireflies glittered. Poly rode beside Adam. In the moonlight the brilliance of her hair was turned to silver. She sat, tall and erect, her height making her seem more than her twelve years. Ahead of them rode the doctor and Joshua; Charles led the procession, a solitary, small figure. The two men were talking and their voices, though not their words, were blown back on the wind.

"Daddy wants to talk to Josh," Poly said, "and I can see he'd rather I didn't listen. And Charles is in one of his hermit moods. I want to talk to you anyhow. Josh and I went for a long walk this afternoon while you were in the lab working, and he didn't tell me one single thing."

"About what?"

"About anything. Adam, I know children are not supposed to be curious, but life isn't as simple as that any more, and I *am* twelve, and after all, I *was* kidnapped."

Adam's sense of relaxation vanished; he felt himself stiffen in the saddle. "Yes, Poly, you were."

"Well, then, don't I have a right to ask a few questions? I don't think Joshua thought I did. Had the right. I mean, it was okay for me to ask *him* questions, even if he wouldn't answer any of them, but I got the idea that he didn't think it was all right for me to ask *you* questions. Why?"

Adam looked not at Poly but at the moonlight dazzling the surface of the ocean. "I'm not quite sure," he said at last.

"Then is it all right if I *do* ask you some questions?"

"You can ask me anything you want to," Adam said, "though I may be like Josh and not be very good at answering. But how about letting me start off by asking you a few things first?"

"Of course." She was so willing, the face she turned to him in the moonlight was so open, that Adam winced.

"Poly, on the plane, when you went into the washroom, you were afraid, weren't you?"

"Yes."

"Why?"

"Father Tom had told me it wasn't safe for him to keep me with him."

"Why?"

"Because of the pa——" she stopped herself. "Because they'd know I was daddy's daughter. And they know I know about what daddy's doing."

"About starfish regenerating their arms?"

"Yes."

"But that's not a secret, Poly. Your father said himself that he was sure other scientists were doing the same experiments."

Poly leaned over her horse with a caressing gesture, putting her head down on its neck. After a moment she sat up straight in the saddle again. "But it's more than that."

"What is it, then?"

"Didn't daddy tell you?"

"He doesn't trust me," Adam said starkly.

"But Adam—"

Adam's voice was savage. "He has every right not to trust me."

"I trust you," Poly said.

It was all Adam could do not to kick his heels into his horse's ribs, to gallop away. He growled, "You're much too trusting for your own good."

"Oh, I don't go around trusting everybody, the way Peggy does. I'm not that much of a child. I know there are people in the world you *can* trust, and people you can't."

"How do you decide which is which?"

"You know with people, or you don't. I don't trust that Kali. I wish you weren't going out to dinner with her."

"So do I."

"Do you have to?"

"Yes, I think I do."

Back in the brush an owl screeched, a shrill, terrifying cry. Poly shuddered. "And I didn't trust the steward on that plane. He was weasely."

"When you went to the washroom—were you afraid of being kidnapped?"

"Not exactly. I didn't really know what I was afraid of. After all, I'd never been kidnapped before. But I guess it was really sort of in the back of my mind."

"You're sure it was the steward who put you in the canvas bag?"

"Adam, if you're kidnapped you don't forget the person who kidnaps you."

"But did you really see him?"

"Yes. I was washing my hands, and I heard the knob of the door turn, but I'd locked it, so I didn't expect it to open. But when it did I saw him in the mirror. He put his hand over my mouth before I could scream. He was so much stronger than I am, in spite of being weasely, that I couldn't even make a noise fighting. And then he put that stuff over my nose and got the gag on me and got me in the sack." She began to tremble.

"I'm sorry," Adam said. "I'm truly sorry to have to remind you of it. Will you let me ask you just a couple more questions?"

"If you need to."

"I do need to. I wouldn't do it to you otherwise, I promise."

Poly gave an oddly grown-up laugh. "Don't sound so agonized, Adam. It's all right."

"Well, what about the steward," Adam asked, almost savagely. "Is he just floating around loose? I mean, he might try to come here or something."

"Really, Adam." Poly sounded impatient. "You must think daddy's very careless or something. Interpol went right after him."

"Have they got him?"

"Yes. Last night. Father Tom called from Madrid."

"But—"

"I don't want to talk about it. I don't want to think about it. It's all over." Tension tightened her voice again.

Adam sighed. "I'm sorry. Just one more thing. When you got to the house, they took you right out of the sack?"

"Yes."

"Who took you out?"

"I don't know, Adam. Don't think Josh and daddy haven't asked me this one over and over again, too. I was still groggy and it was so dark in the room all I could tell was that it was a man, and I couldn't really tell about him, because at first I thought he was terribly fat, and then I felt one of his arms, and it was skinny."

It was Adam's turn to shiver. The moon rode placidly in a cloudless sky, the stars dimmed by the brightness. The sea, too, was calm, the waves rolling in gently, rhythmically. Up on the dunes the grasses and the great wings of the palms were almost still, though the fronds made their incessant scratchy whispering. The air was warm and they rode without sweaters or jackets. But Adam shivered.

Poly looked over at him. "He gave me something to drink. I told you that. And it put me back to sleep. And then, later on, whenever it was, when I was awake and it was all dark and horrible and I was frightened and the door was locked and I started to cry, that man came in—"

"Which man?"

"You know, Adam, I told you at the Ritz, the man who drove us, that beast. And then he blindfolded and gagged me and put me in the car and I knew he'd hurt me if I tried to cry or do anything. And then there I was in front of the Ritz, and you were there, too, and you held me, and I knew it was all going to be all right."

In front of them Adam could see Dr. O'Keefe and Joshua talking quietly, their horses close. Charles was still in the lead, sitting up very straight, a stocky shadow on his little pony. A firefly flew across the beach from the dunes, lit for a moment on Charles's shoulder, then disappeared into the moonlight.

"Adam," Poly said, "why haven't daddy or Josh told me anything about you?"

"I don't know."

"How did you happen to be there on the sidewalk? Were you in the car, too?"

"Yes."

"Were you kidnapped, too?"

Suddenly, almost without his volition, Adam's heels kicked and his horse broke into a trot. He kicked again. The horse started to canter.

As he came up beside Joshua he called out, half choking, "It was Carolyn Cutter I opened the door to!"

He pulled the horse up. Joshua dropped behind, then came up on Adam's other side, so that the boy was riding between the two men. Dr. O'Keefe, at the water's edge, was looking straight ahead, not at Adam, not even at the small figure of Charles placidly riding along a few yards in front. Adam turned toward Joshua who smiled at him brilliantly but did not speak.

Behind them there was a thudding, and Poly's bay came ambling along with what was obviously all the speed it considered suitable. "*Hey!*" Poly called.

"I'm sorry," Adam said. "I have to talk to your father."

"Poly," Dr. O'Keefe said, "go ride with Charles, please."

"But Charles wants to—"

"You don't need to talk to him. Just go ride beside him."

In the moonlight Adam could see Poly glower. But she responded obediently, "Yes, daddy," and trotted the large, disapproving bay so close to the water's edge that an incoming wave rippled against its protesting hooves. Charles turned to her and spoke, at which Poly flung her arms up in the air in an abused fashion and trotted the bay around the pony so that the little boy could be next to the water.

"All right, Adam," Dr. O'Keefe said quietly. "And then she took you to her father."

"You know?"

"Yes. But you had to tell us yourself."

Joshua turned to Adam. "Had you ever seen Carolyn Cutter before you met her in the airport in New York?"

"No."

"How did you happen to speak to her there?"

"I suppose," Adam said slowly, "you might say she picked me up. But it all seemed perfectly natural. What with the fog and everything and planes being canceled and flights deferred, all kinds of people were talking who wouldn't have if everything had been perfectly ordinary."

Dr. O'Keefe asked, "Was it just casual chitchat between you?"

"No. She warned me about—about Canon Tallis. And about you, sir."

"Warned you about what?"

"Well—not anything particular. Just a warning in a vacuum. I don't think I really took it very seriously at first. It all just seemed kind of exciting and an adventure."

"And you thought she was attractive?"

"Yes, sir."

Joshua reached over and patted the neck of Adam's horse, as though in this way he could communicate comfort directly to Adam. "And so she is. So when she knocked on the door . . ."

"She told me she'd help me find Poly."

"You believed her?"

"Well, Josh, I *did* find Poly. She was there, at the Cutters' house."

The older men exchanged glances, and Dr. O'Keefe said, "Yes, Poly's description of the man in the dark room could hardly have been of anyone but Typhon Cutter. But we had to be sure. Now, Adam, will you go back to the moment you opened the door and tell us in as much detail as you can everything that happened until you and Poly were put out of the car in front of the Ritz?"

"Yes, sir. I'll try. But I *was* terribly tired, so I may not get it exactly right. I'll do my best." He looked out over the ocean. The moon made a wide, shining path from water's edge to horizon. Carefully he tried to tell the two men the events of that night that seemed far more than three nights behind him. In spite of the fatigue that had kept him from thinking clearly or acting reasonably his accurate memory again helped him, bringing the events and words of that night up from his subconscious. He looked at the bright swathe of moonlight on water and recalled small details he hadn't even known he remembered, or that, up to this moment, he hadn't remembered. He saw again with his mind's eye the black-and-white room, saw the obesity of Typhon Cutter's body in such repellent contrast to the thinness of arms and legs; he saw again the extraordinary beauty of the young man in the portrait, the young man who had grown into a middle-aged spider.

"If you didn't know it was the same person—how *could* anyone change so completely?"

"The odd distribution of weight is glandular," Dr. O'Keefe

said, "but I don't think it's as simple as all that. He also reflects all the choices he has made all his life long."

"Why," Adam asked, with the abruptness with which he had asked it of Typhon Cutter, "why did Canon Tallis lose his eyebrows?"

For a moment the strained look tightened Dr. O'Keefe's face again. "It was in Korea. He not only withstood torture himself, but he helped the men with him to stand up against it. This was what left the greatest mark on him, not his own suffering, but the pain of others."

"Adam," Joshua said, "when we didn't know where Poly was, and then when we didn't know where you were—if he'd had any hair left it would have turned white."

"Stop, Joshua," the doctor said quietly. "Don't make this any harder for Adam than it is already. Go on, boy."

"Yes, sir." He sighed deeply, unconsciously, talking in a voice so low that several times he was asked to repeat himself. Finally he said, "I think that's about it. I'm glad I've told you. But I think I have to tell you that I'm still confused. I'm still not certain or secure about anything."

Again Joshua patted Adam's horse, saying softly, "That's all right, Adam. Who is?"

"So of course I won't have dinner with Kali tomorrow night. I don't ever want to see her again."

Dr. O'Keefe spoke quietly but firmly. "But I'm afraid you'll have to. When you opened that door to her you started a chain of events for yourself that you can't end quite this easily."

Ahead of them Poly called out, "There's the plane!"

Charles's clear voice came, "Race you!" and his little pony tore across the sand. Poly's bay broke into a resigned trot.

The plane lay on the beach ahead of them like a strange, prehistoric bird in the shadows. Again Adam felt a sense of irrational panic at the idea that Joshua was going to leave. Charles reached the plane the pony's length ahead of Poly. They dismounted and walked their horses over to the softer sand where there was an old barnacled pile that could be used as a hitching post. Dr. O'Keefe turned to the children, leaving Joshua and Adam side by side.

"Adam—"

"Yes, Josh?"

"Feel better?"

"I don't really know."

"You will."

"Okay, if you say so."

"Not if *I* say so. But you will. Even though it's not going to be easy."

Adam set his jaw stubbornly. "I will not have dinner with Kali tomorrow night. I will not have anything more to do with the Cutters."

Joshua spoke tranquilly. "Oh, yes, you will."

"I will *not*."

"Listen," Joshua said, "I'll bet you anything you like that you will."

"I wouldn't put money on it if I were you."

"I'd put more than that on it. When I whistled the Tallis canon you said you'd sung it in choir."

"Till my voice changed."

"I was going to say something, but I'm not. Instead—did you ever hear Tom Tallis use a kind of password phrase?"

"Yes. In Madrid. Twice."

"Recognize it?"

"No. It was poetry, that's all I could tell."

"Yes. Robert Frost. *Two Tramps in Mud Time.* A simple sort of little poem it starts out to be, with the poet out chopping wood and two tramps coming along and resenting it because he's doing for fun what they figure they ought to be paid for. Then comes the last stanza, whammo, a lower cut right to the solar plexus.

> *But yield who will to their separation,*
> *My object in living is to unite*
> *My avocation and my vocation*
> *As my two eyes make one in sight.*
> *Only where love and need are one,*
> *And the work is play for mortal stakes,*
> *Is the deed ever really done*
> *For Heaven and the future's sakes.*

I'm not sure about heaven, but I do feel I have to do my best for the future, and if you're any kind of scientist you will, too. And if that means going out with Kali tomorrow you'll do it."

Adam still sounded stubborn. "As far as I'm concerned, Carolyn Cutter is the past."

"Listen, you told us tonight because of Poly, didn't you?"

Adam sighed again. "I really don't know why I told you. I don't know why anything any more."

"It was Poly," Joshua said with certainty. "At least it would have been for me, and I'm willing to bet it was for you. Adam, I don't know about you, but I can't do anything except because I care about people, because I love people. I can't do it for love of God, like Tom Tallis, or for heaven's sake, as Mr. Frost said. But because I love people I have to act according to it—to the fact that I love them. Maybe this doesn't make any sense. But it's the way I am, and you'll just have to accept it."

Adam said softly, "The way you accepted me?"

"I failed you on that this morning, didn't I? I wanted to push you too far, too fast."

"Don't push me now, then," Adam said.

"Touché. But I have the feeling that there isn't much time. That I don't have the time to give you time. Okay, kid, come on, it's time I shoved off."

13

ADAM, Poly, and Charles stood at the hitching post while Joshua and Dr. O'Keefe checked the plane. When all was in readiness Joshua climbed into the cockpit; as the motor coughed and the propeller began to spin, making the little plane vibrate as though it must fall apart, the doctor came and stood beside the horses, a little away from Adam and the children. The plane wheeled and moved slowly across the sand, gathered speed, bounced once or twice, and then began to climb.

"Sir," Adam asked, "is that plane really safe?"

The doctor laughed. "Doesn't look it, does it? But yes, as safe as the latest jet. Particularly with Joshua piloting it."

They watched the plane as it gained altitude, flying, it seemed from where they stood, directly along the path of moonlight on water, flying further, higher, smaller, until it lost the reality of being an elderly, battered Hawker Hurricane piloted by a young man, and became a silver bird in the night flying to the moon.

Standing beside Adam Poly let out a low, startled cry. "Charles! Don't!"

Adam turned and saw in the moonlight that Charles's face was contorted in a vain effort at control, that tears were silently squeezing out of the tightly closed eyes and down the little boy's cheeks.

Dr. O'Keefe knelt on the sand in order to bring himself to the child's level. "Charles."

Without opening his eyes, Charles moved into his father's arms.

Poly stamped. "I *hate* it when Charles cries."

"Charles," Dr. O'Keefe said again.

Poly whispered fiercely, "He *never* cries unless . . ."

Adam asked, "Unless what?"

"Unless something is awfully . . . wrong."

Charles stood, leaning against his father, still crying silently. Finally he said in so low a voice that Adam could hardly catch the words, "I wish Josh hadn't gone."

Dr. O'Keefe's voice was quiet. "He'll be back in Lisbon almost as soon as we've had time to ride home. He has a good tail wind and the weather is clear all the way."

"Will he call when he gets back?"

"He always does. And I will come in to you and tell you. I promise. He has no important papers on him this time. I have to correlate and code everything he brought me. Come, now, Charles, it's late and you're tired and we must go. You'll ride with me."

Obediently Charles mounted his pony.

Dr. O'Keefe and the little boy led the way, Joshua's horse ambling along just behind them, with Poly and Adam in the rear. They did little talking. Poly was frowning, seeming unduly disturbed, Adam thought, by her brother's behavior. After a while she began to droop in the saddle, saying, "I'm half asleep. Pick me up if I fall off."

Ahead of them both Dr. O'Keefe and Charles sat straight and still and somehow stern. The moon moved across the sky.

As they neared the bungalows Adam saw that someone was standing on the sea wall, waiting, and for a moment fear leaped into his throat, but Dr. O'Keefe raised his arm in greeting.

"It's José, María's husband," Poly said. "He takes care of the horses."

They went directly to bed. As Adam drifted into sleep he heard the phone ring, and then he heard Dr. O'Keefe pause outside Charles's door. "That was Josh, Charles. All's well. Go to sleep now."

In the morning Adam was wakened by Poly coming in with a breakfast tray. His room was flooded with light and warmth and he felt a sense of pure well-being he had been afraid would never return.

"Sit up, lazy," Poly said. "I let you sleep as long as possible. I'm not spoiling you. Breakfast in bed is one thing we always do. I'm going to take Charles his tray and then I'm coming back to talk to you."

Adam grinned at her. "Okay. Forewarned is, I hope, forearmed, though I have only two."

Poly turned at the door. "And the starfish has five. You will have exactly time to wash your face and stuff. *If* you hurry." She made a quick exit, and Adam heard her say, "Move, Sandy."

"Does Mother know you're bothering Adam?"

"She said I could ask him, and *he* said it was okay." Their voices continued in friendly argument as they went into the living room.

Poly returned, saying, "Daddy's out in the lab. You're to go on out as soon as you're ready. Then I'll come for you a little before lunch and we'll go for a swim."

Adam poured hot milk, hot coffee. "Will we see—what's her name?"

"Macrina? Yes. If she comes."

"Doesn't she always?"

"Usually. But not always. Then, after lunch, we'll take you to the village."

"What village?"

Poly sat, crosslegged, on the foot of Adam's bed. "The native village. Where María and José come from."

Adam said, rather uncomfortably, his mouth full of croissant, "I don't have to be taken sightseeing, Poly. I've caused enough trouble for all of you already. I'd really rather stay in the lab and work."

Poly frowned, then gave him a stern and piercing look. "It's not sightseeing, Adam. I assure you that's not our purpose in taking you there."

"Are you going too?"

"If daddy'll let me. He usually does." She got down off the bed. "Okay. I'll come over to the lab and yell for you when it's time for our swim."

When Adam went out to the lab Dr. O'Keefe was sitting at the rolltop desk, writing, but he looked up at the boy's step, saying without preamble, "I want to show you something." He took Adam into the small side lab and to the first of the tanks. In it was a starfish in the process of regeneration. It was not a starfish with part of its own central disc; it was an isolated fragment of arm into which Dr. O'Keefe told Adam he had transplanted nerve rings as he had done with the starfish the boy had already seen. The difference between the starfish in this tank and those in the main lab was that this starfish was not developing normally. This particular combination of arm and nerve ring seemed to be generating into a strange, lumpy, three-armed creature.

Without speaking Dr. O'Keefe moved to the second tank. Here was a lizard who had lost a leg. Something was growing where the leg had been; it was not a lizard leg, but a deformed stump. In the third tank was a frog who had lost a forearm; this, too, was growing back abnormally.

Dr. O'Keefe went into the main lab, sitting down at his desk. Adam stood, waiting. For some time Dr. O'Keefe appeared to study a pencil. Finally he said, "Back in the early sixties scientists were able to start babies, actual human foetuses, in a test tube. For a while they developed normally. Then, and no one knew why, their development went awry. They became deformed; monstrosities. You've probably heard about this."

"Yes, sir."

"Why did this happen?"

"I don't know, sir. I don't think anybody does."

"Why is regeneration a normal thing for starfish? Why, if we transplant nerve rings from the central disc can an isolated arm fragment then organize itself? Why is this also true of frogs and lizards?"

"Well, it's because the augmented nerve supply provides the stimulation."

"Why were the animals in the little lab developing abnormally?"

"I don't know, sir. Mutations?"

"In a very small percentage, yes. But usually, no. Where do you think I get my experimental animals from, Adam?"

"Well, from the beach, from around here . . . I used to collect specimens for Old Doc."

"Yes. The children find a good many for me. They bring me any animal they see, marine or land, that has been injured. The villagers bring me some, too, for which I pay them one escudo for twenty-five specimens. I made it absolutely clear that they were to bring me only the animals that had been accidentally hurt. Then, after the first abnormalities began to develop, I learned that two of the men who work at the resort hotel had been deliberately mutilating the creatures. I had thought that the smallness of the payment would avoid this, an escudo being three and a half cents, you will remember. But it didn't. There always have been and there always will be people who have been corrupted into enjoying any excuse for cruelty."

For some reason Adam thought of the Cutters' chauffeur. He could quite easily imagine Molèc tearing the arm off a lizard.

Dr. O'Keefe continued. "It is from these deliberately mutilated animals that the deformities have come. But it isn't even that simple. I had, for a brief while, a lab assistant who was a brilliant man. He was also one of the most evil human beings I have ever encountered. Every animal he tended, every starfish arm into which he transplanted nerve rings, every frog or lizard into whose wounds he injected augmented nerve supply, developed malformations that were malignant and that devoured the creature on which they grew."

"Why—" Adam asked, "why was he evil?"

"You remember the story of the Third Man?"

"Yes. Josh mentioned it."

"Antibiotics diluted and sold on the black market, and innocent children suffering and dying through this incomprehensible greed. This kind of thing doesn't happen only in fiction. You don't have to read the book or see the movie to come across it. This man, with a brilliant and utterly warped mind, grew fat on underworld black-market corruption."

"Then why did you employ him, sir?"

"I was asked to. In order to convict him."

"Did you?"

"With Joshua's help."

"What happened?"

"He's in Leavenworth."

Adam said, slowly, "So I guess this kind of thing makes enemies?"

Dr. O'Keefe looked at him. "They *are* enemies, Adam. You don't have to *make* enemies of them."

Adam got his stubborn look. "But what about Poly?" Dr. O'Keefe did not answer, and Adam continued. "If you didn't—if you didn't *make* enemies, I mean, even if they *are* enemies anyhow, then would anybody have wanted to hurt Poly?"

The older man's face tightened. "Nothing is easy, Adam. Nothing. And we're all of us in danger from the moment we're born. You've grown up in New York. You know that if you cross a street a truck can run you down. If you ride in the subway and there's a spot of trouble a bullet meant for someone else can find its way into your heart. And if my research, which I had anticipated as a quiet and hermit-like life, so that I could bring my children up in a peaceful and natural way in the midst of an unpeaceful and unnatural world, has, instead, led them into added dangers, then I must accept this for them, as well as for myself, if I believe in what I am doing."

"I'm sorry, sir. I didn't mean . . ."

"That's all right. I just want you to understand clearly why it is so important that what I am doing does not get into the wrong hands. Remember the deformed babies that came of thalidomide being used before enough was known about it? We're just at the very beginning of this, and it cannot be taken out of our hands and misused."

"It's like what you said about the atom?"

"Yes. Like splitting the atom. We're just beginning to learn why the regeneration is sometimes abnormal and malignant. We're just beginning to understand that you cannot change stones into bread. This is not the way miracles are worked, but it's always been a temptation. If what we are doing is taken over by the unscrupulous it can cause unimaginable horror and suffering. Here is power to give life to people, or to devour them. What I am trying to do is to go back about two thousand years in my thinking. Somewhere in the last two thousand years we've gone off. When we began to depend on and to develop *things* in the western world we lost something of inestimable value in our understanding. There's something wrong about trying to heal with a surgeon's knife. There's got to be an alternative to cutting and mutilating and I'm trying to learn it from the starfish. But I'm just at the beginning. And I'm afraid, Adam. If it gets out of my hands—I'm afraid." Dr. O'Keefe clenched his fist and pounded it softly against the papers on his desk. Then he smiled. "All right, Adam. I have work to do here at my desk. You get along with your job until Poly comes to take you for a swim."

It was several minutes before Adam could concentrate on his care of the tanks, but, as he began to put the day's observations down in the files, the discipline of the work took hold of him, and he was able to keep his mind on the job at hand. This was a task that fascinated him, that engrossed him utterly, and he was surprised when he heard Poly's voice and realized that the morning had passed.

Poly stood in the lab, wearing a black two-piece bathing suit that did nothing for her still undeveloped figure.

"Daddy," she asked, "what are the specifications for a fashion model?"

"Oh—thirty-four, twenty-two, thirty-four," Dr. O'Keefe replied absently.

Poly sighed. "Oh, dear. I'm twenty, twenty, twenty."

Her father laughed. "I really think you look better in the red wool, even if it does fight with your hair."

Poly sighed again. "Yes. Okay. I'll change, while Adam's getting into his trunks. Mother says time will take care of this particular problem, and I suppose it will. Was mother gorgeous when she was my age?"

"Frightful," Dr. O'Keefe said. "Much worse than you."

"That's encouraging, at any rate. And I suppose it's a good thing about time, because right now I'd have an awful time choosing between Adam and Joshua, even if Josh *is* too old for me."

Her father laughed again. It was a good laugh, warm and open and loving. "Time seems to be making its inroads already. A few weeks ago you were announcing that you were never going to grow up."

"Oh, I'm over being Peter Pan. Maybe it's jealousy. Knowing that that Kali has her hooks into Adam. Come on, Adam, let's go. I told María I'd be back in time to help serve lunch."

It was another golden day, the sand was gold; gold shimmered from the sun into the blue of the sky, touched the small crests of waves in a calm ocean. Adam and Poly swam out, side by side, until Poly stopped and began to tread water, making the strange, breathy whistling noise that was her call to the dolphin.

It was longer this time; Poly's calling began to sound tired, and Adam had given up and was just about to suggest swimming back, when silver arched out of water in a swift flash, and Macrina came leaping, diving, flying, to meet them. Again there was the ecstatic greeting, Poly with her arms about the great, slippery beast, Macrina giving her marvelous, contagious dolphin smile, so that Adam felt that he was grinning like a fool. After a while Macrina left Poly, came over to Adam and gave him a gentle, inquisitive nudge. For a moment he was frightened. He knew that dolphins were friendly and gentle, that sailors rejoiced at seeing them because they kept away sharks, but Macrina was so large, so alien, that it was all he could do to make himself keep treading water quietly, and to say, "Hello, Macrina."

Macrina nudged him again, then flashed out of the water, dove, disappeared, and came up on Poly's other side.

"She likes you!" Poly cried joyfully. "Macrina, show Adam your flipper."

As she had done the day before, Macrina obediently rolled over and waved her sleek, wet flipper.

At last Adam realized. "The flipper—" he said. "Did she—"

Stroking Macrina, Poly nodded. "Yes. We don't know how it happened. I found her on the beach, flipper torn off, bleeding to death. I ran and got daddy, and he was able to stop the bleeding. Of course we didn't know her then, but she seemed to know that daddy and I wanted to help. Daddy has some big tanks in the village. They're not in a building; the village is around a cove, and there are some pens in the cove. Luckily Father Tom was here, and he helped, and we managed to get her to the village and into one of the pens. Daddy and Father Tom stayed with her all night. As a matter of fact, we could hardly get daddy away for weeks, he ate there with Virbius, he's their chief, and I guess you'd call him their medicine man, too, he's a hundred and forty-nine years old, and he prayed over Macrina and it all worked, the augmented nerve and stuff, and isn't she marvelous and good and beautiful and virtuous and wonderful?"

Macrina rolled over in the water and smirked.

"Okay, Macrina," Poly said. "We've got to go in to lunch now, I promised María. Give my love to Basil and Gregory."

"Basil and Gregory?"

"Her brothers. They're very intelligent. Of course dolphins are, but we think Macrina's family is more so. It's quite obvious they are, isn't it?"

Macrina waited for no further goodbyes. Down, down she dove, and then, a hundred yards away, Adam saw her flash through the air.

"By the way," Poly said. "While you were in the lab that Kali's father called and talked to mother. They're sending the hotel helicopter for you at seven-thirty. I don't know why daddy wants you to go there for dinner. I think it's just awful. But I suppose if he wants you to go you'll have to go."

"Yes." The pleasure ebbed from Adam's limbs. "If he wants me to I have to."

Poly stopped treading water, rolled over onto her back, blew a jet of water upward like a small whale, and floated. "Promise me one thing."

"What?"

"Don't go without saying goodbye to me. I have something to give you, and you *mustn't* leave without it. Promise."

"Okay," Adam agreed. "I promise. What is it? A charm?"

"No," Poly said. "A weapon."

14

AFTER lunch José brought three horses around to the bungalow, and Dr. O'Keefe, Poly, and Adam set off for the village, riding uphill to the plateau with the monolithic slabs of stone. As Joshua had stopped by the great central table the day before, so did Dr. O'Keefe, although he did not dismount. Poly and Adam reined up beside him. Adam's spirits soared, despite the fierceness of the sun.

The doctor was sitting erect on his horse, as though waiting. He caught Adam's inquiring gaze and said, "Virbius, the chief of the village, wished to meet us here. Visitors aren't encouraged there. The people from the hotel have brought only disease and trouble. But you are under my aegis, and he will escort us."

Adam nodded. Dr. O'Keefe continued to sit straight and tall, and Poly was in one of her rare silent moods. Adam looked around, at the great stone table, above which a large golden butterfly was fluttering. The flash of a bird's scarlet wing led his gaze beyond the encircling stones and through the trees that edged the plateau and into a clearing. In the clearing were a few small, white slabs, with light moving over them, and leaf shadows, green, mauve, and indigo.

Again Dr. O'Keefe followed Adam's gaze. "Yes. It's a cemetery. A small one. The villagers have their own, and if anyone does anything as inconvenient as dying at the resort hotel they're whisked back to the mainland as inconspicuously as possible." He held up his hand for silence, and they could hear a rustling in the brush. A yellow-and-black bird flashed across the clearing, followed by a wizened old man on a horse, a dark and shriveled old man, with a few strands of soft, silvery hair. Adam had no doubt that this was Virbius, the chieftain. Poly had said that he was how old? a hundred and forty-nine? Adam knew that the villagers' way of counting time was probably different from the way he had been taught in school, but if Virbius was not a hundred and forty-nine he was certainly the oldest man Adam had ever seen, far older than Old Doc, who, after all, was ninety.

Dr. O'Keefe raised his arm in greeting; Virbius responded, the gesture full of dignity despite the fact that his hand was tremulous with age. Without a word he turned his horse and headed into the brush again. Dr. O'Keefe followed, with Poly and Adam in single file behind him on the narrow path.

They rode through the low brush along the spine of the plateau; the sun was high and hot, so that their shadows were small dark blobs moving along the scrub. Somehow Adam was grateful for the golden warmth that seeped through him, even though his shirt began to cling damply to his body. The blue, almost cloudless sky was so high that there seemed to be between earth and sky a golden shimmering of sunlight. The red of Dr. O'Keefe's and Poly's hair was touched with gold; gold, gold, everything glinted and glimmered, and light as well as heat penetrated Adam's pores.

He had lost track of time (would time ever seem normal, countable, accountable, to him again?) when the path started to descend. Below them lay the straw roofs of the village, the large central hut, with smaller huts raying out from it, the whole village on a promontory about a perfect, natural bay. In the bay fishing boats were anchored, and Adam thought he could see others, small dark specks out at sea. While they were still a fair distance above the village Virbius stopped his horse, raised his arm, this time in a gesture of command, and let out a strange, penetrating whistle. For a moment all the activity in the village seemed to cease, suspended in time. Then women and children scurried into huts; men, who were working on upturned fishing boats, on spread-out nets, moved leisurely but definitely away, disappearing either into the thick jungle growth that edged the village, or into the huts.

Poly turned back to Adam. "Don't be hurt; it's just because it's your first time here. They have to make sure. They've been so abused by the hotel people."

"Poly," Dr. O'Keefe said without turning.

"Sorry, daddy," Poly said.

Virbius started forward, his horse moving slowly, carefully, on the last, steep downward grade. As they came into the village Adam saw that each hut was surrounded by a profusion of flowers that seemed to grow wildly; but, remembering his mother's garden on the Cape, he had a suspicion that they were carefully tended. The fishing boats were large, heavy shells, reminding him of pictures he had seen of Phoenician vessels. All were painted with strange emblems. The most startling boats were stark black or white with prows which reared sharply upward and on either side of which were painted two very wide-open eyes.

Virbius led them directly to the waterfront, to the harbor. He raised his hand and two small boys came running to him, appearing, it seemed to Adam, out of nowhere, to take care of the horses.

A long T-shaped wooden dock let out into the water, and Virbius, moving slowly and stiffly, his great age more apparent than it had been while he was mounted, led the way, keeping always a few paces in front of the others. Ahead of them in the water Adam could see what he realized must be the pens Poly had told him about. As they reached the T at the end of the dock Virbius beckoned to Poly, pointed to one of the pens, and began to speak to the child. Adam stood beside Dr. O'Keefe, looking into the pen in which a dead shark floated. It had obviously been wounded, not by another fish, but by some kind of weapon; a long knife, judging by the wounds. A strange odor came from the water which Adam guessed was something to disguise the smell of blood, and the water itself was murky.

Virbius' words sounded like gibberish with a touch of the Portuguese soft *ssh* and *jjh* added. Poly, head cocked, listened, frowning with concentration. "He says that this is the same shark that attacked Temis." To Adam she explained, "Temis is one of Virbius' great great grandchildren, Adam. Last night the shark attacked one of the children right here in the harbor, and one of Virbius' nephews went after him with a knife and drove him into the pen. The child is all right; his wounds are healing cleanly and there will be only a scar on one leg to show that anything happened. They did everything you told them to about the shark, daddy, but the shark has died. Virbius says that he has prayed neither for nor against him, but that it is justice. The shark died this morning and they only kept him for you to see."

From the dock Dr. O'Keefe took a pole with a large hook and pulled the dead beast in. Then he squatted down at the edge of the pen and examined it carefully.

Virbius had moved along the dock and was standing beside the next pen. Adam followed him. Here the water was a brilliant, clear green, with purple shadows. A small school of tiny fish flashed by in a swoosh of silver. At the bottom sea plants moved, their green, white, rose fronds undulating in a sinuous dance. Swimming ponderously in the pen was a large and extremely cross-looking tortoise. His head was stretched out on the leathery neck to its full length, and he glowered and blinked. Adam could see that one of the four legs had been almost, or perhaps entirely, torn off. It was healing neatly. The turtle turned his head toward Adam, put a scornful nose in the air, and then, with an indignant gesture, retired completely into his shell.

Poly shook with laughter. "He's the snootiest animal I've ever come across. Macrina's fond of him, so I suppose he's all right, but he has no manners whatsoever."

Adam was surprised to hear Virbius let out a thin, dry cackle of amusement as he moved on to the next pen. In this was a shark whose dorsal fin had been ripped off in some kind of marine battle. Small, ugly lumps were appearing where the fin had been.

"Of course we don't *get* many sharks," Poly said, "but we've never had one regenerate normally. I can't even be sorry for them and Josh says I'm a fool about all animals. But not sharks. I hate them. I would far prefer to meet a sting ray coming around a corner, and *they* look like bats out of hell if any beast ever did."

Dr. O'Keefe moved up to join them. "I'm very pleased about the turtle, bad manners or no. One of our most exciting successes has been a sea-gull wing. We would never have managed that without Virbius. While the bird couldn't fly it was all right, but he wanted to use his wing too soon, and only Virbius could control him."

Virbius spoke, and again Poly translated. "He says his gods are very powerful, and they gave him some of their power."

Virbius spoke again, spreading out his hands.

"He says it was the way Father Tom's God gave him of His power the night he stayed up with Macrina. Virbius says they must be good friends."

"Who?" Adam asked. "Canon Tallis and Virbius?"

"No, silly," Poly said impatiently. "Their gods."

Virbius nodded. If he spoke nothing but his own native tongue he understood, Adam guessed, almost everything that was said. And if he understood English it was more than likely that he also understood Portuguese. Adam realized that the old man was no one to underestimate. As a matter of fact, he reminded the boy in many of his mannerisms of a combination of Old Doc and Mahatma Gandhi.

There were two other tanks which were presumably empty at the moment, because neither Virbius nor Dr. O'Keefe went to them. Virbius led the way back up the dock to the village and to the green clearing in front of the central hut. Around the hut and climbing up its walls were flowers of every shade of blue, and Adam noticed that none of the other dwellings had blue flowers; there was every color of red, orange, yellow, but no blue. Virbius squatted down, beckoning to Poly to sit on his right side, Adam on his left. Dr. O'Keefe sat crosslegged opposite the old man.

From the central hut came a woman and a child, a girl perhaps Poly's age, perhaps younger. They bore coconut bowls which they set down in front of the visitors. Poly gave a warm, welcoming grin to the child, which was equally warmly returned, but neither of them spoke.

Virbius raised his hand for silence, although no one was speaking, then bowed over his coconut bowl, murmuring in his native tongue and swaying slightly from side to side. He took the bowl, raised it over his head in a gesture of offering, then sipped from it. Dr. O'Keefe raised his bowl in a similar gesture, and Poly and Adam followed suit. Adam did not know what it was they were drinking; something strange and cool and sharp.

Virbius beckoned to the child, who squatted down on the grass in front of the old man. Adam decided that she was definitely younger than Poly, although already more developed physically. She had straight, lustrous black hair, and a dark skin through which a golden glow seemed to shine, as though she had caught and contained the light in which the island was drenched. She smiled at Dr. O'Keefe, who smiled back, a smile of both compassion and joy. Virbius spoke and Poly translated.

"It is all right?"

Dr. O'Keefe nodded. "Tell them that Josh brought back all the lab reports Father Tallis got in Boston. Everything is perfectly normal."

As Poly spoke the child raised one golden-brown hand, looking wonderingly at the five outstretched fingers.

Adam turned to Dr. O'Keefe.

"Yes. This is Temis, the child the shark attacked six months ago. Her body was badly slashed, and one of her fingers was severed."

Beside him Adam heard a strange sound and looked to see that Virbius was crying, tears rolling unchecked down his wrinkled cheeks. Putting one hand on the child's shoulder the old man stood up, then raised both arms heavenward, calling out in a loud voice. With the tears still streaming he turned to Dr. O'Keefe and embraced him. There were tears in Dr. O'Keefe's eyes, too. Temis stood quietly, smiling.

Poly said to Adam, "We were sure it was all right, but it's good to have all the lab work say so, too. When the shark attacked Temis, Virbius called daddy. I've never seen daddy so upset. He said he wasn't ready, that it wasn't time. The body would heal; that wasn't the problem; it was the lost finger. You couldn't say: let's try, there's nothing to lose. There'd been the deformities. And there'd been the—the horrible malignancies. Father Tom came, and he and Virbius and daddy sat up all night, and then daddy said they'd try. Father Tom stayed to help. He never left Temis, he and daddy and Virbius. And then it happened, Adam, it happened, and it's all right, and Temis has five fingers again." Her eyes filled. "But Adam, if it hadn't been all right—if the new growth hadn't been natural—if it had devoured Temis the way it has some of the animals when things haven't gone right—" she choked and stopped.

Her father took her hand. "Hush, Poly. It's all right." He said to Adam, quietly, "Poly's anguish during this time was making her ill. As soon as we were sure that everything was going as we prayed it would, Tom Tallis took her away with him. The trip to Boston was to take slides and X-rays to a zoologist there, but served as a needed change for Poly, too. When you landed in Madrid instead of Lisbon and had to be bailed out of the airport things were complicated, but Tom managed to get the reports to one of our friends, who in turn got them to Josh. So, in spite of a little unexpected confusion, we have all the final lab reports and clearances."

"And it's all right!" Poly cried, joy driving the tension from her face. "It's all right!"

Dr. O'Keefe said heavily, "Through the grace of God it's all right. I know now that I know nothing, and many men think that I know everything, and this is where the danger lies. If only we had more time—"

Virbius said something, and Poly translated for her father, "He says that time is a dream, but that his gods and Father Tom's are awake."

Dr. O'Keefe put his hand for a moment on the old man's shoulder. Then he and Virbius bowed in silent farewell, and the doctor moved quickly away. Adam and Poly followed him, and as they walked away from the harbor and the village the two little boys came up with the horses, which had been watered and rubbed down.

They rode in silence. The sun was beginning to move toward the horizon. The long fronds of the palms rattled in the evening breeze, their shadows like great, dark birds. Adam's white horse blew gently through her nostrils and her flanks lifted in a patient sigh. But to Adam it was as though everything were bathed in light, as though the golden sun of the island had at last penetrated the darkest reaches of his mind.

He understood now. All the pieces had fallen together to

make a clear and unmistakable picture. He knew why he was important to Mr. Cutter, why anybody even remotely connected with Dr. O'Keefe would be important to all the Mr. Cutters. And he knew why the Mr. Cutters of the world must never be allowed to see Dr. O'Keefe's papers, particularly Dr. O'Keefe's papers on Temis. Unconsciously he heaved a sigh less patient than the old white horse's.

"'Smatter?" Poly asked.

"Nothing. I just wish I didn't have to have dinner with the Cutters this evening."

But it seemed there was no evading the dinner. When they got back his good suit had been pressed and was laid out on the bed with a clean shirt and his most colorful tie, a rather splotchy blue-and-red affair that Adam called his 'Jackson Pollock.'

Mrs. O'Keefe told him, "María chose the tie, so if you don't mind wearing it, Adam, it would make her very happy."

"As long as you think it's okay. I'm kind of fond of it."

He dressed carefully, but more to please María and the O'Keefes than Kali. He would have liked to go to Kali in his lab clothes, already slightly stained, and a symbol of his work, and somehow also a symbol of where he stood. But this, he realized, would be a rather Don Quixote sort of gesture, and not very effective.

Shortly before time for the hotel helicopter to come for him Dr. O'Keefe summoned him to the laboratory.

"Adam, you are probably wondering why I want you to have dinner with the Cutters tonight."

"Well, sir, I suppose maybe it would be wisest if they didn't know I'd made up my mind. I mean, it might be a good idea if they think I'm still willing to work for them."

The doctor looked at him with approval. "Exactly. I hate to ask you to do this, Adam. It's going to be difficult for you. One of your most evident qualities is a direct honesty, and prevarication of any kind isn't easy for you. However, there is an urgent and immediate need for this. Once the results of any experiment are in I have to get them off the island as quickly as possible. The papers on Temis are finally complete. I don't have to tell you how important they are. All the lab reports from Boston are in code, and I will now double code them. This will take me about a week. There is only one man—and he's in Lisbon—who can break the code so that they can get from the Embassy to Washington. During this week I'll keep the real papers on me and leave others, indicating another experiment, in the lab. Josh took a set of these phony papers with him and will be careful to see that the right—or wrong—people get hold of them. Now we come to the problem of getting the Temis papers to Lisbon. Joshua, of course, has been courier many times, but now it's safe neither for him nor the papers. I've used María once, José twice, but it's not fair to ask them again. The Ambassador himself has been errand boy on occasion. Next week it will have to be you. If you can make Cutter think you're willing to play along with him because you think he's right, then you'll be under less suspicion than anybody else. I don't think anything has been discovered about Temis, and it must not be." He stopped, repeated slowly, "It must not."

"I know, sir."

"So I want you to make a date with Kali in Lisbon. I'll give you some papers to give her. They'll look legitimate, and they'll follow the ones I'll appear to be working on this week and that Josh took back to Lisbon with him. We'll talk later about getting the real papers away. The point is that tonight you must appear to be still confused about me: you are *not* confused any longer, are you?"

"No, sir." Adam's voice was firm and confident.

"Let Typhon Cutter do his emotional patriotic act for you. It's very effective."

"Yes, sir. He's already done it. It—it *did* confuse me."

"All clear now?"

"Yes, sir."

"You understand what I am asking you to do?"

"Yes, sir." Adam swallowed. "It will kind of make up for—"

"Not to make up for anything. That's over and done with, and no real harm, thank God. You're doing this for the future."

"*For Heaven and the future's sakes?*" Adam asked softly.

Dr. O'Keefe nodded. "This is where Joshua has been so

remarkable. His love and need *are* entirely one. And while the work has been play for him he has been well aware of the mortal stakes. *Only where love and need are one, and the work is play for mortal stakes, is the deed ever really done for Heaven and the future's sakes.* Think of Joshua tonight if you like. You couldn't have anybody better to follow." Above them they heard a loud droning; Dr. O'Keefe remarked, "They're very prompt," and stood up.

The helicopter dropped clumsily to the beach in front of the bungalows. Poly, running with the other children to say goodbye, called, "You'll get sand in your shoes."

"It'll shake out," Adam answered.

Barefooted, she caught up with him, gently shoving Peggy ahead and saying, "Run look at the helly, Pegs." She whispered to Adam, "I have what I told you I'd give you. Here. Just pretend you're holding my hand."

Charles asked, "What're you whispering about?"

Poly stamped her bare foot against the sand impatiently. "Charles. Please. Oh, do run get Johnny for me, quickly, and let me say goodbye."

"Adam's just going out for dinner," Charles said, but he went after Johnny who, fully dressed, was heading for the water.

Adam put his hand around Poly's firm, thin one. "What is it?"

"Adam, have you ever seen a switchblade?"

"Yes," Adam said, smiling. "Is that what you're giving me?"

Poly scowled darkly. "You're condescending to me."

"I'm sorry; but if it's a switchblade I don't want one and I don't like the idea of your having one."

Poly shook her head impatiently so that her red hair flew about her face. "Okay, I know you coped with gangs on the streets of New York and all that jazz. This isn't an ordinary switchblade."

"What's extraordinary about it?"

"It looks like a switchblade and it works like a switchblade—I'm taking this on hearsay because I've never actually used one. But it's really a kind of hypodermic needle."

"Poly, for heaven's sake—"

"There's a channel in the blade filled with MS-222."

"—what do you expect me to do with it, use it on Kali?"

Again Poly pawed the sand. "She'll probably ask you to go for a moonlight swim, and there have been sharks at the hotel beach this summer, though they won't admit it. I wouldn't put it past that Kali to send you straight into a shark's jaws, and daddy says MS-222 is still the best thing; it knocks them out right away. When the blade is released the capsule of MS-222 is punctured and it goes right in, so you don't have to aim for a vital spot or anything. It's on a belt, and it looks just like an ordinary knife. It's quite flat, so you can wear it under your bathing trunks. You've got them with you, haven't you?"

"Yes. Your mother told me to bring them along."

"Which ones?"

"Just the plain navy ones, Pol. I guess I'm not uninhibited enough to wear the wild ones the way Josh does."

"You promise me you'll wear the belt with the knife?"

Adam knew that he could not hurt Poly by laughing at her intensity. "Well, I don't really think Kali wants to dispose of me. But thanks anyhow, Pol."

Poly pulled at his jacket sleeve. "Promise me you'll never go swimming without it."

"Even when I go with you?"

"Not with me, goosey. Macrina keeps the sharks away. But anywhere else. Promise."

"But, Poly—"

"*Promise.*"

"All right."

Poly heaved a great sigh of relief. "Okay. I know I can trust your word. Goodbye. I suppose I'll be in bed when you get home. I don't really want you to have a good time but I'm going to be polite and tell you to have one. But it's just courtesy. So have a good time." She turned and ran back to the bungalows, not standing on the sea wall to wave and watch him off as he had expected her to. The other children called and waved, and Adam waved back, but he found himself looking beyond them for Poly.

The pilot was Portuguese, and if he spoke English he kept

it a closely guarded secret. Adam was glad for the minutes of silence: no, silence was certainly not the word, for a helicopter is a noisy bird, but for a time of not having to listen to new ideas, of not having to respond.

As they landed on the flat roof of the hotel Kali was waiting and came running to meet him. She flung her arms around him, whispering, "Adam, help me, help me. I've been all wrong about everything. I know now that daddy's doing things that aren't—that aren't right. Adam, what am I going to do?"

15

BEFORE Adam could make any response to this outburst Kali whispered, "Here comes daddy. Hush."

Typhon Cutter looked even more like a spider than Adam remembered. It seemed incredible that this obese mass with the stringy appendages could possibly be father to the beautiful girl at his side. Then the boy remembered the portrait of the angelic young man and wondered if Kali could ever be anything but young and radiant and lovely.

She pressed her fingers quickly against his, a gesture that was both intimate and warning. Adam did not return the pressure and her look flickered quickly over him like a flame.

"Of course," Typhon Cutter was saying, "all the rooms have balconies overlooking the ocean, and our guests, in a primitive setting, nevertheless have every modern convenience."

Kali explained, "Daddy's part owner of the hotel."

They walked through a rooftop bar and lounge, Typhon Cutter gesturing expansively with one thin arm. "I think our service can compare with any of the great hotels in the world. We'll stay up here and cool off before going down to dinner."

In the lounge, long windows opened to the terrace, and there were groups of comfortable chairs and couches around low tables. The walls were painted with lush murals of the native village, so glamorized that it was a moment before Adam recognized it. The mud and straw huts, the fishing vessels, the natural harbor, were all enlarged and garishly ornamented, and the natives themselves wore elaborate leis and looked more as though they came from a tourist's dream of Hawaii than a primitive island off the south coast of Portugal. In one corner of the room was a huge television set around which a group of young people was clustered. The volume was on high. Without looking around Typhon Cutter raised his hand and snapped his fingers, and a uniformed page went running over to the set and adjusted the dials.

At one of the low marble tables sat a solitary man in a dark suit. Adam could see only his back, but it looked somehow familiar.

Mr. Cutter turned toward him, saying, "Dr. Ball hopped over with us. His busy schedule doesn't permit him to get away often, but he's badly in need of the rest. We're flying him back tonight since of course he can't be away over Sunday."

Adam said nothing. Silence, as a matter of fact, was his plan of campaign: to look naïve and innocent and gullible (not too difficult, he realized ruefully); to be swift to hear, and slow to speak. He caught Kali looking at him anxiously, then glancing away as her father turned toward her. Adam felt a hot surge of resentment. He had enough on his hands without coping with a confused Kali. If she'd tumbled to the fact that her father was a stinker she'd have to work it out her own way.

Dr. Ball rose as they reached him, shook hands effusively with Adam, and kissed Kali. Adam found that he enjoyed this latter even less than the handshake.

"Dear boy," Dr. Ball murmured, lowering himself into his comfortable chair. "How delightful to see you again, and in less hectic circumstances than our first meeting. What will you have to drink?" He indicated his own glass.

—Get the prospective victim drunk or drugged, Adam thought. Aloud he said, "I'm not thirsty, thanks."

Kali put a hand lightly and briefly against his knee. "The bartender has Cokes. I'm going to have one."

Dr. Ball urged, "Do join us in our libation."

"Okay, a Coke, then, thank you." Adam realized that a uniformed boy was hovering by Typhon Cutter waiting to take their order. Mr. Cutter nodded at the boy, who went to the bar.

"Now, Adam," Mr. Cutter said, "when last I saw you we had reached a certain understanding, had we not?" Adam said nothing. "You did agree to help me, did you not?" Adam tried to look blank and made a slight gesture of his head that could have been interpreted either as affirmation or negation. An edge of impatience came to Mr. Cutter's voice. "I believe that I made it reasonably clear to you that I am in a position to be useful to the Embassy, and that I feel that it is my duty to my country to help out when I am called upon."

"Yes, sir," Adam said.

"You were understandably tired, but you did agree to help."

"Yes, sir. I would consider it my privilege to help them at the Embassy." This seemed to be a nice, double-barreled response, the Embassy, being in his mind, Joshua.

"Good." Mr. Cutter's voice spun upward, a high, thin, plausible web. "At that time—I am referring to the time of our first meeting—my men, in order to inspire your confidence and insure your cooperation, went to a great deal of trouble and not a little danger to rescue the O'Keefe child from the very organization to which her own father belongs! A great man, but you know how stupid scientists can be. I may say that I personally underwent danger: our enemies are ruthless, so ruthless, indeed, that they do not hesitate to use an innocent child, the child of one of their own members, for their purposes." He paused, waiting.

Adam knew that a further response was indicated here. "I've only been with Dr. O'Keefe a couple of days and everything's all secret and hush-hush around me. Just what *are* their purposes, sir?"

Now Dr. Ball leaned forward, his well-manicured hands spread out on the table. "You have spent these two days in working for O'Keefe, have you not, lad?"

"Well, yes, sir, but . . ."

"Are you aware of the nature of his experiments?"

"Well, to some extent, sir. I mean, I knew before I ever came."

Mr. Cutter asked sharply, "You have actually been working *with* the starfish?"

"Well . . . just cleaning tanks and simple jobs like that, so far."

Dr. Ball put his hand on Adam's knee. It felt heavy, and very unlike Kali's leaf-like gesture. Adam felt his skin crawling. He raised his eyes from the hand to the immaculate white dog collar to Dr. Ball's handsome, smiling face.

"Adam, dear boy," the doctor said, lifting his hand and passing it over dark, well-pomaded hair, "you do realize what O'Keefe is doing, don't you?"

"Well, yes, sir, working on the regenerative process of the arm of the starfish."

"In the starfish—" (—Dr. Ball sounded as though he were in the pulpit, Adam thought) "—and in certain other specified beasts, this is a perfectly natural thing. O'Keefe is taking it beyond the point of nature. But not only is he usurping the prerogatives of the Almighty, he is then allowing his work to get into the wrong hands, hands soiled with the taint of sin."

Adam tried to imagine Canon Tallis saying these words. It didn't work. He mumbled, "I'm afraid I don't understand."

"Un-American hands," Mr. Cutter said. "Hands that do not have their country or its economy at heart."

All Adam could think of at this point was that hands do not have a heart. He shook his head slightly to try to pull his thoughts together. This time he did not have lack of sleep as an excuse for not being alert.

The young waiter put two Cokes down on the marble table, a fresh drink for Dr. Ball, and a drink for Mr. Cutter. The bartender evidently knew, without being told, exactly what Mr. Cutter wanted. "Adam," Typhon Cutter said in his soft, tenor voice, "I am a very wealthy man. I admit to you perfectly openly that I enjoy my money."

Dr. Ball broke in, "But you are a generous man, a very generous man."

"That's not the point. I try to do what I can, of course, and if I have been able to be of some small service to you it gives me great gratification. Eliphaz—Dr. Ball—is on the boards of several hospitals and orphanages and old people's homes as well as attending meticulously to his regular parish duties."

—It's catching, Adam thought. —Even Mr. Cutter's beginning to talk in Dr. Ball's pompous pattern.

Perhaps Typhon Cutter realized this, for he cleared his throat before saying, "All I'm trying to tell you is that although I enjoy my money and the things it can buy, my country comes first. In fact, I love my native land so well that I am willing to live outside it, in voluntary exile, because in this way I am better able to serve. I've been asked by people who must remain nameless to find the results of Dr. O'Keefe's work and to get them into the hands of our own government before unscrupulous agents grab them."

"But, sir," Adam said, trying to sound innocent and reasonable, "Dr. O'Keefe is an American."

"Pink," Dr. Ball murmured, "tinged, alas, with scarlet."

Standard tactics, Adam realized. Accuse those who might well accuse you before they have a chance to get in a word edgewise.

"Adam," Mr. Cutter asked, "how much do you care about your country?"

"Very much," Adam answered with complete honesty.

"Would you make a sacrifice for it if necessary?"

"Yes, sir." Here again he could speak with the ring of truth.

Dr. Ball asked, "Do we have your word of honor that you are willing to work for your native land, no matter how difficult it may be for you personally?"

"Yes, sir." Adam added mentally, —and I'm quite sure that this doesn't mean working for you. It's Dr. O'Keefe who cares about the things you're talking about, not you. You're—you're nothing but a whited sepulcher.

Mr. Cutter put his glass down with a click. "When do you think you can get back to Lisbon?"

"Well—I—I think I could manage it next weekend." Dr. O'Keefe would have the Temis papers ready by then; it would be time for him to go.

"Make a date with Kali."

"Well, yes, sir, that would be my pleasure anyhow." Kali smiled at him and he managed to smile in return.

"Arrange to meet her on Friday. The hotel taxi service schedules a routine Friday morning flight. By then you should know more about O'Keefe's work. And, so that you have more than my word to go on that I have my country's rather than my own interests at heart, you may bring your information directly to the Embassy."

"Oh, good," Adam said with deliberate innocence. "I have a friend there. I could go right to him. Joshua Archer." He turned and smiled at Dr. Ball. "He's a good friend of yours too, isn't he?"

Dr. Ball forced a toothy smile. "Yes, indeed. Indeed, yes. But O'Keefe's work is too important to—if the Ambassador himself is busy we'll see to it that you talk to someone very close to him. This is nothing for mere underlings, no matter how delightful they may be. This is more than a patriotic duty, my son. It is also a very big opportunity for you. It may make all the difference in the world to your entire life."

"Yes," Adam said. "I know."

"Come to me at the rectory as soon as you reach Lisbon," Dr. Ball said. "Perhaps that would be easier for you than braving all those formidable secretaries at the Embassy."

Mr. Cutter rose. "I'll have instructions waiting for you at the rectory. We'll go downstairs for dinner. The air conditioner works passably well in the Coral Room. I don't know what they do with the air conditioners; must get an investigation going. I'll order some good American food; I imagine you're tired of these Portuguese messes. Drink up, Kali girl, Adam must be hungry."

The Coral Room, too, went in for murals. These, Adam gathered, were meant to be of Manhattan, though it was only a faintly recognizable Empire State Building that told him this. The artist, if he had ever been to New York at all, had seen it last in the days of elevateds; one enormous wobbly structure ran right by what appeared to be the main branch of the Public Library, since there were two lions in front of a pillared building approached by an enormous flight of steps.

The fourth wall was French windows leading out to the tennis courts, the pool, and finally the ocean. Adam sat between Kali and Mr. Cutter at dinner, and across from Dr. Ball. Mr. Cutter ordered steak and French fried potatoes, and salad with Thousand Island dressing. "That all right with you, Adam?"

"Oh. Well. Yes, sir. Fine." Anything he could agree with legitimately was fine with him. There was no longer the slightest question in Adam's mind as to who was serving his country, Mr. Cutter or Dr. O'Keefe, and there had never been any question as to who was serving God, Dr. Ball or Canon Tallis. The critical moment Joshua had predicted had definitely been passed. There could be no more holding back. He had chosen sides, whether he liked it or not. At the moment he found to his immense surprise that he was liking it. A new kind of excitement surged through his veins. He felt tingly and alert from toes to fingertips, and ready to go.

There was only one hitch, and it was an unexpected one. Kali's anguished greeting had doubled all the complications. He knew that if Kali needed him he could not reject her plea for help. Joshua had said that his side cared about the fall of the sparrow; Kali, in her frantic cry as Adam climbed out of the helicopter, had become a sparrow.

But how to help her, he pondered, as he chewed his rather tough steak and kept one ear on the conversation. He tried to think what Joshua would do. Joshua would not turn away from anyone who needed him. That was the first thing. After that he would probably play it by ear. Adam only hoped that his ear would come close to being half as true as Joshua's.

What he must do now, he decided, was to manage to sound suspicious about Dr. O'Keefe when Kali was out of the room. He felt a surge of anger. This whole business about Kali was off the schedule entirely. He had written her out of his life except as the daughter of the spider, and here she was, a new and unwanted responsibility, and a sparrow instead of a spideress. Canon Tallis had put Polyhymnia in Adam's charge, and he'd muffed that one. Here, out of the blue again, he was being handed another problem, and this time he must not goof. He wondered if Dr. O'Keefe would have sent him off to dinner at the hotel if he'd known what was going to happen. Joshua, in playing by ear, seemed to have perfect pitch. Adam wasn't at all sure that he himself wasn't tone deaf.

After dessert he had the chance he was looking for. Typhon Cutter said, "Adam, we adhere to the rather old-fashioned custom of the gentlemen's lingering over the port for a brief respite after dinner. We'd be delighted if you'd care to stay with us. You can join Kali in a short while. I believe she has some idea of a moonlight swim."

"Thank you, sir," Adam said. "I don't think I'll have any port but I'd love to stay and talk if I may." Kali sent him a stricken look, and he added, "We'll have time for a swim, too, won't we?"

Typhon Cutter moved his ponderous head so that the folds of pink flesh rolled over his immaculate shirt collar. "Certainly. I've arranged for the helicopter to stand by to take you back whenever you're ready. There isn't any hurry, at this end, at any rate."

When Kali, reluctant and pouting, had left, and the port had been brought, "Sir," Adam asked, looking from one man to the other, "this Dr. O'Keefe—"

"Yes?" Typhon Cutter asked.

"Well, sir, Dr. Didymus, the man I worked for before, you know, he's no slouch, but he didn't—well—"

"Well, what, lad?" Dr. Ball asked in his gentlest voice.

"Well, sir, I know it's only been a couple of days, but all I've done is scrub the lab floors and clean tanks. I mean, junk *any*body could do. I haven't been doing things like that since I was in seventh grade. I mean, it's not Oliver Twist kind of stuff exactly, but it certainly doesn't challenge my *mind*, and he keeps the files locked, and I have a feeling . . ."

"A feeling?" Dr. Ball prompted.

"Well, that he doesn't trust me."

Dr. Ball said smoothly, "It's probably not personal, son. I don't think O'Keefe trusts anybody. And if a man trusts no man, then he cannot trust God."

"I've been very careful," Adam said. "I mean, I've been very discreet. I've just done my job, whatever he's asked me to do, no matter how silly. And I've kept my eyes open, so that I'm getting *some* idea of what's going on, whether he wants me to or not . . ." He paused, frowning slightly.

Dr. Ball raised one pale hand. "Under these circumstances, my son, do you think you *will* be able to get to Lisbon next Friday?"

"Well, yes, sir. Mrs. O'Keefe wants me to do some errands. I mean, shopping, knitting wool and stuff that absolutely anybody could do. And they did say something about the hotel plane. After all, I could have used my mind more if I'd stayed with Dr. Didymus in Woods Hole, no matter how old he is."

Typhon Cutter shifted position in his chair, the topheavy body swinging cumbersomely. "Don't worry. We'll give you a chance to use your mind."

"Yes, Mr. Cutter. I hope so."

"You know what your instructions are?"

"Yes, sir. I'll fly over to Lisbon on Friday, ostensibly to do some shopping for Mrs. O'Keefe. I'll manage to wangle permission to have a date with Kali to give me the extra time I'll need. I'm to go right to the rectory to Dr. Ball."

"How," Typhon Cutter asked slowly, "will the idea of a date with Kali be received?"

"Well, they *know* I like her, sir. After all, she *is* very attractive. I mean, any red-blooded American male . . . And after all, they gave me permission to come here tonight. I mean, it's not as though I were in prison or anything. It's just that the work I've been given seems kind of silly for someone with as much background in marine biology as I have."

Typhon Cutter poured more port. "A reasonable precaution on O'Keefe's part, isn't it?"

"Well, yes, Mr. Cutter, I guess it is."

"All right, Adam. You're a bright lad. Now's your opportunity to use that mind of yours. Keep your eyes and your ears open. You *will* be able to bring us some information, won't you?"

"Yes. I think so."

"Be careful not to arouse suspicions. What you don't accomplish this time can be done next, though we don't have all the time in the world. Remember that."

"I'll remember."

"If you want your swim with Kali we'll excuse you now. She'll be waiting in the lounge. Make your arrangements to meet her on Friday."

"Yes, Mr. Cutter."

Dr. Ball smiled again, rubbing his hands. "Be gentle and understanding with her, dear boy. She's a particular pet of mine."

"Yes, sir. It's been very nice to see you again." He turned with equal courtesy to Typhon Cutter. "It was a wonderful dinner, thank you, sir. Just the ticket." He shook hands with both men, first the steel grip, then the hail-fellow-well-met one.

"Until Friday," Dr. Ball said softly as the boy left. Outside the dining room Adam breathed deeply. So far so good.

16

Kali, already changed to a scanty black bathing suit and a white terrycloth beach robe, was waiting for him in the lounge. "Come on and I'll show you where to dress," she said. "We'll swim in the ocean, not the pool. I want to be sure we aren't overheard. Hurry up." She spoke quietly, quickly, nervously.

As Adam changed to the plain navy blue trunks he remembered Poly's gift. He took it out of the box and looked at it, a canvas belt with a holder for what looked like an ordinary knife. He took the knife carefully out of the sheath and inspected the mechanism for triggering the blade. He couldn't check the blade for the vein filled with MS-222 without releasing both blade and chemical, but it looked as though it would be perfectly simple to manage. Although Adam had never owned a switchblade he had seen several, and he knew how they worked.

He shrugged and put the knife and belt back in the box. If he wore the belt Kali's keen eyes might spot it, and the evening was complicated enough already. He did not worry about needing the knife; Poly was an imaginative kid, still frightened from the kidnapping experience, and Typhon Cutter would hardly allow Kali to swim in dangerous waters.

Then, with his hand already on the doorknob, Adam swung around and went back for the knife. At the corners of his mind he felt that something was wrong with the evening. It seemed as though he had done exactly what he had set out to do, but he had an uncomfortable, nagging feeling that somewhere, somehow, he was being stupid. And a promise is a promise. He had promised Polyhymnia that he would not go swimming without the MS-222, and even if it were not for that small worry at the edge of his consciousness he would have to honor that promise.

He strapped the belt around his waist. The sheath was tapered and made very little bulge under the trunks, which were slightly loose for him in any case. Then he went to join Kali.

She was waiting at the edge of the big pool, herself in a pool of golden floodlight which made her tan glisten. Her black bathing suit was sleek against her supple curves, and cut more deeply in the back than Adam would have thought possible. As she saw him walking down the path toward her she picked up her robe and ran to him, taking his hand. "See why we can't swim here? The pool is full, and I don't dare trust *any*body. Daddy has an enormous organization and I don't know half the people involved in it, though I thought I did."

Across from the pool the tennis courts, too, were floodlit, and a game of singles and a game of doubles sounded in the night, the ping of ball against gut, against the clay of the court. There was calling and laughter from the pool. Ahead of them the ocean lay dark and its murmur was almost lost in the light and sound about the hotel.

As they got to the long ramp leading to the beach, and out of the glare of the floodlights, Kali seemed to relax. She held Adam's hand lightly, instead of clutching. But her voice was still wound with tension. "Oh, Adam, everything's so *awful*!" She moved closer to him, seeking, it seemed, the strength and comfort of his body. "Adam, oh, darling, darling Adam, can I trust you?"

"Trust me how?" he asked cautiously.

They had reached the end of the ramp and stood on the night beach. Kali let her robe drop onto the sand, and turned to Adam, putting her arms tightly around him, leaning her head on his shoulder. "I need your help so terribly."

The light fragrance of her hair brushed against his nostrils. Kali, despite her sophistication, was just as vulnerable as Poly. She might be a few years older, but she was just as helpless against the powers of evil that surrounded them. "How do you need me?" he asked gently.

Kali lifted her head and looked at him. The moonlight fell full on her, so that her skin was milkwhite and her lovely features seemed chiseled out of marble. Her eyes were imploring. "Adam, I know you have no reason to trust me. I wouldn't blame you a bit if you—if you just rejected me now. But please don't."

"I'm not rejecting you, Kali."

"Let's just sit down for a few minutes before we swim and I'll tell you as quickly as I can. All the awful things I've done because daddy told me to and everything." She led the way along the beach, back through the soft sand to the foot of a high dune. Here she sat down, pulling him after her, and lay back. "We can wash the sand off when we go in for our dip. Adam, what would you do if you discovered that your father was doing things—things that were wrong?"

This was something Adam could not possibly imagine. If he had to choose one word to describe his father it would be *integrity*. So he answered, "I don't know." He did not add, "Because it would never happen."

But Kali must have caught the unspoken thought. "I used to think daddy was perfect. I thought that no matter what he did, as long as it was daddy who was doing it, it must be right. But now I know—" she stopped with a sudden intake of breath. "I can't tell you anything more unless you promise me something. I shouldn't have said this much."

For a moment caution returned to Adam. "What do you want me to promise?"

"Oh, nothing difficult. I don't want you to *do* anything or anything. Just promise that you'll never, never, never say anything to anybody in the world about what I'm telling you."

"Why would I want to say anything?"

Kali sat up, looking down at him broodingly. "Adam, I know now that O'Keefe and Tallis and their people are right and daddy's wrong. I'm sure you know it, too. You might want to tell them. O'Keefe and Tallis. But I'm not going to tell you anything they don't already know; I wouldn't put you in a position where it would be your duty to tell them. I promise you. But I couldn't bear—please, Adam, promise me you won't tell them. It's—maybe it's just a matter of pride. I still love daddy, you see. He's still my father. So please just promise me you'll never tell. I can't work for O'Keefe and Tallis or anything. I can't work *against* daddy, even—so please, please promise you'll never tell them any of what I've told you or what I'm going to tell you now." She flung herself at him, pressing her face against his shoulder, so that he could feel her tears hot against his flesh.

"All right, I promise," he said, stroking her back gently as though she were Poly.

She heaved a great sigh of relief. "Oh, thank you. *Thank* you. Adam, daddy only returned Poly to you to get you to work for him. But I guess you know that, anyhow."

"Yes," Adam said.

"And I know daddy's asking you to work for him again." Adam didn't say anything, and Kali continued, "I'm not going to ask you about that. That's your problem, and you have to handle it whatever way you think is right. I know it'll be the right way. Maybe you don't trust me, yet. But I trust you. Implicitly."

She paused, so Adam mumbled, "Thank you."

"You're supposed to go into Lisbon this week, aren't you?"

"Yes."

"And you're supposed to meet me?"

"Well, yes, you know that."

"On Friday, isn't it?"

"Yes."

"I know about the plans, of course, because daddy doesn't know I know about him, and I couldn't ever let him know. He might—Adam, he might hurt *me*. I know now that all he wants is more money and more power, and he doesn't care who's hurt as long as he gets them. There are people in China, for instance, who are willing to give daddy almost anything he wants if they can get hold of O'Keefe's findings. They think people are—what's the word—expendable—and so does daddy. It isn't anything as simple as communism versus democracy. It's power pitting itself against power. So I'm—I'm trapped in the middle. By Friday I ought to know more what I have to do. So if we can just pretend to play along with daddy—and it will just be pretending—we can meet in Lisbon and things ought to be clearer by then. The main thing is that you *have* to keep your promise, Adam. You must *not* tell anybody, not *any*body anything I've told you."

"I'm not in the habit of breaking promises," Adam said.

"I know you're not. But you see, a promise simply doesn't mean a thing in the world to daddy. He'll promise anything in order to get what he wants and break it the next minute without a thought. So I'm—so I just have to make extra sure. It isn't that I doubt you. You're the only person in the world I trust."

"I'm sorry, Kali," Adam said, helplessly. Kali was lying back against the dune, her fair hair spread out on the sand. The moonlight fell full upon her beautiful face and body. He felt a profound longing to protect her, to rescue her from the evil that held her in thrall.

She whispered, so that he could hardly catch the words, "Thank you."

"For what?"

"For being you. It was the best day of my life when our planes got held up by fog and I met you in the airport." She turned her face toward him, then reached out and touched him gently on the cheek, moving so that she was closer to him. Very lightly she put her lips against his, then, abruptly cutting his response, she jumped up, saying, "That isn't fair to you. Come on, Adam darling, let's have a quick dip and then you'd better get on back to the O'Keefes."

Like a naiad she ran swiftly across the sand and into the water, and he followed her, splashing through the waves.

The moon was high and the ocean quiet. It was not long before they were beyond the breakers and into the rhythmic swells. Kali rolled over onto her back and floated, staring up at the moon. "You see, Adam, I think I can help you now. I can't work against daddy, you do understand that, but I think I can help you not to work against O'Keefe. It won't be safe for you to call the apartment when you come in to Lisbon on Friday, so we'll have to arrange to meet somewhere. We could meet for lunch, couldn't we? That would be perfectly natural, wouldn't it?"

Adam, too, was floating, letting the water ripple gently against his body, slap lightly at his cheeks. "That's pretty much what's expected, I think."

"Someplace large and obvious would be our best bet. There's

a good seafood restaurant, the Salão de Chá. Anybody can tell you where it is. Meet me there at one."

"Fine." Adam looked up at the moon. He thought of Joshua in the little plane flying straight along the path of moonlight as though he were heading toward the clear, cold light of the moon itself.

"Adam, I'm so jittery about everything I could jump out of my skin. Let's have a race." She flipped over and faced out to sea.

"What about undertow and stuff?" Adam asked.

"Oh, *Adam*."

"Sorry, but I've learned to treat the ocean with a good deal of respect."

"For goodness sakes, Adam, I'm as used to this beach as I am to my own bathtub."

Adam asked, doggedly, "What about sharks?"

"That's nonsense. Daddy says it's just a malicious story made up by people who'd like to see the hotel lose business. Come on. I'm going. If you're scared you can go in to shore and wait for me." She thrust her body forward in the water. After a moment's hesitation Adam followed.

Kali swam easily and well and she had a head start. Adam was stronger, his arms and legs longer, but he had to work to catch up with her.

Just as he drew even and began to forge ahead he heard Kali scream.

They were in the path of moonlight, now, and in the water beside them he could see a large, dark body. He felt a moment of cold blankness. Then, almost without thinking, he reached for the knife Poly had given him.

17

As Adam's hand touched the sheath he felt himself being butted.

Kali shrieked. "It's a shark! Swim for your life!"

He was butted again.

His next reaction was not on the thinking level. He simply knew that a shark does not butt. A shark turns over on its back, white belly exposed, and attacks. The dark body bumping against him in the night water was not a shark.

"Macrina!" he shouted.

The moment of recognition was not conscious, it was pure and joyful instinct.

Macrina kept butting at him. She was deliberately turning him around and heading him toward land. Kali was already swimming in, cleaving swiftly through the water, not looking back for Adam.

"Thank you, Macrina," Adam said, loudly, hoping that Macrina would understand the intonation if not the words, since he could not, as Poly seemed able to, talk in dolphin language. He turned and headed in to shore, looking back to see Macrina's body, bright with moonlight, flash through the air and disappear into the sea.

Kali stood, knee deep in water, waiting for him. She flung herself into his arms, sobbing and gibbering. "I was going to run for help—and then I saw you swimming in—it was a shark—oh, Adam, I'm terrified of them—oh, Adam, it was so horrible—oh, Adam, oh, oh, oh—"

He held her, patting her gently. As her torrent of sobbing ceased he said, as calmly as he could, for his own legs were quivering and his heart thumping madly against his ribs, "It wasn't a shark. It was a dolphin."

"You're crazy," Kali said. "Look." She pointed to the water and he could see the swift black triangle of a shark's fin moving across the path of moonlight. "That's a shark. A porpoise leaps out of the water. Adam, I don't know why it didn't kill us. You saved me."

"I didn't do anything," Adam said. "We both swam in as fast as we could." But it *had* been Macrina who had butted him. That was it! he realized. Macrina had been warning him of the shark.

"Sharks swim much faster than people. I just don't understand." Kali still clutched at him in a terrified manner.

Adam tried to sound matter-of-fact. Instinctively he knew that he could not tell Kali about Macrina. "Let's just be grateful that we're here and that we're okay. You're shivering, Kali. Get your robe and let's go in and get dressed." He was still acting on an automatic level, his brain arrested, frozen by the icy bath of terror and moonlight.

Kali leaned against him as they walked across the sand to where her robe lay in a small white pool by the ramp. Adam picked it up and held it for her as she got into it, shivering. Strangely enough he felt no desire to take her into his arms now, to hold her, to comfort her, to brush his lips against the fair hair, the delicate mouth. His mind was still suspended; his emotions, too, seemed caught and frozen in the moonlight. Everything about him was calm and cold, but somewhere inside was a small, still voice telling him what to do. His earlier anger at having Kali added to his responsibilities was gone; the moment of joy that had come when he recognized Macrina was gone. He knew that all that was required of him at the moment was to take Kali back to the hotel; then he would be free to go home to the O'Keefes.

Typhon Cutter and Dr. Ball were drinking coffee and brandy in the lounge.

"Dear children," Dr. Ball cooed, "did you have a pleasant swim?"

Kali walked up to her father. "Daddy, there *are* sharks. Adam and I saw one."

Typhon Cutter's voice was unperturbed. "I think that highly unlikely, Kali. Were you in the ocean?"

"Yes."

"I thought you were going in the pool."

"It was too crowded."

Mr. Cutter pulled out a platinum case, extracted a cigarette, and lit it unhurriedly. "I would suggest that, if you think you saw a shark, you follow the hotel rules in future. They are, if you will remember, *my* rules, and I've asked you before to swim in the ocean only during the day time when there is a lifeguard."

"All right, daddy. Sorry. I just thought you'd want to know."

Typhon Cutter swung his cumbersome body toward Adam. "Did you see a shark?"

"Yes, sir. I think so."

"You're not positive?"

"Not a hundred percent, Mr. Cutter. But as far as swimming at the hotel beach is concerned I'd certainly go on the assumption that there *are* sharks."

Dr. Ball stretched and crossed his legs. "A proper scientific attitude, my boy."

"I think I'd better go now," Adam said. "I don't expect anybody'll be waiting up for me, but it's getting late, and I do have to get up early."

He said goodbye to the two men and Kali took him to the roof. Before he climbed into the helicopter she moved close to him. The moonlight shone down on her face and he could not avoid or evade her imploring look. He took her gently into his arms. "See you Friday, Kali. Everything will be all right." She nodded, rubbing her face against his shoulder, then lifted her lips to be kissed.

He was surprised at his reaction, for he seemed to be two separate Adams; one responded fully to the physical excitement of the kiss and to her body pressed against his; the other, and the Adam who seemed at the moment to be in control, was thinking only of Friday, of the dangers and problems involved, and that he must not let himself be blinded by emotion no matter how badly Kali needed him. Indeed, if he was to be able to help Kali at all, he must keep his mind clear and disengaged. After Friday was over would be time enough to think of other things.

He turned away from her firmly and got into the helicopter. As it rose clumsily straight up into the air and then headed east he could see her watching and waving after him.

Again during the homeward journey the pilot did not speak. Adam, jumping down onto the sand, called "Obrigado," which he had picked up as meaning "thank you," and hurried toward the lab where he could see a light still burning in the big room.

Dr. O'Keefe was working at one of the tanks, but went to his desk and sat down, rather wearily, as Adam knocked and entered. "I'm making some hot chocolate over one of the Bunsen burners," the doctor said. "I find if I drink coffee this late at night I'm apt not to go to bed at all. Want to get yourself a cup from the cupboard over there?"

"Thank you." Adam got a cup and set it down beside the doctor's on the counter top. "I'll finish making this, sir."

Dr. O'Keefe looked at him probingly. "How did the evening go?"

Adam stirred the fragrant chocolate. "All right, I think. There's something that bothers me, and I can't put my finger on it." As he said 'finger' he almost dipped his own into the saucepan to see if the chocolate was hot enough, then decided that Dr. O'Keefe might not approve of this distinctly unsterile procedure. There *was* something wrong with the evening, and it was something quite unconnected with Kali. It had been bothering him off and on all during the flight home, although it had been Kali who had been in the forefront of his mind. He wanted very much to tell Dr. O'Keefe about Kali, but he had promised. However, at the moment Kali seemed to be on the periphery of the central problem which was to get the phony papers to Dr. Ball and the real papers to Josh or the Ambassador. On Friday when he met Kali at the restaurant he would make her see that he must tell Dr. O'Keefe. He could understand her feelings about this: Typhon Cutter was her father and she must still love him very much no matter what she had learned about his actions. You cannot suddenly stop loving where it has been the central emotion of your entire life.

"Want to tell me about it now?" Dr. O'Keefe asked, "or would you rather wait until morning?"

Adam decided, from the bubbles at the edge of the saucepan, that the cocoa was hot. "I don't think it'll take too long," he said as he poured. "I can tell you while we have our chocolate."

Dr. O'Keefe reached into a desk drawer and brought out a tin of biscuits. He handed it to Adam, and accepted the steaming cupful.

"I'm not quite sure how to start . . ." Adam took a biscuit.

"Begin at the beginning, go on to the end, and then stop."

That, of course, was the trouble. He could not begin at the beginning, which was Kali's cry for help. So he began with going into the terraced lounge.

"So Ball was there," Dr. O'Keefe murmured.

"He's a whited sepulcher!" Adam said vehemently.

The doctor laughed. "He may be beautiful without, but yes, he's full within of dead men's bones and all uncleanness."

"Then how can he possibly have a church and everything?" Adam asked.

"The scribes and pharisees were respected by a great many people, and a great many of them did a respectable job. I suppose most people see only the outside—he's a great one for rather showy good works—and have no idea of what's within. Go on."

Adam's memory again served him well. He was able to give a detailed account of the conversations in both the lounge and the dining room.

When he had finished Dr. O'Keefe sat twirling a pencil. "It seems to me you did very well. What's bothering you?"

"I wish I knew."

Dr. O'Keefe continued to twirl the pencil, staring at it with concentration. At last he said, "Do you think maybe you feel that it was all too easy?"

Adam looked up, his face alight. "That's it! They believed me too easily. That I'd work for them, and that I didn't trust you."

"It sounds to me as though you'd been pretty persuasive. Why do you think it was too easy?"

Adam said, slowly, "I don't think I'm *that* good an actor. I don't mean that I was bad or anything, I really think I did all right, but—"

"You think there may be a trap somewhere?"

"Yes. But I don't know *why* I think it. It's just a feeling, and I may be all wrong."

Dr. O'Keefe swirled the dregs of hot chocolate in his cup. "No. I think I know why you feel the way you do. Cutter and Ball aren't to be underestimated, and they aren't easily sold a bill of goods, and that's just what you were trying to do, and what you seem to have succeeded in doing, isn't it?"

"Yes, sir."

Again there was a pause, during which Adam wished even more strongly that he hadn't made his promise to Kali. Dr. O'Keefe took both cups to the sink and rinsed them out. "Tom Tallis will be in Lisbon on Friday. That's one good thing. I think you ought to go directly to Tom, rather than to Joshua or the Embassy."

"But what about Dr. Ball—"

"Yes, you'll have to go there first, though I hate to have you with the papers on you when you see him. I'll try to work out a plan between now and Friday. You've blundered into enough danger since you left New York without my sending you into more."

Adam said, "I want to do anything I can."

"I know, Adam, and I'm grateful. But you *are* in my care. If there were anyone else to send to Lisbon—"

"There isn't, and anyhow they expect me, and it would make them suspicious if I didn't come."

Dr. O'Keefe stretched and yawned. "Let's go to bed, boy. We'll sleep on it."

They had turned out the lab lights and shut and locked the door behind them, when Adam said, "Dr. O'Keefe, I forgot to tell you one of the most important things of all."

"What's that?"

"It's Macrina."

Dr. O'Keefe listened, standing quiet and unmoving, as the moon dropped slowly behind the hills. "If Macrina did that for you—"

"But I could be wrong again, sir. Maybe I just thought—"

"No. I don't think there's any doubting what happened.

And each separate event added up makes me realize—" He paused, sighing.

"Realize what, sir?"

"That you *are* the one to go to Lisbon on Friday, no matter how much it goes against the grain for me to send you into what we both know will be danger." The older man's hand dropped onto Adam's shoulder, but it was a touch completely unlike that of Dr. Ball. Whereas Adam had wanted to pull away from Dr. Ball and had had to will himself not to move, Dr. O'Keefe's hand felt like his father's; it seemed to be giving him strength, and determination, and the courage to do whatever it was that he had to do.

"Good night, Adam," the doctor said. "See you in the morning."

18

THE next day was, in a quiet and unexciting way, every-thing Adam had hoped the entire summer would be. Poly brought him his breakfast but was surprisingly reticent and the only question she asked about the evening before was what he had had to eat. Adam wondered if her father or mother had told her to leave him alone. He did his chores in the laboratory, drank coffee with Mrs. O'Keefe while the doctor was busy at his desk; Mrs. O'Keefe knew a great deal about her husband's work and had often assisted him.

Before lunch Poly called for Adam and he went swimming with all the children; they did not see Macrina, which was only partly a disappointment. Macrina would have made him think about the night before and all its implications, and he wanted a day of simple, straightforward work.

In the afternoon Dr. O'Keefe rode over to the village. Adam was left in charge of the laboratory, happy and uninterrupted. Mrs. O'Keefe brought him tea, but left him alone, and he spent the time deep in concentration on the files.

After dinner they sang again, and, as Adam's mind had been held during the day by his concentration on his work, so now the music held him and he relaxed into the singing. When the younger children were in bed he walked with Poly at the edge of the ocean. Poly had slipped off her sandals on the sea wall, and walked silently, teasing her bare toes against the in-coming waves, her white cotton dress blown tight against her twenty-twenty-twenty body. Not quite twenty-twenty-twenty any more, Adam realized. It wasn't going to be long before Poly would be bursting out of childhood as she was already beginning to do out of her dress.

As it grew darker there was a glittering against the dunes and Poly ran, colt-like, across the sand crying, "Fireflies!" and tried to catch the small sparkles between her hands. "Sometimes I catch them in a jar, just to look at for a little while, just to make a small lantern. But I never hold them for very long. I used to think they were tiny stars, but then I found out how cruel they are, and I don't think stars should be cruel."

"Fireflies cruel?" Adam asked with tolerant good humor.

"Oh, *you* know," Poly said impatiently.

"Fireflies have been pretty much left out of my education. All I know is that they're the only source of light that provides illumination without incandescence."

"So far so good." Poly held her cupped hands out to him, and a small startled spark flew out and up. She put her hand in Adam's and pulled him down onto the dune. "Let's sit for a while."

Adam leaned back against the soft, warm sand. How different this was from the night before with Kali. He sighed with relief at the release from tension. Ahead of them the moon was rising. Above, fireflies glittered. "It's really fantastic," he said lazily, looking at one small, moving spark. "Every light man can make is mostly heat. I forget the proportion it is in an electric bulb, but something like ninety-five percent of the energy needed to make an ordinary light bulb for an ordinary lamp in an ordinary house is used up in heat. If we could find out how the fireflies do it, cold light, electricity would cost only a fraction of what it does now. It would be so cheap it would hardly cost anything."

Poly lay back, looking out to sea. "The light and power companies wouldn't like that."

"I think Old Doc was working on it for a while. He used to pay me a penny, way back when I was a little kid, for every ten fireflies I caught for him in a jelly jar. I spent all evening chasing them. Didn't make much money but I had an awful lot of fun."

Poly rolled over, leaning on one elbow and looking at Adam intensely. "Do me a favor and leave fireflies alone."

"Hunh?" Adam turned to look at her.

"Listen," Poly said, still up on her elbow so that she could stare down at him. "Did you know they're divided into different levels or classes?"

"I've told you all I know about fireflies. They don't seem much of a menace to me."

Poly did not laugh. She continued to stare at him with a

serious, probing expression, so that she looked much older than her twelve years. "Well, they are. And they mate by their flashes. A male firefly will give his flash—maybe four flashes, say. And if the female is in the same class or category that he is, she'll answer back with four flashes. But if she's in the class that has three flashes, or two, or five, she won't answer. Unless she's hungry. Then she'll give him back four flashes and when he comes down to her, instead of making love with him she'll eat him."

"What a bloodthirsty fiendess," Adam said lightly.

"That's exactly what I mean. Leave fireflies alone, Adam." She stood up, calling, "Race you back to the house!" and went streaking across the sand.

Sunday morning the whole family went up to the monolithic stones and sat around the large table while Dr. O'Keefe read morning prayer. Then they rode to the native village, Mrs. O'Keefe carrying Rosy in a canvas sling on her back, Dr. O'Keefe carrying Johnny, and Adam riding with Peggy in front of him on the saddle. He had one arm around the little girl and she leaned back against him contentedly and slept.

Virbius entertained them with a lavish and exotic meal, and Poly and Temis rounded up all the O'Keefe children and the village children for a series of dancing and singing games. Adam, sitting next to the doctor, felt lapped in peace and joy.

Friday seemed a long way off. It seemed a long way off all during the week of working in the lab with the doctor, of swimming with the children, of singing in the living room in the evening, of coming to feel that this island and this family was his home. He knew that in actuality Friday was moving closer and looming larger with every passing minute, but he kept it out of his mind until Thursday night when all the children, including Poly, were in bed, and he was sitting in the living room with Dr. and Mrs. O'Keefe. Mrs. O'Keefe was mending a pair of Dennys' shorts, but her face had a watchful, waiting look, and she raised her head as the doctor said, "I've arranged to have the helicopter pick you up in the morning, Adam. You have a hard day ahead of you, and it's a tiring ride by horse over to the hotel."

"Whatever you say, sir." Adam's heart began to beat so that he could feel its thumping.

"You should get to Lisbon around ten in the morning. The plane leaves for Gaea again at six, but you can arrange to miss it. Joshua will fly you back."

Adam smiled with pleasure. "Oh, great. Something really good to look forward to."

"Now, Adam, there hasn't been time for you to learn any Portuguese, has there?"

"Just a few isolated words and idioms."

"Here's a small phrase book you may find useful, then. This is a good street map of Lisbon which will help you to find your way about. In the morning I'll give you the Temis papers. María and José report that the laboratory has been watched all week. One small paper I carefully dropped 'inadvertently' has disappeared. I hope we are leading them away from any thoughts of Temis into thinking I have been experimenting on one of the horses. José has dropped hints of this to the stable boys, and one of the horses has a badly cut hoof. This nonexistent experiment is important enough to excite much interest, but what is more, in the long run it would not work. As for the papers on Temis, we'll try to have them on you for as short a time as possible. María has made a concealed pocket for you to carry them in. She also made a slightly less clever pocket for the phony horse papers. If you are searched this pocket will be discovered first. You are of course aware that you will be followed wherever you go."

"Yes, sir, I figured I would be."

"Know too that someone from the Embassy will have an eye on you. I don't think you yourself will be in any danger, although the papers may be."

"I won't let anything happen to the papers," Adam said fiercely.

"I know, Adam. If I had not come to trust you implicitly I could not allow you to go."

Adam, remembering that until the promise was lifted he could not tell Dr. O'Keefe about Kali, bowed his head.

"Adam will be all right," Mrs. O'Keefe said softly.

Adam looked over at her with gratitude. Dr. O'Keefe continued, his voice quiet, calm, but containing absolute authority. "The first thing you must do when you get to Lisbon is to call Father Tallis. You will be most private in a public phone booth. Now, Adam, you have already learned that it is the unexpected that usually happens."

Adam controlled a shiver that threatened to ripple through his body. "Yes, Dr. O'Keefe. I have."

"We've tried to prepare, as much as possible, for the unexpected, to foresee the unforeseen. I think you're right in your suspicions about Dr. Ball and Typhon Cutter the other night: they're hot on the trail and you're being used as a decoy. I wish I knew what move they're going to make, but I don't. I can only guess that they'll try to keep you from getting in touch with either Joshua or Father and certainly they'd prevent you from getting through to the Ambassador. And the Temis papers are too important to go to anybody else. So, to try to prepare for the unpreparable, we have worked out alternate times and places for you to call Tom Tallis. I'm only grateful that he is able to be in Lisbon instead of Gibraltar or heaven and the bishop know where else."

"Sir," Adam asked, "how did Canon Tallis get involved in this—in this kind of business?"

"Inadvertently and unwillingly. Like most of us."

Adam nodded. "Yes. How am I to get in touch with him?"

"He will be moving all day Friday. I cannot give you a list of where he would be, because it would be too dangerous for you to carry. You'll have to memorize the places where he'll be available at each particular hour. The phone numbers will be no trouble since they'll be, in each case, numbers you can look up in the public phone book. Ready?"

"Yes, sir."

"Until ten-thirty the Russian Embassy." Adam looked startled, but Mrs. O'Keefe smiled serenely, and Dr. O'Keefe continued. "You must try to get him there, because we want the papers off you as soon as possible. Ask for Dr. Fedotov. Don't speak to anybody else."

"How will I be sure—"

"He will identify himself to you through the Frost poem, since it's the only one of the pass codes you know."

"What about the Tallis canon?"

"That's more a trademark than a code. Dr. Fedotov will put you through to Canon Tallis. If all goes well, and there's no reason it shouldn't, you'll be able to give him the papers before you go to the rectory to Dr. Ball. But if anything should happen to prevent your calling or getting to him, after ten-thirty you'll be out of touch until eleven—it does take time to get from one place to another—but between eleven and twelve you can call the Monastery of São Juan Chrysostom. Ask for the *senhor paroco*, Father Henriques."

"The *senhor paroco*, Father Henriques," Adam murmured, memorizing.

"If by noon you still haven't been able to talk to Tom you'll have time at the restaurant when you go to meet Kali. Between one and two-thirty call Rabbi Pinhas. Look in the phone book under the name of Senhora Leonora Afonso. Got it?"

"Yes."

"If you haven't been able to phone by two-thirty—and you should be able, Adam, these are just emergency procedures like the life belts on a plane that you never really expect to use—then from three-thirty to five call Joshua. You have his numbers, don't you?"

"Yes, in my passport."

"Whatever happens don't let anybody get hold of them. I hope long before afternoon you'll be all through with your job. If, by any mischance you're not, in the evening Joshua and Father Tallis are going to the opera. If you have to call them, ask for Dr. Magalhâes and say it is an emergency. Tom Tallis will have left that name, and say that he may get a call. I repeat, Adam, this should be an unnecessary precaution. Now I'll go over the list again."

Adam listened carefully. Mrs. O'Keefe finished patching Dennys' shorts and reached for a sweater of Peggy's. "Poly's growing out of everything," she murmured. "I'll have to go into Lisbon myself soon."

"Got it?" Dr. O'Keefe asked Adam.

"I think so," Adam said. "Until ten-thirty Dr. Fedotov at the Russian Embassy. Between eleven and twelve Father Henriques at the São Juan Chrysostom Monastery. Between one and two-thirty the Rabbi Pinhas, in the phone book under the name of Senhora Leonora Afonso. From three-thirty to five, Joshua. In the evening the opera house, and ask for Dr. Magalhães."

"Good. A friend of Arcangelo's will have the plane ready for you and Joshua after the opera. We can't use Arcangelo any more since Ball saw him with you at the airport. He's now pinpointed as one of our men, so don't try to get in touch with him whatever happens. He can't help you any more, and it would only be putting him in jeopardy."

Adam gave an involuntary shudder because he understood now just how grave the danger to Arcangelo could be. For some reason he remembered the chauffeur, Molèc, and the brutality of the huge hand as it sliced against his knee.

"Arcangelo's a good man," Dr. O'Keefe said, "and absolutely loyal. We'll miss him badly."

Mrs. O'Keefe looked up. "Is it safe for him to stay in Lisbon?"

"Safer than to try to leave."

"Dr. O'Keefe," Adam asked, "is the Rabbi Pinhas the one who was on the plane—"

"Yes. Now, Adam, you'd better get to bed and get a good night's sleep. We'll be waiting for you and Joshua tomorrow night."

"Yes, sir," Adam said. "Good night. Good night, Mrs. O'Keefe."

He lay in bed in the small airy room that had so quickly come to seem like home. A fresh ocean breeze came in the open window. He pulled the blanket up over him, but he was not sleepy. His body was tense and ready to spring, as though he were already in the plane on the way to Lisbon. He ran over in his mind the list of the places he was to call Canon Tallis. Then he tried to project his imagination beyond the unknown quantity of the day and to the trip back to the island with Joshua. But he could see in his mind's eye only the daytime trip the week before, and Joshua sending the little plane into the great, turbulent clouds, his voice rising above the tumult of the elements.

Back in the hills a night bird hooted. Dr. and Mrs. O'Keefe walked past his door on their way to bed. Adam did not look at his watch because he did not want to know how much time had passed. If ever he needed a good night's sleep it was tonight, so that his mind would be clear for whatever might happen the following day. In the next room Charles made a noise in his sleep. Adam wondered if the children would see Macrina when they went swimming, and if Poly would tell Macrina that he was in Lisbon, and if Macrina would care. There was no questioning Macrina's intelligence, but Adam wondered whether or not things mattered to her. How did a fish, even a mammal, show sadness? A crocodile might be supposed to shed tears, if only crocodile tears, but what could Macrina do to show sorrow?

As he thought about Macrina the thoughts got more complicated and more confused and he was in Gaea and he was in Woods Hole and Macrina was sitting at the concierge's desk at the Avenida Palace and Adam was asleep. . . .

Mrs. O'Keefe brought him breakfast in the morning. "Our thoughts will be with you all day, Adam," she said.

"Thank you. I'm glad."

Poly knocked and came in. "Take care of yourself for heaven's sake."

"For heaven's and the future's sake," Adam quoted.

"For my sake," Poly said.

Charles slipped into the room. "Just take care of yourself."

Peggy came running along the corridor, calling for her mother, plummeted into Adam's room, and was barely stopped from leaping up onto the bed and spilling the breakfast tray. "When will Adam be back?"

"Tonight," Poly said tightly.

"Tonight," Charles said, looking at Adam.

Mrs. O'Keefe pulled Peggy up onto her lap. "But late, Charles. Very late. Long after midnight. They should arrive with the dawn."

Charles looked at his mother, at Adam, nodded without speaking, and left the room as quietly as he had entered it.

Mrs. O'Keefe put Peggy down. "Come along, Pol, Peg. Let's give Adam a few minutes to eat breakfast in peace."

The whole family stood on the sea wall and waved as he left in the helicopter.—It won't be long, Adam thought, —before I'm back here and everything will be all right.

It was the same silent pilot who had taken him to dinner with the Cutters, and they whirred across the island with the pilot scowling out the windshield, seemingly wishing to avoid even looking at Adam. They circled the hotel, then flew over the pool and tennis court, and down the beach to a small cement landing strip. The taxi plane was there, and Adam was allowed to get on and settle in his seat, although he was early. There was room for twelve people in the compact cabin, but not much leg room. A pleasant-looking stewardess offered him coffee, but he was suspicious of all stewardesses and not at all sure of anything offered him to drink. He thought he could handle himself and protect the papers in María's special pocket as long as he was wide awake and alert, but he did not want to risk a Mickey Finn and someone searching him between the island and Lisbon. So he smiled politely and said, "No, thanks, I've just had gallons."

"Would you care for a magazine?" she asked in her charming accent. "We have the latest American magazines, *Esquire*, *Mad*—"

"No, thanks, I've brought some work." And he did have a sheaf of magazines Dr. O'Keefe had given him, some American, some English, some European, in a number of which Dr. O'Keefe had articles. The first magazine he opened, an Australian one, had a lead article by T. S. Didymus, and Adam felt that this was somehow a propitious omen.

He read the piece by Old Doc, smiling affectionately at the old man's individual quirks of phrasing. Then he managed to lose himself in various other articles that caught his interest, grateful for the discipline of concentration he had learned at school. Dr. O'Keefe's writing style was spare and clear, with unexpected, vivid illustrations, and a quick sense of humor.

—How could I ever have thought he wasn't okay? Adam wondered, and then remembered that his doubts were all seeded before he met the scientist, and that if it had not been for the New York fog for which Kali was so grateful, he might not be heading for Lisbon and danger now.

But this was purposeless thinking. He shook himself and returned to the magazine, reading until the passengers from the hotel came aboard. A portly, porcine man with a briefcase settled himself beside Adam. The boy kept his nose in the magazine, determined not to be drawn into conversation, no matter how innocent. But the man appeared as averse to chitchat as Adam, opened his briefcase immediately, and set to work on a sheaf of papers, only grunting in assent as the stewardess offered him coffee.

Adam read, holding his mind at bay. He managed not to think of the hours ahead, but discovered that he was not retaining anything from the articles in which he had thought he was engrossed.

They landed at the small airport from which he and Joshua had taken off, and where he had first met Dr. Ball. A limousine was waiting outside to take the passengers into the center of Lisbon, and Adam found a seat, seeking the portly man as a seat companion so that he would be assured of silence.

But the man did not reopen his briefcase. Instead he turned to Adam, smiled pleasantly, and said, "I'm Donald Green of the Singer Sewing Machine Company. Haven't noticed you around the hotel."

Adam did not in his turn introduce himself. Instead he answered politely, "Well, no, sir, I haven't been staying there."

"*Is* there any other place to stay on Gaea?"

"Oh, yes, sir."

"Where? Except for the hotel it seems a jungle as far as I'm concerned."

Adam did not know how to get out of this one. "Well, I have a summer job with a scientist who has a laboratory there." He tensed his body and mind for further questioning.

But Mr. Green of the Singer Sewing Machine seemed satisfied. To Adam's surprise he asked no more questions but went into a eulogy on the merits of his machines and how they were changing the entire life of the Iberian peninsula. "I feel that I'm doing a great service to these people. Tried to get those savages over in the Gaean village interested but was most rudely turned away." Adam mumbled politely and Mr. Green of the Singer Sewing Machine continued to talk about his experiences until the limousine stopped.

"Nice to have met you, sir," Adam said, and strode purposefully down the street as though he knew exactly where he was going.

He did not.

He had no idea.

Dr. O'Keefe had given him a street map of Lisbon, and Adam had studied it. But Lisbon is not the simple chequer board that makes up most of Manhattan; Lisbon is unexpected hills, open squares, closed alleys, a city of twisting, turning, revealing, hiding, light, dark, a city of mystery and beauty and fascination.

And Adam realized that he did not know where anything was in Lisbon. If he could find the Ritz then he thought he could find, in one direction, the Avenida Palace hotel, and, in the other, Joshua's apartment. If he could find the Ritz he could go in and look at the map again, phone Canon Tallis, and figure out how to get to the rectory.

No. He shouldn't go into the Ritz because of Arcangelo. But if he could find the Ritz then he would be able to find someplace else to look at his map and make his phone call. He stopped a man, saying, "Ritz, por favor?"

The man went into a torrent of Portuguese, and Adam simply shook his head. The man spoke slowly and at full volume, but this did not help, and Adam grinned foolishly and shook his head again.

Then a voice came from behind him. "I show you where go."

Adam turned and faced the huge body and coarse face of Molèc.

19

"THIS way," Molèc said, and Adam followed helplessly.

"Não, não," the man who had been trying to direct him called, and pointed in the opposite direction.

Molèc scowled, speaking rapidly and angrily. The man responded shrilly, flung up his hands in exasperation, and strode off.

"Where are you taking me?" Adam demanded.

"Padre Ball."

There was nothing to do but go with him. Molèc led Adam back to where the limousine was just pulling away to return to the airport. Parked nearby was Mr. Cutter's car. Adam would not easily forget this car, and he had no desire to get into it again, but he clenched his teeth and climbed in as Molèc opened the door to the back seat.

—If Mr. Cutter was going to have him meet me why didn't he tell me? Adam thought. —Or is this some kind of test or trick?

He looked out the window, trying to see something he recognized, trying to remember the route, to see street signs, but he realized that as far as finding his way around Lisbon was concerned he was completely helpless. Squares with fountains, sidewalks in mosaic patterns, laundry hanging, fountains splashing, all seemed to flash by him in an unassimilated jumble as Molèc drove.

"Igreja," Molèc said, pulling up abruptly in front of a grey stone cross-topped building on a broad, tree-lined street somewhere on the outskirts of Lisbon, though at which point of the compass Adam did not know. His sense of direction had completely forsaken him. Once he could study the map he would feel a little more secure.

A narrow, cobblestoned street led to a modern villa behind the church, and to this the chauffeur pointed. "Padre Ball."

"Obrigado," Adam said, quitted the Cutters' car and Molèc with a sense of relief, and walked quickly over the cobblestones.

The villa was a handsome one, large, faced with patterned tiles in Venetian red. He rang the bell and the door was opened almost immediately by Dr. Ball himself who grasped Adam's hand in his usual overhearty grip.

"Dear lad, I'm so grateful that you're here safely. So Molèc found you."

Adam retrieved his hand.

Dr. Ball led him along a narrow corridor into a large study. It was a light and cheerful room, filled with books and leather-covered furniture. Although it did not seem to Adam to reflect Dr. Ball's personality at all, it was no doubt the kind of study that the rector thought he ought to have. He sat down at his large, leather-topped desk, indicated a comfortable chair near him, and showed his teeth in a smile. "We should have thought of having Molèc meet you when we talked with you last week, but alas, we did not, and both Mr. Cutter and I felt that a phone call to you would be most unwise under the circumstances, and that we'd just have to trust Molèc to find you. He's a most reliable fellow. Though I'm sure you'd have managed to get to me anyhow, wouldn't you?"

"Well, I think so, sir. As a matter of fact, I didn't see Molèc right away, so I planned to look up your address in the phone book and then figure out how to get to you from the map." —I'll tell the truth whenever possible, he thought, —and when I can't I'll try not to say anything at all.

"Clever boy," Dr. Ball told him. "Are you hungry? Would you like something to eat? What can I get you?"

"Nothing, thank you. I had a good breakfast and I've arranged to meet Kali for lunch."

"Where are you meeting Kali? Perhaps it will simplify things if I show you on the map and tell you how to get there."

"That would be fine. It's a seafood restaurant called the Salão de Chá."

He gave Dr. Ball the map, and the rector spread it out on the desk. "Ah. Ah, yes. Here we are." He indicated a central point. "Here is the Salão de Chá. Here is the rectory. If you will walk three blocks east from here—thus—you will be able to get a number 198 bus which will take you to the Salão de Chá in about ten minutes. Or perhaps it would be simpler just to take a taxi. Yes. Yes, of course. That would be better."

"Well, no, thank you, sir, I think I'd rather take the bus."

"Why, boy? Do you not have enough money?"

Dr. O'Keefe had given Adam a sizable roll. He answered promptly, "Oh, yes, sir, I have the money for Mrs. O'Keefe's shopping, and I have my first week's salary, so I'm fine."

Dr. Ball sniffed. "O'Keefe is not known for overpaying his assistants." He took a wad of bills from his wallet and handed it to Adam. "We took that into consideration, of course, so let it be no problem to you."

"I really don't want the money, sir. I don't care about taxis."

"Kali is not accustomed to ordering inexpensive lunches."

"I can manage."

"My dear lad, I think you should feel free to accept a little payment for what you are doing for us."

"I'd really rather not take any money."

"I appreciate your sentiments, dear boy, but accept it as a loan. If you don't need it you can return it. But you may run into expenses you haven't anticipated."

Further arguing would be suspicious, so Adam took the money, putting it gingerly into his pocket. "About the taxi. I'd really rather take the bus so that I can learn my way around Lisbon a bit; it'll help give me the lay of the land."

"All very well and good if there's time. We shall see. Now for instructions. You have something for us?"

"Yes. Some papers I managed to get from the file when it was unlocked. Shall I give them to you?"

"Oh, no, sonny, no, no, no. It wouldn't do at all for me to have the papers, nor would it be right for me to act as courier. You must understand that. I do what I can to help, of course, but my position naturally limits what it is fitting for me to do."

"Well, then—" Adam let his voice trail off. He had a feeling that Dr. Ball was leading him around in circles with his questions, his bus numbers. The rector was like a well-fed cat who nevertheless enjoys playing with a mouse.

Now Dr. Ball looked at his watch. "Ten forty-five. What time are you meeting Kali?"

"One."

"Very well." An edge came into the voice that made Adam feel that now they were getting down to business; they were through playing games. "Professor Embuste of Coimbra is upstairs. I will take you to him." He rose, looked at his watch, checked it against a clock on the mantelpiece, then led Adam through the quiet house and up a flight of back stairs. "Professor Embuste does not speak English but his French is fluent. Yours?"

"Pretty good."

"Splendid, splendid. Cutter and I were betting on it, though we have an interpreter in readiness. We prefer not to use an intermediary if we can avoid it." He paused on the landing. "If Dr. Embuste is satisfied with what you have for us, you will be free to meet Kali at the Salão de Chá, where you will receive further instructions."

"Further instructions?" Adam asked blankly.

"Surely you didn't think your job would be over when you had delivered the papers? You are not that naïve nor that young."

—And it will give this Professor Embuste more time to go over the papers, Adam thought. Aloud he said, "I really don't think it's a question of naïveté, Dr. Ball. It seems to me that once I've delivered the papers my use is over."

"You may be wanted for questioning." Dr. Ball started up a second, narrower flight of stairs. "Remember that you work closely with O'Keefe. We may need to know more than his progress in the regeneration experiments."

"But what—there's nothing I know—"

"You know his habits. What time he gets up. When he is out of the laboratory. Where he goes. When the files are unlocked."

"I see," Adam said slowly. "It seems to me Joshua would be lots more use to you than I, sir, since he's such a good friend of yours and he's known Dr. O'Keefe so much longer." Perhaps this was a dangerous gambit, but it seemed to go along with the rôle Adam was trying to play.

Dr. Ball cleared his throat, went up two more stairs, paused. "Although our young friend Joshua is not a churchgoer, alas,

I consider that he is still within my parish and therefore my responsibility spiritually. He is lost now, and so, despite my disapproval of his way of life—he is really no fit companion for you—I must never abandon him. I would really prefer it if you did not see him." He hurried up the last few steps, walked down a short hall, knocked briskly at a door and opened it to reveal a small, almost bare room. At a desk sat a man with a sallow, intelligent face. An unshaded light bulb hung over the desk. It reminded Adam of the room in the airport in Madrid.

Without making any introductions Dr. Ball closed the door on Adam and disappeared. Adam could hear his footsteps descending.

The sallow man looked up. "Embuste."

"Adam Eddington," Adam said, looking at the professor.

Professor Embuste glared back, the corners of his mouth turned down in a bitter and unwelcoming expression. Adam was becoming accustomed to being examined, so he stood his ground.

Professor Embuste did not ask him to sit down. Without moving in his chair he said, "The papers, please."

Adam handed them across the desk.

"You will wait," the professor said sourly, "while I look at them."

Adam stood, watching the professor go through the papers, eyes flicking quickly over the formulas. Those eyes, small, close-set, dark in themselves and darkly shadowed, seemed to Adam to be sharp, cruel, and frighteningly intelligent. Minutes moved and Adam did not dare check his watch. He shifted uncomfortably from one foot to the other. But Dr. O'Keefe had prepared the papers well, for Professor Embuste put them down on the desk, looked at Adam, and said, "Very well. You may go. You will receive further instructions at the Salão de Chá."

Adam felt that he could not get out of this small trap of a room quickly enough. He opened the door and came face to face with Dr. Ball. If the rector had descended audibly, he had come back up the stairs in his stocking feet. Putting a finger to lips that were curved in a peculiar smile he led Adam to the front door, then took his hand in the too-strong grip. "My dear good lad, I am immeasurably relieved that all is well. You still wish to take the bus?"

"Yes, please."

"You remember the number?"

"198."

"Bright boy. We will be in touch." Adam's hand was pumped, blessings were rained upon his unwilling head, and he fled down the street.

At the bus stop a lonely young man waited. He wore heavy, horn-rimmed spectacles and carried a pile of books under his arm. He beamed at Adam and said in studied English, "A million pardons, but are you an American?"

"Yes."

"I am a student at the University of Lisbon and am taking courses in the English language and the literature of England and America. It is always my deepest pleasure to talk to students from either of these great countries." The light glinted against his spectacles so that Adam could not see his eyes.

"I'd like to talk to you," Adam said, trying to sound courteous, "but I'm in a terrible hurry. I'm off to meet a girl and the last time we met—well, we had a misunderstanding—so you see—" his voice trailed off.

The bespectacled student waved his books gleefully. "A lover's quarrel! How delightful! So of course I understand that you are not interested in my idle chatter."

Adam was spared a reply by the arrival of a bus, 198, —what luck, he thought gratefully. He smiled, waved courteously, jumped on and ran up the stairs to sit in one of the front seats on the upper deck, then looked down the street. The student was no longer at the bus stop, so presumably had boarded the bus, too, but he did not come upstairs. Adam alternately checked his watch and the map. It was already eleven-thirty, but with luck he would be able to manage a phone call to the São Juan Chrysostom Monastery. He felt a terrible need to be in touch with Canon Tallis. Something about Professor Embuste had frightened him, and although the false papers had for the moment been accepted, the boy knew that the Professor must now be going over them more carefully.

He left the bus, the Temis papers seeming to burn in María's pocket, bumped by several young people who pushed out ahead of him and stood clustered on the sidewalk. He knew the papers had not been touched but he still felt panic. The young people stood talking together animatedly and he was not sure whether or not he was imagining sidelong glances. Some of the glances came from girls, and to this he was moderately accustomed, but was the boy with his back turned the young man with glasses? Was Adam being watched as he walked quickly down the street?

It was not yet twelve. He knew, from the map, where the restaurant was, but to walk there before calling would be cutting the time too close for comfort. He went into a small hotel and found a phone. It was not in a closed booth, but no one, as far as he could tell, had followed him in. He struggled with the phone book and managed with considerable difficulty to find the number for the São Juan Chrysostom Monastery. With the help of the phrase book he was able to give the operator the number, and after a good deal of clicking and clacking he heard a distant ring. Then came a rough voice, and Adam said, "Senhor Paroco, Padre Henriques, por favor."

There was a long pause, during which Adam felt that everyone in the hotel lobby was staring at him. This, he knew, was not likely, and he would not be alert to the people who might really be following him if he was suspicious of everybody else. A gentle voice, an old voice, sounded in his ear: "Padre Henriques."

"Adam Eddington," Adam said. "Canon Tallis, por favor."

"Momento."

A shorter pause. Then the familiar, brusque voice. "Adam?"

"Yes."

"Where are you?"

"Lobby of the Hotel São Mamede."

"How much time do you have?"

"Until one."

"Lunch with Kali then?"

"Yes."

"Are you being followed?"

"I'm not sure. Maybe I'm being too suspicious."

"I doubt it. Leave the hotel and turn right down Rua São Mamede. Go into the coffee shop at number 28, over the oculist. I'll be there as quickly as I can."

A wave of relief broke over Adam as he hung up. He found the coffee shop without trouble, climbing a steep flight of stairs to a long, narrow room filled with small tables. The table by the window was empty and he sat there, looking out over the enormous gold spectacles that signified the oculist's office and shop below. Across the narrow street were more shops, a tobacconist, a music store, a shoe store. Down the street, which seemed purely commercial, he saw the ubiquitous laundry hanging out.

He ordered coffee and tried to appear relaxed and casual, but he could not keep from looking out on the street. He did not know from which direction Canon Tallis would approach, so he would take a sip of coffee and look up the street, another sip and look down the street. He was looking down the street, leaning forward, thinking he saw the canon in the distance, when somebody sat down opposite him, and he turned, thinking he must have been mistaken, to be met by the beaming face of the student from the bus stop.

"But what good fortune to come across you here!" the student cried. "Perhaps I can be of assistance to you. It would be my unutterable delight. Where is your—what do you call it—girl friend?"

"I'm meeting her in a few minutes." Words came quickly, almost without thought, to Adam's lips. "The bus was faster than I'd expected and I don't want to be *too* early. Bad for them to think you're too eager, if you know what I mean."

The student giggled convulsively. "You Americans! You steal our girls right out from under our envious noses. We are all so poor that it is difficult for us on the surface to compete with you."

"And below the surface?"

The student shrugged apologetically. "America is a rich country and life is easy for you. But the ability to love a woman and to please her to the ultimate fullest comes only through centuries of experience and suffering. I think that in the inner matters of the heart you have much to learn." He beamed at Adam as though he had paid him a great compliment.

A dark figure moved deliberately by Adam, and the Canon seated himself at the next table, so that Adam faced him and the student had his back to him. Adam felt a moment of frantic frustration. He had a wild impulse simply to take the Temis papers from María's pocket and give them to the canon then and there. Canon Tallis looked at him, raising what, if he had had hair, would have been eyebrows.

Adam stood up, saying rather loudly to the student, "Well, it was very pleasant meeting you. It's time for me to go to my girl, now." He could not resist adding, "And I assure you that I, too, have more charm than money."

The student burst into roars of laughter, slapping his knee in enormous appreciation. He, too, rose. "Perhaps it would amuse you if I walk along with you and show you some of the particular points of interest."

"But you haven't had your coffee."

The student shrugged and waved his arms in a windmill gesture. "Coffee I can have any time. The chance to exercise my English and simultaneously talk with an American is rare. Where are you meeting this lovely her?"

"At the Salão de Chá."

The student made a face. "The Salão de Chá prefers money to charm."

"Oh, well, you know," Adam said, "girls. I won't eat for a month."

Behind the student's back Canon Tallis' lips moved silently. "Phone." Adam's eyes met his for a brief moment of acquiescence. Then he paid for the coffee and left.

20

THE student chattered gaily about Portuguese architecture, history, wine, cheese, until they reached the restaurant. Adam listened enough to respond intelligently and, he hoped, innocently, but he was busy learning streets, memorizing landmarks. At the entrance to the Salão de Chá they said goodbye, the student pumping Adam's hand with affection, as though they were old friends, Adam trying to sound cordial. He did not know whether the bespectacled young man was one of Cutter's boys or not, but he was inclined to think so. The innocence was too calculated to ring true. And what about Adam's own?

The Salão de Chá was a large restaurant with a fountain in the center, and a balcony. The maître d'hôtel came bustling up to him, saying in English, "May I help you, sir?" Was he that obviously an American?

"I'm meeting a young lady for lunch," Adam said, "but I'm afraid I'm rather early." There was no use in trying to telephone now. He would have to give Canon Tallis time to get to the Rabbi Pinhas, since that was the next place Dr. O'Keefe had told him to call.

The maître d'hôtel was looking through a small black book. "Would you perhaps be Mr. Eddington?"

"Yes."

"Miss Cutter called. She has reserved a table on the balcony. It is more private, there. Would you like to go up and wait?"

"Fine. Thanks." He wouldn't like to go up and wait at all. He wanted to dash back out onto the street and find Canon Tallis; but Canon Tallis was probably on his way to the rabbi's. Adam decided that he would call in ten minutes, so he asked, "Is there a telephone I could use?"

"Yes, indeed, sir. There is one in the gentlemen's lounge upstairs."

Adam thanked him and was escorted up the stairs to the balcony. He sat at the table and tried not to keep checking his

watch. A waiter brought him a carafe of water and asked if he
wanted to wait for the young lady before ordering. It seemed
that everybody in Lisbon knew more about Adam's plans than
Adam himself. He drank a glass of water thirstily and went to
the men's room.

He was relieved to find it empty. The phone was on a table,
the phone book beside it. He looked up Senhora Leonora
Afonso. With the aid of the phrase book again he gave the
operator the number, having to repeat it several times, wasting
time in giving the numbers in French, German, English, and
finally going back to Portuguese. At last he could hear the
phone ringing. Ringing. Ringing. Then a man's voice: "Sim?"
Adam knew that this meant *yes*, but the voice was formidable,
unwelcoming.

"Rabbi Pinhas, por favor."

The voice replied, switching into English (was Adam's accent
as apparent as all that?), "Speaking."

"Canon Tallis, please."

"Who?"

"Canon Tallis. Canon Thomas—I mean John Tallis."

The Rabbi Pinhas—if it was he—said, "I think you must
have the wrong number."

"This *is* the Rabbi Pinhas?"

"Yes, and I am extremely busy. Please check your number
with the operator."

"Sir, this is Adam."

"Young man, look up your numbers more carefully in the
future."

"But sir, I know *you*. You were on the plane when—"

A cross voice cut him off. "Young man, this is most definitely not a restaurant. We serve no meals. I do not wish to be
discourteous to a foreigner, but you must go to someone else
with your problem."

At this apparent non sequitur Adam realized that the rabbi
might not be alone, or able to speak freely. "Sir," he said, "if
you think you'll be seeing Canon Tallis could you pretend I'm
asking you for money?"

"Of course I can't lend you any money, young man. I suggest

you go to the American consul. He is supposed to take care of his nationals."

"Do you expect him soon?"

"Young man, you are taking too much of my time. I am expecting a colleague in a few minutes."

"I'm at the Salão de Chá waiting for Kali. I'll try to call again. I'll be here for at least another hour."

"My dear young man, I lead an extremely busy life and several things have come up. Of course you can't come to see me. I'm going out in half an hour."

"I'll try to call back within half an hour, then," Adam said.

He went back to the balcony, to his table. There, at the next table, was Mr. Green of the Singer Sewing Machine. He saw Adam and smiled pleasantly.

"My young friend! And what are you doing here?"

"Meeting a friend for lunch."

"A young lady, I presume?"

"Well—yes."

"Lucky boy. You may wish me luck, too. I'm hoping to bring off a sizable deal." Mr. Green turned from Adam as two men with dark hair and rather flashy suits came up to the balcony, spoke to them in easy, if heavily accented Portuguese, and settled down to what seemed to be business, paying no further attention to Adam. The boy was inclined to think that Mr. Green's appearance was only an accident. Kali had said that the restaurant was well known, and it seemed a likely place to bring someone if you wanted to clinch a business deal.

He looked at his watch. After one. He felt twitchy. Where was Kali? There was no point in trying to call the rabbi's number again yet. He looked over the balcony to the tables below, to the fountain in the center. The restaurant was filling rapidly now, and when Kali came in it was with a group of other people, so that Adam did not see her at once. Then he caught sight of the familiar shining hair, the slender, expensively dressed body, the self-assured walk. The maître d'hôtel hurried to the girl, ignoring other guests who had come in first, and bent gallantly over her hand. Kali smiled and spoke to him, then moved swiftly through the crowded room and up the stairs.

"Adam, darling, I'm sorry I'm a few minutes late. Oh, how lovely to see you." She kissed his cheek exuberantly. At the next table Mr. Green winked at Adam.

Kali stiffened and leaned over the table, saying in a low voice, "Do you know those men?"

"One of them was on the plane this morning."

"There is absolutely *no* privacy in the world any more. Let's eat something quick and get out. They have a kind of prawn here that's just marvelous. I'll order those and we can pick up some tea later. We'll do some sightseeing first."

"While you're ordering," Adam said, slowly and deliberately, "I have a phone call to make."

"To whom?"

"Just a call. I'll be right back."

He went into the men's room. An elderly gentleman with a white goatee was washing his hands, but left without even looking at Adam. This time the boy managed to get the number over to the operator without trouble, and the phone was answered almost immediately. He recognized the rabbi's voice. "It's Adam."

"Hold on."

A short pause, then Canon Tallis. "Adam?"

"Yes."

"Are you alone?"

"At the moment. I'm in the men's room."

"How long are you going to be with Kali?"

"I don't know. She wants to take me sightseeing."

"Fine. Make one of your stops the São Juan Chrysostom Monastery. I'll have Father Henriques on the lookout for you. He'll ask if he can be of any assistance to you—he speaks excellent French, so you won't have any language problem—and you are to ask him who was the pagan orator who taught law to São Juan. If he simply answers *Libanius* you are to call me at the theater tonight. It's not safe for you to go to the Embassy or to call Joshua this afternoon. Cutter's men are all over the place."

The door to the men's room opened and Mr. Green came in. Adam said, "All right, Susie honey, I understand, but what else do you want me to do?" If the rabbi could play this game so could Adam.

There was a snort at the other end of the line. "Company?"

"Absol*u*tely."

"If he goes on to tell you that John studied theology under Diodore of Tarsus you must manage to get back to the monastery before six, when the doors are locked. I will be there at five-thirty, and will be by the sarcophagus of Princess María Fernanda."

"Anything you say, darling."

Canon Tallis gave another snort and hung up.

Mr. Green grinned conspiratorially. "Quite the young Don Juan, aren't you?"

"Well, you know how it is . . ." Adam replied modestly.

Mr. Green sighed. "Not any more. Those days are gone forever. All I can say is make the most of your hay while the sun shines."

Adam went back to Kali. He still thought that Mr. Green was all right, but he was taking no avoidable risks. Kali was dabbing butter on a bread stick. "I thought you were never coming back," she said crossly. "Who on earth were you talking to?"

"A girl friend."

She glowered as the waiter put a dish of shellfish in front of them. She took her fork and a pick, "Watch," and ripped the meat out of the shell. "I bet it was that Joshua," she said, as Adam tried clumsily to open his shell.

"Joshua who?"

"Don't play innocent. I may not approve of what daddy's doing, but I know what's going on. And I know Joshua. I've seen him dozens of times at Embassy things and he's always been very rude to me. I can't stand him." She spoke in a low and rapid voice, so that Adam had a hard time catching her words.

He leaned across the table and took her hands in his, so that to an observer it would seem like a love scene.

"Adam, I'm scared out of my wits. Daddy's utterly ruthless. He doesn't care how many bodies he tramples over to get what he wants. I'm sorry I sounded all snarly about Joshua. I know he's working with O'Keefe. I guess I'm just jealous of anybody who takes you away from me."

Adam released her hands. "We'd better eat."

"Yes. Let's get out of here. Adam, darling, if it hadn't been for you I'd probably never have questioned daddy. I'd have gone on thinking that anything he did was perfect just because he did it. But after I saw Molèc drive off with you and the O'Keefe child I was—I began to think. There's never been anybody I cared about enough to think about before. I mean, if Molèc drove off with somebody else I wouldn't have given a second thought whether they'd end up dumped in the Tagus or not. But I found myself thinking about you. And then I had to go on and think about all the rest of it." She dropped her eyes as though afraid of having said too much, leaned back in her chair, and began to pick the meat out of the shell with precision. She ate with rapid concentration, and long before Adam had finished she pushed back her chair, saying, "Let's go."

Adam picked up the check and stood up. "How much tip should I leave?"

Kali took the check from him, reached into her own pocketbook and put money down. "Quicker this way. You can pay me back. Come on."

At the next table Mr. Green gave another conspiratorial wink and Adam, giving a foolish grin in return, followed Kali down the stairs. The student spy had been right. The Salão de Chá was interested in money. One of Adam's favorite restaurants in New York was The Lobster on 45th Street, and it was a good deal more reasonable.

"We have to talk," Kali said intensely as they emerged into the crowded street.

"Well, let's do our sightseeing and we'll be able to talk then."

"Where do you want to go?"

"Just the usuals. The Belém Tower and the Jeronymos Monastery and the São Juan Chrysostom, and maybe the Madre de Deus church."

"We can do the Belém Tower and the monasteries without

any trouble; they're all fairly close together along the water-front. What about Mr. Eiffel's tower?"

"I'd like to see that, too. Let's do the things along the Tagus, and then we can do the Madre de Deus and the Eiffel if there's time."

They were standing on the street corner, Kali's hand resting lightly on Adam's arm. Several taxis slowed down suggestively, but she waved them on. "As soon as I see a driver I'm sure of," she said. "It has to be someone who doesn't speak English, so we can talk. How are you for time?"

Adam replied cautiously. "I have until five, maybe. See, there's this shopping I have to do for Mrs. O'Keefe." This he and the O'Keefes had decided to make legitimate for the benefit of anyone following his movements; easy enough, Mrs. O'Keefe had said, since the children always needed socks and underwear.

Kali flagged a taxi and Adam opened the door for her. As she climbed in she spoke in swift and charming Portuguese to the driver, giving him what appeared to be complicated directions. Adam thought he heard her mention the tower and the monasteries. She settled back in the seat. "Only till five? What about dinner? Can we have dinner together?"

"I'm afraid not."

"Why not?"

"I just can't, Kali."

"There has to be a *reason*. Are you having dinner with somebody else?"

"I'm not sure."

Kali gave a little cry and turned toward him. "You still don't trust me!"

"I don't know," Adam said with painful honesty, "whether I trust you or not."

Suddenly, unexpectedly, Kali's eyes filled and she butted her face childishly against Adam's shoulder. Through sobs she choked out, "If you don't trust me . . . if you don't love me . . . I can't bear it. . . . I'll want to die. . . ."

At this weakness, so strange in Kali, Adam was flooded with

a wave of protective tenderness. He held her closely, saying, "It's all right, Kali; it's all right."

Her sobs dwindled and she raised her head, asking like a child, "Is it really all right?"

"Of course."

"And you *will* help me?"

"In every way that I can. But I don't really see how."

Kali's voice rose. "By keeping me with you. By not sending me away." She began the sharp, frantic sobbing again.

"How can I possibly keep you with me? What about your father, anyhow?"

Kali's eyes darkened. "Oh, Adam, it's so awful. I do love him, but I don't want to see him, and I can't help him any more. All he wants O'Keefe's stuff for is money and more money, he doesn't care how it's used. He says there are too many people in the world anyhow and of course he's right but . . . Did you see Ball this morning?"

"Yes."

"Daddy said you were going to have papers from O'Keefe."

"That's right."

"You mean you *did*?"

"Did what?"

"You gave Ball O'Keefe's stuff?"

"No, Kali. I gave it to Professor Embuste."

"That repulsive little shrimp. Adam, you didn't, you couldn't!"

"Couldn't what?"

"Give him—you know—the things you've found out from O'Keefe." Adam was silent, and Kali cried, "The only way I can think of to make you trust me is to stay with you, so you'll know I'm not going to anybody with information. And it's safest for me, too. If daddy finds out I've told you anything he'll kill me."

"But you haven't told me anything."

"I've told you that I know what he's doing."

"But I already know that, Kali."

The taxi stopped. Kali jerked around and looked out of the window. Adam realized that he had been looking at the girl and not at where they had been driving. She said, "It's the Belém Tower. Come on." She spoke again to the driver, saying over her shoulder to Adam as she climbed out of the cab, "He'll wait for us."

They walked down a rough path. "Manueline architecture," Kali said absently. "Let's not go in."

Adam tried to look like an innocent tourist as he faced the great white building jutting out into the water. The tower was something out of Africa, and he could imagine a white-robed man standing at one of the corners (which one would face Mecca?) calling the faithful to prayer.

He could not keep Kali with him, but if she were telling the truth he could not let her go.

Kali turned away from the tower and the water. "All right. I'll tell you something else. I said I couldn't work against daddy, but I can't let you be hurt, either. Because I love you, too, Adam. That's what makes it so awful. If you double-crossed daddy this morning, I mean, if what you gave Embuste wasn't right, he'll be out for blood. He has plenty of people who'd be glad to shoot you down for a small sum—or for past favors. But everybody knows me, and as long as you're with me you'll be safe. Look." Adam could see a dark figure slip into the shadows of the tower. "That's one of daddy's men. I don't know if they've found out anything about you—I don't know what you've done—so I don't know if he's really after you or just keeping tabs. Let's go back to the taxi."

They walked over the gritty pavement. Adam held the cab door open, saying, "Let me think."

"All right, darling, darling." She sat close beside him, so that her thigh touched his, but she did not put her hands on him, and she did not speak. At the Mosteiro dos Jeronymos she led the way silently, walking rapidly around groups of tourists. When she spoke it was quietly, unemotionally, in the polite way of someone showing the sights to a distant acquaintance or the friend of a friend.

"It's a rather austere entrance, but I guess that's all right for a monastery. One of daddy's men is over there, stay close to me. The reddish color of the stone is lovely, don't you think?

Daddy says that the proportions are more harmonized than in any other building in Lisbon except the São Juan Chrysostom. He's looking at us. This is Vasco da Gama's tomb, but they had the wrong man in it for a while or something. Come on, this way. The cloister is famous because it's two-tiered, like the Chrysostom, and they both have these open cells leading off them. I don't know what the monks used them for. Let's go, Adam." The control of her voice slipped. "I want some tea."

Adam took her hand. It was warm and dry, while his, he discovered, was becoming cold with nervousness. "We'll have tea after we've been to the São Juan Chrysostom Monastery."

"Let's skip it. It's very much like the Jeronymos, only smaller, and less ornate."

"I'd still like to see it."

"Adam, you can't be interested in sightseeing *now*."

A sightseeing bus pulled up in front of the monastery, and a group of chattering young people got off. Was that the student with the spectacles again? "If we're being followed," he said, "we'd better act as natural as possible, and it would be natural for me to see the São Ju——"

Kali cut him off. "All right. Maybe you have a point. Let's go."

In the taxi Adam felt his hands getting colder by the moment, beginning to ooze icy moisture. He must not hold Kali's hand and give away his tension.

The São Juan Chrysostom Monastery had fewer tourists than the more famous Jeronymos. It was smaller, less ornate, but there was a purity to it that reached Adam even through his whirling mind. The double cloister soared heavenward, forming a narrow rectangle about a garden with a fountain in the center. In the church itself the light had an underwater-green quality, reminding Adam that the Tagus was just outside. This time Kali gave no tourist's spiel; her face was brooding as they walked slowly, footsteps echoing on the stone floor. They turned into an octagonal bay with a low font in the center, surrounded by seven columns. As they entered by one arch a tiny, elderly priest in a shabby cassock came in by another, bowed, and smiled at them. "May I help you?" he asked, first in Portuguese, then French. Adam answered in French.

"Well, Father, I was studying St. John Chrysostom for a school project once, and I can't remember—what was the name of the pagan orator who taught him law?"

"Show off," Kali whispered.

"Now let me see," the priest said. "That would be Libanius, wouldn't it? It was Diodore of Tarsus who instructed him in theology. I'm delighted at your interest, young man. May I inquire where you're from?"

"New York," Adam said.

"And the young lady? Is she interested, too?"

"No," Kali was impatient. "I'm afraid not. Please, Adam."

The priest smiled at Adam, his faded blue eyes twinkling. "Perhaps you will come another time and let me show you around? I am Father Henriques."

"Thank you, Father. My name is Adam Eddington, and I'll be back as soon as possible, I promise you."

"*Adam*," Kali said. "Sorry, Father, but we have to go."

When they were back in the taxi Adam said, "You weren't very polite."

"If you're not keeeping track of time, I am. Adam, I have to know. Are you going to let me stay with you or not?"

Adam sighed.

"Is it such a horrible prospect?" Kali asked in a low voice. "I did think that you might—that you might care about me a little. I'm not used to telling people I'm in love with them. I'm used to it being the other way around. It's either you or the Tagus as far as I'm concerned."

Looking at her strained face and rather wild eyes, Adam was torn between belief and doubt.

She continued, "I'm not trying to threaten you or say it'll be all your fault if I throw myself into the river. But there isn't any alternative for me. Everything I've ever cared about is all smashed. If you turn me away I don't want to live." Slow tears trickled down her cheeks.

Adam thumped a tight fist into a cold palm. "All right. Look. Tell the taxi driver to take us to Eiffel's Tower."

 **21**

KALI leaned toward the driver obediently and the cab headed back into the city. Adam, straining to look out the window, tried to keep landmarks, street names in his mind, but the problem of Kali kept whirling about, driving away all other thoughts. He could not abandon her either to the Tagus or to the web of steel threads being woven so mercilessly by her father. But he had to go back to the São Juan Chrysostom Monastery, and he had to go there alone.

Why? If he believed that Kali was telling him the truth why wasn't taking her with him to Canon Tallis the best possible thing to do?

He believed her and yet he was not quite sure. A week ago the confiding way she was holding on to his arm would have undone him utterly. Now all he felt was cold, cold inside and out.

"Why are we going to Eiffel's Tower?"

"To give me time to think."

"But you're going to keep me with you?"

"I'm going to try to."

"You're going to take care of me?"

"Yes."

The tower loomed up grotesquely in the street, the observation platform balanced precariously on top of the spindly elevator shaft. It was built, it seemed, out of a small boy's erector set. Adam had never seen the Eiffel Tower in Paris, but he had seen pictures of it, and both were obviously the result of the same rackety imagination. The Lisbon Tower, however, also served a purely practical purpose. Lisbon, like Rome, was a city of steep hills, and the foot of the tower was on one street level, the observation platform on another, and riding the elevator was for many people simply a useful short cut. At any other time Adam would have been immensely pleased with it. Now he gave the wild construction the scantiest attention.

As they waited for the elevator to take them to the upper level he said, "Okay, I think I've got things straight."

"Tell me."

"If you'll do the shopping for Mrs. O'Keefe—it's just socks and underthings for the kids, and I have all the sizes and everything written down—then I can do one other errand at the same time, and then we can meet for dinner."

"What's your errand?"

"Something for Dr. O'Keefe."

Kali frowned as though this was something she needed to ponder about. Finally she said, "I'm sorry, Adam, but how will I know you'll ever come back to me? You could send me shopping and just disappear."

"I give you my word."

"People's words don't mean much to me any more. I need something more tangible than that."

"I don't have anything more tangible. I'll do my errand and then I promise you I'll meet you wherever you say."

Kali thought again. "Have you got your passport with you?"

"Of course."

"Give it to me as a hostage. Then I'll know you can't go off and leave me."

"I thought you trusted me."

"I do. More than anybody else I know. But you see the people I know have been daddy and his people, and I always trusted daddy. So how can I trust anybody? Please, Adam, if you *are* coming back to me there isn't any reason not to give me your passport."

Slowly Adam took the passport out of his breast pocket. Still holding it, he asked, "Where will we meet?"

"At the Folclore, as soon after six as possible. The food's good and you ought to hear some Fado and see some of the folk dancing." She held out her hand. Adam put the passport in it. She began leafing through it. "Oh, Adam, what an awful picture, I'd never recognize you!" Between the next two pages was the slip of paper with Joshua's phone numbers. "What's this?"

"Just some phone numbers. Give it to me."

Kali shut the passport. "Oh, no, I'm going to keep the whole thing."

To make an issue over the numbers would be to give them importance in Kali's mind.

Adam swallowed. His hands felt colder and colder. His feet, too, seemed to be lumps of ice. He was doing what he had promised not to do. He said, "The numbers are just for the errand for Dr. O'Keefe. I'd appreciate it if you'd let me have them."

"Look them up in the phone book." Kali put the passport into her bag. "You don't trust me, Adam. I can't bear it."

Adam felt physically sick. His stomach clenched with fury at his ineptness, with frustration at his inability to do anything right. He did not dare press the issue of the phone numbers further. If he could convince Kali that they were unimportant and if he could get back to the São Juan Chrysostom in time to deliver the Temis papers to Canon Tallis, then he could meet Kali for dinner, get the passport and Joshua's numbers back, and no real harm would be done.

Mr. Eiffel's elevator creaked down and groaned to a stop, disgorging a chattering group of Lisbonese on their way home, and tourists gawking at and commenting on the tower in all languages.

"Come *on*," Kali said, pushing through the crowd into the elevator, pulling Adam after her.

People continued to jam in long after Adam felt capacity had been reached. He could not see the usual comforting sign to tell how many the elevator could safely hold. The air was thick with sweat, smoke, perfume. With each passing second he felt more of a sense of pressure and more as though he were going to be sick. He was pressed close against Kali and she managed to slide one arm confidingly around his waist. He was glad she had not taken the clammy hand that would have given away his intense nervousness that was bordering on fear.

They were standing near the elevator operator and Kali spoke to him in Portuguese, explaining in Adam's ear, "He's an old friend."

"One of 'daddy's men'?"

"*Really*, Adam," Kali said as the door clanged shut. "I

thought I'd made myself clear." Her voice choked up and Adam was afraid his stupidity was going to make her burst into tears there in the crowded elevator.

"I'm sorry." His voice was gruff. He clenched his fists. He *must* keep in control of himself and the situation while he carried the Temis papers and while Kali had the passport with Joshua's phone numbers.

The elevator started to creak upward. People going home from work continued their conversations or stood in stolid fatigue. The tourists exclaimed in excitement, one fat woman giving small shrieks of nervousness at the reluctant jerking of the elevator.

Just as they neared the observation platform there was a groan, a shudder, and they stopped. The operator fiddled with the controls. He said something in Portuguese, then loudly in English, "STUCK."

There was a burst of excited, multilingual talk. Kali said in a clear voice as the fat woman's shrieks grew louder, "It's all right, don't worry, this happens all the time, he'll get it going in a moment. It's perfectly all right, don't get panicky."

The operator broke through her words to call up through the roof. From both the upper and lower levels came shouts of excitement and, evidently, directions, because the operator began jerking at the controls. The elevator dropped a foot and stopped. The fat woman let out a piercing scream.

Adam could feel, particularly among the tourists, a sense of terror compounded by his own. Kali, strangely, seemed less nervous than she had all day. She said something in a very low voice to the operator, but a Frenchman, standing close to them, had evidently heard, because he said, "What was that?"

"I beg your pardon?" Kali asked icily in French.

The Frenchman accused, "*You* told him to stop the elevator."

"Why under the sun would I do that? I'm in just as much of a rush as you are."

"I heard you say *parar*. That means *stop*."

Kali burst into shrill laughter. "Your Portuguese isn't very good, is it? *Para* means *in order to*. I told him to call someone in order to get us out."

The Frenchman looked sourly at Kali. "I don't believe you.

I think we are being forcibly detained." He shouted above the babel, "Start this car at once!"

The operator shrugged. "Stuck."

The fat woman cried shrilly, "Somebody *do* something! *Help!*"

"Madame," the operator said, "I 'ave already press ze alarm button."

From the streets above and below the shouts were louder, as though larger groups were gathering.

Adam felt suffocated. Seconds were passing and the Temis papers still on him. He had to get to Canon Tallis. Above him he could see the floor of the observation platform. If the doors of the elevator were opened he would be able to climb up and out onto the platform.

But when he suggested this to Kali and she spoke again in her fluent, rapid Portuguese, the operator shook his head. "Not safe."

Kali's arm tightened around Adam's waist. "Are you in that much of a hurry? Nobody here eats dinner before nine."

Adam's head reeled, but through his dizziness a high English voice cut, "I was stuck in the lift at Harrod's once, but not for nearly as long as this."

It was stiflingly hot in the elevator with all the jammed-in bodies, and the laughter was beginning to have a hysterical edge that was ready to slip over into panic, and he, in his own panic, was being no help. He could feel his heart pounding. Kali's arm was tight about his waist. The fat lady gave a thin, bubbly scream, but before her hysteria got over the edges of control the elevator gave a groan and a jerk, and the operator, as though he were piloting a plane, brought it to a stop at the upper platform.

Adam, forgetting all courtesy, pushed out, dragging Kali after him. He looked at his watch. Almost six. He swung on Kali, shouting, "You do the shopping. Here's the list. Here's some money." He thrust Dr. Ball's bills into her hand. There. "I'll meet you at the Folclore as soon as I can." Without stopping for any kind of response from her, without giving her a chance to hold him back, he rushed off up the street. An empty cab was passing. He hailed it, and got in, panting. "São Juan Chrysostom Monastery, por favor." He saw that Kali had run up the street after him, but he slammed the taxi door, giving her a vague nod and wave. If she had heard where he was going it was too late now.

He looked from the window of the taxi to his watch and back to the window. The streets were full of people going home, streaming out of stores, hotels, subway stops, their shadows long as the sun began to drop.

The driver wove skillfully around pedestrians, buses, cars. Adam looked at him through the dividing glass, a rough-appearing man in a fisherman's sweater and cap and an unkempt beard. He looked at Adam in the rearview mirror and winked. Adam froze. One of Cutter's men? Had he walked into a trap?

Still with his foot on the accelerator the driver turned to face Adam, gave a jerk to the beard, which came off, revealing Arcangelo. A swift movement and the beard was back in place.

"Arcangelo!" Adam gasped. "What—"

"I've been following you all day," Arcangelo said in his careful English. "So have others."

"But it's not safe for you!"

"You did not recognize me, did you?"

"But it's still not safe. Dr. O'Keefe said—"

"You think I would let those snakes drive me under cover?" Arcangelo swerved scornfully around a bus and turned down a side street. "If anything happened to you Polyhymnia would be unhappy."

Ahead of them a large black car swung out of a side street so that Arcangelo had to jam on his brakes. "*Duck!*" he said suddenly, and in a quick reflex Adam dropped to the floor.

"Molèc," Arcangelo growled between closed teeth. "We are in for what you would call the showdown. Where is the Cutter girl?" He spoke with as little lip motion as possible, then puckered his lips up in a whistle, so that anyone looking back from the dark car ahead would not know he was talking to the passenger. The whistling resolved itself into a melody. The Tallis Canon.

Adam felt a surge of excitement despite his cold hands and

feet. "She's safe. She's shopping. I have to get to the São Juan Chrysostom Monastery before six. Canon Tallis is waiting for me."

"Six now," Arcangelo said. "They are trying to slow us down and I cannot let them know I know who they are or they will know who I am."

"It closes at six."

"I know a side door but we will have to get rid of Molèc." Arcangelo swung around and down a side street, then turned back into the city. Adam raised his head, but Arcangelo said sharply, "Stay down." The boy could not see where they were going, but he could feel that it was a rapid and devious way. The taxi stopped with an abruptness that threw him against the seat in front, and Arcangelo said, "Get out."

Cold though Adam's hands might be, his reflexes were functioning satisfactorily. He grasped the handle of the door and pitched himself into the street. They had stopped at a rank of taxis. Arcangelo was leaning out the window, talking to one of the drivers, and indicated with a gesture of his thumb that Adam was to get into the other cab. As the boy slammed the door Arcangelo said, "He will take you to the São Juan Chrysostom. I will continue to drive so that Molèc will be put off the trail. Go now, quickly."

The taxi shot off. Adam called back, "Arcangelo, take care of yourself."

The taxi driver, a thin young Negro, looked at Adam in the rearview mirror and smiled. Then he began to whistle, softly. The Tallis Canon. Adam joined him. They smiled at each other. Adam knew that he must not make the mistake of thinking that either he or the papers were safe because Arcangelo was taking charge, because he liked the young man who was driving him, but the terror had left the pit of his stomach, and he sat, coiled like a wire, ready at any moment and whenever necessary, to spring.

"São Juan," the driver said, and ahead of them was the beautiful, austere building. They drove past the entrance, the great doors closed, only darkness showing behind the stained-glass windows which were drained of color as light was slowly draining from the sky. They turned the corner and went past the Chapter House. Beyond this was an iron gate that opened to a long, narrow, hedged-in path to the cloister. The driver looked quickly around, stopped, and jumped out. Adam followed him, and together they ran to the gate. The driver pulled at the bell, once, twice, three times. In the distance they could hear it clanging.

Bong. Bong. Bong.

Through the sound of the bell came the sputter of an engine. The driver grabbed Adam and together they pressed into the shadows. A diesel-powered taxi drove up and someone sprang out.

22

IT was Joshua.

"Muito obrigado," he said to Adam's driver, "apresse se," clapped him in a swift, comradely gesture on the shoulder, and turned to Adam. The young driver ran back to his cab. They heard him gun the engine and roar down the street.

Joshua pulled a key out of his pocket and bent to unlock the gate.

"How did you know—" Adam started.

"Kali phoned me. How did she get my numbers?" The gate creaked open. Joshua pulled Adam through, clanged it shut, locked it. When Adam did not answer his question he did not repeat it. They hurried down the path, brushed by early evening shadows cast by the tall hedges. Behind them they could hear the squeal of tires, screech of brakes, slamming of car doors.

"Run." Joshua sprinted ahead, Adam close on his heels. The path turned, leading them to an arched side entrance. Again Joshua bent to the lock. As the door swung open they could hear footsteps pounding down the path. Joshua slammed the door and leaned against it for a moment, panting. "Are the papers still on you?"

"Yes."

Behind them there was a pounding at the door. Joshua pulled Adam away as shots rang out, splintering the heavy wood. "Quick."

The room they were in was so deep in shadows that Adam could see nothing after the light outside. Joshua grabbed his hand and they ran, Adam stumbling, slowing them down, ran through the room, through a corridor illuminated by high, dusty windows, and then out and into the light of the cloister. In the center of the garden the fountain rose high, catching the long rays of sun in a shower of silver. They ran pounding down the echoing stones; their footsteps echoed, and the echo was lost in the crash of heavy feet seeming to close in from all sides.

Ahead of them a hulking form loomed up: Molèc.

"God," Joshua said. He swung Adam around and shoved him into one of the monks' niches as a shot rang out.

Still running, Joshua fell.

Out of the niche beside Adam came Typhon Cutter, and Kali ran swiftly along the cloister and plummeted into his arms. "Well done," Typhon Cutter said, and Adam saw, with a feeling of nausea, the look of adoration she gave her father, the spider weaving his inexorable web in which they were all trapped. How, now, was there any escaping the tightening threads?

Despair burned in the pit of Adam's stomach, then burst into a fierce and controlled anger such as he had never felt before. He stood, crouched like a panther ready to spring.

Another shot.

The gun dropped from Molèc's hand and he gave a scream of rage and pain. Another shot dropped him, writhing, to his knees. Typhon Cutter pulled Kali back into the monk's cell.

Joshua lay, without moving, on the stones a few feet from Adam.

"Stay back!" A voice catapulted across the cloister as Adam started to leap out of the niche into which Joshua had shoved him.

He had no weapon. No gun. He could not help, only hinder. There was, at the moment, nothing to do but obey.

Across the cloister he saw the dark form of Canon Tallis, smoking gun in hand. He thought he saw Arcangelo. A shot rang across the cloister from Typhon Cutter's cell and ricocheted from a stone column.

Adam looked at Joshua's still form, only a shadow as light began to withdraw from the cloister, and let out a cry of anguish and rage.

His cry was echoed in the high shriek of a siren. Turning, he saw Typhon Cutter and Kali slip out of their cell. As they disappeared into the darkening corridor he was after them, and with one leap he flung himself on Mr. Cutter, throwing him to the ground.

"Daddy, don't kill him!" Kali screamed.

Adam's fingers clamped around the wrist that held the gun, his knee was on the bloated stomach.

"No," Kali said. "No." She grabbed the gun from her father and pointed it quaveringly at Adam. He could barely see the gun because the passage was almost entirely locked in darkness. The light filtering dustily through the high windows was above their heads and they were enclosed in shadows. "Let him up," Kali ordered.

Adam looked toward her. In the dim light her face was contorted in a horrible mixture of emotion. If ever she had been beautiful for him she was not beautiful now.

"Let him up," she said again, her voice steadier, "or I'll shoot. I mean it."

Adam lifted his knee from the belly, released his hold on the wrist. Typhon Cutter struggled to his feet as a searchlight swept across the cloister, penetrating the dark reaches of the corridor where the three of them stood, panting.

"The papers," Typhon Cutter said.

"I gave you the papers."

"Not those. You have others. Give them to me." The treble voice soared.

"No," Adam said. "I don't have any papers."

"The gun, Kali."

"No, daddy. No."

If he shouted, Adam thought, they might hear him in the cloister and come. But no sound emerged from his constricted throat.

"The gun."

The muzzle pressed against Adam's chest.

"The papers."

"Go ahead and shoot," Adam croaked, "for all the good it will do you." He expected to hear the explosion of the bullet if, indeed, he heard anything.

But Cutter said, "Kali," and the boy felt, instead of a deadly burst of lead, her long fingers moving over him, coming closer, as she searched, to María's pocket.

Without conscious volition his hand flashed out and slapped across the girl's face, the sound sharp and unexpected and immediately followed by a shot and the crash of the gun dropping from Typhon Cutter's hand.

The shot had not come from Cutter's gun. From where?

Cutter began to back down the passage, holding Kali in front of him as a shield.

Through the darkness came the voice of Arcangelo. "Let them go. My men outside."

Adam reached down in the shadows to look for the dropped gun, but he could not find it. His breath came in painful gasps as his heart thudded against the rib cage.

"Come," Arcangelo said. "It's over. Everything is over. Come."

The searchlight swung around again, and Adam moved toward it and to the cloister that still contained the last rays of the sun, the fountain glistening as it rose toward the sky, Joshua, lying sprawled on cold stone.

With an absolute carelessness and indifference to what was going on around him Adam ran across the pavement to Joshua and knelt by him. Joshua's eyes were open, but he did not see.

"Joshua!" Adam cried. "Joshua!" He put his head against Joshua's chest, listening, listening, and thought he felt the faint thread of a heartbeat. He noticed two uniformed men going by with Molèc bellowing on a stretcher, noticed it only because the sound kept him from listening for Joshua's heart. He pressed his cheek to Joshua's lips to try to feel the faintest breath.

"Adam." It was Canon Tallis' voice.

Adam looked up.

The priest stood there, gun still in hand, with two uniformed policemen beside him. Adam could tell that the canon was thanking them, that he was giving them instructions. When they turned toward Joshua he spoke to them brusquely, and they bowed and moved away.

"Get up," Canon Tallis said to Adam, and the boy stood. The canon knelt beside Joshua. A faint sound came from his lips, the single word, "God." It was also the last word Joshua had said.

Out of the shadows Arcangelo and Father Henriques emerged, Arcangelo looming enormous beside the tiny priest. Canon Tallis looked at them. "Morto," he said.

"No," Adam babbled, "no, he's not dead, he can't be."

"He is dead. Be still," Canon Tallis said. He leaned over Joshua again and it was as though the two of them had gone two thousand miles away, that they were not in the cloister with Adam and Father Henriques and Arcangelo. The canon took Joshua into his arms, holding him close in a gesture of infinite tenderness and love.

Father Henriques touched Adam's arm and drew him away. The three of them, Father Henriques, Arcangelo, Adam, walked slowly along the cold stones of the cloister, their feet muffled in darkness and grief, leaving Canon Tallis with Joshua.

23

W AS it only that the light bulb in Father Henriques' tiny office was dim, like the light bulb in the Avenida Palace, or was the darkness in Adam's mind?

He sat on a straight chair across from Father Henriques and Arcangelo. Their faces were closed and emotionless, as though turned to stone. Adam did not know when Father Henriques and Arcangelo started to talk in low voices, nor when he realized that they were speaking French, until he heard Father Henriques ask, "Arcangelo, how did you know—"

"You think you could keep me away," Arcangelo asked, "when I am needed? You think I will hide in safety when you are in danger?" His voice deepened with emotion. "You think I cannot find out when you try to protect me?"

Father Henriques held up a thin white hand, and Arcangelo rumbled into silence.

A dark shadow moved across the doorway and Canon Tallis came into the office. "The papers," he said without preamble and, as Adam handed them to him, he demanded, "Why was Joshua here? He was to be at the Belém Tower."

Adam stood up, but his knees were trembling so that he sat down again immediately. "He was here because of me."

Then came the questions, Canon Tallis clear, precise, ice cold, Father Henriques gentle but nevertheless touching every raw and open nerve.

It had been again (again and again: would it never end?) the unexpected, the unforeseen that had happened. The papers Adam had delivered to Professor Embuste at Dr. Ball's rectory had indicated a meeting at the Belém Tower. Joshua, working with Interpol and the Lisbon police, was to have been there. Typhon Cutter was to have been led into his own spider web.

"As indeed he was," Father Henriques said. "But not in the way we thought."

And not before Molèc's bullet had found Joshua.

Adam cried in anguish, "I killed Joshua. I believed Kali and

I didn't tell Dr. O'Keefe." He began to gasp through sobs that racked his body. "I let Kali get Joshua's phone numbers and he came to save me—"

Canon Tallis cut him short. "Stop."

"But he would still be alive—"

The canon's voice was quiet, firm as a rock. "You cannot see the past that did not happen any more than you can foresee the future. Come, Adam. We must go."

In the back seat of a police car Adam rode beside Canon Tallis. Two policemen sat in front, talking casually. The last late light of evening had left the sky, so time must have passed, and light from street lamps, shop windows, neon signs, streamed across the mosaic sidewalks. A mule-drawn wagon turned into the street in front of them, a lumbering, cumbersome wagon bearing great red clay jars of wine. The mule ambled along, paying no attention to the honking of the police car. The driver shouted threats at the mule driver, and finally managed to swerve around wagon and mule, almost knocking down an elderly man in a tam-o'shanter who was riding along on a bicycle. The man wobbled precariously, shrieking at the police car and shaking his fist. The policeman leaned out the window and yelled back, zigzagging toward the curb to more shouting from excited pedestrians.

Beside Adam the canon sat still and stern, paying no attention. The driver regained control of the car and himself, and turned down a side street, then down another and darker street where laundry flapped, ghost-like, in the breeze from the Tagus.

The car stopped and the canon got out, beckoning to Adam, crossed to a narrow house faced with blue-and-white tile, and banged a brass knocker against a blue door. Above them a window was flung open and a man with a long white beard and a nightcap stuck his head out.

"A.H. 173–176," the canon said.

"E.H. 269," the man in the nightcap replied.

"ΦΩΣ ἱλαρὸν ἁγίας δόξης ἀθανάτου Πατρὸς, οὐρανίου, ἁγίου, μάκαρος, Ἰησοῦ Χριστὲ, ἐλθόντες ἐπί τοῦ ἡλίου, δύσιν, ἰδόντες φῶς ἑσπερινὸν, ὑμνοῦμεν Πατέρα, καὶ Υἱὸν καὶ ἅγιον Πνεῦμα Θεοῖ," the canon said.

"Ἄξιος εἰ ἐν πᾶσι καιροῖς ὑμνεῖσθαι φωναῖς ὁσίαις, Υἱὲ Θεοῦ, ζωὴν ὁ διδούς. Διὸ ὁ κόσμος σε δοξάζει," the man with the beard replied, and disappeared, pulling the window closed behind him.

It had sounded like Greek to Adam. As a matter of fact, it probably *was* Greek.

The door creaked open and the man in the beard led them into a small side room containing only a high desk and a stool. The canon explained curtly, "Father Metousis is the only one who can break Dr. O'Keefe's code."

The patriarch sat on the stool, steel-rimmed glasses slipping down his nose. He wrote with a scratchy, sputtering nib which he had continually to dip into ink. Adam did not know how long Canon Tallis and he stood there while the old man wrote, thought, wrote, scratched out and wrote again. It must have been more than a few minutes. It was probably less than hours. Time had no meaning: it was not.

Finally Father Metousis handed the papers over.

"Joshua?" he asked.

Canon Tallis nodded. "Tomorrow afternoon."

"Gaea?"

"Yes."

Adam no longer attempted to understand. He swayed. Canon Tallis gestured to him and they left, climbing back into the police car which was waiting outside. "The American Embassy," the canon said, then, dryly, to Adam, "We don't usually have this kind of escort."

At the Embassy a party was in progress. Lights and music filled the night. Uniformed servants were passing trays of champagne, platters of canapés. The canon walked by the open archways that led into the rooms in which the party was being held. At one end of the large room to the right an orchestra was playing, banked by palms. That they could play on the night of Joshua's death, that the world could still turn, the Tagus flow, seemed to Adam incredible.

"Come," Canon Tallis said.

They went up a flight of wide marble stairs. Adam could feel himself climbing, but he could not see: he was blind with rage, and even the brilliant lighting of the room into which he was led could not clear his vision. The kaleidoscopic events of the past hours crackled around him. He stood obediently by Canon Tallis while the echoing shots in the São Juan Chrysostom Monastery sounded in his ears.

He knew that he was being introduced to the Ambassador, and that he was being questioned kindly. He answered, but he did not hear what he said. In the bright room the Ambassador had to repeat a question.

Adam replied, the question slowly filtering through. "Oh. He was with the Singer Sewing Machine Company. I don't think he was one of Cutter's men."

"No," the Ambassador said. "One of ours."

"Poly—" Adam said to the Ambassador, but heard no answer to the name that was now a question. "Charles cried," he said, but when the ambassador, with gentle patience, asked, "What was that, Adam?" the boy only shook his head as though to try to clear it. Then he was able to answer the questions he had already answered once for Canon Tallis and Father Henriques.

Through the open windows of the Ambassador's bright room the singing of summer insects came clearly, and it was as though their buzzing was in Adam's head. The Ambassador was looking through the decoded papers. Later Adam would remember that there had been a transatlantic call to Washington. There were other calls.

Later it would all sort itself out in Adam's memory, questions and answers finally settling like sediment in a test tube. Next to Canon Tallis' steel control the Ambassador seemed excitable, harried, but Adam realized later that although he was undoubtedly the second he was not the first.

"But why did Arcangelo let Cutter and Kali *go*?" Adam exploded once. "Why did he let them leave the São Juan Chrysostom?"

"The police and Interpol were both there. If you remember, they were already at the Belém Tower."

"But how—"

The canon silenced Adam with a stern glance. "When your young taxi driver friend left you and Joshua at the São Juan he went, as Arcangelo had directed him, to Belém."

"But what about Cutter and Kali *now*? Where are they?"

"Free," Canon Tallis said, "in a manner of speaking."

"But—"

The Ambassador sighed. "You are not at home, Adam. Trying someone like Typhon Cutter in a Portuguese court is difficult if not impossible—"

"You mean he can buy his way out?"

Now the Ambassador's voice was hard. "You think *our* courts are entirely free from corruption? Of course Cutter would be able to buy and subvert at least part of the testimony against him. But this is nearsighted oversimplification. Even in America it's difficult to arrest someone on suspicion of intent to commit murder. You have to have real and absolute evidence."

"But Molèc—"

"—is being tried for murder. And will be found guilty. The beast caught in his master's trap. One can't help being sorry for him."

"I can."

"That's evading the issue. He is, in a way, our scapegoat, too. Remember that the Portuguese are not interested in the moral and ethical qualities of expatriates, especially people whose extremely lucrative businesses bring employment and money where it is rather desperately needed. This is worth thinking about."

But Adam was not capable of thought.

The Ambassador continued—or was it before? when? words floated to Adam's mind with no consecutivity: "Has it occurred to you, Adam, that we don't want to air Dr. O'Keefe's experiments in court? The need for silence has not been removed. Has it occurred to you that both the Portuguese and the United States governments would wish to avoid the appearance of an international incident which Cutter would not hesitate to exploit? Something like this, allowed to snowball, could start a holocaust. Is this what Joshua would have wanted?"

"But—"

The Ambassador banged down onto the desk a coffee cup Adam hadn't even realized he was holding so that the dark liquid slopped into the saucer. "We are not going to try to do more than we know we can do. If this seems to you inadequate expediency, try to remember that one battle won today permits us to embark on the next, and then a next, and all the long ones that are to follow." He rose. Was it then, or later? In any case the blinded time in the bright office was finally over and Adam followed the dark, erect form of the canon down the stairs. They left the light and music of the Embassy and climbed into the police car.

"I'll take you back to Gaea," Canon Tallis said.

Adam nodded.

"We'll take Joshua's plane. I'm not the pilot he was, but I'll get us there."

"And Cutter?" Adam repeated, thickly.

"How much were you able to listen to?" There was no censure in the question. "He's been given a week to leave Portugal. He'll lose his property here, and all the money he has tied up in it. His Portuguese operation is over."

Adam clenched his fists. "That's not—" he started savagely.

"No revenge is, Adam."

At the little airport Arcangelo was waiting. He held out the heavy jackets, the goggles, helped strap them in. Then he looked in silent questioning at Canon Tallis, who said, "Father Henriques is bringing Joshua tomorrow. Come with him." He leaned out of the pilot's seat and reached for Arcangelo's hand. "Thank you, Arcangelo. Thank God for you."

Arcangelo shrugged, smiled briefly, went to the propeller. The plane shuddered into life, moved slowly along the runway, jerked, and left the ground.

Once again time was outside Adam, or perhaps it was Adam who was outside time. He sat in the cockpit of the same small plane where Joshua, in the pilot's seat, had sung the "Ode to Joy" as they bucked wildly through the boisterous clouds. Now Canon Tallis sat darkly at the controls, closed in, stern. Above them and around them the stars were thick. Below was a sea of white clouds.

—He's flying this crate much too high, Adam thought fleetingly.

It didn't matter. They would or they would not get to the island, and whichever one it was didn't matter, either.

The plane jerked and dropped. Canon Tallis grimly pulled on the stick and the plane steadied and nosed upward again.

"Why didn't you kill Molèc?" Adam shouted suddenly. He strained for the answer.

"Would that have brought Joshua back?"

With the taste of ashes in his mouth Adam realized that his grief was nothing beside the canon's. He slouched down in his seat as though to avoid the piercing light of the stars. Behind them the moon, just beyond fullness, sailed lopsided and serene. Through a rift in the clouds it made a path upon the water below.

And all Adam wanted to do was to swear, to split the pure and silver air with every blasphemy he had ever heard on the streets. He shuddered, controlled himself, shuddered again. He bellowed, the words coming out like oaths, "She has my passport!"

"Kali?"

"Yes."

"All right. We'll get it."

"I don't want it," Adam cried. "I don't want anything."

To this the canon did not reply. He seemed to be concentrating only on the plane, the stars above, the clouds below.

They moved through space; they must also have moved through time. The clouds were gone and below them lay the vast, slowly breathing surface of the sea. Ahead was the dark shadow of the island. The plane nosed downward, and suddenly along the beach flares were lit, one after another, outlining a runway for the landing.

Dr. O'Keefe was there, with José, María's husband. Four horses were hitched to the barnacled pile.

Canon Tallis climbed stiffly from the plane. Adam unstrapped himself and followed. Beyond the barest greeting there was no talking. Dr. O'Keefe and Canon Tallis rode ahead, Adam and José behind. José spoke no English, but once he looked over at Adam and said softly, "Jhoshuajh . . ." and Adam could see that tears were trickling quietly down his cheeks. Looking at José's tears Adam fought down a reaction to shout, "*Shut up!*" He bowed his head and let the horse carry him along the water's edge, the drumming of the hoofbeats muffled in the sand.

The horses moved with unhurried pace, taking them inexorably through time, through space.

In the bungalows lights were on in the living quarters.

—Make Poly be in bed, Adam thought savagely. —I cannot see her. I cannot see Charles.

They dismounted. The horses followed José, and Adam followed Dr. O'Keefe and Canon Tallis. Only Mrs. O'Keefe was in the living room and she drew Adam to her in a quick, maternal embrace. Adam felt an enormous sob rising within him and pulled from the circle of her arms. She held him not with her arms but with her eyes. "You must not blame yourself."

"It started with the door at the Avenida Palace," Adam said. "If I hadn't opened the door—"

The canon cut brusquely across his words. "Or the fog in New York. Or if I had not asked you to take Poly back to Lisbon. This is foolish talk and must be stopped."

"But he died for me," Adam choked. "I gave Kali his phone numbers and he pushed me into one of the monk's cells and Molèc's bullet hit him."

"He died for us all," the canon said, "and if you love him you will have to stop talking and thinking like this, because what you have to do now is to live. For him, and for us all."

Mrs. O'Keefe moved to the arch that led to the living quarters. "And what you have to do at this particular moment is to go to bed. There will be work tomorrow."

—Work? What work? Adam thought numbly, but he bowed a clumsy good night and went to bed.

24

IN the morning Poly brought Adam his breakfast. She put the tray down on the bed and then stood looking at him steadily and, it seemed to him, accusingly. He had been weighed again and found wanting.

But when she spoke she said only "Adam—" and then, "Adam, I do love you and I'm terribly sorry." At the door she said in a muffled voice, "Daddy and Father expect you in the lab as soon as you're ready."

"The lab?" Adam asked stupidly.

Poly ran her fingers with impatience through her hair. "The starfish have to be tended to. Daddy's work doesn't stop because—" she broke off. A tremor moved across her face like the wind moving upon water. She stamped angrily to regain control. "Why do you think Joshua went rushing off to you when Kali called him? You don't think he thought it was fun and games and the good of his health, do you?"

Adam shook his head.

"All right, why, then?"

Adam banged down his cup. "Starfish and sparrows," he said loudly.

Poly stamped again, "*Okay*, then," and hurried out of the room.

Adam finished the cup of now lukewarm coffee, poured another, drinking slowly, unwilling to leave what seemed the comparative safety of his room. Seeing Poly had been bad enough. He wanted to put off seeing anyone else. Slowly, deliberately, he drained the last drops of coffee and milk from the little pots, picked up each crumb of his roll and ate it. Finally there was nothing to do but get dressed, and since his lab clothes were nothing but chino slacks and a tee shirt he could not prolong the process by more than a few minutes. Then he almost ran through the living room, hurried across the breezeway and into the lab.

Dr. O'Keefe and Canon Tallis were standing by one of the tanks. Dr. O'Keefe beckoned to him.

"Look at this, Adam. This is the tiny fragment of starfish arm we planted with nerve rings several weeks ago. Yesterday I'd about given up on it, but look, there's regeneration beginning. Check the other tanks, will you, please? and let me know if there's anything unusual."

Nobody was behaving as though it were an ordinary day, but nevertheless the work in the laboratory was going on, and this was still a shock to Adam. He took care of the starfish, pointed out new growth on a lizard, wrote up his notes in the files. He worked automatically, adequately, but his mind was no longer out of time as it had been the night before. He was thrust back into time, and therefore into pain.

This time the day before Joshua had been alive. In the short space of twenty-four hours more had happened than it would seem time possibly could take care of. And time hadn't taken care of it. Molèc's bullet had sped through space and time and into Joshua's heart.

"Adam," Canon Tallis said, "will you go over these figures, please? These are from Scotland and we want to see if they gibe with Dr. O'Keefe's findings."

"Sit down to it," Dr. O'Keefe suggested as Adam took the sheaf of papers. "It's important that you check them accurately. You'll find the equations perfectly straightforward, but you'll have to concentrate if you don't want to make errors. We'll see you later."

"All right, sir." Adam had not wanted to come in to the lab to see Dr. O'Keefe and Canon Tallis; now he did not want them to leave. But they went on out, without telling him where they were going. Perhaps to the village to see Virbius or to check the pens there. He did not know. He concentrated on the letters and numbers written in black ink on thin paper. He found that if he was to check them properly he could not think about anything else. At first it was an effort to pay attention to what he was doing; then, as always, the discipline of work took hold of him and he bent over the papers, his lips moving, his bruised mind occupied only with the job Canon Tallis had given him.

He was surprised when Peggy came to call him, hugging him, twining her arms around him lovingly, kissing him over and over again, but not speaking, not explaining the sudden passion of affection.

Mrs. O'Keefe stood in the lab doorway. "Have a quick swim before lunch, Adam. The children are looking for you."

Adam changed to the navy blue trunks, trying not to look at the zebra-striped ones. The children were waiting for him on the sea wall. Poly wore the red bathing suit, but the color seemed drained from it, from her hair. There was no running and jumping over the sand, no delighted leaping into the surf. Peggy held Adam's hand. When she was ankle-deep she let go, saying, "I don't think I'll go swimming today if you don't mind, Adam. I want to go back in with Johnny and Rosy."

Sandy and Dennys sat at the water's edge, letting the small waves wash over them, letting the damp yellow sand sift through their fingers, talking only to each other.

Poly said, "If you'll come with me, Adam, I want to swim out a bit."

"I'll come, too." Charles moved to Adam's other side.

The three of them walked out into the water, not jumping through the waves, simply pushing against them, letting the water break, unheeded, over them, until they were out deep enough so that first Charles could drop down and start to swim, then Poly and Adam.

He did not ask about Macrina. After a while he said, "That's far enough out, Poly," and obediently she stopped swimming and began to tread water. She did not make the breathy, whistling noises with which she usually called Macrina. She simply kept treading water and staring out to sea. Charles lay on his back and floated, his eyes closed against the glare of the sun. Adam dog-paddled between them.

He was about to say, "Okay, kids, we'd better go back in," when there was the familiar flash of silver and Macrina was with them. Poly gave a great cry and flung herself at the dolphin. Charles continued to lie on his back in the water, his eyes closed. Poly's sobs were enormous, racking the thin body in the red wool bathing suit. For a moment Macrina thrashed the water with her tail. Then she gave a shudder and swam slowly around Poly, keeping her head with the great smiling mouth constantly toward the child. The mouth was smiling but there was no doubt in Adam's mind that Macrina, now nuzzling Poly's shoulder, was trying to comfort the child, that Macrina cared. Then the dolphin left Poly and swam over to Charles, nudging at him gently until he opened his eyes, rolled over in the water, and flung his arms around the great, slippery body. When Charles let Macrina go she came to Adam, seeming to look at him questioningly. Then, with a flash of silver, she was gone.

The children swam in. "Come on, Sandy, Dennys," Poly said to the two little boys who were building a sand castle. As they walked across the burning beach to the bungalow Poly murmured, "She's not an anthropomorphic dolphin, she's an anagogical dolphin."

"Hunh?" Adam asked.

"I don't know what it means. It's something Father Tom said once and I made him say it over until I remembered it. I think it's something good."

Canon Tallis and Dr. O'Keefe were not at lunch. The younger children chattered desultorily. Adam tried to choke down a few mouthfuls because Charles was looking at him, and when Adam took a bite, Charles took a bite. Once Mrs. O'Keefe turned to Adam, saying in a steady voice, "The Cutters are at the hotel, Adam. They'll be flying to Spain from here, and then to America. My husband and Father Tallis will go over tonight to get your passport."

Adam bowed his head to show that he had heard, and took another bite.

Mrs. O'Keefe rose. "Do whatever María tells you to, children. I won't be very long. Adam, Poly, Charles, come."

It was only then that Adam noticed that Poly and Charles had changed from their bathing suits to their riding breeches. Mrs. O'Keefe said, "María has laid out your riding clothes for you, Adam. We'll wait outside."

The riding breeches Joshua had given Adam the first night on the island were on his bed, together with a clean white shirt. Lying carefully placed on the shirt was the canvas belt with the switchblade knife containing the lethal dose of MS-222. Adam looked at the knife broodingly. Had María put it there? Had Poly? He stripped off his lab clothes and strapped the knife on under the riding clothes.

Poly led the way inland. Since her storm of sobbing in the ocean and the silent comfort of the dolphin she seemed less tightly drawn. As the horses began to climb Adam realized that they were going to the great golden stones where Joshua had taken him the morning he had arrived on the island, the morning he had failed to notice the small cemetery in the clearing.

When they reached the plateau there were several boys from the village waiting to take care of the horses, and Adam saw that there were already other horses there. Around the great table was a large group of people, some seated on the stones, more standing. A few of them Adam recognized: Virbius was there, with Temis. Rabbi Pinhas was there, and Mr. Green, Father Metousis and Arcangelo. Was the inspector from the Madrid airport sitting on one of the stones by the young taxi driver? Their faces were turned away; he could not be sure.

Canon Tallis held the burial service.

Adam had heard the words before. For his grandparents. For a teacher at school. It was the American words which the canon was using for Joshua. Now the words seemed tangible, material; steeled by the English voice they held him erect on the stone bench where he sat between Poly and Charles.

". . . Remember thy servant Joshua, O Lord," Canon Tallis said, "according to the favor which thou bearest unto thy people, and grant that, increasing in knowledge and love of thee, he may go from strength to strength, in the life of perfect service. . . ."

Charles reached over and took Adam's cold hand in his smaller but equally cold one.

"Unto God's gracious mercy and protection we commit you," Canon Tallis said. "The Lord bless you and keep you. The Lord make his face to shine upon you, and be gracious unto you. The Lord lift up his countenance upon you and give you peace both now and evermore."

They moved from the golden stones across the rough grass and into the clearing where the open grave waited. Charles continued to hold Adam's hand. Once he pressed his face against Adam's shirt. Then he turned and looked back at Canon Tallis. On Adam's other side Poly stood, still as death.

Adam closed his eyes.

It was over.

The group dispersed quietly. It was only as Adam went with Charles to the horses where Dr. and Mrs. O'Keefe stood waiting with Canon Tallis that he realized that Poly had gone from his side, that she was nowhere to be seen.

"Stay with Charles," the doctor said. "We'll look for her."

They waited, and Charles said only, "Don't worry, Adam, Poly's all right."

When Dr. O'Keefe and Canon Tallis returned alone, Charles said, without anxiety, "I think she's gone to the village with Temis. She has to be away from us for a little while."

Mrs. O'Keefe looked at her husband. "Will you ride over and see?"

The doctor nodded. "Tom, come with me. She may need you."

Now there were just the three of them on the plateau, Adam, Mrs. O'Keefe and Charles, and to one side two little village boys staying faithfully with the horses. Adam asked Mrs. O'Keefe, "Would you and Charles be all right if I ride over to the hotel? I'd like to get my passport back myself."

She looked at him. "If this is what you think you want to do, Adam. Charles and I will be fine in any case. But please be home in time for dinner."

Adam agreed absently. He was not thinking of dinner. As he rode toward the hotel darkness closed in on him again. He did not see the sun, or even feel its rays, although he frequently raised his arm to wipe off the sweat that streamed down his face. He rode through darkness and through time. The sun was slipping down the sky toward the west when the path opened out between the hotel landing strip and the tennis courts and swimming pool.

He did not know what he was going to do or say when he saw

Typhon Cutter and Kali. He was not thinking primarily about his passport. This would be easy enough for Dr. O'Keefe and Canon Tallis to get. He only knew that the anger that burned in him would not abate until he had seen Kali, Kali who had deliberately led him into the killing at the São Juan Chrysostom Monastery. Her high, shrill laugh echoed in his ears.

He hitched the tired white horse to a tree at the end of the path, walked past the landing strip, along the beach, up the path between tennis courts and swimming pool, glancing at the courts where two paunchy men were playing. The pool was emptying; only a handful of young people remained splashing in the water, or sitting on the sides of the pool, dangling their legs and sipping Cokes. He almost walked by without seeing a girl in a black bathing suit sitting alone on the diving board. Her head was down on her knees, and her fair hair fell in a graceful sweep across her face.

He went up to her. "Kali."

She raised her head. When she saw him her eyes widened, but she did not move. "What do you want?"

"My passport."

She rose to her feet in a quick, lithe gesture. "Catch me and I'll give it to you," she cried, and gave her high-pitched laugh which rose shrilly almost into hysteria. She dived cleanly into the water, flashed to the end of the pool, climbed up the ladder, ran along the path, down the ramp, and across the beach, Adam following, losing ground, hampered by his riding breeches, his boots.

Kali ran splashing into the water, looking back over her shoulder, laughing. She dove through a wave and started to swim.

Adam pulled off his boots, his trousers, ripped off his shirt and, in underclothes and Poly's canvas belt, he ran into the sea, flinging himself against the waves, thrusting through the breakers, until he could throw himself down and swim. He looked up, panting, to see Kali's arms flashing through the water ahead of him. Each time he looked she was less far ahead.

Then he heard her scream.

His first thought was that it was Macrina.

But the second scream that rang across the water was one of mortal terror.

He saw the shark, the sleek malevolent body, its murky darkness unable to leap to a flash of silver, its only light the sickly white of its belly.

The shark would do for him more than he had dared hope to do.

"Adam!" The scream throbbed against his ears.

He snatched the knife from the sheath, gave a mighty kick that shot him through the water toward the screaming girl, and plunged the knife into the shark.

There was blood in the water, Kali's blood, but the shark was still. Adam took Kali in a one-arm hold and started to swim in to shore. She was limp in his grasp although an occasional scream bubbled from her lips. When he could stand he picked her up. Her arm was ripped and bleeding copiously. He put her down at the water's edge where loose sand would not get into the wounds, and picked up his shirt from the beach, ripping the white material so that he could wrap it around her arm to stanch the blood.

He carried her to the hotel. She was sobbing and beginning to writhe in his arms. He felt neither hate nor love toward her, only an infinite weariness, as though she were a tremendous burden he despaired of ever being able to put down. He tried not to think of the horribly ripped arm.

He endured grimly the clamor of excitement and curiosity that greeted their entrance, pushing blindly through the avid guests toward the elevator, calling, "The doctor, quickly."

The hotel manager rushed after him, wringing pudgy hands. "But what is it? What has happened?"

"A shark," Adam said, grittily. "Get her father. Get a doctor."

In a luxurious room he put her down on the bed. She was white from shock. Her head moved feebly on the pillow. "Adam. Adam. Help."

Typhon Cutter and the doctor arrived together. "What have you done to her?" Typhon Cutter asked, face contorted with accusation.

Adam did not answer.

"He said it was a shark," the manager babbled, "but it couldn't have been a shark, it's not possible that it was a shark."

The doctor undid the bandages Adam had made, looked at Kali's arm. "A shark," he stated categorically. "Get me blankets. Get me hot water bottles." He opened his bag and began to work over the girl.

Typhon Cutter watched sickly. The room was silent except for the movements of the doctor and the sound of the surf outside. The flesh of Typhon Cutter's face had gone greenish and seemed to sag. "In the ocean?"

"Yes," Adam said.

"Why? She knows I have forbidden—"

"I asked her for my passport and she said 'Catch me.' You know how quick she is."

"Yes." The older man's eyes were focused on the girl on the bed, on the doctor's actions. "Then?"

"I hadn't quite caught up with her when I heard her scream."

"The shark had attacked her?"

"Yes."

"How did she get away?"

Adam took off the canvas belt and sheath. "I had a switch-blade with MS-222."

"What?"

"It knocks a shark out faster than anything else."

"You used it to save her?" There was scorn and disbelief in the voice.

"Yes."

"Where is the knife?"

"In the shark." Adam, feeling sick, through with questioning, through with the Cutters forever, started for the door. Typhon Cutter's steel talons shot out and clamped over his arm.

"Wait." A lock of fair hair fell, unheeded, over the older man's forehead. Still holding Adam he asked the doctor, "The arm?"

The doctor shook his head. "Bad. If it were not for the young man and his quick action you would have no daughter at all."

"But what about the arm?"

The doctor shrugged. "There is much damage. A shark's teeth are deadly."

"You're sure it *was* a shark?"

The doctor shrugged again. "I have seen shark bites before. There is no question."

Typhon Cutter, pulling Adam with him, leaned over the bed. "What are you going to do?"

"There is little I *can* do except stop the bleeding and shock. You will have to get her to Lisbon. But even there—" Again the expressive lifting of the shoulders.

Typhon Cutter jerked his head at the manager. "Come." Not relaxing his painful clamp on Adam's arm he went into the corridor. A police officer was waiting outside the door with the hotel detective. Cutter ignored them, although they bowed respectfully, and the detective started to murmur expressions of alarm and concern.

"Get O'Keefe," Typhon Cutter said to Adam. As Adam did not reply the talons increased their pressure. "*I said get O'Keefe.*"

"Why?" Adam asked, beyond caring what he said or did.

"Fool, do you think I don't know that he has worked on human beings in the native village? Go to the telephone. Get him to come. He will do it for you. I will send the helicopter." There was anger in the voice, command in the words, naked pleading in the eyes. Another strand of pale gold hair fell forward, unheeded.

"I'll call," Adam said, "but he may not be there."

"The private line in your office," Cutter snapped at the manager.

They went down the hall, into the elevator, through the lobby: the oily little manager; the uniformed police officer; the detective (still ignored); Cutter, his ponderous body quivering; Adam.

In the lobby the guests were milling around.

"But her arm was ripped off, I saw it—"

"She will bleed to death before anything can be done—"

"Nonsense, it was only a scratch, they said so—"

"It wasn't her arm, it was her leg—"

The police officer shouted for quiet. "Please do not concern yourself. The girl is all right. She disobeyed rules in swimming in the ocean when the lifeguard was not there; she would never have been allowed to go out so far. If you will be sensible there is no danger whatsoever."

The manager echoed him, wringing his hands anxiously. "Everything is all right. There is no cause for alarm. She went out too far." He scurried around to Adam, grasping his hand in an effusion of gratitude. "My *dear* young man—"

"Fool. Come," Cutter said.

The manager put the call through. Charles answered the phone, called his mother. "It's Adam."

"Yes?" Mrs. O'Keefe said. "What is it, Adam?"

"Is the doctor there?"

"No. He's in the village with Poly and Father Tallis. What is it? What happened? Can I help?"

"Kali has been hurt by a shark. Do you know when they'll be back?"

"Some time this evening. I don't know just when. Adam, are you all right?"

The warmth and concern in her voice shook Adam so that he had to lean on the desk for support. But he said, "I'm fine, and I'll be home as soon as I can."

Cutter, who was breathing heavily behind him, said as he hung up, "In the village?"

"Yes."

Cutter snapped at the manager. "Get the helicopter ready." To Adam. "Go to the village and get him."

The police officer held up his hand, speaking to Adam. "There will have to be a statement from you."

The detective finally got in a word. "To absolve the hotel of any blame."

Typhon Cutter's thin voice rose in an angry squeak. "I *am* the hotel. There is no question of blame. She broke hotel rules. *My* rules." Controlling the soaring pitch of his voice he asked Adam, "Why did you have this stuff—whatever it is—on you?"

"You know there have been sharks here. I had the knife with me when Kali and I saw the shark before."

The phone on the manager's desk rang and Cutter pushed the little man aside to reach for it. "Yes? . . . Yes." He put the receiver down. "The helicopter is ready. Bring O'Keefe to her."

Adam said humbly, "I'll try."

"You will do more than try. I will go with you."

"No." Adam's voice was firm. "I'll go alone. Stay with Kali. She may need you."

For a moment Typhon Cutter chewed his lip. "Very well. The pilot is one of my men. If O'Keefe doesn't come he will have my instructions to—"

Adam cut through the threat by walking deliberately past Typhon Cutter and out of the manager's office. Again the procession moved through the lounge, Adam silent, closed in, indifferent to the curiosity, the manager and the detective responding excitedly to the heightening tension of the guests, assuring them that all was well, everything was perfect, the young man was a hero.

The helicopter waited on the roof.

The manager pumped Adam's hand. "Thank you. *Muito obrigado.* Thank you."

As the boy started to climb into the helicopter he paused. "My passport."

Typhon Cutter said, "When you send O'Keefe back."

"No more of that. Now." Adam stood his ground, staring at Cutter's ravaged face. "Do you want Dr. O'Keefe?" The manager, the detective, the police officer murmured. Typhon Cutter reached into his breast pocket and handed over the passport.

Adam climbed into the helicopter. He did not look back. Not in time, not in space. His mind was exhausted to the point where it was bliss to allow it to drift with the noise of the rotors, to relax in the silence of the pilot.

When the helicopter hovered over the village Adam looked down and saw a scurrying of dark shapes. The village emptied, men and women disappearing into the jungle, into the huts. The pilot set the machine down on the greensward in front of the central hut. As Adam climbed out he saw the pilot reaching for his gun, but he felt no fear.

Virbius emerged from his hut, raising his hand in greeting. Adam, too, raised his hand. "Is Dr. O'Keefe here?"

The old man spoke slowly, tremulously, with great effort. "You—wish—speak?"

"Please."

The old man beckoned and Dr. O'Keefe and Canon Tallis came out of the hut, Dr. O'Keefe bending his tall frame to pass through the doorway. As Adam started to speak Dr. O'Keefe called, "Poly—" and she came out with Temis.

Adam told what had happened, while Poly translated for Virbius and Temis. When the boy had finished Dr. O'Keefe questioned him, then stood, as though still listening. Then he looked at Canon Tallis, and their eyes met for a long moment. Dr. O'Keefe nodded.

"Daddy!" Poly cried. "You're not going!"

"Yes. I will have to see the arm for myself. Then, if it is as bad as it seems, I will have to tell Typhon Cutter of the dangers, and then, if he still wishes me to, I will try."

Poly ran to her father and caught his hands in hers. "But you wouldn't try if you didn't think you could do it, would you?"

"No."

"But why are you going, daddy? Why?"

Canon Tallis drew Poly away from her father. "Ask Adam why, Poly."

But she was silent. They stood, looking, while Dr. O'Keefe climbed into the helicopter, still stood looking, half-deafened by the noise of the rotors, until it had droned away, until the night sounds of the village could be heard again. Without a word Virbius sat on the greensward, crosslegged, looking out to the harbor. Canon Tallis sat by him, gesturing to Adam. The two girls stood together, facing the men. Temis raised her hand, looked at the spread-out fingers, dropped it to her side.

Virbius spoke.

Poly said, "He wants to know if you think daddy did right to go."

"Adam?" Canon Tallis asked.

Adam was silent, looking at the village, at the men returning from the jungle, at the women and children emerging from their huts. Evening was coming quickly. The sun had already dropped with the sudden fierceness of the jungle, and the sky over the island was suffused with great streaks of color: rose, raspberry, deepening to mauve, to indigo. Above a date palm a star began to pulse, at first faintly, then growing in brilliance. In the darkness of the surrounding brush fireflies flickered.

"Adam?" Canon Tallis asked again.

"I think he had to go," Adam said unwillingly. He began to shiver and realized that, like it or not, he would again be able to feel heat and cold, sunlight and moonlight.

At a word from the old man, Temis slipped into the hut.

"But why!" Poly demanded passionately. "*Why* did he have to go?"

Adam was silent while Temis came out and draped a softly woven robe about him. Then he said, heavily, "Because of Joshua."

"But she killed Joshua!" Poly cried. "Why should daddy help her now? I don't want to help her! Adam should have let the shark kill her!"

Adam was silent.

"Father!" Poly cried.

Canon Tallis said quietly, "Suppose it had been Adam the shark attacked?"

Tears began to roll down Poly's cheeks. "But Adam's good, and she's—"

Adam stood up, holding Temis' robe about his shoulders. He could not say what he had to say sitting down. "I killed Joshua, too."

"But—"

"Be quiet, Poly," Canon Tallis commanded.

Adam let the robe drop as he clenched and unclenched his fists. "If I hadn't used the knife, or if we didn't try to help Kali now, it would be justice, wouldn't it?"

Verbius nodded, saying the English word, "Justice," nodding again.

"But Joshua—" Adam said. "Joshua—" he broke off.

"It's Joshua I'm thinking about!" Poly cried.

"It was what he always said," Adam choked out, "about the

sparrow. Even Kali would be a sparrow to Joshua. If you're going to care about the fall of the sparrow you can't pick and choose who's going to be the sparrow. It's everybody, and you're stuck with it." He sat down and put his arms about his knees and his head on his arms.

Virbius spoke. When he had finished there was silence until he spoke again, rather crossly, to Poly. She translated.

"He says it is not enough if you pray neither for nor against. He says he will go to his gods and pray. For."

Virbius stood up, tremulously, and went into his hut.

Adam did not know how long he sat there with his head down. When he looked up Temis had gone and Poly had turned away.

Canon Tallis looked at Adam, smiled briefly, but did not speak. Night was coming, but to Adam, as he returned the canon's smile, everywhere there seemed to be light.

At last Poly reached over and took his hand in hers. "I see that daddy had to go," she said. And then, "I love you, Adam."

He held her hand tightly. "I love you, too, Poly."

DRAGONS IN THE WATERS

For Robert Giroux

CONTENTS

1. THE FORK LIFT

THE M.S. *Orion* was tied up at Savannah, Georgia.

Simon Renier, hands in the pockets of his old-fashioned grey shorts, looked at the small white ship with mounting excitement. He would be spending the next week on the *Orion* en route to Venezuela and already, standing on the pier in Savannah, he was farther away from home than he had ever been in his thirteen years.

It was chill this February day, with a thin rain and a biting wind. In a more sheltered part of the dock stood his cousin, Forsyth Phair, with whom he would be traveling, and his great-aunt Leonis Phair, with whom he lived, and who had come with them on the train from Charleston to see them off. Simon looked at the two of them standing under the shelter of the shed and their umbrellas and thought that if he were traveling with Aunt Leonis instead of Cousin Forsyth he would be perfectly happy.

Aunt Leonis was comfort and all-rightness in a precarious world; Cousin Forsyth he had known for barely a month, and while the distinguished-looking middle-aged man was courteous and pleasant he was not outgoing and to Simon he was still a stranger. He looked damp and uncomfortable with the rain dripping off his large black umbrella, and the collar to his dark raincoat turned up. Even the corners of his waxed moustache seemed to droop. The old woman, on the other hand, stood straight as an arrow, unperturbed by the downpour.

"Can't you come, too?" Simon had begged her.

"I'm too tired, child," the old woman had said. "At ninety I've earned the right to my rocking chair and my books. Besides, I have to stay home and take care of Boz." The old dog in pointer years was almost as old as Aunt Leonis. His proud skeleton showed under the still-glossy liver-spotted body, and Simon felt a tightening of his stomach muscles as he realized that the old hound might not be there when he returned.

He turned his face into the rain and moved farther away from Aunt Leonis and Cousin Forsyth, past the gangplank of the *Orion*, and on down the dock. All around him was activity, the tall yellow arms of the *Orion* swinging sacks of seed and grain and rice up onto the ship, to be stored in the hold. Simon watched in fascination as a large station wagon was carefully hoisted up from the dock, swung loose for a moment high in the air, then was lowered gently onto the foredeck.

On the aft deck stood the passengers who had already embarked at Brooklyn or Baltimore, eagerly watching the business of loading the freighter. A few of them waved at him, and he waved shyly back. Then he turned to watch the orange fork lifts buzzing rapidly up and down the dock, the two long tines of their forks fitting neatly into the small wooden platforms onto which bags and bales were piled. Great yellow arms swung out from the *Orion*, dropping heavy ropes which were looped around sacks and platform; the crane raised its burden to the ship's foredeck, and the highly mobile fork lift darted away, moving far more easily than an ordinary tractor, turning on a dime to reach for another load. The sailor managing the long-angled pincers from his glassed-in cab high up on the *Orion* swung the bags and sacks with easy accuracy. Everywhere was bustle, and men's shouting, and the smell of wet wood and the salt wind from the sea. Simon would be almost sorry when they boarded, so fascinating was the loading procedure.

He jumped as he heard a horn, and a Land Rover drove onto the dock, full of children who kept piling out, like clowns out of a car at the circus. Simon found it difficult to keep count, but it appeared to be a mother and father and seven children. After considerable shouting and laughing, the two older children, a girl and a boy, sorted themselves out, managed to get two battered suitcases from the Land Rover, and came to stand not far from Simon. The mother urged the younger children back into the car, out of the rain, and the father, rain dripping off his cap, stood leaning in the window, talking to the mother.

The girl, banging her old suitcase against her knees, dropped it by the gangplank and came on down the dock toward Simon. Her brother followed. She was, Simon guessed, maybe a year older than he was, maybe fourteen, and probably would resent being called a child. The boy looked younger, although he was as tall as Simon, who guessed him to be no more than twelve. Both brother and sister wore yellow slickers and sou'westers, and were considerably drier than Simon, whose fair hair was slicked wetly to his head.

"Hello," the girl said. "Are you going on the *Orion?*" Her accent was not quite foreign, but it was certainly more precise than the soft Southern speech Simon was accustomed to hearing.

"Yes'm. Are you?"

"Yes. At least, Charles and Daddy and I are." She smiled, a swift spreading of sunlight over her face. "How nice to have someone our age. Daddy warned us that freighter passengers tend to be ancient. I'm Poly O'Keefe, pronounced Polly but spelled with one *l*. I'm fourteen. And this is my brother, Charles. He's twelve."

So he had been right. "I'm Simon Renier, and I'm thirteen."

Again Poly smiled, a shaft of light lifting the drab day. "You're not traveling alone, are you?"

He indicated the man and the old woman. Suddenly Cousin Forsyth stepped forward as one of the fork lifts picked up a large flat wooden crate. He watched anxiously as ropes from the *Orion* were looped around it. "Be very careful," he fussed. "It's extremely valuable. It contains an irreplaceable portrait."

The dock hands nodded indifferently as they went about their business. The fork lift backed away from the crate, which was then lifted up in the air and hung swinging between the ship and the dock.

"What's in there?" Poly asked Simon. "Your father looks as though he's about to have a heart attack." The horn of the Land Rover tooted before Simon could answer or correct her. "We have to say goodbye!" Poly cried. "We'll be back in a minute, Simon!" and she and Charles ran across the dock, dodging loading trucks and fork lifts.

Simon watched rather wistfully while there was a tangle of hugging and kissing goodbye. Then he looked up at the *Orion* just in time to see the great crate with the portrait being safely lowered onto the deck, and Cousin Forsyth mopping his forehead with his handkerchief as though it were hot.

Aunt Leonis was still standing in the shelter of the shed and her small, not very waterproof umbrella. Simon ran over to her, skidding on the wet boards. "Where's Cousin Forsyth going?"

"He's off to make sure the portrait isn't going to get banged or crushed. I certainly can't complain about his care of it. He's overzealous, if anything." She put her gnarled old hand on his head. "You're soaking, Simon!"

"Yes, ma'am."

"You'll be boarding in a minute or two. You're old enough to take care of yourself without me, aren't you?"

"Yes, ma'am."

"And don't let Forsyth overprotect you. He can keep that for the portrait. I want you to have some fun."

He leaned lightly against her. "I'll miss you."

"It's time you got out of the nest, child. A nonagenarian is hardly a fit companion for a boy. I'm glad there are other young persons on board."

"Yes, ma'am!"

"I'm going now, Simon. I have a train to catch." She was still taller than he was. She bent down, and he kissed her softly on each cheek. For a brief moment she held him to her. Then she stood upright and gave him a little shove. "Run along, now."

Tears filled his eyes. He did not want her to see. Moving in a blur of tears and rain, he crossed the dock. He paused at the gangplank but the tears would not be held back. Poly and Charles had said their goodbyes and were hurrying along the dock toward him.

No one must see him cry.

He moved on past the gangplank, past the stern of the *Orion*, on to the very end of the dark, slippery dock. He did not see the fork lift, out of control, hurtling toward him.

Someone on deck screamed.

He felt a shove, and then both he and Poly O'Keefe were in the water.

The fork lift ground to a screeching halt, barely avoiding crashing off the dock after them.

The water was icy cold. Their clothes dragged them down.

From the deck of the *Orion* round orange life preservers were thrown into the water for them, but both Simon and Poly had managed to grab on to the pilings of the dock and were clinging to them safely. Dock hands pulled them up out of the chilling water, and they stood dank and dripping in the February rain.

The driver of the fork lift kept explaining that his accelerator had stuck.

The shivering boy and girl were surrounded by the entire O'Keefe family, by sailors and dock hands. Aunt Leonis used her umbrella to get through the mob to Simon. Through chattering teeth he said, "I'm all right, Aunt Leonis. Please don't miss your train."

The old woman turned her sharp eyes on Poly. "I saw. You saved him. If you hadn't thrown yourself at him and got him out of the path of the fork lift he'd be—" She looked at the vicious prongs of the fork lift and did not finish her sentence. She turned to the father of the family. "You will watch out for him, sir? I am gravely concerned."

Dr. O'Keefe replied, "Of course I'll keep an eye out for him. But I don't think you need worry. It was only an unfortunate accident."

Aunt Leonis looked at him sharply, but all she said was, "Where is Forsyth? If he's going to worry about the portrait to the exclusion of the boy—"

The captain of the ship came running down the gangplank, followed by a youngish man with officer's bars on his dark sleeve. "I am Captain van Leyden, and this is my first officer, Mynheer Boon."

Mynheer Boon smiled and draped heavy blankets over Poly and Simon.

Van Leyden said, "Boon will get the children aboard and help them. Order hot tea, too, please, Boon."

Simon held out his hand. "Goodbye, Aunt Leonis." His voice faltered slightly. He hoped that this would be attributed to the cold.

Aunt Leonis shook his hand formally. Then she said to Dr.

O'Keefe, "I do not think that I am being just a foolish old woman." To Poly she said, "I am much obliged to you, Miss—"

"Poly O'Keefe. It wasn't anything."

Aunt Leonis said, "It was."

To Simon's surprise Charles O'Keefe looked directly at the old woman and replied, "Yes. It was."

Miss Leonis's old eyes were clouded with more than age as she watched Simon's dripping, blanket-covered form trudge damply up the gangplank. Poly O'Keefe and her brother and father were ahead of Simon; Forsyth Phair, who had emerged from the ship just in time for farewells, was behind, fussing over Simon in much the same nervous way he had fussed over the portrait. It was apparent that the boy was being taken care of. The nice Dutch officer would see to it that he got hot tea and changed to dry clothes. There was nothing more she could do. She walked slowly along the dark, wet boards of the dock.

Mrs. O'Keefe was trying to herd her excited younger children into the Land Rover. She saw the old woman struggling along, wind tugging at her ancient umbrella. "Is there anywhere I can drop you? A Land Rover's not the most comfortable vehicle in the world, but at least you'll be out of the rain."

Miss Leonis looked at the younger woman, and at the children, who had stopped their chattering and were staring. "Thank you. I should be much obliged if you'd take me to the railroad station. I think I may not have missed my train."

"Sandy, Dennys, help Mrs.—" She paused.

"Phair. Miss Leonis Phair. I can manage quite nicely myself, thank you just the same, young gentlemen." With the help of her now-furled umbrella she pulled herself briskly onto the high seat of the Land Rover.

Mrs. O'Keefe asked, "Can we drive you any farther than the station?"

"Thank you, no. I am taking the train to Charleston."

Mrs. O'Keefe turned around in the car and looked back at her children, then smiled at the old woman. "What with all the excitement at the dock I think it very likely that you've missed your train, and I've been promising the children a visit to Charleston for ages. We'd be delighted to drive you there. Now that my husband has gone off for a month with Poly and Charles, surely everybody else deserves a special treat."

There was a loud noise of agreement.

Miss Leonis looked at Mrs. O'Keefe, who was now smiling serenely. "I am much obliged to you. You are very kind."

"Not at all. It's you who've given us the opportunity for sightseeing, and the weather report promised sun late this afternoon, and the rain's beginning to slacken off already. Do you live right in Charleston?"

"Out in the backwoods." The old woman's next words seemed to be audible thinking, rather than conversation. "I hope I have made the right decision. It is not normal for a young boy to live all alone with an old woman." Then she pulled herself together and spoke briskly, "I would be delighted to give you a conducted tour of Charleston, and then perhaps you will drop me off on your way home—you do live north of Savannah?"

"Yes. Benne Seed Island."

Leonis Phair turned around and stared solemnly at the children. "I hope you young ones have stamina. You may find me difficult to keep up with." There was stifled giggling as she asked Mrs. O'Keefe, "Your husband will keep an eye on Simon?"

Mrs. O'Keefe turned the car away from the dock area and onto the highway. "Of course he will. He's used to having a mob of children to keep track of."

"It will make me easier in my mind. Simon has never been away from home before. And that was not a propitious beginning."

Mrs. O'Keefe said lightly, "If he and Poly needed an intro-duction, that was sure-fire. They're probably the best of friends by now."

Miss Leonis was silent for the next mile. Her gnarled hands held the umbrella handle, and she tapped the steel tip thoughtfully on the floorboards. Then she spoke quietly. "Your daughter saved Simon's life. I shall not forget that."

On the M.S. *Orion*, Simon and Poly in their separate cabins were changing out of their soaking clothes. Simon, alone in the double cabin he was to share with Cousin Forsyth, wondered if Dr. O'Keefe or Charles was helping Poly.

Forsyth Phair had said, "Take a good hot shower, Simon, and wash your hair. That water by the dock in which you chose to swim can hardly have been very clean."

Simon did not reply that the swim had not been of his own choosing.

"And dress in warm clothes. I don't want you coming down with a cold right at the beginning of the trip. I am very susceptible to colds."

"Yes, sir."

"I must go tend to the portrait now. One of the boards on the crate came loose as it was being loaded. Captain van Leyden says that since cabin 5 on the port side of the ship is unoccupied until Caracas, the portrait can be stored there. I certainly wouldn't trust it with the rest of the cargo." And off he fussed.

Simon stood for a long time under the hot shower, not so much to wash off the oily waters as for comfort. The noise of loading and unloading continued outside his portholes; the ship was still safely berthed in Savannah but he felt very far from home. What had seemed like a great adventure only a few hours ago now gave him a cold feeling in the pit of his stomach and an ache around his heart.

He wanted Aunt Leonis.

Not that Cousin Forsyth wasn't kind. But Simon found it odd that it was the middle-aged bachelor who had suggested that the boy accompany him on this voyage.

He got out of the shower, dried, and put on his seersucker bathrobe. Cousin Forsyth had said, 'There's no point in packing winter things. After the first or second day at sea it's going to be summer.'

Simon shivered. His soaking blazer was the warmest thing he had. "Come in," he called to a tap on the door.

It opened to a young man, barely out of boyhood, with dark hair and eyes, who was wearing a white coat. He bore a small tray with a pot of steaming tea, and some buttered rusks with Gouda cheese.

Simon smiled his thanks and asked the young man's name.

"Geraldo Enrique Armando José Ramírez. I am the assistant steward, at your service. You are Simón Renier?"

"Simon Bolivar Quentin Phair Renier. We have the same number of names. I pronounce Simon the English way instead of the Spanish way."

Geraldo poured tea for Simon, put in lemon and sugar. "But you are named after the great General?"

"Yes," Simon said, and shivered.

Geraldo looked at the boy in his inadequate cotton robe. "You have nothing warmer?"

Simon pawed through his suitcase and pulled out a light-weight sleeveless pullover.

Geraldo shook his head. "That is not enough, and it will be tomorrow before I have your wet things cleaned and pressed." He sounded like an old man. "Drink your tea, please, while it is hot. I will return."

The steaming, lemony tea warmed Simon inside and out. He sipped and unpacked and ate the rusks and cheese and unpacked some more, taking care to leave most of the drawer and wardrobe space for Cousin Forsyth. He knew that Cousin Forsyth would have preferred a single cabin, but when they had booked passage the two single cabins on the *Orion* were already taken, one by Poly.

There was, however, plenty of room for two. The bunks were divided by a sizable chest of drawers, and Simon took the bottom drawer. Cousin Forsyth had already put his briefcase on the bunk on the inner wall, so Simon had the bunk under the two portholes. This would have been the bunk of his choosing, and he would not have felt free to take it if Cousin Forsyth had not established himself on the other.

The boy knelt on the bunk and peered through the glass. Cabin 3 was on the dock side of the ship. Sacks of grain were still being loaded deep in the hold. Sailors and dock hands shouted back and forth. Fork lifts skittered about like bugs, beetles with long sharp mandibles. He was not feeling very happy about fork lifts and he turned away. He took his small stack of paperback books out of the bottom of his suitcase and arranged them in a rack where they would be easy to reach from his bunk. Then he put out his face cloth, toothbrush, and toothpaste.

Over the two washbasins was a fan, for which there was no present need. In the radiator the steam was clanking. By the side of each washbasin was a thermos flask in a holder; Simon uncorked his and peered in: ice water. He corked it again, sat down in one of the two small chairs, and poured himself another cup of tea. Then he heard a loud, deep honking: the ship seemed to shake from the vibration, and he realized that the *Orion* was indeed throbbing; the engines were being revved up; they were about to sail.

He knelt on his bunk again and looked out.

On the dock the longshoremen were unhooking the great ropes which held the *Orion* to the pier. Two dark-uniformed sailors pulled the gangplank aboard; two others leapt across the dark gap of water between dock and lower deck. Slowly the dock seemed to recede from the ship; the dark expanse of water dividing ship and land grew wider and wider. Sea gulls swooped about, calling in raucous excited voices. Deep within himself Simon felt an echoing response of excitement. He was at sea, on his way to Venezuela.

He began to whistle, softly, a minor, haunting melody, and then to sing,

> *I met her in Venezuela,*
> *A basket on her head . . .*

He was still looking out and singing softly when Geraldo returned with a heavy navy-blue sweater and a fisherman's cap. "Mynheer Boon is lending you the sweater till it is warmer. The cap is for you to keep. You will need it to keep the sun off your nose as well as the rain off your head." He knelt on the bunk beside Simon, not much larger than the younger boy, and they looked at the activity on the dock becoming small and almost unreal as Savannah drifted farther and farther away.

In schoolboy Spanish, Simon tried to thank Geraldo, and was interrupted by a bang on the door and Poly's voice, "Here we are, Simon!" and she burst in, wearing a long plaid bathrobe which undoubtedly belonged to her father; her short, carroty hair stuck out in spikes from being rubbed dry. Charles, in jeans and a red turtleneck, followed her.

"All right if we come in?" he asked.

"Oh, please do come in," Simon welcomed them, indicating Geraldo. "Do you know—"

"Oh, yes, Geraldo brought me hot tea, too, like a Herald Angel—that's what Geraldo sounds like. I used to spell it with an *H* instead of a *G*." Then she burst into a stream of Spanish so fluent that Simon found it difficult to follow.

Geraldo spoke slowly and carefully to Simon. "You understand that Geraldo begins with a *G*, which is pronounced like an *H* in Spanish? And the other passengers are all having tea in the salon. Mr. Phair would like you please to join them as soon as you're dressed."

At Geraldo's grave courtesy, Poly flushed, the red beginning at her neck and moving up her face to her forehead. "I'm sorry, Simon. I didn't think."

Under his breath Charles said, "Don't show off . . ."

Poly flung around as though to flash a reply to her brother, then stopped herself.

"It's okay," Simon assured her, "really, it's okay. And just as I was feeling smug about my Spanish, too. Teaches me how nonexistent it really is."

"We used to live in Portugal," Poly explained, "on Gaea, an island off the south coast. If you learn Portuguese, which is a stinker, it's easy to learn Spanish. Whereas it's most difficult for someone who speaks only Spanish to learn Portuguese, and—" She broke off. "Am I showing off again?"

Charles sat down on Cousin Forsyth's bunk. "It's second nature," he said, not unkindly. Then he bestowed a singularly sweet smile on his sister, on Simon and Geraldo, a slow blooming of pleasure quite different from Poly's flash of light. "Did you see us sail? Our cabins are starboard, so we almost missed it, what with you and Poly having been so suddenly in the soup."

Simon glanced at the porthole through which he had watched the land, rather than the ship, move slowly away. "It was exciting. I've never been away from home before. Even coming to Savannah was a journey for me."

"Where's home?" Poly asked.

"Near Charleston."

"Charleston, South Carolina?"

Simon's surprised look said as clearly as words, 'Is there any other?' Then he indicated the sweater and cap. "From Geraldo. He's lending me Mynheer Boon's sweater and he's giving me the cap."

Poly spoke to Geraldo in Spanish, but this time it was slowly and carefully so that Simon would understand. "Geraldo, would you tell them, please, that Simon and I'll dress and be right along. And it's a lovely cap."

"I will tell them, Miss Poly." Then he referred to a slip of paper he pulled out of his pocket. "On the passenger list it says Pol—Polyhymnia."

"Poly, please, Geraldo."

Charles grinned. "Polyhymnia's a muse. The muse of sacred music."

Poly pulled the belt to her father's bathrobe tight in a determined gesture. "If any of you calls me anything but Poly there'll be—there'll be murder."

"Not at the beginning of the trip," Charles said.

Geraldo picked up Simon's tea tray. "I will tell them."

"What?" Charles asked. "That there'll be murder?"

"That you will shortly be in for tea."

"Okay." Poly followed Geraldo out, but turned at the door. "I won't be more than five minutes. Hurry, Simon."

Charles asked, "Shall I stay and talk?"

"Please. Please do." Simon took clean underclothes, navy-blue shorts, and a blue cotton shirt from his drawer and went into the shower to dress.

Charles reclined on Cousin Forsyth's bunk. "If you had all the brothers and sisters Poly and I have, you wouldn't have room for modesty. But you're an Only, aren't you?"

Simon compromised by leaving the bathroom door half open. "Yes."

"How come you and your father are taking this trip?"

"Not my father." Simon pulled on his shirt and emerged.

"I didn't think he seemed terribly fatherly. At least not like our father. I get the feeling he's not used to children."

"I don't think he is." Simon sat on the edge of his bunk and pulled on navy-blue knee socks.

Charles, his hands behind his head, looked up at the ceiling of the cabin. "How do you happen to be traveling with him, then?"

Simon pulled the heavy sweater over his head. The rough wool felt comforting. He pulled Geraldo's cap over his still damp hair. His shoes were with his other wet things, so he took a pair of worn sneakers from the bottom of the wardrobe. "Cousin Forsyth offered me the trip, and Aunt Leonis thought it would be good experience for me, since I'm a country bumpkin. I guess you've done a lot of traveling."

"Oh, some, but mostly we've lived on Gaea—the island; the younger kids were born there. Last year we came back to America and moved to Benne Seed Island, but most of us still think of Portugal as home."

Poly appeared in the doorway, now dressed in a plaid skirt and a burnished-orange sweater which just managed not to conflict with her hair. "Daddy's a marine biologist, so islands are very good for his work. C'mon. Let's go brave the lions' den."

Charles rose from Cousin Forsyth's bunk and Simon smoothed the coverlet, almost as anxiously as Cousin Forsyth had supervised the loading of the crated portrait.

Poly helped him. "What would he do if he found Charles had sat on his bunk? Beat you or something?"

"No, oh no, he's very kind."

"It's okay." Charles glanced impatiently at the bunk. "You'd never know anybody'd even sat on it. Let's go. We're expected to meet everybody."

In the salon Geraldo was replacing one teapot with a fresh

one. Poly led the way in; Charles slipped past her and sat on a sofa beside his father. Simon held back at the doorway, shyly looking at the people sitting on sofas and chairs around the tea table. Cousin Forsyth did not greet him; he seemed concentrated fully on the woman pouring tea, a dark, handsome woman, very Spanish-looking, though she turned out to have the incongruous name of Dr. Wordsworth. She and her traveling companion, Dr. Eisenstein, were professors on sabbatical leave from their university. Dr. Wordsworth taught Spanish—so she must be at least half Spanish, Simon thought.

Cousin Forsyth said, "It was indeed a pleasant surprise for me to find the lovely Inés Wordsworth on the *Orion*. We knew each other many years ago when we were both young in Caracas."

Dr. Wordsworth replied with distinct chilliness, "It was not that many years ago, and our acquaintance was slight. *Very* slight."

Cousin Forsyth raised his fine eyebrows, but made no comment, and Dr. Wordsworth went on to explain to the children that Dr. Eisenstein was an anthropologist, going to the Lago de los Dragones in Venezuela, to make what Dr. Wordsworth called an in-depth study of the Quiztano Indians who lived at the far end of the lake.

Poly said with interest, "We're getting off at Puerto de los Dragones, too, and going on to the lake. Daddy's been asked to—" She caught a warning look from her father and hurried on. "I think it's lovely having a town and a lake be places of dragons. I'm very interested in dragons. Of course, one always thinks of St. George and the dragon, and he's my favorite, but did you know that Margaret of Antioch had a dragon, too?" As always when she came close to blundering, she talked too much about something else. "Fork lifts look a little like dragons, don't you think?"

After a slight pause among the company, Cousin Forsyth said dryly, "I hadn't noticed the resemblance."

"Maybe they don't spout fire," Poly said stubbornly, "but they can be as dangerous as dragons. Right, Simon?"

Simon nodded, and continued to observe the passengers and

listen to the conversation. He learned that afternoon tea was not usually served on the *Orion*; this tea party was an impromptu affair; some of the passengers, seeing Geraldo brewing tea for Simon and Poly, had suggested that tea in the salon would be a pleasant and informal way for new and old passengers to meet.

Dr. Wordsworth did not offer tea to the children but began to refill the adult passengers' cups. Simon looked at her hands, which had long, scarlet nails. They were not young hands, and the flashing rings and bright nail polish accented rather than minimized their age. Aunt Leonis did not wear nail polish, and though her nails were horny with age, Simon compared Dr. Wordsworth's hands unfavorably with the old woman's.

Dr. Eisenstein appealed more to Simon—a brown mouse of a woman, brown all over, suit, eyes, the shadows below the eyes; there was considerable brown remaining in the greying hair, which she wore braided in a thin crown on top of her head. Her smile was friendly, Simon thought, and did not exclude the children.

He turned his regard to the three other passengers, two old men and one old woman—all three probably considerably younger than Aunt Leonis, but nevertheless old. Mr. and Mrs. Smith were both plump and beaming; they were from New Hampshire and were en route to visit their granddaughter and great-grandchildren in Costa Rica, and were obviously thrilled at the prospect. Mrs. Smith was knitting a blue baby's bootee, and with her pink cheeks and curly white hair she looked like a magazine illustration of the perfect grandmother.

The last passenger bore the formidable name of Emmanuele Theotocopoulos, and Simon was relieved when they were told to call him Mr. Theo. If Dr. Eisenstein looked like a friendly field mouse, Mr. Theo was small and frail as a sparrow, but he emanated enormous vitality, and he had lively dark eyes and a mop of yellowed white hair which stood out in a thick ruff around his head; he looked, Simon decided, not in the least like a bird, but rather like an aging lion.

Cousin Forsyth's words caught his attention. ". . . a portrait of Simon Bolivar which I am taking to Caracas as a gift to the Venezuelan government."

Simon's shyness was overcome by Cousin Forsyth's proprietary air about the painting. "The portrait has been in our family always. It is the greatest portrait ever painted of the General—and I'm named after him. Simon Bolivar Quentin Phair Renier. The portrait was given to my ancestor, Quentin Phair, by Bolivar himself, and it belongs to my Aunt Leonis—" He stopped short. Cousin Forsyth had bought the portrait from Aunt Leonis, the portrait which otherwise would one day have belonged to Simon. It was no longer Aunt Leonis's. It would never be Simon's.

The grownups had started playing the "Since it's a small world, do you know?" game. Cousin Forsyth and Dr. Wordsworth had once known each other, so it was likely there might be more connections between the passengers.

Mr. Theo asked Dr. O'Keefe, "I suppose this is a very long shot, but one of my oldest friends was in Portugal a couple of years ago, and got involved with a marine biologist there. Could you be the one? Do you know Tom Tallis?"

Poly precipitated herself into the conversation. "He's my godfather! He's one of our very favorite people in the world!"

Simon felt excluded from the excitement shared by the O'Keefes and the old Greek. Who was this man who was so important to them that Poly should be dancing with joy?

Dr. O'Keefe said, "I don't know what we'd have done without Tom. For a priest, he does get himself involved in some extraordinarily sticky situations."

Poly turned to Simon, drawing him in. "He knows everybody in Interpol and Scotland Yard and everything. He's not really a detective, but whenever there's big trouble he gets called in to help."

Dr. O'Keefe said wryly, "Let's hope there'll be no cause on this voyage to send for him. For once in his life he's living quietly as a canon of St. Paul's and being allowed to be a priest."

Mr. Theo nodded. "It would be splendid to have him along just for fun—but I've had my share of excitement—enough to last me for a long time. My doctor was very firm that this is to be a quiet voyage for me. My heart won't take much more wild adventuring."

Dr. Wordsworth came into the conversation. "That's exactly what freighter travel is for—peace and quiet. Ruth and I are exhausted. We slept the clock round last night and feel much the better for it. During the normal academic year I have precious little time for myself."

The tea party was breaking up. Mr. Smith tucked *The Wall Street Journal* under his arm, remarking that they would not see another newspaper until they reached Port of Dragons, and there would probably be only Spanish papers there; it was not a port which attracted many tourists.

Mrs. Smith held up a blue bootee to hide a yawn. "I think I'll have just a wee little rest before dinner. We were all so distressed at the accident. Coming, Odell?"

Mr. Smith helped her up. "I could do with some shut-eye, too. You youngsters may have had the dunking, but it was quite something for us oldsters, too. What a mercy that no real harm was done. Patty and I'll see you later, folks." Arm in arm, walking with legs slightly apart so that they could balance themselves against the slight roll of the ship, Mr. and Mrs. Smith moved like storks out of the salon and into the first cabin on the starboard passage.

Forsyth Phair looked at Simon. "Have you unpacked?"

"Pretty much, sir."

Poly jumped up. "I haven't. Charles, have you?"

"Sort of. I was waiting to see which drawers Daddy wanted."

"Come along then, Charles," Dr. O'Keefe said, "and we'll get things sorted out."

Simon, again feeling somewhat lost, watched them leave.

Dr. Eisenstein rose. "I think I'll check my notes on the Quiztano Indians until time for drinks. We usually meet in here for drinks before dinner, Mr. Phair, and of course as soon as it's warm enough we'll sit on deck for our pre-prandial libation."

"That will be day after tomorrow," Dr. Wordsworth announced in her definite way.

"You are quite sure of that." Forsyth Phair smiled.

"Quite."

Dr. Eisenstein started out and turned toward the port-side passage. "Coming, Inés?"

"Shortly, Ruth."

Mr. Theo retired to the farthest corner of the salon with a book. Simon went close enough so that he could see what it was: a complete Shakespeare, with print so small that he wondered that the old man could read it. But he had put on steel-rimmed spectacles and was smiling at what he was reading, totally engrossed.

Simon did not know what he was supposed to do. Cousin Forsyth was looking through some papers on one of the tables. Dr. Wordsworth was gathering books and embroidery into a needlepoint bag. He felt very young and inexperienced, standing uncomfortably in the middle of the salon. When Cousin Forsyth continued to read, Simon wandered across the room, bumping clumsily into a chair as the ship rolled, and returned to the cabin. It did not seem courteous to Cousin Forsyth to close the door, so he left it open and pulled flowered curtains across the opening; these, he assumed, were for use when the weather was hot and every available breeze was sought. Now they let in a draft which would have been unpleasant had he not been comfortably warm in Mynheer Boon's sweater.

He knelt on his bunk, his cheek to the porthole glass, and gazed out. The rain had stopped but the light was beginning to fade. Land was a dim purple shadow on the horizon. The ocean was dark and mysterious and speckled with white bursts of spume. The sound of water was all around him. The small ship creaked as it pressed through the waves. From somewhere below decks Simon could hear orders being shouted in a guttural Dutch voice; there was male laughter, solid and reassuring.

Outside the open cabin door he heard voices; he had been aware of them for some time without focusing on them.

". . . have nothing to hide." That was Cousin Forsyth, speaking in a warm and intimate way Simon had not heard before.

"Oh, do we not?" Simon recognized Dr. Wordsworth's strong, slightly harsh voice.

"Are you still dwelling on that, my dear? I had almost forgotten. No, I was not referring to that. But I was thinking that the fact that a young man should have fallen in love with a beautiful young girl is nothing that need be hidden. I am charmed that our cabins are adjoining."

"And I am not." Dr. Wordsworth's voice did not soften. "I waited because I wished to speak to you."

Simon cleared his throat, but evidently not loud enough to call attention to his presence, because Cousin Forsyth continued, "Lovely! I wish to speak to you, too."

"And I do not wish that. What I want to say to you is that I will not let you bring up the past. It is dead and buried and I want it to stay that way."

"Are you ashamed to claim acquaintance with me?"

"Acquaintance, F.P." She emphasized the initials. "Nothing more. And I would not speak of shame if I were you."

Simon felt acutely uncomfortable.

Dr. Wordsworth's voice shook with emotion. "I prayed that we might never meet again. I left Caracas and made a new life in a new world. I never should have come with Ruth—"

"Come, come, Inés. It's not so extraordinary that our paths should cross again. Can't this be an opportunity for a new understanding between us?"

She had difficulty keeping her voice low. "After what happened? I haven't forgotten."

"Can't I help you to forget? Can't you? After all this time?"

"I *had* forgotten, until I saw you. I will not allow you to presume on the past," Dr. Wordsworth said with icy control. "We are mere acquaintances. No more."

Phair's voice was tolerant. "How intense you still are, Inés. That has not changed. I hope that before the voyage is over, you may be willing to forget. Meanwhile, of course, I defer to your wishes, though I fail to understand."

"I gave up expecting you to understand anything a long time ago. The past is past. I'll kill you if you rake it up. Have I made this clear?"

Simon heard the door to the next cabin open. "Inés!" called Dr. Eisenstein. "I thought I heard your voice. Have you seen my green notebook?"

Dr. Wordsworth sighed. "Dear Ruth, you're always misplacing things. I'll go look in the salon."

Simon, too, sighed, and looked out to sea. At the horizon the light was soft and rosy, pulsing into green above, and then deepening to a blue almost as dark as the sea. It occurred to him that if he went down to the deck below and walked around or climbed over various pieces of cargo, he could get to the very prow of the ship and pretend to be his ancestor, Quentin Phair, who was indirectly the cause of Simon's being on the *Orion* now, sailing to Venezuela with the portrait of Bolivar.

He huddled into Mynheer Boon's heavy sweater and took courage. Quentin Phair may have been nineteen, a grownup, a man, when he left England to go to Venezuela to fight with Bolivar, but Simon had the same adventurous blood in his veins—he hoped. If Aunt Leonis had been with him, thirteen would have seemed a great deal older than it did when he was with Cousin Forsyth.

The tall radiators were too hot to touch. It seemed improbable that in just a few days the sun would be warm and they might even need to turn on the cabin fan.

"Hello, Simon." It was Cousin Forsyth. "What have you been up to?"

Simon got down from the bunk and stood politely before his cousin. "Looking at the ocean, sir."

"All settled in?"

"Yes, sir, thank you, sir. If you don't mind I think I'll go out on deck." He could not explain to Cousin Forsyth—he would not have needed to explain to Aunt Leonis—that he was going to take a journey into the past and pretend to be his own ancestor, Quentin Phair, setting out from England to the wild and glamorous new world of South America. Quentin was Simon's hero and model, and it was far more splendid to make believe that he was Quentin Phair, the white knight in shining armor, than Simon Bolivar Quentin Phair Renier, who was only a thirteen-year-old boy.

"Be careful," Cousin Forsyth warned, "and be sure that you're in time for dinner. Ship's meals are served promptly."

"Yes, sir. I'll be on time."

He left the cabin and as he walked along the passage he heard the cabin door shut behind him with a firm click. It was difficult suddenly to accept Cousin Forsyth as a man with the complete fabric of a past. Until a few minutes ago Cousin Forsyth had been for Simon only a month old. Before a month ago Simon had never heard of this tall, grave, suave man with whom he was traveling. It seemed unlikely that this close-mouthed, middle-aged person had once been young and in love.

He started down the steps, remembering that only a few hours ago Mynheer Boon had hustled him, blanketed and dripping, across the foredeck with a high sill over which he had tripped, past the crew's quarters and up these same steps which Mynheer Boon had told him were properly called a ladder, though they looked like an ordinary staircase.

From the crew's quarters came sound and smell, both delightful: someone was playing a guitar; someone else was rendering the melody on a flute or recorder. Through a partly open curtain he saw two young sailors lounging on a double-decker bunk. A delicious scent of baking wafted toward him as he passed the galley, and he could see the chef, a young man with round spectacles and a high white hat, taking a tray of steaming pastry out of the oven. The loveliness of the music and the comfortableness of the cooking cheered him. He remembered to step high over the sill and went out on deck into the clean raw wind. Most of the doorways on the *Orion* had sills far higher than those in a house, but the sill to the foredeck was even higher than the others, to keep out the waves in rough weather.

The boy stood on the gently rolling deck, breathing salt air, listening to the music coming sweetly from within the ship, punctuated by the sound of men's voices; he picked his way through the cargo, pausing in the clear evening light to look at the writing on the wooden crates. If it was Dutch he had trouble even in guessing; if it was Spanish he could usually decipher it; there was a lot of equipment for oil wells and refineries. He guessed that most of the bags of grain and seed he had seen being loaded were now stashed away down in the hold.

He moved through the narrow walkways left open between cargo, past the station wagon, two cars, and a large black hearse. He did not like the idea of having the hearse aboard. It was five years since the death of his parents, and he loved Aunt Leonis and was happy with her; nevertheless, the sleek dark hearse was a reminder of death, of grief, of the terrifying precariousness of all life. As he hurried past it he saw a rayed-out shattering in the windshield that looked as though it had been made by a bullet.

Simon shivered, only partly from the blustery wind, and hurried on until he came to the prow of the ship. By standing on one of the bales he could look out to sea. The cold wind blew through the heavy sweater. He pulled the cap down over his eyes and crouched so that he was protected from the wind. If he tried hard enough he could visualize the *Orion*'s great yellow masts holding billowing sails which slapped in the wind, as Quentin Phair must have heard them . . .

But he couldn't. Usually he was able to move deep into a daydream, the intense daydream world of an only child, so real that he heard nothing of what was actually going on around him. But the fact that the Bolivar portrait no longer belonged to Aunt Leonis, that it would never belong to Simon, that it had been bought by Cousin Forsyth, made it difficult for him to plunge deep into his favorite daydream of being the brave and heroic Quentin.

He felt lonely and lost. Poly and Charles were safe with their father; they had forgotten him. He closed his eyes tightly, forbidding tears, and withdrew inside himself, not onto a sailing vessel en route from England to Venezuela, but back to the known world of South Carolina and Aunt Leonis, back in time to the difficult decision to sell the portrait.

This time his concentration was deep. The sounds of the M.S. *Orion* no longer reached him. He was reliving a heavy, humid August evening at Pharaoh, the small cottage on an acre and a half which was all that was left of the once great plantation. Simon and Aunt Leonis sat on the tiny porch to their house—"shack" would have been a more realistic word, though it had once been a solid cottage—fanning themselves in slow, rhythmic movements with palm-leaf fans, rocking in quiet and companionable silence. Boz, the ancient pointer, snored contentedly at their feet. It was not yet dark, and Simon could see an expression of grief move across the old woman's face.

As though his awareness had been a blow, she put her hand up to her cheek. "Night soon," she said quietly. "There'll be a breeze later."

"Aunt Leonis, couldn't I get a job?"

"You're too young."

"But, ma'am, I could work as a field hand or something."

"No, Simon. Education is a tradition in our family, and I am going to see to it that you have yours."

"With you for a teacher, don't you think I'm educated enough?"

"No one is educated enough," Aunt Leonis said. "I am still learning. When I stop learning, you will bury me."

"That will be never, then."

"I'm an old woman, Simon, and ready to meet my Maker. I look forward to it with great anticipation. But I would prefer to be certain that you have mastered Latin, which you are not being taught at school. And next week I intend to start you on Spanish, a language I have forgotten, and which both of us surely should know."

Simon scowled. "I'm not apt to go to Spain."

"You have an ancestor who helped liberate the South American continent."

"And I'm not likely to go to South America."

"I realize that you are insular, child, but things will change, and meanwhile I will not permit you to be lazy."

"No, ma'am. But you've already taught me French."

"Next week we will start Spanish. I still have my old books."

"Buenas noches, señorita," Simon said. "¿Como está?"

"That is hardly adequate, and you are speaking with a French accent. And you are being ugly. Is something wrong?"

"No, ma'am."

They lapsed into silence, and darkness fell with the abruptness of the subtropics. Around them a light wind emerged from nowhere and stirred the Spanish moss in the live oaks.

Aunt Leonis's fan moved more and more slowly until it stopped and rested lightly on the faded black of her dress. "Simon, I will have to sell the Bolivar portrait."

"But, ma'am, you can't! It's your most treasured thing." He was shocked and incredulous.

"It is only a thing, my son, and we must not be bound by material things."

"But, Aunt Leonis—"

"You think that I would let you go undernourished in order to hold on to some oil paint on an old, already decaying piece of wood?"

"Oh, Aunt Leonis, ma'am, let me get a job, please."

"Simon, you are not yet thirteen, and I made a promise to your parents."

"They wouldn't have wanted you to sell the portrait."

"When one nears a century, one surely should have learned not to depend on that which will rust or decay. You are the only person left in my life who has not crossed to the other side of time. I have survived much death, the loss of my only brother, of Pharaoh, of all the other things I used to believe made up the woman who is Leonis Phair. But we are not our possessions. That is one thing I have discovered. I am not sorry that I will be leaving you with no material goods. But I must leave you with enough education so that you will be able to choose the manner in which you will earn your living, and you are not getting that from the local school, particularly if you continue in your wish to be a doctor. You must be able to pass examinations and earn scholarships. I have to supplement your education. You are a good student, Simon."

"Yes, ma'am, but you're easy to learn from. You make it all fun."

Miss Leonis picked up her fan. "I will put a notice about the portrait in the Charleston papers and in *The New York Times*. I am not rushing into this unadvisedly. We have enough money to get us frugally through one more year, and by then we should have found an appropriate buyer." The summer dark was so thick that Simon could no longer see the old lady, but he reached over and took her hand in his. Her hand felt as thin and warm and dry as an old leaf. He knew full well that if she said they would start learning Spanish next week, start they would. He understood with a corner of his mind that Aunt Leonis was an extraordinary old lady, but she had always been part of his environment; now she was home, the rock on which he stood, and he could not look without flinching on another change of life which would be even more radical than the change that followed his parents' death. Without Aunt Leonis, where would he go? Who would he be?

As though following his thoughts, she said, "Quentin Phair's journals, his letters to Niniane, and to his mother in England, are in my jewel box. You might be able to sell them one day. When you are twenty-one they will be yours to read, even in the unlikely event that I am still alive, and who knows what you will learn? They are all that you will find in the box, but they will stand you in good stead. I have honored Quentin Phair's written request not to read letters or journals for six generations, which I consider a wise precaution. Even the most innocent of journals, if they are honest, contain pages which could hurt other people. It will be interesting for you to learn whether you are like him in spiritual as well as physical characteristics."

Simon demurred, "I'd rather read them with you."

"No. My memory stretches back a long way. There may be things in journals or letters which I'd rather not know."

Each month Aunt Leonis put the notice about the portrait in the papers. "We will not sell it to just anybody. It must be somebody who will appreciate and honor it."

On a cold evening in January, Cousin Forsyth Phair appeared.

Simon and Aunt Leonis were indoors, keeping warm by a lightwood fire. The resin-saturated wood burned so brightly that Simon was studying by it. He had finished his regular schoolwork and was doing the Spanish lesson Aunt Leonis had prepared for him. Together they could speak slowly but with moderate fluency, although she still deplored his French accent.

A knock on the door took them both by surprise. Aunt Leonis reached for her cane, and Boz growled deep in his throat. Simon went to the door.

They had learned to do without electricity, so he saw the

man at the door only in the glow of the fire. Aunt Leonis rose rheumatically to her feet and turned on a lamp by the round table which served them as desk and dining table.

"Good evening," the man said. "Is Miss Leonis Phair in?"

"Yes, sir. Who is it, please?"

The man moved past Simon into the circle of lamplight. He was tall and thin and dark and elegant, despite stooped shoulders; his dark hair was greying at the temples and about the ears, and he held a dark hat in his gloved hands. "Miss Leonis Phair?"

She stood facing him, holding her cane as though it were a weapon. "Who are you, sir?"

"I am your cousin, Forsyth Phair. I saw your notice about the Bolivar portrait in *The New York Times*, and I have come to inquire about it."

"Hey, Simon!" It was Poly's voice.

Simon stood up, out of the protection of the lee of the ship. "Here!"

Poly and Charles were halfway across the foredeck and came hurrying toward him. Charles said, "We've been calling and calling."

"I didn't hear you. I'm sorry."

Poly asked, "What are you, deaf or something?"

"I guess I was concentrating."

Charles clambered over a bale and jumped to where Simon was standing in the *Orion*'s prow. "What a great place, Simon! How did you find it?"

"I came looking for a private place. Cousin Forsyth was in the cabin, and I thought people would be coming into the salon."

Poly put her hands on her slender hips and looked around. "You've found it, all right. We'd better check with the captain for protocol's sake, but this is it, Simon, this is absolutely it. I was wondering where we could go to escape the grownups. You're marvelous."

Simon felt himself flush with pleasure. "It's a little cold here unless you crouch down."

"It won't be cold in a couple of days. Hey, did you see that hearse with a bullet hole in the windshield?"

Simon spoke shortly. "Yes."

"Who would want to be driven in a hearse with a bullet hole in the windshield?"

"Who would want to be driven in a hearse, period?" Charles countered.

Simon did not laugh. Instead, he gave a small, involuntary shudder.

"Someone walk over your grave?" Poly asked.

Simon did not answer. He looked out at the foam breaking whitely about the prow.

Charles stuck his elbow into Poly's ribs, and she said quickly, "It's cold out here tonight, all right. Let's go in, Simon. I'm starved. How about you?"

"I'm pretty hungry, I guess."

"Charles and I looked in the galley and spoke to the cook. Dinner is going to be good. He's a super cook. I don't speak much Dutch, but enough to find out what we're eating. Come on."

"Poly thinks she speaks every language in the world," Charles said.

"I *like* languages!"

"Just stop bragging about them. Pride goeth before you know what."

Simon followed the amicably arguing brother and sister. As they approached the doorway they met the captain, dressed in a dark serge winter uniform, who greeted the children with paternal friendliness.

Poly pointed to the prow. "Captain van Leyden, is it all right if we go up there and sit sometimes? We'll be very careful, and we won't be in anybody's hair, and of course we'll stay out of the way when we're in port."

Simon added shyly, "And we can pretend we're setting out to help Bolivar free South America."

"It is all right," Captain van Leyden replied in his precise, guttural English, "as long as you disturb nothing. Do not climb into the cars, or try to open the crates."

"Oh, we won't, we promise, we'll be very careful."

The captain smiled down at them. "We do not often have children aboard."

"Why is that?" Charles asked.

"To be free to take a freighter trip means leisure, and for most people this leisure does not come until after the time of retirement. We usually have no one under sixty-five."

"Our father isn't anywhere near sixty-five," Charles said. "He isn't even fifty."

"No. We have a very young ship this time. There is not much for young peoples to do. I hope you will amuse yourselves."

"Of course we will," Poly assured him. "Everything's marvelous, Captain."

"It is cold, now," the captain said, "and you and Master Simon were chilled this afternoon. You had best go in where it is warmer."

"We're just on our way. Thank you, Captain."

They stepped over the high sill and made their way along the passage and up the steps. Dr. O'Keefe, Dr. Eisenstein, Dr. Wordsworth, Mr. Theo, and the Smiths were in the salon, with Geraldo passing drinks and nuts. Simon did not see Cousin Forsyth.

"Let's go out on the aft deck," Poly suggested, "at least for a few minutes."

They walked down the port passage, past the professors' cabin, past Simon's and Cousin Forsyth's. At cabin 5, Simon paused. "This is where the Bolivar portrait is."

"Is it really famous, Simon?"

Simon pushed the fisherman's cap back on his head. "I never thought about it being famous before Cousin Forsyth came along."

"We have a portrait of our grandmother when she was young and beautiful, but it isn't famous. It's—" She stopped as a voice sounded loudly from cabin 5.

"I will not tolerate carelessness or curiosity." It was Cousin Forsyth's voice, followed by a low, indistinguishable murmur, then, "But you were trying to look at the portrait, don't deny that." The murmur came again, and then Cousin Forsyth's voice was lowered, as it had been while he was talking with Dr. Wordsworth.

"Is there any reason people shouldn't look at the portrait?" Poly asked.

Simon shook his head. "Not that I know of. But it's all crated, so you can't see it."

"He certainly sounded mad at someone. Who do you s'pose?"

"I don't know."

"And wouldn't anyone have to pry open the crate to see the portrait?"

Simon shook his head again. "Beyond me."

"It's made me curious, at any rate," Poly said, but she moved on and rested her hand lightly on the handle of the fourth door. "For those like me who don't like showers, there's a bathtub in here. Geraldo says he'll unlock it for me tomorrow."

Simon asked, "Why is it kept locked?"

"Oh, things are always kept locked in ports, and he's been so busy this afternoon, what with us falling in the drink and all, that he hasn't had time to do anything else." She started to open the door to the back deck, which was reserved for the passengers; there were lights strung up under the canvas awning, and it looked cheerful, if cold.

But just at that moment Dr. O'Keefe called from the head of the corridor, "Dinner's ready, kids. Come along."

The passengers sat at two tables: Cousin Forsyth, Simon, Mr. Theo, and the Smiths at one; the O'Keefes, Dr. Wordsworth, and Dr. Eisenstein at the other. At a third table sat Captain van Leyden, his first officer, Lyolf Boon, second officer Berend Ruimtje, and chief engineer Olaf Koster. The essential second language for these Dutchmen was Spanish, and their English tired easily, so it was simpler for the officers to sit apart from the passengers.

The captain's table was waited on by Jan ten Zwick, the chief steward; Geraldo tended the passengers. Poly was right: the food was plenteous and well prepared.

"I believe," Cousin Forsyth said in his lightly ponderous way—very unlike the way in which Simon had heard him speaking to Dr. Wordsworth—"that the chief reason freighters carry passengers is to afford a good chef for the officers. This is as good a rijstafel as I've ever tasted."

Whatever it was, thought Simon, it was delicious, and very unlike the nearly meatless diet he was accustomed to. He ate with appetite. He would have been happier at the table with Poly and Charles, where conversation was lively, with little bursts of laughter. Poly looked over and winked at him, and he winked back.

"What was that, Simon?" Cousin Forsyth asked.

Simon rubbed his eye. "Nothing, sir." He looked down at his empty plate, then across to the table where the officers were eating. Mynheer Lyolf Boon, the first officer, folded his napkin, said something in Dutch to the captain, and left.

Simon's table had finished dessert, a delectable mixture of apples and flaky pastry, well before the second table, and everyone had moved out of the dining room into the salon for coffee. Simon sat at the far end, on a long sofa under the fore windows. Mr. Theo settled himself in a chair not far off, with his volume of Shakespeare. Cousin Forsyth was talking to the Smiths, and pointing to a card table in the corner of the room near the door to the foyer. Simon closed his eyes, suddenly overwhelmed with sleep.

"Simon . . ." It was a whisper.

He jumped. Poly and Charles stood in front of him. "Oh. Hi. I was just sleepy for a minute."

Geraldo came up with a small tray of half-filled demitasses and a pitcher of hot milk, put it down on the table, and then bustled back to the other passengers.

Poly sat down beside Simon. "I'll pour. Have some, Simon?"

He nodded. "I've never had coffee before. Aunt Leonis and I drink tea."

"You may not like it, then. Put lots of sugar and milk in; then it tastes sort of like hot coffee ice cream."

Simon followed her instructions, tasted, and smiled.

"Oh, Simon," Poly said, her long legs in green tights stretching out under her plaid skirt, "I'm so glad you're you. Suppose you'd been some awful creep? Whatever would we have done, all cooped together like this?"

Simon nodded in solemn agreement. "I'm glad yawl are you, too." Now that he was relaxed, his voice was warm and rhythmic.

Poly flashed her brightest smile. "I like the way you talk, Simon. It isn't all nasal and whiny like some of the Southerners we've met."

"I was born in Charleston." It was a simple statement of fact.

Poly giggled. "Snob."

Simon blushed slightly. "I like the way you talk, too. It isn't British—"

"Of course not! We're American!"

"—It's just clean and clear. Aunt Leonis loves music more than anything in the world, so voices are very important to her. Her voice is beautiful, not a bit cracked and aged. Somebody compared her voice to Ethel Barrymore's—I guess she was some kind of famous actress in the olden days."

Poly poured Simon some more coffee and hot milk. "Hey, look at all the grownups over there, nosing each other out. And we knew about each other right away."

"Well, they didn't almost get drowned together," Simon said. "You saved my life, so that means—"

"It means we belong together forevermore," Poly said solemnly.

Charles was looking across the salon at the adults. "They've forgotten how to play Make Believe. That's a sure way to tell about somebody—the way they play, or don't play, Make Believe. Poly, you won't ever grow too old for it, will you?"

"I hope not." But she sounded dubious.

Simon pushed back a lock of fair hair from his face. "My Aunt Leonis is very good at it. Actually, she's my great-grandaunt, or something. When people get ancient they seem to remember how to play again—although I don't think Aunt Leonis ever forgot. She says you can tell about people—whether they're friend or foe—by your sense of smell, and that most people lose it."

"Fe fi fo fum," Charles intoned, "I smell the blood of an Englishman."

"It's probably our pheromones," Poly said.

"Our what?" Simon asked.

"Pheromones. They're really quite simple molecules, eight or ten carbon atoms in a chain, and what they do is send out— well, sort of a smell, but it's nothing we smell on a conscious level, we just react to it. For instance, a female moth sends out pheromones at mating time, and a male moth comes flying, but he doesn't know *why*, he just responds to the pheromones, and we're not any more conscious of it than moths. At least most of us aren't. Charles is, sometimes." She stopped, then said, "It's obvious that we're children of scientists. Maybe Aunt Leonis's sense of smell is simpler and just as good." She sniffed delicately, and looked with quick affection at Simon. "You smell superb, Simon."

He sniffed in his turn. "You smell right lovely yourself. Maybe it's your red hair."

But Poly sighed. "I haven't worn a hat in years because I keep hoping that if I keep my hair uncovered and let the salt air and wind and sun work on it, maybe I'll bleach out and turn into a blonde. It hasn't shown any signs of happening yet, but I keep on hoping."

"You look right nice exactly the way you are," Simon said firmly.

He might be a year younger than she was, but Poly felt a warm glow. "Look, your Cousin Forsyth is playing bridge with the Smiths and Dr. Eisenstein. That's a funny combination."

Simon looked at the card table. Bridge was another unexpected facet in Cousin Forsyth, who was shuffling with great expertise.

"At any rate," Poly said, "we're certain about Mr. Theo."

"Certain?" Simon asked.

"That he's all right. He's a friend of Uncle Father's and that means he's okay."

"Uncle Father?" Simon asked.

"My godfather. Canon Tom Tallis. You remember, we were talking about him at tea."

"Why do you call him Uncle Father?"

Poly gave her infectious giggle. "Rosy, our baby sister, started it when she was just beginning to talk, and we all took it up. We see more of Uncle Father than we do of our own grandparents, because we live so many thousands of miles apart, but Uncle Father was in and out of Portugal for a while, so he's a sort of extra grandparent for us. And I guess I trust him more than I trust anybody in the world."

Charles said, "But he warns you about that, Pol. He says that no human being is a hundred percent trustworthy, and that he's no exception."

Poly shrugged. "I know, but I trust him anyhow. Trust isn't a matter of reason. It's a matter of pheromones. I trust Simon."

Simon beamed with pleasure. "My Aunt Leonis says that it isn't proper to ask personal questions. But yawl can ask me anything you like."

Poly asked immediately, "How does it happen that you have a portrait of Simon Bolivar in your family, and why're you taking it to Venezuela with Cousin Forsyth?"

Simon's eyes took on the pale grey stare which meant that he was moving back into memory. Aunt Leonis lived as much in the past as in the present, and the games of Make Believe she played with Simon were usually forays into time remembered. Simon, his voice low and rhythmic, said, "My favorite ancestor is Quentin Phair. He was the youngest son in a large family in Kent. In England. In the olden days the eldest son got the title, then there was the army or the navy or the law or the church, and after that the younger sons had to fend for themselves. So when Quentin Phair was nineteen and announced that he was going to South America to help free the continent, his family didn't even try to stop him. He fought with Bolivar, and became his good friend, and the portrait is one painted at the time of the freeing of Ecuador, when Bolivar was at the height of his greatness. Aunt Leonis said that in going to Venezuela the way he did, Quentin really gave up his youth for others."

"But how did you get the portrait?"

"Not me, and it won't ever be mine, now. It came to Aunt Leonis when her brother died, because he didn't have children."

"Yes, but Quentin was English, wasn't he?" Poly asked. "How did the portrait get to South Carolina?"

"Well, when Quentin finally went home to England, his mother had just inherited a sizable hunk of property in the South of the United States, so he offered to come over and see about it for her, expecting to stay only a few weeks."

"But he took over his mother's property and stayed forever," Charles said, as though he were ending a fairy tale.

Simon smiled. "He met a young girl, Niniane St. Clair, and they fell in love and were married."

"What a pretty name," Poly said. "Niniane. She was beautiful, of course?"

"We have a miniature of her. It's very faded, but yes, she was beautiful. And when Aunt Leonis was young she looked just like her. Quentin built Pharaoh for Niniane, and all their children were born there. The landscape must have reminded him of Venezuela, especially in the spring and summer, with all the same kinds of flowers, bougainvillaea, oleander, cape jessamine, and the great, lush, jungly trees. It wasn't tamed and cultivated the way it is now."

"Pharaoh," Poly mused. "It's sort of a pun, isn't it?"

"I like it." Simon was slightly defensive.

"Well, so do I. And the portrait?"

"It's been handed down from generation to generation. It's a very special treasure. Since Aunt Leonis never married, it was to come to my mother as next of kin, and then to me. Only we had to sell it."

"But why on earth would you sell it?" Poly asked.

"We needed the money."

"Oh." Poly flushed slowly, as she had that afternoon when speaking Spanish to Geraldo over Simon's head.

"It was the last of the portraits. Aunt Leonis sold most of them when she had to sell Pharaoh—the big house and most of the furnishings and the silver and the grounds. Her father tried very hard to keep Pharaoh going, but he got into terrible debt, and when he died Aunt Leonis had to sell everything, even the portrait of Quentin Phair. But at least it stayed in the house, over the mantelpiece in the library where it's always hung. I look like him, my ancestor Quentin. I hope that when I grow up I'll be like him."

"If you had to sell Pharaoh, where do you live?" Poly asked.

"Aunt Leonis kept an acre and a bit, and we live in an old cottage. If there's a heavy rain from the northeast, the roof leaks in exactly eight places, which is a powerful lot for a small house. Aunt Leonis has various buckets and pots and pans which she puts out to catch the leaks, and she's managed to work it out so that as the rain hits each pot it plays a different note of the scale, and we have a mighty fine time listening to the different tunes the rain makes."

"Your Aunt Leonis," Charles said, "sounds like the kind of aunt everybody would like to have. Who else would have thought of making something magic about eight leaks in a roof?"

"I sometimes think Aunt Leonis doesn't enjoy it nearly as much as I do, but she never lets on that she'd really rather have the roof repaired. We have a purty little garden patch behind the house, and we have live oaks and water oaks all around to give us privacy—not that we need it; the Yankees who bought Pharaoh are only there a couple of months a year. Sometimes Aunt Leonis and I pretend that we're visiting our cottage, bringing turkey broth and custard to a sick child, and that we really live in Pharaoh, the way Aunt Leonis did when she was young. We have a right fine old time together."

Charles said slowly, "I think I love your Aunt Leonis."

"She's a great believer that all things work together for good. It's Cousin Forsyth who's come to the rescue now. And maybe that's good, but I didn't want her to sell the portrait."

Charles spoke quietly. "I'd guess that she sold it because she loves you more than she loves the portrait."

Simon nodded, and looked across the salon to where Cousin Forsyth was spreading out his cards with a flourish.

Poly's regard followed his. "How does your Cousin Forsyth come into it?"

"Out of the blue, you might say," Simon replied, and told them.

"So you really don't know him very well."

Simon looked across the salon, and thought of the conversation he had heard between Cousin Forsyth and Dr. Wordsworth. "I don't think I know him at all."

2. THE FIRST NIGHT AT SEA

CHARLES and Dr. O'Keefe shared the second double cabin on the starboard corridor, and Poly had the first single cabin, next to theirs. She was in bed, reading, happy with her compact little nest, barely big enough for bunk, chest of drawers, washbasin. On the chest she had propped her favorite travel companion, an ancient icon of St. George battling the dragon, which she had taken from a calendar and mounted on a thin piece of wood. Wherever she had St. George she felt at home, and protected from all dragons, real or imaginary.

A brisk, rhythmic knock came on her door, the family knock, and Charles entered, wearing pajamas and bathrobe. "Hi. What are you reading?"

"*Wuthering Heights.*"

"Would I like it?"

"Not yet."

"I'm not that much younger than you are."

"You're a boy, and you wouldn't like it yet," she stated dogmatically.

Charles let it drop, looked around for a place to sit, and then climbed up onto the foot of her bunk and sat crosslegged, lotus position.

"I like it when you sit that way," Poly said.

"It's comfortable."

"And you didn't even know it was a special position, used by Eastern holy men when they meditate?"

"How would I know? It's a good position for thinking in."

"What do you think of Simon, then?"

Charles smiled his slow smile. "I've never met anybody before who wasn't in our century."

"What do you mean?"

"Aunt Leonis—he belongs to whenever it was she belonged to, and maybe it wasn't a whole century ago, but it certainly isn't now."

"We have to take care of him, then, don't we?"

Charles was silent for so long that Poly thought he was not going to answer. Then he said, "Someone has to. I don't think Cousin Forsyth is going to."

Poly looked interested. "What about Cousin Forsyth?"

"What Simon's Aunt Leonis calls sense of smell—"

"What about it?"

"I'm not sure. Maybe it's not Cousin Forsyth. But my sense of smell is giving me warnings."

"About what?"

"I'm not sure, Pol. I just get a sense of anger, and fear, and it's coming at me from all directions. Too many pheromones."

"Have you spoken to Daddy?"

"Not yet. It isn't definite enough."

Poly looked at her brother with absolute seriousness. "I don't like it when you get feelings."

"I like it if they're good ones."

"But this isn't?"

"It's strange. I've never felt anything like it before. It seems to come from almost everybody, and to have something to do with Cousin Forsyth, and that just doesn't make sense."

"I wish you'd speak to Daddy."

"I will, if anything begins to focus. It's all vague and fuzzy now."

"What about Simon?"

"Simon is our friend," Charles said.

Simon lay awake in his bunk. Cousin Forsyth snored. Simon had never slept in a room with anyone else before. In Pharaoh he and Aunt Leonis each had a private cubicle, his made out of what originally had been a small storeroom. He was afraid to move about lest he disturb Cousin Forsyth. He started to drift into sleep, and woke up with a jerk, dreaming that the fork lift was pursuing him, and the fork lift was alive and wild and hungry, with red eyes and smoke, like a dragon. Simon was prone to occasional nightmares, and at home he would go out to the kitchen and brew a cup of tea, and Aunt Leonis always heard him and came out to him, and they would sit and drink tea and talk until the nightmare had dissolved in the warm light of the kitchen, and he could go back to bed and sleep.

Cousin Forsyth's snoring was rhythmic and placid, but it was not a restful sound.

Then the *Orion* began to rock gently in the night swells of the ocean, and this living movement was as comforting as the lit candle in the kitchen at Pharaoh. Thoughts of fork lifts and dragons receded, and he went to sleep.

In the cottage at Pharaoh, Miss Leonis was reading by the bright light of a resiny fire. On the small table by her side lay her Bible, closed. She was not certain that consulting it had caused her to make her decision to open Quentin Phair's letters and journals, unread for so many generations, instead of waiting to leave them for Simon.

But ever since Mrs. O'Keefe had dropped her at Pharaoh, after an exhausting and stimulating afternoon, she had been restless and unable to settle down. Her sense of smell kept telling her that something was wrong, but not what that something was, except that it had to do with Simon, Simon who was miles away at sea in a small freighter heading into the Caribbean. Had she been right to accept Forsyth Phair's invitation to take his young cousin to Caracas with him? It would be a journey of less than two weeks; they would be returning by plane after leaving the portrait in Caracas. Surely this was an opportunity for Simon which should not be turned down?

—Something is wrong, something is wrong, an inner voice continued to nag. —Simon is in danger.

Had her concern over Simon's future dulled her sense of smell over Forsyth? He had come with documents tracing his descent from one of her great-uncles who had moved out West after the war. She knew that this shared ancestor had undoubtedly played politics with the carpetbaggers, but Forsyth Phair was not to be blamed for that, after all, and perhaps it was old-fashioned prejudice which made her hold this against him.

In any event, Forsyth was a Phair; his nose and chin told her that, the high-bridged, hawk-like nose—though Forsyth's eyes crowded close together, unlike the wide-spaced Phair eyes.

But he had the strong chin softened by an unexpected dimple which usually turned into a formidable cleft by middle age. In Forsyth the cleft was almost a scar. Yes, he was a Phair, and hanky-panky with those who wanted to get rich on the troubles of the South was hardly to be blamed on him. His talk of his life in Caracas sounded serious, and surely it was commendable that he wanted to return the portrait to his adopted country rather than to keep it himself?

And then, Forsyth was the last of the Phairs. Simon was a Renier. The male line of Phairs had been prone to accident and sudden death.

Pride of name, she thought wryly. —Is that part of it?

Pride. Pride was always her downfall. When Simon's mother died she had concealed the fact of her poverty from the Renier relatives. They had wanted the boy to come to them, to his father's people. She had had to battle to keep him, and she respected the Reniers for letting Simon, in the end, make the choice. They would be ready to take him to their hearts when she died. They would see to it that he was properly educated, that he went to medical school. If she had asked them for money they would have given it to her. If she had asked them to buy the portrait they would have bought it—but then she might have lost Simon.

Pride. Forsyth Phair was Simon's one link with his mother's kin, with Miss Leonis, with Quentin Phair; indeed, with the very name of Phair. Not only pride was involved in her feelings here. The dying of a name was as real as the death of a person. If Simon kept in touch with Forsyth Phair it would keep the name alive a little longer.

—I am a foolish, proud old woman, she thought. —In eternity the end of the Phairs makes no never mind.

She was suddenly full of misgivings. Was Forsyth really all that he appeared to be? Had pride of name made her too eager to accept this kind and considerate stranger who had appeared out of the blue?

She fed old Boz, and then walked slowly around the house with him. There had been sunshine in Charleston that afternoon and the air was warmer, but now the sun had set and she was glad to get back to the fire. She reached for her Bible. It opened to Nehemiah, and the first words she read were, "And Tobiah sent letters to put me in fear." This could hardly be construed as a suggestion that she open Quentin Phair's letters and journals; besides, she considered people who opened the Bible, put a pin on a word, and expected an answer to their problem, to be superstitious at the least, and idolatrous at the worst, and she wished to be neither.

"What do you think, old Boz?" She fondled the dog's ear.

The old hound sighed and put his chin heavily on her knee. Then he walked arthritically into her small bedroom, where she kept the carved wooden coffer which had once contained jewels and now held Quentin Phair's journals and letters. After a few moments she followed the dog. She took two of the journals and a few packets of letters from the coffer and returned to the fire.

She took one of the journals out of its oilskin casing and opened it at random. The ink was brown and faded, but the script was elegant and still completely legible. She read, ". . . when I returned from Dragonlake today Umara showed me our baby. It was an extraordinary feeling to take this tiny brown thing in my arms and to know that he is my seed, that his fair skin comes from me. Now 'I have shot my man and begot my man.' I am not the first, nor will I be the last, of the English regiment to leave my seed here on Venezuelan soil, but my Umara is not like the usual women we soldiers meet. Indeed, the Quiztanos seem a race apart as well as a world apart, a gentler world. I do not want to leave my son, my first son, here in this strange place, but I cannot send my Umara home to my mother and cold England. Why am I so unduly disturbed by what, after all, is nothing unusual?"

Miss Leonis closed her eyes. She sat, unmoving, until the fire died down and the room grew cold and the old dog began to whine.

In the cabin next to Cousin Forsyth and Simon the two professors prepared for bed. Dr. Wordsworth was brushing strong black tea through her luxuriant hair; Geraldo left her a pot of

tea in the cabin each evening immediately after he had cleaned
up demitasses and glasses. "I learned about brushing black tea
into my hair at bedtime from an Armenian ballet dancer," she
said, "and I don't have any grey, which at my age is not bad."

Dr. Eisenstein had heard about the black tea before. She
looked at herself in the mirror, not pleased with what she saw.
She reached for her toothbrush. At least she had all her teeth,
which was more than Inés could say. The brownish circles
under her eyes did not vanish when she had enough sleep. The
study lines about her mouth and nose were graven deep; too
much staring into books and not enough living. But when she
could not see herself her inner mirror gave her a younger, more
pleasing image. She did not feel nearly sixty. She brushed her
teeth vigorously, and for a moment she was intensely irritated
by Inés's glossy black tresses.

Dr. Wordsworth patted her cheeks with cotton soaked in as-
tringent lotion. She sighed. "I wish Phair hadn't come aboard
at Savannah. It's brought up a past I hoped I could forget."

"He seems very pleasant," Dr. Eisenstein said.

Dr. Wordsworth's voice was bitter. "If you will remember,
my youth in Caracas was not exactly happy. I've deliberately
tried to forget as much as possible."

"I know," Dr. Eisenstein murmured.

"You don't know. You didn't know Fernando."

"I know what you told me. I know he treated you abomina-
bly and made you very unhappy."

Dr. Wordsworth laughed harshly. "That's putting it mildly. I
don't know why I let myself be talked into coming along with
you on this trip."

"Inés, it's supposed to be a rest for both of us."

Dr. Wordsworth yawned elaborately, patting her wide-open
mouth with her scarlet-tipped fingers. "I'm exhausted, all right.
And I admit to being curious about your Quiztanos. Fernando
was mostly Levantine, but he had a touch of Quiztano in him."

"You're still trying to understand him," Dr. Eisenstein said
softly.

Dr. Wordsworth finished wiping off her face cream and

threw out the astringent-soaked cotton. "No, Ruth. I'm trying to understand myself."

"Then why are you so upset about meeting an old acquaintance?"

"I don't feel logical about my past, and he reminds me of it."

"He appears to be very much of a gentleman, and he plays an excellent game of bridge."

"As long as he doesn't presume on mere acquaintance—"

"I'm sure he won't," Dr. Eisenstein reassured. "Anyhow, it's only a few more days before we debark at Port of Dragons and he goes on to Caracas."

Dr. Wordsworth got under the covers. "I look forward to your Quiztanos, Ruth. Twentieth-century civilization has lost its appeal for me."

Dr. Eisenstein put her notebooks away. She felt a stirring of envy. Fernando may have caused Inés great pain, but at least she had known life and love. There had never been a Fernando in Dr. Eisenstein's life, and she felt the poorer for it.

Simon was awakened by his cousin's stertorous breathing. It was so loud that Simon smiled into the darkness because it seemed a strange and primitive sound to be coming from Cousin Forsyth. He thought of the two professors in the next cabin and wondered if they could hear it through the walls, and what kind of conversation two such different people as Dr. Eisenstein and Dr. Wordsworth would have with each other.

Aft of Simon and Cousin Forsyth was cabin 5, the cabin with the portrait, the Bolivar portrait which was the reason for this journey. The thought that once they left Caracas he would never see the portrait again gave him a sharp pang of regret.

—Pride of possession, he thought. —Aunt Leonis told me to beware of that.

Cousin Forsyth gave an extra-loud snort which evidently woke him up. Simon could hear him turn over in his bunk and start to breathe quietly.

He lay in a strange bed on his way to a strange land. Now that the snoring had stopped he could hear again the soothing sound of wind and wave. He remembered that he had new friends on board. He tried to feel adventurous and brave like Quentin Phair. He tried to feel that one day he, too, might be a hero. The ship rocked like a cradle. He closed his eyes, turned over, and returned to sleep.

3. THE WORD "UMAR"

CAPTAIN van Leyden had teenage children of his own at home in Amsterdam, and he enjoyed the presence of the three young ones on his ship. After breakfast the next day, which pleased and astonished Simon by consisting of platters of sliced Gouda cheese, sausage, salt herring, freshly baked rolls, honey, jam, peanut butter, and boiled eggs, the captain gave them a grand tour of the *Orion*, introducing them to the crew, and then took them up on the bridge. "You may come up whenever you wish," he told them, "except when the pilot is coming aboard. Consider this to be your ship. I can see that you are careful young persons." He instructed them in detail on the use of each of the vast array of instruments, and then showed them his radar machine, of which he was obviously proud. "You see," he explained, "it not only blips around at various distances—ten miles from shore, five miles from shore, and so forth—but look: now you see a photographic representation of sea and shore at various distances—not now, of course; all we see is water. But after lunch you will be able to see Cuba, from the starboard side, and if you wish to come and look at it through the radar machine, you may."

"Oh, we do wish," Poly said. "Thank you, Captain."

"Tomorrow I will have the chief engineer, Olaf Koster, take you all over the engine room. It will be hot and dirty, so please dress accordingly."

"We will."

"You are amused?" he asked them several times.

"We're having a marvelous time," Poly assured him.

"You are not bored?"

She stretched with enjoyment. "I've never been bored in my life. And certainly I couldn't be bored on the *Orion*. Where is the hearse going?"

"To Caracas."

"What about the bullet hole in the windshield?"

"It was sold at what you would call bargain price."

"And all the big boxes and cases?"

"They contain mostly equipment for oil fields, refineries."

"The *Orion* carries almost everything, doesn't she, Captain?"

"We are an all-purpose ship."

"You know that list of cargo on the table in the salon?"

"For the information of the passengers. Jan ten Zwick made the translation."

"Maybe sometimes his English is a little peculiar."

"Peculiar?"

"Well, it says *5 boxes reefers.* What are the reefers, Captain?" Poly was simply curious. She did not think for a moment that the little ship was carrying marijuana.

The captain looked at her in surprise. "Reeferigerators, Miss Poly. They are expensive in Caracas, and not as large as American reeferigerators. If one is successful, one has an American car, or a Mercedes, and one has an American reeferigerator."

Simon and Charles were looking at each other with laughter in their eyes, but all three of them kept polite and straight faces. Poly said, "I see. Thank you. And all the grain down in the hold?"

"That goes to various places. Port of Dragons, for one. We should see the coasts of Colombia and Venezuela by Friday evening—three more days."

Poly looked across the vast expanse of water. "That'll be exciting. But it's even more exciting to be in a small ship in the middle of the ocean and to see no land at all—almost as though we were like Noah."

The captain said dryly, "Noah, I assure you, was very happy to see land."

After lunch the three children went to Simon's place in the prow of the ship. The adult passengers had retired to their cabins for a siesta. On the promenade level two young sailors were swabbing down the deck. Others were running up and down the ladders, carrying ropes, buckets. On the boat deck a young sailor was painting the white rail, while another was polishing the brasses. The sailors smiled or waved at the children while continuing about their business.

In the prow the wind was still chill, and they were well bundled up. Ahead of them, and to starboard, was a shadow of land.

"Cuba," Poly said, "but I don't think we're going to get anywhere near enough to get an idea of what Cuba's like. I wish we could see it better. Geraldo says we'll be close enough to see something on the radar by mid-afternoon."

Simon looked at Cuba, which revealed nothing, and then down at the water, which was a deep dark blue, streaked with white caps. He braced his feet against the gentle rolling of the ship. Around the prow the water looked like fluid marble and he thought it was one of the most beautiful things he had ever seen. "Hey, look, yawl. Liquid marble, sort of the way rock must have been when the earth was being formed, only that was boiling hot, and this is cold." He shivered. Geraldo had given him an extra blanket in place of a coat, and he pulled it more tightly around him and sat on a crate of oil-well machinery in the lee of the wind. "It occurs to me," he said in his old-fashioned way, "that I answered a lot of questions last night, and there are some questions I would like to ask you."

Charles perched in his favorite position on another crate. "Ask ahead."

Poly sat on the deck between the two boys. "We ought to have a name for our place."

Simon's face lit up. "So we should! What?"

"Let's each think about it till after dinner, and then tell each other what we've come up with, and we can decide which name is best. What did you want to ask us, Simon?"

"How come you two're going to Venezuela with your father, and leaving your mother and everybody else behind?"

Charles stared up at the sky, watching the movement of the clouds, and left Poly to answer.

"Well, you know Daddy's a marine biologist, and we used to live on Gaea Island off the south coast of Portugal, and now we're living on Benne Seed Island . . ."

"Yes."

"Well, this isn't for general information, Simon. As a matter of fact, you might call it classified. But Charles and I decided last night that we could trust you."

"Thank you." Simon bowed with grave formality.

"The Venezuelan government asked Daddy if he would come spend a few weeks at Dragonlake and study what's happening to the lake. It's a big source of oil, and you know how important oil is right now."

"Well, no, I didn't."

"What do you and Aunt Leonis heat your house by?"

"Firewood."

"Oh. Well, oil *is* important. People thought it would sort of keep spouting out of the earth forever and ever, and suddenly there's not enough, and Americans are used to having more than enough. So places that have oil are important. But at Dragonlake the oil wells are *in* the lake, the way they are in Lake Maracaibo, and in Dragonlake the fish and other marine life are dying, and if they can't find out what's causing it, Dragonlake is going to be a dead sea. Some people are saying that the dragon has been angered by the oil wells, and is drinking the oil. And maybe that's just a way of saying that if we don't take care of the earth, the earth is going to rebel. Anyhow, when the Venezuelan government asked Daddy, he decided he'd go, and take Charles and me out of school for a month and bring us with him. The reason that it's all top secret is that the oil companies might get upset, so you won't say anything?"

"Of course not."

"Daddy's purportedly going to get some unusual specimens of marine life, and of course he'll do that, too, and Charles and I can help him there. He and Mother say that the trip and working with Daddy that way is an education in itself for Charles and me, and fortunately the principal of our school agreed. And Charles and I are due a proper vacation, aren't we, Charles?"

"Definitely."

"You two are the eldest?"

Charles's face lit up with his slow smile which began with a quirk at the corners of his lips and spread all over his face, focusing in the deep blue of his eyes, the same gentian color as his father's. "We have five brothers and sisters—well, you saw them in Savannah—all younger than we are. If you're used to being with Aunt Leonis, we're usually surrounded by infants, and because we're the eldest, we do try to help out."

Poly added, "It would be impossible for Mother, otherwise, though she was the one who thought of having us go along with Daddy. Say, Simon, what about your Cousin Forsyth, and why didn't you think maybe he was an impostor?"

Charles looked sharply at Poly, but she was looking at Simon.

Simon answered, "He had all kinds of credentials, but I don't think Aunt Leonis would just have accepted them if he didn't have the Phair nose and chin. If you had looked at him, and then at some of the old daguerreotypes Aunt Leonis kept because they weren't salable, you'd know he was kin. He has a swarthy complexion, but otherwise he looks like the Phairs."

"You don't look like him, not one bit. You're blond as Jan ten Zwick."

"My hair comes from the Reniers. My father's family."

"Did Aunt Leonis open her arms and embrace Cousin Forsyth, like the long-lost son, and so forth?"

"Not exactly. She wasn't entirely happy about Cousin Forsyth because he comes from the branch of the family which collaborated after The War."

"Way back with the Nazis?"

"No, no, with the carpetbaggers."

"Simon, what war are you talking about?"

"The War between the States." Simon looked surprised.

Charles and Poly exchanged glances. Poly said gently, "Simon, there have been several wars since then. When you said 'The War' you sounded as though it were the only war."

"Maybe its effects are still felt more at Pharaoh than the other wars . . ."

"But slavery was bad."

"Sure it was bad. But mostly that wasn't what the war was about. Anyhow, we didn't have slaves at Pharaoh."

"You sound as though you'd been there. Why didn't you have slaves?"

"Quentin Phair. After all, he spent a long time with Bolivar fighting for freedom. He could hardly have slaves on his own plantation. It was what might be called a commune today.

Everybody worked together, black and white. All the slaves were given their freedom by Quentin Phair when he built Pharaoh, and then they could choose whether to stay as part of the family, or to go. And it was the same way in my father's family, the Reniers. Their plantation was called Nyssa, and there weren't any slaves there, either."

"You're not telling us that this was typical, Simon?"

"I know it wasn't typical. But it's the way it was for the Phairs and the Reniers, and that's where I come from. And after the war everybody was poor, poor unto starvation."

Poly continued to probe. "If you didn't have any slaves, and everybody worked together, why was everybody so poor?"

"You forget we were an—an occupied country. Like Israel at the time of Christ, or Norway with the Nazis. Pharaoh wasn't burned, the way Nyssa was. The Yankee officers took it over for their headquarters, so the house was saved. But they burned the fields and then they salted them. It took years before the land would yield any crops. If you've lived off the land, by dint of very hard work on everybody's part, and the land is destroyed, then things aren't easy for anybody."

"Oh," Poly said in a chastened way. "That's something I hadn't realized. Every time I think I know it all I get taken down a peg, and I guess that's a good thing. What about Cousin Forsyth's family?"

"They had money and food and clothes and luxuries, and people didn't unless they collaborated with the carpetbaggers. So you see why Aunt Leonis wasn't entirely happy about him. Maybe it *was* like collaborating with the Nazis."

"But the carpetbaggers weren't Nazis. They were us." Poly stopped, then said, "Maybe that's the point. Oh, dear. So what happened with Cousin Forsyth's family?"

"They moved up North, and then out West, and we lost track of them until the evening Cousin Forsyth knocked on our door."

"And it was only a month ago that he came?"

"Yes. He stayed in Charleston at the Fort Sumter while all the arrangements were being made—calls to Caracas, and our booking on the *Orion*, and everything. And all that month Aunt Leonis tried to make me speak only Spanish."

"Have you lived with her all your life?" Poly asked.

Simon's face hardened, and he looked older than thirteen, but his voice was calm. "I've known her all my life and been in and out of Pharaoh, but I've only lived with her all the time for five years—since my parents died."

"Oh, Simon!" Poly reached out to touch him gently on the arm. "I'm so sorry!"

Simon nodded gravely.

"Was it an accident?"

"Well, it seemed to me it was a sort of cosmic one. My mother was dying of cancer, and six months before she died my father—my father had a heart attack. He died. So Mother and I moved in with Aunt Leonis, and she nursed Mother until she died." His voice was stiff and dry.

Poly's chest tightened in sudden panic. She thought she would not be able to bear it if anything happened to her parents. Charleston and Benne Seed Island seemed more than a day away by sea, and suddenly she missed her mother and her younger brothers and sisters so badly that it hurt. If only she could run to a telephone and hear their voices, be reassured of their being—but the telephone was one of the aspects of civilization that Dr. O'Keefe had said he would be pleased to do without for a while.

—No emergency, please, Poly pleaded silently. —Don't let there be any emergency.

Simon's color came back to his cheeks. "Not everybody would have an Aunt Leonis to take over. I'm lucky."

Poly shook herself, shedding ugly thoughts like water. "Let's go to the promenade deck and see what the grownups are doing."

She led the way, and as they passed the door to the cabin with the portrait, she tried the handle. It did not move under the pressure of her hand. "Oh, well, I suppose it would be locked—but if it's so heavily crated and all . . ."

"It's a nice portrait." Simon, too, tried the door. "Bolivar looks handsome, and you can actually see energy in his expression, and a sort of excitement. He looks the way a great hero ought to look."

Poly pushed the handle of the bathroom door, which opened under her pressure to reveal a long, deep tub, almost the size of her bunk. "Oh, wonderful, wonderful, I'll have a gorgeous soak this evening. I don't care if I never see a shower. I love to wallow in a hot tub. In Gaea we had the whole ocean for a tub most of the year round, but it's been much too cold at Benne Seed Island for swimming."

On the promenade deck Geraldo had put out some games for the passengers—a set of rings to toss, and pucks for shuffleboard. Dr. Wordsworth and Dr. Eisenstein, wrapped in blankets, their heads swathed in scarves, occupied two of the deck chairs. Poly led the way out the door, across the back of the deck, and then in the door to the starboard passage. "I have a hunch our two professors don't care much for the companionship of children. You can't have secrets very easily on freighters, and I heard them talking about us after breakfast." She assumed Dr. Wordsworth's voice—strong, pedantic, and with a faint trace of accent. "'What do you make of those three children?'" Her voice changed to Dr. Eisenstein's, gentler than Dr. Wordsworth's, with a touch of Boston. "'They're moderately polite, which is a refreshing change. And they do not have the usual moronic lack of vocabulary and the mumbling speech of the affluent American young.' And Dr. Wordsworth said, 'At least they are keeping out of our hair.' And Dr. Eisenstein said, 'I wish you'd stop reminding me how gorgeous your hair is,' and changed the subject."

Simon and Charles laughed at her accurate mimicry of the two women. They passed Mr. Theo's single cabin, and came to Poly's. She ushered them in.

"I'm hardly affluent," Simon said.

Charles climbed up onto the foot of the bunk. "I know you must be poor as far as money goes. But you're not like most poor people in any other way."

"Most poor people aren't like Aunt Leonis. We're rich in education, and we're rich in tradition. We're very lucky."

Charles nodded. "I don't think we're affluent, either. We're not poor or anything, but marine biologists aren't apt to make millions, and Daddy's always having to buy expensive equipment. The Smiths like us, by the way. Mrs. Smith keeps trying to pat me on the head and tell me what a nice little boy I am, and that they have a great-grandson in San José who's very much like me. She told me, 'You're so courteous and considerate. Not like a little American boy at all.'"

"I hate that!" Poly said vehemently. "We're completely American. And anyhow it implies that all American kids are rich slobs and that's not true."

Simon, leaning against the chest of drawers, agreed gravely. "There are quite a few of us poor slobs, too."

Poly sat on the small space of floor between bed and chest, leaning against the bed. "Tell us more about you and Aunt Leonis. Why are you so poor, as far as money goes?"

"I'm not exactly sure. When my parents were alive I guess we were sort of like you—not rich, not poor. But my father had a newspaper and his business was all in his head, and when he died there just wasn't anything left over, because Mother's illness had already cost so much. Aunt Leonis says that only the very rich and the very poor can afford to be ill. I guess being poor is a lot harder on her than it is on me, because she grew up in the big house at Pharaoh, and she's the one who's gone from riches to rags." He pushed the fisherman's cap up on his head. "Everybody's so nice on this ship," he said, changing the subject, "the captain letting us watch him up on the bridge, and Geraldo giving me this cap, and all. It's almost worth having to sell the Bolivar portrait. Not quite, but almost." He swung around and saw Poly's icon. "What's that?"

"It's St. George and the dragon. I take it with me wherever I go. St. George looks so kind, even while he's being fierce with the dragon."

"Aunt Leonis and I have a dragon—a make-believe one, but he's a good dragon, and protects Pharaoh and our garden. Hey, yawl, that's what we can call our place—the Dragon's Lair!"

He looked so delighted that Poly and Charles immediately agreed that the Dragon's Lair was the perfect name.

"Because there *are* good dragons, like Aunt Leonis's and mine. He eats nothing but Spanish moss, and he sleeps curled around one of the live-oak trees, and whenever there's danger he spouts fire."

Charles asked unexpectedly, "Did he spout fire when Cousin Forsyth came?"

Simon looked uncomfortable. "Why would Cousin Forsyth be dangerous?"

"I don't know," Charles said flatly.

"Even the dragon couldn't keep Aunt Leonis from having to sell the portrait. If it hadn't been Cousin Forsyth it would have been someone else. And Aunt Leonis says that if it had to go, she's glad it's going back to Venezuela where it came from. She says that things know where they belong, and maybe the time had come for the portrait to return to its native land."

Poly scrambled up from the floor. "We've got St. George with us on the *Orion*, and he'll take care of us if we encounter any dragons that aren't as nice as yours." She stretched and yawned. "I think I'll take my bath now, before dinner. Come along and talk to me while it runs. And maybe the cabin with the portrait will be unlocked. I'd like at least to see the case."

"Who'd have unlocked the cabin door in the last fifteen minutes?" Charles asked.

The boys trailed after her, out the door to the aft deck, behind the deck chairs of the two professors, and in through the door to the port passage. Poly opened the door to the bathroom, and leaned over the tub to turn on the taps, then raised her finger to her lips. Simon started to speak, but Poly turned on him. "Shush."

There were voices coming from the cabin next to the tub room, the cabin with the portrait. A heavily accented voice said, ". . . saw the word *Umar*."

"Nonsense. You are mistaken." It was Cousin Forsyth's voice. "And you are spying again."

"I do not spy. But the word *Umar* I saw."

"Impossible."

"You remember—when we were bringing the portrait into

the cabin—there was a loose board which I hammered back into place. That is when I saw it—*Umar*."

"So? A random grouping of letters. It means nothing."

"You think that?"

"Of course. Totally unimportant."

The voices stopped. Poly bent back over the tub and turned on both taps, full force.

"We eavesdropped," Simon said.

"We listened."

"Aunt Leonis says—"

Poly held her hands under the flow of water, adjusting the taps until the water suited her. "Your Aunt Leonis is absolutely right for her world. But this isn't Aunt Leonis's world."

"What do you mean?"

"Simon, this is the end of the twentieth century. Things are falling apart. The center doesn't hold. We don't have time for courtliness and the finer niceties of courtesy—and I've learned that the hard way. Does *Umar* mean anything to you?"

"No."

"Is there something written on the back of the portrait?"

"I don't know. I never looked. Only at the portrait itself. There was never any reason to turn it around."

"That was Cousin Forsyth we heard."

"Yes."

"And the man with him had a Dutch accent. Who helped him with the portrait yesterday?"

"I don't know. It was while we were getting dry after the fork lift—"

Charles sat down on the small white stool which was the only piece of furniture in the tiny tub room. "Don't make too big a thing of it, Pol."

"Am I?" She looked fiercely at her brother.

"I don't know," Charles said.

Darkness fell more quickly at Pharaoh for Aunt Leonis than it did for Simon at sea. In the last of the light she sat on her small, sagging front porch (Simon had kept it from tumbling down altogether) and read her ancestor's journals. Her heart was heavy, and she was not sure why. His was not an unusual story. A virile young man expending his energies in fighting for the freedom of a beleaguered, overtaxed country could hardly be expected to be celibate. Wherever foreigners fight in a strange land they leave their foreign seed, and leave it probably more casually than did Quentin Phair.

"My son grows apace," wrote Quentin. "Each time I manage to get to Dragonlake he seems to have doubled in size. Already he is walking, falling, picking himself up and walking again. Like his Indian cousins he is learning to swim almost more quickly than he is learning to walk. I cannot pretend that he is not mine. I cannot forget Umara and our child. The Quiztanos are not like any of the other natives I have met in my five years here, not like the other Indians, not like the white Creoles, certainly not like the tragic, imported Africans; they are not like anybody. Dragonlake is another world. If I cannot bring my Umara and my son to England—and I cannot; Umara would not be welcomed; she would be insulted, and I will not have that—then it seems to me that when my work is done I must stay here, though I doubt if this battling the royalists will be over before several more years. What is there to take me home to England? I have become used to this country and these people and even this malaria, with which I have been bedridden for the past week. I will go back to Kent briefly—I owe my dearest mama that much. And then I will set sail for the last time and make my home at Dragonlake—if the Quiztanos will have me, and Umara says they will. My fellow officers already think me mad—Simón is the only one who understands, and he only because he is my friend—and so, then, this will be my final madness and I feel cold and strange even while my heart rejoices." Miss Leonis, too, felt cold and strange and there was no rejoicing in her heart. When Quentin wrote those words he had not yet met Niniane; the future toward which he looked with fear and joy was not the future which was to come. He did not know, as Leonis did, the end of the story—or was it the end? Did such stories end with the death of the protagonist?

Or were there further scenes to be acted out before the curtain could fall?

It was too dark to read, and with the setting of the sun the shadows moved in coldly; in her warm coat the old woman shivered, and went indoors to light the fire, followed by Boz, who nudged at her hand. She moved heavily, unable to throw off the thought that Quentin Phair's drama was being continued through Simon Bolivar Quentin Phair Renier, and that Simon was in danger.

Simon, who had accustomed himself to Cousin Forsyth's snoring, slept. He dreamed that he and Dr. Eisenstein were carrying the Bolivar portrait along the edge of a deep lake; they were running, stumbling over hummocks and tussocks, because a dragon was after the portrait. Dr. Eisenstein turned into Mr. Theo, who put the portrait down, put two fingers in his mouth, and whistled loudly. The dragon came hurrying to him, puffing and panting in eagerness, and then Simon and Mr. Theo climbed onto the dragon, who soared into the sky.

It was a nice dream. It had started out to be a nightmare, and then it turned into fun.

In his sleep Simon sighed peacefully.

He woke up shortly after dawn, the memory of his dragon ride fading at the edges of his mind. Cousin Forsyth was still snoring. It would be another hour before Jan ten Zwick or Geraldo would ring the breakfast bell.

He was wide awake. For a while he tried to get back into the dream, but he could not. The dragon who had carried him aloft had vanished with daylight. The dragon had had a name. Mr. Theo had whistled, and when the dragon had come, he had called him by name. What was it? Then he remembered: *Umar.*

That was the word they had heard from cabin 5, and *Umar* meant nothing to him, although it seemed to have considerable import to whoever was talking with Cousin Forsyth. Why was something written on the back of the Bolivar portrait? Did

Aunt Leonis know about it? and if she did, why hadn't she said anything?

—Probably because it doesn't mean anything. Probably because it's unimportant, just as Cousin Forsyth said.

But Poly and Charles had not thought it was unimportant.

He dressed quietly, without waking Cousin Forsyth, slipped out of the cabin, and went to the aft deck.

The air was fresh but no longer cold; the sky was soft with spring. Mr. Theo was out on deck ahead of him, leaning on the rail and looking out to sea.

Shyly, Simon went and stood beside him. Next to the O'Keefes, who were a revelation and a joy to him, he was most drawn to Mr. Theo, who sat next to him at table; and the dream had made Mr. Theo even more of a friend.

"Look, Simon," the old man said, and pointed down at the water. "Flying fish. There. Like little flashes of silver."

"Oh—oh—beautiful!" Simon exclaimed.

They stood in companionable silence, watching the brilliant brief flashings until the school of fish was left behind them. Then Mr. Theo went and sat on one of the cane chairs under the canvas awning, motioning Simon to sit by him. "We are the two early birds today. I wonder if there will be a mouse to catch."

"It's nice enough, just being here with you, Mr. Theo. And I had a dream about you last night."

"Was I an ogre?"

"No. You whistled for your dragon, and we both went for a ride on it."

The old man seemed pleased. "I have always wanted to ride a dragon. I'm sorry I didn't dream it, too."

Simon smiled at him. "You remind me of my Aunt Leonis, and I've been homesick for her."

"It's hardly a compliment to her that I remind you of her. I'm nearing eighty."

"Aunt Leonis is ninety."

"Is she!" He sounded pleased. "And how do I remind you of her, then, since I am such a young chicken in comparison?"

"She likes Shakespeare, too, especially *King Lear* and *The*

Tempest. And she loves music. Dr. O'Keefe says that you're an organist, a famous one."

"Not that famous. But I am only part of a person when I am separated from an organ. Does your Aunt Leonis play an instrument?"

"She used to play the harp, until we had to sell it. And sometimes in the very early morning or in the evening she still plays the flute, though she says she doesn't have the lips or the lungs for it any more. Are you going to read all of Shakespeare while you're on the *Orion*?"

"If I get through half a dozen plays I'll be doing well. I, too, love *King Lear* and *The Tempest*, but right now I'm reading *Romeo and Juliet.* He is like a great organ, that Will, and gives me much solace from being separated from mine. So your Aunt Leonis is ninety, eh?"

"In chronology only. Ninety and not quite a month."

Mr. Theo fumbled in his pocket and pulled out dark glasses which clipped on over his regular spectacles. "I once heard someone say that the job of the very old is to teach the rest of us how to die, and I still feel young enough so that I'm looking for someone older than I to teach me."

"Aunt Leonis does that. I'm the only person she has who hasn't died. She was with my mother when she died, and if someone has to die, it's good to be with Aunt Leonis."

"Methinks she's teaching you how to live," Mr. Theo said, "but of course they're part of each other."

They lapsed into silence, but it was a good silence. After that brief exchange he felt completely comfortable with Mr. Theo. He could, he thought, tell the old man things that he couldn't tell anybody else, the way he could with Aunt Leonis. Aunt Leonis was, he supposed, teaching him about both life and death; she had taught him how to be at least a little less enraged at the thought of death in a world created by a loving God.

After his mother's death the local minister, Dr. Curds, had come to call, and had immediately alienated Simon by talking of this premature death as the will of God.

Aunt Leonis looked down her long, aristocratic nose at the middle-aged man in his dark suit. "I wonder how it is,

Dr. Curds, that you are so certain that you understand the will of God?"

Dr. Curds looked at her with patient gentleness. "You must not fight the Lord, my dear Miss Phair. Trust in his will, and he will send you the Comforter."

"Thank you. I believe that he has already done so. I also believe that my niece's illness and death were not God's will. I doubt very much if he looks with approval on such suffering. It seems to me more likely that it has something to do with man's arrogance and error. However, being mortal and finite, I do not presume to understand God's will, so I am not certain."

Dr. Curds murmured something about it being part of God's plan.

Aunt Leonis replied, "It may be part of God's plan that a young woman should suffer and die, or it may be the work of the enemy."

"The enemy?"

"Don't you believe in the devil, Dr. Curds? I do."

Dr. Curds murmured again, "The Church in these more enlightened times . . . the devil seems a little old-fashioned."

Aunt Leonis raised her left eyebrow. "I haven't noticed many signs of enlightenment. And I am undoubtedly old-fashioned. But I do believe that God can come into the evil of this world, and redeem it, and make it an indispensable part of the pattern which includes every star and every speck of hydrogen dust in the universe—and even you, Dr. Curds."

Despite his grief, Simon nearly laughed.

"Hello there, young Simon. Where were you?"

"Oh—Mr. Theo—I'm sorry. I was remembering."

"You go deep into your memories."

"Too deep, Aunt Leonis says."

"Was that a good one?"

"No. It was bad, except for Aunt Leonis. It was about when a minister came to call on us after my mother died, and he was horrible, and Aunt Leonis put him in his place. Do you believe in God, Mr. Theo?"

"I do. It would be difficult to have lived as long as I have and to think that one can get along without God."

"Well, I'm glad you and Aunt Leonis believe in God."

"Don't you?"

"I'm not as old as either of you, and he let my parents die."

Mr. Theo apparently changed the subject. "Do you know why I'm on the *Orion*, Simon?"

"For a vacation?"

"Partly. My doctor ordered me to go by sea rather than air. But mostly I'm on the *Orion* because I'm going to Caracas to hear the first concerts of the pupil who is dearest to my heart. When she was ten years old she was blinded in a vicious accident. But she didn't moan and groan about God's allowing such a cruel thing to happen. She just went on with her music."

"Am I moaning and groaning?" Simon asked.

"You're not far from it, are you?"

Simon closed his eyes and clenched his fists. Then he relaxed and smiled. "You really and truly are like Aunt Leonis. I'm going to get on with it, Mr. Theo. I really haven't moaned and groaned for a long time. It just isn't possible to do much moaning and groaning around Aunt Leonis. This is the first time I've been away from home, and I guess I've regressed. Mr. Theo, does the word *Umar* mean anything to you?"

"Umar?" Mr. Theo repeated. "No, I don't think it does. Should it?"

"It was the name you called the dragon. Don't say anything about it, if you don't mind."

"Very well, *Umar* shall be between the two of us. There goes the breakfast bell. Are you hungry?"

"Starving."

Cousin Forsyth had made it clear that in the morning after breakfast he wished to have the cabin to himself while he shaved, so Simon wandered out to the promenade deck. The wind was brisk but the sun was warm. Dr. Eisenstein was settling herself in a deck chair with a plaid steamer rug to wrap round her legs, and a straw basket stuffed with academic-looking magazines and several spiral notebooks. Simon took the ring toss and moved to the far end of the deck, but after he had tossed several rings, missing the post with most of them, he realized that she was looking at him. She smiled at him welcomingly and he crossed the deck to her and bowed politely.

"It must be very dull for you young ones traveling with us old folk."

"Oh, no, ma'am, not in the least dull. We're having a lovely time."

"Self-sufficient, eh? Don't need to be amused? What about television?"

"We don't have one, Aunt Leonis and I."

"Most unusual for your generation. What are your interests?"

"Well, ma'am, I'd like to hear about the Indians you're going to visit."

Dr. Eisenstein's eyes gleamed. "The Quiztanos?"

"Yes, ma'am."

"They are of particular interest to the anthropologist because they are one of the very few tribes to remain virtually unchanged in numbers and culture—you see, usually when a country is taken over by a higher civilization, the native strains diminish radically in number, or change from their old ways. Most of the other Indian tribes in this section of South America have either dwindled in number while their culture has deteriorated, or, on the other hand, they have adapted to the ways of the invaders. Los Dragones peninsula was one of the first places on the South American continent to be visited by Spanish explorers in the sixteenth century, but neither the land, which is thick jungle, nor the comparatively small number of Indians invited conquest. And they were not welcoming. According to Dr. Wordsworth's old Guajiro Indian nurse, the legend that the Quiztanos are waiting for a young white savior from across the sea evidently postdates the sixteenth century, possibly even the seventeenth. I'm not boring you?"

"No, ma'am." —But Aunt Leonis makes learning more fun.

"I'm not used to talking to young children."

"I'm not that young, ma'am. I'm thirteen."

"Thirteen, eh? I'll try not to be too dry. But I find it fascinating that long after the Spaniards came, long after the Quiztanos knew white men, and what white men did to the Aztecs, they should acquire a legend about a young white man who will come to them from far away."

"Yes, ma'am. That's right interesting."

"The source of this legend is one of the things I hope to discover when I go to the Quiztano settlement, though I may need a Guajiro contact. Evidently the Quiztanos and the Guajiros have been involved in smuggling together for many generations, and the smuggling trade today is less innocent than it was when the colonists were oppressed by Spain."

Out of the corner of his eye Simon saw Poly and Charles emerge from the starboard passage and stand waiting for him. His mind was more on them than on the Quiztanos, but he maintained his expression of courteous interest.

"Los Dragones peninsula with its almost unpopulated coastline has been easily accessible to small smugglers' boats, especially since the Dutch occupied Aruba and Curaçao in the early years of the seventeenth century."

"Yes, ma'am."

"After the wars of independence, when the border between Venezuela and Colombia cut across the southern side of both the Dragones and Guajiran peninsulas, smuggling became even more active." Suddenly she realized that she did not have Simon's full attention. She turned slightly and saw Poly and Charles in the background. "Your friends are waiting for you. And here comes Inés—Dr. Wordsworth—looking for me."

"Yes, ma'am. Thank you. That was very interesting. I'd like to hear more."

"Would you, honestly?"

"Yes, ma'am. Really and truly."

"We'll get together again, then, shall we?"

"Yes, thank you, ma'am." He left Dr. Eisenstein and he and Poly and Charles repaired immediately to the Dragon's Lair.

Dr. Wordsworth pulled a deck chair beside Dr. Eisenstein. "I see you've found your proper level."

"That's a highly intelligent boy."

"Because he was listening to you ride your hobbyhorse?"

Dr. Eisenstein raised her eyebrows. "You're in a fine mood this morning."

"That blasted Phair. I dreamed about Fernando last night. I haven't dreamed about Fernando for years."

"Try to forget him," Dr. Eisenstein urged. "Anybody who'd let you take the rap for his smuggling activities isn't worth dreaming about."

"Not only his smuggling." Dr. Wordsworth's voice shook with irritability. "Mine, too. You don't seem to understand that smuggling is as natural a part of my background as juggling income tax is with some of our reputable colleagues. My father was a highly successful dealer in jewels, and so was his father before him, and a good part of their business involved smuggling." She looked at a chip on one of her nails. "Poor Ruth. Have I shocked you?"

Dr. Eisenstein spoke with sympathy. "It must have been horrid for you when you found out."

"I didn't 'find out,' as you so kindly put it. I always knew. Our family, like many other early colonials, was forced by the Spanish throne into smuggling as a way of life long before I was born."

The tenseness in her voice made her friend look at her sharply, but all Dr. Eisenstein said was, "It seems somewhat like the problems my own ancestors in New England had to cope with—such as the Boston Tea Party."

"Something like. But for us in South America it was even more intolerable."

"But why so much smuggling?"

"Dear Ruth. You know a great deal about primitive tribes and very little else. Colonists were not allowed to export any products except to Spain. The ships belonged to Spain. All prices were fixed in Madrid—Madrid, mind you—by people who knew nothing of the supply or demand in Venezuela." Her voice was bitter.

—But at least she's not thinking about Fernando. "I do see how unfair it was," Dr. Eisenstein said.

"You know how excellent our wines are, and our olive oil?"

"Superb."

"They were superb in the early days, too, but the colonists were stopped from planting vines and olive trees because they were forced to buy wine and oil from Spain, at high prices. And any interprovincial trade tried by my forebears was exorbitantly taxed. So do you see how smuggling of wine and oil and spices and all the things we ourselves could grow became inevitable?"

"I suppose I do," Dr. Eisenstein said.

"It was not the kind of criminal activity I can see you think of all smuggling as being—unless it's your precious Quiztanos."

"No, no—"

"We never went in for blackmail or extortion. We were not like Fernando, who blackmailed as he breathed. And he was willing to sell anything to anyone—jewels, oil-well parts, wine, drugs, women. He almost sold me, but I preferred jail."

"Oh, Inés." Dr. Eisenstein leaned forward in her deck chair and clasped her small hands about her knees. "Don't keep at yourself this way."

"I want a drink," Dr. Wordsworth said.

"This early?"

"Coffee."

"All right," Dr. Eisenstein said. "I'll ring for Geraldo. How about a game of gin rummy?"

"You're very kind, Ruth," Dr. Wordsworth said. "Sometimes I wonder why you put up with my bad temper. Yes, by all means let's play gin."

It was warm and comfortable in the Dragon's Lair. The breeze had summer in it, and Simon took off his fisherman's cap and let the wind ruffle his hair.

"What were you and the professor talking about?" Poly asked curiously.

"She was telling me about the Quiztano Indians. She's a very nice person. She doesn't know much about children, but once I'd persuaded her I was thirteen and not three she treated me like a human being."

"Look at that sort of olive mist of mountains on the horizon." Poly leaned out to sea and pointed. "That's Haiti. Geraldo the Herald Angel says we're still technically in the Windward

Passage, but once we get to Haiti we'll be in the Caribbean. I'm sort of sorry we aren't stopping in Haiti."

"How about being Norsemen today for a change, Simon," Charles suggested. "There *is* a theory that they actually got to South America."

"They got almost everywhere," Simon said. "May I be Leif Ericson?"

They moved only halfheartedly into their game of Make Believe, and Charles broke out of it to say, "Simon, I went to Pharaoh last night."

Simon raised his left eyebrow in a commendable imitation of Aunt Leonis.

"In a dream."

Poly asked with interest, "Was it a regular dream, or a special dream?"

"A special dream."

Simon asked, "What's a special dream?"

Charles leaned on the rail and gazed down at the churning marble water. "It's hard to describe. It's much more vivid than a regular dream, because it's much more vivid than real life—I mean, when I go to a place in a special dream I see it much more clearly, I'm much more aware than I am most of the time in everyday life."

"Do you have special dreams?" Simon asked Poly.

"No. Charles is the only one. The rest of us just dream common garden-variety dreams."

"Me, too. Except that last night I dreamed that Dr. Eisenstein and I were trying to save the portrait from a horrible dragon, and then Mr. Theo whistled and the dragon turned out to be friendly, like the one at Pharaoh, and Mr. Theo and I rode him up into the sky, and Mr. Theo called him Umar. Charles, please tell me your dream about Pharaoh."

"It was just the way you described it. In the dream it was very early morning, barely dawn, and Aunt Leonis went into the kitchen to make tea in a dented copper kettle."

"Did I tell you about the kettle?" Simon demanded.

"I'm not sure. Maybe. Do you remember?"

"No."

"Anyhow, I'm sure you didn't describe everything in the

kitchen, and I could tell you where each cup and saucer is, each pot and pan. And the way Aunt Leonis was dressed, in an old-fashioned long cotton dress, white, with little blue flowers. Does she have a dress like that?"

"Yes." Simon nodded uncomfortably.

"You see, Simon, when we were on the wharf in Savannah, waiting to board the *Orion*, Poly and I saw Aunt Leonis, remember?"

"Yes."

"And what we see gets recorded in our memory, and most of the time we draw on our memory only in bits and pieces. But when I have a special dream it's all more complete than I could possibly remember."

"She didn't have on the blue and white dress that day."

Charles sighed. "I know. Well. I saw Aunt Leonis going out to the kitchen. You were still asleep. And she said good morning to the kettle, as though it were an old friend, and she talked to it while she filled it with water and put it on to heat; and she talked to the fire while she built it in the stove—paper and wood and then a couple of chunks of coal."

"Yes," Simon corroborated.

"Then, while the water was heating, she went outdoors and spoke to an old tin watering can in the same way, and filled it from an old hose, and then she watered her plants, her camellias and gardenias, only she didn't call them gardenias—"

"Cape jessamine," Simon supplied.

"That's right. And then"—Charles continued to look down at the water, away from Simon and Poly—"then she talked to your mother."

"You mean in the dream it was before my mother died?"

"No. Your mother was dead. But Aunt Leonis was talking to her."

Simon did not speak for a long moment. Then he said, "Yes. I know. She does that. I wish I could. Aunt Leonis says she's so old she's already partly on the other side, and that's why she can talk to things, like the kettle, and to people who aren't here any more, people even longer dead than my mother. She sometimes talks to Niniane."

"Not to Quentin?"

"I think only Niniane, because they're somehow specially close. She doesn't speak about it often, even to me, because she says she knows it makes me uncomfortable, and she's afraid if anybody else hears about it they'll think she's gone dotty from old age. And, she says, maybe she has."

"Do you think she has?" Poly asked.

"She's the most sane person I've ever met."

Charles turned from his contemplation of the sea. "Does it make you uncomfortable, my having dreamed about her that way?"

"Yes. But I'm getting used to being uncomfortable." He tried to laugh.

"Do you mind?"

"No. I don't understand it, but I don't mind. And I want you to come to Pharaoh in real life."

"It couldn't be any more real. But I want to come."

"When we all get back from Venezuela, maybe your parents will bring yawl to visit us?"

"Of course they will," Poly said. "Wild horses couldn't keep us away. We belong together, Simon. You and I almost drowned together, and now Charles has been to Pharaoh, and that makes us family."

"I'm glad," Simon said. "It's very nice to have a family."

After lunch Jan ten Zwick, the chief steward, invited them into his cabin, which was at the starboard end of the foyer, between the salon and the starboard cabins. It was not much bigger than Poly's cabin, but the bunk was higher, and the space underneath was filled with drawers with recessed brass pulls. There was a desk with a portable typewriter, and pictures of Jan's parents and his younger brothers and sisters. The photograph of the father was much as Jan might look in another twenty years—square-featured, a little heavy, with straw-colored hair, and completely Dutch. The mother, on the other hand, was dark and exotic-looking, though overweight. The children were a mixture of dark and fair.

Poly examined the picture of the children assembled about their mother with interest. "Your mother doesn't look Dutch."

"She isn't."

"You look Dutch. You look like your father. But your mother looks—well, not Oriental, maybe Indian."

"She is half Quiztano Indian. Her mother was a Quiztana, my grandmother."

"From Dragonlake?"

"Yes. They are nowhere else, the Quiztanos."

Charles said, "That ought to please Dr. Eisenstein. Isn't she doing an in-depth study of the Quiztanos? You ought to be able to give her a lot of input and feedback and help her finalize her foci."

Jan looked baffled and Poly giggled, explaining, "He's just using educationese jargon. Don't pay any attention. But Dr. Eisenstein probably will want to ask you all kinds of questions."

"Oh, please, please—" Jan spread out his hands imploringly. "I did not think. I would much rather that Dr. Eisenstein does not ask questions. It is a matter of time. I have much work to do. And I think she does not understand my people."

Poly said wryly, "A particularly primitive and savage tribe, didn't she say? Or was it Dr. Wordsworth?"

"It has to be Dr. Wordsworth," Simon said. "I'm sure it wasn't Dr. Eisenstein, not after the way she talked this morning."

"We won't say a word, Jan," Poly promised. "We don't want anybody bloodsucking you."

"She does not understand. We are a very old civilization. We have forgotten more than the New World remembers."

Simon said, "We won't say anything, we promise. But don't you want to set her right about things? Dr. Eisenstein is really interested, she really is."

"There is no point. To people like Dr. Eisenstein and Dr. Wordsworth, different is the same thing as savage."

"I really don't think that's true of Dr. Eisenstein," Simon started, and gave up.

Jan smiled. "It is all right. I am proud of my Quiztano blood."

Poly asked, "Have you been to Dragonlake?"

"Many times, now."

"Jan, we're going to Dragonlake, you know. Would it be

possible for us to meet any of your relatives? Am I asking something awful?"

"No, Miss Poly. I know that you are not like the professors. Geraldo tells me how simpático he finds you. If we are at Port of Dragons long enough I will take you to see my many-times-grandfather, Umar Xanai."

Poly dug her elbow into Simon's ribs. "What did you say your grandfather's name is, Jan?"

"Umar Xanai."

"It's an—an interesting name."

"It is part of my name," Jan said. "I am Jan Umar Xanai ten Zwick. My mother is Umara, after her mother and grandmother. There are many Umars and Umaras among the Quiztanos, Polyheemnia."

"Poly," she corrected automatically.

"But it is a beautiful name, Poly-heem-nia." He sounded the syllables lovingly.

"Maybe I'll like it one day. I don't like it now. Do you like your name?"

"It is important to me. Jan is the name also of my father and of my grandfather, both seafaring men. As you know, Umar is the name of my grandfather."

"Jan, do you speak Quiztano?" she asked.

"A little. A few phrases. It is a deep language."

"How many languages do you speak?"

Charles grinned at Simon. "Here we go again. She's off."

Jan answered Poly. "I speak Dutch, Spanish, which of course is necessary in my work, and a reasonable amount of French, German, and English. It is a constant astonishment to me that well-educated Americans, such as travel with us, should be so unproficient in languages, and show no interest in learning them. I understand from Geraldo that you speak excellent Spanish."

"Well, we lived in Portugal. Simon speaks quite well, too."

"I speak French better, though," Simon said.

Jan pointed to his typewriter, on which he was typing out the menu for the following day.

"Why do you do the menus in French?" Poly asked.

"Because the French have the great cuisines. And for my own amusement." He pointed to the word *rognons* on the menu for lunch, and gave them a very young grin. "I heard Dr. Eisenstein say that she cannot abide kidneys. Our chef cooks *rognons* superbly. I wonder if she will know she has eaten kidneys?"

Poly giggled. "Jan, you're a snob."

Charles said, "So are you."

"Okay, probably I am." —It had to be Jan who was in the cabin with the portrait the day before, she thought. Again she nudged Simon.

Uncomfortably he turned to Jan. "Did you help Cousin Forsyth with the portrait? Getting it into the cabin next to ours and all?"

"Yes. He seems very concerned for it."

"It's valuable, I guess."

"That I quite understand. But it is completely safe on the *Orion*. No one would trouble it."

"Well—of course," Simon said. "I know that. Thank you for letting us come see your room, Jan."

"Es su casa," Jan said.

Poly led the way swiftly to the promenade deck. The Smiths and Mr. Theo were stretched out on deck chairs, wrapped in blankets. "I would have thought it would be too windy for them," Poly muttered, and climbed the steep stairs to the small upper deck with the lifeboats. The captain had showed them how the lifeboats worked, and warned them never to stand in the space between the deck rail and the lifeboats. 'You could slip and fall into the ocean,' he cautioned. 'Always stand by the rail.'

Now Drs. Wordsworth and Eisenstein were briskly walking the small span of deck. Dr. Eisenstein smiled at the children. "This appears to be our only way to exercise, and we have to be careful not to walk into the captain's laundry." She indicated a small line on which flapped several snowy handkerchiefs, undershirts, and underpants.

Dr. Wordsworth added, "Fifteen paces each length, and forty paces the full walk from starboard to aft to port. We are trying to walk at least three miles a day."

"We like to exercise, too," Poly said politely.

Simon and Charles followed her back down the stairs, through passage and foyer, downstairs again, past the galley, where they waved at the chef, and out onto the deck.

Charles asked, "Why didn't you come here in the first place?"

"I called my shots all wrong. I thought everybody'd be in the salon or in their cabins. Now we know who was in the cabin with Cousin Forsyth yesterday. It was Jan. And no wonder he was interested when he saw his name on the back of the portrait."

"But it doesn't make any sense," Simon cried. "Why would one of Jan's names be on the back of the Bolivar portrait?"

"We have to find out."

"Should I ask Cousin Forsyth?"

"No." Charles spoke quickly. "If Cousin Forsyth knows, he certainly wasn't telling Jan yesterday. And he didn't want Jan poking around the portrait, that's certain. I wouldn't ask him if I were you. It's more than just yesterday, and what we heard. I just—well, don't say anything to Cousin Forsyth, Simon. I'm not sure exactly why, but I just know you shouldn't."

Poly said, "Simon, when Charles knows something—I mean, knows it with his pheromones, sort of, not with his thinking mind, then you have to take whatever it is that Charles knows seriously."

"I think I would always take Charles seriously anyhow."

"Simon, you're so nice." Poly took his hand in a swift gesture of affection. "You're too nice for the end of the twentieth century. I worry about you."

"I'm all right, and I'm not very nice."

"Umar," Poly repeated. "Just keep your eyes and ears open. And if there's anything to report . . ."

"Oh, I'll tell you," Simon said. "The portrait has always been a treasure, a happy treasure, and now I feel kind of funny about it and I don't like feeling that way. Why on earth should it have one of Jan's names on it? That makes me feel very peculiar. I wish I could ask Aunt Leonis."

"Daddy says if there's an emergency we could use the radio room," Charles said.

Poly scowled in thought. "This isn't an emergency. Yet."

"Anyhow," Simon said, "we don't have a telephone. That's why Cousin Forsyth just arrived instead of calling. The nearest phone is at the filling station a mile down the road. Is it all right if we don't think about it for a while? Can we be Quentin Phair and Bolivar and his sister again?"

4. A STRANGE GAME OF BRIDGE

BY the third day at sea the blankets were put away and the Caribbean sun was warm on winter-white skin. The captain and the officers had changed from winter serge to summer whites, and Jan told the children that in the afternoon the sailors would fill the pool. The 'pool' was a large wooden box at the end of the promenade deck; it had a lining of heavy plastic, and would be filled with ocean water by a large hose which lay coiled like a boa constrictor aft of the deck. The pool was hardly big enough for swimming, but Jan said the crew enjoyed splashing about in it when the weather was hot, and the passengers were welcome to use it, too.

The breeze was warm and moist. Dr. Eisenstein and Mrs. Smith still carried sweaters, but Simon, Poly, and Charles went to the Dragon's Lair dressed for summer. It seemed as though they had been at sea for weeks. They found it no trouble to keep to themselves, mostly in the Dragon's Lair, leaving the promenade deck for the adults.

"Which I think they actually appreciate," Poly decided.

"It's not that I don't like old people," Simon replied, "but these aren't like Aunt Leonis. But then I don't suppose anybody is like Aunt Leonis."

Poly leaned against a box of oil-well equipment. "It's a wonder we aren't sick and tired of Aunt Leonis. But we aren't—we love her," she added swiftly.

Reassured, Simon nodded. The sun was warming and comforting him. He pulled Geraldo's fisherman's cap forward to keep the sun off his nose. "What do you want to be when you grow up?" he asked the two O'Keefes.

Charles countered, "What do *you* want to be?"

"A doctor. I haven't decided yet whether or not to be a people doctor, or to go into research, to stop heart attacks or cancer from ever happening."

"Then there'd be something else," Poly said. "People do die. We have a life span, just like every other organism."

"It's supposed to be threescore years and ten," Simon said.

"Yes. Okay. I understand. You'll be a good doctor, Simon. I'll come to you."

Charles said, "I want to be a kind of people doctor myself."

"What kind?"

"Well, I don't want to do research, or to be a psychiatrist, and I don't think I want to be a philosopher or a priest—"

"Although my godfather is a priest, remember," Poly said.

Charles continued thoughtfully, as though she hadn't interrupted. "I want to take care of all of a person—body, mind, and spirit. It will probably mean getting several kinds of degrees, a medical one, and maybe a theological one."

"I don't think much of church." Simon looked dour.

Poly said, "That's a lovely dream, Charles, but may I remind you how many years of school are involved?"

Charles smiled his slow, bright smile. "Sometimes I'm glad I haven't inherited Mother's talent for math. If I counted I might never begin. But it's what I want to do and I plan to do it." He spoke with quiet conviction.

Simon nodded, then looked at Poly. "What about you, Pol?"

"I don't know yet. Not that I haven't thought about it. Our grandmother—Mother's mother—is a bacteriologist and a biologist with two earned doctorates; she won the Nobel Prize when she isolated farandolae within a mitochondrion."

"You expect me to understand what you're talking about?" Simon asked.

"Not before you study cellular biology. I don't understand it very well myself. Anyhow, I don't think I want to be a cellular biologist or a chemist or anything. Mother's a whiz at math; Daddy says she could get a doctorate with both hands tied behind her back, but she just laughs and says she can't be bothered, it's only a piece of paper. I'm not sure what I want to be. You and Charles are lucky. I think you'll be a marvelous doctor, Simon."

But Simon scowled ferociously. "What's the point of being a doctor if people die anyhow? If we find the cure for cancer and then people die of something else?"

"Of course there's a point. You can care about people, and

about their lives. And you can help take away pain, and stop people from being frightened. Of course there's a point. You have to be a doctor."

"If I can get scholarships."

"You'll get scholarships," Poly promised grandly. "If you want something badly enough and aren't afraid to work you can usually get it."

"I'll hold on to that thought." He sounded grave. "I wish you were right."

"I'm always right," Poly said, and before the boys could pounce on her she jumped up and ran across the deck.

"She's off to talk to Geraldo," Charles told Simon.

Simon raised his left eyebrow.

"Geraldo is teaching her Dutch."

Simon grinned. "With a Spanish accent?"

"His Dutch is probably pretty good. He's been on a Dutch ship since he was twelve."

Simon's smile vanished. "He's not twelve now."

"No. But he's only seventeen and Poly's fourteen, and Geraldo is the first male friend she's ever had who wasn't lots older. Why do you think she calls him Herald Angel?"

"Because the *G* in Spanish sounds like an *H*."

"You don't think maybe she thinks he looks like an angel? He is extremely handsome."

"I hadn't noticed."

"Oh, come on, Simon. He has beautiful classic features, and beautiful black hair and huge eyes with lashes so long they'd look funny on anybody except a Latin."

"I know Geraldo's nice-looking," Simon said. "And he's our friend, too, not just Poly's."

"True, but it's different."

"Well, it shouldn't be."

"Why shouldn't it be? Come on into this century, Simon."

"I'm not at all sure I like this century. Does your father feel the same way that you do?"

"About what? This century?"

"Poly and Geraldo."

"We haven't exactly discussed it. But Daddy has sharp eyes and ears, and his pheromones work as well as mine."

Simon sighed. "I suppose we could be Quentin Phair and Bolivar for a while, but I don't feel much like that right now. Let's go see if the pool is filled."

In the evenings it was already looked upon as established procedure that after dinner Forsyth Phair would play bridge with old Mr. and Mrs. Smith and Dr. Eisenstein. The first officer, Mynheer Lyolf Boon, often stood behind one of them, kibitzing, though he refused to take a hand.

Simon, Poly, and Charles were sitting quietly in the background, finishing their sweet coffee, and in a pause in their conversation they heard Cousin Forsyth saying in his calm, reasonable way, "I'm not suggesting that we play for enormous stakes, after all. I doubt if any of us has either the money or the gambling instinct. But it's more fun if we play for a penny or two a point—gives a fillip to the game."

Mr. Smith's old voice was slightly quavery. "I'm sorry, Mr. Phair. I do not play for money."

Dr. Eisenstein said, "But for only a penny—"

"Not even for a penny. I enjoy the game, but if you want to gamble, then ask one of the others." He cleared his throat and his dewlap quivered and he mumbled something about his religion forbidding any form of gambling.

Mr. Phair looked pointedly at Mr. Smith's after-dinner drink of whiskey and soda.

Dr. Eisenstein looked toward Dr. Wordsworth, who said sharply, "Sorry, I don't play bridge."

Dr. Eisenstein looked at her in surprise, but did not pursue the matter.

Dr. O'Keefe smiled. "Afraid I don't, either. Never had time for it."

Mr. Theo, when questioned by Dr. Eisenstein, looked up from his book, shaking back his yellowish hair, which had a habit of falling across his face. "You would not want to play with me. I ace my partner's deuce, or whatever you call it. I am better off to stick with *Romeo and Juliet*."

"One of Shakespeare's more inept plays," Forsyth Phair said. "He does not understand the Latin temperament. The death of the young lovers would have increased the enmity between Capulet and Montague rather than making peace."

Mr. Theo made no comment but returned to his reading.

Mr. Phair turned to the first officer, who was leaning against the door frame between salon and foyer. "Mynheer Boon?"

"No, no, thank you, no. I'm on duty in a few minutes."

Old Mrs. Smith looked anxiously at her husband. "Odell, dear . . . couldn't you . . ." Her gnarled hands fluttered over the green felt of the card table.

Mr. Phair shuffled the cards with an expert riffling. "No sweat, as the kids would say." (Poly, Simon, and Charles exchanged glances.) "We'll play as we have been doing, for points. No money. I'd never want to disturb anybody's religious scruples. Now let's see, Dr. Eisenstein, you and I were five hundred points ahead of the Smiths last night. Let's see if we can't give them an even bigger trouncing tonight."

Mr. Smith wiped the back of his neck with his handkerchief, as though the room were extremely warm. As a matter of fact, the evening was breezy and quite cool. Jan ten Zwick, coming into the salon to see if more drinks were needed, noted the curtains blowing straight out from the prow windows, and lowered them.

"Let's go." Simon put down his cup.

"I think I'll go on the upper deck and take a walk," Dr. Wordsworth announced in her penetrating voice. "I find that the Dutch food, delicious though it is, weighs heavily on me, especially that superb pastry. This afternoon I walked 175 laps, and I doubt if it was two miles."

The children rose, and Dr. Wordsworth preceded them to the foyer, then turned down the starboard passage to the aft deck, from which she climbed up to the boat deck.

Poly whispered, "I wonder if the captain's warned her about not standing between the rail and the boats?"

Charles said, "I like to sit there sometimes, with nothing between me and the ocean. But I'm very careful."

"You'd better be." Poly looked around. Dr. Wordsworth had vanished. Geraldo was in the galley washing out the coffeepot, waiting until he could clear the after-dinner coffee cups, and the glasses, and wash up and go to bed. He smiled and waved at them as they turned to go downstairs.

"He's hardly any older than I am," Poly said.

Simon said, "He's a *lot* older than you are."

"Only three years."

"I'm twelve. Do you think Mother and Daddy would let me go to sea?" Charles said. "I'm the same age Geraldo was when he started."

"No."

"Why not?"

"Such things are beyond logic." She led the way down the stairs.

Charles said, "What about Geraldo's parents?"

"We're affluent compared to Geraldo's family. He has a whole lot of brothers and sisters and his parents were relieved when he got a job and they had one less mouth to feed. Listen, what was all that about?"

"All what?" Simon asked crossly, still concentrating on the unwelcome thought of Geraldo being more important to Poly than Simon.

"Around the card table."

"It was about bridge," Charles said reasonably, jumping over the high sill between passage and deck.

"It wasn't just about bridge. They were all trying to pretend that it didn't really matter whether or not they played for money—but it did matter."

"Especially to Mr. Smith." Charles picked his way carefully through the dark shadows between cargo, heading for the prow.

"And Cousin Forsyth," Simon said. He did not understand Cousin Forsyth.

Poly detoured around the hearse. "Adults are strange. And they seem stranger as I start to become one of them."

Simon seated himself on a keg. "I think it's stupid to play games for money, even if you have money to spare. But Cousin Forsyth wasn't suggesting high—watchamacallem—high stakes."

"It was all more important than it was." Poly leaned over the rail and looked at the slightly phosphorescent spume breaking about the prow of the *Orion*. "Which is what's so peculiar about it. Dr. Eisenstein would have liked Dr. Wordsworth to play, and Dr. Wordsworth wasn't having any of it—as though Cousin Forsyth had suggested they play for a thousand dollars a point or something."

Simon thought he knew why Dr. Wordsworth didn't want to play with Cousin Forsyth, and he wished he felt he could tell Poly and Charles about the conversation he had overheard.

Poly continued, "And Mynheer Boon wasn't about to play, either. He sounded almost frightened at the idea, and I don't see why it would be that out of line for an officer to play cards with the passengers for a few minutes. Now, Daddy and Mr. Theo were casual about saying no; it really was just because they aren't much for card games."

Charles leaned back against the rough paint of the rail. "I like Mr. Theo—and thank heavens he said to call him Mr. Theo. I can never remember Theoto—whatever it is."

"Theotocopoulos," Poly said. "I can remember it because it was El Greco's real name, and El Greco's my favorite painter in the world."

"You're a walking encyclopedia," Charles started automatically, then said, "Sorry, Pol, I know you love El Greco." He stared up at the stars, at constellations in completely different positions from those in the sky above Benne Seed Island or Gaea. "Those two professors are a funny combination. Dr. Wordsworth looks like a Spanish opera diva, and Dr. Eisenstein has sort of Norwegian hair, what with those brown-grey braids around the top of her head."

"She's got a very big nose for a Norwegian," Poly said.

"How do you know Norwegians don't have big noses?"

Poly settled herself in a more comfortable position. "As we said, adults are peculiar."

A voice called from the gangway. "Simon! Simon!"

Simon sighed. "Cousin Forsyth. Every time his hand is dummy at bridge he decides he'd better be cousinly about me and send me to bed." He called, "We'll be right in, sir. Don't worry. We won't be more than five minutes."

"I'd prefer you to come now." Mr. Phair moved around boxes and bales, disappeared in the shadow of the hearse.

"All right." Simon rose.

"We'll come, too." Poly stood up, shaking out the pleats of her skirt. "I've got a book I want to finish. Here we are, Mr. Phair. You can go back to your game. *Umar!*"

Mr. Phair's dark form stiffened. "What was that you said?"

"What was what?" Poly sounded over-innocent.

"What you said just now, that word."

"All I said was that we were coming and you could go back to your game and then I yawned." But she grabbed Simon's wrist in a steel-strong clamp. "See you at breakfast, Simon."

5. NOCTURNE

THE passengers of the *Orion* usually retired early. Occasionally Dr. Wordsworth and Dr. Eisenstein lay out on the small back deck for half an hour or so, their deck chairs pulled out from under the shading canvas, so that they could study the stars. They were very serious about this, and it seemed to Simon that they forgot to notice the beauty of the night sky.

But this night they were in their cabin early, Dr. Wordsworth brushing her black tresses with the ritual tea. Dr. Eisenstein, in brown cotton bathrobe, looked up from her notebook. "Inés, what on earth did you mean by saying that you don't play bridge? You know you play a far better game than I do."

Inés Wordsworth did not deny this. "I just didn't want to play with that bunch."

"Why? What's wrong with them?"

"Oh, Ruth, the Smiths are thousands of years old. I got a peek at her passport—she's eighty-one, and he's obviously older. They're sweet and all that, but they're dull old fuddy-duddies."

"What about Phair?"

Dr. Wordsworth knew how to swear picturesquely in a good many languages. She brought all of them into use, while Dr. Eisenstein put down pen and notebook in amazement.

A slow tear trickled down Inés Wordsworth's cheek and she wiped it away furiously. "My God, to think that I was once in love with that desiccated fop!"

"Oh, my dear!" Dr. Eisenstein cried. "I'm so sorry—how dreadful for you."

"Forsyth, forsooth," Dr. Wordsworth said, and blew her nose furiously. "At least it does begin with an *F*."

"You don't mean—you can't mean—Mr. Phair is Fernando?"

"Aren't you being a trifle slow? Fernando Propice: Forsyth Phair: F.P. both, and Propice does mean *fair* in English. And for him I went to jail. Is it so surprising that I tried to put the past behind me?"

"My dear," Ruth Eisenstein said slowly, "of course it is behind you. But it is not good to bury things. They will always erupt and in that way they may even destroy you. I hate to see you in pain, but I think that it may be a very good thing for you to come to terms with the past. It will always be part of you, and until it is acknowledged and put in its proper perspective it will always be able to hurt you."

Dr. Wordsworth lay still in her bunk, looking away from her friend.

Dr. Eisenstein put away her notebook and pen and got into bed.

Still looking away, Dr. Wordsworth said, "You may be right. Thank God he's going on to La Guaira. I'll be better when we get to Lago de los Dragones and your Quiztanos. Perhaps it will do me good to talk about the past. I know you want to help me. I'm very grateful."

"Nonsense." Dr. Eisenstein turned out her light. The curtains were drawn across the portholes and the room was dark and stuffy. That morning Geraldo had folded their blankets and put them on top of the wardrobe. Dr. Eisenstein thought of turning on the fan and decided it was not quite warm enough for her thin blood.

Through the darkness came Dr. Wordsworth's voice, back in control. "Thank God my father was English. My temperament is basically far more Anglo-Saxon than Latin."

Dr. Eisenstein barely stopped herself from laughing. "We have been colleagues for nearly twenty years and I have yet to find an Anglo-Saxon trait in you."

"You've always been deceived by looks. I meet a situation with reason. That is an Anglo-Saxon trait. The Latin crashes into everything with emotion."

"And that," said Dr. Eisenstein, "is a generality."

Jan ten Zwick, still in his white uniform, sat at his desk and finished tallying the day's accounts. His cabin was hot and the fan did little to cool it. His blood, unlike Dr. Eisenstein's, was not thin. And he was disturbed. He decided that he would go up on the boat deck, where Dr. Wordsworth walked laps, and that he would stand in the breeze for a few minutes before going to bed. He locked the drawer where he kept money and records, and left his cabin, crossing the foyer and walking down the port passageway so that he would pass the cabin with the Bolivar portrait.

As he went by, he put his hand against the handle, but the door, as usual, was locked, and the handle did not move to his touch. He had keys to all the cabins, but he did not go in. No use risking further unpleasantness.

—Umar, he thought. —Umar. Why should a Quiztano name be written on the back of the portrait? What else is written there? If that one board had not come loose as we were carrying the case into the cabin, I would never have seen that much. What possible reason could there be for a Quiztano name to be written on the back of a portrait of Bolivar that was given to an American? Umar. Umar. It is very strange. Perhaps I will talk about it to Mynheer Boon.

In his tiny cabin next to Poly's, Emmanuele Theotocopoulos prepared for the night. He read an act of *Romeo and Juliet*—an inept play!—then turned out the light. Within easy reach of his hand—and the cabin was so compact that anything he might need was in easy reach—was a worn music manuscript of Bach organ preludes and fugues. He knew them so well that it was unlikely that he would need to refer to the music. He lay on his back, his mane spread out on the pillow, and let the music fill the cabin. He heard it as he himself had played it during his many years as Cathedral organist; the small cabin grew and expanded until harmony and counterpoint overflowed the ship and spread out into the ocean. He felt relaxed and at peace. He looked forward with joy to Emily Gregory's first public concerts; he felt little anxiety; she was a superb musician, with the depth and power of suffering behind her technique, a musical wisdom far beyond her age. He looked forward to taking her to some of the great restaurants, to being proud of her.

The girl, Poly O'Keefe, just growing out of gawkiness, reminded him of his pupil, despite Emily's black hair and Poly's flame. But they were more or less of an age, moving into adulthood with a kind of steel-spring stubbornness and an otherworldly innocence almost as acute as that old-fashioned boy's, Simon's.

He was both surprised and annoyed to have the great strands of the fugue broken thus by thought: thoughts of the girl he was sailing across an ocean to hear; of the three children on the ship. He was, for no logical reason, worried about his three young traveling companions, and since Mr. Theo was both a Greek and a musician he payed attention to such illogical notions.

He sat up in his bunk. —I am too old to be bothered with children. And there is nothing wrong. They are all quite safe. Dr. O'Keefe is as loving a father as I've ever come across, and Mr. Phair treats young Simon as though he were a piece of Venetian glass. Phair: harrumph: there was something odd going on around that bridge table.

He pushed the unwelcome thoughts away, went back several phrases in the music to pick up the theme, lost it again. It was not only the niggling, irrational worry about the children, or a sense that there had been unexplained tension at the bridge table that was interfering with the music: it was the heat. He realized that they had moved into sultry weather and he was damp with perspiration. He had always disliked hot weather; why hadn't he had sense enough to get on a ship with air-conditioning? He hated air-conditioning, that's why.

The cabin was too small. Even with the door open, the drawn curtains kept out the breeze. The little fan did no more than recirculate warm air. He decided to go out on deck. Dr. Wordsworth was right; they were eating too much and exercising too little. He would make several laps around the deck. It would not be as good exercise as playing a great organ, but it would have to suffice.

Charles sat on his bunk, lotus position, and watched his father getting ready for bed. After Dr. O'Keefe had finished brushing his teeth, and would therefore be able to respond, Charles said, "Are you missing Mother?"

"Very much."

"Poly and I miss her, too."

"I know you do, Charles, but you're enjoying the trip, aren't you?"

"We're having a fabulous time. But you can have two very different feelings simultaneously. You miss her differently from Poly and me, don't you?"

"Yes." Dr. O'Keefe pulled on his pajama bottoms.

"And the kids—Poly and I miss them, but that's different, too."

"I suppose it is, Charles." Dr. O'Keefe turned on the fan over the washbasin.

"And I guess they miss us. But it's really a good kind of missing, because we know it's only for a month, and then we'll all be together again, and maybe we'll love each other more because of not having seen each other all that time."

Dr. O'Keefe stretched out on his bunk. "Maybe we'll appreciate each other more, but I doubt if I could love your mother or any of you kids more than I already do."

"But love always has to grow, doesn't it?"

"Yes, Charles. You're quite right." Dr. O'Keefe had an idea that his son was leading up to something, so he lay back and waited.

"When Aunt Leonis dies, what will happen to Simon?"

"I suppose his Cousin Forsyth would take care of him."

Charles was silent for so long that his father decided the conversation was over, without really having gone anywhere. But Charles said, "There's something wrong about Cousin Forsyth."

"Why do you say that?"

"I don't know. I just know it. The way I know things sometimes."

Dr. O'Keefe did not contradict his son. It was quite true that occasionally Charles knew something in a way not consistent with reasonable fact. It was odd, and it was disturbing, but there was no denying that it happened. "What do you want me to do, Charles?"

"I don't know. It's all vague and foggy. There's something wrong, and I don't know what it is. I wish we weren't getting off at Port of Dragons day after tomorrow and leaving Simon alone with Cousin Forsyth. I'm afraid, Daddy."

Dr. O'Keefe did not scoff. "It's not till day after tomorrow, and I'll keep a close eye on both Simon and his cousin in the meantime."

"Thank you, Daddy. If the worst comes to the worst, could we stay on the ship till La Guaira?"

"I doubt it, Charles. Let's hope there's no reason to."

"All right. I'm not sleepy. I think I'll go talk to Poly for a few minutes."

"Please don't worry her about this, Charles."

"I wasn't going to. But it's hot tonight."

When the boy had left the cabin, his father stared at the ceiling for some time, thinking. Charles's intuitions were too often right for comfort, and he found himself wishing, along with his son, that they were not leaving Simon with Cousin Forsyth when they docked at Port of Dragons. There was something unpleasant about Forsyth Phair, despite his rather Latin courteousness. That bridge game, for instance. It had seemed to Dr. O'Keefe that Phair was baiting old Smith, and enjoying his discomfiture. But why? It also seemed to Dr. O'Keefe that Phair had taken uncommon trouble to learn about his fellow passengers.

—I know that I am well known in my field, he thought, —but Phair knows more about my experiments with starfish than I would expect a layman to know. And I think he suspects that I am going to Dragonlake for more than my own personal interest in marine biology.

But Phair, he hoped, did not know that in one section of Dragonlake starfish were no longer able to regenerate when they lost an arm. Or that on shore there had been reports of death as a result of industrial effluents poured into the lake. Or that there were rich and ruthless industrialists who would resent interference.

He picked up an article on mercury poisoning and tried

to read, but he could not concentrate. Had he been foolish to bring Poly and Charles with him on this journey? Was he bringing them into danger? Had he, in his single-minded devotion to science, underestimated the greed and brutality of those to whom money and power are more important than human life?

He must warn Poly and Charles again not to mention that he was going to Dragonlake at the urgent request of Venezuela.

Mrs. Smith was preparing for bed, brushing her soft, sparse white hair. She took out her dentures and placed them carefully in a dish of water in which she had dropped a cleansing tablet.

Mr. Smith came through the curtains in the doorway.

Mrs. Smith, toothless, lisped, "Thay, Odell, where have you been?"

"Up on deck, having a cigar." He began to undress, folding his clothes carefully.

Mrs. Smith hurriedly cleaned her dentures and fitted them back in her mouth. When she spoke, her speech was clear but her voice was tremulous. "Odell, you made too much of it."

"Too much of what?" He folded down the top sheet and lay on his bunk, reaching for a paperback novel set in Costa Rica.

"Playing for a penny a point. It sounded as though—"

"As though what?"

"We lost last night. It sounded as though you didn't want to pay if you lost . . ."

His mouth set in a rigid line. His voice was tight. "I can't, Patty. Not even . . ."

She sat on the side of her bunk and looked at him across the narrow width of cabin. "Everybody thought it was strange."

"You mean Forsyth Phair thought it was strange."

"All right. But he did."

"I'm sorry, Patty, but I'm like an alcoholic. You know that. I cannot and I will not start gambling again."

"But you're cured. It's been over fifty years since—"

He looked at her over the book. "Patty, you know it cannot be cured. That you of all people should want to tempt me—"

Her soft lips trembled and quick tears rushed to her eyes,

which were magnified by heavy cataract lenses. "I'm sorry, Odell, I didn't mean—but I'd thought the past was over, that we could forget it—and one fear got the better of the other. If Mr. Phair should make the connection—"

Mr. Smith snapped, "I had been gone from the bank and back in the United States for ten years before Forsyth Phair came to work in Caracas. Everybody on the ship knows we are going to Costa Rica to visit our granddaughter and her family. It's a pleasure trip for us, and we've been looking forward to it for months. There's no reason anybody should think of Caracas in connection with me at all, or even know that we ever lived there. You're just imagining things. Mr. Phair will get off at La Guaira with his precious portrait of Bolivar, and we can forget it as though it was all a bad dream."

Mrs. Smith got into her bunk and picked up the baby's bootee, now almost finished. "Oh, Odell, I hope so. I hope so. You paid back every cent of the debt, you've had a good name all these years. Oh, Odell, why does it have to come back to hurt us all over again?"

Captain Pieter van Leyden was on the bridge, but ready to turn the helm over to Lyolf Boon. The sea was calm; he expected no difficult weather conditions, and the report for Port of Dragons was clear. The radar was void of disturbance. Not even a fishing boat marred its serenity.

Lyolf Boon looked at his captain; van Leyden's face was frequently stern; he ran a tight, albeit happy ship. Even though he permitted the guitar and flute and the sound of singing as long as the work was done, and well and promptly done, he seldom smiled or sang himself. At this moment he was frowning, not in an angry way, but as though he was worried about something; and he did not immediately hand the vessel over to his subordinate.

Boon checked the radar, found no cause in sea or sky for anxiety. He had learned early that it was not wise to ask questions of the Master of the *Orion*, so he continued to look at the ship's instruments, finally saying, "An interesting group of passengers this voyage."

"They are a pleasant change from our usual elderly types. I like the children. They are happy, not spoiled or noisy."

Boon agreed. "The girl isn't much now, but give her a few years and she'll have every sailor looking at her."

"A few years and a few pounds." The captain nodded. "Geraldo seems to find her already attractive. Perhaps we should have Jan speak to him—though I do not think Geraldo will overstep."

"Geraldo is a Latin." Boon grinned. "Latins always overstep."

Van Leyden turned away from wheel and instruments, paused at the doorsill, and moved back toward his second-in-command. "There is one passenger—"

Boon waited.

It seemed that van Leyden would leave without completing his sentence, but at last he said, "I will be glad when we reach La Guaira. Not that I have anything to fear personally, but I have met Mr. Forsyth Phair once before—though I think he did not have the same name. It was on my first voyage." He paused. He did not see the sudden look of surprise in Boon's eyes. "He made life extremely difficult for the Master of the ship."

There was another long silence, which Boon broke at last. "He does not seem unusually demanding. Quite the contrary."

Van Leyden shrugged. "On my first voyage—I was only a seaman but I had eyes and ears—Mr. Phair went to the authorities when we docked at La Guaira and made accusations about carelessness in accounting for cargo. In the end it was impossible to prove that my captain had tried to pocket money for oil-well machinery, but it was also impossible for him to prove that he had not. However, I knew my captain. He would never have been caught in any kind of petty thievery or smuggling. The matter was dropped, but my captain wrote out his resignation as Master of his ship, and I will never forget the look in his eyes as he said goodbye to us all in Amsterdam and we knew he would not be going to sea again."

Silence once more. The *Orion* slid quietly through the night.

Van Leyden went on, "The young man made a public apology. 'If I was mistaken in this matter I am truly sorry. But we all know that there is considerable dishonesty over cargo.' I did not feel that this was an adequate apology. I loved and honored my captain."

Boon asked, "How on earth did you recognize him after all these years, particularly if the name is not the same? Are you sure?"

"I would take my oath on it. One does not easily forget one's first voyage, especially such a voyage. The moustache is the same, and the nose and jaw, with that deep cleft. There is the same look to the eyes. The moment I saw him in Savannah, that first voyage of mine flashed before my eyes. I do not think I am mistaken."

"Only a few days more," Boon said, "and he will be gone. But why would he have a different name?"

"Many men find occasion when a change of name is helpful."

"True," Boon agreed. "I can think of one or two myself. Perhaps I should tell you a rather strange thing. Jan ten Zwick came to me just a few minutes ago with an odd story of a Quiztano name painted on the back of Mr. Phair's portrait of Bolivar—not just any Quiztano name, one of Jan's names. He seemed very concerned over this. I told him that it was probably no more than a coincidence, and asked him if he was absolutely certain of what he had seen. Apparently a board came loose on the crate as they were carrying it into the cabin, and he saw *Umar* written there. He said he went back later to verify this, and Mr. Phair came into the cabin and was extremely angry and disagreeable. I thought the whole business totally unimportant, but under the circumstances perhaps it is wise to mention it."

The captain sighed. "Are there still rumors that the Quiztano treasure is somewhere around the Lake of Dragons?"

"There are always rumors. The treasure of Dragonlake is in the lake itself: the oil. But that is not colorful enough for some imaginations. It had not occurred to me that Jan might be wondering about the treasure, but that is possible. He told me once that the Quiztanos are awaiting the return of some Englishman who fought with Bolivar, fell in love with a beautiful Quiztano girl, and disappeared. They've apparently learned nothing from the Aztecs. But I don't pay too much attention to his Quiztano fairy tales."

The captain turned to leave. His face moved in one of his rare smiles. "I am just as happy that we are not carrying an Englishman with us." He looked out to the horizon where sea met sky and no land was to be seen dividing water and air. "In any event, I will be glad when Mr. Phair leaves the ship at La Guaira and takes his portrait to Caracas. I would like to know how he got hold of such a portrait, and what he is being paid for it."

"I understand that he is giving it to the Bolivar Museum in Caracas."

"People like Mr. Phair do not give away valuable things for nothing."

Simon undressed and brushed his teeth and drank a glass of ice water from one of the two thermoses which Geraldo filled morning and night. Cousin Forsyth had not yet come to bed.

Simon knelt on his bunk and looked out his porthole into the warm dark of sea and sky. The ocean was calm, and he could see starlight reflected in the water. They would be at Port of Dragons too soon for comfort, and Poly and Charles would be leaving, and he was homesick for them in advance, which, in turn, made him homesick for Aunt Leonis, for his small cupboard of a room, for the wind stirring the Spanish moss in the live oaks, for old Boz, and for the dragon who was a vegetarian and ate only Spanish moss.

He sighed, pressing his cheek against the porthole frame, and looking out to the horizon where sky and water mingled. The light breeze was wet and salty.

He thought of being on the *Orion* without Poly and Charles and unaccountably shivered. —Am I moaning and groaning again? he asked himself, shook himself slightly, and then sang softly:

> *I met her in Venezuela*
> *With a basket on her head.*
> *If she loved others she did not say*

But I knew she'd do to pass away
To pass away the time in Venezuela,
To pass away the time in Venezuela.

His mother had sung that song to him. Aunt Leonis had given him back the song by singing it, too. At first he had not wanted to hear it, but she had said, "Don't put away the things that remind you of your mother because they hurt, Simon. It will hurt much worse later on if you try to wipe out such memories now."

I gave her a beautiful sash of blue,
A beautiful sash of blue,
Because I knew that she could do
With all the things I knew she knew
To pass away the time in Venezuela,
To pass away the time in Venezuela.

It still hurt, but it was a bearable pain, and it was, at this moment, more nostalgia than anything else; the song was Aunt Leonis's song even more than his mother's, because it was Aunt Leonis, long before Simon was born, who had taught it to his mother.

He lay down on his bunk on top of the sheet. Cousin Forsyth still did not come, and he felt that it would be discourteous to turn out the overhead light and let Cousin Forsyth fumble in the dark. It was hot. Almost as hot as in the summer at Pharaoh. A sadness surrounded him like the breeze, a sadness which had nothing to do with reason.

He thought of going to Poly's cabin and knocking and asking if he could come in and talk for a few minutes, but she had said she wanted to finish a book. Nevertheless, he stood up and pulled on his worn seersucker bathrobe. He left the cabin and went past the galley, through the foyer, and down the starboard passage. He paused at Poly's cabin; the door was open and he could see the light through the flowered curtains, but somehow he hesitated to go in uninvited. He went on, past Mr. Theo's cabin, out onto the back deck, and up the steps to the upper deck. Here he stood between the rail and one of the lifeboats. He remembered the captain's warning, and stepped back slightly, but the sea was calm and was moving with very little roll, and as long as he kept one hand lightly on the rail he would be perfectly safe.

The old song kept going around in his head.

> *When the moon was out to sea,*
> *The moon was out to sea,*
> *And she was taking leave of me*
> *I said, Cheer up, there'll always be*
> *Sailors ashore in Venezuela,*
> *Sailors ashore in Venezuela.*

The melody was minor and haunting and reminded him not of Venezuela, which he still had never seen, but of South Carolina. All those generations ago the land around Pharaoh reminded Quentin Phair of Venezuela, and perhaps Simon would feel a flash of recognition when he stepped on Venezuelan soil, but now he imagined only a small, comfortable shack protected by oak trees hung with moss.

He looked up into the sky and the stars were so close and warm he could almost feel their flame. The stars at home were clear, too, because they were not near any city lights.

He moved, within himself, back in time, as he and Aunt Leonis had so often done together. Now, standing on the *Orion*, on the way from one world to another, he remembered the first days after his mother's death—days he had not thought of since that first year. But his pre-breakfast conversation with Mr. Theo had for no explainable reason brought it all back. Neither Mr. Theo nor Aunt Leonis would want him to moan and groan, and he didn't intend to. But when a memory flickered at the corners of his mind he had learned that it was best to bring it out into the open; and rather than making him sorry for himself, it helped him to get rid of self-pity.

The time of his mother's dying had been a time of limbo; it was not until they left the cemetery that he realized completely that both his parents were dead and that he was starting an entirely new life with Aunt Leonis. After the numbness of shock had worn off, a strange irritation had set in; it was worse than moaning and groaning. The smallest trifle sent him into a rage. Soap slipped out of his fingers onto the floor. His socks wouldn't go on straight. Aunt Leonis overcooked the rice. He was furious with the soap, the sock, the rice, furious with Aunt Leonis.

She remained patient and unperturbed.

The humid South Carolina heat thickened and deepened, and although he was used to the heat and it had never bothered him before, now it added to his anger. 'There's no use going to bed. It's too hot. My head's as wet as though I've been swimming.'

Aunt Leonis looked at him quietly over her half-moon spectacles, then put down her knitting,—she was making him a sweater. 'Let's go for a walk. If there's any breeze around, we'll find it.'

But no breath of air was moving. The night shadows seemed a deepening of the heat. The stars were blurred. The Spanish moss hung limp and motionless from the trees. The old woman and the boy moved under the thick shade until they had left the trees and stood under the wet stars.

'Look at them.' Aunt Leonis pointed skyward. 'They're all suns, sun after sun, in galaxy after galaxy, beyond our seeing, beyond our wildest conceiving. Many thousands of those suns must have planets, and it's surely arrogant of us to think of our earth as being the only planet in creation with life on it. Look at the sky, Simon. It's riddled with creation. How does God keep track of it all?'

'Maybe he doesn't,' Simon had said.

'You're thinking, perhaps, that he didn't keep very good track of your mother and father.'

Simon made no answer.

Aunt Leonis continued to look up at the stars. 'I don't know about you, Simon, but I get very angry with God for not ordering things as I would like them ordered. And I'm very angry with your parents for dying young. It is extremely unfair to you.'

'They didn't do it on purpose,' Simon defended hotly. 'They didn't mean to die. They didn't want to die.'

He was so deep in the reliving of that evening that he did not sense the dark presence moving slowly toward him.

He heard only the old woman's voice. 'I am aware of that. But it doesn't keep me from being angry. Nor you. You've been angry all week, Simon, but you're taking it out on the wrong things. It's better to take it out on God. He can cope with all our angers. That's one thing my long span of chronology has taught me. If I take all my anger, if I take all my bitterness over the unfairness of this mortal life, and throw it all to God, he can take it all and transform it into love before he gives it back to me.'

Simon dug his hands into his pockets. 'If he has all of these galaxies and all of these stars and all of these planets, I wouldn't think he'd have much time left over for people.'

The dark figure moved slowly, silently, closer to Simon.

Unaware, Simon continued to look out to sea. He heard Aunt Leonis, her voice as clear in his memory's ear as though she were present.

'I somehow think he does. Because he isn't bound by time or quantity the way we are. I think that he does know what happens to people, and that he does care.'

'Why did he let my father and mother die, then?'

'We all die to this life, Simon, and in eternity *sooner* or *later* doesn't make much never mind.'

'I don't want you to die,' Simon said.

The dark figure was nearly on him. Hands were stretched out toward him. One quick push would be all that was needed. Simon was standing exactly where the captain had warned them not to stand.

From the shadow of the deck came another figure who

grabbed the arm of the first. The first figure jerked away and turned with incredible speed to streak down the steps and disappear into the shadows.

His pursuer, equally swift, leaped after him.

Simon had heard nothing. He reached across the ocean to the woman who had given him life as much as if she had borne him.

'I'm a very old woman, Simon, and in the nature of things I don't have a great deal longer to live. But I've already so far outlived normal life expectancy, and I'm so fascinated by the extraordinary behavior of the world around me and the more ordered behavior of the heavens above, that I don't dwell overmuch on death. And I'm still part of a simpler world than yours, a world in which it was easier to believe in God.'

'Why was it easier?'

'Despite Darwin and the later prophets of science, I grew up in a world in which my elders taught me that the planet earth was the chief purpose of the Creator, and that all the stars in the heavens were put there entirely for our benefit, and that humankind is God's only real interest in the universe. It didn't take as much imagination and courage then as it does now to believe that God has time to be present at a deathbed, to believe that human suffering does concern him, to believe that he loves every atom of his creation, no matter how insignificant.'

Simon leaned against the guardrail. He whispered, "O God, I wish I believed in you." So even at a distance the old woman's influence worked in him. He sighed deeply, at the same time that he felt strangely relaxed, as though Aunt Leonis had actually been with him there on the deck.

The breeze lifted, lightened, cooling him. He was ready to go back to the cabin. And he felt no need whatsoever for any more moaning and groaning.

Poly lay propped up on the pillows in her bunk. She liked the tidiness and snugness of her little cabin; it gave her a sense of protection and peace. She was finishing the last few pages of *Wuthering Heights* and it was good to be in a warm place while she was feeling the chill wildness of Emily Brontë's Yorkshire.

The O'Keefe rhythmic knock sounded on her doorframe.

"Come in, Charles," she called, and he pushed through the curtains. "Sit on the foot of the bed and wait a sec. I've just got two more pages."

Charles sat, lotus-like, at the foot of the bed, but his face held none of the tolerant merriness of a Buddha. When Poly closed the book with a long-drawn sigh, he said, "Pol, do you think Cousin Forsyth likes Simon?"

"He certainly overprotects him."

"But does he *like* him?"

Poly hesitated. Then she looked directly at her brother. "No. I don't think he does. Does Simon feel it? Has he said anything?"

"No. But Simon is not an idiot. If Cousin Forsyth doesn't like him, he's had lots more chance to sense it than we have."

"I don't think Cousin Forsyth likes children. Period. As a matter of fact, I think he's a xenophobe. But how could anybody not like Simon?"

"You like him because he likes you. Liking someone isn't a reasonable thing. It's a sense, like seeing and hearing and feeling."

Poly nodded. "Yah. Okay. Pheromones. But I still think Cousin Forsyth doesn't much like anybody. Now that you've brought it up, Charles, I've had the feeling since the first night that he wishes we weren't on the ship, taking Simon away from his watchful eye."

"You'd think he'd be grateful to us for getting Simon out of his way."

"He isn't."

"I know he isn't. What I want to know is why."

A timid knock came on the doorframe. Poly called out, "Who is it?"

"Simon."

"Oh, come in, come in."

Simon pushed through the curtains. "I saw your light

was still on and I heard you talking so I thought maybe you wouldn't mind if I came in."

"Of course we don't mind, Simon. Have some bed."

Simon perched on the edge of the bunk. "This is the first hot night, and it's not really hot. Not the way it gets in the summer at home."

"It was cold when we left Savannah," Poly said. "That must be why we feel it. Benne Seed Island gets hotter than this, too, and so did Gaea."

Charles asked, "Simon, is anything wrong?"

Simon looked down at his bare feet—Cousin Forsyth would not approve—and said, "Nothing wrong. I was just going back into the past."

Poly put her hand lightly on Simon's knee. "We're going to miss you when we get off the ship day after tomorrow."

"I don't even like to think about it," Simon said.

"Let's not, then. Let's just remember we have all day tomorrow to be together. Hey, Simon, do you like your Cousin Forsyth?"

Simon did not answer.

"I probably shouldn't have asked."

"Oh, that's okay. I didn't answer because I don't really know. He keeps telling me that I'm like a son to him, and how happy he is that we can be together. But I don't think of him as a father, or even an uncle-ly sort of person, and I don't think he really feels fatherly about me. So that's why I didn't answer. Aunt Leonis has never said that she feels like a mother to me, but I know she loves me. And I don't love her like a mother. I love her because she's Aunt Leonis. And I guess maybe I don't much like Cousin Forsyth. I feel that I ought to, but there's something—I don't know, but I don't think I like him. There."

Charles said, changing the subject in his own calm way, "Speaking of special dreams, I had one last night."

Simon turned and looked at him.

"It was a good one," Charles said reassuringly. "It was one of those brilliant pictures, with all the colors more alive than they ever are when we just see them with the awake eye. I think it must have been Dragonlake—I'm going to check it out with Dr. Eisenstein sometime. I was looking at a great, beautiful lake, with small grass-roofed cabins up on stilts out in the water, and a forest behind. And I saw a dugout canoe with two people in it. One was an Indian, a girl, with huge velvet eyes and delicate features and skin that lovely rosy-bronze color. The other was a young man, not an Indian. In fact, he looked very much like you, Simon, except that he had dark hair and he was grown up. When I woke up I thought, —That was Quentin Phair. It was a beautiful picture. Just one lovely flash and then I woke up."

"It couldn't have been Quentin Phair," Simon said.

"Why not?" Poly asked. "After all, he was in Venezuela for a long time. He could perfectly well have gone to Dragonlake at least once."

But Simon shook his head stubbornly.

"There is a theory," Charles said dreamily, "that somewhere in the universe every possibility is being played out."

"I'm not sure that's a comforting thought," Poly said.

At that moment there came a firm knock, and Dr. O'Keefe came through the curtains. "Here you are, Simon. Your Cousin Forsyth is worried about you."

"I'm sorry, Dr. O'Keefe. I was hot, and I went up on deck for a few minutes, and when I came down I saw that Poly had her light on—"

"That's quite all right, Simon, but maybe you should have told him."

"He wasn't in the cabin, sir, or I would have."

Dr. O'Keefe looked at his watch. "It's nearly midnight. Did you three know that?"

"Heavens, no, Daddy! Go to bed, Charles. Good night, Simon."

Charles untwined his legs. "I've been thrown out of better places than this. Come on, Simon."

Dr. O'Keefe and the two boys left. Poly lay back on her pillows for a few minutes, relaxing, thinking. Then she turned out the light.

Cousin Forsyth was holding out his pocket watch when Simon came into the cabin. The boy let the scolding slide off him, murmured courteous apologies, got into his bunk, and turned off the light. But somehow Cousin Forsyth had turned the evening sour.

Miss Leonis sat in front of the dying embers of the fire. Her hand dangled loosely. It should have been fondling Boz's ear, but she had buried Boz that afternoon, managing with extreme difficulty to dig a shallow hole. She could not lift the old dog to carry him to the grave; despite the gauntness of age he was still too heavy for her; so she dragged him, apologizing for the indignity, until she could push him into the waiting rectangle, barely big enough, and cover his ancient bones with the loose dirt.

Now she was exhausted. She had been too tired to eat. She was too tired to make the effort of taking off her clothes and preparing for bed. A thought fleetingly passed across her mind: —If Simon should need me I am free to go to him without worrying about finding someone to take care of old Boz.

She tried to shake the thought away, but it would not go.

Her empty hand reached for a letter of Quentin's which she had read earlier in the day:

"I am anguished, dearest Mama, at the plight of the poor and ill in this beleaguered country. And our wounded soldiers die of infection or exposure because there is no way to care for them. Manuela—and I do have an eye for beautiful women, Mama—is giving me jewels with which to buy ointments and bandages, but we must depend on generosity from the Continent and England for a great deal. Could you turn your kind heart to our predicament? You will know what we most need—quinine, of course, but you will know what else. And I have a flair for tending wounded men. Had I not been your youngest son I might have been a physician."

This was the Quentin Miss Leonis knew and loved and understood—even the reference to the unknown Manuela was, in this context, understandable; this was the Quentin she had taught Simon to revere.

And she had been wrong.

The next letter held cold comfort:

"Forgive me, dearest Mama, for the long delay in writing, and if my script is somewhat shaky. I have had an adventure which nearly proved fatal. Somewhat over a month ago I was out in the jungle hunting. I had strayed slightly from my companions, and suddenly I heard a horrid rattling and my horse bolted. He is a spirited but nervy creature and it was some time before I could calm him, and by then I was thoroughly lost. I tried to guide myself by shadows and sun, but evidently misjudged most woefully, and by nightfall I had to admit to myself that I was indeed in a plight. I will spare you details, but I survived in solitude and mounting distress for several days, eating roots and berries and drinking water from various streams. Whether from water, or from insect bites, I do not know, but I fell violently ill of an ague. The time came when I knew that I was dying, and I could do naught but welcome death, though I felt sore alone and near to weeping. Then in my delirium I felt that you were with me, your cool hand on my fevered brow. You held my head up and put water to my lips and I opened my eyes and looked into eyes of black flame instead of cool grey water like yours. Somehow or other I had been transported to a small round dwelling smelling sweetly of fresh grass and flowers. I learned when I was stronger that I had been found by a small party of hunters from the Quiztano village—found just in time."

The next letter contained detailed descriptions of the Quiztano village, and then Quentin wrote, "Oh, Mama, what a gift for caring the Quiztanos have in their hands. I was brought back from the very doors of death. Umara says that healing is the Gift of the tribe."

The letter which followed dealt impersonally with politics and battles and had only a parenthesis mentioning a few days spent resting with the Quiztanos because of a brief return of the fever. Then, "Oh, my mother, how I am torn. I never would have believed that my heart could thus be rent in twain. Manuela is ever dear to me, and her father, it seems, begins to look on me kindly; it would be an alliance most suitable and you and Papa would approve. And yet my little Quiztana is deep within my heart. We have a dream of making a place where the wounded can be brought and nursed by these gentle people who in no way deserve the name of savage."

And then, "Am I fickle by nature? I would never have believed so. I love Manuela not one whit less. I never believed it possible to love two people simultaneously, but I find that it is so. I adore my little Umara who brings healing in her small and beautiful hands."

Wearily Miss Leonis let the letters fall from her hand, but her tired mind kept worrying (like old Boz with a bone) over what she had learned. The Quiztano gift for healing was widely known throughout the peninsula. Indians of other tribes, and even some Creoles, brought their injured or desperately ill people to Dragonlake for healing.

The young Englishman was deeply impressed by this vocation, and promised, in his gratitude, to provide the Indians with money if any of them wished to be trained as physicians. This was a promise he was quite capable of fulfilling, for he received jewels not only from Manuela. As Bolivar's victorious forces moved triumphantly through the liberated towns and villages, the General and his officers were greeted not only with flowers, speeches, and songs of welcome, but with jewels, with gold; and Quentin Phair happily received his full share, that being the way of the world. As the liberation of the continent continued he amassed considerable treasure.

Manuela—whoever she was—became betrothed to a fellow officer, and Quentin's conscience was relieved. By now his infatuation with the Indian princess outweighed all else. It became his intention to leave his treasure with his—he called Umara his wife, but as far as Miss Leonis could gather they were not married, at least not in any way that would be considered binding in an English court.

Not long after this there was a bitter entry in his journal. "Why do I tend to idealize, and then get disenchanted? Idolize might be the better word for me to use against myself. It is not my Umara. She is still as lovely and as pure and as good as when I first was brought back to life by her tender hands. But I tried to believe that all the Quiztanos were like my Umara, that they were indeed the Noble Savage—and that is true of some of them, perhaps the majority, but of this I am no longer sure. Others—and Umara's favorite brother is one—have little patience with the gift of healing, and are deeply involved in smuggling—not that I blame them; they have no reason whatsoever to be loyal to Spain, and they have every reason to ignore Spanish prohibitions against foreign trade. So it is natural for them to be an important link in the chain of smuggling luxury goods which would be prohibitive otherwise. All this I understand. But they do have cause for some loyalty to those of us who have been risking life and limb to set their country free, and they appear to care about us no whit more than they love Spain. I begin to doubt if they will really accept me when I come back from England, but I see no alternative. I wonder if I could take Umara and the child and live in Caracas, perhaps?"

But Umara did not want to leave Dragonlake, and when Quentin left Venezuela for Kent he expected to return in a few months, and then to remain with the Quiztanos for the rest of his life. The bulk of his considerable accumulation of treasure would then be used for the education of his son, and though Quentin had decided, despite reservations, to cast in his lot with Umara's people, he planned an English education for his son, and the contradiction implicit in this either had not occurred to him or did not disturb him.

—I thought I knew that all people were a mixture of good and bad, even the best, but I did not expect quite this amount of complication, Miss Leonis thought. —Oh, Niniane, what was it like for you?

The discovery of the young Indian girl in Venezuela must have been a ghastly shock for the young bride in South Carolina, pregnant with her first child. Quentin had told her only that he had lived the typical life of a soldier of fortune, and that he was ready now to settle down and live like an ordinary citizen.

Niniane must have known that her husband's experience was as great as her own innocence, and he quickly made her sure and secure in his love. Few people in the pioneer South of those days would have thought twice about the rights of some South American Indian girl, even had they known about

Umara. Stories like Quentin's were casually accepted and soon forgotten, Miss Leonis thought bitterly, and he must have had no suspicion that the past would have any effect on the present. Pharaoh was built, and they were happy and their affairs prospered. If Umara had anything to do with Quentin's decision to free his slaves, he told no one. And if he had played free and easy with his loves in Venezuela, there was no indication in letters or journals that his love for Niniane was anything but faithful and true.

—And it was, wasn't it, Niniane? Miss Leonis asked. —It was. But fidelity built on broken promises has a shaky foundation.

One week when the mail was delivered, Quentin was in Charleston. Niniane sorted the mail, and was mildly curious when she came to an envelope addressed to Sra. Niniane St. Clair de Phair, an envelope mailed from Venezuela. It must be something to do with the portrait of Bolivar which he was having sent from Caracas.

So she opened the letter, suspecting nothing.

But the letter was from one of Umara's brothers and Niniane's safe world of home and husband was shattered.

With white face and cold hands and heart she learned of Umara and of Quentin's promise to return to Dragonlake. She learned that the Indian girl had died giving birth to a still-born child conceived just before he left Venezuela and his Quiztano wife and little son.

"This is to warn you," Umara's brother continued, "you who took Umara from the heart of her husband, that we will not forget and that we will be avenged. When your so-called husband sent for his portrait of Bolivar—a portrait which rightfully belongs to his son—we made our plans. Know that you are much hated. It was you who made Quentin Phair betray his wife. We will not kill him—that would be too easy, and small satisfaction to us. We understand that in your religion you are told that the sins of the fathers are visited on the children, even for seven generations. Beware. You will find to your sorrow that for you this will be true. This letter has been put into English by Sean O'Connell of the Irish regiment."

Miss Leonis could feel within her own body the storm of

sobs which racked Niniane. Her love for Quentin, and his for her, must have been real indeed, that it had survived such an opening of the past, and that it continued despite horrible proof that Umara's brother had meant his threat. Quentin's and Niniane's first-born son was thrown from his horse and died of a broken neck. He had been alone. There was no reason for anybody, other than Niniane and Quentin, to suspect anything other than accident. They must have lived in terror, and there was nobody with whom they could share their fears. Of their five sons, only the two youngest survived. If Quentin had thought, when he left Venezuela, that a small fortune in jewels would satisfy Umara and her brothers he learned that he was wrong. He had lived by the standards of another age, standards, Miss Leonis thought, still acceptable by far too many people today, and those standards became a boomerang for his undoing. He died of a heart attack before he was fifty. Niniane lived to be nearly ninety-nine.

They must have warned their surviving children, and surely the warning must have been passed from one generation of Phairs to the next. Perhaps at the time of the War between the States, fear of the revenge of the Quiztanos had faded in view of what was going on at home. And then it seemed to have been forgotten; perhaps those who were to carry the warning had been killed in battle. Certainly Miss Leonis's parents had not mentioned it, nor had there been any questioning when her only brother was killed while hunting, by a gun accidentally set off. And perhaps she was overreacting, imagining things in her senility.

No. There had been too many unexplained accidents; the family tree showed the untimely death of a young man in every generation.

She began to pray.

6. THE BOLIVAR PORTRAIT

T HE sun was brilliant and fierce the next morning. Charles was awake before his father, dressed, and went out into the passage, where he bumped into Poly, also up early and wearing her lightest cotton dress. She asked, "Where are you going?"

Charles sighed in his tired, adult manner, and Poly knew that he was concerned. "I'm going to talk to Dr. Eisenstein."

"Dr. Eisenstein!" she exclaimed. Then, "Oh, I see, to ask her about the Quiztanos."

He nodded.

She said, "Well, then, I think I'll go talk to Geraldo."

"What about Simon?"

"He's probably already up in the prow, pretending to be Quentin Phair. He really has a *thing* about that ancestor."

Charles paused at the door to the promenade deck. "He says that it's a Southern trait, particularly among the gentry, or whatever you call them, who don't have any money. After the Civil War they didn't have anything left except their family trees. And Quentin Phair sounds like a good person to live up to."

Now it was Poly's turn to look old for her age. A shadow moved across her face. "Nobody's that good."

They parted, Poly going to the galley, Charles to the deck, where he was pleased but not surprised to see Dr. Eisenstein in her usual deck chair under the canvas awning. She was writing busily in one of her notebooks, but looked up and smiled at him.

"It has been an unexpectedly pleasant part of this voyage to be with you three young ones, nicer for us than for you, I dare say."

"We've liked it very much," Charles said. "We're all used to being with grownups, and we enjoy lots of grownup conversation. May I ask you something?"

She closed her notebook, marking her place with her pen. "Fire ahead."

"The Quiztano village—is it the only one, or are there others?"

"There are, I believe, a few scattered groups in the jungle related to the Quiztanos, but the tribe keeps to the settlement at the lake."

"Are their houses sort of airy grass huts built upon stilts right out into the lake? Do you have any pictures, maybe?"

Dr. Eisenstein reached into her straw carry-all and pulled out a *National Geographic* which opened automatically to a double-spread color photograph.

Charles studied it carefully. It showed a sizable greensward on which were two long screened houses raised slightly from the ground, and a few small round huts on higher stilts. Behind these the darker green of jungle and the shadow of mountain pressed closely. The greater part of the village stretched out into the lake, and consisted of round, airy straw houses with peaked roofs and movable straw screens like those in the long houses. The huts stood stork-like on long thin legs: under most of them, small dugout canoes were tethered. Charles studied it and nodded. "Yes. That's it."

Dr. Eisenstein looked at him questioningly.

But Charles gave no explanation. "There's the breakfast bell. I'm hungry. Aren't you?"

Everybody came to the dining room in summer cottons. The heat seemed to put a damper on conversation. Simon helped himself to cheese and herring and decided that right after breakfast he'd go out to the Dragon's Lair and snooze. If it hadn't been for Cousin Forsyth he'd have slept through breakfast, but Cousin Forsyth was a regular riser and made it clear that he expected Simon to be, too.

But his feeling of heaviness was not only because he was sleepy. After the O'Keefes debarked, would Geraldo talk with him as he did with Poly? Or would Simon feel lost and isolated? He felt lonely and unsure.

Mr. Theo pulled him from his thoughts, speaking softly, only to the boy. "Tell me, young Simon. Would you like to go to a concert with me in Caracas?"

"Oh, sir! That would be marvelous."

At the other table Poly yawned and turned away from one of Dr. Wordsworth's dissertations, this time on the virtues of the Spanish language, and tuned her ear to the officers' table, trying to see how much Dutch she could understand. The men spoke rapidly, so that sometimes she could barely get the gist of the conversation; occasionally she was able to understand entire phrases, and this always pleased her.

Geraldo brought in a platter of ham and eggs.

"Port of Dragons tomorrow," Dr. Eisenstein said. "Hard to believe the days have gone by so quickly. But I feel rested and ready for work. You, too, debark tomorrow, don't you, Dr. O'Keefe?"

"Yes, we do."

Mr. Phair turned in his chair so that he could speak to the other table. "Simon will miss Poly and Charles, will you not, Simon?"

Simon speared a piece of herring. "Yes."

Poly tried to catch Simon's eye, but he continued to look at his plate. She said, "We'll see each other when we get back. That's a promise."

Mr. Phair said, "That is a pleasant thought, Miss Poly, although shipboard romances seldom continue once the voyage is over."

Simon raised his left eyebrow but continued to concentrate on his breakfast.

Charles was firm. "Our friendship will. Simon is our friend forever."

Mr. Phair looked at the Smiths, sitting side by side, eating toast and cheese. "When Simon and I—and Mr. Theotocopoulos, too—debark at La Guaira, Mr. and Mrs. Smith will be the only passengers."

—He'd never deign to call anybody by a nickname, Poly thought. —I'm glad he doesn't know my name is Polyhymnia.

Then a phrase from the officers' table caught her attention.

Lyolf Boon was speaking. ". . . a strange tale brought me by Jan, who had it from Geraldo." She missed the next words, then was sure she understood ". . . tried to push Simon over-board. Jan said that Geraldo swears he was not mistaken. He grabbed the man . . ."

Dr. Eisenstein's voice covered the next words. ". . . and thanks to Inés's perfect Spanish I expect to have fewer problems than if I were traveling alone."

Poly scowled in her effort to hear Boon.

". . . a man in winter uniform, but he slipped out of Geral-do's grasp and disappeared into the ship before the lad could see who it was."

"The Quiztano language is extremely difficult, as . . ."

Poly leaned toward the captain's table.

". . . my winter uniform is missing. That would seem to support Geraldo's tale."

Poly felt a cold chill run up and down her spine. She began to spread jam on a roll in order to conceal her shudder.

She had not heard enough.

She *had* heard enough.

Captain Pieter van Leyden said, "But this is incredible."

Boon said, "That girl is listening."

The captain looked over at the next table, but Poly was talking with Dr. Eisenstein about the Quiztano vowels. Nevertheless, he spoke in a low voice. "If Jan gives it credence I cannot dismiss it offhand. And if your winter uniform has disappeared—when did you notice this?"

"Not until after Jan had come to me. I had no reason to think about it before. Then, since Geraldo had said the man who attempted to push the boy overboard was wearing a winter uniform, I automatically checked my own, partly to prove that the whole thing was a wild tale. If you will remember, it is the second time in a few hours that Jan has come to me with great worry."

Berend Ruimtje, the second officer, was thoughtful. "Jan may look more Dutch than we, but he is part Quiztano. All Quiztanos are superstitious."

Olaf Koster, the engineer, asked, "How does superstition come into this? Geraldo told Jan that the man's arms were outstretched, ready to push, and if he had not been there the boy surely would have gone overboard. A pity Geraldo couldn't identify the man."

The captain spoke slowly and thoughtfully. "Just in case there is a grain of truth in this—which I doubt—we will keep a careful watch on the boy until he debarks at La Guaira. And I would like to see Jan and Geraldo at nine-thirty, sharp."

Immediately after breakfast Charles sought out Jan and firmly closed the door to the compact office/bedroom. The steward was at his desk, typing out the next day's menus. He had a worried look and the furrows between his eyes were deep. Charles began without preamble. "One time when I was talking to Dr. Eisenstein she said something about the Quiztanos expecting a young white man to come to them from over the sea. I didn't think much about it then, but now . . ."

Jan looked at his watch. It was barely nine. "It is a folk story. Why does such ancient folklore interest you?"

"I'm interested in old stories, and in different kinds of peoples. Poly and I told you about our friends, the Gaeans. Lots of people thought they were primitive, too. But—" He paused, appeared to move into a brown study. Jan looked at him expectantly. Finally Charles continued. "I dreamed about it."

"It?"

"The Quiztano village at Dragonlake. I dreamed I was there. I saw a picture of Dr. Eisenstein's this morning, and it's exactly the way it was in my dream. And I've been dreaming about Quentin Phair. Do you know about him? He's Simon's ancestor who was given the Bolivar portrait. I'm sure it's Quentin because he looks like Simon, only older, and with dark brown hair. Maybe it's just because Simon talks so much about his ancestor, and because Poly and I were reading about the Aztecs last year . . ."

Jan asked, "But you think it's more than that?"

Charles looked questioningly at Jan. "These dreams—they aren't regular dreams. They seem to break through barriers of—"

Jan was listening intently.

Charles sighed. "Barriers of time and space. It's as though

a window opened and I could see through, see things people don't ordinarily see."

"I am a quarter Quiztano," Jan said. "Dreams are to be taken seriously. What have you dreamed about Simon's ancestor?"

"I thought I saw him in the Quiztano village. He was dressed the way people used to dress in olden days—velvet and silk and lots more color than nowadays. He was saying goodbye, and all the village had turned out to wish him Godspeed. He was going across the ocean to England, and he stood next to the young Quiztano woman I saw him with in another dream. He promised, in front of everybody, that he would return. Then the dream faded." Charles stopped.

Jan picked up a paper knife and looked at it intently. He said, "We are speaking in private?"

Charles indicated the closed door.

"What we say will not leave this cabin?"

"I promise."

"You are still only a child—but it did happen as in your dream. The Quiztanos are still waiting. When I first came to Venezuela from Holland I made my first pilgrimage to the Quiztano village at Dragonlake, to see my grandfather, and to try to understand that part of me which is not Dutch. Umar Xanai—my grandfather—came to meet me. And so did the Old One."

"The Old One?"

"The Umara."

"Umara?"

With much questioning, Charles learned that the Umara presides over the religious ritual of the Quiztanos. She is trained from birth to hold the Memory of the Tribe, and this Memory, Jan emphasized, is the chief treasure of the tribe—"the Memory and the Gift."

"Greater than the jewels and things Dr. Wordsworth told Dr. Eisenstein about?"

"Without a memory a race has no future. This is what my grandfather told me."

On the day when Jan went first to the Quiztano village, the Umara had come with Umar Xanai to greet him. She was older than anyone Jan had ever seen before. She was so old that it was said that she had spoken to Bolivar himself, although Umar Xanai made it clear that the chronological age of the Umara was not important; it was the extent of her memory which gave the ancient woman her authority.

She had walked slowly to Jan, helped and supported on either side by two young women, one of whom was being trained by her in the Memory, to be the future Umara. When she was close to Jan she stared at him in silence for a long time. Then she shook her head. 'He is not the One. He is not the Fair.'

"So they are still waiting," Jan told Charles. "Whenever a young white man comes to the village the Umara is brought out to see if he is the one."

"Will this happen to me when we go there—if we're allowed to go?"

"She'll come and look at you—the Umara."

"Umara," Charles said. "That's both a name and an office?"

"Yes."

"She's a princess?"

"We do not call it that. You might. You might also say priestess, though that would not be accurate, either. As I told you, the Umara is the Keeper of the Memory of the Tribe, and of the Gift."

"Do you mean treasure?"

Jan shook his head scornfully. "No, no, what treasure there was is long gone. The gift for healing. People from other tribes bring their ill to us, and the people from the barrio, and even people who could afford doctors but who value our gift."

"Do all the Quiztanos have it?"

"Only a handful in each generation. But we watch for it, and when we see it, we help it to blossom."

"We—" Charles mused. "You sound as though you think of yourself as Quiztano."

"When I am in Holland I am as Dutch as anyone. But as we draw near to Venezuela I begin to think Quiztano."

"Can you tell me anything more about the Englishman and the Umara?"

"They had a child, as is the way with such things. When

the boy was still very young, the Fair—for that is what the Englishman was called—sailed for England and promised to return. After he left, the Umara learned that she was to have another child. And there was not a word from the Fair, not a word. She knew he would not return and she died, and the babe with her. And then—my grandfather tells me—the next Umara saw a vision and she said that the Englishman *would* return, and she is still waiting for him. She is very old—we do not even know how old—and very wise, and she says that she will not die until the Fair returns."

Charles looked unhappy. "Is there anything more?"

Jan spread out his hands and stretched his fingers apart. "It is all history, and my grandfather and the Umara are very old and sometimes they get confused and their stories are not always the same. After the Fair did not return and the Umara died—young, young, for the Umaras usually live to be very old—there was talk of revenge, undying revenge, unless the Fair should return. From his son—the one who was a little boy when he left, remember—there have been many descendants. Some have had the Gift, and some have not, and some have left the tribe, strong with other blood. The Umara—she has dreams, too, Charles, dreams like yours. And she says that there is still anger and hate and lust for revenge, and it will not stop until the return of the Fair."

There was a long silence. Jan looked at his watch. Ten more minutes before it was time to go to the captain.

Then Charles asked, "Jan—my dreams—the Umara's—do you think Simon could be the One?"

The morning sun blazed as brilliantly in Pharaoh as on the *Orion*. Miss Leonis moved slowly and sadly through her morning ritual. The kettle did not gleam as brightly as usual. The flowers did not fill the air with their scent. There was an emptiness to the world.

—And all because of one old hound dog, she thought.

She walked the mile to the mailbox slowly. It was not her habit to collect the mail daily, because there was little mail. Simon's Renier relatives wrote him regularly, newsy but undemanding letters. But she had apprised them of Simon's trip to Caracas. The box would undoubtedly be empty. But the walk would mitigate her loneliness.

Usually Boz walked with her. In his youth he had circled about her happily; in his old age he had creaked arthritically along beside her. She could almost feel his presence. She opened the mailbox absently and pulled out a white envelope without realizing that she had expected no mail. Then she came back into herself and looked at the envelope in surprise. It was from her bank, the bank where she had been known all her life, although for most of that life she had had little or no money in it. Whenever she sold a piece of silver or a bit of jewelry, she had deposited the money. The check Forsyth Phair had given her was one of the largest deposits she had ever made.

She opened the letter from the bank. The check, they informed her regretfully, was not good.

She reached out to steady herself on the mailbox. Forsyth Phair's check dishonored? It had—she searched for the phrase—it had *bounced*.

There must be some mistake.

But her heart told her with dull certainty that there was no mistake.

And she had allowed Simon to go off with this—this scoundrel.

Instead of going to her cabin or out on deck after breakfast, Poly sat at the foot of Charles's unmade bunk. Geraldo usually did the cabins fore to aft, and would come to her father's and Charles's cabin before he came to hers. Even if she could not speak to him in front of anybody, she could give him some kind of signal that it was imperative that she talk with him alone, at once.

Charles was not in the cabin, but her father was sitting in the chair and adding to the journal which he expected to send home to Benne Seed Island as soon as they got to Port of Dragons and a post office. Without looking up he asked, "What's wrong?"

"I am in a high state of perturbation."

"That's obvious. What about?"

"If I knew, I mightn't be so perturbed. I don't have intuitions and intimations and revelations like Charles, but I do have sharp eyes and ears, and there's something wrong on this ship."

"What's wrong, Poly?"

"Mr. Smith is afraid of Mr. Phair. Dr. Wordsworth can't stand him. Charles and I don't think he likes Simon. But it's more than that. Do you think the fork lift going after Simon was an accident?"

Dr. O'Keefe spoke in his most reasonable voice. "Why wouldn't it have been an accident?"

"Fork lifts aren't likely to go out of control."

"It is quite possible for an accelerator to jam."

"I suppose so. But I'm worried about Simon."

Dr. O'Keefe sighed. "I was glad to find that Simon was on the *Orion* and that you and Charles would have a young companion, but I think that possibly all three of you are letting your imaginations run riot."

"Charles doesn't imagine things." At that moment Poly decided not to tell her father the fragments of conversation she had overheard until she talked with Geraldo himself. "You know that, Daddy. And what about the portrait? Mr. Phair treats it as though it were far more valuable than I'd think any portrait could be, even a great portrait of Bolivar. He goes in to check it at least three times a day, as though anybody could move it with all that heavy wooden packing case around it."

Dr. O'Keefe smiled. "You do sound in a high state of perturbation, Pol."

"Well, I am. The ship has been marvelous. I've loved every minute of it. But I keep having this funny feeling about getting off at Port of Dragons tomorrow. I'm sorry I'm showing my perturbation so visibly. I'll get along to my cabin now. I was sort of waiting for Geraldo."

"Oh?"

"I need to talk to him. And then maybe I'll need to talk to you." Without further explanation she departed, leaving her father to think that he was glad she would not be on the ship much longer.

When she pushed through the curtains to her cabin, Geraldo was already there. Her bed was made, and the cabin cleaned, and he was just standing there.

He said, "I've been waiting for you. There is something I have to talk about."

After breakfast Simon followed Mr. Theo into the salon. The old man had a music manuscript spread out on one of the tables. He looked up, his attention quickly focusing on Simon.

"Mr. Theo," Simon asked, "do you believe in dreams?"

"Believe, how? That they can predict the future?"

"Not so much the future. The past. I don't mean that they *predict* the past, but that they can pick things up, things that have happened a little while ago, and even a long time ago."

Mr. Theo asked with interest, "What have you been dreaming?"

"I haven't. Charles has."

Mr. Theo raised his bushy brows in question.

"He dreamed that he went to Pharaoh, and he described things I'm sure I never told him, like the dented copper kettle and the way Aunt Leonis talks to it. And then he dreamed about Dragonlake, and he said that he checked it with Dr. Eisenstein and she showed him a picture that was exactly like what he dreamed. What do you think, Mr. Theo?"

The old man threw back his mane. "Charles is not, in my opinion, a romanticizer. I take dreams seriously, young Simon, possibly because in my dreams I am always young and I play the organ as Bach might have played it."

"Is that dreaming about the past?"

"Not in the way you're implying Charles dreams. That sounds to me more like the ripples you see spreading out and out when you throw a pebble in a pond, or the way sound waves continue in much the same fashion. So it seems quite likely to me that there are other similar waves. Strong emotion,

I would guess, either very good or very bad, would leave an impression on the air. And what about radio?"

"That picks up sound."

"And television?"

"Sight."

"And a good radio or television set will give you brilliant sound or a clear picture, and a bad set will be fuzzy and full of static."

Simon pondered this. "You mean, Charles may be like a very, very good set, and in his dreams he picks up things?"

"I don't discount the possibility."

"Okay, then," Simon said. "Neither do I. I'm sleepy this morning. Charles and Poly and I talked till midnight. I think I'll go have a nap."

He left Mr. Theo and went out into the heat of the sun, stretched out in the shadow of a large crate, and went to sleep. He was deep in slumber when he felt a hand on his shoulder, and somebody shaking him. He rolled over and saw Poly, not with Charles, but with Geraldo.

"Wake up, Simon," she said. "Geraldo and I have to talk to you."

The intensity in her voice woke him completely and he sat up.

Geraldo, too, looked solemn and anxious.

"Simon," Poly said, "while you were up on the boat deck last night, did anything happen?"

"Happen? No. Why?"

"Nothing? Are you sure?"

"Yes. I was feeling homesick, and I went up and daydreamed about Aunt Leonis."

"Were you very deep in your daydream?"

"I guess I was. She was almost as real as though we were talking face to face."

"Did you know that Geraldo was up on deck, too?"

"No."

"Well, he was, and he saw a man come toward you, very softly, so you mightn't have heard if you were concentrating. Geraldo said the man crept toward you, and then he put out his arms and he was going to push you overboard; you were standing right between the lifeboat and the rail, weren't you? right where the captain told us not to?"

"Yes, but I had my hand on the rail and the ship wasn't rolling. I was perfectly safe."

"You were right where someone could give you one shove and send you overboard."

"Who would want to do that?"

"I wish I knew," Poly said. "You really didn't hear anything?"

"No. I told you. Who was the man, then?"

"Geraldo saw only his back. He had on a uniform hat, so he couldn't even see his hair. Geraldo ran across the deck and grabbed his arm, and the man was slippery as an eel and ran down to the promenade deck and into the ship and vanished."

"That doesn't make sense. Nobody would want to push me overboard. Geraldo, are you sure you didn't dream it?"

"Geraldo knows the difference between being awake and asleep," Polly said indignantly.

"Then why didn't I notice anything?"

"You do go awfully deep into your dreams, Simon. Both Charles and I have noticed that."

"They're not proper daydreams unless you go deep."

"So you might not have noticed, if you were in the middle of an important part."

"That's true," Simon acknowledged. "But I don't like it. It scares me."

"Simon, do you think maybe the fork lift wasn't an accident?"

Simon put his hands over his ears in an instinctive gesture of rejection. "Stop! Don't talk like that!"

Poly's voice was low and intense. "But if somebody's trying to kill you—"

"No! Why would anybody want to kill me? There's no reason! I'm not important—no, Poly, no!"

Geraldo spoke. "The portrait of Bolivar—Jan told me he saw *Umar* painted on the back."

Simon scrambled to his feet, lifted his arms heavenward, and then flung them down to his sides. "What I think we should do is go and look at the portrait and see exactly what is written on the back, even if we have to get a hammer and chisel to take the crate apart."

"That's a good idea," Poly said, "but do you have a key to that cabin?"

"No."

"I have all the keys," Geraldo reminded them.

"Good." Simon nodded. Now that he had made a decision to act he was brusque and business-like. "Let's go, then."

They went quickly to the galley. Geraldo opened the small cupboard where he kept the keys, each on its own labeled peg. He lifted his hand to the pegs in bewilderment: the key to cabin 5, the cabin with the portrait, was not in its place. "The key—it is gone."

"But who would take it?" Simon asked. "Cousin Forsyth has his own key—"

"Come," Geraldo cried, and ran down the port passage, Simon and Poly at his heels. The passage was empty. Geraldo tried the door handle. It moved under the pressure of his hand. "It is open."

"But it's always locked—" Simon said.

"Like Bluebeard's closet—" Poly started, then closed her mouth as Geraldo opened the door wide.

They looked into the cabin, and then at each other, in utter consternation.

On the floor of the cabin lay the boards from the face of the case, tidily stacked. The back of the case was still in one piece. It was empty.

"The portrait!" Simon croaked incredulously. "It's gone!" He looked wildly about the cabin for the great gold frame, for the familiar face of the General, dark and stern and noble.

For a moment they hovered on the threshold. As Simon started in to look for the portrait, Poly stopped him. "Don't touch anything. There may be fingerprints. Let's go tell Daddy, quickly."

They ran back up the passage, stopped short at the galley.

Jan was hanging the key to cabin 5 on its peg.

"Where did you get the key?" Poly demanded.

Jan turned around, looking surprised. "Mynheer Boon

found it in the salon. He said Mr. Phair had left it lying on his crossword puzzle."

"But this isn't his key, it's Geraldo's."

"I know," Jan said, still looking surprised. "I saw Mr. Phair and he told me he had his key. So I came and looked on the board and saw that the key was missing. What is wrong?"

Poly said swiftly, "Later, Jan, I have to talk to Daddy."

Jan stood by the keyboard, looking after them in puzzlement as they raced through the foyer and down the starboard passage. "Geraldo, I need you to set up for lunch," he called, but Geraldo had disappeared.

7. THE HEARSE

D R. O'Keefe and Charles hurried to the cabin and stood on the threshold, silently looking at the empty packing case.

Dr. O'Keefe said, "You were quite right not to touch anything. We must tell Mr. Phair at once."

He strode along the passage, the others hurrying behind him, to Mr. Phair's cabin. It was empty. "We'll try the salon."

Mr. Theo smiled at them as they came in. He touched his music manuscript. "It's quite warm in here this morning, but I'm afraid that these loose pages might blow overboard."

"Best not to run the risk," Dr. O'Keefe agreed. "Seen Mr. Phair?"

"No. But he's seldom sociable in the morning." Mr. Theo turned back to his music.

"The promenade deck, then," Dr. O'Keefe said. As they left the salon they met Mynheer Boon in the foyer. Dr. O'Keefe asked him, "Have you seen Mr. Phair recently?"

"Not since breakfast."

"But you found the key to the portrait cabin on his cross-word puzzle," Poly said.

"What are you talking about, Miss Poly? I found no key."

Poly looked at Simon and Geraldo in consternation.

"Come," Dr. O'Keefe said, and led them to the promenade deck. "Seen Mr. Phair anywhere around?" he asked casually of the Smiths, who were sunning in deck chairs.

"Not since breakfast," Mr. Smith said. "How 'bout you, Patty?"

"I haven't seen him since breakfast, either. Maybe he's checking on his portrait."

"Quite possibly," Dr. O'Keefe said dryly, and turned to climb the steps to the boat deck, where Dr. Wordsworth and Dr. Eisenstein were briskly taking their morning constitutional. In a calm, unemphatic voice he asked, "We're wondering if you've seen Mr. Phair?"

Hardly interrupting their stride, the two professors assured him that they had not.

Dr. O'Keefe said, "We've tried all the likely places. I'd better go to the captain and tell him about the portrait. Wait for me in the cabin."

"I have work to do, please, sir," Geraldo said. "It is time for me to set up for lunch. Jan will need me."

"I would prefer you to stay with my children and Simon, Geraldo. Jan can do without you for once. I'll explain to him."

"Please, Daddy," Poly asked, "do we have to wait in the cabin? It's so terribly hot. Couldn't we wait for you in the Dragon's Lair? We can stay in the shade and we'll get the breeze."

It was indeed hot. Dr. O'Keefe wiped the back of his hand across his brow. "All right. But go there directly and immediately. And do not leave until I come for you. I want to know exactly where you are."

—He's worried, Poly thought, —more worried than he wants us to know.

"Sir," Simon asked, "who would steal the portrait?"

"And on a small ship," Poly said, "with no place to hide it—and it's a big portrait. It's absolutely mad, isn't it, Daddy?"

"It's very strange. Please go to the Dragon's Lair now and wait for me."

Simon looked white and strained. As they started down the stairs to the lower deck he said, "I'm afraid."

Geraldo spoke reassuringly. "We are with you, and we will not leave you. We know that you love the portrait of Bolivar, that you love it much more than Mr. Phair does."

Poly took Simon's ice-cold hand. "Daddy'll get it back, Simon. After all, it's got to be on the ship." Her grip was firm. "I wish you didn't have to sleep in the cabin with Cousin Forsyth, but I don't think anybody can hurt you there, unless . . ."

"What?"

"You don't think Cousin Forsyth—you don't think he had anything to do with the fork lift?"

"It was an accident. Anyhow, wasn't he on the *Orion* taking care of the portrait?"

"Or last night?" Poly continued.

Charles said, "If only we could begin to guess who the man was."

Geraldo frowned. "It is more difficult because there are many men on the ship who might have been on the boat deck, from your father and the captain to Mynheer Boon and Olaf Koster. If he had been heavy, like Berend Ruimtje, or very short, like the radio officer, or a string bean like the cook . . . I keep trying to recall exactly what he looked like, and all I can see is a shadowy form in a dark winter uniform who might have been one of many people. The only thing which has come to my mind—and about this I am only guessing—is that he was slow in his movements until I caught his arm, and then he moved like lightning. The slowness makes me think that perhaps he was reluctant, that perhaps he was glad to be caught. But this is only a guess."

Simon's heart was pounding with panic. He tripped over the high sill.

"Careful," Poly warned, leading him through the blazing sunlight, strong and life-giving. The breeze kept the heat from being oppressive, and the beauty of the day gave her a sense of reassurance. There had to be some kind of rational explanation for all the irrational events of the last few days.

They walked silently around kegs and boxes, around the station wagon, approached the hearse with the bullet hole in the windshield. Suddenly Poly stopped.

"What's the matter?" Simon asked nervously.

"The hearse—" she whispered. "The doors are open—in the back—look. They've never been open before."

No. The hearse had always been sealed tight as a tomb. But now the double back doors were slightly ajar.

"Geraldo—" Poly whispered. Her hand was as cold as Simon's, and she clutched to get comfort as much as to give it.

Geraldo, followed by Charles, went up to the hearse and opened the doors wide.

Walking slowly, pulling back, but somehow managing to go forward, Poly and Simon followed them. The sunlight was so brilliant that it was difficult to see into the shadows within the hearse.

"Simon—" Poly whispered. It seemed that her voice had vanished.

There was something—someone—in the hearse.

Something—someone—lying there.

Cousin Forsyth.

8. MURDER

FOR Simon the next minutes were a haze of terror.

Poly pulled him roughly away. "We have to get Daddy—"

"Why is he in the hearse?" Simon asked stupidly. "What is Cousin Forsyth doing in the hearse?"

Charles said, "Cousin Forsyth is dead, Simon. There's a dagger in his chest."

Chronology got all upset. Simon could not remember in which order things happened. Geraldo, trained to obey orders, reminded them that Dr. O'Keefe had told them to stay in the prow of the ship.

"But he doesn't know!" Poly cried. "He doesn't know about Cousin Forsyth! We have to tell him!"

Simon was not sure how he and Poly and Charles got to the O'Keefes' double cabin, who had gone for Dr. O'Keefe, where he had been found. Had he brought them to the cabin? Certainly he had told them to stay there until he came for them. They were to lock the door from the inside, and under no circumstances to open it to anybody else.

"It's sort of locking the stable door after the horse has gone," Poly said.

Charles sat cross-legged on his bunk. "Is it? There's a murderer at large on this ship. Someone has already tried twice to kill Simon."

"But I thought it was Cousin Forsyth!" Poly exclaimed. "I thought he wanted Simon out of the way."

"Somebody obviously wanted Cousin Forsyth out of the way." Charles looked at Simon, who was sitting, still and upright, in the small chair.

They all stiffened as they heard a key turn in the lock. They did not know who had access to the key to the cabin besides Dr. O'Keefe and the two stewards. And although they trusted Jan, either the chief steward or the first officer was lying about the key. Simon realized that everybody on the *Orion* was under suspicion, even those he thought of as incorruptible and his friends.

Dr. O'Keefe came in, his face markedly pale under his tan; even the red of his hair seemed more muted by grey than usual.

"Daddy!" Poly jumped up. "Please, please send for Canon Tallis!"

He replied, "I have thought about it, Poly. But I'm not sure that it's fair to ask Tom to come running whenever anything difficult happens."

"But, Daddy, this isn't just something difficult. This is murder. And Simon is in danger."

"Poly, we'll have to wait."

"But you'll go on thinking about sending for him?"

"I'll think about it, Poly, but I doubt if I'll do more than that. Now. The captain wants us all in the salon."

"Just us?"

"All the passengers, plus Jan and Geraldo."

"Jan and Geraldo haven't done anything wrong!"

"I doubt if they have, though Jan's story about the key is not very convincing. In any case, we must all be questioned. The captain will speak to the crew and officers separately. Jan and Geraldo are the ones in closest contact with the passengers. Simon—" Dr. O'Keefe held out his hand.

Simon put his hand into Dr. O'Keefe's.

The passengers were all sitting in the salon much as they had been when Simon, Poly, and Charles were first introduced to them. Dr. Wordsworth was presiding over the teapot; it seemed that disasters produced tea parties. But on that first day it had been cold, with steam noisily pushing through the radiators. Now it was hot. And Cousin Forsyth was not there.

It was stifling. The fans did not seem to stir the air.

Geraldo stood by the door nearest his galley; the tidy arrangements of cups and saucers, cream pitchers, tea- and coffeepots seemed to give him a sense of order and reassurance. Jan ten Zwick stood at the fore windows, his hands clasped tightly behind his back, which was turned to the passengers.

Charles sat on the sofa beside his father.

Simon and Poly stood.

The captain sat, looking somberly at his passengers. Mr. Theo, the Smiths, the two professors looked at him questioningly.

Dr. Wordsworth broke the silence. "Captain van Leyden, why have you brought us here?"

"There has been an unfortunate—a deplorable occurrence." He shook his head at the inadequacy of his own words. "There has been a tragedy." He paused.

Dr. Wordsworth whispered to Dr. Eisenstein, though they could all hear her. "Where's Phair? I thought we were all summoned to the salon."

"Mr. Phair is dead," the captain said harshly.

Dr. Wordsworth dropped the teapot. Tea flooded over the tea tray, onto Dr. Wordsworth, onto the floor.

Mrs. Smith let out a breathy shriek.

Geraldo and Jan began mopping up the floor.

"But he can't be dead," Dr. Eisenstein said. "He was perfectly all right at breakfast."

Dr. Wordsworth patted her orange shorts with her napkin. "How clumsy of me! I'm so sorry. The teapot handle was unexpectedly hot."

"It must have been a heart attack," Mr. Smith suggested.

Mrs. Smith quavered, "But he was so young!"

The captain waited until comparative order was restored. Then he said heavily, "Mr. Forsyth Phair did not die of natural causes. He was murdered."

Mrs. Smith clutched her husband's hand. "No, no . . ."

Dr. Eisenstein said, "But who would—"

Dr. Wordsworth reached with trembling hands for her empty teacup, lifted it, set it back on the table. "It has to be someone on the ship. It may be someone in this room."

"Stop, stop!" Mrs. Smith wailed. "How can you suggest such a thing? Who could possibly have wanted to murder Mr. Phair?"

Mr. Smith put a restraining hand on his wife's knee. "Somebody did, Patty, and that's a fact."

Simon moved almost deliberately into the state of numbness which had protected him at the time of his parents' deaths, although now there was no grief and outrage, only shock. And he had had too much of death; he would be involved in no more. He did not hear what anybody was saying. He did not want to hear. But after a while he felt that somebody was trying to penetrate his shell of protection, and he turned and saw Mr. Theo looking at him, his eyes fierce under bushy brows. Before Simon could drop his gaze Mr. Theo nodded at him reassuringly. It was almost as though Aunt Leonis were with him and expecting him to behave like a man and not like a child.

He listened to the captain telling the passengers about the vanished portrait, about talking on the radio with the police, and when the shocked exclamations had died down, Poly raised her hand for permission to speak, as though she were in school.

Van Leyden said, "Yes, Miss Poly?"

"Aunt Leonis—Simon's Aunt Leonis. She's the only one who might possibly know."

"Know what, Miss Poly?"

"Why Jan's Quiztano name, Umar, is on the back of the portrait. It might give us a clue."

"What? What's that?" Dr. Wordsworth demanded.

Simon closed his eyes and mind during the explanations.

"A detective in our midst," Mr. Theo said in approval. "You could get in touch with Miss Leonis through the radio officer, could you not, Captain?"

"Yes. That is an intelligent suggestion. In any case, I would inform her of—what has happened." The captain nodded. "You would like to speak to her, Master Simon?"

Simon opened his eyes and the captain had to repeat the question.

"Oh, yes, please, sir! But the nearest phone is quite a way down the road at the filling station by the bus stop. There's usually someone there who's willing to drive over to Pharaoh and fetch her."

The captain's grim face relaxed slightly as he looked at the boy who reminded him so strongly of his own fair son at home in Amsterdam. "All right. We will start the wheels turning as soon as possible." He rose and spoke to the assembled group.

"You are free to go where you please, though I expect you not to go below this deck." He looked at Poly and Charles. "It is a hot day, but I do not think that you would wish to go to the prow."

"No," Poly said. "No."

Simon's mind's eye flashed him a vision of the hearse, and the strange still body there, and he shuddered.

The captain dropped his hand lightly on the boy's shoulder. "Come, Simon, we will go to the radio room."

It was over an hour before Aunt Leonis reached the filling-station phone, during which time both Dr. O'Keefe and Mr. Theo made calls, Dr. O'Keefe to Benne Seed Island, Mr. Theo to Caracas, to say he would be delayed but hoped to arrive in good time for Emily's first concert, which was still a full week off. Then he put in a call to England, and for this he asked Simon to step outside. Why would Mr. Theo be calling England? At this moment it did not seem to Simon to be very important. The captain talked again with the police in Lake of Dragons, and put in a call to Holland.

When Aunt Leonis was finally on the phone the captain spoke to her first. He told her, briefly, what had happened, then listened carefully. Then he said, "I am glad that you will come. I know that my government would wish to see this—more than unpleasantness—this dreadful event—resolved as soon as possible. We will make arrangements to have you flown here at your earliest convenience . . . You will come at once? That is good." He handed the headset to Simon.

Aunt Leonis's voice crackled strangely but was quite comprehensible. "I will be with you by tomorrow evening, Simon. I have read Quentin Phair's letters. There was more than *Umar* on the back of the portrait, but we will not talk of it till I arrive." Then static took over and he could make nothing out of the last garbled words.

No matter, Aunt Leonis was coming. There was still horror, but if Aunt Leonis was going to be with them in Venezuela, then somehow she would manage to bring order out of chaos as she always had done.

The O'Keefes were with Mr. Theo in the salon. Simon was being taken care of by Mynheer Boon. Dr. O'Keefe said, "I think it will be better if Simon sleeps with Charles in my cabin, and I'll take his. We may well be detained for a few days in Port of Dragons. You kids will help make the transfer, won't you?"

"Of course, Daddy," Poly said. "Let's find him and get him settled, and then let's put on our bathing suits and splash around in the pool. I'm not being cold-blooded. I just think it would make us feel—feel cleaner."

Mr. Theo nodded. "How many of us will fit in, do you think?" Then he looked at Dr. O'Keefe. "I'm an old man, Doctor, and I've never been very patient. At the end of my life I find that I can't wait for the prudent moment for things. I have to snatch the time when I have it."

Dr. O'Keefe looked at him inquiringly.

Mr. Theo said, "When I suggested to you that we call Tom Tallis in London you felt that we should wait. I must confess, I have called him."

Dr. O'Keefe asked quietly, "And?"

"I was very cryptic. When he got on the phone I said, 'Tom, this is Theo. I will be delayed in getting to Caracas but hope, with help, to be in time for Emily's concert. You will want to come.' Then I hung up."

Poly clasped her hands. "Oh, Mr. Theo, do you think he'll come?"

Mr. Theo said, "Tom and I have known each other since we were both rather wild young men in Paris. It is not my wont to be cryptic. Tom will come." He turned to Dr. O'Keefe. "I hope you're not angry with me for going over your wishes?"

"I think I'm relieved," Dr. O'Keefe said.

The passengers of the *Orion*, with the notable exception of Mr. Phair, were gathered on the aft deck. Mr. Theo, in an old-fashioned one-piece black bathing suit, stood in one corner of the wooden pool and let the rolling of the ship splash salt water over him. Whenever there was a heavy swell the water sloshed over the sides of the pool onto the deck. Simon, Poly, and Charles joined him. The salt water felt cool and delicious.

Mr. and Mrs. Smith found the steep wooden sides of the pool difficult to climb over. They reclined in deck chairs. Mrs. Smith wore white terry-cloth shorts, a white sleeveless shirt, and white sneakers and socks. Despite her softly wrinkled skin she looked as fresh and clean as a kitten.

"It's all right, Patty," Mr. Smith whispered. "He can't hurt us now."

She shuddered. "What a terrible thing to say! Who could have—oh, Odell, I'm frightened, I'm so frightened . . ."

The two professors had pulled their chairs to the opposite side of the deck from the Smiths. Dr. Wordsworth glistened from sun-tan lotion; she wore orange shorts and a flowered halter and her back glowed with copper and was smooth and supple, though the slack muscles of her upper arms betrayed her age. She brought out a white nose guard and put it over her nose to protect it from the sun, adjusted her straw hat to shade her eyes.

Dr. Eisenstein had pulled her chair into the shade of the canvas canopy.

Dr. Wordsworth's whisper was explosive. "Why don't you say it?"

Startled, Dr. Eisenstein looked up from her notebook. "Say what?"

"What I can see that you're thinking."

Dr. Eisenstein looked sad and tired. "No, I'm not, Inés. I'm numb with horror that such a thing could have happened, but I don't think that you had anything to do with it."

"You know that I hated him."

"I know that you're not a murderer."

Inés Wordsworth held out her hands and looked at them wonderingly. "I could have murdered him, I think, if I'd been angry enough. If he'd raked up the past publicly—but he couldn't do that without implicating himself, and to do him justice I don't think he would have. We did love each other once." She let her hands fall into her lap, the nails like blood. "Odd, to admit that I could kill if I were angry enough. But I didn't kill him."

"I know you didn't," Dr. Eisenstein said gently.

Dr. Wordsworth readjusted her nose guard. "Oh, Ruth, I admit I wished him dead that first day he got on the ship—but not this way. A nice lingering death from some excruciatingly painful disease would have been fine with me—so why am I so squeamish about murder?"

"Maybe because the murderer is still on board. It's unbelievable. It can't be one of the passengers—"

"Why not?"

Dr. Eisenstein shook her head. "I find it impossible to believe that *any*body on this ship, passenger or sailor, is a murderer. And yet somebody is."

"Let's hope it's a sailor."

"But a sailor—what could a sailor have against a passenger? someone he's never met before?"

"Quite a few of the sailors are from South America. And I've told you that Fernando Propice, or Forsyth Phair, was involved in all kinds of minor underworld stuff when I knew him, and a leopard doesn't lose his spots. It may be some kind of private smugglers' vendetta."

"That would be understandable, at least," Dr. Eisenstein said. "I suppose the *Orion* will be swarming with police tomorrow morning when we dock."

Inés Wordsworth was white under her tan. Her hands clenched. "Oh, God! the police always look into everybody's background in the case of murder. They'll find out about me."

"Not necessarily. You have an American passport."

"But don't you see how vulnerable I'll be if the police get hold of my record?"

"There's no reason they should."

Dr. Wordsworth relaxed slightly, letting her hands unclench. "Thank you, dear Ruth. Jail once was enough for me. And there are the officers to consider. Lyolf Boon, for instance, watching the bridge games but refusing ever to take a hand. It was F.P. he was watching, not you and the Smiths."

"And the captain," Dr. Eisenstein continued. "You mentioned only last night that the captain was formidably polite with Phair, the kind of rigid courtesy one reserves for someone one heartily dislikes."

Dr. Wordsworth smiled wryly. "In my youth I used to think I might like to be a spy or a secret-service agent. I don't think I'm cut out for it after all. You'd better use some of my sun-tan lotion, Ruth. Your nose is getting red. You get a lot of reflection from the sun even under the canopy. Oh, God! I wish we were with your Quiztanos and all this behind us!"

On the bridge the Master of the ship looked out to sea. Lyolf Boon was at the helm. Van Leyden said, "You were on the bridge this morning. Are you certain there was nothing on the radar?"

"There were the usual fishing ships, but only a few, and they did not approach us; they remained well on the outer range of the radar."

Van Leyden's jaw tightened. "My heart sank when I recognized the man, but in my most extreme pessimism I never thought of murder. It would seem that somebody attempted to steal the portrait, was caught by Phair, who was then murdered, and the portrait removed—do you have any ideas?"

"Jan is the only person we know to have an interest in the portrait. But I cannot bring myself to believe that Jan ten Zwick would murder. But I do not know what his Quiztano blood might make him do."

"Jan is only a quarter Quiztano," the captain said. "He is essentially Dutch."

"In looks. But there are many qualities in him which come from the Quiztanos."

The captain looked broodingly at the radar machine of which he was so proud. "That doesn't make him a murderer."

"Of course not. I didn't mean to imply—but I do not understand why he had the key to cabin 5. And why invent this wild tale of my having found the key on Phair's crossword puzzle? His lying disturbs me greatly. Never before have I known Jan not to tell the truth."

"Nor I," the captain said.

"Geraldo should keep his key cupboard locked."

"I dare say he will from now on. But there has never before been an occasion to be concerned when we have been at sea."

"Perhaps the possibility of further trouble has occurred to Dr. O'Keefe? You remember, he's changing cabins with Simon."

"A wise decision," Van Leyden said. "But I do not wish the boy to be alone at any time until we're certain no one wishes—wishes him harm. I'm not sure that such was in O'Keefe's mind, otherwise wouldn't he himself have shared his cabin with the boy? It seems likely he merely reasoned that it would hardly be pleasant for Simon to sleep alone in that cabin; that's how I'd feel if it were my son. I think, Boon, that we must be careful not to make any assumptions about anything, or anybody."

Boon agreed. "It is a matter for the police."

Van Leyden put his hand heavily on the radar machine. "Yes. It's all going to be very unpleasant. The police will be waiting when we land. And then Miss Phair's plane from La Guaira will arrive by late afternoon tomorrow. I suppose the police will have her met."

"Yes," Boon nodded thoughtfully. "It is all going to be very untidy. Was Phair a U.S. citizen?"

Van Leyden hit the palm of his hand against his forehead. "No, as a matter of fact, he was not." —How easily, he thought, —the *is* has become *was* on our tongues. "He carried a Venezuelan passport."

"How long do you think we'll be detained? This plays havoc with our schedule."

"I wish I could give you an answer. I have no precedent for this experience. I had no fondness for Mr. Phair, but this is hardly the revenge I would have contemplated."

"You would have contemplated revenge?"

Van Leyden looked surprised. "That was merely a figure of speech. My captain did not need a raw young sailor to avenge him. It was, in any case, not my prerogative. It's nearly time for lunch. I doubt if it will be a pleasant meal."

It was not. In the dining room the fans whirred heavily through the silence. The passengers picked at their food. The meal was over early, and nobody lingered in the salon for coffee.

After lunch the children did not know what to do. They

could not go to the Dragon's Lair, past the hearse with its terrible passenger, even had the captain not put the lower deck out of bounds. The adults, instead of repairing to their cabins for a siesta, went out on the aft deck, seeking the breeze, too uneasy to rest. Dr. Wordsworth and Dr. Eisenstein went up to the boat deck and grimly began their pacing, up, down, around, up, down, around.

Poly went off to talk with Geraldo.

Charles followed his father around.

Boon took Simon into his office and showed him a tattered book of pictures of Venezuela. Simon leafed through it politely, pausing to study a large colored photograph, taken from a plane, of Dragonlake, with the Quiztano huts high on their stilts, far out into the lake.

There was a knock on the doorframe and Mr. Theo looked in.

"Come and amuse me, young Simon."

Boon nodded. "I have work to do. I must lock my office." He spoke heavily. "We are locking everything as though we were in port."

Mr. Theo took Simon out onto the deck. "It is hardhearted of me," he said, "but my main concern is that I get to Caracas in time for Emily's concert."

"I guess I feel pretty hardhearted, too," Simon said. "I didn't want him to die or anything, but he did make me feel very uncomfortable, and I didn't want him taking the portrait away from Aunt Leonis and me, and I felt that he was glad to be getting me away from Poly and Charles, and that he didn't want me ever to see them again. And he frightened me."

Mr. Theo asked quickly, "How?"

Simon shook his head slowly. He could not say that it was because Dr. Wordsworth had made him realize that Cousin Forsyth was somebody very different from the elderly bachelor, overly tidy, impeccably courteous, that he had appeared to be during the month in South Carolina. So he said, "He was always quiet and polite, but there was something underneath."

"What?"

"Poly and Charles think he didn't like me, and I think they're right."

The wind blew through Mr. Theo's hair, ruffling it leoninely. "Let us be grateful for this breeze. We may not have it after we dock. Have you noticed how quiet the ship has become? No more music."

"I guess they don't feel like singing."

"The sound of guitar and flute was part of the breathing of the ship. I feel an emptiness."

"Me, too."

"Come on, then. Let us gird up our loins. The captain suggests that I bring you to the bridge. There'll be fishing boats for you to see on his radar machine."

It seemed to Simon that the captain was careful to see that he was always with an adult, never left alone. It was this which made him accept the unpleasant fact that somebody had already tried to take his life, that this somebody might be as interested in disposing of him as of Cousin Forsyth—but why? why? none of it made sense. He began counting the hours until Aunt Leonis would arrive. It was no more than twenty-four hours, now, or hardly more, only a day. But would a frail old woman be able to protect him? Was she, too, coming into danger?

At bedtime Simon felt strange in the O'Keefe cabin, no matter how easy he was with Charles. But Charles was in one of his silences; he seemed to be completely withdrawn from Simon; his face was cold and forbidding.

It was not until the lights were turned off, earlier than usual, that Charles spoke. "Simon, I think I have to talk to you." He paused.

"I'm listening," Simon said after a while.

"What I have to tell you doesn't seem to have much to do with Cousin Forsyth and the portrait, but it does have to do with you." And in a cold, completely emotionless voice he told Simon all he had learned from Jan. "Of course it's all muddled," he concluded. "It's an old story and stories tend to get exaggerated and changed. But too much of it fits in with my dreams, and Jan said the Englishman is called the Fair—Jan said he's always thought of it as spelled F-a-i-r—but it's too close to Phair for comfort, isn't it?"

"Nothing's comfortable," Simon said, "and it does have to do with the portrait, since *Umar* is written on the back."

"Yes, I suppose it does. It's just Cousin Forsyth who doesn't seem to fit in. Simon, I'm sorry."

"It would be more of a shock," Simon said in a small, chill voice, "if Poly and Geraldo hadn't suggested it to me already. I tried to put it away as speculation and dream and not reality. But so much has happened, I don't seem to know which is which any more."

Charles said softly into the darkness, "It doesn't mean Quentin wasn't—wasn't—I know how much he means to you—how you admire—"

The cabin fan whirred softly and steadily.

"It means he wasn't the kind of person I thought he was. And that changes me, too." The breeze lifted and blew gently through the open windows. Then Simon asked, "Do you think somebody killed Cousin Forsyth in order to get the portrait?"

"Maybe. But who? And where did the portrait vanish to?"

"The only person who . . ." Simon paused, said, "Jan . . ."

"If Jan were going to steal the portrait and kill Cousin Forsyth he'd hardly have told me all he did . . . But either he or Mr. Boon is lying about the key."

"All this wanting to be revenged on—on the Phair—I don't really understand."

"I do," Charles said quietly. "You may remember that Poly told you that two years ago a friend of ours was murdered in Lisbon. And Poly and I wanted him avenged, all right. There were several people we hated ferociously. And then we ended up with Daddy having to help the person who was most responsible for his death. So I understand. I just don't understand its going on and on this way."

"No."

"Uncle Father. It's important for him to know all this."

"I suppose so."

"Maybe Quentin had a reason for not coming back, Simon."

"Niniane," Simon said bitterly.

"But you love Niniane. And Aunt Leonis talks to her."

"I'm very confused," Simon said. "Quentin broke his word."

"Words sometimes do get broken, Simon."

"Not Quentin Phair's! I know a lot of politicians nowadays, and even presidents, don't take promises seriously, and even lie under oath, but I was brought up to speak the truth. My father's newspaper was sometimes in trouble because he uncovered truths, and cared about honor. And Quentin Phair was always our ideal of a man of perfect honor, who cared for the truth above all things, and who spent his youth helping to free an oppressed continent."

"Well, he did do that," Charles pointed out. "He spent his youth with Bolivar."

Simon was silent.

After a while Charles suggested, "Why don't you cry?"

"I'm too old."

"Mother says it's silly for men to feel they shouldn't cry at appropriate times."

"Have you ever seen your father cry?"

"At appropriate times."

"Do you consider this an appropriate time?"

"It's a death."

"I don't feel like crying about Cousin Forsyth."

"Quentin. The man you wanted to be like is dead. He never was. As Poly said, he was too good to be true. So maybe if you cry about him, then you'll be ready to find the real Quentin Phair."

"I'm not sure I want to."

Charles pointed out, "He's brought us all into quite an adventure, you'll have to say that much for him."

9. PORT OF CALL

SIMON woke up suddenly, not knowing where he was. The early-morning light shimmered on the white ceiling of the cabin—not the cabin he had shared with Cousin Forsyth, where drawn curtains kept the light to a minimum, where Cousin Forsyth's snores were now only an echo. No. He was in Dr. O'Keefe's cabin. He was in Dr. O'Keefe's bunk.

He raised himself on his elbow and looked across to the other bunk. Charles was lying there, eyes open, staring at the ceiling. When Simon moved he sat up and smiled.

Simon smiled back. But he still felt empty; something was missing; the loss of Quentin Phair was far larger than the loss of Cousin Forsyth. He did not want to talk about it, so he said, "It's not nearly time for breakfast." He stretched. His pajamas were slightly damp with perspiration. The cabin fan was whirring and they had slept without even a sheet.

"The Herald Angel is probably in the galley making early coffee for the Smiths." Charles assumed his Buddha position and lapsed into silence.

Simon broke the silence by asking, "Is he one?"

"The Herald? I think so. You know the clouds we've been watching after lunch? Very light and transparent, and they seem to be throwing themselves into the wind, and we've all said they look as though they're having such fun . . . ?"

"I remember. I've never seen clouds like them before."

"Well, I dreamed last night that Geraldo and Jan both had wings of clouds and that they were flying above the ship—but flying is too heavy a word. It was a lovely dream to have had last night. Geraldo and Jan—they're on the side of the angels, as the saying goes. Don't worry about Geraldo. He won't do anything to hurt Poly."

Simon thought about this for a moment. Then he said, "Thank you, Charles. I've been being jealous. I know Poly's still my friend even if she's friends with Geraldo in a different way. That was a lovely dream."

A shadow moved across Charles's eyes. "They're not always lovely. But Canon Tallis tells me that I may not reject the gift, because God does not give us more than we can bear."

"If there is a God."

"Poly was very upset when Daddy wouldn't cable him."

"God?" Simon asked in surprise.

"Uncle Father—Canon Tallis. But I think Daddy was really very relieved that Mr. Theo just went ahead and phoned. You'll like Uncle Father, Simon."

"I suppose if you and Poly like him, then I will."

"He's not going to be like anybody you've ever met before. One of our friends described him as looking like a highly intelligent teddy bear, but that's not a very good description, because teddy bears are hairy, and he's completely bald—I mean completely, even to having ridges of bone showing above his eyes where most people have eyebrows."

"How come he's completely bald?"

Charles was standing by the washbowl, starting to brush his teeth. He took his toothbrush out of his mouth and spat. "He was tortured, way back in some war—one of those awful ones in the Far East. They used electric shock on him and it was so strong that it killed all his hair follicles, and it almost killed him, but he didn't betray his men."

"He was a soldier?"

"A chaplain. But he went with the men wherever they went. That's the kind of person he is. And that's why Poly wanted Daddy to send for him, and it's also why Daddy didn't want to. Shall we get dressed and go out on deck?"

"Is it all right?" Simon asked. "Your father told us to keep the door locked . . ."

"I think it's all right as long as we stay together. Let's see if the pool is filled. Salt water's much nicer than a shower."

They made their way along the quiet passage. The passengers were still in their cabins behind the chintz curtains. The rest of the ship was silent. No early-morning sounds of laughter, of music. The silence was as oppressive as the heat, and Simon tried to break it by whistling a few bars of "I met her in Venezuela," and broke off in mid-melody, thinking that Quentin might almost have been the man in the song. The song was even more painful now than it had been after his mother's death. The words would not leave him alone.

> *When the moon was out to sea,*
> *The moon was out to sea,*
> *And she was taking leave of me,*
> *I said, Cheer up, there'll always be*
> *Sailors ashore in Venezuela,*
> *Ashore in Venezuela.*

Was that all it had meant to Quentin? It could not have been all. Simon pushed open the screen door to the promenade deck with a furious gesture.

Much of the water in the pool had splashed over the wooden sides during the night. Nevertheless, Simon and Charles chose the foot of cool ocean water rather than the cabin shower. When they had rolled about till they were thoroughly wet, one of the sailors climbed up to the deck and indicated to them that he was going to drain and refill the pool. Simon and Charles got out and stood at the deck rail, looking across the water to a long dim shadow on the horizon.

"South America," Charles said. "It's really very exciting."

But Simon felt nothing but an aching sadness.

He continued to be passed from person to person, never left on his own. He was silently grateful. He did not want to be left alone with his thoughts. His flesh prickled with apprehension. He was sure that Mr. Theo was not a secret murderer. His pheromones told him that Dr. Wordsworth had a violent temper and cause to dislike Cousin Forsyth but that, except in a moment of passion, she would not murder. The carefully stacked wood from the portrait's crate spoke of premeditation, or at least a kind of cool surrounding the murder which he did not think was part of Dr. Wordsworth's personality. But that left everybody else on the ship to be afraid of. Nobody and nothing was to be trusted, not even his memories.

Shortly after ten o'clock in the morning Lyolf Boon took Simon up to the bridge. "You are privileged," Boon said. "The one time the passengers are never allowed near the bridge is when we are taking on the pilot and bringing the ship in to dock. You must stand out of the way and not ask questions."

The captain gave Simon the briefest of preoccupied nods. Simon stood just outside the bridge cabin and watched a small bug of a boat approach them from the direction of land. The bug sidled up beside the *Orion*, and a man sprang out, clambered up a rope ladder, and landed lightly on the lower deck.

"The pilot. Keep out of the way," Lyolf Boon warned Simon. "He'll be up on the bridge in a minute. Stand here. Don't ask questions. The captain has a very short temper when we're docking. Watch, and anything you want to know I'll tell you later."

"Yes, sir." Simon pressed against the rail, where he could see everything and not be underfoot. Ahead of him was the busy harbor of Port of Dragons; above it rose what appeared to be hundreds of tiny shacks crowding up the steep hillside above the harbor. The wind was sultry and saturated with moisture. He pulled Geraldo's cap farther forward to keep his hair from blowing in his eyes, and to shade them from the brilliance of sun on water. Under the cap he could feel perspiration. His shirt began to cling moistly. The weight of the unknown future lay on him as heavily as the heat.

The other passengers stood in little groups on the promenade deck.

"I don't know what's the matter with the pilot," Dr. Wordsworth remarked to the Smiths. "We've been backing and filling in a most inept manner. I gather the captain has a low tolerance for fools. This certainly must have broken his tolerance level."

"It seems to be a problem in parallel parking," Mr. Smith said. "I find parallel parking difficult with an automobile, and it must be far more of a problem for a ship. There's only one berth left free, with a freighter on either side. Port of Dragons surely is a busy harbor."

Mr. Theo and Dr. O'Keefe stood side by side. "The fork lifts are just sitting there," Mr. Theo remarked. "I suppose we won't be allowed to unload anything until the police have been all over the ship. I expect Tom by mid-afternoon."

His words were drowned out by shouting on the dock. Sailors from the *Orion* threw heavy ropes across the dark water between ship and shore; the ropes were caught by longshoremen and hitched around iron stanchions. Slowly the ship inched landward to bump gently against the old tires which were fastened to the wooden pilings of the dock—primitive but excellent bumpers.

On the quay stood a bevy of uniformed officials, talking loudly and with much gesturing and flinging of arms, shouting to the longshoremen, who in turn shouted to the sailors on the *Orion*, until the gangplank was dropped with a clatter and ship and shore were connected. The officials bustled into the ship and disappeared.

Charles said to his sister, "Jan and Geraldo have drinks and cigars set out in the salon."

"For the customs men," Poly said. "Geraldo says they always do, not just when there's a murder. Ouch. That sounds awful, doesn't it? 'Just when there's a murder.' Oh dear, are we getting hardened?"

"Inured, maybe."

"Isn't that the same thing?"

"Not quite. You can get used to something without being hardened. The cigars and stuff aren't just for the customs officers this time," Charles said. "I wonder what they'll do?"

"The customs officers?"

"The police."

Poly said in an overly matter-of-fact voice, "They'd better get Cousin Forsyth out of that hearse and onto some ice pretty quickly. In this weather by this time he stinketh."

Charles asked, "Will they want an autopsy?"

"I suppose so. It's what's done. But there wouldn't seem to be much doubt about the cause of death. Not much point in sticking a dagger into the heart of someone who's already dead, for instance. And the dagger doesn't afford a clue. It's

Venezuelan, the kind that can be picked up in any port, and most of the sailors have them, because they're decorative, and they take them home for presents. Oh, Charles, I've been trying to look at it all objectively, like Uncle Father, but the thing that throws me is that I thought Cousin Forsyth was after Simon, and now—"

Charles spoke quietly. "I still think he was. I have the strongest feeling that if Cousin Forsyth hadn't been got out of the way he might have succeeded in killing Simon."

"You mean maybe someone killed him to save Simon?" Poly asked hopefully.

"I don't know. There are a whole lot of threads and they're all tangled up. But I still think Cousin Forsyth boded no good for Simon." He held up a hand and pointed.

All the passengers hurried to the rail and watched as a short, excited official ran down the gangplank to the dock and began shouting and gesticulating. A large elevator lift maneuvered alongside the *Orion*. The passengers could not see what was happening on the foredeck, but it was obvious from the increased shouting and excitement that it was something important.

A great yellow metal arm reached out across the dock and over the *Orion*. Then it moved slowly back and the hearse, in a cradle of ropes, wavered in the air over the oily water between the *Orion* and the pier. The passengers watched in fascination as the hearse swung back and forth, tilted, righted, and finally, with a bump, was set down on the dock. A second official ran down the gangplank, shouted in unintelligible Spanish to the men on the dock, ran to the first official, shouted some more, and then the two chief officials got into the hearse and it drove off.

"Could you understand what they were saying?" Charles asked.

"Only a few words. It was some kind of dialect. I think they're driving right to the morgue."

Charles poked her, and she looked up to see Boon coming out to the promenade deck with Simon, and then going back into the ship.

Simon hurried toward them. His voice was studiedly casual. "I wish yawl could have been up on the bridge with me. I had to stay way out of the way, and even so, the captain got in a towering rage and yelled all kinds of things in both Dutch and Spanish at Mynheer Boon and the pilot—I couldn't understand a word, but he obviously was giving them Hades. Mynheer Boon says he doesn't really mean it, and this was a difficult docking and everybody is all uptight—I mean, even more than usual." Then he said in a voice so low that they could hardly hear him, "He's gone. Cousin Forsyth."

"Yes, Simon," Poly said. "We saw."

His eyes looked dark in his pale face. "It seemed so strange to think of him being in the hearse when it was swinging there, over the water and the edge of the dock and it tilted and—"

Poly said in a matter-of-fact way, "A freighter doesn't have a hospital, and it was the most prompt and effective way to get him directly to the morgue."

Charles said, "Simon, just remember that Aunt Leonis is coming, that she'll be here before dinner. Do you think you'll be allowed to go to the airport to meet her?"

"The captain says it depends on the local police, but he'll try to arrange it."

"Think about that, then."

The heat bore down.

After lunch the captain came out to the promenade deck and called Simon. "El señor jefe de policía Gutiérrez, chief of police in Port of Dragons, will take you out to the airport to meet Miss Phair." He smiled at the boy. "Come."

Simon followed van Leyden, through the ship, down the gangplank, to an official-looking black car with a seal on the door. A small, potbellied man with shiny dark hair and a per-spiring face was introduced as el señor jefe de policía Gutiérrez. His black waxed moustache was far more impressive than Cousin Forsyth's had been, its points curling up to the middle of his cheeks, but it was the only impressive thing about him. His white summer uniform was wrinkled and dark with sweat, and he was dancing about impatiently.

Simon shook hands. "How do you do, sir?" he queried in careful Spanish.

Simon's Spanish words evidently relieved el señor Gutiérrez, who began to gabble away until Simon stopped him and asked him please to slow down. This appeared to be a difficult request. Sr. Gutiérrez blew a small silver whistle and was almost immediately surrounded by excited subordinates. He exhaled a stream of incomprehensible Spanish, his voice rising to a high pitch. Minions ran in every direction, and then Gutiérrez bowed politely to Simon and said, "We will drive to the airport now, and you will answer me some questions, yes? It will not be difficult for you. Then we will arrange a happy meeting with the elderly lady, yes?"

"Yes, please, sir."

Gutiérrez opened the right-hand door to the front seat for Simon. Then he got in behind the wheel. "I myself will drive so that we will be private." He took out a large silk handkerchief, flicked some imaginary dust off the steering wheel, and mopped his brow.

Simon reached out to make sure that his window was open. The car was a hot box.

Gutiérrez took a cigar from several in his breast pocket—Dutch cigars—and lit up. The smoke made Simon feel queasy, but he tried to think only that he was on his way to meet Aunt Leonis.

Gutiérrez drove rapidly away from the port, waving in a lordly fashion at the soldiers with machine guns who stood formidably at the exit. They drove along a narrow road above the sea.

Gutiérrez snapped, "Where is this portrait of Bolivar?"

"It has been stolen, sir."

"Aha!" said el señor jefe de policía Gutiérrez. "This is what the Captain van Leyden and the señor Boon have told me. The wooden crate was found open, and the portrait had vanished, and all this at sea!"

"Yes, sir."

Gutiérrez drove with his foot down on the accelerator until they were traveling on a lonely road with jungle above them to the left, sea below to the right. "How did this portrait of our General come into your possession?" It was an accusation. Gutiérrez obviously did not think that Simon had any right to a portrait of Bolivar.

But the boy answered courteously. "Not my possession, sir. It belonged to my Aunt Leonis and she sold it to Cousin Forsyth."

"Sold it. Aha! Ahem! Why would she sell such a valuable thing?"

"Well, because it *was* valuable, sir, the only valuable thing she had left, and she had no money."

"Impossible. All Americans are rich." The cigar smoke blew heavily through the car. "If she had no money, how could she have bought such a valuable portrait in the first place?"

"She didn't buy it, sir. It was hers. It has always been in our family."

"Always? Incredible. How would an aged American have had a portrait of Bolivar in her family? This is a most unlikely story." Gutiérrez spoke around the cigar. Simon's nausea began to be acute. "Why do you speak Spanish?"

Simon countered, "Would you prefer me to speak English? It would be much easier for me."

"That is not what I am asking. Where did you learn Spanish?"

"From my Aunt Leonis—sir."

Simon had decided definitely that he did not like el señor jefe de policía Gutiérrez, who gave him no more confidence in the police than had Dr. Curds in the ministry.

"Your cigar is making me sick, sir," Simon said, "and I don't think I can speak any more Spanish for a while."

Gutiérrez frowned his disapproval, but put out his cigar. "You are withholding information."

They drove in silence for perhaps five minutes. Simon felt sweat trickling down his back between his shoulder blades. Gutiérrez's face glistened like melting lard. The landscape widened out and flattened, with a broad savannah between the road and the forest. Gutiérrez made a long U-turn, and there was the ocean on their left, pounding into shore. "We are here," Gutiérrez said.

The airport for Port of Dragons was little more than a short runway along a strip of dirty beach. The surf was pounding in heavily, and the spume was a mustardy yellow instead of white. Everything brassily reflected the heat of the sun. There was a bird's nest in the wind sock. A small plane was parked like a clumsy bird on the airstrip: Aunt Leonis's plane? If so, where was she? Across the airstrip from the ocean was a small wooden shack outside which a soldier lounged, a rifle swung from his shoulder. By the shack a hearse stood, black and shining and hot.

The hearse.

The sun smacked against the bullet hole in the windshield, and light burst back.

"The hearse—" Simon's throat was dry. "Why is the hearse—"

Gutiérrez did not reply. He drew the car close up to the rear of the hearse.

"Is—is Cousin Forsyth—"

"No, no," Gutiérrez answered soothingly. "He is in the morgue. It is all right. Come, I will show you."

"Aunt Leonis—"

"Her plane is not yet in. There are head winds. We have time. Come." He opened his door and pushed himself out from under the wheel.

Simon did not move.

Gutiérrez walked around the car and opened the door on Simon's side. "Come."

Simon pressed back, his bare legs below his shorts sticking to the seat. His dislike of Gutiérrez had turned to anger, and the anger to terror.

Gutiérrez reached in and took his arm in a firm grip. The rotund little man was far stronger than he looked. Simon was hauled forcibly out of the car, yanked from the stuffy, smoky, sweaty heat of the interior into the blazing broil of the sun. Was Aunt Leonis waiting in the shade inside the shack? Was Gutiérrez lying to him? —Please, please, be there.

He struggled to get loose and run to the shack, but Gutiérrez's flabby-looking arms were like iron and he dragged the boy toward the hearse.

The Venezuelan's voice was gentle in contrast to his fingers, which were bruising Simon's arms. "Don't be afraid. Don't fight me and you won't get hurt. I just want to show you something."

The rifle-slung soldier moved swiftly from the shack over the short distance to the hearse and flung open the double doors. Then he and Gutiérrez together picked Simon up bodily and threw him into the hearse and slammed the doors shut behind him.

Simon landed on something. Something pliable.

Someone.

A body.

10. THE BODY IN THE HEARSE

H IS terror was so great that he could not even cry out.
The body gave a very living grunt as Simon almost
knocked the wind out of—who was it? Not Cousin Forsyth . . .

The grunt was followed by muffled sounds, but no words.

Simon was almost thrown to the floor as the hearse began
to move, accelerating rapidly. The shirred lavender funereal
curtains covered the windows, and Simon precipitated himself
across the hearse and struggled to open them, but they were
tacked down. While he was trying to pull them loose his eyes
adjusted to the dim light and he turned to the still-grunting
body on the stretcher.

There lay a man, trussed up like a fowl; a blindfold covered
his eyes, and a gag was rammed into his mouth. With trembling
fingers Simon untied both, to reveal a rather pale face and a
completely bald head.

"Uncle Father!" Simon cried.

Dark eyes widened in surprise. "Who are you? How do you
know me?"

"You're Poly's godfather," Simon said, starting to work on
the knots; he was slowed down by the rocking of the hearse,
which appeared to be traveling much too rapidly for the state
of the road.

"Make haste slowly," Canon Tallis advised as the hearse
jounced over a rut and Simon was thrown against him. "And
while you're working tell me who you are. And keep your voice
down."

"I'm Simon Renier, Simon Bolivar Quentin Phair Renier,
and I've been on the *Orion* with Poly and Charles and Dr.
O'Keefe, and Mr. Theo, too, of course." The terrifying yet
tedious job of loosening the canon's bonds was finally done,
and Simon helped him to sit up.

Canon Tallis pursed his mouth as though to whistle, but his
lips were so sore and bruised from the gag that only a small puff
came out. He asked, "Where's the rest of the family?"

"Home, on Benne Seed Island. Dr. O'Keefe brought Poly and Charles with him when he was asked to spend a month in Venezuela—you really are Canon Tallis?"

The bald man nodded thoughtfully. "Curiouser and curiouser."

"I guess Mr. Theo didn't tell you much when he called you."

"So right."

"But you came anyhow. He said you would."

"When I got an unexpected and extremely cryptic phone call from him, I thought I'd better come see what was up. I shall want you to tell me what *is* up, Simon, but first we'd better try to look out and see where we're going." Between them they managed to loosen a corner of the lavender curtain, which had been tacked down very thoroughly indeed. They peered out. The hearse was bouncing along what was no more than a double rut cut through the jungle. Trailing vines brushed against the windows. A ferocious-looking wild hog tore through the underbrush and vanished into green.

"We're not moving as quickly as it seems," Canon Tallis said. "I wonder if we could get out?" He tried to open the rear doors. "We're locked in. Do you have a knife on you?"

"No, sir," Simon said. "I'm sorry."

"No matter. I doubt if it would help. This is a solid lock, not the thing one would normally expect on a hearse. It may be padlocked from the outside." The hearse jolted and veered violently to one side. "They're not going to be able to drive much farther. Not unless this path turns into a road, and somehow I doubt if it will. Can you tell me quickly what's been happening?"

As quickly as possible, prompted by astute questions, Simon told Canon Tallis what had happened since the fork-lift incident on the dock at Savannah.

The hearse continued to crash roughly through the jungle. Simon thought it was never going to stop. "Are we being kidnapped?"

"It would appear so. Though I'm hardly a kid."

"But why?"

"Somebody is still trying to dispose of you, it would seem."

"And somebody doesn't want you around to clear things up. But that policeman, Gutiérrez, he wasn't in Savannah or on the ship. He couldn't be the murderer. But he did throw me into the hearse."

"Knocking the wind out of me. It does appear to be a rather complex maze, though I begin to glimpse a pattern."

"What, sir?"

"Your not-overly-lamented late Cousin Forsyth seems to have been involved in one way or another with a good many people."

"Is—is Gutiérrez going to kill us?"

"Since he has not already done so, I somehow doubt it. And when I do not arrive and it's noticed that you've vanished there's going to be considerable excitement on the *Orion*."

"But does anybody know you're coming—I mean, for sure?"

"I was puzzled enough by Theo's call to decide to leave London and come, and I was concerned enough to phone a friend of mine, Alejandro Hurtado, chief of police in Caracas, and ask him to make sure that the captain of the *Orion*, as well as Theo, be advised of the time of my arrival. Hurtado told me that he would arrange to have me met, so I somehow doubt if our present plight will go unnoticed by him." He put his hand out suddenly and touched Simon's shoulder. "We're slowing down."

The hearse jounced along for a moment, then came to a lurching halt.

After a moment the doors were flung open. The hearse had stopped in a small clearing where a helicopter was waiting. Gutiérrez peered in at them. "I am so sorry to inconvenience you," he said in his most unctuous manner. "The lips of someone must be closed, so I have taken you hostage." He grabbed Simon, and pulled the struggling boy out of the hearse and into the helicopter. The soldier with the rifle knocked Canon Tallis on the head, stunning him, and then slung the heavy body over his shoulder as though it were a sack of grain, and dumped it into the copter.

Gutiérrez was at the controls. In a moment the incredible noise of the blades deafened Simon, and then they were airborne.

Poly and Geraldo sat in the small shade up on the boat deck. The heat of port was so heavy after the breeze of open sea that even Dr. Wordsworth had given up her daily constitutional. Despite the shade, the white-painted wood of the bench was hot against Poly's bare legs.

"Oh, Herald," she said, "things are so strange and my emotions are so mixed. If nothing had happened Daddy and Charles and I would have left the *Orion* forever, and you'd be getting ready to go on to Aruba and Curaçao and wherever you go before La Guaira, and the portrait would still be in the cabin, and Cousin Forsyth and Simon would still be on board, and Simon wouldn't be off with that oily policeman to meet Aunt Leonis. And yet I can't bring myself to wish that you and I weren't sitting here, being comfortable together."

Geraldo leaned toward her and kissed her.

When they moved apart she said, "I am gorgeously happy. How can I be happy when someone has been murdered?"

"I should not have kissed you," Geraldo said. "Forgive me."

"Why shouldn't you?"

"Because you're still a child."

"I am not!"

"And I am in no position to—oh, you understand, Poly-heem-nia. Sooner or later you will leave the ship and we will never see each other again."

Poly gave him her most brilliant smile. "I know. I can be quite realistic, Geraldo. But this was my first kiss and I will never forget it, ever, not when I am as old as Aunt Leonis."

"I will try to be realistic, too," Geraldo said, but he would have kissed her again had not Dr. O'Keefe called up to them.

Poly jumped guiltily. "I think Daddy feels he has to keep track of us all."

Geraldo touched her cheek lightly with one finger. "I want him to keep track of you."

"Geraldo, have you any ideas?"

He leaned toward her. "Many."

"No, no, silly, about Cousin Forsyth and the portrait."

"There are murmurs about Jan, but I know that it is not Jan."

"Of course not! Jan wouldn't murder."

"But we know of his interest in the portrait, and there is his lie about the key. The crew—everybody—we are all very disturbed. Most of us have worked on the *Orion* for years, and no one is on the ship for the first time this voyage. We find it impossible to believe that there is a murderer among us. But I heard Mynheer Boon defending Jan to Mynheer Ruimtje."

"What about the passengers?"

"It is not you or Charles or your father or Simon," Geraldo said firmly.

"Mr. Theo, Dr. Eisenstein, Dr. Wordsworth, the Smiths. Not one of them is strong enough to have got Cousin Forsyth into the hearse."

"Possibly two could."

"Mr. and Mrs. Smith certainly couldn't."

"The lady doctors?"

Poly pondered this. Dr. Wordsworth looked strong enough. "Wouldn't they have looked suspicious?"

"Anybody would have looked suspicious, if seen."

"It would be rather difficult to lug Mr. Phair from cabin 5, through the ship, out on deck, and into the hearse without being seen."

"He may not have been killed in the cabin."

Poly fondled Geraldo's hand. "If I were the murderer I think I'd have tried to lure Cousin Forsyth out on deck, get him behind the hearse or one of the big packing cases right by it, and done him in there so that I could have got him into the hearse inconspicuously."

Geraldo raised her hand to his lips and kissed her fingers. "You look so funny and adorable playing the detective."

"I'm not playing!"

"Sorry, Polyquita, sorry." He kissed her lightly and rose. "I have work to do, and you must go to your father."

She stood, too. "Simon and Aunt Leonis ought to be here

soon. And my godfather. I know it's childish of me, but I keep feeling that when he gets here everything's going to be all right."

"May it be so," Geraldo said.

Simon and Canon Tallis watched the helicopter disappear, up through a tangle of leaf and vine, trailing long shards of greenery on its runners; the rotors chopped through the entangling jungle until the machine was free and high in the sky.

They had been dumped unceremoniously in a small clearing which would be visible from the air only to someone who already knew about it, and who was a superb pilot.

"In a cinema," Tallis said, "we'd have overpowered them and taken control of the copter."

"What would we have done then?" Simon asked. "Could you fly it?"

"I'm woefully out of practice, but I do have a pilot's license, and desperation can be a good co-pilot. That man knows his jungle and he knows his machine. Unfortunately they took my gun at the airport before they tied me up."

"You had a gun?"

"Something told me to be prepared. However, it seems that I was not prepared enough, or we wouldn't be here."

"Sir, are you all right?" Simon asked.

Canon Tallis rubbed his skull. "I have a nasty egg here, which will probably be a brilliant hue of purple by morning, but otherwise I'm fine."

"I thought he'd killed you."

"For some reason he only wanted to knock me out, and that he succeeded in doing. But no other harm done, thank God."

Green of leaf and vine hid the helicopter, though they could still hear the roar of its blades. Then sound, too, was lost in the enveloping murmur of the jungle. A bird startled Simon with a scream; deep within the tangle of green and brown and olive came a chattering which sounded like monkeys, and probably was.

Simon asked, "Why did they just dump us out here in the middle of the jungle?"

"I think your fat little man—"

"El señor jefe de policía Gutiérrez."

"El señor Gutiérrez for some reason did not want to kill us outright. Odd how squeamish some types can be. The thug with him would much have preferred to shoot me than knock me out, put a bullet through you, and then leave us here for the vultures."

"What are we going to do?" Simon asked.

"Try to survive until Hurtado finds us."

"Will he find us?"

"Hurtado is one of the best policemen in the world. If anybody can find us, he will."

Miss Leonis leaned toward the window in the little one-prop plane and watched the landing at Port of Dragons. Despite her exhaustion from the trip—the bus ride to Charleston, the long flight to La Guaira with a change of plane en route, and the bumpy trip in this old crate—she was excited. She peered out at the stretch of beach beside the runway, full of flotsam and jetsam, driftwood—and, as they came closer and she could see better, old sandals, tin cans, empty bottles. The water looked yellow and rough. Then the ground came up to meet them and they bounced several times and lurched to a stop. Her ancient heart was beating too rapidly; she could feel a flutter in her throat as though a small and frightened bird was caught there. Her hands, despite the heat, were cold.

Several solicitous officials helped her from the plane and set her down on the airstrip. She looked around. She was glad that she had not seen the bird's nest in the wind sock while they were landing; it hardly gave one a sense of confidence. Close to the plane was a low shack, and through the open door she could see a large set of scales, a soldier with a sub-machine gun, and two other semi-uniformed men with rifles. The three of them were playing some kind of card game, slapping cards and silver down on the table, which was spotlighted by the sun and looked even hotter than outdoors.

She felt a presence at her side, turned, and one of the officials who had helped her from the plane was bowing obsequiously. He was rotund and shiny with heat. "Miss Phair?"

She bowed in acknowledgment.

"Señor jefe de policía Gutiérrez of the Port of Dragons police, at your service."

She extended a white-gloved hand and he kissed it.

"I am here to escort you to the *Orion*, where you will be joyfully reunited with your nephew." He led her to an official-looking car with a gold seal on the door. "If you will be so kind as to sit in front with me, perhaps I can get some preliminary questions out of the way on the drive to the ship."

She did not like him. Her heart continued to thud. The car was stiflingly hot and smelled of stale cigar smoke. As he closed the door for her she decided that she was much too tired to speak Spanish, and so she sat and smiled courteously and vaguely at el señor jefe de policía Gutiérrez as he started the car and drove off, immediately firing a barrage of questions at her.

It took him some time to realize that she was not going to respond. Then he hit his forehead with the heel of his palm and moaned, as though to one of his minions, "But she is supposed to speak Spanish!"

The corners of Miss Leonis's mouth quirked slightly. She leaned back in the car and closed her eyes, making a concentrated effort to relax her travel-taut muscles, to slow the rapid beating of her heart. If she was to be of any use to Simon she must rest. Slowly and rhythmically, without moving her lips, she began to recite poetry to herself, Shakespeare's sonnets, her favorite psalms, the prelude to Chaucer's *Canterbury Tales*.

Her head drooped forward and she slid out of poetry and into a light slumber. She paid no mind to el señor jefe de policía Gutiérrez.

Defeated by passive resistance, he drove on.

The captain and Boon were waiting for them on the dock.

"But where is Simon?" Van Leyden demanded.

"Simón? But he has returned to the ship." Gutiérrez smiled at Miss Leonis, at van Leyden and Boon.

"What are you talking about?" Boon asked.

"The English priest was at the airport when Simón and I arrived. He was waiting in an official car sent from the police department of Caracas. When he said that he wished to question the boy immediately I hesitated, of course, but he persuaded me. He is a man of much authority."

"Where are they, then?" Van Leyden tried to keep his voice calm.

"The Englishman said that they would talk on the way back to the ship. His driver was one of Hurtado's top men. How could I refuse? I was outranked. Surely they are here by now? They left half an hour before Miss Phair's plane arrived."

Miss Leonis asked sharply, "Where is my nephew? What is going on?" She felt old and bewildered and her lace parasol did little to keep the heat of the sun from beating down on her.

"It is of no moment, gracious señora," Gutiérrez burbled. "They will of course be here momentarily."

A large black limousine drew up, and a uniformed chauffeur sprang out. "Where is the Englishman?" he demanded excitedly.

What had been confusion now turned to chaos. The limousine ordered by Hurtado had been delayed by a flat tire. When the chauffeur finally reached the airport he was told that his charge had already departed, that he had been met by an agent of Comandante Alejandro Hurtado—but that, declared the chauffeur, was impossible; he was the agent; the comandante had phoned him; he was always Hurtado's official chauffeur in Port of Dragons . . .

Van Leyden looked at his watch. His anger toward the dead man was even deeper than his anxiety; was history going to repeat itself? Was Phair, even dead, going to cause his resignation? He said, calmly enough, "We will wait half an hour. By then the Netherlands consul, Mynheer Henryk Vermeer, may be here. He was vacationing in the hills but he is already en route to Port of Dragons and should be here shortly. In the meantime, Miss Phair, while we are waiting for your nephew and the Englishman we will try to make you comfortable in the ship's salon, which is considerably cooler than the deck. Please be so kind as to follow me." He took her parasol and held it over her until they reached the cover of the ship.

Miss Leonis was not sure that she was not going to faint before she got to the salon. Van Leyden, seeing her tremble, put his arm about her and helped her upstairs and into a comfortable chair where she would get what little breeze there was.

"I do not understand what is happening," she said.

Van Leyden rang the bell for Geraldo. "Miss Phair, when there has been a murder, things are apt to be incomprehensible temporarily."

"Who is this English priest with whom Simon is supposed to be?"

"Is with, I am sure, is with. He is a friend of one of the passengers, who sent for him."

"Isn't it a bit late for a priest?"

"It appears that he has worked for Interpol and has a reputation as someone who can solve difficult problems."

"Let us hope that he can. Would it be possible for me to have some tea?"

"I have already rung for it."

"Thank you. You are very kind."

"Please try to rest, Miss Phair. You have had a difficult journey."

"Yes. Thank you."

"Simon will be most happy to see you. He is a good lad. Ah, here is Geraldo. Tea for Miss Phair, please, Geraldo, and something light to eat. Please excuse me, Miss Phair. I will send Simon to you the moment he arrives." The anxiety with which he looked at his watch as he crossed the threshold belied the confidence in his voice.

Poly hurried out onto the promenade deck and went to Charles, who was reading in the shade of the canvas canopy. "Aunt Leonis is in the salon."

He dropped his book. "What!"

"Aunt Leonis is in the salon."

"Who told you?"

"I saw her."

"Are you sure?"

"We did see her in Savannah, Charles. Who else could it be?"

"Where's Simon, then?"

"If he's not with Aunt Leonis he should be here with us. Have you been in the cabin lately?"

"It's too hot."

"Let's look for him."

Charles closed his book and put it down on his chair. With a worried look he followed his sister.

Simon was not to be found.

Poly said, "It's like when we were looking for Cousin Forsyth and couldn't find him. Do you suppose—"

"No, I don't. Let's go to the captain."

The captain was on the bridge, with Dr. O'Keefe and Mr. Theo. Quietly he told the children that Simon was supposed to have left the airport in a government car with Canon Tallis. He did not say that the Englishman and Simon were already gone when the official chauffeur reached the airport. Instead, he made his voice reassuring. "No, we must not become alarmed too soon. I've had word from el comandante Alejandro Hurtado, chief of police in Caracas, who is coming today. Evidently Comandante Hurtado is an old friend of the Englishman's."

Dr. O'Keefe nodded. "Yes, Tom has friends all over the world. If he has been met by a government official we needn't worry."

But Mr. Theo shook his head so that his white hair flew about wildly. "They should be here if all is well. They should have been here an hour ago."

The captain did not deny this. "Let us not alarm the old lady. It is possible that the government driver is not familiar with the route. They may have lost their way."

"Tom Tallis does not lose his way," Mr. Theo said.

It had to be conceded that something had gone wrong. Canon Tallis and Simon ought to be on the *Orion* and they were not and there had been no word from or about them.

Walking up and down the promenade deck Gutiérrez wrung his hands. His face streamed with sweat like tears. "But it is impossible, impossible," he kept repeating.

Van Leyden told the assembled passengers and Aunt Leonis, "Vermeer will be here any moment. Hurtado is flying in from Caracas and will arrive after dinner. They will order everything." His face was pale and all the lines seemed to have deepened.

Dr. Wordsworth whispered to Dr. Eisenstein, "This must be hell for van Leyden." She drained her glass and shook the remaining ice.

Dr. Eisenstein whispered back, "And for the old lady. She must be wild with anxiety over the boy."

Van Leyden said, "I think that we should all go to the dining room now. The cook has prepared an excellent meal for us. We must eat, you know."

Mr. Smith took his wife's hand. "This is more than Phair's murder, Patty."

"That nice young boy." She squeezed his hand. "I hope he hasn't come to any harm."

Poly said, "I'm not hungry."

Charles answered, "Neither am I. But the captain's right. We have to try to eat."

Passengers and officers ate in strained near-silence. All fragments of conversation sounded unusually loud, though voices were kept low. When Dr. Wordsworth asked, "Pass the salt, please," in a quiet voice, everybody jumped.

Miss Leonis sat in Simon's place. Cousin Forsyth's chair had been taken away. She ate a little because she knew that she had to, but she did not talk. She was silent not only because she was exhausted, and worried beyond belief about Simon, but because she bore the burden of Quentin Phair's journal, and she did not want to talk until she knew who it was she should talk to. The O'Keefes, she knew, were as anxious about Simon as she was. She had spent an afternoon with Mrs. O'Keefe and the younger children. She trusted the O'Keefes. It might be that she should talk to Dr. O'Keefe. She would wait and see. The two professors and the Smiths she sensed to be preoccupied with problems of their own which might include the disappearance of Simon and the English canon, but went beyond them. The old Greek organist she felt to be a friend; he obviously cared about Simon, and it was he who had sent for the Englishman. He was attentive to her in a quiet, unobtrusive way, not talking, but seeing that her teacup was filled, that she had salt and pepper, butter.

At the other table Charles whispered, "Where is Aunt Leonis going to sleep?"

Poly answered, "Geraldo says they've booked rooms for her and for Uncle Father at the Hotel del Lago in Port of Dragons. Charles, where are they? Simon and Uncle Father?"

"I wish I knew."

Jan came into the dining room and whispered to the captain, whose somber face relaxed slightly. He spoke to the assembled company. "Vermeer and Hurtado are both here. May I ask you, please, to stay in the dining room after dinner, just for a short while, until I know their wishes?" He bowed and left, speaking in a low voice to Jan, who closed the glass doors between dining room and salon, thereby cutting off the breeze. The passengers waited in tense silence, which Mr. Theo broke.

"If this Comandante Hurtado is a friend of Tom Tallis's he'll find Tom and Simon in short order."

Miss Leonis looked at him gratefully.

Geraldo hovered, refilling their water glasses. "Perhaps I should bring coffee?" he suggested.

"It's too hot," Dr. Wordsworth said.

Then Jan reappeared. His expression seemed to have set into a heavy mask of apprehension. Now that he was not smiling, Charles remembered that Jan's usual expression was a pleasant smile.

"Captain van Leyden would like to see you all on the promenade deck. It is cooler than the salon. We will serve coffee there, Geraldo."

"Yes, sir."

The colored lights around the awning on the promenade deck were lit, giving it a carnival appearance in macabre contrast to the mood of the assembly. On shore, small lights blinked on in the huts, moving in the wind and trembling like Christmas-tree lights up the mountainside. A single, very bright star pulsed in the blue-green sky. The dock was brightly lit with bulbs on cords stretched from warehouse to warehouse, and from telephone and light poles. Under one of the light poles was an ancient Hispano-Suiza, highly polished, parked beside a large black limousine.

The captain and two men rose to greet the passengers. They had been sitting at one of the small tables on which stood a bottle of Dutch gin and three small glasses.

Van Leyden made the introductions. The consul, Henryk Vermeer, was a heavy, straw-haired, bulldog of a man in crisp white shorts, crested blazer, and solar topee. Charles heard his father whisper to Mr. Theo, "He looks more like an Englishman in India than a Dutchman in Venezuela."

Mr. Theo whispered back, "Did you see the Hispano-Suiza? Bet it's his."

The comandante from Caracas, Alejandro Hurtado, was tall for a Latin, a dark man in dark clothes, with a dark, sharp jaw which would be purply-black almost immediately after he had shaved.

Vermeer shook hands all round, beaming affably, as though this was a purely social occasion. Hurtado revealed no expression whatsoever, but he looked at each passenger intently when he was introduced, as though memorizing name and face.

—I'm glad I have no secrets to hide from him, Poly thought as Hurtado bowed over her hand. —And I'm glad he looks a hard person to fool.

Gutiérrez was not there.

"Where is Simon?" Aunt Leonis demanded of Hurtado.

Simultaneously Mr. Theo asked, "Where is Tom Tallis?"

In the dimness of the jungle evening Canon Tallis rubbed his hand wearily over the painful lump on his bare pate. "Now, Simon, we had better prepare for the night. Are you a hand at camping?"

"No, sir. Camping wasn't exactly Aunt Leonis's thing."

"Not exactly mine, either, but necessity is an excellent teacher." The priest had taken off the dark jacket of his clerical suit and had rolled up his shirt sleeves. "The first thing to do is to collect enough dry wood for a fire, heat or no heat. It's a good thing we're shaded here; my unprotected head sunburns overeasily. First thing tomorrow I'm going to have to make some kind of head covering—my panama is somewhere in that hearse."

"I can make a sort of hat for you, sir," Simon said, "that's something I know how to do, by weaving palm fronds together."

"Good lad. I shall be much obliged. You do that, and I'll try to get a fire going."

"But why do we need a fire, sir, when it's so horribly hot?"

The canon smiled. "Not for warmth, certainly, though we may be grateful for it during the night. If we can keep smoke going up through the trees it will be an indication of our whereabouts which could be spotted by a helicopter—Gutiérrez is not the only one with a whirlybird. I'm certain that Hurtado will have the jungle searched."

By the time the canon had a small fire burning in the center of their clearing, Simon had woven him a passable head covering which he tried on at once.

"Yes, this will do admirably tomorrow."

He should have looked ludicrous—his bald head covered by the green palm hat, his clerical collar formally about his throat, his arms scratched and bleeding in several places from his endeavors. But all Simon thought was, —I know why Poly loves him. He does make me feel that everything's going to be all right.

In their little clearing it was already night. The canon squatted by the fire, carefully feeding it, "as I wish I could feed the two of us. Tomorrow we'll have to look for nuts and berries, and maybe we can crack a coconut between a couple of stones. But we'll have to be careful. I'm no expert on the edible roots of the Venezuelan jungle."

"Maybe I can help there," Simon said. "We have a lot of the same plants at home, sir, and Aunt Leonis and I eat a lot of wild stuff."

"Good, then. The two of us make an intrepid pair. All shall be well. Now, what I would like us to do this evening, to quell the pangs of hunger, is to go over in detail everything you have already told me, and more. Don't be afraid to repeat yourself. Remember that nothing you can tell me is trivial, no matter how unimportant it may seem. If I can get a clear picture of what went on at sea, possibly I'll have an idea about my unexpected reception at the alleged airport, and why you and I have been dumped here like two babes in the wood. Whose mouth has to be kept closed by Gutiérrez, and why? Start with—no, let's go even further back. Start with the arrival of Cousin Forsyth at Pharaoh."

On the promenade deck of the *Orion* the passengers sat in a stiff circle. Geraldo had brought out the coffee tray, and had been asked by the Dutch consul to serve cognac and liqueurs, and to make lemonade for Poly and Charles.

Miss Leonis, too, chose lemonade. "Where is that little policeman who met me?" She disposed of Gutiérrez by her tone of voice.

"Gutiérrez. I have taken over the case," Hurtado said calmly.

"I'm so glad!" Mrs. Smith clasped her small hands together. "He was trying to question us in such a bullying way."

Dr. Wordsworth said, "He appeared to be the kind of small-town policeman who immediately gets puffed up with the enormity of his own insignificance."

"Murders and missing persons are hardly in his line." Vermeer beamed. "A little smuggling here and there is more the kind of problem he comes up against. More cognac, my dear madame?" He gazed admiringly at Dr. Wordsworth's dark good looks.

"Thank you, no." She gave him a bright smile.

Deftly, Hurtado led the conversation in what seemed a casual way, ably seconded by Vermeer. In a short time they had found out a good deal about the passengers. Hurtado began questioning Dr. Eisenstein about the Quiztano Indians. "It is interesting, is it not, that you should be planning to visit these people who seem, in some way, to be connected with the stolen portrait?"

"And therefore, possibly," Vermeer said jovially, "with the murder."

"I cannot understand it!" Dr. Eisenstein exclaimed. "Why would a Quiztano name be written on the back of Mr. Phair's portrait?" She turned to Miss Leonis. "He bought the portrait from you, I believe?"

"Yes," Miss Leonis said, "but I am afraid I can tell you nothing."

"My dear madame," Vermeer pursued, "nothing?"

"Nothing. I have undertaken this journey because I, too, need information."

Hurtado noted the determined set of the old woman's jaw, the bone showing clearly beneath the soft, finely wrinkled skin.

Dr. Eisenstein continued, "And why didn't Jan tell me that he's part Quiztano, when he knows that the entire purpose of this trip for me is to visit the settlement on Dragonlake?"

"You did not ask him?" suggested Vermeer.

"But who could guess? He looks completely Dutch."

"True, true," Vermeer agreed amiably. "On a happier occasion you and I must chat, my dear doctor. I, too, am interested in the local Indians, and I have found Jan most helpful. Perhaps, later on, I can be of service to you."

"Oh, thank you!" Dr. Eisenstein said. "There are so many things I would have liked to ask Jan."

"It would have been so interesting for all of us," Mrs. Smith said. "When we lived in—" She stopped herself in horror, putting her pudgy hand up to her mouth.

Vermeer asked with sociable interest, "When you lived where, Mrs. Smith?"

"Ver—Vermont. Burlington, Vermont."

Hurtado said, "Your Spanish is excellent, Mrs. Smith, both yours and your husband's. I congratulate you."

"Thank you . . ." Mrs. Smith began to knit rapidly.

"Did you learn your Spanish in Vermont?"

Mr. Smith took off his spectacles and began to polish them. "We frequently visit our granddaughter and her family in Costa Rica."

"You've never been to Venezuela before?" Hurtado asked.

"Certainly we have been to Venezuela." Mr. Smith put on his spectacles. "When we come to South America we always spend a little time visiting and sightseeing in places other than Costa Rica—which is where we learned to speak Spanish. Although our grandson-in-law speaks excellent English."

"Your grandson-in-law is Costa Rican?"

"Yes."

"And yet your accent is that of Caracas," Hurtado said.

Mrs. Smith burst into tears.

Vermeer sprang to his feet and held a large white linen handkerchief out to her. "My dear madame, please do not upset yourself so! What has happened?" He patted her clumsily on the shoulder.

"I can't bear it!" Mrs. Smith sobbed. "I can't bear being terrified of being found out like this!"

"Patty!" Mr. Smith tried to stop her.

"My dear madame," Vermeer said, "found out about what? You have nothing to fear as long as you speak the truth."

Hurtado held up a hand to stop Vermeer. He spoke in his quiet, unemphatic way to the weeping woman. "Would you like to speak to me alone?"

She shook her head. Her soft old face was streaming with tears. "I'd like everybody to hear. It's better that way."

"Patty, please—"

But she could not stop.

—Why doesn't Hurtado take her away? Poly wondered, and then answered her own question. —She might not talk unless she does it right now, right here. But it's horrible.

Charles reached out and took his sister's hand and held it tightly.

Miss Leonis had thought that she was beyond embarrassment. But she was not. She looked at Mr. Theo, who was scowling ferociously at Hurtado.

"He's an honorable man, my Odell." The words flowed from Mrs. Smith like her tears. "A fine man. No one finer. But when we were young he had a problem, a gambling problem."

Mr. Smith stood up, knocking over his chair, and moved away from them. Vermeer moved swiftly toward him, but Mr. Smith only went to the rail and looked out to sea. Vermeer said, "My good man, if this has nothing to do with the murder it will quickly be forgotten by us all."

Mrs. Smith dabbed at her eyes. "He worked in a bank in Caracas. He had a fine position for a young man. We were doing well, I was teaching English, and we had a lovely little house in Macuto—that's a suburb, a nice one. Then—he lost a lot of money and he—he borrowed from the bank."

"Borrowed?" Hurtado asked.

"He told me—he told me what he had done. I made him go immediately to the president of the bank, and he paid it back, Odell did, with interest. He worked hard and he paid back every penny. He wasn't asked to leave his job; the president of the bank was like a father to us, and everything was all right, and ever since that one time there's been nothing, nothing, he's never gambled again, ever, and he was vice-president of the bank in Burlington, they gave him an engraved silver tray when he retired, it was all behind us . . ."

Dr. Eisenstein, who was sitting nearest Mrs. Smith, tried to stop her. "Dear Mrs. Smith, why are you telling us all this? There's no need."

"There is, there is. We had forgotten it. It was past. But then there was that night at bridge—you can't have forgotten that night."

"No."

"Maybe he suspected—"

"Who suspected?" Hurtado asked.

"Mr. Phair. Maybe he suspected about Odell, and was testing. I don't know how he found out—how would he find out?"

"People like Mr. Forsyth Phair have a way of finding out things," Dr. Wordsworth said, and was given a sharp nudge by Dr. Eisenstein.

"However he found out, he found out, and he went to Odell."

"Mr. Phair went to your husband?" Hurtado prompted.

"Yes. He went to Odell."

Mr. Smith turned from the rail and moved back into the light. "He threatened me. He said that if I did not pay him he would tell everybody what had happened, and he would spread the story in Costa Rica, and it would hurt our grand-daughter—" He stopped. Then he said, very quietly, "I told him that as far as I was concerned he could jump overboard. I do not want the past reopened. I do not want our granddaughter to think less of me. I do not want anybody hurt. But I will not live under the constant threat of blackmail. I knew that if I were to give him money the demands would never stop. So I had a motive for murdering him. But I did not."

"Of course you didn't!" his wife cried. "You couldn't have."

"Of course, of course," Vermeer said, full of cordiality. "Do have a drink, Mr. Smith. We all wish you well."

Hurtado looked at his watch. "This will be all for tonight. I am grateful to you, madame." He bowed. "If you will all be equally forthright we will sift this matter through in no time. Miss Phair, it would be my pleasure to escort you to your hotel."

She nodded acquiescence.

"I will see the rest of you after breakfast. Out here, or in the salon, whichever is cooler."

"Señor comandante," Dr. Wordsworth said, "may I suggest that the murder and the theft may not have been committed by one of the passengers?"

"My dear lady, I am quite aware of that. I shall be questioning the officers and crew after you have retired." He spoke affably enough, but there was admonition behind his words. "Vermeer, come with me, please. I will return you to your small appliance which will surely not seat three of us."

Miss Leonis moved numbly between the two men, who helped her down the gangplank. Hurtado seated her carefully in the limousine, saying, "The hotel, alas, is not air-conditioned, but I think you will find it reasonably cool."

"Thank you. Heat does not bother me. My only concern is Simon."

"He is my concern, too, madame. I will pick you up after

breakfast, say ten o'clock. That will give you an opportunity for a good rest."

"I am much obliged. I realize that what happened on deck tonight was probably a good thing—but—do you have any idea as to the whereabouts of my nephew and the English canon?"

"Believe me, Miss Phair, I'm as anxious to find them as you are. Tom Tallis is an old friend. And a highly competent man. If Simon is with him, he is in good hands."

"Do you think they are together?"

"At this moment I see no reason to doubt it."

Vermeer said, "We will try to find the supposed chauffeur who met Tallis. It should not be too difficult."

Miss Leonis asked, "You think that someone impersonated the official chauffeur and then kidnapped Simon and Canon Tallis?"

Hurtado said, "It is as plausible a theory as we have right now. My chauffeur thinks that his flat tire was not accidental."

"And the wool was pulled over Gutiérrez's eyes?"

"So it appears."

"Forgive me, señor comandante, I do not believe in teaching professionals their own business, and if you're not telling me all that you are thinking I quite understand. But I don't think that Gutiérrez is a fool, although I agree with Dr. Wordsworth that he has a somewhat enlarged estimation of his own importance."

"Quite," Hurtado said.

"And I do not trust him."

"Why not, Miss Phair?"

"Sense of smell. A long life has sharpened mine."

"I will bear that in mind. But please try to let us do the worrying, Miss Phair. I shall not be going to bed tonight. But you must rest."

"Yes," she said. "I know that. Señor comandante, I wish to go to Dragonlake tomorrow."

He looked at her, his eyes for a fraction of a second betraying astonishment. "Madame, it is a difficult trip."

"Will you make arrangements for me, please?"

Vermeer began to protest, but Miss Leonis cut him off. "Since I am not under suspicion for murder, theft, or kidnapping, there is no reason you should not allow me to go. If you would care to accompany me, Mr. Vermeer, that would be my pleasure."

Hurtado looked at Vermeer with a slight nod. "It shall be arranged, madame. But you will be kind enough to tell us why you wish to make this excursion?"

"There is, after all, a Quiztano name on the back of a portrait which once belonged to me. And I have a feeling that it may help us to find Simon and your friend."

The limousine drew up before the broad patio of the hotel. Hurtado and Vermeer escorted her into the lobby. The chauffeur carried Miss Leonis's suitcase to the desk.

"My dear madame." Vermeer beamed. "The comandante and I have not eaten. Would you care to join us for a small collation?"

"Thank you, no. The ship's dinner was more than adequate. I should like to be shown directly to my room."

Hurtado said, "Of course. But there is one question I would beg you to answer first. What is written on the back of your portrait of Bolivar?"

She answered, "It once had painted on it, *For my son, born of Umara.* Time, or effort, or both, have blurred and faded the writing, so that now the only letters that show clearly are U M A R."

"What does this mean—Umar, or Umara?"

"Umara is always the name, the inherited name, of the princess of the Quiztanos."

"How do you know this?"

"It is written in Quentin Phair's journal, and referred to in his letters to his mother, and to his wife, Niniane."

"You have these letters?" Hurtado asked.

"I do."

"With you?"

"Yes. In his will Quentin Phair requested that they not be read for six generations. It had always been my intention to leave them for Simon, but during the days since Simon and Forsyth boarded the *Orion* I have dishonored Quentin's request and read the letters and journals. It is because of this, as you can see, that I wish to go visit the Quiztanos tomorrow."

Hurtado said, "I assume that you felt you could give Dr. Eisenstein no information because you did not wish to confide in the assembled company."

"I would have had no right to make such a confidence."

Hurtado's voice was quiet and courteous. "But you will tell us what is in the letters and journals?"

"I will tell you, perhaps, after tomorrow."

"We may have to ask you for the letters and journals."

"I understand. But I am not yet ready to give them to you. They are extremely personal."

"Madame, a policeman is completely impersonal."

"I am not a policeman. But I will not withhold from you anything which might help you in your inquiries." She poked in her reticule and drew out a small bundle of documents. "These are the papers which Forsyth Phair gave me to establish himself as a member of the branch of the family which moved North, and then West, after the War between the States. I would appreciate it if you would check on them for me."

Hurtado held out his hand. "Certainly."

Vermeer asked, "Do you have any reason to doubt the authenticity of these documents?"

"Yes."

Hurtado raised his brows.

"The check Mr. Forsyth Phair gave me for the Bolivar portrait—money which was to see me through the rest of my days—was a piece of paper, no more. Since it was for a large sum of money it was investigated by the bank. The check is worthless. If the man were not dead I would suspect him of absconding with my nephew, and I would place a rather large bet that he is somehow behind Simon's disappearance. There's no doubt that Forsyth Phair, whoever he was, was murdered, is there?"

"No doubt at all."

"Now I wish to retire," Miss Leonis said. "You will, of course, phone me at any time during the night if there is news of Simon?"

"Of course, Miss Phair. Mynheer Vermeer will call for you after breakfast. You are fortunate in your choice of escort.

Vermeer is somewhat of an anthropologist and knows Drag-onlake and its Indians as deeply as anyone who is not a native of this area. The Quiztanos do not welcome strangers to their village, but Vermeer is known to them as a friend."

"Thank you." She bowed gravely. "That is the first piece of good news I have had in a long time."

"I trust you will rest well." Hurtado called the night clerk and asked him to see Miss Phair to her room.

"*A demain, madame.*" Vermeer bent over her hand.

"Good night, gentlemen."

They watched after her. Her walk was stiff with fatigue, but her body was erect.

In his pajamas, Charles went to Jan's cabin.

The steward looked troubled. "It is not good for you to be too much with me."

"Am I bothering you? I'm sorry."

"No, no, it is not that. I know that I am under suspicion."

"That's nonsense."

Jan ran strong, blunt fingers through his fair hair. "I did not murder him. But it is true that I am the only one to have a special interest in the portrait. Mynheer Boon says he never saw the keys, and this I do not understand because he gave them to me to return to Mr. Phair."

"I don't understand either," Charles said.

"I know only that I am suspected."

"Who suspects you?"

"Hurtado. He is the one who is important. I am not worried about Gutiérrez. I know his type. While he was questioning us in the salon he pocketed half the cigars—he's worse than the customs men—and blew and blustered at us but he did not know what he was doing. But Hurtado is different."

"I hate it, I hate it!" Charles cried with vehemence, more like his sister than himself. "I know you didn't kill Cousin Forsyth, but I can't bear to think that *anybody* on the *Orion* could have done it."

"Nor I," Jan said. "It is a bad business. I do not know how it will end."

As Charles crossed the foyer to go to his cabin, el señor co-mandante Hurtado came briskly up the stairs. "Young man, I must talk with you."

Charles waited.

"Shall we go to your cabin?"

In the cabin Charles looked at the bunk in which Simon had spent only one night. He asked, "Where are Simon and Canon Tallis?"

Hurtado lowered himself onto the chair and regarded Charles with his steel gaze. "I wish that I could tell you, Charles. But they are not off my mind for one moment. Tom Tallis is my friend." He touched his breast pocket and indicated a small two-way radio. "If there is any news we will know at once. Now, Charles, I want you to tell me about your dreams."

"How do you know about my dreams?"

"You seem to have discussed them with a good many people."

Slowly Charles crossed his legs. "Dreams are—dreams. They aren't evidence. They don't hold up in court."

"We're not in court. Anything may be important. A reaction to a dream may give me the clue that I need. It may help me to find Simon and Tallis as well as the murderer."

Charles closed his eyes. "All right, I'll tell you. If Canon Tallis phoned you from London to make sure that you would know he was coming, that tells me two things."

"And they are?"

"That you are his friend. And therefore to be trusted. And also that he must have suspected something might happen. He takes my dreams seriously, by the way."

"I take most things seriously," Hurtado said.

When Charles had finished talking, his voice as unemphatic as Hurtado's, the comandante said, "I would like you to tell this to Miss Phair."

Charles nodded.

"If she were not old, and exhausted from travel and worry, I would take you to the hotel tonight. But that will not do. I will pick you up first thing tomorrow morning."

"You're going to take me to her, rather than bringing her to the *Orion*?"

"You are an intelligent boy. Yes. I have reasons. Get to bed now. Perhaps you will dream."

"Perhaps I will," Charles said. He did not sound happy.

Simon and Canon Tallis lay on the rough ground of their clearing. They had tried to soften it with leaves and grasses, but it was still hard and uncomfortable. Their fire burned brightly. But they were grateful not so much for the warmth as for the light. Around them the jungle was alive with noise. Some of the noises Simon recognized from South Carolina, but there were new and strange noises which he had never heard before, breathings and cluckings and hoots. Once he sat upright in terror as the firelight was reflected in two large amber eyes.

Canon Tallis put another piece of wood on the fire. "We have just about enough till morning; then we'll have to collect more."

"What was that?" Simon asked.

"Some jungle creature. I don't think that we'll be disturbed as long as we stay right here and keep the fire going. We'll take turns sleeping. You try to sleep now, and when I get too sleepy to be alert I'll waken you."

"I don't think I'm sleepy," Simon said.

"No. But close your eyes and perhaps sleep will come."

"Do you have any ideas who took the portrait, and who killed Cousin Forsyth, and why Gutiérrez kidnapped us?"

"It appears to me that they are all connected," the canon said.

"Do you think that my ancestor—Quentin Phair—do you think he really did go to Dragonlake and fall in love with the Umara, and then leave her?"

"It seems likely."

"I wish it didn't."

"All human beings break promises, Simon."

"Not Quentin Phair."

"The Quentin Phair of your dreams wasn't a real person."

"No, but—I was brought up to believe that a gentleman does not break promises."

"That's not a bad way to be brought up. It's good to take

promises seriously. Then we're not apt to make or break them lightly. I would guess that your ancestor did not make his promise lightly, but that when he got away from Venezuela and Dragonlake it was almost as though he were waking from a dream. Dragonlake may well have seemed more like a figment of his imagination than anything else, once he reached cold and reasonable England. And then when he came to the North American New World and met Niniane the dream must have seemed even further away. I do not say that this excuses him, but perhaps it does explain him?"

"I guess so. You mean, he didn't break the promise in cold blood. It was what Aunt Leonis would call a sin of omission rather than commission?"

"Quite."

From somewhere in the jungle came the scream of a small animal, a series of hooting calls, a cry that sounded like shrill laughter. "Not much like Piccadilly," the canon murmured. "Do try to close your eyes and rest for a while. No use both of us staying awake all night. We'll do better at solving the murder and getting ourselves out of this predicament if we get some rest."

Simon closed his eyes. He had expected that the canon would lead them in prayer, rolling out pompous words as Dr. Curds had been wont to do. But if the canon did any praying it was in silence. Simon suspected that he had prayed before the boy lay down, but he could not be sure. But Canon Tallis, he understood, prayed the way Aunt Leonis prayed, and this kind of praying was something he respected, even if he did not understand it.

He tried to listen to the fire rather than the noises outside their small clearing. After a while he slid into a doze.

While the boy slept Canon Tallis took a sharp stone and slowly and carefully sharpened the end of a strong branch into a rudimentary spear.

# 11. THE LAKE OF DRAGONS

CHARLES and Aunt Leonis sat at a small round table on the terrace of the Hotel del Lago, eating breakfast. Hurtado had urged them to speak as openly and fully as possible; one never knew what small clue might lead to the murderer, or the whereabouts of Simon and Tallis. Then he left them alone and stood at the far end of the terrace. He had his back turned to them, and had taken himself out of earshot of their conversation, but they both knew that any untoward movement or word would not escape him.

After a while they forgot him.

"You dreamed true," Miss Leonis said when Charles had finished. "It is all in the letters and the journals."

"You've read them?"

"After the accident with the fork lift, which you took as seriously as I did, I kept having the feeling that something was wrong, that I should not have allowed Simon to go with Forsyth—so, yes, I read them. And I learned more than I wanted to know about Quentin Phair. He was not the white knight *sans peur et sans reproche* I was brought up to believe him to be—though neither was he a scoundrel. For all his folly and over-idealism he was a man of uncommon valor, vision, and a great deal of charm." She poured herself another cup of lukewarm tea. "I do not understand why Hurtado has no news of Simon."

Charles said, "If he's with Canon Tallis he's all right."

Miss Leonis beckoned to Hurtado, who joined them. "Have you found anything out about the papers I gave you last night?"

"Madame, I am not a magician."

"I am over-impatient. Forgive me."

"I understand your concern. I should have information on the papers for you by this evening."

"Good. It occurs to me that it might also be wise for you

to call the museum in Caracas and see if Forsyth did make arrangements there about the portrait."

Hurtado looked at her with admiration. "One of my men has already been instructed to do so."

"Sir," Charles said, "wouldn't it be a good idea for Aunt Leonis to go to Dragonlake?"

Miss Leonis smiled at the boy. "I am going. This morning. Mynheer Vermeer is to accompany me. He'll be here shortly?"

"He's waiting in the lobby," Hurtado said. Then he looked directly at Charles. "What did you dream last night?"

Charles's face closed in. Miss Leonis and Hurtado waited. Finally the boy said, "There may be something in one of the Quiztano dwellings which Aunt Leonis ought to see."

"And what is that?" Hurtado asked.

"I didn't dream clearly enough. If Aunt Leonis is going there, she can look."

"Will I be able to?" the old woman asked.

"If what I think is there is there, and if you are meant to see it, you will be able to," Charles said.

Hurtado spoke in a deceptively gentle voice. "Young man, you do understand that if I wish to, I can make you tell me whatever it is that you dreamed?"

Charles gave an unexpected smile. "You're Canon Tallis's friend. So I know there are certain things you won't do."

Hurtado's jaw did not relax. "I wouldn't be too certain of that."

Charles said, "You know that I can't tell you something deadly serious when I'm not sure. When Aunt Leonis gets back from Dragonlake, then I'll tell you."

Hurtado said, "The two of you are a pair. I'm surprised that you are not the nephew; you will tell me what you feel like telling me when you feel like telling me." He snorted. "Please understand that a man has been murdered, the murderer is at large, and we do not know where Simon and Tom Tallis are."

"I do realize that," Charles said somberly. "That's why I can't tell you anything which might be misleading."

"Let me be the judge of that," Hurtado said.

Charles only shook his head. "Tonight."

Hurtado tucked Aunt Leonis into the Hispano-Suiza beside the benevolent Vermeer, who wore, instead of his solar topee, an English straw boater. Miss Leonis had on the thin blue and white dress described by Charles, an ancient leghorn sun hat, and carried her lace parasol.

Vermeer started the engine, revving it fiercely, then nosed uphill, through a narrow street, the houses brightly painted with warm, sunny colors, reds, oranges, yellows, and cooler summer colors, varied shades of greens and blues. Despite her anxiety, Miss Leonis looked about with pleasure.

Vermeer pointed. "If you look through the open doors you can see courtyards and gardens. I live in such a house. It's very pleasant, though hotter in summer than a Dutchman is accustomed to." He drove around the corner into a large square, with a rococo bandstand, flowering cactus, tall, lush trees, towering palms. "Plaza Bolivar." After the cool beauty of the plaza they drove through what appeared to be the main street. Vermeer pointed out bank and post office.

"All the soldiers and policemen with guns," Miss Leonis said, "in front of the bank and the post office, and there—that policeman controlling traffic with his rifle slung and ready—is this the custom in Port of Dragons?"

"Port of Dragons is close to the border, and bandits come across too often for comfort. There's also a sizable band of Cubans in the hills, and the city officials are afraid of revolution."

"With reason?" she asked.

Without answering, Vermeer turned the car and drove rapidly down a long street of brightly colored row houses; suddenly the houses began to be separated and set in flower-filled gardens, and then they drove past prosperous and beautiful villas cheek by jowl with shacks made out of rusty corrugated metal and a few planks. The well-kept and imposing houses became fewer and farther apart, and without warning they were driving through a camp of rickety shacks. A sour and acrid stench assailed their nostrils.

"It looks like a refugee village." Miss Leonis held her handkerchief to her nose.

"It's not. It's the barrio—*ciudad de pobres*—the poor of Port of Dragons."

"Is this—exceptional?"

"Oh, no, you will find this everywhere."

"I understand why you did not answer my question about revolution," she said. "At home we see a few shacks, but never a whole city of them like this. They certainly can't be waterproof."

"They're not."

"What happens in a heavy rain?"

Vermeer's perpetual grin seemed to widen. "A lot of them wash into the sea."

The grin did not deceive her. "How do you stand it?"

He shrugged. "I do what I can. It is not enough."

She looked at the shacks. They seemed to steam in the heat. The laundry hung limp and dirty-looking on the lines.

"There's no easy answer," Vermeer said. "At La Guaira the government built several beautiful high-rise buildings on the waterfront. The people moved out of their shacks and into the apartments, and shortly thereafter most of them moved back to the shacks, where they can have their goat and their garden patch and where the home, bad as it is, is theirs."

A group of naked children with bloated bellies waved at the car. Miss Leonis and Vermeer waved back.

Then the barrio was behind them, and Vermeer drove along a super-highway through a scrubland not unlike some of South Carolina. Vermeer said it was called *monte*. On either side of the highway were booths where Indians were selling touristy gifts—though Miss Leonis wondered how many tourists would come here; it was hardly a resort area. There were also a number of booths with roofs of palm and banana leaves where native men were stopping to drink.

Miss Leonis disciplined herself to observe what was going on around her and not to think about Simon, or what was going to happen when they reached the Quiztano village. She asked, "What are they drinking?"

"Coconut milk." Vermeer slowed down as they passed the next stand, so she could see that the milk was not sold out of the coconut but was poured in and out of two pitchers. "They add sugar water and ice, so that the coconut milk gets dirty and diluted."

She watched as the server hacked several coconuts open with a machete, unplugged them, poured the milk into one of the pitchers, and threw out the coconut with all its meat.

"It looks highly unsanitary," Miss Leonis said as Vermeer accelerated. "But the countryside reminds me of home. No wonder Quentin Phair was happy to stay in North America. We don't have these tall cactus trees, but we do have the palms, and the oleander and bougainvillaea."

The highway narrowed and they drove through a village which Vermeer told her was typical of the area. It was gaudy and crowded, houses, shacks, villas, all crammed in together with no plan or pattern. In the center of the town was a square with a big, beautiful church. In front of the carved wooden doors was a little huddle of old men and women in black.

Miss Leonis regarded it carefully. "In North Florida where some of Quentin Phair's property was, there is Spanish architecture, too."

Vermeer pointed. "Pigs."

She looked, and several large pigs were wandering around the central fountain of the square. Shops crowded out onto the street, with Christmas-tree lights still strung up—possibly, she thought, —they never take them down.

"The houses are interesting," Vermeer said. "Look at that one, so shabby and poor—and yet you can see through the open door that the furniture is new and chrome. And it has always seemed strange to me that the largest and most prosperous villas front directly onto the street, just like the shacks, instead of facing the river, which flows behind them."

"What kind of people live here?" Miss Leonis asked. "And what do they do for a living?"

They left the village and drove across a long suspension bridge. "Most of them are involved in the oil industry in one way or another," Vermeer said, and ahead of them they could see what appeared to be hundreds of round oil tanks.

Suddenly the lake was on their right and Miss Leonis drew in her breath in surprise. Far into the lake sprouted the tall metal towers of oil wells. Vermeer drew up to the shore and stopped his Hispano-Suiza with a flourish, sprang out, and opened the door for Miss Leonis.

She stood beside him under the completely inadequate shade of her parasol. She felt that she was in some kind of hell. Not only was the heat fierce, but excess gas from one of the wells burst in flame from a pipe just a few feet away. Around the spouting flame, heat quivered visibly in the air. Nearby were several official-looking buildings outside which armed soldiers lounged.

Miss Leonis said, "I can see why there have to be men with rifles. All these oil wells must represent millions and millions of dollars. If there should be a revolution it would be quite a coup, and the United States would be just as upset as Venezuela. We depend on all that oil. No wonder even the traffic cops seem ready to shoot on the slightest provocation."

Vermeer nodded. "There is great wealth here. Next to Maracaibo it is the greatest wealth in Venezuela. Nor should one forget that the oil wells provide a reasonable standard of living for a great many people who would starve otherwise."

Miss Leonis looked down at her feet where black sludge oozed heavily out of the lake. "It looks to me as though the oil industry is raping the lake."

"That is for people like Dr. O'Keefe to decide. One thing I have learned in three years at Port of Dragons is that there are no easy solutions."

"It's like something out of Dante's Inferno," she said. "Some of those towers look as though they might be able to stride across the water like robots."

"I have had nightmares of them legging across the land and through the town," the Dutchman said. "But it makes me think of the English H. G. Wells rather than Dante. Shall we continue our journey now? I thought it a pity not to show you the oil wells since our route goes right by them."

They got back in the car. Miss Leonis settled herself. "I am glad to have seen the oil wells, although I do not find them reassuring. And I feel in need of reassurance."

The road narrowed, so that two cars would have had difficulty in passing. The *monte* pressed in on it. Through trees on their left, Miss Leonis could see glimpses of the lake. They were beyond the oil wells now, and the water shimmered in the sunlight.

She pulled her leghorn hat forward to shade her eyes from the glare. Her heart ached. There should have been word of Simon by now. Perhaps she and Charles were both wrong to hold back information; they could have no idea what might mean something to Hurtado; and Vermeer had a keen intelligence behind his idiotic grin.

Vermeer turned toward her. "Only a few miles now, and then we will make the rest of the journey in a canoe."

"Splendid."

"You do not object to the canoe?"

"My dear young man, I was canoeing in the cypress-black waters around Pharaoh long before you were born. I can tell an alligator from a log. In an emergency I am still a good swimmer."

"Perhaps, during the next few minutes, you will tell me why this trip to Dragonlake is so important to you?"

"I will tell you," she said.

For the first time Vermeer looked at her without a smile.

On the *Orion* Hurtado moved from passenger to passenger, officer to officer, sailor to sailor. His jaw appeared to grow darker with each interview, but his eyes retained their sharpness, and his expression remained impassive. He spent more time with Jan than with anybody else.

In the jungle Simon and Canon Tallis struggled to keep their fire going.

"Will we have to spend another night here?" Simon asked.

"It's possible. Not to worry about it now. We managed last night."

"Some of those animals came pretty close to us."

"We'll have to keep the fire going."

"Do you think anyone's seen our smoke?"

"The jungle is extraordinarily thick and our smoke is fairly thin."

"What kind of animals do you think they were last night?"

"Could be many different kinds, from wood mice to wild boar."

"Snakes?"

"We have to watch for snakes as we collect wood, Simon. I don't think they'll bother us at night. How about looking for some more berries? Our frugal breakfast seems a long time ago."

"All right, sir."

Canon Tallis handed him one of the two spears he had fashioned during the night. "You're not apt to need this as long as you're careful, but you might as well take it with you. And do not go out of sight of the fire. Better to be hungry than separated."

"Is it going to be all right, sir?"

Canon Tallis adjusted his palm sun hat. "In terms of eternity, of course it is going to be all right."

"But in terms of right now?"

"No use borrowing trouble, Simon."

"You think Hurtado will find us?"

"Yes. I do think that he will find us. But I can't promise that he will."

Simon turned away. "Aunt Leonis doesn't make promises unless she's positive, either. But if you think he's going to find us that's good enough for me. I'll try to find us more berries. If I climb up and get a coconut do you think we can get into it?"

"I think so," the canon said. "I've found two good flat rocks we could use for crushing purposes."

"We're really managing very well, aren't we?"

"We're an extraordinary pair."

"Aunt Leonis is going to be very worried about us, and so are Poly and Charles and Mr. Theo. I'm very glad your señor comandante Hurtado knows about us."

Miss Leonis sat in the center of a large dugout canoe. Vermeer was in front, and occasionally turned around to nod reassuringly. A young man from the Quiztano village sat in the stern and paddled deftly and swiftly. He was long-limbed and fine-boned, and the golden-bronze of his skin seemed to be lit from within. He wore a short orange tunic, belted in leather, with a knife case. The acanthic folds of his eyes slanted up toward the temples on either side, reminding her of the eyes of young warriors in early Greek sculpture.

He told them that his name was Ouldi, and that he had been sent by Umar Xanai to guide them, and that he spoke English and Spanish. But that was all the information he gave them. His face was as impassive as Hurtado's, and he paddled swiftly and in silence, his oar knifing the water without a splash.

The trip on the lake was cooled by a light wind which ruffled the water. If Miss Leonis had not been beset by anxiety and misgivings she would have enjoyed it. Now that they were nearly there she felt herself trembling in anticipation. She could not escape the thought that Simon might be the next young Phair to be cut down. She tried to eradicate this horror by thinking of Charles: What did he expect her to see at Dragonlake? Could it possibly be Simon?

"Look." Vermeer pointed.

Ahead of them in the lake, small round buildings on high stilts stretched out in the water, somewhat like the oil wells. But where the oil wells had seemed alien and sinister, the Quiztano village appeared to her to be natural and delightful. —It is probably very much the same way it looked when Quentin first came here, she thought.

It was certainly exactly as he had described it. Her old eyes rested on the pleasant scene almost with a sense of *déjà vu*. Half of each circular building was enclosed by a panel of loosely woven straw screening. As they approached the house farthest out in the water Miss Leonis saw a young woman slide the matting around so that the interior of her dwelling would be protected from the sun. All around the circumference of the small and airy building, flowers were blooming. The whole village, she realized, was bright with flowers. The roofs of the small dwellings, like those of the coconut sellers, were covered with palm or banana leaves. Small boats were tied to the slender pilings of many of the dwellings.

Ouldi paddled swiftly toward the shore, past the stork-like dwellings, under several of them. On shore many canoes were pulled up onto the beach out of the water, and she could see a sizable group of people assembled to watch their arrival. No sign of Simon.

Four young men detached themselves from the group and ran splashing through the water to pull the canoe high up onto the sand. Vermeer jumped out, holding out his hands in greeting.

Ouldi, still expressionless, picked Miss Leonis up and set her down gently on the beach. She stood there and looked about her. Had she really expected to see Simon; not really; it was a forlorn hope. If it had been Simon, Charles would have been more definite. Then what did he expect her to see?

There were not as many houses on land as in the water; a few of the round, stilted dwellings, and, most impressive of all the buildings, two long rectangles with flower-filled verandas. Between the two large buildings, in the center of the greensward, was a large statue. From a distance she could not tell whether it was carved from wood or stone; it was the figure of a woman, inordinately tall, flowing in graceful lines from earth to sky, so that it seemed to belong to both. Quentin had mentioned the statue of a goddess, and that her religion was important to his Umara, and it seemed to him no worse than any other form of worship. Religion, to Quentin, was woman's work.

Behind the greensward the jungle reached upward to become a mountain, looming high into the sky. There was a fresh, flower-scented breeze blowing through the village, and a sense of calm and cleanliness. Though the stilted dwellings had a light and windswept look, they were far more substantial than the hovels in the barrio. The mountain itself protected the village, rather than overwhelming it.

The villagers reflected the exuberant colors of their flowers; the young men wore short, colored tunics; on the older men the tunics were longer. The women wore flowing, brightly patterned gowns; everywhere was poinciana scarlet, jacaranda azure, laburnum flame.

—No wonder Quentin could plan to make his life here.

Vermeer was shaking hands with the assembled group, and seemed to know some of them intimately. He bowed low to an old man in a long white robe who came from one of the round dwellings on the greensward. The old man embraced Vermeer, kissing him first on one cheek, then on the other, and thirdly, ceremoniously, on the forehead.

The Dutchman returned the three kisses with joyful formality. "I greet you, Umar Xanai. And I bring to you one who has news of the long-gone One. Her name is Miss Leonis Phair, for she herself is of the line of the Phair."

The old man bowed courteously. "You bring us news, Señora Phair?"

She shook her head. "Sir, I come hoping for news. Do you know where my nephew is?"

Umar Xanai replied, "We know nothing of a nephew. We await the Phair."

Miss Leonis's disappointment was acute, but she said only, "Yes, I know. That is why I am here. I have come to find the past. And now I look for Simon, Simon Bolivar Quentin Phair Renier, a descendant of your Phair."

The old chieftain gestured and two young men ran lightly up the steps to the larger of the round houses and returned with a chair made of young trees laced together with vines. When Miss Leonis was seated one of the young men took her parasol and shaded her with it, while a boy barely past childhood, no older than Simon, fanned her with a palm leaf. Again Umar Xanai bowed over her hand with Western courtesy.

She stiffened as she saw a litter being carried out of the dwelling from which her chair had come. On the litter was a small figure in a silvery-blue robe.

Ouldi said in his rather flat voice, "It is the Umara. She is so old now that she can no longer walk. She eats and drinks little. She spends her time in fasting and prayer."

The Umara was attended by two women in long gowns of silvery-blue, like moonlight. The litter was carried close to Miss Leonis's chair and she could see that the woman sitting on it was indeed very old, much older than she herself. The skin did not have the interior glow of the other Quiztanos, but was the grey-brown of a coconut. She wore a turban and Miss Leonis suspected that she had little or no hair. Her skull showed clearly through the almost transparent skin. Her eyes were sunk deep in their sockets, but they seemed to pierce.

Umar Xanai beckoned to Ouldi. The young man hurried to him, and the old chief dropped one arm lightly on the shoulders of Ouldi's orange tunic. "Your escort, Señora Phair, is one of my great-grandsons."

"Several greats, I should say," Vermeer remarked. "Ouldi is barely out of boyhood."

"You should not worry so much about the bindings of time," the old man said, then turned to Miss Leonis. "Ouldi has just returned to us. He has been away at the big university. Our friend Vermeer arranged for it. So, Ouldi, now you will serve as interpreter. I am too old for long conversing in strange tongues. And the Umara tires even more easily."

The ancient Umara spoke a few words, and began to laugh.

Ouldi said, "She says that she was told that an Old One was coming, and she laughs because the Miss Phair is so young." He stopped, cocking his head to listen as the Umara spoke again, this time with no laughter. "She wants to know if you have the memory that goes beyond death."

"Perhaps."

Ouldi listened again, his head on the slender stalk of neck cocked like a bird's. "She wants to know where the Phair is."

Miss Leonis was surprised to have Vermeer speak to her without even a trace of a smile. "Please be careful how you answer," he said.

She turned to Ouldi, thought for a moment, then said, "I do not know where he is, and this causes me much anxiety."

The Umara nodded in satisfaction at her response. "Again we have sent hunters out to look for him. As they found him before, so they will find him now."

"The jungle is very large," Miss Leonis said. "How will they know where to look?"

"They will go to where they found the Phair the first time."

"And if he is not there?"

"He will be there. Already we have had messages that smoke has been seen. He will be there."

Despite her misgivings, Miss Leonis caught hope from the strength of the Umara's conviction.

The ancient woman continued, "And now we two must speak alone together. You will come to my dwelling, with Ouldi to speak for us." She waved her stick-thin arm imperiously and the litter was raised. The two moonlight-clad women came immediately to her side; now Miss Leonis noted that, though both seemed to her to be young, there must be over a generation separating them. She guessed that they were being trained in the duties of the Umara, from whose point of view anybody under a hundred must be young.

Ouldi helped Miss Leonis rise from the low and supple chair which had been gentle to her tired bones. He spoke in the strange liquid syllables of Quiztano, which reminded Miss Leonis of flowing water and which was completely different from the flat intonation with which he spoke English. The two youths who held parasol and fan moved along with them over the greensward, which was soft and springy under their feet. She moved as though in a dream. Perhaps fatigue and the automatic anesthesia of over-anxiety accounted for her lack of emotion at this extraordinary situation.

She asked, "What are the two long rectangular buildings on either side of the statue?"

"They are the Caring Places, the Caring Places of the Phair."

"What does that mean?"

Ouldi repeated, "They are the Caring Places. For those who are dying. For those who are ill and may, with care, recover."

She stopped. The two youths with parasol and fan quickly stepped back to shade her. "What did my ancestor—the Phair—have to do with all this?"

"It was his thought that the Quiztanos should have special places in which to provide care. We have always had the Gift, but the idea of the Caring Places came from the Englishman, and it was with him that we made the first one."

Miss Leonis looked at the great statue. She could see now that it had originally been carved of wood, but it was so old that the wood had acquired the patina of stone. The face was serene; the lips were quirked in a slight smile which gave a feeling of delight. The carved eyes, however, were as dark and enigmatic as Ouldi's. "What—who—is—?"

Ouldi looked up at the statue and returned its smile. "Until I went away for my studies I understood better than I understand now. She is the one through whom we see the stars and hear the wind."

"Your goddess?"

"Perhaps I would call her that now, though I think I would be wrong. For she is not what she is; and she is more than she is. We do not worship her or pray to her as some of the people in the cities pray to their plaster saints in the gaudy churches. The Umara prays through her, and so does Umar Xanai."

"And the rest of you?"

"Prayer, too, is a gift. We do not all have it. But we benefit from those who do."

Still Miss Leonis did not move toward the dwelling of the Umara. She looked at the two long airy Caring Places. "These—we would call them hospitals today, would we not?"

Ouldi laughed, but there was no pleasure in his laughter. "I think not. When I was at the big university I got a terrible pain in my side and I was taken to the hospital and my appendix was removed. I would not want anybody I love to be ill in a big city hospital. No. These are Caring Places."

"Two Caring Places for a small village—are the Quiztanos often ill, then?"

"Seldom, seldom. We are strong and live long, not as long as the Umara, for we do not have her need and promise to keep, but long, long."

"But who are the Caring Places for, then?"

"For any who may need them. When the Phair and his Umara started them it was for those injured in the wars—liberator or royalist, it did not matter. Many men who were left to die lived because they were brought to us for caring. And those who died did not die alone. We helped them make the journey from here to there."

"Us—we—you talk as though you had been there."

"It is part of the Memory," Ouldi said. "I share in it."

Miss Leonis looked again at the statue. "There isn't war here now. Who is in the Caring Places?" She looked toward the long buildings. The porches were bright with flowers, and the screens were adjusted to provide shade.

Ouldi followed her gaze. "Those who are ill, hungry, filled with the diseases of poverty and starvation. There are some ill from the fish in the far section of the lake. You must have driven by the barrio?"

"Yes," Miss Leonis said. "What happens when the Caring Places are full?"

Ouldi shook his head. "They often are, but they hold as many as we can care for at one time. The people from the barrio come to us; they bring their babies to us. They know that we will care for them and help them make the journey through the valley of death if that is the destination."

"Who does the caring?"

"Those men and women of the Quiztanos who have the Gift, those who have been called to give their lives to the Caring Places. One must be very strong to go through the other side of night with the dying and then return."

"And Quentin Phair—he started all this?"

"I don't know about Quentin, but the Phair started many things," Ouldi said, "both good and bad. He made promises and broke them and there are those who are still angry."

"Here, among the villagers?"

"No. The Umara and Umar Xanai will not permit anger and hate to remain in our midst. Each generation there are those who leave here and make their way in the cities. Some of them have been filled with a sick desire for vengeance, and although they are no longer Quiztanos, they drink and talk about the Quiztano revenge and their lost heritage. Hatred is not the way to bring the Phair back."

She said, "You have left this village and gone to the city and you did not stay there—you returned."

"I am betrothed to an Umara."

"Would you have returned otherwise?"

"I think that I would. At the university I learned much, including that I do not like much of what is supposed to be civilization. Now, Señora Phair, I have talked with you for too long. We must not keep the Umara waiting." He took her arm and urged her forward. When they reached the Umara's dwelling place he gestured to the youths with parasol and fan to wait outside, and helped Miss Leonis up the steep steps. The Umara's two waiting women were adjusting the screens to provide the maximum shade and breeze, and as they slid the screens around, a shaft of sunlight pierced the interior and spotlighted a man's face.

Miss Leonis felt her heart thud crazily within her chest.

The man was not alive. It was a portrait. The portrait of Simon Bolivar.

Hurtado and Vermeer sat on the boat deck.

"You saw the portrait yourself?" Hurtado asked the Dutchman.

"Yes. It is a fine portrait, and an excellent likeness of Bolivar in his prime."

"And on the back?"

"*For my son, born of Umara*. Actually, one had to know that that was what was there. It looked to me as though someone had tried to sand and chip the words away. The wood on which the portrait is painted is thin in places and some of the letters were cut so deep that it would have been impossible to eradicate them without cutting into the portrait. Only the letters U-M-A-R are still clear."

"How did the old lady explain them?"

"She said that until she had read the journals and letters there was no reason to be curious. Unless one has heard of the Quiztanos at Dragonlake, U-M-A-R is only a meaningless jumble of letters. She said that she had thought it might be the mark of the artist."

Hurtado's jaw seemed to darken. "I need to talk to her."

Vermeer nodded sympathetically. "She could not have made the trip back."

"Are you positive?"

"I myself felt her pulse. It was weak, and far too rapid, and very uneven. Her zeal to learn the truth was greater than her strength. And she is half ill with anxiety over the boy."

"With cause. I have learned that Forsyth Phair died two years ago in Salt Lake City, Utah. The passport and all else that the impostor gave the old woman are excellent forgeries. So it is conceivable that the murderer murdered the wrong man."

Vermeer rubbed his nose. "The plot thickens."

"The murderer may not have known that Phair was an assumed name, and it may have been a Phair he was after."

"The ancient Quiztano vendetta against all Phairs?"

"I am a Latin, Vermeer, and I take such things more seriously than you do. Hate does not die easily around here. Nor the passion to bring past crimes to judgment. Don't forget that there are at this moment Israelis in Argentina tracking down Nazis."

"Yes. That too is a long time to hold hate."

"Hate dies less easily than love. How did the Quiztanos explain the portrait in their village?"

Vermeer said, "I would like a beer. How about you?"

Hurtado rose and went to the call bell.

When he sat down again, Vermeer said, "Umar Xanai said that they do not know how the portrait came to them."

"Oh?"

"It was brought to the village, it seems, by a fisherman who has Quiztano blood. He could not or would not tell them how he got it."

"Could not?"

"According to Umar Xanai, he was in a state of terror. All he wanted was to unload the portrait."

Both men were silent as they heard steps. Jan climbed up from the promenade deck. "You rang, sir?"

"Yes, Jan, two beers, please." Vermeer's smile sprang back to his face. He looked after Jan, running down the steps, and asked, "What are you going to do about him?"

"Jan? Tonight, nothing."

Vermeer said, "It was Jan who took me for my first visit to the Quiztanos, otherwise I shouldn't have been welcomed. I feel that I am betraying my friend."

"If he is innocent he has nothing to fear. If he is involved in smuggling—"

Vermeer cut him off. "No. I can't think of Jan as belonging to the world of smugglers, even the more innocent kind."

"Is there an innocent kind?"

"The early smuggling—tea, sugar, spices—I cannot think of such goods in the same category as drugs and chemicals."

"What about the art racket?"

"Art what?"

"Racket. An American idiom."

"It's bad. But it's still not quite as contemptible as drugs, as antibiotics and steroids cut with poisons, as chemicals misused to destroy life for the sake of greed. Smuggling is far worse today than it used to be."

"It is a sin to steal a pin."

"What?"

"An English idiom. Smuggling is smuggling. One step leads to another."

"Jan has not stolen a pin."

"How well do you know him?" Hurtado asked calmly.

"I thought I knew him extremely well, but of course I see him only when the *Orion* puts in at Port of Dragons, and when he takes me out to Dragonlake—but I have always sensed in him a deep innocence."

"Perhaps that very innocence makes it possible for someone less innocent to use him for less than innocent purposes."

"Gutiérrez?" Vermeer suggested hopefully.

"Have you got anything on him?"

"Not yet. Remember, I'm only a consul, and I don't have an army of policemen and detectives and secret-service people at my beck and call."

"You might be interested to know that he has flown the coop."

"Has what?"

"An English idiom. I sent for him this morning and was told that he has gone to visit his mother, who is very ill. Marvelous convenient how mothers can get ill when the heat is on—another English idiom."

"Where is this alleged mother?"

"In one of the small villages deep in the jungle. He preempted a helicopter. No telephone, of course. He cannot be reached."

Vermeer pulled up one of his knee socks and straightened the garter. "He has a reputation for knowing the jungle well, including places that can be reached only by canoe or copter. I prefer to think of oily little Gutiérrez involved in dark doings rather than one of my compatriots. Jan does have a Dutch passport. No, no, he wouldn't do anything to hurt van Leyden."

"It will look bad for van Leyden if someone on his ship is dealing in narcotics on the side."

"Narcotics is only a small part of it. Chemicals, including mercury."

"Mercury. Yes," Hurtado said. "You know, Vermeer, if Dr. O'Keefe had been murdered I could have understood it better than Phair."

"Because it is an ill-kept secret that he has been brought to Venezuela to investigate Dragonlake?"

"There have been several cases of mercury poisoning among the people who live near one of the chemical plants. The oil wells are the obvious pollutant, but not necessarily the most dangerous one."

"Industrial effluents containing mercury absorbed by fish which are then eaten by the people of the barrio? Yes, I've heard. Ouldi said something."

"It's one of the nastier forms of poisoning, with neurological damage and intense pain." Hurtado looked grim. "I'd better have O'Keefe watched, then. Does he have any idea he may be in danger?"

"He's no fool." Vermeer suddenly looked as grim as the policeman.

Jan appeared with a tray, two bottles of beer, and two glasses. He set it down on the bench between the two men. Instead of leaving immediately he asked anxiously, "Is there any news of Simon?"

"Not yet," Hurtado said.

Miss Leonis sat on the veranda of the Umara's house. The Umara had been placed on a low couch, and Umar Xanai sat on the floor, as did Ouldi. A large round tray was set on a low table between them. It contained a graceful bowl of fruit, and a corresponding pitcher of a cool and delicious drink which seemed to have been made from a combination of fruits and herbs.

Umar Xanai passed a glass of the pale-green beverage to Miss Leonis. "This is a restorative. It will give you strength and calm your heart."

She sipped it appreciatively. "Thank you. I had not realized quite how tired I am from my journeyings."

The Umara spoke in her strange, ancient voice, and Ouldi translated. "Your journey through time as well as space?"

Miss Leonis sipped again. "Yes. I am learning that I share in your Memory. It is our loss in my world that we no longer value the memory of our people."

Umar Xanai replied, "Those who do not share in the Memory are only a part of themselves. It is good that you have come to fulfill what has been lost."

Miss Leonis sighed. Her heart pained within her. As she sipped the cool liquid the grey look receded from her face, but her eyes were dark with pain.

Ouldi said, "The Phair is safe. The Umara promises."

Miss Leonis bowed. "I am grateful. And grateful, too, for your kindness and hospitality. I understand from Mynheer Vermeer that you do not encourage strangers."

Umar Xanai replied, "We have a work to do. It is easily misunderstood. If the wrong people come with modern investigations we might be forbidden to do our work—or they might want us to make it bigger, and that would destroy it. And then"—he pointed toward the great carving—"she would no longer smile."

Miss Leonis set down her empty glass. Her breathing was no longer agony, but it still rasped. "It is very kind of you to keep me here tonight. The trip back to Port of Dragons would have been too much for me. And I am not sure when—or if—I will be able to leave."

Umar Xanai smiled. "It is our honor to have you with us, for as long as need be. We knew that you were coming to Venezuela even before the Dutchman made the arrangements for you today, so we have been expecting you."

"How did you know?"

"Jan, the steward on the *Orion*. I have in my Memory a picture of his Quiztano grandmother when she was young and beautiful and in love with the big blond youth from Holland. Jan has become dear to my heart with his love of the Quiztano part of his heritage. He knows our way of sending messages—a whistle here, the beat of a drum there, another whistle, and it is quicker than your modern machines."

"How did Mynheer Vermeer make the arrangements for today?"

"Thus. Through Jan. Jan feared the trip would overtax you, so even before you arrived we had made preparations for you to stay." A twinkle came into the old man's eye, and he spoke swiftly to Ouldi, the liquid syllables bubbling like a brook in early spring.

Ouldi said, "Grandfather says that you will be more comfortable here than at the new so-modern hotel. Always at night a breeze comes over the lake and the forest lends us the coolness of its shadows and the mountain gives us the strength of its peace. And"—he gestured toward the statue—"she gives us her blessing."

"Your Lady of the Lake," Miss Leonis said.

Ouldi translated, "Not of the lake only. She speaks to us not merely of the waters, but of the wind and the rain and the mountain and the stars and the power behind them all."

Miss Leonis looked out over the peaceful scene. "I, too, trust the same power."

The Umara, who seemed to have fallen asleep, spoke.

Ouldi listened carefully. "She says that this Power is the Power which has all Memory. Even her Memory is as nothing compared to the Memory of the Power behind the stars."

Miss Leonis said, "To be part of the memory of this power is for life to have meaning, no matter what happens." She had based her life on this faith. She could not begin to doubt it now.

Simon and Canon Tallis sat by their fire.

"But you don't think we're going to have to stay here more than one more night, do you?"

"No, Simon. If nobody has found us by tomorrow morning I think we will have to start heading toward the sea. We've run out of edible berries within moderate radius of our campsite. But you did nobly indeed to get us those coconuts. I was beginning to feel dehydrated."

"So was I," Simon said. "I don't think anything has ever tasted so good." He looked at his scratched hands. His thighs were scraped from the descent from the high tree. Why did the coconuts have to be at the very top? But they still had two coconuts for morning.

Tallis said, "I've been given too many warnings about the water in South American streams and rivers to risk drinking, no matter how clean that nearby stream may look. There are tiny organisms which bite and then lay eggs in one's bloodstream, for instance, which cause a slow death. It's not worth the risk."

The dark seemed to increase around them. Simon broke the silence to ask, "When Quentin Phair came to see about his mother's inheritance in North Florida and Georgia and South Carolina, was it like this?"

"It was probably more like this than like the country you grew up in. Our ancestors braved considerable danger without making any fuss about it."

"We're not making much fuss, are we?"

"You're not," Canon Tallis said. "I'm doing a good deal of grunting and groaning over my physical exertions. I'm woefully out of condition. Now, Simon, you take the first watch tonight, and I'll sleep for an hour or so. Don't hesitate to wake me if you see or hear anything."

"Are you ever frightened?" Simon asked as the canon arranged himself on his bed of moss and fern. He was a large man, a little too heavy. His bald head caught and reflected the light from the fire.

"Frequently."

"Are you frightened now?"

"No. There doesn't seem to be any particular reason to be frightened. But I am tired from our labors. Good night, Simon."

"Good night, Uncle Father." Simon noticed that the priest kept his wooden spear under his hand.

The night seemed even more alive with sound than had the

night before, or perhaps his ears were more attuned to it. He thought he could even hear insects moving along the rough bark of the tree trunks. The birds settled down for the night, but more noisily than the canon. They seemed to be passing along messages to each other. He was sure he recognized the chittering of monkeys, although they had seen none. The day had been brightened by the wings of birds, but the only animals they had seen were a kind of squirrel, and many lizards of varying sizes.

Simon stiffened and put his hand on his own spear as he saw two eyes reflecting their firelight. He threw another piece of wood on the fire, but he couldn't use too much wood or it wouldn't last until morning. The eyes retreated.

Simon looked over at the canon, whose body was relaxed. The palm-leaf hat was over his eyes. He was breathing quietly, not snoring, but the relaxed breathing of sleep.

The boy turned and the eyes were there again, this time closer. He took a stick and stirred the fire, but the eyes did not go away. He took a small stone and threw it as hard as he could. Whatever beast it was, it moved heavily, with a crackling of twigs, but retreated only a few inches. The eyes looked small and ugly in the firelight, but Simon did not think the animal was as small as the eyes would indicate. He tried staring it down. The eyes blinked, but opened again. There was a small snap of twigs as the beast moved forward until Simon could see what it was: a wild boar.

With trembling hands he grabbed the spear, shouting, "Go away!"

Canon Tallis was awake and on his feet in seconds, holding his spear lightly in his right hand.

There was a horrendous noise of grunting, screeching beast, and the canon shouting, "Out of the way!"

Simon stepped back, spear in hand, ready to move in, but keeping out of the way of the canon's feet. The snarling of the animal was the most repellent sound he had ever heard, but then the snarling changed to a scream which was worse. The canon, too, was breathing heavily with effort. His spear was deep in the boar, but the animal thrashed wildly and with enormous strength, and Simon could see that the canon was beginning to tire.

Suddenly the boar turned so that Simon, putting all his weight into his action, could thrust his own spear into the leathery hide.

But the raging beast was stronger than both of them, although it no longer wanted to attack. With two spears buried deep in its flesh it burst away from them and crashed into the forest.

"Will it come back?" Simon panted.

Canon Tallis was taking great gulps of the dark, humid air. "I doubt it. I think we wounded it pretty badly. That was good work, Simon. I'm not sure I could have kept up much longer. Are you all right?"

"Yes, sir."

"You're a brave boy." Canon Tallis stretched one leg toward the fire. The dark cloth of the trousers was ripped from thigh to ankle, and blood dripped on the ground.

"Oh, sir, he hurt you!"

The canon examined an ugly gash along his calf. "It's only a flesh wound. But I ought to wash it."

"Not the stream," Simon said. "It would be as dangerous as drinking it."

"Bright lad. You're quite right. I'll let it bleed a bit, and the blood itself will clean it. See if you can gather me some clean ferns and I'll stanch the blood with them."

When the wound was covered with fresh green, and the bleeding stopped, the canon said, "I doubt if either of us will do much sleeping for the rest of the night. Let's go over, once more, everything we know about the theft of the portrait and the murder of the Phair. Each time you tell me, you remember something new."

Dr. Wordsworth and Dr. Eisenstein were playing cards in the salon. All the portholes were open and the fans going but it was still hot and stuffy. Dr. Wordsworth slammed down her cards.

"I'm going to Hurtado."

"Inés, no!"

"I should have gone immediately and I was too involved in myself, as usual, to realize."

"But why? What good will it do?"

"Don't you see that if Hurtado knows Phair was involved in smuggling, it may be of immense importance?"

"Yes, I suppose it may be, but then you will have to tell him . . ."

"Everything. It's all right. As far as society is concerned, my time in jail has paid my debt, and my life has been impeccable since. I left for the United States as soon as I got out of jail and not a thing that I've done in my new country cannot be looked at in the light of the sun. And my American passport will help." She stood up. She looked tall and elegant in a long white skirt slit up the sides to show her shapely legs. She smiled at her friend. "Hurtado is a man. When I dressed for dinner I think I already knew what I had to do."

"Would you like me to come with you?"

"No. Thank you. Though he will probably want to talk with you afterward. You've known me longer than most people. So perhaps you'd better stay here and be available."

"Of course. You're very brave, Inés."

"Hurtado may think it a trifle late." Dr. Wordsworth left the salon.

Miss Leonis lay in the fragrant dark of Dragonlake. The high dwelling was, as Umar Xanai had promised, far cooler than the hotel had been. Air flowed beneath, above, through. She could hear the water lapping gently against the pilings of the dwelling huts in the lake. Somewhere nearby a night bird was singing sweetly. Whatever she had been given to drink had indeed helped her. For a while she had thought that her overtaxed heart was giving out, that she was going to die then and there among a strange people in a strange land with Simon who knows where.

Now she thought that she would be able to hold on until Simon was found at any rate and some of the confusions were straightened out—not only about Forsyth Phair, but about Simon and the Quiztanos.

But why was her portrait of Bolivar in the Umara's dwelling place? It still stood there, although she could not see it in the dark.

—They will not be satisfied with the portrait, she thought. —They want Simon. What are we to do?

12. THE RETURN OF THE PHAIR

Iɴ the morning el señor comandante Hurtado assembled the passengers and told them that he had arrested Jan for the theft of the portrait and the murder of Forsyth Phair.

Simon slept fitfully toward morning. When he woke up, the canon was putting the last few twigs on the fire. His face looked flushed and feverish.

"Sir, are you all right?"

Tallis indicated his leg. "It seems to be a bit infected."

"Can you walk on it?"

"I don't think so, Simon."

"Well, then," Simon said after a moment, "I'd better try to find us some berries and stuff for breakfast. We've got another coconut, so we won't get dehydrated. I'll have to go a little farther afield for the berries, sir."

"Not until daylight."

"No, sir."

"And then stay within voice hail, Simon. It would be very easy to get lost. Call out every few seconds, and I'll call back."

"Yes, sir. I will. I'm sorry about your leg. Does it hurt much?"

"A bit."

"You were like St. George killing the dragon last night."

"A far cry, I'm afraid."

"You were close enough to St. George for me. Wild boars are probably more dangerous than dragons. Hurtado or someone should be along to find us any moment now."

"Yes, Simon. They ought. It should be daylight soon."

Miss Leonis rose early at Dragonlake, as she did at Pharaoh. She awoke feeling refreshed, although her heart still seemed to rattle like a dry leaf.

With considerable effort she dressed in her blue and white dimity, and folded the soft gown she had been given to sleep in. Then she climbed carefully down the steps of the Umara's dwelling place and walked across the greensward to the lake's edge. Her breath came in small, shallow gasps.

Umar Xanai was there before her, alone, sitting in Charles's favorite position.

The old woman sat down silently, slightly to one side and behind him. Around her she could sense the sleeping village. Someone was moving on the porch of one of the Caring Places. Soon Dragonlake would be awake. All around her she heard bird song. A fish flashed out of the lake and disappeared beneath the dark waters. Above her the stars dimmed and the sky lightened.

When the sun sent its first rays above the mountain, Umar Xanai rose and stretched his arms upward. He began to chant. Miss Leonis could not understand the velvet Quiztano words, but it seemed clear to her that the old chieftain was encouraging the sun in its rising, urging it, enticing it, giving the sun every psychic aid in his power to lift itself up out of the darkness and into the light. When the great golden disc raised itself clear of the mountain the chanting became a triumphal, joyful song.

At the close of the paean of praise the old man turned to the old woman and bent down to greet her with the three formal kisses.

She asked, "You are here every morning?"

He nodded, smiling. "It is part of my duties as chief of the Quiztanos."

"To help the sun rise?"

"That is my work."

"It would not rise without you?"

"Oh, yes, it would rise. But as we are dependent on the sun for our crops, for our lives, it is our courtesy to give the sun all the help in our power—and our power is considerable."

"I do not doubt that."

"We believe," the old man said quietly, "that everything is dependent on everything else, that the Power behind the stars has not made anything to be separate from anything else. The sun does not rise in the sky in loneliness; we are with him. The moon would be lost in isolation if we did not greet her with song. The stars dance together, and we dance with them."

Miss Leonis smiled with joy. "I, too, believe that. I am grateful that you help the sun each morning. And when the moon wanes and the sky is dark—you are with the dying moon, are you not?"

"When the tide ebbs and the moon is dark, we are there."

"My tide is ebbing."

"We know, Señora Phair."

"It will be an inconvenience to you. I am sorry."

"Señir Phair, it is part of our Gift. We will be with you."

"I am not afraid."

"But you are afraid for the Phair."

"I am afraid for Simon."

"Do not fear, Señora Phair. You have come to redeem the past."

"That is not in my power," she said sadly.

He looked at her calmly. "You will be given the power."

"I can make no decisions for Simon."

"But you will allow him to make decisions for himself?"

"I have always tried to do so. I will not try to influence him by telling him that I will not be returning to South Carolina. I wish I shared your certainty that he is all right."

Umar Xanai nodded calmly. "He will be here before long. The Englishman with him has been hurt, and has to be carried. A litter will be made for him in the same way that a litter was once made for the Phair."

"How do you know all this?"

He smiled, all the wrinkles in his tan face fanning upward. "We have our own ways of seeing. They will be found today, your boy and his friend. I am not sure when. But today."

"I am grateful."

"Come." With amazing agility he sprang to his feet. "It is time that we broke our fast. You have need."

Miss Leonis accepted his strong hand; she could not have risen without him. "Thank you. I am grateful to have a few more days. It would ease me if I could be certain about Simon. Can you keep me going that long?"

He looked at her steadily. "You will have that much time.

It is our Gift. Sometimes when we have sent out young men to the cities, to the hospitals and medical schools, the Gift is laughed at. Sometimes our young men laugh, too, and do not return."

"I know." She sighed. "The Great God Science. It has failed us, because it was never meant to be a god, but only a few true scientists understand that."

Again he smiled. "There are things that you must teach us, Señora Phair. The young Umaras seek time with you."

"They will teach me, too."

He held out his arm to support her, and together they walked slowly back to the village.

To the passengers on the *Orion* it seemed even hotter and more humid the second day in port than it had the first.

But now that Hurtado had made an arrest, the unloading of the ship began. No one was allowed on the foredeck, though the passengers could watch through the windows in the salon. One of the sailors sat in his high cab and manipulated the levers which controlled the great yellow cranes. From the promenade deck the passengers could see the station wagon hover over the dock, as the hearse had hovered, then drop down gently, all four wheels touching earth simultaneously.

Dr. Wordsworth and Dr. Eisenstein left the salon for the deck, seeking what little breeze there was. They leaned on the rail and watched a large crate swing onto the waiting mandibles of a fork lift. "They know what they're doing," Dr. Wordsworth said with considerable admiration.

Dr. Eisenstein turned from the dock and toward her companion. "Inés, do you really think it was Jan?"

"Hurtado's no fool," Dr. Wordsworth said, "but I confess I was surprised. However, since I've been unable to come up with a prime suspect myself, I have to assume that he knows what he's doing."

"But after what you told him about Mr. Phair being Fernando—"

Despite the heat Dr. Wordsworth shivered. "Interesting,"

she remarked casually, "how heat can affect one like cold. Hurtado was extraordinarily courteous with me. I have great respect for him. But has it occurred to you that what I told him may have been what he needed to put his finger on Jan?"

"But Jan is so open and friendly, and almost as vulnerable and innocent-seeming as Geraldo."

"Don't you realize, Ruth, that the innocent and the vulnerable are the very ones preyed upon by types like F.P.?"

"But Jan—!"

"I don't like it, either. But I'm grateful it's over."

Dr. Eisenstein glanced at the chair where she had put her straw bag of notebooks and academic periodicals. "Mr. Hurtado says we will be allowed ashore, soon. I'm glad he wasn't too hard on you last night."

Dr. Wordsworth laughed, a more spontaneous laugh than her companion had heard in some time. "Hurtado is an intelligent and successful and highly desirable man. I think he found me attractive—though if he had suspected me of murder that would have made no difference. But, do you know, Ruth, it's funny, theatrical Vermeer I'm drawn to. Human beings are the most peculiar of all creatures."

Dr. Eisenstein smiled. "The feeling between you and Mr. Vermeer appears to be mutual."

"Here you go, matchmaking again. No, Ruth. Vermeer beams on the entire world and only he knows what goes on behind that smile. And I certainly have no desire to lose my heart to a Dutch consul in an obscure backwash of a country which is no longer mine."

"He knows a lot about anthropology—"

"Which makes up for all deficiencies in your eyes. Oh, I know he's not the idiot he appears. But all I meant was that Hurtado has the machismo and it doesn't even touch me. I'm sorry about Jan. I liked him. But Fernando Propice was a master at corrupting innocence."

Dr. Eisenstein put a restraining hand on Dr. Wordsworth's arm. "Look—"

Jan, his face pale, was walking down the gangplank, somewhat awkwardly, because he was handcuffed. A policeman walked in front of him, another behind him. The two women watched as he was pushed into a police car and driven off.

There had been scant pickings for breakfast, or for lunch, as Simon and Canon Tallis carefully called the bare handful of berries that made up their meals. They drank the milk from the last coconut, and chewed on a few greens which Simon recognized as being like the edible greens around Pharaoh, picked by Aunt Leonis and cooked with a little white bacon. But cooked greens and greens raw are quite different; these tasted bitter, though at least they contained a little water and were worth chewing for that alone, for the coconut milk did little to assuage their thirst. Simon knew that if it had not been for Canon Tallis, he would long ago have cupped up water from the brook.

"If Gutiérrez is the type I think he is," the canon said, "he would choose a place with no safe water supply. Murder by indirection is what he's after."

"We've got to have something more to eat," Simon said. "I'll have to go a little farther."

"No, Simon. You went beyond voice range last time, and almost got lost."

"But I didn't get lost. I got back."

"You might not, the next time. It's not worth the risk of being separated. I know neither of us cares if we never see another coconut, but we can survive on them for a while longer, if you'll climb another tree. And by tomorrow I'll be able to walk."

Simon knew that Canon Tallis did not think much of the boy's chances of surviving alone in the jungle. —And I've never been a Boy Scout or anything, he acknowledged. —Aunt Leonis and I have led very sedentary lives.

He could recognize a water moccasin or a rattler or a coral snake. He did not think much of his ability to fight off a wild boar singlehanded.

By mid-afternoon it was apparent to both of them that the priest's wound was worsening. Despite frequent fresh dressings of cool leaves the wound became steadily more inflamed and suppurating. The flush of fever rose boldly in the canon's cheeks.

He reached up to the woven sun hat covering his bald pate. "I think I must have a touch of sun."

"You have fever, sir."

"Yes. Perhaps I have."

"You're not going to be able to walk by morning, sir."

The priest did not answer. Around them the jungle noises seemed to increase, to draw closer. They heard hoots, clucks, cackles; hisses, screeches, growlings.

"They smell my wound," Canon Tallis said. "If Hurtado has not found us by tomorrow you had better leave me here and head for the sea. Do you know how to guide yourself by sun and wind?"

"I've never had to, but—as you said—necessity makes a good teacher. I'll do my best to—" He broke off as there was a crescendo of noise and activity, and a sudden screeching of birds flying high up into the air above the jungle. Near their clearing twigs crackled, leaves rustled, a branch creaked.

Then, above them, Simon saw eyes, great obsidian eyes in a cat-shaped face. The body was spotted, and rippled with muscles tensed to spring.

"Run!" Canon Tallis ordered. "Simon, run!"

Blind with terror, Simon ran.

Geraldo would not leave his hot box of a galley. He stood at the sink and washed cups and saucers which did not need washing. His face was stained with tears.

Poly hovered. "I know he didn't do it, Herald."

Tears gathered again in Geraldo's dark eyes. He blew his nose.

"But"—Poly asked hesitantly—"why did he lie about the key to cabin 5?"

"Jan does not lie."

"You still think he's covering up for somebody?"

Geraldo shrugged.

"You think he'll go on covering even if he's hanged for it—or whatever they do in Venezuela?"

Geraldo hunched his shoulders upward again.

"And the portrait—" Poly said. "How did the portrait get off the *Orion* and into the Umara's house at Dragonlake?"

"It could be done," Geraldo said slowly. "A fishing boat could come close enough so that a strong swimmer could get to the *Orion* unseen."

"Unseen by radar?"

"Yes. It is possible."

"And then what?"

"From the lower deck, where the pilot comes on, from there the portrait could easily be lowered into the water. And you said that it is painted on wood."

"That's what Simon said."

"So it would float."

"But wouldn't the salt water hurt it?"

"Perhaps not if it were only for a short time and if it were to be cleaned off immediately."

Poly looked at him admiringly. "You've really thought it all out, haven't you?"

"It seemed necessary."

"Have you told Comandante Hurtado?"

Again Geraldo shrugged. "I did not think that it would help Jan."

"You mean, it's something Jan could have done?"

"Jan—or the man who tried to push Simon overboard. And I have no doubt that the señor comandante could figure this much out for himself. He does not need me to tell him."

"But we don't know what he said to Jan, or what Jan said to him."

"We know enough. Jan was not quiet. He was heard. He swore he had nothing to do with it, any of it."

"And Simon and Uncle Father?"

The tears began to flow down Geraldo's cheeks. He spoke over a sob. "I do not understand the comandante Hurtado. I thought he was a man of wisdom. Why has he not found them and brought them to the *Orion*? We do not even know if they are alive."

Poly put her hand over Geraldo's mouth. "Stop! Stop!" She wondered at her own dry eyes.

Charles sought out Hurtado, and was finally summoned up onto the bridge, where the policeman had been talking with the captain.

"You want to see me?" Hurtado asked.

"Yes, please. I had a dream last night."

Hurtado wiped his hand over his somber jaw. "It is late for dreams."

"Please—I saw a man being handcuffed, and it was not Jan, because Jan was crying, crying for the man."

"Who was it, then?"

"It was a man in a winter uniform, with his cap pulled down. I do not know who it was. But it was not Jan."

"Your dreams do not tell you enough."

"But my dreams have never lied. And it was not Jan who was being handcuffed, because Jan was there, weeping for whoever it was."

Hurtado spoke heavily. "Charles, I have to trust the evidence."

"But it was not Jan, I know it was not Jan."

Hurtado reminded him, "You yourself said that dreams do not hold up in court. I'll speak to you later, Charles. I have work to do."

"Simon and Uncle Father?" Charles asked. "Have you found them?"

Hurtado looked over the boy's head, not meeting the blue eyes. "A party of Quiztanos is searching for them, and they can move in the jungle where no white man can manage."

"But you think they're all right?"

Now their eyes met. "I will not think otherwise."

Simon did not know how long or how far he ran in his panic, crashing through underbrush, not thinking of scorpion or snake, not feeling the lash of vines cutting across his face. At last the density of the jungle itself stopped him. He had run into a wall of trees and bushes laced together by vines.

He stood still, panting, his heart thudding wildly. Sweat suddenly poured out of him, while his mouth and throat were parched.

He had run away.

He had run away from Canon Tallis with his wounded leg. He had run away from whatever kind of wildcat it was which had been about to leap on them.

He had abandoned Canon Tallis, incapable of protecting himself, left him to be killed. He had thought only of saving his own life.

Suddenly he was furious, furious with Quentin Phair.

—If you hadn't run away from Dragonlake I'd never have run away from Uncle Father. If you'd been where you ought to be, then I'd never have deserted my friend. It's your blood in my veins that's responsible—

No. He could hear Aunt Leonis as clearly as though she were there in the jungle beside him. 'Ultimately your decisions are yours, Simon. You have a goodly heritage, but it is up to you to live up to it. Quentin Phair cannot make you brave in an emergency. You have to condition your own reflexes of braveness.'

If Quentin Phair could not make him brave, neither could he make him a betrayer.

—But I'm blood of your blood, Quentin, he thought bitterly.

His anger ebbed, leaving him spent and heavy of heart. He began to walk. He had no idea in what direction he had run, or if he was heading toward or away from the clearing. He was afraid of returning to the clearing, afraid of what he might find there. But he had run away, there was no evading that, and the only thing left to do was to return. He knew that it would be too late, but it was still what he had to do.

Shortly after lunch Gutiérrez appeared. His mother had recovered from her illness; the sight of her son had given her renewed strength.

Vermeer, staying on the *Orion* in Hurtado's absence, greeted him effusively, rejoicing over the miraculous recovery of el señor jefe de policía Gutiérrez's beloved mother, "and I am happy to tell you, my dear Gutiérrez, that Hurtado has made a definitive arrest. All our troubles are over."

Gutiérrez's surprise was as enlarged as Vermeer's sympathy. "But who can it be? Never have I known so complex a problem!" When Vermeer told him, he said, "Of course, I should have guessed. I have been suspecting that young man of indulging in smuggling for some time, but could not pin anything definite on him."

"Smuggling as well as murder and theft and kidnapping!" Vermeer exclaimed.

Gutiérrez rubbed his pudgy hands together. "It explains much."

"Does it? Why does smuggling explain the murder?"

"The Bolivar portrait," Gutiérrez said. "That is an extremely valuable portrait. If Jan were caught stealing the portrait by Mr. Phair, then he would be forced to dispose of him. There is much profit to be made from stolen art treasures."

"You think Jan was part of a ring of art thieves?"

"It is likely, is it not?"

"And what about the boy and the Englishman?"

Gutiérrez moved his face into distressed lines. "They have of course been found?"

"Not yet. We know more or less where they are; the Quiztanos saw smoke in the interior of the jungle, and a party is out looking for them. We expect them to be found shortly."

"A happy issue to all our problems," Gutiérrez said, but he did not sound happy. "Pray do excuse me, señor consul, but I must get back to my job. I wanted to come directly to the *Orion*, but now there is work to be done, all the daily routines to be picked up."

When Gutiérrez had bustled off, greeted at the gangplank by what seemed to be hundreds of waiting minions, Vermeer went out onto the dock and spoke to a man who was lounging in the shade of his truck.

During the afternoon the pain in Canon Tallis's leg had become so acute that he knew he was not going to be able to keep it from the boy much longer. As his fever mounted, his mind began to remind him of a movie camera; sometimes everything was close up, clear, each detail visible; then the camera would move back so that all was far away. When he became aware of the beast in the tree above them, crouched to spring, he viewed it as from an incredible distance, as through the wrong end of a telescope. He knew that he could not run. He heard himself calling to Simon to run, and then he crossed himself and prepared to die.

His life did not flash before him—after all, he was not drowning—but he had a quiet feeling of pleasure that his life had been rich in experience and friendship and the love of God.

He closed his eyes.

Then he heard a thwack, and a scream, and a thud, and the wildcat dropped from the tree, dead, an arrow piercing its heart.

The Smiths sat in the shadow of the canvas canopy on the promenade deck. "That nice Jan," Mrs. Smith said. "It is hard to believe."

"Not many people who knew us in Burlington would ever have suspected that I was once so involved in gambling that I nearly ruined our lives."

"But—murder! I cannot see Jan as a murderer."

Mr. Smith patted her hand gently. "The human heart is too often an ugly thing, Patty. There are not many gentle souls like you. If it hadn't been for you I *would* have ruined us."

"I knew what you were really like," Mrs. Smith said. "You're a good man, Odell, and I love you."

"You've made me what I am, Patty. You gave me the courage to stand up to Phair and refuse to be blackmailed. I love you, too, and just as much as I did fifty years ago."

They sat holding hands, and smiling at each other, and did not even notice Dr. Eisenstein looking at them with a rather wistful expression.

It was blunder and stubbornness and sense of smell and possibly pheromones which guided Simon until finally he broke out of the undergrowth and into the clearing. The jungle closed quickly over his tracks.

The fire was there, no more than smoldering ashes.

That was all.

No Canon Tallis. No beast crouched to spring, ruby eyes gleaming.

Simon's heart began to pound again. Could this be someone else's clearing?

No. This was the branch from which the puma—or whatever it was—had prepared to attack. This was the small pile of green wood and leaf mold he had collected for the fire. There were the coconut husks. These were the beds of grass and fern which they had made, Canon Tallis's still bearing the imprint of his body. And there was the palm-leaf hat Simon had woven for the priest.

For a moment Simon had a horrible vision of wildcat, lion, leopard, snake, scorpion, vulture, all feasting on the ample body of the priest.

But something would have been left: white clerical collar, silver cuff-links, belt. Or buttons; there would at least have been a button. He scrabbled about on the ground.

Nothing.

Absolutely nothing.

He sat back on his heels in perplexity.

What to do?

Then he stiffened. In the distance he heard a motor, completely incongruous amid the jungle sounds. But it was approaching, and it came from above. Leaf and vine had quickly closed over the tearing by Gutiérrez's helicopter. The smoke signal which might once have penetrated the green was dead ash. If this was a helicopter sent out by Hurtado there would be nothing to see.

The sound came closer, high above his head, then lower, lower.

He began to tremble. Only Gutiérrez or one of his men would know how to get here without a signal from the ground, and a landing strip.

The noise of the rotors was deafening.

Monkeys screeched, birds flew up in the air. Then there was a sound of ripping and the helicopter dropped through the vines. The blades quivered to a stop.

Simon pressed back into the surrounding tangle of jungle, but there was no point in running away. This time there was to be no escape. He had abandoned Canon Tallis and anything that happened to him now was his own fault. He waited.

Gutiérrez climbed out of the machine.

He was followed by the soldier with the rifle who had thrown Simon into the hearse and the priest into the copter.

Simon did not move. He would have welcomed boar or wildcat.

"Where is he," Gutiérrez demanded, "the Englishman?"

"I don't know."

"What you mean, you don't know?"

"I don't know," Simon repeated.

Gutiérrez grabbed him by the arm. Simon tried to jerk away, but he could not.

The soldier kicked him in the belly. "Where is he?"

The wind was knocked out of Simon. He gasped like a fish out of water. He saw the boot raised to kick again.

He closed his eyes.

When Hurtado reached the dock at Port of Dragons, a message was waiting for him. A man who seemingly had been asleep all day in his hammock had received a message from the Quiztano village. The English priest had been found, and the boy was not with him.

Vermeer and Hurtado were closeted in the captain's quarters. "This is serious," Hurtado said. "You actually told Gutiérrez that smoke was seen in the jungle?"

"I did."

"Vermeer, I do not understand you."

Vermeer's smile had a slightly fixed look. "I did not forget what you said. It was the only way I could think of to force Gutiérrez's hand."

Hurtado wiped the back of his fist across his sharp blue jaw. "Gutiérrez left the *Orion*, went to the police barracks, got in a small police car, and took off. One of his subordinates reports that Gutiérrez was called to meet someone at the airport."

"You have called the airport?"

"Gutiérrez did, in fact, go there. He stopped only long enough to collect one of the soldiers who hangs about the place, and preempt a helicopter."

"Are you having him followed?"

"Vermeer, I am only a policeman. He has a good start on us. I have three helicopters out, but I cannot cover the entire jungle. If Gutiérrez has gone back to his mother's village there'll be no tracing him."

Vermeer asked, "Alejandro, what else is on your mind?"

"Tom Tallis has been found. He has a badly injured leg, where he was gored by a wild boar."

"And the boy?"

"We don't know where the boy is."

"But why?"

Hurtado told him.

"Tallis is with the Quiztanos?"

"Yes. His leg is evidently in bad shape."

"But what about Simon?"

"The Quiztano party has gone back into the jungle to look for him. He evidently ran in terror. He will have left traces. But they must find him quickly. There are dangers in the jungle."

Vermeer said, "Alejandro, you have to get hold of Gutiérrez."

"Why is Gutiérrez so important at this moment?"

"I have a hunch that he has something to do with the kidnapping, and that he and the murderer are—what do you say—"

"In cahoots," Hurtado said. "An American idiom. It is possible. But why do you say 'the murderer' that way?"

"I am not at all convinced that you have arrested the right man."

Hurtado's dark eyes sparked. "As you tried to trap Gutiérrez, so have I tried to trap the murderer. Jan has everything against him. But I am convinced of his innocence."

At Dragonlake, Miss Leonis and Canon Tallis tried to hide their anxiety about Simon. Tallis lay on a chaise longue made of young trees and vines in the same way as Miss Leonis's chair. It had been placed on the porch of Umar Xanai's dwelling. The crude couch was amazingly gentle to his tired and aching body. His leg wound had been cleaned and dressed and he had quickly withdrawn his first request to be taken immediately to a hospital. The agonizing pain was gone and if he did not attempt to move he was quite comfortable. The hectic flush had left his face.

Miss Leonis's chair had been placed so that they could talk easily. The life of the village flowed about them like a cool stream. Birds sang. On the porch of one of the Caring Places they could see a young Quiztano male in a bright, belted tunic, helping a little boy to walk. At the far end of the porch a young Quiztano woman, in softly patterned, flowing robe, tended an old man.

"I have muscles I never even knew existed," Tallis said. "Why didn't they put me in one of their hospitals?"

"Caring Places," she corrected. "You have a wound, but it's not that serious, now that it's been cleaned and the infection controlled. Umar Xanai says that you were absolutely right not to touch the water in the stream. It's full of lethal amoebae."

"What have the Quiztanos used on me? I cannot tell you how much better I feel."

She smiled. "They have ministered to me, too. They have ointments and powders which have been used by them as far back as the Memory goes. I would guess that what they put on your wound must be some equivalent of an antibiotic. After all, penicillin comes from bread mold."

"It was like a dream," he said, smiling. "There I was, my leg being cleaned and dressed by a gorgeous young creature who told me that she has her M.D. from the university in Caracas. Quentin Phair would be pleased."

"Yes. I think he would. I hope that Niniane would be pleased, too."

He changed the subject. "I noticed that the young men who rescued me carried bows and arrows, or spears, not firearms."

"The Umara and Umar Xanai do not permit firearms, and those who wish to use them leave the tribe."

"The Umara and the old chieftain—they rule together?"

"I believe the Umara carries the ultimate authority. They are a strange and fascinating people, and I hope that I am not putting too much trust in them when I expect them to find Simon."

"They found me."

"But this is not the first time on this journey that Simon has come close to death."

"It would seem to me," Canon Tallis said, "that Simon has been saved for a purpose. And if he has been saved for a purpose, he will be all right now."

"He should not have run away from you."

"I ordered him to."

"But you were wounded and helpless."

"He couldn't have helped. What use two of us dying? And your lad is no coward. He was extraordinarily brave and resourceful about the boar."

She shook her head slowly. "He shouldn't have run."

Canon Tallis said gently, "Miss Leonis, all we must concentrate on now is having Simon found and brought here to us."

"He will try to get back to the clearing. Once he comes to himself he will know he shouldn't have run, and he will try to get back."

"The Quiztanos have returned to the clearing, and they will ray out from there. They will be able to follow his tracks no matter how quickly the jungle covers them for untrained eyes."

"It will be night in a few hours."

Tallis corrected her. "It will not be night for a few hours. We will pray that during that time Simon will be found."

She sighed. "Sometimes I think I am prayed out."

"I doubt that."

She looked at him, at his bald head, his warm, dark eyes, at the lines of pain on his face, pain which did not come only from his injury. "I have learned that no is an answer to prayer, and I have come to accept a great many noes. I cannot accept a no about Simon."

"You will accept what you have to," the priest said quietly. "Meanwhile, you must hope. Simon is to be saved for a purpose. That is the best help you can give those who are looking for Simon. Prayers of hope."

"Yes." She shut her eyes. For a long time the two of them, the middle-aged priest and the old woman, remained in silence. The sounds of the village mingled gently with their quiet. From the lake came splashing and the laughter of children. From somewhere behind them came a woman's voice raised in song almost as clear and high as a bird's, and her song was joined by bird song. The breeze lifted and moved through the trees with a sound like rain.

After what seemed an eternity, Miss Leonis opened her eyes. Canon Tallis was looking at her, his dark eyes compassionate. She asked him, "Do you know who murdered the man who called himself Forsyth Phair?"

"Yes. I think I do."

"It was not Jan?"

"No. Not Jan."

The afternoon sun beat down on the *Orion*. Dr. Eisenstein nodded in her deck chair.

Dr. Wordsworth poked her. "Ruth. Come look at this." She pointed down at the dock.

Dr. Eisenstein pulled herself out of her chair and went to the rail; she laughed with pleasure as she saw a man asleep in a rope hammock which was slung under the side of a large truck, so that the man slept in the shadow of the truck as comfortably as between two trees.

"We should take a nap, too," Dr. Wordsworth said.

"But Englishmen detest a siesta."

Dr. Wordsworth stretched slowly, languorously. "My English blood grows thinner by the hour. I have discovered that I love my country. Why doesn't Hurtado let us leave the ship? Vermeer said that permission should come through any moment."

Dr. Eisenstein moved to the shade of the canvas canopy. "It does seem odd. I understand that Dr. O'Keefe has been allowed off."

"Official business," Dr. Wordsworth said. "He's here at the invitation of the Venezuelan government, and now that Jan has been apprehended I guess it was easy enough to relax regulations for him. He went off with several pompous-looking officials."

"Where did you learn all this?"

"Vermeer. Oh, Ruth, I wish there was something we could do."

"Do you want to play cards?"

"I mean about finding Simon. Let's go take a siesta."

Dr. Eisenstein leaned back in her chair. "I was having one when you woke me up."

"Sorry. Go back to sleep."

Dr. O'Keefe returned to the *Orion* hot and depressed. Charles and Poly were not in their cabins. Poly, he assumed, would be with Geraldo. He undressed and took a cold shower. His preliminary investigations of the lake had not been encouraging, and the Head of Department who accompanied him had not been optimistic. Most worrying was a chemical plant from which O'Keefe guessed that a dangerous amount of mercury was escaping into the lake, although "Any amount is dangerous," he said to his guide, a distinguished-looking man from Caracas with the incredible name of Geiger, pronounced Hay-hair.

Geiger told him that to keep the poison from infecting the lake would be enormously expensive. He himself was highly alarmed because the chief of public health had reported cases of mercury poisoning.

"And I very deliberately drove you through the barrio," Geiger told O'Keefe. "You have seen for yourself what conditions are like there, and you will guess that there may well have been other cases which have not been reported. Life is less important to the business barons than their profit sheets."

It was going to be difficult to shake up this greed so that a beautiful lake would not be destroyed, taking along with it a great many human lives.

"What about the water by the Quiztano settlement?"

"It is unpolluted thus far, but unless the industrial effluents are expelled elsewhere it is inevitable that the whole lake will suffer. We are further handicapped by the fact that there are many people in high official positions who consider that the people of the barrio are themselves pollutants, and that if a great many of them should happen to die off, it will be helping to curb the population explosion."

"I gather that you do not sympathize with this view?" O'Keefe asked.

Geiger shook his head. "No, but it makes it more difficult for us to impress the business barons with the seriousness of the situation. Add to this that many foreign powers have interest in our oil wells and chemical plants, and you will see that our efforts could be turned to provoke an international incident."

"But you will make the efforts anyhow?"

Geiger nodded. "This is why we asked you to come. Words from a man of your reputation will hold more weight than anything one of our own scientists could say."

—Greed, Dr. O'Keefe thought angrily, as he stood under the cold shower. —Is the same kind of greed behind the murder of Phair and the kidnapping of Simon and Tom?

When he was dressed in clean shorts and shirt he went to check on his children. Geraldo told him that Poly had gone back to her cabin, and he found her there, scowling at her little icon.

She looked up. "St. George isn't killing dragons any more, is he, Daddy? He's not going to be able to save Simon and Uncle Father. He's only a piece of paper pasted on wood. I hate him."

Dr. O'Keefe said, "You never thought your icon was a miracle-worker, did you?"

"No. But it used to make me feel that dragons could be killed if there was a St. George around."

"Don't you still feel that way?"

"Most of the St. Georges I know have been killed by the dragons. Like Joshua. And Quentin Phair was never a St. George at all. Daddy, if Simon and Uncle Father are all right we should have heard by now."

"This isn't like you, Poly," her father said. "The worst thing you can do for them is to give up hope."

"Okay. I'll try to hold on. You'd better go look in on Charles. I think he's upset about something."

"Where is he?"

"In the cabin."

Dr. O'Keefe left his daughter and walked up the starboard passage to the cabin. He looked in and saw Charles lying face down on his bunk.

Dr. O'Keefe touched him lightly on the shoulder. "Charles."

Charles turned over and startled his father with his pallor. His eyes were red from weeping.

"Charles, what is it?"

"It has been an appropriate time for a man to cry," Charles said.

He turned over, and once more buried his face in his pillow. Dr. O'Keefe watched him for a few moments, then left. When his children were very small there was usually something which he could do to ease whatever was troubling them. Both Poly and Charles had moved beyond that stage, and he felt helpless and heavy of heart.

He went to the salon, looking for Mr. Theo.

Simon crouched, eyes closed, waiting for the boot to kick him again. It was not going to be an easy way to die, and he was certain that the soldier was going to kill him.

Then he heard a *twing* and a shout.

He opened his eyes and the soldier was dancing about in pain, an arrow through the hide of his boot and into his foot.

From every direction, it seemed, came bronze young men in bright tunics, carrying spears, and bows and arrows.

If Gutiérrez knew the jungle, so did the Quiztanos. In single file they walked through what appeared to be impenetrable undergrowth. Gutiérrez was marched between two of the Indians, as was the soldier whose boot had so nearly killed Simon. The arrow had been removed.

Gutiérrez screamed and howled and cursed. He was the chief of police of Port of Dragons. The Indians would pay for this. Here he was, rescuing Simon, didn't the fools realize that he, with his helicopter, had found the boy first and was there to save his life? and for this he was treated like a criminal. They would all shortly be behind bars.

At last he ran out of wind.

The soldier moved along without emotion. His rifle had been taken from him and left in the copter. If the arrow had hurt his foot he gave no sign.

Simon walked with a young Indian, who identified himself as Ouldi and told him that Canon Tallis and Aunt Leonis were waiting for him. After that there was little conversation.

The trip through the jungle used all their lung power and concentration. Simon followed in Ouldi's footsteps, and it took every ounce of his failing strength for him to keep up. The heat of the jungle which hardly affected the Indians had Simon streaming with sweat. His mouth was so dry that the dryness was pain. Occasionally Ouldi reached a hand out to help him through a difficult place.

Simon tried to conceal the fact that he was so exhausted he was not certain one foot would continue to follow the next. His breath came in short gasps. He had a stitch in his side which threatened to double him up. Just as he was about to pant out to Ouldi a plea for a moment's rest, the undergrowth cleared, the trees and shrubs were behind them, and they faced the deep blue of Dragonlake.

Two large open wooden boats were waiting on the beach. Ouldi told Simon to get into the first. Gutiérrez and the soldier were hustled into the second, and Gutiérrez again began to scream threats and abuse. Instinctively Simon put his hands over his ears.

"It is all right," Ouldi assured him. "He cannot hurt you now. He will be taken directly to Port of Dragons where Mynheer Vermeer and the police from Caracas will be waiting."

"Señor Hurtado?"

"His men. Señor Hurtado is at Dragonlake. And we have the information he and Mynheer Vermeer were seeking. Gutiérrez"—Ouldi spat the syllables—"he was not born with that fine name. One look at him and I could tell that he is an Indian from across the border—"

"Not Quiztano—"

"No, no, a tribe of short stupid people who have almost completely vanished because they have betrayed their own ways. They have no Memory. As for that Gutiérrez, he is a smuggler."

"But he's a policeman."

"So? Not all policemen are Hurtados, any more than all consuls are Vermeers. Being a policeman simplified his dirty work—very dirty."

Simon looked at Ouldi with respect. "Canon Tallis suspected he might be into something like that." He gazed somberly as the boat with Gutiérrez and the soldier was rowed away.

Four Indians were in the boat with Simon and Ouldi. They rowed swiftly, in the opposite direction from the other boat. Ouldi sat in the prow, his back turned to the water so that he was facing Simon. "We are glad you have come, little brother."

"I'm glad, too. You saved my life. Gutiérrez wasn't rescuing me. That soldier was going to kill me and Gutiérrez wasn't about to stop him. You came just in time." His throat was so parched he could scarcely speak.

Ouldi took a small skin bag from his belt and handed it to Simon. "There are only a few swallows, but that is all you should have right now."

The swallows were sheer bliss, and Simon handed the empty skin to Ouldi with gratitude.

The Indians rowed strongly and swiftly but it seemed a long time before Simon saw ahead of them the round dwellings on high stilts stretching out into the lake. It was exactly as Charles had described it, exactly like the picture he had seen in Jan's book.

"Uncle Father—Canon Tallis—is really there? And Aunt Leonis?"

Ouldi smiled slightly. "How many times do I have to tell you? Yes, they are there." The boat swept past the dwelling farthest out in the lake. Ouldi pointed toward it proudly. "That is my dwelling. That is where I will bring my betrothed on the night when we two are made a new one."

When the boat neared the beach he held up his hand for silence.

A large group was assembled. Simon looked about eagerly, but at first he could not see Aunt Leonis or Canon Tallis. Hurtado was clearly visible standing a little apart from the Indians, with his dark hatchet face and city suit.

Ouldi jumped from the boat and helped pull it ashore, then held out his hand to Simon, who jumped out onto the soft sand.

From the clearing a young girl came running out of the large central building, her patterned dress flowing like butterfly wings. She carried a goblet which she offered to Simon. It was half filled with a pale liquid.

"We know that you are still thirsty," Ouldi said, "but you have been very long without enough water, and so you must drink only a little at a time. This will help."

He drank thirstily, and the golden liquid cooled and healed his throat far more than water would.

"Thank you," Simon said. "It has helped." He gave the goblet back to the girl.

"Now," Ouldi said. "It is the moment."

The group on shore had turned away from Simon and the boats and were looking back to the greensward. Simon followed their gaze, past an enormous stone-grey statue of a beatifically smiling woman, to a litter being carried by two young Indians. A small figure was crouched on the litter; at first he thought it was a child. Beside the litter walked two women, one middle-aged, one young. When the litter came closer he realized that the small figure was not a child but a very old woman, much older than Aunt Leonis.

A man in a long white tunic, with white hair down to his shoulders, detached himself from the group and went up to the litter and spoke briefly to the occupant, who raised her hand imperiously, and spoke in a cracked, almost whispering voice.

The man returned a few words, and Ouldi whispered to Simon, "Umar Xanai and the Umara."

The litter bearers carried the old woman up to Simon.

He felt a strange constriction in his chest. He held his breath until he thought his lungs would burst, but his grey eyes met the probe of her dark ones. He felt that he was moving out of time and into eternity, that this meeting of eyes would never end, that time had stopped and would never begin to flow again.

Then the ancient Umara spoke three words in a language completely foreign to Simon, a language fluid as water.

Umar Xanai came to her and asked her something in the same deep, dark tones.

Again she spoke three words.

The words were whispered from person to person, and then the whole village burst into cries, cries which had a harmonious, musical quality, cries which were certainly sounds of joy.

And then Simon saw Aunt Leonis, standing in the background, next to Canon Tallis, who had been carried out on his light and flexible couch. Simon ran to them, and then he and Aunt Leonis were holding each other, and he was crying, and so was she, and they held each other and rocked back and forth as they had not since the night Simon's mother had died, but this time the tears were tears of joy.

So it was some time before he realized that Ouldi was speaking to him, trying to get his attention, speaking formally for the whole village. "She says that you are the One. The Umara says that you are he for whom we wait."

Simon pushed the words away. "No, no. I'm only Simon Renier, from South Carolina, tell them, Ouldi, please, I can't possibly be the one . . ."

Ouldi repeated calmly, "The Umara says that you are the One."

"Aunt Leonis—Uncle Father—"

Ouldi kissed Simon ceremoniously on each cheek and then on the forehead. "We welcome you, Phair."

"I'm Simon. Simon Bolivar Renier."

Umar Xanai stepped forward, giving Simon the three ritual kisses. "You are the Phair."

"Oh, Aunt Leonis, Uncle Father, please tell them!" Simon cried. "I'm not—you mustn't let them think—"

Umar Xanai said, "The Phair promised that he would return. Now the Phair has kept his word and the long waiting is over."

"But he was a grown man," Simon protested, "and I'm only a boy." There was a darkness before his eyes which was only partly the darkness of approaching night.

"You are blood of his blood," Umar Xanai said.

Simon paused, then said slowly, "Yes. I am. I, too, have run away when it was my obligation to stay."

"And now you have returned," Umar Xanai said.

The Umara had been sitting impassively on her litter. Now

she gestured again and the bearers brought her back close to Simon. She put her small and ancient hands up to his face and gave him the three kisses of benediction. Then she gestured regally toward her dwelling place and the bearers carried her away.

"Aunt Leonis—"

"Yes, Simon."

"Well, tell them, ma'am, please tell them."

"What do you want me to tell them, Simon?"

"That I am not Quentin Phair."

The old woman looked at the chieftain. "I think they understand that."

"And Aunt Leonis, I couldn't possibly just stay here and leave you to go back to Pharaoh all alone."

"I'm not at all sure that I could make the trip back to Pharaoh, Simon. I'm too old for jet travel. I don't think that my heart could stand the journey back."

"But Boz—what about Boz? We can't just desert Boz!"

"Boz is dead, Simon."

The boy put his hands over his eyes. No. It was too much. Bitter tears forced their way through his fingers.

He felt a gentle but firm pressure on his shoulder, and Umar Xanai said, "It is late, and the Phair is tired from his ordeal. He needs refreshment and rest. He will be ministered to by one of the Umaras, and then he will spend the night with Ouldi in his dwelling. Tomorrow, when he is rested, he will see more clearly."

"What am I to do!" Simon cried. He turned desperately to Umar Xanai. "Sir, Quentin Phair is my ancestor. He is long dead. I am his descendant. I have all—all his faults."

Umar Xanai smiled placidly. "And you have returned to us, as you promised you would. The Umara recognized you as the One. We welcome you."

Hurtado and Tallis remained on the beach after the village had settled down. The dark night of the jungle was heavy around them.

"But there are hardly any insects," Hurtado exclaimed. "What do they do?"

"Whatever it is, if they could bottle it they could make a fortune," Tallis replied.

"You really are all right?" Hurtado asked. "Don't you think you should see a doctor?"

"I have. And these people with their Gift have something that hasn't been around in modern medicine for a long time. Whatever they used on my wound has completely taken away the infection. I'm convinced that I could walk on my leg now, but they will not permit it, and I trust their judgment. Hurtado, if you wish to remain my friend you will say nothing about their Caring Places."

"There is really no reason why I should say anything," Hurtado said. "Vermeer, too, would take it ill, and I wish to remain friends with both of you. So Vermeer was right about Gutiérrez. There are two young men, of Quiztano blood, who are willing to testify against him."

"An unpleasant character," Tallis understated. "He certainly never expected that Simon and I would survive the jungle. And we nearly didn't."

"But it doesn't get us any closer to finding the murderer."

"Doesn't it? I rather think it does. From all the bits and pieces I've gathered, I've been able to get a pretty clear picture."

Hurtado looked at him and waited. Tallis's face gleamed whitely in the starlight.

"We know that Forsyth Phair was not, in fact, Forsyth Phair, but Fernando Propice, a Venezuelan of mixed blood, largely Levantine, long involved in smuggling, extortion, and any nasty business that came to hand. Right?"

"Correct," Hurtado agreed.

"And that no bank in Caracas has either a Forsyth Phair or a Fernando Propice on the records."

"Correct."

"The murderer, I would guess, dabbled in smuggling and got involved with Propice, who tried to drag him in further than he wanted to go. The murderer wanted out, and the only way out was to dispose of Propice."

"And who is this person? Do you know, or is it all guesswork?"

"It's largely guesswork."

"Are you going to let me in on it, or do I have to find out in my flatfooted way?"

Tallis's smile gleamed. "Phair/Propice was the boss in this smuggling operation; he was almost making it. Gutiérrez was his sidekick. The murderer got tangled with them, but he didn't want to kill anyone, or to get involved in drugs or chemicals. When he told Gutiérrez that he no longer wanted to play his game, Gutiérrez took off with Simon and me and told the man that he would kill us if he didn't keep his mouth shut. The murderer, being more squeamish than Gutiérrez, was forced to keep quiet to avoid further bloodshed."

"Go on."

"Back to Propice. It seems more than likely that what little Quiztano blood remains in his veins went back a long time—to Quentin Phair, in fact."

"I know that's what the old lady thinks."

"Umar Xanai and the Umara corroborate this. They knew him to be an evil and vindictive man, like Edmund in *Lear*, dwelling on rights he felt he ought to have, and willing to do anything to get what he thought he deserved. At one time he took himself to Dragonlake to claim the jewels Quentin Phair had left the Umara, and which Propice thought were his due."

"What did happen to the jewels?"

"They were sold and the money used for education—universities, medical schools. So Propice felt abused there, too. As Quentin's heir, he was due everything that befits the heir—the long-spent fortune, the portrait, of course the portrait, and the ancient grudge."

Hurtado looked across the lake at the peaceful stork-like dwellings. Violence and vengeance seemed out of place. He sighed. "I think you're probably right, Tom. There are natures warped enough actually to be more proud of the ancient grudge than any other part of the inheritance. And it fits in with what Dr. Wordsworth told me. But you still haven't pointed to the murderer. Half of Venezuela would have a motive."

"Simon gave me the first clue with the story of the key to cabin 5."

"The cabin with the portrait, yes. And Jan's foolish lie. Geraldo is convinced that Jan is lying to protect someone."

"I think that Jan did not lie."

"Then—?"

"Boon did."

"Where's your evidence?"

"I don't have enough. But Boon's winter uniform vanished. A winter uniform is less visible in the tropical dark than summer whites. It would have been easy for Boon to weigh it down and dump it on the bottom of the ocean. The key story was an attempt—a successful one, as it turned out—to implicate Jan, and so was the planting of the portrait here."

"How did he manage that?"

"Easily enough. If he was on the bridge in the small hours of the night he could have lowered it into the water without being seen."

"So could anybody else."

"It was Boon who was alone on the bridge, the only one watching the radar scan. A fishing boat could easily come right up to the *Orion*; the portrait could be lowered, and no one the wiser."

"This is guesswork."

"Back to Propice for a moment, then. It's all part of the pattern. He paid or blackmailed someone to run Simon down with the fork lift, and that little scheme was foiled by Poly. So then Propice ordered Boon to push Simon overboard. Boon probably refused to kill, and then Propice threatened him until he thought he had no choice."

"Geraldo's talk of reluctance," Hurtado said. "Yes, it fits."

"I see Boon moving slowly to the boy with a heavy heart—for he appears to be a foolish rather than an evil man, Alejandro. And when Geraldo stopped him and he did not have to complete an action which was totally repugnant to him, he decided the only way out was to kill Phair."

"What about the portrait?"

"It's probably Propice's hold over him. If Boon didn't play

along, Propice would pin him for smuggling, easy enough to do if he was already in Propice's and Gutiérrez's net. My theory is that Boon intended his smuggling to be a strictly on-shore business. It seems that his tastes are fairly expensive and he wanted to pick up a little extra cash. Also, he knows something about art."

"Plausible," Hurtado said. "We're fairly certain the art ring is centered in Port of Dragons."

"It probably seemed innocent enough at first. But the innocent don't stay innocent when they think they can stay on the edge of crime. Drug dealers aren't worried about anybody's conscience, nor would it concern a Gutiérrez that Boon would try not to do anything which would reflect on the Master of the ship."

"You have a vivid imagination, Tom," Hurtado said. "Imagination does not hold up in court."

"No, but you agree with me," Tallis said. "You arrested Jan on the gamble that the murderer would then betray himself. Or that he would not let someone else hang. I think your gamble will pay off."

"There's not much time."

"I don't think Boon will let Jan take the rap. He got into deeper waters than he intended, and he ran scared. I think he will stop running."

"He'd better stop soon, then. I can play for time only so long. What we have to do is find a way to turn imagination into evidence." He looked about him through the velvet dark. "This is an incredible place."

"Not so incredible as all that. We who have spent our lives in cities tend to forget that human beings were not meant to live in anthills. Only insects can manage to survive in such conditions. And our work does not often take us among the innocent, Alejandro. We have been over-exposed to the darker reaches of the human heart."

Hurtado continued to look out over the lake to the dwellings. "They expect the boy to remain here."

"Yes."

"They don't really think that he is Quentin Phair?"

"They don't think about such things the way we do. Because Simon is Quentin Phair's direct descendant, he partakes in his ancestor and can fulfill his destiny."

"They won't force him?"

"Alejandro," Tallis said, "this is simply something I don't want to think about tonight. It strikes me as being a far more difficult problem than finding the murderer of Propice, for which you really don't need me. As soon as you had all of the information you would have put two and two together exactly as I have done. But Theo sent for me, and I came, and I think that I came because of Simon."

"A boy you'd never heard of?"

"He needed me, Alejandro. He has been far more wounded than I, and it occurs to me that perhaps the Quiztanos are the only ones who can complete the healing."

"He appears perfectly healthy."

"He has been wounded in spirit. He attempted to hold on to an idol—and when he was forced to see him as a human being who lied and lusted and was as other men, it was like having the rug pulled out from under him. He has been exposed to murder; he has almost been killed himself; it has all been too much for him."

Hurtado said, "He has to grow up sometime."

"He is doing precisely that, Alejandro."

"What about the old lady?" Hurtado asked.

"She is dying."

"I see. Yes, it will be difficult for the boy. But surely you can't think that staying here is a possibility."

"Why not?"

"Tom, these people are—for all Vermeer says—a primitive Indian tribe."

"You do sound like a city boy. Would you want your son, had he been through what Simon has been through, to live in Caracas? Or New York? Or Charleston? Haven't you seen something healthy in this place?"

"He'll revert," Hurtado said. "He'll be no better than a savage."

"And we? How much better than savages are we?"

"Oh, have it your own way," Hurtado said. "When will you be ready to be moved?"

"By tomorrow. But I must stay here until my mind is at ease about Simon. Forty-eight hours together in the jungle can forge a close friendship."

The next day had the timeless quality of a dream for Simon. Ouldi took him through the village, through the Caring Places.

Simon stood in the cool interior of the Caring Place for the dying. There were two long rows of low beds, twelve on each side. Only two of these were empty. By most of the beds a Quiztano was seated, holding the hand of the dying person. The air was fragrant with flowers. Here was no horror, only an ineffable sense of peace.

"I'm not sure—" Simon whispered.

"Not sure of what?"

"That I'm strong enough. I'm afraid of death."

"That is all right," Ouldi said. "So am I. I have been out in the world and I have learned fear and lost faith. So I have returned to Dragonlake to lose fear and regain faith. That will happen to you, too."

Several of the Indians started to sing. "A soul is going," Ouldi said. "It is being sung into the land of the blessed. But many of those who are brought here to die do not die. They get well, and they take some of our peace and some of our caring with them."

"And my ancestor started all this?"

"With the Umara."

"Everybody here is so *good*!"

But Ouldi shook his head. "No. We are as other people. Some good, some bad. Many leave Dragonlake and choose the material goods of the world."

"Ouldi, what am I to do?"

"You will do what is right. I am trying to hide nothing from you. It is a constant struggle for us to keep to the Quiztano ways. If you become one of us it will be your struggle, too, will it not? You would not wish us to change?"

Simon shook his head. "My ancestor started these Caring

Places. No, I would not want you to change, Ouldi. I would be the one to have to change."

"Not as much as you think."

"Gutiérrez—you said he turned his back on the ways of his people?"

"Not only Gutiérrez. All of that particular tribe. And they learned to like to kill. Not to eat, not for life, but to destroy."

"What's going to happen to him?"

Ouldi moved his shoulders sinuously. "He is an evil man. He will be made to pay."

Simon shuddered. "And Jan? What about Jan?"

"Jan did not kill. The Englishman knows that."

"But who did?"

Ouldi shrugged. "I do not know his name. But it is someone Jan thought of as a friend. He will be sad. Come, I still have much to show you."

The passengers stood on the promenade deck of the *Orion*, all leaning on the port rail and looking down at the dock. Geraldo had summoned them together, saying that the captain, el señor comandante Hurtado, and Mynheer Vermeer wished to speak to them. Everybody watched as a dark car drew up.

"Look!" Mrs. Smith cried. "It's Jan!"

Jan left the car, crossed the dock, and ran up the gangplank to the *Orion*. He did not look at the passengers.

Charles moved to his father. Dr. O'Keefe took his son's hand in his own.

"Daddy, Charles," Poly said, "has Jan been cleared?"

"Wait. No doubt we'll find out what's going on in a minute."

Dr. Eisenstein looked relieved. "I couldn't bring myself to believe that Jan would murder."

"Someone did," Dr. Wordsworth said, "and I would like to know who it was."

They all turned as they heard the screen door into the ship close with a light slam. Vermeer came out onto the deck, affable as usual. Dr. Wordsworth took a step toward him, then stopped.

"Ladies and gentlemen," he said. "Perhaps you all saw

someone getting out of a car just now? And now you want to know what is going on, and why you have been asked to come together here. It is my sad duty to inform you that Mynheer Boon went to the captain last night and confessed to the murder of Mr. Phair."

The facts were very much as Canon Tallis had guessed. The straw that broke the back of Boon's resistance was a hint from Hurtado that Simon had been murdered. It was this last horror which finally caused Lyolf Boon to go to van Leyden.

"How terrible for Jan!" Poly cried.

Dr. O'Keefe said, "But at least he's been completely cleared."

"But Mynheer Boon! He was Jan's friend!"

Vermeer said, "Gutiérrez threatened to kill Simon and Canon Tallis unless Boon kept his mouth shut."

Dr. Wordsworth said, "From what you have been telling us it would seem that if Boon had not killed Propice, then Propice might well have succeeded in finding a way to dispose of Simon?"

"It is quite possible."

"Then, although it wasn't exactly a murder of self-defense, it was in order to stop Simon from being murdered?"

Vermeer beamed. "That will be taken into consideration, I'm sure."

Mr. Smith asked, "But the smuggling?"

"He will have to pay for that. He was into the art racket, as Hurtado calls it. But Propice and Gutiérrez were trying to get him involved in chemicals."

"So for that, too," Dr. Wordsworth said, "he had no way out except to remove Propice?"

"He refused to deal with drugs or chemicals. Yes. Propice would undoubtedly have destroyed him one way or another had he remained alive."

"And that, too, will be taken into consideration?" Dr. Eisenstein asked.

"I would assume so."

"But there would still have been Gutiérrez," Mr. Smith said.

"There would. Mynheer Boon had—as my friend Hurtado said—painted himself into a corner."

Dr. Wordsworth asked, "Did Gutiérrez know that Boon had killed Phair?"

"He guessed. He accused him, hoping in this way to avoid what Hurtado calls the rap."

"I hate Gutiérrez!" Poly cried. "He's a beast! He didn't care whether he killed Simon and Uncle Father or not. He was just using them to hurt Mynheer Boon. Gutiérrez and Propice made Mynheer Boon do—be—something he never should have been."

Mr. Smith said heavily, "That first breach of honesty which can lead to so much disaster . . ."

Dr. Wordsworth reached out and took his hand with unexpected solidarity. "We've been lucky, you and I, Mr. Smith. We've managed to break away from bondage."

Mr. Theo said, "Thank God Simon and Tom are all right. That's what we have to think about. What about the captain, Vermeer?"

"As long as Boon's smuggling was done ashore, and not on the ship, the captain cannot be implicated. The Bolivar portrait was Propice's first wedge. But we have the portrait. It was not only to implicate Jan that Boon sent it to the Quiztanos. It was the only place he could think of where it would not be taken by the art-smuggling ring he was trying to get free of. So we have the portrait, and I think the captain will have no problem. This is one of Mynheer Boon's greatest concerns."

Dr. Wordsworth asked, "What's going to be done with the portrait?"

"Miss Phair and the Quiztanos wish it to be given to the Bolivar Museum."

"Which had not been Mr. Phair's intention."

"It had not."

Poly whispered to Charles, "I sort of wished Simon could keep the portrait."

"Aunt Leonis is right about things knowing where they belong," Charles said in an exhausted and withdrawn manner.

Vermeer clapped his hands together. "Now, my dear friends, I have good news and an invitation. You are all free to go into town or wherever you would like, until five o'clock this afternoon, when you are all requested to return to the *Orion*."

Dr. Wordsworth's conditioned reflex was outrage at any curtailment of liberty. "Why?" she demanded.

Vermeer beamed on her. "Cars will be waiting to take the entire company out to the Quiztano settlement at Dragonlake, where a feast is being prepared. This will be an excitement for my fellow anthropologist, will it not, Dr. Eisenstein?" After the exclamations had died down, he said, "My dear doctors, I should count it my extreme privilege to accompany you today and be your guide if you will permit."

Dr. Wordsworth bowed graciously.

Vermeer turned his sunshine on the old Greek. "Mr. Theoto—uh—Mr. Theo, a car will come to take you to the Cathedral, for as long as you desire to play the organ. Will you be ready in half an hour?"

"In five minutes," Mr. Theo said.

Poly asked anxiously, "Simon and Uncle Father are really all right, really and truly all right?"

Vermeer's smile seemed to reach completely around his head. "Really and truly." Then he looked at her father. "May I have a word with you, sir?"

"Of course. In my cabin?"

"Please." Vermeer turned to Dr. Wordsworth. "I will call for you ladies in a quarter of an hour."

Despite the heat, he shut the door to Dr. O'Keefe's cabin. "If there is anything my government can do to assist you in your investigations, Doctor, we will be glad to."

"Thank you."

"You know that there have been cases of mercury poisoning near Dragonlake?"

"Yes."

"What can you do?"

Dr. O'Keefe ran his hand worriedly through his hair. "I am a scientist and not a politician. But I will use every big gun I have. And Tallis has friends with influence who will bring their weight to bear. Even Dr. Eisenstein may be useful.

People all over the world are rebelling against the results of greed. Perhaps we are ready for a test case, and the problems at Dragonlake involve at least half a dozen nations."

"The Quiztanos do not want publicity."

"We will keep it to the minimum. But they will do what has to be done to save the lake and the people of the barrio."

"Few industrial magnates in Europe or America will worry about what is happening to a small tribe of Indians most of them have never even heard about."

"We will do everything we can to stop the deterioration of the lake," Dr. O'Keefe said heavily. "I am grateful for your help."

"My Quiztano friends understand what is going on. They have an example of the problem in one of their Caring Places right now."

"Mercury poisoning?"

"Yes. A child from the barrio. Yes, they will help. I am a realistic man, Doctor, I know how difficult it is going to be, but I also believe that if just in one place we can win the battle over greed and callousness, that one victory may swing the tide over the entire world."

"We'll try," Dr. O'Keefe said. "We will certainly try."

The scene being enacted in the captain's quarters was not exactly as it had been in Charles's dream, but it was close enough. Lyolf Boon was in his summer whites. His face was turned to Jan, a face nearly destroyed with anguish and weeping. Jan, too, wept. Hurtado wore his most expressionless mask. Van Leyden had moved beyond tears. But the *Orion* was still his. He was still Master of his ship. Despite his pain over what Lyolf Boon had been forced to do, his relief washed over him like a clean salt wave from the sea.

Throughout the entire ship there was both sorrow and relief. It was not a happy ending to the story, but at least it was an ending. When van Leyden told the crew that he alone would remain on the ship, and that the rest of them were free to go to the festivities at Dragonlake, the atmosphere lifted. As van

Leyden returned to the bridge he heard the sweet tone of a flute playing a haunting minor melody.

The evening sun poured its benediction over the Quiztano village; the water was golden, and the greensward, too, was touched with gold. A long ray of sunlight spotted the ancient Umara at the foot of the great carving. She gave her blessing to the festivities of the evening, but she herself would remain in prayers of gratitude for the return of the Phair.

The canoes were pulled up onto the beach, and the villagers were waiting for the boats bearing the passengers and sailors from the *Orion.*

Canon Tallis had graduated from his litter to a chair and a cane. Miss Leonis sat beside him. They had little need of conversation. They had moved into the companionship of mutual understanding. She knew, with gratitude, that Tallis would stay at Dragonlake until after her death. She wished that she, like the Umara, could spend the evening in solitude and prayer. —But there is an eternity awaiting me for that, she thought.

As though she had spoken aloud, Tallis rested his hand lightly on her shoulder.

A shout arose as the first boat was sighted, and then what appeared to be a small fleet appeared in the sun-flecked water.

Poly was in the first boat, and she rushed ashore and flung her arms ecstatically around Canon Tallis, around Simon, around Aunt Leonis, and, without thinking, around Umar Xanai, as though he were a dearly beloved grandparent. "Oh, thank you, thank you! We were afraid we were never going to see Simon or Uncle Father again!"

The old chieftain's eyes lit with pleasure. "You are their friends. We welcome you." He looked about him until he saw Charles, who had gone to Canon Tallis and was standing silently by him. "You are the true dreamer?"

"Sometimes my dreams are—special."

"We are grateful to you."

"I haven't done anything."

"You have dreamed true." Then he spoke to the assembled

company. "We have invited you to be with us tonight because you are friends of the Phair, and he has asked that you be present at our celebration of his return."

"His what!" Poly's voice rose incredulously.

"The Phair has come back to us, to make his life with us, as he promised us that he would."

"But Simon is not Quentin Phair!"

"He bears his blood. He is part of the Memory."

"Simon!" Poly cried. "No! You're not staying here, not for good!"

Canon Tallis looked down at Charles. The boy was pale. The priest took his hand, and it was cold. "Charles, are you all right?"

"I don't think I want to grow up."

"But you already have, haven't you?"

"Simon!" Poly cried. "Aunt Leonis! Explain to them!"

"Explain what?" Miss Leonis asked.

"That Simon must return with you to Pharaoh."

The old woman shook her head. "I will not be returning to Pharaoh."

"Simon's going to be a doctor!" Poly cried. "He can come live with us, we'd love to have him, wouldn't we, Daddy?"

Simon held up his hand. "I have thought about this, Poly. I must stay."

"Why?"

"Because it is what I must do. I ran away from Uncle Father when we were in the jungle and the wildcat was about to attack us—"

"Simon," Canon Tallis said, "you're making too much of that."

"No. It has made me understand a lot of things. About human beings. About Quentin. About myself." He smiled at Poly, then at Canon Tallis and Charles. "The Quentin Phair I made into a god was much less real than she is." He indicated the great carved figure. "I am learning to love him now like a real person. And that's a good thing, I think. There's also the matter of the revenge, of Cousin Forsyth's wanting to kill me. Now that he is dead, perhaps the idea of revenge will die, too. But it might not, as long as there are people like Gutiérrez left in the world. If I stay, then the Phair has returned, and the revenge will be finished. And"—he pointed to the Caring Places—"Quentin Phair started these. I have his work to continue. I'm going to be a doctor, and I have a great deal to learn. When the time comes I'll go to Caracas to medical school, or maybe back to the United States. But I have plenty to learn right here. A new language, for one thing."

Umar Xanai raised his arms. "Rejoice with us! Come, we have prepared a celebration." He drew the groups together with great embracing gestures, then led the way toward the center of the greensward, where a long colorful cloth had been spread across the grass. It was laden with bowls of fruit, platters of salads, pitchers of assorted drinks.

Dr. Eisenstein quivered with pleasure and excitement. "This is more than I dared hope for in my wildest dreams."

Dr. Wordsworth said, "It took a murder. So my Fernando has for once done a good deed."

Mrs. Smith said, "I'd like to forget him, but I'm not sure it's possible."

Mr. Theo looked at the beaming Vermeer bearing down on the group, and turned to Dr. Eisenstein. "Will you do me the pleasure of sitting with me at this feast, Ruth?"

She glanced at Dr. Wordsworth and Vermeer, and took Mr. Theo's arm. "Thank you. Did you enjoy your time at the Cathedral?"

"I have washed myself clean with music. That is a superb organ. Tomorrow evening, before we sail, the captain and Mynheer Vermeer have arranged for me to play for the passengers—for those of you who enjoy music."

"What a privilege," Dr. Eisenstein said. "I don't know much about music. My loss. And then you'll be sailing tomorrow night, Theo." He nodded. "I'll miss everybody." She sounded wistful. "But perhaps we'll be able to see the O'Keefes. You know, I'm not in the least sorry for Gutiérrez, but I feel for Boon."

"We all do. But it's a sorry lesson for us that one can seldom dabble only in the shallow waters of crime. There's always someone to pull us in deep."

Dr. Eisenstein looked at her travel companion laughing with Vermeer. "It takes a lot of courage to get out. Perhaps Boon will be able to start a new life when he has served his term."

"It's Simon who's starting the new life."

"Is this really serious?"

"Oh, yes. Simon is a serious boy."

Dr. Eisenstein looked about. "I think I envy him," she said.

Poly sat on the cool green grass between Geraldo and Jan. "It is good that you can be with your people tonight, Jan," she said.

Jan's face had a prison pallor that made it seem as though he had been jailed for more than just over twenty-four hours. "I do not think that I could be anywhere else. I need to be healed."

Geraldo nodded solemnly, then took Poly's hand in his. "It is good that you are staying in Port of Dragons, Polyquita. You will be able to see Simon."

"Oh, Jan—Geraldo—I am so confused about Simon. Do you think he's making a terrible mistake?"

Geraldo kissed her hand. "It is not a decision the world would understand. But it is like Simon."

Poly looked gratefully at Geraldo. "Charles says Simon doesn't belong in our century."

The strain was ebbing slowly from Jan's face. "It has always seemed to me that the Quiztanos do not live in time at all. When I am here I forget clocks and bells and all the things which occupy me when I am being Dutch."

Poly looked across the greensward to where Miss Leonis was sitting. "What about Aunt Leonis?"

Jan said, "She will rest her bones in Dragonlake."

"You mean, she's dying?"

"She is an old woman, Polyquita, and her work is done." Geraldo raised Poly's fingers to his lips and kissed them gently. "It will be easier for me to let you go when we sail tomorrow night because I know that Simon will need you and Charles and your father. It will not be easy for Simon."

Jan said, "But he will become a healer, and the world is in need of healers."

"But the world won't know about him if he stays in Dragonlake!"

Jan's face relaxed into his old smile. "You think that matters, Miss Poly? I am part Quiztano, and I know the things that truly matter—and so do you."

Simon sat between Umar Xanai and Ouldi. On the old chieftain's other side was Aunt Leonis, with Mr. Theo by her. She looked as frail as old glass, and yet her expression was full of peace.

She looked at him and smiled, calmly and reassuringly.

Not everybody was seated, but Umar Xanai picked up a piece of fruit as a signal that the feast was to begin. Then he rose and spoke:

> *Power behind the stars*
> *making life from death*
> *joy from sorrow*
> *day from night*
> *who heals the heart*
> *and frees the lake*
> *of dragons and all ill*
> *come feast with us*
> *that we may share your feast*
> *with all we touch.*

Then he bowed his head silently.

When he looked up, Miss Leonis spoke:

"Thou didst divide the sea through thy power; thou breakest the heads of the dragons in the waters. Thou broughtest out fountains and waters out of the hard rocks; the day is thine, and the night is thine; thou hast prepared the light and the sun. Oh, let not the simple go away ashamed, but let the poor and needy give praise unto thy Name." She did not bow her head, but looked briefly up at the sky, then out over the lake, and closed her eyes.

"Lady, Señora Phair," Umar Xanai said, "we are as one."

All around them conversation and laughter rose like butterflies in the evening air. Above the lake the sky was flushed with color. The shadow of the mountain moved slowly over the greensward, cooling the air.

Simon looked about him at the assembled company. The intensity of the past days had broken the conventions of time and he felt that all the passengers of the *Orion* were old and treasured friends, and he was filled with love for them. He looked at Canon Tallis, sitting at the feast, with Charles between the priest and Hurtado.

—He has freed me to love Quentin as he really was, Simon thought gratefully. —So I must love him as he really is, too, and not make up another idol.

—I am older now, he thought. —And perhaps it is because I have come into the right time and place for me. Where Cousin Forsyth would have destroyed, I must learn to continue what Quentin began.

Tallis looked at the untouched plate in front of Charles. "You're not eating."

"I'm not hungry," Charles said.

Hurtado said, "My plate is already empty. You need food, Charles."

"I'll try."

"By the bye, Charles, any time you want a job in the Venezuelan Secret Service, just let me know."

Charles forced a smile. "It's not my line of work, Señor Hurtado. Dreams are not an advantage to a policeman. And I get too involved. I'm feeling very sad."

"Not as sad as Jan. Or the captain. They trusted Boon."

"I know. Jan is with Poly and Geraldo. They'll help."

"You must help, too," Tallis said.

"I know. I'll try."

"For that, then, you will need food." Hurtado piled his own

plate high. "Tom, I understand that the O'Keefes have five more children at home. Surely they don't need Charles. Don't you think you could arrange to have Charles given to me?"

Now Charles's smile was real. "I'll always be your friend, Señor Hurtado."

Simon ate and drank. His responsibility to Quentin had become real, at last. Time redeemed had broken the limitations of time.

Ouldi lifted a pitcher and poured clear liquid into Simon's glass, into Umar Xanai's, then raised his own glass. "To the return of the Phair."

Simon raised his glass and drank deeply. Then he looked around until he saw Poly with Geraldo and Jan, Canon Tallis with Charles and Hurtado. They were all looking at him. So was Aunt Leonis.

In the jungle behind them a bird broke into an ecstatic trill. Water rippled gently against the shore, against the pilings of the dwellings reaching out into the lake. The breeze lifted. In the sky shadowed by the mountain a star pulsed into brightness.

Simon raised his glass to the assembled company. "It is good to be home," he said.

A HOUSE LIKE A LOTUS

For Robert Lescher

ONE

Constitution Square. Athens. Late September.
  I am sitting here with a new notebook and an old heart.
Probably I'll laugh at that sentence in a few years, but it is serious right now. My sense of humor is at a low ebb.

I'm alone (accidentally) in Greece, and instead of enjoying being alone, which is a rare occurrence, since I have six younger siblings, I am feeling idiotically forlorn. Not because I'm alone but because nothing has gone as planned. What I would like to do is go back to my room in the hotel and curl up on my bed, with my knees up to my chin, like a fetus, and cry.

Do unborn babies cry?

My parents are both scientists and for a moment I am caught up in wondering about fetuses and tears. I'll ask them when I get home.

The sun is warm in Constitution Square, not really hot, but at home, on Benne Seed Island, there's always a sea breeze. Late September in South Carolina is summer, as it is in Greece, but here the air is still and the sun beats down on me without the salt wind to cool it off. The heat wraps itself around my body. And my body, like everything else, is suddenly strange to me.

What do I even look like? I'm not quite sure. Too tall, too thin, not rounded enough for nearly seventeen, red hair. What I look like to myself in my mind's eye, or in the mirror, is considerably less than what I look like in the portrait which now hangs over the piano in the living room of our house on the beach. It's been there for maybe a couple of months.

Nevertheless, it was a thousand years ago that Max said, 'I'd like to paint you in a seashell, emerging from the sea, taking nothing from the ocean but giving some of it back to everyone who puts an ear to the shell.'

That's Max. That, as well as everything else.

I've ordered coffee, because you have to be eating or drinking something in order to sit out here in the Square. The Greek coffee is thick and strong and sweet, with at least a quarter of the cup filled with gritty dregs.

I noticed some kids at a table near mine, drinking beer, and I heard the girl say that she had come to stop in at American Express to see if her parents had sent her check. "It keeps me out of their hair, while they're deciding who to marry next." And the guy with her said, "Mine would like me to come home and go to college, but they keep sending me money, anyhow."

There was another kid at the next table who was also listening to them. He had black hair and pale skin and he looked up and met my eyes, raised one silky black brow, and went back to the book he was reading. If I'd been feeling kindly toward the human race I'd have gone over and talked to him.

A group of kids, male, definitely unwashed, so maybe their checks were late in coming, looked at me but didn't come over. Maybe I was too washed. And I didn't have on jeans. Maybe I didn't even look American. But I had this weird feeling that I'd like someone to come up to me and say, "Hey, what's your name?" And I could then answer, "Polly O'Keefe," because all that had been happening to me had the effect of making me not sure who, in fact, I was.

Polly. You're Polly, and you're going to be quite all right, because that's how you've been brought up. You can manage it, Polly. Just try.

I'd left Benne Seed the day before at 5 a.m., South Carolina time, which, with the seven-hour time difference, was something like seventeen hours ago. No wonder I had jet lag. My parents had come with me, by Daddy's cutter to the mainland, by car to Charleston, by plane to New York and JFK airport. Airports get more chaotic daily. There are fewer planes, fewer ground personnel, more noise, longer lines, incomprehensible loudspeakers, short tempers, frazzled nerves.

But I got my seat assignment without too much difficulty, watched my suitcase disappear on the moving belt, and went back to my parents.

My father put his hands on my shoulders. 'This will be a maturing experience for you.'

Of course. Sure. I needed to mature, slow developer that I am.

Mother said, 'You'll have a wonderful time with Sandy and Rhea, and they'll be waiting for you at the airport, so don't worry.'

'I'm not worried.' Sandy is one of my mother's brothers, and my favorite uncle, and Rhea is his wife, and she's pretty terrific, too. I'd be with them for a week, and then fly to Cyprus, to be a general girl Friday and gofer at a conference in a village called Osia Theola. I've done more traveling than most American kids, but this time, for the first time, I'd be alone, on my own, nobody holding my hand, once I left Athens.

Athens, my parents kept telling me, was going to be fun, since Rhea was born on the isle of Crete and had friends and relatives all over mainland Greece and most of the islands. Sandy and Rhea were both international lawyers and traveled a lot, and being with them was as safe as being with my parents.

Why hadn't I learned that nothing is safe?

'Write us lots of postcards,' Mother said.

'I will,' I promised. 'Lots.'

I wanted to get away from my parents, to be on my own, and yet I wanted to reach out and hold on, all at the same time.

'You'll be fine,' Daddy said.

'Sure.'

'Take care of yourself,' Mother said. 'Be happy.' Underneath her words I could almost hear her saying, 'Don't be frightened. I wish I could go with you. I wish you were a little girl again.'

But she didn't say it.

And I'm not. Not anymore. Maybe I'd like to be. But I'm not.

My family knew that something had gone wrong, that something had happened, but they didn't know what, and they respected my right not to tell them until I was ready, or not to tell them at all. Only my Uncle Sandy knew, because Max had called him to come, and he'd flown down to Charleston from Washington. This was nothing unusual. Sandy, with or without Rhea, drops in whenever he gets a chance, popping over to the island en route to or from somewhere, just to say hello to the family.

Fortunately, I'm the oldest of our large family, including our cousin Kate, who's fourteen, living with us and going to school with us on the mainland. So no one person comes in for too much attention.

Mother put her arm around me and kissed me and there were questions in her eyes, but she didn't ask them. Flights were being called over the blurred loudspeaker. Other people were hugging and saying goodbye.

'I think that's my flight number—' I said.

Daddy gave me a hug and a kiss, too, and I turned away from them and put my shoulder bag on the moving conveyor belt that took it through the X-ray machine. I walked through the X-ray area, retrieved my bag, slung it over my shoulder, and walked on.

On the plane I went quickly to my window seat and strapped myself in. The big craft was only a little over half full, and nobody sat beside me, and that was fine with me. I wanted to read, to be alone, not to make small talk. I leaned back and listened to the announcements, which were given first in Greek, then in English. A stewardess came by with a clipboard, checking off names.

'O'Keefe. Polly O'Keefe. P-o-double l-y.' My passport has my whole name, Polyhymnia. My parents should have known better. I've learned that it's best if I spell my nickname with two *l*'s. Poly tends to be pronounced as though it rhymes with pole. I'm tall and skinny like a pole, but even so I might get called Roly Poly. So it's Polly, two *l*'s.

Another stewardess passed a tray of champagne. Without thinking, I took a glass. Sipped. Why did I take champagne when I didn't even want it? Not because I don't like champagne; not because I'm legally under age; but because of Max. Max and champagne, too much champagne.

At first, champagne was an icon of the world of art for me, of painting and music and poetry, with ideas fizzing even more brightly than the dry and sparkling wine. Then it was too much champagne and a mouth tasting like metal. Then it was dead bubbles, and emptiness.

I drank the champagne, anyhow. If you have a large family, you learn that if you take a helping of something, you finish it. Not that that was intended to apply to champagne, it was just an inbred habit with me. When another stewardess came by to refill my glass I said, "No, thank you."

A plane is outside ordinary time, ordinary space. High up above the clouds, I was flying away from everything that had happened, not trying to escape it, or deny it, but simply being in a place that had no connection with chronology or geography. All I could see out the window was clouds. No earth. Nothing familiar. I ate the meal which the stewardess brought around, without tasting it. I watched the movie, without seeing it. About halfway through, I surprised myself by falling asleep and sleeping till the cabin lights were turned on, and first orange juice and then breakfast were brought around. All through the cabin, people yawned and headed for the johns, and there are not enough johns, since most of the men use them for shaving.

Window shades were raised, so that sunlight flooded the cabin. While I was eating breakfast I kept peering out the window, looking down at great wild mountains. Albania, the pilot told us: rugged, dark, stony, with little sign of habitation or even vegetation.

A dark and bloody country, Max had said.

Then we flew over the Greek islands, darkly green against brilliant blue. Cyprus. After Athens, I would be going to Cyprus.

I had a sense of homecoming, because this was Europe, and although we've been on Benne Seed Island for five years, Europe still seems like home to me. Especially Portugal, and a small island off the south coast called Gaea, where the little kids were born, and where we lived till I was thirteen.

Then we moved back to the United States, to Benne Seed Island. Daddy's a marine biologist, so islands are good places for his work, and Mother helps him, doing anything that involves higher math or equations.

Being brought up on an isolated island is not good preparation for American public schools. Right from the beginning, I didn't fit in. The girls all wore large quantities of makeup and talked about boys and thought I was weird, and maybe I am. Some of the teachers liked me because I'm quick and caught up on schoolwork without any trouble, and some of them didn't like me for the same reason. I don't have a Southern accent—why should I?—so people thought I was snobby.

The best thing about school is getting to it. We all pile into a largish rowboat with an outboard motor, and running it is my responsibility. I suppose Xan's taking over while I'm away. Anyhow, we take the boat to the mainland, tie it to the dock with chain and padlock around the motor. We walk half a mile to the school bus, and then it's a half-hour bus ride. And then I get through the day, and it's bearable because I like learning things. When we lived in Portugal, there was no school on Gaea, and we were much too far from the mainland to go to school there, so our parents taught us, and learning was fun. Exciting. At school in Cowpertown, nobody seemed to care about learning anything, and the teachers cared mostly about how you scored on the big tests. I knew I had to do well on the tests, but I enjoy tests; our parents always made them seem like games. So I did well on them, and I knew that was important, because I will need to get a good scholarship at a good college. Our parents have made us understand the importance of a good education.

Seven kids to educate! Are they crazy? Sandy and Dennys will probably help, if necessary. Even so . . .

Charles, next in line after me, will undoubtedly get a good scholarship. He knows more about marine biology than a lot of college graduates. He's tall—we're a tall family—and his red hair isn't as bright as mine.

Charles and I were the only ones to get the recessive red-hair gene. The others are various shades of ordinary browns.

Alexander is next, after Charles, named after Uncle Sandy, and called Xan to avoid confusion, since Sandy and Rhea come to Benne Seed so often. Xan is tall—of course—but last year he shot up, so that now he's taller than I am. It's a lot easier to boss around a little brother who's shorter than you are than one who looks over the top of your head, is a basketball star at school, is handsome, and adored by girls. We got along better when he was my *little* brother. He and Kate team up against the rest of us, especially me. Kate is beautiful and brown-haired and popular.

After Xan is Den, named after Uncle Dennys. He's twelve, and most of the time we get along just fine. But every once in a while he tries to be as old as Xan, and then there's trouble. At least for me.

Then come the little kids, Peggy, Johnny, and Rosy. Because I'm the oldest, I've always helped out a lot, playing with them, reading to them, giving them baths. They're still young enough to do what I tell them, and to look up to me, and to accept me just as I am. And I feel more like myself when I'm playing on the beach with the little kids than I do when I'm at school, where everybody thinks I'm peculiar.

Under normal circumstances I would have been delighted to get away from the family and from school for a month. Mother tries not to put too much responsibility on me, and everybody has jobs, but if Mother's in the lab helping Daddy work out an equation, then I'm in charge, and believe me, all these brethren and sistren have about decided me on celibacy.

The plane plunged through a bank of clouds and the stewardess called over the loudspeaker that we were all to fasten seat belts and put seats and tray tables in upright position for the descent into Athens. I kept blowing my nose to clear my ears as the pressure changed. With a minimum of bumps, we rolled along the runway. Athens.

I joined the throng leaving the plane, like animals rushing to get off the ark.

I followed the others to baggage claim and managed to get my suitcase from the carousel by shouldering my way through the crowd. As I lugged the heavy bag toward the long counters for customs, I heard loudspeakers calling names, and hoped I might hear mine, but nobody called for Polly O'Keefe.

The customs woman peered into my shoulder bag; she could have taken it, as far as I was concerned. But I couldn't refuse the bag, which Max sent over from Beau Allaire, without someone in the family noticing and making a crisis over it. It was gorgeous, with pockets and zippers and pads and pens, and if anybody else had given it to me I'd have been ecstatic.

The customs woman pulled out one of my notebooks and glanced at it. What I wrote was obviously not in the Greek alphabet, so she couldn't have got much out of it. She handed it back to me with a scowl, put a chalk mark on my suitcase, and waved me on.

I went through the doors, looking at all the people milling about, looking for Uncle Sandy and Aunt Rhea to be visible above the crowd. I saw a tall man with a curly blond beard and started to run toward him, but he was with a woman with red hair out of a bottle (why would anybody deliberately want that color hair?), and when I looked at his face he wasn't like Sandy at all.

Aunt Rhea has black hair, shiny as a bird's wing, long and lustrous. I have my hair cut short so there'll be as little of it to show as possible. Daddy says it will turn dark, as his has done, the warm color of an Irish setter. I hope so.

Where were my uncle and aunt? I'd expected them to be right there, in the forefront of the crowd. I kept looking, moving through groups of people greeting, hugging, kissing, weeping. I even went out to the place where taxis and buses were waiting. They weren't there, either. Back into the airport. If I was certain of anything in an uncertain world, it was that Sandy and Rhea would be right there, arms outstretched to welcome me.

And they weren't. I mean, I simply had to accept that they were not there. And I wasn't as sophisticated a traveler as I'd fooled myself into thinking I was. Someone else had always been with me before, doing the right things about passports, changing money, arranging transportation. I'd gone through passport control with no problem, but now what?

I looked at the various signs, but although I'd learned the Greek alphabet, my mind had gone blank. I could say thank you, *epharisto*, and please, *parakalo*. *Kalamos* means pen, and *mathetes* means student, and I'd gone over, several times, the phrase book for travelers Max had given me. I'm good at languages. I speak Portuguese and Spanish, and a good bit of

French and German. I even know some Russian, but right now that was more of a liability than an asset, because when I looked at the airport signs I confused the Russian and Greek alphabets.

I walked more slowly, thought I saw Sandy and Rhea, started to run, then slowed down again in disappointment. It seemed the airport was full of big, blond-bearded men, and tall, black-haired women. At last I came upon a large board, white with pinned-up messages, and I read them slowly. Greek names, French, German, English, Chinese, Arabic names. Finally, P. O'Keefe.

I took the message off the board and made myself put the pin back in before opening it. My fingers were trembling.

DELAYED WILL CALL HOTEL SANDY RHEA

They had not abandoned me. Something had happened, but they had not forgotten me. I held the message in my hand and looked around the airport, where people were still milling about.

Well, I didn't need someone to hold my hand, keep the tickets, tell me what to do. I found a place where I could get one of my traveler's checks cashed into Greek money, and then got a bus which would take me to the hotel.

It was the King George Hotel, and Max had told me that it was old-fashioned and comfortable and where she stayed. If Max stayed there, then it was expensive as well as pleasant, and that made me uncomfortable. I wouldn't have minded my father paying for it, though marine biologists aren't likely to be rolling in wealth. I wouldn't even have minded Sandy and Rhea paying for it, because I knew Rhea had inherited pots of money. But it was Max. This whole trip was because of Max.

It was in August that Max had said to me, 'Polly, I had a letter today from a friend of mine, Kumar Krhishna Ghose. Would you like to go to Cyprus?'

Non sequiturs were not uncommon with Max, whose thoughts ranged from subject to subject with lightning-like rapidity.

We were sitting on the screened verandah of her big Greek revival house, Beau Allaire. The ceiling fan was whirring; the sound of waves rolled through all our words. 'Sure,' I said. 'But what's Cyprus got to do with your Indian friend?'

'Krhis is going to coordinate a conference there in late September. The delegates will be from all the underdeveloped and developing countries except those behind the Iron Curtain—Zimbabwe, New Guinea, Baki, Kenya, Brazil, Thailand, to name a few. They're highly motivated people who want to learn everything they can about writing, about literature, and then take what they've learned back to their own countries.'

I looked curiously at Max, but said nothing.

'The conference is being held in Osia Theola in Cyprus. Osia, as you may know, is the Greek word for holy, or blessed. Theola means, I believe, Divine Speech. We can check it with Rhea. In any case, a woman named Theola went to Cyprus early in the Christian era and saw a vision in a cave. The church that was built over the cave and the village around it are named after her, Osia Theola.'

I was evidently supposed to say something. 'That's a pretty name.'

At last Max, laughing, took pity on me. 'My friend Krhis is going to need someone to run errands, do simple paperwork, be a general slave. I've offered you. Would you like that?'

Would I! 'Sure, if it's all right with my parents.'

'I don't think they'd want you to miss that kind of opportunity. Your mother can do without you for once. I'll speak to your school principal if necessary and tell him what an incredible educational advantage three weeks on Osia Theola will be. It won't be glamorous, Polly. You'll have to do all the scut work, but you're used to that at home, and I think it would be good experience for you. I've already called Krhis and he'd like to have you.'

Just like that. Three weeks at Osia Theola in Cyprus. That's how it happened. That's the kind of thing Max could do. Now that I thought about it, it seemed likely that Max had paid for my plane fare, too.

The week in Athens, before the conference, was something Max said I shouldn't miss, and my parents agreed. I had never been to Greece, and they were happy for me to have the opportunity.

We were all less happy about it by the time I left Benne Seed than when the plan was first talked about, Max enthusiastically showing us brochures of Athens and Osia Theola, the museums, the Acropolis. Those last weeks before I flew to Athens, my parents looked at each other when I came into a room as though they'd been talking about me, but they didn't say anything, and neither did I.

And now I was on a bus, sitting next to a family who were talking loudly in furious syllables. The man wore a red fez, so I assumed they were Turkish, and Turkish is a language I've never even attempted. During the drive I began to feel waves of loneliness, like nausea, until I was certain the hotel wouldn't have a reservation for me, and what then? I certainly wasn't going to call South Carolina and ask someone to come rescue me.

But I was welcomed, personally, by the manager, and given a message which said the same thing as the one at the airport.

I liked the hotel, which reminded me a little of hotels in Lisbon. But I felt very alone. I followed the bellman to my room. He opened the door, put my bag down on the rack, flung open doors to closets, to a big bathroom, opened floor-length windows to the balcony.

"Acropolis," he said, pointing to the high hill with its ancient, decaying buildings, and I caught my breath at the beauty. Sounds of the present came in, contradicting the view: bus brakes, taxi horns, the wail of a siren. I stood looking around, first at the view, then at the room, which was comfortably European, with yellow walls, a brass bed, a stained carpet, and an enormous bouquet of mixed flowers on a low table in front of the sofa.

After a moment I realized that I'd forgotten the bellman and that he was waiting, so I dug in my purse for what I hoped was the right amount of money, put it in his hand, saying, "*Epharisto*."

He checked what I'd given him, smiled at me in approval, said, "*Parakalo*," and left, closing the door gently behind him.

The sunlight flooded in from the balcony, warming me. Despite the heat, I felt an odd kind of cold, like numbness from shock. I unpacked, spreading out notebooks and paperbacks on the coffee table to establish my territorial imperative. No photographs. Not of anybody.

Whenever I stepped out of the direct sunlight, the inner cold returned. And a dull drowsiness. Although I had slept more on the plane than I had expected, it was a long time since I'd actually stretched out on a bed. The early-afternoon sun was streaming across the balcony and into my room, but my internal time clock told me I was tired and wanted to go to bed.

Max had suggested that I get on Greek time as soon as possible. 'Take a nap when you get to the hotel, but not a long one. Here.' And I was handed a small travel alarm. 'I won't be needing this anymore, and it weighs hardly anything. Sleep for a couple of hours after you arrive, and then go to bed on Greek time. It'll be easier in the long run.'

I didn't want Max's alarm clock, and I didn't want Max's advice, no matter how excellent. If it hadn't been for the telephone, I'd have gone right out, defiantly, and wandered around Athens. But I couldn't do anything until I'd heard from Sandy and Rhea.

'Do you still love me?' Sandy had asked.

'Of course I do.'

'It was I who introduced you to Max.'

'I know,' I had said.

It all seemed a very long time ago. And yet it was right here in the present. I had crossed an ocean and still I couldn't get away from it.

The sunlight fell on the bed. I stretched out in its warmth, lying on my side so that I could see the Acropolis. I looked across twentieth-century Athens, across hundreds of years to a world long gone. To the people who lived way back when the Parthenon was built, who worshipped the goddess Athena, what had happened to me wouldn't be very cosmic. To the other people in the hotel, also maybe looking out their windows from the present to the past, it wouldn't seem very important, either.

'It's all right.' Sandy had his arms about me. 'You have to go all the way through your feelings before you can come out on the other side. But don't stay where you are, Polly. Move on.'

There was a knock on the door, and I realized I had been hearing Sandy's voice in a half dream. I sat up.

"Who is it?"

"Some fruit, and a letter for Miss O'Keefe."

I opened the door to a young uniformed man who bore a large basket of fruit, which he put down on the dresser. "With the compliments of the manager." He handed me an envelope. "We neglected to give you this when you arrived."

"*Epharisto.*" I shut the door on him and ripped open the envelope. One page, in the familiar, strong, dark handwriting. "Polly, my child, take this week in Athens in the spirit in which it is given. Forgive me and love me. Max."

I crumpled up the letter. Flung it at the wastepaper basket. The phone jangled across my thoughts.

It was Sandy, sounding as close as when he called at home, ringing South Carolina from Washington.

"Polly, you're there!"

"Sandy, where are you? What happened?"

"Still in Washington. An emergency. Sorry, Pol, but in my line of work you know these things do happen."

His work has more to it than meets the eye. He and Rhea don't just work with big corporations and their international deals. It's top-secret kind of stuff, but I know it has something to do with seeing that underdeveloped nations don't get ripped off, and when tensions rise in the Middle East or South America or Africa they're often sent there to ease things. Rhea and Mother are close friends, and I have a hunch she tells Mother a good bit, but the most I've ever got out of Mother was an ambiguous 'They're on the side of the angels.'

I said to Sandy, "I know these things happen, but are you going to come?"

"Of course we're coming. I'll be dug out by Monday night, with Rhea's help, and we've changed our flight to Tuesday. We should be with you in plenty of time for dinner, three days from now. Will you be all right?"

"Sure," I said without much conviction. But Sandy always makes me feel that I can manage anything, and I didn't want to let him down. "Do Mother and Daddy know?"

"Do you want them to?" he asked. It was a challenge.

I accepted it. "No. They might worry." Funny. We've been given a lot of independence in many ways, we've had more experience than a lot of kids, and yet we're also in some ways very overprotected. They *would* worry.

"Do you have enough money?" he asked.

"Max gave me three hundred dollars in traveler's checks. Daddy gave me two hundred. I'm rolling in wealth."

"Good. Don't blow it all the first day. But make a reservation on the roof restaurant of your hotel tonight, and just sign for your dinner. There's a superb view."

"There's a superb view from my room," I said. "I can see the Parthenon."

"Good. Max is an old friend of the manager. I knew you'd get one of the best rooms."

"It's very European and comfortable. Sandy, it's got to be expensive."

"Forget it," he said briskly. "It's peanuts to Max. Check with the concierge and get yourself a ticket for a bus tour or two and see the sights. Don't waste these days till Rhea and I join you."

"I won't. I'm not a waster, you know that."

"That's my Pol. You all right?"

"I'm fine," I said, which meant, I accept your challenge, Sandy. I'll be fine in Athens on my own. I'm not a child.

"See you Tuesday," he said. "I love you, Polly."

"I love you, too. See you."

When we hung up, I lay down on the bed, fighting the tears which Sandy's voice had brought rushing to my eyes. Sandy believes that things have meaning, that there are no coincidences, so I had to suppose there was some meaning to his being detained in Washington. Maybe it was to knock my pride down, to remind me that I might have seen a good bit of the world but I'd never been completely on my own before.

I went into the bathroom and took a hot, soaky bath; wrapped myself in two large, thick towels and sat at the open window to dry and look at the view. In the distance the Acropolis and the bright stones of the Parthenon were dazzling. In the foreground were the streets of Athens, with tropical trees which reminded me of home.

When I was dry I put on a cool cotton skirt and top and looked at my watch, which I'd changed to Greek time on the plane. Just after 2 p.m. I went to the balcony again to set myself in time and space.

The great city was spread out before me. And I wondered: What do the old gods, the heroes in the *Iliad* and the *Odyssey*, think of the cars and buses and gas-and-oil-smelling streets of today, or the modern hi-rise buildings going down to the harbor and stretching up the mountainsides? Piraeus, the port, and Athens are one vast city. In the days of Homer, what did all this look like? Were there great plains between the city and the harbor?

I went down to the lobby and made a reservation for dinner on the roof. The restaurant didn't open till eight, and the concierge looked at me as though he thought I was gauche when I asked for an eight o'clock reservation, so I put on my most aloof look and told him that I had jet lag and wanted to get to bed at a reasonable hour, which, after all, was true. Then I checked on Sandy and Rhea's reservation, and of course they'd already taken care of changing it. I asked about tours, but there were so many I decided I was too tired to choose until I'd had a good night's sleep, and I just went out of the hotel and across to Constitution Square.

I passed three evzones. Rhea had talked about them—Greek soldiers still dressed in the same colorful costumes they wore in Turkish times, white-skirted tunics with vivid splashes of red. They were marching briskly along, looking ferocious, and suddenly I had a police-state kind of feeling. But all around me everybody was bustling, hardly turning to stare, and I heard a lot of American accents and saw women in pants, which I should have thought would be too hot in this weather, and men with cigars—the ugly Americans Max had talked about. We didn't see that many Americans when we lived on Gaea, but we were in Lisbon often enough for me to have to face the fact that we aren't very much loved. Most of the shops around Constitution Square seemed to be entirely for the benefit of American tourists, junky gift shops, phony icons, sleazy clothes, and pictures of American credit cards on the glass fronts of the doors. One souvenir shop had a sign reading, "Welcome, Hadassah," and was recommended by some Jewish Association. I wouldn't have been surprised to find a shop window with a commendation by the Pope, or another by the World Council of Churches. I didn't like it. But that was judgmental of me. I still didn't like it.

Most of the Americans seemed to be clustered in the cafés on the sidewalks across from the Square. There was one big café which appeared to be used exclusively by kids my age, or not that much older, all dressed exactly alike in jeans, with backpacks which were dumped on the ground by their tables. In the Square itself, where I went to sit, there were some Americans, but also many Greeks, relaxing and drinking coffee and reading papers.

The light was the way Sandy and Rhea had described it, blue and gold, alive with color. I'd thought they were just rhapsodizing, and that nothing could beat the blue and gold of south Portugal and Gaea, but this was really different, more dazzling, with a quality of brilliant clarity, so that I could almost see Apollo driving the chariot of the sun across the sky. And in this light I could believe in Pallas Athena, could see her eyes, the same blinding blue of the sky.

Max said my eyes were that color, and that's unusual in carrottops.

Max was, theologically, heterodox. Religion, Max said, is divisive, and went on to cite the horrors going on between Christians and Moslems in the Middle East, between Hindus and Buddhists in Sri Lanka, between Protestants and Catholics in Ireland. If we could forget religion, Max said, and remember God, we might have a more reasonable world.

Max liked reading aloud, and had read to me from books written in the very early days of Christianity, works by Gregory of Nyssa and Basil the Great and Clement of Alexandria, because their world was like ours, changing rapidly, with the Roman Empire falling apart around them.

'Listen to this,' Max said one winter night when we were eating supper in front of the library fire and the northeast wind was beating against Beau Allaire. 'Clement of Alexandria:

Now the fables have grown old in your hands, and Zeus is no longer a serpent, no longer a swan, nor an eagle, nor a furious lover.

Isn't that superb?'

I turned away from Max in my mind. No more furious lovers. I was no Semele.

Max's house, Beau Allaire, is built of soft pink brick and surrounded by three-story white verandahs, a house built for shade and breeze. It is at the far end of Benne Seed Island from our house, just past Mulletville, which used to be a functional fishing village till a developer came in and started an expensive housing development, now that islands are becoming status symbols. It's a cocktail-partying place, cheek by jowl with what's left of the original village. There's a causeway from Mulletville to the mainland, and a school bus comes to take the development kids to Cowpertown—those who don't go off to boarding school. Beau Allaire is set on a hundred acres, but even so, Max is not happy about the development on what used to be an almost private island.

Between Mulletville and our house are two privately owned plantations and a state wildlife preserve, so we're moderately isolated. Benne Seed is shaped like a crescent moon, the Mulletville and Beau Allaire point of the moon much closer to the mainland than our point. Our house and Beau Allaire are in all ways at opposite points of the compass. Beau Allaire is a great house, often photographed for books on Southern architecture. Our house was once a motel, but Benne Seed is really not a tourist-type island, or we wouldn't be there. There's a tricky undertow, and swimming isn't safe unless you know the waters well.

Mother and Daddy rebuilt the falling-down motel, dividing the rooms so each of us kids would have our own bedroom and there'd be a few extra for the uncles and aunts and other visitors. Mother and Daddy's bedroom was what had originally been the office and lobby, with a big screen porch off it, facing the ocean. Our rooms were off on either side, and the ocean side was all screens in summer, with enormous storm windows for winter. There were two wings, one for Daddy's labs, with cases of starfish and lizards and squid and various kinds of octopuses and a medium-size computer for Mother; the other had a big long living room, a big dining room, and a good kitchen. The wings made a kind of court, where we had swings for the little kids, and a picnic table under an ancient water oak. The wood of the house was weathered, so that it was a soft, silvery grey, and behind it were great, jungly trees, full of Spanish moss and mockingbirds. We were fairly high up on the dunes, so there was a long wooden ramp which led down to the beach. It was comfortable and informal.

Beau Allaire was formal. The Greek revival columns rising up the three full stories emphasized the height of the ceilings. It was by far the most elegant of the three plantation houses, and the best kept up. The other two were owned by Northerners who were seldom there and probably used them as tax write-offs. Max has always had several yard men, and a couple living over the garage to take care of things and clean the silver—and everything else of course, but there is a great quantity of silver. All the doorknobs, for instance, are silver. 'They come from my mama,' Max said, 'and I treasure them.'

There are Waterford chandeliers and candelabra, and paintings by Max, and also by Picasso and Pissarro and even a Piero. And portraits. Southerners do seem to have a great many portraits, and Max had more than most.

But, until last Christmastime, Beau Allaire was no more than a name to us.

Early winter was miserable, cold and rainy and dank. In Cowpertown it seemed as though the sun never shone, and the fluorescent lights at school glared. Nobody turned on any strobe lights for me. And I certainly didn't have that inner luminosity Max saw in the portrait of me in the seashell, a luminosity which Max brought out in me. December was grey day after grey day, with fog rolling in from the sea, so bad that Daddy wouldn't let us take the boat to Cowpertown but drove us the fifteen or so miles to Mulletville to take the school bus from there, and we hated that.

And then Sandy and Rhea came for Christmas, and Uncle Dennys and Aunt Lucy, bringing Charles with them. It was wonderful having Charles home for three weeks. He's by far my closest sibling. But when Uncle Dennys and Aunt Lucy decided that Kate needed to live with a family and stop being an only child for a few years, they suggested that Charles go to Boston as a sort of exchange, partly because they didn't want to be completely without children, and partly because Charles is a scientist, or will be, and the science department at Cowpertown High leaves a great deal to be desired.

It was our turn to have everybody for Christmas. One of the good things about being back in the United States is getting together for holidays. Almost all of us. Daddy's parents are dead, and his family is pretty well scattered. But there are Mother's parents, who are also scientists. Our grandfather is an astrophysicist, and our grandmother a microbiologist. Then there're Sandy and Rhea. And Dennys and Lucy. Dennys and Sandy are twins, and very close. Mother's youngest brother, the one Charles is named after, is off somewhere on some kind of secret mission, we don't know where. Anyhow, when the larger family is gathered together, it makes for a full house. This past year our grandparents didn't come, because our grandfather was just getting over pneumonia. We missed them, but it was a lot of people, in any case.

The morning after everybody arrived, Sandy and I were alone in the kitchen, because Daddy had taken everybody else out in his cutter to show them around the island. Sandy and I warmed our toes at the fire and had one last cup of cocoa made from some special chocolate he and Rhea'd picked up in Holland.

The phone rang, and I answered it. 'Sandy, for you.'

'Me? Who on earth would be calling me here? I told Washington under no circumstances . . .' he muttered as he took the phone. *'Max!'* His voice boomed out with pleasure.

When he finished talking (I washed the dishes to give him privacy), he rubbed his blond beard and smiled. 'Polly, I'd like you to meet a friend of mine. I think you'd get on.'

Sandy knew things at school were not going well for me. He'd pumped me thoroughly, and it was not easy for me to keep anything from my favorite uncle. 'Who? Where?'

'A painter. A very good painter. And not far from here, at the other end of the Island, Beau Allaire. Want to drive over with me?'

I'd go anywhere with Sandy. 'Sure. Now?'

'Anything else on your social calendar?'

Coming from Xan, that would have been snide. From Sandy it was okay. 'I didn't know anybody was living at Beau Allaire.'

'Max has been back only a few weeks. I want to find out what on earth has brought Max to Beau Allaire.'

We drove through the stark December day. We never have snow on Benne Seed, but winter can be raw.

'Max's family built the hospital in Cowpertown,' Sandy said. 'It's named for Max's sister, Minerva Allaire Horne, who died young and beautiful. But I suppose you know all about that.'

I shook my head. 'No. Only that it was given by a family with pots of money and Daddy says it's an unusually good hospital for a place like Cowpertown. He knows some of the doctors there. And he and Mother were saying it was too bad nobody lived in Beau Allaire.'

'Max has had it kept up. The land is rented for cotton. And there are gardeners and two old-time Southern faithful retainers, Nettie and Ovid, like characters out of a movie. Max usually comes for a week or so each winter, but Beau Allaire hasn't really been lived in for years. Max said she was staying all winter. Wonder why.'

'She?'

'Maximiliana Sebastiane Horne. The parents gave both daughters absurdly romantic names. Minerva Allaire—Allaire was the mother's name and the plantation came from her—was always known as M.A., and Maximiliana Sebastiane is called Max, or Maxa, or sometimes Metaxa. Metaxa is a rather powerful Greek brandy, and it's not a bad name for her.'

We drove up a long driveway of crushed shells, lined with

great oaks leaning their upper branches over the drive till they touched and made a green tunnel. The car crunched over the broken shells. As we drew near, I saw the graceful lines of a verandah, and Sandy pointed out the beautiful fanlight over the door. 'And eleven chimneys, count them. The architect was well aware of the dampness that can seep into an island house.'

We got out of the car and started toward the door just as a sports car pulled up behind us. Out of it emerged a tall woman wearing a dark green velvet cape lined with some kind of soft, light fur, with the hood partway up over midnight-black hair. Her light grey eyes were large and rimmed darkly with what I later learned was kohl.

'Good enough for Isak Dinesen, good enough for me.'

Isak Dinesen was a Danish writer who used to be famous, and Max said that the wheel would turn and she'd come into her own again.

Now Max held her arms out, wide, and so did Sandy, and they ran and embraced each other. It was theatrical, but it was also real, and I envied the freedom that allowed them to be so uninhibited. I stood watching their pleasure in each other, feeling that I shouldn't have come in old jeans and a yellow sweater that was too small for me.

After a moment Sandy and the woman broke apart, and he introduced me. 'Max, this is Polly O'Keefe, my sister's first-born. Pol, this is Maximiliana Sebastiane Horne.'

I held out my hand. 'Hello, Mrs. Horne.'

She took my hands in hers, and from her hands I realized that she was older than I'd thought. 'Max, please, or Maxa. I'm not Mrs. Horne. My husband was Davin Tomassi, but I had already made a start as a painter when we married and he wanted me to keep my own name.'

He *was*. So she was a widow.

'Come in, come in, don't stand out here in the cold.' She opened the heavy front door, which creaked. 'I'll have to get this oiled,' she said, leading us into a large hall.

Sandy took my elbow. 'Look at this hall, Pol, it's an architectural gem, with a groin-vaulted plaster ceiling and beautifully proportioned woodwork.'

It was gorgeous, with the walls papered a color I later learned was Pompeian red.

Max opened another door, to a long, high library, the kind of room we'd love to build onto our house, where we've long ago run out of book space. But this wasn't a beach-house room. It was so high-ceilinged that there was a ladder which could be moved along a wooden rail so the books on the top shelves could be reached. There was a fireplace with a wood fire burning, though the room still smelled and felt damp. The mantelpiece was Georgian and beautiful, and over it was a portrait, in a heavy gold frame, of a young woman with black hair, wearing a low-cut ivory gown. She was so lovely it made you draw in your breath, and I assumed it was Max when she was young.

Max took off her cloak and flung it over a mahogany and red-velvet sofa, then went to the wall near the fireplace and pulled on a long, embroidered piece of cloth. A bellpull. I'd read about bellpulls, and when our TV worked I'd seen them in plays with Victorian settings, but this was the first one I'd seen in real life.

I studied the portrait again, and Max said, 'My sister, Minerva Allaire. M.A. was truly beautiful.' She perched on a low chair with a hassock covered in petit point. She wore narrow black pants and a black cashmere cardigan over a white, softly ruffled blouse. And yet, while I knew she was quite old, older than my parents, she did not seem old, because a tremendous, sunny energy emanated from her.

There was a knock on the door and a woman came in, a woman who somehow went with the house and the bellpull. She was stocky and had grey-brown hair, short and crisply curly. She bowed elaborately. 'Madame rang?'

Max laughed. 'Don't be dour, Ursula. It's damp and cold and this house hasn't been lived in for thousands of years.'

'Madame would like some consommé?' the woman suggested.

'Consommé with a good dollop of sherry,' Max agreed. 'And some of Nettie's benne biscuits.'

Sandy asked, 'Max still bullying you, Urs?'

The woman smiled, and the heaviness in her face lightened. 'What would Max be like if she didn't bully us all?'

'Ursula, this is my niece, Polly O'Keefe. Pol, this is Dr. Heschel.'

I'd thought she was some kind of servant, a housekeeper.

She shook hands with me, a good, firm clasp. Her fingers were long and delicate and tapered, but very strong. 'I'm glad to meet you, Polly. Your Uncle Dennys and I are colleagues.'

Well, then, she had to be a neurosurgeon. I took another look.

Sandy said, 'The world of neurosurgery is small. Dennys and I, as usual, both have connections with Max and Ursula. Davin Tomassi was a colleague of mine. So, separately, we've known Max and Urs for a long time. We'll have a terrific reunion.'

Dr. Heschel asked eagerly, 'Dennys is here, too?'

'The whole kit and caboodle of us. I don't know if the name rang a bell with you, Urs, but Polly's father is the O'Keefe who's done such amazing work with regeneration. His lab is now full of squid and octopuses. I suppose I have to take it on faith that their neurological system resembles ours.'

Dr. Heschel flung out her arms. 'Good Lord, when we left New York and came to Benne Seed I thought we were coming to the wilderness, and here is not only Dennys but a scientist I've long wanted to meet. Before I get overexcited, I'd better get out to the kitchen and see about that consommé.'

'We'll have a party,' Max said as the doctor went out. 'We'll bring Beau Allaire back to life with a real party.'

Sandy and Max talked about mutual friends all over the world until a frail old black man came in, carrying a silver tray which looked much too heavy for him. He wore rather shiny black trousers and a white coat. He put the tray on a marble-topped table in front of a long sofa, looked at Max with loving concern, and left.

Dr. Heschel sat in front of the tray and handed out cups of consommé in translucent china. I thanked her for mine.

'Call her Ursula,' Max ordered. 'She gets enough doctor-this and doctor-that in New York. People treat neurosurgeons as though they were gods. And many of them fall for it.'

Dr. Heschel—Ursula—responded mildly: 'Your iconoclasm takes care of that.'

'Are you on vacation, Urs?' Sandy asked her.

'Leave of absence.' And, as though to forestall further questioning, she added, 'I was overdue a sabbatical. I'm glad to see you still have your beard, Sandy.'

'I grow tired of it,' he said, 'but it's the best way to tell Dennys and me apart. We still look very much alike. Max, show Polly some of your paintings.'

Max shrugged, so that her thin shoulder blades showed sharply under the cashmere. It looked to me as though she needed a doctor handy, though an internist would likely have been more help than a neurosurgeon.

'Most of my best stuff is in museums or private collections,' Max said. 'Contrary to opinion, I do have to earn a living. M.A.'s untimely death caused my father to start a hospital in her memory, and that's where the money went. Not that I begrudge it.'

Sandy gave a snort and turned it into a sneeze.

'You ran through a good bit on your own.' Dr. Heschel —Ursula—smiled.

'True, and I enjoyed it. But now I have to work for the finer things of life.' She looked at both of them and burst into laughter. 'Like many filthy-rich people, I tend to cry poor.' She smiled at me. 'Never believe people who tell you they have no money, Polly. People who don't have it seldom mention the fact. People who do, tend to be embarrassed about it, and so deny it, especially in front of someone like Sandy, who spends his life fighting the big international megacorps. Come on, and I'll show you some of my work.'

'Don't forget the painting of Rio Harbor,' Ursula said.

'First I want to show her my self-portrait.' Max drained her cup and put it back on the tray. 'Come on.'

I followed her into the big hall and up a curving staircase and then into a room which was as large as the library.

There was a huge, carved four-poster bed, with a sofa across the foot. I turned and saw another high fireplace, with a large, white fur rug in front of it, and I could imagine Max, in black, lying on the white rug and staring into the fire. The fire was laid, and there was a copper bucket of fat pine beside it. The far end of the room had a big desk, a chaise longue, some comfortable chairs upholstered in smoky-rose velvet. A long wall of French windows opened onto the verandah and the ocean view.

On the wall over the desk was a portrait. I knew it was Max because she'd said so. She was as young in this picture, or almost, as the girl in the portrait in the library, and they did look very alike, with the same dark hair and light grey eyes and alabaster skin. Max was thinner than M.A., and she was looking down at something she held in one hand. A skull.

It reminded me of etchings of medieval philosophers in their studies, with skulls on their desks and maybe a skeleton in the corner, contemplating life and death. It was a beautiful painting. A shaft of light touched the skull, and the shape of bone was clean and pure.

'I was a morbid young woman in many ways, Polly, and felt it would do me no harm to cast a cool eye on my own mortality. It did keep me from wasting time as I might otherwise have done. I've had an interesting life, and I've had my fair share of vicissitudes, but it hasn't been dull and it hasn't been wasted. What are you going to do with yourself when you finish your schooling?' She sat on the foot of the chaise longue.

'I don't know,' I said.

'Where do your interests lie?'

'Almost everywhere. That can be a real problem. I'm interested in archaeology and anthropology and literature and the theatre. I pick up languages easily. I'm not a scientist, like my parents.'

'But you're intelligent.'

'Oh, yes. But I haven't found my focus.'

'You've got a couple of years,' Max said. 'When the time comes, you'll find it.' She got up. 'Come, I'll show you the picture that Urs likes.' On the way she pointed out some of the other pictures. A Hogarth. A de Chirico sketch. A Van Gogh.

'Fortunately, the Islanders don't know how valuable they are—just Maxa's junk. Even with Nettie and Ovid living over the garage, we aren't immune to burglars. If I'm short of cash, I sell one of the pictures. I do have very extravagant tastes.'

The painting of Max was what is called representational. The one of the harbor at Rio was expressionist, I think, with vivid colors which looked one way straight on and another if you glanced sidewise.

'Why isn't this in a museum?' I was awed by it.

'Because I won't let it go,' Max said. 'I have to keep a few things. Urs wants to buy it, and if I sold it to anyone it would be to her.' She looked at the painting. 'She'll get it soon enough.'

We went back out into the hall, and as we started down the stairs I saw something on the landing I hadn't noticed on the way up, a wood carving on a marble pedestal, of a man, with his head thrown back in laughter and delight.

'That's the Laughing Christ of Baki.' Max paused. 'I had a reproduction made. The original is life-size and gives the effect of pure joy. It's probably nearly ten thousand years old.'

'The Laughing Christ?'

'The Bakians simply assumed, when the missionaries told them about the Son of God, that it was their statue, which had never before had a name. Anthropology is one of my hobbies, Polly. Someday I'll show you the sketch books I've made on my travels. This statue is one of my most favorite possessions.'

'I love it,' I said, 'I absolutely love it.'

We went on downstairs and back to the library, and Max had another cup of consommé, complaining that Nettie hadn't put enough sherry in it. 'She disapproves. Nettie and Ovid are growing old, and I'd like to get someone to help them, but they won't hear of it. Urs likes to cook, and Nettie and Ovid come in after dinner and do the washing up, and they bring us our breakfast. Nettie is a firm believer in a good breakfast, grits and fried tomatoes and eggs and anything else she thinks she can get me to eat.'

'You could do with a few more pounds,' Sandy said.

Max sat on a low chair and stretched her legs out to the fire.

'So you and Rhea are here for Christmas, Sandy? How can you take all those children?'

'Very happily,' Sandy said. 'We'd hoped to have children of our own, but that didn't happen to be possible.'

'Oh, God, Sandy, I'm sorry.' Max put her hands to her mouth.

'It's probably just as well in our line of work,' he said. 'We have to travel too much of the time. And with all our nephews and nieces, we don't do too badly.'

I'd wondered about Sandy and Rhea not having kids of their own.

He looked at his watch. 'We'd better go, Pol.'

Max put her hand very lightly on my shoulder. 'Come back and see me, little one, and we'll talk about anthropology.'

'All right,' I mumbled. But I knew I wouldn't. Not unless Max called me. And she did.

But not until she and Ursula had joined the throng for Christmas. As soon as Mother and Daddy heard that Max and Ursula were at Beau Allaire, and about the connections with Sandy and Dennys, they invited them for Christmas.

'Max won't come,' Sandy said.

But she called and accepted the invitation. 'So Urs will have someone to talk neurosurgery with.'

'Granted,' my Uncle Dennys said, 'Ursula Heschel has overworked ever since I've known her, but it still seems atypical of her and Max to come here in the dead of winter. In the spring when the azaleas are out, yes, but not in December.'

'It's quiet,' Mother said.

'True, it's quiet. But I'm the one who's the researcher. Ursula's a superb surgeon.'

'You're right, Dennys,' Sandy said. 'There's something odd about it.'

Christmas was cold and clear and perfect. The sun glinted off the Atlantic. We had fires going in both the living and dining rooms. The little kids played outside with their new toys, so the rest of us could have some reasonable conversation indoors. Dennys, Urs, and Daddy talked about the mysteries of the brain, and Daddy took them off to the lab. It does seem weird to me that the octopus and the human being share so much of the neurological system.

Max, Mother, Rhea, and Lucy talked about the state of the world, which as usual was precarious, and about the state of American education, which was deplorable.

'Kate is getting an education just living in this zoo,' Aunt Lucy said while we were gathered in the kitchen basting the turkey and doing various last-minute things.

Kate was nibbling the candied grapefruit peel we'd made a few days before. 'Cowpertown High's okay. I'm learning plenty.'

'And going to all the dances?' Aunt Lucy asked.

'Enough,' Kate said. She could have said 'all.' Kate always had half a dozen boys after her whenever there was a dance, and I knew that Mother and Daddy felt responsible for her and worried about whichever boy was driving and whether or not booze or joints had been sneaked in. But Kate had sense enough not to drive home with anyone who was stoned, and she had already called twice to ask someone to come for her. Though we didn't tell Lucy and Dennys.

If Mother and Daddy worried about Kate being popular and successful, they worried about me being alone too much. It was okay. I didn't want to go. Kate loves parties and dances and barbecues, and she gets bored if she doesn't have a lot to do. Not me.

We'd put all the extensions in the table. Max had brought over an enormous damask banquet cloth, and with candles and oil lamps lit and the Christmas tree lights sparkling, it looked beautiful. The little kids all behaved reasonably well, and no one threw up. It was a good Christmas.

And then Max and Ursula asked us for New Year's Eve—the grownups, plus Charles and me.

Charles had grown taller, though he wasn't quite as tall as Xan, but he was still my special brother Charles who understood me better than anyone else. We spent hours up in our favorite old live-oak tree, talking, catching up. I was going to miss him abysmally when he went back to Boston; in my eyes, Kate was not at all a fair exchange for Charles. But at least Charles was still here for New Year's Eve, and Beau Allaire was a perfect place for a party.

All the verandahs were full of light as we drove up, and the great columns gleamed. Nettie and Ovid passed hot hors d'oeuvres, and there was lots of conversation and laughter. We played charades. Sandy and I were the best at pantomime, and Mother and Max were best at guessing, but we all threw ourselves into the game and had a lot of fun.

As all the clocks began to chime midnight, Ovid opened a magnum of champagne, and after a toast we all put our arms about each other's waist, standing in a circle, and sang *Auld Lang Syne*. When we were through, Ursula put an arm around Max, tenderly, protectively. And I thought I would like to be protected like that.

Sitting in Constitution Square, being warmed by the sun, I did not want to think about Max. But that was not very intelligent of me. What I needed to do was to think about Max objectively, not subjectively. I'm enough of a scientist's daughter to know that nothing can be thought about completely objectively. We all bring our own subjective bias to whatever we think about, but we have to recognize what our bias is, so that we will be able to think as objectively as possible.

Daddy had said that he could not even study his lab creatures totally objectively, because to observe something is to change it.

That was certainly true. Max had observed me. And changed me.

I had finished two cups of the thick, sweet coffee, and that was more than enough. I put my pen and journal back in the shoulder bag, crossed the street to the hotel, went up to my room, and napped. It seemed that all I wanted was sleep, and not just because of jet lag. Sleep is healing, Sandy said, and when I woke up, I did feel better. I had one foot in Athens and the present, and although the other foot was still across the Atlantic and dragging in the past, at least Max had made me aware of how complex we can be, so it did not surprise me to be in both worlds simultaneously.

The problem was that I could not comprehend the vast span of Max's complexity. My parents are, as human beings go, complex, but also moderately consistent. I can count on them. And the bad people I've met have been so bad that I could count on them being bad, which does simplify things. But shouldn't I have learned that life is neither consistent nor simple? Why did it surprise me?

I looked at the travel alarm I'd put on the bed table. Nearly eight. Just time to dress and go up to the roof for dinner. I took a book so I wouldn't be lonely. I love to eat and read, but in a family like ours I don't often have the opportunity—only if I'm sick enough to stay in bed, which doesn't happen often, and when it does, I'm usually too miserable to read.

Sometimes, when I went over to Beau Allaire, Max and I ate together, with books open beside us on the table, and didn't talk, unless one of us wanted to read something to the other. We usually ate in the screened part of the back verandah, rather than in the formal, oval dining room. A breezeway went from the screened porch to the kitchen, which was slightly separated from the rest of the house, in the old Southern manner.

'Pol, listen to this,' Max said. 'It's by a physicist, J. A. Wheeler. He says: "Nothing is more important about the quantum principle than this, that it destroys the concept of the world as 'sitting out there,' with the observer safely separated from it by a 20-centimeter slab of plate glass. Even to observe so minuscule an object as an electron, we must shatter the glass."' She made a movement with her hand as though breaking through glass, and her face was bright with interest as she looked up from the book, blinking silver eyes against the light of the candles in the hurricane globes. 'We cannot separate ourselves from anything in the universe. Not from other creatures. Not from each other.'

But I had put the glass up between Max and me, erected a barrier, so that we could no longer touch each other.

I got up to the restaurant at two minutes before eight, and the doors were just opening. I was the only person there, though people did begin to trickle in after a few minutes. It was a beautiful, open-air restaurant, with lots of plants, and candles on all the tables. I had a waiter who spoke good English, so I didn't try to practice my Greek. He was concerned that I was all alone, so I told him about Uncle Sandy and Aunt Rhea and that they would be with me on Tuesday.

This seemed to reassure him, and he began explaining the menu to me, and I didn't think it would be polite for me to tell him that I had a Greek aunt and was used to Greek food. Anyhow, I liked his taking care of me, and he was a kind of surrogate uncle for an hour or so.

Two couples came in and were seated at tables between me and the view of the Acropolis, and I think one man thought I was staring at him when all I was trying to do was see the Parthenon.

Dinner tasted good, really good. And that in itself was a big improvement. I ordered fruit and cheese, and my waiter told me that if I lingered over dessert and coffee I'd see, if not hear, the *son et lumière* show at the Acropolis.

I ate slices of pear with Brie, a French rather than a Greek dessert. I don't have a sweet tooth and I'm not fond of baklava or any of the other pastries dripping with syrup. Spreading the soft Brie on a crisp slice of pear, I felt a presence behind me, thought it was the waiter, and turned.

It was the black-haired kid who'd raised his eyebrow at me while we were sitting in Constitution Square. And he was tall. Taller than I.

"Hi, Red," he said.

If Sandy and Rhea had been with me as planned, I'd have ignored him. Though likely if I'd been with Sandy and Rhea he wouldn't have spoken. I intensely dislike being called Red.

"Saw you walk over to the King George from the Square this afternoon," he said. "I'm Zachary Gray, from California. You *are* American, aren't you?"

"Yes." Did I really want to talk to this guy?

"May I sit down?"

"Feel free." I still wasn't sure.

"What's your name, and where're you from?" he asked. He was really spectacular-looking, with black eyes and long black lashes. I envied him those lashes, though I'm happy with my own eyes. Kate would have fallen all over him.

I didn't exactly want to fall over him, but I decided I did want him to sit down. "I'm Polly O'Keefe, and I've come from an island partway between Savannah, Georgia, and Charleston, South Carolina."

"You don't have a Southern accent. Almost English."

"Middle Atlantic," I corrected him. "I spent a lot of my childhood in Portugal." Max's accent was softly Southern, not jarringly, just a gentle, musical rhythm.

"So, what're you doing all by your lonesome in Athens? Are your parents with you?"

"My parents are home on Benne Seed Island. I'm here for a week, and then I'm going to Cyprus. What're *you* doing here?"

"Just bumming around. I'm taking a year off from college to wander around Europe and get some culture."

He didn't look like the typical American backpacker. He looked like money, lots of money.

The waiter came over and Zachary greeted him. "Hello, Aristeides. This young lady's a friend of mine."

"Yes?"

I almost told Aristeides I'd never seen him before in my life, but I shut my mouth on the words. I was lonely. And being picked up by a desirable young man was a new experience.

Zachary ordered a bottle of retsina. "It's a white wine, soaked over resin. It tastes like the Delphic Oracle."

Rhea looks down her nose at retsina.

But Zachary went on: "There are other Greek wines which are much better; I just happen to like it. Aristeides, by the way, means someone who is inflexibly just."

"You speak Greek?" I asked.

"A few words and phrases. You pick it up."

A waiter's name which means 'inflexibly just' would be fine to set down in that journal I was supposed to be keeping for school. "How do you happen to know Aristeides?"

"I like good food and pleasant places to eat it in. And Athens is my favorite city. I infinitely prefer it to Paris or London or Rome. How come you're going off to Cyprus right at the beginning of the school year? You don't look like a dropout."

"I'm not. It's an educational trip. I'm going to be a gofer at a conference in Osia Theola."

"How'd you get chosen for the job?"

"I'm not afraid of hard work."

Zachary said, "Your parents must trust you, to let you come this way all alone and stay all by yourself at a hotel in Athens."

"They do trust me," I said. I didn't think it necessary to say they had no idea I was all alone in Athens.

"So where's this place on Cyprus?" he asked.

"Osia Theola. It's a small village with a conference center in what used to be a monastery."

"Maybe we'll have a chance to get better acquainted before you go. I decided when I spotted you this afternoon that you were someone I wanted to know."

How to respond to this? Kate would have known exactly the right thing to say. I didn't.

"I'm glad your parents put you in the King George. You'll be safe here." His tone was condescending. "What's on your agenda for tomorrow?"

I replied firmly, "I'm going on a bus tour." I didn't want this Zachary taking too much for granted.

"No, no, not a bus tour," Zachary said. "They're the pits. You're coming with me." He sounded very sure of himself. "I just happen to be free for the next couple of days, and I'll give you the million-dollar tour."

Aristeides brought the wine and two glasses and looked at me questioningly.

"No, thank you," I said to him. "Not after I spent all last night on a plane and my internal clock is all mixed up."

Zachary started to protest, so I added, "I'm underage, any-how," and Aristeides nodded at me and took my glass away, then poured some for Zachary, who held the glass out to me. "Take a sip at least."

Because of Rhea's taste in wines, I'd never had retsina.

Maybe my tastes are low, but I liked it; it made me think of pine forests, and Diana walking through fallen needles, her bow slung over her shoulder.

Aristeides moved away to serve another table, and Zachary looked at me over the rim of his glass. Zachary really was in Athens on his own, while my being by myself was because of some kind of crisis in Sandy and Rhea's work. And I was suddenly grateful that my parents cared enough about me so that I was not like this Zachary, or the other kids checking in at American Express for their money while their parents did whatever parents do who just want their kids out of their hair.

"How old *are* you?" Zachary asked.

"Nearly seventeen."

He leaned toward me. "It's hard to tell by looking at you. I'd have thought you were older, except that your blue eyes are a child's."

"I'm not a child."

"Thank God. Tell me about this Benne Seed Island where you live. It sounds as though it's out in the boonies."

"Benne Seed makes the boonies look metropolitan," I said. "But isolation is good for Daddy's work."

"What does he do?"

"He's a marine biologist," I said briefly. We've learned never to talk about Daddy's experiments, because they're in an incredibly sensitive area and in the wrong hands could be disastrous. But Zachary seemed to expect me to say something more, so I added, "My father needs a lot of solitude for experiments that take a long time to show any definitive results."

"Isn't that hard on you? How do you feel about all that solitude?"

I shrugged. "I have six younger brothers and sisters, so it isn't all that solitary."

He nearly swooned. "Seven kids! What got into your parents? You Catholic or something?"

I shook my head. Sometimes I wondered myself what had got into my parents. It seemed to me that when we were living on Gaea they felt they had to repopulate the island all by themselves so we'd have people to play with.

Who, of all of us, would I send back? Not even Xan, who's the one who rubs me like sandpaper.

From my seat I still had a good view, despite the middle-aged man who thought I was looking at him, and suddenly the walls of the Acropolis were lit by soft, moving lights, shifting from pale rose to green to blue. "Look," I said.

Zachary turned around in his chair, and back. "It's pretty vulgar." (Rhea would have agreed with him there.) "But I'll take you tomorrow night if you like."

Again, I didn't know what to say. Yes? Kate says boys don't like it if you're too eager. The only person I'd ever dated was Renny, and I'm not sure having pizza with Renny even qualified as a date. He was an intern, and I was a kid who listened to him talk.

I pushed the thought of Renny away. If I was going to go out with Zachary the next day, I ought to know something more about him. "When you finish getting culture and go back to college, where are you going? What are you planning to be?"

"One at a time," he said. "I'm going back to UCLA, and I'll be studying law. My pa's a corporate lawyer, and I mean a multinational corporate lawyer, with his finger in pies on every continent."

As I thought: money. I watched the lights shimmer on the hillside and then blink off.

"I'm taking this year off to find out what I really want. I'll tell you what I want right now. I want to spend tomorrow with you."

With me. This extremely gorgeous-looking young man wanted to spend the day with me. It sounded a lot better than going on a bus tour with a lot of people I didn't know. I wasn't sure I trusted Zachary. But I didn't have any reason to trust a lot of strangers on a bus, either.

"Here we are, both on our own"—Zachary reached across the table and lightly touched the tips of his fingers to mine—"and I think we can have a good time together."

Not only had I not mentioned to Zachary that my parents had no idea I was on my own, I also did not tell him about Sandy and Rhea.

He went on. "When I saw you in the Square this afternoon
you reminded me of a wild pony, ready to shy off if anybody
frightened you. You still have that look, as though you might
suddenly leap up from your chair and vanish. You're sophisticated enough to be eating alone on the roof of the King
George and yet you have an innocence I haven't seen in anyone
your age in I don't know how long."

For want of anything better to say, I murmured, "I've lived
on islands most of my life."

"I was expecting to take off for Corfu tomorrow, but I'd
much rather stay here and show you around. I'll rent a car so
we can go off into the countryside."

I was flattered. I suspected my cheeks were pink. Kate collects
male animals as I collect specimens for Daddy, going out in the
boat to get squid or whatever he needs. Nobody anywhere near
my age had ever wanted to spend a day with me before. "That
sounds like fun. But I think right now I'd better go to bed and
get a good night's sleep if I'm to be awake for you tomorrow."

"I'll take you to your room," he said.

"No. Thanks. I'll go myself."

"Don't you trust me?"

I shook my head. "It isn't you."

"You *are* a wild little animal," he said. "I'm not a wolf."

I stood up. "What time shall we meet tomorrow?"

"Ten okay?"

"Sure."

"I'll pick you up. What's your room number?"

"I'll meet you in the lobby."

"Okay, okay, pretty Pol, I suppose you have every right to be
suspicious of some guy who's just picked you up. I'm staying
at the Hilton, by the way, because it has a better view. Wait till
you see it. Lobby of the King George. Ten a.m. tomorrow."

"I look forward to it," I said. I was glad I'd already signed
for my meal, so I could just walk away, without looking back.

The view from my room at night was as beautiful as it had
been in the full sunshine, although the *son et lumière* show was
long over. I looked at the ancient stones and wondered what all

those centuries did to our own troubled time—put it in more cosmic perspective perhaps? But even if the Acropolis speaks of the pettiness and brevity of our mortal lives, while our lives are going on they matter.

The ancient stones seemed lit from within. Sometimes I think the past has its own radiance. I turned from the balcony, switched on the lights, and ordered my breakfast for the next morning, hanging the breakfast chit on the outside of the door. Breakfast in the room was my Uncle Sandy's suggestion. He and Rhea like to keep their mornings quiet when they're traveling, and I thought I might like that, too—continental breakfast, *café au lait* and croissants, and a book. It sounded good to me.

The bed had been turned down while I was at dinner, and it looked so comfortable that I got undressed right away and climbed in, pushing the pillows up behind me, dutifully writing in the journal for school. Most certainly the day in Athens had not been in the least what I had expected. No Sandy and Rhea; instead, a boy called Zachary. That was not the kind of thing to write down. I thought for a moment, then described the view from my room and mentioned Aristeides, the inflexibly just, to prove that travel is truly educational.

And then the phone rang.

I was not entirely surprised to have it be my Uncle Dennys calling from Boston. Sandy and Dennys have the special closeness of twins.

All Dennys wanted to know was that I was okay, that I wasn't lonely or frightened. He and Sandy use the long-distance phone as though it were local. They both feel that it's very important to keep in touch. And I suppose they can both afford it. Nevertheless, it awes me. He asked, "What are your plans for tomorrow?"

"I'm going sightseeing."

"All alone?"

"No, I met this guy from California who knows a lot about Athens, and he's going to show me around."

"Are you sure he's okay?"

"Who can be sure about anyone? I can take care of myself."

"Sure you can, Pol, but be careful."

"I'll be careful. Don't worry."

"Sorry Sandy got held up, but maybe it'll be good for you to have this time on your own."

"Don't tell Mother and Daddy—"

"Never fear. Sandy's already made me promise. Strikes me he's being more protective of them than he is of you."

"He just wants me to grow up," I said.

"You will. You already are, in many ways." We said goodbye, and I felt warmed by Dennys's call. Sandy had promised me that what Max had called him about wouldn't go any further, he wouldn't tell anyone, even his twin. And I knew he hadn't.

When I put the phone down I looked at my school journal and decided I was too tired to write any more. I slid down in bed and turned out the light. It was cool enough, with the balcony windows open to the night breeze, for me to snuggle under the covers. I plummeted into sleep, and slept deep down dark for a couple of hours, and then woke up and felt myself floating to the surface. At first I thought I was in my familiar bed at home. But I heard street noises instead of the surf rolling and the wind in the palmettos. I was alone in a hotel in Athens. Sandy and Rhea were still in Washington, but Zachary Gray was not far away in the Hilton. Amazing.

What time was it at home? Never mind. I'd better get body and mind on Greek time. I leaned on my elbow and peered at the travel alarm. Midnight. I lay down. Wrapped the covers about me. Too hot. Pushed them down. Too cold. Slipped into half sleep. Half dream.

Renny.

Queron Renier.

(With a name like Queron, who wouldn't be called Renny?)

Like Zachary, Renny was tall, taller than I. Most of the kids at Cowpertown High were shorter. Zachary was sophisticated and exotic. Renny was serious and nice-looking in a completely unspectacular way. His light brown hair bleached in the summer from sun and salt water. His grey-blue eyes peered behind thick lenses in heavy frames. In the dream he was standing beside me on the open verandah at Beau Allaire, wearing his white doctor's coat, with his stethoscope dangling out of his pocket, looking like a young doctor on TV. He said, 'An intern's life is hell,' the way he had said it to me at least a dozen times, but in a tone of voice that belied his words. Renny loved being an intern. He loved the hospital and everything about it. When I first met him I assumed that he was at the M. A. Horne Hospital because it was the only place he could get. Renny is from Charleston, and there are bigger hospitals in Charleston. There are bigger hospitals in Savannah and Jacksonville. Or Richmond or Baltimore.

In the dream he sat on the white rail of the verandah. 'You watch out for this guy who's picked you up. I don't trust him.'

'I can handle him,' I said.

'You're much too sure of yourself, Polyhymnia O'Keefe. Pride goeth before a fall.'

'I'm not really sure of myself,' I said. 'It's just a front.' It was. I'm sure of myself as far as my brain is concerned. I've got a good one, thanks to my genetic background. But in every other area of life I'm insecure. I can talk easily and comfortably with adults, but not with kids my own age.

'Watch it,' Renny said, his voice echoing in the dream. 'Watch it . . . watch it . . .'

His warning woke me and brought me back from Beau Allaire to my bed in the King George. I was hot, so I got up and went out onto the balcony, and the night sky was that extraordinary blue which was deep behind the stars. Greek blue. Blue and gold by day; blue and silver by night. I wondered how much human nature had actually changed in the thousands of years since the Acropolis was built, and if all that had happened to me was so extraordinary after all.

I'd seen Renny every week or so during the past winter and summer. Going out with him for barbecue or pizza on his rare free evenings, and listening to him talk about tropical medicine, was a good antidote to not being asked to a dance at the Cowpertown High School, but that's all it meant, until a couple of weeks ago.

Renny was still an antidote, but for something far more cataclysmic than not being asked to a dance, or watching my cousin Kate go off with a bunch of kids, usually including Xan, while I stayed home. Kate is everything Mother and Daddy would have liked me to be. She's not short, but she's shorter than I am, and when she goes to a dance she doesn't loom over the boys. And she's beautiful, full and beautiful. I'm no longer the same measurement all round; I have reasonable curves both in front and behind, which is a big improvement over the pole I used to be, but Kate has pheromones which draw boys to her like honey. I wasn't exactly jealous of Kate; I didn't even want to change places with her; I was just wistful.

The light on the Acropolis was different now than it had been earlier, a deeper, darker blue, with many of the city lights extinguished around it, though not all. Cities never go completely to sleep. While they are alive, that is. I stood looking at the pearly light on the stone until I was chilly. Then I went back to bed. Edges of dawn were outlining the windows as I slid into sleep. I didn't wake up till there was a knock on the door.

Breakfast. I was wide awake in an instant. Breakfast in Athens. I grabbed my bathrobe and rushed to open the door. A nice young waiter who looked like pictures of Greek statues carried in a breakfast tray which he took out to the balcony. There was a pot of coffee, a pitcher of hot milk, a dish with croissants and toast, jam, honey, and butter.

When we lived on Gaea and school was whenever Mother and Daddy decided we should start lessons, breakfast was unhurried, too. We fixed trays and ate in our rooms and emerged into the day when we felt like it, some of us getting up at dawn, some not till seven or even eight. But at Benne Seed we were on a schedule; we had to get to the mainland in time for that school bus. So, though Mother set breakfast out and we were free to get our own and eat it whenever we liked, we couldn't help bumping into each other. If Mother and Daddy could have gone on teaching us I might have loved Benne Seed as much as I loved Gaea. It was Cowpertown and the high school which depressed me. The island itself was home.

So breakfast alone in Athens reminded me of breakfast on Gaea, though it was much more elegant. I thanked the waiter

in Greek which was, if not flawless, at least understandable, and
he beamed at me. "*Parakalo*," he said, and then he pointed to
the Acropolis with the morning light bringing the stones to
life, gabbled at me in Greek, beamed again, and left.

The telephone rang, jolting me. I went back to the room and
answered, and why was I surprised when it was Zachary Gray?

"I just wanted to make sure we were getting together today."

He was worried about *me* backing out? "Of course."

"Have you had breakfast?"

"I'm having it right now, out on the balcony, enjoying the
view."

"We'll have lunch together somewhere, then, though I want
you to see the view from my balcony first. Can you be in your
lobby at ten sharp?"

I looked at my watch. It was just after eight. "Sure. See you
at ten."

The sun was so bright as it slanted across the balcony that I
hitched my chair back into the shadows so I could see to read
without being half blinded. The croissants were crumbly and
delicious, and the *café au lait* was good, much better than the
sweet thick stuff. Instead of reverting to childhood, having
breakfast alone in Greece as we used to do in Portugal, I suddenly felt very grownup. Absurd. Why did it take being alone
in Athens to make me feel mature enough to look at human
nature and feel part of it? Not better. Not worse. Just part.

I was reading a book Sandy had given me, about Epidaurus,
where he was planning to take me. There's a magnificent theatre there, though we were going to be too late in the season
to see any plays. And there were holy precincts in Epidaurus
where, back in the high days of Greek civilization, people were
brought to be healed, some with physical ailments, some with
mental ones. There were really interesting things in the book.
The snake pit, for instance. Those snakes in the pit where really
sick mental patients were put weren't just snakes, which would
have been enough to send them out of their minds for good;
they were snakes with a strong electric charge. So it was, you
might say, the first electric-shock treatment, and probably no

more inhuman than any kind of electric-shock treatment. I wondered what Renny would think of it.

The brilliant sun dazzling off the stones of the buildings and onto my stretched-out legs and arms was a shock treatment in its own way. My spirits lifted, and I took the last bit of apricot jam and licked it off the spoon.

The sun tingled against my legs, which had a good tan from summer. Unlike a lot of redheads, I do tan, as long as I'm careful and do it slowly. I also have long, straight toes, probably because I've worn sandals or gone barefoot most of my life. Feet are usually not the prettiest part of the body, but my feet were one of the things I could feel pleased about.

In Epidaurus, before sick people could go into the sacred precincts for healing, they had to stay outside the gates to pray, to be purged of bad feelings, anger, resentment, lack of forgiveness. Only then could they go in to the priests.

I looked at the words: *anger, resentment, lack of forgiveness,* and in the brilliant light the letters seemed to wriggle on the page like little snakes. I needed that purging. Nobody could get rid of all those bad feelings but me, myself. The warmth of the sun on the balcony, and those words leaping off the page at me, had made me see that much. Or maybe it was getting away from everything and everybody so I could see it in perspective.

'You'll like Krhis Ghose,' Max had said, showing me a snapshot of a thin man who looked something like Nehru. We were up on the second-floor verandah outside her bedroom, where she had comfortable Chinese wicker furniture, and the breeze from the ocean, plus the ceiling fan, plus mosquito coils, kept the insects to a minimum.

'Is he a Hindu or a Moslem?'

Max fanned herself slowly with an old-fashioned palm-leaf fan. 'A Christian. One who actually *is* one. A person of total integrity. Why we get along so well I'm not sure, but I count him among my closest friends.'

'How did you meet?'

'In Bombay. Much against my will, I was dragged to a lecture Krhis was giving on the connection between religious intolerance and land boundaries. And instead of being bored,

I was fascinated, and we went out with him afterwards and talked all night. He's come through hell. Saw his wife and child shot. God, they do keep shooting each other in that part of the world. But he's come out on the other side, somehow or other. Without bitterness.'

You could not go into the sacred precincts in Epidaurus with bitterness in your soul. Inner and outer illnesses were seen as part of each other, and both patient and priest participated in the healing. The Greeks understood psychosomatic, or holistic, medicine long before they were heard of in the West, where we've tended to separate and overspecialize. In Epidaurus, healing was an art, rather than a science.

Sandy and Dennys say it's an art for Daddy, too, and that's why he's had such remarkable results in his experiments on regeneration.

Ursula Heschel was fascinated by Daddy's work, and when she and Max came over for dinner, she and Daddy always spent time together in the lab. Xan and I both helped in the lab, feeding the animals, cleaning the tanks, and I had to wash down the floor with a hose once a day. Max was interested and intelligent, but Ursula was the one who truly understood. She and Daddy really hit it off.

Once in January, Daddy and Ursula went to Florida to a lab there specializing in the nervous system of the octopus. In February they went together to Baltimore, where Daddy was giving a paper at Johns Hopkins. They had lots in common.

Xan said once, 'It's a good thing Ursula Heschel is much too old for Dad.'

'What are you talking about?'

'They sure like each other. Kate's noticed it. But Mother doesn't seem jealous.'

'They're just friends. There isn't any reason to be jealous.'

And indeed Mother, rather than being jealous, often suggested asking Max and Ursula to dinner.

But if Urs, as it were, belonged to Daddy, Max belonged to me. And my parents encouraged the friendship. Mother said, 'I expect too much of you, Polly. The oldest always gets too

much responsibility foisted on her. I should know. Of course
you can go over to Beau Allaire this afternoon.'

If the car wasn't free I'd go to Beau Allaire right from school,
taking the bus from Cowpertown to Mulletville and walking
over from there, and then later on, Mother would come for me,
or Urs would drive me home.

Max had called and asked me for tea early in January. The
uncles had left, Charles had gone back to Boston with Dennys
and Lucy, and Kate had stayed with us. The house was back
to its normal population. School had started again and was as
stultifying as ever, and I was glad to be going over to Beau
Allaire, but a little shy, driving over by myself. I'd got my license on my sixteenth birthday. One of the good things about
Cowpertown High was the driver's-ed course, though Mother
and Daddy said that driver's ed and similar courses were one
reason why the science department was nearly nonexistent, and
why no languages were offered.

As I climbed the steps to the front entrance to Beau Allaire,
Max flung open the door and welcomed me in. Nettie and
Ovid were setting out tea in the library. I didn't see Ursula.

'Urs went into Charleston on a consultation,' Max explained.
'They don't have a neurological service at M. A. Horne, more's
the pity. It would keep Urs busy. Dennys introduced her to
the chief of neurology at Mercy Hospital and one would
have thought Dennys had given him pure gold. In a sense,
he did. People flock to New York to see Ursula. They'll flock
to Charleston just for a consult. *Maintenant.*' She spoke to
me in French. 'Did you bring your homework with you as I
suggested?'

I replied in Portuguese: 'It's here, in my canvas bag.'

'Not Portuguese,' Max said. 'That *was* Portuguese, wasn't
it?'

'Yes, and it's the language I speak best,' I answered in
German.

She laughed. 'I concede. You're good at languages. Let me
see some of your schoolwork.'

I pulled out my English notebook. On the bus from school
to the Cowpertown dock, I'd written a sketch of the natives on

Gaea, comparing them with the Indians we'd met when Daddy took Charles and me with him for a month when he was doing research in Venezuela.

'That's good, Polly,' Max said, to my surprise. 'You really give a flavor of the people you're writing about, but you haven't fallen for the Noble Savage trap. You look at them with a realistic eye. Where did you get your gift for writing?'

'I didn't know I had one. Daddy used to write when he was young, and Mother says he should go over his journals and have some of them published. But he's too busy.'

'If he's that good, he should make time,' Max said. She began leafing through my English notebook. 'You use imagery well. That's a good snow metaphor, *soft flowers that perished before they reached the ground*. Where have you seen snow?'

'Sometimes it snowed in Lisbon. And we've seen snow when we've stayed with our grandparents in New England.'

'Good. I didn't think you could have written that if you hadn't seen it. Does your English teacher appreciate you?'

'She gives me B's. She thinks I'm showing off when I write about Lisbon and other places we've been.'

'Are you?'

'No. When she wants a description of a place, I have to write about places I know.'

'True. But I can see that it might seem like showing off to your English teacher. What's her name?'

'Miss Zeloski.'

'Hardly a good South Carolina name. Who are your favorite poets?'

Sandy and Rhea often give me poetry for Christmas. This year it was a small volume of seventeenth-century writers. I loved it. 'There's someone called Vaughan, I think. I love the way he *relishes* words.'

'And Miss Zeloski?'

'If anything rhymes, Miss Zeloski says it's old-fashioned. She likes poetry that—that obfuscates.'

Max leaned back on the sofa and laughed. 'And I suppose she likes all that garbage full of genital imagery?'

'Not at Cowpertown High. The PTA has its eye out for obscenity.'

'*Go and catch a falling star*,' Max said. '*Get with child a mandrake root.*'

'She doesn't like John Donne. I think he scares her.'

'Too real?'

'That's not what she calls it. But yes. I think she's afraid of reality. So if the poetry doesn't mean anything, she doesn't have to cope with it.'

Max climbed up on the library ladder and pulled a book off one of the top shelves and read a few lines. 'e. e. cummings.'

'I love him,' I said. 'Sandy and Rhea gave me one of his books for my birthday a few years ago.'

'Not cool enough for your Miss Z.?'

'Too cool.'

Max climbed down from the ladder, and refilled my cup. It was a special tea, smoky, and we drank it without anything in it. I liked it. I liked Max. I liked talking with her. At home, everybody (except my parents) was younger than I, and our conversations were limited. And at school I didn't have any real friends. It wasn't that I was actively unpopular, I just didn't have anyone special to talk to. Mostly I felt I was walking through the scene, saying my lines reasonably well, but not being really in the show. At school I tried to play the role that was expected of me, as best I could. With Max, I was myself.

She laughed at me gently. 'What a snob you are, Polly.'

'Me?' I was startled.

'Why not? It's obvious that school bores you, and that there's nobody to challenge you, teacher or student.'

'A lot of the kids are bright.'

She cut me off. 'Go ahead and be a snob. I'm a snob. If you didn't interest me I wouldn't give you the time of day. Being a snob isn't necessarily a bad thing. It can mean being unwilling to walk blindly through life instead of living it fully. Being unwilling to lose a sense of wonder. Being alive is a marvelous, precarious mystery, and few people appreciate it. Go on being a snob, Polly, as long as it keeps your mind and heart alert. It doesn't mean that you can't appreciate people who are different from you, or have different interests.'

Max made me not only willing to be Polyhymnia O'Keefe but happy to be.

It was, oddly enough, through Max that I began seeing Renny. He called me early one evening late in January.

Xan shouted, 'Hey, Polly, it's for you. Some guy.'

I ambled to the phone. Sometimes kids in my class call me to ask about homework.

'Is this Polly O'Keefe?'

'Yes.'

'You don't know me. I'm Queron Renier, and I'm a distant cousin of a friend of yours, Simon Renier, the one who's staying in Venezuela.'

'Well, hello,' I said. 'It's nice to hear from you.'

'I'm an intern at the M. A. Horne Hospital in Cowpertown, and I thought maybe we could get together.'

Interns usually move in sometime in early July. This was January. 'Well, sure.' I didn't sound wildly enthusiastic.

'I haven't called before because I'm basically a shy guy. But I was talking with an outpatient who's a friend of yours. I guess she saw I was lonely, and somehow or other I mentioned that I'd heard of you through Simon but I hadn't felt free to call—'

'Who was it?' I was curious now.

'A Mrs. Tomassi.'

It took me a moment to remember that Max's husband's name was Tomassi. 'Max!'

'I guess. She lives on Benne Seed at Beau Allaire—'

'What was she doing at the hospital?'

A pause. 'She was just in for some blood tests.'

I wanted to ask what for, but Daddy has talked to us often enough about confidentiality, and I knew that Renny wouldn't tell me.

He said, 'Well, could we get together sometime? Take in a movie in Cowpertown or something?'

'Sure.' I realized I wasn't being very hospitable. 'Would you like to come to dinner? Do you have anything on, your next evening off?'

'It's tomorrow,' he said. 'It's sort of short notice, but no, I don't have anything on.'

'Well, good. Come on over. Do you have access to a motorboat?'

'Nope.'

'Well, come by the causeway, then. It's a lot longer, but if you don't have a boat it's the only way. We're the far end of the island.'

'No problem.'

'About six?' I gave him directions, hung up, and then double-checked with Mother.

'Of course it's all right,' she said. I knew she was worried that I didn't bring friends home the way the others did.

Renny was nice. Everybody liked him. Kate made eyes at him, but fortunately she really was too young for him. Fourteen, after all. Anyhow, Renny and I got on well. He was almost as shy as I was, and I think he was grateful to have someone he could be purely platonic with. I mean, he hardly saw me as a sexpot. But he asked me to go out for something to eat, and see a movie, on his next free evening.

I saw Max the day after Renny came for dinner. She called me to come over after school, to do my homework at the long table in the library, and stay for an early supper.

Ursula was in the library, too, sitting in her favorite chair, deep in some medical journal.

'So how did you like my nice young intern?' Max asked.

'You described him,' I said. 'Nice.'

'Not exciting?'

'He just came over for dinner with the family. It was kind of a mob scene. But he was able to cope with it, and that says something.'

'Hm.'

'Max, why were you having blood tests?'

Ursula looked up from her journal but said nothing.

Max replied shortly, 'When one is my age, every time one sees a doctor, one has to have a million tests.'

'Why did you need to see a doctor?'

'When one is my age, it is prudent to have regular medical checkups.'

'Renny called you Mrs. Tomassi.'

'It was, after all, my husband's name.'

'You never use it.'

'Therefore it gives me a modicum of privacy, of which there is very little around here. And stop prying. It is not a quality I like.'

'Weren't you prying about Renny?' I countered.

'At my age, prying is permissible. Not at yours. Please treat me with the respect I deserve.'

Ursula put her journal down and stood up, stretching. 'I'm off to finish up in the kitchen.'

'Need any help?' I asked.

'No thanks, Pol. Nettie and Ovid already think I'm displacing them. I do try not to hurt their feelings, and I'm more than grateful to have them wash up. It's a dream of a kitchen, and cooking has always been therapy for me.'

At Beau Allaire it wasn't always easy to remember that Urs was at the top of her profession. She seemed to enjoy acting the housekeeper.

'I take outrageous advantage of Urs,' Max said, as the doctor shut the library door. 'But she doesn't have to let me.'

'Well, she loves you.'

'So, are you going to see Renny again?'

'Yup.'

'When?'

'He's not on call on Thursday. We're getting together.'

'He's coming to the Island for dinner again?'

'No. I'm going out with him.'

This seemed to please Max. And that surprised me. Max did not strike me as the matchmaking type.

Ursula came in with a decanter of sherry and said she'd fixed a good French peasant stew for dinner and it could sit on the back of the stove till we were ready. 'Like Nettie and Ovid, I tend to ignore the electric stove and use the old wood-and-coal one. I suppose I'll be grateful for the electric stove come summer.' She poured a small glass of sherry for Max, half glasses for herself and for me, and put the crystal stopper back in the decanter. 'You're good to spend so much time with us, Polly.'

'Good! You've rescued me! You've no idea how lonely I've been.'

'I do,' Max said. 'I grew up at Beau Allaire I, too, went

to school in Cowpertown. You were probably luckier on your Portuguese island, where you were the only Americans, the only Europeans, really, and had to make your own company.'

I nodded. 'I was lots less lonely than I am here. It's not the island—I love Benne Seed.'

'Too bad you and Kate don't hit it off better. M.A. and I made life under the Spanish moss bearable for each other.'

'Kate and Xan are the ones who get along. And Kate's wildly popular at school.'

'You're not?' Ursula's voice was gentle.

'I think the other kids think I'm weird.'

'You're brighter than they are,' Max said, 'and that's threatening.'

'A couple of guys in my grade killed a tortoise the other day,' I said, feeling sick all over again. 'I mean deliberately, and I could have killed them. I wanted to, it was awful, but then I realized that the tortoise was already half dead so it was better to let them finish the job, and everybody laughed because I was making such a case of it.'

'Kate and Xan, too?' Ursula asked.

'They weren't there. Xan would have stopped them.'

Ursula spoke reassuringly. 'Don't worry, Polly. You'll have friends, too, even if you have to wait till you get to college and meet more people. You're friend material, and once you have friends you'll keep them for life.'

Renny had borrowed a motorboat from one of the doctors, which saved us nearly an hour. He took me to a Greek restaurant, Petros', near the dock, which shared a run-down sort of boardwalk with a seafood restaurant.

Renny and I sat in a booth and he told me about his special field, tropical medicine, especially in South America.

That surprised me. I looked at Renny sitting across from me, and there was something solid about him. His blue-grey eyes behind the thick lenses were amused. 'I inherited the Renier myopia,' he said. He'd have been good casting for a young doctor on a soap opera. If I'd been asked to guess what he was going to specialize in, I'd have said orthopedics, or maybe general surgery.

No. South American amoebas and parasites.

'What about India?' I asked, because I've always wanted to go to India. 'Aren't there vast quantities of amoebas and parasites there?'

'Yes, but I'm particularly interested in some parasites which are found largely in South America. They get into the bloodstream, and—to try to simplify a long procedure—eventually invade the heart.'

'Doesn't sound nice.'

'Isn't. The parasite Trypanosoma enters the body usually through the bite of an insect. There are two types of Trypanosoma problems I'm interested in—Chagas' disease and Netson's. Netson's disease is even more lethal than Chagas', particularly to someone with no immunities. When it gets to the heart, ultimately it kills, and thus far we don't have any successful treatment. More important than treatment is finding a means of prevention.'

'Hey. Is there any of this disease around here?'

'No, no, don't worry. So far, it's found almost exclusively in South America. None indigenous to North America.'

Behind Renny was a large poster of the Acropolis, the Parthenon prominent. Despite the Greek decor, the menu was Italian. But I had no idea, that first pizza with Renny, that I'd ever be going to Greece.

'So how come you're interning at M. A. Horne in Cowpertown if you're so interested in South American diseases?'

'Because Bart Netson's on the staff of M. A. Horne. He's my immediate boss.'

When I looked totally surprised, he grinned. 'I have the feeling you suspected that M. A. Horne was at the bottom of my list when I applied to hospitals.'

I could feel myself flushing. I had once again jumped to conclusions. I had judged Renny quickly and unfairly. 'Offhand, a small general hospital off the beaten track doesn't sound like a number-one choice. I didn't know about this Netson or his disease. Why is *he* at M. A. Horne?'

Renny laughed, a nice, hearty laugh. 'He was born in Charleston but spent most of his childhood in Argentina because his father was in foreign service. He came back to Charleston to medical school and married an Allaire. He spends a couple of months each year in South America doing research. He's published a lot of good material, probably the best in the field of tropical medicine, and it's prestigious for M. A. Horne to have him. They're heavily enough endowed to give him pretty much whatever he wants.'

'So he's a sort of cousin of Max's?'

'Has to be. Her mother was an Allaire.' He cut two more slices of pizza and put one, dripping cheese, on my plate. 'Polly? If I go on riding my hobbyhorse, we'll miss the movie.'

'That's okay. I'd rather talk.'

He looked eager. 'Sure?'

'Sure. I'm interested. I wouldn't think you'd have many patients coming into M. A. Horne with South American diseases.'

'You'd be surprised.' He took a large bite of pizza and a swig of milk. 'With the continuing flood of refugees from South American countries, some of them coming in via Cuba and Florida and filtering up through Georgia, we get quite a few. And because of Bart Netson, their problem is recognized more quickly than in other places. For instance, a mild case of conjunctivitis plus a fluctuating fever isn't usually equated with a parasite.'

'Conjunctivitis? You mean pinkeye?'

'The vector—the biting insect—often bites the face at the mucocutaneous junction—'

'Translate.'

'The lip, or the outer canthus of the eye.'

'How'd you get involved?' It did seem an odd choice for a perfect Southern-gentleman type like Queron Renier.

'I spent a couple of summers working in a clinic in Santiago. Eventually, I want to go back.'

'Like a missionary?'

He shook his head. 'To do research. A lot of good medicine has, in fact, come from medical missionaries who give their lives to help people nobody else gives a hoot about—millions of people worn down and living half lives.'

'So how'd you get to Chile and this clinic?'

He looked over my head at one of the Greek posters. 'I met a girl from Santiago while I was in college. Jacinta was over here taking pre-med courses and stayed on for medical school. It was through her I got the summer jobs in Chile.'

'You were in love with her?' He nodded. 'And vice versa?'

A shadow crossed his face. 'To some extent. But there wasn't any future for us.'

'Why not?'

'For one thing, Jacinta was Roman Catholic.'

'Would that really matter?'

'To her, yes. And she came from a big Chilean family, and she was engaged to someone there. They still arrange marriages.'

'She sounds like an independent type. Why'd she accept it?'

'Who knows? Maybe she liked the guy. Maybe he had enough money for her clinic.'

'And you don't want me to ask you any more questions about her.'

'It's okay,' Renny said. 'I've pretty well got her out of my system.'

'But you're still into tropical medicine.'

'Yeah. I guess I'm grateful to her for that. I really am fascinated by it.'

And he was still bruised over the Chilean girl.

'Jacinta's interning in Louisiana,' he said. 'I might bump into her if I ever get back to Chile. But she'll be married by then. They make good baklava here. Want some?'

'Too sweet. You go ahead.'

After we finished eating, he drove back to the dock and we got into the motorboat. About halfway to the Island, he cut the motor and kissed me, which Kate had given me to understand was mandatory, whether the guy really liked you or not. I hoped that Renny liked me. He kissed nicely.

'I'm glad your friend made me call you,' he said.

That was Renny, and I liked him, as the older brother I'd always wanted, even if I got a little tired of tropical medicine. And maybe I was helpful to him in getting his Chilean girl out of his system.

The view of the Acropolis from the balcony at the King George was very like the poster at Petros' in Cowpertown. I took longer over breakfast than I'd expected, looking out at the view, reading bits from the book on Epidaurus (Sandy would expect me to have done my homework), relaxing in the warm morning sunlight.

So I had to dress in a hurry to get down to the lobby by ten. Not difficult. I don't have a large wardrobe to choose from, unlike Kate, who could barely get all her clothes plus herself into her room at Benne Seed. Well, Kate's an Only, and if I had that many clothes I'd have a terrible time deciding what to wear.

I put on a blue-and-white seersucker dress and my sandals and was ready when Zachary pulled up in a diesel taxi with flames coming out the tail pipe. I remember thinking the car was on fire when I first saw a diesel taxi in Lisbon.

I felt simultaneously warm with excitement and frozen with shyness as I sat by this extremely handsome young man on the drive to the Hilton. Zachary did the talking, so I didn't have to worry about what to say. "And listen, Red"—as we drew up to the Hilton—"uh—Pol—about coming up to my room—it's perfectly okay—I mean, I'm not going to try anything or anything like that. So just relax."

His room was on the eleventh floor of the Hilton, "in the best curve of the building," he told me as we went up in a very swift elevator. He led me through his room and right out onto the balcony, and I caught my breath in awe and delight. He had a view not only of the strange, flat-topped hill with the Parthenon but also a wide vista of the harbor at Piraeus, with the Aegean Sea to the left. And there was a high, stony mountain rising out of cypress trees, topped with a stone belfry, and then a large, white building, probably a monastery. It was far more spectacular than the view from the King George, or the poster at Petros'.

I had let my breath out in what was almost shock at the vast sweep of gloriousness. He gave me a proprietary smile. "Told you it would wow you."

It did. But the funny thing was that despite the staggering

magnificence of the view, I liked my old hotel better than the Hilton.

As though reading my thoughts, Zachary waved toward the room. "The decor is pure Hilton, and a Hilton is a Hilton is a Hilton. However, my pa has connections, and the view redeems it. And the bathroom is European, black marble, with a tub made for people who prefer baths to showers."

"Like me," I said.

"I can't start the day without a shower. Okay, what now?"

"The Acropolis, please, if you haven't been there too many times."

"The Acropolis, pretty Pol, can't be visited too many times. We'll just grab a cab."

"Can't we walk?"

"We could, if we had nothing else to do all day. I want to drive out in the country with you, and then come back to Athens, and maybe go to the Plaka to one of my favorite small tavernas." He was planning to be with me the whole day. I felt a thrill of pleasure ripple over me. I glanced at him out of the corner of my eye. He was just as gorgeous as I thought, and at least two inches taller than I.

It was a glorious end-of-summer day. Despite Zachary's chatter about the terrible pollution which was destroying the Parthenon and other ancient sites, and which gave him allergies, to me the air was clear and crisp and invigorating. It would be romanticizing to say it was like Gaea, because Gaea had as much fog and dampness as any other island, but it was like Gaea as I remembered it.

Zachary insisted on paying the entrance fee for both of us, and I was not happy about this. I didn't want to be beholden to some guy I had just met who came from the world of megabucks. I pulled out my Greek money and my booklet of traveler's checks, but he brushed me aside and got our tickets and I couldn't very well arm-wrestle him in the middle of the throng. I followed him through the gates, along with a lot of other tourists. Many were bunched together in groups, with guides herding them like sheep.

Zachary pointed to a cluster of Japanese tourists slung with cameras. He nudged me. "They say that Japanese tourists really aren't pushy. They just get behind a German." He laughed, then said, "Or don't you approve of ethnic jokes?" Just at that moment we saw a big, red-faced man in lederhosen pushing his way through the crowd.

"See?" Zachary said. But the man opened his mouth and called to someone, and he spoke in pure middle-American. "Ouch." Zachary made a face. "Corn belt. What does he think he's trying to prove? No wonder most of the world hates us. Come on, Pol. If you think there's a mob today, you should see it in midseason." He took me by the hand.

I pulled back, looking at the scaffolding partly concealing a beautiful building. "Not so fast."

He stopped. "Okay, listen, this is really interesting. They're literally inoculating the stone with antibiotics to try to slow down decay. The Caryatids—you know what Caryatids are?"

Max had seen to it that I would not come to Greece unprepared. "Female forms, sort of like columns, holding up a roof."

I think Zachary was slightly annoyed that I knew about Caryatids. (Kate had said to me, 'Listen, Polly, guys don't like it if they think you know more than they do.' 'I *do* know more than they do.' 'You don't need to show it.') "Okay, then," Zachary said, "they're trying to restore the Caryatids which hold up the Erechtheion. That's what all the scaffolding is for. And that's why the Parthenon is roped off, because all those tourists' feet were wearing down the marble. Okay, Red, c'mon. The Theseum is one of my favorites. What gets me is knowing that all this beauty was destroyed not so much by the erosion of time, and normal wear and tear, as by war, and greed, and man's stupidity. It really makes me more anti-war than some of the more obvious things, like nuclear stockpiling. Lots of these fallen columns were destroyed by people scavenging for metal."

"What for?"

"Guns. Cannons."

I shuddered. "You mean they really destroyed gorgeous temples just to get a small quantity of metal?"

"That's exactly what I mean."

"And Lord Elgin, all those marbles he took—" I looked

around. "I suppose he really thought he was saving them from the Turks, but shouldn't they be back now where they belong? At least those which didn't get lost when that ship sank?" Why don't you shut up, Polyhymnia. You're showing off how much you know again, reeling back the tape of what Max taught you.

Zachary knew I was showing off. But he was nice about it. "You've done your homework, haven't you? That's okay. Lots of Americans don't know anything about what they're gawking at, and don't really care. Like my pop. He has a fancy camera and takes hundreds of slides, and when he gets them home he can't even remember where he was when he took the pictures." He led me to a marble bench in the shade of an ancient olive tree. "Let's sit for a minute, and watch the crowd go by, okay? You know, Red—"

"Don't call me Red."

"Polly. You really intrigue me. You aren't like any girl I've ever met."

Was that good? He made it sound good.

"You said you're nearly seventeen—"

I nodded.

"I'd say you're nearly thirty and nearly twelve. And there's something virginal about you. Nice contrast to me. But don't worry. I won't do anything to hurt you. Trust me."

Did I trust this guy? I was not in a trusting frame of mind. But I didn't have to trust him to enjoy being with him.

"Are you?" Zachary asked.

"Am I what?"

"A virgin."

I hesitated. She who hesitates is lost.

He gave me a long, scrutinizing look. "Still waters run deep, eh?"

I tried to recover myself. "That is not a question you should ask somebody you have just met. It is not an acceptable question."

He actually looked discomfited. "Sorry. Sometimes my curiosity gets the better of me. And you make me intensely curious, pretty Pol."

"I don't play around," I said. "Not ever."

"Sweetie, I never thought you did. Not for a minute. Whatever you did, and with whomever, would be totally serious." He touched my arm lightly. "I didn't mean to upset you. Shall we change the subject?"

"Please." I was trembling.

We got up and started to walk along again, brushed by tourists who were hurrying to catch up with their groups. If there was going to be any further conversation between us, he would have to start it. I wanted to tell him to take me back to the hotel, but my voice was lost somewhere deep down inside me.

After a while he spoke in a quiet, normal way. "The Parthenon is probably more beautiful to us today than it would have been when it was built, because now it's open to the Greek light that plays on the marble and brings it to life. In the old days, when it was complete, the main body of the building, the sanctuary that housed the goddess, was enclosed and had no windows, so the only light came from the doorway."

"Wait, please." I dug into my shoulder bag. "Let me get some of this down, so I can write about it in the journal I have to take back to school."

"Now you sound like a little kid again. Why bother? Teacher'll spank you if you don't?"

"I said I'd do it." I opened the journal and made a couple of notes. My hand was steady.

"You might add," Zachary said, "that despite their brilliance, the Greeks were limited in their architecture, because they never discovered the arch. With the arch you can support lots more weight, and that's why the great cathedrals can be so spacious."

Writing furiously, I said, "You certainly know a lot."

"I'm not stupid. I got kicked out of several prep schools because I was bored. But if I'm interested in something, I learn about it. Okay, take your notes and then we'll go on. We can come back to the Acropolis another day. It's so overwhelming you can't take too much at a time."

I wrote down what Zachary had said, and I wondered about the Greeks and their gods. Why had they closed in the Parthenon, so that the goddess Athena had been hidden?

Zachary surprised me by picking up on my thoughts. "Odd, isn't it, Pol, how all the different civilizations want to box God in. The ancient Hebrews wanted to hide the Tabernacle in the Holy of Holies, so the ordinary people couldn't see it. Christians are just as bad. Peter wanted to put Jesus, Moses, and Elijah in a box on the Mount of Transfiguration."

We had come to another bench, and I sat down; it was not easy to write standing up, and the notes I had taken were an untidy scrawl.

"I'm an atheist, obviously," Zachary said.

I looked up at him. "For an atheist, you seem to know a lot about religion."

"That's why I'm an atheist."

Maybe it was because Zachary was older than the kids I went to school with that he did not seem to be afraid to talk about ideas. I was far more comfortable with ideas than with ordinary social conversation.

Athena was the Greek name for the goddess. The Romans called her Minerva. Max's sister was Minerva Allaire. This was the kind of conversation Max delighted in.

The sun was hot, the same sun which beat down on these stones and other people thousands of years ago.

"Penny, Pol," Zachary said.

"Oh—just wondering what it would be like to worship a goddess." Was that a Freudian question?

"You a feminist?"

"Liberation for all," I said. "The Greeks had a pantheon of gods of both sexes, didn't they?" I put the notebook in my bag. "Why am I suddenly famished?"

"Breakfast was a long time ago." Zachary took my hand to pull me up. "I've ordered the car for eleven. We'll drive to Delphi and have lunch at a xenia. Know what a xenia is?"

Sandy and Rhea and I would be staying at xenias. "Greek-run inns." ('You don't have to show off all the time,' Kate said.)

"Ever been in one?"

"I just arrived yesterday."

"Okay, c'mon, let's go."

The car was an old VW Bug, a bit cramped for our long legs.

"Sorry about this rattletrap," Zachary said. "It was all I could get at the last minute."

"We have a Land-Rover on Benne Seed." Daddy could drive it over the dunes, and it didn't get stuck in the sand the way an ordinary car would. "This is a lot less bumpy than that."

Zachary drove too fast. I buckled my seat belt tightly. I'd much rather have puttered along and looked at the countryside. But I kept my mouth closed.

Zachary was a new experience for me, and I didn't want to turn him off by saying the wrong thing. If he was intrigued by me, I was certainly intrigued by him. I couldn't figure out why he had picked me, out of all the kids in Constitution Square. But the fact that he had certainly did something for my ego.

I think I expected Delphi to be bigger and grander than it turned out to be. It's a small village on top of a mountain, facing a great valley and what appears to be a large lake but is actually part of the Bay of Corinth. We stopped at a small xenia set in the midst of gardens built on several levels, with the roofs of the lower levels planted with grass, trees, flowers, so that the xenia seemed part of the hillside. If Delphi was smaller than I'd expected, it was also lovelier, and the mountains were higher and grander. I was overwhelmed by the mountains.

The xenia served only one dish, a lemony chicken that was delicious. But again I felt tongue-tied.

"What's wrong, Red?"

"Polly."

"Polly. 'What's wrong?'"

"Nothing."

"Come on. I know better than that. Someone's hurt you."

"You can hardly get to be my age without being hurt."

"You're a constant surprise to me. When I relax into thinking of you as a child, you turn into a woman, wounded."

"Don't be romantic."

"Don't you want to talk to me?"

"Of course I want to talk to you. What've we been doing all day?"

"Chatting. Showing off how much we both know. With a few minor exceptions, we haven't been talking."

Well. He was more sensitive than I'd realized.

"So, shall we talk?"

Out of desperation, I asked, "Why don't *you* talk?"

"About what?"

"Well, why are you in Greece instead of college? It's not just for the culture."

"Little Miss Smarty-pants. No. It's not."

"So who wounded *you*?"

As though stalling for time, he signaled the waitress for the check. "I got dumped by a girl I liked, and I deserved to be dumped. As is my wont, I showed off, tried to prove what a big shot I am, and when she really needed me I let her down. I don't like accepting that about myself." Suddenly his face crumpled. Then he was back in control. "My self-image took a beating. Hey, Red, I don't talk about myself like this, not with anybody. What've you done to me?"

This time I didn't tell him not to call me Red.

He went on. "So it seemed wise to take some time off, to find out more about who I am, what I want to be."

"Have you been finding out?"

"No. As usual, I've been running away. It hit me a couple of days ago in Mykenos. I've been running so I wouldn't have to stop and look at myself. Do I want to be a lawyer, part of an enormous global corporation, like Pa? I always thought I did. Putting growth and profit over the interests of any nation. Multinationals are not accountable to anybody. That's Pa's world. Do I want to inherit it?"

It occurred to me that the world which Zachary stood to inherit was the world which Sandy and Rhea were devoting their lives to fight. Sandy and Rhea put the interests of human beings above the interests of corporations, and I knew they'd upset several global oligarchies.

"Do you want to inherit that world?" I asked.

"It's power," he said.

"Power corrupts."

"Well, Red, I don't know, I just don't know. It's easier to face your own weaknesses in a context of money and power than looking in the mirror in the morning while you're shaving. If you have enough money, and enough power, nothing else matters. Pa's never loved anything except money. He and Ma endured each other—she died a couple of years ago. The extent of their conversation was, 'I need another ice cube.' Or, 'Where shall we go for dinner?' I doubt if they ever slept together much after I was conceived. What about your parents? Do they still have sex?"

He'd revealed too much about himself, I thought, so he had to turn it on me. My voice was cool. "They sleep in the same bed. What they do in it is their own affair."

Zachary paid the bill, putting out what seemed to be a very small tip. "Let's get out of here and climb up to the stadium."

It was quite a climb, and Zachary got out of breath. If he was wandering around Europe finding out who he was and what he wanted to do, he must have been doing it in taxis and rented cars and expensive hotels. I felt sorry for him. But he also represented a world which was ruthless, where money mattered, and not people. We'd had to leave Portugal because of that world, because of people coming to Gaea and trying to get hold of Daddy's work on regeneration and exploit it, long before it was safe. I liked Zachary, and not just because he liked me; there was just something about him that appealed to me. But I was also frightened by the world in which he'd grown up. Mixed feelings. As usual.

The stadium was impressive, with many of the original marble seats intact, carved right out of the hillside. We sat looking at the mountains looming above us, at the valley far below, caressed by the golden air. The land was very dry and bare-looking. There were a few trees, but very little grass, and that was parched and brown. But this was only part of a great cycle, Max had told me. In the winter the rains would come and the earth would be green again.

I didn't like it when Zachary asked me about my parents' sex life. I'm not like Rosy, of course. At four, Rosy still thinks of

Mother as an extension of herself. I don't. But still, I want Mother to be Mother, Daddy to be Daddy.

Max, in a different way from Zachary, also separated my parents from me, seeing them with her clear grey eyes in a way that I had never seen them.

'Your mother's restless,' Max said, one rainy winter day when we were sitting in the library.

'Oh?' Mother, restless?

Max got up from the long sofa and put more fat wood on the fire. 'She's been a good mother to all of you, but it's beginning to wear on her. She's got a fine brain, and not enough chance to use it.'

'She helps Daddy a lot in the lab, does all the computer stuff.'

'Yes, she does, and that's a saving grace, but it's not her own thing.'

'She's going to finish her Ph.D. as soon as Rosy's in school.'

'Easier said than done. You do a great deal, too much, I think, but you'll be out of the nest soon. The boys aren't going to be that much help.'

'Everybody helps out,' I said. 'Everybody has chores.'

'Most of it still falls on your mother,' Max said. 'She's so tired and so restless she's ready to do a Gauguin and walk out on all of you.'

'But she won't—' The idea was preposterous.

'No. She won't. Your Uncle Sandy told me that your mother suffered as an adolescent because her own mother was beautiful and successful in the world of science—didn't she win a Nobel Prize?'

'Yes, for isolating farandolae within mitochondria.'

'Your mother felt insufficient because of your grandmother, and she didn't want the same thing to happen to you, to make you feel you had to compete. So she's held herself back, and it's beginning to tell. She *will* get to her own work, eventually, but eventually no doubt seems a long time away.'

I stared into the fire. Now that Max had pointed out that Mother was restless, I could see that it was true.

'Your mother is a truly mature human being, and they're rare. She's learned to live with herself as well as with your father, and believe me, your father's no easy person. He may be a genius, but single-minded scientists tend to let people down.'

'Daddy doesn't—'

She cut me off. 'Of course he does. We all do. You won't grow up until you learn that all human beings betray each other and that we are going to be let down even by those we most trust. Especially by those we most trust.'

I didn't like this, but it had the ring of truth. And I didn't like that, either.

'If we put human beings on pedestals, their clay feet are going to give way and they are going to come crashing down, and unless we get out of the way, they'll crush us.'

And I didn't get out of the way.

I hardly heard Max. 'Your mother has the guts to stick it out on this godforsaken island with amazing grace. Your father's work is important, and it demands isolation and considerable secrecy, but it's hard on the rest of you.' She continued to squat by the fire, poking at the smoldering logs. The fat wood caught and its bright flames soared. Satisfied, Max sat back. 'Your parents have one thing going for them. They love each other.'

My response was again a reflex. 'Of course.'

Max turned from the fire and smiled at me, her loveliest smile. 'There's no "of course" about it. Lots of married people barely tolerate each other. People stay together because of the children, or for financial convenience. Divorce is expensive. But your parents love each other. They're lovers, and that's probably incomprehensible to you, but it's a wonderful thing indeed.' The fire was blazing brightly now, and she got up and sat next to me on the sofa. 'It worries your mother that Kate goes to all the school dances and you don't.'

I shrugged. The wind beat the rain across the verandah and against the library windows. 'I don't like disappointing her.'

Max put her arm around my shoulders. 'You don't disappoint her. She just doesn't want you to have the same kind of difficult adolescence that she did. But she weathered it. You will, too.'

'I suppose.'

'Polly, love, having it easy is no blessing. To my mind, it hinders maturing.'

Zachary and I climbed down from the stadium to the sacred precincts and the theatre. I wanted to be able to walk in awe, here where so many extraordinary mysteries had gone on thousands of years ago. It was here that people came to consult the Delphic Oracle in times of emergency. How lonely the Oracle must have been, speaking only in riddles, with no one to understand her except the priests, who may or may not have translated correctly what she was saying.

The guides were herding their groups like goats—sheep at the Acropolis; why did I think of them as goats in Delphi?— and shooting facts at them in German, English, French. The noise cut across the clarity of the air. Noise pollution is as destructive as any other.

If I focused on one of the guides I could translate what he was saying. But the facts were delivered with the boredom of repetition.

"Apollo was worshipped here," Zachary said, "and Dionysus. Light and dark, reason and fecundity, waxing and waning like the moon."

We were standing on a green knoll. Across the valley were the great, dark mountains. The sky moved upward into a vanishing vastness of blue.

"I'm an Apollo worshipper," Zachary said. "Or would be if I lived in Greek times. Apollo, the god of reason."

"You strike me as being rather Dionysian," I said. The name Dennys comes from Dionysus, but my Uncle Dennys is both sober and reserved. Sandy says it's because Dennys spends his time with the unfathomable mysteries of the human brain.

Zachary bowed. "Thank you. I take that as a compliment. But I don't want you to think about philosophy. I want you to pay attention to me."

"Even you can't compete with all this."

He took my hand. "*Avanti!* Let's go."

It was a good day. Confusing, but good. Zachary made me feel I wasn't just a gawky, backward adolescent who didn't even need a bra till I was fourteen, but that I was mature, and attractive to him.

We went to the *son et lumière* show at the Acropolis, which somehow had less magic close up than it had had from the roof of the King George the night before. Then to the Plaka for a late supper, a small place Zachary had discovered that wasn't touristy. Good food and Greek music and lots of laughter in the air. I decided that I was meeting Sandy's challenge pretty well. *Very* well.

After the meal, we sipped small cups of the sweet Greek coffee and I was sorry the day was almost over.

"Polly, I haven't had this good a time in ages. You don't put any pressure on me. You take me as I am. Dare I ask you to spend tomorrow with me?"

Dare *he*? I hadn't dared dream that he would. "Dare ahead."

"We'll do something fun. Take a drive. Have a picnic. I'll pick you up at ten again, okay?"

"Fine." What would I have been doing if Zachary hadn't picked me up? Going on that bus tour and feeling sorry for myself?

Max had once said, 'We cannot afford the luxury of self-pity.' Self-pity is destructive, I do know that. But Zachary made it very easy for me not to need the luxury.

In the taxi he leaned toward me and brushed his lips against mine, then kissed me, gently. "That's not your first kiss," he said.

No, but it was different. I was different.

He kissed me again. "Polly, I don't know what you're telling me."

"Good night," I said firmly as the taxi drew up in front of the hotel. "And thanks, Zachary. It's been a good day, a really good day."

Back in the room, I undressed and bathed and then wrapped myself in towels and sat at the desk, getting my journal for school finished for the day. How would Miss Zeloski translate what I had written? I wrote about what I had seen, but not that I had been with anybody.

Then I took a postcard from the stationery folder and wrote the family. Wrote a separate card to Charles. And to Renny.

There was one postcard left. Should I write Max and Ursula?

I shut the folder.

Writing the journal for Miss Zeloski was as much fun as it was work. Even if I didn't tell her about being with Zachary in Delphi, I enjoyed writing about Apollo and Dionysus.

Max had shown me some sketchbooks she'd made in Greece. Line drawings not of the present but of the past—Semele and the swan; Jason being brought up by the centaur Chiron; Orpheus with his harp.

There were other notebooks I'd loved looking through, each one dealing with a special place and time. The Bushmen of southern Africa, a race of tiny people who had come, Max thought, originally from Egypt. The Schaghticoke Indians from the part of New England where my grandparents still live and where I was born. The nomads, or Numidians, of North Africa.

Max had not been familiar with Gaea, so I showed her some more pieces I'd written about the native Gaeans. I didn't go into anthropology, just wrote about the way they lived, accepting some things from the twentieth century, rejecting others. She liked my Gaean pieces, and so did I.

It was nevertheless a complete surprise the day she called and suggested I come over for supper, that she had something to show me.

'Let's go to the bedroom,' she said. 'I've a good fire going, and with the February northeaster blowing, it's the warmest room in the house. It can be colder on Benne Seed Island than in the Arctic.'

'Where's Urs?'

'Shopping on the mainland. Planning something special for supper.'

I paused on the landing, as usual, to look at the Laughing Christ. There was no way one could feel self-pity in front of that absolute joy. Even in laughter the face reflected a tolerance and forbearance that made me ashamed of my own tendency toward judgmentalness.

Max paused, too. 'I'm glad you like him.' We went on up the stairs. The long windows in Max's room that led out onto the verandah were closed, and though we could hear the wind sweeping around the house, the fire was comforting.

'What do you have to show me?' I asked.

She smiled at me, the firelight bringing out silver glints in her eyes, then moved slowly to her desk and got an envelope, which she handed to me. It was addressed to Polyhymnia O'Keefe, c/o Maximiliana S. Horne. It had come from a travel magazine, not an important one, but still a real magazine, and they had accepted one of my pieces on Gaea. I wouldn't get any money, but I'd get two complimentary copies of the magazine. I couldn't believe it.

Max laughed and took my hands and swung me around, and I saw an ice bucket on a stand near the fireplace. 'This calls for a celebration.' She put a napkin over the bottle and uncorked it gently. 'The idea that the champagne cork should pop up to the ceiling is insulting to good champagne.'

We lay on the rug in front of the fire, and after a while Ursula came in and joined us. She brought a bowl of shrimp which had been caught that afternoon, and some spicy sauce. It was lovely. One of the happiest times I'd ever known.

And I was happier at home, too. The fact that I hated school no longer seemed important. Max was my teacher, as Mother and Daddy had been my teachers on Gaea. And because I was learning, and felt happy about it, I was more patient with the little kids. I helped get them ready for bed without being prodded, read to them if Mother was working with the computer in the lab. I let Kate borrow my favorite necklace for one of the school dances. Xan and I didn't spat as much as usual.

And at least a couple of times a week I did my homework over at Beau Allaire. When I'd finished with the written stuff, Max would pull a book down from one of the library shelves and have me read aloud to her. 'You're going to have more than

one option when you come to choose a career. You have a lot
of acting ability.'

'I'm too ugly.'

'You aren't ugly at all. You have the kind of face that comes
alive when you're speaking. Why would I want to paint you if
you were ugly? I'll take you over Kate, any day.'

Max taught me to see the world around me with her painter's
eye. Now I noticed not only the loveliness of a new moon seen
through a fringe of Spanish moss, I saw also the delicacy of a
spider's web on the grass between two tree roots, saw the little
green lizard camouflaged under a leaf. And this seeing the
particular wonder of the ordinary was reflected in what I wrote
for school, but if Miss Zeloski noticed it, she didn't particularly
like it. And Miss Zeloski was the one who gave the grades, and
I had to get good grades.

'Why?' Max demanded. 'One does not live by grades alone.'

'I want to go to a good college, and I need to get a scholarship. After all, there are seven of us to educate. So grades
matter.'

Max put the back of her hand to her forehead in a swift
gesture of apology. 'Of course. Stupid of me. Like most people
who've never had to worry about money, I can be very dense.
So. How do we win Miss Zeloski? Get her to give you A's
instead of B's? What does Miss Zeloski *want*? That's the first
question you have to ask. You don't have to compromise in
order to please her. Find out what she's looking for, and then
give her that in the very best way you possibly can.'

'I don't want to give Miss Zeloski anything.'

'You really dislike her, don't you?'

'She grades unfairly.'

'You are very opinionated, Polly. Part of becoming a mature
woman is learning compassion.'

'I know I'm opinionated. I'm sorry.'

'Don't be sorry. Just think. You talk about being odd man
out. How do you think Miss Z. feels?'

It took me a while to answer. 'Lonely.'

'And maybe insecure. And that may help explain why obscure
poetry is comforting to her. I'll bet she loves footnotes and all

the vines of the groves of academe. The next time she gives you a free writing assignment, give her a well-documented essay. It'll be good discipline for you.'

It was. Max made me see the fun of cross-referencing, of finding out, for instance, what was happening in the world of science when Montaigne was writing his essays, and what the lineup of nations was, and who was painting, and what was the popular music of the day. And it worked. Miss Zeloski didn't seem such a bore to me, and her nasal Southern accent didn't grate so, and she gave me A's.

Max taught me to understand that Miss Zeloski was far lonelier than I was. She taught me to see that some of the kids who drank and slept around were lost and groping for something they couldn't find. But she didn't have much patience with those who hunted down animals and birds. 'Sadism isn't limited to the rich and corrupt. One doesn't tolerate it even when it comes from ignorance and stupidity.' Then, 'Come out on the porch. I brought in a Cape jessamine bud this morning. It's blooming in a small crystal bowl and the air is full of its scent and the promise that spring is just around the corner.'

Through Max's eyes I saw more than I'd ever seen before.

One beautiful early-spring evening, Max and Ursula came to dinner. Daddy and Urs went to the lab, as usual. When dinner was ready, Mother sent me to call them. As I came to the screen door, I heard my name and stopped.

'You mustn't let Polly bother Max,' Daddy was saying. 'Polly has Max confused with God, and she'll give her no peace if Max goes on encouraging her.'

Ursula laughed, her warm, sane laugh. 'I dare say God gets no peace, either, and I'm sure he continues to give encouragement.'

'Max has certainly brought out the best in Polly.'

I realized I'd done enough eavesdropping, and banged on the door to call them in to dinner.

At dinner Kate and Xan were talking about tryouts for the school spring play, open to everybody in the high school. It

was always a Shakespearean play, and this year was going to be
As You Like It.

Xan said, 'They chose that because there are so many female
parts. They never get enough guys.'

'Oh, come on, Xan,' Kate urged. 'If you try out, you'll get
any part you want.'

'It'll interfere with tennis.'

'No, it won't,' Kate said. 'They schedule rehearsals so it
doesn't interfere with anything.'

I knew she'd talk him into being in the play. And she'd
probably be Rosalind.

Max asked, 'What are you going to try out for, Polly?'

I used Xan's ploy, which hadn't worked for Xan. 'I'll be
practicing for swimming.'

'I told you,' Kate said, 'the rehearsals are during school
hours. You could have one of the boys' parts if you want, Pol.
They always have to use girls, too.'

I saw Max and Ursula look at Kate, then at each other.

Daddy said, 'I don't think Polly needs to limit herself to
male roles.'

'Oh, I didn't mean—' Kate said. 'It's just that she's tall and
they need tall girls to play men.'

I'd tried out for the play the year before, and had a walk-on.
Even so, it was the most fun I'd had from school the whole
year.

'Do you get a choice of whom you try out for?' Ursula asked.

Kate said, 'Well, you can ask.'

Xan said, 'I'll try out if Polly will.'

'Oh, sure,' I said. 'At least I can paint scenery.' I did not
mention that I had no intention of trying out for the backstage
crew; I was going to try out for Rosalind or Celia. Miss Zeloski
did the casting.

In March, Beau Allaire was brilliant with azaleas in great banks
around the house. Max's gardener got extra help, and the
grounds rivaled the great gardens in Charleston. The magnolia
trees were heavy with waxen white blossoms. The camellias
were exceptionally brilliant. All the long windows were open

to the verandahs and the ocean breeze and the singing of the mockingbirds.

On the day of the tryouts I got home from school to find a normal kind of chaos. The little kids had friends over and were shouting out on the swings and slide. The lab door was shut, with an old hotel DO NOT DISTURB sign on it, which meant Mother was doing something tricky with equations on the computer and needed to concentrate.

I called Max. 'I have news.'

'Good?'

'Terrific.'

'Come on over and tell me. Urs is in Charleston and I was going to call you anyhow. You beat me to it.'

I didn't want to disturb Mother about the Land-Rover, but Xan said go ahead, he'd tell Mother as soon as the lab door was open again. So I headed for Beau Allaire, singing at the top of my lungs.

Max was out on the steps, waiting for me. 'So what's this big news?'

'I'm going to play Celia in *As You Like It*.'

She flung her arms wide, then gave me a big hug. Then pulled back. 'Who's playing Rosalind?'

'One of the seniors.'

'What about Kate?'

'A shepherdess.'

Max laughed. 'I'm delighted about Celia, absolutely delighted. She has some splendid lines. With the right director, Celia can be almost as good a role as Rosalind.' She pulled me into the hall. 'Let's go up to my verandah. There's a lovely breeze.'

On the landing we paused to look at the statue of the Laughing Christ. 'He approves,' Max said. 'He thinks you're terrific.'

When we got out on the verandah I sat at the glass-topped table to get my homework out of the way. Max curled up on the cushioned wicker couch and read till I'd finished. When she saw me putting my books away, she said, 'Your parents have done a good job with you, Polly. And they've taught you something contrary to today's mores, that instant gratification is a snake in the grass.'

'What do you mean?' I zipped up my book bag.

'When you eat a meal, what do you eat first? What do you eat last?'

'I eat what I like least first, and save what I like best till last. Why?'

'Because people who eat the best first, and then likely can't finish the meal, are apt to be the same way with the rest of their lives. Fun first, work later, and the work seldom gets done.'

I giggled.

'What's funny?'

'A couple of years ago when we spent Christmas in New England with the grandparents, I was asked out to dinner with some friends who had a daughter my age, and they had turnips. Ugh. So I ate mine up, fast, so I could get rid of them and get to the rest of the dinner. And the mother saw me, and beamed at me, and said how wonderful it was that I liked her turnips so much, and before I could say anything, she gave me another great big helping. I was almost sick.'

Max laughed. 'Don't let it stop you from saving the best. When you came in today you sat right down and did your homework, not putting it off till later.'

'Well, as you said. If I put it off, I won't get it done.'

'What about your classmates?'

I pondered briefly. 'Some do the work. Some don't.'

'How do *they* expect to live?'

'I don't think they think much about it. I think about it, but I haven't got anywhere.'

'You'll do all right, whatever you choose. Wait.' She disappeared into the bedroom and came back with a book.

'Listen to those mockingbirds,' she said. 'They sound right out of the Forest of Arden.' She riffled through the pages. 'Here. This is practically my favorite line in all of Shakespeare, and it's Celia's: *O wonderful, wonderful, and most wonderful! and yet again wonderful! and after that, out of all whooping!*'

'It's going to be fun,' I said. 'Rosalind has a line I love: *Do you not know I am a woman? when I think, I must speak.*'

'A bit chauvinist,' Max said.

'Maybe men ought to speak more than they do?' I suggested.

'Stay here,' Max said again, and disappeared once more, but

instead of coming back with a book, as I'd expected, she came with a bottle of champagne. 'Nettie and Ovid have left some salad for us in the icebox,' she said.

We never got to it. We kept reading bits and pieces from *As You Like It*, and then some other plays, sad ones, funny ones. I'd never before realized just how alive Shakespeare is, how very present.

When I got home I parked in the shed at the end of the lab wing. I felt tingly, and as though the ground was about a foot lower than it ought to be. I walked to the dunes and stood looking down at the water. Then I turned back to the house and heard the phone ring. It wouldn't be for me, so I didn't pay any attention. When I reached the lab, Daddy was standing in the doorway.

'Come on in the lab for a minute, Polly.'

I went in and sat on one of the high stools.

'I just answered the phone, and it was Max, very apologetic because she was afraid she'd given you too much champagne and shouldn't have let you drive home.'

I could feel that my cheeks were flushed. 'You always let us have a little wine when you have it.'

'There is such a thing as moderation. I'm grateful to Max for calling me, but surprised she let you drink so much.'

'We didn't have that much.' How much had we had? I had no idea. Max kept filling my glass before it was empty, and I certainly wasn't counting.

Daddy sat on the stool next to mine. On the high counter was a pad full of mathematical scribblings: Mother's writing. Daddy moved the pad away. 'Max was concerned enough to call to see that you were safely home.'

I felt deflated. And defensive.

'You're a minor, Polly, and you're not accustomed to drinking, and it's very easy to have too much without realizing it.'

'Please don't make a case out of it, Daddy. Max isn't in the habit of giving me too much to drink. We were celebrating.'

'Celebrating what?'

'I'm going to play Celia in *As You Like It*. It's a really good role.'

'That's wonderful news, honey. Just don't overcelebrate next time. Have you told Mother?'

'I haven't had a chance to tell Mother.'

'She's reading to the little ones. Why don't you go tell them? And send Xan out to me if you see him. He hasn't cleaned the lizard tanks.'

I cleaned my share of the tanks in the morning before school so I wouldn't have it hanging over me. Xan probably does a better job than I do, but he leaves it till last thing. He does it—I don't think he's forgotten more than once—but he puts it off.

'Okay. Daddy—'

'What, my dear?'

'I'm not drunk, really. It's as much excitement about getting a part in the play as anything. Xan's playing Jaques, by the way, but he couldn't care less.'

'And Kate?'

'She's one of the shepherdesses.'

'Is she disappointed?'

'Yes. But I didn't have even a walk-on when I was Kate's age.'

Daddy put his arm around me. 'We hoped that Kate would be a friend for you, a girl you could have fun with.'

'Kate's okay.'

He pulled me closer. 'Polly, you don't have to compete with Kate in any way. Not in looks, not in talent, not in school. I wouldn't have you be any different. You don't need to prove anything, to anybody. I truly don't have favorites among my children, but you are my first child, and very special. I love you.'

I returned his hug. 'You're special, too.' And I wished that there were more times when Daddy and I could have time alone.

Daddy and Ursula went to Charleston together the next week, and I think they talked about all that champagne, because there wasn't any more after that. At least when Ursula was there. And, as a matter of fact, the next time Max brought out champagne was the day after the production of *As You Like It*. The performance was in mid-April so as not to interfere with all the academic stuff that accumulates in the last semester.

As You Like It was a big success, and I even got my own curtain call, and everybody said what a pity it was to put in all that work for one performance. But it was worth it, at least for me.

Max called me over to celebrate. Ursula had been to see me play Celia but had flown to New York in the morning for some kind of big consultation. Max brought out a bottle of champagne, but we had only one glass each, and with it a lot of fried chicken which Nettie had fixed for us, and a big casserole of okra, onions, and tomatoes. I don't like okra, I think you have to be born to it, and I told Max I was eating it first to get it out of the way.

That weekend there was a school dance, and I went with the guy who played Orlando. Rosalind was going steady with another senior. We were to meet at the school, so I drove Xan and Kate. Xan was going stag, and he said he didn't trust Kate's date to bring her home.

If Daddy wanted me to have a warning about booze, I got it. The girl who played Phebe got sick all over herself.

'Go help her clean up,' Xan said disgustedly. 'The kids she came with are all stoned, and so's Kate's so-called escort.'

Kate came and helped me.

Not that Cowpertown High is full of alcoholics and junkies. Just a few, like any other high school. But even a few is too many.

After we got Phebe moderately tidy, Xan and Kate wanted to go home. I was actually having a good time with some of the kids from the play, who seemed aware of my existence for the first time. The boy who played Oliver was dancing with me when Xan came over, followed by Kate, who was followed by half a dozen boys. I didn't want to leave, but I was the one with the driver's license. And maybe it was better to leave while I was doing well and wasn't what the Cowpertowners still call a wallflower.

We talked about the dance the next night at dinner, and I suppose it was a good and maybe unusual thing that we *could* talk with our parents.

'Pot is an ambition damper,' Xan said in his most dogmatic voice.

'You're right,' Daddy agreed. 'But on what do you base your conclusions?'

'The kids who use pot regularly aren't doing much, and they don't seem to care.'

Den put in, 'I'm pitching in the next game between Mullet-ville and Cowpertown. Y'all coming?'

Kate picked up on Xan's last remark. 'They didn't learn their lines for *As You Like It*, and they simply dropped some of the light cues. The shepherdesses were practically in the dark.'

'Hey, you should see me do the double flip.' Johnny tried to get our attention.

Xan cut across his words. 'It hasn't helped the tennis team.'

'Any addiction's a bad thing,' Daddy agreed.

Peggy said loudly, 'We're going to have an addic sale at school.'

'Xan's addicted to tennis,' Den said.

'When do you think I'll be old enough to wear a bra?' Peggy shouted loudly enough so that she was finally heard.

'A long time, if you're anything like Polly,' Xan said, and went on, 'I don't want to be addicted to anything. I don't want some chemical to be in control of my body. Or mind.'

'A lot of kids are smoking,' Kate added. 'Not just pot. Cigarettes.'

'Yukh.' Den made a face. 'With all the pollution we have no choice about breathing, why add to it?'

'Smoking's gross,' Peggy said.

'More rice and gravy, please, *please*.' Rosy jogged Mother's arm.

'We can't do anything about acid rain,' Xan continued as though there had been no interruptions or interpolations, 'or red tides, but we don't have to put gunk into our lungs on purpose.'

Den grinned at me. 'Or does he mean on porpoise?'

At least Xan and Kate hadn't called me Puritan Pol.

Later, while we were brushing our teeth, Kate asked me, 'Have you ever tried pot?'

I shook my head. 'Minority me.'

'I don't like it. Don't worry, I haven't smoked here, it was last year in Boston. I hated it. You know what, I think it's more square to try pot than not to. I hope your parents don't think Cowpertown is unique. It's no worse than any place else.'

'I know,' I agreed.

'And at least we have swimming and crew almost all year round. And Shakespeare. You were really good, Pol.'

That was nice of Kate, and I thanked her. Playing Celia had done me no harm at school.

I was in my Celia costume, but I was not in the Forest of Arden the kids had made with branches of trees hung with Spanish moss. I doubt if there was Spanish moss in the real Forest of Arden, but it was a pretty set.

Renny was dressed in the forest-green costume Orlando had worn. I was dreaming. In Athens, I was dreaming of Renny, who led me under a tree which became enormous, looming up through the roof of the stage at the end of the school gym.

Why Renny, in Athens, two nights in a row?

Why not Renny?

I saw him maybe every other week. Sometimes we went to the movies, if anything decent was showing in Cowpertown. Usually we sat in our booth at Petros' and talked. The place smelled of cheese and tomatoes and a whiff of fish from the other restaurant on the dock. Renny went on and on about his pet South American diseases. He talked to me about medicine as though I could understand everything he said. He thought I was terrific as Celia, and he'd had to get someone to cover for him in order to come see the show. I liked the way he never put me down. I liked the way he kissed me, giving, rather than taking.

Sometimes he talked about his girl, Jacinta, in Chile. They'd really had a big thing going. Someone would have to do a lot of measuring up to get Renny's attention. Sometimes when he kissed me I understood that steady, sturdy Renny could unleash a lot of passion at the right moment, and with the right person. I was safe, because I was too young.

I wasn't too young with Max, and that's one reason I loved being with her. Chronology didn't enter into it. Max was as young as I was, and I was as old as Max. And when Ursula was there, I was treated as an equal.

I had emerged from my dream of Renny into that half-waking, half-sleeping state where thoughts are not really directed but shift around like the patterns in a kaleidoscope. I slid deeper into sleep, thinking to myself about the glory that was Greece and the grandeur that was Rome.

I woke to the glory that was Greece, about five minutes before breakfast was brought and set out on the balcony. It was another blue-and-gold day. I had a date with a young man who would set my cousin Kate reeling. I felt moderately reeling myself.

Zachary and I started off by going to the museum, because he said it was mandatory. There was far more than I could absorb in an hour, though it wasn't quite as overwhelming as the Prado in Madrid. Nevertheless, it was a city museum, and it would take days to see everything. There were some marvelous, very thin gold masks, ancient, thousands and thousands of years old, and yet they reminded me of faces in Modigliani paintings. We saw the statue of the Diadumenus. He seemed to be tiptoeing with life, even though parts of the statue were missing.

Zachary kept checking his watch, and after exactly one hour he said, "Okay, that's enough culture. Let's go."

"Where?"

The VW Bug was waiting for us, and as he opened the door for me, he said, "A funny old place called Osias Lukas."

"What's that?"

"It's an old monastery tucked into a cup in the hills, and there are good picnic places nearby."

"Osias Lukas—Blessed Luke?"

"Yes. His chapel was built in the tenth century, I think, and there are some nice icons. And the mosaics have been well restored. It's a small enough place so you can see it all and not get saturated. Osias Lukas was a monk who, allegedly, was a healer."

Why do I dislike so intensely the skepticism, the self-protectiveness, of *allegedly*? It's part of the legal jargon Zachary was inheriting, but it still strikes me as a cowardly word.

Max's attitude about theology makes more sense to me than Zachary's dogmatic atheism. Max was always willing to take a metaphysical chance, Sandy said once; she was an eager observer, tolerant of human foible, open to the unexplainable, but nobody's fool.

We stopped at the entrance of Osias Lukas to buy postcards for me to send home. There was a comfortable feeling to the cluster of buildings nestled against the hills, protected from weather and the anger of the gods. I wondered if people had truly been healed by Osias Lukas. Ursula, who didn't talk about religion, agreed with Daddy and Dennys that not only attitude but faith had done almost unbelievable things in the way of healing. They were scientists, properly skeptical, but open.

I wondered if Osia Theola in Cyprus was going to be anything like this protected place. Osia Theola, Max had told me, was reported to have been given the divine gift of truth after she had seen her vision. People still came to her church to pray, to seek the truth.

'Superstitious, perhaps,' Max said, 'but if one should go to the cave of Osia Theola to seek the truth, one would need to be extremely brave.'

"Daydreaming?" Zachary asked me. We were standing in the chapel and I was looking at the fresco over the altar without seeing it.

"I was just thinking Theola and Lukas might have liked each other."

"They were nearly a thousand years apart," Zachary said.

I thought I'd better not say that people like Lukas and Theola probably weren't bound by chronology.

Suddenly we were surrounded by a group of Japanese tourists, and Zachary said, "Come on, let's get out of here. The Hilton has packed us a super picnic, and I know a good spot."

We sat on a hillside overlooking water and sky. Zachary made me feel amazingly happy about myself.

Then he spoiled it by pulling me to him and kissing me, much more of a kiss than I wanted. I pulled away.

"Why not?" he asked.

"We don't even know each other."

"So?"

"Getting to know people takes time."

"But we make music together. You like me, don't you?"

"Very much."

"And you told me you aren't a virgin."

I pulled further away. "I didn't say that."

"Your silence did. Or am I wrong? Are you a virgin?"

Silence was admission, but I could not speak. My throat was dry, my tongue tied.

He put one hand on my cheek and turned my face toward him. "Did it hurt you very much? Was the guy a bastard?"

I moved my head negatively against the pressure of his hand.

"Sweet Polly. Someone has hurt you, and you're putting a hard shell of protection about your wound. But unless you break the shell, the hurt can't be healed. And I'm speaking from very painful experience."

I nodded. Blinked. I would not cry. Would not.

"I won't do anything you don't want me to do," Zachary said. "You're beautiful, Polly."

Max had made me see that inner beauty was better than outer beauty, that it could, indeed, create outer beauty.

'You shone as Celia,' she said, 'in that depressing gym, on a dreadful stage, with appalling lighting. You had a radiance nobody else in the cast even approached.'

We were in her studio, which was a separate building to the north of the house, with the entire north wall made of glass. I was sitting for the portrait in the seashell. 'You have elegant bones. Tilt your head just slightly to your right. Beautiful slender wrists and ankles, like princesses in fairy tales. Bet Cousin Kate envies them.'

I didn't think Kate envied anything about me.

'Don't move,' Max said. 'What splendid eyes you have, like

bits of fallen sky, and wide apart, always suggesting that you see things invisible to lesser mortals.'

Ursula, coming in with iced tea, heard her. 'Don't turn the child's head.'

Max paused, paintbrush in hand, a dab of paint on her nose. 'It can do with a little turning. She still underestimates herself.'

Ursula put the tea down and came to stand behind Max, looking over her shoulder at the painting, nodding approval.

Max said, 'Enough for today, or I'll start overpainting.'

Playing Celia and having my portrait painted were definitely doing something for my ego.

It was a beautiful painting when she finished. Even if I didn't recognize the Polly Max saw in the seashell, I knew that the painting was beautiful. Max brought it to my parents.

'It's a superb painting,' Daddy said, 'but we can't possibly accept something that valuable. It's much too great a gift.'

Max smiled calmly at his protestation. 'It's little enough. You O'Keefes have made a winter which could well have been the winter of my discontent into a stimulating and pleasant one.'

Daddy looked at her, a brief, diagnostic glance. 'It's a beautiful picture, Maxa. We're more than grateful. Where shall we hang it?'

Well, it ended up in the living room, on the wall over the piano. We keep a light on by the piano because of the beach humidity, to keep it dry enough to stay in tune, so the portrait was well lit, and it dominated the room. The little kids said, 'Polly's eyes keep following us wherever we go.'

Xan and Den made rude remarks, which I did not take personally. Kate said, 'I don't know why nobody's ever painted a portrait of me.' She said it several times, once in front of Max, but Max simply smiled and said nothing.

About a week after the portrait was hung, we had the first really hot weather of the season, so that as soon as we came home from school we put on shorts and sandals. At dinner the little kids were wriggly, and the moment they'd finished eating, Mother said they could go out and play and she'd call them in for dessert.

As soon as they had gone outdoors, Xan asked, as though he had been waiting, 'Do you think it's good for Polly to spend so much time with those dykes?'

What?

Daddy paused with his fork halfway to his mouth, looking at Xan. 'Who're you talking about?'

Xan looked at Kate, and Kate looked at Xan.

Kate said, 'Well, some of the girls were talking to me at recess, and I didn't like what they said about Polly.'

'Kate, what are you talking about?' Daddy demanded.

Again Kate and Xan looked at each other. Xan said, as though sorry he'd started whatever it was he was starting, 'Some of the guys said Polly looked really pretty as Celia, with makeup on.'

'I don't wear makeup,' I said.

'Well, that's part of it,' Kate said. Kate didn't wear much makeup, but she wore some. I had no idea what she and Xan were looking at each other for. I asked, 'Why do you two keep looking at each other as though you had some secret?'

'It's no secret,' Xan said.

'What, then?'

Xan looked down at his plate. 'You do spend a lot of time over at Beau Allaire.'

'Why not?' I demanded. 'I'm welcome there. I'm happy there.'

Again Xan and Kate exchanged glances. 'Of course we know Polly isn't,' Kate said.

'Isn't what?' I demanded. 'I don't know what you're getting at.'

'Don't you?' Xan asked.

Daddy said, 'Xan, is this something you really want to talk about?'

Xan flushed a little. 'I'm sorry, but if Polly doesn't know people are talking, I think she ought to know.'

'Who's talking? About what?' And suddenly I didn't want to know.

'Some of the girls from Mulletville,' Kate said.

Xan went on, 'Mulletville's right near Beau Allaire and you're always there with Max and Ursula and everybody knows they're—'

'Shut up!'

Mother tried to calm things down. Xan and Kate, I'm surprised at you. What "everybody knows" is usually gossip, vicious gossip.'

'I know it's vicious,' Kate said. 'I hate it.'

'I don't like hearing glop about my sister,' Xan said.

'You punched that guy,' Kate said.

Den got into the fray. 'All you and your friends think about is sex and who has it with who, and who does what. It's sick.'

Daddy banged a knife against the table. 'This conversation has already gone too far. Xan, you know what we think about gossip, either listening to it or spreading it.'

'But, Dad, I thought you ought to know. Polly—'

'Stop him,' I said. 'How can you let him say vile things about our friends? They're your friends, too, aren't they?'

Daddy replied quietly, 'They are indeed our friends. Ursula Heschel is one of the finest people and one of the most brilliant surgeons I've known. You've always been interested in the brain, Xan. And your father's a neurosurgeon, Kate, and Ursula's friend.'

'And Max is one of Sandy's closest friends,' I cried. 'Sandy introduced us to them.'

'Sandy makes mistakes, like everybody else,' Xan snapped.

Den pushed away from the table. 'May I be excused? This conversation is gross.'

'Yes, go, Den, by all means,' Daddy said. When Den had left, he turned back to Xan and Kate. 'Do you think your Uncle Sandy would introduce Polly, or any of us, you two included, to people he didn't trust and respect?'

Kate and Xan looked down at their plates.

'Do you think Mother and I would have them here so often if they weren't our friends?'

'I'm really sorry,' Kate said. Xan and I talked about it, a lot, and we thought you ought to know what people—'

I interrupted. 'It's a good thing the little kids are outside. I'm glad they aren't hearing this garbage. Den was right to leave.'

Mother absentmindedly passed the salad to Daddy, who tossed it. 'Sandy knew we had a lot in common with Max and Ursula. That's what makes friendship. Like interests. Your father and Ursula have nourished each other this winter.'

'And Max has nourished me,' I said. 'She's made me believe in myself.'

'Sure, she flatters you,' Xan said, 'paints your portrait, swells your head—'

Daddy cut him off. 'Xan, are you feeling well?'

'I have a sore throat. What's that got to do with it?'

'After we finish eating, I'm going to take your temperature. And I would remind you that a morbid interest in people's sexual activities is as perverse as anything else.'

'We're sorry,' Kate said.

Mother added, perhaps trying to bring this ugly conversation back to normal dinner-table talk, 'Possibly the high divorce rate has something to do with a tendency to equate marriage with sex alone, instead of adding companionship and laughter.'

'Ursula and Max aren't married.'

'Alexander!' Daddy was getting really angry.

When Xan gets hold of a subject, he can't let go. 'Lesbianism does exist. I should think you'd be worried about Polly.'

We all spoke simultaneously. I said, 'Leave me out of it.'

Mother said, 'Xan, I think you're feverish.'

Kate said, 'We're just trying to protect Polly.'

Daddy said, his voice so quiet we had to stop talking in order to hear, 'Don't you have any faith in Polly? Or our ability to understand and to care? Of course lesbianism exists, and has since the beginning of history, and we have not always been compassionate. I thought it was now agreed that consenting adults were not to be persecuted, particularly if they keep their private lives private. We human beings are all in the enterprise of life together, and the journey isn't easy for any of us. Xan, come with me. I want to take your temperature. Polly, you can bring in dessert and call the others.'

Xan had a fever of 102°. He was coming down with a strep throat. He went to bed with penicillin instead of dessert.

'That explains it,' Daddy said. 'I'd better keep a close watch on the rest of you. Polly, will you come out to the lab with me, please?'

I followed him. He gazed into one of the starfish tanks, jotted something down on a chart, then sat on one of the high stools. 'I don't want you to be upset by what Xan and Kate said.'

I perched on the other stool, hooking my feet around the rungs. 'I am upset.'

'In this world, when two people of the same sex live together, assumptions are made, valid or not.'

'I hate the Mulletville girls. They think they're better than anybody else, and they love to put people down. They didn't like it that I got Celia in the play, and they didn't like it that I was good. None of them got anything but walk-ons.'

'You think they're getting back at you for succeeding?' Daddy asked.

'Sure. I've been the bottom of the pecking order. They don't want me to move up.'

'Polly, I don't want this to affect your friendship with Max and Ursula.'

'Don't worry. It won't. It hardly affects my feeling for the Mulletville girls, either. It was already rock-bottom.'

Daddy hugged me and I burst into tears. 'It's your first encounter with this kind of nasty-mindedness, isn't it, Pol? Island living has kept all you kids more isolated than you should have been.'

'That's fine with me.' I reached for the box of tissues behind the Bunsen burner.

'No, Polly, you live in a world full of people of all kinds, and you're going to have to learn to get along with them.'

'I suppose.'

'And, Polly, I don't want you to worry about any gossip about you. You're a very normal sixteen-year-old.'

'Am I?'

'You are. You're brighter than a lot of your peers, you're physically a slow developer and intellectually a quick one.'

I said, 'I'm not a lesbian, Daddy, if you're worried that I'm worried about that.'

'Sure?'

'Sure.' I pressed my face against his firm, comfortable chest. 'But I wish we were back in Portugal.'

'We aren't. And even in Portugal, time would have passed; you'd still be in the difficult process of growing up.'

'I've got some history reading to finish,' I said. 'I'd better go do it.'

'All right, love. But don't let all of this get out of proportion. Put at least some of it down to strep throat.'

'Sure. Thanks, Daddy.'

Xan did not give me his strep throat, but he had planted an ugly seed, uglier than strep. Talking about Max and Ursula the way he had was a far cry from the remark Xan had made weeks ago, that it was a good thing Ursula was older than Daddy. That, at least, made a certain amount of sense.

But the seed was planted.

While we were little, Mother and Daddy were anything but permissive parents. The little ones don't get away with much. But once we get well into our teens—and that meant Xan and Charles and me, and Kate, while she was with us—they moved into a hands-off policy. If we hadn't learned from all they had tried to teach us when we were younger, it was too late.

And what we'd learned was as much from example as from anything they said. Our parents were responsible toward each other as well as toward us. What's more important, they loved each other. Max didn't need to tell me that. I knew it. It was solid rock under my feet. And love means that you don't dominate or manipulate or control.

Xan missed a few days of school. Den was the only one to catch anything from him, but Daddy was watching us all, and Den lost only a day. The rest of us were all right, as far as strep was concerned.

What Xan and Kate said shouldn't have made any difference. I should have thrown it away, forgotten it. Or I should have asked Daddy when we were out in the lab together if he believed what they'd said about Max and Ursula. But I didn't ask him. And what's said is said. Xan's and Kate's words were like pebbles thrown into the water, with ripples spreading out and out . . .

It kept niggling at the back of my mind.

I didn't want to think about sex. The male population of Cowpertown High was still in intellectual nursery school. Renny didn't want me to be anything but a kid sister to him. Who else was there?

Friday night I couldn't sleep. Finally I got up and went into the kitchen to make myself something warm to drink. We'd put away the winter blankets, and the night was cool. Mother was already there, in her nightgown, waiting for the kettle to boil.

'I'm making herb tea,' she said. 'Want some?'

'I'd love some,' I said, 'as long as it's not camomile.'

'I don't like camomile either, unless I have a very queasy stomach.'

'My stomach's queasy,' I said, 'but I still don't want camomile.'

'Why is your stomach queasy, honey?'

'What Xan said.'

'What, that Xan said? Xan says a lot.'

'Xan and Kate. About Max and Ursula.'

Mother got two cups from the kitchen dresser and fixed our tea. 'I hoped Daddy'd relieved your mind about that.'

'It keeps coming back.'

She handed me a steaming cup, and we sat at the kitchen table. The windows were partly open and the steady murmur of the ocean came in, and the wind moved through the palmettos, rattling them like paper.

Mother slid one of the windows closed. 'Xan and Kate are both fourteen. At that age, children tend to have a high interest in sexual activity, because they're just discovering themselves as sexual human beings. Their interests do widen after a while, as yours have.'

'When I was fourteen, I hardly knew lesbianism existed, and I wasn't particularly interested.'

'You and Xan are very different people. You and Kate, too. For one thing, if you'd heard upsetting gossip at school, you'd have come to your father or me privately. You wouldn't have brought it up as dinner-table conversation.'

'Xan thinks anything's okay for dinner-table conversation.'

'That's partly our fault. We encourage you to talk about what's on your minds. You've always been interested in an unusually wide variety of topics. What do you and Max talk about?'

'Philosophy. Anthropology. Lately she's been on a binge of reading the pre-Platonic philosophers. She says they were the precursors of the physicists who study quantum mechanics.'

'Shouldn't that tell you something?'

'Tell me what?'

'Where your interests lie. And Max's.'

I couldn't hold the question back any longer. 'Mother, do you think Max *is* a lesbian?'

Mother sighed and sipped at her tea. Outside, a bird sang a brief cadenza and was silent. 'The point I thought I was making is that what's important to you about Max is her interest in ideas. She's someone who appreciates and encourages the ideas you have. You might not have tried out for Celia if it weren't for Max.'

I couldn't leave it alone. Maybe I'm more like Xan than I realized. 'But if she *is* a lesbian, wouldn't that worry you and Daddy—I mean, that I'm over at Beau Allaire so often?'

Mother sighed again. She looked tired. Daddy had been off to Tallahassee with Ursula. Mother had stayed home with us kids. Daddy had been promising her a few nights in Charleston, to go to the Dock Street Theatre, to the Spoleto Festival, but there hadn't seemed to be time. Or money. Charleston may not be New York, but theatre tickets aren't cheap anywhere. The neurosurgeon Dennys had introduced Ursula to, who also knew Daddy, had offered his guesthouse, which put it in the realm of possibility. It just hadn't happened. Daddy traveled around, to medical meetings, and Mother stayed home.

'Polly,' she said, 'there are a great many areas in which Daddy and I simply have to trust you kids. We have to trust that how Charles lives his life while he's in Boston is consistent with the values we've tried to instill in all of you, just as Dennys and Lucy have to trust Kate while she's with us. When Kate and Xan—and you—go to a school dance, we have to trust you not to give in to peer pressure and experiment with alcohol or with drugs you know to be harmful and addictive. We've been grateful and perhaps a little relieved when Kate has called us to come get her, rather than drive home with someone who's been drinking, and I suspect Dennys and Lucy feel the responsibility for Charles as strongly as we do for Kate.'

'Kate's got good sense.'

'And so do you. And that's why we trust you; and we trust Max and Ursula not to do or say anything that would harm you. Has our trust been justified?'

'Yes.' I nodded agreement. This was how Mother and Daddy thought. This was how they behaved.

'If they were pulling you away from other people, then we'd think that was not a good influence. But you've been happier in school, haven't you?'

'Yes.'

'You've been asked to be in the chorus, haven't you?'

'Yes.' I did not tell her that the teacher who taught chorus went into ecstasies because she said I had 'the pure voice of a boy soprano.'

'You're getting more phone calls from your classmates. Things are generally easier for you.'

'Yes.' I'd hardly realized it consciously, but it was true. Except for those snobs from Mulletville.

Mother continued. 'Trusting people is risky, Polly, we are aware of that. Trust gets broken. But when I think of Max and Ursula, I don't feel particularly curious about their sex lives, one way or another. They're opening a world of ideas for you, ideas you're not likely to bump into at Cowpertown High. I'm sorrier than I can say that there's been ugly gossip from the Mulletville girls and that the gossip has touched you. You're young to bump into this kind of gratuitous viciousness, but it hits us all sooner or later. I've had to sit out a good bit of gossip about your father and female colleagues.'

'But it wasn't true!'

'No, it wasn't true, Polly. That's the point I'm making. If you can, try to forget Xan and Kate's fourteen-year-old gossip.'

Now I sighed. 'I'll try. But I wish they'd kept their big mouths shut.'

'So do I, Polly, so do I.'

She had not told me whether or not she thought Max was a lesbian. But perhaps that was part of the point she was making.

April, turning into May, was Benne Seed's most gorgeous weather. We had a few summer-hot days, but mostly it was sunny and breezy and the air smelled of flowers and the sky was full of birdsong. Kate made a tape of a mockingbird to take home.

Daddy and Ursula drove down to Florida again, overnight. Daddy was to give a paper on new developments in his experiments with octopuses, with Ursula giving another paper about how it could be applied to neurosurgery on human beings. I found myself wishing that Xan was still concerned about Daddy and Ursula.

Max called when I got home from school, as she almost always did when Ursula was away. I drove over; Urs and Daddy had taken Ursula's car; a Land-Rover's not great for long distances. And suddenly, when I was about halfway to Beau Allaire, the fog rolled in from the ocean, and the outlines of the trees were blurred, and the birds stopped singing. There was a damp hush all over the island. Turning on the headlights just made visibility worse, and the fog lights didn't help much. I slowed down to a crawl, and was grateful to arrive safely at Beau Allaire. We went right up to Max's room, which is always the pleasantest place when the wind swings to the northeast. When the sun is out on the Island, it's warm, even in winter.

When the sun is hidden by fog, it feels cold, even if the thermometer reads 80°.

We were sipping tea when Mother called, to make sure I'd arrived safely and to say that the visibility at our end of the island was nil. She agreed without hesitation when Max suggested I spend the night and go to school in the morning on the bus with the kids from Mulletville.

That was the only part I didn't like. I looked into the fire so Max wouldn't see my face.

But she saw something. 'Your mother's confidence in me means more than I can say. But—'

'But what?' I asked, still looking away from her.

'For some reason you're not happy about going to school with the Mulletville contingent.'

'They're all snobs, and anyhow, I'm needed at home to handle the boat.'

'And you don't want the students from Mulletville to know you spent the night here.' Her voice was flat.

'If the fog lifts, I'll get up early. Anyhow, I have to get the car home—Mother didn't think of that.'

'What she was thinking of was your safety. When your father and Ursula get back, Urs can drop him off here and he can drive your Rover home.' I didn't say anything, but I turned to look at her, and her eyes were bleak, the color of ice, and the shadows under them seemed to darken. 'I hope this isn't going to compromise you any more than you've already been compromised.'

I stared back at the fire. 'I don't care.'

I could hear Max draw in her breath, let it out in a long sigh. 'It's taken a long time for gossip to reach you, hasn't it? I expected it to raise its ugly head long before this.'

'Gossip is gossip. Mother and Daddy take a dim view of it. The girls from Mulletville are the bitchiest group at school.'

Max sighed again, and I turned once more to look at her, lean and elegant, stretched out on her side, leaning on one elbow. 'I'd hoped this conversation wouldn't be necessary. Urs said it would be, sooner or later, since the world considers personal privacy a thing of the past. Have you noticed how, whenever there's a tragedy, the TV cameras rush to the bereaved to take pictures, totally immune to human suffering?'

'Well—our TV doesn't work—but I know what you mean.'

'And I'm avoiding what I need to say. You're pure of heart, Polyhymnia, but most of the world isn't. I wish Urs were here. She could talk about it more sanely than I, so that it wouldn't hurt you. We—Ursula and I—have been lovers for over thirty years.'

I stared down at the white fur of the rug. If Max wanted to avoid this conversation, so did I.

'When people think of homosexuals they usually think of—Ursula and I have had a long and faithful love.'

In my ears I heard Xan's words about two dykes. It didn't fit Max and Ursula. Neither did the words I heard at school, gays and faggots and queers.

'I love you, Polly, love you like my daughter. And you love me, too, in all your amazing innocence.'

There was a long pause. I hoped the conversation was over. But Max went on. 'Ursula'—she paused again—'Ursula is the way she is. She's competed in a man's world, in a man's field. There are not many women neurosurgeons. As for me—'

—I don't want to know, I thought. —Keep this kind of thing in the closet where it belongs. That's what doors are for. It doesn't have anything to do with me.

'We'd better go downstairs,' Max said. 'I asked Nettie and Ovid to set the table on the verandah.'

I followed her. Instead of going directly out to the verandah, she paused at the oval dining room, switching on an enormous Waterford chandelier which sparkled like drops of water from the ocean.

Mother and Daddy have eaten in the oval dining room at Beau Allaire. When I ate with Max and Ursula, it was supper, not dinner—sometimes if it was chilly, on trays in the library, or sometimes on the big marble-topped table in the kitchen. Ursula kneaded dough on that table, and the kitchen usually held the fragrance of baking bread.

'Nettie, really!' Max exclaimed, and I saw that two places had been set at the mahogany table, which, like the room, was oval.

As though she had been called, Nettie came in through the swing door which led to the breezeway and the kitchen. 'Verandah's too damp, Miss Maxa. Table's wet. Fog's thick.'

'Fine, Nettie,' Max said. 'You're quite right. We'll eat here.' She sat at the head of the table and pointed to the portrait over the long sideboard, a portrait of a man, middle-aged or more, stern and dignified, with white hair and mustache, a nose which was a caricature of Max's, and a smile which made me uncomfortable.

Ovid came in and lit the candles on the table and in the sconces on the wall.

'My papa.' Max nodded at the portrait and her smile matched the smile on her father's face. I felt cold, chillier than the dampness the fog brought in.

'Looks like him,' Max said. 'Spitting image, as they say. It's not a bad piece of work. One has to admire the artist's perception which transcends the stiffness of his technique. What do you think?'

I couldn't very well say, 'His smile gives me the creeps.' I said, 'He looks rather formidable.'

'Formidable? Oh, he was.'

Nettie and Ovid came in with silver dishes, cold sliced chicken, hot spoon bread, served us, and withdrew.

Max said, 'When my sister and I were little, we used to think God looked like Papa, and I suspect he fostered the idea. Papa liked being God. You don't make as much money as Papa did without a God complex. Beau Allaire belonged to Mama, and Papa got a job in the family bank. He was a big frog in a little pond, but he made the money not only to keep up Beau Allaire but to build a hospital. And he had no hesitation in shoving people aside if they got in his way. After all, isn't God supposed to do whatever he wants?'

That wasn't the way I thought of God. Or the way I thought Max thought of God.

She took her fork and spread spoon bread around on her

plate. 'I wonder if God ever feels guilt? The M. A. Horne Hospital is Papa's big guilt offering. Urs sees God as a benevolent physician. That's a better image than mine. The only way I can get rid of the false image of Papa as God is to think of the marvels of creation. The theory now is that everything in the universe, all of the galaxies, all of the quanta, everything comes from something as small as the nucleus of an atom. Think of that, of that tiny speck, invisible to the naked eye, opening up like a flower, to become clouds of hydrogen dust, and then stars, and solar systems. That softly opening flower—I visualize a lotus—is a more viable image of God for me than anything else. I keep the portrait of Papa to remind me that God is *not* like him.'

I liked the image of the gently opening lotus. I didn't like the man in the portrait.

Ovid came in with a bottle of wine in a napkin and poured a glass for Max. 'This will help your appetite, Miss Maxa. You need Nettie's good spoon bread.' Then he put a very small amount in my glass and filled it up with water. My talk with Daddy was still clear in my mind. That was plenty for me.

'M.A. and I were only eleven months apart, and were more like twins than just sisters. Not that we didn't think for ourselves, but there wasn't anything we couldn't tell each other. She was the younger, and when we were four or five years old our mother died—she had a weak heart—and that made us closer than ever. Mama's portrait is the middle of the three across from you.'

I looked at the three gold-framed portraits. The middle, and largest, was of a fragile-looking woman, almost beautiful, but too washed-out to make it. She was not vivid like Max, or translucent, like M.A. in the portrait in the library. 'She looks pretty. But tired.'

Max laughed, not a happy laugh. 'Papa was a tiring man. Our maternal grandfather, our Allaire grandfather, must have been equally tiring. Poor Mama. Her name was Submit, and her two sisters, in the portraits on either side of her, were Patience and Hope. Which gives you an idea of the frame of mind of our Allaire grandmother. Mama's calling us Minerva

Allaire and Maximiliana Sebastiane may have been her way of getting even. She died before we had much chance to know her, but she was affectionate and gentle.'

Ovid came to take away our plates, checking that Max had eaten most of her meal. Nettie followed him with salad, delicate greens from the Beau Allaire greenhouse.

'Keeping this enormous house with inadequate help killed Mama. I have one wing completely closed off, but while Papa was alive, all the rooms had to be ready at a moment's notice. Papa did not make his business deals on the golf course, he made them here in the oval dining room, over port.' She paused. 'The portrait's uncannily like him. I don't think the artist realized how accurate he was.'

We sat in silence for a while. Then she said, 'I'm not really a portraitist, but every once in a while there's someone I know I must paint—like you. Ursula's never allowed me to paint her, but she can't stop me from making sketches.'

Nettie came in, bearing *crème brûlée*, which she put in front of Max, beaming. When she went back to the kitchen, Max laughed, a nice laugh this time. 'Nettie feels she must compete with Urs. Bless Urs. She has to make godlike decisions all the time, but she has more genuine humility than anyone I've known. She picks up her scalpel and she holds life and death in her hands. No wonder she comes home from the hospital and bakes bread and creates casseroles and listens to Pachelbel and Vivaldi.' She served me a luscious dish of *crème brûlée*. 'Bless Nettie, too. I'm far better served than I deserve.'

When we had finished dessert, Max suggested we go upstairs again. The fire had died down, and she rebuilt it, then sat on the rug, head on her knees, watching the fat pine take flame. 'As soon as we were old enough, M.A. and I became Papa's hostesses. After Mama died, he got a good housekeeper, but M.A. and I sat with him in the dining room every night, were with him when he entertained business guests. I think it was expected that eventually we would marry from the guest list. Money tends to marry money. And when Papa snapped his fingers, we did whatever he wanted us to do. He wasn't beyond hitting us if we didn't obey promptly. M.A. was deathly afraid of him. I suppose I was, too, but I pretended I wasn't. I talked back to him, and he liked that. One didn't show fear in front of Papa.'

Something in Max willed me to turn from the fire and look into her eyes, grey, like the fog, the silver glints dimmed. She spoke in a low, chill voice. 'Papa was a lecherous old roué. It killed my mother. But she submitted, poor darling, until her heart gave out, living with a man completely unprincipled. He killed M.A., too. He hated women, I think, but he wanted them. All of them. One night when I was away, he . . . She got away from him and ran out into the rain, and died of pneumonia. And anguish. I will never forgive him.'

I shuddered. The fog seemed to be creeping into the room. It did not seem like May.

'Sorry, Polly, darling Polly. Hate is a totally destructive emotion, I know that. But I hate him. I hope you will never have cause to hate anyone as I hate Papa. I would like to forgive him, but I don't know how.'

I stole another look at her. Her eyes burned, and I thought she had fever.

'It's extraordinary how I can hate Papa—and at the same time acknowledge that in my youth I wasn't unlike him, completely indiscriminate in my affairs after my marriage broke up. What I did had little connection with love. And then I met Ursula. Blessed Ursula, who loved me and healed me. We have been good for each other. Nourishing. As your parents nourish each other.'

Max comparing herself and Ursula to my parents? Was that possible?

'Sandy trusted me enough to bring you over to me. I value that trust. I want never to hurt you. And I already have, haven't I? Or vicious gossip has. People are assuming that because you are very dear to me, you are like me. The world being the way it is, they'd assume it even if I was straight as a pin.'

'Never mind,' I said clumsily. 'They're stupid.' I thought of the girls from Mulletville who thought they were better than anybody else. To put themselves up, they had to put other people down.

Max said, 'I love you as I would have loved the daughter I couldn't have. You don't need a mother, you have a fine one. But every adolescent needs someone to talk to, someone to whom she is not biologically bound, and I serve that purpose. We are alike in our interests, you and I, but not in our ways of expressing our sexuality.' She looked straight into my eyes. 'Don't be confused about yourself. You're not a lesbian. I know.'

I suppose, looking back on it, that it was brave, maybe even noble, of Max to tell me all this.

She took a long brass wand and blew into the fire. The flames soared. She put the wand back, speaking as though to herself. 'Bad hearts run in the Allaire family. Mama. M.A. My little—' She broke off. 'I have a heart as strong as an ox. What irony.'

I didn't understand the irony.

A sudden crash of thunder cut across my thoughts. Almost daily thunderstorms are part of summer on Benne Seed Island. Five minutes of lightning and thunder and rain and the air would be cleared. This sudden storm would dissipate the fog.

'Your father and Urs are friends, Polly. I don't know whether or not they've talked about this, because it isn't within the context of their interests, but I suspect your father knows.'

I suspected that both my parents knew. That they knew before Xan and Kate brought it up at dinner.

Max said, 'I asked Ovid to light the fire in the green guest room to cut the damp. We'll just wait till this storm is over.' She took a soft wool blanket from the chaise longue and tucked it around me. I was overwhelmed by great waves of sleep, a reaction of shock from what Max had told me.

'Little one,' she said softly. 'Let it go. You don't have to bear it with me. It's over. You have a terrifying ability to enter into the experience of others, that's why you're such a good little actress. You feel things too deeply to bear them unless you can get them out of yourself through some form of art.'

I closed my eyes and her words drifted away with the smoke.

When I woke up, it seemed that a light was shining in my eyes. The fog had cleared, and the moonlight was coming through the windows. By its ancient light Max was looking at me, her eyes as bright and savage as a gull's.

But her voice was gentle. 'Time for bed.'

I staggered to my feet and followed her to the green guest room. The fire had died down to a glow, but it had taken the damp away, and the breeze coming in from the window was summery. I slipped into bed, and Max tucked the covers about me. I drifted back into sleep.

In the morning I got up early, drank a glass of milk, drove the length of the Island to our house, and took the boat across the water to Cowpertown and the school bus.

Stubbly grass was prickling against my cheek, and a hand moved gently across my hair. I opened my eyes and looked up at Zachary.

"Have a nice nap?"

I sat up and pushed my fingers through my hair. "I guess I'm not quite over jet lag yet. Sandy says it takes a day for each hour."

"Sandy? Who's Sandy?" he asked suspiciously.

"My uncle. He and Aunt Rhea are coming into Athens tomorrow, late afternoon, I think."

"Are you going to ditch me for them?"

"We do have plans . . ."

"Will you at least spend the day with me, Sleeping Beauty?"

I probably looked a mess, with grass marks on my cheek and my hair sticking out in all directions, and here he was asking me to spend another day with him. "I'd love to spend the day with you."

"You cried out in your sleep," Zachary said. "Listen, about whoever it was who hurt you, remember I've been hurt, too. It's not a nice feeling. It takes the already shaky ego and shrivels it, like putting a match to a plastic bag. I'm not pushing you, Polly, but it really might help if you talked about it."

I shook my head. "Thanks, Zach, I don't want to talk about it till I have it all sorted out."

"Sometimes talking helps sort things out."

"I'm not ready. You talk if you want to. I'm sorry you got hurt. I do care."

"You do, don't you? Thanks, Pol, but I'm a selfish bastard and I deserved anything I got. I lived by sophomoric mores, Number One all the way. In my world, love affairs were taken with incredible seriousness, which ought to mean at least an expectation of permanence."

"Doesn't it?"

"Ha. Totally serious can mean a few days, and then along comes someone over the horizon who has more money or more prestige, and whoops, musical chairs, change partners. You know how, at cocktail parties, the person you're talking to is looking over your shoulder, in case there's somebody more important to talk to?"

I didn't. I'd never been to a cocktail party.

"In my world they're looking over your shoulder while they're making love, and it's musical chairs again." He sounded bitter.

"Are you talking from experience?" I asked.

"Pretty Pol, in experience I am old enough to be your grand-father." He put his head down on my lap, and I ran my fingers through his silky black hair. Another first for me. I was amazed at how natural it seemed.

"You're lucky, Red," he said. "My parents don't know any-thing about trust. They never trusted each other, and they never trusted me. And I've never trusted them. And your parents trust you, enough to let you come to Greece all alone, not because they want to get rid of you, but because they trust you. I mean, that's pretty incredible."

Even though my parents didn't know I was in Greece all alone, their trust in me, and in the rest of us, was indeed pretty incredible. And that trust had been betrayed, and I hoped they'd never have to know the extent to which it had been betrayed. Part of growing up, I was discovering, was learning that you did not have to tell your parents everything.

Did Mother and Daddy carry trusting us to an extreme?

What choice did they have? The three little ones were the only ones young enough to be monitored twenty-four hours a day. Den was in junior high, the rest of us in high school. We did have curfews, and if there was a valid reason we couldn't make them, they trusted us to phone. When Xan and Kate were late, twice, without calling, they were given a 10 p.m. curfew for the month, which meant no going to Cowpertown after school hours. From their point of view, that was only an inch away from capital punishment. They complained the entire time, but they kept the curfew.

If I'm a slow developer, Kate's a rapid one. I knew that she'd gone a lot further with boys than I had, not that I'd had much chance, and that this concerned Mother and Daddy. And sometimes Xan seems older, as well as taller, than I. But how much did Mother and Daddy know about string bean Xan? He was already six three, and good-looking, and a little arrogant, and he brought home straight A's and was star of the basketball team and president of his class. But did they know him?

And how much did they really know about me? When I went out with Renny, Mother and Daddy knew what our plans were, whether we were going to drive, whether Renny had borrowed a boat. They probably suspected that Renny kissed me good night. Did they trust us blindly?

How could Max ever trust anybody again, after what her father did? And yet she trusted.

And I knew that there wasn't any other way to live. You simply cannot go around sniffing suspiciously at everyone and everything, expecting the worst. At least, Mother and Daddy couldn't. And, by gene and precept, neither could I.

'People are trustworthy only by virtue of being trusted,' Daddy had once said.

Having your parents trust you is a pretty heavy burden.

On the other hand, I trusted my parents.

"What're you thinking?" Zachary asked.

"Oh, trusting people. Letting them down."

Zachary patted my thigh. "I can't imagine you letting anybody down."

I ran my fingers through his hair again. "You don't know me very well." The thought flashed across my mind that I had let Max down. I pushed it away.

Zachary yawned. "We'd better be getting back to town. I've made reservations on the roof of the Hilton. We'll have drinks outside first, and I've reserved a window table. The view is better than the food, though the food's not bad. Rather bland, to please unexperimental Americans. You can even get a hamburger." He eased out of my lap, stood up, held out his hand to me, then took one finger and touched my cheek. "So soft," he murmured. With the tip of his finger he circled my eyes, then leaned toward me and kissed me.

I pulled away, and started toward the car.

"What's the matter?" he asked. "You know our chemistry's explosive."

"Chemistry's not enough."

"Why not?" I didn't answer. "If you gave in once, why not now, when you know things are really fizzing between us?"

"I said," clenching my jaw, "chemistry's not enough." I picked up the picnic basket and put it in the car.

Zachary ran after me. "Hey, wait up. Was I being offensive?"

"You might call it that."

"Well, listen, Pol, hey, listen, I'm really sorry. Okay?"

"Okay." I still sounded pretty chilly.

"You're going to have dinner with me tonight? I'll be good. Promise. Okay? I've never met anyone like you, and I've learned, honest I have, it's a mistake for me to think you're going to react like anyone else. I don't want you to. I like you the way you are. So you will have dinner?"

"Sure. Dinner will be fine."

I'd never had anyone pleading to have dinner with me before. If I needed affirmation, Zachary was providing it.

The view from the roof garden of the Hilton was as spectacular as the view from Zachary's balcony. I ordered lemonade, and Zachary had a Metaxa sour.

Metaxa. Urs often called Max that.

"Have a sip?" Zachary asked.

I shook my head.

"Polly, I'll see you tomorrow?"

He was saying it, and I still didn't quite believe it, that he really wanted to be with me three days in a row. "I'd love to."

"And after tomorrow, what? Am I ever going to see you again?"

"Who knows? It's a small world."

"I'd like to be friends with you forever. I want to know there's something permanent in human relations."

I sipped my lemonade. "I'm not sure there is."

He signaled the waiter for two more drinks. "I'm the one who's the cynic, not you. What about your parents? They sound pretty permanent to me."

"As things go in this life, I guess they are."

"And that's what you're looking for?"

"Ultimately. But not for a long time. I have to get through college and figure out how to earn my living."

"And you're going to wear your chastity belt all that time?"

"I don't know," I said. "If I've learned nothing else, I've learned that you never know what's going to happen. But right now, tonight, in Athens, I'm wearing my chastity belt." I thought I'd better be firm about that, for myself as much as for Zachary.

The maître d'hotel summoned us then, and took us to our table. After we'd ordered, Zachary said, "I wish I knew who he was, this guy who hurt you so much. He's made you put your armor on so there isn't even a chink. Why are you rejecting me?"

"I'm not rejecting you. We've just met, and already we're friends. I could have been very lonely, and you've been wonderful."

He smiled at me across the table. "If you ever take off that chastity belt, Polly, it'll be for real."

He walked me back to the King George and kissed me gently just before I got in the elevator. I took another long, hot bath, to help me unwind. Got into bed and read. I realized that I missed the family, even Xan.

He had come into my room one night while I was reading

in bed, knocking first, which is a tradition. Our rooms are our own.

'Yah?' I didn't sound very welcoming.

He stuck his head in the door. 'I'm sorry about the other night.' He was so tall that he almost had to bend down to get in the door. His wrists and ankles showed past his pajama sleeves and legs, and he was skinny, because of having shot up so quickly.

'What other night?'

'You know. What Kate and I said about the Mulletville kids and stuff. About Max and Ursula and you. I'm really sorry.'

'Okay.' But it wasn't okay, and I didn't sound or feel gracious. Maybe eventually Max would have told me all that she'd told me, but it mightn't have hurt so much.

'I hate those Mulletville kids,' Xan said. 'It's not *fair*.'

He sounded so vehement that he reminded me of my little sister Peggy, who frequently stamped and said, 'It isn't *fair*,' and Mother would reply, 'We never told you life was fair.' 'But it *ought* to be,' Peggy would insist.

Max had said once, 'The young have an appalling sense of justice. Compassion doesn't come till much later.'

Was I looking for justice without compassion? I'm not even sure what justice would be. If the milk has soured, there's no way to make it sweet again.

Now I said to Xan, 'Since when did you expect things to be fair?'

He hovered in the doorway. 'Can I come in?'

'Sure.' I closed my book, a finger in it to mark the place, to give him a hint that I didn't want him to stay long.

'I had a long talk with Dad.'

'Did you?'

'In the first place, I shouldn't have listened to the Mulletville kids. In listening to them, I was encouraging them.'

I shrugged. 'I listen to gossip, too.'

'About me?'

'People don't gossip much about you.'

He sat on the foot of my bed. Because I'm the oldest, I have the room farthest from the main part of the house and

Mother and Daddy's room. I have a combination desk/chest of drawers. A chair. A closet for my clothes. And a view of the ocean through an enormous chinaberry tree, which is a favorite of redbirds.

Xan said, 'Dad told me that Ursula is very highly thought of, and he feels privileged to be her friend, and Max's.' He looked at me and added, 'At least all this has taught me something.'

'What?'

'I used to think of lesbians as being different from other women, kind of freakish. I didn't think they were like other people, like Ursula Heschel doing a good job. I mean, being a neurosurgeon is tough.'

And Ursula managed it without playing God. She came home and baked bread. And took care of Max.

Xan said, 'We do gossip and bitch at school about things we really don't know about. I'm as bad as Kate. What I want to say is, I'm really sorry we brought it up. Being sick was no excuse.'

'Forget it,' I said.

Xan stood up. 'It's hard to keep your head on straight in a world like this.'

'You're right,' I agreed. 'It's not easy.'

'You're not still mad at me?'

'No.'

On the whole, I thought, Xan kept his head on straighter than I did. I decided I'd write him a postcard all his own, not just a family one.

I woke up in the night hearing sirens. Greek sirens. I do not like sirens, anywhere. They mean police and fire and violence. They made me feel very alone in a hotel in a strange city. I comforted myself with the thought that Sandy and Rhea would be with me in time for dinner, and it might be a good idea if I made a reservation for a table at the roof restaurant.

Zachary and I were going to meet in the morning, drive out in the country again, and take the ferry ride from Itea, at the foot of Mount Parnassus, to Aegea, and wouldn't be back till late afternoon. Was it because I was seeing Zachary in a new country, with home far behind me, that we had come to know each other so quickly? It took weeks and weeks of seeing Renny before we could talk the way Zachary and I had talked in only two days. I had mixed emotions. In a way I would almost be glad to say goodbye to him when Sandy and Rhea came, because he did have a powerful effect on me, and it scared me. And at the same time it would be a wrench to leave someone forever who had appeared when I really needed rescuing.

Zachary knew that I expected Sandy and Rhea, but not that I'd expected them to be at the airport to meet me, that these days alone in Athens were not part of anybody's plan. If I still believed in guardian angels, I'd suspect it had all been prearranged for my benefit.

Max sometimes talked about the delicate balance between a prearranged pattern for the universe and human free will. 'Sometimes our freedom comes in the way we accept things over which we have no control, things which may cause us great pain and even death.'

I didn't understand then that she was talking about herself. We were sitting on the verandah, overlooking the ocean. The wisteria vines were in bloom, the blossoms moving from pale lavender to deep dark purple. Pungent scents from flowers and herbs wafted toward us.

She changed the subject. 'I wonder how long Benne Seed will be the kind of lovely island it is now? If the other two plantations should ever be sold, there'd be more developments like Mulletville, only bigger.'

'I'd hate it,' I said. 'Daddy'd hate it. He'd have to look for another island.'

'I don't think it'll happen for a while. Spring and early summer, before the long heat sets in, are as lovely here as any place in the world. I'm not sure why I love Beau Allaire. I was never happy here. M.A. and I came out in Charleston, but most of the time Charleston seems as far from Benne Seed as New York. And I've spent far too much of my life on that asphalt island. Maybe that's why I love to come here. But I'd die of loneliness, intellectual loneliness, if I had to live on Benne Seed for long.'

The idea that Max might not stay on the Island was horrible, but why had I ever thought her return to Beau Allaire was permanent? I remembered Sandy and Dennys questioning her coming, thinking there was something odd about it. But I felt that I, too, would die of loneliness without Max to talk to. 'You're not leaving, are you?' When she did not reply, I asked, 'Is Ursula's sabbatical over?'

Max looked down at her hands, lightly folded, pale against her dark dress. 'No, Polly. And no, I am not going back to New York.'

During the normal pattern of Max and Ursula's year, Urs took August off and they traveled abroad together. In the winter, Max went off by herself to paint, to check on Beau Allaire, to get away from the city.

'And,' she added, 'from Ursula. We're both dominant personalities, and people who love each other need to be apart periodically. I have my own studio on Fifty-seventh Street, but even a city as big as New York can be too small. And I enjoy travel more than Urs does. Even though it's getting daily more difficult, and one expects planes to be late, connections to be missed, trains to stop for hours instead of minutes, I still love it. Two years ago I spent a month in Antarctica. I nearly got frostbite on my aristocratic nose, but I was totally fascinated by that wild, cold world. I wanted to bring Urs back a penguin, but only if I could bring back a square mile of its environment.'

For a while I was embarrassed when Max talked about Urs, but she was so matter-of-fact that it stopped bothering me. She talked about Urs as anyone would about a good friend. Slowly I began to forget Xan and Kate's gossip, even to forget what Max had told me. As Mother had pointed out, it was not where Max's and my interests lay.

Mother and Daddy seemed to take it for granted that I might go over to Beau Allaire a couple of times a week. I got my chores in the lab done in the early morning, helped with the little ones as much as possible, once a week stripped the beds and put the sheets through the washing machine. What time was left, apart from school, was my own.

Max and Ursula came across the Island to have dinner with

us every few weeks. And if Xan and Kate heard any more gossip, they didn't say anything. Sometimes I wondered about Max's husband, Davin Tomassi, and why they'd married, and what had happened. I asked Mother one day when we were taking sheets off the line, smelling of ocean and sky.

'I don't know much about it,' Mother said. 'I gather Max and Davin remained very good friends, and kept in touch until he died. Max is a very complex human being. A very fine one.'

The phone rang. In the middle of the night, in the King George Hotel in Athens. Groggily, fearfully, I reached for it, heard a thick male voice asking for Katerina, got an apology for disturbing me. I'd have been furious if I hadn't been half awake, anyhow. Even so, it scared me. Phone calls in the middle of the night aren't usually good news.

I'd thought it might be about Max.

One warm May afternoon I was over at Beau Allaire. Ursula and I had gone for a swim. Max said she didn't feel up to it and I thought Ursula's glance was anxious.

But the two of us had a fine swim. We knew the tides and undertows and so were able to go out beyond the breakers. When we got back to the house, Max was on the verandah, curled up in the wicker swing, a pile of her old sketchbooks beside her, one open in her lap.

Ursula picked up a sketchbook Max had filled when they were on safari, shooting with cameras, not guns. Ursula had the camera, Max the sketchbook, and had filled it with pictures of wildebeests, honey badgers, lions, elephants, giraffes.

'Get dressed,' Max said sharply. 'I don't want sand and salt water all over my sketchbooks.' Then she smiled at us, her special, slow smile which made me feel—oh, not just that Max was fond of me, but that being Polyhymnia O'Keefe, just as I was, with red hair and legs that were too long for me, was an all right thing to be.

I changed in the green guest room, which was beginning to be 'Polly's room,' and went back to the verandah. Urs was in the kitchen, 'doing something elegant with chicken and fresh dill,' Max told me.

I picked up another African sketchbook, this one filled with people rather than animals, pencil drawings of Africans doing tribal dances. Pygmies. Bushmen. Matabeles.

Another sketchbook. From Asia. More odd dances, people wearing masks, leaping about fires. 'What's it about?' I asked.

'Aggression,' Max said. 'Getting rid of it legitimately. We don't, nowadays, we sophisticated peoples. As society evolved, we began to repress the destructive, aggressive instincts we needed to acquire back when we were living in caves and trees and had to protect ourselves from wild animals—or wild people. What do you do about your own anger?'

'I chop wood,' I said. 'That's the good old-fashioned way of getting it out of your system, but it works.'

Max pointed to a pen-and-ink sketch of naked people dancing. They had long legs, and long slender necks, and Max had given them a wild rhythm. 'They're acting out their feral feelings in a way which doesn't endanger society. Kids in inner cities, or even places like Cowpertown, don't have any legitimate way of working out their aggressions. Not too many of them—in the South, at least—chop wood.'

'Benne Seed gets mighty cold, and we use a lot of wood. I can split a cord as well as Xan.'

'Even the old scapegoat'—Max riffled through the pages —'was a useful device whereby people could dump their sins onto the animal, and not be crushed under a burden of neurotic guilt.' She put down the sketchbook, picked up a pad, and began sketching me. 'If I had it to do again, I'd be an anthropologist. Who is it who said the proper study of mankind is man?' I didn't know the answer, and she went on, 'We all have our own burdens of neurotic guilt. Sketching helps me get rid of mine.'

I reached for another sketchbook. It was filled with water-color paintings of brilliant, jungly-looking birds, flashing color in deep-green forests, and then more people, wearing masks and dancing.

To my surprise, Max grabbed the sketchbook. 'I don't like those paintings.'

'Where were you when you did them?' I asked, not understanding why she was so vehement.

'Ecuador.'

Ecuador. In South America. 'Were you in the jungle?'

'For a while.' She pulled out another sketchbook. 'Now look at these sketches, Polly. It's from my last China trip.'

'When were you in Ecuador?' I persisted.

'Last year. Look, here's the Great Wall of China. It's almost unbelievable, even when you're looking right at it.'

I looked, not at Max's drawings of the Wall, but at Max herself, her pallor, her thinness. And the pieces of the puzzle suddenly fitted together. This was why Max had come home to Beau Allaire, why Ursula was on leave of absence from her hospital in New York.

If I'd seen Urs alone, I'd have asked her if my guess was right, but there wasn't a moment. Once Urs called to us that dinner was ready, the three of us were together the whole time, and then they both waved me off when I left for home. I wished the Land-Rover hadn't been available, so I could have asked Urs to drive me.

As soon as I got back, I checked in, and then went out to the lab and called from the phone there, called the hospital in Cowpertown and left a message for Renny to call me. I'd never done that before.

I took the hose and sluiced down the cement floor of the lab, so I'd be there to grab the phone when it rang. I was cleaning one of the tanks when he called.

'What's up, Polly?'

I perched on one of the high stools; the telephone was on the wall above a shelf full of beakers and jars and a lot of lab paraphernalia. 'Max was in Ecuador last year. Has she got one of your awful parasites?'

A pause. Then, 'Thousands of Americans go to South America every year.'

'Max was in the jungle, not on a cruise ship.'

Renny was silent.

'Listen, I know all about doctors' confidentiality, but you've talked to me a lot about your field, and unless you tell me I'm wrong, I'm going to assume that Max got infected while she was in South America, and this thing is going to kill her. Is killing her.'

Renny said, 'Polly.' And then, 'Look, I can't talk on the phone. Where are you?'

'In the lab. There's no one around.'

'Pol, I can't talk about it at all. You know that.'

'Then it's true. Okay, I know I'm not next of kin, I have no legal right to ask. But Max is my friend. She matters to me.'

Renny sounded very far away. 'If Mrs. Tomassi wanted you to know, she'd tell you.'

'That's telling me. Thanks.'

'What are you going to do with it?'

'Nothing. You're right. If Max wanted me to know, she'd tell me herself. But I want to talk to you, please. Not about Max. You've talked to me plenty about vectors, and parasites circulating in the blood of the host in Trypanosomal form.'

'You know too much about too many things,' Renny said.

'You don't have to talk to me about Max. Just talk to me about Netson and his research.'

'I suppose I owe you that much. It's all my fault that you guessed. I'm not on call tomorrow evening.'

He'd borrowed a boat, so we went to Petros' as usual. Renny had brought an article by his boss in the *New England Journal of Medicine*, and I skimmed it, then went back to read more slowly. Clinically, the patient experiences a recurrent fever. The Trypanosomal organisms go through some kind of change, but eventually they get back in the bloodstream and invade the heart. In the case of people like Max (though we never mentioned her name) who have no immunities whatsoever, severe heart disease develops. Even with people who have lived for generations in areas where the disease is endemic, about ten percent of the population end up with congestive heart failure, and sudden cardiac arrest is common.

'How did Max find out she had Netson's?' I handed him back the *New England Journal*. Renny began leafing through it, not answering.

I felt angry and frustrated, and at the same time I respected his attitude. I spoke slowly, quietly. 'You don't have to tell me. I can figure it out. Max is no fool, and Ursula is a doctor, even if tropical medicine isn't her field. But she must have heard of these diseases, and Max is an omnivorous reader. If she had a bite on the eyelid, followed by conjunctivitis while she was in Ecuador, she'd have suspected. One of the foremost specialists in tropical diseases is her cousin, on the staff of M. A. Horne, which was started with her father's money. Ironic, isn't it?'

Renny looked at me over the magazine, but said nothing.

I went on. 'So it would be a logical thing for her to come home to confirm a diagnosis she and Ursula already suspected, and to stay here, because Dr. Netson's in Cowpertown, and Beau Allaire is home. And Ursula's on leave of absence, to be with Max until—' My voice broke, and I looked at Renny. He did not contradict me, so I knew I was right, if not specifically, at least generally. For a moment a wave of nausea broke over me. I fought it back. 'Isn't there any treatment?'

'Nothing satisfactory.' Renny spoke reluctantly. 'We're trying primaquine in the dosage suitable for malaria. And there's a nitrofurazone derivative that shows promise. But if there's organ damage, it's irreversible, at least at present.'

'What about a heart transplant?' I suggested.

'They're chancy, at best, and contraindicated in Netson's. Polly, I've told you more than I should.'

'You haven't said a word about Max. You've just talked to me about a disease in which you're particularly interested. If Max weren't involved, you could have said everything you've said to me, and it wouldn't have hurt. That's the difference.'

His voice was heavy. 'She's a special lady. A real lady, and there aren't many around nowadays. I truly admire her. I wish there were something I could do for her. You're lucky to have her for a friend.'

'Yes. I know.'

We didn't finish our pizza. Petros came and asked us if anything was wrong with it, and we assured him it was fine, but he wanted to make us another, on the house, and finally I convinced him I didn't feel well.

Renny asked him for the check. 'Polly, sweet. I'm sorry.'

'I know.'

'For all the breaks we've been getting in medicine, there's still a lot we can't do anything about.'

My voice was brittle. 'Nobody ever promised us life was going to be safe. Everybody dies, sooner or later.'

'Would you want not to?' Renny asked. 'To go on in a body growing older and older, forever? Even if we could keep the body in reasonable shape, would you want to live forever?'

'Yes,' I said, and then, 'No. Forever would be crippling. One would never have to do anything, because one could always do it tomorrow.' *One could*—I'd picked that up from Max, as so much else. 'But not extinction. I can't imagine Max being annihilated.'

Renny didn't say anything, and I didn't want him to, because he's an intern, and I knew what he'd say. At least I'm older than Renny in that way. He can take on faith that there are mitochondria and farandolae, and that there are quarks and quanta, even though they can't be seen. Well, so can I. My parents are scientists, after all. But I can also take on faith that Max is too alive to be extinguished by anything as—as banal as death.

Renny paid for the pizza. 'Polly—'

I looked at him.

'Can you keep . . . what you've guessed . . . to yourself?'

'I'll try. If I don't see Max for a couple of days, maybe I'll get it all into some kind of perspective. I'm not very good about hiding things from people I care about.' Max had guessed immediately that I'd heard gossip about her and Urs. But this was different. I'd have to keep her from knowing that I knew.

We drove to the dock and jumped into the small motorboat. Halfway to Benne Seed, Renny cut the motor as usual, but instead of kissing we looked up at the stars.

'In the life span of a star,' I said, 'our lives are less than a flicker, whether we live for ten years or a hundred.'

'In the life span of the universe,' Renny said, 'that life of a star is less than a flicker.' And then he kissed me. And I wanted him to. Just as it was beginning to build, he broke off. 'Time to take you home.'

Heavy with unwanted knowledge, I went to my room, saying that I had a lot of reading to do for school. Which was true. Exams were coming up, and I had to do well.

And my room was full of Max. The little crystal bird she'd given me for the opening of *As You Like It* was on my desk, by the window, where it caught and refracted the light sparkling off the ocean. Over my desk chair was flung a Fair Isle sweater Max had loaned me one early spring night when it had grown unexpectedly chilly, and then told me to keep because she didn't need it anymore. On my bed table were books she'd taken down from the library shelves at Beau Allaire and given me to read.

Now that I knew all that I knew, I couldn't understand why it had taken me so long to realize just why it was that Max had come home to Beau Allaire.

But I learned that I was capable of keeping a secret.

Max and Ursula did not know that I knew.

In the King George Hotel in Athens I woke up with tears on my cheeks, and the sound of the redbird in the chinaberry tree in my ears. The sound faded into the night noises of a city, and I knew that I had been crying about Max. Suddenly I heard a soft rain spattering on the balcony floor, and a cool breeze came in. And I went back to sleep.

In the morning the sky was even more brilliantly blue and gold than it had been, with no heat haze, and a cool breeze.

Zachary called while I was having breakfast, the Fair Isle cardigan over my shoulders. He explained that we'd need to make an early start if I wanted to be back in time for dinner with Sandy and Rhea. "Can you be in the lobby at nine?"

"Sure, why not?"

"Leave a message for your uncle and aunt, that you may not be back when they arrive. When are they getting in, by the way?"

"I'm not sure. Uncle Sandy just said in plenty of time for dinner."

"Okay, then, he doesn't expect you to hang around. I'll have you back at the King George in good time to bathe and change. Just leave them a message."

"Will do." Sandy would certainly not want me to hang around.

"That was quite a downpour we had during the night," Zachary said. "Did it wake you?"

"I heard it." It was mixed up in my mind with the redbird in the chinaberry tree and my conversation with Renny. "But now we've got the most glorious day of all." I had carried my coffee cup from the balcony to the telephone in the bedroom, and took a swallow. It was cooling off. "See you at nine."

The air was dry and warm when we started off in the VW Bug, which was beginning to seem like a familiar friend. Zachary'd brought another picnic basket, not from the Hilton this time, he said, but very Greek: cold spinach pie, feta cheese, wrinkly dark olives, taramasalata, cucumber dip.

"And I got them to make me some fresh lemonade at the Hilton. I don't suppose you want to greet your uncle and aunt with wine on your breath."

"I'm not much of a drinker," I told him.

"There's a difference between having an occasional glass of wine and being an alcoholic."

"Of course. But I'm still a minor, in case you've forgotten, and I've seen enough of the results of the abuse of alcohol to be very wary of it."

He looked at me with open curiosity. "Not your parents?"

"Heavens—no!"

"Who?"

I didn't say Max. It was a while before I realized that sometimes she drank too much. She frequently switched from wine to bourbon. 'It's good for elderly hearts,' she said.

I asked Renny if it was all right for her to drink bourbon, and he said that to an extent Max was right, that a moderate amount of whiskey actually dilated the arteries. And he added that it was a painkiller. He gave me another of Netson's articles to read, this one way over my head, but I gathered that in the last months of the disease there is a good deal of acute pain, and the damaged heart muscle will not tolerate ordinary painkillers.

One evening when Max and I were alone at Beau Allaire she talked to me about her husband. We were sitting at the table out on the verandah, and she was sipping bourbon. Only the slight flush to her cheeks made me realize that she was drinking more than usual, but there was nothing ugly about it.

'I married Davin Tomassi in good faith,' she said. 'I wanted family life, wanted children, and I thought Davin and I could make it. He was the gentlest man I have ever known, and occasionally he could get through all my blocks and inhibitions, but not often. God knows it wasn't Davin's fault there was no miracle. He was infinitely patient. And when I got pregnant—oh, God, how we rejoiced. But the baby was born with the Allaire weak heart, and lived only a few days. After that—it was apparent things weren't going to work out for us as husband and wife. That was my worst time, after I left Davin. I fell apart in the ugliest possible way. Then I met Urs. And was able to be friends with Davin again. I will always love Davin, in my fashion, and be grateful to him.' She put her hands to her cheeks, and her fingers trembled. 'I think I want you to go home now, Polly. I'm tired.'

I left. It had been almost as hard for Max to tell me about her marriage as it had been for her to tell me about her father and M.A. I wondered when she was going to tell me that she was dying.

The next time I was at Beau Allaire, Ursula was there, and I managed a few minutes with her in the kitchen (Max didn't give us much time alone, basically because Max didn't want to be alone). 'Urs, I don't mean to pry, and I know Max doesn't want to talk about it, and nobody told me, I mean Renny didn't say anything, but I guessed—'

Ursula turned from the stone sink. 'Did you? I thought you might have. How much do you know?'

'That Max has Netson's disease, and that there's no cure.'

Ursula wiped her hands carefully. 'Oh, Polly child, this is a lot for you to handle, and you're in too deep now for you to turn your back on Max and withdraw.'

Withdrawing had not occurred to me. 'Can't anything be done to help her?' I knew the answer, but Ursula was older and more experienced than Renny.

'Not much. When Bart Netson confirmed the diagnosis I don't think she realized how much she was going to have to endure. With some people it's just a slow wearing down of energy, and then quick heart failure. It's being much slower with Max; she's very strong. The pain is bad, and getting worse. I'm grateful to you, child, for all you do to help Max. You're both friend and daughter to her. Did she tell you that she and Davin had a little girl?'

'Yes.'

'That was a devastating blow to Maxa, seeing what appeared to be a perfect infant, and then watching it wilt and die. You're Max's child, Polly, the child she couldn't have, and that's an enormous burden to put on a sixteen-year-old. What have we done to you, Max and I?'

'You've made me alive,' I said quickly.

'I worry about you.' She turned back to the stone sink. 'I hope we're not—I hope we're not destructive to you.'

'Constructive,' I said quickly. 'Sandy brought me to Beau Allaire to meet you, just me, remember? He wouldn't have, if he hadn't known I needed you and Max.'

'Bless you.' Ursula refilled the kettle and put it back on the stove. 'Bless Sandy. Dennys, too. They're good friends.'

Mother went to Charleston with Ursula, at last, to go to the Spoleto festival in the afternoon while Urs was consulting at Mercy Hospital, and then go out to dinner, and back to the festival in the evening. She came back glowing.

The following week Max said, 'It's your turn, Pol. Urs has to go back to Charleston to see Ormsby—there are times I could kill your Uncle Dennys for offering Urs to him—but Urs needs the stimulation, so I'm simultaneously grateful. There's an interesting play on at the Dock Street Theatre in the evening.'

'When?'

'Tomorrow. We've already cleared it with your parents. Urs will be getting her hair trimmed, so we'll kill two birds with one stone and get yours styled.'

'You're not coming?' Of course she wasn't coming. She wasn't up to it, and I knew it.

'Not this time. You go with Urs and have fun.'

Ursula and I stayed in the Ormsbys' guesthouse, which was a separate building behind the house and had been the kitchen in the old days. There was a comfortable sitting room over-looking the garden, a bedroom with twin beds, a bathroom, and a tiny kitchenette, so the guests could be self-sufficient. The furniture was antique and beautiful—Mrs. Ormsby was an interior decorator—and there was air-conditioning.

We said hello to Mrs. Ormsby, who was welcoming and chatty and asked about Daddy and then Uncle Dennys, and talked about getting Mother into Charleston more often, and wouldn't Ursula be interested in serving on some commit-tees? 'And how is Maximiliana doing?' she asked, a tentative note coming into her voice.

'As well as can be expected.' Ursula's tone was carefully noncommittal.

'I wish we could help, my dear,' Mrs. Ormsby said.

Suddenly and for the first time I realized that Ursula was bearing Max's death on her own shoulders, bearing it for Max as well as for herself. And I had a faint glimmer of what that death was going to mean to Ursula. Max had said that they had been together for over thirty years. That was longer than Mother and Daddy had been married. How would either of my parents feel if they were watching the other die? I couldn't quite conceive it. Now, as I watched and heard Ursula being courteous and contained, some of her pain became real to me.

Mrs. Ormsby, returning to her social, light voice, told us there was iced tea in the fridge, and a bottle of white wine.

We thanked her and then went to the hairdresser, chic and undoubtedly exorbitantly expensive. I felt a little odd, having my hair styled. Kate's chestnut hair is curly, and even when she nibbles at it with the nail scissors, it looks just right. If I hack

at mine with the nail scissors, it looks exactly as though I've
hacked at it with the nail scissors. Mother usually cuts it.

'Cut it short, please,' I said to the stylist, 'as short as possible.'

'Why so short?' he asked.

'It's an awful color, and the shorter it is, the less of it.'

'If I could make up a dye the color of your hair, half my
ladies would come flocking. You have a beautiful neck. We will
show off your neck to the best advantage.'

(Kate's reaction when I came home was, 'Golly, Polly!'

Xan said, 'Gosh, Pol, what'd they do? You look almost
pretty!'

'She *is* pretty,' Mother said.

Max simply made me turn round and round, looking at me
critically from every angle, nodding with satisfaction.)

I could hardly believe it myself. When the stylist was through
with me, my straight hair actually lay in soft curves, capping
my head.

Ursula's hair looked nice, too. 'Max found Dominic for me,'
she said. 'If Max didn't see to it that I go to a good stylist,
she knows I wouldn't bother. After all, a surgeon's hair is
frequently concealed under a green surgical cap.'

When we left the hairdresser, Ursula went to the hospital
and I went to the art gallery, where there was an interesting
exhibition of women painters: Rosa Bonheur, Berthe Morisot,
Georgia O'Keeffe. O'Keeffe. Hm. Two *f*'s. I liked the way it
looked. My parents had not objected when I put the extra *l* in
Polly, but I doubted if they'd let me get away with putting an
extra *f* in O'Keefe.

I'd gone back to the cottage to change, and was delayed
by Mrs. Ormsby, so I was a few minutes late and Ursula was
waiting for me. She was evidently known by the people who ran
the restaurant, and the waiter was smiling and respectful. 'We
have the *moules marinières* that you like, Dr. Heschel.'

'Splendid, François. I think you'll like the way they prepare
them here, Polly.'

'Fine.'

She did not order wine. We had Vichy water. 'This place is

small enough to be personal, and I've got in the habit of eating here when I'm in Charleston. Did you have a good afternoon?'

'Terrific. It's ages since I've been in an art gallery.'

'Sometime I'm going to take a real sabbatical. But it's been good for me to keep my hand in during all these months. Norris Ormsby called me in today on an interesting and tragic case, a young woman in her thirties who has had a series of brain tumors. Benign, in her case, is a mockery. After her first surgery, some nerves were cut, and her face was irrevocably distorted, her mouth twisted, one eye partly closed. A few days ago another tumor was removed, and several more smaller ones were discovered. I agreed with the decision not to do further surgery. She said that she is looking with her mind's eye at the tumors, willing them to shrink, *see*ing them shrink. And she quoted Benjamin Franklin to me: *Those things that hurt, instruct.* An extraordinary woman. A holy woman. She looks at her devastated face in the mirror and, she says, she still does not recognize herself. But there is no bitterness in her. She sails, and as soon as she gets out of the hospital she plans to sail, solo, to Bermuda. At sea, what she looks like is a matter of complete indifference. My patients teach me, Polly. Old Ben knew what he was talking about, and it's completely counter to general thinking today, where we're taught to avoid pain and seek pleasure. Pain needs to be moved through, not avoided.'

Ursula was referring to her own pain, I thought. And Max's. And mine.

'Why is hurting part of growing up?' I demanded.

'It's part of being human. I've been watching you move through it with amazingly mature compassion. You've been the best medicine Max could have. Well, child, it's a good thing the play is a comedy. This is more than enough heaviness.'

We spent two hours in the theatre laughing our heads off. Then back to the guest cottage. Ursula went into the main house to have a drink with the Ormsbys, and I got ready for bed, and read until she came in. She took a quick shower, and then got into the other twin bed, blowing me a kiss. 'Sleep well, child. I've enjoyed our time together.'

'Me, too. It's been wonderful.'

'We'll have a bite of breakfast at seven, and then drive back to the Island before the heat of the day. Sleep well.'

'You, too. Thank you. Thanks, Urs.'

Urs wasn't Max. But she was still pretty special.

"Who?" Zachary asked as we drove toward Mount Parnassus.

"Who what?" I asked stupidly.

"Who's abused alcohol, to make you so uptight about it?"

"Zachary, I go to high school, okay? Occasionally I get invited to dances. Kids sneak in booze and drink themselves silly. You have no idea how much time I spend holding kids' heads while they whoops, or mopping them up afterwards if they don't make it to the john. It's enough to make me join the WCTU."

"What on earth is the WCTU?"

I giggled. "The Woman's Christian Temperance Union."

He didn't think it was funny. "Your parents aren't teetotalers, are they?"

"No. But they're moderate."

"Anything good can be abused. I know that from very personal experience. But I've learned that I am capable of temperance, and temperance means moderation, not abstinence."

"Okay, okay, I'm not arguing with you. Moderation in all things, as the immoderate Greeks said."

It was from Max that I'd heard about the Greeks talking about being moderate. It was, she said, because temperamentally they were totally immoderate. Starting a war over Helen of Troy is hardly moderate. The vast quantity of gods and goddesses isn't very moderate, either.

We'd talked comfortably over a cup of tea, Ursula making cucumber sandwiches for us, and then I sat at the table on the verandah, and did my homework, while Ursula sat in the white wicker swing, reading a medical journal, and Max sketched. When I was through—it wasn't a heavy-homework night—I left my books and papers on the table and went to stand by Max, looking down at her sketchbook. A sketch of me. One of Ursula. Several sketches of hands.

'Polly—'

Something in her tone of voice made me stop.

'Urs tells me that you know.'

Ursula let the magazine slip off her lap onto the floor, but did not bend down to pick it up. The swing creaked noisily from its hooks in the ceiling.

'Yes, Max, I know.'

'Because of Renny, I suppose—'

'He never talked about you—'

'No, he wouldn't. He just talks about tropical diseases ad infinitum. And you're no fool. Dear, square Renny. I'm glad he's assisting Cousin Bart. Glad you have him for a friend. I'd hoped to spare you, Polly, at least a little longer.'

'No, no, I'd rather—' I started, and trailed off inadequately.

'Not many people have the privilege of being given time to prepare for death. I can't say that I'm ready to die—I'm still *in media res* and I have things I'd like to paint . . . things I'd like to do—but I'm beyond the denial and the rage. I don't like the pain.'

'Oh, Max—' I looked helplessly at Ursula.

Urs glanced at Max, rose, picked up the journal, and dropped it in the swing. 'I'm off to the kitchen. Come and join me in a few minutes, Polly.'

'Little one,' Max said. 'There are worse things than dying. Losing one's sense of compassion, for instance; being inured to suffering. Losing the wonder and the sadness of it all. That's a worse death than the death of the body.'

I was silent. Trying to push back the dark lump of tears rising in my throat.

'I don't know how long I have left,' Max said. 'Bart doesn't know. I'm strong as an ox. My heart is not going to stop beating easily. But it's been an immensely interesting journey, this life, and I've been given the child of my heart to rejoice me at the end.'

She stood, pushing up from her seat with her hands, and I was in her arms, tears streaming down my cheeks. She wiped them with her long fingers. 'Dear, loving little Pol. But it's better this way, isn't it? Out in the open?'

I nodded, pushing my fingers in my pocket to look for

Kleenex. She put a handkerchief in my hand. 'Max, I don't want to go to Cyprus.'

'Nonsense.' Her voice was brusque. 'I am not going to allow my plans for the education of Polyhymnia O'Keefe to be disrupted.'

I wanted to ask, 'Will you be here when I come back?' I mumbled, 'I still don't want to go.'

She smiled at me. 'You'll go, Polly, if only for me. You won't disappoint me. Now. Go help Ursula. And let's have a merry meal. I've had a rich life, Polly, and I'm grateful indeed.' She gave me a gentle hug, then a small shove, and I went out to the kitchen.

I could ask Urs what I couldn't ask Max. 'Urs, if I go to Cyprus, will Max be . . . will Max be alive when I get back?'

'I can't answer that, child. I don't know. There are no tidy answers to Netson's. But things aren't going to get better.'

'I don't want to go.'

'You must. You know that. Part of growing up is learning to do things you don't want to do.' She looked at me gravely. 'Child, I promised Norris Ormsby I'd go back to Charleston next week. Just this once more. I've made it clear that it's the last time. Max won't ask you to stay with her, now that she knows that you know. She won't want to burden you. But I'm going to ask you to come stay with her overnight. Are you up to it?'

'Yes,' I said.

'It's a lot to ask of you. I know that.'

'You don't need to ask. I want to be here.'

'You're a strong child, Polly.'

—It's all a front, I wanted to say, but I didn't. And I didn't mind when Ursula called me child. I'd have hated it from anyone else.

She handed me a plate of cold chicken and ham. 'I hope you're not going to regret these months since Sandy brought you over to Beau Allaire as his Christmas present to Max and me.'

'Never!' I cried. 'I've learned more in these past months than I've ever learned in school. I could never regret them.'

'Never' is a long word.

"Am I never going to see you again, after I take you back to the hotel this afternoon?" Zachary asked.

"It's been wonderful being with you," I said. "I've had a marvelous time. I'll write you postcards from Cyprus."

"I want more than postcards. You really do something special for me, Polly, you really do. Do you honestly enjoy being with me?"

"I wouldn't be with you if I didn't." Zachary evidently didn't even suspect that I was anything but a social success in Cowpertown and that having a young man after me was a totally new experience.

"Mount Parnassus isn't that far beyond Delphi, O goddess mine," he said, "but I won't trace any of our route. Did you do your homework?"

"Sure." In my mind's eye I saw Max sitting with me on the verandah swing, showing me pictures and sketches, got a whiff of her perfume, of Beau Allaire's flowers in the spring. "Mount Parnassus is sacred to Dionysus, and the Thyiads held their Bacchic revels on one of the summits."

"I'd like to have a Bacchic revel with you." He took one hand off the steering wheel and pulled me close to him. I must have stiffened. "Relax, pretty Pol. I'm not going to hurt you."

I did relax during the ferry ride. We stood on deck and the light of sun on water was so brilliant it was almost blinding. The sea was choppy, white-capped, with a high wind which dried the spray as fast as it blew up at us. To our right was a barren coast of stony mountains, with only a little scrubby-looking vegetation on the lower slopes. I wondered if it had been greener for the Dionysian revels; I could hardly imagine them on hard, bare stone.

The sea got choppier and choppier as we approached land, and the sky more lowering. "It rained last night," Zachary said. "I forbid it to rain today."

But as we got back in the Bug to drive off the ferry, big raindrops splattered against the windshield. Zachary swore. Then, "There's a place nearby where we can have a glass of tea and see what the weather's going to do."

The small restaurant he took me to was right on the shore, and we could watch the rain making pockmarks on the water. The waiter seemed sorrowful but not surprised when Zachary asked for tea and nothing else, and while we were drinking it the skies opened and dumped quantities of water, and then, abruptly, stopped.

"I have a rug for us to sit on," Zachary said. "I think we can drive on and have our picnic." The sun was out, and the wet flagstones outside the restaurant were steaming.

The wind was still strong, and it was a wild, warm, early afternoon of swiftly shifting clouds which went well with the grandeur of the scenery. Zachary drove to a grove of ancient pines, from which we had a view of a crumbling temple, the stone shining and golden in the post-storm sunshine.

Zachary spread a rug over the rusty needles, and we ate comfortably, protected by the trees, which swayed in the wind, sounding almost like surf. Zachary popped a wrinkled little olive into his mouth, and then lay down, looking up at the blue sky through the green needles of the pines, a high, burning blue with golden glints.

I looked at one of the crumbling columns. "It's so old—"

"And gone," Zachary said, putting his dark head in my lap. "As our own civilization will soon be gone. It's a never-ending cycle of rise and fall, rise and fall. Except that there's a good possibility we'll end it." He spat out the olive seed. "With the new microtechnology, there'll be less than a fifteen-second lapse between the pressing of the button and the falling of the bombs. All those bomb shelters people have built, my pa among them, will be useless. There won't be time to get to them. When it happens, it'll happen without warning."

I pushed his head off my lap. "Shut up."

"Ow." He rubbed his head and put it back on my lap. "It might happen now, in the next few seconds. A light so bright we'd be blinded, and heat so intense we'd be incinerated before we realized what had happened. It wouldn't be a bad way to go, here, with you."

I pushed at his head again, but he didn't move. It's one thing to contemplate one's mortality realistically, another to wallow in melodrama. It was almost as though this strange young man was deliberately inviting disaster.

"Don't be an ostrich," he said, "hiding your head in the sand."

"I'm as realistic as you are, but it doesn't do any good to dwell on the horror. Nobody wants it, and it doesn't have to happen."

"Give a child matches, and sooner or later he'll light one."

"We had an essay contest, not just our school, but the whole state, on how to prevent nuclear warfare, and I wish the President of the United States would listen to the kids."

"Did you win?" Zachary asked.

"I was a finalist. At least I was able to speak my piece. And we have to live as though there's going to be a world for us to live in."

"What's the point of making plans?"

I countered, "What's the point of *not* making plans?"

"We're at the end of our civilization, let's face it."

"Oh, Zach." Absently I began to run my fingers through his hair. "Think of all the groups who decided they knew exactly when the end of the world was coming, because of the lineup of planets, or some verse from Revelation, and dressed up in sheets to wait on some mountaintop for Judgment Day. Or had big Doomsday parties. And refusing to live, because it wasn't worth it when the end of the world was so close, and even selling their property—and then, when the world didn't end at the predicted moment, there they were."

"I'm not selling my property," Zachary said. "You needn't worry about that. Just in case, I'll hang on to what I have."

"You can't take it with you."

"I'll keep it till the last second. I've got five thousand dollars in traveler's checks with me right now."

I did not like this aspect of Zachary. I'm realistic enough to know the possibilities for the future, but there are some positive ones, too, as I reminded Zachary. There are people like Sandy and Rhea whose work is about diametrically opposite to Zachary's father's, though I didn't mention that. A lot of doctors are refusing to take part in emergency medical-disaster planning, making it clear that it's unethical to delude people into false beliefs that there are any realistic mechanisms of survival after an atomic war. More and more people are rising up against nuclear stockpiling. At home. Abroad. We don't have to blow up the planet.

Max said once, 'We do make things happen by what we think, so think positively, Polly, not negatively. When you think you are beautiful, you are beautiful. If you believe in yourself, you will do well in your life's work, whether you choose acting or writing or science.'

It was a warm summer evening and we were out on the verandah upstairs, off Max's room, watching night fall. The sky over the ocean was rosy with afterglow, which Max said was more subtle than the sunset. The ceiling fan was whirring gently. In the purply sky above the soft rose at the horizon a star came out, pulsing softly so that it was more like the thought of a star than a star, and then there it was, followed by more and more stars.

Max pointed to the sky. 'The macrocosm. Stars beyond countless stars. Galaxies beyond galaxies. If our universe is finite, as many astrophysicists believe, there may be as many universes as there are galaxies, floating like tiny bubbles in the vastness of space.'

'Tiny bubbles?'

I was sitting on a low stool at Max's feet, and she reached out her fingers and massaged the back of my neck gently. That's where I get tired when I write a lot, and I'd just finished my last long paper of the year for Miss Zeloski.

'The last time Urs and I were at your house, Rosy and Johnny were blowing bubbles, lovely little iridescent orbs floating in the breeze. And when one thinks of the macrocosm, and then the microcosm, size makes no never-mind, as Nettie would say.' She laughed gently. 'Is a galaxy bigger than a quark? I lean more and more on the total interdependence of all creation. If we should be so foolish as to blow this planet to bits, it would have repercussions not only in our own solar system but in distant galaxies. Or even distant universes. And if anyone dies—a tree, a planet, a human being—all of creation is shaken.'

How different that was from Zachary. Frightening, but in a completely different way, because it gave everything meaning.

'Never think what you do doesn't matter,' Max said. 'No one is too insignificant to make a difference. Whenever you get the chance, choose life. But I don't need to tell you that. You choose life with every gesture you make. That's the first thing in you that appealed to me. You are naked with life.'

And wasn't that what drew me to Max, that abundant sense of life?—pointing out to me the fierce underside of a moth clinging to the screen; fireflies like a fallen galaxy on the dunes in front of our house; the incredible, pulsing life of the stars blooming in the night sky, seeming to cling to the Spanish moss on the old oaks.

I looked at the crumbling golden columns near Zachary's picnic spot, the chipped pediments, and thought that Max would see in them not the death of a civilization but the life. I got up and walked slowly toward the temple, and Zachary followed me.

He dropped his doom talk. "When am I going to see you again?"

"Uncle Sandy has plans to take me to various places for the rest of the week, and then I'm off to Cyprus."

"I like Cyprus. I'll come see you there."

"No, please, Zachary. I'm there to do a job, and I'm not going to have time for anything else."

"How long is this job?"

"Three weeks." We'd reached the temple, and I sat on the still-damp stone of a pediment with a lotus-leaf design. Did the Greeks think of the lotus as flowering into an entire universe?

Zachary counted off on his fingers. "Three weeks, okay, I may go to Turkey for a while, then. How're you getting home after the conference?"

"Cyprus Airlines to Athens, then on to JFK in New York, and then to Charleston."

"You change planes in Athens?"

"Of course."

"How long do you have between planes?"

"Nearly three hours."

"I'll meet you at the airport, then, and we can have a bite together and a chance to catch up. When we get back to the hotel, write me down your flight numbers."

"Okay, that would be fun." I tried not to let on just how thrilled I was that he didn't want to drop me when Sandy and Rhea arrived.

He touched my nose, then my lips with his finger. "I can't imagine anything nicer than fun with you, Polly. You're like a bottle of champagne just waiting to be uncorked. Or don't you like that analogy?" I had turned away, and he pulled me back. "I didn't mean to hurt you, sweet Pol. Since you haven't told me anything, I can't help blundering." He pressed my face against his shoulder, gently.

It was nearly seven when we got back to the hotel. Zachary insisted that I give him the Cyprus Airlines flight number, so I let him into my room just long enough to check my ticket and write down the information for him. He was looking around the room, and I'm sure it gave him the impression the O'Keefes are a lot richer than we are. But I didn't explain.

He kissed me goodbye, and electricity vibrated through me. But we don't have to act out everything we feel. I'd learned that much.

"I've got to call Uncle Sandy's room. Thanks, Zach. These have been good days for me. Really good. Thanks."

"Believe me, the pleasure was mine. And this is not goodbye, Pol, you're not going to be able to get rid of me this easily."

I hoped he would be at the airport to meet me at the end of my three weeks in Cyprus. But I thought I'd better not count on it.

I rang Sandy and Rhea's room, and he answered. "Polly! We arrived about an hour ago and got your message. Glad you were off doing something. Been having a good time?" There was both question and challenge in his voice.

"Yes. I have. I met a guy from California—did Uncle Dennys tell you?"

"He mentioned it."

"I've been off sightseeing and doing things with him."

"Not too much, I hope?"

I laughed. "No fault of his, but no, not too much."

"My, you sound grown up."

"It's about time," I said. "I hope it's all right that I went ahead and made a reservation for dinner on the roof at nine. I thought that might be easiest for you—"

"It's just right," he said. "Rhea's napping, but I'll wake her up in time. See you at the restaurant."

I soaked in a warm bath. Zachary had been an escape route in many ways. I could forget that Sandy was likely to ask me questions. Some of the questions had no answers. But there were other ones which I was going to have to respond to, and I wasn't ready. I felt as though a splinter of ice had lodged deep in my heart. While I was with Zachary I was able to forget it, but now it was there, chilling me.

I stayed in the tub as long as possible, but it didn't thaw anything. Then I dressed in the one dressy thing I'd brought with me, a soft, floaty geometric print of mauves and blues and lavenders, which softened my angles and brought out the blue of my eyes and made my hair look less orange. Rhea had given it to me for Christmas, and I'd worn it for the New Year's Eve party at Beau Allaire, and for Zachary when we went to the Hilton for dinner. Rhea knew how to buy clothes which were just right for me.

At nine sharp, I was standing in front of the elevator, and when I got to the roof, Sandy and Rhea were waiting. I hugged them, rubbing my face against Sandy's soft golden beard, smelling Rhea's familiar, exotic scent, embraced by them both. For a fleeting moment Rhea reminded me of Max. They both had black hair. They were both tall. They both had fine bones. They knew how to dress. But that was it. Max's eyes were silver, and Rhea's like dark pansies. Max was thin, and Rhea was slender. Max vibrated like a plucked harp, and Rhea was serenely quiet. Max, with her acute awareness of life, was dying, and Rhea still had her life ahead of her.

We were shown to a table with a good view, one of Aristeides' tables. He greeted me like an old friend, and I introduced him to Sandy and Rhea.

"You seem to have made yourself very much at home," Sandy said.

Rhea smiled at me approvingly. "We're proud of you for managing on your own so well. Of course we knew you would."

Sandy and Aristeides spent quite a while discussing the merits of various dishes, and when Rhea said something in Greek Aristeides was delighted, repeated everything in Greek, rattled off a list of wines, and approved of Rhea's choice. It was not retsina.

During dinner, Sandy and Rhea told me that after they had visited some of Rhea's relatives they'd been invited to tour the islands on a friend's yacht, and then they had a job to do. They didn't tell me what or where, but I was used to secrets. A lot of Daddy's research was secret, too.

Rhea and Sandy were even more cosmopolitan than Max, and I was only Polly, the island girl, but I was completely at ease with them.

Zachary came with the after-dinner coffee, appearing at Sandy's elbow and introducing himself.

"I thought you might like to see who it is who's been escorting Polly these past few days." He looked handsome in dark pants and blazer and a white shirt.

Rhea invited him to sit down, and I could see they thought I'd done pretty well, until Zachary mentioned his father's corporation, and something in Sandy's eyes clicked, like the shutter of a camera. Then he switched the conversation to my job in Osia Theola, and the tension evaporated, and we talked comfortably. Zachary flattered Rhea without being obvious, and was politely deferential to Sandy. He shook hands with them as we parted, kissed me on the cheek, and said, "Be seeing you, Pol," and left us.

Sandy laughed slightly. "Your young man doesn't suffer for lack of funds."

Rhea spoke gently. "You can't blame him for his father."

"True. I'm glad you had a good time with him, Polly."

Sandy had rented a car big enough for the three of us and our luggage. As I left my room and my balcony I felt a sudden pang of homesickness for this place where I had been for only a few days.

Sandy came to my room to see if I needed anything. "Set?"

"I think so. The flowers are pretty well wilted, but I've put the rest of the fruit in a plastic bag—I thought we might want it while we're driving."

"Good thought." He sat down on the sofa. "I talked with your parents last night." Sandy and Dennys must have astronomical phone bills, but still I was surprised. "Everyone's fine, and I gave them a good report on you. They haven't heard from you yet, it's too soon."

"I've written every day, at least a postcard."

"They're aware that mail takes at least a week or ten days. Should I have phoned when you could talk with them?"

I shook my head, slowly.

"And I talked with Ursula and Max. We could call again, if you like, so you could talk."

I shook my head again, bent to pick up my shoulder bag.

"Max is weaker, Urs says, and in a good bit of pain." It was more a question than a statement.

I slung the bag over my shoulder. We'd had all the big conversations on Benne Seed. I had nothing to add.

Sandy went to the door. "Someone will be up for your bag in a moment. We'll meet you in the lobby." His voice was even, not condemning, not judging.

"Okay." I sat down to wait. I didn't want to leave. I wanted to be going somewhere with Zachary. I'd been devastated when Sandy and Rhea were not at the airport to meet me. Now I'd be delighted if they were delayed for another week.

A knock on my door. Time to go.

Rhea insisted that I sit in front with Sandy since she was so familiar with the countryside. I told them what Zachary and I had done, where we'd gone, and they approved.

"He wasn't very thorough. One hour in the museum. And I'll have to go back to Delphi, and Osias Lukas. It's all so overwhelming—there's far more than I can manage to see in a week."

"And you don't want to get saturated," Sandy said. "Just a

sip here, a taste there, and you'll know what you want to drink of more deeply the next time. And there'll be a next time, Polly, maybe not for the next few years, but you have travel in your blood, and Greece will draw you back. Now, my loves, my plan for today is this. We'll stop in Corinth for lunch and a little sightseeing, and go on to Nauplion for the night. Then tomorrow we'll push on to Epidaurus. We'll spend a good part of the day there, and then we'll have to head back to Athens to get you on your plane to Cyprus."

"We'll stick to a fairly easy pace," Rhea added. "Sandy and I are in the mood to putter along, enjoy things without pressure. All right?"

"Fine. Absolutely anything's fine. Charleston is the farthest I've been from Benne Seed in years, and I've missed Europe."

Rhea leaned over the seat. "Have you read Robinson Jeffers's play about Medea?"

"Max had me read it, along with a lot of Aeschylus and Sophocles."

"How did you get along with all that classicism?"

"With Max's help, pretty well." I didn't want to talk about Max, but with Rhea and Sandy it was impossible not to.

Sandy and Rhea were much more thorough sightseers than Zachary. "If we want to plummet Polly back thousands of years," Sandy said, "Mycenae's the place."

It was. As we drove steadily uphill, the sky clouded over, and as we approached Mycenae, the wild grey of the sky seemed to go with the stark and ancient magnificence. Max had shown me her sketchbooks of Greece, but they hadn't prepared me for the reality. She'd taken me through a good bit of Sophocles, some of which I thought was absolutely fantastic and some of which was boring, and I knew that the Acropolis of Mycenae was the setting for his plays.

We parked the car and walked through the stone gates at the top of the mountain. Sandy grasped my arm. "Do you realize, Pol, that these are the gates through which Agamemnon and Orestes walked? Come on, I'll show you the place which is thought to be where Clytemnestra murdered Agamemnon in his bath. You'll read Sophocles differently after this."

I reached for his hand. "Why are human beings so violent?"

"We can be tender, too," he said, "and we can laugh at ourselves. Didn't Max give you any comedies to read?"

"I think we just didn't get to them."

"Perhaps she thought they were too bawdy?" Rhea suggested.

Sandy laughed. "I doubt that. Max is committed to opening Polly's eyes."

But Max's plans for the education of Polyhymnia O'Keefe had been interrupted before we got to the comedies.

In the xenia in Nauplion, Sandy and Rhea had a large corner room, facing the Bay of Argos. From their balcony we could see a Venetian fortress. My room, next to theirs, overlooked the water, and the sound of wind and waves was the sound of home, but wilder, because here the sea beat against rock, not sand. But it was still the familiar music of waves, and I slept.

I was in a small boat in the wide stretch of water between Cowpertown and Benne Seed Island. The waves were high and the boat was rocking, but I wasn't afraid. I held a baby in my arms, a tiny little rosy thing, but it wasn't Rosy, or any of my younger siblings. It had no clothes on, and I held it close to keep it warm. Above us a seagull flew.

And then something seemed to be hitting at the wooden sides of the boat, and I looked over to see what it was—

—And Sandy was knocking on my door in the xenia in Nauplion and calling, "Wake up, sleepyhead. Come and have breakfast with Rhea and me on our balcony."

"Be right there," I called.

But I dressed slowly, still partly in the dream, which had been strangely beautiful. Bending down to fasten my sandal strap, I remembered, with somewhat the same windswept clarity as in the dream, that last evening with Max, when we sat drinking lemonade before dinner and she had talked about her baby again. Her little girl had been born in the same month that I had, and just the day before, though a lot of years earlier. Max's voice as she said this was cool and calm, with the barest hint of sadness. Birds were chirping sleepily in the oaks, and the rolling of the breakers was hushed. The air was heavy with humidity, and heat lightning flickered around us. But Max seemed relaxed, and the pain lines which were permanently etched in her forehead seemed less deep than usual, and her grey eyes were not shadowed.

She put her hand gently over mine as she said that sometimes when one gives something up completely, as she'd given up the thought of ever having another child, then God gives one another chance, and God had done that for her, in me.

And she said that, said God.

So that was what the dream was about, I thought, and perhaps it had come to me because I went to sleep with the sound of the sea in my ears. But why was I holding the baby?

'Dreams are messages,' Max said. 'But don't get faddy about them. Take them seriously, but not earnestly. It can be a form of self-indulgence if you overdo it.' Nettie came and refilled our glasses. I think Nettie was always delighted when Ursula was away, but Nettie also loved Max, and knew that Max needed Ursula.

When Nettie had withdrawn to the kitchen quarters, Max said, 'Don't be sorry for me, Polly. I've had a good life. I'm not a great painter, but I'm a good one, and I've had more than my fair share of success. I have few regrets. Not many people can say that.' We were silent for a while, listening to the evening sounds around us. A tiny lizard skittered up the screen. Summer insects were making their double-bass rumblings. 'There isn't anything that happens that can't teach us something,' she said, 'that can't be turned into something positive. One can't undo what's been done, but one can use it creatively.' She looked at me and her eyes were sea-silver. 'I'm glad I had the experience of having a baby. I wouldn't undo it, have it not have happened. The only thing is to accept, and let the scar heal. Scar tissue is the strongest tissue in the body. Did you know that?'

'No.'

'So I shouldn't be surprised if it's the strongest part of the soul.'

Perhaps, when the ice thawed, the scars on my soul would heal.

But had Max's? Once again I thought of the portrait of her

father, of the smile on his face which gave me chills. Did healed scars ever break open again? Get adhesions? Could one get adhesions on the soul?

I fastened the second sandal strap and went to join Sandy and Rhea on their balcony, where wind from the sea blew the white tablecloth so that it flapped like a sail.

The theatre in Epidaurus was impressive all right, great stone seats built into the mountain. It must have seated tens of thousands. Rhea and I climbed to the top row to test the acoustics, and Sandy stood in the center of the stage and recited "The Walrus and the Carpenter." We'd thought we were the only people there, till a group of kids rose up from the seats and began applauding. They drifted off, and Rhea and I climbed down and took the stage. She recited a passage from *Antigone*, in Greek, which made me shiver. I didn't understand more than a few words, but the Greek rolled out in glorious syllables.

"Your turn, Polly," she said.

Uncle Sandy called down, "Do one of your speeches from *As You Like It*."

"Oh, do," Rhea urged. "We were so sorry we couldn't be there for the performance. Only one performance for all that work!"

"It was worth it," I said. "Okay, here goes." I stepped to the exact center of the stage, where the acoustics were supposed to be perfect. I chose a speech early in the play, where Rosalind is about to be banished by Celia's father, who was just about as nasty as Max's father. But Celia stands up to him, defending Rosalind. She reminds him that after he had taken the dukedom and banished Rosalind's father

> *I did not then entreat to have her stay;*
> *It was your pleasure and your own remorse.*
> *I was too young that time to value her;*
> *But now I know her: if she be a traitor,*
> *Why so am I; we still have slept together;*
> *And wheresoe'er we went, like Juno's swans,*
> *Still we went coupled and inseparable.*

Sandy and Rhea applauded, and Rhea said, "That was superb, Polly. If I'm ever in need of a defender, I'll take you."

Sandy said, "The Elizabethans understood friendship. This pusillanimous age seems afraid of it. You can have sex with someone without commitment, but not friendship. You were excellent, Pol. Have you thought of acting as a career?"

"I've thought of it. Max says I read aloud well, but I doubt if I'd have a dream of making it on Broadway. Or even at the Dock Street."

"You made friendship real again. Did any of the kids misinterpret?"

"Of course. The Mulletville girls. Miss Zeloski talked about affluence going along with intellectual deprivation. I think she was pretty upset that it was the kids with affluent backgrounds who made the nastiest cracks." I did not add that the cracks were particularly nasty because of Max, though they never actually mentioned her name.

"In a world where pleasure rules, people tend to be under-developed in every other way. Your Miss Zeloski sounds like a good teacher."

"She is," I said, "though it took me a while to realize it."

"Let's go on to the sacred precincts," Sandy suggested. "There's a lesson in compassion."

"It's a sort of B.C. Lourdes," Rhea explained, "dedicated to the god Aesculapius."

"I gave Polly a book about it." Sandy galloped down the high marble stairs as agilely as Xan.

When we got to the sacred precincts, we stopped talking. We saw dormitories for sick people, saw the special baths in which they were given healing waters. In the museum we saw ancient surgical instruments, and Sandy remarked that some of them were like those in Dennys's office.

When we left the museum he said, "They knew a lot about psychology, those old Greeks. One of their medicines for healing was comedy. The patients sat just where we were, and on the stage the best actors of the day played comedies— Euripides, and other less well known playwrights. They were exceedingly bawdy—Shakespeare would have been right at home—and exceedingly funny, and laughter does have healing qualities."

"Miss Zeloski said that Shakespeare was bawdy, but never dirty."

"True." Rhea nodded. "The Greeks were way ahead of the present world in many ways. I'm proud of my ancestry." I thought I saw Sandy give her a look, a signal. She went on, "I'm rather tired and I think I'll just sit and rest for half an hour. Then it'll be time for lunch. You two go on."

"You all right?" Sandy sounded concerned, so maybe it wasn't a signal after all.

"I take longer to get over jet lag than you do. I'm fine, and I'll be famished for lunch."

"Okay, Pol?" Sandy asked.

"Sure." We wandered along the path together. I was glad there weren't many other tourists that morning, because the ancient stones, even the air we breathed, filled me with awe.

We stood near the site of the snake pit. "You read the book on Epidaurus I gave you?" Sandy asked.

"I finished it last night."

"A patient couldn't get through the outer gates until all bitterness and self-pity and anger were gone. The belief was that healing wasn't possible until the spirit was cleansed. I think you're better, Polly, but not all the way. Am I right?"

I nodded.

"What are you holding on to? What can't you let go?"

I turned away from him.

He followed me.

"Zachary said I'd put a hard shell around myself."

"That's more perspicacious than I'd given him credit for. Hardness doesn't become you."

"I know."

"I'm not asking you to forget, Polly, because you're never going to forget. What you have to do is remember, with compassion, and forgive."

My voice trembled. "Uncle Sandy, I don't like having a piece of ice stuck in my heart. It hurts!"

"Sit here in the sun," he said, "and let it thaw. I'll be back for you in a few minutes. I'm going to see how Rhea's doing."

He was leaving me for Rhea just as Ursula had left me—

Stop it, Polyhymnia O'Keefe. That's plain self-pity, self-indulgent self-pity. None of that.

I sat where Sandy had left me, on an uncomfortable stone bench. I closed my eyes, and a vision of the dream from the night before came back to me, unbidden. I was in the boat, protecting the baby, and the seagull flew over us.

And the seagull was Max.

Ursula had called Daddy to tell him she was going to Charleston for one last consultation with Dr. Ormsby, and asked if I could go over to Beau Allaire to stay with Max. Nettie and Ovid roomed over the garage, and it was not a good idea for Max to be completely alone. Ursula would be back as early as possible on Saturday.

'Do you want to go?' Daddy asked me. We were in the lab, and it was September-hot; sometimes it seems September is the hottest month of all. Daddy wore shorts and a white T-shirt. I had on shorts, too, and a halter top, and I'd just scrubbed down the floor and cleaned my tanks.

'Max shouldn't be alone.' I looked at him. I'd talked with him about Max, and he'd treated me as an intelligent adult. I didn't want him to treat me as a child now.

He didn't. 'I've talked with Dr. Netson, and he doesn't expect any radical problem in the immediate future. But this disease is unpredictable, so if Max should show any kind of alarming symptoms, call him at once. Or call Renny. And of course, call me.'

'Okay, but you don't think there will—'

'No, Pol, I don't think so. Your mother and I are very fond of Max and Ursula, and I'm glad we can help, even a little. Max has given you a lot, in self-confidence particularly.'

Daddy was sitting in an old leather chair that was too battered, even, for our house. I perched on the sagging arm. 'Daddy, people are so complicated!'

'That hasn't just occurred to you, has it, Pol?'

'No. But Max and Ursula seem particularly complicated.'

'In a way, they are. But, you know, I prefer their kind of complication to some of the cocktail-partying, wife-swapping, promiscuous lives of some of the people in Cowpertown.'

'And Mulletville.'

'Yes. Many of them are on third or fourth marriages. Love has to be worked at, and that's not popular nowadays.'

'I'm glad you and Mother don't worry about being popular.'

'We do work at our marriage. And it's worth it.'

'And I'm glad you trust me,' I said.

'Over the years, you've proven yourself to be trustworthy.'

'I hope I'll never let you down.'

He pulled me onto his knees. 'You will,' he said gently. 'It's human nature. We all let each other down. I may be putting too much responsibility on you, in allowing you to go over to Beau Allaire to stay with a very ill woman.'

'I want to go.'

'I know you do, and I'm glad you do. Your mother and I have always given you a great deal of responsibility, and you're a very capable young woman. Just remember, call me if there's even the slightest sense of emergency.'

'All right.'

But I didn't get a chance to call.

On Friday I piloted everybody home in the boat, then packed my overnight bag. Mother was going to drive me to Beau Allaire because Daddy had some kind of meeting to go to and would need the Land-Rover.

'Just call on Saturday morning when you're ready, and I'll be over.'

'Urs said she might be able to bring me home.'

'Whichever. Just remember, it's no trouble for me.'

She dropped me outside the house, waited till Ovid opened the door, waved, and drove off.

Ovid led me through the house and onto the back verandah. The ceiling fans were whirring, but the air was oppressive.

Max held out her hands in greeting. 'Heavy electrical storms forecast, with possible damaging winds. I lost a great oak in the last storm, and I don't want to lose any more. Nettie has fixed a cold meal for us and left it in the fridge. She and Ovid feel the heat, and I told them to take the evening off. We'll leave the dishes in the sink and they'll take care of them in the morning.'

We watched Ovid retreating toward the kitchen, a slight figure in his dark pants and white coat, and cottony hair. Then I regarded Max and was grateful that the pain lines were not deep.

Ovid came back in to refill the pitcher of lemonade, then said good night to us and left. I wondered if he and Nettie knew how ill Max really was.

She took a long drink and put her glass down. 'Do you believe in the soul, Polly?' Max never hesitated to ask cosmic questions out of the blue.

'Yes.' I thought maybe she'd turn her scorn on me, but she didn't.

'So, what is it, this thing called soul?'

This scarred thing, full of adhesions. 'It's—it's your *you* and my *me*.'

'What do you mean by that?'

'It's what makes us *us*, different from anybody else in the world.'

'Like snowflakes? You have seen snow, haven't you—yes, of course you have. All those trillions of snowflakes, each one different from the other?'

'More than snowflakes. The soul isn't—ephemeral.'

'A separate entity from the body?'

I shook my head. 'I think it's part. It's the part that—well, in your painting of the harbor at Rio, it's the part which made you know what paint to use, which brush, how to make it alive.'

Max looked at the silver pitcher, sparkling with drops, as though it were a crystal ball. 'So it's us, at our highest and least self-conscious.'

'That's sort of what I mean.'

'The amazing thing is that one's soul, or whatever one calls it, is strongest when one is least aware. That's when the soul is most aware. We get in our own way, and that diminishes our souls.' She pushed up from her chair and headed toward the table, which was already set with silver and china. 'Be an angel and bring the food out to the verandah.'

We ate comfortably together. Max had a book with her and began leafing through it, looking for something. 'There's a passage our conversation reminds me of . . .'

'What?'

'In the Upanishads—a series of Sanskrit works which are part of the Veda. Here it is, Pol, listen: *In this body, in this town of Spirit, there is a little house shaped like a lotus, and in that house there is a little space. There is as much in that little space within the heart as there is in the whole world outside.* Maybe that little space is the reality of your *you* and my *me*?'

'Could I copy that?' I asked.

'Of course. I've been watching that little space within your heart enlarging all year as more and more ideas are absorbed into it. Some people close their doors and lock them so that nothing can come in, and the space cannot hold anything as long as the heart clutches in self-protection or lust or greed. But if we're not afraid, that little space can be so large that one could put a whole universe in it and still have room for more.' She stopped and her hand went up and pressed against her chest, and I could see pain dimming the silver in her eyes.

'Get me some whiskey. Quickly.'

I ran into the house and into the dining room, turning on the lights. The Waterford chandelier sparkled into bloom. I hurried to the sideboard and got the decanter of bourbon, with its silver label, turned out the light, ran back to the verandah, and poured Max a good tot.

She drank it in a gulp, so quickly that she almost choked, then sighed and put the glass down. 'It works, and quickly. I'm sorry, Pol, I don't like you to see me in pain.'

I reached across the glass top of the table and put my hand on hers. It was hot and dry. Mine was cold.

'Don't be afraid, little one. I'm all right. These episodes are bad, but they don't last.' She reached for the decanter and poured herself some more.

'You're sure I shouldn't call—'

'Polly. I'm all right. There's nothing anyone can do. Don't
fret. The pain's much better.'

I took our plates out to the kitchen, rinsed them, and left
them in the sink for Nettie and Ovid. I thought that maybe
I should try to call Daddy, and then decided that it would
make her angry. When I got back to the verandah, dark was
falling. The long evenings of summer were behind us. Night
was closing in early, though the shadows of evening still held
the humid heat of the day.

Max was leaning back in her chair, and there was just enough
light for me to see that the look of pain had eased. She took a
sip of bourbon and put her glass down. 'It leaves me tired,' she
said. 'Let's sit here for a while and watch the stars.'

I sat across from her, glancing at the unlit candles in their
hurricane globes. 'Do you want any light?'

'No. Even candle flame adds to the heat. Look, there's a
star.'

The wind was rising, but it was not a cooling wind. The
gentle whirring of the paddle fan, the slow rolling of the waves
across the sand, the chirring of locusts, were hot, summer
sounds. A seagull screamed.

'Another star,' Max said. 'All the galaxies, the billions of galaxies—the possibility of billions of island universes—floating
like bubbles in a great spacious sea—'

'There's the Big Dipper,' I said, relaxing a little.

'The Great Bear,' Max said. 'I talk about the unimportance
of size, the microcosm as immense as the macrocosm—but
then I think of Beau Allaire sitting on a small island on an
insignificant planet—how can God keep track of it all? Do you
think God really does count the hairs of our heads?'

'Yes.'

'Why?'

'I don't know why. It's just what I think.'

'At least you don't give me glib answers. If human beings can
program computers to count astronomical figures, why should
God do less? If there isn't a God who cares about our living and
dying, then it's all an echoing joke. I don't want my life to be

a bad joke, so I have to believe that God does care. That there is a someone who began everything, and who loves and cares.' She shivered. 'Funny, how intense heat can make one break out in gooseflesh, just like cold. Let's go up to my room. It's cooler there. Why don't you get ready for bed, and I will, too.'

We paused on the landing, as always, to look at the statue of the Laughing Christ. The light touched the joyous face, and there was compassion in the eyes.

While I was changing in the green guest room, thunder began to rumble in the distance. The air was so thick with humidity you could squeeze it. The sky flickered faintly with electricity.

Max's nightgown was ivory satin, so lovely it could have been worn as an evening dress. She sat on the white rug, her hands about her knees. A Chinese screen was in front of the fireplace, gold background with flowers and herons painted on it.

'You've grown over the summer,' Max said. 'You're going to be tall.'

My old seersucker nightgown was too short. 'Not too tall, I hope.'

'You come from a tall family, and you carry it well. Don't ever slump. That just makes one look taller. Hold your head high, like royalty.'

The light from one of the lamps glinted off the decanter of bourbon and onto Max's glass, half full of amber liquid. I hoped that she knew how much she should drink. Then I noticed a bottle of champagne. 'I really don't need anything,' I said awkwardly. 'There's more lemonade if I get thirsty.'

'I've already uncorked the champagne,' Max said. 'Hold out your glass.'

I picked up the tall fluted glass which was on the hearth in front of the Chinese screen, held it out, and she poured. I thought her hand was a little unsteady, and I was concerned.

Why should I worry about that decanter of bourbon, or that maybe Max was drinking too much? If she was dying and it eased the pain, what difference did it make?

But it did. It did make a difference. This was not the Max I knew, the Max who made me believe there were wide worlds open for Polyhymnia O'Keefe.

Thunder again. Low. Menacing.

'To you,' Max said, her voice slurring. 'To all that you can be.' Some of her whiskey spilled on the rug.

I wanted to throw it at the Chinese screen. This could not be Max, this woman with her hand clutching the decanter of bourbon.

She poured herself more. Her eyes were too bright, her cheeks too flushed.

Lightning flashed again, brightening the flowers on the screen. 'That's too close,' Max said as the thunder rose. We could hear the wind whipping the trees. 'I'm afraid, oh, little one, I'm so afraid . . .'

Not of the thunderstorm.

'Afraid of the dark. Afraid of nothingness. Of being alone. Of not being.'

This was naked, primordial fear. I wanted to call Daddy, but what would I say? Max is drinking too much and she's afraid of dying?

Lightning again, but this time there were several seconds before the thunder. 'Are you afraid?' Max whispered.

'No. I don't mind thunderstorms as long as I'm not alone.'

A slow wave of thunder rolled over her response. 'I need an affir'—her words slurred—'an affirmation. An affirmation of being.' She picked up her glass. I glanced at the decanter and saw that it was half empty.

Oh, Max, I wailed silently, I wish you wouldn't.

She bent toward me, whispering, 'Oh, my little Polly, it's all so short—no more than the blink of an eye. Why are you afraid of Max? Why?'

Her breath was heavy with whiskey. Her words were thick. I was afraid. I didn't know what to do, how to stop her. How to make her be Max again.

In the next flash of lightning she stood up, and in the long satin gown she seemed seven feet tall, and she was swaying, so drunk she couldn't walk. And then she fell . . .

I rolled out of the way. She reached for me, and she was sobbing.

I scrambled to my feet. Ran. I heard her coming after me. I turned at the landing, rushed down the stairs, heard her unsteady feet, then a crash, and turned to see that she had knocked over the statue.

I ran on, panting, past the dining room, slipped in my bare feet on the polished floor, and almost fell. I reached out to steady myself, and my hand hit the light switch, and the crystal chandelier bloomed with light, and the light touched the smile on the face of the portrait of Max's father.

'Pa!' she screamed out, staggering toward me, carrying the statue. 'Damn you! Damn you! I'm just like you, damn you!'

I pushed open the heavy front door and burst out into the pelting rain.

I ran up the long drive, hardly realizing I had on only my nightgown. The crushed shells hurt my feet but did not slow me down. My nightgown was drenched and clung to my body. I felt a sharp pain in my foot. Rain streamed from my hair and into my eyes, so that the headlights of an approaching car were nearly on me before I saw them, and heard the shells crunching under the tires, and veered to the side of the road.

Brakes were slammed on. The car stopped. A window was opened and someone looked out. 'Polly!'

It was Ursula.

'Something told me—' She flung open the door. 'Get in, child.'

Ursula would take care of everything.

I stumbled into the car.

'Child, what happened?'

'Max is drunk—oh, Urs, she's—drunk—and I got away from her and ran. She . . . she ran after me, she knocked over the statue of the Laughing . . . and the light came on and hit the portrait of her father, and . . .' I babbled on, hardly knowing what I was saying.

'Oh, Max,' Ursula said. 'Oh, Max.' She started the car again and drove up to the house. 'Wait here, child.' She ran indoors. I heard her calling, 'Max! Max, dear, it's Urs. Where are you?' And the door slammed on her words.

TWO

IN the morning, before time to take me to the airport for my plane to Cyprus, Sandy came into my room. Once again he suggested that I might want to call the United States. "Phoning anywhere from Cyprus isn't easy." He didn't say, 'Do you want to call the family?' or 'Do you want to call Max?' and I think he was leaving all options open.

I just said, "No, thanks." And then, because I felt that I was being ungrateful and ungracious, I said, "I think it's time I cut the umbilical cord."

"From your family?" he asked. "Or from Max?"

I fumbled in my suitcase, refolding a blouse.

"I should have realized," Sandy said, "how young and vulnerable you are. You're so mature in some ways it's easy to forget how inexperienced you are in human relationships. You idolized Max, and that is always the prelude to disaster."

—I speak five languages, I thought irrelevantly, and it doesn't make any difference at all.

He put his hand over mine. "The toppling of your goddess was nothing I could have conceived of, and I do not in any way condone what happened. But it was an aberration, a terrible one, and it was nothing that had anything to do with the Max I have known for twenty years."

I shut the suitcase, clicking the latches.

"Do you know, Polly, can you guess, what it must have cost Max to call me, to tell me what happened, what she did? The fact that she could do that tells me just how much she loves you, not in any erotic way, but as her child."

I heard, and I didn't hear. I rolled up the cardigan, the Fair Isle cardigan I'd brought in case it turned chilly, and put it in the shoulder bag.

"Your parents do not know what happened, because you didn't tell them, and that speaks well."

For me? For my parents? For Max?

"I think you will be able to forgive what happened, Polly.

I'm not sure they would be able to. And they would blame themselves."

"They didn't have anything to do with it."

"I know that. But your parents wouldn't." He paused, looking at me. "Ursula says that Max has stopped drinking entirely, except for what Urs gives her for pain, and she doesn't want that but Netson has ordered it. I realize that nothing can take back what happened, what Max did. But would you want never to have known her?"

"I don't know."

"Perhaps where I hold Max most at fault is in letting you worship her. But you are a contained person, Polly, and I doubt if Max realized the extent of your adoration. Maybe you didn't, either."

I nodded, mutely.

"You're all right, Polly." He rubbed his hand over his beard. "Nearly ready?"

"Yes. Thank you, Sandy. I've loved these days with you and Rhea. Thank you."

"No thanks needed. You are very dear to us." He pulled me to him, kissed my hair. "Have you been keeping that journal for school?"

"Every day. I try to describe things, not only the ancient sites, but little things, like the men with braziers standing on the street corners in Athens selling roasted corn. That surprised me. I think of corn as being only American."

"We bring our worlds with us when we travel, we Americans." He gave me his rough, Uncle Sandy hug. "You bring the scent of ocean and camellias."

"That's nice. Thank you."

"And that young man, Zachary, who seems so taken with you, brings the smell of money and power. To the Zacharies of this world, Turkey, Pakistan, Kuwait are interchangeable. They exist only for their banks and insurance companies and megabucks. When money is your only concern, there isn't any difference between Zaire and Chicago."

"Hey," I protested, "you and Rhea don't even know Zachary.

He's just like all the other kids who hang around Constitution Square."

"With his father's corporation behind him? Don't be naïve, Polly. I'm glad you had him to escort you around till we got here. I think he was good for you in many ways, but I'm just as glad you're never going to see him again."

"Wait a minute!" I said. "You saw him just that once. I spent three days with him. He's my friend." But I remembered, too, Zachary's saying that even if he expected the world to end he'd hold on to his property. "He's complicated. Sure, he has lots of money, but there's more to him than that."

"You're willing to let Zachary Gray be complicated?"

"Of course."

"But not Max?" Sandy looked at me, a long, slow look from under those bushy blond eyebrows. I turned away from him and picked up my suitcase.

I kissed Rhea goodbye, and Sandy drove me to the airport. I was very glad he was with me. I didn't know about the airport tax of sixty drachmas, and I'd deliberately used up all my drachmas because in Cyprus I'd be using Cypriot pounds. Sandy paid the tax and then helped me get a traveler's check cashed into Cypriot money.

"Have a good time in Cyprus. Don't work too hard. Have fun."

I waved after him, and then there was a great shoving getting on the bus that whizzed across the airfield to the plane; then everybody jostled to get off, and then pushed to get up the steps to the plane—no jetway for the small plane to Larnaca. There was no attempt at queuing, and lots of people simply jammed their way into the line. A small amount of consideration was given to very old women and those with infants.

Finally I got onto the plane and into my seat, next to two Greek women. The hostess gave us landing cards to fill out, and the two women told me, with a lot of signs, that they did not know how to fill out their cards. So I did it for them. I had to put down their ages, and I was astonished to find out they were a great deal younger than they looked. The older, one of the grandmothers people made way for, was exactly Mother's age. With white hair pulled into a knot on top of her head, and wrinkles around her eyes and mouth, she looked old enough to be Mother's mother. Mother's hair is still chestnut brown, and she swims a lot, and her body is strong and supple. It was a vivid contrast.

In filling out their landing cards, I learned that they lived in England and were coming home to Cyprus for a visit. They spoke only a few words of English, and they did not know how to read or write. They beamed and nodded their thanks, and then began talking together in Greek as I filled out my own landing card.

Larnaca was a comparatively small, quiet airport, though no Greek-speaking public place is really quiet. So I was grateful indeed to see a man who looked like Nehru waiting for me. He introduced himself, told me to call him Krhis, took my suitcase, and led me to a battered old Bentley. At home it would have been snobbishly chic. Here, it was just functional.

"I'm glad your plane was a few minutes late," Krhis said. "I had a flat tire on my way in. This old wagon's not going to hold up forever. It's good to have you with us, Polly. The rest of the staff is already at the Center. Virginia Porcher and I have been here for a week, both resting and planning. And now we will all—the staff—have three days together before the delegates arrive. Did you lunch on the plane?"

"Yes. Thanks."

"Was it edible?"

"More than. There was something I thought was turkey which turned out to be smoked fish and it was really good."

He turned slightly and smiled at me. "You do not mind, then, eating the foods of the country you are in?"

I smiled back. "Not all Americans insist on hamburgers."

"Yes. Maxa told me you were a cosmopolitan young woman. Dear Maxa. How is she?"

I had a moment to think while he maneuvered the car around a donkey cart. If Max had not told Krhis anything was wrong, obviously she didn't want him to know. I said, carefully, "She hasn't been very well this winter. That's why she's been staying at Beau Allaire."

With a loud honking, a smelly bus provided another diversion as it forced Krhis over to the side of the road and roared past. He said, "Maxa tells me you have a gift for languages."

"Oh, I love languages." Now I could be freely enthusiastic. "I speak Portuguese, because we used to live in Portugal, and I speak Spanish and French and a bit of German, and Gaean, which probably won't be much use to you, but it was the language of the natives on the island off the south coast of Portugal where Daddy had his lab."

Again the slight turn, the gentle smile. "But Portuguese and Spanish will be helpful. We'll have a delegate from Angola, where many people still speak Portuguese. And another from Brazil. And two or three are from the Spanish-speaking countries of South America. However, all the delegates must have some facility with English, as it will be our common language."

He drove down a dusty road lined with tired-looking trees. It was as hot as Cowpertown in midsummer. Krhis said, "We won't see much of Larnaca today. It's on a salt lake as well as the ocean, and suffers from having the new superimposed on the old without much thought. Luxury hotels are sprouting like mushrooms."

What I saw of Larnaca looked rather barren. There were a few expensive-looking villas, a big oil refinery, and then we drove through several sizable villages, with low white houses surrounded by flowers and surmounted by dark panels for solar heating. We passed several working windmills, too. An island like Cyprus has both sun and wind, and the villages were making good use of them.

"You are the oldest of several children?" Krhis asked.

"Seven," I said. "We're old-fashioned and unfashionable."

"And you help?"

"We all do."

"But, as Max pointed out, the oldest bears the brunt of the work. She is very fond of you." He paused. "It is too bad she was not able to have children of her own."

I looked down at my hands, still summer-tan. "Yes. She—

she—" Did he know about the lost little baby? "She wanted children."

"And now she has you. That is good. I had hoped she might be able to come with you. She would love Osia Theola—and our varied and various delegates. She has a great gift with people, does she not?"

I murmured agreement.

"With Max there are no barriers of race or culture. Or age. You are her friend as well as her child."

I did not reply, but leaned back against the seat and closed my eyes.

The humid heat and the rhythm of the car eased my thoughts, and I was dozing when Krhis said, "We are here." I opened my eyes as we drove through gates of golden stone, and we were at the Conference Center.

It was much bigger than Osias Lukas, not nestled in a cup in the hill, but perched on the side of the mountain. We entered a great, dusty courtyard surrounded by a cloister. There was a two-story building, a tallish rectangle forming part of the wall to our right, with arched doors and windows with eyebrow-like carvings over them. Krhis drew up in front of it.

"Now that the village is becoming a resort, the monastery grounds are not as quiet as they used to be. Tourists come to see the church and the fountain house and tend to wander all over."

I sat up and looked around at the gracious arches of the cloister, with glimmers of sun on sea sparkling in the distance.

Krhis continued, "It is a delight to us that the village church is within the monastery grounds—see, just ahead of us, the tall bell tower? You will see weddings and funerals and baptisms. The village is still small enough so that its life goes on, as it has done for centuries, and we who come here for conferences are, as it were, tourist attractions for the villagers. We'll be a strange group, but Osia Theolians are friendly and welcoming. Ah, here comes Norine." His face lit up.

A young Chinese woman, tiny and delicate, came hurrying to greet us, shook my hand with a firm grip, insisted on getting my suitcase out of the trunk while I stood awkwardly by, towering over her.

"Norine Fong Mar, Polly O'Keefe," Krhis introduced us. "Norine is one of my colleagues in London and is associate director of this conference."

"I am from Hong Kong," Norine said, "but lately I've spent more time in England than at home. Follow me." She set off at a rapid pace.

I hoisted the shoulder bag and followed her across the dusty compound, almost having to run to keep up, despite my much longer legs. We went past the church and then veered to our left, to the center of the grounds, where there was a small octagonal stone building with open, arched sides and a domed roof.

"The fountain house," Norine said. "Very old. The only new building in the Center is the Guest House, and it is in the old style and doesn't stick out like a sore thumb." We went along a narrow path with roses blooming on either side, and the air smelled of roses and salt wind. The only roses on Benne Seed Island were at Beau Allaire, and grew there because the gardener was constantly watering and tending them.

Norine headed for a long, white building with a red-tiled roof, the blinding white of the stucco walls muted by flowering vines. Bougainvillea I recognized, and oleander; but the other flowers were new to me. It was much hotter on Cyprus than it had been in Greece, and I could feel sweat trickling down my legs. I'm used to heat; even so, it was *hot*.

Norine beckoned me imperiously, and I hurried to catch up. She opened a door leading to a long corridor. Over her shoulder she said, "Your roommate is from Zimbabwe. She's the youngest of the women delegates, and we thought you'd enjoy each other. But you'll have the room to yourself for these next few days." She spoke with a crisp English accent, more fluently than Krhis, whose words came slowly, thoughtfully. She was dressed in a denim skirt and white shirt and exuded efficiency.

She opened the next-to-last door on the left, which led into a pleasant room with twin beds, two desks with shelves for books, and two narrow chests of drawers. It was what I imagined a college dorm would be like, except for the dim bars of light on the floor, filtering through the closed shutters, which spoke of the tropics.

Norine heaved my bag onto one of the beds, then opened the shutters. The windows were already wide open, and I followed her onto a balcony which looked across terraced gardens to the Mediterranean Sea. It was different from Greece, but equally glorious.

"You like it?"

"It's absolutely lovely!"

She beamed at me, then glanced into the room. "See, you have been sent coals to Newcastle."

Not understanding, I looked into the room and saw a vase of hothouse flowers on the desk by the window. A small white envelope was clipped to one of the stems. I opened it and pulled out a card, and read: JUST SO YOU WON'T FORGET ME. ZACHARY.

I could feel myself blushing. Nobody had ever sent me flowers before; the ones at the King George had come from the management and didn't count. I put my face down to sniff them to hide my hot cheeks.

Norine laughed. "It seems that someone likes you. I may call you Polyhymnia? You will call me Norine?"

"I'd love to call you Norine, but call me Polly, please, Polly with two *l*'s."

"But Polyhymnia is a Greek name and she was one of the Muses—"

"I know, but plain Polly takes a lot less explaining."

"As you like." She sounded disappointed. "Since you are here first, you will have the choice of bed, desk, chest. You would like the window side?"

It was hardly a question. Fortunately, I *would* like the window side. "Thank you."

She looked down at the beds, which were unmade, showing mattresses with grey-and-white ticking. A bed pad, sheets, pillowcase, towel, facecloth, were in a neat pile in the center of each bed. "It will be very helpful, Polly, if you will make the beds. Most of the delegates will have been traveling for many hours and will be very tired."

I can't say that making beds is my favorite job in the world, but I'm certainly used to it. I've done it often enough at home, particularly before the little kids were old enough to do their own. "Of course, I'll be glad to," I said.

Norine handed me a key on a leather thong. "This is the master key. We keep the rooms locked, because sometimes the tourists come snooping around, not realizing that this is a dormitory. They are not dangerous, only a nuisance, particularly those who go in for topless bathing. It upsets the villagers." I nodded. "If you are tired, don't try to make all the beds this afternoon. Just a few. You can finish tomorrow, or the next day. We are sorry it is so unseasonably hot. This heat wave began today. We hope it will break before the delegates arrive." She pulled open a desk drawer, and there was a box of matches and a mosquito coil. Norine started to explain, but I told her that I knew all about mosquito coils. Even with screens everywhere, the little kids are constantly running in and out, so we have to use mosquito coils a lot.

"Okeydokey, that is good. You can help me explain them to the delegates. This heat has brought the insects out, the night ones especially. Even with the coil, you will have to pull the shutters to at night." She snapped on a fan that was on the inner desk. "It helps a little. When you are in your room, you can leave the door open for cross-drafts. Now I go for my siesta. The staff will have a meeting at five o'clock this afternoon, before the evening meal. I will come for you to show you the way."

"Thank you."

As briskly as she had come in, she left, and I could hear her clip-clopping along the tile floor of the long corridor.

I moved back to the desk with the bouquet of flowers from a florist. Even if Norine was right, and sending flowers to a flower-filled place like Osia Theola was coals to Newcastle, I was thrilled with them. I checked to see that they had enough water, and moved the vase so that they would not get the direct heat of the sun. Then I looked around the room. There was an open closet near the entrance, and on the shelf above it were grey wool blankets. I doubted that we'd need them, unless the weather changed radically. There were four wire hangers on the rod, and I was glad Max had told me to bring hangers of my own. 'You'll have plenty at the King George, but not in Osia Theola unless I'm very much mistaken.'

The sun was streaming into the room from the balcony, which ran the length of the building, with high, stucco dividers between each room for privacy. There were two folding canvas chairs leaning against the wall, and I opened one and stretched out. I looked appreciatively at the view, across terraces planted with vegetables and vines, and windmills turning in the breeze; and then my gaze traveled on to the sparkling of the sea below. It was too hot to stay out in the sun for long, so I went back into the room, sniffed the fragrance of Zachary's flowers, and then unpacked, putting my notebook on the desk nearest the window; my books on the shelf; my underclothes in one of the chests of drawers; hanging my clothes in my half of the closet, leaving the four wire hangers for my roommate from Zimbabwe.

Once I was completely unpacked, I made up the two beds in my room. Then I took the master key and went into the hall, and opened the door of the room next to mine. It was stiflingly hot. I opened the windows while I made the beds. By the time I had done that room, and two others down the hall, I was dripping with sweat. I decided that in this heat four rooms, eight beds, were enough for a while. I felt suddenly very lonely, and at the same time I was grateful that I was going to have these first few days in the room by myself. I've never had a roommate. Mother says there are so many of us it's important that we each have our own room, even if it's no more than a cubicle.

I opened my notebook and started to describe the room and the view, to paint in words the Conference Center of sun-gilded stone and ancient buildings. Since the notebook was for school, I didn't mention Zachary's flowers.

I wrote about Krhis, Kumar Krhishna Ghose, with his gentle tan face with the long lines moving down from his eyes, and the smile that belied the sadness. Why wouldn't he be sad? seeing his family shot and killed. He hadn't pushed me to talk on the drive from Larnaca, and the silences between us had been good silences.

I described Norine Fong Mar, from Hong Kong, tiny and bossy. Krhis wasn't bossy at all, so perhaps he needed an assistant who was. Krhis was quiet; there was no static. Norine had considerable static. She was not calm inside, like Krhis. I wasn't, either.

Miss Zeloski, I thought, was going to enjoy my notebook. And if it hadn't been for Max, Miss Zeloski and I would never have become friends.

I shut the notebook. I was as hot as though I were at home. My fingers were making smudges on the paper. I went back to the balcony. There were no screens, just the long windows and the wooden shutters. I pulled the deck chair into the shade of the divider and stretched out. The light breeze from the sea, and the moving air from the fan in the room, met and blew across me. I slid into sleep.

The breeze from the Mediterranean blew over me, blew through the window of the car in which I was sitting. No. Not the Mediterranean breeze, but a stronger wind from the Atlantic, spattering me with raindrops as I sat huddled in Ursula Heschel's car, parked outside Beau Allaire. I sat there in the humid hothouse of the car and waited. What else could I do? It was still pouring, although the electrical storm had passed over. I couldn't walk very far—I noticed blood and saw that I'd cut my foot on a broken shell, a deep, ragged gash. All I had on was a too-small, very wet nightgown.

I felt tired as though I had been running for hours. A wave of sleep washed over me, and I gave in to it, as into death.

Ursula woke me. 'Polly. Child. You'd better come in.'
I didn't want to wake up.
'Polly. Come.'
'I want to go home.'
'No,' Ursula said.

'Please. I want to go home.'

'I can't take you this way. Your nightgown is soaked. Your parents are expecting you to spend the night here.'

'No.'

'Polly, child, I know that you are shocked and horrified by what happened. I am, too.'

I couldn't hear Ursula's shock, or any but my own. 'Please take me home.'

Ursula got in the driver's side of the car and sat beside me but did not touch me. 'Child, I'm sorrier than I can say for what Max—'

A funny little mewling noise came out of me, but no words.

'Poor child. Poor little one.' Ursula lifted one hand as though to pet me, then drew back. 'It wasn't Max doing any of—of what she did. It was pain and alcohol and fear . . .' I didn't answer, and there was a long silence. Finally Ursula spoke in a low voice. 'Max, unlike the true alcoholic, will not sleep it off and forget what happened. She will remember everything. I wish she *could* forget. I wish you could.'

I looked at her.

'Come.' Ursula spoke with her authoritarian doctor's voice. I followed her in. I didn't see Max.

'What's wrong with your foot?'

I looked down, and there was blood on the soft green of the Chinese rug. 'I cut it, on a shell, I think.'

Ursula took me into the kitchen, washed my foot, and bandaged it. Warmed some milk. I took a sip and nearly threw up.

'I'm going to give you a mild sedative,' she said.

'No—Daddy—'

'I agree with your father. I do not use a sedative unless I consider it absolutely necessary. You *must* get some sleep.'

I don't remember how we got from the kitchen to the green guest room. It was as though fog had rolled in from the ocean and obliterated everything.

'I've brought you a nightgown,' Ursula said, and helped me into it, much simpler than Max's satin one, but more elegant than my old seersucker.

Did she kiss me good night? I don't think she touched me.

The sedative must have been working. Everything was blurred. I thought I heard someone crying, but I wasn't sure whether the sound came from me or from Max.

I closed my eyes.

Saw Max running after me with the Laughing Christ cradled like a baby in her arms, saw the statue fall, crashing, down an endless flight of stairs—

My scream woke me.

A woman came hurrying toward me from the path which ran just below the balconies. "Hoy! What's wrong?"

I looked at her in confusion as she jumped up onto the balcony. "I think I had a nightmare."

"This heat is enough to give you one. You're Polly O'Keefe, aren't you? I'm Virginia Porcher." She pronounced it the French way, Por-shay.

"Oh—Mrs. Porcher—I love your writing—"

"Not Mrs. Porcher. Virginia. Or Vee, as most people call me. We're all on a first-name basis here. You'll understand why when you hear the last names of some of the delegates—they make me understand why most people pronounce my last name as though it were the back porch. Simplify, simplify. And I understand you prefer being called Polly to Polyhymnia?"

I smiled at her. "Wouldn't you?"

"I think you could probably carry Polyhymnia, but I sympathize. Polly. Krhis tells me you'll be helping me with the writing workshop, among your many other chores."

"Yes, anything I can do to help, anything at all."

"I expect there'll be a good deal. I hope this heat breaks. It's not at all seasonable. It's usually pleasantly warm during the day, and cool at night, by late September. Weather all over the world seems to be changing drastically. Why don't you come along to my room? Since I'm a workshop leader, I have the privilege of a room to myself. Krhis will have a folder for you at the staff meeting, but I thought you might like a preview of the schedule." She was chatting away, giving me time to wake up, to move out of the horror of the nightmare.

Virginia Bowen Porcher, one of my favorite writers, who

wrote novels about people who were flawed but with whom you could identify, dealing with all aspects of the human being, the dark as well as the light, but never leaving you in a pit of despair. And in the simplest possible words and images she wrote poems which seemed almost light on the surface, and then, when you backed away from them, the fact that they were neither light nor simple kicked you in the teeth. Max compared Porcher's work to Mozart. When I told Miss Zeloski that Virginia Porcher was leading a workshop, that in itself was enough to get Miss Zeloski to urge the principal to let me take the month away from school.

And here Virginia Porcher was asking me to call her by her first name, and looking—well! Now that I had recovered enough from the nightmare to look at her, I saw that she had red hair. Not blatantly red like mine; it was much more subtle. But still, it was red. She had green eyes, really green, as my eyes are really blue. She wore a full cotton skirt with a tiny millefiori print, and a peasant blouse.

Meeting one of your favorite writers in the world can be scary. It's so easy to be let down. But I felt elated. I liked her, liked her as well as admired her. And she had red hair.

Her room was almost identical to mine. One of the twin beds was covered with books and papers. "My filing system." She picked up a blue folder, opened it, and handed it to me, and I looked at the typed schedule. Three workshops in the morning, with an hour before lunch for swimming. An hour for lunch, an hour for rest, and three more workshops in the afternoon. The evening meal. An evening program. A full schedule, indeed. The writing workshop was the first one of the day, at nine in the morning.

"This weather knocks out swimming at noon." Virginia Porcher sat on her bed, indicating the desk chair for me. "It's a twenty-minute walk to the sea, and it's much too hot under the broiling noonday sun. I've been taking my swim at bedtime, but Krhis won't be able to come with me now that the staff is all here. He'll have his hands full. This is a glorious place for a conference, isn't it?"

I nodded, looking around the room. On one of the desks was a picture of a man with dark hair and a kind, sensitive face. He must be her husband. He looked like the right kind of person to be married to one of my favorite writers.

"My sister-in-law, who's holding the fort at home, asked, 'Why Cyprus?' and I told her it's more or less a mean point geographically for the delegates. But, also, if the conference were being held in—say, Detroit—I wouldn't have accepted the invitation to lead a workshop. Krhis says you've had a week in and around Athens?"

"Yes. The *Iliad* and the *Odyssey*—all the Greek myths—everything means much more to me than it did. I'm overawed."

"That's a good reaction. So am I. No matter how many times I come to Greece or the islands, I'm swept out of the limited world of technocracy and into the wildness of gods and goddesses and centaurs and nymphs. We'll have a full moon this weekend and you'll understand anew why the moon has so often been an object of worship. The moon goddess, beneficent while she is waxing, harsh while she is waning. Astarte fascinates me. She was a Syrian goddess, but her worship spread to Greece. Aphrodite is, I guess, her Greek counterpart, though she isn't as much associated with the moon. So. How is Ursula Heschel?"

That startled me. "Fine, I guess. You know her?"

"I'm one of her more remarkable miracles. I had an aneurism which would have been inoperable before microsurgery, and even with all science now knows, it was a risky business. It was a long surgical procedure, and a very long recovery, and Ursula and I became friends. And then, of course, I met Max. And through Urs and Max I met Krhis Ghose when he was in New York. A conference like this tends to be very small-worldy. You're here because of Max, aren't you?"

"Yes." Beneficent while waxing, harsh while waning.

"How old are you?"

"Nearly seventeen. I'm a slow developer."

Virginia Porcher stretched out long, suntanned legs, wriggling her toes under the sandal straps. "I was, too. Still am.

Some people say that we slow developers end up going further than the quick-flowering ones."

I nodded. I hoped she was right.

"Are you interested in writing?"

"I don't think so. I enjoy it, but I'm not passionate about it. I like acting, really a lot, but I know it's an awfully chancy field. What I'm best at is languages, but I don't want to be a teacher, and I don't think I want to be a simultaneous translator at the UN because I'm an island girl."

"Manhattan's an island."

"Oh. I guess I mean small islands with low-density population."

She laughed, a nice, warm laugh, not at all *at* me. "You still have time. Sometimes it's not an advantage to have too many talents." She reached down to scratch a bite on her leg. "Watch out for the bugs here. They're not bad during the day, but they're monstrous at night, and they love American blood."

"I'm pretty used to bugs," I said. "Benne Seed Island's off South Carolina—so I'm used to heat, too."

"You'll find"—she nodded—"when the delegates arrive that you'll be spending these next weeks with people who have experienced a great deal of life under conditions where personal freedom as we know it is hardly even a dream. When I fuss because the bathwater here is tepid, it chastens me when I remember that some of the delegates don't even have indoor plumbing. This dormitory building is going to seem wildly luxurious to most of them." She stood up. "I've got work to do now before we meet at five. By the way, a word of warning." I paused by the door. "The tap water here is quite saline, and you won't be able to drink much of it. And this heat that clamped down on us today isn't supposed to let up for a while. There's a little shop outside the monastery gates and up the hill where you can buy sodas. And if you have any other questions, trivial or cosmic, don't hesitate to ask me."

"Thanks," I said, still feeling too shy about calling Virginia Bowen Porcher by her first name to call her anything. "Thanks a lot."

I took the master key and made up the beds in three more

rooms. Even though I opened the windows, I was still streaming with sweat, so I went back to my room and sat at the desk
to record meeting Virginia Bowen Porcher in my journal for
Miss Zeloski.

For Miss Zeloski? Max. Even though Max would never read it,
the journal was also for Max.

Because of Max's insight into someone she'd never even met,
I was able to see Miss Zeloski as someone who hadn't had many
breaks in life, someone who'd wanted a family, and children,
and instead lived alone. Or, as I found out when Max prodded
me, not alone but with an elderly father she supported and
cared for. She was intelligent, and she'd probably have been
a good college English teacher, but here she was, stuck in
Cowpertown because of her father, teaching a lot of kids who
weren't particularly interested in all she had to give. I hadn't
been, until Max opened my eyes. I'd been as bad as the rest.

Here, in Osia Theola, I was on my own, making up my
own mind about the people I was meeting, and learning that
making up my own mind, just me, Polly, wasn't even possible.
As I tried to describe Virginia Porcher to Miss Zeloski, I was
seeing not only through my own eyes but through Max's, and
through Miss Zeloski's. And that was all right, too, because it
gave an added dimension to what I was writing.

Left completely to myself, how much would I have noticed
beyond the fact that Virginia Porcher had red hair? Would I
have seen the kindness with which she drew me out of the
nightmare?

But I didn't write about the nightmare, the Laughing Christ
falling, falling.

I described the papers on Virginia Porcher's bed, and the
small typewriter on the desk, with a pile of manuscripts beside
it. I wished I'd dared ask her if she was working on a new novel.

I told Miss Zeloski she probably was, and that what struck
me most was how natural she was, not a bit a prima donna, but
as simple as her own work. As deceptively simple?

Norine Fong Mar called for me a little before five, as promised. "Okeydokey, time to go." She wore, now, a long yellow cotton print dress with a Chinese collar, the skirt slit, with braid at the sides, and looked far more exotic than when I had first met her.

The meeting was in the golden stone building by the monastery gates. We gathered in a sizable room on the second floor, where Krhis was already sitting by a table, with Virginia Porcher next to him. She smiled at me and patted the chair by hers.

"Vee tells me the two of you had a good talk," Krhis said.

"Yes. She showed me the schedule and helped fill me in." She had done far more than that, but I was embarrassed to say, "She was wonderful." Could I let her be wonderful, and human, too?

"Good." On the table by him was a pile of blue folders, and Norine handed me one.

"Here you are. One of our delegates is already here, Omio Heno from Baki. There are only two days a week when he can fly out, so he will be with us this weekend."

"I'm not sure where Baki is," I said.

Krhis answered, "It's one of those numerous islands north of Australia. It used to belong to Australia, and there are still many Britishers there in supervisory positions. Omio is in his mid-twenties, and very talented."

Norine added, "His English is considerably better than that of many of the delegates, and he devours books as we send them to him. He works in adult education, not an easy job, as the level of literacy is still very low on Baki."

Virginia Porcher suggested, "Perhaps the Australians wanted to keep it low. Educate them, and they'll cause trouble?"

Krhis smiled, shaking his head. "That's too facile. However, Omio got into considerable difficulty all round when he insisted that the native women be allowed to learn to read and write. He ran into walls of prejudice, but he finally got his coeducational classes. When Omio sees something as right, he won't stop till he gets it. He's quite a lad." He paused as we heard heavy footsteps, and a large, dark-skinned woman came in. Krhis and Norine rose to greet her, and she kissed them both, then came to shake hands with Virginia Porcher and me.

Krhis introduced us. "Milcah Adah Xenda is our storytelling expert. Millie, Vee is our writing-workshop leader."

The large woman—wide, rather than tall—smiled. "Yes, I know Mrs. Porcher's work." She spoke with an accent which was partly guttural, partly French. I couldn't place it. "We're lucky to have you."

"Thanks, I'm lucky to be here. And I'm Vee, please."

"At home in Cameroon, in the college where I teach, I'm called M.A.," Milcah Adah Xenda said. "Krhis calls me Millie, and I like that."

"Millie, then," Virginia Porcher said.

M.A. How ironic. I was glad we were going to call her Millie. I did not need to be reminded of Minerva Allaire.

Milcah Adah's handclasp was firm and dry, despite the heat. When she sat down, the chair creaked under her, but she exuded calm and comfort. She wore a loose cotton shift, and space shoes.

"Polly is going to help Vee in her workshop," Krhis said, "be with Norine in the office, and do all kinds of odd jobs. If you need special errands run, that's one of the things Polly is here for."

"I'm not much for running myself." Millie bathed me with her smile, which was not a quick flash but a slow spreading of appreciation.

I decided that I'd be happy to run anywhere for Milcah Adah Xenda, and that I would like to be young enough to climb in her lap. The fact that she came from Cameroon explained her accent; Cameroon used to be French. I liked her voice, which had a deep quality to it, like the night sky at home at Benne Seed when it is warm and the stars are blurred.

We heard more feet on the stairs, and two people came into the room. One was a woman, black, though a darker, more purply black than Millie, and tall, much taller than I am. She wore a loose robe of brown with a pattern in rust and black, and a turban, which made her seem even taller than she was, and she looked formidable.

Behind her came a man who surprised me simply because he looked so ordinary, like my father, or my uncles, or anybody I might meet at home. He had brownish hair with a touch of mahogany, not red, just warm, and nice eyes; they reminded me of Sandy's.

Krhis made the introductions. The immensely tall woman was Bashemath Odega and she came from Kenya. It was easy to think of Milcah Adah as Millie; but I couldn't conceive of giving Bashemath any kind of nickname.

Millie said, glancing at her folder, "You're the expert in childhood education?"

"That sounds very impressive," Bashemath said. "It's what I teach, and what I care about."

"And this is Frank Rowan," Krhis continued. "He's the publisher of a small educational press in Istanbul, and he will give the delegates hints on starting their own presses—difficult, but not impossible."

Bashemath Odega and Frank Rowan evidently knew each other, because Bashemath said, "We're running a small independent press, thanks to Frank. We're constantly on the edge of bankruptcy, but that's not Frank's fault." Her voice was deep, more guttural than Millie's.

Krhis introduced me as a colleague, not just a kid who'd been given a chance to be a gofer. Everybody was on a first-name basis, as Virginia Porcher had said, and I understood I'd have to get over my hesitancy. Would I ever feel really comfortable calling Virginia Porcher Vee? But already I felt so close to her that Mrs. or Madame Porcher sounded not only formal but unfriendly.

Krhis called the meeting to order. I liked him. I trusted him, though I tried to remind myself that trusting people is dangerous. I watched him, with his coffee-colored skin and dark, grieving eyes, but no self-pity in the lines that moved downward, and I knew that Max loved him, and that he loved Max, and that there was a lot about human relations I didn't understand, and that maybe I was going to have to move through a lot of time before I was going to be able to understand.

Millie kept wiping her face with a large handkerchief. Bashemath fanned herself regally, with an odd-looking fan of ivory and feathers. Frank Rowan kept pushing his spectacles back up his nose, a gesture which reminded me of nearsighted Renny. If it had not been for the sea breeze coming in the arched windows, the heat would have been unbearable. The walls of the room were the same sun-soaked stone that was found almost everywhere in the old part of the monastery grounds.

Krhis discussed the schedule and explained that he would like us all to be at all the workshops, to encourage and support the delegates. "Your presence is important to the morale of the group." Then he smiled and told us that it was nearly time for supper, and that there would be fresh lemonade in the cloister while we waited for the meal.

Norine whispered to me, "Wait just a minute, Polly. I'd like to take you down to the office and show you how to use the mimeo machine. Vee and Bashemath both have some things they'd like you to run off."

Krhis and Millie went out together, followed by Virginia Porcher. Bashemath turned to Frank and I heard her mutter in a dark whisper, "If Krhis throws one of his ecumenical religious services, he can count me out. I'm here for early-childhood education. Period."

I couldn't hear Frank's murmured response because Norine was buzzing, "Fresh lemonade is even more of a treat here than wine. It's not the lemons—there are plenty of those—but the bottled water which is an expensive luxury." Then she called to Frank and Bashemath, "Be careful of the steps, okeydokey? They've been worn down through the centuries, and they're slanting and slippery."

"Right-o," Frank called back, and I noticed that he was limping.

I followed Norine down the steps and into the office, which was a small room on the first floor.

"Do you know how to type?" she asked.

"I'm slow, but I can do it if I take enough time."

"Have you ever typed a stencil?" She handed me a sheet of purply, carbon-like paper.

"No. We have a photocopy machine at school."

"You Americans take for granted a lot of luxuries the rest of the world can't even contemplate. When you type a stencil you have to be careful, because you can't correct mistakes. Here's some stuff Vee would like to hand around to the delegates. You don't have to run it off now. There isn't time before dinner. Tomorrow morning, okeydokey?"

"Sure." Then I asked, "Why does Frank limp?"

"He lost a leg a few years ago. He and his wife were taking their children to the United States so they could go to high school there, and as they were driving to New York to fly back to Turkey, they were in a terrible automobile accident, and his wife was killed, and Frank lost a leg."

"How awful."

"Funny games fate plays," Norine said. "Frank's spent most of his life in the tinderbox of the Middle East, but tragedy hits him when it's least expected, in the safe United States. His children are in college now. The eldest graduates next year."

So Frank was probably a little older than my parents—but I'm not good about chronology.

Norine showed me how to work the mimeo machine, once I'd done the stencil. "How are you coming on the beds?" she asked me.

"I've done quite a few."

"The staff members have already done theirs, of course. You can tell the staff rooms because the names are on the doors." She pulled a tissue from a box on her desk and wiped her forehead. "Lemonade?"

"I'm ready," I said. I was parched. I followed her out of the hotbox of the office. Across the compound a breeze was blowing from the sea.

In the cloister a table was covered with a blue-and-white cloth. It was on the Mediterranean side of the long walkway, where open arches gave onto vistas of the village and the sea. A young man stood by a small table on which there was a large pitcher and a tray of glasses.

"I bear refreshment for your thirst on this island, which is welcoming us as warmly as my island of Baki. I am Omio

Heno." His voice was warm and rhythmic, his speech slightly overprecise. He poured me some lemonade.

Omio turned to me. "Krhis wrote me you would be here, all the way from the United States, and so young."

Don't rub it in, I thought. I took the glass he handed me. "I'm nearly seventeen." He looked very young himself. Mid-twenties, Krhis had said. Like Renny.

He smiled, showing perfect white teeth. His skin was so dark that it was a surprise when light brought out copper glints. His palms were pale pink, and so were the soles of his feet, showing a rim of pink between foot and sandal. His hair was fine and black, curling softly. He moved like a dancer, and Norine (who was to become my great source of information) told me later that one of the special pleasures I had to look forward to was Omio performing some of the traditional Bakian dances.

"And blue eyes so beautiful," he said, "like the first blue of sky after sunrise on a fine day."

I could feel the telltale blush. I had been given more cause to blush since I flew to Athens than in all the time on Benne Seed Island and at Cowpertown High. "Thank you." And then, "How long did it take you to get here?"

His smile widened into even more brightness. It was the kind of smile some people might have used to show off, but with Omio it seemed pure, spontaneous delight. Now he burst into a laugh and pointed at his wristwatch. "Time got changed on me so many times, lo back, lo forth, I don't know how long it has taken. A jeep, a bus, a train, four planes, two buses, and here I am."

I smiled back. "You speak very good English."

"I spent a year in London working with Krhis. I was given a scholarship and lo, I learned more than in the rest of my life, though we have many English-speaking people on Baki, more, almost, than Bakians. I learned also in London that I do not like English weather and that Baki is my home, and although we Bakians are thought of as primitive, we also have old wisdom. I work hard to teach people to read, to write, and most importantly to think, so that we will know how to hold on to the old wisdom, and not let it degenerate into superstition.

I am writing down the stories of my people, how the world began and is held up on the spout of a great whale."

"I'd love to see what you've written."

His smile shone again. "One day, then, I will show you." (When we know each other a little better, I thought the 'one day' meant.)

Krhis called us to the table and we stood around it holding hands the way we do at home. Holding hands around the table is the best way to keep the little kids quiet, but there's more to it than that, and I liked holding Virginia Porcher's hand on my right, Omio's on my left.

Krhis suggested, "*Saranam?*"

I did not know what he meant, and evidently neither did Virginia Porcher, but the others lifted up their voices to sing in beautiful harmony.

> *Receive our thanks for night and day,*
> *For food and shelter, rest and play,*
> *Be here our guest, and with us stay,*
> *Saranam, saranam, saranam.*

It was beautiful. Two Cypriote women standing in the background beamed and nodded appreciation.

We pulled out our chairs and sat down. There was a big pitcher of water on the table, and another of red wine. Krhis poured some of the wine into his glass, then filled it with water. "I'm afraid the wine is rather rough, and the water is salty. Mixed together, they are quite potable." He took out a large white handkerchief and patted his brow, although he did not look hot. "This is an unusual heat wave. And I have become acclimated to England."

Omio smiled at him. "In England I froze, lo, into the very marrow. This is like home."

Norine passed around a basket of bread. "You may find this a little sour, but it is baked fresh every day and is very good. They do not serve butter except at breakfast, okeydokey?" She indicated two small dishes. "This spread is made from olives, and this from cucumber. Very good on the bread." She nodded at me, and I helped myself and passed the dishes to Virginia Porcher. Vee. I would have to start thinking of her as Vee.

A platter of what looked like onion rings was passed around. "It is octopus," Norine explained. "It is a little rubbery, but quite tasty."

One of the Cypriote women passed the platter to Virginia— Vee—who helped herself. "*Epharisto*, Tullia."

Fortunately I'd eaten octopus before, though not at home. I watched Millie take a tentative taste and try not to make a grimace. Frank Rowan, living in Istanbul, was obviously used to it, and helped himself lavishly.

Bashemath took a middle-sized helping and looked gravely at me. Why should eating octopus be worse than eating shrimp or any other kind of fish? As I ate mine, I thought of Ursula and Daddy and Dennys, and their mutual interest in the octopus because of its nervous system.

The sour bread was good, and so was the bowl of salad Tullia brought us. I drank half a glass of mixed wine and water. For dessert we had fruit.

"This is simple, typical Cypriote fare," Krhis said, "but to me it is enjoyable."

After Tullia and her younger helper ("Her name is So-phonisba," Virginia Porcher whispered to me) had cleared the table, refusing to let us help, Krhis suggested that we stay out in the cloister to catch the breezes. "And we should teach Vee and Polly some of our songs. We will do a lot of singing together, and many of the delegates will look to you to help them with songs they are not familiar with."

"*Saranam*," Omio said, and turned his smile on me. "It is an Indian song Krhis brought to us, but we have made many of our own verses."

"Sing a verse through for us," Krhis suggested.

With no self-consciousness Omio lifted up his voice.

> *For this small earth of sea and land,*
> *For this small space on which we stand,*
> *For those we touch with heart and hand,*
>   *Saranam, saranam, saranam.*

He sang it until we all had memorized the words and the melody, and then dropped his voice to a rich bass accompaniment. Millie lifted hers in a descant. It was piercingly, painfully beautiful.

Almost too beautiful. I ached with unshed tears. Bashemath said suddenly, "Here's one we all know, and it will be good for all of us to hear it in the various languages of the delegates." I wasn't quite sure what I expected, but I was totally surprised when in her smoky voice she sang *Silent Night* in Masai. She sounded both tender and formidable. When she had finished, she bowed to Frank Rowan.

"I'll sing it in Turkish," Frank said. Although the words were foreign, he still sounded very American. Then he bowed to Norine. The familiar words sounded strange in Chinese, pitched rather higher than we were accustomed to, and with a gentleness I had not felt before in Norine.

Then came Omio, with his voice like black velvet, the Bakian words coming out softly, like an ancient lullaby. It was amazing how different the same song could sound. I'd been bored with *Silent Night* from overexposure, so that I could no longer even hear it, and suddenly, in this hot late September night in a cloister in Osia Theola, with the breeze barely stirring, it was alive and new.

I listened to Omio sing and felt tears come to my eyes, and looked at Vee and she was blowing her nose. I wondered what memories the familiar carol brought to her, and to the others of the staff. What was Christmas like in Kenya? Cameroon? For me, the familiar melody brought back Mother baking Christmas cookies with all of us, even the littlest ones, helping (hindering) her, and the smell of turkey and stuffing, and childhood, when my parents were Olympian and their love could solve all problems and keep us safe, and there was nothing on earth I couldn't talk to them about.

I looked around the circle of people; faces were unguarded, and when I saw Millie put her hands over her face, I turned away quickly, feeling that I was violating her privacy, and my glance fell on Frank Rowan and his eyes were bright with tears, and I turned away again, wondering if he was remembering Christmas when his children were little and his wife was alive. I looked at Norine, who sat with her hands tightly clenched in her lap, her eyes closed, no longer the efficient leader, but a woman with her own memories, her own griefs. I had not lived long enough to have learned the coming to terms with life which I felt from these people, but I thought of New Year's Eve at Beau Allaire when everything had been as shining and beautiful as the Christmas tree, and we had sung carols and played charades, and champagne was sparkling and didn't hurt anyone—but now I hurt, and I couldn't get out on the other side of that hurt.

Vee said (and was it *Silent Night* that was helping me to think of her as Vee?), "Polly, can you sing it in German?"

I nodded, and started, "*Stille nacht, heilige nacht,*" and while I was singing, there were no memories, nothing but the song for these people who were already becoming close to me.

Krhis said, when I was through, "Sing it in French, Vee. Millie, you'll use one of the native dialects?"

Millie nodded, and Vee sang in French.

When she was through, Millie lifted her voice in her clear soprano, as easily and joyously as a bird. Everybody had sung at least reasonably well; nobody flatted, or swooped, or sang nasally, but Millie's voice was extraordinary, and we were mesmerized. She sang with a complete lack of self-consciousness.

I had thought I had the tears well under control. But the pure effortlessness of Millie's singing made me choke up, and tears slipped down my cheeks. I got up quietly and went to one of the open arches and stood looking at moonlight making a wide path on the sea, then jumped down from the high sill to the sand below, walking along until I came to an ancient-looking tree shadowing the remnants of a wall. I stepped into its darkness and sobbed.

An arm came around my shoulders, and I was drawn to a lean, masculine body, smelling a musky, pungent smell. It was Omio.

"I'm sorry—I'm sorry—" I gasped.

"It is all right. Lo, many of us have brought wounds with us, and Millie's singing opened them and brought healing tears. Do you have a handkerchief?"

Omio's presence stilled the storm of tears. I dug in my pocket and found a tattered piece of Kleenex. "I'm sorry—"

"It is all right. Norine has provided punch and macaroons, and we'd better go back before we are missed."

When we got back to the cloister, everybody was drinking punch from tiny paper cups and munching macaroons. Nobody mentioned my absence.

Krhis asked, "You like to sing, Polly? Does your family enjoy it?"

"We love it. We used to sing more when we were all littler and had less homework, but when there are nine people in a family, singing is something everybody can do."

Norine said, "You have a nice voice, Polly. While we are working in the office tomorrow, we can do some singing as well."

Vee announced that she was going for a swim, and did anybody want to come?

"Sorry," Frank said. "The walk's a bit much for my inanimate leg."

"Not tonight for me, Vee," Krhis said. "Now you will find other swimming partners. But I beg all of you, and ask you to emphasize it to the delegates, do not go alone. There are strong tides and undertows. But the water is refreshing, and the walk at night will not be too hot."

Only Omio and I wanted to go. I was used to all kinds of undertows, and I felt sticky, and the idea of a swim at night in the Mediterranean was enticing. It had grown dark while we were singing, the sudden, subtropical dark I was used to on Benne Seed. Vee said, "Krhis is right that we should stick together. Polly and I live next door to each other, at the far end of the dormitory building. Let's meet just outside, at the laundry umbrella, and I'll show you the way."

Omio told us that he was on the second floor, and he'd be ready in two minutes.

"Make it ten," Vee said.

It didn't take me more than a couple of minutes to get into my suit, so I went out the back door of the building and walked toward the laundry umbrella, which was like an empty tree, with one pair of bathing trunks (probably Krhis's) hanging like a single leaf. When everybody arrived, it would fill up.

As I stepped toward it, my foot slid out of my thong and I stepped on a pebble. A sudden pain shot up my leg.

Just as the sharpness of a broken shell sliced into my foot, as I was running away from Beau Allaire.

I did not see Max in the morning after Ursula bound my cut foot and made me spend the night at Beau Allaire. I woke around five, dressed, and slipped out of the house. But I no longer wanted to go home.

It was cool, before the sun was up; little webs of dew sparkled on the grass, which was kept green by constant sprinkling. I walked slowly down the drive because my cut foot hurt, and because the crushed shells crunched noisily. Ursula, I knew, got up early, so I walked carefully, as though that would keep her from looking out a window and seeing me. I was fleetingly grateful that her window, like Max's, faced the ocean, and not the front of the house with the gardens and the long curving drive. And even if Nettie and Ovid were already in the kitchen, that, too, faced the water.

The drive wound around until the house was no longer visible. It seemed miles until I got to the road with its smoother surface. I turned and headed toward Mulletville and the causeway. How was I ever going to make it with my cut foot? Periodically I stopped and sat at the side of the road until I had the energy to move on. I did not want anybody in Mulletville to see me, but only the fishermen would be up, and they wouldn't care. The development people would all still be in bed.

I heard a car behind me and stepped to the side of the road. The car slowed down and someone called out, 'Hey, hon, want a ride? Look as if you could use one.'

It was a boy from Mulletville who went to Cowpertown High, called Straw because of his sun-bleached hair and his stubby, almost-white lashes. He went with a rough crowd, kids who smoked and drank a lot. Why on earth was he up and out so early? He was older than I was; I think he'd had to repeat a couple of years. I'd never had much to do with him, and didn't want to see him now, and I hoped he wouldn't recognize me. But he did.

'Hey, aren't you Kate's sister?'

'Kate's my cousin,' I said.

'So what's your name, Kate's cousin?'

'Polly.'

'Where you coming from?'

'I'm going,' I said. 'To Cowpertown.'

'Y'are?' He lit a cigarette and dangled it in the corner of his mouth.

'To the M. A. Horne Hospital. I cut my foot, and I have a friend there who's an intern. He'll fix it for me.'

'You sure looked hagged out. Hop in. I'll drive you into Cowpertown, as far as LeNoir Street, and maybe you can get another hitch from there. I have a Saturday job at Diceman's Diner, so I can't take you any further. I'll be sacked if I'm not there in time for the breakfast crowd.'

So that's why he was up. I got in beside him. I had no choice. I hoped he'd go on enjoying the sound of his own voice. He was, I was pretty sure, one of the guys who'd killed the tortoise. But I needed the ride into Cowpertown. I'd never make it on foot.

'Kate sure is pretty,' he said.

After a pause, I agreed. 'Yah.'

'You don't look like her.' He flicked ashes out the window.

'We can't all be that lucky,' I said.

He looked at me instead of the road. 'Hey, how'd you cut your foot?' He glanced down. The cut had broken open, and blood was seeping through the bandage. It probably looked a lot worse than it was.

'On a shell,' I said, 'a broken shell.'

'Why, you poor little thing.' He took his hand off the steering wheel and patted my thigh. 'Hurt much?'

'Some.' I'd just as soon he kept his hands on the wheel and his attention on the road.

'I got a good first-aid kit. Want me to fix it up for you?'

'No, thanks. My friend at the hospital will take care of it.'

His hand reached for my thigh again, rhythmically patting. I stood it as long as I could, then pulled away.

'What's the matter?' His hand came down hard, and I winced.

'I told you. My foot hurts.'

'Why don't you let me make it feel better?' He tossed his cigarette out the window.

'It's my foot that hurts, not my thigh.'

'You don't like Straw, hunh?'

I remembered his face, full of lust for killing, as he battered the tortoise. No, I didn't like him. 'I don't know you very well.'

'Well, now,' he drawled, 'maybe Kate's right after all.'

'About what?' I should have kept my mouth shut.

'You.'

If I knew one thing, it was that Kate hadn't talked to Straw about me. He'd never been one of her dates. He'd never come home with her for dinner. He wasn't her type. But he came from Mulletville, and he dated Mulletville girls. I pushed away from him as far as possible.

'So what's Kate's cousin doing at this end of the island?'

I didn't answer.

'You've been at Beau Allaire, haven't you?'

I looked down at the blood drying rustily on Ursula's bandage.

'We know all about those dames at Beau Allaire, and what they do. You've been with them. You're like the way they are, and that's why you don't like me.'

'Let me out,' I said.

He jammed on the brake, throwing me forward. 'You really want to get out?'

'Yes.'

'Don't have an attack. I'll get you to LeNoir Street.' He stepped on the gas pedal, and his hand came at me again, and I pulled away. 'What's the matter, honey? You really don't like Straw?'

What arrogance. This guy thought every girl in school was after him.

'You like dames, is that it? Can't make it with a guy?'

I shut my eyes, clamped my lips closed. He kept his foot on the gas pedal. The car rocked as he whizzed around a curve with a screech of tires. I didn't care if it turned over.

I opened my eyes as I felt the car slow down and we drove through the outskirts of Cowpertown, then onto LeNoir Street with its post office and banks and stores. Again he slammed on the brakes. 'Here we are.'

'Thanks.'

'I feel real sorry for Kate. She's a nice girl. Norm—'

I opened the door and jumped out, and the pain shot sharply from my foot through my body into my head, sending yellow flashes across my eyes.

Straw drove off with another rubber-smelling screech.

I was still a long way from M. A. Horne, which was at the farther end of LeNoir Street, a good three or four miles, too far to walk on a bleeding foot. I stumbled along, not knowing what to do, until I saw a phone booth.

I would call Renny.

I was jerked back into the present as I heard a sliding of sand and stones. Omio came leaping down from the top of the hill, wearing bathing trunks and a short terry jacket.

I couldn't stand Straw's hands on me, but I had liked Omio's arms around me as I cried under the old tree.

The door opened, and Omio greeted Vee by handing her a flashlight. "You may need it to warn drivers of our presence."

"Thanks, Omio, what a good idea. Half the drivers here are crazy and drive these windy roads as though they were the Los Angeles Freeway. And cars drive English-fashion, on the left, when they're not in the middle of the road, so we'll walk on the right."

She led us along the path which ran below the balconies of the dorm, and there was the tree I had fled to, and now that my eyes were not blinded by tears I could see how beautiful it was. "What is it?"

"A fig sycamore. I don't know how old it is, but hundreds of years. It's the most beautiful tree I've ever seen, and I keep trying to write poems about it, but thus far they elude me."

The moonlight turned trees and branches to silver. "Full moon, day after tomorrow," Omio said.

Vee started downhill. "Careful. It's rocky and rough, and we don't want any sprained ankles."

Below the monastery complex we came out on a road that ran through the lower part of the village. There were a few shops, closed for the night; what looked like a small bank; a taverna, with people sitting outside, laughing and talking. Music came from within, and light spilled out onto the road.

"Osia Theola is on its way to becoming a resort," Vee said, "since the old resort towns, like Famagusta, are now Turkish. If I were a millionaire I'd buy Osia Theola and save it from the tourists—as well as the Turks; it's anybody's guess as to who's the most destructive."

I said, recalling Max's teaching, "Poor Cyprus. It's always being taken over and ruled by somebody. The Italians were here before the Turks, and the Turks before the English, and now in the north the Turks have come again."

"That's the way of the world," Omio said. "Baki has always been prey to stronger, less peaceable peoples. Now there are more Australians and English than Bakians."

"And yet England," Vee said, "was overrun by Vikings and Normans. The Picts and Angles and indigenous inhabitants were ruthlessly wiped out. Genocide isn't new to this century."

We turned off the main village street onto a dirt road which ran past more tavernas, narrowed to a path cutting through walls of high grasses, and turned sharply at a boatyard. The sea was on our right. "Not far, now," Vee said, "and we'll come to a good place to bathe, beyond the village, but before the hotel, where it's too crowded for my liking. I've found an unused bit of beach. There's a wide band of stones between the sea and the sand, and I've been trying to move them aside to make a path to the water, but they keep washing back."

"You've been here awhile?" Omio asked.

"For a week, resting. Doctor's orders, and orders I was happy to comply with. I've slept and swum and worked on my new novel with no interruptions or outside pressures."

So she *was* writing a novel. I wished I dared to ask her what it was about.

Omio and I followed the path she had made through the stones. I slipped and almost turned my ankle, but Omio caught me. The stones were not very big, and they were rounded from water, but they were still uncomfortable to step on. Although the cut on my foot had healed, the stone near the laundry umbrella had reminded me that there was further healing needed, and it seemed that I could feel the skin stretching around the scar as I stepped into the water.

Omio dropped down and swam out, cleanly, barely tossing up spray. Vee and I followed. The water was cool, not cold, just right for getting cooled off. The sky was misty with stars.

"Don't go too far out," Vee called. "Krhis is right about the undertow. This is one of the safest places, better than the beach up at the hotel."

Omio was a superb swimmer, like most island people, but he turned around and came back toward us, then veered off and swam parallel to the land, up toward the lights of the hotel. I would have liked to swim with him, but thought it would not be courteous to Vee, who swam well but not quite as well as I did, since I've been in and out of water all my life.

She stood inside the stones, shaking water out of her ears. "Good thing we've both got drip-dry hair."

Omio had turned again and was swimming back. "He's a nice lad," Vee said. "I'm glad he's here early. You'll enjoy him. He's been through a lot, and he holds no bitterness. You'll find that's true of most of the delegates. I suspect Norine will fill you in on some of their histories. It's probably one of the most varied groups we'll ever encounter, geographically, physically, every way."

Omio had swum back to us and was running through the shallow water with great leaps, splashing silver spray.

"What energy!" Vee exclaimed. "Why can't you bottle it and give some to me? Come on, kids, we'd better go on back. Breakfast's at seven-thirty and we all need our sleep."

I felt comfortably cool after the swim, but the walk back

to the dormitory building was all uphill, and I was sweating
again by the time we reached the monastery. At Beau Allaire,
Max has a white coquina ramp going over a jungle of Spanish
bayonets and crape myrtle, down to the beach. At home we
run along our cypress ramp over the sand dunes and across a
lovely long stretch of beach. At Osia Theola we were going to
have to work for our swim.

Norine was waiting at the dormitory building, waving to us.
"Polly," she said, "I have a phone message for you."

My heart thumped. "For me?"

"Yes. While you were swimming, some young man called.
Zachary Gray. You know him?"

I hadn't told Norine who the flowers were from. "Yes."

"He wanted to make sure you'd arrived safely. He said to
give you his love, and he'll call again."

"Oh—thanks." I could not help being pleased, and showing
it. Then I said good night to Vee and Omio, thanked Norine
again, and we all went to our rooms. I took a lukewarm bath
and lay back in the tub, dazzled by Zachary's flowers, by his
call.

The bedroom was hot. I lit the mosquito coil and opened
the shutters and lay down on the bed to read for a while. At
home there are screens everywhere, and windows open to catch
the breeze. Max had told me that when she and M.A. were
growing up at Beau Allaire, not many people had screens, and
they slept under white gauze mosquito nets. A mosquito net
would not be a bad idea at Osia Theola.

The coil went out without my realizing it, and instantly I
was attacked by invisible, soundless insects. I slapped at them,
struck a match, and relit the coil. Realized I was going to have
to close the shutters. I was bitten on the legs, the arms, the
face.

I slammed the shutters closed. Scratched my legs. Rubbed
my eye. Could feel it hot and itchy. I remembered Renny telling
me that the vector, the biting insect which put Trypanosomas
into the bloodstream and ultimately the heart, frequently
enters the body with its lethal poison by biting the corner of
the eyelid. I had a moment of utter panic.

Nonsense, Polly. You come from a family of scientists. Use

your mind. Chagas' and Netson's diseases are endemic in South America, not in Cyprus. They don't exist in Cyprus.

I rubbed my eyelid again. Looked in the mirror. The lid was red and puffy. Absurd. But I felt infected.

Idiot. Renny would have warned me if there was any Netson's in Greece or Cyprus. Max would never have arranged the trip. Ursula would not have allowed it. Daddy wouldn't even have considered it. There are plenty of biting bugs at home, nasty red bugs, shrilling mosquitoes, no-see-um bugs which bite and the bites puff up like the one on my eyelid and get red and feverish but are unimportant. That's the kind of insect these Cyprus bugs were, just like the Benne Seed no-see-ums, itchy and horrid but not dangerous. Nobody would have a conference center where insects were a threat to life.

My heart began to beat less fearfully.

But it was hot. My sheet was wet. The fan was blowing a warm draft over me, doing no more than recirculating hot air. I put down my book and turned out the light; even the filament of the light bulb added to the heat of the room.

The coil burned slowly, its end barely glowing, so that I knew it was still lit. I was not being bitten anymore. I turned on my stomach, spread-eagled. The cool waters of the Mediterranean seemed eons ago; I was bathed in perspiration.

And I wanted Renny to sit by me on the bed and reassure me, tell me I needn't worry about the bite on my eyelid.

How do you feel when you know that an insect bite on the corner of your eyelid means death to your heart? What a funny little muscle to hold life and death in its pumping.

But this wasn't that kind of insect, that kind of bite.

I wanted to run to Renny, the way I had run when I fled Beau Allaire.

I called the hospital. 'I'd like to speak to Dr. Queron Renier, please. It's an emergency.'

'Who is calling, please?' The operator had my most unfavorite kind of Southern accent, nasal and whiny.

'Well—could you just say it's Polly?'

'Just a minute, hon. I don't know if he's in.'

Of course he was in. He'd be in his quarters or on the floor. I waited. The nasal voice came again. 'He's not answering. May I leave him a message?'

I looked at the number of the phone in the booth, gave it to the voice on the other end of the line. 'Please . . . please try to find him. Please, it's urgent,' I said. I could not control the trembling of my voice.

I would have to wait for Renny to call.

Suppose, for some reason, he wasn't at the hospital? How long should I wait? And what then? I leaned against the wall of the phone booth and I wasn't sure how long I could stand up.

The part of LeNoir Street where Straw had left me was mostly shops. A few dusty palmetto trees drooped in the morning sun. My breath fogged the glass of the phone booth, and I opened the door. A few people walked by. A few stores opened. I waited. Waited.

Half an hour.

I couldn't stay in the phone booth all day.

I would have to go somewhere, do something. The night before, I had wanted to go home. Not now. I couldn't go home.

I crouched over, as though I had cramps, and heard a funny noise, like an animal's, and looked around to see what was making the noise, and it was coming from me. I pushed my hand against my mouth and it stopped.

Oh, Renny. Renny, help.

The phone was silent. I had been there for an hour. The street was waking up.

I had to go somewhere and there was nowhere to go. My foot throbbed, and blood continued to seep through the bandage. Numbly, not even thinking, I started away from the phone. I was a few yards down the street when it rang.

I rushed back.

Grabbed the phone off the hook. 'Hello?'

'Polly?'

'Oh, Renny, Renny—'

'Where are you? What's wrong?'

I heard myself wailing. 'My foot's cut, and I'm bleeding all over the phone-booth floor—'

Renny's voice was sharp. 'Polly. Calm down. Tell me where you are, and what's wrong.'

'I'm in a phone booth on LeNoir Street near the post office. Can you come for me, oh, please, Renny, please—'

'*Where* on LeNoir Street? Polly, don't get hysterical, this isn't like you.'

I looked around. 'Two blocks south of the post office. I'm right by a hearing-aid place. I'm bleeding—'

'All right,' Renny said. 'I've just finished making early rounds. I'll be there in ten minutes.'

I gave a sob, but there were no tears with it; it was so dry it hurt my throat. 'Hurry—please—'

The ten minutes I waited for Renny seemed longer than the hour before the phone rang. He drove up in his old green car, and I stumbled out of the booth. He hurried around to open the car door for me, and I almost fell in.

'Let me see that foot.'

I leaned back against the shabby seat. Stuck my foot out at him.

'Who bandaged it for you?'

'Ursula Heschel.'

'Polly, what happened?'

'I cut it on a shell.'

His fingers worked the bandage free. 'That's a nasty cut. How did you get here?'

'I walked partway, then I got a hitch.'

'A hitch?'

'Renny.' My voice was heavy. 'Hitching's a federal offense in my family. But I couldn't walk.'

'No, Polly, you couldn't.' He opened the glove compartment and rummaged among maps and dark glasses and a can opener and pulled out an Ace bandage. 'This will do until I can get you to the hospital and dress your foot. Then I'll take you home.'

Now the tears came, spurting out, as sudden as a summer storm. 'No, no, Renny, no, I don't want to go home, I can't go home, no—' I was being incoherent and hysterical and I have never in my life been incoherent or hysterical.

Renny shut the glove compartment, took my foot and

wrapped it in the Ace bandage, then shut the door and went around to the driver's seat. He got in and sat down, waiting for me to get under control. 'Polly, what happened?'

I shook my head, and again that awful animal noise came out of me, but this time it flowed out with tears, and it was easier to stop.

Renny started the car.

'Renny, I don't want anybody to see me. Some of the doctors know Daddy—'

'I have no place to take you except the hospital,' Renny said. 'We'll go in through Emergency.' He drove in silence along LeNoir Street. The shops gave way to houses, at first close together, then set back from the street, larger and farther apart. The street curved around to the hospital driveway. He drove to the back. Opened the door for me. 'Try not to put too much weight on that foot.'

We went in through the Emergency entrance. There were only a few people in the waiting room, and the nurse at the desk was sipping from a Styrofoam cup. Renny greeted her, saying that he was taking a patient to have her foot bandaged. I don't think she even looked up from her magazine.

'It was a heavy night in Emergency.' Renny led me into one of the examining cubicles. 'It's all quiet now.'

'Are you on Emergency rotation?'

'No. Urology. Word gets round in a small hospital. How did you cut your foot?'

'I told you. On a broken shell.'

'Where?'

'Max's driveway.'

'When?'

'Last night.'

'Where were you going?' He was bathing my foot, holding it in a bowl of water, pink from my blood.

'I was running.'

'Where?' He swabbed the cut with disinfectant and I cried out. 'Where, Polly?'

'Away.'

His strong fingers held my foot, holding the cut so that the bleeding stopped. 'This was last night?'

'Yes.'

'Did you go home?'

'No. No. I couldn't. Then I got up early to—to come to you.'

Renny pressed a gauze pad against the cut, then taped it. 'You'll have to stay off that foot today.'

'All right.'

He was perched on a small white stool, keeping his hand around my foot. 'I do have to take you home, you know.'

'No. No!' My voice rose.

'Shhh,' he said. 'Unless you can give me a good reason, a real reason not to, I'll have to take you home or call your parents to come get you.'

'No.' This time I kept my voice low. 'I can't. I can't talk to them.'

He stood up, put his hands on my shoulders, looked into my eyes. 'You'd better tell me whatever it was that happened.'

'I can't.' I leaned toward him so that I could press my face against his white coat. Renny had been to our house once when Max and Ursula were there for dinner. He knew Max that way, and as an outpatient. I could not tell him.

'You were with Max and Ursula?'

'With Max, so she wouldn't be alone while Urs was in Charleston.'

'Oh, Polly—' He sighed. 'When did Ursula come in on this?'

'While I was running away from—she was driving home from Charleston. Oh, Renny, Max was drunk. She was in terrible pain and she was drunk. I've never seen anybody drunk that way. She didn't really know what she was—'

His arms came tightly around me. I didn't have to tell him any more. And then he asked me who'd picked me up to drive me to Cowpertown, and I told him about Straw and his ugly insinuations.

'The creep,' Renny murmured, 'the crude creep.' His arms were protecting, reassuring. 'The first thing you need is some sleep. I'm going to call a friend of mine, one of the nurses here. She's on duty now, but I'll get her key. Wait.'

'Don't tell her.'

'Shhh. I won't tell her anything.'

'Don't tell anybody—not Mother or Daddy—'

'I won't tell anybody.' He shut the door of the examining cubicle behind him.

While he was gone I lay back on the black examining table, which was too short for me. It was covered with white paper that crinkled if I moved, so I lay still. I was half asleep when Renny came back.

'All right, Polly, let's go.'

He led me along a back corridor, down some stairs, and out a side door. We got back in the car and drove to one of the streets around the hospital which had once been a street of rich people in big houses and was now funeral parlors and rooming houses. He pulled up in front of a Greek revival house with heavy white columns and none of the airy grace of Beau Allaire. We went up the steps to a side verandah, and Renny opened the screen door, then took a key and opened the inner door. He led me through a small living room and out onto a screened porch where there was a double bed, a green wicker chair and stool, a cherry chest, completely out of place with the rest of the porch furniture, with a few drawers pulled half open.

'Nell wasn't exactly expecting company.' Renny pulled down the white Marseilles bedspread.

A small, cold part of my mind was wondering who Nell was, and why Renny was so familiar with her. He was rummaging through one of the open drawers.

I sat down.

He turned to me, holding out a shorty nightgown. 'Get undressed and put this on.' He flicked a switch, and the ceiling fan started to turn. In the hospital it had been cool. 'Some of the apartments have air-conditioning,' he said, 'but Nell sleeps out here half the year. I'll be back in five minutes.'

I undressed, put on Nell's nightgown, and got into bed. The floor of the sleeping porch was painted green, the wooden ceiling was green, and the green of a huge magnolia tree pressed against the screen. With the fan moving the air, it gave the effect of coolness.

Renny came in with a mug. 'Chicken broth,' he said. 'I don't want to give you any caffeine or anything cold.'

I put my hands around the mug. It must have been well

in the nineties outdoors, but my hands were cold, and the warmth of the mug felt good.

'I have to get back to the hospital.' He sounded reluctant. 'Polly, I don't know what to do. You've had a bad shock. I think I should call your parents.'

'No. I don't want them to know.'

'You're not going to tell them?'

'No,' I repeated, 'I don't want them to know.'

Renny sat on the edge of the bed beside me. 'You're going to have to go home sometime.'

'They think I'm with Max and Ursula. I was to call Mother when I was ready to go home.'

'Will you still do that?'

'I don't know. Not yet.'

He got up and walked to the door, then turned back. 'When Max and Ursula find you gone and realize you aren't coming back, won't they call your parents?'

I sat up in bed, put my head on my knees. That had not occurred to me. 'Would they?'

'Likely.'

'But what would they say?'

'They might just want to know if your parents know where you are.'

'Will you call them?' I asked. But then they would know that Renny knew. And Max would have to see Renny when she went into Cowpertown for blood tests . . .

I got out of bed and followed Renny. 'I'll call.'

He nodded, pointing toward a desk in the corner of the rather drab room. On it, among a clutter of mugs and a coffeepot and a bowl of lilies, was a phone. Renny asked, 'Do you want me to go?'

'No. Stay. Please.' I dialed. —Don't let it be Max who answers. Don't let it be Nettie or Ovid. Let it be Urs.

It was. I said, 'Ursula, this is Polly. I just want you to know I'm all right. I'm with a friend, not at home, so don't call home, please. I need to sleep. I'm very tired. Goodbye.' I spoke quickly, not giving her time to say anything, though in the background, behind my words, I heard, 'Thank God. Where are you? I need to see you, to talk.' —No, Ursula. You don't need to see me. There's nothing to say. Go to Max.

I put the phone down and went back out to the porch.

Renny leaned against the doorframe. 'I get off at five. I'll come to you then. I'm sorry, Polly, so sorry—' He bent down and kissed me on the cheek.

I slept. Woke, with my eye itching. Rubbed it. Felt hot. The sheet was wet. I opened my eyes. Mostly my right eye. The left was swollen nearly closed.

I was in Cyprus, and I'd been bitten on the eyelid. I turned on the light, got up, and stared in the wavery mirror. It looked as though someone had socked a fist into my eye.

There was no Netson's in Cyprus. Anyhow, it was only my eyelid that was inflamed. No conjunctivitis.

I got back into bed. My room at home wasn't even half the size of this one, but it was all mine. After my roommate came, it would be very different. So I got out of bed, opened the shutters, and stepped out onto the balcony. The insects drove me back into the room before I could appreciate the loveliness of the night. I curled up, pulling the sheet just over my toes, and slept.

I woke to someone walking up and down the corridor, ringing a bell. Norine, I guessed, though there was only the staff, Omio, and me, to rouse. There was going to be no oversleeping at this conference.

I met Vee as I came out my door. "Polly, what on earth has happened to you?"

"The no-see-um bugs got me."

She scratched her arm. "Me, too, though not in as sensitive a place. Did you use the bug coil?"

"Yes, but for a while I tried to keep the shutters open to catch the breeze. Believe me, I shut them fast."

She leaned over to look at my eye. "I think one got you on a vein, right there at the corner of your lid. Does it hurt?"

"No, it's just uncomfortable."

"It *is* a temporary affliction, if that's any comfort; it'll go away in a day or so. The bugs are much worse in this humid heat than they were last week." She scratched again, bending down to her ankle. "Do you have a can of spray in your room?"

"No, just the coil."

"I'll find you some for this evening. It helps if you spray the shutters. Not so many of the little horrors get through the slats."

We walked the rose-lined path to the dining area of the cloister. The sun was already uncomfortably hot. Norine exclaimed over my eye and said she'd give me some witch-hazel pads to help bring the swelling down.

For breakfast there were packets of instant coffee in a wicker basket, and a big pitcher of hot milk. A platter of eggs was brought in by Tullia. There was a loaf of bread still warm from the oven, a big bowl of jam, and a smallish pat of butter each. I wondered how much refrigeration they had in the kitchen, which was simply the enclosed end of the cloister.

While we were still eating, the bells in the tower began to ring, and we could see people coming in through the gates to go to church. A young woman was carrying a baby in a long white dress; a man in a dark suit, face flushed with heat, had his arm about her. They were followed by a group of beaming people.

"A baptism!" Vee cried in delight.

As the people went into the church, most of them turned to stare at us sitting around the breakfast table.

Omio's delighted laugh pealed out. "Wait till the rest of the delegates arrive!"

Bashemath said in her solemn way, "We are already a circus for them."

Vee, Frank, and I were the only Caucasians. Krhis was Indian, Norine Oriental, Bashemath and Millie were African, and Omio was—I wasn't sure—Micronesian?

Omio wore a brightly patterned garment that was something between a kilt and a loincloth, and an ordinary cotton T-shirt. "At home, in the old days, we wouldn't have worn the shirt," he explained to me. He reached out one long finger, pale at the tip, and touched my inflamed eyelid. "Poor Polly, when we go swimming this evening, lo, the salt water will be good for it."

Norine passed the warm milk. "After breakfast, Polly, I'd like you to help me in the office. And I have the medicine chest with the witch hazel there."

Bashemath said, "You have the papers I want duplicated?"

Norine nodded. "And I showed Polly how to use the mimeo."

When we got to the office, Norine took a bottle of witch hazel from a tiny cooler. She rummaged in drawers until she found a gauze pad, which she soaked with the cold witch hazel. "Hold it to your eye."

I had forgotten my eyelid at breakfast. Now I was very aware of the itching and swelling. It was so inflamed that the witch-hazel pad warmed up quickly, and Norine wet it again. It felt marvelously soothing, and I thanked her.

"Any time you get a chance during the day, wet the pad and hold it to your eye, okeydokey? Now, are you ready?" She pointed at the typewriter.

"I'm afraid I'll be very slow."

Norine was busily looking through some files. "That is all right as long as you are accurate."

I sat down at the typewriter and typed, very carefully, a series of forms of poetry, lines of iambic pentameter, tetrameter, trochaic and anapestic measures. There were examples of meters, everything explained in the simplest way possible. Somehow or other I managed to make a passable stencil.

Norine looked at it, and nodded. "Okeydokey, now run it off."

I managed that, too, though I ended up with purple ink on my fingers and somehow or other got a purple streak down one leg.

"You can type Bashemath's stencil this afternoon," Norine said. "If you try to do too much at once, you begin to make mistakes." She indicated a wooden file box filled with cards. We were to check over the names and addresses of each delegate, and assign them rooms in the dormitory building, trying to choose suitable roommates for each.

"I have already picked your roommate, as I told you," Norine said, "because she is the youngest woman delegate—not yet thirty."

Not yet thirty sounded quite old to me.

"It is best if we put people of different languages together. That way they'll have to speak English. Here, you see, we will not put Andres, from Brazil, with Gershom, from Angola, because they would be tempted to speak Portuguese. Andres can room with Nigel from Bombay."

Norine did most of the choosing, and I stuffed blue folders for everybody, marking their names and room numbers on the cover.

When we had finished, Norine soaked the gauze pad in witch hazel again, and I was ready for it.

"You like Omio?" she asked.

"Very much."

"He has great talent. And the Bakian affectionateness. You are acquainted with peoples of different races and colors?"

"Reasonably. We lived on an island off the south coast of Portugal when I was a child, and we were friends with the Gaeans. And I spent a month in Venezuela and saw a good bit of the Quiztanos."

"Omio speaks better English than some of the other delegates, and has no small estimation of himself. Bashemath is an interesting person, a fine educator. There was big trouble for her when she left home for her first conference. While she was gone, her husband's friends urged him to go back to the old ways and take another wife. When she got home, the other woman was putting Bashemath's own children to bed. But you have seen Bashemath. The other woman did not stay long."

I had seen Bashemath. "It must have been awful for her."

"It was. She is required at her university to attend a certain number of conferences, but after that she did not leave home again for two years."

Norine was something of a gossip. And I listened. I listened avidly. Was I being like Xan and Kate listening to the Mulletville girls? Not entirely. Norine relished her stories, but she was not being vicious.

Now she laughed her rather tinny laugh. "Bashemath could certainly frighten me away if she wanted to. She is a real warrior. Now Millie is quite different. She is a dear person, is Milcah

Adah. She, too, has been through much grief. All her family died during an epidemic. Millie nursed them, buried them, and by some fluke did not get ill herself. She nursed children who had been taken to the hospital, and it was discovered what a fine storyteller she is. A rare person, if a little sentimental. Here, let me soak that pad again."

The cool pad felt so good I would have liked to pat it all over me.

When I took it away from my eye, Norine peered at me. "The swelling is going down. Are you thirsty?"

"Parched." At home there's always lemonade and iced tea in the fridge.

She went again to her little cooler, pulled out a bottle of ginger ale, got two paper cups from the file cabinet. The fizzy coolness helped my thirst but did nothing to dry my sticky clothes. Even my feet were sweaty, and my wet sandal straps had made stained marks across my foot.

"We'll work on the table assignments now," Norine said. "We like to rotate the seating, so that people can get to know each other, and also to prevent cliques from forming. A conference experience like this can produce intense friendships."

We put numbers in a small wooden box for the delegates to draw. "This heat wave is absurd, positively absurd," Norine said. "It's a good thing many of our delegates come from hot climates. I think Vee feels the heat more than the rest of us, and she's prone to headaches if she's overstressed. You have read her books?"

"I love them."

"She is a fine writer. And it takes her mind off her husband."

What did she mean? "Is he alive?"

"Unfortunately." She looked at me. "This is of course in confidence, Polly."

"Okay," I said uncertainly.

"He is French, Henri Porcher. There was an American grandfather, I believe, from one of those inbred Southern families, who late in life married a distant cousin in Paris, a singer. There was a latent strain of insanity, violent insanity, in the Porchers. Until ten years ago, Henri seemed free of it. But then he got an encephalitis virus, which evidently triggered it, and he has been institutionalized ever since."

"Oh—how awful—"

"He is in a hospital in Switzerland, and Vee is able to be with us because her sister-in-law spells her. Henri is very dependent on Vee, and if she visits him daily he is less violent. Poor man, he is like a wild animal. I suppose, legally, Vee could divorce him, but Vee being Vee, of course she won't. Krhis says that in his own irrational way Henri still loves her. She is brave. Now"—Norine was brisk efficiency again—"we have done a good morning's work."

"I know," I agreed. I was already learning much from the staff.

At lunch we were served by the younger woman, Sophonisba. Omio whispered to me, "Look at her gold tooth. It's a status symbol."

Millie entertained us with stories, a few from her native Cameroon, others from different countries, and had us all in stitches. When Bashemath was really amused, her laughter was a deep booming. Frank had a hearty, contagious laugh. Even Krhis was shaking with laughter.

"The delegates have a treat in store," he said at the end of the meal. "Now, my dears, it is siesta time, and it is so hot—104° in Nicosia, and not that much cooler here—we will take the afternoon off, and have our meeting after the evening meal instead. I think that will be more comfortable for us all."

I walked with Millie along the pebbled path that led to the dormitory building. "You were terrific," I said.

She smiled. "When we are listening to stories, then it is the story center of the brain which is functioning, and the pain center is less active. I go into the children's wards of hospitals, where there are children in great pain. When I am telling them stories they laugh and they cry and in truth their pain is less. Mine, too." Again she smiled at me, and then at two old men with long hoses who were watering the flowers, and who smiled back, nodding and bobbing, looking curiously at Millie and me and the others coming along behind us.

I turned on the fan in my room, and I think it did help a

little. I changed the water for Zachary's flowers, then stretched out on the bed with a book, and got up to a gentle knock. It was Vee, with a can of bug spray. "I got this for you from Norine. There's supposed to be some in each room."

"Oh, thank you."

"See you anon," Vee said, and went to her room.

I finished making the beds on the first floor, and did three rooms on the second floor, then decided to go back to my room for a nap.

I left the shutters wide open, and while sunlight streamed in, so did the breeze from the sea. Whatever the stinging insects were, they weren't bad during sunlight. I sprawled out on the bed and slept.

When I woke up I could hear snoring from the room on the other side of me, not Vee's, Millie's. I got up and went into the hall, and all the doors were closed. I walked softly in my crepe-soled sandals, out into the brilliant sunlight. Just walking along the path made me perspire. I went into the office and typed the stencil for Bashemath, suggestions about teaching small children to read and write. When I had finished, sweat was stinging my eyes, trickling down my legs. I went into the compound and the sun blasted at me like a furnace.

The church bells were quiet, but the doors were open, leading into darkness. I slipped in, standing in the back until my eyes adjusted to the shadows. The light filtered in gently, touching an icon here, a statue of the Virgin there. I sat on one of the stone steps leading down into the nave.

There was a screen covered with icons dividing the main body of the church from the sanctuary. A little old man was polishing candlesticks, and when he turned and saw me his face lit up with a smile as though he had been expecting me. He came up to me.

"Come, little," he said, "come, *despina*," and led me down the steps into the church and to a wooden seat hollowed with age. I sat and watched him as he puttered about. He took a sprig of green from a stand in front of a statue, a flower from a vase before an icon, picking here and there, until he had a tiny bouquet, which he handed me, beaming.

"*Epharisto.*" I was a little embarrassed. I hoped it was all right for him to give me flowers taken from icons and statues.

"*Parakalo*, little, *parakalo, kyria.*"

I held the bouquet to my nose, and it was pungent and lemony-smelling.

He pointed to a statue which I had thought was a Virgin and child, but as I looked more closely I saw that the child wore a crown and carried a cross like a scepter, and that the woman was wearing red velvet. The old man spoke in Greek, and I thought he was telling me that this was Blessed Theola and her vision of Christ.

He beamed on me again and pointed to the lower section of the church. "Cave. Eight hundred, eighteen hundred old, *kyria.*" He switched back to Greek, and I kept nodding at him, catching words and phrases about Theola and truth, and he gestured urgently toward the cave.

I followed him and stood in the entrance to the cave, peering into darkness. Was it here that Theola gave people the truth about themselves? Max had said that Theola was gentle and did not give people more than they could bear.

I stood there, and the only truth to come to me was that I was still in the darkness of confusion, about myself, and everybody. I allowed Zachary Gray, whom I had known only a few days, to be complicated and contradictory. Why couldn't I allow it in anybody else? Why couldn't I allow it in myself?

"*Kyria? Despina?*" The old man was looking at me anxiously.

"*Epharisto.*" I smiled at him and turned away from the cave and returned to the wooden seat he had first offered me.

"*Parakalo.*" He picked up a candlestick and polishing rag. I sat there for quite a long while, holding the little bouquet to my face. There was something healing about the pungent smell. Then the bells began to ring, so I got up and left quickly, waving goodbye and thanks to the old man, and wandered across the courtyard to the cloister.

Omio was there before me, in the refectory section, sitting at a table and writing in a notebook, with another book beside him. He looked up and beckoned to me. "I promised I'd show you this." He pointed to the big notebook and pulled out a chair for me, watching me while I leafed through the pages.

He had set down in this book the stories of his people, first in Bakian, then in English. The stories were lavishly and beautifully illustrated in bright watercolors. Many of his paintings and sketches reminded me of Max's notebooks. Max would love this book of Omio's.

"Why does this man have so many wives?" I looked up from a story of a man with seventeen wives.

He laughed. "Seventeen is, lo, excessive, is it not? But to have more than one wife was the old way. On Baki there used to be many more women than men, so the kindest thing to do with all the extra women was to marry them. Every Bakian woman had a family to care for, and to be cared for by. My grandmother was, lo, my grandfather's fifth wife, and the most beautiful. The children—there were many—thought of each other as whole brothers and sisters. If a woman did not have enough milk after childbirth, there was always another to suckle the baby." He smiled his merry smile.

"We were lucky on Baki." He put his hand down on the book, his long forefinger with the delicate pink nail pointing to a picture of a baby being held by a white man in a dog collar. "In some places the missionaries made the men get rid of all but one of their wives. Do you think Jesus would have wanted that?"

I shook my head. "It doesn't show much concern for the leftover wives."

"In Baki, the missionaries who came to us were warm of heart, and said only that when the children grew up, each, like my father, like me, should have one wife only. And this made reason because, with, lo, the new medicines they brought us, fewer male children died, and there were no longer many women needing men. They—the missionaries—wanted the women to cover their breasts, but they said little to those who went around as usual. They believed that, as time went on, we would move into their ways."

"Did you?"

He smiled. "We are still moving. The missionaries who came to Baki understood that differences need not separate. But they were followed by others, the military people, for instance, and their families. Some of their ways were good ways. But there were ways, too, which we did not understand."

There was a tightness in his face which I had not seen before. "Tell me—"

Omio looked at me with his dark eyes, which were usually so merry but now were simply dark, the pupil hardly darker than the iris. "I'm not sure you will understand."

"I can try."

"Our ways are so different."

"Please."

"On this far island of Baki there came, lo, many Australian and many English people. We felt very fortunate when my father got a job working in the big military hotel they built. These people called themselves Christian, you understand."

I did not.

"Although many people, my family included, welcomed them, they did not think they had to treat us as they treated each other. When my father displeased them in any way, they beat him. One time they beat him so that he bled on his back, and then salt was rubbed into him. My mother bathed him and bathed him, making more blood to come to wash away the salt, and then took him down to the sea because the salt in seawater is healing. But I heard his screams."

I looked down at the open page to hide my horror; he had painted birds and butterflies, vivid and happy. "How could you be Christian, then?"

He put his hand down on mine. "Oh, I think we could be. I think we were Christian, lo, long before the missionaries came, although we did not know to call it so. We knew only that the maker of the great whale came to us and was part of our lives, and the missionaries called this person who loved and cared for us by the name of Jesus. And we were glad to have a name for the part of the maker we had not known by name before." He turned the page, and there was a painting of the statue which had become so familiar to me at Max's, the stone carving of the man laughing in sheer delight.

If Max had ever told me that the statue was Bakian, I had forgotten. Seeing it in Omio's book was like the slap of a rough ocean wave. I had last seen the statue in Max's arms as she ran down the stairs after me.

Omio said, "The missionaries who were our friends called it the Laughing Christ. Some of the others called it a heathen idol."

"Oh—Omio . . ." From Omio's painting it was evident that the actual statue was much larger than Max's copy, but the loving delight was the same. Had Max put the statue back on the landing? I looked at the joyous face and pressed my hand against my mouth to stifle a sob.

I hardly heard Omio. I was hearing, seeing, Max.

He said, "My father told me we must learn to love such people, because they must be sick in their minds, and only love could heal such sickness. When people have great power, lo, they become very sick, and must be loved as we love those who are dying. It was not easy, my Polly, after I had seen my father's back and heard his screams."

Suddenly he put his hand under my chin and looked hard into my eyes. I could not hide my confusion and pain. "My Polly," he said gently, "let us not hold on to past wounds. You don't have to bear it with me. I see you entering into the hurt of others, and I love you for it, but you must try not to carry too much."

His words echoed Max's the night she told me about her father, and the echo almost undid me.

He went on. "I do not think it is love if it is too easy. Have you not yet lived long enough to need to love someone who is not easy to love? Surely you have known people who have done wrong things and need to be healed."

I bowed my head and a tear dropped onto the page. Quickly I took a tissue from my pocket and blotted it, where it had fallen on the foot of the Laughing Christ. I looked up and saw Bashemath and Millie walking toward us. I could not speak to them. I ran to one of the open arches and jumped down, ran blindly to the shadows of the fig sycamore.

I could hear Omio running after me, but I could not see him for the blinding tears. His arms went around me.

"You are not crying about my father." I blew my nose, shaking my head. "What is causing your tears?"

I could not tell him. I wiped them away with the palms of my hands.

"Who has hurt you?" he asked. When I did not answer, but shook my head again, he kissed both my eyelids, the still slightly puffy one first, then the other.

Renny had kissed my eyelids, too. Young Doctor Renier, with his stethoscope and white jacket and all-American face, couldn't have been more different from Omio, and yet they were alike in their experience, and my nonexperience.

When I woke up in the green shade of the sleeping porch of Nell, the nurse, she was sitting looking at me. 'I'm home only for a few minutes,' she said. 'I hope I didn't frighten you.'

'No.' A mockingbird was singing sweetly in the magnolia tree.

'I just need to get a few things. I'm doing a double shift, covering for a friend. Renny asked me to fix you some more broth. Here it is, donax soup. It'll cure all ills.'

'Thank you.' Even in my state of shock I was impressed by Nell's offering of donax soup. The tiny shells are no longer easy to find, so it was a real gift. 'Thank you, a lot.'

'Renny'll be back a little after five. He's a good man. He'll be a good doctor, but that doesn't make a good man. Renny's good.'

'I know.'

She stood looking down at me. 'You're just a child.'

I moved my head negatively against the pillow. 'Not now.'

'Whatever it is, whoever it was, it'll pass, you'll get over it. People have bad things happen but they survive.' She turned away from me, took some things out of one of her drawers. 'You'll be okay?'

'Yes. Thanks for taking me in.'

'Make yourself at home. Wander about the place. There isn't much to it. But you'll be here when Renny gets back?' She was afraid I was going to run away. But I'd already run away. There wasn't any place else to run.

'I'll be here.'

After she left I managed to drink the donax soup with its delicate ocean flavor. At first I thought I was going to throw up, but I didn't, and I got it all down. For some reason that seemed important, if only for Nell's generosity in giving me such a rare delicacy. Then I wandered around a little. There was only the large sleeping porch, and a living room with a couch, where she probably slept in winter, and a kitchen and bath. It was obvious that Nell rented it furnished.

I went back to the porch. To bed. Nell's bed.

Nell had given me donax soup, something special. Renny, too, always gave to me. He didn't take. Straw wanted to take. Max—

I started to cry, but crying was exhausting, and I fell into sleep in the middle of a sob. I woke up as I heard Renny letting himself in, hurrying to the porch.

'Did you sleep?'

'Yes.'

'Nell make you some broth?'

'Donax soup. That was really nice of her.'

'Nell's a nice person. A good nurse.' He perched on the bed beside me. 'I want to take you home, Polly.'

'No. Not yet. I need to—I'm too confused, Renny. I can't see my parents till—'

He stroked my hair back from my forehead. 'Why are you confused, Polly? Tell me.'

'Straw—' I said, knowing that I was incoherent, but not knowing how to make sense. 'He killed a tortoise, with some other guys, and he liked doing it—'

'Polly, honey, what's that got to do with it?'

'If you try to *take* love, it's as bad as—as bad as that.'

'Don't let someone like that creep upset you.'

'It's just that—he tried to *take*—and it doesn't work that way—it has to be given—'

'Hush,' he said, 'hush. Yes, it has to be given.' And he kissed my eyelids again, then my lips, the way he did when he cut the motor on the boat when we'd been together. And the kiss continued on past the point where he usually broke off. Then, slowly, he pulled away.

I groped for him, as though I were blind. 'Renny, please, please—' My lips touched his.

And he was kissing me again, and slipping the shorty night-gown over my head. His strong and gentle hands began to stroke me, his hands, his lips, his tongue.

Gentle. Not frightening. Knowing what he was doing. I felt my nipples rise, and it startled me.

'Shhh,' Renny whispered. 'Shhh, it's all right, don't worry, just relax and listen to your body.'

He was slow, rhythmic, gentle, moving down my body,
down . . .
and I was nothing but my body
there was a sharp brief pain
brief
and then a sweet spasm went through me
and I seemed to rise into the air
no more pain
just the sweetness
the incredible
oh, the
and then Renny, panting
I pressed him hard against me.

He kissed my eyelids in the darkness, under the fig sycamore. "We'd better go back to the others," he said. Omio said.

Bashemath and Millie were drinking tea, sitting at the table. I hoped I didn't look as though I'd been crying. Norine came toward me. "Where were you, Polly?" she accused. "That same young man phoned you again, and I couldn't find you."

Bashemath said, in her calm, deep voice, "She doesn't have to tell you whenever she goes for a walk, Norine."

"Well, you missed him once more," Norine said to me.

"Is he going to call again?" I asked.

"He didn't say."

I wasn't sure whether I wanted him to or not. This world of Osia Theola was a completely different world from Athens, and Zachary seemed alien to it. Still, I was glad he had called. I was glad he had sent flowers.

"Tea, Norine?" Millie asked. "Polly?"

"No, thank you," Norine said. "I have work to do."

"Do you need me?" I asked. "I've typed Bashemath's stencil. Shall I run it off?"

"Not now, Polly. I'm going over some of my lectures."

"Then I'd love some tea," I said.

Norine trotted across the dusty compound to the office, and Bashemath got a mug, and Millie poured me tea from the large pot on the table.

Millie said, "There are some hot peppers by the dormitory building. I've picked a few, to add to the dinner tonight. This food is good, but not overly seasoned."

Bashemath spoke, following her own train of thought. "Do not let Norine bother you with her sharp ways. She has a heart of gold."

"She doesn't bother me," I replied. "And I'm here to work."

"But not to be overworked."

"Oh, I'm not, and I like work."

Omio drained his mug. "We're not likely to have another free afternoon. How about a swim? Or is it too hot?"

"Much too hot," Bashemath said.

"I don't swim. I'm afraid of crocodiles," Millie said.

Omio laughed. "But this is Cyprus, not Cameroon."

"Nevertheless," Millie said firmly, "no. Thank you."

"I'd love a swim," I said.

"Let's meet under the fig sycamore." Omio smiled at me.

He was there, waiting for me, and we started downhill. "Polly, forgive me."

"For what?"

"I have given you, lo, a romantic picture of Baki. It is not only the Christians there who have done bad things. If the missionaries were not overly concerned about whether or not the women covered themselves, it was because they were more concerned about the black magic, the witchcraft. Using hateful, hurting magic was as bad as beating a man and rubbing salt in the wounds. Worse. It could kill. We Bakians and the Christians were alike, some good people, turning the heart to love, others wicked, turning to greed and power."

He was holding my hand, swinging it, as we walked. I said, "I guess everybody's like that." And then I asked, "Does your Laughing Christ always laugh?"

His hand squeezed mine. "It is said that in time of great disaster tears fall from his eyes. My great-grandfather is supposed to have seen him cry before a tidal wave which killed many of our people. I have seen only the laughter, and there have been bad things in Baki. But if I ever saw him cry, I think I would be very afraid."

Did the statue on Max's landing ever weep?

We left the houses of the village and moved quietly along the path protected by high walls of grasses plumed with pale fronds, bleached by the fierce sun. And then we came to a tiny pasture I hadn't noticed the night before in the dark. In the pasture were the most beautiful little goats I'd ever seen, with soft, silky hair, and long, drooping ears. We stopped and admired them. They looked at us with great, startled eyes, then went back to grazing.

When we reached the place which Vee had tried to clear of stones, Omio sat down in the water and began to throw stones far up on the shore, to make the path wider. I joined him, throwing the rounded stones as far as possible.

"If we keep at this a little every day," Omio said, "we will keep the path open. I think Vee has tender feet. She is a poet."

That seemed rather a non sequitur, but I thought it likely that Vee did have tender feet, or she wouldn't have bothered to move the stones. My cut foot was not that tough, either. I was glad of the path.

When we had finished throwing what Omio decided were enough stones, he said, "Last night you held back because of

Vee, and that was nice of you. But I think you swim well. Let's race." And he splashed into the water and threw himself under a breaker.

I followed. I have learned that it is not a good idea for a girl to beat a man in a race, even though I think that's stupid. However, I did not have to hold back with Omio. It was all I could do to keep up with him.

"How do you come to swim so well?" he asked while we were splashing into shore. The sun was low on the horizon; evening came early to Cyprus; and the sky was flushed with a lovely light.

"I've lived on islands most of my life. We swim a lot."

Omio took my hand, and we walked on up the beach. "You are promised?" he asked.

"What?"

"You have a boyfriend? A special one?"

"No."

"In Baki, by your age, a woman is at least promised."

"In my country I'm considered too young. At least my parents would certainly think so."

Omio swung my hand. "It's time we went home." He gave me his shining smile. "It is home, isn't it?"

Yes. Already the monastery was home.

After the evening meal, with the dark closing in, Krhis said that we would stay in the cloister for the staff meeting instead of going to the upper room. He had each of the staff members talk a little bit about what they planned to do. Bashemath expected to have everything ready for a book fair, posters and all, by the first weekend. Millie hoped they'd be telling their own stories. Frank talked about the hope for small presses, and then, at his urging, Millie sang for us, and then Norine suggested that Omio do one of the Bakian dances.

Without embarrassment, Omio stood up and stripped off his T-shirt, kicked off his sandals. Then he moved into a dance which started with his entire body undulating in slow rhythm. Then the tempo accelerated until Krhis began to clap, joined by Frank, then Millie and Norine. Then Omio squatted low to the ground, with one leg, then the other, stretching out, somewhat like Russian Cossack dances, but much more quickly, incredibly quickly, and then he rose, rose, until he was leaping high into the air, fingers stretching him taller, higher . . .

Then the clapping began to come more slowly, winding him down. He was glistening with sweat, breathing in short, panting gasps, and the clapping changed from being an accompaniment to the dance, to applause.

"Lo, now we must sing *Saranam*." His voice was breathless, and he looked to Millie, who started singing.

> *In the midst of foes I cry to thee,*
> *From the ends of earth, wherever I may be,*
> *My strength in helplessness, O answer me,*
> *Saranam, saranam, saranam.*
>
> *Make my heart to grow as great as thine,*
> *So through my hurt your love may shine,*
> *My love be yours, your love be mine,*
> *Saranam, saranam, saranam.*

"What does it mean, 'saranam'?" I asked.

"Refuge," Norine said.

"God's richest blessing," Millie added.

Krhis said, "There is no English equivalent."

Frank laughed. "There doesn't need to be. Saranam says it all, loving, giving, caring."

Omio said, "I think it is like a Bakian word which means that love does not judge."

Vee added, "Love is not love which alters when it alteration finds."

"What's that?" Bashemath asked.

"Shakespeare, from one of the sonnets."

"Shakespeare?" Millie asked.

"Sonnets?" asked Bashemath.

Suddenly I realized that things I'd taken for granted, as part of my background, were unknown to people of other cultures.

"Shakespeare is probably our greatest writer in the English

language," Vee said, "and the sonnet is a form of poetry. I'll talk about it in one of the workshops. I even hope to have people writing sonnets."

Another thing I realized was how little I knew about Vee. I knew from her poems and novels that she had loved, and passionately. Because of Norine I knew she had an insane husband. There were a few chinks my imagination could fill in, but I realized something else that evening. I realized I was too young to understand much that had happened in the lives of these people who had quickly become my friends.

We finished the lemonade, which was tart and lovely, and Krhis sent us off to bed. I walked across the compound with Omio and Vee.

"Too late for a swim," she said. "Ah, well, we'll make time tomorrow."

"Too bad Frank can't come with us," I said.

Vee nodded. "He does swim at home, in a pool. He misses it."

"Lo, he is a kind man, is Frank," Omio said.

"Yes," Vee agreed. "I wonder if someone who has never suffered, known loss and pain, is capable of true kindness?"

Omio took my hand. "We find much true kindness here in Osia Theola."

I watered Zachary's flowers, which were thirsty in this heat, then wrote in my school journal till my eyes drooped with sleep. Got into bed and turned out the light. Could smell the punky odor of the mosquito coil. Could smell the bug repellent I'd sprayed on the shutters. My eye was still itchy, so I guessed closing the shutters was worth it. Under my door I could see a line of yellow from the hall, where the light burned all night. A faint glow filtered through the shutters, and I longed to be able to open them to the sky and the night birds and the sound of the sea. I turned on my stomach. My pillow was hot, so I pushed it onto the floor. I thought of Omio coming to find me under the fig-sycamore tree, and I felt his lips brushing my eyelids.

I woke up in a puddle of sweat. I could not hear the dull whir of the fan. There was no line of light under the door. Because the power tended to go out on Benne Seed whenever all the development people ran their air-conditioners, I guessed that the power in the monastery maybe had gone off because all the fans were on. I peered at the travel alarm. Ten past three.

I got up and drew open one shutter just enough so that I could slip out on the balcony. The sky was filled with stars. There were no lights on in the village. So the power was off there, too. No one was stirring. Except the mosquitoes.

I withdrew and got back into my damp bed. I could hear Millie snoring, and her snore was so different from her glorious voice that it made me giggle. Millie looked as though she should have a baby in her arms. Norine had said that all Millie's family had died. Children, too?

I would have liked to have Millie come in and sit by me and stroke my hair back from my forehead and sing to me, one of the verses from *Saranam*, maybe.

But I was not Millie's child.

And I wasn't a child anymore. It felt lonely.

Mother came in to me the night Renny brought me home, and sat on the bed by me, reaching her hand out to smooth my hair. 'Renny didn't tell me how you cut your foot.'

'I was running barefoot on Max's driveway, like an idiot. It was lucky Renny dropped by.' That was the story I'd cooked up and sold to Renny.

'Why would Renny have dropped by?'

'He's Max's doctor, peripherally. He assists Netson.' That would hold water if she checked it out.

'But you're upset about something other than your foot.'

Usually I could tell anything to Mother. I told her when that gross kid exposed himself to me while we were standing in line at the school cafeteria. Something smooth and slightly damp touched my hand and I turned, and there he was, sticking himself out at me. It was nasty, and I felt dirty, but it didn't really have anything to do with me, or even that stupid boy. And Mother could tell me that the same thing had happened to her, and she had felt like me, dirty, and wanting to take a bath.

But this wasn't something outside me that essentially didn't have anything to do with me. And I couldn't say a word.

Mother didn't try to use a can opener on me the way some mothers might. She just sat by me, stroking my hair, waiting. But I didn't speak. I closed my eyes. When she thought I was asleep, she left.

Renny, in a way, provided a smoke screen.

He called first thing in the morning, saying that he was coming over to Benne Seed to check my foot. Daddy could perfectly well have checked my foot. Mother could have checked my foot. It didn't need a doctor. But Renny came, midmorning, and Mother brought him into the living room, where I was sitting in the comfortable leather chair with my foot up on the footstool. The rest of the kids were swimming, and they'd evidently been told not to bug me, because they'd pretty well left me alone, even Xan and Kate.

Mother brought Renny and me some iced tea, then left us, saying she was in the middle of baking bread. Unlike Ursula, Mother did not bake bread often, and it was usually a sign that she was disturbed.

As soon as she had gone, Renny wanted to know where I was in my menstrual cycle, and was relieved when I told him I was just over my period. Then he was full of rather incoherent apologies. He rebandaged my foot, saying that it was healing nicely. 'Nell sends her best—' He sounded awkward.

'What about Nell?' I asked.

'Nell's a good friend.' He sounded surprised. 'She's engaged to one of the male nurses, and they're both friends of mine.'

Why did that make me feel better about Nell? And a little ashamed about having asked Renny.

He put my foot down on the stool. 'Did you think I was sleeping with Nell?'

'I didn't know.'

'What with the general promiscuity in Cowpertown—and other places—I can hardly be surprised that it crossed your mind. However, Polly, if I had been, I wouldn't have taken you there. I don't sleep around. I'm a Renier. My relationship with Jacinta was not celibate. But I'm a lot older than you. Sweet Polly, what happened between us mustn't happen again. It mustn't happen with you at all, not with me, not with anybody, until you're older and ready to make a real commitment.'

'I'm not planning to sleep around, either,' I said stiffly.

He studied my bandaged foot. 'It's hard to remember you're only sixteen, you seem so much older in so many ways—' He let his breath out gustily. 'Polly, you're very attractive. Don't you know I've plain lusted after you all summer? And yesterday it got the better of me, because—'

'You didn't seduce me, Renny. I wanted it.' —And no, I had no idea you lusted after me. No idea at all.

'I wanted it, too. But I shouldn't have.'

I looked down at his hand, lying on the stool near my foot, and shoulds and shouldn'ts meant nothing at all.

Renny took our empty glasses and put them on the table. He was being very Renier.

'Renny. Stop. I'm glad what happened happened with you. But I'm—' I choked up.

'Oh, Polly honey, I'm sorry. I know you're hurting. I'm sorry.'

Max was there between us, but neither of us mentioned her name.

Daddy came in to me that evening after I was ready for bed. 'Foot feeling better?'

'It's fine. Renny checked it this morning.'

'Mother told me. Polly, is something wrong between you and Renny?'

'No. Renny's a good friend.'

'Are you sure?'

'Sure.'

'What about you and Max?'

'What about me and Max?'

'Mother said Max called today and you wouldn't come to the phone.'

'Renny said I shouldn't walk on my foot.'

'Was that the only reason?'

'Daddy, I was getting too dependent on Max.'

'What made you realize it?'

'Renny . . .'

'Max is a dying woman. You can't just drop her like a hot coal.'

'Daddy, I was like a kid, idolizing Max. It wasn't good.'

'No, Polly, idolatry's never good. But Max and Ursula have been a good influence on you. You've been doing admirably in school, and you've been particularly pleasant to have around the house. I wish Xan did his jobs in the lab as diligently as you do yours. Did anything happen to make you decide you were too dependent on Max?' He was looking at me, not his daddy-look, but diagnostically, trying to see through what I was saying to what was really wrong. But he didn't see.

'It was just time.'

'Did anything happen to upset you when you stayed at Beau Allaire?'

'Max drank too much.'

'Was she in pain?'

'Yes.'

'Why didn't you call me?'

'I don't know—'

'People with too much alcohol in them are always unpleasant, though to a certain extent it's understandable with Max. How much too much did she have?'

'Daddy, she was *drunk*.'

'It's not good to idolize people, Pol, you're right. I don't condone Max's drinking, but you have to allow even the people you most admire to be complex and contradictory like everybody else. The more interesting somebody is, the more complex.'

'Sure.'

'You don't have to like it, honey, but you do have to understand it.'

'Okay.'

Daddy stood up. 'All right, Polly. I'm sorry Max showed you

her clay feet. If you want to talk about it further, remember, Mother and I are right here.'

'Yes. I'm glad. Thanks.'

He left, and in a few minutes I heard a knock on my door. Xan's knock.

I didn't want to talk to him. So I just let him knock.

The soft knocking on my door roused me. I got out of bed and opened the door onto darkness.

"It's Millie," came her gentle voice, with a slight tremor. "My fan's off—I think the power's out—"

She followed me into the room, holding my arm, and then sat on the first bed. "Do you think something's wrong?"

Millie was obviously afraid, so I said, reassuringly, "It's just a power failure."

"You don't think it's some kind of emergency?"

"No, Millie, I think it's okay." Suddenly I realized that while a power outage was to me a sign of poor electricity, to Millie it could mean that a power plant had been bombed, it could mean a military coup, an attack on civilians— "I'll go check." I got up and slipped out onto the balcony. Nothing but normal night sounds. But Cyprus was an island of many emergencies, of being overrun by Italians, Turks, British, and, within the memory of everybody there, the Turks again. Millie came from a world of emergencies, of small countries fighting to get out from under the domination of foreign powers. I understood why she would be so afraid that she would fumble through the darkness to make contact with someone in the next room.

I went back in. "Everything's okay. All quiet. I'm sure it's just the power going off because it's so hot and everybody's got fans on, and probably air-conditioners at the hotel."

"Thanks, Polly dear. Thanks. I'll go back to bed now."

I lit a match and helped her back to her room, standing in the doorway until I heard her bed creak and she called good night. I went back to bed, but there was no sound from Millie's room, no comfortable snoring. I wondered what she was remembering.

I got up early enough to finish making the beds, and then I still had time to go into the church for a few minutes before breakfast. I went deep into the interior, to the dark entrance of the cave.

A shadow moved, and I turned to see Vee coming toward me. "I always drop in when the doors are open," she said. "It's a very special place." I nodded. "Osia Theola is indeed kind in what she lets us know about ourselves. She tells me that I am stronger than I think I am. I've bought a little icon of her to take home. There are some nice ones in that little shop up the hill." We were silent for a while. Then Vee asked gently, "What does Theola tell you?"

"She warms the cold place in my heart," I said. "She's helping the ice to thaw."

"But you have a loving heart, Polly, that's one of the first things I noticed about you. I'm glad Theola's making you realize it." She laughed a little wistfully. "Some people would call this the rankest superstition. But is it? What happens in a place does leave its imprint. Even today the sites of the concentration camps have a bone-chilling cold, no matter how hot the day. Osia Theola left love here, and we can catch it from her."

The ancient sacristan came up to us then, with two tiny bouquets. He, too, must have picked up the largeness of love from Blessed Theola, because he warmed us with it.

We left the candlelit church and went to breakfast.

I had been right about the power failure. Krhis announced that the power had gone off largely because of the air-conditioning at the hotel and that the power company promised to have it back on by noon.

Tullia served us fresh, hot bread, her toothless smile lavished on us as though we were her honored guests. Sophonisba brought us eggs, smiling so that her front gold tooth reflected the light.

I was sitting with my back to the monastery grounds, facing the sea, so I did not see anyone coming until I noticed people's heads turning, and I turned, too, and there was Zachary.

"Found you at last, Polly," he said, coming up the steps. He smiled at the tableful of what must have seemed to him very strange people. "I'm Zachary Gray, a friend of Polly's," he said. "I got here last night, just in time for the blackout at the hotel. I wonder if I could steal Polly for lunch today?"

"Oh, no, Zach—" I protested. "I have work to do."

Krhis looked at Norine, who looked at me, then said, "I'll need Polly in the office for a while this morning, but there's no reason she can't be free by eleven. And we won't need her again till two."

"That's fine," Zachary said. "I'll be back for you at eleven."

"Won't you stay and have a cup of coffee?" Krhis suggested.

"No, thanks. I've some things to do back at the hotel. I'm off to Mykonos tomorrow, so this is my only chance to see Polly till I meet her plane in Athens."

At that, Omio gave Zachary a sharp look. I did not think they would get on. Zachary represented a good many things Omio was fighting, and while somebody like Sandy could see this clearly and still get along courteously with Zachary, I was not sure about Omio.

"I'll rent a sailboat or a kayak for us," Zachary called as he jumped down the steps. "Nice to have seen all of you."

"Very good-looking," Millie said.

"He is the young man who has kept calling?" Norine accused rather than asked.

"Yes." And who sent me flowers. And made me feel special. I was excited to see him, and yet he seemed a slightly discordant note in this place and with these people. But I didn't wish he hadn't come.

"An old friend?" Norine asked.

"No, I met him while I was in Athens."

"You want to go out with him?" Bashemath asked.

"Well—he was very kind to me in Athens."

"It'll be a kind of culture shock," Vee said, "leaving the monastery and going to—oh, another world, with the beach full of topless bathers, and people sitting around the pool drinking and ignoring the real, unchlorinated water."

"If he takes you swimming," Omio said severely, "don't go out too far. And don't be late."

"I won't be," I said. "I'll have to be back at two to help Norine."

"And then, later, we'll have our swim," Vee said.

Zachary picked me up promptly at eleven, in a rented car.

"Do you have your bathing suit?"

"I can get it."

"Do, and hurry. I've made our reservations for lunch at one, and I thought we'd have a swim and a sail first."

He'd rented a cabana for me to dress in and suggested that we swim in the pool.

"No, thanks. I don't like chlorine and I do like salt water."

"All those rough waves—" But we went in the ocean. Zachary swam moderately well. He did the strokes correctly, but he had no stamina. After a few minutes he splashed into shore. I followed him, and started to tell him a little about the conference staff, but it was obvious that he wasn't interested in the people or the worlds they came from.

"Do your parents know this mixed kind of group you're with?"

"Of course."

He headed toward the pier. "I've rented us a kayak. All the sailboats were taken, okay?"

"Sure, a kayak's fine." Anything would have been fine with me, even a rowboat. I could still hardly believe that Zachary had come all this way to see me.

The kayak was waiting at the little landing dock. Zachary and the attendant helped me in, and Zachary sat behind, holding the double paddle used for this little play boat. The attendant said something in Greek that I could not quite understand, but I think he was warning us to be careful not to go beyond the white ropes strung from red buoys which enclosed a sizable section of water.

"You're a help to me, Polly," Zachary said. "You help me think clearly. I'd predicated my life on being a corporate lawyer.

If I don't want that, what do I want? I couldn't be a doctor, I faint at the sight of blood. Listen, Red—" He splashed with the paddle instead of feathering. "I talked with my pop on the phone, and he knows your aunt and uncle."

"He does!"

Zachary nodded. "Not personally. Reputation. He says they're dangerous."

"They're not—"

"Hey, hold it, don't rock the boat, you'll have us in the soup."

"Sorry." My jerky movement had set the little craft rocking, but it stabilized quickly. "Sandy and Rhea—"

"Don't you see, Pop has to think that way? Megabucks is the only game he knows, and people who care about people get in his way. If you want to put a highway through a village, you can't be concerned about the people in the village whose homes are going to be destroyed."

"Is that your world?" I asked. "Do you really want that?"

"No, Polly, I don't. That's why I wanted to be with you today. I'm glad Dragon Lady gave you at least three hours off." He put the paddle across the thwarts and we drifted gently. "I wanted to tell you that I've decided to stop puddling around Europe. I'm flying home—after we've had our reunion in Athens airport—and I'm going back to college."

"That's wonderful!" Then I looked around us at the softly slapping water. "We're outside the white ropes."

"That's okay. I went way out this morning. And the sailboats all go out." He pointed to half a dozen colorful sails. "I'll paddle us back in a minute. Right now I need to talk. The problem is, Polly, I'm going back to college, but I'm not sure I still want to be a lawyer and take over Pop's world."

"Sandy and Rhea are lawyers," I reminded him.

"I'm not sure I'd have the guts to do what they're doing. I'm learning that I do have limitations."

"Sure," I said, "we all do, but given the chance, we can go beyond our limitations."

"Do I want to? At least, do I want to put my life on the line? People like your uncle and aunt are in danger, do you realize that? People like my pop, particularly those with even more money and power than my pop, are pretty ruthless about wiping out people who get in the way. They look down on lawyers who care about human life as stupid sentimentalists."

"Rhea and Sandy aren't sentimental!" I didn't like this conversation. I looked around and all I could see was water and a couple of sailboats in the distance. The tide, I thought, was going out, and we'd drifted rapidly. "Zachary," I said, "I don't see the hotel."

He looked around. "Okay, we'll go back." He picked up the paddle. "The thing is, Polly, you've really made a difference in the way I think about things. I've never been close to my pop, never loved him, but I thought his way of life was a realistic one and that I had every right to inherit power and prestige. But here he is, middle-aged, with ulcers, not happy, and not knowing how to do anything but make bigger and bigger deals. I don't think that's what I want to look forward to."

"I'm glad, Zach, very glad." I didn't think I could take much credit for his decision. It must have been under the surface all the time, waiting to break through. But I was glad it had.

He went on. "I want to thank you, Polly. I'm not sure what I'm going to do with my life, but you've turned it completely around." He rested the paddle again and bent forward to kiss me. It stopped being just a kiss and began to be more, and suddenly I wasn't sure how much I believed of all he'd just said. He drew back slightly, breathed, "Oh, Polly, come—" He put his hand behind my head to draw me closer.

"No, Zach—" The boat started rocking violently.

"Watch it!" And suddenly we were in the water. We came up sputtering. I grabbed at the kayak as it began to slip away from us.

"Now look what you've done!" he shouted.

I didn't answer. He was thrashing about, tiring himself. "Here!" I called. "Here! Hold on!"

He grabbed at the overturned kayak and managed to get a grip. If it had been a canoe, I could have turned it over and got in. It's not so easy with an overturned kayak. "Tread water for a minute," I said, "and let me try to right the kayak." Without saying anything, he let go, and I got under the gunwales and pushed, kicking as hard as I could, and to my relief the little play boat was light enough so that I could flip it over. The paddle was gone. "Do you think you can climb back in?" I asked.

"I doubt it. I'm not the athletic type. Do you want to try? Then maybe you can pull me in. I'll hold on and try to keep it level for you."

Even without the paddle, we'd be better off in the boat. Zachary's stamina was not going to last long. But when I tried to pull myself up over the gunwales, Zachary lost his grip. "Zach! Hold on!"

He splashed back to the kayak, and grabbed at the side, almost overturning it again. This was not going to work. I looked around for the sailboats, but although I saw a couple, they weren't in hailing distance, and they were too far off for anybody to notice us. We couldn't stay in the water for several hours till Norine missed me and someone came to look for us.

Zachary realized this, too. "If I let go and dog-paddle again, do you think you can get in without my help?"

"I'll try." I didn't say it would be easier without his 'help.' I was almost in the kayak when suddenly he grabbed at it and I lost my balance and slid back into the water. Fortunately, the boat did not overturn again. But the little boat was made for the quiet waters around the dock, within the boundaries of the ropes, not for the open sea. I didn't think Zachary knew much about boats. Left to myself, I could have managed to clamber in without overturning it, but Zachary was in a silent panic, and whatever I did, he was going to undo by grasping at the sides, or letting go and risk being swept away by the undertow.

"I can't see the hotel," he said. I'd already told him that.

"Listen, Zach." My voice was urgent. "Let me try once more to climb in. Tread water, but make sure you don't drift away."

"I'll try."

He let go and began to dog-paddle. I put one hand on either gunwale for balance and had almost heaved myself in when I heard him cry out. He had already drifted two lengths of the boat. I dropped back in the water, still holding the kayak with one hand, because it would be madness to lose it, and kicked as strongly as I could in his direction. "Zachary! Swim! Try to swim toward me!" The distance between us began to widen, and I could see that he was floundering, moving arms and legs aimlessly and futilely. I was going to have to let the kayak go in order to get him, and then what? We could never make it back to the kayak together; he simply didn't swim well enough. And we certainly couldn't even think of trying to make it to shore against the tide.

I wasn't ready to die.

But I couldn't save myself and let Zachary drown.

Why not? If I didn't save myself, we'd both drown, and what good would that do?

"Polly—"

"Don't thrash, Zachary," I shouted. "I'm coming." I let go of the kayak.

"Polly!"

I had one arm around Zachary and was kicking to keep afloat. He was pulling me down. I couldn't go on holding both of us up for much longer.

"Polly!"

It wasn't Zachary calling me. Zachary was an exhausted, dead weight.

"Polly!"

"Here!" I shouted. "Here, Omio, here!"

"Keep calling, so I don't lose you."

"Here! Here, Omio, here!"

And suddenly I saw a rowboat, a lovely, solid rowboat, with Omio at the oars. He saw us and pulled the boat to us with strong, sure strokes.

"Get Zachary in first," I said.

Omio rested the oars, reached out one strong arm, then both, as he realized that Zachary could do little to help himself. Somehow or other, Omio pulling, me pushing, we managed to get him into the rowboat. Then Omio's hands were stretched down to me, and with his help I heaved myself up, and flopped into the bottom of the boat, panting. "The kayak—" I whispered.

"Forget it," Omio said fiercely. Then he turned to Zachary.

He let out a long stream of invective in Bakian. If I had thought Bashemath's anger could be terrifying, I was not prepared for Omio's.

"I'll pay for the kayak," Zachary said.

"And could you have paid for Polly's life? Do you know if I had been five minutes later you'd both have been dead? Would you have made everything right by paying for the funeral?" He was an avenging angel in his anger.

I was still gasping for breath. "How did you—how did you know?"

"I was worried. And Vee said she smelled danger, and told Frank, and he went with us to the hotel, and we were told you'd gone out in a kayak. But there weren't any kayaks in the roped-in area. So Frank suggested I take the rowboat. He and Vee will be waiting for us." He was rowing with strong, smooth strokes. Even so, it seemed a long time before we could see shore and the hotel. "Where did you think you were going?" Omio asked Zachary.

Some of Zachary's confidence had returned, though his face was pallid. "I was thinking of emigrating to Syria with Polly. It was farther than I realized."

"It is not funny." Omio still sounded enraged.

"Oh, come on," Zachary said. And then, with one of his lightning switches, "I was an arrogant fool, and I'm beyond apology."

"I would not have any harm come to Polly," Omio said.

Vee and Frank were waiting at the landing dock, their faces lighting in relief as they saw us.

Omio drew the rowboat skillfully up to the dock, and the attendant helped me out.

"Thank God you're safe," Vee said.

"What happened?" Frank asked.

Zachary spoke swiftly, before Omio could say anything. "I misjudged the tide and lost my bearings."

Omio burst out, "And lost the kayak. Polly was holding him up in the open sea. They couldn't have lasted much longer."

I discovered that I was trembling. Frank put out a hand to steady me.

"We'll take you home," Omio said.

"Polly is having lunch with me," Zachary said.

Omio leapt onto the dock. "Polly is not going anywhere with you."

For a second I thought he and Zachary were going to get into a fight. Frank stepped between them, and I said, "I think I'm too tired to eat. I'm going to get my clothes on." And I walked away from them, went to the cabana, and changed. I was still very shaky.

When I had my dress back on, sandals on my feet, I returned to the hotel, where they were sitting at one of the terrace tables, waiting. The three men rose as I approached. Zachary said, "Polly, please forgive me for having been such a monstrous fool."

Frank stopped his apologies. "Polly's exhausted, and we need to get her to bed."

Zachary did not argue. "I'll call you, Polly, if you're willing to speak to me again. I'll never be such a chauvinist idiot—"

"It's okay, Zachary," I said.

Frank borrowed Zachary's rented car to drive us home, and I was grateful. I wasn't at all sure my wobbly legs would have made it. Of course we'd missed lunch, but everybody was still in the refectory. Norine looked up in surprise.

"Omio and Frank will explain," Vee said. "I want to get Polly to her room and into bed."

Without saying anything, and somehow inconspicuous despite her great height, Bashemath fell into step beside us.

"There was a near-catastrophe," Vee said. "Polly needs a hot bath and bed."

"It won't be a very hot bath," Bashemath said.

"Even lukewarm would be heavenly."

When we got to the room, the fan was whirring, so the power was back on. "Go along," Vee said to me. "I'll tell Bashemath what happened."

The water was at least warm, and felt wonderful, and I lay back and relaxed for a long time, almost dozing once or twice, till my twitching muscles let go their panic tightness. Then it occurred to me that Vee and Bashemath might be waiting, so I got out and dried myself and put on my nightgown.

Only Bashemath was in the room. "Vee's gone to see about getting some hot soup for you."

I sat, facing her dignified presence. "Omio saved my life."

"And Vee and Frank. It was Vee who had the knowing that there was something wrong, and Frank who had the wisdom to take her seriously."

"How did Vee know?"

"Vee is a poet. Sometimes poets still have the ancient knowings."

I was grateful to Vee, to Frank. "But, Bashemath," I said, "it was Omio who came with the boat and got us out of the water. I was tiring—we were almost drowning—I couldn't have held on much longer."

"But you had left the little boat and were holding up this strange young man—"

"What else could I do?"

"What else?" She turned to answer a knock. Norine came in, carrying a kettle of something which smelled delicious. Millie followed with bowls, and Frank with spoons. Omio and Vee came in together. Norine set the kettle down on the empty desk.

"Get into bed, Polly. We will spoil you this afternoon, okeydokey? You and your rescuers will have some of this good soup Tullia has prepared, and then you will sleep. Someone will bring you tea, and you can come to the afternoon meeting, okeydokey?"

"Very okeydokey," I said. Every bone and muscle ached, but I was so full of the love of these people I had not even met a few days ago that it didn't matter. Norine ladled out a rich soup full of vegetables and fish, and Vee and Frank and Omio and I ate. I was ravenously hungry. Back at the hotel, I had thought I would never want to eat again.

Norine noticed Zachary's flowers, which were drooping despite my ministrations. "These are completely wilted. Do you want me to throw them out for you?"

It seemed like throwing Zachary out, but Norine didn't know that, and it didn't make much sense to keep dead flowers, so I told her to go ahead.

When we'd finished eating, everybody stood up to leave, except Millie, who came and sat by me. "I will give Polly a back rub. She will sleep better. Roll over, little one." I hardly heard the others leave. Millie's hands were strong yet tender, and she seemed to know which muscles I had strained.

When I was half asleep, Millie drew the sheet up over me, and then started to sing, not *Saranam*, or any of the songs she'd sung to the group with her miraculous voice, but a song with an odd, minor melody, and words I didn't understand but which weren't unlike Gaean.

And I realized that she was singing to me as her baby, that for this moment I *was* Millie's baby—perhaps one of the children she had lost—and I was lapped in her love.

When I woke up she was gone, and my muscles were no longer tense, but the scar on my foot was pulling painfully. Why?

Renny had come to look at my foot again on Sunday. He called on Monday after school, though he didn't come over because I said my foot was fine, and he called again on Tuesday. When Xan yelled to me on Wednesday, 'Hey, Pol, telephone, I think it's Renny again,' I said, 'Look, if you keep calling they'll know something's wrong.'

'Something *is* wrong.'

'Okay, but I don't want them worried.'

'Aren't they?'

'I guess, but they don't know what about, and I don't want them to know.'

It was that evening Sandy called from Washington and said it just happened that he had to go down to Cape Canaveral to see someone and he'd drop off at Benne Seed on the way if we'd meet his plane in Charleston on Friday. This is the kind of thing Sandy does, so nobody thought anything about it. We were accustomed to having him or Rhea drop in on us from all kinds of places.

But when we were alone together, which wasn't until Saturday afternoon, he said, 'I need some exercise. Let's go walk on the beach.'

We took our sandals off and splashed along the water's edge. He said, 'Max called me.'

'Max?' I, too, had simply taken Sandy's coming for granted.

'She told me to come, because you needed me.'

We had splashed a little farther into the water, and an unexpected wave wet Sandy's rolled-up pants, so we turned toward the dunes. Finally I asked, 'Why did she say that?'

'She told me what happened. Do you want to talk about it?'

I was not prepared to have Sandy know. I was not prepared for him to have come to Benne Seed because Max had called him. 'You won't say anything to Mother or Daddy?'

'You haven't said anything?'

'No.'

'Are you going to?'

'No.'

'Are you trying to protect them?'

I didn't know who I was trying to protect.

'Polly, you've had a lot of responsibility, helping your mother with the little ones, helping your father in the lab, doing all kinds of jobs most kids your age haven't had to do. You're very mature for your age in many ways—'

'And very immature in others,' I finished for him. 'Please, Sandy, I don't want you to say anything to Mother and Daddy.'

He looked at me for a long time. At last I let my eyes drop. 'All right.' He turned toward a large sand dune, climbed partly up it, and sat down in a tangle of scuppernong grapevines. 'I think I'd just as soon not say anything to them about it myself. The problem is, Polly, you made Max into a god.'

'I know that.'

'Can't you let her be a little human?'

I didn't answer.

'Are you being fair to Max?'

Sandy, like Ursula, was considering Max and not me. 'Was Max being fair to me?'

'No. But two wrongs never make a right.'

'What am I doing wrong?' Did he somehow know about Renny?

But he said, 'It's not what you're doing wrong. It's what you're not doing. Max wants to talk to you.'

I shook my head and looked into the vines as though looking for the dark fruit of the scuppernongs.

'Polly.' He waited till I looked at him. 'Max is dying.'

I nodded, again dropping my glance.

'Perhaps you're too young,' he said, as though to himself. 'Too overwhelmed. You need time. But I'm not sure there's enough time.' I did not answer. He slid down from the dune, and I followed him back to the water's edge. 'Your mother is inviting Max and Ursula to dinner tonight. It's the natural thing to do, since we've been friends for years and I haven't been here since Christmas.'

'I don't want them to come.'

'I understand that. And I don't know whether or not they will come.'

I got up and headed for the house. I could not see Max. I could not. I'd have to get out of it somehow.

But when I got home Mother was on the phone. It was Urs saying Max wasn't feeling well. Sandy took the Land-Rover and went over to Beau Allaire. Renny called to ask me to go out for pizza. He was able to borrow a boat, so we went, as usual, to Petros', and sat in our usual booth. Max was between us. What had happened on Nell's green sleeping porch was between us.

'Polly, I don't want you to get the idea that making love is a casual, one-time thing.'

'It wasn't casual, it was wonderful.'

He put his hand over mine. 'I'm glad it was wonderful. For me, too. If my parents knew what happened between us, they'd think I should ask you to marry me, but that wouldn't be a good idea. I have a lot more studying to do, and so do you. You're much too young. But, Polly, please don't let—'

I stopped him. 'Renny, don't worry about me. I'm not going to make a habit of throwing myself at guys. How often do I have to tell you? Please get off your guilt trip.'

Our pizza was put before us, steaming and bubbly with

cheese and anchovies and peppers. 'Renny the Square. That's me. But the Reniers believe that there *is* right and wrong, and a world without restraints is going down the drain.'

'Hey, Renny, I do have restraints.'

'What?'

'My family. My parents. And'—my voice was very low—'Max.'

'Max!'

'Max acted without restraints.'

'Okay,' Renny said. 'I'm glad you see it that way.'

I didn't know whether to hit or hug him. 'Maybe I acted without restraints with you, but I still thank you.'

He cut the pizza and put a slice on my plate. 'Oh, Polly, I don't know what to say.'

'Don't say anything. And don't let it spoil our being good friends.'

But everything was changed. He couldn't even talk about his pet South American diseases without our both thinking of Max.

'When you get back from Cyprus,' he said, 'you'll have had a million new experiences, and you'll have been separated by all that space and time—'

'I'll write you postcards,' I said.

In the boat on the way back to the Island he cut the motor as usual and bent to kiss me, then stopped.

'Why?' I asked.

He held me so tightly that it hurt. 'Not tonight, Pol. I'm not sure I could hold back.'

And he was right, Renny was right. He had wakened my body.

And Omio had saved that wakened body. I had been attracted to Omio from the very first evening. But now it was more, much more.

I lay there, half awake, thinking about Omio, when he knocked on my door and came in with a glass of iced tea.

I sat up. "Oh, Omio, thank you, thank you."

"It's only cold tea," he said.

"Not the tea. *Me*. My life. If it hadn't been for you, I'd be in a watery grave. I nearly was."

He put my glass down on the table between the beds and took my hands. "It was Frank, and Vee, as much as I, who saved you, Polly, but it has made you—lo, a part of me, a part of my own life."

"I'll always be grateful."

He was fierce. "I do not need gratitude. I do not want it. This is not our way." He smiled. "But we are friends forever in the mind of God, so I have brought you something." And he handed me the painting of the Laughing Christ from his notebook.

"But you can't take a page out of your book!" I protested.

"I will paste in another after I am home. I want you to have this so that you will always remember me."

"I would always remember you, no matter what."

"Lo, we need something we can touch or see," Omio said.

I wasn't sure how I felt about the painting of the Laughing Christ. Omio had no way of knowing that it could remind me of anybody except himself. I looked at it, and saw a double image, the face of sheer joy and Max carrying the statue, her face distorted with whiskey and fear.

"What is it?" Omio asked.

"Nothing."

"I have hurt you."

"No—no—it's not you at all."

"That young man, that Zachary?"

I shook my head. "Not Zachary. Omio—if I take this, I need to give you something, and I don't have anything."

"A picture of yourself? A snapshot?"

"I don't go around carrying pictures of myself. Well—I do have my school ID card, but it's an awful picture like most ID cards."

"But I may have it?"

"Sure, if you want it." Actually, it wasn't that bad a picture, or I wouldn't have dreamed of giving it to him. I got up and went to the desk and took it from my school notebook. I handed the picture to him.

He smiled. "Yes. That's my Polly." He opened his wallet. "You won't need it when you get back to school?"

"I can get another." It was all I had to give to Omio, and I wanted him to have something of me.

"Good, then, I will put it here, next to—" And he indicated a snapshot of a blond, fair-skinned girl with curly golden hair. On her lap was a dark-skinned baby boy, with a surprising mop of that fair hair.

"Who are they?" I asked curiously.

He looked surprised. "My wife and baby. When I married a girl who was born in England, I knew that I had truly forgiven, all the way deep in my heart, what had been done to my father."

My lips felt the way they do when the dentist has pumped them full of novocaine. "I didn't know you were married."

His eyes widened. "But, my Polly, I showed you my pictures that first night."

"No."

"How could I not? I showed them to Krhis, I know. Our little one was born since I last saw Krhis, and is named after him."

I got up and took the picture of the Laughing Christ to my desk and propped it up. But now I saw no laughter in the face, no joy. "Norine will be wanting me," I said. "I've got to get dressed."

"Polly, you really did not know that I have a wife?"

I shook my head.

"Why does it make such a difference?"

I shrugged. "It doesn't."

He put one hand lightly on my shoulder. "I am married to one wife, and I will be true to her. But that does not mean that no one else can touch my soul."

"No," I said. "Please go, Omio. I have to dress."

He dropped his hand. "To deny friendship is unlove." And he left.

Why was I making such a big deal out of Omio's not telling me he was married? He thought I knew. He wasn't trying to keep anything from me. He truly thought I knew. And why should it matter, anyhow? We'd be together for three weeks, and then Omio would go back to Baki, and I'd go back to Benne Seed, and maybe we'd write a couple of times, and that would be that.

But Omio had kissed my eyelids under the fig-sycamore tree. Omio had pulled me out of the sea. Yet, despite my own imaginings of his kisses, his touch, I knew that Omio had never kissed me as Renny had kissed me in the boat on the way back to Benne Seed. Omio knew restraints.

We were in Osia Theola. Theola's love, and her perception of truth, were restraints. Krhis was a restraint.

I worked in the office with Norine for the rest of the afternoon. If I seemed preoccupied or upset, she put it down to the accident with Zachary. She kept me busy with the ancient mimeograph machine, and I did my best to run off stencils without getting completely covered with purple ink in the process.

"I hope Frank is not getting too fond of Vee." She frowned.

"Does he know? About her husband?"

"She does not make it a secret. Neither does she talk about it."

"Well—at least they can be friends." As I could be friends with Omio. To deny friendship is unlove, he had said.

Norine's hands slowed down as she was feeding paper into the machine. "Without friends, we would not survive."

And I knew nothing about what had hurt Norine.

The phone rang, and she answered it in her usual brisk manner. "I'll see," I heard her say. "She may not wish to speak with you." She turned to me, her hand over the mouthpiece. "It is that young man who has caused so much trouble. You don't have to speak to him." She shook her head.

But I moved toward the phone. "I think I'd better. He's got to be feeling terrible."

Maybe my concern over Zachary's feeling was, under all the circumstances, inconsistent of me.

He was, indeed, contrite, and I had it in me to be sorry for him, and agreed to meet him in Athens between flights.

Norine had left me alone, saying that she had to speak to Sophonisba and Tullia.

"Hey, Pol, you know I'm really sorry, don't you?" he asked. "I mean, I know it was my fault we went in the soup, not yours."

"It's okay," I said, and that was all I could think of to say to Zachary. The funny thing was, it *was* okay. I could let Zachary be the way he was and it didn't really bother me.

Was it because I didn't really care about him that much? He'd been terrific while I was in Athens; I'd had fun with him; he'd done marvels for my ego. But despite his talk about our chemistry being so great, it really wasn't. He didn't do things to my pheromones the way Renny did. Or Omio. I was going to be able to say a casual goodbye to Zachary, whether on Cyprus or in Athens airport; it wasn't going to make a ragged scar in my life.

I liked him, but I didn't love him. And that was very confusing, because I certainly hadn't sorted out what love is.

"Hey, are you there?" he asked. The phone was crackling as though we were talking long-distance.

"I'm right here. But I have work to do, Zach."

"But is everything okay with us? I haven't ruined it all?"

"No," I said. "It was an accident."

"So you don't mind if I meet your plane in Athens?"

"No, I don't mind a bit. It will be fun."

"Can you sound a little more enthusiastic?"

"Sure, Zach, I'm still kind of tired."

"I'm just grateful that you're not dumping me," he said. "See you in Athens."

I hung up and went back to the recalcitrant mimeograph machine, getting even more ink on myself. I didn't notice when Krhis came into the office until he spoke.

"Polly?"

I looked up from the machine and wiped my inky fingers on a rag. "Oh, Krhis. Hello."

"You are doing a good job, Polly, being very helpful."

"Thank you. I'm loving every minute of it."

"Despite your accident with the kayak?"

"Thanks to Omio—and Vee and Frank—nothing terrible happened."

"Norine is afraid we're working you too hard."

"Oh, no! I was afraid I wasn't working hard enough!"

"I am glad indeed that Max arranged for you to come to us."

I fiddled with the machine, spilling more ink.

"Polly, whenever I mention Max, you withdraw. Is something wrong?"

"Yes," I said, "but since Max didn't tell you—"

"What is it? Would you be betraying a confidence by telling me?"

I blurted out, "Max is dying. Maybe I am betraying a confidence, but oh, Krhis, she's afraid, and maybe you could pray for her—"

I could see a shadow of grief cross his face. "I will pray."

"She has an awful South American disease, transmitted by an insect bite. It affects the heart, and it's slow and painful. And lethal." I managed to keep my voice level.

He accepted without question what I said. "I'm glad you told me." He took my hands and looked into my eyes. "I think Maxa would be glad, too."

"I'm glad you know," I said. "Oh, Krhis, I'm very glad you know."

He squeezed my hands gently. "You are covered with ink. Go back to the dormitory, where there is warm water to wash it off."

I nodded. Left.

Krhis's prayers would not save Max's life. But they were nevertheless very important.

Omio came up to me as I walked along the path with the roses.

"I'm inky." I held out my purple hands. "Don't touch me."

"My Polly, you have been beaten, and you are still bleeding, and, lo, I have rubbed salt in your wounds."

I shook my head. Tears rushed to my eyes. "I'm being very silly."

"Is it that Zachary? Has it something to do with him?"

"No!"

"But you have been hurt. When I gave you my picture of the Laughing Christ, I hurt you. If you do not want to keep it, I will not be offended."

"No. Please. I want to keep it."

"Lo, I am glad then, of that. Before you came to Cyprus, someone hurt you?"

"Yes. But I'm not thinking straight about that, either."

"Are we still friends?"

"Of course." I closed my eyes, and the slanting rays of the sun made dancing dots behind my eyelids. "I don't know what's the matter. It doesn't have anything to do with you."

"Doesn't it? That does not make me happy." His fingers lightly touched mine. "We of Baki are still close to the old ways. It was always understood that it was possible to love more than one person at a time, without dishonor."

I nodded, looking at our shadows, which were lengthening on the hot ground.

"And," he said, "Jesus was more forgiving to those who made mistakes in love than to those who judged each other harshly and were cold of heart."

"Your picture"—I tried to speak over the lump in my throat—"of the Laughing Christ will not let me forget that. Omio, I do have to go wash off all this ink."

"And then we will meet Vee under our fig-sycamore tree. She is ready to go swimming."

I got most of the ink off before going to the tree, where Omio and Vee waited.

"Sure you're up to it?" Vee asked me.

"Sure. I had a good nap this afternoon." And my foot no longer hurt me.

When the water came in view, Omio stopped us. "Look!" he exclaimed. The moon rose above the water, waxing full and beneficent, while on the other horizon the great orb of golden sun slid down into the darkness behind the sea's horizon. I had never before seen the end of day and the beginning of night greet each other. We were caught in the loveliness between the two.

"Oh—joy!" Vee breathed.

Above us the sky was a tent of blues and violets and greens, with just a touch of rose, and we were enclosed in it. We walked slowly until we got to the path Omio and I had made through the encircling ring of stones.

"What a splendid job," Vee said. She bent down to the stones and searched until she had found four small round white ones. She put them in the pocket of her terry robe. "One for each of us. And one for Frank. Whenever there is a full moon we will hold our moon stones and think of Osia Theola, and the rising of the moon and the setting of the sun. Now, children, you go ahead and race."

"Just one quick one," I said. We swam parallel to the shore, and I could tell that Omio was constantly checking me.

"I'm a good swimmer, Omio, you don't have to worry."

He swam beside me. "If you were not a good swimmer, lo, you would by now be washed up on some strange shore, and that—young man with you." He used a Bakian word I did not understand, but I knew it was not complimentary. He went on. "I do not want him meeting you in the airport. I, too, have time between planes. I will stay with you to take care of you. If you will let me."

I did not answer that. I tried to turn it into a joke. "He can't take me kayaking in Athens airport."

"He is not good for you," Omio said. "He wants too much. He is someone who takes. He does not give."

Those words were an echo of something, but at that moment I could not remember what.

"We'd better swim back to Vee," I said, and we turned toward shore.

When we got back to her, Omio asked, "Will we be able to have our afternoon swim tomorrow, when the delegates are all here?"

"We'll manage," Vee said. "We need the exercise. Don't worry about it now. We have today to rejoice in, and this moment of sheer loveliness."

"Don't you have a saying?" Omio asked. "That we should live every day as though we were going to die tomorrow and as though we were going to live forever?"

"It's an old adage," Vee said, "but a good one. Let's have another swim."

The water was caressing as I swam, this time with Vee. The sunset was deepening, and Omio called out and pointed, and we saw great bursts of lightning zagging behind clouds which were all the way across the Mediterranean.

"Shouldn't we get out?" I asked. "Isn't it dangerous?"

Vee reassured me. "It's all right. The storm is over in Lebanon and Syria, so far off we can't even hear the thunder."

But we swam for only a few minutes longer, then turned into shore. Vee put on her robe and pulled two of the stones out of the pocket, giving one to Omio, one to me. Moon stones.

We walked slowly through the steamy evening, up the sand and stones of the hill, pausing to say good night to the little goats. Omio leaned over the fence, and one of the goats came and nibbled on his fingers, and he stroked the soft ears. Then we walked on. Omio did not take my hand.

After dinner we stayed in the cloister. Krhis said that a bus would meet the first load of delegates in the early morning. There would be delegates coming in on three different planes. And our lives would change radically as we were joined by thirty or more different people from all over the world except behind the Iron Curtain.

"But you will be amazed at how quickly you come to know them," Krhis said, "how soon they will seem like family, as we are family around this table."

"But there will be four or more tables," Norine said, wiping her face. The breeze was hot, the air so heavy it was tangible.

"This heat has got to break soon," Krhis said, "and then I will insist on swimming at the scheduled time, Vee, please, in the middle of the day."

Vee put her hands together, bowing. "Yes, master."

Then we sang for a while, ending with *Saranam.*

> *For those who've gone, for those who stay,*
> *For those to come, following the Way,*

Be guest and guide both night and day,
Saranam, saranam, saranam.

Omio walked with me back to the dormitory and down the length of the long hall to my room. My room alone for this one last night. As I turned to open the door, he took my hands. "Would you want never to have had these days together, before everybody comes, never to have become friends?"

"Of course not. It's been marvelous."

"Isn't it still marvelous? It will go on being marvelous when lo, we are a large instead of a small family."

Omio had never promised me anything except friendship, and that was still his offering to me. The intensity of the experience with the kayak was part of that friendship. I had been greedy, grasping. Everything Renny had warned me of I had fallen for, if not actually, at least potentially. I felt small and chastened.

Chaste. Chastened.

Omio looked at me questioningly.

"It's still marvelous," I said.

Would I want never to have met Max? Never to have had my horizons expanded? Would I truly want to eradicate all of the good times because of one terrible time? Yes, it was terrible, Max insane with alcohol and pain and fear. But would I wipe out all the rest of it for that moment of dementia?

If I wanted Max as goddess, as idol, then, yes, I would have to destroy it. But not if I wanted Max as a human being, a vibrant, perceptive human being, who saw potential in me that I hardly dared dream of. Not if I wanted Max as she was, brilliant but flawed. Perhaps the greater the brilliance, the darker the flaw.

And what about Ursula? Surely Ursula had given me the best, with open generosity, not threatened by Max's love of me.

Why was I able to feel compassion for Zachary, who was selfish, who belonged to a world of power and corruption, and who had nearly killed me? Why didn't I want to wipe Zachary out?

And now I knew that I no longer wanted to wipe Max out. To wipe Max out was to wipe out part of myself.

"Good night, my Polly," Omio said.

I got ready for bed and worked on my school journal. I was in the middle of a sentence when there was a great flash of lightning, coming through the slats in the shutters, followed immediately by thunder, and the heat-breaking storm struck.

I closed my notebook. This was not the kind of violence one could write through.

There was a knock on my door and Millie came in. "You all right, Polly?"

"Yah, fine. This is going to break the heat."

"You're not afraid?"

"No."

"Would you like me to stay with you for a few minutes, till the worst is over? These storms never last long." Millie was nervous over man-made power failure, but not of a storm caused by nature. She had come to me, not because she was afraid, but because she thought I might be. "Yes, please, Millie," I said.

The lights went out.

Millie reached over and took my hand.

"Ahoy!" We heard Frank's voice outside, and he came in with a flashlight and a handful of stubby candles.

"Krhis has these for all of us." He came in, and we saw that Vee and Bashemath were with him. He lit candles for us, placing them on desks and chests of drawers. In a moment Norine came in and Vee beckoned her to join her on the spare bed.

Millie began to sing, her voice unwavering through the crashing of the thunder. Khris came and stood in the doorway, looking at us with his gentle smile, and Norine pulled him in and Omio offered him one of the desk chairs.

"All of us sing," Millie ordered, and we sang until the storm was over, and cool air came in, even through the cracks of the shutters. Bashemath stood up and yawned, and said good night.

"Yes, it is time," Krhis said. "Tomorrow will be a busy day."

Frank held out his hands to Vee. Omio left with them.

Krhis stood looking down on me sitting on the bed. "Bless you, Polly. Good night."

I felt somehow as though at last I had been allowed past the outer gates of Epidaurus, and into the sacred precincts.

Millie stood and stretched. "Good night, little one. It's cooler."

"Much. We may even need our blankets."

"You'd better not open the shutters, anyhow. Did you light your bug coil?"

"I will."

Millie bent down and kissed me, then went to her room.

I lit the coil, blew out the candle which remained. The darkness was lifted by the lightness in the air.

I was suddenly wide awake, because the power had come back on and the lights in my room were bright. I got up and turned them off, pushed the shutters open to a lovely cool breeze. Through the wall I could hear Millie snoring—safe, comfortable snores.

I slipped outside and the breeze was fresh, not burdened with moisture. I was not attacked by insects. The full moon was low in the sky, streaked by swiftly moving clouds. The storm in Osia Theola was over, but in those troubled lands across from us the electrical storm was still playing.

"Polly—"

I looked over the balcony and saw Omio.

"You're awake—"

"I was sound asleep," I said, "but when the power came on, my lights woke me."

"Come and sit on the wall by the fig sycamore for a while."

The stones hurt my bare feet, but I made it to the crumbling remnant of wall and sat looking at the moon sliding below the horizon. Omio sat beside me, and when I shivered in the cool breeze he drew me to him to keep me warm.

Whatever it was I had silently been demanding of Omio I was no longer demanding. I was happy sitting beside him, watching the night sky. I loved him, but I loved him as a friend, as I loved Max as a friend. The clean feeling of love blew through me with the breeze. I sighed with a joyful kind of relief.

Omio's arm tightened about me. "Is everything all right with us, Polly?"

"Everything is fine. I'm sorry I was such an idiot."

"It was not Omio," he said. "It was whoever hurt you."

"I was very confused."

"And now?"

"It's okay," I said wonderingly. "It's all right!"

"We are true, good friends?"

"True, good friends."

He kissed me, gently, on the cheek, and we climbed back up to the balconies, and he waited until I was in the room, drawing the shutters not quite closed.

I slept and dreamed. I went into the church and Osia Theola's cave. Inside the cave my littlest brother and sister, Johnny and Rosy, were blowing bubbles, and the bubbles with their iridescent colors illumined the darkness of the cave. Then I saw that each bubble was filled with stars, with galaxies, countless galaxies; each bubble was an island universe.

The cave was gone, the little ones were gone, and all I could see was the loveliness of the bubbles, universes glowing softly with the life of all creation.

And then I saw a hand, and all the bubbles were in the hand, which was holding them, tenderly, lovingly.

And in the dream I understood that this was Blessed Theola's vision of love.

I woke up even earlier than usual, feeling rested and refreshed. I dressed and hurried out into the clear air. The sun was warm, not hot; the day sparkled. Nobody was about, not even the old men eternally watering the roses.

I thought I heard sounds in the direction of the church, and moved across the compound. There was an early-morning service going on, and I stood in the doorway, watching the people standing quietly, their heads covered. I listened to the Byzantine chanting of the priest.

I felt a presence behind me, and it was Krhis.

We turned away from the church together. "Krhis, would it be possible for me to make an overseas call?"

"We can try." He did not sound surprised.

We went to the office, and he dialed several times, spoke to three different operators, finally gave the phone to me and left me alone. I gave the operator the number. There was a long, blank pause, and then the sound of distant ringing. And then a voice. "Hello?"

"Urs—"

"Yes, who is it?"

I had no idea what time it was at home. It didn't matter. "Urs, it's Polly. Max—may I speak to Max?"

Ursula's voice sounded hollow, with an echo following it. "Just a moment, child." . . . *moment, child.* The echo came faintly.

I waited. Waited.

And then Max's voice. "Polly?" . . . *Polly?*

"Max, I love you. I just wanted to call and tell you I love you—" I stopped because I could hear my own voice distantly echoing back what I had said.

"Oh, Polly, forgive me—"

"Me, too, forgive me, too—"

Forgive . . . forgive echoed back.

"I'm so glad you called" . . . *you called.*

"I love you, Max, I love you" . . . *love you.* "I have so much to tell you—" But before the echo had a chance to repeat my words the connection was cut and the phone went dead.

It was all right. I had said what I needed to say.

Krhis was waiting outside. He didn't ask me who I had needed to phone so suddenly. We walked slowly across the compound to the refectory part of the cloister. The cold place within me that had frozen and constricted my heart was gone. My heart was like a lotus, and in that little space there was room enough for Osia Theola, for all of Cyprus. For all the

stars in all of the galaxies. For all those bubbles which were
island universes.

In the cloister everybody was gathering for breakfast.

"Polly!" Norine called. "We will be very busy today. All the
delegates must come into the office, and we will check them
off and give them their blue folders and room assignments . . ."

She paused for breath and Omio took my hand and pulled
me to the chair next to his.

"Saranam," he said.

AN ACCEPTABLE TIME

For
Dana, Bér & Eddie
Ron, Annie & Jake

CHAPTER 1

SHE walked through an orchard, fallen apples red and cidery on the ground, crossed a stone wall, and wandered on into a small wood. The path was carpeted with leaves, red, orange, gold, giving off a rich, earthy smell. Polly scuffed along, pushing the toes of her running shoes through the lavish brightness. It was her first New England autumn and she was exhilarated by the colors drifting from the trees, dappling her hair with reflected amber and bronze. The sun shone with a golden haze through a muted blue sky. Leaves whispered to the ground. The air was crisp, but not cold. She hummed with contentment.

The trees were young, most no more than half a century old, with trunks still slender, completely unlike the great Spanish-moss-hung water and live oaks she had left less than a week before. Apples from a wild seedling had dropped onto the path. She picked one up, russet and a bit misshapen. But the fruit was crisp and juicy and she wandered on, eating, and spitting out the seeds.

Now the path led her toward a forest of much older trees, towering maples, spruce, and pine. Reaching above them all was an ancient oak, with large, serrated leaves of a deep bronze color, many still clinging tenaciously to the branches. It was very different from the Southern oaks she was used to, and she had not recognized it as one until she learned her mother and uncles had always called it the 'Grandfather Oak.'

'When we first moved here,' her grandmother had explained, 'most of the oaks were gone, killed by some disease. But this one survived, and now our land is full of young oaklings, all evidently disease-resistant, thanks to the Grandfather Oak.'

Now she looked at the oak and was startled to see a young man standing in its shadows. He was looking at her with lucid blue eyes which seemed to hold the light of the day. He wore some kind of white garment, and one hand was on the head of a tan dog with large, pricked-up ears, outlined in black.

The young man raised his hand in greeting, then turned and walked quickly into the forest. When she reached the great tree, he had disappeared from sight. She had thought he might speak to her, and she was curious.

The wind had risen and played through the pines, sounding almost like the rolling of the breakers on the beach at Benne Seed Island, off the coast of South Carolina, where her parents still were, and which she had left so short a time ago. She turned up the collar of the red anorak she had taken from the generous supply that hung on pegs outside her grandparents' kitchen door. It was her favorite because it fitted her well and was warm and comfortable, and she liked it because the pockets were full of all kinds of things: a small but very bright flashlight; a pair of scissors; a notepad in a leather binder, with a purple felt pen; an assortment of paper clips, safety pins, rubber bands; a pair of dark glasses; a dog biscuit (for what dog?).

She sat on a great flat glacial rock, known as the star-watching rock, and looked up at white clouds scudding across the sky. She sat up straighter as she heard music, a high, rather shrill piping of a folk melody. What was it? Who was making music out here in the middle of nowhere? She got up and walked, following the sound, past the Grandfather Oak, in the same direction as the young man with the dog.

She went past the oak and there, sitting on a stone wall, was another young man, this one with lustrous black hair, and skin too white, playing a penny whistle.

"Zachary!" She was totally startled. "Zachary Gray! What are you doing here?"

He took the whistle from his mouth and shoved it into a pocket in his leather jacket. Rose from the wall and came toward her, arms outstretched. "Well met by sunlight, Miss Polly O'Keefe. Zachary Gray at your service."

She pulled away from his embrace. "But I thought you were at UCLA!"

"Hey." He put his arm around her waist and hugged her. "Aren't you glad to see me?"

"Of course I'm glad to see you. But how did you get here? Not just New England, but here, at my grandparents'—"

He led her back to the wall. The stones still held warmth from the autumn sun. "I called your folks in South Carolina, and they informed me you were staying with your grandparents, so I drove over to say hello, and they—your grandparents—told me you'd gone for a walk, and if I came out here I'd probably find you." His voice was relaxed; he seemed perfectly at home.

"You drove here from UCLA?"

He laughed. "I'm taking an internship semester at a law firm in Hartford, specializing in insurance claims." His arm about her waist tightened. He bent toward her, touching his lips to hers.

She drew away. "Zach. No."

"I thought we were friends."

"We are. Friends."

"I thought you found me attractive."

"I do. But—not yet. Not now. You know that."

"Okay, Pol. But I can't afford to wait too long." Suddenly his eyes looked bleak. His lips tightened. Then, deliberately, he gave her one of his most charming smiles. "At least you're glad to see me."

"Very glad." Yes. Delighted, in fact, but totally surprised. She was flattered that he'd gone to the trouble to seek her out. She had met him in Athens the previous summer, where she had spent a few days before going to Cyprus to be a gofer at a conference on literature and literacy. It had been an incredibly rich experience, full of joy and pain, and in Athens Zachary had been charming to her, showing her a city he already knew well, and driving her around the surrounding countryside. But when he had said goodbye to her in the airport after the conference had ended, she had never expected to hear from him again.

"I can't believe it!" She smiled at him.

"Can't believe what, Red?"

"Don't call me Red," she replied automatically. "That you're here."

"Look at me. Touch me. It's me, Zach. And what are *you* doing here?"

"Going for a walk."

"I mean, staying with your grandparents."

"I'm studying with them. For a few months, at any rate. They're terrific."

"I gather they're famous scientists or something."

"Well, Grand's a Nobel Prize laureate. She's into little things—sub-sub-atomic particles. And Granddad's an astrophysicist and knows more about the space/time continuum than almost anybody except Einstein or Hawking."

"You always were a brain," he said. "You understand all that stuff?"

She laughed. "Only a very little." She was absurdly glad to see him. Her grandparents were, as she had said, terrific, but she hadn't seen anyone her own age and hadn't expected to.

"So why are you doing this instead of going to school at home?" he asked.

"I need lots more science than I could get at Cowpertown High, and getting to and from the mainland from Benne Seed was a real hassle."

"That's not the only reason."

"Isn't it enough?" It would have to be enough for Zachary, at least for now. She looked away from him, across the star-watching rock, to an autumn sky just turning toward dusk. The long rays of the sun touched the clouds with rose and gold, and the vivid colors of the leaves deepened. A dark shadow of purple moved across the low hills.

Zachary followed her gaze. "I love these mountains. So different from California mountains."

Polly nodded. "These are old mountains, ancient, worn down by rain and wind and time itself. Perspective-making."

"Do you need perspective?"

"Don't we all?" A leaf drifted down and settled on Polly's hair.

Zachary reached out long, pale fingers and took it off. "It's the same color as your hair. Beautiful."

Polly sighed. "I'm just beginning to be reconciled to my hair. Given a choice, I wouldn't have chosen orange."

"It's not orange." Zachary let the leaf fall to the ground. "It's the color of autumn."

—Nice, she thought. —How nice he can be. "This is the first time I've seen autumn foliage. I've always lived in warm climates. This is—I don't have any words. I thought nothing could beat the ocean, and nothing does, but this—"

"It has its own glory," Zachary said. "Pop's living in Sausalito now, and the view from his house can overwhelm, all that incredible expanse of Pacific. But this, as you say, gives perspective and peace.

"Your grandparents," he continued, "offered tea and cinnamon toast if I could find you and bring you back."

"Sure." She jumped down from the wall. As they passed the Grandfather Oak, she asked, "Hey, who was that blue-eyed guy I saw here a few minutes ago?"

He looked at her. "I thought he was someone who worked for your grandparents, a caretaker or gardener or something like that."

She shook her head.

"You mean they take care of this whole place themselves?"

"Yes. Well, a neighboring farmer hays the fields, but he's older, and this man was young, and he didn't look like a farmer to me."

Zachary laughed. "What do you think a farmer looks like? I grant you, this guy had a kind of nobility."

"Did you talk to him?"

"No, and that was, as I think about it, a little weird. He looked at me, and I looked at him, and I was going to say something, but he gave me this look, as though he was totally surprised to see me, I mean totally, and then he turned and walked into the woods. He had this big-eared dog with him, and they just took off. Not running. But when I looked, I didn't see them." He shrugged. "As I said, I thought he must be a caretaker or whatever, and a lot of those types are sort of surly. Do you suppose he was a poacher? Do you have pheasants or quail?"

"Both. And our land is very visibly posted. It's not big enough to be called a game preserve—most of the old farms around here were a hundred acres or less. But my grandparents like to keep it safe for the wildlife."

"Forget him," Zachary said. "I came out here looking for you and I've found you."

"I'm glad. Really glad." She smiled at him, her most brilliant smile. "Ready to go?"

"Sure. I think your grandparents are expecting us."

"Okay. We'll just go back across the star-watching rock."

"Star-watching rock?"

She stepped onto the large flat glacial rock. Patches of moss grew in the crevices. Mica sparkled in the long rays of the descending sun. "It's always been called that. It's a wonderful place to lie and watch the stars. It's my mother's favorite rock, from when she was a child."

They crossed the rock and walked along the path that led in the direction of the house. Zachary walked slowly, she noticed, breathing almost as though he had been running. She shortened her pace to match his. Under one of the wild apple trees scattered across the land the ground was slippery with wrinkled brown apples, and there was a pungent, cidery smell. Inadvertently she moved ahead of Zachary and came to a low stone wall that marked the boundary of the big field north of the house. On the wall a large black snake was curled in the last of the sunlight. "Hey!" Polly laughed in pleasure. "It's Louise the Larger!"

Zachary stopped, frozen in his tracks. "What are you talking about? That's a snake! Get away!"

"Oh, she won't hurt us. It's only Louise. She's just a harmless black snake," Polly assured Zachary. "When my uncles, Sandy and Dennys, were kids—you met Sandy in Athens—"

"He didn't approve of me." Zachary stepped back farther from the wall and the snake.

"It wasn't *you*," Polly said. "It was your father's conglomerates. Anyhow, there was a snake who lived in this wall, and my uncles called her Louise the Larger."

"I don't know much about snakes." Zachary retreated yet another step. "They terrify me. But then isn't this snake incredibly old?"

"Oh, she's probably not the same one. Grand and I saw her

sunning herself the other day, and she's exactly like the old Louise the Larger, and Grand said there hasn't been a black snake like Louise the Larger since my uncles left home."

"It's a crazy name." Zachary still did not approach, but stayed leaning against a young oak by the side of the path, as though catching his breath.

—It's a family joke, Polly thought. Zachary knew nothing about her family except that it was a large one, and she knew nothing about him except that his mother was dead and his father was rich beyond her comprehension. Louise later. "Ready?"

His voice was unsteady. "I'm not walking past that snake."

"She won't hurt you," Polly cajoled. "Honestly. She's completely harmless. And my grandmother said she was delighted to see her."

"I'm not moving." There was a tremor in Zachary's voice.

"It's really okay." Polly was coaxing. "And where you have snakes you don't have rats, and rats carry bubonic plague, and—" She stopped as the snake uncoiled, slowly, luxuriously, and slithered down into the stone wall. Zachary watched, hands dug deep into the pockets of his leather jacket, until the last inch of tail vanished. "She's gone," Polly urged. "Come on."

"She won't come out again?"

"She's gone to bed for the night." Polly sounded her most authoritative, although she knew little of the habits of black snakes. The more tropical snakes on Benne Seed Island were largely poisonous and to be avoided. She trusted her grandmother's assurance that Louise was benign, and so she crossed the wall and then held out her hand to Zachary, who took it and followed tentatively.

"It's *okay*." Polly tugged at his hand. "Let's go."

They started across the field to what Polly already thought of as home, her grandparents' house. It was an old white farmhouse which rambled pleasantly from the various wings that had been added throughout the centuries. Like most houses built over two hundred years ago in that windy part of the world, where winters were bitter and long, it faced south, where there was protection from the prevailing northwest winds. Off the pantry, which led from the kitchen to the garage, was a wing that held Polly's grandmother's lab. Originally, when the house had been part of a working dairy farm, it had been used as a pantry in which butter was churned, eggs candled.

To the east was the new wing, added after Polly's mother and uncles had left home. It held an enclosed swimming pool, not very large, but big enough for swimming laps, which had been strongly recommended for her grandfather's arthritis. Polly, like most children brought up on islands, was a swimmer, and she had established, in only a few days, her own pattern of a swim before dinner in the evening, sensing that her grandparents liked to be alone in the early morning for their pre-breakfast swim. In any case, the pool was large enough for two to swim in comfortably, but not three.

The downstairs rooms of the old house had been opened up, so that there was a comfortable L-shaped living room, and a big, rambly area that was kitchen/sitting room/dining room. Polly and Zachary approached the house from the north, climbing up onto the tiered terrace, which still held the summer furniture. "I've got to help Granddad get that into the cellar for the winter," she said. "It's too cold now for sitting outdoors for meals."

She led Zachary toward the kitchen and the pleasant aromas of cooking and an applewood fire. Four people were sitting around the oval table cluttered with tea cups and a plate of cinnamon toast. Her grandmother saw them and stood up. "Oh, good. You did find each other. Come on in. Tea's ready. Zachary, I'd like you to meet my old friend Dr. Louise Colubra, and her brother, Bishop Nason Colubra."

The bishop stood up to shake hands with Zachary. He wore narrow jeans and a striped rugby shirt and his thinness made him seem even taller than he was. He reminded Polly of a heron. He had strong, long hands and wore his one treasured possession, a large gold ring set with a beautiful topaz, in elegant contrast to his casual country clothes. "Retired," he said, "and come to live with my little sister."

Little indeed, in contrast to her brother. Dr. Louise was a small-boned woman, and if the bishop made Polly think of a heron, Dr. Louise was like a brown thrush in her tweed skirt and cardigan. She, too, shook hands with Zachary. "When Kate Murry calls me her old friend, I wonder what the 'old' refers to."

"Friendship, of course," Polly's grandmother said.

"Dr. Louise!" Polly took her place at the table, indicating to Zachary that he should sit beside her. "We saw your namesake!"

"Not the original Louise the Larger, surely?" The doctor took a plate of fragrant cinnamon toast and put it in front of Zachary.

"I'm sorry." Zachary stared at the doctor. "What's your name?"

"Louise Colubra."

"I get it!" Zachary sounded triumphant. "Colubra is Latin for snake!"

"That's right." Polly looked at him admiringly. Zachary had already shown himself to have surprising stores of knowledge. She remembered him telling her, for instance, that Greek architecture was limited because the Greeks had not discovered the arch. She went to the kitchen dresser to get mugs for herself and Zachary. "My uncles named the snake after Dr. Louise."

"But why Louise the *Larger*?"

The bishop smiled. "Louise is hardly large, and I gather the snake is—larger, at least, for a black snake, than Louise is for a human being."

Polly put the mugs on the table. "It's lots easier to explain Louise the Larger with Dr. Louise here, than back at the stone wall."

A kettle was humming on the wood stove, its lid rising and falling. Polly's grandfather lifted it with a potholder and poured water into the teapot. "Tea's pretty strong by now. I'd better thin it down." He put the kettle back on the stove, then poured tea for Polly and Zachary.

The bishop leaned across the table and helped himself to cinnamon toast. "The reason for our unceremonious visit," he said, swallowing, "is that I've found another one." He pointed to an object which sat like a loaf of bread by Polly's grandfather's mug.

"It looks like a stone," Polly said.

"And so it is," the bishop agreed. "Like any stone from any stone wall. But it isn't. Look."

Polly thought she saw lines on the stone, but they had probably been scratched as the old walls settled, or frost-heaved in winter.

But Zachary traced the stones with delicate fingers. "Hey, is this Ogam writing?"

The bishop beamed at him in delight and surprise. "It is, young man, it is! How do you know about it?"

"One of my bosses in Hartford is interested in these stones. And I've been going so stir-crazy in that stuffy office that I've let him rattle on to me. It's better than medical malpractice suits"—Dr. Louise stiffened—"and it *is* interesting, to think maybe people were here from Britain, here on the North American continent, as long ago as—oh, three thousand years."

"And you flunked out of all those fancy prep schools," Polly said wonderingly.

He smiled, took a sip of tea. "When something interests me, I retain it." He held out his cup and Polly refilled it.

She put the teapot down and tentatively touched the stone. "Is this a petroglyph?"

The bishop helped himself to more cinnamon toast. "Um-hm."

"And that's Og—"

"Ogam writing."

"What does it say?"

"If I'm translating it correctly, something about Venus, and peaceful harvests and mild government. What do you think, young man?"

Zachary shook his head. "This is the first Ogam stone I've actually seen. My boss has some photographs, but he's mostly interested in theory—Celts, and maybe druids, actually living with, and probably marrying, the natives."

Polly looked more closely. Very faintly she could see a couple of horizontal lines, with markings above and below them. "Some farmer used this for his stone wall and never even noticed?"

Her grandmother put another plate of cinnamon toast on the table and removed the empty one. The fragrance joined with that of the wood fire in the open fireplace.

"Two hundred years ago farmers had all they could do to eke out a living. And how many farmers today have time to examine the stones that get heaved up in the spring?" her grandfather asked.

"Still our biggest crop," Dr. Louise interjected.

Polly's grandfather pushed his glasses up his nose in a typical gesture. "And if they did see markings on the stones and realized they weren't random, they wouldn't have had the faintest idea what the markings were about."

His wife laughed. "Did you?"

He returned the laugh. "Touché. If it hadn't been for Nase I'd have continued in ignorant bliss."

Dr. Louise smiled at him. "Your work does tend to keep your head in the stars."

"Actually, Louise, astrophysicists get precious little time for stargazing."

"Where did you find this rock, Nase?" Mrs. Murry sat at the table and poured herself some tea.

"In that old stone wall you have to cross to get to the star-watching rock."

"Louise the Larger's wall!" Polly exclaimed, thinking that it was natural that the bishop should know about the star-watching rock; it had been a special place for the entire Murry family, not only her mother.

The bishop continued, "The early settlers were so busy clearing their fields, it was no wonder they didn't notice stones with Ogam markings."

"Ogam is an alphabet," Zachary explained to Polly. "A Celtic alphabet, with fifteen consonants and some vowels, with a few other signs for diphthongs, or double letters like *ng*."

"Ogam, however," the bishop added, "was primarily an oral, rather than a written, language. Would your boss like to see this stone?"

"He'd drop his teeth." Zachary grinned. "But I'm not going

to tell him. He'd just come and take over. No way." He looked at his watch, stood up. "Listen, this has been terrific, and I've enjoyed meeting everybody, but I didn't realize what time it was, and I've got a dinner date back in Hartford, but I'd like to drive over again soon if I may."

"Of course." Mrs. Murry rose. "Anytime. The only people Polly has seen since she's been here are the four of us antiques."

"You're not—" Polly started to protest.

But her grandmother continued, "There aren't many young people around, and we've worried about that."

"Do come, any weekend," Mr. Murry urged.

"Yes, do," Polly agreed.

"I don't really have to wait for the weekend," Zachary said. "I have Thursday afternoons off." He looked at Polly and she smiled at him. "Okay if I drive over then? It's not too much over an hour. I could be here by two."

"Of course. We'll expect you then."

The Murry grandparents and Polly accompanied Zachary out of the kitchen, past Mrs. Murry's lab, and through the garage. Zachary's small red sports car was parked next to a bright blue pickup truck.

Mr. Murry indicated it. "Nase's pride and joy. He drives like a madman. It's very pleasant to have met you, Zachary, and we look forward to seeing you on Thursday."

Zachary shook hands with the Murrys, kissed Polly lightly.

"What a nice young man," Mrs. Murry said, as they went back into the house.

And in the kitchen the bishop echoed her. "What a delightful young man."

"How amazing," Mr. Murry said, "that he knows about the Ogam stones."

"Oh, there've been a couple of articles about them in the Hartford papers," Dr. Louise said. "But he does seem a charming and bright young man. Very pale, though. Looks as if he spends too much time indoors. How do you know him, Polly?"

Polly squatted in front of the fire. "I met him last summer in Athens, before I went to the conference in Cyprus."

"What's his background?"

"He's from California, and his father's into all kinds of multinational big business. When Zachary bums around Europe he doesn't backpack, he stays in the best hotels. But I think he's kind of lonely."

"He's taking time off from college?"

"Yes. He's in college a little late. He didn't do well in school because if he's not interested, he doesn't bother." A half-grown kitten pushed out of the cellar, stalked across the room, and jumped into Polly's lap, causing her to sit back on her heels. "So where've you been, Hadron?" Polly scratched the striped head.

Dr. Louise raised her eyebrows. "A natural name for a sub-atomic physicist's cat."

The bishop said, mildly, "I thought it was a variant of Hadrian."

"Or we were mispronouncing it?" Mrs. Murry suggested.

He sighed. "I suppose it's a name for a sub-atomic particle or something like that?"

Dr. Louise asked, "Kate, why don't you and Alex get another dog?"

"Ananda lived to be sixteen. We haven't been that long without a dog."

"This house doesn't seem right without a dog."

"That's what Sandy and Dennys keep telling us." Mr. Murry turned from the stove and began drawing the curtains across the wide kitchen windows. "We've never gone out looking for dogs. They just seem to appear periodically."

Polly sighed comfortably and shifted position. She loved her grandparents and the Colubras because they affirmed her, made her believe in infinite possibilities. At home on Benne Seed Island, Polly was the eldest of a large family. Here she was the only one, with all the privileges of an only child. She looked up as her grandfather hefted the Ogam stone and set it down on the kitchen dresser.

"Three thousand years," he said. "Not much in galactic terms, but a great deal of time in human terms. Time long gone, as we limited creatures look at it. But when you're up in a space shuttle, ordinary concepts of time and space vanish. We still have much to learn about time. We'll never leave the solar system as long as we keep on thinking of time as a river flowing from one direction into the sea." He patted the stone.

"You've found other Ogam stones?" Polly asked.

"I haven't. Nase has. Nase, Polly might well be able to help out with the translations. She has a positive genius for languages."

Polly flushed. "Oh, Granddad, I just—"

"You speak Portuguese, Spanish, Italian, and French, don't you?"

"Well, yes, but—"

"And didn't you study some Chinese?"

Now she laughed. "One day, maybe. I do love languages. Last summer I picked up a little Greek."

Mrs. Murry lit the two kerosene lamps which flanked the pot of geraniums on the table. "Polly's being modest. According to those who know—her parents, her uncles—her ability with languages is amazing." Then, to Polly's relief, she changed the subject. "Louise, Nase, you will stay for dinner, won't you?"

The doctor shook her head. "I think we'd better be heading for home. Nase drives like a bat out of hell at night."

"Now, really, Louise—"

Mrs. Murry said, "I have a large mess of chicken and vegetables simmering over the Bunsen burner in the lab. We'll be eating it for a week if you don't help us out."

"It does seem an imposition—you're always feeding us—"

The bishop offered, "We'll do the dishes tonight, and give Polly and Alex a vacation."

"It's a bargain," Mr. Murry said.

Dr. Louise held out her hands. "I give in. Alex. Kate." She indicated the Ogam stone. "You really take all this seriously?"

Mr. Murry replied, "Oddly enough, I do, Celts, druids, and all. Kate is still dubious, but—"

"But we've been forced to take even stranger things seriously." Mrs. Murry headed for the door. "I'm off to get the casserole and finish it in the kitchen."

Polly shivered. "It's freezing in the lab. Grand was showing me how to use a gas chromatograph this morning but icicles trickled off the end of my nose and she sent me in. Uncle Sandy calls me a swamp blossom."

Dr. Louise smiled. "Your grandmother's machinery is all for show. Her real work is up in her head."

"I couldn't get along without the Bunsen burner. Why don't you go for a swim, Polly? You know the pool's the warmest place in the house."

It was Polly's regular swimming time. She agreed readily. She loved to swim in the dark, by the light of the stars and a young moon. Swimming time, thinking time.

"See you in a bit." She stood up, shaking a reluctant Hadron out of her lap.

Up the back stairs. The first day, when her grandparents had taken her upstairs, she had not been sure where they were going to put her. Her mother's favorite place was the attic, with a big brass bed under the eaves, where her parents slept on their infrequent visits. On the second floor was her grandparents' room, with a grand four-poster bed. Across the hall was Sandy and Dennys, her uncles' room, with their old bunk beds, because on the rare occasions when the larger family was able to get together, all beds were needed. There was a room which might have been another bedroom but which was her grandfather's study, with bookshelves and a scarred rolltop desk, and a pull-out couch for overflow. Then there was her uncle Charles Wallace's room—her mother's youngest brother.

Polly had had a rather blank feeling that there was no room in her grandparents' house that was hers. Despite the fact that she had six brothers and sisters, she was used to having her own room with her own things. Each of the O'Keefe children did, though the rooms were little bigger than cubicles, for their parents believed that particularly in a large family a certain amount of personal space was essential.

As they climbed the stairs her grandmother said, 'We've spruced up Charles Wallace's room. It isn't big, but I think you might like it.'

Charles Wallace's room had been more than spruced up. It

looked to Polly as though her grandparents had known she was coming, though the decision had been made abruptly only three days before she was put on the plane. When action was necessary, her parents did not procrastinate.

But the room, as she stepped over the threshold, seemed to invite her in. There was a wide window which looked onto the vegetable garden, then on past a big mowed field to the woods, and then the softly hunched shoulders of the mountains. It was a peaceful view, not spectacular, but gentle to live with, and wide and deep enough to give perspective. The other window looked east, across the apple orchard to more woods. The wallpaper was old-fashioned, soft blue with a sprinkling of daisies almost like stars, with an occasional bright butterfly, and the window curtains matched, though there were more butterflies than in the wallpaper.

Under the window of the east wall were bookshelves filled with books, and a rocking chair. The books were an eclectic collection, several volumes of myths and fairy tales, some Greek and Roman history, an assortment of novels, from Henry Fielding's *Tom Jones* to Matthew Maddox's *The Horn of Joy*, and on up to contemporary novels. Polly pulled out a book on constellations, with lines drawn between the stars to show the signs of the zodiac. Someone had to have a vivid imagination, she thought, to see a Great and Little Bear, or Sagittarius with his bow and arrow. There was going to be plenty to read, and she was grateful for that.

The floor was made of wide cherrywood boards, and there were small hooked rugs on either side of the big white-pine bed, which had a patchwork quilt in blues and yellows. What Polly liked most was that although the room was pretty it wasn't pretty-pretty. Charles, she thought, would have liked it.

She had turned to her grandmother. 'Oh, it's lovely! When did you do all this?'

'Last summer.'

Last summer her grandparents had had no idea that Polly would be coming to live with them. Nevertheless, she felt that the room was uniquely hers. 'I love it! Oh, Grand, I love it!'

She had called her parents, described the room. Her grand-parents had left her to talk in privacy, and she said, 'I love Grand and Granddad. You should see Granddad out on his red tractor. He's not intimidating at all.'

There was laughter at that. 'Did you expect him to be?'

'Well—I mean, he knows so much about astrophysics and space travel, and he gets consulted by presidents and important people. But he's easy to talk to—well, he's my grandfather and I think he's terrific.'

'I gather it's mutual.'

'And Grand isn't intimidating, either.'

Her parents (she could visualize them, her mother lying on her stomach across the bed, her father perched on a stool in the lab, surrounded by tanks of starfish and octopus) both laughed.

Polly was slightly defensive. 'We do call her Grand and that sounds pretty imposing.'

'That's only because you couldn't say Grandmother when you started to talk.'

'Well, and she did win a Nobel Prize.'

Her father said, reasonably, 'She's pretty terrific, Polly. But she'd much rather have you love her than be impressed at her accomplishments.'

Polly nodded at the telephone. 'I do love her. But remember, I've never really had a chance to know Grand and Granddad. We lived in Portugal for so long, and Benne Seed Island might have been just as far away. A few visits now and then hasn't been enough. I've been in awe of them.'

'They're good people,' her father said. 'Talented, maybe a touch of genius. But human. They were good to me, incredibly good, when I was young.'

'It's time you got to know them,' her mother added. 'Be happy, Polly.'

She was. Happy as a small child. Not that she wanted to regress, to lose any of the things she had learned from experience, but with her grandparents she could relax, completely free to be herself.

She grabbed her bathing suit from the bathroom and went

along to her room. Downstairs she could hear people moving about, and then someone put on music, Schubert's "Trout" Quintet, and the charming music floated up to her.

She left her jeans and sweatshirt in a small heap on the floor, slipped into her bathing suit and a terry-cloth robe, and went downstairs and out to the pool. She hung her robe on the towel tree, waited for her eyes to adjust to the dim light, then slid into the water and began swimming laps. She swam tidily, displacing little water, back and forth, back and forth. She flipped onto her back, looking up at the skylights, and welcoming first one star, then another. Turned from her back to her side, swimming dreamily. A faint sound made her slow down, a small scratching. She floated, listening. It came from one of the windows which lined the north wall from the floor up to the slant of the roof.

She could not see anything. The scratching turned into a gentle tapping. She pulled herself up onto the side of the pool, went to the window. There was a drop of about five feet from the window to the ground. In the last light, she could just see a girl standing on tiptoe looking up at her, a girl about her own age, with black hair braided into a long rope which was flung over her shoulder. At her neck was a band of silver with a stone, like a teardrop, in the center.

"Hi," Polly called through the dark glass.

The girl smiled and reached up to knock again. Polly slid the window open. "May I come in?" the girl asked.

Polly tugged at the screen till it, too, opened.

The girl sprang up and caught the sill, pulling herself into the room, followed by a gust of wind. Polly shut the screen and the window. The girl appeared to be about Polly's age, and she was exotically beautiful, with honey-colored skin and eyes so dark the pupil could barely be distinguished.

"Forgive me," the girl said formally, "for coming like this. Karralys saw you this afternoon." She spoke with a slight accent which Polly could not distinguish.

"Karralys?"

"Yes. At the oak tree, with his dog."

"Why didn't he say hello?" Polly asked.

The girl shook her head. "It is not often given to see the other circles of time. But then Karralys and I talked, and thought I should come here to the place of power. It seemed to us that you must have been sent to us in this strange and difficult—" She broke off as a door slammed somewhere in the house. She put her hand to her mouth. Whispered, "I must go. Please—" She seemed so frightened that Polly opened the window for her.

"Who are you?"

But the girl jumped down, landing lightly, and was off across the field toward the woods, running as swiftly as a wild animal.

CHAPTER 2

THE whole incident made no sense whatsoever. Polly put on her robe and headed for the kitchen, looking for explanations, but saw no one. Probably everybody was out in the lab, where it was definitely too chilly for a swamp blossom in a wet bathing suit and a damp terry-cloth robe.

Her parents had worried that she might be lonely with no people her own age around, and in one day she had seen three, the blue-eyed young man by the oak—though he was probably several years older than she; Zachary; and now this unknown girl.

Upstairs in her room, the stripy cat was lying curled in the center of the bed, one of his favorite places. She picked him up and held him and he purred, pleased with her damp warmth.

"Who on earth was that girl?" she demanded. "And what was she talking about?" She squeezed the cat too tightly and he jumped from her arms and stalked out of the room, brown-and-amber tail erect.

She dressed and went downstairs. The bishop was in the kitchen, sitting in one of the shabby but comfortable chairs by the fireplace. She joined him.

"What's the matter?" he asked.

"I'm just puzzled. While I was swimming there was a knock on one of the windows, and I got out of the pool to look, and there was this girl, about my age, with a long black braid and sort of exotic eyes, and I let her in, and she—well, she made absolutely no sense at all."

"Go on." The bishop was alert, totally focused on her words.

"This afternoon by the Grandfather Oak—you know the tree I mean?"

"Yes."

"I saw a young man and a dog. The girl said the man with the dog had seen me, and then something about circles of time, and then she heard a noise and got frightened and ran away. Who do you suppose she was?"

The bishop looked at Polly without answering, simply staring at her with a strange, almost shocked look on his face.

"Bishop?"

"Well, my dear—" He cleared his throat. "Yes. It is indeed strange. Strange indeed."

"Should I tell my grandparents?"

He hesitated. Cleared his throat. "Probably."

She nodded. She trusted him. He hadn't had a cushy job as bishop. Her grandparents had told her that he'd been in the Amazon for years, taught seminary in China, had a price on his head in Peru. When he was with so-called primitive people he listened to them, rather than imposing his own views. He honored others.

She was so concerned with her own story that she was not aware that what she had told him had upset him.

"Polly," he said, "tell me about the young man with the dog." His voice trembled slightly.

"He was standing by the Grandfather Oak. He had these intensely blue eyes."

"What was the dog like?"

"Just a big dog with large ears. Not any particular breed. I didn't see them for more than a few seconds."

"And the girl. Can you describe her?"

"Well—not much more than I just did. Long black braid, and dark eyes. She was beautiful and strange."

"Yes," the bishop said. "Oh, yes." His voice was soft and troubled.

Now she saw that something had disturbed him. "Do you know who she is?"

"Perhaps. How can I be sure?" He paused, then spoke briskly. "Yes, it's strange, strange indeed. Your grandfather is right to discourage trespassers." His eyes were suddenly veiled.

Mr. Murry came in from the pantry, heard the bishop's last words. "Right, Nase. I'm quite happy to have deer and foxes leaping over the stone walls, but not snoopers. We've had to put a horrendously expensive warning system in the lab. Louise is correct, most of Kate's equipment hasn't been used in decades. But the computers are another story." He headed for the wood stove, turned to Polly. "The lab has been broken into twice. Once a useless microscope was taken, and once your grandmother lost a week's work because someone—probably local kids, rather than anyone who knew anything about her work—played around with the computer." He opened the small oven of the wood stove and the odor of freshly baked bread filled the kitchen. "Bread is something Kate can't make on the Bunsen burner, so this is my contribution, as well as therapy. Kneading bread is wonderful for rheumatic fingers."

Mrs. Murry and Dr. Louise followed him into the kitchen. Mrs. Murry lit candles in addition to the oil lamps, and turned out the lights. Dr. Louise put a large casserole of Mrs. Murry's chicken concoction on the table, and Mr. Murry took a bowl of autumn vegetables from the stove, broccoli, cauliflower, sprouts, onions, carrots, leeks. The bishop sniffed appreciatively.

Mrs. Murry said, "The twins used to have a vast vegetable garden. Ours isn't nearly as impressive, but Alex does amazingly well."

"For an old man, you mean," Mr. Murry said.

"Except for your arthritis," Dr. Louise said, "you're in remarkably good shape. I wish some of my patients ten or more years younger than you did as well."

After they were seated, and the meal blessed and served, Polly looked at the bishop. His eyes met hers briefly. Then he glanced away, and his expression was withdrawn. But she thought he had barely perceptibly nodded at her. She said, "I've seen a couple of odd people today."

"Who?" her grandfather asked.

"You're not talking about Zachary!" Dr. Louise laughed.

She shook her head and described both the young man with the dog, and the girl. "Zachary thought he was a caretaker, maybe."

The bishop choked slightly, got up, and poured himself some water. Recovering himself, he asked, "You say that Zachary saw this young man?"

"Sure. He was right there. But he didn't talk to either of us."

"I hope he wasn't a hunter," Mr. Murry said. "Our land is very visibly posted."

"He didn't have a gun. I'm positive. Is it hunting season here or something?"

"It's never hunting season on our land," her grandfather said. "Did you speak to him? Ask him what he was doing?"

"I didn't get a chance. I just saw him looking at me, and when I got to the tree he was gone."

"What about the girl?" Mrs. Murry probed.

Polly looked at the bishop. His eyes were once again veiled, his expression noncommittal. Polly repeated her description of the girl. "I really don't think they were poachers or vandals or anything bad. They were just mysterious."

Her grandfather's voice was unexpectedly harsh. "I don't want any more mysteries."

The bishop was staring at the Ogam stone sitting on the kitchen dresser, along with assorted mugs, bowls, a gravy boat, a hammer, a roll of stamps.

Mrs. Murry's voice was light. "Perhaps they'll be friends for Polly?"

"The girl's about my age, I think," Polly said. "She had gorgeous soft leather clothes that would cost a fortune in a boutique, and she wore a sort of silver collar with a beautiful stone."

Mrs. Murry laughed. "Your mother said you were finally showing some interest in clothes. I'm glad to note evidence of it."

Polly was slightly defensive. "There hasn't been any reason for me to wear anything but jeans."

"Silver collar." The bishop spoke as though to himself. "A torque—" He was busily helping himself to vegetables.

Mrs. Murry had heard. "A torque?" She turned to Polly. "Nason has a book on early metalwork with beautiful photographs. The early druids may have lived among Stone Age people, but there were metalworkers at least passing through Britain, and the druids were already sophisticated astronomers. They, and the tribal leaders, wore intricately designed torques."

"The wheel of fashion keeps coming full circle," Dr. Louise said. "And how much have we learned since the Stone Age as far as living peaceably is concerned?"

Mr. Murry regarded his wife. "There's a picture of a superb silver torque in Nason's book that I wish I could get for you, Kate. It would eminently suit you."

Polly looked at her grandmother's sensible country clothes and tried to visualize her in a beautiful torque. It was not impossible. She had been told that her grandmother was a beauty, and as she looked at the older woman's fine bones, the short, well-cut silver hair, the graceful curve of the slender neck, the fine eyes surrounded by lines made from smiles and pain and generous living, she thought that her grandmother was still beautiful, and she was glad that her grandfather's response was to want to get his wife a torque.

Mrs. Murry had taken a blueberry pie from the freezer for dessert, and brought it bubbling from the oven. "I didn't make it," she explained. "There's a blueberry festival at the church every summer, and I always buy half a dozen unbaked pies to have on hand." She cut into it, and purple juice streamed out with summer fragrance. "Polly, I can't tell you how pleased I am that your Zachary turned up. It must have been hard for you to leave your friends."

Polly accepted a slice of pie. "Island kids tend to be isolated. My friends are sort of scattered."

"I've been lucky to have Louise living only a few miles away. We've been friends ever since college."

Yes, her grandmother was lucky to have Dr. Louise, Polly thought. She had never had a real female friend her own age. She thought fleetingly of the girl at the pool.

Polly and the bishop did the dishes together, and the others went to sit by the fire in the living room, urged on by Mrs. Murry, who said they all spent too much time in the kitchen.

"So, island girl," the bishop said, "is all well here?"

"Very well, thank you, Bishop." She wanted to ask him more about the man with the dog and the girl at the pool, but it was clear to her that the bishop was guiding the conversation away from them. She took a rinsed plate from him and put it in the dishwasher.

"My sister has taught me to wash everything with soap, even if it's going in the dishwasher. Be careful. The plates are slippery."

"Okay."

"Your young man—"

"Zachary. Zachary Gray."

"He didn't look well."

"He's always pale. Last summer in Greece when everybody was tan, Zachary's skin was white. Of course, I don't think he goes out in the sun much. He isn't the athletic type."

"How was last summer?" The bishop wrung out a sponge.

Polly was putting silverware in the dishwasher basket. "It was a wonderful experience. I loved Athens, and the conference on Cyprus was worth a year at school. Max—Maximiliana Horne—arranged it all. And she died just before I got home."

He nodded. "Your grandparents told me. You're still grieving."

She dried the knives, which were old silver ones with the handles glued on and could not be put in the dishwasher. "It was harder at home, where everything reminded me of Max. Did you know her?"

The bishop let soapy water out of the sink. "Your Uncle Sandy told me about her. They were great friends."

"Yes. Sandy introduced me to her." Unexpectedly her throat tightened.

The bishop led the way to one of the shabby chairs by the kitchen fireplace, rather than joining the others in the living room. Polly followed him, and as she sat down Hadron appeared and jumped into her lap, purring.

"Bishop, about the young man and the girl—"

But at that moment Dr. Louise came into the kitchen, yawning. "Dishes all done?"

"And with soap," the bishop assured her.

"Time for us to be getting on home."

Polly and her grandparents went outside to wave the Colubras off, and the stars were brilliant amidst small wisps of cloud. The moon was tangled in the branches of a large Norway maple.

The bishop climbed into the driver's seat of the blue pickup truck and they took off with a squeal of tires.

Polly's grandmother turned to go back into the house. "We're going for a quick swim. I'll come and say good night in a while." It had already become a comfortable habit that after Polly was in bed her grandmother would come in and they would talk for a few minutes.

She took a hurried bath—the bathroom was frigid—and slipped into a flannel nightgown, then into bed, pulling the quilt about her. She read a few pages of the book her grandfather had given her on white holes, cosmic gushers, the opposite of black holes. Her grandparents were certainly seeing to her education. But perhaps it was no wonder that her grandfather had not noticed stones in his walls that had strange markings.

When her grandmother came in, she put the book down on the nightstand, and Mrs. Murry sat on the side of the bed. "Lovely evening. It's good that Nase is living with Louise. Your grandfather and I feel as though we've known him forever. He was a fine bishop. He's tender and compassionate and he knows how to listen."

Polly pushed up higher against the pillows. "Yes, I feel I could tell him anything and he wouldn't be shocked."

"And he'd never betray a confidence."

"Grand." Polly sat up straight. "Something's been bothering me."

"What, my dear?"

"I sort of just got dumped on you, didn't I?"

"Oh, Polly, your grandfather and I have enough sense of self-protection so that if we hadn't wanted you to come we'd have said no. We've felt very deprived, seeing so little of our grandchildren. We love having you. It's a very different life from what you've been used to—"

"Oh, Grand, I love it. I'm happy here. Grand, why did Mother have so many kids?"

"Would you want any of you not to have been born?"

"No, but—"

"But it doesn't answer your question." Mrs. Murry pushed her fingers through her still damp hair. "If a woman is free to choose a career, she's also free to choose the care of a family as her primary vocation."

"Was it that with Mother?"

"Partly." Her grandmother sighed. "But it was probably partly because of me."

"You? Why?"

"I'm a scientist, Polly, and well known in my field."

"Well, but Mother—" She stopped. "You mean maybe she didn't want to compete with you?"

"That could be part of it."

"You mean, she was afraid she couldn't compete?"

"Your mother's estimation of herself has always been low. Your father has been wonderful for her and so, in many ways, have you children. But . . ." Her voice drifted off.

"But you did your work and had kids."

"Not seven of them." Her grandmother's hands were tightly clasped together. Then, deliberately, she relaxed them, placed them over her knees.

Polly slid down in the bed to a more comfortable position. Suddenly she felt drowsy. Hadron, who had taken to sleeping with Polly, curled in the curve between shoulder and neck, began to purr.

"Women have come a long way," her grandmother said, "but there will always be problems—and glories—that are unique to women." The cat's purr rose contentedly. "Hadron certainly seems to have taken to you."

"A hadron," Polly murmured sleepily, "belongs to a class of particles that interact strongly. Nucleons are hadrons, and so are pions and strange particles."

"Good girl," Mrs. Murry said. "You're a quick learner."

"Strange particles . . ." Polly's eyes closed. —You'd think human beings would be full of strange particles. Maybe we are. Hadrons are—I think—formed of quarks, so the degree of strangeness in a hadron is calculated by the number of quarks.

"Were druids strange?" She was more than half asleep. "I don't know much about druids." Polly's breathing slowed as she pushed her face into the pillow, close to Hadron's warm fur. Mrs. Murry rose, stood for a moment looking at her granddaughter, then slipped out of the room.

In the morning Polly woke early, dressed, and went downstairs. No one was stirring. The ground was white with mist which drifted across the lawn. The mountains were slowly emerging on the horizon, and above them the sky shimmered between the soft grey of dawn and the blue which would clarify as the sun rose.

She headed outdoors, across the field, which was as wet with dew as though it had rained during the night. At the stone wall she paused, but it was probably too early for Louise the Larger. Polly continued along the path toward the star-watching rock. She had pulled on the old red anorak, and she wore lined jeans, so she was warm enough. She looked up at the sky in surprise as there was a sudden strange shimmering in the air. Then there was a flash as though from lightning, but no thunder. The ground quivered slightly under her feet, then settled. Was it an earthquake? She looked around. The trees were different. Larger. There were many more oaks, towering even higher than the Grandfather Oak. As she neared the star-watching rock she saw light flashing on water, and where the fertile valley had been there was now a large lake.

A lake? She reeled in surprise. Where had a lake come from? And the hills were no longer the gentle hills worn down by wind and rain and erosion, but jagged mountains, their peaks capped with snow. She turned, her flesh prickling, and looked at the rock, and it was the same star-watching rock she had always loved, and yet it was not the same.

"What's going on?" she asked aloud. Wreaths of mist were dissipating to reveal a dozen or more tents made of stretched and cured animal skins. Beyond them was an enormous vegetable garden, and a field of corn, the stalks recently cut and gathered into bunches. Beyond the cornfield, cows and sheep were grazing. On lines strung between poles, fish were hanging. Between stronger poles, beaver skins were being dried and stretched. In front of one of the tents a woman was sitting, pounding something with mortar and pestle. She had black hair worn in a braid, and she was singing as she worked, paying no attention to Polly or anything going on around her, absorbed in the rhythm of the pestle and her song. She looked like a much older version of the girl who had come to the pool.

In the distance Polly heard the sound of a drum, and then singing, a beautiful melody with rich native harmony. The rising sun seemed to be pulled up out of the sky by the beauty of the song. When the music ended, there was a brief silence, and then the noises of the day resumed.

What on earth was happening? Where was she? How could she get home?

She turned in the direction where the Murry house should have been, and coming toward her was a group of young men carrying spears. Instinctively, Polly ran behind one of the great oak trees and peered out from behind the wide trunk.

Two of the men had a young deer slung onto their spears. They continued past her, beyond the tents and the garden and the cornfield and pasture. They wore soft leather leggings and tunics, similar to the clothes worn by the girl who had come to Polly at the pool.

After they were out of sight on the path she leaned against the tree because her legs felt like water. What was happening? Where had the huge forest behind her come from? What about the lake which took up the entire valley? Who were the young men?

Her mind was racing, reaching out in every direction, trying to make some kind of sense out of this total dislocation. Certainly life had proven to her more than once that the world is not a reasonable place, but this was unreason beyond unreason.

Up the path came a young man with hair bleached almost white. He carried a spear, far larger than those of the hunters. At the haft it was balanced by what looked like a copper ball about the size of an apple or an orange, and just below this was a circle of feathers. She hid behind the tree so that he would not see her, dressed in jeans and a red anorak.

In one of the great oaks a cardinal was singing sweetly, a familiar sound. A small breeze blew through the bleached autumn grasses, ruffled the waters of the lake. The air was clear and pure. The mountains hunched great rugged shoulders into the blue of sky, and early sunlight sparkled off the white peaks.

She drew in her breath. Coming along the path toward her was the girl she had seen at the pool, her black braid swinging. She carried an armful of autumn flowers, deep-blue Michael-mas daisies, white Queen Anne's lace, yellow golden glow. She walked to a rock Polly had not noticed before, a flat grey rock resting on two smaller rocks, somewhat like a pi sign in stone.

The girl placed her flowers on the rock, looked up at the sky, and lifted her voice in song. Her voice was clear and sweet and she sang as simply and spontaneously as a bird. When she was through, she raised her arms heavenward, a radiance illuminating her face. Then she turned, as though sensing Polly's presence behind the tree.

Polly came out. "Hi!"

The girl's face drained of color, and she swirled as though to run off.

"Hey, wait!" Polly called.

Slowly the girl walked toward the star-watching rock.

"Who are you?" Polly asked.

"Anaral." The girl pointed to herself as she said her name. She had on the same soft leather tunic and leggings she had worn the night before, and at her throat was the silver band with the pale stone in the center. The forefinger of her right hand was held out a little stiffly, and on it was a Band-Aid, somehow utterly incongruous.

"What were you singing? It was beautiful. You have an absolutely gorgeous voice." With each word, Polly was urging the girl not to run away again.

A faint touch of peach colored Anaral's cheeks, and she bowed her head.

"What is it? Can you tell me the words?"

The color deepened slightly. Anaral for the first time looked directly at Polly. "The good-morning song to our Mother, who gives us the earth on which we live"—she paused, as though seeking for words—"teaches us to listen to the wind, to care for all that she gives us, food to grow"—another, thinking pause—"the animals to nurture, and ourselves. We ask her to help us to know ourselves, that we may know each other, and to forgive"—she rubbed her forehead—"to forgive ourselves when we do wrong, so that we may forgive others. To help us walk the path of love, and to protect us from all that would hurt us." As Anaral spoke, putting her words slowly into English, her voice automatically moved into singing.

"Thank you," Polly said. "We sing a lot in my family. They'd love that. I'd like to learn it."

"I will teach you." Anaral smiled shyly.

"Why did you run off last night?" Polly asked.

"I was confused. It is not often that circles of time overlap. That you should be here—oh, it is strange."

"What is?"

"That we should be able to see each other, to speak."

Yes, Polly thought. Strange, indeed. Was it possible that she and Anaral were speaking across three thousand years?

"You do not belong to my people," Anaral said. "You are in a different spiral."

"Who are your people?"

Anaral stood proudly. "We are the People of the Wind."

"Are you Indians?" Polly asked. It seemed a rude question, but she wanted to know the answer.

Anaral looked baffled. "I do not know that word. We have always been on this land. I was born to be trained as—you might understand if I said I was a druid."

A native American who was a druid? But druids came from Britain.

Anaral smiled. "Druid is not a word of the People of the Wind. Karralys—you saw him yesterday by the great oak— Karralys brought the word with him from across the great water. You understand?"

"Well—I'm not sure."

"That is all right. I have told you my name, my druid name that Karralys gave me. Anaral. And you are?"

"Polly O'Keefe. How do you know my language?"

"Bishop."

"Bishop Colubra?"

Anaral nodded.

"He taught you?" Now Polly understood why the bishop had been concerned when she talked to him about Anaral and Karralys. And it was apparent that he had not told her grandparents or his sister everything he knew about the Ogam stones and the people who walked the land three thousand years ago.

"Yes. Bishop taught me."

"How do you know him?"

Anaral held out her hands. "He came to us."

"How?"

"Sometimes"—Anaral swung her black braid over her shoulder—"it is possible to move from one ring to another."

Polly had a vision of a picture of an early model of a molecule, with the nucleus in the center and the atoms in shells or circles around it. Sometimes an electron jumped from one shell or circle to another. But this picture of the movement of electrons from circle to circle in a molecule didn't help much, because Anaral's circles were in time, rather than space. Except, Polly reminded herself, time and space are not separable. "You came to my time yesterday," she said. "How did you do it?"

Anaral put slim hands to her face, then took them down and looked at Polly. "Karralys and I are druids. For us the edges of time are soft. Not hard. We can move through it like water. Are you a druid?"

"No." Polly was definite. "But it seems that I am now in your time."

"*I* am in my time," Anaral said.

"But if you are, I must be?"

"Our circles are touching."

"Druids know about astronomy. Do you know about time?"

Anaral laughed. "There are more circles of time than anyone can count, and we understand a few of them, but only a few. I have the old knowledge, the knowledge of the People of the Wind, and now Karralys is teaching me his new knowledge, the druidic knowledge."

"Does the bishop know all of this?"

"Oh, yes. Do you belong to Bishop?"

"To friends of his."

"You belong to the scientists?"

"I'm their granddaughter."

"The one with the crooked fingers and lame knees—Bishop tells me he knows something about time."

"Yes. More than most people. But not about—not about going back three thousand years, which is what I've done, isn't it?"

Anaral shook her head. "Three thousand—I do not know what three thousand means. You have stepped across the threshold."

"I don't know how I did it," Polly said. "I just set out to walk to the star-watching rock and suddenly I was here. Do you know how I can get back?"

Anaral smiled a little sadly. "I am not always sure myself how it happens. The circles overlap and a threshold opens and then we can cross over."

As Anaral gestured with her hands, Polly noticed again the Band-Aid anachronistically on Anaral's finger. "What did you do to your finger?"

"I cut myself with a hunting knife. I was skinning a deer and the knife slipped."

"How did you get that Band-Aid? You don't have Band-Aids in your own time, do you?"

Anaral shook her head. "Dr. Louise sewed my finger up for me, many stitches. That was more than a moon ago. It is nearly well now. When I could take off the big bandage, Bishop brought me this." She held up the finger with the Band-Aid.

"How did you get to Dr. Louise?"

"Bishop brought me to her."

"How?"

"Bishop saw me right after the knife slipped. The cut was deep, oh, very deep. I bled. Bled. I was scared. Crying. Bishop held my finger, pressing to stop the blood spurting. Then he said, 'Come,' and we ran—Bishop can really run—and suddenly we were in Dr. Louise's office."

"You don't have anybody in your own time who could have taken care of the cut for you?"

"The Ancient Grey Wolf could have. He was our healer for

many years, but he died during the cold of last winter. And his
son, who should have followed him, died when the winter fever
swept through our people a few turns of the sun ago. Cub,
the Young Wolf, who will become our healer, still has much
to learn. Karralys of course could have helped me, but he was
away that day, with the young men, hunting."

"Karralys is a druid from Britain?"

"From far. Karralys is he who came in the strange boat,
three turns of the sun back, blown across the lake by a hurricane of fierce winds. He came as we People of the Wind were
mourning the death of our Great One, felled by an oak tree
uprooted in the storm, picked up like a twig and flung down,
the life crushed out of him. He was very old and had foretold
that he would not live another sun turn. And out of the storm
Karralys came, and with him another from the sea, Tav, who
is almost white of hair and has skin that gets red if he stays out
in the sun."

Tav. That must be the young man with the spear.

"Where did they come from, Karralys and Tav?"

"From the great waters, beyond the rivers and the mountains. And lo, at the very moment that Karralys's boat touched
the shore, the wind dropped, and the storm ended, and a great
rainbow arched across the lake and we knew that the Maker of
the Stars had sent us a new Great One."

"And Tav?" Polly asked.

Anaral continued, "Tav was in the canoe half dead with fever.
Even with all their skill, Karralys and Grey Wolf had a hard
time bringing the fever down. Night after night they stayed
with Tav, praying. Cub, the Young Wolf, was beside them,
watching, learning. The fever went down with the moon and
Tav's breathing was suddenly gentle as a child's and he slept
and he was well. They are a great gift to us, Karralys and Tav."

"Is Tav a druid?"

"Oh, no. He is a warrior. He is our greatest hunter. We have
not had to worry about having enough meat since Tav came."

Polly frowned, trying to sort things out. "You were born
here, in this place?"

"Yes."

"But you're a druid?"

Anaral laughed. "Now. That is what I am called now. For this I was born. And Karralys has trained me in his wisdom. And now there is danger to our people, and Karralys thinks you have been brought across the threshold to help us."

"But how could I possibly—" Polly started.

There was a sharp sound, as of someone stepping on and breaking a twig, and Anaral was off, swift as a deer.

Polly looked around, but saw no one. 'You have been brought across the threshold to help us,' Anaral had said. What on earth did she mean? And how was Polly to get back across the threshold to her own time? Without Anaral, how could she possibly get home?

She ran after the other girl. Polly had long legs and she ran quickly, but she was not familiar with the path, which zig-zagged back and forth, always downhill. Anaral was nowhere to be seen.

Polly continued on, past the village, around the garden and the cornfield, across the pasture, and then picked up a path which led through a grove of birch and beech trees. She followed it until it opened out at a large flat stone, not quite as large as the star-watching rock. But in this terrain which had been covered by glaciers the topsoil was thin, the bones of the earth close to the surface. She continued on, listening, as she heard water plashing. Then she was standing on a stone bridge under which a small brook ran. She had been here before during her exploring, and it was a lovely place. Trees leaned over the water, dropping golden leaves. She was surrounded by rich October smells, decomposing apples, leaves, hickory nuts, acorns, pinecones, all sending their nourishment into the earth.

And suddenly she realized that the trees were the trees of her own time, not those of a primeval forest. She was home.

CHAPTER 3

In her own time. Weak with relief, Polly sat on the stone bridge, dangling her legs over the brook, trying to return to normalcy.

—Why do northern trees shed their leaves? she asked herself. —Is it to reduce their exposure to extreme cold?

That sounded sensible, and she wanted things to be sensible, because nothing about the morning had been sensible, and inside her warm anorak she felt cold. She got up and continued along the path, looking for the slim girl with a heavy dark braid. But Anaral had been in that other time, not the now of Polly's present. Nevertheless, she pushed along the path cut through low bushes, and on to a high precipice, from which she could look over the swampy valley to the hills beyond.

Her uncles, Sandy and Dennys, had cut paths through the brush when they were young, and the wildlife had more or less kept them open. She would need to come out with clippers to cut back some of the overgrowth. She stood on the high rock, looking westward. The landscape rippled with gentle color, muted golds now predominating, green of pine suddenly appearing where fallen leaves had left bare branches.

Then, below her, down where the bed of the brook should be, she saw a flash of brightness, and Bishop Colubra appeared out of the bushes, wearing a yellow cap and jacket and carrying a heavy-looking stone. A steep path led down the precipice which would have been easy to follow had it not been criss-crossed by bittersweet and blackberry brambles that caught at her as she plunged downhill toward the bishop, scratching her legs and hands, catching in her clothes.

The bishop was hailing her with pleasure, holding out the stone, and explaining that he hadn't been looking for Ogam stones but there was one, right there in an old stone wall, and wasn't it a glorious morning?

"Bishop!" she gasped as she came up to him. "I've been back!"

He stopped so abruptly and completely that the air seemed to quiver. "What?"

"I crossed the threshold, or whatever Anaral calls it. I went back to her time."

His voice was a whisper. He looked as though he were about to drop the stone. "When?"

"Just now. I've just come out of it. Bishop, while it was happening it was all so sudden and so strange I didn't have time to feel anything much. But now I think I'm terrified." Her voice quavered.

He put the stone down, touched her arm reassuringly. "Don't be terrified. It will be all right. It will work out according to God's purpose."

"Will it?"

"I didn't expect this. That you— You saw her yesterday, at the pool?"

Polly felt cold, though the sun was warm. "She says that she and Karralys—he's the one by the oak—she says that they can cross the thresholds of time because they're druids."

"Yes." The bishop kept his hand on Polly's shoulder, as though imparting strength. "We've lost many gifts that were once available." He bent down to pick up the stone. "We'd better head back to your grandparents' house. This is the shortest way, if you want to follow me." He was definitely wobbly on his long, thin legs, trying to tuck the stone under one arm so that he could balance himself with the other, reaching for small trees or large vines to help pull himself along. They came to another curve of the brook and he stopped, looked at the water flowing between and around rocks, and made a successful leap across, dropping the stone, which Polly retrieved.

"I'll carry it for a while," she offered. She followed the old bishop, who scurried along a nearly overgrown path, then turned sharply uphill, scrabbling his way up like a crab. At their feet were occasional patches of red partridge berries. A spruce branch stretched across their path, and he held it aside for Polly, continuing along his irregular course until he pushed through a thicket of shadblow and wild cherry, and they emerged at the star-watching rock.

"Bishop," Polly said. "This—what happened—it's crazy."

He did not speak. The sun rose higher. A soft wind moved through the trees, shaking down more leaves.

"Maybe I dreamed it?"

"Sometimes I don't know what is dream and what is reality. The line between them is very fine." He took the Ogam stone from her and set it down on the star-watching rock. Folded his legs and sat down, indicated that she was to sit beside him. "Tell me exactly what happened."

"I got up early and went for a walk, and as I came near the star-watching rock, everything changed. The ground quivered. I thought it was an earthquake. And then I saw that the trees, the mountains—the trees were much bigger, sort of primeval forest. And the mountains were huge and jagged and snow-topped."

He nodded. "Yes."

"And I know you've been there—back—"

"Yes."

"Is it real?"

He nodded.

"Do my grandparents know about this? Dr. Louise?"

He shook his head. "They don't believe in such things."

"They believe in the Ogam stones."

"Yes. They're tangible."

"But haven't you told them?"

He sighed. "My dear, they don't want to hear."

"But, Bishop, you took Anaral to Dr. Louise when she cut her finger."

"How do you—"

"Anaral told me."

"Yes. Oh, my dear. I didn't know what to do. I didn't stop to think. I just took her and ran, and thank heavens Louise was in her office."

"So she does know."

He shook his head. "No. I told her, and she thought I was joking. Or out of my mind. I've tended periodically to bring in waifs and strays for her to mend, and she thinks Annie was just another. Because that's what she wants to think. Have you had breakfast?"

"No."

"Let's go on back to your grandparents' and have some coffee. I need to think. Thursday is All Hallows' Eve . . ."

Halloween. She had completely forgotten.

He scrambled to his feet. Picked up the Ogam stone. "That may partly explain—the time of year—"

"Bishop, my grandparents don't know you've done what I did—gone back three thousand years?"

"Do you realize how extraordinary it sounds? They've never seen Karralys or Anaral. But you've seen them. You've crossed the threshold. If you hadn't, would you believe it?"

He was right. The whole thing did sound crazy. Time thresholds. Three thousand years. Circles of time. But it had happened. She didn't see how she and the bishop could have dreamed the same dream. "Bishop—how long have you been going—going back and forth? Between then and now?"

"Since last spring. A few months after I came to live with Louise."

"How often?" —Often enough to teach Anaral to speak English, she thought.

"Reasonably often. But I can't plan it. Sometimes it happens. Sometimes it doesn't. Polly, child, let's go. I really feel the need to confess to your grandparents, whether they believe me or not."

"They're pretty good at believing," Polly said. "More than most people."

The bishop shifted the stone from one arm to the other. "I never thought you'd become involved. I never dreamed this could happen. That you should—I feel dreadfully responsible—"

She offered, "Shall I carry the Ogam stone?"

"Please." He sounded terribly distraught.

She took the stone and followed him. When they crossed the wall that led to the field, Polly saw Louise the Larger watching them, not moving. The bishop, not even noticing the snake, scrambled across the wall and started to run toward the house.

Polly's grandparents were in the kitchen. Everything was reassuringly normal. Her grandfather was reading the paper.

Her grandmother was making pancakes. Breakfast was usually catch-as-catch-can. Mrs. Murry often took coffee and a muffin to the lab. Mr. Murry hurried outdoors, working about the yard while the weather held.

"Good morning, Polly, Nason." Mrs. Murry sounded unsurprised as they panted in, Polly scratched and disheveled from her plunge down the precipice. "Alex requested pancakes, and since he's a very undemanding person, I was happy to oblige. Join us. I've made more than enough batter."

"I hope I'm not intruding." The bishop seated himself.

Polly tried to keep her voice normal. "Here's another Ogam stone. Where shall I put it?"

"If there's room, put it beside the one Nase brought in last night," her grandmother said. "How many pancakes can you eat, Nase?"

"I don't know. I'm not sure I can eat anything. I don't think I'm hungry."

"Nason! What's wrong? Don't you feel well?"

"I'm fine." He looked at Polly. "Oh, dear. What have I done?"

"What have you done?" Mr. Murry asked.

Polly said, "You didn't do anything, Bishop. It just happened."

Mrs. Murry put a stack of pancakes in front of him, and absently he lavished butter, poured a river of syrup, ate a large bite, put down his fork. "I may have done something terrible."

"Nason, what's going on?" Mr. Murry asked.

The bishop took another large bite. Shook his head. "I didn't think it would happen. I didn't think it could."

"*What?*" Mr. Murry demanded.

"I thought the time gate was open only to me. I didn't think—" He broke off.

"Polly," her grandfather asked, "do you know what all this is about?"

Polly poured herself a mug of coffee and sat down. "The man by the oak, the one both Zachary and I saw, lived at the time of the Ogam stones." She did her best to keep her voice level. "This morning when I went off for a walk, I—well, I don't know what it's all about, but somehow or other I went through the bishop's time gate."

"Nase!"

The bishop bent his head. "I know. It's my fault. It must be my fault. *Mea culpa*."

Mrs. Murry asked, "Polly, what makes you think you went through a time gate?"

"Everything was different, Grand. The trees were enormous, sort of like Hiawatha—*this is the forest primeval*. And the mountains were high and jagged and snow-capped. Young mountains, not ancient hills like ours. And where the valley is, there was a large lake."

"This is absurd." Mrs. Murry put a plate of pancakes in front of her husband, then fixed a plate for Polly.

"Nason!" Mr. Murry expostulated.

The bishop looked unhappy. "Whenever I've tried to talk about it, you've been disbelieving and, well—disapproving, and I don't blame you for that, so I've kept quiet. I wouldn't have believed it, either, if it hadn't kept happening. But I thought it was just me—part of being old and nearly ready to move on to— But Polly. That Polly should have—well! of course!"

"Of course what?" Mr. Murry sounded more angry with each question.

"Polly saw Annie first at the pool." The bishop used the diminutive of Anaral tenderly.

"Annie who?"

"Anaral," Polly said. "She's the girl who came to the pool last night."

"When you were digging for the pool," the bishop asked, "what happened?"

"We hit water," Mr. Murry said. "We're evidently over an aquifer—an underground river."

"But this is the highest point in the state," Polly protested. "Would there be an underground river this high up?"

"It would seem so."

The bishop put down his fork. Somehow the stack of pancakes had disappeared. "You do remember that most holy places— such as the sites of the great cathedrals in England—were on ground that was already considered holy before even the first pagan temples were built? And the interesting thing is that under most of these holy places is an underground river. This house, and the pool, are on a holy place. That's why Anaral was able to come to the pool."

"Nonsense—" Mrs. Murry started.

Mr. Murry sighed, as though in frustration. "We love the house and our land," he said, "but it's a bit farfetched to call it holy."

"This house is—what?—" the bishop asked, "well over two hundred years old?"

"Parts of it, yes."

"But the Ogam stones indicate that there were people here three thousand years ago."

"Nason, I've seen the stone. I believe you that there is Ogam writing on them. I take them seriously. But I don't want Polly involved in any of your—your—" Mr. Murry pushed up from his place so abruptly that he overturned his chair, righted it with an irritated grunt. The phone rang, making them all jump. Mr. Murry went to it. "Polly, it's for you."

This was no time for an interruption. She wanted her grand-parents to put everything into perspective. If they could believe what happened, it would be less frightening.

"Sounds like Zachary." Her grandfather handed her the phone.

"Good morning, sweet Pol. I just wanted to tell you how good it was to see you yesterday, and I look forward to seeing you on Thursday."

"Thanks, Zach. I look forward to it, too."

"Okay, see you then. Just wanted to double-check."

She went back to the table. "Yes. It was Zachary, to confirm getting together on Thursday."

"Something nice and normal," her grandfather said.

"Is it?" Polly asked. "He did see someone from three thou-sand years ago."

"All Hallows' Eve," the bishop murmured.

"At least he'll get you away from here," her grandmother

said. "Strange, isn't it, that he should know about the Ogam stones."

Polly nodded. "Zachary tends to know all kinds of odd things. But what happened this morning is beyond me."

The bishop said gently, "Three thousand years beyond you, Polly. And, somehow or other, I seem to be responsible for it."

Mr. Murry went to the dresser and picked up one of the Ogam stones. "Nason, one reason I've tended to disbelieve you is that, if what you say is true, then you, a theologian and not a scientist, have made a discovery which it has taken me a lifetime to work out."

"Blundered into it inadvertently," the bishop said.

Mr. Murry sighed. "I thought I understood it. Now I'm not sure."

"Granddad. Please explain."

Mr. Murry sat down again, creakily. "It's a theory of time, Polly. You know something about my work."

"A little."

"More than Nase, at any rate. You have a much better science background. Sorry, Nase, but—"

"I know," the bishop said. "This is no time for niceties." He looked at Mrs. Murry. "Would it be possible for me to have another helping of pancakes?" Then, back to Mr. Murry: "This tesseract theory of yours—"

Mrs. Murry put another stack of pancakes on the bishop's plate.

Mr. Murry said, "Tessering, moving through space without the restrictions of time, is, as you know, a mind thing. One can't make a machine for it. That would be to distort it, disturb the space/time continuum, in a vain effort to relegate something full of blazing glory to the limits of technology. And of course that's what's happening, abortive attempts at spaceships designed to break the speed of light and warp time. It works well in the movies and on TV but not in the reality of the created universe."

"What you ask is too difficult," the bishop said. "How many people are willing to take lightning into their bodies?"

Mr. Murry smiled, and to Polly it was one of the saddest smiles she had ever seen. "You are," her grandfather said.

The bishop said softly, "*It was as if lightning flashed into my spirit . . . and with the light such a profound peace and joy came into my heart. In one moment I felt as if wholly revitalized by some infinite power, so that my body would be shattered like an earthen vessel.*" He sighed. "That's John Thomas, a Welshman in the mid-1700s. But it's a good description, isn't it?"

"Very good," Mr. Murry agreed. "But it also shocks me."

"Why?" the bishop asked.

"Because you know more than I do."

"No—no—"

"But you don't know enough, Nase. You've opened a time gate that Annie—Anaral, whatever her name is—seems to be able to walk through and which has drawn Polly through it, and I want it closed."

Close it! How could it be closed!

The door had been opened, and the winds of time were blowing against it, keeping it from closing, almost taking it off the hinges.

"No!" Polly cried, stopping her grandfather in midsentence. "You can't forbid me to go to the star-watching rock!"

Her grandfather sighed heavily. "What a lifetime of working with the nature of the space/time continuum has taught me is that we know very little about space, and even less about time. I don't know whether you and Nase have actually gone back three thousand years, or whether those young snow-capped mountains are some kind of hallucination. But I do know that you're in our care, and we are responsible for you."

The bishop poured more syrup onto his pancakes. "Certainly some of the responsibility is mine."

Polly looked into his eyes, a faded silver that still held light, but there was nothing of the fanatic, of the madman, in his steady gaze.

Mr. Murry said, "Nase, you've got to keep Polly out of this. You don't know enough. We human creatures can make watches and clocks and sensitive timing devices, but we don't understand what we're timing. When something has happened—"

"It doesn't vanish," the bishop said. "It makes waves, as sound does. Or a pebble dropped into a pond."

"Time waves?" Polly suggested. "Energy waves? Something to do with E = mc²?"

Nobody responded. Mr. Murry started clearing the table, moving creakily, as though his joints pained him more than usual. Mrs. Murry sat looking out the window at the distant hills, her face unreadable.

"I don't know what to do about this." Mr. Murry turned from the sink to look directly at Polly. "When we told your parents we'd love to have you come stay with us, it never occurred to your grandmother and me that you might get involved with Nase's discoveries."

"We didn't take them seriously enough," her grandmother said. "We didn't want to."

"Under the circumstances," her grandfather said, "should we send Polly home?"

"Granddad!" Polly protested.

"We can't keep you prisoner here," her grandmother said.

"Listen." Polly was fierce. "I don't think you *can* send me away. Really. If I'm into this tesseract thing that Bishop Colubra has opened—because that's what's happened, isn't it?—then if you try to take me out of it, wouldn't that do something to—maybe rip—the space/time continuum?"

Her grandfather walked to the windows, looked out across his garden, then turned. "It is a possibility."

"If time and space are one—" the bishop suggested, then stopped.

"So it might," Polly continued, "rip me, too?"

"I don't know," her grandfather said. "But it's a risk I'd rather not take."

"Look"—the bishop clapped his hands together softly—"Thursday is All Hallows' Eve. Samhain, as Annie and Karralys might call it. The gates of time swing open most easily at this strange and holy time. If Polly will be willing to stay home just until after Thursday night—"

"Zachary's coming Thursday afternoon," Polly reminded them. "I can't very well tell Zachary that I can't go anywhere with him because Bishop Colubra's opened a tesseract and somehow or other I've blundered into it." She tried to laugh. "Is Zachary in it, too?"

The bishop shook his head slowly. "I think not. No. His seeing Karralys when he came to our time is one thing. Going through the time gate himself is quite another."

"If Zachary hasn't gone through the time gate, then he's not in the tesseract?"

"I think not," the bishop repeated. "Nor is Louise, even if—whether she believes it or not—she saw Annie."

"Polly," Mr. Murry queried, "you're *sure* Zachary saw this person?"

"Well, Granddad, yes."

Her grandfather had the hot water running, and he held his hands under the tap, nodding slowly. "Going somewhere with Zachary should be all right. Away from here, but not too far away. Nowhere near the star-watching rock."

"Just lie low till after Samhain," the bishop urged. "And don't go swimming unless one of your grandparents is with you."

She nodded. "Okay. Samhain. What does that mean?"

"It's the ancient Celtic New Year's festival, when the animals were brought down from their grazing grounds for the winter. The crops were harvested, and there was a great feast. Places were set at the festival dinner for those who had died during the previous year, as a sign of honor and faith in the continuing of the spirits of the dead."

"It sounds like a sort of combination of Halloween and Thanksgiving," Polly said.

"And so it was. Pope Gregory III in the eighth century dedicated November 1 All Saints' Day, and October 31 was All Hallows' Eve."

"So," Mr. Murry said dryly, "the Christian Church, and not for the first time, took over and renamed a pagan holiday."

The phone rang again, interrupting them. Mr. Murry went to it. "Yes, Louise, he's here. It would seem that somehow or other Polly walked into three thousand years ago this morning, if such a thing is to be believed . . . No, I find it difficult, too . . . Yes, we'll call." He turned back to the table.

"My little sister is a doctor," the bishop said.

"All right, Nason. We know your sister is a doctor."

"I made the mistake—if it was a mistake—Annie cut her finger deeply, badly. It needed stitching, and Cub, the young healer, is not experienced enough, and Karralys was away, so I brought Annie home with me."

"To now—to the present?" Incredulity, shock, and anger combined in Mr. Murry's voice.

"Just long enough for Louise to fix her finger. I took her right back."

"Oh, Nase." Mr. Murry groaned. "You can't play around with time that way."

"I couldn't play around with Annie's finger, either."

"Did Louise go along with you in this—this—"

"She wasn't happy about it, but there we were in her office and—to tell you the truth—she had never seen Annie before, so it didn't occur to her to think in terms of three thousand years ago. Her first reaction was that Annie needed help, and quickly, so she did what had to be done. When I told her who Annie was, she didn't really believe me, and I didn't press the point. She just told me to get Annie back to wherever or whenever it was she came from as quickly as possible."

"Nason." Mr. Murry stood up, sat down again. "This isn't *Star Trek* and you can't just beam people back and forth. How did you do it?"

"Well, now, I'm not exactly sure. That's part of the problem. Don't shout at me, Alex."

"I'm beyond shouting."

"Granddad." Polly tried to calm things down. Now that her grandparents were taking charge, the adventure began to seem exciting rather than terrifying. "Your tesseract thing—what you've been working on—space travel—it's to free us from the restrictions of time, isn't it?"

"Yes. But purely for the purpose of extra-solar-system exploration. That's all. We don't know enough to play around with it, as I know from my own experience."

The bishop spoke softly. "We climbed the Matterhorn because it was there. We went to the moon because it was there. We're going to explore the farther planets in our own solar system and then in our own galaxy and look toward the galaxies beyond because they're there. I didn't come to live with Louise with any idea of finding Ogam stones, but when I found one—well, I was interested because they were there."

"Here," Mr. Murry corrected.

"Here. I may have been foolish. But neither did I expect what has happened to Polly. Child, can you lie low till the weekend? Yes, go off somewhere on Thursday with your young man. Not that I think there's any real danger. But don't go to the star-watching rock—can you wait until Sunday?"

"I don't know." Polly looked troubled. "I don't know if that would do any good, because the first time I saw Anaral it was right here, last night while I was swimming."

The bishop held up his long, thin hands in a gesture of disclaimer, shook his head. Sunlight flashed off the topaz in his ring. "I'm sorry." Then he looked at Polly. "Or am I? We may be on to something—"

"Nason!" Mr. Murry warned.

Mrs. Murry hit the palm of her hand softly against the table. "This is Polly's study time. I think a little return to normalcy would be a good thing. There are some books up in her room she needs to look at."

"Good," Mr. Murry said. "Perhaps this morning was just an aberration. By all means let's try to return to normal."

Polly rose, went to the bishop. "This Ogam writing. You said it's an alphabet. Do you have it written down? I mean, so that I could make sense of it?"

"Yes. At home."

"Could I see it, please?"

"Of course. I have what may be no more than my own version of Ogam in a notebook, but it's helped me translate the Ogam stones. I'll bring it over this afternoon."

Mrs. Murry started to intervene, then closed her mouth.

"Thanks, Bishop," Polly said, and turned to go upstairs.

Up in her room Polly simply sat for a few minutes in the rocking chair, not reaching for the books. What she would have liked to do was go out to the star-watching rock. She was no longer afraid of being trapped in past time. Somehow the threshold was open to her, as it was to Anaral. But her grandparents would be upset and angry. Would it truly help if she stayed around the house until after Thursday?

Polly turned toward her night table and reached for the books. Studying for her grandparents was a tangible reality, a relief after the almost dream world of the lake and village of three thousand years ago. Yes, she wanted to learn Ogam. If Anaral could learn English from the bishop, Polly could learn Ogam.

Meanwhile, she would study. The Murrys were more demanding than her teachers at Cowpertown High had been, and she was delighted at their challenge.

She turned to the first book in the pile. All the books had been marked with slips of paper. The first was by John Locke, a seventeenth-century philosopher—she knew that much, thanks to Max, who had frequently augmented whatever Polly was given at Cowpertown High. These were Locke's impressions of America, idyllic and, she thought, a little naïve. But Locke was writing from the far past (though only centuries ago, not millennia) when the new continent was fresh and still uncorrupted by the accumulated evils of the Old World. The naked Amerindians seemed to Locke to live a life as innocent as Adam and Eve in the Garden. They lived without external laws, did not buy or sell or pile up wealth. They were, Locke implied, without shame, not burdened by the guilts of the past.

The book on her lap, Polly rocked, thought. There was no evidence that there had ever been Celts or druids on these shores when the early settlers landed. Had they been assimilated into the local tribes, as Karralys and Tav seemed to have been taken into Anaral's people? Gone back to Britain? If there really were druids in New England three thousand years ago, what had happened to them?

She sighed, opened the second book to the page her grandmother had marked. It was by Alexis de Tocqueville, writing in the troubled period of Andrew Jackson, when the Indians were treated with terrible unfairness, and yet Tocqueville wrote that the settlers in America "had arrived at a state of democracy without having to endure a democratic revolution" and that they were "born free without having to become so."

Still true? Polly thought of herself as having been born free, and yet in the short span of her life she had witnessed much abuse of freedom. Surely the lusts and guilts and greeds of the Old World had taken root in the New. And despite her affection for the natives of Gaea, for the Quiztano Indians in Venezuela, she was leery of the concept of the "noble savage." People, in her experience, were people, some good, some bad, most a mixture.

Next in the pile was *Lectiones geometricae*, published by Isaac Barrow in 1670, and despite Polly's proficiency with languages she could not concentrate on the Old Latin, so she put it aside for when she could focus better. She read a marked chapter in a history of the sixteenth century, learning that Giordano Bruno had been burned at the stake for heresy, including the proposal, horrifying to the Church establishment of those days, that there are as many times as there are planets.

—And even one planet, Polly thought, —has many time zones, and when we try to cross them too quickly we get jet lag. And even in one zone, time doesn't move at a steady rate.

She remembered a day of lying in bed with flu and fever, every joint aching, and the day dragged on and on, far longer than an ordinary day. And then there was a New Year's Eve party at Max's beautiful plantation house, Beau Allaire, with Max sparkling as brightly as the crystal chandeliers, and there had been singing and charades and the evening passed in the twinkling of an eye. Poor Giordano Bruno. He was probably right about time. How many people have been burned at the stake for being right?

Then came a book by an eighteenth-century philosopher, Berkeley. She sat with the book unopened on her lap. Max had talked to her about this philosopher, who was also a bishop (was he anything like Bishop Colubra?), who had had the idea, amazing in his day, that the stairs outside his study were not there unless he was aware of them, that things had to be apprehended to *be*. 'The anthropic principle,' Max had called it, and had seen it as both fascinating and repellent.

If Polly did not believe that she had seen and talked with Anaral, would that keep the other girl in the past where she belonged? Would it close the threshold? But she had seen Anaral, and there was no way she could pretend that she hadn't. The threshold was open.

Last in the pile was a copy of the *New England Journal of Medicine* with an article by her grandmother on the effect of the microscopic on the macroscopic universe. What might seem to have been a random assortment of books was beginning to reveal a pattern, and the pattern seemed to Polly to have something to do with Anaral and the Ogam stones, though she did not think that her grandmother had had either Anaral or the Ogam stones in mind when she had chosen the readings, any more than she had had Polly in mind when she redecorated the bedroom.

Polly studied for a couple of hours, making notes, absorbing, so that she would be able to answer her grandparents' questions. She was fully focused in the present moment, and she did not know what made her look at her watch. It was after eleven. One of her jobs was to drive to the post office for the mail. If something was needed for lunch or dinner, her grandmother would leave a note with the outgoing mail.

She went downstairs. No one in the living room or kitchen. Her grandmother's lab door was closed, but Polly knocked.

"What?" came the not very gracious response.

"It's Polly. Is it all right if I get the mail and go to the store?"

"Oh, Polly, come in. I didn't mean to snarl. I suppose it's no use wishing Nase had never retired and come to live with Louise." Her grandmother was sitting on her tall lab stool. There was an electron microscope in front of her, but the cover was over it and looked as though it had not been removed in years. She wore a tweed skirt, lisle stockings, a turtleneck, and a cardigan—a down-to-earth country woman. And yet Polly knew that her grandmother delved deep into the world of the invisible, the strange sub-microscopic world of quantum mechanics. Her grandfather looked most comfortable in an old plaid flannel shirt, riding his tractor; and yet he had actually gone into space, orbiting the earth beyond the confines of the atmosphere. Her grandparents seemed to live comfortably in their dual worlds, the daily world of garden, kitchen, house, and pool, and the wider world of their scientific experiments. But Bishop Colubra had thrown them completely off course, Bishop Colubra and Polly's own unexpected journey through time.

"Grand?"

"I don't know, Polly. I don't know what your parents would say . . ." Her voice trailed off.

"Just to the post office and the store, Grand. I didn't want to go without asking you."

Her grandmother sighed. "Have I been living in a dream world? The only piece of equipment in my lab that gets any real use is the obsolete Bunsen burner, because it's become family tradition. Like your grandfather, I've been doing thought experiments." As Polly looked at her questioningly she continued, "Alex and I have sat in our separate worlds, doing experiments in our minds."

"And?" Polly prodded.

"If a thought experiment is capable of laboratory proof, then we're apt to write a paper about it, and then either we or another scientist will put it to the test. But quite a few thought experiments are so wildly speculative that it will be a long time before they can be proven."

Which was more of a dream? The thought experiments in the minds of her grandparents and other scientists? Or the world of three thousand years ago which was touching on their own time?

The lab was damp. Polly wondered how her grandmother stood it. The floor was made of great slabs of stone. There was a faded rag rug in front of two shabby easy chairs, and the lamp on the table between them gave at least an illusion of warmth. Only the permeating cold grounded her in present reality. "Grand?"

"What is it, Polly?"

"The post office?"

"I suppose so. We can't keep you wrapped in cotton wool. I'm not even sure what we're afraid of."

"That I'll get lost three thousand years ago? I don't think that's going to happen."

"Neither do I. I still haven't given it my willing suspension of disbelief. But just the post office."

"We're out of milk."

"All right. The store. But check in with me when you get back."

"Sure."

Polly would keep her word and go only to the post office and the store. What she wanted was to talk to Anaral again. Go to the Grandfather Oak and see Karralys and his dog and hope that this time he would stay and talk with her.

Thursday was All Hallows' Eve and Bishop Colubra took it with great seriousness. Samhain. A festival so old that it pre-dated written history. Polly's skin prickled, not with fear now, but with expectation, though for what she was not sure. All she knew was that she was touching on that long-gone age as it rose out of the past to touch on another age, a present that was perhaps as brutal as any previous age, but was at least familiar.

Her grandparents' car was elderly, and it took a few tries before the engine turned over and she shifted into reverse and pulled out of the garage. She went to the post office, to the store, speaking to the postmistress and the checkout girl, who were curious and friendly and already knew her by name.

When she got home, her grandmother had left the lab and was making toasted cheese sandwiches for lunch. They had just finished eating and were putting the dishes away when they heard a car pull up noisily. Bishop Colubra.

"Just a quick visit," he said. "Louise made me promise to come right back. I just wanted to bring Polly my Ogam notebook." He sat down at the table, indicated the chair next to him, and spread out the book between them.

It was tidily and consistently done, vocabulary, and simple rules of grammar, and a few phrases and idioms. "Druids had a vast amount of information in their memories after long years of training, but Ogam was an oral language rather than a written one. What I have here is in no way pure Ogam. It's what Anaral and Karralys and the People of the Wind speak today—their today, that is."

In three columns he had listed words used by Anaral's people before Karralys and Tav came; then there were words which were strictly Ogam and which Karralys and Tav had brought to the language; plus a short column of words which were still recognizable today; such as mount, glen, crag, bard, cairn.

"You can read my writing?" he asked.

"Yes, it's lots clearer than mine."

"Fascinating, isn't it, to see how language evolves. I wonder how many of our English/American words will still be around in another thousand years or so." He stood up. "I must go."

Polly picked up the notebook. "Thanks a lot, Bishop. I'm glad you've written out the pronunciation phonetically." She turned the pages, nodding, while he stood on one leg, scratching his shin with the other foot, looking more like a heron than ever.

"It's pretty arbitrary of me to call it Ogam, but it seems simplest. The language has evolved fairly easily, a sort of lingua franca."

"Bishop, you did teach Anaral to speak English?"

"Shh." He put his foot down and glanced at Mrs. Murry, who was feeding the fire, and at Mr. Murry deep in an article in a scientific journal. He leaned over the chair toward Polly. "She's very bright. She learned amazingly quickly."

"But you've spent a lot of time with her."

He glanced again at her grandparents, sighed deeply. "This is no time for secrecy, is it? Yes. Whenever the time gate has opened for me, I've gone through. But you—" He shook his head. "I have to go." He ambled toward the pantry door. "You will stay close to your grandparents?"

She, too, sighed. "Yes, Bishop. I will."

CHAPTER 4

POLLY spent several hours with Bishop Colubra's Ogam notebook. In the late afternoon her grandmother went swimming with her. Nothing happened. Anaral did not come. The evening passed quietly.

On Tuesday the bishop asked her over for tea.

"Go along," her grandmother said. "I know you're going stir-crazy here, and even though I don't think anything will happen while I'm with you, refusing to believe that three thousand years ago can touch directly on our own time, I'm just as happy to have you away from the pool."

"You don't need the car?"

"I'm not going anywhere. Louise's house is no distance as the crow flies. Our land is contiguous with hers. But by car you have to go down to the main road, drive west a couple of miles, and then turn uphill to the right the first chance you get."

The phone rang. Zachary. Obviously wanting to talk. "Polly, I'm just so glad to be in touch with you again. You're like a bright light in these filthy days."

"Autumn seems pretty glorious to me."

"Not in an office that's a small box with no windows. I can't wait to see you."

"I'm looking forward to it, too."

"Polly, I don't want to hurt you."

Her grandmother had left the kitchen and gone out to the lab, leaving Polly alone with the phone. "Why should you hurt me?"

"Polly, it's my pattern. I hurt every girl I get involved with. I hurt you last summer."

"Not really," she protested. "I mean, it turned out all right."

"Because your friends came and rescued us after I'd upset that idiot little canoe. But you're right. That was minor, compared to—"

He sounded so desperate that she asked, gently, "Compared to what, Zach?"

"Polly, I'm a self-protective bastard. All I think of is my own good."

"Well, don't we all, to some extent?"

"To some extent, yes. But I take it beyond some extent."

"Hey, are you at work?"

"Yah, but don't worry, I'm alone in my box and things are slow today. I'm not goofing off. There's nothing for me to do right now. I just want to say that I'm going to try really hard not to hurt you."

"Well. Okay. That's good."

"You don't believe me."

"Sure I believe you, that you're not going to hurt me."

"No, what I mean is, how self-serving I am. Listen. Once I was with a girl I really liked. Her grandfather was sick, dying, really, and we went to the hospital to get blood for him, and she was upset, of course, really upset. And there was a little kid she knew there, and the little kid was having a seizure—well, Polly, the thing is that I really don't know what happened because I ran out on it."

"What?" She kept her voice gentle.

"I ran away. I couldn't take it. I got into my car and drove off. I just left her. That's the kind of putrid stinker I am."

"Hey, Zach, don't put yourself down. That's in the past. You wouldn't do it again."

"I don't know what I'd do, that's the point."

"Listen, Zachary, don't get stuck in the past. Give yourself a chance. We do learn from our mistakes."

"Do we? Do you really think so?"

"Sure. I've made plenty. And I've learned from them."

"Good, then. All I wanted to say is that I think you're terrific, and I want us to have a good time on Thursday, and I don't want to do or say anything to hurt you."

"We'll have a good time on Thursday," she promised.

"Okay, then. Till Thursday. I'm glad you're on this earth, Polly. You're good for me. Goodbye."

She was baffled by his call. What on earth was he afraid he would do that would hurt her? She shrugged, went out to the pantry, and took the red anorak off the hook, knocked on the lab door. "Grand, can I help with anything before I go?"

"Not a thing. Just be back in plenty of time for dinner. I'm sorry to be having an attack of mother hen-ism, but I can't wipe out your experience of crossing a time threshold just because it's totally out of the context of my own experience."

"I keep asking myself—did it really happen? But, Grand, I think it did."

"Go have tea with Nase." Her grandmother's voice was slightly acid. "Perhaps he'll see fit to tell you more than he's told us."

As Polly drove up the hill to Dr. Louise's yellow house, surrounded by maples and beeches dropping yellow leaves, the bishop came out to meet her, led her in, took the red anorak.

Dr. Louise's kitchen was smaller than the Murrys', and darker, but large enough for a sizable oak table by the window, and brightened by a surprising bouquet of yellow roses as well as copper pots and pans. The bishop took something lopsided out of the oven.

"Alex's breadmaking challenged me. This is supposed to be Irish soda bread, but I don't think it's a success."

"It'll probably taste wonderful," Polly said, "and I'm hungry."

The bishop put the bread out, with butter, jam, and a pitcher of milk. "Tea, milk, or cocoa?"

"Cocoa would be lovely. It's cold today."

"Perfect autumn weather, pushing sixty. Sit down, be comfortable."

Polly sat, while the bishop puttered about making two steaming mugs of cocoa, slicing the soda bread, which did indeed taste better than it looked, especially with homemade rose-hip jelly.

"What happens to what's happened?" Polly asked him.

"It's a big question," the bishop said. "I seem to have found one time gate. There may be countless others."

"What was going on three thousand years ago?" she continued.

"Abraham and Sarah left home," the bishop said, "and went out into the wilderness. But there were already Pharaohs in Egypt, and the Sphinx was asking her riddles."

"What else?"

"Gilgamesh," the bishop continued. "I think he was around then."

"But he wasn't from anywhere around here."

"Uruk," the bishop said. "Way on the other side of the world. And there was Sumerian poetry, lamenting the death of Tammuz, the shepherd god." He sliced more bread. "Tammuz's mother was the goddess Innini. Let me see. Back to Egypt. That wasn't anywhere around here, either. The great pyramid was built at Giza. The Cheops pyramid conforms in dimensions and layout to astronomical measurements—like Stonehenge, in astronomy, if not in architecture. The stars have taught us more than we realize." He was rambling on happily. "I wonder what it would be like on a planet where the atmosphere was too dense for the stars to shine through? This bread isn't that bad, after all."

"Bishop, please." Polly smoothed jam onto her bread. "Maybe you've told my grandparents, but how did you meet Anaral and Karralys? When?"

"It started last spring." The bishop folded his legs and made himself comfortable, a piece of bread and jelly in his hand. "I'd never before been so unbusy in my life, and I was wandering around looking for odd jobs to do and came across an old root cellar behind the barn where Louise parks her car. At least, it was called a root cellar, and in the days when it was assumed that one could protect oneself from a nuclear attack some of the old root cellars came into reuse as bomb shelters."

"Fat lot of help they'd be," Polly said.

"Louise never bothered with hers. She always said that when she retired she'd have a garden and put it back to its original use, a storage place for tubers. But the thing is, some of the old root cellars were not built as root cellars."

"What, then?"

"They were dug centuries before the people we know as the first settlers came over from England, and they were dug to be holy places, where the priests or druids or whoever they were could go to commune with the dead, and with the gods of the underworld. They believed that those who had died were still available for advice and help, back for countless generations."

"Oh, I like that," Polly said. "Do my grandparents have a root cellar?"

"They used to, but when they put in the pool it got dug up, so I had only Louise's to excavate, and I spent weeks on it, with a trowel, then a shovel. And there I found the first of the Ogam stones, and the only one not on your grandparents' land. Over the years, the root cellar had filled in with leaves, loose dirt, other debris, and this had protected the stone. The writing on that first one was far clearer than those I've found in the stone walls."

"What did it say?"

"It was a memorial marker honoring our foremothers."

A car door slammed outside, and Dr. Louise came in, calling, "Hallo, I'm earlier than I thought I'd be. I hope there's tea left for me."

"Plenty," the bishop said. "I made a large pot, and Polly and I've been drinking cocoa instead."

Dr. Louise shucked off her heavy jacket and then her white coat, both of which she hung on deer antlers to the side of the door. "I inherited the antlers with the house."

Polly laughed. "You don't strike me as a hunter."

"Hardly." The doctor helped herself to bread and butter. "Nase, you're really becoming domesticated in your old age. This isn't half bad."

"It looks better now than when I took it out of the oven."

"Bishop," Polly said softly, "please go on."

"If I am right about root cellars, and of course I may not be, they were ancient time devices, a way the druids could commune with their past, with their gods, with powers of both good and evil long lost to us. You might call the root cellar a three-thousand-year-old time capsule."

"Have you been watching too much TV?" Dr. Louise asked.

"It's probably affected my metaphors," her brother agreed. "All spring the root cellar kept drawing me, but also sending me out. I found other Ogam stones in Alex and Kate's stone walls, worked on translating their hieroglyphs. Found three in a small cairn of stones near your star-watching rock, Polly. I knew there was something special about the star-watching rock. That it was a place of power. Benign power."

Polly said, "It was always a special place to my mom and her sibs. Go on, please, Bishop."

"In mid-June, as the days lengthened toward the summer solstice, an early heat wave hit us, and the root cellar was cool, so I spent more time there. Not digging anymore. Just sitting. Often moving beyond thought into the dark and timeless space of contemplation."

"I was afraid you were becoming a pagan," Dr. Louise remarked with irony.

"No, Louise, no. I was not then and am not now turning to the old gods. No, the God I have tried to serve all my life is still good enough for me. Christ didn't just appear as Jesus of Nazareth two thousand years ago, don't forget. Christ is, will be, and certainly was at the time the druids dug the root cellar three thousand years ago, just as much as now. But we rational and civilized people have turned our backs on the dark side of God because we are afraid of the numinous and the unexplainable. Forgive me, I'm preaching. I've spent so much of my life giving sermons that it's a habit I find hard to break."

"You're a good preacher," Dr. Louise said with sisterly pride.

"So, please," Polly urged.

"Midsummer's Eve," the bishop continued, "I was in the root cellar. When I called it a three-thousand-year-old time capsule, I was in a way joking. It's a metaphor that seems right. You see, what happened was that I was in the root cellar, and then, without transition, I was on the star-watching rock, and there was Anaral."

"And—"

"That first time we couldn't understand each other, except by gestures. I jumped to some conclusions, because she obviously wasn't an ordinary girl. There was a dignity, a nobility about her that set her apart. But it was a while before we knew each other's language well enough to communicate and I could truly believe that I had moved through a great deal of time."

"Bishop," Polly asked, "can you just go in and out of the time gate whenever you want to?"

"Oh, no." He shook his head. "I'm not sure how it happens when it happens. There is a feeling, just as you said, of lightning, and the earth quivering, if not quaking, and something seems to happen to the air. After that first time it has never again been from the root cellar, always from the star-watching rock. I go there and wait, and sometimes Annie or Karralys will come to me. But there will be weeks when nothing happens."

Dr. Louise said, "Thanks for the tea. I have some charts to go over."

The bishop was stiff. "I know it offends you, Louise. I try not to talk about it in front of you."

"That's not the solution, either," the doctor said. "I keep wondering what Polly's family would make of your madness." She turned to Polly. "Are you going to tell them about this?"

"Of course. But not yet. I need to understand more, first. And I don't want to worry them."

"You may have to," the doctor said.

The bishop's eyes were closed, as though he was listening. "One of the stones from the cairn by the star-watching rock had a lovely rune on it. *Hold me in peace while sleeping. Wake me with the sun's smiling. With pure water slake my thirst. Let me be merry in your love.* That's a simplicity that's gone, at least in our so-called higher civilization."

"Don't knock our civilization," his sister warned. "Cataracts used to make people blind, and still do, in many parts of the world. Your lens implants have you seeing like a much younger man."

"That's technology, not civilization." The bishop was testy. "I'm grateful every day that I can read and write. I don't underestimate knowledge. But we get into trouble when we confuse it with truth."

"All right, Nase."

"Truth is eternal. Knowledge is changeable. It is disastrous to confuse them."

"My dear, I don't," Dr. Louise said. "But I can conceive of your adventures as having little to do with either knowledge or truth. They're beyond reason. And now I'm afraid they've made Kate and Alex terribly upset."

"I'm sorry," the bishop said. "I didn't expect Polly to become involved. If I've been closemouthed up till now, it has been not only because of your distaste for what has been happening but because I thought it was my own, unique adventure. I never expected that Polly— I simply have to have faith that all this has meaning."

Dr. Louise sighed, rose. "I really do have to go over charts."

Polly, too, stood. "I'd better get on back. I promised I wouldn't be late."

She drove off down the long dirt road. The tree frogs were singing their autumn farewell to summer. A few lingering insects chirred away. Above her flew a great gaggle of geese, honking their way south. Their haunting cry was new to Polly, and she found it both exciting and sad. On either side of the road, bushes were red and rust-colored. There was some dry-looking goldenrod and joe-pye weed. As she turned into a curve, she could see the hills shadowed in purple. Low hills weathered by centuries. Comforting hills.

When her grandmother came in to say good night, Polly was deep in Bishop Colubra's notebook.

"This Ogam's really not too difficult, as long as I don't try to connect it to Latin or Greek roots but think of it as a made-up language."

"Polly." Her grandmother sat on the edge of the bed. "It is my hope that you are not going to have any opportunity to speak this language."

"I love languages, Grand. They're fun. You know how Granddad loves to do his puzzle in the paper every day? It's the same sort of thing."

Her grandmother ruffled her hair. "I want you to have fun, my dear, but not to get yourself into any kind of danger. I hope you'll have fun with Zachary on Thursday. But he strikes me as a complex young man, and I'm very uncomfortable with the idea that you think he's seen someone from the past."

"I find it pretty uncomfortable, too."

"And you'll stay away from the pool and the star-watching rock?"

"Yes. We will." Polly sighed, then indicated the pile of books still on her bed table. "I went through the parts you marked and took notes. I love learning from you, Grand."

"You don't miss school?"

"I didn't much like it. I was used to being taught by Mother and Daddy when we lived on Gaea, and the Cowpertown school was pretty boring after that. I wasn't that great at school. Okay, but not great."

"Your mother must have understood that. School was disastrous for her till she went to college."

"I find that hard to believe."

"Believe it."

"But she's so brilliant."

"She's good at the difficult stuff, but not with the easy, and I guess you're not unlike her in that."

"Well—maybe. Like Zachary, I'm better if I'm interested. The only teacher I really liked left. And last year I could go to Beau Allaire and do homework there and Max could make it interesting."

"Her death must be a great grief to you." Her grandmother touched her gently on the knee.

"Yes. It is. But Max would want me to get on with life, and that's what I'm trying to do. But I do miss . . ." For a moment her voice trembled.

"Max was very close to Sandy and Rhea, too. Sandy says her death has left a big hole in their lives."

"I guess the planet is riddled with holes, isn't it? From all the people who've lived and then died. Do the holes ever get filled?"

"That's a good question."

"Grand, those people I saw when I went back—Anaral and— Maybe you don't want to talk about it?"

"Go on."

"They've been dead maybe three thousand years." She shuddered involuntarily. "What about their holes? Are the holes just always there, waiting to be filled?"

"You have always tended to ask unanswerable questions. I don't know about those holes. All I know is that Max gave you great riches, and we would, all of us, be less than we are if it weren't for those we love and who've loved us who have died." Her grandmother rose, bent down, and kissed Polly. "Good night, my dear. Sleep well."

Polly woke up, freezing. Her quilt had slid to the floor. She was caught in a dream, not quite a nightmare, of Zachary driving along a winding road in the bishop's blue pickup truck. She was in the back of the truck and icy rain was drenching her. Every time Zachary hit a bump, she was nearly thrown out. To one side of the road was a cliff, to the other a drop down to a valley far below. The truck hit a bump and—

She woke up. Hadron's warm body was not by her. She picked up the quilt and huddled under it. Her feet were like ice. There was no way she was going to be able to escape the dream and go back to sleep until she warmed up.

The meaning of the dream was apparent to her. It was simply her reaction to Zachary's phone call and had, she thought, no particular meaning of its own. She had dreamed of the rain chilling her because the quilt had slid off the bed and she was frozen. The wind hit against the house, emphasizing the cold.

The pool. It was by far the warmest place in the house. Forgetting her promises, forgetting for the moment the reason for them, aware only that she was shivering, she tiptoed downstairs. All the fires were banked. The house was cold. She opened the door to the room with the pool and was met with a humid warmth and a green smell from all the plants which flourished there.

Moonlight was coming through the skylights. The plants hanging in the windows made strange shadows. Then, as her eyes adjusted, she saw an unexpected shadow, a darkness in one of the poolside chairs. Someone was sitting there.

Terrified, she reached for the light switch and the room was flooded with light.

Anaral leapt from the chair like a wild gazelle, more frightened than Polly. Surely Anaral's world knew electricity only as lightning unleashed and dangerous.

Polly's heart stopped pounding in her throat. "Lights. Electric lights. Don't be afraid."

Anaral capsized, rather than sat back down. "Bishop told me about lights. Yes. Still, it frightens me. No one can hear us?"

"Not if we're quiet. How did you get here?"

"I came from our great standing stones to this place of water in a box." Anaral was referring to the pool, the pool that was over an underground river. "Where your water in the box is in your time circle, in my circle it is our most holy ground, the stones that stand over the scent of water. I lay on the sarsen and I thought about you and I called myself to you. And I came." She looked at Polly with a delighted smile. Then she got up and walked slowly around the room, looking at the poolside chairs, the stationary bike Polly's grandmother used when the weather was too inclement for walking outside. "Bishop says you live in house. We are in house?"

"Yes. This is the new wing, built for the pool—the water in a box." Of course Anaral would know nothing about a house or its contents.

Anaral picked up a paperback book lying on a small table by the chair where she had been sitting. "One day Bishop brought book to show me. Bishop says you have stories in books."

"Many stories."

"Karralys says that for stories the writing has to be more—more full than ours, less simple."

"Yes, more complex."

Anaral touched her forehead. "Druids have stories here. Many stories. We keep the memory. Without our memory we would be—less. I do not know the word."

"Our books are like keepers of the memory. In them we have the stories of many people, many times, many cultures."

"Cultures?"

"People who live in different circles of place, as well as time."

Anaral nodded. "You are certain you are not a druid?"

Polly laughed. "Positive."

"But you have gifts. You cross the threshold of time. To do that requires much training, and Karralys was concerned that, though I have the training, no threshold was open to me. But then I saw Bishop before he did, and now I am practicing using the gift and the training by coming to you. And you crossed into my time."

Polly spread out her hands. "I don't know how I did it, Anaral. I haven't any idea. I don't know if I could ever do it again."

"Karralys has been to many places, to many different times. I have crossed only one threshold, seen only you and Bishop. Karralys says that there is meaning that you have come, meaning for the pattern."

"What pattern?"

"The pattern of lines drawn between the stars, between people, between places, between circles, like the line between the great stone and the water in a box."

Polly thought of the book of constellations in her room, with the lines drawn between the stars.

Anaral looked at her, smiling. "It is nice, what I sit on."

"A chair."

"At the great stones there are chairs, but very different, carved out of stone. This holds my body with more ease."

Polly wondered what Anaral would think of the rest of the house, of the bedroom, the kitchen. All the things that Polly took for granted, hot running water, toilets, refrigerators, microwave, food processor—would they seem like miracles to Anaral, or would she think them magic, perhaps evil magic? "Anaral, I'm very glad to see you, even in the middle of the night. But—why have you come?"

"To see if I could," Anaral said simply. "Everybody else was asleep, so I could practice the gift all alone. I came and I called you. To know you. To know why you can come to my circle of time. To know if you have been sent to us by the Presence."

"The Presence?"

"The One who is more than the Mother, or the goddess. Starmaker, wind-breather, earth-grower, sun-riser, rain-giver. The One who cares for all. Karralys says that it happens only once or twice in a pattern where the lines touch so that circles of time come together with the threshold open in both directions. When this happens, there is a reason."

"Have you asked the bishop?"

"Bishop, too, says there is a reason. But he does not know what. Do you?"

Polly shook her head. "Haven't the foggiest."

"The—"

"I don't know the reason, Anaral. But I like you. I'm glad you're here. I would like to get to know you better."

"Friends?"

"Yes. I'd like to be friends."

"It is lonely for druids, sometimes. Friends care for each other."

"Yes."

"Protect each other?"

"Friends do everything they can to protect each other."

"But it is not always possible." Anaral shook her head. "In a terrible storm, or when lightning starts fire, or when other tribes attack."

"Friends try," Polly said firmly. "Friends care." She felt deeply drawn to Anaral. Was it possible to develop a real friendship with a girl from three thousand years ago? "I would like to be your friend, Anaral."

"That is good. I am your friend." Anaral stood up. "Bishop calls me Annie."

"Yes. Annie."

"I willed for you to wake up, to come here, to water in a box. And you came. Thank you."

"The quilt fell off my bed. I was cold." Quilt. Bed. It would make no sense to Anaral.

"You came, Polly. Now I go." Anaral went to one of the north windows. "See? Now I know how to open it." She jumped lightly down and ran off into the night.

Polly looked after her until she disappeared into the woods. Then she closed the window. She stayed by the pool for several more minutes, but nothing happened. The water was quiet. She sat in one of the poolside chairs, wondering, until she grew drowsy and her eyelids drooped. She was warm now. Even her toes. Had Anaral been part of a dream? She went upstairs. Perhaps she would understand more in the morning.

She woke later than usual, dressed, and went downstairs. Her grandfather was sitting at the table drinking coffee and doing his puzzle. Polly poured herself half a cup of coffee, filled it with milk, and put it in the microwave. For the moment she had forgotten her bad dream, forgotten going down to the pool to warm up, forgotten Anaral's visit. "This does make *café au lait* much easier. I hate washing out a milky saucepan."

"Polly." Her grandfather looked up from the paper. "Tell me what you know about time."

She sat down. "I don't know that much."

"Tell me what you know."

"Well, there's the—uh—the space/time continuum, of course."

"And that means?"

"Well, that time isn't a separate thing, apart from space. They make a thing together, and that's space/time. But I know that there isn't any time at all if there isn't mass in motion."

Her grandfather nodded. "Right. And Einstein's famous equation?"

"Well, mass and energy are equivalent, so any energy an object uses would add to its mass, and that would make it harder to increase its speed."

"And as it approached the speed of light?"

"Its mass would be so enormous that it couldn't ever get to the speed of light."

"So in terms of space travel?"

"You can't separate space travel from time travel."

"Good girl. So?"

"I don't know, Granddad. How did I go back three thousand years?" Suddenly she remembered Anaral's visit the night before, but this was not the moment to talk about it.

The pantry door opened and her grandmother came in.

Her grandfather said, "That's the billion-dollar question, isn't it?"

"And I seem to have broken Einstein's equation. I mean, didn't I get there faster than the speed of light? I mean, I was here, and then I was there."

"Department of utter confusion," her grandfather said.

Mrs. Murry sliced bread and put it in the toaster. "One theory I find rather comforting is that time exists so that everything doesn't happen all at once."

"What a picture!" Polly had ignored the microwave timer's ping. Now she opened the door, took out her cup, and sat at her place. Hadron got up from his scrap of rug at the fireplace, greeted her by twining about her legs, purring, then returned to the warmth.

Mrs. Murry took the bread from the toaster and put it on a plate in front of Polly. "Eat."

"Thanks. Granddad's bread makes wonderful toast."

Her grandmother continued, "Your grandfather and I have lived with contradictions all our lives. His interests have been with the general theory of relativity, which is concerned with gravity and the macrocosm. Whereas I have spent my life with the microcosm, the world of particle physics and quantum mechanics. As of now these theories appear to be inconsistent with each other."

"If we could find a quantum theory of gravity," Mr. Murry said, "we might, we just might resolve the problem."

Polly asked, "Would that explain the space/time continuum?"

"That's the hope," Mrs. Murry said, and turned to answer the phone.

And now Polly remembered her dream. Zachary. She hoped it would be Zachary on the phone.

But her grandmother said, "Good morning, Nason . . . Yes, we're all here in one place and one time . . . That's dear of you, but why don't you two come here? You know you and Louise like to swim . . . Nase, I like to cook . . . No, don't bring anything. See you this evening."

She turned to her husband and Polly. "As you gathered, that was Nason. Louise has filled him with chagrin and remorse, as a result of which she hasn't been able to talk him out of feeling that he can protect Polly from the past if he's here with her, which is certainly logic nohow contrariwise. They're coming over for dinner."

Mr. Murry smiled. "That was at least partly his motivation in calling."

His wife smiled back. "Cooking has never been Louise's thing. She's a perfectly adequate cook, but it's not foremost on her mind."

"And Nase has rather gourmet tastes," he added.

"And you're a terrific cook," Polly said.

Her grandmother flushed. "Oh, dear, it does look as though I was fishing for a compliment."

"A well-earned one," her husband said.

"I enjoy cooking. It's therapy for me. Louise's therapy is her rose garden. You may note, Polly, that we don't have any roses."

"Accept it graciously, my love," her husband said. "You're a good cook."

"Thanks, dearest." She sat down, elbows on table, chin in hands. "Polly, there is the matter of your parents."

Polly looked at her questioningly.

"Your grandfather believes that you are right, that it would not be safe to take you out of the tesseract, to send you back to Benne Seed. And if I didn't take his fear seriously, you'd be with your parents right now."

"How far can I go?" Polly asked. "How far away from the time threshold?"

Her grandfather folded his paper. "I'm not sure. About ten or so miles, I'm guessing. Maybe more. Maybe as far as Anaral and her people ranged. But not up in a plane. Not across the country."

"Well, I really am in the tesseract." And she told them about Anaral's visit.

Her grandparents gave each other troubled looks.

"Don't tell Mother and Daddy," Polly urged. "Not yet. We don't know enough. It sounds too impossible."

Her grandfather said, "If I know your father, he'd come and get you and there'd be no reasoning with him. And that could be fatal."

"I hate secrets," her grandmother said. "But I agree it would be best to keep silent for a few days."

"Till after Halloween," her grandfather said.

"Tomorrow," her grandmother added.

"Samhain," Polly said.

"We'll tell them everything on Sunday when they call," her grandmother said.

Both grandparents looked at Polly, and then at each other, unhappily.

The morning passed without incident. Polly spent an hour with her grandmother in the lab, till her toes grew too cold. Then she went to her room, to sit at her desk and write out responses to some of the questions her grandmother had asked her. She found it unusually difficult to concentrate. At last she shut her notebook and went downstairs. It was time for a brisk walk before lunch.

She had promised not to walk across the field to the woods and the star-watching rock, so she walked along the dirt road the house faced. Originally it had been one of the early post roads, but with the changing of demographics it was now only a lane. The garage led to a paved road, with farms above, a few dwellings below. The lane wandered along, past pastures, groves, bushes. It was a pleasant place to walk, and Polly ambled along, picking an assortment of flowering autumn weeds.

When she got home, Dr. Louise had called to say that she had an emergency and would not be able to get away for dinner. Could they come the next day? Nase very much wanted to be with Polly on Thursday.

Thursday came, crisp and beautiful. The autumn days were perfect, blue and gold, with more and more leaves falling. Polly worked with her grandfather in the morning, studying some advanced mathematics. Around eleven he took off for town to get his chain saw sharpened, and her grandmother as usual was in the lab.

She walked to the end of the lane and back. A little over a mile. Then she crossed the field to the stone wall. She would go no farther than that. Surely just to the stone wall should be all right.

Louise the Larger was there, basking in the sun. Polly was used to all kinds of odd marine animals, and her father had once had a tank of eels for some experimental purpose, but she knew little about snakes. Polly looked at Louise, lying placidly in a puddle of golden light, but did not feel enough at ease to sit down on the wall beside her.

As though aware of her hesitancy, Louise raised her head slightly, and Polly thought the snake nodded at her kindly before sliding down into the wall and out of sight. Or was she anthropomorphizing, reading human behavior into the snake?

Snake in Ogam was *nasske*. It was on the bishop's vocabulary list. So that meant that the people who used that language knew about snakes. She continued to stare at the wall, but when there was no sign of Louise after a few minutes, Polly sat down. The stones felt warm and comforting. This was as far as she could go without breaking her promise. The breeze ruffled the leaves remaining on the trees which leaned over the wall, making shifting patterns of light and shadow. The day was gold and amber and russet and copper and bronze, with occasional flashes of flame.

A rustling sound made her turn around and there, on the other side of the wall, stood the tow-headed young man, holding his spear. He beckoned to her.

"I can't come. I'm sorry, I promised," she explained, and realized that he could not understand her.

He smiled at her. Pointed to himself. "Tav." She returned his smile.

"Polly," she replied, pointing to herself.

He repeated after her, "Poll-ee." Then he looked up, pointed at the sun, then pointed at her hair, and clapped his hands joyfully.

"I'm just an old carrot top." She blushed, because he was obviously admiring her hair.

Again he indicated the sun, and then her hair, saying, "*Ha lou*, Poll-ee."

She visualized a page of Bishop Colubra's notebook. *Ha lou* was a form of greeting. Easy enough to remember. The bishop's notebook had contained various greetings used throughout the years: hallo, hello, hail, howdy, hi. The negative, *na*, was also simple. *No* in English, *non* in French, *nicht* in German, *nyet* in Russian. The *n* sound seemed universal, she thought, except in Greek, where the *neh* sound meant *yes*.

Tav beamed, and burst into a stream of incomprehensible words.

She smiled, shaking her head. *"Na."* She did not have the vocabulary to say 'I don't understand.'

Carefully, tenderly, he placed his great spear on the ground. Then he sat beside her on the wall. Pointed to the sun. *"Sonno."* Then, with utmost delicacy, his fingertips touched her hair, withdrew. *"Rhuadd."* He held out his hand, spoke a word, and touched his eyes. Spoke again, and touched his nose. He was teaching her words of Ogam. Some of the words, such as *sun* and *red,* she recognized from Bishop Colubra's vocabulary list. Others were new to her. Polly was a quick study, and Tav laughed in delight. After they had worked—or played—together for half an hour, he looked at her and spoke slowly, carefully. "You, *sonno.* Tav"—he touched his pale hair—"*mona.* You come tonight."

She shook her head.

"It is big festival. Samhain. Music. Big music. Much joy."

She could understand him fairly well, but she could not yet put enough words together to explain to him that she had promised not to cross the wall, not to go to the star-watching rock. And did Tav understand that they were separated not only by the stone wall but by three thousand years?

Suddenly he leaped to his feet. Louise had come out of her hiding place. Tav reached for his spear.

"No!" Polly screamed. "Don't hurt her! She's harmless!"

If Tav did not understand her words, he could not miss her intent. She thrust herself between the snake and the young man.

He put down the spear, careful not to bruise the feathers.

"I would only protect you," he told her, in sign and body language as much as in words. "Snake has much power. *Mana* power, good power, but sometimes hurting power."

Fumblingly, Polly tried to explain that Louise was a harmless black snake, and a special one, a family friend.

Tav let her know that Louise's friendship was good. "You are gift. The Mother's gift. You will come? Tonight?"

"I cannot. I—" What was the word for promise? Or for grandparents? Mother was something like *modr*. "Mother says no." That was the best she could do.

He laughed. "Mother sent you! You will come!" He bent toward her again and delicately touched her hair with the tips of his fingers. It was like a kiss. Then he picked up his spear and walked along the path in the direction of the star-watching rock.

Polly went back to the house. His touch had been gentle, pleasing. He had actually compared her red hair to the sun. Her fear of him had vanished. But she also felt confused. Why had he been ready to kill Louise? Did he really think the snake was about to strike? What had he meant by good power and hurting power? His intent had certainly not been to kill for killing's sake, but only to protect her.

At lunch she told her grandparents about Tav. They listened, made little comment. It was evident that they were deeply concerned. "I won't cross the field to the stone wall again," she promised. "But he was nice, really he was."

"Three thousand years ago?" her grandfather asked wryly.

Her grandparents did not scold her for going to the stone wall. They were all unusually silent as they ate lunch.

P ROMPTLY at two, Zachary drove up in his red sports car. It struck Polly again how sheerly felicitous he was to behold, like Hamlet, she thought, Hamlet in modern dress. Black jeans and a pale blue cashmere turtleneck, his black jacket over his arm. Dark hair framing a pale face. Tav had likened Polly to the sun, and himself to the moon. Although Zachary's hair was dark as Tav's was fair, he was far more a moon creature than a sun creature.

He greeted her grandparents deferentially, pausing to sit and tell the Murrys a little about his work in the law office in Hartford. "Long hours at a desk," he said. "I feel as though I've come out from under a stone. But I'm lucky to have got an internship, and I'm learning a lot."

Again he was making a good impression, she thought.

"I've done some research on this Ogam stuff," he said. "As a language, it isn't that difficult, is it? It really does look as though this land was visited three thousand years ago, long before anyone thought. Primitive people weren't nearly as primitive as we'd like to think, and they did an incredible amount of traveling to all kinds of places. And druids, for instance, were not ignorant savages who did nothing but slit the throats of sacrificial victims. They could navigate by the stars, and as a matter of fact, their knowledge of astronomy was astounding."

"Bishop Colubra would agree with that," Polly said.

Her grandparents were polite, but not enthusiastic.

Zachary said, "I'd really like to talk with the bishop. My boss, whom I've been pumping, is erudite and dull."

Mr. Murry smiled. "Let's keep Polly in the twentieth century." But his smile was strained.

Zachary said, "Fine with me. Is there someplace around here we can go?"

As far as she knew, the village consisted of post office, store, church, filling station, and a farm-equipment place.

Her grandfather suggested quickly that they go to the country club, that he'd already called ahead to arrange a guest pass. Polly knew that her grandfather occasionally played golf when he needed to talk to a colleague without fear of being overheard. "It's a lovely drive," he told Zachary, "especially right now when the colors are still bright. But there's not much going on at the club this time of year if you're not a golfer."

"My pop is," Zachary said. "I plan to take it up when I'm rich and famous."

"The swimming pool is closed for the winter. But you can get a soda and there are some nice walks." It was obvious that he wanted them away from the house. And that, under the circumstances, was understandable.

"Do I look okay for the country club?" She was wearing jeans and a flannel shirt.

"You're fine," Zachary and her grandparents assured her simultaneously.

"But take a jacket," her grandmother added.

Polly and Zachary went out through the pantry and she took the red anorak off one of the hooks. Zachary pointed to the door to her grandmother's lab. "What's in there?"

"Grand's lab."

"Can we have a peek? I'm really honored to have met your grandmother, Pol, and I'd love to see where she works."

"Just a peek." She opened the door. "It's verboten to go into the lab without Grand, but she won't mind if we just look."

Zachary peered in with interest, looking at the counter with its equipment. "What's that?"

"It's an electron microscope."

"What's it for?"

"Oh, lots of things. It proved, for instance, the existence of a plasma membrane bonding each cell, separating it from the internal environment. But I don't think Grand's used it in years. Most of her work is in her head."

"Your parents are scientists, too, right?"

"My father's a marine biologist. That's why we've tended to live on islands. My mom does all his computer work. She's a mathematical whiz." She stepped back and shut the door carefully.

Zachary had not parked his car in the driveway but had left it on the dirt road which the house faced, so they walked across the lawn. "Listen," he said. "I didn't mean to turn you off with that phone call."

"You didn't." But she looked at him questioningly.

He was looking at the house. "This is beautiful, your grandparents' place. We don't have any houses anywhere near this old in California."

"I love it," she said. "I'm really happy here."

"I can understand that." He held the car door open for her. As they started off, he pointed to the wing. "Hey, is that a swimming pool?"

"Yah, a small one. The doctor recommended it for Granddad's arthritis."

"That's terrific. It's the best exercise in the world, my doctor says. Is there good skiing around here?"

"Yes. Do you ski?"

He drove slowly along the dirt road. "Oddly enough, I do. Being a totally non-kinetic person, I'm not very good at it, but given time, I might improve. You ski?"

"I've spent my life in warm climates. But Grand says she'll go skiing with me this winter."

Once they were out on the highway, Zachary's driving reminded her of Bishop Colubra's, though it was probably a little less erratic.

"Gad, the fall's glorious," he said. "A couple of my prep schools weren't far from here. But the colors always catch me in the throat. Look at that golden tree there. There aren't many elms left. Isn't it gorgeous?"

"That it is. And there's one maple we see from the kitchen windows that's almost purple. I've never seen autumn colors before and I'm overwhelmed."

"I'm glad you were here a week ago. It's past its first glory now," Zachary said, "but it's still breathtaking."

"Here we are." Polly pointed to a sign that indicated the long driveway to the country club. At the top of the hill was a large white building with a gracious view across the valley—that valley which had been covered by a lake three thousand years ago.

Zachary led her into the bar, where he asked her what she wanted. "Don't worry, sweet Pol. I'm driving, so I'm having a Coke. Do I remember that you like lemonade?"

"You do. How nice of you to remember."

"There's not much about you I've forgotten." He ordered their drinks and they sat on high bar stools and the slanting autumn sunlight reached through the windows and touched Polly's hair. Zachary whistled. "I'd forgotten how gorgeous you are."

She could feel herself blushing. She understood that she was far better-looking now than she had been as an early adolescent, but she did not think of herself as beautiful, or even pretty, and now both Tav and Zachary were telling her that she was.

"You were lovely last summer in Greece," Zachary said, "but you're even better now. I'm glad I was able to find you."

"Me, too." She sipped at her lemonade, which was nicely tart. It had been an amazement to her the past summer in Athens that Zachary had wanted so much of her company; it was still an amazement to her.

"What do you do with yourself all day?"

"Oh, lots of things. Grand and Granddad worry about my being bored, but the days slide by so full it's hard to realize at bedtime that another day has passed."

"Full of what?"

"I study with my grandparents in the mornings. I hike. I swim. We've had friends over for dinner. It may not seem exciting, but it's just what I need." It didn't sound exciting as she told it, but although Zachary had surprised her by knowing about the Ogam stones and, even more surprising, had seen Karralys, she was not ready to tell him about Anaral or Tav.

Then he reached into his leather pouch. "I brought you a present."

"An unbirthday present!" Polly exclaimed. "Terrific."

He handed her something flat and rectangular wrapped in

wrinkled pink tissue paper. She removed the paper and there was a picture, backed by a thin piece of wood, of an angel, immensely tall, with great wings, bending protectively over a small child.

"A guardian-angel icon! It's beautiful! Thank you!"

"I found it in a funny junk shop in Turkey, not long after I left you at Athens airport last summer. When I looked back to wave at you, you looked so sort of lost that I thought then that you needed a guardian angel. So, when I saw this, it made me think of you, and I got it, and thought I'd give it to you if ever we met again, and here we are."

"Thanks, Zachary. Really. Thanks a lot."

"It's not an original or anything. I don't suppose it has any real value."

"I love it." She put it carefully into the largest of the anorak pockets. "It was really nice of you to think of it."

"Why do you sound so surprised? Is it because it's a picture of an angel?"

"Well—sort of."

"I suppose I made it quite clear that I don't believe in anything."

She nodded.

"Take what you can get. Right now. Because that's all there is. That's still my policy. But I had a grandmother who really believed in angels, and that they care for us." He stopped, drained the dregs of ice from the bottom of his glass. "She loved me. Me, Zachary, not some projection."

"Grandmothers are marvelous. Mine is. And Granddad, too."

"I didn't know my grandfather that well. Pa's parents died young. The ones I knew were Ma's parents, and they lived near us. My grandfather was a champion polo player, but he was thrown from his horse and his spine was crushed. And Grandma went right on believing in angels—and in me—while he cursed from his wheelchair till the day he died. Another lemonade?"

"No, thanks."

"Shall we just drive around and see what we can see?"

"Sure. That would be nice."

For the first few miles he was silent, and Polly thought that Zachary had just revealed to her, in talking of his grandparents, more than he had been willing to show when they were together in Athens. She glanced at his face, and it seemed very thin.

"Have you lost weight?" The question slipped out before she realized that it was a personal one and shouldn't be asked.

"Some. Look, that maple's completely bare." He whistled a few notes, then said, "If autumn comes, can winter be far behind?"

"Where's the whistle you had the other day?" she asked.

"Oh, I gave it to one of the office boys. I found it used too much wind." He apologized quickly. "Sorry, Polly, sweet, sorry. I spend my days in an office, ruining my eyes and getting no exercise. At this point I don't know why I'm doing it, but I still seem to want to learn all about insurance and all the legal ramifications." He turned off onto a side road that wound through a pine forest.

"What about college?" she asked.

"I hope I can go back next semester. I'm not sure I think a college degree is really necessary, but law schools do. It's a rough world out there, and I've always been determined to equip myself for it, and college is part of the deal."

A plane droned by, far above them. She looked up but could not see it. It must have passed overhead before its sound followed it. Their road turned sharply uphill.

"What about you, Polly?"

"What about what?"

"You *are* planning to go to college?"

"Sure."

"Planning to be a scientist?"

"I don't know. I'm interested in a lot of things. One problem is—well, Max said I have too many options."

"Are you over it?"

"Over what?"

"Your friend's death."

"Zachary, you don't get over someone's death. Ever. You just learn to go on living the best way you possibly can."

"I got over Ma's death." He sighed.

Did he? Really? she wondered. And what about the grandmother who had believed in him? "I don't want to get over Max's death. She'll always be part of me and I'll be—more—because she was my friend."

"Oh, Polly." He took his hand off the steering wheel and reached out to touch her shoulder gently. "You teach me so much, and I love you for it, Polly. Polly, if I'm going to see as much of you as I want to these next few months, there's something I ought to tell you." Then he fell silent. The road came out of the woods, went past a farm, and then offered them a wide view across a valley to ranges of mountains beyond, a far more spectacular view than her grandparents' gentle one. He pulled the car over, stopped it, and sat there, staring out.

She waited. Decided he was not going to tell her whatever it was, when he said softly, "Polly, if I died, would you get over me?"

She turned to look at him.

"I've always been my own worst enemy, and now it's coming back at me." She saw his eyes fill with sudden tears.

"Zachary. What is it?"

"My heart. It's never been very good. And now—"

She looked at his white face, at the slight blueness about his lips, at his eyes trying to blink back tears. She reached out to touch him.

"Don't touch me. Please. I don't want to cry. But I don't want to die. I'm not ready. But I've only got—oh, nobody will be specific, but it's not likely I'll make it to law school."

"Oh, Zachary." She sat, not touching him, honoring his wish. "What about open-heart surgery?"

"It wouldn't help that much."

"If you take care of yourself, don't work too hard . . ."

He shook his head, reached up, and fiercely rubbed away his tears with the heel of his hand.

"Oh, Zach—"

"See, I'm hurting you just by being. I don't mean to use emotional blackmail. Polly, sweet, what I'm doing is living as though I'm going to go on living. Working in Hartford this semester. Planning on going back to college. To law school. My doctors say that's the best thing. Take it moderately easy, but live while I can. So what I'd really like is to see you sort of on a regular basis. Would that be possible?"

"Well, of course, Zach." Words seemed totally inadequate.

He started the car again and took off, far too fast. He'd said that he didn't want to die, that he wasn't ready. He'd said that he didn't want to hurt her. "Slow down a bit, hey?" she suggested.

He took his foot off the accelerator and drove at a more moderate speed. In silence. She did not break it because there was nothing to say. When they got to her grandparents' land, he turned onto the dirt road the house faced and stopped his car by the wing with the pool.

"I've been horrible," he said. "I'm sorry."

"You haven't been horrible."

He groped toward her to kiss her and she let his lips touch hers, then gently turned away. She felt deep sympathy for him, but kissing out of sympathy could only lead to trouble.

Instead of trying to kiss her again, as she expected, he stared out the windshield. "Hey, who's that girl?"

She stared, but saw nobody. "Who?"

"She just went around the corner of your pool." He pointed.

"Who?" Polly asked again.

"A girl with a long black braid. She turned and ran."

Polly stared. There was the white wing of the addition, with lilacs planted beneath the windows, their leaves turned grey with autumn and slowly dropping to the ground. There was nobody there.

Zachary explained, "She was just walking toward your pool. A good-looking girl. But when she saw me and I smiled at her, she took off. Like a deer."

Anaral. It had to be Anaral Zachary had seen. There was nobody else it could be. First Karralys and now Anaral—why?

"Is it someone you know?" he asked.

"Well, yes, but—"

"Listen, I didn't mean to upset you by telling you about myself. I'm sorry."

Of course she was upset. Upset in all directions.

"Polly, you know the last thing I want in the world is to hurt you. But I thought you ought to know about me. I know I've often been self-destructive, but I didn't expect—" Again his dark eyes were bright with tears. Fiercely he blinked them back. "I'm sorry. This isn't fair of me. I'd better take off, and I'll see you again soon—maybe this weekend?"

She nodded slowly. Now Zachary had seen Anaral. What would her grandparents think? Bishop Colubra? She unfastened her seat belt. She was badly shaken, both by what Zachary had told her about his heart and by his having seen Anaral. Her ears were cocked for the Colubras. Perhaps if they drove up, Zachary would talk with the bishop. "Listen, are you busy this evening? Could you stay for dinner?"

"Tonight?"

"If that's okay. Dr. Louise and Bishop Colubra are coming, and Bishop Colubra knows Anaral really well—the girl you saw." Dr. Louise, she thought, might be able to check on Zachary's doctors, see if there might be some better hope for him.

"No, sorry. I wish I could, I really do. But I promised my boss I'd have dinner with him and let him go on about Ogam. Fortunately, he doesn't try to order dinner in Ogam. He'd drop a gourd if he knew I'd seen an Ogam stone."

—If he knew Zachary had seen a girl from Ogam days . . .

"I'm free on Saturday," he continued. "Shall I come on over?"

"Yes, please do."

"Maybe we'll just go for a walk around your grandparents' place. It'll be good just to be with you. But now I really need to get back to Hartford."

Zachary got out of the car and came around to her. "Don't worry overmuch, pretty Pol. I'm not going to drop dead on you. That wouldn't be fair. I do have some time left." He hugged her briefly, and he felt painfully thin. The Colubras had not come, and probably weren't even expected for another hour.

It was All Hallows' Eve. Samhain. That made a difference. At least she was sure that the bishop would think that it did. Samhain must be why Zachary was able to see Anaral. And yet he had seen Karralys, too. Was it that, as the time of Samhain approached, the doors started opening?

She walked slowly round the house, scuffing fallen leaves, walked around the wing with the pool. The house faced south. The wing was on the east end, with windows on all three sides and skylights north and south. She crossed to the field by the northeast corner, although she was not going to cross the field. She would not go near the stone wall.

Coming across the field toward her was the young man with the intensely blue eyes. He did not have the dog with him this time, but a grey wolf. When he saw Polly, he spoke to the wolf, who turned and ran back across the field and disappeared into the woods.

Mesmerized, Polly stood still and waited. He walked toward her unhurriedly, smiling slightly. There was no telling how old he was. Certainly older than she, but there was a serene agelessness to his face.

"Karralys—"

He nodded. "You will be Poll-ee." Like Anaral, he spoke slowly and carefully, with an indeterminate trace of accent. Probably Bishop Colubra had taught him English, too. "It is time we talked. I am sorry Anaral didn't summon me when you came to us."

She stared at him. "Who are you?"

"As you said. Karralys."

"A druid?"

He nodded gravely.

"You came from England—from Britain?"

Again the slight nod. The blue of his eyes was serene.

"Why did you come?"

"I was banished."

She looked at him in astonishment.

"For heresy," he said quietly. "You have heard of punishment for heresy?"

"Yes." She thought of Giordano Bruno being burned at the stake for his understanding of time, and also because he did not believe that planet earth was the center of all things. She wondered what Karralys's heresy could have been, that he had been expelled from Britain and sent so far from home. What did druids believe?

He said, "I have been here, on this land, for what you would call three years. It is good land. Benign. The great underground river flows from the place of our standing stones"—he waved toward the wing—"to the lake, with its beneficence. I believe this land, these mountains, the lake, to be the place where the Presence has called me to be. When I was banished, I held on to the hope that there was a reason for my leaving home and that I would find a new home waiting for me, and so I did. The Presence calmed the storm that blew me here, and the promise of the rainbow came, and I knew that I was where I was meant to be." He smiled at her. "And you? You, too, were banished?"

She laughed. "No, not banished. I needed more education than I could get at the local high school, so my parents sent me here. But it wasn't banishing. It's wonderful here."

"I, too, find it wonderful." Above Karralys, high in the sky, flew an eagle. "Here you have"—he pointed to the addition with the pool—"water that is held in on all four sides, and it is in the same space as our great standing stones, our most holy place, even more holy than the rock and the altar by the lake. But for you the lake is gone, and the great stones, and there is no snow on the hills. I see you, and I wonder."

"I wonder, too."

"Bishop Heron—"

"Bishop Colubra." She laughed with delight that Karralys, too, thought of the bishop as a heron.

"Yes. He is, I believe, a kind of druid."

The eagle soared up, up, until it was lost in blue. Polly watched it disappear, then asked, "Bishop Colubra's spent lots of time with you?"

"When he can. The threshold does not always open for him, and he cannot leave his own circle. He is wise in the ways of patience and love. He has turned his loss to compassion for others."

—What loss? Polly wondered fleetingly.

But Karralys continued, "He has much knowledge of the heart, but he does not understand why it is that you were able to see me by the oak tree, or why the young man saw me. He does not understand how it is that you walked into our time."

"I don't understand, either."

"At Samhain, more is possible than at other times. There has to be a reason. Anaral says you are not a druid."

"Heavens, no."

"There has to be a reason for you to have come. Perhaps the Heron opened the time gate especially for you."

"But I'm not the only one. Oh, Karralys—" She took in a deep gulp of fresh air. "Karralys, Zachary was here with me just a few minutes ago, and he saw Anaral."

Karralys looked shocked, frozen into immobility. "Who saw Anaral?"

In her urgency, Polly sounded impatient. "The one you saw by the oak tree. His name is Zachary Gray. He's a young man I met last summer in Greece."

"In—"

"Greece. It's far away, in the south of Europe, near Asia. Never mind. The point is, he's someone I met last summer, but I don't know him very well. He told me, this afternoon, that his heart is giving out, that he's going to die. And then he saw Anaral."

Karralys nodded several times, soberly. "Sometimes when death is near, the threshold is open."

Suddenly Zachary's words rang frighteningly true. She had not completely understood or believed him before. Now she did. "But he hasn't crossed the threshold."

"No," Karralys said. "No. He has glimpsed us when we have crossed the threshold and come into your circle. But you—you have come into our circle, and that is a very different thing."

"But—" She was not sure what she wanted to ask.

"When we are in your circle, we are not invisible," Karralys said. "People do not expect to see us, so we are translated, as it were, to people of your own time."

"You mean, people don't know what—who—they've seen? I mean, I didn't, when I saw you by the oak tree."

"Exactly," Karralys said.

"And when I first saw Anaral, at the pool, I thought she was just some girl—"

"Yes."

"But then, when I was walking to the star-watching rock, and everything changed, and I was in your time . . ." Again her voice trailed off.

"There is a pattern," Karralys said. "There are lines drawn between the stars, and lines drawn between places, and lines drawn between people, and lines linking all three. It may be that Zachary is indeed as you are."

Polly frowned. "It does seem weird that his boss should be so interested in Ogam stones. But, Karralys, what about Dr. Louise? She saw Anaral."

"That was by chance, by emergency. Anaral does not fit into her worldview, so she does not believe. But you, Polly. You must be part of the pattern. There is a strong line drawing you from your circle to ours. I am afraid for you."

"Afraid? Why?"

"You have spoken with my countryman? Tav?"

"Yes." She smiled. Both Zachary and Tav thought her red hair was beautiful. Tav tried to teach her Ogam and it was a game and they had laughed and been happy.

"You must not speak with him."

"Why not? I've been studying Bishop Colubra's notebook of Ogam, and Tav taught me some more."

"The hand that feeds the chicken ends up wringing its neck."

"What?"

"If Tav likes you, and you like him, it will be even harder."

"What will be?"

"Do not cross the threshold again. There is danger for you."

"I don't understand."

"Anaral has come to you too often. She is very young, and

she must learn not to waste her power. Speak with the Heron. Tell him. Tell him about this—his name again, please?"

"Zachary. Zachary Gray."

"He alters the pattern. Tell Bishop Heron. You will?"

"Yes." Suddenly she remembered the bishop saying that Zachary did not look well. Dr. Louise had said that he was too pale.

"I must go." Karralys bowed to her, turned, and walked away across the field. She watched after him until she heard a car drive up, too fast, skidding on the macadam as it came to a stop. Bishop Colubra.

The bishop and Dr. Louise had brought their bathing suits, but they all sat around the table and listened as Polly told them about Zachary. About Karralys.

"I didn't totally believe Zachary—about his heart being that bad, until Karralys . . ." Her voice faltered.

"Now, wait," Dr. Louise said. "I'd like to speak to his doctor. Someone in the last stages of heart failure doesn't work in a law office or drive around in sports cars. He'd be pretty well bedridden. He looks pasty, as though he doesn't get outdoors enough, but he doesn't look as if he's on his deathbed."

"He didn't say he was actually on his deathbed," Polly said. "He didn't give any time limits. Only that he wasn't likely to make law school. And that's at least a couple of years away."

"It still sounds a little overdramatic to me."

"Well, I thought so, too, but Karralys—"

Dr. Louise spoke sharply. "Karralys is not a physician."

"He's a druid," the bishop said, "and I take him seriously."

"Really, Nason. I thought you were more orthodox than that."

"I'm completely orthodox," the bishop expostulated. "That doesn't mean I have to have a closed mind."

"Since when has this odd faith in druids been part of your orthodoxy? Weren't they involved in the esoteric and the occult?"

"They strike me as being a lot less esoteric and occult than modern medicine."

"All right, you two," Mr. Murry broke in.

"And if you're going to have a swim before dinner," Mrs. Murry suggested, "have it. Did you two squabble when you were kids?"

"We drove our parents crazy." Dr. Louise smiled.

The bishop rose. He was a good foot taller than his sister. "But on the big things, the important things, we always stuck together. By the way, Louise, St. Columba speaks of Christ as his druid. You scientists can be terribly literal-minded. There's really not that much known about druids, and I think they were simply wise men of their time. Caesar considered that all those of special rank or dignity were druids."

"Nase, let's go swimming." Dr. Louise was plaintive.

"Of course. I'm running off at the mouth again. Alex, shall I change in your study?"

"Fine. And Louise can have the twins' room. I'll just go out and bring in some more wood for the fire. It's a never-ending job."

"I'll set the table," Polly said.

Her grandmother was washing broccoli. "First thing tomorrow morning I'm going to take those Ogam stones off the kitchen dresser and put them outside somewhere. I'd move them tonight, but Alex and Nase—Nase particularly—would object."

"Why?" Polly asked. "I mean, why move them?"

"The kitchen dresser's cluttered enough already. Large stones are not the usual kitchen decor. And if that Ogam writing was carved into them three thousand years ago, they may have something to do with Anaral's and Karralys's ability to come to our time and our place. And your ability to go to theirs. I'll go out to the lab and get the casserole. It's one of my Bunsen Burner Bourguignons."

As the door closed behind her grandmother, Polly remembered that Karralys had warned her of some kind of danger. In her concern for Zachary she had forgotten, and she did not take it very seriously because she could not believe that Tav with his laughter as he taught her Ogam, with his fingers gently kissing her hair, was any kind of menace to her.

She opened a drawer in the kitchen counter and pulled out table mats, which she began to place on the table. Slowly she added silver, china, glasses. Had she ever studied English history? She thought back to some of the books, historical novels mostly, that she had read. Britain, she remembered, was made up of a lot of warring tribes in the early, pre-Roman days, and they impaled the heads of their enemies on poles and, yes, had practiced human sacrifice, too, at least in some of the tribes. Ugh. That was a time long gone, and a way of seeing the universe that was completely different from today's.

She was folding napkins as her grandmother came in, bearing a steaming casserole.

"Grand, do you have an encyclopedia?"

"In the living room. It's the 1911 Britannica, which was supposed to be particularly fine. It's totally obsolete as far as science goes, but it should be all right for druids, if that's what you want to check out. It's on the bottom shelf, to the right of the fireplace."

Polly got the encyclopedia, the D volume. There was only one page on the subject of druids. But yes, there was a mention of Caesar, the bishop was right. Druids went through extensive training, with much memorizing of handed-down wisdom. Anaral had told her that.

Her grandmother called from the kitchen, "Found anything?"

Polly took the volume and went into the kitchen. "Some. Druids studied astronomy and geography and whatever science was known in their time. Oh, and this is fascinating. There's a suggestion that they might have been influenced by Pythagoras."

"Interesting, indeed." Her grandmother was slicing vegetables for the salad.

"Oh, listen, Grand, I like this. Before a battle, druids would often throw themselves between two armies to stop the war and bring peace."

"Armies must have been very small," her grandmother remarked.

Polly agreed. "It's hard to remember in this overpopulated

world that two armies could be small enough for a druid to rush in and stop war."

"They were peacemakers, then," her grandmother said. "I like that."

Polly read on. "Oak trees were special to them. I can see why. They're the most majestic trees around here. That's about it for information on druids long ago. Later on, after the Roman Empire took over, druids and Christians didn't get along. Each appeared to be a threat to the other. I wonder if they really were."

"Even Christians are threats to each other," her grandmother said, "with misunderstandings between Protestants and Catholics, liberals and fundamentalists."

"Wouldn't it be great," Polly suggested, "if there were druids to throw themselves between the battle lines of Muslims and Christians and Palestinians and Jews in the Middle East, or Catholics and Protestants in Ireland?"

"And between Louise and Nason when they spat," her grandmother said, as the doctor and her brother came downstairs in bathing clothes, carrying towels.

Polly put the encyclopedia away. She had learned a little something, at any rate.

The bishop, evidently continuing a train of thought, was saying, "The people behind the building of Stonehenge were asking themselves the same questions that physicists like Alex are asking today, about the nature of the universe."

Mr. Murry was coming in with a load of wood in a canvas sling. He set it down beside the dining-room fireplace. "We haven't come up with a Grand Unified Theory yet, Nase, not one that works."

The bishop ambled toward the pool, his legs showing beneath his robe. "The motive was certainly religious—behind the building of Stonehenge, that is—more truly religious than the crude rituals and 'worship services' that pass for religion in most of our churches today."

"Coming from one who has spent his life in the religious institution, that's a rather sad remark," his sister commented.

The bishop opened the door, speaking over his shoulder.

"Sad, perhaps, but true. And not to be surprised at. Come on. I thought we were going swimming."

"And who's holding us up?" The two of them went through the door to the pool, shutting it carefully behind them.

Mr. Murry put a sizable log onto the fire.

"Polly looked druids up in the encyclopedia," Mrs. Murry said. "The article wasn't particularly enlightening."

"We need more than an encyclopedia to explain Nase's opening a time threshold." Mr. Murry blew through a long, thin pipe and the flames flared up brightly. "And Polly's involvement in it. It's incomprehensible."

"It's not the first incomprehensible thing that's happened in our lifetime," his wife reminded him.

"Have things ever been as weird as this?"

Her grandmother laughed. "Yes, Polly, they have, but that doesn't make this any less weird."

Mr. Murry stood up creakily. "Polly's friend Zachary strikes me as adding a new and unexpected component. Why is this comparative stranger seeing people from three thousand years ago that you and I have never seen?"

"Nobody told him about her," Mrs. Murry said, "so he didn't have time to put up a wall of disbelief."

"Is that what we've done?"

"Isn't it? And isn't it what Louise has done?"

"So it would seem."

"Remember Sandy's favorite quotation? *Some things have to be believed to be seen?* Louise doesn't believe, even though she's seen. Zachary, it would seem, has no idea what—or who—he has seen."

Mr. Murry took off his glasses and wiped them on his flannel shirt, blew on them, wiped them again, and put them on. "Why on earth did I think that old age would mean less unexpectedness? Wouldn't a glass of wine be nice with dinner? I'll go down to the cellar and get a bottle." In a moment he came back up, carrying a rather dusty-looking bottle. "There's a dog barking outside."

There was—a dog barking with steady urgency.

"Dogs bark outside all the time," his wife said.

"Not this way. It's not just ordinary barking at a squirrel or a kid on a bike. He's barking at our house." He put the bottle down and went out the pantry door. The dog kept on barking. "It's not one of the dogs from the farms up the road," he said as he returned. "And it doesn't have a collar. It's sitting in front of the garage and barking as though it wants to be let in."

"So?" Mrs. Murry was wiping off the bottle with a damp cloth. "Do you want me to open this to give it a chance to breathe?"

"Please. Louise thinks we ought to have another dog."

"Alex, if you're going to let the dog in, for heaven's sake let it in, but remember we have company for dinner."

"Polly, come out with me and let's study the situation. I agree with Louise. This house doesn't feel right without a dog. A dog is protection." He walked through the pantry and garage, and Polly followed him. In the last rays of light, a dog was sitting on the driveway, barking. When they appeared, it stood up and began wagging its tail hopefully. It was a medium-to-large dog, with beautiful pricked-up ears, tipped with black. There was a black tip to its long tail. Otherwise, it was a soft tan. Tentatively it approached them, tail wagging. Mr. Murry held out his hand and the dog nuzzled it.

"What do you think?" he asked Polly.

"Granddad, it looks like the dog I saw with Karralys." But Karralys had had a wolf rather than a dog with him that afternoon. She could not be sure.

"He looks like half the farm dogs around here," her grandfather said. "I doubt if there's any connection. He's a nice-looking mongrel. Thin." He ran his hands over the rib cage and the dog's tail wagged joyfully. "Thin, but certainly not starved. We could at least bring him in and provide a meal."

"Granddad." Polly put her arm about her grandfather's waist and hugged him. "Everything is crazy. I went back three thousand years, and Zachary saw Anaral, and—and—you're thinking of adopting a stray dog."

"When things are crazy," her grandfather said, "a dog can be a reminder of sanity. Shall we bring him in?"

"Grand won't mind?"

"What do you think?"

"Well, Granddad, she's pretty unflappable, but—"

"I don't think a dog is going to overflap her." Mr. Murry put his hand on the dog's neck where a collar would be, and went into the garage, and it walked along with him, whining very softly, through the pantry, and into the kitchen, just as the Colubras were coming in the other direction, wrapped in towels.

"I see you're taking my advice about another dog," Dr. Louise said.

"Oh, my." Bishop Colubra's voice was shocked.

Mrs. Murry looked the dog over. "He seems clean. No fleas, as far as I can tell, or ticks. Teeth in good condition. Healthy gums. Glossy coat. What's wrong, Nase?"

"I'm not sure, but I think I've seen that dog before."

"Where?" his sister asked.

"Three thousand years ago."

CHAPTER 6

THE silence in the kitchen was broken by Dr. Louise drumming on the table.

Mr. Murry put a bowl of food by the pantry door. "Are you sure?"

The bishop rubbed his eyes. "I could be wrong."

Hadron, asleep on his scrap of rug, watched with one suspicious eye. The dog ate hungrily, but tidily. When it was finished, Hadron minced over to inspect the bowl, licking it for possible crumbs, while the dog stood, wagging its long tail.

Mrs. Murry took an old blanket out to the garage. "He can stay there for tonight. If he's a dog from three thousand years ago, I don't want him to . . ." Her voice trailed off.

Dr. Louise laughed. "If he's from three thousand years ago, do you think keeping him either in or out of the house would make any difference?"

Mrs. Murry was chagrined. "You're right, of course. But somehow I feel he's freer to come and go if he's outside. For tonight, at any rate. Tomorrow we'll see. This evening we're going to sit around the table and eat a civilized meal with a very nice glass of burgundy." She washed her hands. "All right. We're ready. Let's gather round."

The kitchen curtains were drawn across the long expanse of windows. The fire in the open hearth crackled pleasantly. The aroma of Mrs. Murry's casserole was tantalizing. It should have been a normal, pleasant evening, but it wasn't.

"Bishop, tell us about the dog, please," Polly asked.

He lifted his glass of wine so that the light touched the liquid and it shone like a ruby. "I'm getting old. I'm not sure. I'm probably wrong. But Karralys has a dog like that."

"Yes," Polly agreed. "The first time I saw Karralys, by the big oak, there was a dog with him."

"Was it that dog?" her grandfather demanded.

"That kind of dog, with big ears tipped with black."

"You're sure Karralys has a dog?"

"Yes. Why?" the bishop asked.

"It just seems very unlikely. Three thousand years ago there were very few domesticated dogs. There were wolves, and dog-wolves. But domesticated dogs were just beginning to be mentioned in Egypt."

"We don't know exactly how long ago Karralys lived. Three thousand years is just a convenient guess. Anyhow, how do you know?"

"I'm a fund of useless information."

"Not so useless," his wife said. "This dog appears to have no wolf blood. It's unlikely your Karralys would have had a dog like this."

"Unless," the bishop said, "he brought him to the New World with him?"

"What's all the fuss?" Dr. Louise raised her eyebrows. "If you're seeing people from three thousand years ago, why get so excited about a dog?"

"It's one more thing," the bishop said. "I think it's a sign."

"Of what?" His sister sounded impatient.

"I know, I know, Louise, it's against all your training. But you did take care of Annie, you have to admit that."

"I took care of a girl whose badly lacerated finger needed immediate attention. She wasn't that different from all the other fallen sparrows you seem to think it's your duty to rescue."

"Louise," Mrs. Murry said, "I find it hard to believe that Nase actually brought Anaral to your office and that you treated her as an ordinary patient."

"As an ordinary patient," Dr. Louise said firmly. "Whether or not the girl whose finger I took care of was from three thousand years ago or not, I have no idea."

"You told me to take her back," the bishop said.

"To wherever. Whenever."

"Louise, it all started in your root cellar with the first Ogam stone."

"I'm only a simple Episcopalian," Dr. Louise said. "This is too much for me."

"You aren't a simple anything, that's your problem." The bishop looked over to the Ogam stones on the dresser. "And noting the fall of the sparrow is an activity not unknown to you, Louise. Maybe you should come to the star-watching rock with me. Maybe if you crossed the time threshold—"

Dr. Louise shook her head. "No, thanks."

The bishop's plate was empty and he took a large helping from the bowl Mrs. Murry held out. The quantity of food he managed to put away seemed in direct disproportion to his long thinness. "This is marvelous, Kate. And the wine—you don't drink this wine every night?"

Mr. Murry refilled the bishop's glass. "All in your honor."

The bishop took an appreciative sip. "The words on the Ogam stones, if I have deciphered them correctly, are peaceable, gentle. Memorial markers. And occasionally something that sounds like part of a rune. The one Polly carried in for me, for instance: *Let the song of our sisters the stars sing in our hearts to*—and there it breaks off. Isn't it beautiful? But, alas, in Annie's time, as now, sacred things were not always honored. Words—runes, for instance—were sometimes misused. They were meant to bless, but they were sometimes called on for curses. And they were used to influence weather, fertility, human love. Yes, runes were sometimes abused, but it was never forgotten that they had power."

"You're lecturing again," his sister commented.

But Polly, interested, asked, "You mean the old rhyme 'Sticks and stones may break my bones but words can never hurt me' is wrong?"

The bishop agreed. "Totally."

Mrs. Murry pushed her chair back slightly and Hadron, taking this as an invitation, left his place by the hearth and jumped into her lap.

The bishop continued, "That little rhyme doesn't take into account that words have power, intrinsic power. *I love you.* What could be more powerful than that small trinity? On the other hand, malicious gossip can cause horrible damage."

Mr. Murry said, "If Dr. Louise tells me I look awful, my joints are going to feel hot and inflamed."

"Whereas, happily, I can say you're doing very well indeed," Dr. Louise said.

"Swimming definitely helps," Mr. Murry said, "but we do respond to suggestion."

Dr. Louise pursued her own train of thought. "I'm an internist, not a cardiologist, but I'd like to have a look at Zachary. I thought he seemed a charming young man and I don't like the sound of this."

"He's coming over on Saturday," Polly said. "I'd like you to see him, too, Dr. Louise, I really would."

"Is he a special friend of yours?" she asked.

"He's a friend. I don't know him that well. I don't even know him well enough to know whether or not he's likely to exaggerate. I know he was scared."

"One of the Ogam stones"—the bishop frowned slightly, remembering—"goes: *From frights and fears may we be spared by breath of wind and quiet of rain.*"

"Is a rune a sort of prayer?" Polly asked.

"If one truly believes in prayer, yes."

"Like the Tallis Canon?" she suggested.

"*All praise to thee my God this night*"—the bishop nodded—"*for all the blessings of the light.* Yes, of course. And then there's: *Let all mortal flesh keep silence.* Oh, indeed, yes."

Mrs. Murry brought the salad bowl to the table. "What a conversation for a group of pragmatic scientists—with the exception of you, Nase."

"Alas." Bishop Colubra took a piece of bread and wiped up his gravy. "Bishops all too often limit themselves to the pragmatic. And there are times when pragmatism is essential. The trouble is that then we tend to forget that there's anything else. But there is, isn't there, Louise, even in the most pragmatic of sciences?"

"Louise has a fine reputation as a diagnostician," Mrs. Murry said, "and—am I right, Louise?—her diagnoses are made not only from observation and information and knowledge but also on a hunch."

Dr. Louise agreed.

"Intuition." The bishop smiled at his sister. "The understanding of the heart, rather than the mind."

"You were always wise, big brother." Dr. Louise suddenly

sounded wistful. "You were the one I could always turn to for reason when things got out of hand. And now I'd think you've gone completely off your rocker if these eminently sane people sitting around the table didn't take you seriously. And Polly, who strikes me as a most sensible person, is having the same hallucinations that you are."

"Mass hallucinations—though two people are hardly a mass," Mrs. Murry said. "It's a possibility, but not a likelihood."

"I wish I didn't feel so outraged," Dr. Louise apologized. "It's making me inordinately grumpy. When Nase brought Annie to me, did I just move into his hallucination? If it weren't for that possibility, I could wipe the whole thing out and return to my rational world."

Mrs. Murry took the casserole to the counter and brought back a bowl of fruit. "I couldn't eat another thing," Polly said, "not even an apple. Anyhow, I like our funny-looking gnarled ones better than these pretty ones."

The bishop reached into the bowl and helped himself.

No one wanted coffee and Dr. Louise rose and announced that it was time to go home.

Polly and her grandparents went outdoors to give the Colubras the traditional farewell. The northwest wind was cold, but the sky was high and clear, the stars dazzling like diamonds. The Milky Way streamed its distant river across the sky.

The bishop raised his face to the starlight. "How many millions of years are we seeing, Alex?"

"Many."

"What is the nearest star?"

"Proxima Centauri, about four light-years away."

"And how many miles?"

"Oh, about 23 million million."

The bishop's breath was cloudy in the light over the garage door. "Look at that star just overhead. We're seeing it in time as well as space, time long gone. We don't know what that star looks like now, or even if it's still there. It could have become a supernova. Or collapsed in on itself and become a black hole. How extraordinary to be looking at a star in this present moment and seeing it millions of years ago."

Dr. Louise took her brother's arm affectionately. "Enough fantasizing, Nase."

"Is it?" But he got into the car, behind the steering wheel.

"Louise shows both courage and trust to let Nason drive," Mrs. Murry murmured.

Dr. Louise, getting into the passenger seat, laughed. "He used to fly a lot, too."

"Terrifying thought," Mrs. Murry said.

They waved as the bishop took off in a cloud of dust.

"Well, Polly." Mrs. Murry sat on the side of her granddaughter's bed.

"Grand, there isn't any point keeping me cooped up. Zachary saw Anaral just outside the pool wing, he really did, even if we find it strange. And I saw Karralys." She thought of Karralys's warning, but said firmly, "I don't think there's any danger."

"Not from Annie or Karralys, perhaps. But wandering about in time doesn't strike me as particularly safe."

"It really isn't wandering about in time," Polly persisted. "It's just one particular sort of circle of time, about three thousand years ago, to now, and vice versa."

"I don't want you getting lost three thousand years ago."

"I really don't think that's going to happen, Grand."

Mrs. Murry gently smoothed back Polly's rumpled hair. "Bishop Colubra suggested that you not go to the star-watching rock till after the weekend. Please abide by that suggestion. For my peace of mind. And not to the stone wall, either."

"All right. For you."

Her grandmother kissed her good night and left. The wind continued to rise and beat about the house. One of the shutters banged. Polly heard her grandparents getting ready for bed. She herself was not sleepy. Anything but sleepy. She shifted from one side to the other. Curled up. Stretched out. Flopped over onto her back. Sighed. Insomnia was something that very seldom troubled her, but this night she could not sleep. She turned on her bed lamp and tried to read, but she could not keep her mind on the book. Her eyes felt gritty, but not sleepy. She could not get comfortable in bed because something was drawing her out of it.

The pool. She had to go to the pool.

—Nonsense, Polly, that's the last place in the world you should go. You promised. Don't be crazy.

But the pool kept drawing her. Maybe Annie was there. Maybe Annie needed her.

—No. Not the pool. She lay down, pulled the quilt over her head. —No. No. Go to sleep. Forget the pool.

And she could not. Almost without volition, she swung her legs out of bed, pushed into her slippers. Went downstairs.

When she got out to the pool, the moon, which was only a few days off full, was shining through the skylights, so there was no need to turn on the lights. She pulled off her nightgown and slid into the water, which felt considerably colder than it did during the day. Swam, backstroke, so that she could look up at the night sky, with only a sprinkling of the brightest stars visible because of the moonlight. Then she swam the length of the pool underwater, thought she saw metal glistening on the bottom of the pool at the deep end.

She dove down and picked up something hard. Shining. It was a silver circlet with a crescent moon. At first she thought it was a torque, but there was no opening, and she realized that it was meant for the head. She put it on over her wet hair, and it felt cool and firm. Took it off and looked at it again. She did not know much about jewelry, but she knew that this small crown was beautiful. What was a silver crown with a crescent moon doing in her grandparents' pool?

She got out of the water, wrapped a large towel around herself, and sat down to dry off before going to her cold bedroom. She still felt wide awake. In the moonlight she could see the big clock at the far end of the pool. It was not quite midnight. She put on her warm nightgown, intending to go right back upstairs. But the silver circlet caught the light and she picked it up and looked at it again, and once more placed it on her head, with the crescent moon in the center of her forehead.

The webbing of her chair no longer felt soft and resilient under her, but hard, and cold, and a sharp wind was blowing.

She shuddered.

She was sitting on a stone chair, slightly hollowed, so that her hands rested on low arms. A circle of similar chairs surrounded a large altar, similar to the one before which Anaral had sung her song of praise to the Mother, but several times bigger. Behind each chair was a large standing stone. The place was reminiscent of pictures she had seen of Stonehenge, except that at Stonehenge there were no thrones or jagged mountains in the background, no snow on peaks white with moonlight.

She should never have gone to the pool.

Her breathing was rapid, frightened. Her heart thumped painfully. Karralys was sitting on one of the thrones, about a quarter of the way around the circle from Polly. He wore a brass torque set with a stone she thought was a cairngorm, which reminded her of the topaz in Bishop Colubra's ring. He wore a long robe that looked like white linen but was probably very soft, bleached leather. His dog was beside him, sitting upright, ears pricked at attention, his dog which looked like the dog Mr. Murry had brought into the house. Anaral was at his right, wearing a silver circlet similar to the one Polly had found in the pool and which was still on her head.

Across the altar from Karralys was Tav, who wore a short, light tunic, a wildcat skin over one shoulder, and leather straps around his wrists and upper arms. His great spear was leaning against his chair. There were several other men and women, some young, some old, many wearing animal skins or cloaks of feathers. Only Anaral and Polly wore the silver circlets. The chair at Karralys's left was empty.

The moon was setting directly behind the standing stone that backed Karralys's chair, and above the moon was a bright star. No, not a star, Polly thought; a planet. She started to speak, to question, but Anaral raised a hand to silence her.

In the background there were more people, and she heard the low, almost subliminal throbbing of a drum. In the distance the sound was echoed. Otherwise, there was silence. All the faces in the circle were grave. Expectant.

Karralys and Anaral rose and went to the outside of the circle, where a large fire was laid in a shallow pit. Anaral gave Karralys a flintstone and he struck a spark and ignited the fire. The two druids raised their arms in a wide gesture of praise, and together they danced slowly and majestically, first around the now blazing fire, and after that around the circle of standing stones. Then, one by one, each person in the circle took a brand and lit it from the fire, and handed it to one of the people who were outside the circle.

When the passing of the fire was complete, there was a burst of song, rich in harmony, joyous in melody. Polly's heart soared with the voices of the people in and around the circle, so that she forgot her fear. Slowly the song died away into a gentle silence.

Then Karralys spoke in his low, ringing voice. "The year has been kind." He indicated the empty chair next to his. "The Ancient Grey Wolf was full of years and was gathered to the ancestors on the sixth day of the moon during the night. His spirit will continue to care for us, joined to the spirits of all of the People of the Wind who are among the stars but whose concern is never far from us." A soft breeze touched Polly's cheeks, moving over the great circle of standing stones. Behind them shadows swayed, purple, silver, indigo, shadows of men and women so tall that they seemed to reach to the stars. Polly could not understand all of what was said, but she felt wrapped in loving strength.

Karralys continued, "The Cub is still young, but he has the gift, and he will learn under the guidance of those who have gone before."

A young man, indeed very young, wearing a grey-wolf skin, rose. "And from you, Karralys." He turned around slowly, bowing to the assembly.

Then Tav spoke, standing and leaning on his great spear. The moonlight touched his hair and turned it to silver. His grey eyes glinted silver. Moonlight touched the ruffling of feathers on his spear. "We have honored the ritual. The fire burns. It flames as brightly as the head of the one who has been sent us by the Mother." He indicated Polly, and his face was solemn.

"Tav, you assume too much and too quickly," Karralys chided.

"The Mother has kept her promise," Tav said. "And so have I. She has come." Again his spear pointed toward Polly.

"You brought her." Karralys spoke sternly.

"I did what the Mother bade. I put the diadem on the altar and she translated it to the place of sacred water."

"Time is fluid at Samhain," Karralys said. "This may not have been the Mother's will."

"Listen to me." Tav leaned forward earnestly. "The Mother speaks in the dark, in the waters, in the womb of the earth. She is never to be understood directly."

"She does not ask for blood!" Anaral's voice rang out clearly.

"No," Tav agreed. "The Mother does not want the blood of her children. *Her* children. Hear me! This sun-headed child is not one of hers, nor of ours. She has been sent us so that the Mother may be nourished and her demand fulfilled."

Tav spoke more rapidly than Karralys and the implications of his speech did not fully reach Polly because she was struggling to understand the Ogam phrases. If she listened carefully she could make out each word, but it took several beats before the sentences had meaning. The fire had something to do with Samhain, a sacred fire that was passed to each family of the tribe. The dancing had been beautiful and serene, and the singing had been pure joy, taking away her fear, but now Tav was bringing in a different note, a somber note, and her skin prickled.

"And what does the goddess say?" Karralys demanded.

Tav looked up at the moon. "The goddess says that there is danger for us. Grave danger. There has been no rain for the People Across the Lake. Last week a raiding party took sheep from us, and two cows. Their drums tell us that their crops wither. The earth is dry and must be nourished."

Karralys replied, "Ah, Tav, it is not blood that our Mother demands, nor do the gods across the lake. What is asked from us is nurture, our care for the crops, that we not overuse the land, planting the same crops in the same place too many years in a row, not watering the young shoots. Our Mother is not a devouring monster but a loving birth-giver."

"And for such strange ideas you were sent away from home. Excommunicated." The moonlight struck against Tav's eyes.

"And you, Tav? Why were you sent from home?" Karralys demanded.

"You have not forgotten that there was a time when there was no rain, and the little people from the north came and stole our cattle. Our own crops withered, as the crops of the People Across the Lake are withering. Then I understood that blood was demanded, not the blood of a lamb, but real blood, human blood. A raider came by night and I fought him in fair combat and I took him. And so we had the necessary sacrifice. I put him on the altar, yes, I put him on the altar because you would not, nor would you permit the others. I, only I, obeyed the Mother. And so we had the blood that brought the rain, though I was expelled for taking upon myself the sacrificial role of a druid. And so we were both sent away—you for refusing, I for doing what you should have done. Blood was demanded by the Mother then, and it is demanded now. If we do not take care, tribes who are stronger than we are will come and drive us away from our land."

Anaral rose. "Tav, here on my land you and Karralys have lived together in harmony for three turns of the sun. Do not start the old quarrels again, especially on this night."

Tav's voice was urgent. "There will be more raids. And we ourselves have had no rain since the last moon."

"Our crops are harvested. Corn was plentiful." Karralys smiled.

"The water of the lake is low. The rivers run dry. Even our underground river which gives water to our crops flows less swiftly."

"As always at this time of year. When the winter snows come, the rivers will be refilled."

"The winter snows may not come," Tav warned, "if the earth is not given what she demands."

"Tav." Karralys looked at him sternly. "Why bring up again what was resolved when we became one with the People of the Wind? Those of this land who have welcomed us into their lives forbid such sacrifice. As do I."

"There are other peoples, across the lake, beyond the mountains, who do not think as you do, or as the People of the Wind. We must protect ourselves. Can you not hear the drums which echo ours and are not merely an echo? It is the People

Across the Lake. Do you think they will stop at one small raid? Please understand. I know you do not like the sacrifice. Nor do I." He looked at Polly and his face was anguished. "But unless we obey, our land is doomed."

Behind Karralys the moon slipped below the great standing stones, leaving the star to shine brightly just above it, almost like a jewel touching his fair hair.

Tav's voice grated with urgency. "Will one war spear be enough if others want our land?" He raised his great spear. "And why, Karralys, why have we been sent this sunlit stranger?"

"Sunlit, yes," Karralys said. "Life, not death."

"A time gate has been opened," Anaral said.

"And why? A time gate opens once in how many hundred years? Why now? Why here? And when the time is needful?"

Anaral rose again. "She has been sent for good, not ill. This girl and also the old Heron. They have come for our good. We must treat them with courtesy and hospitality until we understand."

"I understand!" Tav cried. "Why are your ears closed?"

"Perhaps it is your ears that are closed," Karralys reprimanded gently.

"I long for home," Tav said. "Around our standing stones were poles and on the poles were the skulls of our enemies. Blood ran from the altar into the ground and the summers were gentle and the winters short. Here we wither from the heat of the sun, or our bones are brittle from the ice and cold. Yes, we have been treated gently by the People of the Wind, but their ways are not the old familiar ways. And now a time gate has been opened and if we are not careful it will close again, and we will have lost the one we have been sent."

Behind Karralys the star, too, was slipping below the great stone. He rose, walked slowly around the table, and took the silver circlet from Polly's head. "Go home," he commanded. "Go home."

CHAPTER 7

S HE jerked upright, as though out of sleep. She looked around. There was no silver circlet with crescent moon. She wore only her damp nightgown. The pool rippled in the starlight. The moon was gone. The distant sound of the village church bell came to her, twelve notes, blown and distorted by the wind. She shivered.

All she knew was that it had not been a dream.

When Polly woke up, it was broad daylight and the sun was streaming into her room. She lay in bed debating. How could she explain to her grandparents what had happened to her? On Samhain. All Hallows' Eve. It was over. Today was Friday, All Souls' Day.

She heard them coming up from the pool. She dressed and went downstairs, feeling weary and anxious. Coffee was still dripping through the filter into the glass carafe. She got a mug from the dresser. The Ogam stones were still there. She wondered where her grandmother was going to take them. She waited till the coffee had stopped dripping, then filled her mug and added milk. She was too tired to make *café au lait*.

Her grandparents came downstairs and into the kitchen. Greeted her. Then: "What's the matter?"

She started to spill out her story.

"Wait," her grandfather said, and poured himself a cup of coffee and sat at his place.

Her grandmother, too, sat down. "Go on."

They listened without interrupting. They did not tell her she should not have gone down to the pool. When she had finished, they looked at each other.

"We'd better call Nase," her grandfather said.

While they were waiting for the bishop, they had breakfast. Mrs. Murry had made oatmeal the night before, and it was on the back of the stove, hot, over a double boiler. Automatically she set out brown sugar, raisins, milk. "Help yourselves."

"I don't like the implications of this," Mr. Murry said. "There seems to be no way we can protect Polly, except by chaining her to one of us."

They stopped talking as they heard urgent barking outside. Mr. Murry put his hand to his forehead. "I'd almost forgotten—" He went out through the pantry door and came in with the dog, who pranced about excitedly. "Polly, is this Karralys's dog?"

"I think so."

Mr. Murry shook his head, went back out to the garage, and returned with the blanket, which he put down near the wood stove. The dog flopped down on it, tail thumping, and Hadron leaped upon him, playing with his tail as though with a mouse. The dog sighed with resignation.

"Three thousand years don't seem to make much difference to Hadron," he said. "Somehow I find that comforting. But maybe I'm grasping at straws."

The bishop arrived with Dr. Louise. "I want to make sure that sanity outweighs my brother's fantasy," she said. "I don't have to be at the hospital for another hour."

"The dog's still here." The bishop petted the animal's head, stroked the great ears.

"He was with Karralys last night," Polly said, "whenever last night was . . ."

"Have you had breakfast?" Mrs. Murry asked.

"Long ago," Dr. Louise replied.

The bishop looked at the stove. "Very long ago."

Mrs. Murry handed him a bowl. "Help yourself, Nason. It's only oatmeal this morning."

He filled his bowl, heaped on brown sugar and raisins, added milk, and sat at the table. "I find it comforting that the dog is here. I'm sure he's protection. Now, Polly, tell me exactly what happened last night. Don't leave anything out."

"I couldn't sleep," she started, "and it was as though the pool was pulling me. I can't explain. I knew I shouldn't go to the pool. I didn't want to go to the pool. But it kept pulling me. And I went."

The bishop listened carefully, eating all the while, looking up as she described the silver circlet with the crescent moon. "Surely," he said, "a symbol of the moon goddess. You said Annie had one, too?"

"Yes."

"The moon goddess. And the Mother, the earth. What we have, you see, is a mixture of Native American and Celtic tradition. They overlap in many ways. Go on."

After a while Mr. Murry interrupted, "You say that Karralys and this other person—"

"Tav."

"—have been here, in the New World, only three years?"

"I think so, Granddad. That's what Anaral and Karralys both said."

The bishop nodded. "Yes. That's what they told me. I've paid less attention to time than to the trip. Karralys and Tav came in a boat. Of course that would not be possible now with the lake long gone, along with the rest of the melt from the glaciers. But three thousand years ago it is quite possible that one could have come first across the ocean, and then by the rivers—and probably what are merely brooks and streams now would have been sizable rivers then—and so get to the lake and to this place. What do you think, Alex?"

"Possibly," Mr. Murry agreed. "Once they'd landed on this continent, they could probably have made their way inland in some kind of small boat."

"It's the ocean crossing that's hard to understand," Dr. Louise said.

"People did cross oceans, remember," her brother said. "Navigating by the stars. And the druids were astronomers."

The bishop helped himself to more oatmeal. "Go on, Polly."

When she had finished, the bishop's bowl was again empty. "All right. So you were part of the Samhain remembrance of the People of the Wind."

"And Karralys and Tav were assimilated by the native people—the People of the Wind?" Mr. Murry asked.

"Karralys became their new leader," the bishop said. "He and Tav were blown across the lake by a hurricane, which in itself would have seemed an omen." He took a handful of raisins.

"Karralys and Tav were each sent from Britain for opposite heresies—Karralys for the refusal to shed blood, and Tav not so much for shedding it as for performing the sacrifice that should have been done by a druid. Tav believed that human sacrifice was demanded, that the earth cried out for blood, and he acted accordingly."

"Polly. Blood." Mr. Murry's voice was heavy. "He's thinking of Polly."

Until her grandfather put it thus baldly, Polly had not quite absorbed the import of Tav's words the night before.

Mrs. Murry asked, "Was blood sacrifice part of the druidic ritual?"

"It's not been proven," the bishop said. "There is a theory that it was believed the Earth Mother demanded blood and that each year, perhaps at Samhain, there was a human sacrifice. If possible it was a prisoner. If not, then someone, usually the weakest in the tribe, would be laid on the altar and blood given to the ground."

Polly shivered.

"What about the skulls?" Dr. Louise asked.

"That, I understand, was common practice among some of the tribes. The skulls of the enemies were placed on high poles in a circle around the altar or the standing stones. Remember, these were Stone Age people and their thinking was very different from ours."

"Bloodthirsty," Dr. Louise stated.

The bishop asked mildly, "Any more bloodthirsty than incinerating people with napalm? Or hydrogen bombs? We appear to be bloodthirsty creatures, we so-called human beings, and peacemakers like Karralys are in the minority, I fear."

"Meanwhile," Mr. Murry demanded, "what about Polly?"

"Samhain is over," the bishop said. "Karralys was able to send Polly safely home."

"You think the danger is over?"

The bishop nodded. "It should be. The time has passed."

The dog rose from the blanket and came over to Polly, sitting beside her and laying his head on her knee. She put her hand on his neck, which felt strong and warm. His hair, while not long, was soft.

The bishop nodded again. "Karralys and Annie will protect Polly. Karralys has sent his dog."

Mr. Murry spoke sharply. "It is not necessarily the same dog. I don't want Polly to see them again, not any of them. And as soon as your time gate is closed, I want Polly away from here."

"But, Granddad, if the time gate is closed, then there isn't any problem, and we don't have to worry about the tesseract one way or the other."

The bishop agreed, then said, "Samhain is over. This is All Souls' Day, when we remember those who have gone before. It is a quiet day when we can let our grief turn to peace."

"Nason." Mr. Murry's voice grated. "What do we do now? Can you guarantee that the danger to Polly is over?"

The bishop gazed at a last raisin in his bowl as though searching for an answer. "I don't know. If it weren't for that young man, Zachary."

"What about him?"

"His part in all this, whatever it is, has not been played out."

Mrs. Murry asked quietly, "Is Polly still in the tesseract?"

Again the bishop stared at the raisin. "There are too many questions still unresolved."

"Is that an answer?"

"I don't know." The bishop looked at Mr. Murry. "I don't understand your tesseract. Polly has been through the time gate, and if I am the one who opened it—forgive me."

"Bishop," Polly interrupted, "Tav. What about Tav?"

"Tav has reason for concern. There are neighboring tribes which are not as peaceable as the People of the Wind. There have been several summers of drought, far more severe across the lake, where there is no underground river to be tapped for irrigation. Raids have already begun. This land is eminently desirable. Tav is ready to fight to protect it."

"Is Karralys?" Mr. Murry asked.

"I'm not sure." The bishop rubbed his forehead. "He seeks peace, but peace is not easy to maintain single-handed."

Mr. Murry went to the dresser. "I wish you'd never found the Ogam stones, or opened the time gate."

"It was—it was inadvertent. It was nothing I planned."

"No? You opened the time gate thoroughly when you

brought Annie to Louise." Mr. Murry's voice was level, but it was an accusation nevertheless.

Dr. Louise said quickly, "She would have lost the use of her forefinger. Infection would probably have set in if I had not used antibiotics. What might seem like a simple slip of the knife could well have proved fatal."

Mrs. Murry smiled slightly. "Brother and sister do stick together when push comes to shove," she murmured to Polly. "Anyhow, Alex, you and I were fascinated, disbelieving but fascinated, until Polly was involved."

Mr. Murry asked, "Is it safe for us to send Polly home to Benne Seed Island?"

"No—" Polly started, but the bishop interrupted, raising his hand authoritatively.

"I think not yet. Things have to be played out. But meanwhile we will keep her safe here. One of us must be with her at all times to prevent a recurrence of last night."

"Not you, please, Nase," Mrs. Murry said. "Sorry, but it's you who opened the gate."

"You're probably right," the bishop conceded, "but you, my dear. And Alex. Just be with her."

"What would happen," Mr. Murry suggested, "if you sealed up the root cellar?"

"Nothing, I fear. It was simply the closest root cellar to the star-watching rock, and the place of your pool. These are the holy places."

"Holy?" Dr. Louise asked.

"Sacred. We have lost a sense of the sacredness of space as we have settled for the literal and provable. We remember a few of the sacred spaces, such as Mount Moriah in Jerusalem, or Glastonbury Abbey. Mount Moriah was holy before ever Abraham took Isaac there. So was Bethel, the house of God, before Jacob had his dream, or before the Ark of the Covenant was briefly located there, according to Judges."

"Nase," his sister said softly, "you're getting in the pulpit again."

But he went on, "One theory is that such sacred spaces were connected by ley lines."

She interrupted, "Nase, what on earth are ley lines?"

"They are lines of electromagnetic power, well documented in England, leading from one holy place to another, lines of energy. I suspect that there is a ley line between the root cellar and the star-watching rock, between the star-watching rock and the pool."

"What faddish rubbish," his sister said.

But Polly remembered Karralys talking about lines between the stars, lines between places, between people. It did not seem like rubbish.

"It can become a fad," the bishop told his sister, "but that doesn't make the original holiness any less holy."

"I don't want you falling for fads in your old age," Dr. Louise warned.

"Louise, I didn't ask for any of this. I wasn't looking for Ogam stones. But they can hardly be classified as rubbish. I had no idea that your root cellar was in fact not a root cellar at all. I didn't expect three thousand years to be bridged by Annie. But Annie is a lovely, innocent creature, and I feel a certain—a distinct—responsibility toward her."

"How can you be responsible for someone who has been dead for approximately three thousand years?" Dr. Louise demanded. "Her story is already told. Kaput. Finished."

"Is it?" the bishop whispered. "Is it?"

Dr. Louise went to the door. "I have to get along to the hospital. But I think it might be a good idea for all of you to come over to our house for lunch and perhaps the rest of the day. The greatest risk to Polly seems to come from right around here, and I think there's a certain safety for her from being with us pragmatists, who may well keep Nase's time gate closed because basically we still don't give it our willing suspension of disbelief."

This plan was readily agreed to, although there was considerable argument about whether or not Polly should be allowed to ride in the pickup truck with the bishop.

"There are no time gates on the highway," the bishop said. "We'll go directly to your house, Louise, and Kate and Alex can come right behind us."

"Why can't Polly go with Kate and Alex?"

"I feel responsible."

"Nase, you're the last person she should be with."

But the bishop was persistent and finally it was agreed that Polly could ride with him as long as he stayed within the speed limit and the grandparents followed directly behind him.

"I'll be home for lunch," Dr. Louise said. "I'll pick up some cold cuts on the way."

Polly climbed into the truck after the bishop. The dog whined and barked, not wanting to be left behind.

"Go," Mr. Murry ordered the dog. "Go to wherever you came from."

The bishop started the ignition. "Polly, I'm sorry."

She sighed. "Don't be. It wasn't anything you planned, and, Bishop, it may be scary, but it's also exciting."

"I wish I had something to give you for protection, a talisman of some kind."

She had put on the red anorak. Now she felt in the pocket and pulled out Zachary's icon. "Zachary gave me this yesterday afternoon."

The bishop took it, keeping one hand lightly on the steering wheel. "A guardian-angel icon! It's delightful, utterly delightful!"

Behind them the Murrys honked, and the bishop lightened his foot on the accelerator and gave the icon back to Polly. "It's a reminder that there are powers of love in the universe, and as long as you respond with love, they'll help you."

She put the icon back in her pocket. "Once my Uncle Sandy gave me an icon of St. George and the dragon."

"And it didn't stop bad things from happening?" the bishop suggested. "An icon is not meant to be an idol. Just a reminder that love is greater than hate."

"Do you really and truly believe that?"

The bishop nodded calmly. Then he said, "You know a good bit of physics, don't you?"

"Is that a sequitur?"

"Indeed. Do you know what physicists call the very different interactions between the electromagnetic, the gravitational, and the strong and weak forces?"

"Nope."

"The *hierarchy* of interactions. Hierarchy was the word used by Dionysius the Aeropagite to refer to the arrangement of angels into three divisions, each consisting of three orders. Today the physicist arranges the fundamental interactions of matter into hierarchies instead. But it does go to show you that at least they've heard of angels."

"Why does it show that?"

"Your grandfather pointed it out to me."

"Does that mean he believes in angels?"

"Perhaps. I do, though not that they look like that beautiful angel in your icon. What is the first thing that angels in Scripture say when they appear before somebody?"

"What?"

"*Fear not!* That gives you an idea of what they must have looked like."

Once again the Murrys honked. Again the bishop slowed down, then turned up the hill to Dr. Louise's house in a burst of speed, stopped, and turned off the ignition. The Murrys drew up beside him.

They sat around Dr. Louise's kitchen table. "It's by far the warmest place in the house," the bishop said.

Polly felt a wave of unreality wash over her. In a way, she was as much out of the world staying with her grandparents, or here in Dr. Louise's kitchen, as when she moved into Anaral's time. Her grandparents were isolated in their own, special, scientific worlds. Their house was outside the village. She could go for days without seeing anyone else if she did not go to the post office or the store.

At home, although the O'Keefes' house on Benne Seed Island was as isolated as her grandparents' house, school and her siblings kept her in touch with the real world. How real was it? Drugs were a problem at Cowpertown High. So were unwed mothers. So was lack of motivation, a lazy conviction that the world owed the students a living.

She suddenly realized that although there was a television set in her grandfather's study, they had not turned it on. The radio was set to a classical music station. Her grandparents read the papers, and she assumed that if anything world-shattering was happening they would tell her. But she had, as it were, dropped out since she had come to them.

She looked at her grandparents and the bishop. "Zachary's coming tomorrow. What are we going to do about Zachary?"

"I want Louise to see him," Mrs. Murry said.

"She's not a cardiologist," Mr. Murry warned.

"She's been a general practitioner for so long in a place where there are few specialists that she has considerable knowledge based on years and years of experience."

"All right, I grant you that, but I suspect that Zachary would like us to treat him as normally as possible. His seeing Annie may have been an aberration. Or it may not have been Annie he saw at all."

"Who else could it be?" Polly asked.

They all looked up as they heard an urgent barking outside. The bishop went to the door, opened it, and in came the dog, tail wagging, romping first to Mr. Murry and Polly, then the others.

The bishop put his hand on the dog's head. "We can't escape the past, even here."

"He's a perfectly ordinary dog." Mr. Murry was determined. "I'm still not certain he's anything but a stray."

"He's protection," the bishop said. "Don't take that lightly."

The dog pranced to Mrs. Murry and leaned his head against her knees. Absently she fondled the animal's ears. "We don't seem to have much choice about keeping this creature."

"You have been chosen." The bishop smiled. As though in response, the dog's ropy tail thudded against the floor. "Now you should name him."

Mr. Murry said, "If we name him, we're making a commitment to him."

"But we are, aren't we?" Polly asked.

Her grandmother sighed lightly. "So it would seem."

Polly added, "And Dr. Louise said you needed another dog."

The bishop suggested, "Would you like to name him, Polly?"

She looked at the dog, who, while he did not seem to belong to any known breed, was handsome in his own way. His tan coat was sleek and shiny, and the black tracing around his ears gave him a distinguished look. His rope of a tail was unusually long, tipped with black. "He ought to have a Celtic name, I suppose. That is, if he has anything to do with Karralys."

"He may be just a stray." Mr. Murry was not going to give in.

"Ogam. How about calling him Ogam?"

"Why not?" Polly's grandmother asked. "Naming a dog is a normal, ordinary thing to do, and we need normal, ordinary things right now."

The dog settled at Polly's feet, snoring lightly and contentedly.

"Okay, Polly," her grandfather said. "Let's have some normal, ordinary lesson time. What is Heisenberg's uncertainty principle?"

She sighed, relaxing into the world of particle physics, which, strange as it was, was a welcome relief. "Well, if you're measuring the speed of a particle, you can't measure its position. Or if you measure its position, you can't measure its speed. You can measure one or the other, but not both at the same time."

"Right. How many quarks does a proton have?"

"Three. One of each color."

"Position?"

"Two up quarks and one down quark."

"And quarks are—"

"Infinitely small particles. The word *quark* is out of *Finnegans Wake*."

"So Murray Gell-Mann, who named them, obviously read Joyce. I find that rather comforting."

So did Polly. Working with her grandfather was ordinary and normal, but it was not ordinary and normal to be sitting in Dr. Louise's kitchen.

Her grandparents felt the dislocation, too. The lesson petered out. Her grandmother took the wilting bunch of roses from the table and emptied the water from the vase. "I'll just go throw these on the compost and see if there are a few more to bring in."

Mr. Murry looked at his granddaughter. "You all right?"

"Sure. Fine."

"If I go out to the garden with your grandmother, you'll stay right here?"

"I won't go anywhere."

"Nor I," the bishop promised.

"We'll be only a few minutes."

As the door slammed behind Mr. Murry, the bishop said, "What happened last night—"

"It was very frightening."

"*It* was frightening?" he asked. "Are *you* frightened?"

"A little."

"A little is not enough. We can't have you going through the time gate again."

Polly looked down at the dog. Ogam. His black nose was shiny. His eyes were closed, and he had long, dark lashes. "I went through the time gate last night because I went down to the pool and put on the silver circlet."

"Don't do it again."

"Of course not, Bishop. But the first time I went through I was just walking along on my way to the star-watching rock."

"I wish you could go home."

"Bishop, I'm in a tesseract. Granddad believes it could really hurt me if I were taken out."

"He's probably right. Does he believe that Tav would put you on the altar for a sacrifice?"

"I don't know. I'm not sure I believe it."

"Believe it, child. The idea of blood sacrifice is gone from our frame of reference, but it's not that much different or worse than things that go on today. What else is the electric chair or lethal injection than human sacrifice?"

"We're told that it's to protect society," Polly said.

"Isn't Tav trying to protect his society in the only way he knows how? He believes that if the Mother isn't appeased, his land and his people are going to be taken over by stronger tribes."

"Tav likes me," Polly said softly.

"Who could help it?" the bishop asked. "His liking for you will just make it harder for him to do what he believes he is called to do. Do you understand? He has to obey the Mother whether he wants to or not."

"She doesn't sound very motherly," Polly said.

The bishop continued, "I don't want to speak this way in front of your grandparents. They're already distressed enough, and if it would be seriously harmful to you to send you away, there's no point in upsetting them further."

"I agree," Polly said, "and I promise not to do anything stupid."

"Now. About Zachary."

"I don't understand what he has to do with all this."

"Karralys may be right. If he's near death—"

"I don't think death is imminent, or anything. But he's scared."

"Of?"

"Death. He's frightened of death."

"Yes." The bishop nodded.

"He thinks death is the end. Poof. Annihilation."

"And you, Polly?"

"I can't imagine Max entirely gone from the universe. I don't need to know *how* she is being, somehow, Max—learning whatever it is she needs to learn, doing whatever she's supposed to do. But I can't just imagine her totally wiped out."

"What you believe is what I, too, believe," the bishop said. "It is enough."

The Murrys returned then, Mrs. Murry carrying a few yellow roses which were still blooming in a sheltered corner. She cut their stems, put them in the vase, and set it on the table. They were all on edge, out of place, trying to make normal that which was not normal.

"At least you take it seriously," Polly said. "You don't think the bishop and I are out of our tree."

"We would if we could," her grandmother said.

"I just wish"—Mr. Murry spread out his gnarled hands— "that we could be in this with you."

Dr. Louise came in with two brown paper bags, which she set down on the table; then shucked off her outer clothes, hanging them on the antlers. "Bread—not as good as yours, Alex, but reasonable. And an assortment of cold cuts."

The bishop unpacked the bags, setting out plates of bread and meat, while Dr. Louise took condiments from the refrigerator, and a pitcher of milk. "I'll make tea," the bishop offered.

They sat around the table, making sandwiches. —And we don't know what to say, Polly thought.

Dr. Louise sighed.

"All Souls' Day," the bishop said. "Always a poignant day for Louise and me."

There was a silence, and Polly looked questioningly at her grandparents. Mrs. Murry spoke in an even voice. "It was on this date that Louise's husband and baby boy, and Nason's wife, were killed in a train accident. Louise survived. Nason was away."

"It was a long time ago." Dr. Louise's expression was calm. "I was pregnant again and I miscarried. I thought I had lost all that made life worth living, but Nason kept prodding me, and I went to medical school, and I have had a good life. I *have* a good life."

"And I," the bishop said, "with friends who keep the stars in their courses for me, and a faith in God's loving purpose and eventual working out of the pattern."

"And all this?" Dr. Louise asked. "This three-thousand-year-old time capsule you've opened up, what does this do to your faith?"

The bishop smiled. "Why, widens it, I hope."

Dr. Louise laughed softly. "Nason, if you'd been a druid, you'd probably have been excommunicated for heresy, just like Karralys."

"Yesterday's heresy becomes tomorrow's dogma," the bishop replied mildly, and Polly thought once again of Giordano Bruno.

After lunch they went for a walk in the woods behind Dr. Louise's house, Ogam close at their heels, occasionally tearing off in great loops, but always circling back. "Behaving just like an ordinary dog," the bishop said. "Bless Og."

"He may give you a sense of security, Nase," Dr. Louise said, "but he reminds me of the reason we're keeping Polly here all day, and that's something I'd rather forget."

They found some beautiful pale pink mushrooms, saw the bright red clustered berries of jack-in-the-pulpit, and tried to pretend they were focused on a nature walk. The rising wind

and their own restlessness drove them in. The bishop made tea
from a selection of herbs in the garden. They played Botticelli
and other word games, but they could not concentrate. When
the sun slipped behind the mountains, Mr. Murry stood up.
"It's time we went home. We'll keep a close eye on Polly. And,
as you say, Nase, Samhain is over. Keep the dog here."

But not long after they were home there was a sharp, demanding bark outside.

"He stays in the garage," Mrs. Murry said.

They had a quiet dinner, with music in the background.
Afterwards Polly helped her grandfather with the dishes. When
they were through, he suggested, "Let's go for a brief stroll
around the house."

They put on anoraks and as soon as they were out of the
house Og pranced up beside them. "We always used to walk
our dogs three times around the vegetable garden," her grandfather said. "We might as well continue the tradition. It helps
keep the woodchucks away. I've plowed and composted half
the garden, but we still have some good broccoli and sprouts
and carrots and beets. The twins' garden was magnificent.
After they left home for college they grew Christmas trees
for a while, but when they were all sold I found I wanted a
vegetable garden again. What time is your young man coming
tomorrow?"

"Around two, I think."

Og chased off into the field and Mr. Murry whistled and he
turned and ran back to them. "Good boy," Mr. Murry praised,
"though whistling was a reflex. I should have let you go." He
stood, raising his face to the sky. It was a clear night, with the
Milky Way a river of stars. Polly tipped her head to look for
the North Star.

"I can understand how people could see a big dipper or a
little dipper," she said, "but not bears. And maybe if you draw
lines between those stars you could make a crooked chair for
Cassiopeia." —Ley lines between stars?

"There's Orion's belt," her grandfather pointed. "See those
three bright stars?"

"Belt, okay," she said, "but I don't see Orion the hunter.

Some night, could we have a plain old-fashioned astronomy lesson?" As she spoke, a falling star streaked across the sky and went out in a flash of green light.

"Of course. Let me do a little brushing up. It would be nice to have a dog again. It ensures a night walk, and that means a chance to look up at the sky."

"Granddad, where do you think Og came from?"

"I really don't think he came from three thousand years ago. We often have stray dogs in the village, dumped out of cars by people going back to the city."

"People don't do that!"

"People do. They have a puppy or a kitten for the summer and then, on the way back to the city, they let their summer pet loose. Maybe the city's got into their bloodstream and they're under the illusion that country dogs and cats can fend for themselves. I phoned around to see if anybody's lost a dog, but thus far, nobody has. He's a sweet dog. But he's going to sleep in the garage tonight. Not in the house."

Mrs. Murry came into Polly's room, wearing her nightclothes. "Polly, love. I'm glad this is a double bed. I'm going to sleep with you."

"Grand, it's all right. I won't leave. I won't go downstairs. I promise."

"Your grandfather and I will feel better if I'm in here with you."

"But you won't be as comfortable—I'll keep you awake—"

"Please. For our sakes."

"Okay, Grand, but I really don't think it's necessary. I mean, it's fine with me, but—"

Mrs. Murry laughed. "Indulge your grandfather and me. We just want to make sure one of us is with you." She got into bed beside Polly. "Let's read for a while."

Polly picked up a book, but she could not concentrate. After half an hour her grandmother kissed her good night and turned over on her side to sleep. Polly switched off the light, but she was not sleepy. Hadron was stretched out between them, purring sleepily.

Again the pool was pulling her. Pulling. This time she would resist. She pressed up against her grandmother's back. Was it Tav's influence, pulling her toward the pool and the past as the moon pulls the tide?

Polly stiffened. No. No. She would not go to the pool. If she got out of bed, her grandmother would waken, would stop her.

What Tav cared about was protecting the land, the flocks, the people, and Polly could not help feeling sympathy for that. When the O'Keefes had had to leave the island of Gaea, with its golden beaches and azure waters, it had been because of developers, because of greed and corruption, and people lusting for money and power and ignoring the loveliness of the island, the birds and the animals and the natives, who lived much as they must have many centuries earlier. And Benne Seed Island was already being developed, and soon it, too, would be irrevocably changed, with no thought for the birds whose habitat had been the jungly forest, or for the great trees two and three hundred years old.

Is it all greed and corruption? she asked herself. We've become an overpopulated planet. People need places to live.

But the condos and resort hotels were for the rich, not the poor. Nobody was building condos in the Sahara or the Kalahari deserts. Not yet.

But three thousand years ago the planet was not overpopulated. There was land enough for everybody. Was drought really bad enough to send tribes away from their home places and into land that belonged to others? Wasn't the history of the planet one of people taking over other people's lands? Didn't Jacob and his people take over the land of Canaan? The Romans and then the Saxons and then the Normans took over the British Isles, and then the British took over India, and if some of the American colonists wanted to live in peace with the Indians, others didn't. Others took over.

She sighed. There were no easy answers.

The pull of the pool had lessened. Polly nestled against her grandmother and went to sleep.

CHAPTER 8

POLLY slept late, and when she got up, both her grandmother and Hadron were gone. She hurried downstairs.

She had a stubborn determination to see this adventure through. All her senses were unusually alert. The smell of danger was in the air, and she had a strong feeling that, even if she wanted to, there was no way she could run away from whatever awaited her.

Could Tav really sacrifice her without Karralys's or Anaral's consent? They would never give it. They were the leaders of the tribe, and surely they would be listened to.

She sipped her coffee thoughtfully. Her grandparents came in from the pool. Her grandfather dressed and then came to the table with the morning paper. When her grandmother went out to the lab, bearing her cup of coffee, the dog came leaping in, jumped up, and greeted Polly and her grandfather. Then went to Hadron and licked the cat, who flicked his tail indifferently. Polly idly watched the big dog and the half-grown cat. Hadron had jumped to his feet and was thoroughly and diligently washing Og's face while the big dog sat patiently.

"Granddad, look."

He smiled at the two creatures. "Our animals have always been friends, but this is remarkable. I have a feeling we aren't going to be able to get rid of Og, and oddly enough, I don't want to. I wish I could hold on to the thought that he's only an ordinary stray." He picked up a ballpoint pen and began doing his crossword puzzle.

Dr. Louise arrived shortly after lunch. Clouds were scudding across the sky, and although it was warm in the sun, the wind was brisk.

"Where's Nase?" Mrs. Murry asked.

"I don't know where Nase is." Dr. Louise looked troubled. "He took off in hiking boots right after breakfast and said he'd meet me here."

"I think we have enough Ogam stones." Mrs. Murry glanced at the two on the dresser, which she still had not removed.

"I don't think he was looking for Ogam stones. He seemed unusually preoccupied. You know, Kate, it's really rather foolish, my coming here. I can't very well ask that young man to let me listen to his heart, and I'm not one for long-distance diagnoses. I need to know his history, talk to his doctor. But I, too, feel the need to protect Polly. I don't have office hours on Saturday, and I have only one patient in the hospital, and I promised Nason I'd meet him here."

"I'm glad you've come," Mrs. Murry said, and Polly echoed her.

"And I'm curious," Dr. Louise acknowledged. "I think all this is folly, but at the same time I'm curious." She laughed at herself, then glanced at Polly, who was finishing the luncheon dishes. Mr. Murry was out, chopping more wood, a never-ending task, and they could hear the rhythmic stroke of his axe. The dog was with him, and occasionally barked in sheer exuberance. "Nothing new, I hope, Polly."

"No. I just wish the bishop were here."

"Why?"

"I want to ask him about blood."

"What about blood?"

"Well, I know that blood is important in all cultures. And in lots of Eastern religions women have to be set apart, away from everybody else, during their menstrual periods, because they're thought to be unclean."

"Maybe not unclean as you're thinking of it," the doctor said. "Remember, sanitary napkins and tampons are inventions of this century." Polly looked at her questioningly. "My grandmothers, and women before them, used old sheets, any old linens. Back in the Stone Age there weren't any cloths to use. Having women set apart during their periods was a simple sanitary measure, and a ritual that was often looked forward to, when women could be together and rest from the regular backbreaking work. It was a time of rejuvenation, of peace and prayer."

"I hadn't thought about that," Polly said. "I guess I took a lot for granted. But weren't men convinced that women were—I think I read somewhere—separated from God at that time?"

Dr. Louise smiled. "You will have to ask Nase about that. All I can tell you is that superstition has been around as long as human beings."

Polly still had a dish towel over one arm. "Okay. Yes. But what about blood sacrifice?"

"I suppose I think it's superstition," Dr. Louise said. "The earth doesn't need human blood in order to be fertile."

"But what about—what about—"

"What, Polly?" her grandmother urged.

"Well, Jesus. Aren't we supposed to believe that he had to shed his blood to save us?"

Dr. Louise shook her head decisively. "No, Polly, he didn't have to."

"Then—"

"Suppose one of your siblings was in an accident and lost a great deal of blood and needed a transfusion, and suppose your blood was the right type. Wouldn't you want to offer it?"

"Well, sure . . ."

"But you'd do it for love, not because you had to, wouldn't you?"

"Well, yes, of course, but . . ."

"I'm a doctor, Polly, not a theologian, and lots of Christian dogma seems to me no more than barnacles encrusting a great rock. I don't think that God demanded that Jesus shed blood unwillingly. With anguish, yes, but with love. Whatever we give, we have to give *out of love*. That, I believe, is the nature of God."

"Okay," Polly said. "Okay. That's good. I don't quite understand it, but it makes some kind of sense." She looked at Dr. Louise and thought that she must be a good doctor, someone you could truly trust with your life.

"Polly," her grandmother said, "why these specific questions?"

"Oh—well—Tav does seem to believe in some kind of blood sacrifice."

"Tav lived three thousand years ago," her grandmother reminded her. "He didn't know what was going to happen a thousand years later."

There was the sound of a car outside on the lane, and the toot of a horn. Ogam barked, telling them about it, tail swishing back and forth, ready to greet the guest.

Mrs. Murry patted his head, "Thanks, Og," and turned toward the door. "Must be Zachary."

"Bring him in," Dr. Louise suggested, "and we'll give him a cup of tea."

Once again Zachary had parked his car on the lane. He kissed Polly in greeting, then said, "Thanks for letting me come. It means a lot to me."

"It's good to see you. Come on in and say hello."

"Who's here?"

"My grandparents—though Granddad's working outdoors. And Grand's friend Dr. Louise. You met her."

"Yes. Nice. A bit formidable maybe, but nice. What kind of doctor is she?" They went in through the garage.

"An internist. But, she says, she's basically a country doctor, and they're almost a lost breed. Endangered, at any rate."

They passed Mrs. Murry's lab and climbed the three steps to the kitchen just as the kettle began to sing. Mrs. Murry went to the wood stove. "Hello, Zachary. Will you join us for a cup of tea?"

"Thanks. Tea would be fine. Hello, Dr. Colubra. Nice to see you again." Zachary shook hands courteously, then sat at the table.

Mrs. Murry poured tea. "Sugar? Lemon? Milk?"

"Just as it comes, please."

She handed him a cup. "It's another superb autumn day. Do you and Polly have plans?"

Zachary was wearing jeans and a bulky Irish-knit sweater, and new-looking running shoes. "I thought we might go for a walk."

"Oh, good. If you drive to the ski area, there are several excellent walking trails."

"Polly says there are good places to walk right around here."

"There are, but . . ."

—Now what? Polly thought. —How are they going to keep us away from here?

Mrs. Murry was busy adding more water to the teapot. "I gather there's a good movie on in town if you're interested. It's only half an hour's drive."

"No, thanks," Zachary said. "I can go to a movie anytime, and what I really want to do is just amble around and talk with Polly."

Polly perched on the stool by the kitchen counter, where her grandmother sat to chop vegetables, and waited. She knew she ought to say something, make some reasonable suggestion, but her mind was blank. How could she explain her trips to Anaral's time? Zachary had no idea that the girl he had seen was from the past, and if Polly cared anything about him, she would see to it that he didn't get drawn further in.

"Zachary," Mrs. Murry said, "I'm simply going to have to ask you to take Polly somewhere else for your walk. As I said, there are some good hiking trails near the ski area."

Zachary put down his cup. "That was excellent tea. Mrs. Murry, is something peculiar going on? Does it have something to do with that guy with the dog or the girl I saw the other day that Polly was so mysterious about?"

"Anaral? In a way, yes."

"I don't mean to push, but could you explain?"

Dr. Louise stood up, took her cup to the sink, rinsed it, and put it in the rack. "All right, Zachary. You would like an explanation?"

"Yes. Please."

"My brother, who is a retired bishop, has accidentally opened a time gate between the present and three thousand years ago, when there were druids living with the native people of this land." Her voice was calm, without emphasis. "The girl you saw on Thursday is a druid and belongs to that time. Her people are largely peaceable, but one of the Celts who came here from Britain believes that the Earth Mother needs human blood to stop the drought which is driving other tribes to this part of the world, tribes which are not peaceable."

Zachary stared at her and burst into laughter. "You're kidding!"

"Would that I were."

"But that's—"

"Crazy?" Dr. Louise smiled.

"Out of sight."

Dr. Louise continued, again in a cool, academic way. "It seems that there is at least one person back in that long-gone time who feels that Polly would be just the right human sacrifice. Naturally, we are not eager for Polly to be drawn through the time gate and into danger."

There was what seemed to Polly a very long silence. Then Zachary said, "This is absolutely the most off-the-wall—"

Mrs. Murry said, "You did see Anaral."

"I saw a beautiful girl."

"Describe her."

"She had a long black braid. And honey-colored skin, and eyes that weren't quite slanty, just—"

"A little exotic?" Dr. Louise suggested.

"Definitely. I'd like to see her again."

"Even if it means going back three thousand years?"

"That's an extraordinary suggestion," Zachary said, "especially coming from a—a—"

"A physician. Who totally rejects everything she's said, and yet on another level has to admit the possibility."

"Why? It's impossible."

"A lot of things my forebears would have considered impossible, such as television, or astronauts, or much of modern medicine, are now taken for granted."

"Still—"

"Polly has been through the time gate. So has my brother. My brother may be eccentric, but he's no fool."

Mrs. Murry's voice, too, was quiet. "We don't want Polly in any kind of danger, real or imaginary. Perhaps the imaginary danger is the most frightening because it is the least understood."

Zachary looked at Polly, raising his brows at the story he was expected to take seriously.

Polly said, "Well, I know it sounds crazy, but there it is."

"In which case," Zachary touched her arm lightly, "I'd still like to go for that walk with you. I gather this time gate is somewhere on your land?"

"Yes. By the star-watching rock, where we were the other day. But also by the swimming pool. That's where you saw Anaral."

"A swimming pool hardly seems the likeliest place for a time gate, or whatever you call it." He sounded slightly dazed.

"The pool is over an underground river, and three thousand years ago there wasn't a pool, and there wasn't the house. It was a great circle of standing stones."

"If I didn't know you're an intelligent person, I mean highly intelligent—do you believe all this?"

"I've been there. Then."

"So—I can't just wipe it out, can I?" Suddenly he laughed. "I'm intrigued. Really intrigued. You think the girl I saw actually lived three thousand years ago?"

"Yes," Polly said.

"Mrs. Murry? Dr. Colubra?"

"It appears to be a possibility," Mrs. Murry said.

"Who knows, then?" He sounded suddenly wistful. He looked at Mrs. Murry and Dr. Louise. "Polly may have told you I'm having some problems with my health."

"She told us that your heart is troubling you," Mrs. Murry said.

"And my life expectancy isn't good. If I'm to take all you've been saying seriously, maybe it would be a good idea for me to drop back three thousand years."

"Not with Polly." Mrs. Murry was firm.

"Zach—" Polly was tentative. "Would you let Dr. Louise examine you—listen to your heart?"

"Sure," Zachary said. "But I don't think you"—he turned courteously to Dr. Louise—"can find much beyond a murmur and some irregularity."

"Probably not," Dr. Louise agreed. "I have my stethoscope with me, but that's all. Shall we go into the other room?"

Zachary followed her out, and Polly turned to her grand-mother. "He's right, I guess. I mean, she can't find out much just this way, can she?"

"I doubt it. But Louise has a sixth sense when it comes to diagnosis. Polly, can't you suggest to Zachary that you go to the club, or hike by the ski trails?"

"I can suggest," Polly agreed, "but I don't think Zach's up to much in the way of hiking."

When Dr. Louise and Zachary came back, the doctor's face was noncommittal. "Zachary obviously has excellent doctors," she said, "who are doing everything I'd recommend. Now, my dears, I need to make a move-on. What are your plans?"

"We could amble along the lane toward the village," Polly suggested.

"Ambling is fine with me," Zachary said. Then, to Dr. Louise, "Thank you very much, Doctor. You're very kind." And to Mrs. Murry: "Would it be possible for us to have tea and some of that marvelous cinnamon toast when we get back?"

"Quite possible. Polly, just walk on the lane and the road to the village, please."

"Yes, Grand." She and Zachary went out through the pantry and Polly took the red anorak off the hook. "Are you warm enough?" she asked.

"Sure. This sweater is warm enough for the Arctic. Polly, I wish your doctor friend had been able to give me some good news. She didn't say anything."

"Well—as you said—she didn't have anything except her stethoscope."

"Polly, do you believe in angels?" He turned to follow her as she started down the dirt lane.

"I don't know. Probably." —But not, she thought, that they're fairies with magic wands who can hold back bullets or make new a maimed heart.

"I wish my grandmother were still alive—the one who was willing to let me be me, and didn't load all kinds of expecta-tions on me. I've gone along with the expectations. I could follow in Pop's footsteps if I had a life expectancy in which to do it. Now I'm not sure that's what I want. Maybe there's more to life." He turned as there was a sound behind them and Og dashed to Polly, waving his tail, jumping up in joy.

"Down, Og," she said severely, and the dog obediently dropped to all four feet.

"Hey!" Zachary stared at Og. "Where'd that dog come from? I mean, haven't I seen him before?"

"Yes." Polly looked directly at him. "Remember that man you saw under the oak tree the day you came looking for me?"

"Yeah. He had a dog."

"This dog." Polly tried to keep her voice as dry and emotionless as Dr. Louise's.

"So how come he's here, obviously thinking he belongs to you?"

"Well. He just sort of appeared."

"What do you mean?"

"What I said. That's how my grandparents always get their dogs."

"Crazy." Zachary shrugged.

"Maybe," Polly said. "The thing is, he's come through the time gate, too."

Zachary sighed exaggeratedly, then looked again at Og, who stood by Polly, long tail moving gently back and forth. "Dogs going through time gates? That's as nuts as anything else."

"Yes," Polly agreed.

"He's sort of odd-looking. Reminds me of some of the dogs on the Egyptian friezes. Well, if he's three thousand years old, that would explain it all, wouldn't it?" He laughed, a short, unamused sound. "Does he have a name?"

"We're calling him Og, mostly. It's short for Ogam."

"It suits him, somehow." Zachary plucked a blade of grass and chewed on it. "Polly, this dog—it's just another sign. I want to go back to that place—the star-watching rock—and that oak tree—and the stone wall where I met you."

"I can't go there, Zach. I promised." Og nudged his head under her hand, and she scratched between his ears.

"I just have this strong feeling that if we go there, there will be things I need to find out."

"I don't think so, Zach. There are things to find out just walking along here. This is a beautiful place." She paused to watch a small stream, not more than a trickle, sliding under some water willows.

Suddenly fierce, he said, "I don't give a bloody zug if it's beautiful. What I want to know is if there's some way I can live a little longer. I don't think that's likely here, in this time. I don't like the way your doctor friend very carefully didn't say anything. But I saw her face. I saw the look in her eyes."

"You're projecting," Polly said firmly. "She didn't say anything because she didn't have enough to go on."

Just past the small stream there was a faint path to their left, probably made by wildlife. "Let's go this way," Zachary said.

"It doesn't go anywhere. It'll just end up in underbrush." Polly didn't remember having seen the small path before, but it ran roughly parallel to the orchard and the field that led to the stone wall.

"Polly." Now Zachary's voice was soft. She followed him along the path in order to hear, Og at her heels. "I want to see what all this Ogam stuff is about. If somehow I could go back three thousand years, what would happen? Would I be the same me? Or would my heart be okay?"

"I don't know." Polly watched Zachary push through browning blackberry brambles. Then the path widened out slightly and wound between grassy hummocks and across the ubiquitous glacial rocks.

"Am I right?" Zachary asked. "Is this path going toward the star-watching rock?"

"I've never been on it before. I don't think it goes anywhere."

He reached back and caught her hand. "Polly. Please. I need you to help me."

"This isn't going to help. Come on. Let's go home." She tried to release her hand.

"Polly. Please. Please. Don't pull against me. I need you to help me. Please."

Og had run on ahead of them, and circled back, tail swishing happily.

"See, the dog thinks everything's okay," Zachary said.

Now the path went under some wild apple trees and they had to bend low. Then it opened up and joined the path at the stone wall. Louise the Larger was lying there in the sunlight, but they were on the far side of the stone wall and Zachary hurried away from her, along the path to the star-watching rock.

"No, Zach, come back!"

Louise raised her head and several inches of body and began weaving back and forth.

"No, Zach!" Polly repeated. "Zach! Come back!"

But he was continuing along the path, calling, "Polly! Please! Don't desert me now!"

Og pushed against her, growling slightly, but she could not let Zachary go alone. Stumbling a little, she ran after him. "Zachary, this is foolish. Nothing's going to happen."

"Okay, so if nothing happens, we'll just go back for tea." He stopped, breathing rapidly and with effort. His face was very pale, bluish around the lips. He reached out his hand for hers, and she took it.

Under their feet the ground seemed to tremble. There was a faint rumble, as of distant thunder. The air about them quivered with concealed lightning.

"Hey! Polly!" Zachary's voice soared with surprise.

The trunks of the trees thickened, the branches reached upwards. Ahead of them, sunlight glinted off water.

"Well," she said flatly, "it's happened."

"What's happened?"

"We've gone through the time gate. Look at the trees. They're much older and bigger. And that's a lake that fills the whole valley. And look at the mountains. They're younger and wilder and there's still lots of snow on their peaks. I guess in geological terms the Ice Age wasn't so long ago."

Zachary stared around at the primeval forest, the jagged mountains. "Maybe I've had a heart attack and died?"

"No, Zach."

"In which case," he continued, "you'd have to be dead, too."

"No, Zachary. We aren't dead. We're three thousand years ago."

"So in our time we'd be dead, wouldn't we?"

"We're alive. Right now."

"I don't feel any different." He breathed in, deeply, disap-
pointedly. "Hey, and the dog's still with us."

Polly put her hand on his arm as she saw Anaral running
toward them.

"Poll-ee! Go back! It is not safe!" She looked suddenly at
Zachary, her hand to her mouth. "Who—"

"Zachary Gray. He saw you the other day. I guess you saw
him, too."

Zachary stared at Anaral. "Who are you?"

Anaral's eyes were veiled. Polly answered, "She's a druid."

"Holy zug."

"Go back, both of you. It's not safe."

"What's not safe?" Zachary demanded.

"Last night there was a raid. Several of our best sheep and
cows were taken."

"What's that got to do—" Zachary started.

Anaral continued. "Tav is wild, and not only Tav. We are all
in danger. Raiders may return at any moment."

"Tav?" Polly asked.

"Tav is not the only one who is ready to fight for our
land. Karralys fears that there will be much blood shed. You
understand?"

"No," Zachary said.

Polly still could not conceive of having fun with someone
you were planning to sacrifice.

Anaral looked at her. "You understood what was being
said—" She paused, looking for words. Continued, "—around
the council table?"

"Most of it, I think."

"What did you understand, please?"

"I think—I think Tav believes that the Mother—Mother
Earth?"

"Yes."

"That she demands a blood sacrifice, and that I have been
sent—" Her skin prickled. "Do you and Karralys—?"

"No. Not us. For us, the Mother is loving and kind. Karralys,
too, believes that you have been sent."

"Sent?"

"Not for the shedding of blood. Karralys lies on the great altar rock and prays, long, long, and he says the pattern is not yet clear."

"Hey, what are you talking about?" Zachary demanded.

"Well." Polly's face was stark. "Tav believes—perhaps—that the earth demands blood in order to be fertile, and that my blood . . ." Her voice trailed off.

Anaral said, "Karralys says that there is—is problem—across the great water where he and Tav come from. He says it used to be that the shedding of the blood of a lamb was—was—" She stopped.

"Enough?" Polly suggested. "Sufficient?"

"Yes, and the lamb was thanked, and mourned for, and then there was a great feast. But there came a time of no rain—you remember, Tav told—"

"Yes."

"The lamb's blood was not suff—"

"Sufficient."

"Sufficient. Rain did not fall. Crops died. People were hungry. And after Tav killed the man and his blood was spilled on the ground, rain came."

Zachary asked, "Do you think that was why the rain came?"

"No. We People of the Wind do not try to tell the Presence what to do, but to understand and use what is given, whether it seems good or bad. Some of my people think that there may be other gods across the water, gods who are angry and have to be—"

"Placated?" Zachary suggested.

Anaral looked at him questioningly.

Polly said, "The gods will be mad at you unless you give them what they want?"

"Yes."

Zachary scowled. "But you think your god loves you?"

Anaral smiled. "Oh, yes. We do not always understand our part in the working out of the pattern. And you see, it is possible for people to work against the pattern, to—to tangle the lines of love between stars and people and places. The pattern is as perfect as a spiderweb, and as delicate. And you"—her level gaze rested on Zachary—"we do not know where you fit in the pattern, which lines come to you, or which lines are from you, or where the lines that touch you touch us."

Og, who had been standing quietly by Polly, moved to Anaral, and she reached down and patted the dog's head. "Karralys has sent him to you. I am glad. Now go. Please go. To your own place in the spiral." She turned from them and ran swiftly away.

"Wow," Zachary said. "Let's go after her." He took a few hurried steps.

"No, Zach. Let's go home."

"Why?"

Polly was impatient. "You heard Anaral."

"Yes, and I'm fascinated. I want to know more."

"Zachary, it isn't safe."

"Surely you don't believe anybody is going to sacrifice you."

"I don't know what to believe. I know we should go home." She walked in the direction of the house, or what should be the direction of the house, but the trees continued to tower above them.

From behind one of the great oaks came a low whistle, and she froze. Og pressed against Polly's legs, ears up and alert, tail down and motionless.

"Poll-ee." It was Tav's voice. He appeared from behind the tree, and Og's tail began to wave. "You've come."

"Who's that?" Zachary was startled. "I can't understand a word he's saying."

"It's Tav," Polly said, "and he's speaking Ogam."

"I know that." Zachary sounded irritated. "It's much faster than when my boss tries it."

Polly turned back to Tav, and despite Anaral's warning, she was absurdly glad to see him. "He's a Celt, a warrior from ancient Britain." Og was pressed close against Polly, but he was not growling. His long rope of a tail was swishing back and forth.

Tav, holding his great spear firmly, pointed at Zachary. "Who?"

"His name is Zachary." Polly spoke slowly in Ogam, sounding out Zach-a-ry carefully. "He is from my time."

Tav raised his eyebrows. "Zak?"

"Zachary."

"But we do not need another one!" Tav's eyes were wide with surprise. "Why would the goddess send another one? I do not understand." The sun turned his pale hair to silver.

Zachary interrupted, "What's he saying?"

Behind them came the throb of drums, low, menacing. Og's tail dropped, and he began to growl, his hair bristling.

Tav listened. "There is danger. Go back. Do you know that we have had a raid and some of our best animals taken?"

"Yes," Polly said. "I'm sorry."

"Go home," Tav said. "Quickly."

"I'm not going back," Zachary muttered.

Tav ignored him. "Oh, my Poll-ee, there will be another raid. You must go. I do not understand why this one"—he looked at Zachary—"this Zak one, has been sent."

The sound of the drums grew louder, closer. Og barked.

Polly turned to Tav. "I don't know how to get him to go back."

Tav shook his spear. "Go, then, Poll-ee. Go."

But suddenly the beating of drums was upon them, was joined by shouting, screaming, closer, louder, and up the path from the direction of the lake burst a group of men wearing skins, with feathers in their dark hair. Two of them were dragging Anaral with them, and two of them held Bishop Colubra. Anaral was screaming, and the bishop was shouting, trying to free himself.

Into their midst leapt Tav with his great war spear, one man against a mob. Polly grabbed a branch from the ground and rushed after him. Og crouched low and then launched himself at one of the men who held Anaral. He let her go, clutching at his throat. But she was still held in the other warrior's arms. Polly hit at him with the branch, which was dry and broke off ineffectually. She began kicking, hitting, clawing, biting, whatever she could do to free Anaral. She must have seemed such an extraordinary apparition in her red anorak and with her flaming hair that she almost wrenched Anaral away from the warrior before he thrust her roughly to the ground.

"No!" Anaral screamed. "Go home, Poll-ee!"

The men were shouting, singing a high-pitched melody, each line ending with a shrill *"Hau!"*

Suddenly the bishop began to sing, too, his voice quavering but clear. *"Kyrie eleison! Christe eleison! Kyrie eleison!"*

There was a beat of silent surprise, then the clamor began again as the People of the Wind came running from all directions, carrying spears, clubs, bows and arrows, shouting as they rushed the raiders. The noise and confusion made Polly reel, but she continued her wild fighting.

Then, seemingly out of the blue, came Karralys, bearing a staff, trying to thrust it between the two groups. "Stop!" he was shouting. "Stop this madness!"

"You can't stop it!" Tav shouted back. "They have Anaral and the Heron!"

Polly was grabbed from behind and heaved up into the arms of one of the raiders. She grabbed at his hair, knocking his feathers askew. Og leaped to her defense, and was felled by the blow of a heavy club.

"Help!" Polly shrieked. "Help!" Then a hand slapped roughly against her mouth, and she bit at it. "Help!"

Now Karralys was thrusting with his great staff fiercely, and his young warriors were shouting, too, and there was nothing but chaos and terror.

Polly wrenched her head free of the man's hand. "Help!" she screamed again.

Then there was a strange hush, still as the eye of a hurricane. A harsh cry of terror. The raiders holding Anaral and the bishop let go abruptly, and to Polly's amazement they turned and ran away. She herself was dumped on the ground. She picked herself up and saw Louise the Larger slithering along the path, red tongue flickering.

As suddenly as it had begun, it was over.

The raiders were running away, bumping into each other in their fear.

The battle had been noisy and rough rather than lethal. The wounded were gathered together.

The raiders were in long, swift canoes, and were already well out into the lake, paddling fiercely.

Among the People of the Wind was a woman whose hair was white and who had a broken arrow still stuck in her shoulder. Karralys looked around and saw Polly. "Our Eagle Woman is hurt and cannot help with the wounded. Cub and I will have to have some assistance. What we need is a steady hand and head." He looked at her questioningly.

"Sure, I'll do what I can," Polly said. "I'm not afraid of blood." She looked around for Zachary but did not see him anywhere. Meanwhile, she was obviously needed. She turned to Karralys, who introduced her to a young man who had a grey-wolf skin over his shoulder, the young man who had been at the circle of standing stones on Halloween—Samhain.

"This is Cub, our young healer."

"I have not the experience of Karralys or the Old Wolf," the young man said. "I will be grateful for your help."

She did whatever Karralys and Cub told her to do when they took the arrow from Eagle Woman's shoulder, which had been broken from the impact. She clenched her teeth while they worked, and Polly kept wetting a soft piece of leather and wiping the sweat from her face. Then they moved on to set broken bones, stanch blood from a few wounds.

Mostly what was required of Polly was to hold a bowl of clean water and replenish it from the lake after each use. One of the raiders was laid out with a concussion, and Karralys had him stretched out on a bed of moss, covered with skins to keep him warm. Another had been left behind with a compound fracture of his leg, and Polly helped hold his head while Karralys and Cub set the leg. It was a bad break, and the young raider clutched her in pain. Cub gave him something to drink, telling him it would ease the pain, then poured a thick greenish liquid into the wound where the jagged bone had broken through the skin, explaining that this would help prevent infection.

When the leg was set and bound between two splints, the young raider was able to talk. Polly had difficulty in understanding him, and Karralys translated for her. "He says their crops have failed. There is no corn. Their grazing grounds are parched and the earth is dry and hard. They will not have enough to eat this winter. They will raid us again, with more men this time. They have no choice, he says. If they do not take our land and our crops and herds, they will starve."

"Couldn't they just come ask you to share with them?" Polly asked.

Karralys sighed. "That is not how it is done."

"Well." Polly sighed, too. "At least nobody was killed."

"This time," Karralys said. "Thank you for your help, Poll-ee." He glanced over at the white-haired woman, who was still among the wounded, her shoulder held immobile by a stiff leather sling. "Eagle Woman is our—" He paused, searching for the right word.

"Medicine woman?" Polly suggested. "Witch doctor? Shaman?"

Karralys shook his head. None of these words had any meaning for him. "From what the Heron tells me, I think she is something like what you call doctor, and that you have no one like Cub, who is healer. She has knowledge of herbs and the cure of fevers and chills, and helps Cub nurse the sick or hurt. But the wound in her shoulder will keep Eagle Woman from work for some time. The bone is shattered where the arrow penetrated. You have done well. You did not need to turn away. You have training in the care of wounds?"

Polly shook her head. "I come from a large family, and when we lived on Gaea—an island far away—where there weren't any doctors, when anybody was hurt or sick I helped my parents. Karralys, where is Zachary?" She had followed Zachary out of a sense of responsibility, and now she had no idea where he was.

"Zak?"

"He was with me, the one I told you about, who saw Anaral.

He was with me, and then when the fighting began, I forgot about him."

Karralys looked troubled. "He is here?"

"That's why *I'm* here," Polly said. "I tried to stop him—but then I couldn't let him come alone, so . . ."

"I do not understand why he is here," Karralys said.

"Neither do I."

"He is an unexpected complication. He may change the pattern."

"Karralys." Polly pondered the question. "If Zachary and I have come to your time, couldn't that change what happens in our time?"

"Yes," Karralys replied calmly. "The future is often changed by the past. There may indeed be many futures. But someone blundering into our time who is not part of the pattern may tangle and knot the lines."

"Unless," Polly questioned, "he is part of the pattern?"

"It is possible," Karralys said. "If it is so, then it will not be easy."

"But where is he?"

Anaral came up to them, hearing the question. "Zak? He is all right. He is with Bishop."

Polly then remembered that Dr. Louise had said her brother had gone off wearing hiking boots. Had he crossed the time threshold, knowing that he would be needed?

Anaral had brought a clean bowl of water so that Karralys and Polly could wash their hands. The druid looked at Polly gravely. "You were a very great help. You are brave."

"Oh, I didn't do anything much."

"Your hands have the gift," Karralys pronounced. "You should serve it. Now we must join the others at the standing stones. They will be waiting."

They sat on the stone chairs within the great ring of stones—Polly, Anaral, Karralys, Cub, Tav, Zachary, the bishop, and several others of the People of the Wind.

Polly still had a feeling of nightmare from the strange battle between two small armies, or bands of people—they could hardly be called armies. But if the skirmish had ended differently, Anaral could very well have been taken by the raiders.

And what about Bishop Colubra? What would have happened if the raiders had taken the bishop? How would that have affected the circles of time? She shook her head. What mattered right now was that she had helped Cub and Karralys with the wounded, and she had to understand that although this clash of two tribes was over, there was more danger to come.

She looked around at the circle of men and women, the leaders of the People of the Wind. Each one wore an animal skin or bird feathers or something representing a specific role in the affairs of the tribe. Eagle Woman was in her chair, her face white but composed, her arm held immobile by a leather sling and cushioned on a bed of moss and fern.

The bishop was sitting across from Polly, and beside him was Zachary, pale as alabaster. Karralys sat in his stone chair, looking unutterably weary. He wore the long white robe and the torque with the stone the same shade as the topaz in the bishop's ring. Og was lying beside him, bruised from the raider's blow, but, Karralys assured them, no bones were broken.

"The snake," Tav said. "How was it that the snake came to end the fighting?"

Karralys looked at Polly. "We have few snakes, and they are revered as gods. That you should have called a snake—you did call this snake?"

"No!" She was astonished. "I just shouted for help."

"But immediately the snake came."

"It had nothing to do with me," Polly protested. "Maybe she was just coming—on her way somewhere."

"A snake does not willingly come through lines of battle," Cub said. "You called, and she came."

Tav hit the butt of his spear against the hard ground. "The snake came for you before, at the wall, when I was first speaking with you. She is your friend, that is what you said."

As Polly started to protest, again Karralys raised his hand. "It must have seemed to the raiders that you called the snake, that you had special help from the goddess, and that you yourself had special powers."

"*Archaiai exousiai*," the bishop said.

It was Greek, Polly knew, something about powers. The bishop had called out the Kyrie. Could not Louise have come as much for that as for her own cry for help? Or was it not, most likely, coincidence that the snake had come along the path at just that moment?

"Principalities and powers," the bishop said. "It would have looked to the raiders as though you could call on the principalities and powers." He spoke gaspingly, as though he could scarcely breathe.

"Bishop!" Anaral's voice was sharp with anxiety. "Is something wrong?"

All attention was drawn to the bishop, who was breathing in painful gasps. The rapid fluttering of his heart could be seen through his plaid shirt.

Cub rose and went to the bishop. "Heron, our dear, it would please me if you would let me try to slow the beating of your heart. It is fast, even for a bird."

The bishop nodded. "Of course, Cub. It would be a great inconvenience to everybody if I died now, and it might produce a paradox that would distort the future."

Cub knelt beside the bishop, placing one hand under the plaid shirt, firmly against the bishop's chest.

Polly saw Zachary's eyes lighten with interest and hope.

Karralys watched Cub intently, nodding in approval.

Tav looked from Cub to Karralys, then to Zachary. Zachary had disappeared during the fighting, and it seemed to Polly that Tav was looking at him with scorn.

But instead of accusing Zachary he demanded, "Where did the snake go?"

"Louise the Larger," the bishop panted.

"Hush, Heron," Cub said, and pressed his palm more strongly against the old man's chest. Cub's own breathing was slow and rhythmic, and the pressure of his hand reinforced the rhythm.

"Where?" Tav repeated.

"Hey," Zachary said. "Translate for me, Polly."

"They're talking about the snake," Polly said. "Tav wants to know where she went."

Zachary said, "I saw her going along the path there, and probably she went three thousand years into the future."

"You—" Now Tav's voice was definitely accusing.

Zachary's fingers were white as he held the sides of the stone chair Karralys had assigned him. "You're talking much too fast for me to understand you, but if you want to know why I wasn't in that beer-parlor brawl with you, I wouldn't have been any help. I have a weak heart and I'd just have been in the way." He spoke with stiff pride.

Quickly Polly translated as best she could for Tav and the others.

Cub withdrew his hand from the bishop's chest. "There. That is better."

"Yes, my son," Bishop Colubra said. "I could feel my heart steadying under your hand. I thank you."

"Is he all right?" Anaral asked anxiously.

Cub nodded. "His heart is beating calmly and regularly now."

"I am fine," the bishop said. His breathing had steadied with his heart, and he spoke normally. "Now we must think what to do next."

"Please," Zachary said. "I saw that kid"—he indicated Cub—"steady the old man's heart. I saw it. Please. I want him to help my heart."

Polly spoke in Ogam to Cub.

"Yes. I will try. Not now. Later, when we are back at the tents," Cub assured her.

"He will try to help you," Polly translated for Zachary, "later."

"The snake," Tav insisted. "The snake who came for Poll-ee—"

"No—" Polly started to deny again.

But the bishop held up his hand. "Yes, Tav. We must not forget Polly's snake."

"But she's not—"

Karralys addressed the bishop. "Can you explain?"

"I'm not sure. You said that for you the snake is sacred?"

"We revere the snake," Karralys agreed.

"And the People Across the Lake? They ran from the snake."

"True." Karralys leaned on his elbow, his chin on his hand. "They did not retreat just because we fought well."

Tav said, "They thought that if Poll-ee could call the snake, then she could cause the snake to do them great harm. That is how I would feel." He looked at Polly and she remembered his first reaction to Louise.

She spoke directly to him, then turned to the others. "Louise—that is what we call her—is the first harmless snake I've ever met. Where I came from before I went to live with my grandparents, the snakes were mostly very poisonous."

The bishop said, "The Anula tribe of northern Australia associates a bird and a snake with rain."

Karralys shook his head. "The People Across the Lake have different traditions from ours, but as far as I know, they do not believe that snakes can bring rain. But neither they nor we would kill a snake."

Eagle Woman said, "The kindred of the snake would come and cause harm in vengeance. If we kill a snake because otherwise it would kill us, or by accident, we beg pardon of the snake's spirit."

Tav pointed his spear at Zachary, and all eyes turned in his direction.

"This is Zachary Gray," Polly said.

"He is from your time spiral?" Cub asked.

"He is the one who saw Anaral," Karralys explained, "because he is near death."

"What's he saying?" Zachary asked.

Polly was grateful that Zachary could not easily understand Ogam. No matter what he said about his heart and his brief life expectancy, she was certain he was not ready to hear anyone talking about his imminent death. She tried to make her face expressionless as she turned to him. "Karralys wants to know where you're from."

"California," Zachary said.

Tav stood. "Karralys, you fought well."

"I did not want to fight," Karralys said. "What I wanted to do was stop the fighting."

"They would have taken Anaral and Poll-ee, and the Heron, too."

"And so I fought. Yes, we fought well. But they were more than we, many more, and if the snake had not come—"

"Bless Louise the Larger," the bishop said.

Karralys's blue eyes brightened. "Is that not enough for you, Tav? That Polly was sent to us by the goddess for this?"

"I was so certain," Tav murmured. "But perhaps he—" He looked at Zachary.

"Hey!" Zachary's voice was urgent. "Slow down! I'm not quick with languages like Polly. What are they talking about?"

"Well—" Polly prevaricated. "We were outnumbered by the raiders—"

"We? Are you part of this 'we'?"

She looked around the circle of stone chairs protected by the great standing stones. "Yes." She was one with Anaral and Karralys and Tav and Cub and the others. And so was the bishop. He had proven that.

Tav looked at her hopefully, and the paleness of his eyes was not hard or metallic, like a sky whitened and glaring from too much sun, but tender and cool, like the lake. "You were right when you told me the snake was your friend. Perhaps I have been wrong about the Mother's needs."

"You are wrong, indeed." Karralys stood. "Bishop Heron. Polly, Zak. You must go. Now, while there is still time."

The bishop looked around. "I don't think we can."

"Why not?" Cub asked.

"I may be wrong, but I do not think the time gate is open."

Karralys looked startled. He went to the central flat altar stone and climbed up on it, then lay down on his back, arms outstretched, eyes closed. Motionless. Time seemed to hang suspended. No one spoke. The People of the Wind seemed to have moved into another dimension where it was possible for them to wait infinitely. The bishop sighed. Zachary restlessly shifted position. Polly tried not to move, but began to be afraid that her legs would cramp.

At last Karralys sat up, slowly shaking his head. "The threshold is closed."

CHAPTER 9

IT was getting dark. The sun slid down behind the standing stones. A northwest wind blew cuttingly.

"Perhaps we should go someplace warm and make our plans?" the bishop suggested.

Karralys raised a hand for attention. "There is a fire and a feast being prepared. We need to celebrate our victory—and then be sure that we have people keeping watch all through the night."

"And collect all our weapons." Tav moved away from his chair. "The feast, and our thanks to Poll-ee."

"It was only Louise the Larger," Polly insisted. "It had nothing to do with me."

"We will talk later about the time gate." Karralys started toward the lake and the tents.

Zachary shouted after him, "Wait!"

Karralys paused.

"I don't understand your time gates," Zachary said, "or how I could possibly be here, but I saw that kid in the wolf skin—"

"Cub. Our young Grey Wolf."

"I saw him calm the old man's heart."

"The bishop," Polly amended.

"Please. I don't want him to forget me."

Karralys looked at Zachary compassionately. "He will not forget you. Now. Come with me."

At the lake a great bonfire was blazing, so bright it almost dimmed the stars, which were coming out as night deepened. The wounded men and women were attended by other members of the tribe so that they would not be left out of the celebration, and the two raiders were there, too. The man with the concussion had regained consciousness, and Eagle Woman had been placed next to him. Despite her arm and shoulder held in the sling, and the fact that her lips were white with pain, she was watching him with care.

"The dark of his eyes is back to normal," she said. "He will be all right."

Polly, the bishop, and Zachary were given seats on skins piled near the star-watching rock. Near them was the young raider with the broken femur, and Anaral sat by him, helping him to eat and drink. Behind them, the oaks rose darkly and majestically, their great branches spreading across the sky, with stars twinkling through the branches as an occasional bronze leaf drifted down. Across the lake, the mountains loomed darkly, their snow-covered peaks just beginning to gleam as the moon prepared to rise. The shore where the People Across the Lake had their tents was invisible in the distance.

Karralys stood at the water's edge and raised his arms to the sky. "Bless the sky that holds the light and life of the sun and the promise of rain," he chanted, and one by one the other council members joined him, echoing his song.

"Bless the moon with her calm and her dreams. Bless the waters of the lake, and the earth that is strong under our feet. Bless those who have come to us from a far-off time. Bless the one who summoned the snake, and bless the snake who came to our aid. Bless the east where the sun rises and the west where it goes to rest. Bless the north from where the snows come, and the south that brings the spring. Bless the wind who gives us our name. O Blesser of all blessings, we thank you."

He turned from the lake and smiled at the people gathered around skins spread out on the ground. A deer was being roasted on a spit, and a group of young warriors danced around it, chanting.

"What're they singing about?" Zachary asked Polly.

"I think they're thanking it for giving them—us—its life."

"It didn't have much choice," Zachary pointed out.

Perhaps it didn't, but Polly felt a graciousness in the dance and in the singing.

"When's that kid going to feel my heart?"

"Soon," Polly assured him. "At the right time, Zachary, please trust him."

Bowls of vegetables were spread out, with fragrant breads, wooden and clay dishes of butter and cheese. Half a dozen girls and boys, long of limb and slim of body, nearing puberty, began passing food around. Two young warriors carved the deer, and an old woman, wearing a crown of feathers with an owl's head, poured some kind of pale liquid into small wooden bowls; she had been one of those in the stone circle.

Anaral brought bowls to Polly, Zachary, and Bishop Colubra. As he accepted his, Zachary tentatively touched Anaral's fingers, looking at her with eyes which seemed unusually dark in his pale face. Anaral withdrew her hand and returned to the young raider, holding his head so that he could drink. Polly noticed that on the stone altar there was a great bouquet of autumn flowers, set amidst squash, zucchini, eggplant, all the autumn colors arranged so that each seemed to brighten the others.

"It's crazy," Zachary muttered to Polly. "Here we're sitting and stuffing our faces as though we'd won some kind of great battle, and those goons who rowed off across the lake could come back any minute and slaughter us all."

The bishop replied, "I think Karralys is aware of their intentions, but he also knows that the human creature needs special celebrations. The rites themselves cannot give life. Indeed, they can be hollow and meaningless. The heart of the people is what gives them life or death."

"Is this all in honor of some god?" Zachary asked.

"It is a form of thanks to the Presence."

"What presence?"

The bishop spoke softly. "The Maker of the Universe."

"Oh, zug," Zachary grunted.

"Not necessarily." The bishop smiled slightly. "Sacred rites become zug, as you so graphically put it, only when they become ends in themselves, or divisive, or self-aggrandizing."

Polly saw a young man with a spear standing at the head of the star-watching rock, looking across the lake. A woman with a bow and arrow stood at the path which led to the standing stones. There were probably others on guard where they were not visible to her. Karralys was not leaving his people unprotected. He moved about, from group to group, greeting, praising, and wherever he went, Og went with him.

After the young people had cleared the food away, there was singing and dancing, and the moon rose high and clear, casting a path of light across the lake.

Karralys and Anaral led the dancing, at first moving in a stately and gracious circle, then dancing more and more swiftly.

"You know, that girl is beautiful," Zachary remarked. "Things haven't improved in three thousand years. By the way, I think that Neanderthal is interested in you."

"Who?" Polly asked blankly.

"That tow-headed guy with bow legs and monkey arms."

He meant Tav. Perhaps Tav's legs were not quite straight. Perhaps his strong arms were long. But he was no Neanderthal. Polly prickled with indignation but held her tongue. She was uncomfortable both with Zachary's obvious fascination with Anaral and with his jealousy of Tav's interest in her. She kept her voice quiet. "I don't think it's a very good idea for either of us to get involved with someone who's been dead for three thousand years."

"They're not dead tonight," Zachary said, "and neither are we. And if I can lengthen my life expectancy by staying here, then I'll stay. Anyhow, didn't the bishop say the time gate was closed? We're stuck here, so we might as well make the best of it."

Cub approached them, spoke to Zachary. "I would feel your heart. There is, I think, trouble there."

Zachary turned toward Polly. She explained. Zachary looked at her with anxious eyes. "Please, tell him to go ahead."

Cub slid his hand under Zachary's shirt, closed his eyes, breathed slowly, slowly.

"Well?" Zachary asked impatiently.

Cub raised his hand for silence. He kept his hand on Zachary's chest for a long time, feeling, listening. Then he raised his eyes to Polly's. "There is bad damage there. The Ancient Wolf might have been able to repair the hurt. I will do what I can, but it will not be enough."

"But the bishop's heart—"

"Bishop's heart is only old, and he is not used to being in

the middle of a battle. But this—" Slowly he removed his hand from Zachary's chest. "This demands skills I do not yet have. But perhaps we should not take hope away from him."

"What's he saying?" Zachary demanded. "I wish he'd slow down."

Polly replied carefully, "He says that your heart has damage, as you know, and that it will not be easy to fix."

"Can he fix it?"

"He will do his best."

Zachary moaned. Put his face in his hands. When he looked at Polly, his eyes were wet. "I want him to be able to fix—"

"He will do his best." Polly tried to sound reassuring, but she was getting impatient.

Cub said, "Each day I will work on the strangeness I feel within his heart. The rhythms are playing against each other. There is no harmony."

"What?" Zachary demanded.

"He will work with you every day," Polly said. "He really is a healer, Zachary. He will do everything he can."

Cub frowned with worry. "Perhaps if Karralys—" He looked at his hands, flexing the fingers. "Now I must go see to the others who have been hurt."

"What do you think?" There was renewed eagerness in Zachary's voice. "I'd be glad to stay in this place even with no showers or TV or sports cars or all the stuff I thought I was hooked on. I guess I'm more hooked on life."

"He's a healer," Polly repeated.

The drums were increasing their rhythms, and the dancers followed the beat. Tav came and took Polly's hands and drew her into the circle of dancers, and the touch of his strong hands did something to her that Zachary's did not, and she did not understand her reaction to this strange young man who thought she had been sent by the goddess as a sacrifice to the Mother.

Dr. Louise's words about sacrifice flicked across her mind and were wiped away as Tav took her hands and swept her into the circle of the dance.

When she was panting and almost out of breath, he took her to the edge of the lake, his arm tightly about her. "I cannot let you go."

Still caught up in the exhilaration of the dance, she asked, "What?"

"It is very strange, Poll-ee. The Mother is usually clear in her demands. But now I am confused. The drought across the lake is bad. If they do not get rain, not just a little rain, but much rain for those who have taken our cattle—if there is no rain, they will come again, and they are many, and we are few, and we will not be able to defend ourselves."

"But you were marvelous," Polly exclaimed. "You dashed in single-handed and you fought like—" If she likened him to one of the heroes of King Arthur's court, it would have no meaning for him. So she just repeated, "You were marvelous. Brave."

He shrugged. "I am a warrior. At least I was, at home. There had to be warriors. Here we have been so away from other tribes that only the drought has brought back an understanding that land must be protected. Land, and those we love." He reached out his hand and gently touched hers, then withdrew.

Polly sighed. "I wish people could live together in peace. There's so much land here. Why do they want yours?"

"Our land is green and beautiful. We have had more rain than across the lake. We use the water of our river to—" As he tried to explain, she understood that the People of the Wind used some form of irrigation which the People Across the Lake did not. Even so, there had not been enough rainfall. If the winter snows did not come, everybody would suffer. "When you came, it seemed clear to me that the goddess had sent you. But now there is not only the old Heron who came before you but this strange young man who is as white of skin as I am white of hair."

"Do you pray for rain?" Polly asked.

Tav laughed. "What else have we been dancing and singing about?"

Of course, she realized. All ritual for the People of the Wind was religious.

"To dance and sing is not enough," Tav continued. "We must give."

"Isn't your love enough?" The question sounded sentimental as she asked it, but as she looked at the moon sparkling off the lake, she understood dimly that the love she was thinking about was not sentimental at all but firm and hard as the star-watching rock.

Tav shook his head. His voice dropped so low that she could scarcely hear. "I do not know. I do not know anymore what is required." As his words fell into silence, the soft wind gently stirred the moonlit waters of the lake. He spoke again. "There are many women of the People of the Wind who are beautiful, who would like to please me, to be mine. But none has brought me that gift without which everything else is flat. That gift! Now I look at you and the mountains are higher, and the snow whiter on the peaks, the lake bluer and deeper, the stars more brilliant than I have ever seen them before."

Polly tried to put what she wanted to say into Ogam. Tav reached out his hand and smoothed out her frown. "Tav, it is very strange. I don't understand anything that is happening. When you touch me, I feel—"

"As I feel?"

"I don't know. What I feel has nothing to do with—" She touched her forehead, trying to explain that her reaction had nothing to do with reason. "But"—she looked at his eyes, which were silver in the moonlight—"you still think the Mother wants blood, my blood?"

Tav moaned. "Oh, my Poll-ee, I do not know."

"I don't think the Mother—" She stopped, unable to think of a word for "demand" or "coerce." —Nearer our time, she thought, —one name for the goddess was Sophia, Wisdom. A divine mother who looks out for creation with intelligence and purpose.

She shook her head, realizing that even if she could put what she was thinking into Ogam, it was not within Tav's frame of reference.

Tav took both her hands. "We must go back to the others, or they will wonder—"

She had hardly realized that the singing had changed. No longer were the drums sounding the beat of a dance. The song was similar to the one Polly had heard that first morning when she crossed the threshold to the People of the Wind, but now it was gentler, quieter, almost a lullaby.

"We sing good night." His arm about her, Tav returned her to where Bishop Colubra and Zachary were sitting. Anaral was behind them, with the young raider. The singing drifted off as, one by one or in pairs, people went to their tents.

Karralys came to the bishop, his long white robe pure as snow in the moonlight, the topaz in his torque gleaming. "It will be my honor if you will share my tent. And, Zak—"

"Zachary."

"And you, too, Zachary."

Anaral left her tending of the raider and took Polly's hand. "And you will come with me."

Anaral's tent was a lean-to of young saplings covered with cured skins. It backed against a thick green wall of fir and pine and smelled fresh and fragrant. There were two pallets of ferns covered with soft skins. Anaral handed Polly a rolled-up blanket of delicate fur. Polly took off her red anorak and sat down on one of the fern beds.

Anaral squatted beside her. "Tav is, well, Poll-ee, you must know he is drawn to you."

Polly wrapped the fur blanket around her. "And I to him, and I don't understand how I could be."

Anaral smiled. "Such things are not understood. They happen. Later, if two people are to be together for always, then understanding comes."

"Is there going to be a later?" Polly asked. "I know the threshold is not open now, but I—I do need to get home to my own time. Before"—she could hardly bring herself to articulate it—"before I have to be sacrificed to the Mother."

"That will not happen," Anaral protested. "There will be rain."

"Across the lake?"

"Across the lake."

Polly said, "If it hadn't been for Tav this afternoon when the raiders came—"

"And the others."

"But Tav leapt in and fought when he didn't know if the others were coming. And it was, oh, in a strange way it was exciting."

"You were a warrior, too," Anaral said.

"I just wasn't going to let those strange men carry you off."

Anaral sighed. "And I am grateful. To Tav. To you. And Karralys."

"He tried to stop the fighting," Polly said. "But when he couldn't, he fought as well as Tav did."

"We People of the Wind"—Anaral sighed again—"we have always been what the bishop calls paci—paci—"

"Pacifists," Polly supplied.

Anaral nodded. "It is the drought that has changed things. If it would only rain! The Old Grey Wolf told us that there was drought many years ago and that we—my people—came here to this fertile place because our own grounds were parched, the grasses brown instead of green, the cattle with their bones showing, the corn not even making its tassels. We have been in this place since the Old Wolf was a baby. We cannot just leave and let the People Across the Lake take our home. Where would we go? Beyond the forest there are now other tribes. If only the goddess would send rain!"

"Do you think the goddess is withholding rain?" Polly asked.

Anaral shook her head. "It is not in the goddess's nature to destroy. She sends blessings. It is us, it is people who are destructive." She left the tent abruptly.

In a few minutes she returned with a wooden bowl full of water, and a soft piece of leather for a washcloth. She wet the leather and gently washed Polly's face, and then her hands, and it was as much a ritual as the banquet and the singing and dancing had been. She handed the bowl to Polly, who understood that she in her turn was to wash Anaral. When Anaral took the bowl out to empty it, Polly felt as clean as though she had just taken a long bath. She lay down on the fern bed, wrapped in the soft fur blanket, and slid into sleep.

When she woke up, she thought at first that she was at home with her grandparents. But there was no Hadron sleeping beside her. She reached out her hand and touched hair, not the fur of the blanket, but living hair, and Og's moist nose nuzzled into her hand, his warm tongue licked her fingers. She was comforted and lay listening to the night. The quiet was different from the quiet of her own time, where the soughing of the wind in the trees was sometimes broken by the distant roar of a plane going by overhead, by a truck on the road a mile downhill from the house. Here the lake covered the place where the road was, and she could hear small splashings as an occasional fish surfaced. There was also a sense of many presences, that the People of the Wind surrounded her. Her eyes adjusted to the dark and she could see Anaral's curled-up form on the other pallet, hear her soft breathing.

Polly sat up carefully. It was cold, so she put on the red anorak and crept out into the first faint light of dawn, Og following her. Stars still shone overhead, but the moon had long since gone to rest, and there was a faint lemon-colored streak of light on the horizon far across the lake. She saw someone sitting on a tree trunk, facing the lake, and she recognized Bishop Colubra by his plaid shirt. Quietly she walked to him.

"Bishop—"

He turned and saw her, and invited her with a motion to sit beside him.

"The time gate—"

He shook his head. "It is still closed."

"Yesterday, when Dr. Louise came over, she said you'd gone off in hiking boots—"

He looked down at his feet in laced-up leather boots. "I thought I'd better be prepared."

"You mean you knew—"

"No. I didn't know. I just suspected that something might happen, and if you came to this time and place and couldn't get back, I wanted to be here with you."

"Are we going to be able to get home? To our own time?"

"Oh, I think it's highly likely," the bishop said.

"But you aren't sure?"

"My dear, I'm seldom sure of anything. Life at best is a precarious business, and we aren't told that difficult or painful things won't happen, just that it matters. It matters not just to us but to the entire universe."

Polly thought of the bishop's wife, of Dr. Louise's family. She did not know that Karralys was there with them at the lakeside until he said, "Zachary is not in the tent."

Karralys stood with his back to the lake, looking down at Polly and Bishop Colubra. "I do not wish to raise an alarm. You have not seen him? He has not spoken to you?"

"No," both the bishop and Polly replied.

"I had hoped he might be with you. Wait here, please. I will check the other tents. If Zachary should come to you, please keep him here till I return." He turned away from them, walking rapidly. Og looked at Polly, licked her hand, then took off after Karralys.

"Bishop," Polly said softly, "Zachary is terrified of dying."

"Yes." The bishop nodded.

"And he thinks his best hope is here, in this time. So I don't think he'd go off anywhere. He tries to be so glib about everything, but he's frightened."

The bishop's voice was compassionate. "Poor young man, with his house slipping and sliding on sand."

Polly said, "If it was my heart, and I was told I had only a year or so to live, I'd be afraid, too."

"Of course, my dear. The unknown is always frightening, no matter how much we trust in the purposes of love. And I do not think that Zachary has that trust. So the dark must seem very dark to him indeed."

"It can seem pretty dark to me, too," Polly admitted.

"To all of us. But to you, and to me, there is the blessing of hope. Isn't there?"

"Yes. Though I'm not exactly sure what my hope is."

"That's all right. You've lived well in your short life."

"Not always. I've been judgmental and unforgiving."

"But on the whole you've lived life lovingly and fully. And I suspect that much of Zachary's life has been an avoidance of life. Now *I'm* sounding judgmental, aren't I?"

Polly laughed. "Yes, well. Being judgmental has always been a problem for me. And Zachary's the kind of person who just seems to get judged. If he weren't so sort of spectacular, people probably wouldn't care."

They looked up as Karralys returned, his face grave. "I cannot find him. And the raider is gone, too, the one whose head was nearly broken. Brown Earth, he is called. His pallet was by Eagle Woman's, but Cub gave her a potion to ease her pain and she is still asleep."

The bishop asked, "You think Zachary and the raider went off together?"

"It is possible the raider took him as hostage," Karralys suggested.

"But how would they get away? You had watches posted at all points."

Karralys sat down beside Polly on the fallen log. "Those across the lake move as silently as we do. Brown Earth could have gone into the forest and come out to the lake from another direction. There are many miles of shoreline."

"But the raider couldn't have taken Zachary if he was unwilling," Polly objected. "Wouldn't he have yelled and made a noise?"

Karralys appeared to be studying a bird who was flying low over the lake. "We went through the raider's clothes. We took away his knife. He had no arrow, no poison to make Zachary helpless." Suddenly the bird swooped down and flew off into the sky with a fish.

"But why would Zachary have gone with him?" Polly was incredulous. "Karralys, he thought his hope for life was here, that Cub could help his heart. He wouldn't just have gone off."

"No one knows what that young man would or would not do," Karralys said. "Is he not—"

"Unpredictable," the bishop supplied.

"Well, yes," Polly agreed, "but this doesn't seem reasonable."

"Many things that people do are unreasonable," the bishop pointed out. "Now what should we do?"

The lake was bathed in a radiant light as the sun rose, and with the sun the rich singing of the morning song. "I will ask the others," Karralys said. "Then we shall see."

Karralys went around the compound asking people singly, in pairs, in small groups, Og at his heels, whining a little, anxiously. There was consternation over the disappearance of the raider, more than over Zachary.

Eagle Woman berated herself. "I should have heard him. Normally, my ears are tuned—"

"Normally, you do not have a shoulder that has been pierced by an arrow," Karralys said.

"And the young man—where can he be? Cub told me his heart sounded like a dry leaf in the wind."

"We will call council at the great stones," Karralys said. "Meanwhile, we must get on with the day's work. We will continue to keep watchers posted to look out for canoes, or perhaps an attack from the forest."

Polly and the bishop were asked to join the group in the circle within the ring of standing stones.

"If they think they can use this Zak—" Tav started.

"Zachary."

"—as a hostage, they are wrong. He is worth nothing to us."

"He is our guest," Karralys said quietly. "Under our hospitality."

"I do not understand why he came," Tav said. "I fear that he will bring us grief."

"We are still responsible for him."

Cub turned to Karralys anxiously. "If they treat him roughly, I do not think his heart will stand it."

"That bad?" Eagle Woman asked.

Cub looked at her soberly.

"Then," Tav deliberated, "it was just as well he did not fight yesterday?"

"It might have killed him," Cub said.

"He is young for his heart to be so feeble," a man wearing a red-fox skin protested.

"Perhaps he had the child fever with the swollen joints that weakens the heart," Cub suggested.

—Rheumatic fever, Polly thought. —Yes, that sounded likely.

"Enough," Tav said. "What are we going to do? Why did the raider take him? Of what use can he be—except as a hostage?"

"If it is as a hostage," Karralys said, "we will hear from them, and soon."

There seemed nothing more to discuss. Karralys dismissed the council, doubled the watch. Polly helped Anaral make bread in an oven made of hot stones. She looked around for Og but did not see him. He must be with Karralys, she thought.

"This goddess," Polly mused, "and the Mother. Are they one and the same?"

Anaral punched down the risen dough. "To me, and to Karralys, yes. To those who are not druids—Tav, for instance—the goddess is the moon, and the Mother is the earth. For some, it is easier to think of separate gods and goddesses in the wind, in the oaks, in the water. But for me, it is all One Presence, with many aspects, even as you and I have many aspects, but we are one." She placed the bread in the stone oven. "It will be ready when we return."

"Where are we going?" Polly asked.

"To the standing stones. In that place is the strongest energy. That is why council is always held there."

The standing stones. Where, three thousand years in the future, Polly's grandparents' house would be, and the pool which could not be dug as deeply as planned because there was an underground river.

"Below the place of the standing stones"—Polly followed Anaral away from the tents and the lake—"there is water?"

"A river. It runs underground and then comes up out of the earth where it flows into the lake. But its source is beneath the standing stones."

"How do you know?"

"It is the old knowledge."

"Whose old knowledge?"

"The knowledge of the People of the Wind. But Tav would not take my word for it, so I gave him a wand of green wood and told him to hold it straight in front of him, and not to let it touch the ground, and then I asked him to follow me. He thought I was—what does Bishop call it? Oh, yes, primitive. But he followed me, laughing, and holding the wand. And when we got to the standing stones, he could not keep it still, he could not keep it off the ground. It leaped in his hands like a live thing. Then he knew I told true."

When they got to the standing stones there was someone lying on the altar. With a low cry, Anaral hurried forward, then drew back. "It is Bishop talking with the Presence."

While Polly watched, the bishop slowly pushed himself into a sitting position and smiled at her and Anaral. Then he returned his stare to some far distance. "*But, Lord, I make my prayer to you in an acceptable time,*" he whispered. "The words of the psalmist. How did he know that the time was acceptable? How do we know? An acceptable time, now, for God's now is equally three thousand years in the future and three thousand years in the past."

"We are sorry," Anaral apologized. "We did not mean to disturb your prayers."

The bishop held out his hands, palms up. "I have tried to listen, to understand."

"Who are you trying to listen to?" Polly asked.

"Christ," the bishop said simply.

"But, Bishop, this is a thousand years before—"

The bishop smiled gently. "There's an ancient Christmas hymn I particularly love. Do you know it? *Of the Father's love begotten*—"

"*E'er the worlds began to be.*" Polly said the second line.

"*He is alpha and omega, He the source, the ending*—" the bishop continued. "The Second Person of the Trinity always was, always is, always will be, and I can listen to Christ now, three thousand years ago, as well as in my own time, though in my own time I have the added blessing of knowing that Christ, the alpha and omega, the source, visited this little planet. We are that much loved. But nowhere, at any time or in any place, are we deprived of the source. Oh, dear, I'm preaching again."

"That's okay," Polly said. "It helps."

"You've had good training," the bishop said. "I can see that you understand."

"At least a little."

He slid down from the great altar stone. "Zachary," he said. "Do you think he's all right?"

"That I have no way of knowing. But whatever all this is about, our moving across the threshold of time in this extraordinary way has something to do with Zachary."

"How could it?" Polly was incredulous.

"I don't know. I have been lying here contemplating, and suddenly I saw Zachary, not here, but in my spirit's eye, and I knew, at least for a flash I knew, that the true reason I had gone through the time gate was for Zachary."

Anaral dropped to the ground, sitting cross-legged. Polly leaned against one of the stone chairs. "For his heart?"

The bishop shook his head. "No, I think not. I can't explain it. Why go to all the trouble to bring us three thousand years in the past for the sake of Zachary? I don't find him particularly endearing."

"Well, he can be—"

The bishop continued, "But then I think of the people Jesus died for and they weren't particularly endearing, either. Yet He brought back to life a dead young man because his mother was wild with grief. He raised a little girl from the dead and told her parents to give her something to eat. He drove seven demons out of Mary of Magdala. Why those particular people? There were others probably more deserving. So, I ask myself, what is there that makes me think I have crossed three thousand years because of Zachary?"

Polly plunged her hands into the pocket of the red anorak. None of this made any sense. Zachary was peripheral to her world, not central. If she never saw Zachary again, her life basically would not be changed. Her fingers moved restlessly in the anorak pockets. She felt something hard under her left hand. Zachary's icon. She pulled the small rectangle out, looked at it. "I guess Zachary could use a guardian angel."

"A great angel and a small child." The bishop, too, looked at the icon. "The bright angels and the dark angels are fighting, and the earth is caught in the battle."

"Do you believe that?" Polly asked.

"Oh, yes."

"What does a dark angel look like?"

"Probably exactly like a bright angel. The darkness is inner, not outer. Well, my children, go on about whatever it is you need to do. I will stay here and wait."

"You are all right, Bishop?" Anaral asked.

"I am fine. My heart is beating steadily and quietly. But I probably should not fight in any more battles." He glanced at the sun, which was high in the sky, then clambered up onto the altar again and lay back down. The shadow of one of the great stones protected his eyes from the glare.

Polly followed Anaral back to the compound.

There was an unease to the day. The normal routines were carried on. Fish were caught. Herbs were hung out to dry. Several women, each wearing the bright feathers of her bird—a finch, a lark, a cardinal—were making a cloak of bird feathers.

Cub called to Polly, "I may need your help."

Polly had forgotten the second raider, the very young man with the compound fracture, whom Anaral had tended so gently the night before. Now he was lying under the shade of a lean-to. His cheeks were flushed and it was apparent that he had some fever. Cub squatted down beside him. "Here," he said, "I have some of Eagle Woman's medicine to help take away the fever. It is made from the mold of bread and it will not taste pleasant, but you must take it."

"You are kind," the young raider said gratefully. "If you had been wounded and taken prisoner by my tribe, we would not have cared for you in this way."

"*Could* you have cared for me?" Cub asked.

"Oh, yes, our healer is very great. But we do not waste his power on our prisoners."

"Is it a waste?" Cub held out an earthen bowl to the raider's lips and the lad swallowed obediently. "Now I must look at the leg. Please, Poll-ee, hold his hands."

Polly knelt by the raider. Anaral had followed her and knelt on his other side. Polly found it hard to understand him, but she got the gist of what he was saying in a language that was more primitive than Ogam. "What is your name?" She took his hands in hers.

"Klep," he said. At least, that is what it sounded like. "I was born at the time of the darkening of the sun, of night coming in the morning as my mother labored to bring me forth. Then, as I burst into the world, the light returned, slowly at first, and then, as I shouted, the sun was back and brilliant. It was a very great omen. I will, one day, be chief of my tribe, and I will do things differently. I, too, will take care of the wounded and not let them die." He gasped with pain, and Polly saw Cub bathing the broken and raw skin with some kind of solution. Anaral turned away while Polly held Klep's hands tight, and he grasped her so hard that it hurt. He grimaced against the pain, clenching his teeth to keep from crying out. Then he relaxed. Turned and looked at Anaral. "I'm sorry."

She smiled at him gently. "You are very brave."

"And you are doing well," Cub said. "I will not need to hurt you any more today."

Klep let out a long breath. "I hear that Brown Earth, my companion, is gone from you, and also one of yours. Or is he one of yours, with the pale skin and dark hair?"

"He is not one of ours," Cub said. "He comes from a far place."

Anaral asked eagerly, "Do you know where they are?"

Klep shook his head. "Not where they are, or how they left. Your medicine made me sleep like a child and I heard nothing."

Cub asked, "Do you think Brown Earth took Zak with him?"

"I do not know. Would this Zak want to go?"

"We don't know," Anaral said. "It is very strange."

"We don't understand," Polly said.

"If I knew anything," Klep assured them, "I would tell you. I am grateful. Brown Earth has a big mouth. It may be that he has made promises."

"Promises he can keep?" Cub asked.

"Who knows?"

"Rest now," Cub ordered. "Anaral will bring you food

and help you to eat. I will be back this afternoon to put fresh compresses on your leg."

They reported their conversation to Karralys.

"It solves nothing," he said, "but you have been helpful. And Klep may yet be helpful, who knows? Thank you. Eagle Woman sends her thanks to you, Polly. Cub will need you again when he dresses her shoulder. Anaral"—he smiled gently at the girl—"is a nourisher, but she cannot take the sight of blood."

"It is true," Anaral agreed. "When I cut my finger, I screamed. Poor Bishop. But I will be glad to help Klep eat."

"We are glad you are here, Polly," Karralys said. "And we wish you could return to your own time. You must wish that, too."

Polly shook her head. "Not until we find Zachary. And not until there is rain."

The attack came during the night. Og woke Polly, barking loudly. Anaral was up in a flash, spear in hand. Polly followed her. Torches cast a bloody glow over the fighting people, and at first Polly could not tell which were the People of the Wind and which were the raiders. Then she saw Og rushing to Karralys's aid, jumping on a raider who had a spear at Karralys's ribs. Og clamped the man's wrist in his jaws, and the spear fell.

Then Polly felt something dark flung over her, and she was picked up like a sack of potatoes. Her screaming mingled with the general shouting. She tried to kick, to wriggle free, but her captor held her tight as he ran with her. She could not tell in which direction they were going. She heard the snapping of twigs underfoot. Felt branches brushing by. Then at last she was put down and the covering removed from her head. They were on the beach, out of sight of the village. Trees reached almost to the lake's edge. The moon was high, and she gasped as she saw Zachary standing by a shallow canoe.

"Zach!"

"You brought her," Zachary said to her captor. "Good."

"Get in the canoe," Zachary said. His face was white and pinched in the moonlight, but his voice was sharp.

"What is this?" Polly demanded.

"It's all right, sweet Pol, really it is," Zachary reassured her. "I need you."

She drew back. "I'm not going anywhere."

Her captor's hands were around her elbows and she was propelled toward the canoe. He was not Brown Earth, the raider who had had the concussion, but an older man, muscled, heavy.

"He won't hurt you, as long as you don't make a fuss. I promise," Zachary said. "Please, Polly." He was cajoling. "Just come with me."

"Where?"

"Across the lake."

"To the people who are trying to take our land?" Her voice rose with incredulity.

"Our land?" Zachary asked. "What do you care about it? It's three thousand years ago. You don't know anything about the People Across the Lake. They aren't enemies."

"They attacked us."

He overrode her, speaking eagerly. "They have a healer, Polly, an old man, wise, and full of experience. Brown Earth saw Cub."

"Cub will help you."

Zachary shook his head. "He's too young. He doesn't know enough. The healer across the lake has power. He can make me better."

"Fine," Polly said. "Go to him. But leave me out of it."

"I can't, Polly love. I would if I could. But they want to see you."

"Me? Why?"

"Because you called the snake and it came. They think you're some kind of goddess."

"That's nonsense. Anyhow, how can you understand what they're saying?"

"If I can get them to speak slowly enough, I get the gist of things. I'm not good at Ogam like you, but I get enough. And sign language can be very effective," Zachary said. "How else do you think Brown Earth got me to go with him? Please, Polly, please. I don't want him to have to hurt you."

"You'd let him? I thought you cared about not hurting—ouch!" Her captor's hands tightened about her arms like a vise.

"Please, Polly, just come, and everything will be all right."

"Take your hands off me," Polly snapped. She opened her mouth to scream for help, but her captor silenced her with a rough hand. From the village she could hear sounds of shouting, so probably her cry would not be heard. Her captor shoved her toward the canoe. He was taller than she was, and full of brawn. To try to fight him was folly. At the moment it seemed the simplest thing to get into the canoe, to go with Zachary and the raider, to see what all this was about.

The raider pushed the bark off the narrow beach, grating it over the pebbles, then leapt in lightly, barely causing it to sway.

Zachary reached out to touch Polly's knee. "I'm sorry, Polly. You know I don't want to hurt you. You know that." His face was drawn and anxious. "They sent this goon with me because they were afraid I mightn't bring you. I'm the one they don't trust, not you. You'll be treated well, I promise you, just like a goddess. And that's what you are to me, even if I think of you as a goddess differently from the way they do."

She sighed gustily. "Zachary, when the fighting's over and I'm missing, they'll be frantic."

"Who will?"

"Karralys, and Anaral. The bishop, Tav. Cub. Everybody."

Her captor made two guttural sounds, which Polly interpreted as "Let's go." He pointed, and they could see several longer canoes moving swiftly across the lake.

The battle, then, was over, though Polly had no idea who had won, who had been hurt, or even killed. Swiftly she leapt into the water and sloshed toward shore, but her captor was after her and grabbed her before she could reach land.

"You have no right to take me against my will," she struggled to say.

He did not reply. He picked her up and carried her back to the canoe.

"Polly! Don't do that again!" Zachary sounded frantic.

Polly struggled to catch her breath, which had been nearly squeezed out of her by the strong arms of the raider.

"Polly, don't deny me my chance. Please. I know their healer can help me."

"But there's a price on it?"

"They just want me to bring you to them because they think you're a goddess."

Polly shook her head. "I'm no goddess. I didn't call Louise. She just happened to come. I don't have any magic powers." She held on to the side of the canoe as the raider paddled swiftly. "Does he have a name?"

Zachary laughed. "It sounds something like Onion, I think, but their language isn't pure Ogam. Lots of grunts and noises and arm waving. Polly, I'm sorry I had to get you this way, truly I am, but I didn't know how else. I need you. If you come with me, then their old healer will fix my heart."

—*Fix it*, she thought wearily. —He's used to having money fix everything. And not everything can be fixed.

Suddenly they were surrounded by other canoes, and paddles were held aloft triumphantly, and those without paddles raised their hands above their heads, clapping.

"See?" Zachary gave her his most charming smile. "See how happy they are to see you?"

Once ashore, she was greeted by an old man with a face full of fine wrinkles, like the lines of an etching. He held out his hands to Polly and helped her out of the canoe. "Poll-ee."

She nodded.

"Tynak," he said. "Tynak greets Poll-ee." He led her across the narrow beach and then over grass that crunched dryly under her feet. He took her to a lean-to, where there was a couch of ferns, similar to Anaral's fern beds. Tynak indicated that Polly was to sit, and he himself squatted back on his heels.

Speaking with Tynak, who had an authority that declared him to be the leader of the People Across the Lake, was not easy, but Polly managed to learn that the battle had been no more than a cover-up for her abduction. No one had been seriously wounded, no prisoners taken, other than Polly.

Zachary stood just outside the lean-to, and the old man summoned him in with a smile so faint that there was no joy in it, but rather a sense of solemnity.

"See, I've brought her, Tynak," Zachary said. "Now will the healer fix my heart?" He put his hand to his chest and looked eagerly at the chief.

Tynak embarked on a long, vehement speech which Polly could not follow. His language was mostly short, sharp syllables, and he was speaking quickly. She understood only isolated words: goddess, rain, anger. But nothing coherent fitted together.

She looked out at a land far drier and browner than that of the People of the Wind. What grass there was between beach and lean-to was brittle. The leaves of the trees drooped dryly, drifting listlessly to the ground. Over the lake the sky had a mustardy-yellow tinge at the horizon, staining the night. The air was so humid that the farther shore was not even visible. Only the mountains rose out of the murk. They were higher, looked at from this side of the lake, and their peaks held more snow. The melting of the additional snow might be what would help keep the land of the People of the Wind fertile and green. The moon shone hazily through drifting clouds.

Tynak rose and turned to Polly, indicating that she was to follow him. He was much shorter than she had realized when he met the canoe. His legs were short sticks under a skin tunic. But he moved with authority and dignity. She followed him across a compound of tents, many more than on her side of the lake. There were people moving about. Tynak spoke and what she understood was that in the daytime the sun was no longer gentle, but was hot and burning. He took her toward what should have been a cornfield of stalks that had been harvested and cut down but which, in the moonlight, were dark midgets, barely tasseled. Tynak spoke again, more slowly, and she thought he was telling her that his people were kind to the land, treated it with respect, but it had turned on them.

He looked at her with small, very dark eyes, and told her that without rain they would starve.

He led her back to the lean-to and showed her a rolled-up fur covering in the corner. Then he bowed to her and left, signaling to Zachary to come with him.

A few minutes later one of the young women of the tribe brought Polly a bowl of some kind of stew, put it down by her, then looked at her shyly.

Polly thanked her, adding, "I am Polly. You are—"

The girl smiled. "Doe." Then she hurried away.

Polly saw that the tribe was gathered around a fire, sharing a meal together from which she was excluded. Why? The raiders had been included in the feast of the People of the Wind. But Klep had said that the People Across the Lake treated their prisoners differently from the way the People of the Wind did.

She ate the stew, which was passable, because she knew she needed to keep up her strength. Probably the meat from which the stew was made came from one of the beasts stolen from the People of the Wind. Then she sat, knees drawn up to her chin, thinking. She realized that the People Across the Lake might have had no feast, no meal, without what they had taken during the raids made on the more fortunate people whose land was still fruitful. She had seen poor or primitive people before, but never those who were starving.

She lay down, knowing that she needed to rest, but every muscle was tense, and the singing and shouting of the tribe kept her awake. It was not the happy singing of the People of the Wind; rather, it was a plaintive chant. Were they worried about Klep, who had been taken prisoner—Klep, who was to be their next leader?

She lay with her eyes closed, trying to rest so that she would be ready for whatever was in store, feeling within herself a desperate quietness. It was inconceivable that she should be trapped three thousand years in the past, that she might never get home. And yet here she was, a prisoner.

Because of Zachary.

But Zachary had not closed the time gate.

No, but he had brought her here, across the lake. Zachary

was too terrified of dying to think of anything or anybody else. In his case, what would she have done? She did not know. She closed her eyes and drifted off into a state between waking and sleeping. In her half dream she felt a strange security, that she was surrounded by love that came to her from across the lake, from the People of the Wind, from the bishop and Anaral, Karralys, Tav, even from Klep, who knew where she was and who she was with far better than the others. She turned on her side, relaxing into the protection of their love.

In her half sleep she saw Tav, and looked into his silver eyes, saw his fair, thick lashes, his mop of pale hair. He was questioning her, affirming that she was a goddess to the People Across the Lake, and wanting to know how they captured her. Longing for the reality of his presence, she slid more deeply into sleep.

"Zachary and one of the men kidnapped me."

She saw Tav's outraged scowl. "Why would anyone, even that Zak, do such a thing?"

Polly murmured, "Klep was right when he said that maybe Brown Earth promised something to Zachary."

"Promised what?" Tav demanded.

"Zachary was promised that their healer would fix his heart if he brought me to them."

"But Zachary should never have done that!" Now it was Anaral who was angry.

"I guess if you think you're going to die, and you're told someone can keep you alive, that becomes the only thing you can think of. Anyhow, I'm sure he doesn't believe that there's any kind of threat to me. I mean, they wouldn't hurt someone they think is a goddess, would they?"

"They will not do anything until the moon is full," Tav said. "And oh, Poll-ee, we will not let them do anything to you. Klep is grateful to you for having helped set his leg, for having held his hands against the pain."

"He is nice," Anaral said softly. "He is good."

"He says that his honor is bound to you, to help you, and to help us free you." Polly shifted position, holding on to the dream, not wanting to wake up. In the dream Tav leaned

toward her and placed his fingers gently over her ears. Then he
touched her eyes, her mouth. "We give you the gift of hearing,"
he said. "Klep sends you the hearing of the trees."

"We give you the gift of hearing," Anaral said softly. "I give
you the gift of hearing the lake, for I know that you have much
love of water."

"And I"—Tav's voice was soft—"I give you the gift of understanding the voice of the wind, for we are the People of the
Wind, and the Wind is the voice of the goddess. Listen, and
do not be afraid."

"Do not be afraid," Anaral repeated.

"Do not be afraid." Their words echoed in her ears as she
turned again on the hard earth and slid out of the dream into
wakefulness. She tried holding on to Tav's promise that nothing would happen to her, but despite her own affirmation that
the People Across the Lake would not do anything to harm
someone they thought to be a goddess, an inner voice told her
that to these people, whose land was devastated by drought,
the sacrifice of a goddess would be a sacrifice of great power.

She lay on the fern pallet, pulling the fur rug over her. She
wanted to recover the comfort of the dream but she could
not. Her mind began searching for ways of escape. She was a
strong swimmer. She had swum all her life, and her stamina
and endurance were far greater than ordinary. There had even
been a suggestion that she try for the Olympics, a realistic
suggestion, considering her capabilities, but she agreed with
her parents that it was a competitiveness she did not want.
She thought about the lake and realized that the distance was
too great, especially in cold water. Her grandparents' pool was
heated and was barely seventy-two or -three degrees. The lake
would be much colder. Unless it was her last hope, she would
not attempt the lake.

Where was Zachary while she was isolated in this small
lean-to? The sound of people singing and shouting was fainter.
She knelt on the rug and could see several groups leaving the
fires and going to their tents. The feast, if, indeed, it had been
a feast—for what? the coming of the goddess?—was over.

The darkness was tangible. She felt it as a heavy pressure on her chest. —But this is fear, she thought. —If I can only stop being afraid.

She shuddered. How were sacrificial victims killed? With a knife? That would be the quickest, the kindest way . . .

She breathed slowly, deliberately. There was no sound from any of the tents. The water of the lake lapped gently against the shore. She listened. Tried to remember the gifts Tav and Anaral had given her in her dream. There was the gift of listening to the water. Hush, the water said. Hush. Hush. Peace. Sleep.

The wind lifted, stirred in the trees, rattling dry leaves. The lean-to was attached at the back to the trunk of a great oak. The branches overarched the skin roof, adding their protection. In the summer when the tree was fully leafed, the lean-to would be protected from the sun. Klep had sent her the gift of hearing the trees. She listened, with a certainty that indeed gifts had been sent to her, blowing in the wind across the dark waters of the lake. She heard a steady throb, like a great heart beating. The rhythm never faltered. It was an affirmation of steadfastness. The oak was older than any trees in her own time. Hundreds of years old. It *was*, and its being was a strange comfort.

Last she turned to Tav's gift, cherishing it, the gift of hearing the voice of the wind, and she listened as the wind stirred gently among the dry leaves above her. Touched the waters of the lake, ruffling its surface. Reached into the lean-to and brushed against her cheeks. She heard no words, but she felt a deepening of comfort and assurance.

She slept.

When she opened her eyes, it was daylight. Tynak was squatting by her, looking at her. Behind him, the dawn light was rosy on the water. The sun was rising behind the snow-capped mountains that shielded the People of the Wind. But now, as Polly looked at the mountains from the far side of the lake, they seemed wild and menacing. Around the compound, people were stirring, and she could smell smoke from the cook fires.

Long rays of light reached into the lean-to, touched Polly.

Tynak held up one hand, pointing. At first she had no idea what he was indicating with his ancient finger. Then she realized that it was her hair. Tynak had never seen red hair before. At night it would not have shone as it did in the long rays of sunlight. She did not know how to explain that red hair was not particularly unusual in her time, so she smiled politely. "Good morning."

"Klep—" There was urgency in Tynak's voice.

She spoke slowly. "Klep has a broken leg. Our healer is taking care of it. He will be all right."

"He will return?"

"I don't know about that. I don't know what happens with prisoners."

"He must return! You are goddess, we need help."

"I'm not a goddess. I'm an ordinary human being."

"You called snake. It came."

"I'm sorry. It didn't have anything to do with me. I don't have that kind of power. I don't know why she came. It was just coincidence." She hoped he could understand enough of her faltering Ogam to get the gist of what she was saying.

"Snake. Who is?"

"Louise is just an ordinary black snake. They're harmless."

"Her name?"

"Louise the Larger."

Tynak grunted, gave her an incomprehending look, then turned and without speaking further left the lean-to. In a few minutes he returned with a wooden bowl full of some kind of gruel.

She took it. "Thank you."

"Can you call rain?" he demanded.

"I wish I could."

"You must try." His wrinkled face was kind, sad, in no way sinister or threatening.

—Even in my own time, she thought, —where we think we have so much control over so many things, we haven't succeeded in forecasting the weather, much less controlling it. We, too, have droughts and floods and earthquakes. We live on a planet that is still unstable.

"You will try?" Tynak prodded.

"I will try."

"Where you come from, you have gods, goddesses?"

She nodded. Because of her isolated island living, she had had little institutional training in religion. There had been no available Sunday schools. But family dinner-table conversation included philosophy and theology as well as science. Her godfather was an English canon who had taught her about a God of love and compassion, a God who was mysterious and tremendous, but not to be understood as "two atoms of hydrogen plus one atom of oxygen make water" could be understood. A God who cared about all that had been created in love. And that included all these people who had lived three thousand years ago. Bishop Colubra, too, believed in a God of total love. And so, despite her pragmatism, did Dr. Louise.

Anaral had talked of the Presence. That was as good a name as any. "We believe in the Presence," Polly said firmly to Tynak. "The One who made us all and cares about us."

"This Presence wants sacrifice?"

"Only love," she said. But perhaps that was the greatest sacrifice of all.

"This Presence sends rain?"

"Not always. We have droughts, too."

"Where you come from?"

—When, she thought, but nodded. It was impossible to explain.

Did she have anything from her own time which would be impressive to Tynak? She felt in the pockets of the red anorak. Yes, she had several things, artifacts, that might seem to Tynak to have power. Her fingers touched Zachary's icon. She pulled it out. Held it in front of Tynak. Zachary had bought the icon for her because he cared about her.

Tynak stared at the icon intently, almost fearfully, then looked at her questioningly.

She pointed to the child in the icon, then to herself. Then she pointed to the angel, and stretched out her arms as though embracing all of Tynak's compound, the tents, the lake, the great snow-capped mountains on the far side.

Tynak took the icon from her and again stared at it, then

at Polly, then back to the icon. He pointed to the angel, his fingers touching the great wings. "Can fly?"

"Yes."

"Goddess?"

Polly shook her head. "Angel."

He sounded the word out after her. "An-gel. Angel will help you?"

She nodded.

"Angel will let no harm come to you?"

"Angel loves me," she replied carefully.

He nodded several times. Turned the icon over, looked at the plain wood of the back, turned it so that he was looking at the angel and the child again. "Where you get?"

"Zachary gave it to me."

"Zak. Zak. You speak now to the Zak."

She held out her hand for the icon. "Please give it back to me."

He pulled his hand away, still holding the icon.

"Please give it back," Polly repeated, and reached for it.

"No! Tynak keep an-gel power."

Why did she care so much about keeping the icon? If she tried to grab it away from him, others would come to his rescue immediately. She stared into his dark eyes. "Angel has good power for me. Bad power for you."

"Not so. I take an-gel. I take your power."

It was absurd to feel so threatened by Tynak's taking the icon. It was nothing more than a painting on wood. Zachary had said that it had no value. But it was affirmation that he cared about her, that he meant it when he promised that he never wanted to hurt her. Her voice shook. "Bad power for you." She could only repeat herself.

She stopped as she heard a low growl. Wet and dripping, Og bounded toward her.

"Og!" She was almost as glad to see him as she had been to see Tav.

He was at her side, baring his teeth at Tynak.

"Give." She reached for the icon again. "See? Good power for me. Bad power for you."

Tynak put the icon into her hand and walked away, very quickly.

Og licked her hand gently and she burst into tears.

CHAPTER 10

OG's frantic efforts to lick her tears away made Polly laugh, and she wiped her hands across her eyes. "Oh, Og, am I ever glad to see you! How did you get here?" Perhaps Anaral or Tav or Karralys had brought Og most of the way in a canoe. There was no way of guessing. She was just warmly grateful that the dog was with her.

She looked at the icon of the angel and the child. Undoubtedly, Tynak had never seen a painted picture before. If she had a camera with her, one of those instant ones, and took his picture, that would surely convince him of her power. But she didn't have a camera.

Og growled slightly and she looked up to see Zachary in his elegant hiking outfit, incongruous in this ancient village devastated by drought.

"Polly, sweet, are you okay?"

She looked at Zachary, at his pale face, his darkly shadowed eyes. "You kidnapped me."

He put his hand against one of the poles that supported the lean-to. "Polly, don't you understand? I needed you. I needed you terribly."

"Why didn't you just ask me?"

He dropped down to sit beside her on the fern pallet. "I didn't think you'd come."

"But you didn't even try. You let that man kidnap me."

"Oh, sweet Pol, don't call it that. They made it very clear to me that the healer wouldn't come near me if I didn't bring the goddess to them."

"You know I'm no goddess."

"They don't."

"Zachary." She looked straight at him. "You do understand that Tynak is planning to sacrifice me in order to get rain?"

"No, no, he'd never go that far." But suddenly Zachary looked very uncomfortable. "You're a goddess. He just wanted to have you here because you have power." He looked at Og.

"And you do, don't you? The dog has come to you, and Tynak would think that was terrific power, wouldn't he?" He was talking too much, too fast.

"Zachary, would you let Tynak sacrifice me?"

"Never, never, Polly." He looked at her pleadingly. "Polly, I want their healer to help me."

"At this price?"

"There isn't any price."

"Isn't there? My life for yours?"

"No, no. Tynak thinks you're a goddess." Zachary ran his fingers through his dark hair. "Listen, Polly, this Tynak made it clear to me that the healer wouldn't touch me unless you—okay, that's the problem. I couldn't understand what he wanted. Can you understand him?"

"A little."

"You're angry with me."

"Why wouldn't I be?"

"Polly, you have my icon. You do care about me. Tynak said the healer would help me if you came here. You're a goddess, don't you understand?"

She shook her head. Looked at him. He was tragic and handsome, but she had a sinking feeling that he would do anything to get what he wanted. A big thing, this time: life.

"Don't you want me to live?" He was pleading.

"At my expense?"

"Polly, stop exaggerating."

"Am I?"

Zachary stood up. "Polly, I wanted to talk to you, but I can see there's no point while you're being unreasonable. I'm going back to Tynak. I'm staying in his tent. And in case you're interested, there are skulls on poles in his tent." His voice was tight and defensive. "You've brought me back in time to this place where the people are hardly more than savages. I think you should feel a certain sense of responsibility."

"If they're savages, why do you have so much faith that their healer can help your heart?" she asked.

"Ah, Polly, I can't stand to have you mad at me! I thought we were friends."

Friends? She was not sure what a friend was. She thought of her conversation with Anaral about friendship, about how friends cared for and tried to protect one another. Friendship was a two-way street. She wished Zachary would go away and leave her alone. She put the icon back in her pocket, the icon Zachary had given her because his grandmother believed in angels. Bishop Colubra, too, believed in angels. If the bishop could believe in angels, so could she. Not in the angel painted on the icon, but in real powers of love and care. The icon was not a thing in itself, but an affirmation.

For Tynak it was a thing in itself.

"Have you seen the healer today?" she asked Zachary.

"Seen him and spoken—if you can call it that—with him. He's very old. Older than Tynak. He has long, skinny arms, and enormous, strong-looking hands. Listen, Polly, you will help me, won't you? You will?"

He was frantic, out of his mind with terror, she knew that. But she also knew that his denials that Tynak was going to use her as a sacrifice were hollow. She felt a deep pain in her chest.

"See you." Zachary tried to sound casual. Turned away from her and left.

The sun was well above the horizon and slanted warmly against the lean-to. It was going to be a warm autumn day. Indian summer? She slid out of the anorak. Tav had said that nothing would happen until the full moon. Day after tomorrow, she thought. Many things could change between now and then.

She left the lean-to and walked across the compound, Og by her side. People looked at her curiously, cautiously, even fearfully, but no one spoke to her. She felt as though her red hair were on fire. There were many surreptitious glances at Og. These people were not used to dogs, at least not to domestic dogs. Perhaps they thought Og was part of her magic. Perhaps that was why Og had been sent across the lake to her. Og was protection, the bishop had said. She needed his protection.

The sun beat down with a sulfurous glare. It was hot, actually hot, but a strange heat. The sky was yellowish, rather than blue, and her one hope at this moment was that this odd weather meant a storm was coming, and rain.

Whenever she approached a group of people, conversation stopped. Og nudged her, pushing her gently in the direction of the lean-to, so she went back.

At noon, when the sun was high, Doe brought her a bowl of broth and some heavy bread, but did not stay. Polly ate and lay down on the pallet, hands behind her head, staring up at the skins of the roof, trying to think, but her thoughts would not focus. She rolled up the anorak to make a pillow and raise her head so she could see out of the lean-to, across the compound, and to the lake.

Zachary had said that there were skulls in Tynak's tent, that these Stone Age people were savages. But were the people of her own time any less savage? Within her grandparents' memories, Jews and gypsies and anyone who was thought to be a danger to Aryan supremacy were put in concentration camps, gassed, made into soap, used for medical experimentation. At more or less the same time in her own country Japanese people who were American citizens were rounded up and put into America's own version of concentration camps. Surely they were not as brutal as the German ones, but they were as savage as anything on either side of the lake.

She thought then of Bishop Colubra lying on the great capstone and praying, and she closed her eyes and tried to let her mind go empty so that she could be part of his prayer. He and Karralys knew that she and Zachary were here. They had sent Og to her. She hoped that they were praying for her. She knew that they cared, that they would never abandon her. Tav would rescue her.

But there was still an aching hurt in her heart.

In the late afternoon, thunder rumbled from the mountains across the lake, and lightning flashed. The clouds came down in a curtain, but across the lake, not on Tynak's side. It looked to Polly as though the People of the Wind were getting a good shower. The smell of rain was in the air, and it was a summer smell. The air continued to be hot and heavy.

Tynak came to her again.

She sat on the anorak, to protect the icon. Og sat beside her. Tynak pointed to the dog and looked at her questioningly. "Animal?"

"He's a dog. Dog."

"Where comes from?"

"He belongs across the lake. We think he came across the ocean with Karralys—the druid. The leader."

Tynak pointed to the storm that still played across the lake. "Power. You have power. Make rain."

Polly shook her head.

"Earth must have rain. Blood, then rain."

"A lamb?" Polly suggested.

"Not strong enough blood. Not enough power."

Only Polly had enough power for a successful sacrifice. A sacrifice must be unblemished. Tynak was afraid of Polly's power. He had considered the possibility of sacrificing Zachary, he told Polly, but Zachary might not provide enough power to appease the anger of the gods and bring rain to this side of the lake, and return Klep to his people.

"You promised to help Zachary's heart," Polly tried to remind him, pressing her hand against her heart.

Tynak shrugged.

"You promised Zak that if he brought me to you, your healer would help his heart," she persisted. "Do you not have honor? Do you not keep your word?"

"Honor." Tynak nodded thoughtfully. "Try." He left her.

She stared after him, wondering if the healer indeed had enough of the gift of healing to give new life to a badly damaged heart.

Doe brought her another bowl of stew in the early evening. Polly ate it and sat listening. The wind moved in the branches of the oak behind her. Sultry. Too hot for this time of year. The village was quiet. Tynak had left her unguarded, probably because there was no place for her to go. The forest menaced behind her. The lake was in front of her.

The water rippled softly. The wind seemed to call her, to beckon. She was not sure what the wind was trying to tell her. The moon rose. Close to full, so close to full. The village settled down for the night. Fires were extinguished or banked. There was no sound except for the stirring of the wind in the trees, ruffling the surface of the lake. The village was asleep.

Og rose, nudged her. Went to the edge of the lean-to, looked at Polly, tail barely moving, waiting. Then he went to the edge of the lake, put one paw in, looked back at her, put his paw in the water again, looked back, wagging his tail. Finally she understood that he wanted her to go into the lake. To swim. She slipped out of her shoes and socks, jeans, sweatshirt, and left the lean-to in cotton bra and underpants. Og then led her along the lake side, farther and farther away from the tents.

There was no sound from the village. Sleep lay heavy over the compound. The snow on the mountains across the lake was luminous with moonlight. Polly followed Og, trying to be quiet. She could not move silently, like Tav and Anaral. Twigs crackled under her feet. Vines caught at her. Now there was no more beach. The forest went right down to the water's edge. She tried not to brush against branches. Tried not to cry out when twigs or stones hurt her bare feet.

Finally Og slid into the water, again looking back at Polly to make sure she was following him. She walked into the lake, trying not to splash. She slipped into the water when she was knee-deep. Og swam steadily. The water was cold. Bitter cold. On the surface it had been warmed by the unusual heat of the day, but underneath it was cold, far colder than her grandparents' pool. The brazen sun had warmed it just enough so that it was bearable. She followed Og, swimming strongly but not frantically. She had to swim steadily enough so she would not get hypothermia, but not so hurriedly that she would tire before she got across the lake.

The water was quiet. Cold. Cold. She swam, following Og, who moved at an even pace so she could keep up with him without straining. But as they swam, her body felt colder and colder, and her skin prickled with goose bumps. She trusted

Og. He would not have led her into the lake if they weren't going to be able to make it to the other side. She had swum all her life. She could swim forever if she had to.

They swam. Swam. Polly's arms and legs moved almost automatically. How long? How far was it? Now, even in the light of the moon, she could not see Tynak's village, which she had left behind her, nor could she see across the lake, except for the snow-capped mountains.

She felt her breath coming in gasps, rasping in her throat. She was not going to make it. She tried to look for land ahead of her, but her eyes were dazzled with exhaustion and all she saw was a flickering darkness. She went under, gulped water, pushed back up. Og looked over his shoulder, but swam on. Her breathing was like razor blades in her chest. She tried to call, "Og!" but no sound came out of her throat. Her legs dropped. She could not go on.

And her feet touched the rocky bottom.

Og was scrambling onto the shore, barking.

And Tav was rushing across the beach to greet her. He splashed into the water, followed by Karralys and Anaral. The bishop hurried to meet them, bearing a fur robe. Anaral took it from him and wrapped Polly's wet body in warmth.

She was in Tav's strong arms. He carried her into Karralys's tent.

She was safe.

A bright fire was built in a circle of stones in the center of the tent. The smoke hole had been opened and blue tendrils of smoke rose up and out into the night. Anaral brought Polly something hot to drink, and it warmed the cold which had eaten deep into her marrow.

"Did you have rain this afternoon?" she asked.

"Yes. Rain came," Karralys said.

Polly sipped at the warm, comforting drink. She was still shivering with cold and Anaral brought another fur rug to wrap around her legs. Bishop Colubra reached out to touch her wet head. She was so exhausted that she lay down, wrapped in the warm fur, and fell into a deep sleep.

Whether it was strain from the swim, or from something in the warm drink, she moved immediately into dreaming. In her sleep she was the center of a bright web of lines, lines joining the stars and yet reaching to the earth, from her grandparents' home to the star-watching rock to the low hills to the snow-capped mountains, lines of light touching Bishop Colubra and Karralys, Tav and Cub, Anaral and Klep, and all the lines touched her and warmed her. Lines of power . . . Benign power.

Then the dream shifted, became nightmare. The lines were those of a spiderweb, and in the center Zachary was trapped like a fly. He was struggling convulsively and ineffectually, and the spider threw more threads to tie him down. Zachary's screams as the spider approached cut across her dream.

She woke up with a jerk.

"Are you all right?" Anaral asked anxiously.

"You need more sleep," Tav said.

She shook her head. "I'm okay."

"Blessed child"—the bishop's voice was caressing—"we know about Zachary's abducting you. Can you tell us more?"

"Well." She was still chilled to the marrow. "I don't think I can leave Zachary there." It was not at all what she had expected to say.

"Polly." Bishop Colubra spoke gently but commandingly. "Tell us."

Briefly she reviewed her attempted conversations with Tynak, with Zachary.

When she had finished, Tav leaped to his feet in rage. "So this Zak took you to save his own life."

"Heart," she corrected.

"He was willing to have you die so he could live," Anaral said.

Polly shook her head. "It isn't that simple. I don't think he admitted to himself what he was doing."

"Why are you defending him?" Tav shouted.

"I don't know. I just know it isn't that simple." But hadn't she accused Zachary of the same thing? "I think I have to go back."

"No. It will not be allowed," Tav expostulated.

"You are here. Safe. Stay," Anaral urged.

"Why do you have to go back, Polly?" the bishop asked.

Her reasons sounded inadequate, even to herself. But a vision of Zachary trapped in the web kept flicking across her inner eye. "My clothes are there. Zachary's icon is in my anorak pocket, and Tynak thinks it has great power. He tried to take it from me once, but I hope he's afraid of it now. And if I don't go back, I don't know what will happen to Zachary." She shook her head as though to clear it. "I really don't know why I have to go back. I just know I have to."

Tav pounded with the butt of his spear against the hard ground of the tent. "What happens to this Zak does not matter. It is you. You matter. I care about you."

"I can't make rain for them, Tav," she said. "And if there isn't rain they will attack you again. You said that yourself." She wanted to stretch out her arms to him, to have him take her hands, draw her to him, but this was no time for such irrational longings.

"Karralys—" she started, but Karralys was not there.

"He has gone to the standing stones," the bishop told her. "Didn't you see him leave? He gestured for Og to stay here in the tent, and then he went out."

"But he will come back?" Polly asked anxiously.

"He will come back," Anaral assured her. "It is the place of power. He needs to be there."

Polly bit her lip, thinking. "If Tynak believes I have goddess-like powers, he'll hold off. The icon had a terrific effect on him, Bishop. What else have I got?" She thought. "Well, there's a flashlight in the anorak pocket, one of those tiny ones with a very strong light. And a pair of scissors. And a little notebook and a pen. And some other stuff. Tynak will never have seen any of those before."

"Notebook and pen?" Anaral asked. "Like Bishop's? To write with?"

"Yes."

"Karralys is the only one I know who can write, and he writes only on rock or wood. And his real wisdom is not written. It is kept here." She touched first her forehead, then her heart. "What do I have to give you? Oh, look! Bishop gave me this after I cut my finger." She reached into a small pouch at her side and brought out a gold pocketknife. "It would not be much good for skinning a deer, but it is quite sharp. And I have another one of these." And she gave Polly a Band-Aid.

"Stop!" Tav shouted. "No! Polly is not to go back!"

"Tav, I have to."

"You swam. How far you swam! Not many people could swim across the lake, all that way, even in summer. You are here. We will not let you go."

"I have to." She sounded her most stubborn.

"Polly," the bishop said, "you have not yet given us a real reason."

"I can't just leave Zachary there to be slaughtered."

"Why not?" Tav demanded.

"I can't. If Tynak thinks I'm a goddess, maybe I can stop him."

Tav shook his head. "You. They will sacrifice you."

"No," Polly said. "To them, I am a goddess." She wished she was as certain as she sounded.

The bishop's face twisted, as though from pain. "Polly is right. She can't leave Zachary to be a meaningless sacrifice. No matter what he has or has not done, that is not what Polly does."

"No!" Tav cried.

Karralys returned, pushing aside the tent flap. "Bishop Heron is right. Polly is right. We cannot let the young man be sacrificed. It will not bring rain, and we would have sold a life and gained nothing."

"Polly's life," Tav said.

"It is never expedient that one man should die for the sake of the country," the bishop said.

"We will gather all our warriors together—" Tav started.

"They are many more than we are," Karralys pointed out.

"I won't have people fighting over me. People would get hurt or killed. It wouldn't do any good, Tav. You mustn't even think of it. You had rain here today. Maybe there'll be another storm, one across the lake. That's what we need."

Karralys said, "Because of the position of the mountains and the currents of wind, we have rain here far more often than across the lake. But it is possible that rain will come, not just a storm, but a rain all over the lake and shores."

"Yes," Polly agreed. "Rain. Not fighting. Rain."

Karralys looked at her thoughtfully. "I lay on the capstone and listened. The stars are quiet tonight. I hear only that Zachary is to be saved."

"I don't understand." Tav's voice was savage.

"Nor I," Karralys replied. "I know only what I hear."

Polly asked, "You consult with the stars?"

Karralys frowned. "Consult? No. I listen."

"For advice?"

"No, not so much for advice as for—" He paused.

"Direction?" the bishop suggested.

"No. In the stars are lines of pattern, and those lines touch us, as our lines touch each other. The stars do not foretell, because what has not happened must be free to happen, as it will. I look and listen and try to understand the pattern."

The bishop nodded. "The story is not foretold. The future must not be coerced. That is right."

Karralys looked at Polly gravely. "If you are going to return to Zachary, it is time."

Tav turned to the bishop. "You would send Polly back?"

"There is no *would*," the bishop said.

Polly looked at him, nodding. "It is what I am going to do."

Tav said, "Then I will take you in my canoe."

Anaral said, "You will need something warm to wear. I will give you my winter tunic."

"Thanks," Polly said. "I'll need it."

"I go with you, Tav," Anaral continued. "I have talked much with Klep, hoping to find a way to rescue Polly. He has told me of a small island not far from the village, hidden by the curve of the land. From there it is only a short paddle."

"Klep!" Polly had almost forgotten the young man with the broken femur. "Is he better?"

Karralys smiled. "He is better. His fever is gone. The broken flesh is healing cleanly. But it will be weeks before he can walk."

"Perhaps Polly should talk with him," Anaral suggested, "before she goes back to his tribe."

Karralys nodded in approval. "Yes. That would be good. Tav, can you and Cub bring him?"

"Can't I go to him?" Polly asked. "Wouldn't that be easier? Won't it hurt him to be moved?"

"Tav and Cub will be careful. The fewer people know you are here, the better."

Tav was already gone. Anaral detached the leather pouch from her waistband and removed a handful of small stones. Dropped them on the ground at her feet and looked at them where they lay. "If we lose one, we lose all." Her voice was soft. Bent down to touch another stone. "If we save one, all things are possible." Touched another. "The stars will guide. Trust them." And another. "The lines between the stars are reflected in the lines between the sacred places and in the lines that cross time to join people." She looked up, blinking, as though waking from a dream.

Karralys smiled at her. "The stones are well read."

Anaral smiled back. "They read true."

"Annie, dear"—the bishop looked at her searchingly—"these are not fortune-telling stones?"

"No, no," Karralys said quickly. "The stones do not tell us what is going to happen, or what we are to do, any more than the stars. They speak to us only of our present position in the great pattern. Where we are now; here. Sometimes that helps us to see the pattern more clearly. That is all. This worries you, Heron?"

"No," the bishop said. "I trust you, Karralys. You and Annie."

Polly said, "Some kids in my school got really involved in fortune-telling and the future and stuff, and my parents take a very dim view of that kind of thing."

"I, too," Karralys said. "Only Anaral reads stones, that they may not be misused."

They broke off as Tav and Cub came into the tent, bearing Klep between them, his broken leg stretched motionless between two oaken staves. Gently they set him down before the fire, which still burned brightly, illuminating the interior of the tent. When he saw Polly, he smiled in relief.

"You are all right?" Klep asked.

She smiled back. "Now that I'm thawed, I'm fine."

"You swam the whole way?"

"I grew up on islands," Polly said. "I've swum all my life."

"Even so," Klep said, "it is a long way."

Polly grimaced. "Don't I know. I thought I wasn't going to make it."

"And you are going back?"

She squatted beside him. "Klep. Tell me. If I don't go back, what will happen to Zachary?"

He in turn asked, "We had no rain today, on my side of the lake?"

"No. Not a drop."

He made an unhappy grunt. "There will have to be a sacrifice."

"Zachary?"

"Yes."

"But they will wait till the full moon?"

"Yes."

"Two nights from now," Karralys said. "Polly, Og will go with you. If you need help, send him. Like you, he swims like a fish. However, Polly, know that we are with you. The lines between the stars and between us are like—like—"

"Telegraph lines," Bishop Colubra supplied. "This won't mean anything to you, Karralys. But in our time we can send words across lines."

"Faxes," Polly suggested.

"If you will keep your heart open to us, Polly, the lines, too, will be open."

"Karralys!" The bishop pulled himself up, waving his arms. "I have just had a thought!" He looked around the tent, letting his gaze rest on Klep, then returned to Karralys. "You don't want to keep Klep here as a prisoner of war or a slave, or anything like that, do you?"

"No. He is free to go as soon as he is healed."

"If he is well enough for Tav and Cub to have brought him

here, he is well enough to be put in the canoe with Polly. Let us send him back with her. Then she will be the goddess who has rescued Klep."

Klep burst into delighted laughter. "That is splendid! But how strange. I do not want to go." He looked at Anaral, and she returned his gaze steadily, and the line of love between the two of them was almost visible.

"But you will go," Karralys said. "What Bishop Heron has thought of is perfect. And if you, Klep, are to be the next leader of your tribe, the sooner you return, the better."

"I am very young." Klep reminded Polly of her brother, next in age to her, Charles, with his wisdom, unusual for his age, and his lovingness.

"Your Old One still has years to live," Karralys assured him. "We will send two canoes. Polly is too tired to go alone with Klep. Tav, you will paddle Polly and Klep. Cub, you will go with Anaral. When the canoe is near enough shore for Polly to bring it in, you, Tav, will join Anaral and Cub."

"We must hurry," Klep said, "to be there before dawn."

It all happened so quickly that Polly barely had time to think, only to accept that the bishop's plan was the best possible under the circumstances. She was given a warm sheepskin tunic to wear, which she put on gratefully. Klep was placed in the bottom of one of the canoes. Polly sat in the bow, with Og curled at her feet. Tav took the stern. Anaral and Cub got into a slightly smaller canoe.

They pushed out into the dark water. Polly turned once to wave to the bishop and Karralys. Then she turned her face toward the dark horizon.

CHAPTER 11

T HE two canoes moved silently across the lake. Tav and
Cub paddled in rhythm, making no sound of splashing as
the paddles dipped cleanly into the lake, thrusting the canoes
forward.

Klep lay silently, looking at the sky, the velvet dark sky untouched by city lights. The stars were there, but dimmed by a
faint mist, and a few patches were blotted out by clouds. Polly
huddled into Anaral's sheepskin garment. The night air was
cold, and she was still chilled from the long swim.

She turned around and looked at Tav, his muscles rippling
gently as he paddled. There was no way she could think as Tav
thought. She could conceive with her mind a world of gods and
goddesses, of Mother Earth, but she could not understand it in
her heart, except as part of the glorious whole.

"Tav," she whispered.

"Poll-ee?"

"If Tynak decides that I—that I am to be the sacrifice to the
Mother—"

"No." Tav was emphatic. "I will not let that happen."

"But if there is no rain?"

"I will not let Tynak hurt you."

"But if I come back to you and the People of the Wind, and
the drought continues, if there isn't any more rain, what would
you do then?"

The silence was palpable.

"Tav?"

"I do not know." His voice was heavy, and for a moment his
paddle faltered with a slight splash. "My training is that of a
warrior. At home, across the great water, there were people we
had captured from neighboring tribes. The Mother did not ask
us for anyone dear to our hearts."

"But you still believe that the Mother needs blood to be
appeased?" Tav would not know what she meant by appeased,
which she had substituted for the unknown Ogam word, so

she amended, "The Mother needs blood or she will be angry and withhold rain?"

"I do not know," Tav said. "The Mother has been good to us. Karralys with his knowledge of the stars brought us safely across the great water, but the winds were kind. Then we were given a canoe, bigger than this one, and the wind and rain blew us along rivers and into the lake and to the People of the Wind. The storm ceased and the rainbow came. I did not die. Karralys is a healer. We blessed the Mother, and she blessed us, but now the rain is being held back, and even though our land is still green, we will not be able to protect it if the drought continues across the lake. I thought I understood the Mother and I have tried to be obedient to her ways. But now I do not know. I do not know."

Polly thought, —I don't know, either, about the Creator I believe made everything.

She glanced at the sky and between wisps of clouds the stars shone serenely.—But if I knew everything, there would be no wonder, because what I believe in is far more than I know.

"Why, my Poll-ee"—Tav interrupted her thoughts—"does this Zak want so much to see the healer across the lake when the far greater healer is with us?"

"The greater healer?"

"Karralys," Tav said impatiently. "Did you not know?"

"Cub—"

"Cub has the tribal knowledge of healing. And his hands are learning the gift, as you saw with Bishop."

"Yes."

"But it is Karralys who has—how do I say it—who has made Cub's gift to grow."

Now that Tav was telling her this, it became obvious. Why had she not realized it? Zachary had been so focused, first on Cub, then on the healer across the lake, that Karralys had been pushed out of her thoughts. "I was stupid," she said.

"There has been much happening," Tav defended her. "Hsh. We are nearly there."

Never before had the Mother asked for anyone dear to his heart, Tav had said. She held those words to her own heart.

She wanted him to touch her, to tell her that he could care for and protect her, never let anyone put her on the altar to be sacrificed. Could Tav keep his promise to protect her from Tynak? He was as confused in his own way of thinking as she was in hers, and their ways were so alien that it was impossible to think of them as being connected by one of the lines that patterned the stars and the places of benign power and the love between people.

If she could not understand his belief that the earth demanded blood, would he not be equally horrified by the slums of modern cities, by violence in the streets, drug pushing, nuclear waste? How could the star lines be connected to urban violence and human indifference?

The two canoes drew together. Anaral reached across to hold Polly's hand in a gesture of comfort as well as a way of bringing the two canoes together.

Tav stood, balancing carefully, then transferred to the other canoe. Both canoes rolled slightly, but no more. When Tav was seated, he handed a paddle to Polly.

"You can turn the canoe?" he asked.

"Yes."

"If you will paddle equally to the right and toward shore, you will reach Tynak's village."

"Right."

"Klep." Anaral's voice was soft. "Give your leg time to heal. Do not use it too soon."

"I will be careful," Klep promised. "Do you be careful, too. Oh, be careful, be careful." There was a world of meaning in his repetition.

"I will," Anaral assured him. "I will."

"Hold out your paddle," Tav told Polly.

Not understanding, she did as he asked. He used her paddle to pull the two canoes so that she and Tav were side by side. With one finger he gently touched her lips and it was the most marvelous kiss she had ever been given. She reached out and touched his lips in return.

"Ah, my Poll-ee. Go." He gave her paddle a quick shove.

Polly waited, watching, while the canoe with Tav, Anaral, and Cub headed back across the lake.

Klep's voice was warm and soft. "Tav would draw a line between the two of you."

Polly turned the canoe around, facing in the direction Tav had told her Tynak's village would be. "You think he loves me?"

"Loves? What is loves?" Klep asked.

Was it in Bishop Colubra's notebook? "When two people really want to be together, they love each other."

"Love," he repeated. "To join together?"

"Yes. When you love someone, you would do anything to help. It is like being friends, but much more."

"The lines between you," he said, "they grow short, the way the line between Anaral and me came close, close, and now it is being pulled." He looked longingly in the direction of the canoe with Anaral in it.

"Yes. That is love."

"You love?"

"Yes. Lots of people."

"Love who?"

"Oh, my parents and my grandparents and my brothers and sisters."

"But you do not join together with them as one."

"No. That is different. My mother and father, they are one, that way. And my grandparents."

"You and Tav?"

She shook her head. "You have to know someone for more than a few days. If things were different—" —If three thousand years didn't separate us. If totally alien views of the universe didn't separate us, if, if . . . "If we had a lot of time together, then maybe."

"Anaral and I have not a lot of time, but the line is strong."

Yes. Klep and Anaral reached out for each other as Polly would reach out for Tav, but Klep and Anaral were not separated by thousands of years, and if Anaral was a druid, Klep would one day lead his tribe, having been born under a great omen.

"If rain comes, if my people no longer steal cattle and sheep from your people . . ."

Romeo and Juliet all over again—or presaging—the People Across the Lake versus the People of the Wind? "I hope it will work out for you," Polly said. "It would be"—she had no word for suitable, or appropriate—"right."

"I would make short the line between Anaral and me in a way I have never known before."

There was no word for love in Klep's vocabulary, but Anaral would teach him.

They were nearing the shore. Polly could see a shadow, someone standing there, waiting. She drove the paddle deep into the water and sent the canoe sliding up onto the pebbly sand. She jumped out and pulled the canoe far enough onto the shore so that it would not slide back into the lake. Og was at her side.

The shadow came toward her. It was Tynak.

"I have brought Klep to you," she said.

She was a goddess.

She simply smiled at Tynak when he questioned her. "I have brought him to you. Isn't that enough?" She was surprised at the haughtiness in her voice.

As for Klep, he, too, smiled and said nothing. Pushing himself up with his arms, he looked about his village, and Polly recognized anew how much larger it was than the village of the People of the Wind. Tynak summoned four young men, who carried Klep to his tent, and it was one of the largest tents on the compound. Tynak and Polly followed, Polly making sure that Klep's leg was not jolted. Og trotted by her side, occasionally reaching out to nudge her hand. He was not going to leave her.

Klep was placed on his pallet, over which hung a great rack of antlers, even larger than the one in Dr. Louise's kitchen.

"When daylight comes," Tynak said, "the healer will look at your leg."

Klep replied, "My leg is good. She"—he indicated Polly —"has the healing powers of the goddess."

Polly had stopped feeling goddess-like.

Klep asked, "You are cold?"

Even in Anaral's sheepskin garment, she still felt the cold from the lake. Drawing herself up again, she ordered Tynak, "Have someone bring me my coat." Not only would it feel comforting and familiar, but she wanted to know whether or not Tynak had taken Zachary's icon.

He spoke to one of the men who had carried Klep. "Quick!" And the man ran off swiftly.

Klep spoke to Tynak. "Across the lake, I was well treated."

Tynak nodded. "Brown Earth told us the same."

"I was not treated as a prisoner or an enemy. I was treated as a friend."

Tynak shrugged. "Trust easily come by can vanish as easily."

Klep asked, "Where is the young man, Zak?"

"In my tent. See, I am treating him with kindness."

"He is well?"

Again Tynak shrugged. "The healer will tell."

The man came back with Polly's red anorak, and she put it on over Anaral's tunic, feeling in the pockets. The icon was gone. That was not surprising. She pulled out the flashlight and shone it directly in Tynak's eyes. "Give me my angel," she demanded.

Tynak put his hands to his eyes in terror.

She turned the flashlight off, then on again. "Give me my angel."

Tynak shook his head, though the flashlight had shaken him badly.

Polly kept it shining into his eyes and he turned away. "The icon of the angel has no power in itself. The power of the angel is for me." She touched her chest. "If you try to keep it, it will turn against you."

"Tomorrow," he promised. "Tomorrow."

Where had he hidden it?

She flicked off the flashlight. "Light that does not burn," she said.

She turned the flashlight on again, not to blind Tynak with its beam, but to give more light to the tent, and she could see that there were beads of sweat on Klep's forehead and upper lip. The trip across the lake and then to his tent had been hard on him. Polly pointed to him with the light. "He needs rest. Someone should be near in case he calls."

Tynak understood. "Doe will stay."

"I want to go now," Polly said. "I am tired and wish to rest." She moved toward the tent flap, Og beside her.

Tynak bowed and escorted her back to the lean-to, taking care not to get too close to Og. They were followed by two of the men who had carried Klep, not Brown Earth, but Onion and another man, squat and strong. Tynak spoke to them rapidly and sharply. Then he bowed and turned back toward Klep's tent. The two men stationed themselves on either side of the lean-to. She was being guarded. She had proven that she could escape, and Tynak was going to see that this would not happen again.

Polly went into the lean-to and pulled on her jeans under the sheepskin tunic. She was shivering with exhaustion as well as cold. She zipped up the anorak, then wrapped herself in the fur. She was so tired that she almost fell down on the pallet. Og lay beside her, warming her.

When she woke to daylight, Tynak was again squatting at the entrance to the lean-to, watching her, eyeing Og, who was sitting up beside Polly, his ears alert. Her two guards had drawn respectfully away a few yards, but they were still there. It was one day off full moon.

She sat up, regarded Tynak in silence for a moment, then demanded in a tone she hoped befitted a goddess, "Bring me my angel. Now."

He looked at her and his eyes were crafty.

She felt in the anorak pockets and pulled out the notebook and pen. She opened the notebook, which must have been used by her grandfather, for the first pages were filled with incomprehensible equations in his scratchy writing. She held them up to Tynak. Then she turned to an empty page, and took the cap off the pen. She was no artist, but she managed a recognizable likeness of the old man. She held it out to him. Snatched it back as he reached for it.

"Power," she said. "It has great power. Bring me angel icon. Bring me Zachary. Bring me healer."

He stood. Held out his hand again. "I-con?"

"Picture of you is not icon. You bring me angel icon, I give you picture. Pic-ture."

His hand reached for it.

"Not now. When you come back with angel."

He left, walking with what dignity he could. The two guards drew in closer to the lean-to. After a few minutes Polly was brought a bowl of gruel by Doe, who looked fearfully at the dog. Polly took the bowl, said, "Thank you," and put her hand on Og's neck. "He won't hurt you."

Og's tail swished gently back and forth. Doe smiled, not coming closer, but standing and watching Polly. It was obvious that she would have liked to talk if she could. Polly thought that it was not only Og or the language difficulty. She suspected that Tynak had forbidden conversation.

"Klep says careful," Doe warned. "Careful."

One of the guards peered at them.

"Thanks," Polly said softly as the girl hurried away.

She ate the gruel, which was dull but nourishing. It made her appreciate her grandmother's oatmeal. Would she ever have that again? She put the bowl down at the entrance of the lean-to and waited. Waited. The great oak trunk behind the lean-to rose up high into the sky, much higher than the Grandfather Oak. Polly listened, and seemed to hear the heartthrob of the huge tree, the sap within the veins running slowly as it drew in for the winter. Patience. Do not fear. A star-line touches my roots and my roots are under you.

The wind stirred the branches. Ruffled the waters of the lake. It was a warm wind, unseasonably warm. Listen to the heart of the oak. We are with you. Last night the water carried you safely. Trust us.

Yes, she would trust. The universe is a *universe*. Everything is connected by the love of the Creator. It was as Anaral had said: it was people who caused problems. And the dark angels who were separators added to the damage.

She waited. Og lay beside her, his tail across her legs. Suddenly he jumped to his feet, tail down, hair bristling.

Tynak.

He handed Polly the icon. She took it and put it back in her anorak pocket, then drew out the notebook and tore out the page on which she had sketched Tynak, and gave it to him.

He held it up, looked at it, turned the page over, saw only the blank page, and turned back to the sketch. Touched himself, touched the piece of paper, then put it carefully in his tunic. Satisfied, he gestured that she was to follow him. "Leave—" He gestured toward Og.

"No. Og goes with me."

Tynak shook his head, but set off across the compound, looking back to see that Polly was following him. Several paces behind Polly, the two guards moved silently. Og walked slightly in front of her, putting himself between Polly and Tynak.

The chief of the People Across the Lake led her to a tent considerably larger than the others. The flap was pegged open, and she could see inside. Zachary had been right: on poles stuck deep in the earth of the tent were skulls. Zachary was there, and an old man, far older than Tynak, thin and brittle as a winter leaf. But his face had a child's openness, and his eyes were kind. He looked at Og questioningly, and Polly gestured to the dog that he was to lie down.

"Where have you been?" Zachary's voice shook with anxiety. "We were frantic. Where were you?" He rose from his pallet, his hair slightly damp, his eyes dark with fear. When she did not answer, he gestured to the old man. "This is their healer. He won't touch me without you."

Polly looked at the old man and bowed slightly. He smiled at her, and it was a child's smile, radiant and without fear. He pointed at her hair, nodding, nodding, as though both surprised and satisfied. Then he looked at Tynak, pointed again at Polly's hair.

Zachary said, "They think your red hair is another sign that you are a goddess. They go in for a lot of signs, these people. Now will you get the old man to take care of me?"

"You may examine Zachary's heart," she said, and the role of goddess was not comfortable. She pressed her hand against her own chest, then pointed to Zachary's.

The old healer indicated that Zachary was to lie down. Then he knelt beside him. He took Zachary's wrist in both his hands, touching it very lightly, just above the palm, listening intently, his eyes closed. Occasionally he lifted his fingers from Zachary's pulse, lightly, seeming to hover over his wrist like a butterfly, or like a dragonfly over the waters of the lake. Then the fingers would drop again, gently.

After a while he looked up at Polly with a slightly questioning regard. She nodded, and he looked at Zachary again, indicating that he was to remove his jacket and shirt.

Obediently, Zachary complied, fingers shaking, then lay back down. The old healer knelt and bent over him, holding his hands stretched out about an inch above Zachary's chest, moving his fingers delicately, cautiously, in concentric circles. After a long time he touched the tips of his fingers against Zachary's skin. The healer waited, touching again, then hovering. Polly could almost see wings quivering. His palms pressed against Zachary's chest. The old man leaned so that his whole weight was on his hands. After a moment he lifted his hands and sat back on his heels, his body drooping. His whole focus had been intensely on Zachary for at least half an hour.

He looked at Polly and shook his head slightly. "Big hurt in heart."

Zachary cried out, "Can you fix it?"

The healer spoke to Tynak and Polly could not understand him, except that he was saying something about Klep.

Tynak said, "You, goddess, did help Klep. Help this Zak."

Polly gestured. "I only held Klep's hands while Cub set his leg. I would help if I could, but I have no training as a healer." She could not tell whether they understood her or not.

The old healer indicated that he wanted to see her hands. Polly held them out, and he took them in his, looking at them, back, front, nodding, making little sounds of approval. He held out his own hands again, then indicated that he wanted Polly to hold her hands over Zachary's chest as he was doing.

"Stay," she said firmly to Og, and knelt beside the healer. He put his hands over hers, and together they explored the air over Zachary's chest, and she felt a strange tingling in her palms, and her hands were no longer ordinary hands, and they were not functioning in ordinary time. She did not know how long their four hands explored, moved, touched Zachary's heart without ever touching his skin. Slowly, discomfort moved into her hands, and a feeling of dissonance.

The old healer raised his hands, and suddenly Polly's fingers were icy. She looked at the healer. "Power," he said. "Good power. Not enough."

"What's he saying?" Zachary demanded.

"He's saying that together we have good power."

"You're not a doctor," Zachary said. "Does he know what he's doing?"

"Yes. I think he does." She wondered what Dr. Louise would feel.

"You really do?"

"Zachary, these people don't think in the same way that we do. They look at healing in a completely different way."

"So am I healed?"

She looked at the old man. "Is he better?"

"Better. Not—"

"His heart?"

The old healer shook his head. "Better, but not—"

"What's he saying?" Zachary demanded anxiously.

"He says your heart is somewhat better, but it is not cured."

"Why not?"

"He says there is not enough power."

Zachary seemed to shrink. "Why not?" His voice was thin, a child's wail.

The healer rose and beckoned to Polly. She followed him, calling over her shoulder to Zachary, "I'll be back." Og was at her heels like a shadow as she and the healer went to Klep's tent.

He greeted them, smiling. "The healer says I am—am a marvel."

"You're healing well," Polly agreed. "You're young and healthy. You'll be fine in a few weeks, as long as you do what Anaral says, and take care of yourself."

The healer spoke to Klep, then bent to look at his leg, nodding in approval.

Klep said, "He wants you to know that you helped. But Zak's heart is bad."

"I know," Polly said. "Oh, Klep, he is so frightened."

"Healer has helped. If he had more power, he could help more. Why is Zak so afraid? Life is good, but where we go next, that is good, too."

"Zachary doesn't believe that," she said.

"He thinks it is bad?"

"No. He thinks it's nothing. That he'll be gone."

Klep shook his head. "Poor Zak. Healer will try again. Try to help."

Could he, Polly wondered, when doctors with all their modern tools of surgery could not? But that the old man was truly a healer in some way she did not yet understand was certain.

There was nothing specific for her to do. Wherever she went, the two guards were in the background, not approaching her, but keeping her in sight all the time. She walked around the village with Og, but the villagers were nervous about the dog and shot fearful glances at Polly. She did not understand why the fear was also angry, but there was no mistaking their antagonism.

She did not know what was on Tynak's mind. He spent a long time in his tent with Zachary, and came out, looking at the sky as though seeking a sign.

Doe brought Polly her lunch. She drew away, but did not leave. Polly asked, "Why must I eat alone?"

Doe shook her head, glanced at the guards. "Tynak."

"Why are people afraid of me?"

"Goddess." Doe's eyes were troubled. "Where rain?"

Shortly after lunch Tynak came to the lean-to. "Angel?" he asked.

Polly brought the icon out of her anorak pocket and held it up so he could see it, but did not give it to him.

"An-gel has power?"

"Yes. For me. Good power."

Tynak pulled the sketch out from under his tunic. "Power."

"Power is mine," Polly said firmly.

"Mine." Tynak put the sketch away. It was crumpled, as though he had shown it to many people. "Come." He beckoned, and she followed him, Og at her heels. Tynak led her past the village, along a narrow path through the forest of great and ancient trees, until they came to a clearing. All the trees that surrounded the clearing were completely defoliated. Not a single leaf was left clinging to the branches. The trunks and limbs were dark and bare and somehow sinister. The trees farthest from the clearing held a few fading yellow leaves, so pale as to be almost white, and one by one they were drifting listlessly to the ground. In the center of the clearing was a large rock with a flat top, slightly concave. Tynak went up to it, and Polly followed him. There was a foreign chill to the air. Polly felt an oppressiveness on her chest, so that she gasped for breath. On the rock were rusty stains.

Polly pointed. "What?"

"Blood," Tynak said.

Blood. Dried blood. So this was where sacrifices had been made, and where Tynak was considering a new sacrifice.

Og growled, low and deep in his throat. Polly put her hand on his head and tried to still the apprehension which prickled her skin.

"An-gel protect?"

She tried to look haughty. "Yes." Quickly she pulled out the notebook and pen and made another sketch of Tynak, not as good as the first, because her hands were shaking in her hurry, but still recognizable. She reached in her pocket for the scissors, and cut the picture in half. Then she looked at Tynak. "Power."

Tynak clutched his chest as though she had actually hurt him.

Polly put the pieces together, shut the notebook, and put it back in her pocket.

Tynak was visibly shaken. "An-gel give knife with two blades?"

"Angel guards me. Og guards me. Why are you bringing me here?"

"Place of power."

"Bad place," Polly said.

"Good power. Makes rain. Makes Zak's heart good."

"I want to talk to Zak," Polly said sharply.

Tynak gave her a sly, slantwise look. "Goddess's blood has much power. Tomorrow full moon. Power."

She had to ask directly. "Does Zachary know?"

"Know what?"

"About this place? About—" She swallowed painfully. "About my blood giving the healer more power."

"Zak knows. Zak wants."

"Suppose," Polly said, "I am not here tomorrow? Suppose the angel takes me away?"

Tynak glanced at the two guards standing uneasily at the outside of the circle. "No. Angel not take you away."

"And if it rains before tomorrow?"

Tynak clapped his hands. "Good. More power."

"And the healer will help Zachary?"

Tynak shrugged. "If healer has enough power, will help."

Og's growl was low and deep and menacing.

"Stop," Tynak said.

She pressed her hand against Og's head. Tynak would not hesitate to kill Og. If it would make it easier for himself, or for whomever he would order to capture Polly, to drag her to this clearing with the terrible stone, to add her blood to the blood that had been shed there through the years—yes, Tynak would kill Og if he thought that would lessen her power. Og, if he was not killed first, would not let Polly be taken without a fight. But Og could not hold out against an entire tribe. She looked at Tynak and decided that the only reason he had not already killed the dog was a superstitious fear that Polly's and the angel's powers would wreak vengeance.

What was there to do? Her heart was thumping painfully, heavy as a stone. Was that how Zachary's heart felt all the time?

Tynak turned away from the dreadful rock and led her back to the lean-to. The two guards drew near again. One had a bow and arrow, the other a spear. She might be a goddess. She was also a prisoner.

After Tynak left, she walked out of the lean-to, passing between the guards, and they followed her, silently, as she went to the lake. "Go, Og!" she cried, and the dog ran into the lake and swam rapidly. She swung round on the two young men, stopping the one who was fitting an arrow to his bow. "No!" she ordered.

The two men looked at each other, not knowing what to do. When one hefted his spear, she hit his arm sharply. She was sure that they had been told not to hurt her. Her blood was too valuable to be spilled other than ritually. She watched until Og was barely visible, certainly out of range of arrow or spear, swimming strongly away from them. Then she went back to the lean-to, and the young man with the bow and arrows hurried away, no doubt to report to Tynak.

She had sent Og off and that was all she could do.

She sat on the pallet. Did Zachary know what he was doing? Had Tynak somehow promised him that the healer could cure him if he had just a little more power and Polly's blood would give him that power? She did not know him well enough to guess whether or not in his extremity he would willingly, knowingly let her be killed in the hope that his heart could be mended.

She thought of the healer holding his hands over Zachary with the delicacy of a butterfly, of her own experience of the healer holding his hands over hers, as warmth flowed through them. There had been incredible power and beauty in the old man's hands. Could he be a healer and yet with his healing hands take her blood to enhance his power? Could benign power and malign power work together? Mana power and taboo power were each an aspect of power itself.

Well, she, Polly, meant nothing to the healer. He operated from a completely different view of the universe from hers. And she could not superimpose her mores on him.

There were skulls in Tynak's tent.

She was three thousand years from home.

She tried to breathe slowly, calmly. Tried to pray. Bishop Colubra had made it quite clear that although Jesus of Nazareth was not to be born for another thousand years, Christ always was. She turned to the words of a hymn that had long been a favorite of the O'Keefe family:

> Christ be with me,
> Christ within me,
> Christ behind me,
> Christ before me,
> Christ beside me,
> Christ to win me,
> Christ to comfort
> and restore me.

She lay back on the pallet, her hands behind her head, looking up at the leather roof of the lean-to. In the bright sunlight, patterns of oak branches moved across it in gentle rhythm. Hsh. Breathe softly, Polly. Do not panic. The sap moving like blood in the veins of the oak followed the rhythm of the words.

> Christ beneath me,
> Christ above me,
> Christ in quiet,
> Christ in danger,
> Christ in hearts of
> all that love me,
> Christ in mouth of
> friend and stranger.

Would Bishop Colubra call it a rune? A rune used for succor, for help, and she was calling on Christ for help.

Danger. She knew that she was in danger. From all sides. The healer needed more power for Zachary's heart. Tynak needed power for rain.

Christ in hearts of all that love me.

Right now she was more aware of her grandparents, of the bishop and Dr. Louise, than she was of her parents and brothers and sisters, who knew nothing of what was going on. The bishop, Karralys, Annie, Cub, Tav. They were across the lake, waiting. They loved her. They held her in their hearts. What would they think when Og came? They would know that she had sent him. What would they do?

Christ in mouth of friend and stranger.

Karralys and Anaral were no longer strangers. They were friends. Cub was like a little brother. Tav. She was in Tav's heart. Klep had talked of the lines between himself and Anaral, between Tav and Polly. Love.

Stranger.

Tynak was still a stranger. There was no line between Polly and Tynak. But there was between Polly and the healer. Surely the loving power of Christ had been in those delicate hands as they explored Zachary's pulse, breath, heartbeat.

And was there a line between Polly and Zachary? Did one choose where the lines were going to go? If Zachary was truly willing to attempt to save his own life by urging that Polly be sacrificed, what happened to the line? Where was Christ?

She was sure that the bishop would say that there was no place where Christ could not be.

Where was Christ in her own heart? She felt nothing but rebellion, and rejection of the clearing in the woods with the terrible stone.

She thought of Dr. Louise's words about a blood transfusion. If she could save one of her brothers or sisters by offering all of her blood, would she do it? She did not know. A thousand years away, that blood had been freely given. That was enough. She did not have to understand.

A light breeze, warm, not cold, slipped under the lean-to

and touched her cheeks. Little waves lapped quietly against the shore. The oak tree spread its powerful branches above her. Beneath the ground where she lay, the tree's roots were spread from the trunk in all directions. Lines of power. Tree roots reaching down to the center of the earth, to the deep fires that kept the heart of the planet alive. The branches reached toward the lake, pointed across the lake to where people who loved her were waiting. The highest branches stretched up to the stars, completing the pattern of lines of love.

The breeze moved in the oak tree. A leaf drifted down to the roof of the lean-to and she could see its shadow. She listened, and a calm strength slowly began to move through her.

Her peace was broken by the two guards summoning her. The one with the spear banged it on the ground. The one with the bow and arrow reached down to pull her up. She shook him off and stood, putting her anorak on over the sheepskin tunic, though the day was warm. The two men looked in awe as she pulled up the zipper. Here was a showing of power she hadn't even thought about. She reached her hand into the pocket to make sure the icon was there.

If she knew their names, they would have less power over her. "I am Polly." Not goddess: Polly. "You are?" She looked questioningly at the man with the bow and arrow. "Polly. You?"

"Winter Frost," he said reluctantly.

"And you?" She looked at the man with the spear. "Polly. You?"

"Dark Swallow."

"Thank you, Winter Frost, Dark Swallow. You have beautiful names." Even if they did not understand her words, she could convey something with her voice.

Dark Swallow led the way. Polly followed behind him, wishing that Og were trotting along beside her, at the same time that she was visualizing Og swimming ashore, letting the People of the Wind know that she was in trouble. But what could they do? They were a small tribe, less than half the size of the People Across the Lake.

Her steps lagged and Winter Frost prodded her with his bow.

They were taking her to the clearing in the forest, the clearing where the surrounding trees had lost all their leaves, where the great bloodied rock waited. But it was daylight, full daylight. They would do nothing until night and moonrise. Even so, she hung back, and Winter Frost prodded her again.

Tynak and the healer were there. Tynak nodded at the guards, who retreated well out of the open circle, waiting. Tynak and the healer both spoke at once, then Tynak, then the healer, a scrambling of staccato words which Polly found it impossible to understand.

"Slow," she urged them. "Please speak more slowly."

They tried, but still she caught only words and phrases. They kept repeating until she understood that they were asking her if she, a goddess, was immortal. If she was placed on the sacrificial rock, and if her blood was taken so that the healer's power was augmented, would she be dead, really dead, or would she, as a goddess, rise up?

She held out her hands, palms up. "I am mortal, like you. When I die, I am dead, like anybody else." Did he understand? They looked at her, frowning, so she tried again. "This body— it is mortal. If you take my blood from me, this body will die."

The healer took her hands in his, which trembled slightly. When he had held them over Zachary, they had moved like a butterfly, but they had not trembled. He looked carefully at the palms of her hands, then the back, then the palms again.

"Do you really believe," she asked, "that my blood will give you enough strength so that you can cure Zachary's heart? You are a healer. Do you really believe that you need my blood?"

There was no way he could understand her, but she asked anyhow. He shook his head and his eyes were sad.

Suddenly she had an idea. She took Anaral's little gold knife out of her anorak pocket and opened it. Quickly she made a small cut in her forearm, held it out to the healer so that he could see the blood which welled out of the cut. "Will that do?"

With one finger he touched a drop of blood, held his finger to his nose, to his mouth.

"Not enough!" Tynak shouted. "Not enough!"

Polly continued to hold her arm out, but the healer shook his head. She remembered that Anaral had given her a Band-Aid as well as the little knife. She felt for it in her pockets, opened it, and put it over the small cut. Both the healer and Tynak stared, wide-eyed, at the Band-Aid.

But the Band-Aid was not particularly impressive power. If they cut her throat—was that how they did it? or would they go for her heart itself?—there was no Band-Aid powerful enough to stanch the blood, stop it from draining her life away.

She said, "I want to speak to Zachary."

"Zak wants not," Tynak said. "Not to talk with you."

She spoke with all the hauteur she could summon. "It makes no difference whether Zachary wants to talk to me or not. I wish to talk with him." She turned away from the two men to the path which led away from the clearing.

There were the two guards barring her way.

She turned imperiously. "Tynak."

Tynak looked at the healer.

The healer nodded. "Take to Zak."

Zachary was sitting in the shadows within Tynak's tent. The flap was open, and light hit the whiteness of skulls on poles, emphasized the whiteness of Zachary's face.

"I told you not to bring her here," he said to Tynak.

Tynak and the healer simply squatted at the entrance to the tent. Polly stood in front of Zachary.

"Go away." He looked down at the packed earth.

"Zachary. Why don't you want to see me?"

"What's the point?"

"Tonight is full moon."

"So?"

"Zachary. I need to know. Do you want them to put me on the rock and sacrifice me so that the healer can get the power of my blood?"

"Of course I don't want that! But they won't do it. You're a goddess."

"Zach, you must know they're planning to sacrifice me for my blood."

He shrugged. Looked away.

"Look at me."

He shook his head.

"How do you feel about this?"

He raised dark, terrified eyes. "I don't go in for all that guilt stuff."

"But you'll let them take my blood?"

"How can I stop them?"

"You really think my blood will give the healer power to help your heart?"

"Don't be silly. It's for rain."

"But you think the healer will use the power to make you well?"

"Who knows?"

"Zachary, you're willing to let me die?"

He shouted, "Shut up! I don't have anything to do with it! Go away!"

She turned away from him so abruptly that she faced one of the skulls, almost bumping into it. There had once been flesh on those white bones, eyes in the sockets, lips to smile. But whoever had once fleshed the skull was three thousand years gone, as was Tynak, as was the healer.

If Zachary stayed there at her expense, if she died, and if Zachary lived, he, too, was three thousand years gone.

It did not ease the pain of knowing that he was willing to let her be sacrificed.

CHAPTER 12

THE sun burned like a bronze shield. A strange heat reflected from its fires, touching the water with a phosphorescence. It was hotter than it had been when she swam across the lake. The guards kept glancing in her direction. Now that Og had escaped, the guards would be even more careful with Polly.

This was the Indian summer she had been told about, Indian summer that came in November with a last reminder of summer before the long cold of winter. But this was hotter than she had expected Indian summer to be. Hotter than it should be? Perhaps weather patterns were different three thousand years ago. Across the lake, lightning played, and thunder was always in the background, an accompaniment to the steady beating of the drums, Tynak's people drumming for rain, the sound intensified hour by hour. For rain, or for sacrifice?

The pallet of ferns was soggy with heat and humidity. She pulled it to the entrance of the lean-to, hoping for a breath of air. Lay back with her eyes closed. A warm breeze touched her gently. In her mind's eye she saw her room which had once been Charles Wallace's room. Looked out the window to the view of field and woods and the low, ancient hills that gave her a sense of assurance that the jagged mountains did not. She moved her imaging to her grandmother's lab, where she was always cold; tried to feel her feet on the great stone slabs that formed the floor, chilling her toes. Then in her mind's eye she looked out the kitchen window to see her grandfather on his tractor. Saw Bishop Colubra at the stone wall, Louise the Larger coiled up in the warm sunlight. Saw Dr. Louise in her daffodil-colored sweater walking across the field toward her brother.

In this manner she moved through three thousand years. In eternity, her own time and this time in which she was now held, waiting, were simultaneous. If she died in this strange time, would she be born in her own time? Did the fact that she had been born mean that she might escape death here? No, that didn't work out. Everybody in this time died sooner or later. But if she was to be born in her own time, wouldn't she have to live long enough to have children, so that she would at least be a descendant of herself? Karralys understood riddles such as this one. Polly shook her head to try to clear it.

Energy equals mass times the speed of light squared. What did Einstein's equation really mean? Did her grandfather understand it? Her grandfather, at home in her own time—her grandmother, Dr. Louise, they must all be frantic with anxiety. Dr. Louise would not know what had happened to her brother, who had gone off in hiking shoes.

And on this side of time, across the lake, the bishop, Karralys, Tav, Cub, Anaral, what were they doing? If Og had reached them, they would be asking each other how they could help; they would be trying to make plans.

Leaves drifted down onto the skins of the lean-to. The air was so heavy with humidity that she felt she could reach out and squeeze it.

She looked up as she heard a strange, dragging sound, and coming toward her was Klep, supported on one side by the old healer, on the other by a young warrior; Klep, hopping on his good leg.

"Klep!" she cried out. "You'll hurt your leg!"

The healer and the warrior gently placed him down next to Polly. His face was ashen, and beads of sweat broke out on his forehead.

"Klep! What have you done? You shouldn't have come!" Polly knelt by him.

"I have spoken with Tynak," Klep whispered.

The healer gestured at the warriors, who glanced wonderingly at Klep, then drew back several paces. Then the healer knelt on Klep's other side and examined the broken leg, lifting the compress of mosses on the wound where the skin was cleanly healing but was still pink and new-looking. He held his hands over it, shaking his head and mumbling. "There is fever again. He should not be upset," Polly understood him to say. "In his tent he did fret, fret . . ." He held his hands over the leg, glanced at Polly, nodded. She held her hands out, too, just over his. The healer withdrew his right hand to place it over Polly's, not touching, hovering delicately. Again she felt the tingling warmth, and then a strange heat, as though they were drawing the fever out of Klep's inflamed skin. Then the heat was gone and there was a sense of color, of gold, gold of sky in early morning, gold of butterfly wings, gold of finch in flight.

The pinched look left Klep's face, and his whole body released its tension. He looked gratefully at the healer and Polly. "Thank you. I am sorry to have caused trouble. I had to come." He looked pleadingly at the healer, who squatted back on his heels. "I have spoken with Tynak," Klep said again. "He has said that you have caused the rain across the lake with the angel you took from him."

"I didn't take the angel from him," Polly pointed out. "He tried to take it from me."

"He is angry and he is fearful. He says that you are withholding rain from us, and the people are angry."

With Klep, Polly could not understand every word, but enough to get the gist of what he was saying.

"I don't control the rain," she said. "I want it to rain here as much as you do."

The healer murmured, but Polly guessed that he was saying that a broken leg was easier to heal than anger.

Briefly Polly closed her eyes. Her voice shook. "I thought when Zach kidnapped me it was for me to be the sacrifice so the healer would fix his heart."

The healer shook his head. "No, no." And from his mumblings she guessed that it was Tynak who had prevented the healer from working with Zachary until Polly came. A healer heals.

Klep said, "That is what Zak thought, what Tynak wanted him to think, maybe what he still thinks. But the people do not care one way or the other about Zak. They are tired of raiding to get food. They want the sacrifice so there will be rain."

Polly thought of Anaral singing her hymn of joy to the Mother after she had placed the flowers on the altar, of the People of the Wind greeting morning and evening with harmony. "Your god demands sacrifice and blood or the rain will be withheld?"

Klep said what she took to mean "For each person the god is different."

"There is a different god?"

"No. Each person sees differently."

"Klep, what do you believe?"

"That you are good. That you have nothing to do with rain or drought. That your blood is your life and, while it is in you, you will use it for good. But the power is when you are alive, not when you are dead and the blood has spilled on the ground." He added, "Anaral says I am a druid," and smiled.

Polly was listening intently, translating Klep's words as he spoke into words she could comprehend.

"The healer has much power," Klep continued. "I have seen him bring back life where I thought there was none. But even he cannot bring your blood back into you if it is spilled out of your body."

The healer spoke. His vocabulary was far more in his hands than in his mumbling and this time she could not understand what he was saying.

Klep translated, "Go back to your own place."

"I wish I could."

Klep turned to the old healer. They spoke together for a long time, and Polly could not understand what they were saying. Finally Klep nodded at the healer and turned to Polly. "Tonight, when the moon rises, there will be much noise, many people. We will help you get to the lake, stop the arrows and spears, so you can swim."

"You can do this?"

Klep was fierce. "There will be no sacrifice. The healer has great power. No one would dare throw a spear at him, no one would dare try to stop him in any way. He will protect you as you run to the water."

It was a slim hope, but it was a hope. She did not think she could make the swim again, but better to drown than be put on that terrible altar rock. "Thank you. I am grateful."

"You were good to me," Klep said. "Your People of the

Wind were good to me. I would become one with Anaral. From you I have learned much. I have learned that I love. *Love*. That is a good word."

"Yes. It is a good word."

"What I do, I do not do just for you, though I hope I would do what I do even if it were not for Anaral. But if you are sacrificed, do you think the People of the Wind would let me see Anaral, to love? Do I learn *love* and then let *love* be sacrificed along with you?" Again his brow beaded with sweat. "You will swim?"

"I will swim." She tried to sound certain, for Klep's sake.

The healer spoke again.

Klep said, "You have the gift. The healer says you must serve it."

"Tell the healer I will try to serve the gift." As surely as Dr. Louise had done, all her life, so would Polly try to do.

Klep nodded. Looked out at the village, where people talked in small groups, the sound ugly, menacing. "I will stay with you. I cannot do much, but my presence will help."

The healer looked at Polly. "Will stay."

Surely the healer's presence would keep the people from coming to the lean-to and dragging her out, at least until the full moon rose. And the very fact that these two men, the young and the old, were with her, cared enough to stay with her, filled her with warmth.

She asked, "Klep, what about Zachary? I came back across the lake with you because of Zachary."

"Zak? Oh, he is of no importance."

She did not understand. She repeated, "But I thought I was to be sacrificed so that his heart could be mended."

"That is—" Klep searched for words. "That is not in the middle. Not in the center."

Well, yes. She could understand that Zachary was peripheral. But did he know it?

"If rain comes, if the people are quiet, then the healer—" Klep glanced at the ancient man, who remained squatting back on his heels, as comfortable as though he were in a chair. "He will try to help Zak, because he is healer. Where there is brokenness, he must heal. Tynak wanted you to think that Zak was important because he thought the line was drawn close between you. That you—that you *loved* him."

"No, Klep—"

"I know that the line is between you and Tav, not Zak."

Again she shook her head. "Where I came from, it is too soon. I may sense a line between Tav and me, but love—" She could not explain that not only was she not ready to give her heart to Tav or anyone else, that she had much schooling ahead of her, that in her time she was too young, but also that her time was three thousand years in the future. Perhaps in the vast scheme of things three thousand years wasn't much, but set against the span of a single lifetime it was enormous.

Thunder rumbled. She looked across the lake and saw dark sheets of rain.

Klep looked at it. "Ah, Polly, if you could bring rain here!"

"Oh, Klep, would that I could!"

The healer remained squatting on the ground just inside the shadow of the lean-to. The strange light gave a greenish cast to his face and he looked like an incredibly ancient frog. His voice was almost a croak. "Healer will not let healer go." His ancient eyes met Polly's. Not only was he offering her his considerable protection, he was calling her a colleague.

Groups of villagers were muttering, hissing, sounding like a swarm of hornets, looking toward the lean-to but not coming close. Had it not been for Klep and the healer there, with her, for her, she was not sure what would have happened.

The storm across the lake moved away, farther away, and the brazen sun glowed through angry clouds. The heat was wilting the leaves which were left on the trees and they drifted down, sickly and pale.

Polly closed her eyes. Felt a hand touching hers, an old, dry hand. The healer. A cool wind began to blow, touching her cheeks, her eyelids. The waters of the lake rippled gently against the shore. The angry people fell silent.

Slowly the sky cleared. The thunderheads dissipated. But the sound of drums continued.

The day dragged on. Klep slept, lying on his side, breathing like a child, hand pillowing his head. The healer, too, lay down, and his eyes were closed, but Polly thought that he was not asleep, that he was holding her in a still center of quiet. She could feel her blood coursing through her veins, her living blood, keeping her mind, her thoughts, her very being held in life.

Would she give up that blood willingly?

Where was Zachary? Was he still greedily grasping at life, any kind of life, at any expense? There was no willingness in him, no concern, except for himself. Did he really understand what he was demanding?

There was no sunset. The daylight faded, but there was no touching of the clouds with color. It simply grew darker. Darker. Cook fires were lit. The muttering of the people began again. Here the full moon would not lift up above the great trees of the forest as it did for the People of the Wind, but would come from the lake, rising out of the water.

She heard with horror a hissing of expectation. Tynak strode into the center of the clearing, looking first across the lake, then turning around, looking beyond the compound to the heavy darkness of the forest and the clearing with the bloody stone.

A thin scream cut across the air. It was a scream of wild terror, so uncontrolled that it made Polly shudder. It was repeated. Was there already someone at the terrible altar stone, someone facing a sharp knife? She tried to find the source of the scream.

She saw Zachary struggling, screaming, held by two men of the tribe. He was trying to break away from them, but they had him firmly between them, taking him toward Tynak.

A faint light began to show at the far horizon of the lake.

"No!" Zachary screamed. "You can't kill her! I didn't mean it! I didn't! You can't do it, you can't—" He was babbling with terror. "I'll die, kill me, kill me, you can't hurt her—" He saw Polly, and suddenly he was convulsed with sobs. "I didn't mean it! I was wrong! Oh, stop them, somebody, stop them, let me die, don't let them hurt Polly—"

Tynak came up to him and slapped him across the mouth. "Too late."

Zachary was shocked into silence. He tried to pull one hand away to wipe his mouth, but the two men held his arms, and a trickle of blood slid down his chin.

"The sacrifice must be unblemished," Tynak said. "You are not worthy."

Polly was as cold as when she had swum across the lake. Not only her body seemed frozen, but her thoughts, her heart.

The healer stood, helping himself up by pressing one hand against Polly's shoulder. Then he kept it there, in a gesture of protection.

Klep pushed himself up into a sitting position. Polly saw, without really taking it in, that he had a curved knife at his belt, which he now took out and held firmly.

"Tynak, I warn you," he started, but Tynak raised his hand threateningly. With his position of authority as chief of the tribe he did not need a weapon. And Klep, with his broken leg held stiffly between two staves, could not move.

Tynak gestured contemptuously to the two guards who held the struggling Zachary. They dropped him as though he were a dead beast. He fell to the ground, whimpering. The guards came to Polly. They looked at the healer, but he did not take his hand from her shoulder. Polly did not recognize these men, who were not Winter Frost or Dark Swallow. Murmuring what sounded like an apology, one of the guards moved the healer's hand, not roughly, then jerked Polly away.

"Stop!" Klep shouted. "Stop!" But he could only watch in frustration and rage as the men dragged Polly toward Tynak.

"Tynak!" Klep warned. "If you hurt her, it will be disaster for the tribe!"

"Blood!" the people screamed. "Blood for the gods! Blood for the ground, blood for rain, blood for growth, blood for life!" The wind rose, making the flaring torches smoke. The moon began to lift out of the lake, enormous, red as blood. Polly thought her heart would stop beating. The people shouted, stamping their feet rhythmically in time to the drums, in time to their calls for blood. Zachary's thin wails were no more than a wisp of smoke. "Blood!" the people chanted. "Blood! Blood!"

Slowly Polly was being dragged across the compound and toward the path through the forest that led to the terrible stone.

Zachary lurched to his feet and threw himself at Polly. One of the guards struck him and he fell again to the ground, mewling like a sick child.

"Look!" Klep cried, his shout rising above the noise of the mob. "Tynak! People! Look to the lake! Do you not see!"

There were shouts of surprise, of terror.

Polly looked, struggling to stand upright. Silhouetted against the great orb of the moon was a large canoe, with carved and curved ends. As the canoe came closer, she could see two men in it. Holding a great paddle was Karralys, with Og standing proudly by him. Standing in the prow was Bishop Colubra, with Louise the Larger twined about his arm in great shining coils.

"See!" Klep cried triumphantly. "The goddess has called and they come! Do you dare touch the goddess?"

The guards released Polly, recoiling in fear.

"Bishop! Karralys!" Polly raced to the shore.

Tynak was not far behind her.

The bishop and Karralys were dark silhouettes against the sky.

Polly splashed into the water, trying to drag the canoe to the shore. Tynak gestured, and Dark Swallow and Winter Frost pulled the canoe up onto the pebbly beach.

Suddenly the moon was obliterated by a black cloud which spread rapidly across the sky, blotting out the stars. The wind gusted, sending smoke guttering from the torches. Cries of fear and confusion came from the people.

"An omen!" Klep called. "Heed the omen!"

Karralys sprang from the canoe, then helped the bishop out. The old man's legs were wobbly, and he leaned on the druid. Louise the Larger clung to him in tight coils. The healer came up to them, peering first at Karralys, then at the bishop, whose face was suddenly illuminated by a startling flash of lightning.

It was followed almost immediately by thunder, rolling wildly between the two chains of mountains, those of the People of the Wind and those of the People Across the Lake.

Then the rain came, at first spattering in heavy drops into the water, onto the beach, the skins of the tents. Then it came in great sheets, almost as though the waters of the lake were rising to meet the rain clouds.

When Karralys and Tav had been blown by the storm to the People of the Wind, the rainbow had arched across the sky and been seen as an omen. Rain had been threatening for days and now it had come, but the People Across the Lake did not accept it as a natural result of clouds and wind patterns, a storm born of a cloud blown by a wind that veered around and came at them from the east, followed by down-drafts producing great charges of static electricity which birthed fierce bolts of lightning and roaring thunder. The storm was seen by the People Across the Lake as a wonder brought by the bishop and the snake, by Karralys and the dog, and by Polly, who had summoned them.

"To the tents!" Tynak cried, and people began to run, women gathering up their children, scurrying across the compound. Tynak held his face up to the rain, his mouth open, swallowing rain in great gulps.

The healer led the bishop to Polly's lean-to, and she and Karralys followed.

"Oh, Bishop," she cried. "Oh, Karralys, thank you. And you, too, Louise, Og. Oh, thank you."

Klep was already soaked by the downpour, and Karralys helped the healer and Polly drag the young man to shelter.

Zachary was still huddled on the ground, the rain pelting down on him. Nobody seemed to notice him.

Polly looked at the bishop. Everybody was dripping rain. Louise the Larger had retired to the farthest corner of the lean-to. The lightning flashed again, hissing as it struck water. When the thunder came, she ran out to Zachary. "Zach. Get up. Come."

"Let me die," he moaned.

"Don't be dramatic. Come on. It's raining. There isn't going to be any sacrifice."

Zachary tried to burrow into the hard ground. "Let me alone."

She pulled at him, but he was a dead weight and she could not move him. "Zach. Get up."

Karralys was at her side. Between them they raised Zachary to his feet.

"Come on, Zach," Polly urged. "Just get away from the lightning." She flinched as it struck again, thunder roaring on top of it.

Karralys helped her drag Zachary to the lean-to. When they let him go, he fell to the ground and curled up in fetal position.

"Leave him be," Bishop Colubra said gently.

The rain continued to sweep from the lake across the village. The lean-to was small protection, but the rain was warm. Lightning arrowed down, striking into the lake, onto the rocks of the shore. There was a horrible cracking sound, and then a crashing, which echoed as loud as the thunder.

"A tree," Klep said. "The lightning has hit a tree."

Slowly the storm moved off. Polly counted five beats between lightning flash and thunder, then ten. Then the lightning was only a general illuminating of the sky at the horizon; the thunder was only a distant rumbling.

Tynak came to them, holding his palms out to show that he was weaponless, and bowed to Karralys. Then to Polly. "You brought rain." His voice was awed.

"No, Tynak. Rain came. I did not bring it."

But there was no way she could make Tynak believe that the rain had not come because of her powers. Polly was a goddess who brought rain.

She did not like the role of goddess. "Bishop," she implored.

The bishop was sitting on the pallet. The clouds had gone with the storm, and a flash of moonlight entered the lean-to and struck the topaz of his ring. "It is enough that the rain has come," he said to Tynak. "We do not need to understand."

"You are healer?" Tynak asked.

"Not as your healer is healer, or as Karralys. But that has been my aim, yes."

Tynak looked at him, looked past him to Louise the Larger coiled in the shadows, then nodded at Karralys. "You will come?"

Karralys nodded. "Polly, too."

"Where?" Polly asked.

"To hold council," Karralys said. "It is meet."

"Zachary—"

"Zachary will wait." There was neither condemnation nor contempt in Karralys's voice.

"Bishop Heron," Karralys said, "it is fitting that you come, too." He held out his hand to help the bishop to his feet.

"I go, too," Klep announced. Klep had authority. Ultimately he would be the leader of the tribe. Winter Frost and Dark Swallow were summoned to help him.

"Klep," Polly demurred, "you promised Anaral you'd be careful. This is going to be terribly hard on your leg."

"I go," Klep insisted.

There was still a tension of electricity in the air. Clouds were building up again, scudding past the brilliance of the moon so that light was followed by shadow, shadow by light, making strange patterns as they walked. When they reached the end of the path that led to the clearing, they were blocked. A great oak, the tree the lightning had struck, lay uprooted across the path. There was no way they could get across it to the clearing with the rock.

Karralys went to the felled tree, putting his hand on the enormous trunk. Og leaped up to stand at his side. Tynak drew back, but only slightly, standing his ground.

"This tree will do for our meeting place," Karralys said.

"The goddess"—Tynak bowed toward Polly—"she has great and mysterious powers."

"I am not—" Polly started, but Karralys raised his hand and she stopped.

Karralys's eyes regarded her calmly, their blue bright as sapphires in the moonlight. "Polly, it is fitting that you tell Tynak the terms of our peace."

She looked at him, totally unprepared. His face was serene. The stone in his torque burned like fire. She swallowed. Breathed. Swallowed.

Then she turned to Tynak. "There will be no more raiding. If you are hungry, if you need food, you will send Klep, when he can walk again, to speak with Karralys. The People of the Wind are people of peace. They will share what they have. They will show you how to irrigate so that your land will yield better crops. And if, at some time, they are in need, you will give to them. The People of the Wind and the People Across the Lake are to live as one people." She paused. Had he understood?

He stood beside Karralys, nodding, nodding.

She continued, "To seal this promise, and with Anaral's consent, she and Klep will be"—there was no word for "marry" or "marriage"—"will be made one, to live together, to guard the peace. Klep?"

"That is my wish." Klep's smile was radiant.

Tynak stood looking at Polly, at Karralys, who was leaning against the fallen body of the great tree, at Klep held upright between Winter Frost and Dark Swallow.

Polly said, "These are our terms. Do you accept?"

"I accept." Tynak suddenly seemed old.

"Klep?"

"I accept. Gladly. Anaral and I will seek to bring peace and healing to both sides of the lake."

Polly felt a small nudge in her ribs. The healer was poking her. "Blood," he said.

She nodded. She did not know why she understood what he meant, but she did, perhaps because of childhood stories about blood brothers and sisters. She took the gold knife the bishop had given Anaral, then opened the notebook to a fresh page. She flipped out the blade, which was bright and clean. Looked at Tynak. "Hold out your hand."

Without question, he held his hand out to her. She took the knife and nicked the flesh of the ball of his middle finger, then squeezed it till a drop of blood appeared. This she smeared on the clean page of the notebook.

"Karralys?" He, too, without question, held out his hand,

and she repeated the procedure, then blended the two drops of blood on the page.

"This is the seal and sign of our terms of peace." She took the page, then reached for the scissors and carefully cut the page in half, so that there was mingled blood on each piece of paper. One piece she handed to Karralys, the other to Tynak. Then she took the cut sketch of Tynak and handed him one half and gave the other to Karralys. "This is the sign that you will never break the peace. If you do, Karralys has your power."

Again Tynak clutched his chest as though in pain.

"Karralys will never hurt you," Polly said. "Only you can hurt yourself." She felt infinitely weary. "I would like to go now. Back across the lake."

The healer nudged her. "Zak."

She was too tired to think of Zachary. "What?"

The bishop reminded her. "There is the matter of Zachary."

She leaned against the fallen tree. She was too tired even to stand any longer.

The bishop continued, "You came back here to the People Across the Lake because of Zachary. However, you can forget about him now if you wish."

"Can I? Oh, Bishop, can I?" She never wanted to think of Zachary again. But she pushed away from the fallen tree. "We'll go back to him. I suppose he's still in the lean-to."

The procession moved back toward the village, Winter Frost and Black Swallow supporting Klep so that he could hop without any strain to his injured leg. People were beginning to emerge from their tents. The air, cleansed by the storm, felt fresh and fragrant. Now they looked at Polly with wondering awe.

Zachary was still huddled under the lean-to. She knelt down beside him, put her hand to his cheek, turning him so that she could look into his eyes.

He squeezed his eyelids tight.

She turned to the bishop. "I think he's decompensated," she said. "I mean, I think he's beyond us."

"No," Bishop Colubra said. "Never say that, Polly."

The healer knelt on Zachary's other side.

Zachary whimpered.

The bishop said, "Often an alcoholic can start to recover only when he's gone all the way to the bottom. When there's no place to go but up. Zachary's self-centeredness was an addiction just as deadly as alcoholism." He bent over the stricken young man. "Open your eyes." It was a stern command.

Zachary's eyelids flickered.

"Sit up," the bishop ordered. "You are not beyond redemption, Zachary."

Zachary moaned, "I was willing to let Polly die."

"But not when it came down to it, Zach!" Polly cried. "You tried to stop them."

"But it was too late." Tears gushed out.

"Look at me! I'm here! There will be no sacrifice!"

Now his terrified gaze met hers. "You're all right?"

"I'm fine."

He sat up. "I'll die if it will help you, I will, I will."

"You don't need to, Zach. There is peace now on both sides of the lake."

"But what I did—I can't be forgiven—" He looked wildly from Polly to Tynak to the bishop.

"Zachary." The bishop spoke softly but compellingly. "William Langland, writing around 1400, said, 'And all the wickedness in the world that man might work or think is no more to the mercy of God than a live coal in the sea.'"

Zachary shook his head. "I went beyond—beyond mercy." He gasped, and the blueness around his lips deepened. The healer reached out and placed his palm on Zachary's chest. As Cub had steadied the bishop's breathing, so the healer steadied Zachary's.

"Help him," Tynak commanded. "It would be a bad omen to have a death now."

Karralys knelt and lifted Zachary so that the young man lay against his chest. With one arm he supported him. His right hand reached under Zachary's wet clothes, and he nodded at the healer. The old man opened Zachary's jacket and shirt, baring his chest. Then his hands joined Karralys's, hovering delicately, as though his ancient fingers were listening. Karralys breathed slowly, steadily, so that Zachary's limp body, held firmly against the druid's strong one, could feel and catch the rhythm. He looked at the bishop. "Please."

The bishop, too, knelt, placing his long, thin hands over Zachary's chest.

The healer nodded at Polly.

She lifted her hands, held them out, and then she was caught in the restoring power of the healer and Karralys and the bishop, their hands not touching, but tenderly moving over Zachary's pale and flaccid chest. Again Polly felt the golden tingling, and then a stab of acute pain went through her body like lightning, eased off, leaving her weak and trembling. Again came the warmth, the gold.

Karralys's hands seemed to have a life of their own. They hovered like bird wings, like a firebird. His eyes changed from their serene blue to the burning gold of the stone in his torque and the faint lines in his face deepened. He was far older than Polly had realized. She felt that her hands, her eyes, her mind, her whole body was caught in the electric power which Karralys and the healer and the bishop were sending through Zachary. They were, she felt, mending his heart, but far more than his heart. The depth of the healing was not merely physical but poured through the core of Zachary himself.

Time shimmered. Stopped. Polly was not sure that she was breathing, or that her heart was beating. Everything was focused on Zachary.

Tynak let out a hissing sound and time began again. Polly could feel the steady beating of her heart. The tingling warmth left her hands, but this time they were not cold but warm, and dry. Karralys sat back on his heels, Zachary still leaning against him.

"It is well," the healer breathed.

Karralys smiled. "It is well."

The bishop rose, looking down at Zachary. "It is well."

Now Polly, too, sat back. "Zachary?"

The blue was gone from his lips. "I—I—" he stammered.

"Hush," the bishop said. "You don't need to say anything." He looked at Karralys. "His heart?"

"It will do," Karralys said. "It is not perfect, but it will do."

"Much power," the healer said. "Great, good power." He looked at Og, who was sitting watching, ears pricked high; at Louise the Larger, who was lying quietly, coiled into a circle. "All work together. Good."

"Am—am—am I all right?" Zachary's voice trembled.

"Not perfect," the bishop said, "but Karralys tells us that your heart will do."

"Yes. Yes." A touch of color came to his cheeks. "I don't know what to say."

"Nothing."

"But I was willing to let Polly die, and you still helped me."

"You will not do Polly, or any of us, any good by holding on to your guilt. You will help by taking proper care of yourself. There is more to be renewed than your heart."

"I know. I know. Oh, this time I know."

"Come." Karralys stood. "The storm is over. Now there is rain." The clouds deepened and rain fell, soft, penetrating rain, quenching the thirst of the parched earth. Now winter wheat could be planted, the ground prepared for spring. "Let us cross the lake," Karralys said. "Anaral, Cub, Tav are all anxiously waiting."

Tynak and the healer escorted them to the canoe. Klep, helped by Winter Frost and Dark Swallow, stood on the shore and waved goodbye.

"To Anaral you will give my love." Now that Klep had learned the word "love," his face glowed with joy each time he said it.

The healer raised his arm in blessing.

"Come," Tynak said to the healer and Klep. "At the sixth of the moon we will invite them—all the tribe—for a feast. They will not mind that the food has come from them."

Karralys laughed, and Winter Frost and Dark Swallow splashed into the water, pushing the canoe until it floated free.

Cub and Anaral were waiting eagerly to greet them and ran into the lake to help pull up the canoe. Once ashore, Polly found that she was trembling so that she could hardly walk.

Cub put his arm around her and led her into Karralys's tent. "You have given too much." He helped her onto one of the fern beds.

Where was Tav, she wondered.

The bishop looked at her lovingly. "The virtue has been drained from her. It will return."

"I don't want to be a goddess anymore," Polly said.

Anaral brought her a warm drink, and she sipped, letting it slide down her throat and warm her whole body.

"Klep—" Anaral asked.

"He is all right," Polly assured her.

"Truly all right?"

"He has moved his leg more than he should, but he's all right. He loves you, Annie."

A gentle drifting of color moved over her cheeks. "I am so glad, so glad." She reached out and pressed Polly's hand.

Polly returned the pressure, then looked around for Tav, and realized that not only did she not see Tav, she did not see Zachary. "Where's Zachary?" she asked.

"With Karralys." Cub squatted by Polly, taking her wrist in his gentle fingers, letting it fall only after he was satisfied.

"Don't let him come here," Polly implored.

Cub looked at her questioningly.

"I don't want to see him." If she had to do it all over again, she would do the same thing. She would go back across the lake. She would hold her hands with the healer and Karralys and the bishop over Zachary's heart. But now it was done; it was done and there was nothing left except an exhaustion that was far more than physical.

The bishop smiled at Polly. "I have a great question that will never be answered: Did the time gate open for me, and then for Polly, because of Zachary?"

Karralys entered as the bishop spoke. "Who knows for whom the time gate opened." His voice was quiet. "What has happened here, in this time, may have some effect we do not know and cannot even suspect, here in my time, or perhaps in yours. Let us not try to understand the pattern, only rejoice in its beauty."

Was Zachary part of the beauty, Polly wondered. But she was too exhausted to speak.

"Cub." Karralys turned. "Will you go to Zachary, please, and stay with him?"

Cub nodded and left, obediently, just as Tav burst into the tent.

"Poll-ee!" He rushed to her.

"Tav!"

Tav knelt on the packed earth in front of her, raised one hand, and gently touched her lips. "Are you all right?"

"I'm fine."

"Truly?"

"Truly, Tav." There was a deep sadness in her heart. She would not see Tav again, and that was grief.

"And that Zak?" Tav demanded.

"He is all right, too."

Tav scowled. "He would have let you be killed."

"But he didn't."

"He wanted to."

"Not really, Tav."

"He is not worth one hair of your head."

Anaral nodded. "I am still very angry with him."

"Annie," the bishop chided gently. "You do not think that all that Polly went through was for the sake of Zachary's physical heart."

"I don't know." Anaral's voice was low. "It is Poll-ee I care about. Not Zachary."

"Don't care?"

"Bishop! Maybe his heart"—she touched her chest—"is better. But what about the part of his heart that would let Poll-ee be sacrificed, her life for his?"

"Change is always possible," the bishop said.

Anaral looked rebellious. "For Zak? Who helped kidnap Poll-ee? Who would have let her be put on the altar stone? Who would not have stopped the knife? Can he change? Can he?"

"Can you truly say that change is not possible? Can you refuse him that chance? Can you say that only his physical heart was healed?"

Tav growled, "He would have harmed my Poll-ee."

"Zachary hit bottom," the bishop said. "It was an ugly bottom, yes. But in the pit he saw himself."

Tav pounded his spear angrily on the ground.

The bishop continued, "Now it is up to him."

Anaral scowled.

The bishop smiled. "Your anger won't last, Annie. You are warm of heart."

"Poll-ee is back." Tav reached out again to touch her. "Poll-ee is back. That is all that matters. I do not think about that Zak. I think about Poll-ee, and that the rain has come."

"Yes."

"And now you will go." He held his hands out to her with longing.

She sighed deeply. "To my own time, Tav. If the threshold is open."

"And Zachary?" Tav demanded. "Do you have to take him with you?"

At last Polly laughed. "Do you want him here?"

Tav scowled. "He did not want my Poll-ee out of obedience to the Mother, or for any good save his own."

The bishop looked around the tent. "When Zachary saw Annie, he entered the circles of overlapping time. *Behold, I have set before you an open door, and no man can shut it.*"

"Words of power," Karralys said.

"Yes," the bishop agreed. "From John's Revelation."

"And is the door to stay open, Bishop?" Anaral asked.

"No, Annie. No. But it was wide open when Polly made the decision to return across the lake to Zachary, and you must honor that decision." He turned to Polly. "You were very brave, my dear."

"I wasn't brave. I was terrified."

"But you went ahead and did what you had to do."

Og reached out and licked her fingers. Cub opened the tent flap and came in with Zachary. "It is time?"

Polly looked at Zachary and felt nothing. No anger. No fear. No love.

"Yes," Karralys said. "It is time."

Zachary stood between Karralys and Cub, his face pale, but there was no blueness to his lips. "I don't know what to say."

"Then don't speak," Karralys said.

Zachary looked from one to the other. "What I did was beyond apology."

"You were out of your mind with self," Karralys said. "Now you must understand that though your life has been lengthened, ultimately you will die to this life. It is the way of the mortal."

"Yes," Zachary said. "I know that. Now."

"And in you there is still much healing to be accomplished."

"I know." Zachary was as subdued as a small child after a spanking. But he was not a small child. "I will try." He turned to Polly. "May I come see you?"

Her hand stroked Og's head. "No, Zachary. I'm sorry. I don't want to see you again. It wouldn't be a good idea, for either of us." Her voice was level, emotionless. She had had to go back across the lake for Zachary. But what had to be done had been done.

"But—"

"There are things which you have to learn alone," Karralys said. "One is that you have to live with yourself."

"I don't like myself," Zachary said.

"You must learn to." The bishop's words were a command. "From this moment on, your behavior must be such that when you go to bed at night you will be happy with what you have done during the day."

"Can that happen?" Zachary asked. He looked at Polly. "Can it?"

"Yes, Zachary. It can happen, if you will let it."

Louise the Larger slid across the packed earth, out of the tent.

"Follow her," Karralys ordered.

Tav went to Polly, spoke longingly. "I must let you go?"

"From your presence," Karralys said. "Not from your heart."

"Now I know," Tav said softly, "I was wrong about the

Mother. The Mother asks the sacrifice of love. You have shown me that." He touched Polly's lips with his finger and turned quickly away.

Anaral stretched her hands out toward Polly but did not touch her. "We will always be friends."

"Always."

"And Klep and I will hold you in our hearts."

"You will be in mine."

"The lines of love cross time and space." But a tear slid down Anaral's cheek.

Karralys turned toward Polly, took both her hands in his. "We will never forget you."

"Nor I you."

"And, Bishop Heron, when you came to us through the time gate you started it all."

The bishop smiled. "I, Karralys? Oh, I think not."

At the entrance to the tent, Og barked impatiently.

Karralys stroked Og's head, then said, "I will send Og with you, Polly. You and your grandparents have need of a good guardian dog, and Og is that."

Again Og barked, imperiously.

"Come." Bishop Colubra led the way out of the tent. Polly followed him, and Og nudged his cold nose into her hand. Behind them, the lake shimmered. The white peaks of the mountains reached sharply into the sky.

When they reached the stone wall, Louise the Larger was lying in a warm splash of sunlight. She raised herself up, then slithered down between the rocks.

Polly looked around. The trees were their own young trees, the Grandfather Oak overshadowing them all. The snow-capped mountains were gone, and the ancient hills lay quietly on the horizon. She was back in her own time.

Someone must have been keeping watch. The Murrys and Dr. Louise came running through the apple orchard, across the field, running to greet them. There was much hugging, tears of relief, joyous barking from Og.

Zachary stood quietly apart.

Then Polly's grandparents urged them all into the kitchen, the warmth, the scent of applewood and geraniums and freshly baked bread. Polly and the bishop started to speak at once, telling their own versions of what had happened. Zachary stood in silence.

Then Dr. Louise had her stethoscope out, listening to Zachary's heart. "There appears to be a slight murmur," she said at last. "I'm not sure how much clinical importance it has. Certainly it is not a perfect heart. You will need to check in with your own doctors as soon as possible."

"I will. But there's a difference. I can breathe without feeling I'm lifting weights. Thanks, Doctor. All of you." He went to Polly and took both her hands. "Polly." He looked at her, but said nothing more. She waited, letting him hold her hands. He opened his mouth as though to speak, closed it, shook his head.

"You will—" she started. Stopped.

"Yes, Polly. I will." He withdrew his hands. "I'd better go now."

Polly said, "I'll go out to the car with you."

The bishop put his hand on Zachary's shoulder. "It will not be easy."

"I know."

"Remember that the lines of love are always there. You may hold on to them."

"I will. Thanks."

"God go with you."

"I don't believe in God."

"That's all right. I do."

"I'm glad."

Polly walked with Zachary through the garage and to the lane where he had parked his car. He got in. Rolled down the window.

"Polly." She looked at him. He shrugged. "Sorry. Thanks. Words aren't any good."

"That's okay. Just take care." She plunged her hands into the anorak pockets and her fingers touched Zachary's angel icon. She pulled it out.

"You still have my icon."

"Yes. I always will."

She put the icon back. The bishop came out, walking rapidly across the lawn on his heron's legs. "Come, dear one. Let's go into the house."

"Goodbye," Zachary said. "Polly. You have on that sheep-skin tunic."

She ran her hands lightly over the warm fleece that hung well below the anorak. "Anaral's tunic. I can't return it, can I?"

The bishop smiled. "She would want you to have it. For herself and Klep. For the good memories."

Zachary looked at Polly. At the bishop. Rolled up the window, started the ignition. Waved one hand. Drove off.

The bishop put his arm around Polly and they started back toward the house, to all these people Polly loved. But there were others she loved, too, and she would never see them again.

"What happens to what's happened?" she asked the bishop.

"It's there. Waiting."

"But the time gate's closed, isn't it?"

"Yes. But that can't take away what we've had. The good and the bad."

Again her fingers touched the angel icon. She looked across the fields to the low shoulders of the ancient hills. It seemed that flickering dimly behind them she could see the jagged snow-topped peaks of mountains.

They went into the house.

APPENDIX

HOW LONG IS A BOOK?

1973 or 1974

WHEN we remark that a child is unusually gifted, it is important that we remember what this means. It means, quite literally, that the child has been given a gift, and that the gift, misused, can be taken away. It means that if the child (or adult) is to keep the gift, the child must become a servant, and we live in an age when it is considered humiliating to be a servant.

However, there is no more noble or exciting or exacting a vocation than to serve a gift, and the parent or teacher can be enormously helpful here, not in teaching the child to write or paint or make music (for gifts are given and cannot be taught), but in helping to provide the climate in which the child and the gift can collaborate.

Each work of art (and whether the work is major or minor makes no difference) has its own life, quite apart from the artist, and what the Work does is to come to the artist and say: "Write me." Or "Paint me." or "Play me." And then what the artist does is to listen to the work, heed it, and try to serve it.

Far too much that passes for art in all fields nowadays smacks of manipulation; the artist possesses and controls the work, does not listen to it, cannot comprehend it, and so no real collaboration between artist and work is possible, and the book or picture or piece of music never really comes to life, is, in fact, abortive.

"Service is humiliating. Work is degrading." If we really believe this, and get our children to believe it, there will be no more stories written, no fairy tales told, pictures painted, songs sung. But there is a difference between being a servant and being a slave, between work and drudgery.

We live in a *do it yourself* society, but art is not a do it yourself activity. If we allow ourselves to be led by this cult, we limit ourselves to that fragment of ourselves which we can know, control, and dictate, and which is nervous about anything as wild and free as art.

I have not been happy thinking consciously about work which has always been spontaneous, but children ask me questions, in letters and in person, and I have felt that I ought not to evade the questions but try to answer them as honestly as I can. Mostly I answer in terms of my own stories, because these are the books they ask the questions about, and the only books I have any right to make categorical statements about.

Children are not afraid to ask questions.

"How old are you?" "How much money do you make?" "Are you married?"

Most of their questions are reasonably easy to answer—with the exception of the question which is asked more often than any other: "How long did it take you to write this book?"

It's a more complicated question than it might seem, because there are three totally different answers, and they are all valid.

The first and easiest answer is that a book takes from the moment I am born to the moment when the editor takes the final, final, final revisions out of my hand and says, "This is it, Madeleine. You can't make any more changes."

The second answer is more difficult. A book begins when the idea for it is first acknowledged by my conscious mind—but I have a suspicion that it has been a small seed growing in my creative unconscious long before my conscious mind is aware of it.

For instance, when did I begin to write *A Wrinkle in Time*? The first consciousness of an idea for that book came during a camping trip we took from the Atlantic to the Pacific, southerly, and from the Pacific to the Atlantic northerly. One day, while we were driving through the Painted Desert—which is just about as much out of this world as any of the planets I described in *Wrinkle*—the words: Mrs Whatsit, Mrs Who, Mrs Which, popped into my mind. Where they came from I do not know. All I know is that they arrived, unbidden and unexpected, and I turned to our three children in the back of the car and said, "Hey, kids, I just thought of three wonderful names, Mrs Whatsit, Mrs Who, and Mrs Which. I'll have to write a book about them."

At my feet in an old wooden box were piles of magazines and half a dozen or so paperback books which I was reading at night by flashlight. Most of the books were by mathematicians or physicists—I had just discovered that although lower math has always been and still is incomprehensible to me, higher math is exciting. I was reading these books not just to learn the various theories of the creation of the universe, the theories of relativity, of quantum, but because in the writing of Sir James Jeans, of Einstein, Planck, I got a vision of a universe in which I could believe in God. I was struggling through a period of agnosticism, and the theological books I read simply turned me further from belief. But in the writings of the great scientists and mathematicians I saw a reverence for the beauty and pattern of the universe, for the mystery of the heavenly laws which argued much more convincingly to me of a loving creator than did the German theologians. My response to these books certainly had something to do with the story I began when we got home and I went to my typewriter and set down, "It was a dark and stormy night."

In *A Wrinkle in Time* I was trying first and foremost to tell a good story, because that is my business; I am a story teller and nothing else. But like it or not, I was also writing about a universe governed by the kind of loving God in which I hoped to believe. I thought of it as a heretical book, which, in hindsight, is really pretty funny.

But when did I begin it? Long before our ten week camping trip. This trip was to be, for my husband and me and for our children, the bridge between two very different lives. We were going to leave the small and comfortable world of a tiny New England village, and move to New York and the vast world of city and the theatre. When the trip was over, Hugh almost immediately went off on tour with a play. "What are you going to do?" my mother asked me, "all alone with the children?" "I'll write a book," I said—which is always my way out of a problem.

So I wrote *Wrinkle*, mostly alone in the country while the children were in school, partly on weekends in the city when Hugh's play moved to New York and the children and I drove down to the city to be with him on weekends and look for an apartment. All of this affected the book, and I still don't know just when the writing began.

The book I'm working on now, tentatively called *The Bolivar Portrait*, first thrust itself into my conscious mind four years ago when my husband and I were on a freighter trip. Our freighter was a small, Royal Netherlands ship, with space for twelve passengers, but carrying only six. We were fascinated by the compact little vessel and its cargo; it carried an assortment of grains and seeds; oil well equipment; four cars; two used hearses for delivery in Caracas—and one of these had a bullet hole in the windshield. We were given a list of cargo, roughly translated into English, and one item was *5 boxes reefers*. We asked the Captain, "What *are* these reefers." "Reefer–igerators."

Our first stop was Maracaibo, Venezuela. One of the pleasures of freighter travel is seeing ports where no cruise ships go—I can't imagine a cruise ship putting in at Maracaibo. Another pleasure is wandering up and down the dock and watching the various freighters loading and unloading. Two ships down from ours was a rusty-looking ship with a German flag, but registered in Monrovia, Liberia. We learned from one of our crew that this ship paid very high salaries to its crew, but carried no insurance for them, and if someone were to be hurt or become ill, he'd just be dumped at the nearest port, with no one caring whether he lived or died. There was something definitely sinister about this German-African ship, and it wasn't just my story-teller's imagination. Everybody felt it.

We had a lot of cargo to load and unload in Maracaibo, so the next day all six of us passengers hired two cars to drive out to Lake Maracaibo, about an hour away. The other two couples were pleasant and interesting; a retired professor of dairy farming from Laramie, Wyoming, and his wife, both well up in their eighties; and a couple just our age, with children the age of our children. Carter was an oil man from Houston, and was particularly interested in seeing the oil fields in Lake Maracaibo.

In Maracaibo itself, where we stopped to go to the bank and the post office, I got my first glimpse of the radical discrepancy between rich and poor in the third world. Also, in banks and post-office, at traffic intersections, were policemen or soldiers carrying sawed-off shotguns. We learned later that this is because Maracaibo is only a few miles from the Columbian border, and Colombian bandits come across the border to rob banks and create disorder. And Castro has men up in the hills, trying to infiltrate and start a revolution.

The drive out to Lake Maracaibo was fascinating, along a modern super-highway, alongside of which were occasional strings of booths, with Indians selling native jewelry, sandals, hammocks. There were a good many lean-tos where fresh coconut milk was sold; it looked delicious, but highly unsanitary, so we didn't try it; the coconut was chopped in half with a machete, and the milk poured back and forth between two tin pitchers which looked as though they had never been washed.

We drove through small villages with gayly painted stucco houses (North America could learn something from South America about the use of colour), a few shops, a movie theatre, an outdoor café, and a rococo church.

The lake, when we reached it, took me by surprise. I knew we had gone to look at oil wells, but I was unprepared to see a huge lake with oil wells in the water, stretching for a hundred miles in one direction, fifty in the other. It was like something out of a science fiction story. I was shocked and horrified. We stood on the shore, trying not to step into the black sludge that oozed up to our feet. I turned to Hugh and whispered, "It's rape."

So there is the setting for a story of international intrigue: a Dutch freighter; a dock with a sinister German ship registered in Africa; a town full of shotguns; a glorious lake slowly being killed.

So, that day, I remembered a family story I had not had cause to recall for a long time. A hundred and fifty odd years earlier my great great great great grandfather, Miller Hallowes, left his native England and went to South America to fight with Simon Bolivar for the liberation of that great continent. Miller Hallowes was nineteen years old, and the fourth son; in England the first son got the title; the second and third sons got the army and the church; and the fourth son often went adventuring. Miller Hallowes fought with Bolivar for eleven years, and became his close friend and aide de camp.

At the end of eleven years active service he went home to England on leave. His mother had recently inherited some property in what is now north Florida and part of Georgia, so he went to the northern hemisphere of the new world to take care of his mother's affairs. He intended to stay a couple of weeks; instead he fell in love with a young girl and with the undeveloped country, married, and remained on his plantation, which he called Bolingbroke, until the end of his days. The land must have reminded him of Venezuela—the flora and fauna are very similar. In February the flowering trees bloom, and the land is bright with bougainvillea and oleander and the wings of herons and cranes. The skies are blue and the wind is warm and salty from the sea.

One of Miller Hallowes' most treasured possessions was the last portrait of Bolivar ever painted, given his friend as a token of friendship and esteem, and it was handed down in the family as a great treasure. The South American hero was worn with battle when the portrait was painted; he was already ill, with his skin yellowing; but the man in the portrait is a superb example of the beauty which comes from experience and pain; his posture is noble, his face lean and finc-drawn, the eyes deep and sad and wise.

Not very long ago Aunt Sally, the last of the Hallowes, was living in poverty which was worse than genteel. Finally she had nothing left to sell but the Bolivar portrait, so she spoke to my uncle Bion, an artist, and my cousin Carol, married to an artist, and asked them to arrange a sale for her—but not to just anybody—the portrait had to go to the right person, someone who would value and honour it.

One night at the opera Carol and her husband were discussing the portrait and how to find the right buyer; a man in the box next to theirs had been lending Carol his opera glasses, and during intermission he said, "I beg your pardon—I couldn't help overhearing your conversation. I have spent my entire working life in Venezuela, and I would like to buy the portrait and give it to the Venezuelan government."

And that is what happened. When our freighter anchored in La Guaira, the port for Caracas, Hugh and I made a pilgrimage to the Bolivar museum to see the portrait.

So the setting and the story began to come together in my mind. A man and a boy are sailing to Venezuela to give the portrait of Bolivar to the Venezuelan government. The man is murdered and the portrait vanishes. The story begins.

But someday when someone asks me, "How long did it take you to write this book?" do I say that it began then, when I was in Maracaibo, four years before I put pen to paper on a plane flying home after having given a talk in Seattle? When Hugh and I took that first freighter trip I was working on the first draft of what became *A Circle of Quiet*, working mostly out on deck, and struggling to keep pages of typescript from blowing overboard. The next book that came to me was *A Wind in the Door*, and after that, *The Summer of the Great-Grandmother*, which will be out this coming winter.

So is answer three the right one? Is the stretch of time from the struggle with the first page, always the most difficult to write, to the last revisions, always the most difficult to stop writing—is this the length of time it takes to write a book?

I don't know. In a way *The Bolivar Portrait* began long before I was born, when Miller Hallowes said goodbye to England and went to help Bolivar in South America, for a book has a life of its own. It is not the private property of the writer. With each book I write I am becoming more aware that the book has come to me, introduced itself, as it were, and said, "I have chosen you to write me. Do you think you can do it?" Sometimes I am sure that I can not, but once a book has picked me, it will not let me alone until I sit down and try to get it on paper.

A writer is both inventor and discoverer. An inventor takes inventory of that which is already there. A discoverer dis-covers—uncovers—that which is already there. It is said that Michael-Angelo looked at a block of marble and felt that his job was to release that which was trapped inside. One time the great sculptor, Brancusi, was ill with pneumonia in his studio in Paris. He knew that he was close to dying, and he was ready to die; he felt that his work was done, and that he could go in peace. In his studio was a large block of wood which he had been planning to carve, and which now would remain untouched, and he was content to leave it that way. One morning he woke up and looked across the studio at the block of wood, and it had put forth a small green twig, with a tiny, furled leaf, and he took this as a sign that he was not supposed to die. He was supposed to get well and carve whatever was waiting for him within that block of wood. And he did.

The artist of any discipline is the servant of his work, and this is true no matter what the degree of talent. I am unhappy about writers, particularly writers of books for children, who think that they can manipulate and control words, and who cash in on the latest fad. I am convinced that there is no subject which is in itself tabu, and that any subject which is demanded by the book itself must be respectfully written in the story. A subject becomes tabu when it is not needed, when it is not intrinsic, when it is put into the story because it is fashionable—sex—drugs—the occult. There are in certain children's books today scenes which are literally obscene—ob-scene—that which should be off stage. The writer of children's books should be neither above nor below studying the Greek dramatists.

The idea of service has never been less popular than it is today, and this may be partly because people who serve have often been abused by their masters. A book is a hard task master, but not an abuser. Once a book has come to me and demanded to be written, it will not leave me alone. It wakes me up in the night. It occasionally makes me burn dinner. And it invariably pushes me further than I want to go. It laughs at my simple little plots. Characters I never dreamed of appear out of the blue and demand to take part in the action, and change it around. Characters I thought I knew intimately do things I wouldn't have believed they were capable of doing. (Aunt

Olivia shot her beloved Ron, deliberately shot him dead! I could not believe it, but it happened, and it had to happen. She had no alternative.) I have learned, the hard way, that the book knows better than I what it ought to be, and my job is to listen to it, listen, listen, and try to do to the best of my ability what it tells me to do, go where it tells me to go. Then, at its best, writing becomes a collaboration between two partners, which is what the relationship between master and servant ideally ought to be. A book is a hard task master, lordly, arrogant, but not a slave driver. What it wants to do is to pull me up, make me write better than I know how; what a book wants is to make me a collaborator, not a slave.

I have never wholly served a book, but trying to do so is the greatest joy I know.

When I wrote *A Wrinkle in Time* I was vaguely aware that the book was pushing me in a direction I had never taken before. It was my ninth book—two of the earlier ones never got published—and it was the first time that I had moved into fantasy, or science fiction, in order to try to say things which cannot be said in the language of provable fact. I believed in the book, and when the first rejection came it was a painful one. I was not prepared for nearly two years of rejections. One publisher said that she might be rejecting an *Alice in Wonderland*, but she was afraid of it. Several frankly hated it. Many thought that it was much too difficult for children, but didn't quite think it was for adults. And I had a number of offers of publication if I would make the book easier, so that children could understand it, if I would change the plot, if I would make of the book something different. I was tempted, very tempted. *A Wrinkle in Time* came at the end of a decade of rejections, and along with the impulse to write a book comes the impulse to share it. A book which is not published and read is stillborn. I was very tempted. *Meet the Austins*, which also had taken nearly two years to find a publisher, was not yet out, because the publisher who had finally accepted it was afraid to publish it because there was a death in it. I desperately wanted to be published. I am sure that pride comes in here as well as the need to be read. I spent a great deal of time writing when other wives and mothers were making pie crust and mopping the kitchen floor, and I was not justifying this time by publication and money, and I felt defensive and looked-down on. My temptation to do what the publishers asked for was made even more acute by my agent's and my husband's thinking that perhaps I ought to change the book, that I was being stubborn.

I was perfectly willing to rewrite for years if a publisher got the book, understood what it was trying to make me do, and wanted me to strengthen and deepen. I was not afraid of work.

But stubborn or no, plain pig-headed or not, there was something in me which would not let me change the basic pattern of the book; I could not dishonour the integrity of the work, and if that sounds pompous I can't help it, because there are no other words to say what I mean. It was the integrity of the book itself which kept me from whittling it down into less than it was. When Farrar, Straus, and Giroux finally accepted it, I did a good deal of work, but it was work I could do with courage and joy, because they understood what the book wanted me to do.

If I am not sure when a book begins, I am even less sure when the writing of it ends. I know that it doesn't end when I finish the second or third draft and timorously give it to my editor, for there will be at least several more months work on it, and sometimes a year or more. Then there comes a stomach-dropping moment when the editor firmly takes the manuscript from my hands and says, "That's it. No more rewriting." If the editor did not do this I would still be on my first novel, because I know that the book is never finished, is never fully served.

But it is said that the difference between the dabbler and the real painter is that the real painter knows when to stop painting. I let my editor take the manuscript away from me because I know that I have come to that point in a book where I have done as much as I can do at this particular moment in my experience. I hope that in the next book I can go further, but with this book, this is as far as I can go.

Is the book finished now? Definitely not. It is really only beginning. A book is not born until it is read. Readers grossly underestimate their rôle in the making of a book. It is easy to understand that a play cannot come alive without actors and an audience, that a great symphony cannot come into being if the orchestra plays to an empty hall. It may be a little less easy to understand that a book cannot come to life without a reader. First, the writer has to collaborate with the story, and then the reader has to perform exactly the same function, and if the reader *cannot* collaborate with the story, then the writer has not served the work.

A great work of art never ends. Shakespeare's plays are still being created, not only in the playing of them on the stage, but in the reading of them in the study. My Shakespeare professor at college, whose enthusiasm for the bard was so bright that most of us couldn't help catching fire from her flame, said that there were two of Shakespeare's plays she had never read, because she couldn't bear to have read all of Shakespeare.

When my children read the books I had loved best as a child, and fell equally in love, these books were being recreated. I read *The Secret Garden* aloud to a cluster of little girls one rainy Saturday, and they hung on every word—little girls in a small New England village wholly identifying with another little girl who had been born in India and went to a house of a hundred rooms in Yorkshire. Together at bedtime we recreated *The Wind in the Willows*. Mole and Rat and Toad were as alive in New England as they ever were in Old England. Alone, the children went through L. M. Montgomery, shared with me their discovery of the Narnia chronicles.

Now I am seeing re-creation (we sometimes forget that this is what recreation really means) again, as I read to my grandchildren, the songs from Shakespeare's plays, nursery rhymes, *Peter Rabbit*, fairy tales. Their response and the response of all children, is necessary to keep these stories alive, to keep them from having an end.

And here the teacher, the librarian, the parent, the publisher, all have a tremendous responsibility. First of all, you must read each book you are going to offer to children in any of the media available to you—and I know what a mammoth task this is, and that it is probably impossible for any one person to read everything. But it is important to read as much as you possibly can, because if you, yourself, are not moved, in your own heart, to collaborate with it, then it is not worth offering to the children. I am very much against censorship, but it is, in a sense, inevitable, because we practise a kind of censorship simply in what we choose for children.

And please keep open hearts. Try to listen to each book as the writer has listened. Many adults were *not* moved to collaborate with *A Wrinkle in Time*. Sometimes a book for children makes demands which frighten the adult. I have been having the pleasure of corresponding with several college students at various institutions of higher learning, who have re-read *Wrinkle* and been moved to write to me to share their enthusiasm. From two very different young men, at two very different universities, I had letters last spring after they had read *A Wind in the Door*. Both said that they probably liked it better than *Wrinkle*, and both warned me not to be surprised if the book proved too difficult for adults. One added, *A Wind* is as odd today as *Wrinkle* was ten years ago.

Wrinkle almost never got published. A rejection the Monday before Christmas had me so discouraged that I asked my agent to send it back: "It's too peculiar. Nobody's ever going to see it." So he sent it back to me, reluctantly, but he sent it. It would never have been published if my mother hadn't been with us for Christmas, and if I hadn't been giving her a small party, asking some of her old friends to come to see her. One of them said to me, "Madeleine, you must meet my dear friend John Farrar." At that moment I was against all publishers, and was contemplating learning how to make pie crust. But she went to a good deal of trouble and set up an appointment for me with Mr. Farrar, so I went down to his office, rather gloomily, but with my much-rejected manuscript under my arm.

Did you know that when a publisher is in doubt about a manuscript, the manuscript is apt to be sent to a librarian for an opinion? Farrar, Straus, and Giroux couldn't quite make up their minds, my agent told me, and were sending my book to a librarian. I felt pretty depressed. I had hoped against hope that they would like the book, and would take it, and the wait that seemed endless would end. The librarian reported promptly, and the book was accepted. It wasn't until later that my editor told me what the report was: it was succinct, all right. It said: "I think this is the worst book I have ever read. It reminds me of *The Wizard of Oz*."

So when I ask you to read a book with open hearts, I mean that I hope that you will be tuned to the truth which is beyond provable fact. Don't be afraid of open doors and windows. Does the book have the ring of truth? Or is the writer too much in control, too limited by personal prejudice? Please don't be fooled by the emperor's new clothes. As you read a book, see if it carries you along into collaboration with it. It is our own responses which guide us in knowing what to offer our children. The best part of our lives involves collaboration—the collaboration of man and woman, friend and friend, grown up and child, teacher and student, book and reader.

How long is a book? It is as long as it is being read.

REGINA MEDAL ACCEPTANCE SPEECH

1984

I'VE known for a great many years that librarians are a writer's best friends, the ones who really understand the struggle and the failures and the hopes, the ones who encourage. So being here today means something very special to me. It is not only that the Regina Medal is a great and deeply appreciated honor, which it is, but it is also an affirmation of something that goes back more than twenty years, to the time when I received nothing but rejection slips, and found that, when I got offers of publication if I would change my manuscript in a way which would diminish it, I could not do it. It was not so much that I would not as that I could not. And I am glad that I could not.

During the long period of rejection for *A Wrinkle in Time*, which was my eleventh book to be written, my seventh to be published, I wrote in my journal, "I'll rewrite for months for an editor who understands the book and wants me to deepen it, to make it better, but I cannot mutilate it. I cannot."

When Farrar, Straus, Giroux finally took the book, I did do a good bit of rewriting for an editor who understood it and wanted to make it better, and that was a joy. Rewriting, five and even ten times, for an editor who wants to get the best possible book out of me may be a chore, may take months, but it is a happy chore. And rewriting and revising has taught me that my job as a story teller is to listen: a story has its own life. A good editor, and I have been blessed with several good editors, including my husband, also knows how to listen to the story, and sometimes hear things the writer is temporarily deaf to.

Last week I had the fourth or fifth conversation with a woman who is seriously interested in making a movie of *The Arm of the Starfish*. The standard Hollywood contract contains a clause giving the producer freedom to change character and theme, and that is something I cannot sign. I have seen too many beloved books distorted, even ruined, to turn one of mine over to Hollywood with no restrictions. As a matter of fact, I had decided that I would simply never sell a book to the movies; I'd wait till I was dead and then let Hollywood have its way. Then I saw the movies of books by several dead writers who had not been around to defend themselves or their books, and so I decided that if I could possibly have a protective finger in the pie, it might be a good idea.

Four years ago Norman Lear sent his assistant, Cathy Hand, to New York to talk to me about making a movie of *A Wrinkle in Time*, and I wasn't very interested. But Cathy suggested that we have lunch at Windows on the World, and I had never had lunch at Windows on the World. So I went to meet her. She was a delightful, enthusiastic young woman. I told her right off that not only could I not sign that clause, but I had to have a clause in reverse saying that the company could *not* change character and theme. She went back to Hollywood. My outrageous demands were accepted. She came back to New York and offered me some money for the property. I said, "That's not enough." She said, "Do you need money?" I answered, "No, but I need to know that you're serious about this movie. I won't believe you're serious unless you double your offer." I paused and added, "And I want ten percent, too." And I got everything I asked, went home to my husband, and said, "I'm not as stupid as I thought I was."

The story of the Wrinkle movie is still unfinished. There have been several screenplays written, including three by me. It has to be in production by the end of July, or it reverts back to me, or they have to buy it again. At this point I'm not making any predictions, Hollywood is a mystery to me.

But, having once broken down the barrier of that infamous clause giving the producer the right to change character and theme, I was aware, and so was Hollywood, that I really mean it when I say that character and theme matter more to me than money.

So, last week, the woman who wants to produce *Starfish* was trying to find out what I would allow to be changed, how I would react to updating. I told her that of course it would have to be updated; marine biology has gone further in the understanding of regeneration in starfish and other creatures than it had in 1963 when I was writing the book, and new knowledge would have to be reflected in the film. And of course a book is written to be read; it has to be translated, and sometimes radically, for the screen. But it has to *say* the same thing that the book says.

"Could Mrs. O'Keefe have a different number of children?" she asked.

"No. The children appear in several books. Changing the number of people in a family changes all the family patterns."

"Well, then, Can Kali smoke?"

"Why not? She likely would. Adam is a scientist; he wouldn't."

"Does Joshua have to die?"

"Yes," I answered firmly. "Joshua has to die."

"Why?" she asked.

"Because that's what happened," I answered.

Joshua is a particularly important character to me, for a good many reasons. When I started *The Arm of the Starfish* I was setting out to write an international thriller, with lots of intrigue. My young protagonist, Adam, was to spend the summer on an island off the coast of Portugal, working with an American marine biologist, Dr. O'Keefe. But before he leaves the airport in New York Adam is already caught in a web of intrigue, and once he lands in Lisbon, gets even more deeply enmeshed. Dr. O'Keefe's young daughter, Polly, is kidnapped while in his care; things go from bad to worse; he has not slept for three nights; and finally he is allowed to go to sleep in the Ritz Hotel in Lisbon. When he wakes up, a young man called Joshua is sitting in a chair, regarding him thoughtfully. Adam is very surprised to see Joshua. Madeleine was very surprised to see Joshua. There was no Joshua in my plot.

I had a choice as a writer, then. I could say, "Out, Joshua, I have a nice tightly-knit plot, and you aren't in it." Or I could go back to page one and start again and make room for Joshua and that's what I did, and I can't imagine the book without Joshua. But how he got to the Ritz Hotel in Lisbon that morning I can't tell you. But I had a suspicion that when he appeared so unexpectedly, and so named, that in the end he was going to have to give his life, and so it was.

And that's how it is. When something happens in a story, that's what happens.

The woman from Hollywood was not satisfied with this. "But Joshua was *good*," she said.

"Yes," I agreed.

"But doesn't that imply protection?" she asked.

"No," I replied. And it occurred to me that the only person to offer complete protection in mortal terms was Satan. That was the third temptation he offered Jesus. Worship me, and you can have it all, all the kingdoms of the world, and everybody in it, without the pain, without being abandoned by your friends, without the cross. Complete protection.

And that is not, in mortal terms, how it works.

It's a problem every generation struggles with. When our children saw their father play the father in *The Diary of Anne Frank* they were deeply disturbed. In one scene when the Franks are hiding in the attic in Holland and hear a noise downstairs, the father goes down to investigate, and they are terrified, knowing that he may get caught, that they may never see him again. And the mother drops to her knees and says the 121st psalm, all of it, that great cry for protection, ending, "The Lord shall preserve your going out and your coming in from this time forth and even forevermore." And the Lord didn't. The Nazis found the Franks and they were taken to a concentration camp and they all died there, except the father. Anne died there.

And our children cried, "But she was good. She didn't do anything wrong."

And so we got into long discussions about free will, and how that has over and over again led to pain, to the wicked flourishing and the innocent suffering. The whole book of *Job* struggles with the question, and comes to no answer. God asks Job, "Where were you when the morning stars sang together, and all God's children shouted for joy?"

And, as so often happens, I am caught in contradiction and paradox. Because I also believe in prayers of protection. A young woman in Nashville, Tennessee, said to me, "Madeleine, I want you to know that I pray for you every day, because your books have made you vulnerable, and you need protection." I am grateful for the prayers of protection which are made in my behalf; I believe in them. So how can I reconcile Joshua's death, Anne Frank's death, the untimely deaths of so many others, drastic illnesses, accidents, with all that I hope, all that I believe?

Sometimes things that happen give me glimmers of an answer, not a limited, finite answer, but a glimmer. One of these glimmers came on the Wednesday before this past Thanksgiving. You may remember that on the Sunday night before, a great many people all across the country watched *The Day After*. I was not happy with this television movie, not only because it was not a very good movie, nor because it did not begin to show the horror of a real nuclear war, but because I do not think that it is a good thing to send out on the airwaves a story which is totally negative, which offers no hope. Like a great many people I was affected by the movie, unhappy about it.

One of the advantages of living in New York City is that people tend to come to it, either en route somewhere, or to visit, and that Wednesday before Thanksgiving people happened to drop in at the library of the Cathedral of Saint John the Divine where I work. One was a young Korean woman who is a TWA airline hostess; one was a woman I'd met a few weeks earlier when I was speaking at St. Scholastica College in Duluth, Minnesota; one was a professor from Wheaton College, in Illinois. On Wednesday at 12:15 p.m. there is always a mass at the Cathedral, and I suggested to my friends that they join me, and then go out to lunch afterwards with the priest and talk, as is our custom, and everybody thought this was a good idea. During his homily Jonathan, the priest, mentioned *The Day After*, and wondered what the Christian response should be to any kind of disaster, war, earthquake, flood, tornado.

We went out to lunch, and I mentioned a letter I'd received

that morning, in which the writer asked, "Is God going to let us blow ourselves up?"

Mel, the professor from Wheaton, said, "I'd like to tell you something that happened to Jerome Hines, the opera singer. He's a friend of mine, and he told me this. About twenty years ago he was on a tour of Russia, singing Moussorgsky's opera, *Boris Godunov.* He had gone to the trouble of learning the long opera in the original Russian, and he was the first non-Russian singer ever to sing it in Russian. He also felt that the traditional ending to the opera, where Boris loses his crown, and rolls off his throne in anguished defeat, is not consistent with Moussorgsky's music, which is triumphant, and he played the scene as triumph, not defeat.

At the last performance in Moscow the opera was to be televised. But when Hines got to the theatre there were no cameras, and he was told that the television had been called off because Khruschev was going to attend the performance.

All the time Jerome Hines had been in Russia, the name *Khruschev* kept coming into his heart, with a strong feeling that he should pray for him. And so he had prayed. That night he sang superbly, in Russian, and at the end of the opera instead of throwing down his crown and rolling off the throne, he held the crown high over his head in a gesture of triumph. The audience went wild with enthusiasm.

Khruschev came backstage to see him, with an interpreter, to tell him how much he had enjoyed the performance. As Khruschev turned to leave, Jerome Hines said to him in Russian, "God bless you, sir." Khruschev simply looked at him a moment in silence, then left.

There's a mighty time difference between Moscow and Washington, and Khruschev couldn't have been home more than half an hour when the phone rang. It was the line connecting Washington and Moscow, and it was John F. Kennedy telling Khruschev to get out of Cuba. It was the Cuban missile crisis. And Khruschev pulled out of Cuba.

What might have happened if Jerome Hines had not been praying for Khruschev, if he had not taken the trouble to learn the opera in Russian, if he had not played the end as triumph, rather than defeat, if he had not said to the atheist head of an atheist country, "God bless you, sir"? No free will was being tampered with, and yet God was still being part of the story, offering opportunities which could have been rejected either by Hines or Khruschev. That's my only answer to the paradox of God's love and human suffering, and it's not so much an answer as it is a question and a hope. It is the question and the hope I look towards in my stories as I try to serve them, to listen to them, and then to go back to page one, if necessary, when a Joshua arrives.

Last winter, spring, and summer, I spent writing two full 350 pages of a book about Vicky Austin. It wasn't until I had finished the complete second draft that I realized that the book was not meant to be about Vicky Austin at all, but about Polyhymnia O'Keefe, who first came to me in *The Arm of the Starfish*, and who loved Joshua deeply. She appears again in *Dragons in the Waters*. Changing the protagonist of a book is no mere matter of changing names. Poly and Vicky are very different people, with different families, growing up in different geographical parts of the world. But Poly has the intellectual sophistication and the total social naïvete that was needed for what this book wanted to say. The theme of *A House Like a Lotus*, in three rather pompous words, is idolatry, disaster, and redemption. It will be out next autumn. It has now gone through five complete revisions, and many scenes have been written and rewritten more times than I can count.

So the honor I am receiving today is an affirmation that it is right to listen to the book, to go where it takes me, even if it is in directions I never expected to go. It is also a warning that I must not compromise, be cheap, capitulate to subtle pressures, and I am grateful for that warning.

A few years ago my bishop was in India, in the Koralian part of India, to which St. Thomas himself is supposed to have brought Christianity. The bishop celebrated mass for thousands, preached for thousands, and was warmly and lovingly received. When it was time for him to leave, he asked his interpreter to tell him how to say "Thank you" in the language of the people who had welcomed him so warmly. The interpreter had a long discussion with another interpreter, and finally turned to the bishop saying, "We do not have a word for thank you. Thank you is something you do."

So I do not have a word for thank you. But I will try to make my thank you to you something I do, as I go back to the typewriter and try to listen to the book.

SHAKE THE UNIVERSE

1987

L AST May I visited a 5000-year-old village near Xi'an, China. It had recently been discovered and excavated, and a roof and walls had been put around the entire village in order to protect it. Although it was a "primitive" village, the mud dwelling houses were solid and far more comfortable habitations than many I've seen in the barrios and *favelas* of South America, or in our own North American inner cities, for that matter. Research showed the village to have been originally that of a matriarchal society, agrarian and peaceable. At the grave site the head women of the tribe were buried in the center, with the men on either side, along with artifacts that appeared to be musical instruments, as well as cooking vessels beautified with artistic designs. These seemed to indicate a society dominated by women, a society concerned with music and art, with the expression of pattern and order.

A thousand or so years later, this society had shifted to a patriarchy: the head man was buried in the center of the grave, with his women on either side of him, along with primitive instruments of war.

It is a bit simplistic to say that when women guide the way of life society is peaceable, and there is time for music and beauty and things of the spirit; and that when men are in charge there is war, and the tribal dances become war dances rather than patterns of beauty in appreciation of the loveliness of nature—the sun by day, the moon and the stars by night.

Simplistic or not, that is the basic pattern throughout history.

So part of the calling of women as we move out of the last years of the 20th century and into the 21st is to revive a spirituality of creativity that is not afraid of the strange beauty of the underwater world of the subconscious, and to help men out of the restricted and narrow world of provable and limited fact in which society has imprisoned them.

My role as a feminist is not to compete with men in their

world—that's too easy, and ultimately unproductive. My job is to live fully as a woman, enjoying the whole of myself and my place in the universe.

Throughout the past several centuries, women have been allowed to remain in touch with the intuitive, the nurturing, the numinous—the spiritual, if you will—whereas men have been forced to limit themselves to the rational (which is not very rational, after all), and are offering their children and grandchildren a planet raped by war, stupidity, and greed.

This is a masculine point of view against which I have consciously rebelled since I was 12 years old and sent to an English boarding school where we were taught all the masculine virtues: be brave; do not cry; do not show emotions; be morally virtuous; do it yourself; never ask for help; be good and obedient and the world will be perfect. It didn't take much imagination to see that the world that was the outcome of these masculine virtues was anything but perfect. Hitler was already in power. In England we saw the great arms of the antiaircraft lights sweeping the sky as Britain prepared for war.

It was easy for me to rebel because I was clumsy at sports, daydreamed during class, wrote stories when I should have been doing homework. But I did learn one valuable lesson from that school in the spring of the year when we were given little garden plots to cultivate. We were allowed to bring the produce of our gardens in for tea, so most of the kids planted lettuce and tomatoes and radishes and watercress and cucumbers. My garden partner and I planted poppies, nothing but poppies. Our illegal reading had included *Bull-Dog Drummond* and *Fu Manchu*, from which we learned that opium comes from poppies, and that opium gives one beautiful dreams. So we had poppy leaf sandwiches and poppy flower sandwiches and poppy seed sandwiches and went to bed with flashlights and dream books under our pillows.

We found out quickly that we didn't need our poppy sandwiches for our dreams; but what we were doing, intuitively rather than consciously, was rebelling against the fragmented, basically masculine world of the adults. We were allowed no time for daytime dreaming. Daydreaming was suspect. If I locked myself in what at that school was known as The James for five minutes of privacy, after two minutes would come a knock and a sharp British voice: "Madaleen, what are you doing in there?" If we wanted privacy, it was assumed that it was for some nasty, perverse reason. So we had to make use of our nighttime dreams. With our dream books we were trying to reconcile intellect and intuition, conscious and subconscious minds. In our youth and naïveté we were struggling toward what I believe to be truly feminine spirituality.

It is no coincidence that the root word for heal, health, whole, and holy, is hale, as in "hale and hearty." If we are healed we are healthy; if we are healthy we are whole; if we are whole we are holy—that is all being holy means. And in our own blundering way my garden partner and I were struggling to be holy. The worst thing you could call anybody at that school was "pi," short for pious, and I am still suspicious of piosity. Holiness is something else again.

How do we become, much less remain, whole and holy in a world that tears and fragments?

When my husband of 40 years died six months ago, it was as though I had been amputated or split in two. But death—unless it is murder, accident, suicide—is not an unnatural part of the whole journey of life. Death cannot take away anything that two lovers have had. Grief can be acute, and yet clean.

It is my blessing to have living with me in my apartment in New York my 17-year-old granddaughter, a freshman in college, and an 18-year-old friend of hers from high school. We have got into the delightful habit of having multigenerational dinner parties about every other week. A Sunday ago we ranged in age from eight months all the way up to me, with at least one person representing every decade in between. This Sunday we'll drop down to four months for the youngest. Then we jump to nine years, 13 years, 17, two 18s, five young men and women in their twenties, two in their thirties, two in their forties. (Do we have anybody in the fifties this time? I'm not sure.) And up to Madeleine and the sixties. These evenings have somehow or other been generated spontaneously, and they are full of good conversation, and often music if we have performers among the group. Nobody pays any attention to how old anybody is. There is certainly no attempt to try to have as many men as women, or vice versa. I do the cooking; the kids do the cleaning up. There is an amazing kind of wholeness and laughter and lovingness that, to me, at this period of my life, is an icon of feminine spirituality.

Thus feminine spirituality must seek wholeness, holiness. Women have made great strides in this century. My grandmother was a suffragist, and now we take the vote for granted. Of course we can and do compete in the worlds of business, government, medicine. Less obvious but more important is the fact that now most women nurse their babies; in 1947 I had to fight for my right to nurse my first baby.

I went to a small village and an old-fashioned general practitioner to have my second baby, because I wanted my husband with me, and I wanted to deliver my child by natural childbirth. Remember that at that time most obstetricians were men. I, listening to my body, knew what was natural and easiest; male doctors did not. Childbearing in this century was a sterile and lonely business until women raised their voices. Today, natural childbirth with the father participating in the marvelously creative act of birth is becoming the normal procedure. In 2002 I hope that men will play an even more active part in the process of birth and the nurturing of children, touching the baby as it emerges into the world, being in fact midhusbands.

At the time of my marriage in 1946, I was working in the theater and had published two novels, so my husband more or less knew what he was getting, and that he was expected to do his fair share of the housework and taking care of the children. My husband was an artist, an actor; I doubt if I'd have made it for 40 years with a man in the business world. Today the sharing of household duties is becoming more and more the norm regardless of a man's occupation.

This change to "what comes naturally" in our domestic arrangements reflects a change in our spirituality that is a turning away from the rational and explicable to a new understanding of paradox and contradiction in our expressions of the meaning of life. The women mystics, who had been carefully swept under the carpet by a patriarchal church, are being rediscovered. There is 14th-century Julian of Norwich, who saw the entire universe in "the quantity of an hazelnut," and Hildegard of Bingen, an abbess in the Middle Ages who likened herself to "a feather on the breath of God."

Women are being ordained in the Episcopal Church, and there is much heated discussion of such a breakthrough in the Roman Catholic Church; and I have met several women rabbis. Far more important than the fact of ordination (no small triumph) is that these women are given the opportunity to free the churches and temples from a narrow vision of creation and our place in it, and that they may reveal a Creator who is—as I heard a friend say recently—exquisite. Suddenly the word burst open for me: ex-quisite—that which is on the other side of and outside the question.

How many people visualize God as looking like Moses— long beard, white nightgown—and Moses in a bad temper, at that? Male. Chauvinist. Punitive.

I want a Creator who is exquisite.

When we human beings opened the Pandora's box of the atom, a completely new vision of the universe was revealed, a universe that burst forth from a sub-subatomic particle (as physicist Stephen Hawking sees it) into all the countless galaxies exploding farther and farther into space. This universe is totally interdependent; nothing happens in isolation, and nothing can be observed objectively because to observe something is to change it. In an article on astrophysics, I came across the phrase "the butterfly effect," and what is meant by this is that if a butterfly should happen to fly into my office and somehow be hurt, the effect of that accident would be felt in galaxies billions of light-years away.

The universe as the physicists see it is also a world of randomness, of chance, which seems to upset some people. But if we lived in a determined universe, we would have no free will, no share in the writing of the story. I am far happier in an indeterminate universe than a determined one; it offers far more possibilities for spiritual growth and development.

To live in an open and undetermined universe with courage and grace seems to me to epitomize feminine spirituality, and it is the way we are going to have to go if we are to survive as a human race. We must stop reverting to the grave site with the man in the middle, his women on either side, along with the weapons of war. But unless we listen to our planet, unless we listen to our bodies, unless we listen to our spirits, society may plunge back to that world once again—autonomous, independent, destructive, and basically subhuman.

Feminine spirituality accepts interdependence, and is not threatened by questions that have no definitive answers. The world of subatomic particles is a world of paradox, of chance and pattern, randomness and purpose, the tangible and the mystical. It is a vision of creation that demands great courage, spiritual courage, a new kind of courage that women are going to have to be strong and patient enough to teach to men. To look at something is to change it. To hurt a butterfly is to shake the universe. To love is to be vulnerable. To attempt anything—music, love, art—is to risk failure, and that takes a kind of courage I believe to be uniquely feminine. This openness to change, interdependence, questions with no easy answers, vulnerability, and risk is the feminine spirituality that is desperately needed if the human race is to reach the year 2002.

SMITH COLLEGE 50ᵀᴴ REUNION SPEECH

1991

WHAT a privilege it is to be gathered here together, fifty years after graduating from Smith. I remember as an undergraduate looking rather snobbily at the women coming back for reunion, *except* those coming for their fiftieth and on up. These women had a wisdom in their faces and in their demeanors that showed us they had truly lived their lives. We respected them. If growing older meant to be like them, it wasn't such a bad thing after all.

Well, here we are. And we *have* done a lot of living and a lot of maturing. In fifty years of postgraduate life we have moved into being who we are—and liking it. For many of us it hasn't been easy, nor did Smith teach us to expect it to be. Some of us have lost husbands, children, close friends. Some of us have chosen the career of wife, child bearer, nurturer. Some of us have gone single mindedly after a career. Some of us have chosen the double task of doing both, and, as one of these, I know it hasn't been easy.

I have the joy of living with my two granddaughters who are going to college in New York. One night a group of students was gathered around the dinner table, and one young woman said that her Women's Studies professor had told them that day that any woman who married and had children and who *wrote* was a martyr.

My granddaughter Charlotte looked at me, asking, "Gran, were you a martyr?" And I replied, "No, Charlotte, I chose my own conflicts. Believe me, they were conflicts, but I chose them, so there's no way I can be a martyr."

Smith, thank heavens, didn't teach us to be martyrs, but to be women free to make our own choices.

Perhaps the best thing my four years at Smith did for me was to help prepare me to live the rest of my life with courage and hope. One of the advantages of going to a women's college is that we learned self-esteem. Whatever there was to be done, we did. If there was a magazine to be started, we started it. If there was an office up for election, one of us was elected. What we did, we did well, and that gave us confidence. I left college and went to New York with the assumption that of course all doors were open to me—and that's a good attitude to have. If you think doors are going to be open, they're likely to be open. If you expect them to be closed, they're likely to slam in your face.

Smith was certainly an open door for me when I arrived as a freshman as wet behind the ears as a freshman can be. I came to Smith after six years of boarding school, and while I was moderately proficient academically, I was a slow developer in every other area. I did know what I wanted from my education, and I was determined to get it, and what I wanted did not include boredom. Freshman year I signed up for a survey of Greek and Roman history, which I expected to be fascinating. It wasn't. The professor wasn't interested in the human beings who had lived and suffered and rejoiced during those years, all he wanted was dates. So, at midyear, I applied to drop the course without credit. At that time, a freshman could not drop a course without going before a faculty board. So I appeared dutifully before the board and was asked why I wanted to drop the course. I replied truthfully but tactlessly, "Professor X has ruined Greece for me. I'm darned if I'll let him ruin Rome." This did not please the board, but they did let me drop the course and I took something more interesting. I learned to be more tactful when I wanted to drop a course that I felt was a waste of time, and I managed to talk a number of professors into marvelous little seminars, such as a course in piano composition—I was an English major. And during my four years at Smith I did get a marvelous education, and one that has stood me in good stead. Perhaps the best thing my Smith education has done for me has been that I have been able to go on learning, to do research in areas where I have no background, to dare to try new subjects.

As an English major of course I took Mary Ellen Chase's Survey of the Novel. It was a very popular course, and crowded. Early on Miss Chase gave us a quiz. There were a hundred questions, and I didn't know the answer to most of them. One question was, "What color dress did Jane Eyre have on when she met Mr. Rochester?" What Miss Chase was doing with this quiz was trying to weed out the sheep from the goats, but I was too naïve to understand that, and I was outraged. I stalked up to the desk and took several sheets of quizzes and in a white heat I wrote, "Dear Miss Chase, I don't know the answer to most of these questions, but I have read the books, and I'll tell you what I think of them." When I got back my essay she had written at the bottom, "Take no more quizzes," and we got on wonderfully and I learned a great deal from this superb teacher who was so aflame with excitement over her subject that we couldn't help catching fire, too. And I suspect that there are quite a few of us here tonight who remember her famous lecture in John M. Green hall where she divided writers into "majah, minah, and mediocah."

When we came to Smith there was no literary magazine, so I decided that that was an error that needed to be rectified, and I went to the authorities to get permission to start a college literary magazine. Having received the blessing from Laura Scales, I think it was, I looked around campus for the girl I thought would be best able to take care of all my financial worries and leave me free for art. I picked a girl called Betty Goldstein, and she was terrific. She got ads from all the shops on Green Street and everywhere else, and we ran in the black right from the start. She was also domineering and would tell me exactly what my editorial policy ought to be and what I should do, and I would look at her and say, "Betty, you're marvelous," which was true, and "Betty, I couldn't do without you," which was true, and then I did whatever I wanted, and we were both happy. Later on, after graduating from Smith, she married and became Betty Friedan.

My Shakespeare and seventeenth century literature professor was Esther Cloudman Dunn, another magnificent teacher. She sat up on her little platform with her beautiful white hair, her beautiful English complexion, her well cut English tweed suits which, when she sat down, came up well above her knees, so that we could see her long pink woolen underpants all the way.

That is why, when I started to do some public speaking, I wore long dresses. Her love of Shakespeare was so great that she told us that there were two of Shakespeare's plays she had never read, because she couldn't bear to have read all of Shakespeare.

And she taught me one invaluable lesson as a writer. She was talking about the audiences of Shakespeare's day, and how the part of the theatre which we call the orchestra was where the people from the street stood, and if they didn't like what was going on on stage they threw rotten vegetables, rotten eggs, rotten fruit at the actors. So all of Shakespeare's plays start with an attention getter: *Hamlet* starts with a ghost, *Macbeth* with three witches, *Twelfth Night* with a shipwreck, and only after he has caught the audience's attention does Will go on to one of his soliloquies, such as Oh, that this too, too solid flesh would melt. If he'd started with that—rotten eggs! So I learned that when I start a novel, I need an attention getter right on the first page. I might not get rotten eggs without it, but I wouldn't have a reader.

So there were many academic joys for us, and a lot of growing up, for me at least, as well as learning to accept myself as I am, rather than wanting to be someone else I could never be. Falling in and then out of love. Making some lifetime friends, and learning what friendship is all about. And then graduating, still wet behind the ears, but at least a little drier than I had been four years earlier.

Now it is fifty years later, and if anyone had been able to bring a television set onto campus and shown us the evening news from almost any one of those fifty years we wouldn't have believed it. The Second World War we understood; we were already in the middle of that, and we knew that Hitler had to be stopped. But nothing prepared me for my sense of horror when we dropped not one, but two atom bombs on cities full of ordinary people, not fighting armies, but families, children, old people. Would we have believed planned obsolescence, people being taught to make things less well than they can be made? And what about men walking on the moon? Since I've been a science fiction reader from childhood on, that was one of the easiest, as well as one of the most exciting for me.

What would we have thought of Watergate? Irangate? Savings and loans banks going down because of human stupidity and greed and corruption? Would we have believed that we would sit in front of our television sets and watch a war start in the middle east?

Technologically there has been more advance in the fifty years since we graduated than in all the years, all the centuries before them. Some of it has been marvelous and some of it has been terrible. Babies who would have died in 1941 now live and grow up to be healthy adults. People see, and I'm one of them, who in 1941 would have gone blind, so I'm not about to put down the wonders of technology. But there's technocracy, too, and I'm far less happy with that. Nor am I happy with our litigious society, nor the radical general drop in vocabulary. We think because we have words, not the other way around. It was easier for us to read Shakespeare than it is for students today, simply because the vocabulary available to us was far greater than it is today.

When we opened the heart of the atom in our rush to get the atom bomb ahead of Hitler we also opened an entirely new way of looking at the universe, and this has given us wonders as well as horrors. My theological reading for quite a while has been particle physics, quantum mechanics, astrophysics, because these disciplines are dealing with the nature of the universe, and that is what theology is all about. Who are we? Why are we here? Do we make a difference? These are questions we all ask as children and should never forget to ask, and it is the scientists who are asking them most clearly now.

Back when the world was in its fifties and we were in our thirties I read a book of Einstein's in which he said that anyone who was not lost in rapturous awe at the power and glory of the mind behind the universe was "as good as a burnt out candle." There's my theologian, I thought. Saint Alfred! And I went on to read Planck and his quantum theory, discovering with joy that higher math is much easier for me than lower math. Lower math lost me in fourth grade when I was taught, as fourth graders still are taught, that zero times three equals zero. If I have three apples and I multiply them by zero, why are they going to vanish? But that is what you are taught in fourth grade: those three apples are going to vanish. So I wiped out lower math as being philosophically untenable, and it took me another twenty years to discover higher math. Obviously I didn't take any math courses at Smith.

Probably what has impressed me most in my reading of physics is the interrelationship of all things; nothing happens in isolation; everything affects everything else. Because this particular group of us is here tonight, we are going to be different than we would be if it was a different group. A favorite phrase among physicists is "the butterfly effect." What is meant by that is that if a butterfly should fly in here and somehow be hurt, the effect of that accident would be felt in galaxies hundreds of light years away, the universe is that closely interconnected. So here we are living on a planet that is by and large in opposition to the nature of the universe, with our wars, many in the name of religion, our divisions, antagonisms, judgmentalisms. But for this weekend we are gathered together as the class of 41, and that gives us a wonderful kind of unity. Perhaps by the time we return for our seventy-fifth reunion we'll really have reached maturity and wisdom. Meanwhile we're still in media res, many of us still working and enjoying it, taking time for children and grandchildren and family and friends. I'm very happy that we're all here this evening; I believe that it matters that we are here together, and I hope you do too.

CHRONOLOGY

NOTE ON THE TEXTS

NOTES

CHRONOLOGY

1918   Born Madeleine L'Engle Camp (named for a great-grand-mother, Madeleine L'Engle) in New York, New York, on November 29, to Charles Wadsworth Camp and Madeleine Hall Barnett Camp. Father, born in 1879 in Philadelphia, Pennsylvania, is a Princeton-educated journalist and the author of thrillers including *Sinister Island* (1915) and *The Abandoned Room* (1917). Mother, born in 1881 in Jacksonville, Florida, is a concert pianist (trained in Berlin) with crippling stage fright that precluded a career. Parents married in 1906 and live in rented apartment on East 82nd Street, spending summers at Saint-Gaudens Artists' Colony, Cornish, New Hampshire, and Jacksonville, Florida, ancestral home of L'Engles and Barnetts. They regularly invite artist friends, including Metropolitan Opera singers, to Sunday dinners, where mother will play piano while guests gather round to sing. Father works as a foreign correspondent, and then enlists in U.S. Army as second lieutenant and is deployed to France in early 1918. On December 13, mother writes: "My dearest husband— If you could see your little flower of a daughter, I am sure you would forgive her for not being a boy. . . . Have you any idea yet when you are coming home?"

1919   Father returns from wartime military service in May. In summer, family visits maternal grandmother Caroline Hallowes L'Engle Barnett ("Dearma") in Florida, staying at her seaside cottage, Red Gables, where, as L'Engle will later claim, she is awakened for a first glimpse of the stars.

1920–25   Father publishes a number of books with Doubleday, Page, including story collections *The Gray Mask* (1920) and *The Communicating Door* (1923), and novels *The Guarded Heights* (1921), *The Hidden Road* (1922), and *The Barbarian* (1925). In addition, a number of films are released based on father's work, including *Love Without Question*, based on *The Abandoned Room* and directed by B. A. Rolfe (April 1920); *A Daughter of the Law*, directed by Jack Conway and based on short story "The Black Cap" (November 1921); *Hate*, directed by Maxwell Karger and based on short story of the same name, released by Metro Pictures

(May 1922); and *The Signal Tower*, directed by Clarence Brown and based on an article (July 1924). Father's run of genre-fiction publishing successes and film-rights sales fails to solidify his literary reputation or to stabilize family income, which depends heavily on mother's skill as a stock market investor. In New York, Mary McKenna O'Connell—beloved English nanny known as "Mrs. O," or simply "O"—joins Camp household. Later recalls: "Father wanted a strict English childhood for me, and this is more or less what I got—nanny, governesses, supper on a tray in the nursery, dancing lessons, music lessons, art lessons . . ." In 1923, L'Engle writes her first story: "It was about a little G-R-U-L because that's how I spelled 'girl' when I was 5." The next year, enters first grade. Spends the next three school years attending small private schools in Manhattan.

1926   Taken by father to Metropolitan Opera to hear *Madama Butterfly* and *Pagliacci*. Having reacted intensely to the tragic ending of *Madama Butterfly*, weeps uncontrollably before *Pagliacci* begins and is abruptly escorted home. Begins lifelong practice of journaling.

1927–29   Studies at Miss Chandor's School, New York, for fourth and fifth grades. Receives father's old Remington Portable typewriter as gift; will continue to write on it into the 1950s. After overcoming teacher's accusation of plagiarism, wins Lower School poetry prize for "Portraits," published in May 1929 issue of school literary magazine *The Torch*. In fall, enrolls for sixth grade at Todhunter School for Girls, New York (Eleanor Roosevelt, then the first lady of New York State, serves as associate principal and teaches the eleventh and twelfth grades), where Margaret Clapp, later president of Wellesley College, encourages writing interest. Responds by writing and illustrating a sequel to the *Odyssey*.

1930   Having suffered losses in stock market crash of previous October, family breaks up New York apartment and leaves for open-ended stay in France, living luxuriously for a time on a reduced budget at the Château de Publier, near Lake Geneva. Father's declining health, and the promise of fresh mountain air, is a secondary factor in the decision to move, as is the chance to visit Barnett family members living in France. In summer, enjoys French countryside and is deeply affected by Lucy Maud Montgomery's *Emily of New Moon*, a story about another aspiring young writer. In late summer, is driven by parents to Le Châtelard, a boarding school in Montreux, Switzerland, and left without warning to study there for the next three years.

1931   Chafes at Le Châtelard's regimented, English boarding school–style environment and for the most part is an indifferent student. In spring, after reading *Bulldog Drummond* and *Fu Manchu*, plants poppies in student garden and places flowers under pillow at night in hopes of experiencing exciting, opium-induced dreams. Is punished for various minor transgressions by being required to copy Milton's *Il Penseroso* numerous times. Recurring flare-ups of iritis compound academic woes.

1932   Does well in history and music but is judged overall to be an inattentive and undisciplined student.

1933   Family returns to the U.S. in summer, moving in with ailing maternal grandmother, Dearma, in Jacksonville, Florida. Enrolls at Ashley Hall, Charleston, South Carolina, for ninth grade, where teachers encourage writing. Joins Riding Club. Chosen for student council and for role of "Second Shepherd" in Christmas play.

1934   While at Huckleberry Camp in Connecticut during the summer, writes in journal: "I, Madeleine L'Engle Camp, do solemnly vow this day that I will climb the alpine path and write my name on the scroll of fame." Submits poems to *Good Housekeeping*, unsuccessfully, as "Elizabeth Applegate Martin" (fraternal grandmother's name). On September 12, Dearma dies in Jacksonville. Returns to Ashley Hall, where she is elected assistant editor of literary magazine, *Cerberus*.

1935   In June, plays Sir Andrew Aguecheek in student production of *Twelfth Night*. In September, at father's urging, returns to Ashley Hall as a junior, having agreed to stay on for extra year to compensate for academic time lost while in Switzerland; she had hoped to graduate in three years. Becomes editor of *Cerberus*. Elected junior class representative on the student council, as well as to the student council board, a coveted position, but loses both offices after playing a prank on a fellow student, writing fake love letters to her from a supposed suitor.

1936   Sends poems to Archibald Rutledge, the poet laureate of South Carolina. Takes college entrance exam preparatory course in Jacksonville, making friends with fellow student

Patricia Collins (later Cowdery) to whom she will dedicate *A Wind in the Door*. As senior, regains position on student council board; serves as yearbook and literary magazine editor. Takes lead roles in plays. At urging of Ashley Hall principal Mary McBee, applies to Smith College. In October, learns father is gravely ill. Rushes home to Jacksonville, but is too late to say farewell. Charles Wadsworth Camp dies, October 30, of pneumonia, caused, L'Engle will later assert, by the aftereffects of World War I combat exposure to mustard gas; Camp had also, for many years, been a heavy drinker.

1937   In spring, elected student council president. Wins Poetry Prize. Her yearbook quote is "My library was dukedom large enough," from Shakespeare's *The Tempest*. Graduates from Ashley Hall. On July 9, sails for England and France with mother; receives news of Smith acceptance later that month. Late September, enrolls in Smith. Begins writing daily postcards to her mother in Jacksonville, a practice she will keep up for decades.

1938   In November, plays "Old Shepherd" in Smith College Dramatics Association's production of Jean Cocteau's *The Infernal Machine*.

1939   With classmate Marie Donnet, cofounds French House, on-campus francophone residence, and lives there until graduation. Declares English as major. Takes "Descriptive and Narrative Writing," a seminar officially open only to seniors, taught by visiting novelist Leonard Ehrlich. In "Types of English Prose Fiction," hears English professor Mary Ellen Chase, lecturing in her strong New England accent, divide all English literature into three categories: "Majah, minah, and mediocah." In October, helps revive, and edits, student literary magazine, *Opinion*.

1940   On April 17, play *This Is Leap Year* performed in workshop at Smith. Spearheads the revival of *Smith College Monthly* and serves as its editor-in-chief from first issue (of October 31) until graduation, also contributing stories and poems. Disagrees with managing editor Bettye Naomi Goldstein (later Betty Friedan) over Goldstein's desire to tilt editorial focus from literature to politics. December 5–6, her three-act play *Recital* performed at Smith.

1941   June 16, graduates cum laude from Smith College. Commencement speaker, Princeton music professor Roy D.

Welch, declares: "A new Dark Ages seem to be preparing. . . . This class graduates at a moment when men and women must take sides, . . . [when] all those who are not vigorously for a cause are unmistakably against it." Spends summer in Cape May, New Jersey, acting in a summer-stock theater company. Returns to New York, sharing Greenwich Village apartment with Smith friend Marie Donnet and two other friends; mother, who had hoped L'Engle would return to Florida, provides financial help with the understanding that a spare bedroom will be kept for her use, and also gives L'Engle family furniture that had been in storage since their move to Europe in 1930. Studies acting with Morris Carnovsky. In the fall, "The Mountains Shall Stand Forever," a short story that anticipates first novel (*The Small Rain*), published in *The Matrix: A Magazine of Creative Writing*. Teaches English to Jewish refugees at Rodeph Sholom Temple, New York.

1942   Volunteers for the American Theatre Wing, selling war bonds at Broadway theaters. Acting as de facto agent, Donnet sends *Ilse*, a play, to actress, director, and founder of New York's Civic Repertory Theatre Eva Le Gallienne, boldly urging the latter to produce it in New York. In June, Le Gallienne writes that she is interested in *Ilse*, but that the ending needs revision, and encourages L'Engle to continue writing. Spends summer working at Straight Wharf Theatre in Nantucket, Massachusetts. In September, meets Le Gallienne and actress Margaret Webster and joins the Civic Repertory Theatre as ensemble actor and Le Gallienne's personal secretary. Begins writing first novel, *The Small Rain*, while playing understudy role in Thomas Job's *Uncle Harry*, starring Le Gallienne and Joseph Schildkraut.

1943   On January 9, announces intention in letter to mother to be known professionally as "Madeleine L'Engle," a possibility once suggested by father and now strongly encouraged by Le Gallienne. Moves with Donnet to apartment on Twelfth Street with more roommates (and no spare room for mother). *Uncle Harry* closes in May. Returns to Straight Wharf Theatre for summer, where Donnet is acting as the manager and produces two of L'Engle's plays, *'Phelia* and *The Christmas Tree*. Neither does well. In August, publishes "Summer Camp," a short story, as Madeleine L'Engle, in *New Threshold*, which also features fiction by Bernard

Malamud and an essay by Eleanor Roosevelt. In the fall, goes on tour with *Uncle Harry*. Falls out with Donnet, who moves out of their apartment.

1944   In June, Vanguard Press offers a $100 advance for *The Small Rain*. Takes summer off to revise. In December, publishes two short stories: "Vicky" in *Mademoiselle*, and "The Shades" in Grinnell College literary magazine, *The Tanager*, the latter story cast as a translation from the French by fictive author Germaine Courtmont.

1945   In January, has walk-on part in Webster's Broadway production of Chekhov's *The Cherry Orchard* at New York City Center. Meets fellow cast member Hugh Hale Franklin (born in 1916 in Muskogee, Oklahoma), who plays Trofimov, and embarks on on-again, off-again romance. In January, *The Small Rain* published by Vanguard Press; hailed by *The New York Times* as "evidence of a fresh new talent." Begins revising play *Ilse* as a novel. Moves into her own, smaller, apartment on West 10th Street. Hugh proposes in the beginning of December. Later in the month, *The Tanager* publishes "Evening of a Governess," a short story based on observations of New York's socially prominent Warburg family, to which childhood friend April Warburg belongs.

1946   On January 26, marries Hugh Franklin at St. Chrysostom's Church in Chicago while touring together in Philip Barry's *The Joyous Season*, starring Ethel Barrymore. In March, novel *Ilsa* published by Vanguard Press to favorable reviews, the *Chicago Tribune* observing, "Miss L'Engle has the happy gift of never being obvious." Novel's critical portrayal of southern society offends some Florida family members. In summer, couple purchases tumbledown eighteenth-century farmhouse in Goshen, Connecticut, initially as weekend and summer retreat. At mother's suggestion, they name it "Crosswicks" after Chesterfield County, New Jersey, village where her father spent his childhood. Begins work on novel *And Both Were Young*, a story set in a Swiss boarding school.

1947   June 28, daughter Josephine Morrison Franklin born. Franklins live at 32 West 10th Street, with Leonard Bernstein, then director of New York City Symphony, as upstairs neighbor. With Hugh often away on tour, childhood nanny Mrs. O periodically returns to help out with childcare (Mrs.

O will visit for a few weeks every year, also serving as caregiver and confidante to mother on her visits north from Jacksonville). Spends summer at Crosswicks with Josephine, revising *And Both Were Young* at the request of editor Beatrice Creighton at Lothrop, Lee & Shepard so it can be published as a juvenile novel.

1949   In spring, *And Both Were Young* becomes first published work of teen fiction. Most notable change to the original draft is the metamorphosis of a same-sex crush between two schoolgirls into more conventional boy-girl romance. On December 4, *And Both Were Young* is chosen by *The New York Times* as one of "10 best children's books of 1949."

1950   Works on *Camilla Dickinson*, a coming-of-age novel set in present-day Greenwich Village about romance between teens from emotionally troubled families.

1951   In May, *Camilla Dickinson* (first announced under the title *The Fourteen Days*) published by Simon and Schuster. In the fall, after a series of nerve-wracking professional disappointments, Hugh abandons acting career and the Franklins leave New York to live year-round in Goshen, Connecticut.

1952   March 24, son Bion Barnett Franklin born. In spring, Hugh takes first amateur acting role in Goshen Players' production of Kurt Weill–Maxwell Anderson musical *Knickerbocker Holiday*. Franklins purchase and operate Food Market, the local general store, and join the Church of Christ, Congregational. Directs church choir and with Hugh organizes annual Christmas pageant.

1953   In the spring, takes on first acting role for Goshen Players as the Duchess of Plaza-Toro in Gilbert and Sullivan operetta *The Gondoliers*. On October 4, in personal journal in which story ideas are routinely recorded, sets down detailed definition of geometer's concept of the "tesseract."

1954   In spring is deeply troubled by Army-McCarthy hearings conducted by United States Senate's Subcommittee on Investigations: "Not one mention of Oppenheimer's conscience made. Not once was it suggested that perhaps morally he hesitated to make possible a weapon that could destroy our world entirely, that could cause the ghastly murders of billions of people." With Hugh, codirects

Goshen Players double-bill composed of Gilbert and Sulli-van operetta *Trial by Jury* and *Ballad for Americans*, a patriotic cantata with lyrics by John La Touche and music by Earl Robinson originally commissioned by the Federal Theatre Project.

1955   In spring, produces and directs Bedřich Smetana comic opera *The Bartered Bride* for Goshen Players, also taking minor role. In the fall, hospitalized for several weeks with colitis.

1956   Two completed manuscripts for novels, *Rachel* and *A Winter's Love*, make the rounds of publishers without success.

1957   In spring, directs and writes lyrics for Goshen Players' spring production of *Come to the Ball*, an original musical inspired by Oscar Wilde comedy *Lady Windermere's Fan*, with music by Chopin, Delibes, and Offenbach. In May, thanks to persistent efforts of new literary agent, Theron Raines, *A Winter's Love* is published by J. B. Lippincott. Longtime friends Liz Dewing and Arthur Richmond both die suddenly, leaving behind seven-year-old daughter Maria Dewing Richmond (born July 25, 1949), who comes to live permanently with Franklin family and is later adopted.

1958   In spring, plays Countess de la Fère in Victor Herbert–Henry Blossom operetta *The Red Mill*, with Hugh as the American tourist. In need of greater privacy, builds writing studio over garage that becomes known as The Tower. On November 29, her fortieth birthday, receives latest rejection of *The Lost Innocent*, a sequel to *Camilla Dickinson*, prompting distressed thoughts of "stop[ping] this foolish-ness and learn[ing] to make cherry pic." Begins writing *Meet the Austins*.

1959   In late spring, family embarks on ten-week cross-country road trip, visiting Hugh's relatives in Oklahoma and various national parks en route to California. Reads books on physics and cosmology, and while driving through Arizo-na's Painted Desert spontaneously has idea for three "Mrs W" characters and other first glimmerings of *A Wrinkle in Time*. In fall, returns with children to New York City as primary residence and there rejoins Hugh, who had earlier resumed his professional Broadway stage career in the role of Hector Hushabye in George Bernard Shaw's *Heartbreak House* at the Billy Rose Theatre on Broadway. They take up temporary quarters at the Dauphin, an old hotel near Lincoln Center, while searching for an apartment.

1960   On February 1, family moves into a spacious apartment at 105th Street and Broadway, then considered a dodgy neighborhood. Raines begins to submit to publishers first draft of novel titled *Mrs Whatsit, Mrs Who, and Mrs Which*. Volunteers as part-time teacher at children's school, St. Hilda's and St. Hugh's, an Upper West Side Manhattan Episcopal preparatory school, where Edward Nason West, Canon Sacrist of the Cathedral Church of St. John the Divine, is also school chaplain. In fall, enrolls in Columbia University fiction writing course taught by novelist and critic Caroline Gordon. At the behest of actor and director Herbert Berghof, begins adaptation of *Letters of a Portuguese Nun*, a 1669 epistolary romance by Claude Barbin, into a play. In November, *Meet the Austins*, a fictionalized account of the stresses surrounding the family's efforts to integrate Maria into family, published by Vanguard Press. Portrayal of their group dynamic becomes a long-standing source of unhappiness within family.

1961   In January, following repeated rejections, Farrar, Straus and Giroux acquires *Mrs Whatsit, Mrs Who, and Mrs Which*, which publisher John Farrar says he loves but also fears will have negligible sales.

1962   On January 1, Ariel Books, the juvenile imprint of Farrar, Straus and Giroux directed by Hal Vursell, publishes novel now titled *A Wrinkle in Time*, with a striking abstract cover design by Ellen Raskin. Reviewers wrestle with the novel's unconventional nature; *Publishers Weekly* writes, "The book is considerably more thought-provoking than the average space tale, and it is beautifully written." *The Horn Book* calls it "a confusion of science, philosophy, satire, religion, literary allusions, and quotations. . . . I found it fascinating. To children who read and reread C. S. Lewis' fairy tales I think it will be absorbing. It makes unusual demands on the imagination and consequently gives great rewards." And the *Saturday Review* writes: "It has the general appearance of being science fiction, but it is not. . . . There is mystery, mysticism, a feeling of indefinable, brooding horror. . . . One feels that this book quests desperately for something it never quite touches. It is original, different, exciting—and in some parts frustrating."

1963   Visits Portugal with Hugh, gathering material for never-realized film adaptation of *Letters of a Portuguese Nun* that later morphs into novel *The Love Letters*. In March, *The Moon by Night* (the second Austin family novel, about a cross-country family car trip) published by Ariel Books. On March 11, *A Wrinkle in Time* is announced as winner of 1963 John Newbery Medal. Accepts Newbery at American Library Association meeting in Chicago on July 15 ("For a writer of fiction to have to sit down and write a speech, especially a speech in which she must try to express her gratitude for one of the greatest honors of her life, is as difficult a task as she can face"), joined by Ezra Jack Keats who receives Randolph Caldecott Medal for the equally groundbreaking picture book *The Snowy Day*. Begins strenuous speaking career with appearances in Rochester, New York, Chicago, Cleveland, Akron, and San Francisco.

1964   Makes speaking trips to Texas, Louisiana, and Virginia, among other places. In June, writes in *The Horn Book*: "Those of us who work with words are dealing with an instrument so powerful that it leads us out into an ever-expanding universe. . . . We are trying to speak a universal language—what Erich Fromm calls 'the forgotten language,' the language of fairy tale, dream, parable, myth." On August 26, addressing hundreds of library book buyers at the 1964 New Books Preview, sponsored by the Library–Public Relations Council and held at New York's Statler Hilton, in a lecture provocatively titled "The Mystery of the First Law of Thermodynamics, or, Trading Stamp Sex," argues that literature must challenge the reader's imagination rather than simply give everything away (as in a burlesque show), and that librarians, not censors, are the best guides for readers seeking knowledge and insight in a scary, mysterious world. In September, *The 24 Days Before Christmas* (third Austin family novel) published by Ariel Books.

1965   On February 25, begins work as volunteer librarian (and effectively writer-in-residence) at the Cathedral Church of St. John the Divine, New York, receiving steady stream of visitors including adult and child fans of her novels and later, as writings about art and spirituality proliferate, of spiritual seekers as well. Canon West's office adjoins the library, resulting in near-daily communication and a deepening friendship. In March, *The Arm of the Starfish*, inspired in part by her 1963 visit to Portugal, published by Farrar, Straus and Giroux; *The New York Times* praises this "tense, tricky, well-plotted [book with] all the stuff of which adult spy novels are made. . . . A superior junior novel with a sharp, contemporary point: 'You cannot be uncommitted, Adam, believe me, you cannot.'" And Emily Maxwell, in *The New Yorker*, calls it "a well-above-average teen-age mystery, pleasantly worldly, with a fine sense of suspense and a light seasoning of romance and science fiction." In fall, *Camilla Dickinson* reissued as *Camilla* by T. Y. Crowell Co.

1966   In June, daughter Josephine marries Alan William Jones, an Episcopal priest. In October, *The Love Letters* published by Farrar, Straus and Giroux. Gives up teaching duties at St. Hilda's and St. Hugh's as speaking schedule intensifies.

1967   In September, *The Journey with Jonah*, a verse play for young readers illustrated by Leonard Everett Fisher, published by Farrar, Straus and Giroux.

1968   *Prelude*, an adaptation for young readers of the opening chapters of *The Small Rain*, published by Vanguard Press early in the year. Mother travels north from Jacksonville to spend first of four summers at Crosswicks. In May, *The Young Unicorns*, the fourth Austin family book and a novel set in and around Cathedral Church of St. John the Divine and capturing the atmosphere of contemporary urban teen gang violence, published by Farrar, Straus and Giroux. On June 20, first granddaughter Madeleine Saunders (Léna) Jones born.

1969   In April, *Dance in the Desert*, picture book illustrated by Symeon Shimin, published by Farrar, Straus and Giroux. In June, wins Austrian State Literary Prize for *The Moon by Night*. On August 22, second granddaughter, Charlotte Rebecca Jones, born. In December, *Lines Scribbled on an Envelope, and Other Poems* published by Farrar, Straus and Giroux.

1970   On January 5, Hugh begins fourteen-year run as the silver-haired Dr. Charles Tyler on daytime television soap opera *All My Children*. In spring, with writer Sidney Offit, leads after-school writing workshop for Harlem teens at the Cathedral. In November, at request of the Children's Book Council, New York, writes "Intergalactic P.S. 3," an original short story printed as a keepsake for Children's Book Week that anticipates *A Wind in the Door*.

1971   In March, novel *The Other Side of the Sun* published by Farrar, Straus and Giroux. On June 5, stepdaughter Maria Franklin is married. In summer, mother, in failing health, travels north from Jacksonville for extended stay at Crosswicks; dies there on July 28 at age ninety. In December, wins the Austrian State Literary Prize for *Camilla*.

1972   In March, *A Circle of Quiet* published by Farrar, Straus and Giroux, first of four inspirational memoirs collectively titled "The Crosswicks Journal." On October 27, gives first of many lectures, "A Good Picture Is Worth a Thousand Stories," at Wheaton College (Illinois) at the Writing and Literature Conference and meets fellow speaker Luci Shaw, who becomes close friend and later will publish L'Engle's religious writings at Harold Shaw Publishers. In indication of closeness of friendship with Canon West, is elected fellow member of the Order of St. John of Jerusalem.

1973   In May, *A Wind in the Door* published by Farrar, Straus and Giroux; *Kirkus* writes: "The audacity of Ms. L'Engle's mytho-scientific imagination and her undoubted storytelling abilities keep the reader involved in Meg's quest, but one wonders whether its chief appeal doesn't lie in the all too natural desire to believe that our difficulties, like the Murrys', are personal attacks by the forces of cosmic evil," while *The Horn Book* faults the novel for allowing philosophical reflection to overwhelm fantasy and for lacking the "consistency and the believable motivation needed to keep fiction from becoming dogma."

1974   In November, *The Summer of the Great-grandmother* (Crosswicks Journal, volume 2) published by Farrar, Straus and Giroux.

1975   In April, elected to thirty-member Authors Guild Council along with Roger Angell, Elizabeth Janeway, Toni Morrison, and Erica Jong.

1976   In April, *Dragons in the Waters* published by Farrar, Straus and Giroux; *The New York Times* in its favorable assessment notes: "There is enough adventure in 'Dragons in the Waters' to make Nancy Drew and her chums squirm." In September, *Spirit and Light: Essays in Historical Theology*, coedited with William B. Green in tribute to Canon West, published by Crossroad/Seabury Press.

1977   On April 17, grandson Edward Augustus Jones born. On May 23, in Wheaton College commencement address, calls her first childhood viewing of the night sky "enormously important to me, because intuitively I realized that night is as important as day; and [because this led] to making one realize that the intuition is as important as the intellect." On May 27, delivers Smith College commencement address. On August 3, Hal Vursell, editor of *A Wrinkle in Time* and *A Wind in the Door*, dies at age 68. On November 15, at a panel discussion sponsored by the Children's Book Council at New York's Gotham Hotel, comments on the attention to detail that has become a hallmark of her precedent-setting touring career, advising fellow writers "not to neglect the Midwest," to "make your inscriptions personal," and "answer your mail. A handwritten letter to a young fan will result in an avalanche of word-of-mouth publicity that will eventually mean sales." *The Irrational Season* (Crosswicks Journal, volume 3) published by Seabury Press in December.

1978   On January 7, the Madeleine L'Engle Collection is dedicated at Buswell Library, Wheaton College. Wheaton's Marion E. Wade Center had previously acquired the papers of C. S. Lewis, J.R.R. Tolkien, and Dorothy L. Sayers. On March 30, receives University of Southern Mississippi Medallion, delivering acceptance speech entitled "The Freedom of Service in the Life of a Writer" in which she declares: "It takes courage for us to move from the safe world of provable facts into the unknown area of the questions that . . . cannot be answered in the language of provable facts. Nothing really important can be." In July, *A Swiftly Tilting Planet* published by Farrar, Straus and Giroux; *Kirkus* expresses impatience at story's "irksomely superior Murry family"; *Newsweek* calls it "well-written, imaginative, and exceedingly complex, evoking the timeless conflict of good and evil with a detective element thrown in." In August, *The Weather of the Heart: Poems* published by Harold Shaw.

1979   Continues intensive U.S. speaking schedule, also traveling to Argentina, Israel, and Cyprus for a two-week conference with writers from developing nations. On May 27, son Bion marries Laurie Jane Stratton. In fall, Farrar, Straus and Giroux releases *A Wrinkle in Time*, *A Wind in the Door*, and *A Swiftly Tilting Planet* as a boxed set, the "Time Trilogy," with new jacket designs by Leo and Diane Dillon.

Norman Lear's T.A.T. production company acquires film rights to *A Wrinkle in Time*. In October, *Ladder of Angels: Scenes from the Bible Illustrated by Children of the World* published by Seabury Press, inspired by a children's art contest conducted by Jerusalem mayor Teddy Kolleck. *The Weather of the Heart* wins the National Religious Book Award.

1980   On February 1, departs by freighter with Hugh for Cape Town, South Africa. In May, *A Ring of Endless Light* (fifth Austin family novel) published by Farrar, Straus and Giroux. Accepts National Book Award on May 1 in children's paperback category for *A Swiftly Tilting Planet*. On May 17, receives Honorary Doctor of Letters from Gordon College, Wenham, Massachusetts, the first of seventeen honorary degrees. In July, *Walking on Water: Reflections on Faith and Art* published by Harold Shaw. In November, *The Anti-Muffins* (the sixth Austin family novel, illustrated by Gloria Ortiz) published by Seabury.

1981   On February 18, awarded Smith College Medal. In March, elected vice president of Authors Guild of America. On July 29, accepts a Newbery Honor at the American Library Association conference in San Francisco for *A Ring of Endless Light*.

1982   In February, flies with Hugh to Hong Kong to board cruise ship bound for Singapore, Sri Lanka, Bombay, Djibouti, and other ports. On shipboard, revises *A Severed Wasp*, a sequel to first novel *The Small Rain*. In August, *The Sphinx at Dawn: Two Stories* (illustrated by Vivian Berger) published by Seabury Press.

1983   On January 5, *A Severed Wasp* published by Farrar, Straus and Giroux. In April, a revised edition of *And Both Were Young* published by Delacorte Press. In May, *And It Was Good: Reflections on Beginnings*, L'Engle's meditation on the creation story and the first book of what will be known as the "Genesis Trilogy," published by Harold Shaw. On November 16, delivers lecture "Dare to Be Creative!" at the Library of Congress. Hugh retires from role on *All My Children* due to hearing loss.

1984   On January 21, daughter Maria marries for the second time, to John Rooney. On April 1, during Lent, delivers one of several occasional sermons at the Cathedral, speaking about her recent experience as a juror in a Manhattan criminal case concerning assault in the second degree and reflecting on the true meaning of atonement: "at-oneness with God." In late April, accepts Regina Medal of Catholic Library Association in Boston. In July *The Small Rain* republished by Farrar, Straus and Giroux with new author introduction. In November, *A House Like a Lotus* published by Farrar, Straus and Giroux; *Library Journal* writes that the "characterization of both Max and Polly is superbly delineated, showing the very human complications of love and friendship. Conversation here takes a sometimes oppressively philosophical bent, but it is still a pleasure to read a leisurely, often powerful, novel for teens about people who think," and *The New York Times* calls it "a cosmopolitan, romantic novel." In December, on behalf of Authors Guild, protests Peoria, Illinois, board of education's attempt to remove three books by Judy Blume from district school libraries. Letter, which is cosigned by Katherine Paterson, Virginia Hamilton, Natalie Babbitt, Milton Meltzer, Uri Shulevitz, William Steig, and Elizabeth George Speare, asserts that board's actions "teach a poor lesson, one of intolerance, distrust, and contempt [for the values] protected by the First Amendment."

1985   January 4–6, leads silent retreat at Holy Cross Monastery, West Park, New York. In the spring, begins two-year term as president of Authors Guild of America, working closely with Judy Blume, Robert K. Massie, and others on First Amendment issues. On April 25, tells students of Rodeph Sholom Day School, New York: "The great thing about getting older is that you don't lose all the other ages you've been."

1986   Initiates successful Authors Guild lobbying effort in opposition to Federal Tax Reform Act of 1986 provision that attempts to bar authors from taking legitimate deductions for annual business expenses. In April, travels to China with Hugh. On May 18, receives honorary Doctor of Letters from Smith College. On June 2, Hugh is diagnosed with bladder cancer and two days later undergoes surgery that reveals the cancer has spread. The same month, *A Stone for a Pillow: Journeys with Jacob*, the second book in the Genesis trilogy, published by Harold Shaw. On September 26, Hugh dies of cancer at Charlotte Hungerford Hospital, Torrington, Connecticut. In September, Farrar, Straus and Giroux publishes *Many Waters*, about which Susan Cooper writes in *The New York Times*: "Analogies between the Flood and the possibility of nuclear destruction are suggested from time to time, but no didactic conclusion is forced out of them. . . . Miss L'Engle is above all a skillful storyteller." On November 23, receives National Council of Teachers of English ALAN Award for lifetime achievement as a writer for teens.

1987   In September, twenty-fifth-anniversary signed limited edition of *A Wrinkle in Time* published by Farrar, Straus and Giroux. In November, religious poetry collection *A Cry Like a Bell* published by Harold Shaw.

1988   Hires Sheila Brighton as first of a series of personal assistants to manage overbusy schedule. Struggles with eye- and knee-related health issues but without curtailing lecture commitments. On February 4, takes part in reading sponsored by PEN American Center, "Breaking the Silence: The Current Situation of Writers and Journalists in South Korea," with Edward Albee, Susan Sarandon, and Max Apple. In October, *Two-Part Invention: The Story of a Marriage* (Crosswicks Journal, volume 4) published by Farrar, Straus and Giroux, presenting idealized account of her marriage. On November 29, celebrates seventieth birthday with gala event held at Diocesan House, Cathedral Church of St. John the Divine, during which she wears crownlike "head lei" brought by friends from Hawaii.

1989   In January, *Sold into Egypt: Joseph's Journey into Human Being*, the final book of the Genesis trilogy, published by Harold Shaw. Renovates Manhattan apartment, now shared by granddaughter Charlotte Jones while attending college, and begins writing on desktop computer, which proves problematic at first because it is too cumbersome to be taken along on still-numerous speaking trips. Resumes part-time teaching at St. Hilda's and St. Hugh's. In November, *An Acceptable Time* published by Farrar, Straus and Giroux; *Kirkus* writes: "L'Engle is still an able practitioner of time travel, yet . . . here, the conceptual feats are not quite so original, invigorating, or accessible. But her storytelling skill (a blend of practiced writing and theological roving) will carry even nonbelievers along while—in her attempt to reconcile pagan with Christian belief—the notion that Christ existed long before the historical Jesus is superbly debated."

1990   On January 3, while vacationing in Mexico, receives word
        of death of Edward Nason West. Returns to New York to
        deliver eulogy at St. John the Divine, then leads annual
        writing workshop and silent retreat at Holy Cross Monas-
        tery before flying to Japan to address the Tokyo Women's
        Conference. On April 17, receives Kerlan Award from the
        University of Minnesota and in Kerlan Award Lecture
        recalls: "When I was pushing forty, living in a two hundred
        plus year old farmhouse, trying to raise three young chil-
        dren, to write, to cope with rejection slips, I asked again all
        the cosmic questions I had asked as a teen-ager. . . . Then,
        by some chance . . . I stumbled on a book of Einstein's, in
        which I read that 'any one who is not lost in rapturous awe
        at the power and glory of the mind behind the universe is
        as good as a burnt out candle,' and in Einstein I found my
        theologian." In summer, travels to southern California and
        Vancouver; then to Denmark, Holland, England, and the
        Soviet Union, returning September 3. In September, *The
        Glorious Impossible*, a picture book retelling the life of
        Christ, illustrated with reproductions of Giotto frescoes at
        Scrovegni Chapel, Padua, published by Simon and Schus-
        ter. On October 10, gives public reading at St. Paul's
        Church, New York; ruefully notes surge in challenges to *A
        Wrinkle in Time* by members of the Religious Right.
        Objections typically focus on supposed references to witch-
        craft and the ecumenical perspective that equates the con-
        tributions to mankind of Jesus Christ with those of secular
        visionaries such as Albert Einstein and J. S. Bach. Death of
        Canon West prompts L'Engle to search for spiritual con-
        nections beyond the Cathedral, notably at All Angels'
        Church, a mission-focused Episcopal church founded in
        1846 originally to serve the free black community of New
        York's Seneca Village.

1991   On May 17, delivers Class of 1941 fiftieth-anniversary
        address at Smith. On May 31, gives Wellesley commence-
        ment address, urging graduating seniors to "use fully the
        Apollo, the intellect, which is a great glory, and rejoice
        equally in Sophia, the wisdom which makes the intellect
        creative instead of destructive." In early summer, spends
        two weeks at University of Oxford for C. S. Lewis confer-
        ence, then travels to Paris. On July 28, is seriously injured
        in car crash in San Diego, California; released from hospital
        on August 5 but must cancel all fall events. On December

28, writes to May Sarton for upcoming eightieth-birthday tribute: "You were the first real writer I met. Eva Le Gallienne introduced us when you came into New York at a time when my personal world had fallen apart, and you and Miss LeG, simply by being who you were, helped put me back together."

1992 In January, travels to Antarctica with son Bion and his wife Laurie and gathers material for *Troubling a Star*, a Vicky Austin fantasy. Trip also inspires *Penguins and Golden Calves*, a reflection on the spiritual life. In February, is elected member of Century Association, an august New York arts club to which her father once belonged and that had only recently opened to women. On March 27, family opera based on *A Wrinkle in Time*, with music, lyrics, and libretto by Libby Larson, premieres at Opera Delaware. In October, novel *Certain Women* published by Farrar, Straus and Giroux.

1993 From February 22 to March 2, tapes audiobook of *A Wrinkle in Time* in New York studio for September release by Listening Library. In March, *The Rock That Is Higher: Story as Truth* published by Shaw Books. On December 28, undergoes knee replacement surgery.

1994 On June 13, flies to Seattle for start of six-week visit to Pacific Northwest to teach writing workshop and see friends, including David Somerville (the model for Bishop Nason Colubra in *An Acceptable Time*) and publisher Luci Shaw. In September, *Troubling a Star* (the seventh Austin family book) published by Farrar, Straus and Giroux. On December 4, preaches during advent service at the National Cathedral in Washington, D.C., reflecting on the meaning of Christmas: "The thing that has struck me was the birth of Christ—God giving up all power and becoming absolutely vulnerable. That was an incredible act of love and an incredible sacrifice. If I see a bug on the floor, and limit myself to the life of that bug, that would be nothing in comparison to what God gave up in coming to live with us."

1995 Serves as second "Writer in Residence" (after Susan Minot) at Hearst's *Victoria* magazine, a yearlong affiliation (but not an actual residency) with this upscale lifestyle monthly for women that obliges her to make a series of written contributions and public appearances. During summer, tours west coast of Ireland en route to the Children's

Literature New England–sponsored conference "Writing the World: Myth as Metaphor," at Trinity College, Dublin, where she delivers a lecture titled "Mythic Realms of Gods and Heroes." Afterward, visits Isle of Iona, the Holy Island of Lindisfarne, Beatrix Potter and William Wordsworth's Lake District cottages, and London. In late summer, flies from New York to Juneau, Alaska, for weeklong cruise with Bion and Laurie. Crosswicks Cottage, a light-filled, one-story house just across the road from longtime family home, is renovated to eliminate need to climb stairs.

1996   In February, undergoes foot surgery related to aftereffects of knee replacement. On February 12, is called "grand dame of religious fiction in both the general-interest and the religion marketplaces" in the introduction to *Publishers Weekly*'s Spring Religion Books roundup. In May, is excited by first glimpse of recently discovered Hale-Bopp Comet while on annual religious retreat at Laity Lodge Center for Christian Learning, Leakey, Texas. The same month, *Penguins and Golden Calves: Icons and Idols in Antarctica and Other Spiritual Places* published by Shaw Books and *A Live Coal in the Sea*, a sequel to *Camilla*, published by Farrar, Straus and Giroux. In June, *Glimpses of Grace: Daily Thoughts and Reflections*, coauthored with Carole F. Chase, published by Harper San Francisco. In August, granddaughter Charlotte Jones marries John Voiklis.

1997   In January *Mothers and Daughters*, a collection of prayers and prose excerpts with photographs by Maria Rooney, published by Northstone Books. In May, at Laity Lodge, again views Hale-Bopp Comet, now at its brightest having recently passed perihelion. In June, *Friends for the Journey*, a memoir of friendship coauthored with Luci Shaw, published by Servant Publications. On July 1, U.S. space shuttle Columbia blasts off with copy of *A Wrinkle in Time* brought on board by astronaut Dr. Janice E. Voss, who credits book with having inspired her career. In July, works on novel about Meg Murry as forty-year-old mother coming to terms with the complications of her seven children's lives. Still walking with a cane following foot surgery and with all three grown children living in Connecticut, stays close to home in late summer, tending new vegetable garden at Crosswicks. Returns to New York and the Cathedral library in the fall. In September, *Bright Evening Star: Mystery of the Incarnation*, a memoir of religious faith,

published by Harold Shaw. Receives World Fantasy Awards
Life Achievement Award but does not attend World Fan-
tasy Convention (October 30–November 2) at London's
International Hotel.

1998   In February, spends two weeks in Santa Barbara, then all of
April at Laity Lodge. Novel in progress, now about Meg
Murry in her fifties, to be called *The Eye Begins to See*, after
Theodore Roethke line, "In a dark time, the eye begins to
see." On July 1, receives American Library Association's
Margaret A. Edwards Award for lifetime achievement as
writer for teens, in Washington, D.C., then travels west for
writing workshop in British Columbia, then to Oxford and
Cambridge to speak at C. S. Lewis centenary celebration.
Miracle on 10th Street and Other Christmas Writings published by Harold Shaw. On November 29, is presented with
copy of *The Swiftly Tilting Worlds of Madeleine L'Engle*, a
festschrift secretly two years in the making as an eightieth
birthday surprise, edited and published by Luci Shaw, with
contributions by Katherine Paterson, historian Thomas
Cahill, and others.

1999   On February 21, becomes great-grandmother of son of
Charlotte and John Voiklis. On April 1, granddaughter
Léna Jones marries Rob Roy. In May, breaks hip; has hip
replacement surgery in October. On December 17, son
Bion Franklin dies of complications from alcoholism, at age
47.

2000   In March, *A Full House: An Austin Family Christmas*
(eighth Austin family book) published by Farrar, Straus and
Giroux, and *Mothers & Sons*, with photographs by daughter
Maria Rooney, published by Harold Shaw. *A Wrinkle in
Time* ranks 23 on American Library Association's 100 Most
Frequently Challenged Books list, 1990–99, the first period
for which records are kept; it drops to 90 a decade later.

2001   In February, picture book *The Other Dog*, illustrated by
Christine Davernier, originally written in the late 1940s
and inspired by the experience of dog-sitting for Eva Le
Gallienne, published by SeaStar. On March 15, in *New York
Times* interview, after describing self as "lightly Episcopalian," names Daniel and Revelation as favorite portions of
Scripture: "They're both high fiction, and I am a fiction
writer." In September, Farrar, Straus and Giroux releases
boxed set of all four Murry family novels as the "Time

Quartet." In October, *Madeleine L'Engle Herself: Reflections on a Writing Life*, compiled by Carole F. Chase, published by Shaw Books. Is no longer able to make public appearances.

2002   In early February, suffers cerebral hemorrhage. Remains fully aware and after nearly three months of rehab regains limited mobility with help of walker and wheelchair. In June, tells an interviewer: "My books are not bad books to die with. What I mean by that is that when I read a book, if it makes me feel more alive, then it's a good book to die with." On August 23, television adaptation of *A Ring of Endless Light* broadcast on Disney Channel with James Whitmore in the role of Grandfather.

2003   Spends winter months in New York, venturing to Broadway to see *Hairspray*, *42nd Street*, and *Tea at Five*; then to Crosswicks for spring and summer. Days filled with family, books, quiet reflection, and TV game shows.

2004   On April 12, *The New Yorker* publishes "The Storyteller," a profile by Cynthia Zarin that challenges veracity of autobiographical writings, including L'Engle's long-held assertion that father died of mustard gas poisoning during World War I. Long-awaited four-hour television mini-series based on *A Wrinkle in Time* airs on ABC television beginning May 10. In November, back in New York, suffers fall requiring hospitalization. Undergoes physical therapy in Connecticut and does not return to New York. Receives National Humanities Medal but is too ill to attend November 17 White House ceremony. In December, moves into Rose Haven nursing home, Litchfield, Connecticut.

2005   *The Ordering of Love: The New and Collected Poems* published by Shaw Books in March.

2007   Dies on September 6 of natural causes at Rose Haven nursing home. On November 28, a Choral Evensong and Holy Eucharist commemorating her life is celebrated at the Cathedral Church of St. John the Divine, where her ashes are interred in the Cathedral Columbarium.

NOTE ON THE TEXTS

This volume contains four novels by Madeleine L'Engle: *The Arm of the Starfish* (1965), *Dragons in the Waters* (1976), *A House Like a Lotus* (1984), and *An Acceptable Time* (1989). An appendix collects four articles and essays relating to these novels. A companion Library of America volume collects *A Wrinkle in Time, A Wind in the Door, A Swiftly Tilting Planet,* and *Many Waters,* along with deleted passages from *Wrinkle* and five related speeches and essays. These eight novels, which L'Engle called the Kairos books, were published under various rubrics during L'Engle's lifetime, including as the Time Trilogy and the Time Quintet (which included *An Acceptable Time*). Library of America presents them arranged into two quartets: the Time Quartet, featuring Meg Murry and her siblings; and the Polly O'Keefe Quartet, featuring Meg's daughter Polly.

L'Engle was personally involved in supervising the texts of all her books through galley proof stage at the publisher; often, she made extensive alterations at proofs, but these usually consisted of correcting punctuation or style that had been standardized by a copy editor back to her original intention. For example, a letter of October 11, 1965 (now in the FSG Records at the New York Public Library), from L'Engle's agent, Theron Raines, to her editor at Farrar, Straus and Giroux, Hal Vursell, states, "Madeleine points out that she made no author's alterations on STARFISH. She said that she merely changed back to her own style, words and punctuation which had been altered in her manuscript by the copy editor. Therefore, would you see that this $69.21 [charge for alterations to the galley] is credited to her."

THE ARM OF THE STARFISH

The Arm of the Starfish was published in June 1965 by Ariel Books, the children's imprint of Farrar, Straus and Giroux. A paperback edition was published in January 1980 by Dell Laurel-Leaf. There has not been a British edition. The first American edition is the source of the text in this volume.

DRAGONS IN THE WATERS

Dragons in the Waters was published in 1976 by Farrar, Straus and Giroux. A paperback edition was published in August 1982 by Dell

Laurel-Leaf. There has not been a British edition. The first American edition is the source of the text in this volume.

A HOUSE LIKE A LOTUS

A House Like a Lotus was published in November 1984 by Farrar, Straus and Giroux. A paperback edition was published in December 1985 by Dell Laurel-Leaf. There has not been a British edition. The first American edition is the source of the text in this volume.

AN ACCEPTABLE TIME

An Acceptable Time was published in November 1989 by Farrar, Straus and Giroux. A paperback edition was published in December 1990 by Dell Laurel-Leaf. There has not been a British edition. The first American edition is the source of the text in this volume.

APPENDIX

"How Long is a Book?" is an unpublished lecture written in 1973 or 1974, while L'Engle was beginning to write *Dragons in the Waters,* then titled *The Bolivar Portrait.* The source of the text in this volume is an unpublished typescript provided by L'Engle's estate.

The piece printed here under the descriptive title "Regina Medal Acceptance Speech" was published in *Catholic Library World* (July/August 1984), pp. 29–31, which is the source for the text used here.

"Shake the Universe" was published in *Ms.* (July/August 1987), pp. 182–84, 219, and is the source of the text used here.

The piece printed here under the descriptive title "Smith College 50th Reunion Speech" from 1991 was never published. The source of the text used here is a typescript in the Madeleine L'Engle Papers at Wheaton College (Series 8, Box 305, folder 6).

This volume presents the texts of the original printings and typescripts chosen for inclusion here, but it does not attempt to reproduce features of their typographic design. The texts are presented without change, except for the correction of typographical errors. Spelling, punctuation, and capitalization are often expressive features, and they are not altered, even when inconsistent or irregular. The following is a list of typographical errors corrected, cited by page and line number: 18.12, friends was; 34.12, Legion; 73.34, excitedly.; 87.1–2 (and *passim*), Saô; 102.25, "'Come; 110.31, octive; 132.33, Verbius'; 155.34, be be; 170.19, "Yes."; 171.7 (and *passim*), Magalhâes."; 176.3, "Nâo,

nâo,"; 177.33 (and *passim*), Salâo da Chá."; 183.2, Sao; 184.16, too rose.; 190.34, Bélem; 190.35–36 (and *passim*), Madre do Dios; 264.8, nearly; 306.13, There many; 330.18, imaged; 373.11, lions; 382.10, him.; 403.13, wrinked; 422.26, *vue*.; 516.23, A. J.; 482.21, began."; 520.20, "Beene; 558.24, Kate?"; 559.35, fun.'; 573.14, "Sure.; 575.16, precursers; 607.15, Women's; 667.35, Trypanozomas; 673.2, examing; 769.34, up?; 782.26–27, Polly "She's; 803.8, was a dark; 878.11–12, People of the Wind; 988.2, sir."?; 988.24, idolotry,; 990.3, Xian.

NOTES

In the notes below, the reference numbers denote page and line of this volume (the line count includes headings, but not rule lines). No note is made for material included in the eleventh edition of Merriam-Webster's Collegiate Dictionary, except for certain cases where common words and terms have specific historical meanings or inflections. Biblical quotations and allusions are keyed to the King James Version; references to Shakespeare to *The Riverside Shakespeare*, ed. G. Blakemore Evans (Boston: Houghton Mifflin, 1974). For further biographical background, references to other studies, and more detailed notes, see Charlotte Jones Voiklis and Léna Roy, *Becoming Madeleine* (New York: Farrar, Strauss and Giroux, 2018); Suzanne Bray (ed.), *Dimensions of Madeleine L'Engle: New Critical Approaches* (Jefferson, NC: McFarland & Co., 2017); Leonard S. Marcus (ed.), *Listening for Madeleine: A Portrait of Madeleine L'Engle in Many Voices* (New York: Farrar, Straus and Giroux, 2012); Marek Oziewicz, *One Earth, One People: The Mythopoetic Fantasy Series of Ursula K. Le Guin, Lloyd Alexander, Madeleine L'Engle, and Orson Scott Card* (Jefferson, NC: McFarland & Co., 2008); and Luci Shaw (ed.), *The Swiftly Tilting Worlds of Madeleine L'Engle* (Wheaton, IL: Harold Shaw, 1998).

THE ARM OF THE STARFISH

2.1–2 *For Edward Nason West*] Edward Nason West (1909–1990), Episcopal priest, Canon Sacrist at the Cathedral Church of Saint John the Divine, New York, and L'Engle's longtime confessor and confidant. The author delighted West by modeling Canon Tallis on him.

2.3–5 ΚΑΙ ΟΣΟΙ ΤΩ . . . ΑΥΤΟΥΣ] Galatians 6:16a: "And as many as walk according to this rule, peace be on them."

3.2 Kennedy International] John F. Kennedy International Airport, the New York metropolitan area's largest airport, originally known as Idlewild and renamed in memory of the assassinated American president in December 1963.

3.27 Woods Hole] Woods Hole Oceanographic Institution in Cape Cod, Massachusetts. Since 1930, a private, nonprofit research and education center concerned with all aspects of marine science.

3.29   Didymus] A possible reference to Thomas the Apostle (according to tradition, died 72 C.E.), also known as Didymus and as "Doubting Thomas" for his initial skepticism on hearing the news of Christ's resurrection.

4.36   Eddington] Homage to Sir Arthur Stanley Eddington (1882–1944), British astrophysicist and philosopher of science.

6.1   Kali] The Hindu warrior goddess of death, time, and fertility.

6.5   Gaea] Variant of Gaia, the ancient Greek earth goddess. L'Engle's island is fictional.

6.27   Canon Tallis] Named for the Tallis Canon, a musical setting composed by Thomas Tallis (c. 1505–1585) for Psalm 67, and first published in the Archbishop of Canterbury Matthew Parker's *Psalter* (1567). L'Engle sang the Tallis Canon for grace at dinner.

12.25   Cape] Cape Cod (see note 3.27).

13.17   NO SMOKING] Smoking was allowed on most commercial airliners until the late 1980s.

13.33   Hayden Planetarium] At the American Museum of Natural History in New York. Founded in 1933, the original planetarium was demolished in 1997; its successor opened in 2000 as part of the museum's Rose Center for Earth and Space.

15.18   Prado] The Museo Nacional del Prado. Founded in 1819, Madrid's most important art museum, home to the world's finest collection of Spanish art.

16.1–2   Nike sites] The United States Army and the North Atlantic Treaty Organization (NATO) deployed Nike anti-aircraft and anti-missile defense systems throughout Western Europe during the Cold War years.

22.4–8   "*But yield who will . . . is to unite . . .*"] "Two Tramps in Mud Time" (1936), lines 65–66, by Robert Frost (1874–1963).

27.5   "Está bien para mi, también."] Spanish: I'll have the same.

31.37–38   a large painting of St. Andrew and St. Francis] *St. Andrew and St. Francis* (c. 1595) by El Greco (1541–1614). El Greco's two subjects were indeed separated by more than a millennium of chronological time: Andrew the Apostle (first century C.E.) and St. Francis of Assisi (1181 or 1182–1226).

32.32   *cordon bleu*] The Cordon Bleu cooking school was founded in Paris in 1895 and known thereafter as a citadel of classical French cuisine.

33.22–23 *"My avocation and my vocation . . . in sight,"*] Frost's "Two Tramps in Mud Time," lines 67–68 (see note 22.4–8).

34.12–13   French Légion d'Honneur ribbon] Canon West, the model for Tallis, was a Chevalier of the Legion of Honor as well as an Officer of the Order of the British Empire, Officer of the Order of Orange-Nassau (Netherlands), and Knight Commander of the Royal Order of St. Sava (Yugoslavia).

37.6   caravelle] A relatively small commercial jetliner developed in France in the 1950s.

44.7   The Hotel Avenida Palace] Lisbon's first luxury hotel, which opened in 1892.

45.1–2   the Fort] Castelo de São Jorge, the Moorish fortress built atop the highest of Lisbon's seven hills.

45.30–31   Interpol] International Criminal Police Organization, a world body founded in 1923 to foster cooperation among the police forces of more than 190 member nations.

51.29   Molèc] Molech, the name in the Bible for the Canaanite god who required child sacrifice.

53.18   Typhon] In Greek mythology, the youngest son of Gaia and Tartarus, and a hideous monster with a head made up of one hundred snakes. After unsuccessfully challenging Zeus for supremacy, he was consigned to the Netherworld for eternity.

60.24   Korea] The Korean War (1950–53) fought between the forces of North Korea (with Soviet and Chinese backing) and South Korea (and their chief ally the United States).

65.19   *meu bem*] Portuguese term of endearment meaning "honey."

66.30   Joshua] Name rendered in the Hebrew Bible first as "Yehoshua," then as "Yeshua," and which later entered Latin as "Iesus" and English as "Jesus."

70.4–5   Brooks Brothers–style suit] Quintessential American businessman's attire from a New York clothing emporium founded in 1818.

80.2   Respighi's *The Birds*] Work for small orchestra (1928) by the Italian composer and violinist Ottorino Respighi (1879–1936).

82.39   Baal] In the Bible, a Canaanite storm (and fertility) god.

83.1   Eliphaz] One of Job's three false friends in the Bible.

83.1   St. Zophar's] Another of Job's three friends.

86.38   Jeronymos Monastery] Mosteiro dos Jerónimos, the vast, architecturally distinguished former monastery commissioned in 1497 by Portuguese King Manuel I (1469–1521) and featuring lavish ornamentation commemorating Portugal's role in the Age of Discovery, which began during Manuel I's reign and continued to the eighteenth century.

87.1–2   São Juan Chrysostom Monastery] L'Engle invented this monastery, named for John Chrysostom (c. 349–407), the archbishop of Constantinople considered to be an important Early Church Father.

87.4   Belém Tower] Tower built in the early sixteenth century on a small island in the Targus River to bolster Lisbon's defenses.

87.4–5   Manueline architecture] Highly ornamented late Gothic style of Portuguese architecture dating from the early decades of the sixteenth century.

87.7   Henry the Navigator] Portuguese prince Henry the Navigator (1394–1460), foremost patron of Portuguese explorers during the Age of Discovery and a major proponent of the transatlantic slave trade.

90.5   Palisades Park] A popular New Jersey amusement park across from Manhattan that operated from 1898 to 1971.

92.17   *The Third Man*] Novella by Graham Greene (1904–1991) written as a treatment for the Carol Reed film noir of the same name released in 1949, with a screenplay by Greene. The plot concerns the apparent murder of a scientist who had been stealing penicillin from military hospitals and diluting it for the black market.

92.18   Late Late Show] From the mid-1950s, a name used for television programs that broadcast pre-1948 American feature films late at night.

93.25   Mordred] In the Arthurian legend, King Arthur's nephew who fought against his uncle at the Battle of Camlann, at which Arthur was mortally wounded.

95.12   Tallis Canon] See note 6.27.

99.16   Macrina] St. Macrina the Elder (before 270–c. 340 C.E.), Byzantine Christian patron saint of widows and protector against poverty. Mother of St. Basil the Elder and grandmother of St. Basil the Great, St. Gregory of Nyssa, St. Peter of Sebastea, and St. Macrina the

Younger (c. 330–379 C.E.), who was a nun whose exemplary ascetic life became a source of inspiration for adherents within the Roman Catholic, Eastern Catholic, and Eastern Orthodox churches.

110.17–20   *All praise to thee . . . almighty wings.*] First of twelve verses of a hymn written by Anglican bishop Thomas Ken (1637–1711) to be sung to the melody of the Tallis Canon (see note 6.27).

110.25   "Arkansas Traveller."] Jaunty tune composed by Colonel Sanford C. Faulkner (1806–1874) that was the official state song of Arkansas from 1949 to 1963.

111.1–2   'Come Unto These Yellow Sands'] Ariel's song, in Shakespeare's *The Tempest*, I.ii.375–87, which was set to music c. 1695 by Henry Purcell (1659–1695) as well as by many later composers.

124.15–16   Back in the early sixties . . . in a test tube.] L'Engle here indulges, albeit presciently, in science fiction. While human ova were first harvested laparoscopically in 1970, the first "test tube baby" was not born via the process of in vitro fertilization until 1978.

128.38   Virbius] Roman forest god.

132.32   Temis] Variant of Themis. In Greek mythology, a daughter of Uranus and Gaea and the Titan goddess of natural law and divine order.

139.3–5   *Only where love . . . future's sakes.*] Frost's "Two Tramps in Mud Time," lines 69–72 (see note 22.4–8).

140.1   MS-222] Tricaine methanesulfonate (also known by the acronym TMS), a muscle relaxant used for anesthesia and sedation and for the euthanization of fish intended for human consumption.

146.5   "Pink," . . . scarlet."] Cold War–era shorthand for an individual with communist or other left-of-center political leanings.

147.23   elevateds] Elevated trains.

147.25   lions] Two marble lions, affectionately known as Patience and Fortitude, flank the Fifth Avenue entrance of the New York Public Library's central building.

170.11–12   *senhor paroco*] Portuguese: lord parish priest.

170.17   Pinhas] Variant of Phinehas, Exodus 6:25; a grandson of Aaron who was distinguished for his zeal against idolatry.

173.25   *Esquire*] From 1933, an upscale men's fashion and lifestyle magazine.

173.26   *Mad*] Irreverent monthly for young readers launched in 1952.

176.26   "Igreja,"] Portuguese: Church.

176.34   "Obrigado,"] Portuguese: Thank you.

179.4   Embuste] Portuguese: trick or lie.

179.4   Coimbra] The University of Coimbra, Portugal's oldest university, founded in Lisbon in 1290 and moved two centuries later to the city for which it is named.

182.33   Hotel São Mamede] Casa de São Mamede, a hotel converted from an eighteenth-century Lisbon mansion that has operated since the 1940s.

188.33   *Libanius*] Libanius of Antioch (314–394 C.E.), revered Greek Sophist and rhetorician.

189.5–6   John studied theology under Diodore of Tarsus] Diodore, bishop of Tarsus (died c. 390 C.E.), an ardent defender of Christianity against Roman emperor Julian I's attempts to revive paganism, and the teacher of John Chrysostom (see note 87.2–3) and theologian Theodore of Mopsuestia (c. 350–428 C.E.).

189.8–9   sarcophagus of Princess María Fernanda] Possibly the Portuguese Infanta Maria Ana Fernanda (1843–1884), the eldest daughter of Queen Maria I, who is actually buried in Dresden Cathedral in Germany.

190.35–36   Madre de Deus] Igreja Madre de Deus, a Lisbon convent founded in 1509 by Queen Leonor de Viseu and rebuilt after the 1755 earthquake in the Baroque manner. It was closed in 1868 and reopened in 1965 as a museum.

191.2   Mr. Eiffel's tower] The Elevador de Santa Justa, an elevator connecting the two levels of streets in the city designed by Raul Mesnier de Ponsard (1848–1914), a protégé of Gustave Eiffel, which opened to the public in 1902.

197.31   Folclore] Portuguese: Folklore.

197.32   Fado] Passionate style of Portuguese folk music traditionally sung to string accompaniment in pubs and cafés.

200.21   Harrod's] Harrods, luxury London department store founded in 1824.

204.3   "Muito obrigado . . . apresse se,"] Portuguese: Thanks very much . . . hurry!

210.34   A.H.   173–176] A.H. is short for the *Anglican Hymn Book*, published in 1868. The first lines of the four hymns alluded to by Canon Tallis are, respectively: "What are these in bright array?"; "Oh happy saints, who dwell in light"; "Lord of the Church, we humbly pray"; and "How beauteous are their feet."

210.35   E.H. 269] "O Gladsome Light" (see following note) is hymn 269 in *The English Hymnal* of the Church of England, published in 1906.

210.36–211.4   ΦΩΣ ἱλαρὸν ἁγίας δόξης . . . σε δοξάζει] The Phos Hilaron, called in Latin "Lumen Hilare" and in English "O Gladsome Light," an ancient Christian hymn written in Koine Greek: "O Light gladsome of the holy glory of the Immortal Father, / the Heavenly, the Holy, the Blessed, O Jesus Christ, / having come upon the setting of the sun, having seen the light of the evening, / we praise the Father, the Son, and the Holy Spirit: God. / Worthy it is at all times to praise Thee in joyful voices, / O Son of God, Giver of Life, for which the world glorifies Thee."

211.11   Metousis] Metousiosis is the Greek equivalent of transubstantiation, or the change of substance by which the bread and wine in the Eucharist become the very body and blood of Christ.

221.27–38   ". . . Remember thy servant . . . now and evermore."] From *The Book of Common Prayer* of the Episcopal Church.

DRAGONS IN THE WATERS

233.1   DRAGONS IN THE WATERS] Psalm 74:13: "Thou didst divide the sea by thy strength; thou brakest the heads of the dragons in the waters."

234.1   *For Robert Giroux*] Robert Giroux (1914–2008) joined Farrar, Straus as an editor in 1955 and was later made a partner as well as the firm's chairman. Giroux edited L'Engle's books for adult readers published by FSG, and the two became close friends. In a letter dated January 29, 1973, about the newly published *A Wind in the Door*, Giroux wrote her: "I now understand kything and I wish there were more of it in the world. I'm also keeping an eye out for fewmets . . . The book is rich and deep and fine, and I'm a better person for having read it. Thank you."

237.11   Phair] According to the OED, 'phair' or 'phare' is an old word meaning "beacon" or "lighthouse."

246.27–28   *I met her in Venezuela . . . her head . . .*] Opening lines of "Venezuela," a song composed in 1918 by John Jacob Niles (1892–1980), based on a sailors' ditty heard in Boulogne, France.

249.21   Benne Seed Island] Invented island off the South Carolina coast.

250.24–25   Puerto de los Dragones] Although this port city is an invented place, the *Orion* would have passed through the Bocas del Dragón ("Dragon's Mouths") straits on its way to landfall in Venezuela.

250.30   Margaret of Antioch] Also known as Margaret the Virgin. Christian saint now thought to be legendary and said to have been swallowed alive by Satan in dragon guise only to be disgorged when contact with the cross she held irritated the dragon's innards.

252.28   Interpol] See note 45.30–31.

261.10   Niniane] The Lady of the Lake in Arthurian legend, also sometimes called Viviane or Nimue. Also St. Ninian (fifth century C.E.), an apostle from Briton to the Pictish people in modern Scotland.

269.4   Uncle Father's] Term of endearment coined by L'Engle's granddaughters for Canon Edward Nason West (see note 2.1–2).

277.2–3   "And Tobiah sent letters to put me in fear."] Nehemiah 6:19.

284.14   Lake Maracaibo] Body of water variously characterized as a tidal bay, lagoon, or lake, located in an oil-rich region of western Venezuela.

290.14   things know where they belong] In *A Circle of Quiet* (1972), L'Engle attributes this quote to Edward Nason West, whom she refers to by his fictional name, Canon Tallis.

291.15–16   Things are falling . . . center doesn't hold.] Cf. "The Second Coming" (1919) by William Butler Yeats (1865–1939), line 3.

298.31   Guajiro] Also known as the Wayuu; largest group of indigenous people in Venezuela.

328.34–329.15   *I met her in . . . time in Venezuela.*] See note 246.27–28.

375.6   even presidents don't take promises seriously] The Watergate scandal culminated in the resignation of President Richard M. Nixon (1913–1994) on August 9, 1974, while L'Engle was writing this novel.

387.24 "Make haste slowly,"] Classical adage, adopted as a motto by the Roman emperor Augustus (63 B.C.E.–14 C.E.) and the Medici family of Renaissance Florence, among others.

388.4–5 "Curiouser and curiouser."] From Chapter 2 of *Alice's Adventures in Wonderland*.

399.9 Hotel del Lago] Maracaibo's most luxurious hotel, which opened in 1953.

400.5 Hispano-Suiza] Luxury automobile manufactured by the Barcelona-based La Hispano-Suiza Fábrica da Automóviles until World War II.

414.20 *sans peur et sans reproche*] French epithet, meaning "fearless and above reproach," which was first applied to Pierre Terrail, Seigneur de Bayard (1473–1524), a French knight who fought under three kings of France.

416.5 leghorn hat] A finely plaited, brimmed straw hat.

430.3 "The plot thickens."] A saying first recorded in *The Rehearsal* (1671), a satirical play by George Villiers, 2nd Duke of Buckingham (1628–1687).

430.10–11 Israelis in Argentina tracking down Nazis.] The most famous instance of this was the capture by Israeli agents of Nazi SS officer Adolf Eichmann in Buenos Aires in May 1960.

435.11–12 tiny organisms] *Trypanosoma*, one-celled parasites that cause a variety of fatal diseases, including sleeping sickness and Chagas disease. In *A House Like a Lotus*, Dr. Queron Renier identifies *Trypanosoma* as a special research interest. See note 537.5–6.

481.30–482.1 "Thou didst divide the sea . . . unto thy Name.] This version of Psalm 74 comes from the 1928 Book of Common Prayer, verses 14, 16–17, and 22. See also note 233.1.

A HOUSE LIKE A LOTUS

485.1 A HOUSE LIKE A LOTUS] Taken from the first chapter of *Chandogya Upanishad*, one of the oldest Hindu religious texts: "In this body, in this town of spirit, there is a little house shaped like a lotus . . ."

486.1 *For Robert Lescher*] Robert Lescher (1929–2012) succeeded Theron Raines as L'Engle's literary agent.

495.22   King George Hotel] Luxury Art Deco–style hotel that opened in 1936.

495.37   Beau Allaire] Invented place. In French, *allaire*, meaning "cheerful" or "glad," can be a woman's name; *beau* means "beautiful."

502.6   Hadassah] International women's Zionist organization founded in 1912.

502.9   World Council of Churches] An ecumenical fellowship of Eastern and Western Christian churches formed in 1948.

503.4–6   *Now the fables . . . a furious lover.*] From Clement of Alexandria (c. 150–c. 215 C.E.), *Protrepticus* ["Exhortation to the Greeks"], Chapter II.

507.37   groin-vaulted] Ornate architectural ceiling treatment achieved by the intersection of two barrel vaults at right angles to one another.

509.3–4   Dr. Heschel] Likely homage to Abraham Joshua Heschel (1907–1972), Polish-born American Jewish philosopher, theologian, and educator, and a friend of L'Engle's.

512.17   Baki] Another invented place.

516.23   J. A. Wheeler] John Archibald Wheeler (1911–2008), American theoretical physicist and educator who popularized the terms "black hole" and "wormhole."

516.24–34   "Nothing is more important . . . each other.'] John Archibald Wheeler, "From Relativity to Mutability" (1973).

525.15   Pride goeth before a fall.'] Cf. Proverbs 16:18.

530.27   *Maintenant.*] French: Now.

532.3–4   '*Go and catch . . . mandrake root.*'] First two lines of "Song" by John Donne (1572–1631).

537.5–6   some parasites . . . South America] The parasite-borne fatal illness for which Queron Renier wishes to devise preventive measures is the same one that in *Dragons on the Waters* Canon Tallis warns Queron's cousin Simon Renier about as the pair are struggling to survive in the jungle.

541.17   Plaka] Oldest section of Athens, located at the foot of the Acropolis and for that reason known as the "Neighborhood of the Gods."

542.24 Erechtheion] Acropolis temple dedicated to Athena and Poseidon, built 421–406 B.C.E. On the north side of the temple, the famous "Porch of the Maidens" is supported by six caryatids.

542.27 Theseum] Exceptionally well-preserved Athenian temple dedicated to Hephaestus, once called the Theseum under the mistaken belief that the temple housed the remains of Athenian hero Theseus.

542.38 Lord Elgin] Thomas Bruce, 7th Earl of Elgin (1766–1841), regimental commander and diplomat, appropriated for Britain a substantial portion of the original marble friezes and other sculptures that adorned the Parthenon.

559.33–34 *O wonderful, wonderful . . . all whooping!*] *As You Like It*, III.ii.191–193.

559.35–36 *Do you not know . . . I must speak.*] *As You Like It*, III.ii.249–250.

565.22 Diadumenus] Diadoumenus, or "diadem-bearer," a winner of an athletic contest, a favorite subject of the classical Greek sculptor Polykleitos (fifth century B.C.E.).

565.32 Osias Lukas] Walled Byzantine monastery of St. Luke, located in Boeotia, Greece.

575.34 Dock Street Theatre] Historic Charleston, South Carolina, theater founded in 1736.

575.34 Spoleto Festival] Since 1977, an annual spring performing arts festival in Charleston, South Carolina.

591.34 Itea] Gulf of Corinth port and resort town at the foot of Mount Parnassus.

605.33 *moules marinières*] French: mussels.

606.15–16 *Those things that hurt, instruct.*] From *Poor Richard's Almanack*.

607.15 Woman's Christian Temperance Union] A pro-temperance organization founded in 1873, whose membership peaked during the 1920s.

613.22–23 many universes] An early proponent of this idea was Hugh Everett III (1930–1982), a graduate student of John Archibald Wheeler (see notes 516.23 and 516.24–34).

619.15–16 Robinson Jeffers's play about Medea] American poet Robinson Jeffers's (1887–1962) 1946 adaptation of Euripides's *Medea* was a triumph in its initial New York run with Judith Anderson in the title role. Hugh Franklin, L'Engle's husband, played the role of Aegeus, king of Athens

622.30–36   *I did not then . . . inseparable.*] *As You Like It*, I.iii.69–76.

628.8–11   *In this body . . . world outside.*] See note 485.1.

635.28   Larnaca] Southern coastal Cyprus city and site of the island's only airport.

651.1   Milcah Adah] Milcah married the Hebrew patriarch Abraham's brother Nabor, and is thought to have been the daughter of another of Abraham's brothers, Haran (cf. Genesis 11:29). Adah is the name of both one of Esau's wives and one of the wives of Lamech, father of Noah (cf. Genesis 4:19–23 and 36:2).

652.4   Bashemath] In Genesis 36:2–3, daughter of Ishmael and another of Esau's three wives.

656.12   *"Saranam?"*] Variant of Sharanam, Sanskrit for "to surrender to" or "take refuge in" the creator.

657.7   *Epharisto*] Greek: Thanks.

657.7   Tullia] Possible reference to Tullia (79 or 78–45 B.C.E.), the only daughter of the Roman orator Cicero (106–43 B.C.E.), whose burial place is said to have been marked by an eternal flame.

657.22–23   Sophonisba] Carthaginian princess (c. 200 B.C.E.) who, during the Second Punic War, poisoned herself rather than be captured by the victorious Romans.

681.33   *despina*] Greek: lady; it can also refer to the Virgin Mary.

682.3   *Parakalo*] Greek: You're welcome.

682.3   *kyria*] Also Greek for "lady," derived from *kyrie*, meaning "lord."

719.36–38   we should live . . . forever?"] Cf. sayings attributed to St. Augustine (354–430 C.E.): "Take care of your body as if you were going to live forever, and take care of your soul as if you were going to die tomorrow," and to Mahatma Gandhi (1869–1948): "Live like you were to die tomorrow but learn as if you were to live forever."

AN ACCEPTABLE TIME

727.1   AN ACCEPTABLE TIME] Psalm 69:13: "But, Lord, I make my prayer to you in an acceptable time."

728.1–3 *For Dana . . . Jake*] Six of L'Engle's godchildren: Dana A. Catharine, former student of L'Engle's at St. Hilda's & St. Hugh's School, New York, and her adopted goddaughter; Catharine's sons Bernardo-Ruiz Catharine and Eduardo Filipe-Ruiz Catharine, whom L'Engle considered "grand godsons"; Ron and Annie Melrose, and their son Jake.

736.29 Louise Colubra] L'Engle modeled this character on her life-long friend Dr. Patricia ("Pat") Collins Cowdery (1920–2003), to whom she dedicated *A Wind in the Door*, in which Louise Colubra makes her first appearance.

736.30 Bishop Nason Colubra] Although L'Engle chose her friend Canon West's middle name as this character's first name (see note 2.1–2), she modeled Bishop Colubra on David Somerville (1915–2011), sixth Anglican bishop of New Westminster and eighth metropolitan of British Columbia, and a tenacious advocate for full church participation by women, gays, and lesbians.

744.20 Matthew Maddox's *The Horn of Joy*] Invented author and novel first referenced in *A Swiftly Tilting Planet*.

746.2–3 Schubert's "Trout" Quintet] Piano Quintet in A Major, D. 667 (1819), by Franz Schubert (1797–1828).

765.19 thresholds of time] In 1935, Albert Einstein (1879–1955) and Nathan Rosen (1909–1995), building on Einstein's general theory of relativity, proposed the existence of "bridges" in time-space, the cosmic shortcuts later named "wormholes" by John Archibald Wheeler (see note 516.23).

772.3–8 "*It was as if lightning . . .* mid-1700s.] Experience recorded on March 2, 1757, by John Thomas, in Carmarthenshire, Wales, during the Welsh Methodist Revival.

773.3 "Time waves?"] More accurately "gravitational waves," or slight ripples in space-time caused by the behavior of black holes, as predicted in Einstein's general theory of relativity and first observed in 2016 by the Laser Interferometer Gravitational-Wave Observatory (LIGO).

777.19–20 Locke's impressions of America] *Two Treatises of Government* (1689) by John Locke (1632–1704).

777.36–778.3 Alexis de Tocqueville . . . become so."] Alexis de Tocqueville (1805–1859), *Democracy in America*, Book 1, Chapter 1.

786.4 Uruk] Ancient Sumerian city in modern-day Iraq.

786.6   Tammuz] Sumerian god of fertility; like Persephone, he descended to the underworld for six months of the year, to be reborn in the spring.

786.7   Innini] Variant of Innana or Ishtar; the Sumerian goddess of fertility, love, sex, beauty, war, and power, who had a major temple in Uruk.

786.26   bomb shelters] In the U.S., the 1960s Cold War years were the heyday for building such structures, including many installed as underground bunkers in suburban residential backyards.

797.5–7   "One theory . . . happen all at once."] Comment often attributed to Einstein, but see Ray Cummings's (1887–1957) science fiction novel *The Girl in the Golden Atom* (1922): "'Time,' he said, 'is what keeps everything from happening at once.'"

817.8   St. Columba] St. Columba (521–597 C.E.), Irish missionary monk who brought Christianity to Scotland and founded the abbey on the Isle of Iona where the Book of Kells was later created.

819.5   Oak trees were special to them.] According to Pliny the Elder (23–79 C.E.) in *Naturalis Historia* XVI: "The Druids never perform any of their rites except in the presence of a branch of [an oak tree] . . . In fact, they think that anything that grows on it has been sent from heaven and is a proof that the tree was chosen by the god himself."

820.26–27   *Some things have to be believed to be seen?*] English poet Ralph Hodgson (1871–1962), "Queer—Queer," in *The Skylark and Other Poems* (1959).

838.28   napalm] Flammable liquid systematically used as a weapon by the U.S. military during the Vietnam War.

840.31   Glastonbury Abbey] An influential abbey founded by seventh-century Britons in Somerset, United Kingdom, that was once thought to house the final resting place of King Arthur.

840.39   ley lines] Supposedly purposeful alignments of natural landforms and sacred man-made structures like Stonehenge, first posited in 1921 by amateur British archaeologist Alfred Watkins in *The Old Straight Track: Its Mounds, Beacons, Moats, Sites and Mark Stones*.

841.30–31   willing suspension of disbelief] British poet, critic, and theologian Samuel Taylor Coleridge's (1772–1834) formulation for the moratorium on everyday logic required of readers of fiction.

843.2   Dionysius the Aeropagite] L'Engle here understandably confuses the first-century C.E. Athenian judge whom Paul the Apostle converted to Christianity (cf. Acts 17:34) with the fifth- or sixth-century Christian philosopher and theologian who, having encouraged the confusion himself in order to burnish his reputation, came to be known as Pseudo-Dionysius the Aeropagite. The latter's seven authenticated works include *Celestial Hierarchy* and *Ecclesiastical Hierarchy*.

845.22–23   *Finnegans Wake*] Last major work (1939) of Irish writer James Joyce (1882–1941). The sentence "Three quarks for Muster Mark!" provided the name of the elementary particle.

845.24   Murray Gell-Mann] Murray Gell-Mann (b. 1929), American physicist who was awarded a Nobel prize in 1969 for his work on elementary particles.

849.1   Botticelli] Guessing game in which players take turns trying to identify a famous personage by posing a series of fact-based yes-or-no questions.

867.10   *Kyrie eleison! Christe eleison! Kyrie eleison!*] Christian prayer transliterated from the original Greek, beginning: "Lord, have mercy."

872.1   *"Archaiai exousiai,"*] Greek: Ancient powers, or ancient authorities, as in Mark 6:7: "And he called the twelve [apostles] and began to send them out two by two, and gave them authority over the unclean spirits."

874.15   Anula tribe] L'Engle may have derived this information from James George Frazer (1854–1941), *The Golden Bough: A Study in Magic and Religion* (1890, revised 1900).

891.11–12   *But, Lord . . . an acceptable time*] Psalm 69:13.

891.25–28   *Of the Father's love . . . the ending—"*] Variant of "Of the Father's Heart Begotten," Christmas carol based on the Latin poem *Corde natus* ("Heart Begotten") by Aurelius Prudentius (348–413? C.E.).

892.19–21   He brought back . . . wild with grief.] Cf. Luke 7:11–17.

892.21–22   He raised a little girl . . . something to eat.] Cf. Mark 5:21–43.

892.22–23   He drove seven demons . . . Mary of Magdala."] Cf. Mark 16:9 and Luke 8:2.

911.20–22   Japanese people . . . concentration camps.] An estimated 120,000 people of Japanese ancestry were forcibly detained from 1942 to 1946 on orders from President Franklin D. Roosevelt after Japan's attack on Pearl Harbor.

917.30–31 "It is never expedient . . . country,"] Here the Bishop
reverses Caiaphas' infamous declaration in John 11:50: ". . . it is expedient for us, that one man [Jesus] should die for the people, and
that the whole nation perish not." L'Engle had previously parsed the
moral implications of Caiaphas's position in *A Circle of Quiet* (1972).

937.13–33 Christ be with me . . . stranger.] From "St. Patrick's
Breastplate," a long prayer attributed to St. Patrick (late fifth century
C.E.), rendered in English by Irish hymnodist Cecil Frances Alexan-
der (1818–1895).

962.23–24 *Behold, I have set . . . shut it.*] Revelation 3:8.

APPENDIX

974.22 last portrait of Bolivar ever painted] An 1825 portrait by
Ecuadorian painter Antonio Salas (1795–1860).

976.38–977.1 Aunt Olivia shot her beloved Ron] In L'Engle's novel
The Other Side of the Sun (1970).

982.6 the Regina Medal] The Catholic Library Association's lifetime achievement award for distinguished work in the field of children's literature, awarded since 1959.

983.9 Norman Lear] American television writer and producer and
First Amendment advocate (b. 1922) who in 1977 acquired film rights
to *A Wrinkle in Time*.

983.9 Cathy Hand] Catherine Hand, creative director in the office
of Norman Lear's production company and later producer of the
2018 Disney film adaptation of *A Wrinkle in Time*.

987.4 Jerome Hines] American operatic bass (1921–2003) whose
forty-one-year career with New York's Metropolitan Opera (1946–87)
was the longest of any principal singer in that company's history.

987.6–7 Moussorgsky's opera, *Boris Godunov*] *Boris Godunov*, opera
by Russian composer Modest Mussorgsky (1839–1881), which pre-
miered in 1874.

990.3 a 5000-year-old village near Xi'an, China] Banpo, which contains several Neolithic settlements, is no longer considered by archae-
ologists to have evidence of a matriarchal society.

991.28 *Bull-Dog Drummond*] The first (1920) of nineteen British
novels featuring Hugh "Bulldog" Drummond—"detective, patriot,
hero and gentleman"—created by H. C. McNeile (1888–1937), writing as "Sapper," and continued by two successors until 1969.

991.29   *Fu Manchu*] Dr. Fu Manchu, a Chinese master criminal and archvillain featured in English novelist Sax Rohmer's (1883–1959) *The Mystery of Dr. Fu Manchu* (1913), twelve sequels, and several film adaptations.

994.5   "the quantity of a hazelnut,"] In *Showing of Love* (c. 1395) by English mystic Julian of Norwich, which is considered to be the first book in English by a woman.

994.7   "a feather on the breath of God."] An image Hildegard used frequently in her letters to describe herself.

994.25   Stephen Hawking] Stephen William Hawking (1942–2018), English physicist, futurist, writer, and director of research at the Centre for Theoretical Cosmology at the University of Cambridge.

997.36   Mary Ellen Chase's] Smith College English professor and novelist (1887–1973).

998.20–21   Laura Scales] Laura Woolsey Lord Scales (1879–1990), dean of students at Smith College during L'Engle's undergraduate years.

998.32   Betty Friedan] Born Bettye Naomi Goldstein (1921–2006), American feminist writer and advocate best known as the author of *The Feminine Mystique* (1963).

998.34   Esther Cloudman Dunn] Smith College English professor (1864–1977) whose specialty was Shakespeare and the Elizabethan period.

1000.1   Watergate? Irangate?] The political scandal that culminated in the resignation of President Richard M. Nixon on August 9, 1974, came to be known as Watergate after the name of a Washington, D.C., office, hotel, and apartment complex where the Democratic National Committee had its headquarters, and where a botched burglary in June 1972 exposed the first evidence of a broad pattern of White House–directed illegal activities. After Watergate, affixing "gate" to the end of a name became a way to signal an association with a scandal in the news. "Irangate," also called the Iran-Contra Affair, was an illegal secret deal made by officials of the Reagan administration in 1985 to sell arms to Iran (in contravention of a ban on arms sales then in force) in order to covertly funnel a portion of the proceeds to the anti-Communist fighters, or Contras, in Nicaragua.

1000.32–33   "as good as a burnt out candle."] Paraphrase from *The World as I See It* (1949) by Albert Einstein (1879–1955).